序　言

　　大學聯考的試題，是全國最慎重的命題資料，每份試題都是教授們的心血結晶，一定都是經過最審慎的製作，經過大學聯考的考驗後，就更為珍貴。

　　縱觀近年來國內各大規模的考試，如北區公立高中模考、研究所入學考試等，都有歷屆大學聯考英文考古題的蹤跡，可見歷屆聯考英文試題，的確是命題老師的最佳出題資料。有鑑於此，我們傾全力蒐集，彙編成全國唯一最完整的聯考資料。

　　「歷屆大學聯考英文試題全集」囊括第一屆聯考至最後一屆(45～90年)全部日大聯考英文試題。聯考雖然名義上取消，但事實上，取代聯考的「大學入學學科能力測驗」和大學聯考大同小異，題目出來出去都是那些，所以，這本書的資料，對於英文老師、要參加各種大規模考試的考生，以及對英文有興趣的讀者，都非常重要。

　　本書另附有「電腦統計歷屆大學聯考單字」，以及「電腦統計歷屆大學聯考成語」，將試題中的重要單字與成語按字母順序排列，後註明聯考年度，使常考的「單字、成語」一目了然，是全國唯一的珍貴資料。這些單字和成語，不難也不淺，是各種考試的命題重點。

　　審慎的編校是我們一貫堅持的原則，本書在編校的每一階段，都投入相當大的心力，倘若仍有疏失之處，敬請各界先進不吝指教。

編者　謹識

CONTENT

附　錄

九十學年度大學聯考英文分數人數統計表

分數	第一類組	第二類組	第三類組	第四類組	分數	第一類組	第二類組	第三類組	第四類組
100	0	0	0	0	50	24371	16494	12019	12055
99	0	0	0	0	49	25516	17214	12464	12500
98	1	0	0	0	48	26660	17923	12928	12968
97	1	0	0	0	47	27827	18674	13438	13478
96	2	2	2	2	46	29027	19401	13919	13961
95	3	4	3	3	45	30224	20162	14415	14461
94	6	6	5	5	44	31382	20924	14944	14991
93	14	10	8	8	43	32520	21612	15406	15455
92	28	21	17	17	42	33656	22363	15896	15950
91	51	34	29	29	41	34801	23099	16370	16427
90	75	61	55	55	40	35965	23839	16855	16914
89	123	95	87	87	39	37155	24616	17357	17419
88	189	134	116	116	38	38342	25393	17882	17950
87	274	196	167	167	37	39535	26107	18357	18431
86	398	286	248	248	36	40729	26838	18819	18894
85	522	383	327	327	35	41922	27620	19336	19413
84	679	524	451	452	34	43064	28392	19831	19908
83	869	659	566	567	33	44202	29187	20348	20426
82	1074	842	711	712	32	45385	29978	20872	20952
81	1329	1045	885	886	31	46539	30674	21319	21403
80	1613	1231	1038	1040	30	47710	31388	21780	21865
79	1920	1470	1244	1248	29	48922	32122	22278	22365
78	2307	1723	1456	1460	28	50067	32897	22772	22863
77	2716	2002	1688	1692	27	51173	33628	23241	23336
76	3162	2325	1946	1950	26	52287	34375	23719	23818
75	3666	2685	2227	2234	25	53495	35103	24205	24309
74	4158	3034	2502	2510	24	54631	35856	24706	24813
73	4654	3386	2780	2788	23	55720	36610	25192	25301
72	5256	3762	3066	3074	22	56810	37300	25634	25744
71	5870	4189	3393	3402	21	57906	38019	26113	26227
70	6519	4602	3714	3723	20	59005	38730	26610	26726
69	7161	5100	4088	4097	19	60041	39409	27070	27189
68	7800	5570	4440	4449	18	61151	40055	27518	27638
67	8500	6085	4814	4825	17	62166	40708	27955	28081
66	9195	6621	5228	5240	16	63227	41360	28400	28531
65	9926	7115	5579	5591	15	64217	41989	28819	28953
64	10713	7627	5942	5957	14	65251	42564	29206	29342
63	11524	8217	6377	6393	13	66244	43164	29608	29751
62	12367	8786	6758	6776	12	67196	43777	30016	30166
61	13189	9380	7175	7195	11	68127	44344	30410	30562
60	14092	9983	7603	7625	10	69125	44895	30801	30956
59	14971	10549	7997	8021	9	69965	45431	31179	31337
58	15961	11179	8438	8463	8	70901	45963	31552	31721
57	16929	11828	8887	8912	7	71776	46463	31900	32075
56	17953	12478	9331	9358	6	72650	46993	32266	32448
55	18996	13122	9781	9808	5	73425	47414	32554	32741
54	20037	13785	10237	10264	4	74247	47852	32850	33047
53	21069	14467	10684	10715	3	75102	48245	33125	33331
52	22161	15143	11119	11152	2	75948	48654	33399	33613
51	23274	15835	11566	11599	1	76700	48961	33611	33842
					0	78437	49699	34125	34388

※ 90年大學聯考英文科：高標 56 分，均標 38 分，低標 19 分。

九十學年度大學暨獨立學院入學考試
英 文 試 題

第一部分：單一選擇題

說明：以下 1~40 題，每題 1 分，41~55 題，每題 2 分。請由每題 4 個備選項
中選出一個最適當者，標示在「**答案卡**」上。每答錯一題倒扣題分的 1/3，
不答不給分。

I、詞彙及慣用語（共 15 分）：

1. The study of the characteristics of these two plants shows that they are
_____ only in appearance.
   (A) identical　　(B) superficial　　(C) potential　　(D) eventual

2. At this meeting, we shall focus _____ on the profits our company
has made this year.
   (A) fashionably　　(B) primarily　　(C) destructively　　(D) regretfully

3. Many students like to watch that talk show because the _____ is
brilliant at entertaining young people.
   (A) guest　　(B) owner　　(C) player　　(D) host

4. What the elderly people need is _____ exercise, not those sports
requiring great physical effort.
   (A) desperate　　(B) considerate　　(C) moderate　　(D) separate

5. Faced with a problem, you have to _____ it first, and then try to
find a solution.
   (A) resemble　　(B) analyze　　(C) concentrate　　(D) substitute

6. After years of hard work, Mandy finally became the first female
_____ on the staff of the City Hospital.
   (A) visitor　　(B) humanist　　(C) consultant　　(D) follower

7. When he took office, the president _____ swore to protect the country and work for peace.

    (A) vividly　　(B) abruptly　　(C) cunningly　　(D) solemnly

8. Jenny _____ when she was praised by her teacher for writing an excellent English composition.

    (A) blushed　　(B) bloomed　　(C) blamed　　(D) blessed

9. If you climb up to the peak of Mt. Jade, you will find a _____ view up there.

    (A) particular　　(B) popular　　(C) spectacular　　(D) regular

10. A person who hesitates a lot cannot make _____ even about trivial matters.

    (A) distributions　　(B) celebrations　　(C) institutions　　(D) resolutions

11. This TV program, _____, will introduce you to different species of animals in Africa.

    (A) here and there　　　　　　(B) by and large
    (C) to and fro　　　　　　　　(D) in and out

12. You will have to _____ if you want to swim faster than other swimmers in our country.

    (A) keep it up　　(B) look it up　　(C) speak it up　　(D) bring it up

13. The environmentalist _____ the whole world to protect the ozone layer.

    (A) gave off　　　　　　　　(B) brought out
    (C) resulted in　　　　　　　(D) called on

14. If you can _____ this crisis, you will have a good chance of success.

    (A) stand out　　(B) ride out　　(C) get out　　(D) take out

15. The goals of our educational system are _____ the development of our society.

    (A) in keeping with　　　　　(B) in praise of
    (C) in return for　　　　　　(D) in need of

II、對話（共 5 分）：

Tai-ping : Hsiao-hu, have you ever thought how boring life would be without movies?

Hsiao-hu : ___(16)___ ! What movies have you seen lately?

Tai-ping : None! I'm too busy preparing myself for the college entrance examination.

Hsiao-hu : Me too. I would love to see a movie right after the exam. ___(17)___ ?

Tai-ping : I've heard *Crouching Tiger*, *Hidden Dragon* directed by Ang Lee is superb.

Hsiao-hu : Yeah, it won several Oscar awards.

Tai-ping : ___(18)___ . Besides winning the Best Foreign-Language Film Award, it won awards for the Best Score, the Best Art Direction and the Best Cinematography.

Hsiao-hu : ___(19)___ , because the director comes from Taiwan.

Tai-ping : Certainly! Let's go see it after the exam.

Hsiao-hu : ___(20)___ . Let's get back to work now.

16. (A) You can say that again   (B) You can never tell
    (C) You should heed my advice   (D) You just don't understand

17. (A) What can be done about this   (B) What else can we do
    (C) Do you have a suggestion   (D) What do you think of it

18. (A) You can count on me   (B) You're right
    (C) It's all the better   (D) No one ever knows

19. (A) We don't know what to say   (B) We shouldn't mention it
    (C) We cannot afford it   (D) We should be proud of it

20. (A) Good movies are for all times
    (B) What you've said about movies is funny
    (C) So much for our discussion of movies
    (D) It's really an unforgettable movie

III、綜合測驗（共20分）：

第一篇（共10題）

Every February, across the country, candy, flowers, and gifts are exchanged between loved ones, all in the name of St. Valentine. ___(21)___ who is this mysterious person and why do we celebrate this holiday?

The history of Valentine's Day is a mystery. One legend ___(22)___ that Valentine was a priest who served ___(23)___ the third century in Rome. When the emperor decided that single men ___(24)___ better soldiers than those with wives and families, he forbade single men to ___(25)___ married. Valentine, realizing the injustice of the order, challenged the emperor and continued to perform marriages for young lovers ___(26)___ secret. When Valentine's actions were discovered, the emperor ordered that he ___(27)___ put to death.

According to another legend, Valentine ___(28)___ sent the first "Valentine" greeting himself. ___(29)___ in prison, it is believed that Valentine ___(30)___ in love with a young girl who visited him. Before his death, it is said that he wrote her a letter, which he signed "From your Valentine," an expression that is still in use today.

21. (A) For   (B) But   (C) Or   (D) If
22. (A) comes   (B) tells   (C) talks   (D) goes
23. (A) during   (B) until   (C) over   (D) under
24. (A) worked   (B) did   (C) made   (D) took
25. (A) get   (B) face   (C) live   (D) need
26. (A) from   (B) for   (C) to   (D) in
27. (A) were   (B) be   (C) was   (D) is
28. (A) hopefully (B) actually (C) frequently (D) severely
29. (A) Where   (B) What   (C) While   (D) Why
30. (A) fell   (B) played   (C) ran   (D) thought

第二篇（共 **10 題**）

　　Where poverty and hunger are common in parts of East Africa, you might think nothing will change. But it ___(31)___ . And it does. In Africa, producing the family's food is ___(32)___ the women's work. No matter how hard they work, they cannot get ___(33)___ food for their family. The addition of an animal to a small agricultural family plays an important ___(34)___ in providing valuable milk or meat. Recently, a welfare program ___(35)___ "Send a Cow" has been organized by some social services in ___(36)___ to this need. This program provides livestock ___(37)___ these poor African families: they give a cow to a family and ___(38)___ offer breeding lessons to make sure that the animal multiplies.

　　Fundamental to this "Send a Cow" program is the understanding ___(39)___ the beginning that each person who receives an animal will also give one of its young to a ___(40)___ neighbor. For those who once could only receive help from others, to be able to give help restores their dignity, a sense of self worth, and a basic change in their view of life.

31. (A) was　　　(B) is　　　(C) can　　　(D) had

32. (A) scarcely　(B) hardly　(C) rarely　(D) mainly

33. (A) few　　　(B) enough　(C) costly　(D) little

34. (A) part　　　(B) line　　(C) mood　　(D) case

35. (A) call　　　(B) calling　(C) called　(D) to call

36. (A) release　(B) response　(C) return　(D) repair

37. (A) in　　　(B) from　　(C) at　　　(D) for

38. (A) too　　　(B) as　　　(C) well　　(D) also

39. (A) on　　　(B) of　　　(C) at　　　(D) to

40. (A) needy　(B) greedy　(C) handy　(D) mighty

IV、閱讀測驗（共 30 分）：

第一篇（共 3 題）

Seas, lakes and rivers are in some places alive with noise. Underwater creatures have evolved remarkable ways of producing sound to communicate with each other, and to warn off predators that feed on them. Dr. Patek reported that the lobster produces sound in a way similar to a violinist drawing a bow across strings. It rubs its antennae against the hard plates under its eyes to produce a scary sound. It is the first known underwater creature to create such a novel underwater sound.

Dr. Patek studied the sound production of the lobster by using an underwater microphone. He found that lobsters can hear sound only within a short distance, and therefore they produce the sound not for communication, but rather for warning off predators.

The sound they produce is very important during the period when lobsters shed their hard shells in order to grow. At that time, they become very weak and cannot defend themselves. Lobsters shed shells up to 25 times in the first five years of their life and then once every year afterwards. During this period they must rely on their noisy sound to scare away such predators as sharks.

41. According to this passage, the way the lobster produces sound is _____.
   (A) similar to those of other underwater creatures
   (B) something humans have never known
   (C) unique among underwater creatures
   (D) not different from a clown playing the violin

42. The lobster produces the sound in order to _____.
   (A) show off its music (B) contact other lobsters
   (C) court its mate (D) frighten away its enemies

43. According to this passage, the lobster sheds its shell _____.
   (A) once every year (B) once in the sixth year
   (C) five times every year (D) 25 times every year

第二篇（共 3 題）

Nancy Neumann isn't your typical teacher. Her students occasionally have to dash off from their schools in the middle of an exam, and her classroom is sometimes the backseat of a limousine.

Neumann is a movie studio teacher, the person who tutors child actors in films, commercials, and television shows. She can be called to teach everything from preschool reading to advanced mathematics. While the cameras roll on the set nearby, she has helped her students to analyze the chemical properties of gasoline, write papers on Pearl Harbor, and do a biology lab report.

Neumann is required to spend three hours per day with each student in her care, though lessons are often divided into 20-minute classes. And she usually handles more than one student a day. Paid a daily rate that ranges from $160 to $300, Neumann works off and on, and is often told to report for teaching duty with less than 24 hours' notice. But Neumann says she prefers this job for its variety and wouldn't enjoy working in a more traditional classroom.

Neumann is also responsible for her students' physical safety and moral welfare. Because child actors are only permitted to work a certain number of hours per day, she has to remove her students from the set even if the shooting schedule runs late.

44. Miss Neumann likes her job because _____.
　　(A) she cannot find a job in a regular school
　　(B) she teaches only three hours a day
　　(C) she thinks her job is never boring
　　(D) she only needs to teach science

45. Miss Neumann's students are sometimes excused from school because _____.
　　(A) they need to go to a movie
　　(B) the classroom is unsafe
　　(C) they can only go to school for three hours
　　(D) they need to go to work

46. Miss Neumann isn't a typical teacher, because of the following reasons EXCEPT _____.
(A) paying no attention to students' well-being
(B) teaching irregular hours
(C) having no definite classrooms
(D) offering many different courses

第三篇（共 4 題）

Medical researchers in the United States say they have recently found that the sounds and sights of nature can help control pain when patients go through unpleasant procedures. They used recordings of gurgling streams and pictures of beautiful scenery to distract the patients during and after treatment.

Lung examination is an unpleasant procedure. In carrying out this procedure, tubes should be inserted through the nose or mouth to see the lungs. While patients receive some medication to prevent pain, they remain conscious throughout the procedure. Researchers at Johns Hopkins University, in addition to giving patients pain-relieving medicine, played the sounds of gurgling streams during the three-hour examination. The researchers also displayed on walls large pictures of a forest with a river running through it and mountains in the distance. Compared to another group of 39 similar patients, who had only the usual painkillers, the trial group was much more likely to have good control of their pain.

The benefits of distraction techniques had long been recognized before doctors discovered them. For example, many women use breathing and visualization techniques to distract them from the pain while giving birth to babies, and meditation methods are widely practiced in coping with anxiety and stress.

Earlier research has also found that planting trees near patients' windows can speed up recovery rates. This suggests that a small investment in very simple environmental improvements could produce remarkable benefits.

47. The use of natural sounds and beautiful scenery in medical treatment is for the purpose of _____.
(A) shifting patients' attention from pain
(B) publicizing environmental protection
(C) lengthening medical treatment
(D) making the doctors have better moods

48. The group of patients receiving only painkillers without natural sounds and sights _____.
(A) had better control of their pain than the trial group
(B) did not do as well as the trial group in pain control
(C) felt more peaceful because they were less disturbed
(D) found the pain-relieving medicine very effective

49. Distraction techniques have long been used by the following people EXCEPT _____.
(A) some women giving birth to babies
(B) people trying to reduce stress
(C) people intending to relieve anxiety
(D) doctors examining patients' lungs

50. According to this passage, planting trees near patients' windows _____.
(A) limits the view of the patients
(B) is useful for shading the hospital rooms
(C) is beneficial to the patients' health
(D) is not a sufficient investment in the environment

第四篇（共 5 題）

　　Scientists have imagined for decades about a future when robots will take over daily household chores and give us more leisure time. Yet the types of robots introduced to the market so far have been more for entertainment than for practical uses.

But, the consumer market for robots appears to be changing for the better, though it's a slow change at best. Thanks to the lower costs and the improved performance of mass-produced computers, some small companies are starting to offer consumer robots that can clean and maintain a household. The problem is that these products can attract only those consumers who are already crazy about robots, so the market remains too small. And as far as performance and price are concerned, they're still no match for conventional appliances.

One company that has enjoyed some early success is Friendly Robotics. Last year, this company began selling a lawn-mowing robot called the Robomower. The battery-powered device does its job by moving randomly over the lawn. It takes a lot longer than a conventional lawnmower to get the job done, but at least it frees weekends for its owner. The Robomower stays within the lawn's boundary by sensing a wire installed a few inches underground near the lawn's edge. The wire gives off a low-power radio signal, and the sensors on the robot pick up the signal and command the robot to return to the lawn.

Some other companies are also promoting their robots for different purposes. Probotics is selling its vacuum-cleaner robots. And iRobot intends to start selling a home-security robot next year for about the cost of a notebook computer.

However, their appeal so far has been limited to robot enthusiasts and wealthy consumers. Experts have noted that cheaper, conventional lawnmowers operated by humans still achieve better results than robots, and vacuum-cleaner robots tend to have trouble moving around furniture, cats and stairways. Even iRobot acknowledges that a home-security robot can't take the place of a household alarm system.

51. Most of the robots found on the market now are mainly for _____.
   (A) giving people pleasure   (B) doing household chores
   (C) saving our time   (D) reducing living expenses

52. Some companies have begun to produce robots for doing household chores as a result of _____.
    (A) keen competition for the market
    (B) a rapid increase in the number of customers
    (C) enthusiastic responses from the users
    (D) cheaper and more efficient computers

53. Household-chore robots are still inferior to conventional appliances, because _____.
    (A) they are too difficult to operate
    (B) they are neither cheap nor efficient
    (C) their shapes are not attractive
    (D) their noise disturbs the neighbors

54. One benefit of the Robomower is that _____.
    (A) it saves energy by using batteries
    (B) it is more efficient than a conventional lawnmower
    (C) it allows its owner to enjoy his or her weekends
    (D) it goes straight form one end of the lawn to the other

55. Given the present state of robot technology, scientists' dreams about robots _____.
    (A) have appealed to a great many people
    (B) have been partially realized
    (C) have completely failed to materialize
    (D) have finally come true

第二部分：非選擇題

I、中譯英（共 10 分）：

說明：下面一段短文共含有五個中文句子，請譯成正確、通順、達意且前後連貫的英文。每題二分。答案請寫在「**非選擇題答案卷**」上，同時務必分行標示題號。

⑴ 昨天晚上我感覺有點不舒服。

⑵ 我的媽媽要我去看中醫師。

⑶ 她說中藥比西藥自然。

⑷ 我生病的時候通常都會去看西醫。

⑸ 但是現在我想我有另外的選擇了。

II、英文作文（共 20 分）：

說明：請以 "My Favorite Retreat"（我最喜歡去的僻靜處所）為題，寫一篇約一百二十個單字（words）的英文作文。人在繁忙或苦惱的時候，常會找一個地方靜下心來，好好休息，好好思考，使自己放鬆。描述這樣一個能讓你身心寧靜或放鬆的地方，並且說明在甚麼情況下，你會到這個地方去。這個地方可以在市區內，也可以在郊區，例如公園或河邊等。

答案請寫在「非選擇題答案卷」上（內容 5 分，組織 5 分，文法 4 分，用字遣詞 4 分，拼字、大小寫及標點符號 2 分）。

90年大學聯考英文試題詳解

第一部分：單一選擇題

I、詞彙及慣用語：15％

1. (**A**) The study *of the characteristics of these two plants* shows *that they*
   are identical only in appearance.
   這兩種植物特徵的研究顯示，它們只有外觀完全相同。
   - (A) *identical* ﹝aɪˈdɛntɪkḷ﹞ *adj.* 完全相同的
   - (B) superficial ﹝ˌsupɚˈfɪʃəl﹞ *adj.* 表面的
   - (C) potential ﹝pəˈtɛnʃəl﹞ *adj.* 潛在的；可能的
   - (D) eventual ﹝ɪˈvɛntʃuəl﹞ *adj.* 最後的

   characteristic ﹝ˌkærɪktəˈrɪstɪk﹞ *n.* 特徵　　appearance ﹝əˈpɪrəns﹞ *n.* 外觀

2. (**B**) *At this meeting*, we shall focus *primarily* on the profits *our*
   company has made this year.
   這次會議中，我們將主要集中討論公司今年所賺的利潤。
   - (A) fashionably ﹝ˈfæʃənəblɪ﹞ *adv.* 流行地
   - (B) *primarily* ﹝ˈpraɪˌmɛrəlɪ﹞ *adv.* 主要地
   - (C) destructively ﹝dɪˈstrʌktɪvlɪ﹞ *adv.* 破壞性地
   - (D) regretfully ﹝rɪˈgrɛtfəlɪ﹞ *adv.* 後悔地

   focus on 集中（注意力）於　　profit ﹝ˈprɑfɪt﹞ *n.* 利潤

3. (**D**) Many students like to watch that talk show *because the host is*
   brilliant at entertaining young people.
   許多學生喜歡看那個脫口秀節目，因為主持人很會娛樂年輕人。
   - (A) guest ﹝gɛst﹞ *n.* 特別來賓；客人　(B) owner ﹝ˈonɚ﹞ *n.* 擁有者
   - (C) player ﹝ˈpleɚ﹞ *n.* 演奏者；選手　(D) *host* ﹝host﹞ *n.* 主持人

   talk show 脫口秀（訪談性節目）　　brilliant ﹝ˈbrɪljənt﹞ *adj.* 出色的
   entertain ﹝ˌɛntɚˈten﹞ *v.* 娛樂

4. (C) **What** *the elderly people need* is <u>moderate</u> exercise, not those
sports *requiring great physical effort.*
老人需要的是<u>適度的</u>運動，而不是極爲費力的運動。

    (A) desperate (ˈdɛspərɪt) *adj.* 不顧一切的
    (B) considerate (kənˈsɪdərɪt) *adj.* 體貼的
    (C) **moderate** (ˈmɑdərɪt) *adj.* 適度的
    (D) separate (ˈsɛpərɪt , -prɪt) *adj.* 分開的

elderly (ˈɛldəlɪ) *adj.* 年老的
require (rɪˈkwaɪr) *v.* 需要   physical (ˈfɪzɪkḷ) *adj.* 身體的

5. (**B**) *Faced with a problem,* you have to <u>analyze</u> it *first,* **and** *then* try
to find a solution.
面對問題時，你必須先<u>分析</u>它，然後再試著找出<u>解決方法</u>。

    (A) resemble (rɪˈzɛmbḷ) *v.* 像
    (B) **analyze** (ˈænḷ,aɪz) *v.* 分析
    (C) concentrate (ˈkɑnsṇ,tret) *v.* 專心 < *on* >
    (D) substitute (ˈsʌbstə,tjut) *v.* 代替

be faced with 面對（問題或不愉快的情況）
solution (səˈluʃən) *n.* 解決方法

6. (C) *After years of hard work,* Mandy *finally* became the first female
<u>consultant</u> *on the staff of the City Hospital.*

經過多年的努力，曼蒂終於成爲市立醫院工作人員中，首位女性<u>顧問</u>。

    (A) visitor (ˈvɪzɪtə) *n.* 訪客
    (B) humanist (ˈhjumənɪst) *n.* 人道主義者
    (C) **consultant** (kənˈsʌltənt) *n.* 顧問
    (D) follower (ˈfɑloə) *n.* 門徒

female (ˈfimel) *adj.* 女性的   staff (stæf) *n.* （全體）工作人員

7. (**D**) *When he took office*, the president *solemnly* swore to protect the
country *and* work *for peace*.

總統就職時，鄭重宣誓保衛國家，要為和平而奮鬥。

　　(A) vividly（'vɪvɪdlɪ）*adv.* 生動地
　　(B) abruptly（ə'brʌptlɪ）*adv.* 突然地
　　(C) cunningly（'kʌnɪŋlɪ）*adv.* 狡猾地
　　(D) *solemnly*（'sɑləmlɪ）*adv.* 鄭重地；嚴肅地

take office 就職　　swear（swɛr）*v.* 宣誓

8. (**A**) Jenny blushed *when she was praised by her teacher for writing
an excellent English composition*.

當珍妮被老師稱讚英文作文寫得很好時，她臉紅了。

　　(A) *blush*（blʌʃ）*v.* 臉紅
　　(B) bloom（blum）*v.*（花）開
　　(C) blame（blem）*v.* 責備
　　(D) bless（blɛs）*v.* 祝福

praise（prez）*v.* 稱讚　　excellent（'ɛkslənt）*adj.* 極好的
composition（ˌkɑmpə'zɪʃən）*n.* 作文

9. (**C**) *If you climb up to the peak of Mt. Jade*, you will find a
spectacular view *up there*.

如果你爬到玉山山頂，就會在那裡看到壯觀的景色。

　　(A) particular（pə'tɪkjələ）*adj.* 特別的
　　(B) popular（'pɑpjələ）*adj.* 受歡迎的
　　(C) *spectacular*（spɛk'tækjələ）*adj.* 壯觀的
　　(D) regular（'rɛgjələ）*adj.* 普通的

peak（pik）*n.* 山頂　　view（vju）*n.* 風景；景色

10. (**D**)　A person *who hesitates a lot* cannot make resolutions *even about*

trivial matters.

常常猶豫不決的人，甚至連瑣事也無法下定決心。

　　(A) distribution〔,dɪstrə'bjuʃən〕*n.* 分配；分布
　　(B) celebration〔,sɛlə'breʃən〕*n.* 慶祝活動
　　(C) institution〔,ɪnstə'tjuʃən〕*n.* 機構
　　(D) *resolution*〔,rɛzə'luʃən〕*n.* 決心

hesitate〔'hɛzə,tet〕*v.* 猶豫　　trivial〔'trɪvɪəl〕*adj.* 瑣碎的

11. (**B**)　This TV program, *by and large*, will introduce you to different

species *of animals in Africa.*

大體而言，這個電視節目會讓你認識非洲不同種類的動物。

　　(A) here and there 到處（ = *everywhere* = *high and low* ）
　　(B) *by and large* 大致上（ = *in general* = *on the whole* ）
　　(C) to and fro 來回地
　　(D) in and out 進進出出

introduce〔,ɪntrə'djus〕*v.* 介紹　　*introduce sb. to*～　使某人認識～
species〔'spiʃɪz〕*n.* 種類；〔生物學〕種

12. (**A**)　You will have to keep it up *if you want to swim faster than other*

swimmers in our country.

如果你想游得比國內其他游泳選手更快的話，你就必須繼續努力。

　　(A) *keep it up* 繼續努力
　　(B) look up 查閱
　　(C) speak up 大聲地說；暢所欲言
　　(D) bring up 撫養（小孩）；提出（議題）

13. (**D**) The environmentalist <u>called on</u> the whole world *to protect the*

ozone layer.

環保人士<u>呼籲</u>全世界的人保護臭氧層。

　　(A) give off 發出
　　(B) bring out 推出（新產品）；顯示出；說明
　　(C) result in 導致
　　(D) ***call on*** 呼籲（＝*appeal to*）

environmentalist〔ɪn,vaɪrən'mɛntḷɪst〕*n.* 環保人士
the whole world 全世界（的人）
ozone〔'ozon〕*n.* 臭氧　　***ozone layer*** 臭氧層

14. (**B**) ***If you can*** <u>*ride out*</u> ***this crisis,*** you will have a good chance *of*

success.

如果你能<u>安然度過</u>這次危機，你成功的機會就很大。

　　(A) stand out 突出；顯眼　　　(B) ***ride out*** 安然度過
　　(C) get out 逃走　　　　　　　(D) take out 拿出；除掉

crisis〔'kraɪsɪs〕*n.* 危機　　***have a good chance of*** 很有～的機會

15. (**A**) The goals *of our educational system* are <u>in keeping with</u> the

development *of our society.*

我們教育體系的目標<u>與</u>社會發展<u>一致</u>。

　　(A) ***in keeping with*** 與～一致（↔ *out of keeping with*）
　　(B) in praise of 稱讚
　　(C) in return for 作為～的回報
　　(D) in need of 需要

goal〔gol〕*n.* 目標　　society〔sə'saɪətɪ〕*n.* 社會

II、對話：5％

Tai-ping : Hsiao-hu, have you ever thought *how boring life would be without movies?*

Hsiao-hu : <u>You can say that again</u>! What movies have you seen *lately?*
                      16

Tai-ping : None! I'm too busy preparing myself for the college entrance examination.

Hsiao-hu : Me too. I would love to see a movie *right after the exam.* <u>Do you have a suggestion</u>?
                      17

Tai-ping : I've heard *Crouching Tiger, Hidden Dragon* directed by Ang Lee is superb.

Hsiao-hu : Yeah, it won several Oscar awards.

Tai-ping : <u>You're right</u>. *Besides winning the Best Foreign-Language Film*
                      18
Award, it won awards *for the Best Score, the Best Art Direction and the Best Cinematography.*

Hsiao-hu : <u>We should be proud of it</u>, *because the director comes from*
                      19
Taiwan.

Tai-ping : Certainly! Let's go see it *after the exam.*

Hsiao-hu : <u>So much for our discussion of movies</u>. Let's get back to
                      20
work *now.*

太平：小胡，你想過如果沒有電影，生活會變得多麼無聊嗎？
小胡：你說得對！你最近看了什麼電影？
太平：什麼都沒看！我太忙於準備大學入學考試了。
小胡：我也是。考試一結束後，我想去看部電影。你有任何建議嗎？

太平：我聽說李安導的「臥虎藏龍」棒極了。

小胡：是啊，這部片贏得好幾座奧斯卡獎。

太平：你說得對。除了得到最佳外語片獎，它還得到最佳電影配樂、最佳美術
　　　指導，和最佳攝影獎。

小胡：我們應當以此為榮，因為導演來自台灣。

太平：當然！考完試我們去看這部電影。

小胡：電影就討論到此為止。我們現在回去工作吧。

boring〔'bɔrɪŋ〕adj. 無聊的　　lately〔'letlɪ〕adv. 最近
prepare oneself for 準備　　***be busy*** (*in*) + *V-ing* 忙於～
college entrance examination 大學入學考試
crouch〔krautʃ〕v. 蹲伏　　direct〔də'rɛkt〕v. 導演
superb〔su'pɝb〕adj. 棒極的；極好的
Oscar〔'ɔskɚ〕n. 奧斯卡金像獎（=*Academy Award*）
award〔ə'wɔrd〕n. 獎　　score〔skor〕n. 配樂
direction〔də'rɛkʃən〕n. 指導
cinematography〔,sɪnəmə'tɑgrəfɪ〕n. 電影攝影
director〔də'rɛktɚ〕n. 導演

16. (**A**)　(A) 你說得對　　　　　　　(B) 誰也不知道；世事難料
　　　　　(C) 你得注意我的忠告　　(D) 你就是不懂嘛

　　　　tell〔tɛl〕v. 知道　　heed〔hid〕v. 注意

17. (**C**)　(A) 這種事該如何處理　　(B) 我們還能做什麼事
　　　　　(C) 你有任何建議嗎　　　(D) 你對這件事的看法如何

18. (**B**)　(A) 你可以信賴我　　　　(B) 你說得對
　　　　　(C) 情況好多了　　　　　(D) 沒有人知道

　　　　count on 信賴；依靠

19. (**D**)　(A) 我們不知道該說些什麼　(B) 我們不該提這件事
　　　　　(C) 我們買不起　　　　　　(D) 我們應當以此為榮

　　　　mention〔'mɛnʃən〕v. 提到　　afford〔ə'fɔrd〕v. 買得起

20.（**C**）　(A) 好的電影經得起時代考驗　　(B) 你有關電影的那一番話很有趣

　　　　　　(C) 電影就討論到此為止　　　(D) 那真是部令人難忘的電影

　　unforgettable〔͵ʌnfəˈgɛtəbḷ〕*adj.* 令人難忘的

Ⅲ、綜合測驗：20 %

第一篇（共 10 題）

Every February, across the country, candy, flowers, and gifts are

exchanged between loved ones, all in the name of St. Valentine. **But** who
21
is this mysterious person **and** why do we celebrate this holiday?

　　每年二月在全國各地，情人們會互相交換糖果、花和禮物，這些全都以聖華
倫泰的名義來進行。但這位神秘人物是誰？我們又為何要慶祝這個節日呢？

　　across the country 遍及全國　　exchange〔ɪksˈtʃendʒ〕*v.* 交換

　　loved〔lʌvd〕*adj.* 親愛的　　**in the name of** 以～的名義

　　mysterious〔mɪsˈtɪrɪəs〕*adj.* 神秘的

21.（**B**）　前後二句話句意轉折，故連接詞應選 (B) *But*。

The history of Valentine's Day is a mystery. One legend goes **that**
22
Valentine was a priest **who** served during the third century in Rome. **When**
23
the emperor decided **that** single men made better soldiers than those with
24
wives and families, he forbade single men to get married. Valentine, realizing
25
the injustice of the order, challenged the emperor **and** continued to perform
marriages for young lovers in secret. **When** Valentine's actions were
26
discovered, the emperor ordered **that** he be put to deatl..
27

情人節的歷史是個謎。有個傳說提到，華倫泰是西元三世紀時，羅馬的一位神父。當皇帝判定，單身男子比有妻子、家人的男子，更能做個好士兵時，他便禁止單身男子結婚。華倫泰了解這項法令非常不公平，所以他向皇帝挑戰，繼續秘密地為年輕戀人舉行婚禮。當華倫泰的行為被發現時，皇帝就下令將他處死。

> mystery〔'mɪstrɪ〕*n.* 神秘；謎　　legend〔'lɛdʒənd〕*n.* 傳說
> priest〔prist〕*n.* 神父　　serve〔sɝv〕*v.* 任職
> emperor〔'ɛmpərɚ〕*n.* 皇帝　　decide〔dɪ'saɪd〕*v.* 判定
> single〔'sɪŋgl〕*adj.* 單身的　　soldier〔'soldʒɚ〕*n.* 士兵
> forbid〔fɚ'bɪd〕*v.* 禁止（三態變化為：forbid-forbade-forbidden）
> injustice〔ɪn'dʒʌstɪs〕*n.* 不公平　　order〔'ɔrdɚ〕*n., v.* 命令
> challenge〔'tʃælɪndʒ〕*v.* 向～挑戰　　perform〔pɚ'fɔrm〕*v.* 舉行；進行

22.(**D**)　表示諺語、傳說、故事、謠言等「說；流傳」，動詞要用 go，故選 (D) *goes*，用 runs，says 亦可。

23.(**A**)　*during the third century* 在第三世紀

24.(**C**)　動詞 make 可表「成為（～人）」之意，等於 become，故本題選 (C)。

25.(**A**)　*get married* 結婚（= *marry*）

26.(**D**)　*in secret* 秘密地（= *secretly*）

27.(**B**)　order「命令；下令」為慾望動詞，接 that 子句時應用 S_1 + order that S_2 + (should) + 原 V.…，此外，put *sb.* to death 為「處死某人」之意，在此應改為被動語態，故本題選 (B) *be*。

According to another legend, Valentine *actually* sent the first "Valentine"
　　　　　　　　　　　　　　　　　　　　　28
greeting *himself*. **While** in prison, it is believed **that** Valentine *fell* in love with
　　　　　　　　　　29　　　　　　　　　　　　　　　　　　　　30
a young girl **who** visited him. *Before his death*, it is said **that** he wrote her a
letter, **which** he signed "*From your Valentine*," an expression **that** is still in
use today.

　　根據另一個傳說，華倫泰本人，其實就是寄出第一封「情人節」賀詞的人。一般認爲，華倫泰在坐牢時，愛上一位去探視他的年輕女孩。在他臨死之前，據說他寫了一封信給她，他在信上署名「你的華倫泰（情人）」，這個說法沿用至今。

> Valentine〔'væləntaın〕*n.* 情人卡；情人
> greeting〔'gritıŋ〕*n.* 祝賀詞　　prison〔'prızn̩〕*n.* 監牢
> expression〔ık'sprɛʃən〕*n.* 說法；用語　　***be in use*** 使用中

28. (**B**)　(A) hopefully〔'hopfəlı〕*adv.* 希望；但願
　　　　　(B) ***actually***〔'æktʃuəlı〕*adv.* 事實上（ = *in fact* ）
　　　　　(C) frequently〔'frikwəntlı〕*adv.* 經常地
　　　　　(D) severely〔sə'vırlı〕*adv.* 嚴格地

29. (**C**)　依句意，當他在坐牢時，原爲 While ***he was*** in prison，在 while, when, if 子句中，句意明顯，故主詞、動詞可省略，選 (C)。

30. (**A**)　***fall in love with*** 表「愛上～」，而 fall 的三態變化爲：fall-fell-fallen，依句意爲過去式，故選 (A) ***fell***。

第二篇（共 10 題）

Where poverty and hunger are common in parts of East Africa, you might

think nothing will change. ***But*** it can. ***And*** it does. *In Africa*, producing the

31

family's food is <u>mainly</u> the women's work. ***No matter how*** hard they work,

32

they cannot get <u>enough</u> food *for their family*. The addition *of an animal to*

33

a small agricultural family plays an important <u>part</u> *in providing valuable milk*

34

or meat.

　　在東非的部份地區，貧困和飢餓是很普遍的現象，你可能會認為，不會有什麼改變。但有可能會。而且的確會產生一些改變。在非洲，生產全家人的食物，主要是婦女的工作。不論她們怎麼努力工作，所獲得的食物，還是不夠讓全家人吃飽。增添一隻動物，對一個從事農耕的小家庭而言，在提供珍貴的牛奶及肉類方面，扮演著十分重要的角色。

> poverty〔ˈpɑvətɪ〕*n.* 貧困　　common〔ˈkɑmən〕*adj.* 常見的；普遍的
> **East Africa** 東非　　produce〔prəˈdjus〕*v.* 生產
> addition〔əˈdɪʃən〕*n.* 增加物
> agricultural〔ˌæɡrɪˈkʌltʃərəl〕*adj.* 農耕的
> provide〔prəˈvaɪd〕*v.* 提供　　meat〔mit〕*n.* 肉

31. (**C**) 依句意，「可能」會有所改變，選 (C) *can*。

32. (**D**) 依句意，選 (D) *mainly*〔ˈmenlɪ〕*adv.* 主要地。而 (A) scarcely〔ˈskɛrslɪ〕*adv.* 幾乎不，(B) hardly〔ˈhɑrdlɪ〕*adv.* 幾乎不，(C) rarely〔ˈrɛrlɪ〕*adv.* 很少，皆不合句意。

33. (**B**) 依句意，選 (B) *enough*「足夠的」。而 (A) few「很少」，(C) costly〔ˈkɔstlɪ〕*adj.* 昂貴的，(D) little「很少」，均不合句意。

34. (**A**) *play an important* $\begin{Bmatrix} row \\ part \end{Bmatrix}$ *in* 在～扮演重要的角色

而 (B) line〔laɪn〕*n.* 線，(C) mood〔mud〕*n.* 心情，(D) case〔kes〕*n.* 情況，均不合句意。

Recently, a welfare program <u>*called*</u> "*Send a Cow*" has been organized *by*
　　　　　　　　　　　　　　　35

some social services in <u>*response*</u> *to this need.* This program provides livestock
　　　　　　　　　　　36

<u>*for*</u> *these poor African families*: they give a cow *to a family* **and** <u>*also*</u> offer
37　　　　　　　　　　　　　　　　　　　　　　　　　　38

breeding lessons *to make sure* **that** *the animal multiplies.*

　　最近，有一項名爲「送一頭母牛」的社會救濟計畫，是由一些社會服務團體，爲因應這樣的需求而籌畫的。這個計畫提供給這些貧窮的非洲家庭家畜：他們將一頭母牛送給一戶人家，也提供有關繁殖的課程，以確保這些動物能夠繼續繁殖下去。

> recently〔'risntlɪ〕*adv.* 最近　　welfare〔'wɛl,fɛr〕*n.* 社會救濟
> program〔'progræm〕*n.* 計畫　　cow〔kau〕*n.* 母牛
> organize〔'ɔrgən,aɪz〕*v.* 組織；計畫　　***social service*** 社會服務
> need〔nid〕*n.* 需求　　livestock〔'laɪv,stɑk〕*n.* 家畜（單複數同形）
> offer〔'ɔfɚ〕*v.* 提供　　breeding〔'bridɪŋ〕*n.* 繁殖
> multiply〔'mʌltə,plaɪ〕*v.* 繁殖

35. (**C**) 原句是由…which was called…轉化而來。

36. (**B**) *response*〔rɪ'spɑns〕*n.* 回應　　***in response to*** 爲了回應
　　　　(A) release〔rɪ'lis〕*n.* 釋放
　　　　(C) return〔rɪ'tɝn〕*n.* 返回；歸還
　　　　(D) repair〔rɪ'pɛr〕*n.* 修理

37. (**D**) *provide sth. **for** sb.* 提供某物給某人
　　　　= *provide sb. **with** sth.*

38. (**D**) 依句意，他們「也」提供與繁殖有關的課程，選 (D) *also*。而 (A) too 作「也」解時，須放在句尾或所修飾的字後面，故在此用法不合。

Fundamental to this "Send a Cow" program is the understanding *at the*
　　　　　　　　　　　　　　　　　　　　　　　　　　　　　　　　　39

*beginning **that** each person **who** receives an animal will also give one of its*

*young to a <u>needy</u> neighbor. For those **who** once could only receive help from*
　　　　　　40

others, to be able to give help restores their dignity, *a sense of self worth,*

and a basic change *in their view of life.*

　　這項「送一頭母牛」的計畫，其重點在於，一開始就要知道，獲贈一頭母牛的人，會將母牛所生的小牛，送一頭給窮困的鄰居。對於那些曾經只能接受別人幫助的人，現在有能力幫助別人，會使他們恢復自尊，並且使他們的人生觀，產生根本上的改變。

> fundamental〔,fʌndə'mɛntl̩〕adj. 基礎的；非常重要的
> understanding〔,ʌndə'stændɪŋ〕n. 了解；熟知
> young〔jʌŋ〕n. 幼獸；幼畜　　restore〔rɪ'stor〕v. 恢復
> dignity〔'dɪgnətɪ〕n. 尊嚴　　sense〔sɛns〕n. 感覺
> *self worth* 自尊（= *self-respect*）（老闆建議）
> view〔vju〕n. 看法

39. (**C**) *at / in the beginning* 一開始（= *at first*）

40. (**A**) (A) *needy*〔'nidɪ〕*adj.* 窮困的　　(B) greedy〔'gridɪ〕*adj.* 貪婪的
　　　　　(C) handy〔'hændɪ〕*adj.* 方便的　　(D) mighty〔'maɪtɪ〕*adj.* 強有力的

Ⅳ、閱讀測驗：30 %

第一篇（共 3 題）

　　Seas, lakes and rivers are *in some places* alive with noise. Underwater creatures have evolved remarkable ways *of producing sound to communicate with each other*, ***and*** to warn off predators *that* feed on them. Dr. Patek reported ***that*** the lobster produces sound in a way similar to a violinist drawing a bow across strings. It rubs its antennae *against the hard plates under its eyes to produce a scary sound*. It is the *first* known underwater creature *to create such a novel underwater sound*.

　　在某些地方，海洋，湖泊和河流充滿著聲音。水底生物已經進化出一種很棒的方式，牠們能發出聲音，來互相溝通，並且警告以牠們為食的掠食者不得靠近。根據派德克博士的報告指出，龍蝦發出聲音的方式，和小提琴家在弦上拉琴的方式很相似。龍蝦會對著牠眼睛下面堅硬的甲殼，磨擦牠的觸角，產生可怕的聲音。這是第一個為人們所知，會產生如此新奇的水底聲音的水底生物。

alive〔əˈlaɪv〕adj. 充滿的 <with>
underwater〔ˈʌndəˌwɔtə〕adj. 水底的　　creature〔ˈkritʃə〕n. 生物
evolve〔ɪˈvɑlv〕v. 進化形成
remarkable〔rɪˈmɑrkəbl̩〕adj. 卓越的
produce〔prəˈdjus〕v. 製造；產生　　**warn off** 警告～不得靠近
predator〔ˈprɛdətə〕n. 掠食者　　**feed on** 以～為食（= live on）
lobster〔ˈlɑbstə〕n. 龍蝦　　**be similar to** 和～類似
violinist〔ˌvaɪəˈlɪnɪst〕n. 小提琴家　　bow〔bo〕n. 弓
draw a bow 拉弓　　string〔strɪŋ〕n. 弦
rub〔rʌb〕v. 磨擦　　antenna〔ænˈtɛnə〕n. 觸角（複數是 antennae）
plate〔plet〕n.〔動〕（爬蟲類、魚類的）甲；殼
scary〔ˈskɛrɪ〕adj. 可怕的　　novel〔ˈnɑvl̩〕adj. 新奇的

Dr. Patek studied the sound production *of the lobster* by *using an underwater microphone.* He found *that* lobsters *can hear sound only within a short distance,* **and** *therefore they produce the sound not for communication, but rather for warning off predators.*

　　派德克博士使用一支水底麥克風，研究龍蝦如何發出聲音。他發現龍蝦只有在近距離才聽得到聲音，所以牠們發出聲音，不是為了要溝通，而是為了警告掠食者不要靠近。

production〔prəˈdʌkʃən〕n. 產生
microphone〔ˈmaɪkrəˌfon〕n. 麥克風
distance〔ˈdɪstəns〕n. 距離　　rather〔ˈræðə〕adv. 更確切地說

The sound *they produce* is *very* important *during the period* **when** *lobsters*

shed their hard shells in order to grow. At that time, they become *very* weak

and cannot defend themselves. Lobsters shed shells *up to 25 times in the first*

five years of their life **and** *then once every year afterwards. During this period*

they must rely on their noisy sound *to scare away such predators as sharks.*

在龍蝦要脫殼的生長期間，牠們所發出的這種聲音是非常重要的。在那個時候，牠們變得非常虛弱，無法保衛牠們自己。龍蝦在牠們生命週期的前五年脫殼高達二十五次，之後就每年一次。在這段期間，牠們必須依賴牠們吵雜的聲音，以嚇走像鯊魚之類的掠食者。

period〔'pɪrɪəd〕*n.* 期間　　shed〔ʃɛd〕*v.* 脫（殼）
shell〔ʃɛl〕*n.* 殼　　defend〔dɪ'fɛnd〕*v.* 保衛
up to 高達　　afterwards〔'æftəwədz〕*adv.* 之後
rely on 依賴（＝*depend on*＝*count on*）
scare away 嚇走（＝*frighten away*）　　shark〔ʃɑrk〕*n.* 鯊魚

41.(**C**) 根據本文，龍蝦發出聲音的方式＿＿＿＿＿＿。
　　　(A) 和其他的水底生物很類似　(B) 人類還不知道
　　　(C) 在水底生物中是很獨特的　(D) 和小丑拉小提琴沒有什麼不同

unique〔ju'nik〕*adj.* 獨特的　　clown〔klaʊn〕*n.* 小丑
play the violin 拉小提琴

42.(**D**) 龍蝦發出聲音是為了＿＿＿＿＿＿。
　　　(A) 炫耀牠的音樂　　　　　(B) 聯絡其他的龍蝦
　　　(C) 追求牠的伴侶　　　　　(D) 嚇走牠的敵人

show off 炫耀　　contact〔kɑn'tækt〕*v.* 聯絡
court〔kort〕*v.* 追求；求愛　　mate〔met〕*n.* 伴侶
frighten away 嚇走　　enemy〔'ɛnəmɪ〕*n.* 敵人

43.(**B**) 根據本文，龍蝦＿＿＿＿＿＿。
　　　(A) 每年脫殼一次　　　　　(B) 第六年脫殼一次
　　　(C) 每年脫殼五次　　　　　(D) 每年脫殼二十五次

第二篇

Nancy Neumann isn't your typical teacher. Her students *occasionally* have to dash off *from their schools in the middle of an exam,* **and** her classroom is *sometimes* the backseat *of a limousine.*

南西‧諾伊曼不是一般人心目中典型的老師。有時候，她的學生必須在考試考到一半，急忙離開學校，而有時候，她的教室是在豪華大轎車的後座。

typical (ˈtɪpɪkḷ) *adj.* 典型的　　occasionally (əˈkeʒənḷɪ) *adv.* 偶爾
dash off 急忙地離開　　backseat (ˈbæksit) *n.* 後座
limousine (ˈlɪməˌzin) *n.* 豪華大轎車

Neumann is a movie studio teacher, *the person* **who** *tutors child actors in films, commercials, and television shows.* She can be called to teach everything *from preschool reading to advanced mathematics.* **While** *the cameras roll on the set nearby,* she has helped her students to analyze the chemical properties *of gasoline,* write papers *on Pearl Harbor,* **and** do a biology lab report.

諾伊曼是一位電影製片廠的老師，也就是要負責指導電影、電視廣告及電視節目中的童星。她可能必須被叫去指導學齡前的閱讀到高深的數學。當攝影機在片場附近拍攝時，她已經幫忙她的學生分析汽油的化學特性，寫關於珍珠港的報告，以及做一份生物實驗室的報告。

studio (ˈstjudɪˌo) *n.* 製片廠　　tutor (ˈtjutɚ) *v.* 指導
child actor 童星　　film (fɪlm) *n.* 電影
commercial (kəˈmɝʃəl) *n.* (電視、廣播的) 商業廣告
preschool (ˈpriˈskul) *adj.* 學齡前的
advanced (ədˈvænst) *adj.* 高深的　　camera (ˈkæmərə) *n.* 攝影機
roll (rol) *v.* 運轉　　set (sɛt) *n.* 攝影場；片場
analyze (ˈænḷˌaɪz) *v.* 分析　　chemical (ˈkɛmɪkḷ) *adj.* 化學的
property (ˈprɑpɚtɪ) *n.* 特性　　gasoline (ˈgæsḷˌin) *n.* 汽油
Pearl Harbor 珍珠港　　biology (baɪˈɑlədʒɪ) *n.* 生物

Neumann is required to spend three hours *per day with each student in her care*, ***though*** *lessons are often divided into 20-minute classes*. ***And*** she *usually* handles more than one student *a day*. *Paid a daily rate **that** ranges from $160 to $300,* Neumann works *off and on*, ***and*** is *often* told to report *for teaching duty with less than 24 hours' notice*. ***But*** Neumann says *she prefers this job for its variety **and** wouldn't enjoy working in a more traditional classroom*.

諾伊曼被要求一天要花三個小時照顧一個學生，雖然課程常常被分成好幾堂二十分鐘的課程。而且她一天通常要應付不只一個學生。她斷斷續續地工作，每天的薪水從一百六十元到三百元不等，她還常常在不到二十四小時之前被通知，要上班教課。但是諾伊曼說她偏好這個工作，因為它有變化，比較不喜歡在一個比較傳統的教室裡工作。

require〔rɪ'kwaɪr〕*v.* 要求　　***in one's care*** 託付給某人
divide〔də'vaɪd〕*v.* 分割＜*into*＞
handle〔'hændl〕*v.* 應付；處理　　daily〔'delɪ〕*adj.* 每天的
rate〔ret〕*n.* 價格　　range〔rendʒ〕*v.* 範圍（包括）
range from A to B 範圍從 A 到 B 都有
off and on 斷斷續續地（＝*on and off*）
report for duty 報到上班　　notice〔'notɪs〕*n.* 通知
variety〔və'raɪətɪ〕*n.* 變化　　traditional〔trə'dɪʃən̩〕*adj.* 傳統的

Neumann is *also* responsible for her students' physical safety ***and*** moral welfare. ***Because*** *child actors are only permitted to work a certain number of hours per day*, she has to remove her students *from the set **even if** the shooting schedule runs late*.

　　諾伊曼也負責她學生的人身安全和心靈健康。因為童星一天能工作的時數是有限的，所以即使拍攝的進度落後，她也必須帶她的學生離開片場。

> responsible〔rɪ'spɑnsəbl̩〕*adj.* 負責的
> **be responsible for** 為～負責
> physical〔'fɪzɪkl̩〕*adj.* 身體的
> moral〔'mɔrəl〕*adj.* 精神的；道德的
> welfare〔'wɛl,fɛr〕*n.* 安康；福祉　　**moral welfare** 心靈健康
> permit〔pɚ'mɪt〕*v.* 允許　　certain〔'sɝtn̩〕*adj.* 特定的
> remove〔rɪ'muv〕*v.* 帶走　　shoot〔ʃut〕*v.* 拍攝
> schedule〔'skɛdʒul〕*n.* 時間（表）；計畫（表）
> run〔rʌn〕*v.* 變得（＝ *become*）

44.（**C**）諾伊曼小姐喜歡她的工作是因為＿＿＿＿＿＿。
　　(A) 她沒辦法在一般的學校找到工作
　　(B) 她一天只教三個小時
　　(C) 她從來不認為她的工作無聊
　　(D) 她只需要教科學

45.（**D**）諾伊曼小姐的學生有時候被准許從學校離開是因為＿＿＿＿＿＿。
　　(A) 他們需要去看電影　　　　(B) 教室不安全
　　(C) 他們只能上學三個小時　　(D) 他們需要去工作
　　excuse〔ɪk'skjuz〕*v.* 准許～離開

46.（**A**）諾伊曼小姐不是典型的老師，是因為以下的理由除了＿＿＿＿＿＿。
　　(A) 不注意學生的健康　　　　(B) 教學時間不規律
　　(C) 沒有一定的教室　　　　　(D) 提供許多不同的課程
　　well-being〔'wɛl'biɪŋ〕*n.* 健康；福祉
　　irregular〔ɪ'rɛgjələ〕*adj.* 不規則的
　　definite〔'dɛfənɪt〕*adj.* 一定的

第三篇（共4題）

Medical researchers *in the United States* say they have *recently* found *that* the sounds and sights *of nature* can help control pain *when* patients go through unpleasant procedures. They used recordings *of gurgling streams* **and** pictures *of beautiful scenery* to distract the patients *during and after treatment.*

美國的醫學研究人員聲稱，他們最近發現，自然界的聲音和景象，有助於抑制病人接受痛苦療程時，所產生的疼痛。他們使用潺潺流水聲的錄音，和優美風景的圖片，來轉移病人在治療期間及治療後的注意力。

researcher〔ri'sɜtʃə〕n. 研究人員　　sight〔saɪt〕n. 景象
go through 經歷　　unpleasant〔ʌn'plɛznt〕adj. 不愉快的
procedure〔prə'sidʒə〕n. 程序　　recording〔rɪ'kɔrdɪŋ〕n. 錄音
gurgling〔'gɜglɪŋ〕adj.（水）潺潺而流的
stream〔strim〕n. 溪流　　scenery〔'sInərɪ〕n. 風景
distract〔dɪ'strækt〕v. 使分心；使轉移注意力
treatment〔'tritmənt〕n. 治療

Lung examination is an unpleasant procedure. *In carrying out this procedure*, tubes should be inserted *through the nose or mouth* *to see the lungs.* **While** patients receive some medication *to prevent pain*, they remain conscious *throughout the procedure.* Researchers *at Johns Hopkins University*, *in addition to giving patients pain-relieving medicine*, played the sounds *of gurgling streams* *during the three-hour examination.* The researchers *also* displayed *on walls* large pictures [*of a forest* *with a river running through it* **and** *mountains in the distance.*] *Compared to another group* [*of 39 similar patients*, *who had only the usual painkillers*,] the trial group was *much* more likely to have good control *of their pain.*

　　肺部檢查是個痛苦的過程。在進行這項檢查時，導管必須鼻子或嘴巴插入，以便觀察肺部。雖然病人會服用藥物來避免疼痛，但他們在整個檢查過程中仍然是清醒的。約翰霍普金斯大學的研究人員，除了給病人服用止痛藥外，也在為時三小時的檢查過程中，播放潺潺的流水聲。研究人員還在牆壁上展示大型的圖片，圖片中有河流蜿蜒而過的森林，遠方有群山矗立。和另一組三十九名情況類似，但只服用一般止痛藥的病人比起來，這個試驗組更能有效地抑制疼痛。

lung〔 lʌŋ 〕n. 肺　　　　**carry out** 執行

tube〔 tjub 〕n. 管子　　　insert〔 ɪn'sɝt 〕v. 插入

medication〔,mɛdɪ'keʃən〕n. 藥物（= *medicine*）

prevent〔 prɪ'vɛnt 〕v. 防止　　conscious〔'kɑnʃəs〕adj. 清醒的

in addition to 除了～之外（= *besides*）

pain-relieving〔'pen,rɪ'livɪŋ 〕adj. 減輕痛苦的

pain-relieving medicine 止痛藥（= painkiller〔'pen,kɪlɚ 〕）

display〔 dɪ'sple 〕v. 展示　　**run through** 流過

in the distance 在遠方　　compare〔 kəm'pɛr 〕v. 比較

trial〔'traɪəl 〕n. 試驗　　　**trial group** 試驗組

be likely to + V. 可能

The benefits *of distraction techniques* had long been recognized *before* doctors discovered them. *For example*, many women use breathing and visualization techniques [*to distract them from the pain* **while** giving birth to babies,] **and** meditation methods are *widely* practiced *in coping with anxiety and stress.*

　　這種注意力轉移法的好處，在醫生發現之前，早已被認定。舉例來說，許多婦女使用呼吸調節法及視覺法，來轉移生產時的痛苦，而冥想則廣泛被運用在應付焦慮及壓力方面。

benefit（'bɛnəfɪt）*n.* 好處　　distraction（dɪ'strækʃən）*n.* 分心

technique（tɛk'nik）*n.* 方法

recognize（'rɛkəg,naɪz）*v.* 認出；承認　　breathing（'briðɪŋ）*n.* 呼吸

visualization（,vɪʒʊəlaɪ'zeʃən）*n.* 視覺化

give birth to 生（孩子）　　meditation（,mɛdə'teʃən）*n.* 冥想

practice（'præktɪs）*v.* 運用　　***cope with*** 應付（＝*deal with*）

anxiety（æŋ'zaɪətɪ）*n.* 焦慮　　stress（strɛs）*n.* 壓力

Earlier research has *also* found ***that*** *planting trees near patients' windows*

can speed up recovery rates. This suggests ***that*** *a small investment in very*

simple environmental improvements could produce remarkable benefits.

　　早期的研究還發現，在病人的窗前種樹，可以加快病人康復的速度。而這也顯示，花點小錢稍微改善環境，可以產生驚人的效果。

research（'risɝtʃ）*n.* 研究　　plant（plænt）*v.* 種植

speed up 加速　　recovery（rɪ'kʌvərɪ）*n.* 康復

rate（ret）*n.* 速度　　suggest（sə'dʒɛst）*v.* 顯示（＝*show*）

investment（ɪn'vɛstmənt）*n.* 投資

environmental（ɪn,vaɪrən'mɛntl̩）*adj.* 環境的

improvement（ɪm'pruvmənt）*n.* 改善

remarkable（rɪ'mɑrkəbl̩）*adj.* 驚人的

47. (**A**) 利用自然界的聲音和美景於醫學治療上，是為了 ＿＿＿＿＿＿。

　　(A) 轉移病人對疼痛的注意

　　(B) 宣傳環保的概念

　　(C) 延長醫療時間

　　(D) 讓醫生心情更愉快

shift（ʃɪft）*v.* 轉移　　attention（ə'tɛnʃən）*n.* 注意力

publicize（'pʌblɪ,saɪz）*v.* 宣傳　　lengthen（'lɛŋθən）*v.* 延長

48.(**B**) 只服用止痛藥,而沒有接受自然聲音及景象治療的這組病人,＿＿＿＿。

(A) 比試驗組更能抑制疼痛

(B) 在抑制疼痛上,並沒有試驗組來得有效

(C) 感到更平靜,因爲他們受到的干擾比較少

(D) 發現止痛藥相當有效

peaceful (ˈpisfəl) *adj.* 平靜的　　disturbed (dɪˈstɜbd) *adj.* 受到干擾的
effective (ɪˈfɛktɪv) *adj.* 有效的

49.(**D**) 注意力轉移法長久以來被以下人士所使用,除了＿＿＿＿＿＿。

(A) 一些生產的婦女　　　　　(B) 想減少壓力的人

(C) 想減輕焦慮的人　　　　　(D) 幫病人檢查肺部的醫生

reduce (rɪˈdjus) *v.* 減少　　relieve (rɪˈliv) *v.* 減輕
examine (ɪɡˈzæmɪn) *v.* 檢查

50.(**C**) 根據本文,在病人的窗外種樹＿＿＿＿＿。

(A) 會遮住病人的視野　　　　(B) 對於讓病房蔭涼是很有用的

(C) 有助於病人的健康　　　　(D) 對於環境上的投資是不夠的

limit (ˈlɪmɪt) *v.* 限制　　shade (ʃed) *v.* 遮蔭
beneficial (ˌbɛnəˈfɪʃəl) *adj.* 有益的　　sufficient (səˈfɪʃənt) *adj.* 足夠的

第四篇(共 5 題)

Scientists have imagined *for decades* about a future *when robots will take over daily household chores **and** give us more leisure time.* Yet the types *of robots introduced to the market so far* have been *more* for entertainment *than for practical uses.*

　　科學家們數十年來一直在想像,未來機器人將可接管日常家務事,給我們更多閒暇時間。然而,到目前爲止,被引進市面上的機器人種類,娛樂用途多於實際用途。

decade〔'dɛked〕*n.* 十年　　robot〔'robət〕*n.* 機器人

take over 接管　　household〔'haʊsˌhold〕*adj.* 家庭的

chores〔tʃɔrz〕*n. pl.* 瑣事；雜事　　leisure〔'liʒɚ〕*n.* 閒暇

entertainment〔ˌɛntɚ'tenmənt〕*n.* 娛樂

practical〔'præktɪkl̩〕*adj.* 實際的

But, the consumer market *for robots* appears to be changing *for the better,* ***though*** *it's a slow change at best.* Thanks to the lower costs **and** *the improved performance of mass-produced computers,* some small companies are starting to offer consumer robots *that can clean and maintain a household.* The problem is ***that*** *these products can attract only those consumers **who** are already crazy about robots,* ***so*** the market remains too small. ***And*** *as far as performance and price are concerned,* they're *still* no match for conventional appliances.

但是，機器人的消費市場似乎越來越看好，雖然這充其量是個緩慢的轉變。由於大量生產的電腦，成本較低、性能也有所改善，有些小型公司正開始供應消費者，能夠打掃、維護家庭的機器人。問題在於，這些產品只能吸引那些，已經對機器人著迷的消費者，所以市場仍然太小了。而且，就性能和價格而言，它們還比不上傳統的家電用品。

appear〔ə'pɪr〕*v.* 似乎（＝*seem*）　　***at best*** 充其量

performance〔pɚ'fɔrməns〕*n.* 表現；性能

mass-produced〔'mæsprə'djust〕*adj.* 大量生產的

consumer robot 消費者可購買使用的機器人（非專業、工廠使用的用途）

maintain〔men'ten〕*v.* 維持　　***as far as～is concerned*** 就～而言

match〔mætʃ〕*n.* 對手　　***be no match for*** 不是對手；比不上

conventional〔kən'vɛnʃənl̩〕*adj.* 傳統的

appliance〔ə'plaɪəns〕*n.* 家電用品

One company *that has enjoyed some early success* is Friendly Robotics. *Last year*, this company began selling a lawn-mowing robot *called the Robomower*. The battery-powered device does its job *by moving randomly over the lawn*. It takes a lot longer *than a conventional lawnmower* to get the job done, *but* *at least* it frees weekends *for its owner*. The Robomower stays *within the lawn's boundary* [*by sensing a wire* *installed a few inches underground near the lawn's edge*.] The wire gives off a low-power radio signal, *and* the sensors *on the robot* pick up the signal *and* command the robot *to return to the lawn*.

已享有初期成功的公司之一是友善機器人公司。去年,這家公司開始銷售一款會割草的機器人,稱為「割草機器人」。這款裝置以電池為動力,會在草坪上隨意移動,進行割草的工作。它完成工作所需的時間,比傳統的割草機要長很多,但至少能使主人空出週末的時間。「割草機器人」能保持在草坪的範圍裡,是藉著感應安裝在草坪四周地下幾英吋的電線。這條電線會發出低量的無線電信號,而機器人的感應器會接收這個信號,並命令機器人回到草坪上。

robotics〔roˋbɑtɪks〕n. 機器人學;在此為公司名稱
lawn〔lɔn〕n. 草坪   mow〔mo〕v. 割(草)
mower〔ˋmoɚ〕n. 割草機   battery〔ˋbætərɪ〕n. 電池
power〔ˋpauɚ〕n. 電力;動力   v. 以~為動力
device〔dɪˋvaɪs〕n. 裝置   randomly〔ˋrændəmlɪ〕adv. 隨意地
boundary〔ˋbaundərɪ〕n. 界限;範圍   sense〔sɛns〕v. 感應
wire〔waɪr〕n. 電線   install〔ɪnˋstɔl〕v. 安裝
underground〔͵ʌndɚˋgraund〕adv. 在地下   edge〔ɛdʒ〕n. 邊緣
give off 發出   signal〔ˋsɪgn̩〕n. 信號
sensor〔ˋsɛnsɚ〕n. 感應器   *pick up* 接收(= *receive*)
command〔kəˋmænd〕v. 命令

Some other companies are *also* promoting their robots *for different purposes*. Probotics is selling its vacuum-cleaner robots. *And* iRobot intends to start selling a home-security robot *next year for about the cost of a notebook computer*.

其他有些公司，也在促銷不同用途的機器人。普羅機器人公司（Probotics）正在銷售他們的吸塵器機器人。而 iRobot 公司也打算，明年開始銷售一款住家保全機器人，價格和一台筆記型電腦差不多。

promote〔prə'mot〕v. 促銷　　purpose〔'pɝpəs〕n. 用途
vacuum〔'vækjuəm〕n. 眞空　　***vacuum cleaner*** 吸塵器
security〔sɪ'kjurətɪ〕n. 安全；保全
notebook computer 筆記型電腦

However, their appeal *so far* has been limited *to robot enthusiasts and wealthy consumers*. Experts have noted *that cheaper, conventional lawnmowers operated by humans still achieve better results than robots, **and** vacuum-cleaner robots tend to have trouble moving around furniture, cats and stairways*. Even iRobot acknowledges ***that** a home-security robot can't take the place of a household alarm system*.

然而，它們的吸引力，至今只侷限於機器人迷和有錢的消費者。專家也注意到，由人操作的、比較便宜的傳統割草機，仍然比機器人更好用，而吸塵器機器人在傢俱、貓咪，和樓梯四周移動常會有困難。甚至連 iRobot 公司都承認，住家保全機器人還是不能取代家庭的警報系統。

appeal〔ə'pil〕n. 吸引力　　enthusiast〔ɪn'θjuzɪ,æst〕n. 狂熱者
note〔not〕v. 注意到　　operate〔'ɑpə,ret〕v. 操作
achieve〔ə'tʃiv〕v. 達到　　***tend to + V.*** 容易；傾向於
stairway〔'stɛr,we〕n. 樓梯　　acknowledge〔ək'nɑlɪdʒ〕v. 承認
take the place of 取代（= *replace*）　　alarm〔ə'lɑrm〕n. 警報

51. (**A**)　目前市面上大部分的機器人主要都是用來 ＿＿＿＿＿＿。

(A) 提供人們娛樂　　　　　　(B) 作家事

(C) 節省我們的時間　　　　　(D) 減少生活費

expense〔ɪk'spɛns〕*n.* 費用　　***living expenses*** 生活費

52. (**D**)　有些公司已開始生產機器人來做家事，這是由於 ＿＿＿＿＿＿。

(A) 市場競爭很激烈　　　　　(B) 顧客人數快速增加

(C) 使用者反應熱烈　　　　　(D) 電腦比較便宜，而且更有效率

keen〔kin〕*adj.* 激烈的　　competition〔ˌkɑmpə'tɪʃən〕*n.* 競爭

enthusiastic〔ɪnˌθjuzɪ'æstɪk〕*adj.* 熱心的；熱烈的

response〔rɪ'spɑns〕*n.* 反應

53. (**B**)　家用機器人仍然不如傳統的家電用品，這是因為 ＿＿＿＿＿＿。

(A) 它們太難操作

(B) 它們既不便宜又沒有效率

(C) 它們的外型不吸引人

(D) 它們製造的噪音會打擾到鄰居

inferior〔ɪn'fɪrɪɚ〕*adj.* 較差的 < to >　　shape〔ʃep〕*n.* 外型

disturb〔dɪ'stɝb〕*v.* 打擾

54. (**C**)　割草機器人的好處之一是 ＿＿＿＿＿＿。

(A) 它使用電池，所以節省能源

(B) 它比傳統的割草機更有效率

(C) 它讓主人能夠享受週末

(D) 它可以從草坪的一邊直直走到另一邊

energy〔'ɛnɚdʒɪ〕*n.* 能源　　straight〔stret〕*adv.* 直地

55. (**B**)　以機器人的科技目前狀態看來，科學家對於機器人的夢想 ＿＿＿＿＿＿。

(A) 已經吸引了很多人　　　　(B) 只實現了一部分

(C) 完全無法實現　　　　　　(D) 最後終於實現

given〔'gɪvən〕*prep.* 假設有　　present〔'prɛznt〕*adj.* 目前的

state〔stet〕*n.* 狀態　　***appeal to*** 吸引（＝*attract*）

partially〔'pɑrʃəlɪ〕*adv.* 部分地　　***fail to*** ＋ *V.* 無法

materialize〔mə'tɪrɪəlˌaɪz〕*v.* 實現（＝*realize*）

第二部分：非選擇題

I、中譯英：**10％**

1. 昨天晚上我感覺有點不舒服。

   I felt a little (bit) uncomfortable last night.

2. 我媽媽要我去看中醫師。

   My mother $\left\{ \begin{array}{l} \text{wanted} \\ \text{asked} \end{array} \right\}$ me to $\left\{ \begin{array}{l} \text{go to / go see} \\ \text{see / visit} \\ \text{consult} \end{array} \right\}$ a Chinese $\left\{ \begin{array}{l} \text{herbalist.} \\ \text{doctor.} \end{array} \right\}$

3. 她說中藥比西藥自然。

   She said (that) Chinese medicine was more natural than western medicine.

4. 我生病的時候通常都會去看西醫。

   I usually $\left\{ \begin{array}{l} \text{go to / go see} \\ \text{see / visit} \\ \text{consult} \end{array} \right\}$ a (western) doctor when I $\left\{ \begin{array}{l} \text{feel} \\ \text{am} \end{array} \right\}$ $\left\{ \begin{array}{l} \text{sick.} \\ \text{ill.} \end{array} \right\}$

5. 但是現在我想我有另外的選擇了。

   But now I think (that) I have $\left\{ \begin{array}{l} \text{another choice.} \\ \text{an alternative.} \end{array} \right\}$

II、作文範例：**20％**

My Favorite Retreat

Everyone has his or her favorite place to hide, and I am no exception. The place I consider to be my favorite retreat is my room. It is a miniature wonderland where I can go to get away from it all.

My room is not lavishly furnished. In fact, it is furnished with a bed, desk, computer and bookshelf, just like any teenager's room. My bookshelf is heavily laden with history books and English novels. Whenever I feel down or discouraged, I would go into my room to read about the exploits of some great people and how they overcame the obstacles. It makes me realize that my troubles are so minute compared to theirs. I can also surf the Internet or play computer games all in the comfort of my own room.

When I am locked away in my room, I can be left alone to think in peace. There, I can study, play or daydream. I can really rediscover myself there. That is why my room is my favorite retreat.

retreat〔rɪˈtrit〕n. 僻靜處所　　***be no exception*** 不例外
miniature〔ˈmɪnɪətʃɚ〕adj. 縮小的
wonderland〔ˈwʌndɚ͵lænd〕n. 仙境　　***get away from*** 逃避
lavishly〔ˈlævɪʃlɪ〕adv. 豪華地
furnish〔ˈfɝnɪʃ〕v. 給（房子、房間）裝置（家具等）
bookshelf〔ˈbʊk͵ʃɛlf〕n. 書櫃
be laden with 充滿（ = ***be full of*** ）
down〔daʊn〕adj. 情緒低落的
exploit〔ˈɛksplɔɪt〕n. 英勇事蹟　　obstacle〔ˈɑbstəkl̩〕n. 障礙
minute〔maɪˈnjut〕adj. 微小的
compare〔kəmˈpɛr〕v. 比較< *to* >
surf the Internet 上網（ = ***go to the Internet*** ）
lock away 把…鎖藏起來　　***in peace*** 平靜地
daydream〔ˈde͵drim〕v. 做白日夢
rediscover〔͵ridɪˈskʌvɚ〕v. 再發現

心得筆記欄

八十九學年度大學聯考英文分數人數統計表

分數	第一類組	第二類組	第三類組	第四類組	分數	第一類組	第二類組	第三類組	第四類組
100	0	0	0	0	50	30560	21434	14509	14560
99	0	0	0	0	49	31765	22193	14955	15008
98	0	0	0	0	48	32978	22955	15423	15477
97	0	1	1	1	47	34185	23733	15890	15945
96	0	2	2	2	46	35343	24460	16305	16364
95	3	3	2	2	45	36545	25226	16773	16834
94	9	6	5	5	44	37826	25964	17212	17275
93	15	17	15	15	43	39077	26660	17657	17722
92	32	35	32	32	42	40256	27402	18101	18171
91	54	53	48	48	41	41537	28186	18572	18647
90	94	92	78	78	40	42721	28867	18987	19067
89	143	135	112	112	39	43917	29622	19440	19521
88	234	223	184	185	38	45144	30338	19880	19963
87	360	326	268	269	37	46346	31066	20322	20409
86	512	466	382	383	36	47525	31764	20752	20842
85	697	658	541	542	35	48716	32474	21169	21263
84	920	867	713	714	34	49841	33159	21599	21698
83	1200	1103	895	896	33	50967	33828	21973	22076
82	1538	1384	1129	1131	32	52121	34537	22390	22500
81	1959	1714	1387	1391	31	53288	35189	22790	22902
80	2410	2059	1647	1652	30	54455	35891	23218	23337
79	2838	2412	1920	1925	29	55586	36555	23604	23723
78	3373	2844	2247	2252	28	56698	37157	23976	24097
77	3940	3267	2568	2573	27	57838	37766	24349	24472
76	4554	3701	2906	2914	26	58909	38378	24717	24844
75	5203	4209	3274	3284	25	59977	38991	25074	25206
74	5920	4745	3672	3684	24	61064	39561	25430	25564
73	6705	5283	4067	4081	23	62048	40130	25763	25899
72	7427	5868	4483	4499	22	63132	40679	26121	26259
71	8268	6444	4862	4879	21	64153	41186	26437	26579
70	9153	7070	5305	5322	20	65214	41706	26758	26906
69	10024	7725	5782	5802	19	66223	42241	27067	27218
68	10930	8403	6258	6279	18	67175	42773	27382	27537
67	11897	9074	6708	6729	17	68066	43214	27659	27819
66	12812	9726	7137	7159	16	69033	43674	27945	28107
65	13774	10456	7612	7638	15	69984	44155	28236	28407
64	14754	11138	8077	8104	14	70938	44575	28501	28678
63	15783	11856	8540	8569	13	71772	44990	28743	28926
62	16873	12540	8990	9022	12	72607	45399	28977	29164
61	17879	13255	9441	9474	11	73520	45817	29221	29414
60	19058	13958	9875	9908	10	74359	46224	29451	29655
59	20094	14691	10344	10378	9	75085	46531	29608	29815
58	21186	15423	10812	10846	8	75897	46890	29813	30039
57	22362	16167	11286	11321	7	76640	47233	30005	30246
56	23457	16949	11766	11802	6	77463	47598	30223	30472
55	24630	17706	12227	12264	5	78031	47856	30383	30640
54	25805	18481	12715	12756	4	78740	48150	30540	30805
53	26992	19233	13168	13211	3	79467	48447	30702	30980
52	28180	19939	13617	13663	2	80122	48754	30872	31162
51	29375	20681	14066	14114	1	80561	48933	30972	31266
					0	82392	49798	31395	31739

八十九學年度大學暨獨立學院入學考試
英　文　試　題

第一部分：單一選擇題

以下 1~40 題，每題 1 分，41~55 題，每題 2 分。請由每題 4 個備選項中選出一個
最適當者，標示在「**答案卡**」上。每答錯一題倒扣題分的 ⅓，不答不給分。

I、**對話（共 5 分）：**

1. **Tom** : Excuse me, but I can't seem to find my luggage.
   Clerk : _____
   Tom : Flight 007, North Western Airlines.
   (A) When did you arrive, Sir?
   (B) How could I help you, Sir?
   (C) What color is your luggage, Sir?
   (D) Which flight were you on, Sir?

2. **Bill** : I can't believe it! I haven't seen you for years.
   Mike : Yeah, what have you been up to?
   Bill : _____ How about you?
   Mike : I'm now a free-lance writer.
   (A) I'm going to buy some groceries.
   (B) I'm going to get married in two weeks.
   (C) I've been working for a trading company.
   (D) It's good to see you.

3. **Nancy** : Hello, I'd like to know the number for Jane Isateck.
   Operator : _____
   Nancy : Sure, Isateck. I as in Irene, S as in Susan, A as in Adam,
   T as in Tom, E as in Eric, C as in Charles, K as in Karen.
   Operator : Thank you, one moment please.... The number is 883-4733.
   (A) What's your last name?
   (B) Could you repeat the last name, please?
   (C) I don't know how to spell your last name.
   (D) It's an unusual name, isn't it?

4. **Clerk** : How are the shoes?
   Mary : They're too loose. I need one size smaller.
   Clerk : ＿＿＿＿＿＿＿＿＿＿＿
   Mary : O.K.
   Clerk : I'm sorry, but your size is sold out.
   (A) Let me check if we have that size available.
   (B) But they look so nice on you.
   (C) I don't think we have anything smaller.
   (D) Why don't you try them on first?

5. **Carol** : Take a look at that dress. It's gorgeous.
   Judy : ＿＿＿＿＿＿＿＿＿＿＿
   Carol : Oh my! I didn't notice it! That's too much!
   (A) Yeah, it's gorgeous and the price is good, too.
   (B) Yeah, but look at the price! NT$50,000!
   (C) Yeah, it's pretty but it's not my style.
   (D) Yeah, it's lovely. You should buy it.

II、詞彙及慣用語（共 15 分）：

6. Although Martha had been away from home for a long time, when she came near her house, everything suddenly became ＿＿＿＿＿＿＿＿.
   (A) functional　　(B) impulsive　　(C) emotional　　(D) familiar

7. It was obvious that this young artist's latest work was ＿＿＿＿＿＿＿ much better than any other work in the exhibition.
   (A) definitely　　(B) optionally　　(C) occasionally　　(D) initially

8. Since the contestants were all very good, the competition for the first prize was ＿＿＿＿＿＿＿.
   (A) sincere　　(B) fierce　　(C) radiant　　(D) efficient

9. The company decided to put the plan into operation because it was the most ＿＿＿＿＿＿ one.
   (A) addictive　　(B) likable　　(C) pleasant　　(D) feasible

10. The owner was demanding. He expected nothing but _____ from his employees.

    (A) laziness　　(B) impatience　(C) perfection　　(D) ignorance

11. The reason for designing the special bus lane is to _____ the traffic flow, not to slow it down.

    (A) accommodate　(B) discount　(C) facilitate　　(D) influence

12. In many novels and films, step-mothers are often _____ as wicked women.

    (A) stereotyped　　(B) isolated　(C) irritated　　(D) decorated

13. Among the high-risk group of heart disease are people with a _____ for fat-rich foods.

    (A) preference　　(B) reflection　(C) sympathy　　(D) frequency

14. There was no doubt that the candidate was popular, because he had won a _____ victory in the election.

    (A) helpless　　(B) landslide　(C) thoughtful　(D) permanent

15. Technological changes will _____ lead to a change in human relationships.

    (A) suspiciously　(B) generously　(C) earnestly　(D) inevitably

16. After a lengthy discussion, the experts finally _____ with suggestions for resolving the economic crisis.

    (A) set up　　(B) caught up　(C) came up　　(D) gave up

17. These batteries are not good. _____ they will last only for two months.

    (A) At best　　(B) In advance　(C) In contrast　(D) At least

18. The sale of the company's new product is overwhelmingly good. It has _____ two million dollars so far.

    (A) carried on　(B) kept up　(C) brought in　(D) consisted of

19. Einstein was considered one of the greatest scientists of the 20th century _____ his influence on the study of physics.

    (A) in exchange for (B) in spite of　(C) on behalf of　(D) in terms of

20. When the landlord opened the door, he looked me _____ before asking who I was.

(A) back and forth　(B) up and down　(C) to and fro　(D) off and on

III、綜合測驗（共 20 分）：

第一篇（共 10 題）

People have different ideas about what exactly is being on time and being late. These ideas also differ from ___(21)___ , and from country to country. ___(22)___ , in the United States, it is very important to be on time for ___(23)___ occasions. The only time it is socially ___(24)___ to be late is when going to a friend's party. A person usually tries to arrive about 5 minutes ___(25)___ the invitation time, so that the host would have a little extra time to prepare for the guests. This ___(26)___ being "fashionably late." Any time ___(27)___ than that is considered impolite, because it keeps the host and other guests ___(28)___ .

Being on time goes ___(29)___ ways. One should also not arrive early for a friend's party, because it would rush the host. ___(30)___ , when going to a doctor's appointment, it is usually good to arrive earlier than the appointment because there are usually forms that need to be filled out by the patient.

21. (A) head to toe　　　　　　(B) hour to hour
　　(C) top to bottom　　　　　(D) time to time

22. (A) For example　(B) In addition　(C) In case　(D) For good

23. (A) hardly any　(B) simply none　(C) almost all　(D) nearly every

24. (A) acceptable　(B) accessible　(C) attainable　(D) admirable

25. (A) while　(B) before　(C) after　(D) when

26. (A) called　(B) is called　(C) has called　(D) calls

27. (A) later　(B) sooner　(C) faster　(D) earlier

28. (A) to wait　(B) waiting　(C) to be waited　(D) have waited

29. (A) either　(B) neither　(C) each　(D) both

30. (A) Then　(B) And　(C) So　(D) However

第二篇（共 **10** 題）

　　When Jerry Siegel and Joseph Shuster were just teenagers they developed that heroic character known as Superman. ＿＿＿(31)＿＿＿ was a clever idea to create a person faster than a speeding bullet and ＿＿＿(32)＿＿＿ leap tall buildings in a single bound. Children ＿＿＿(33)＿＿＿ were fascinated by Superman and bought ＿＿＿(34)＿＿＿ of comic books with stories of his heroic acts. Soon other products ＿＿＿(35)＿＿＿ the Superman symbol hit the market, and ＿＿＿(36)＿＿＿ long before the superhero was the star of his own television show.

　　Superman's great popularity ＿＿＿(37)＿＿＿ his originators very rich, but it didn't. ＿＿＿(38)＿＿＿ Mr. Siegel and Mr. Shuster invented the superhero, it was the company they ＿＿＿(39)＿＿＿ for that actually made the money. The genius of the creators was not rewarded, and ＿＿＿(40)＿＿＿ most of their lives these two men made barely enough to survive.

31. (A) Such　　　　　(B) None　　　　(C) Either　　　　(D) It
32. (A) paid to　　　 (B) able to　　　(C) unlikely to　　(D) forced to
33. (A) somewhere　　 (B) nowhere　　 (C) everywhere　　 (D) wherever
34. (A) thousands of hundreds　　　　(B) hundreds of thousands
　　(C) hundreds and thousands　　　 (D) thousands and hundreds
35. (A) sending　　　 (B) buying　　　(C) asking　　　　(D) bearing
36. (A) it could be　 (B) it wasn't　 (C) it has been　 (D) it hasn't been
37. (A) should have made　　　　　　 (B) had made
　　(C) should make　　　　　　　　　(D) had been made
38. (A) Unless　　　　(B) Since　　　 (C) Although　　　 (D) Because
39. (A) looked　　　　(B) searched　　(C) waited　　　　(D) worked
40. (A) for　　　　　 (B) at　　　　　(C) on　　　　　　(D) about

IV、閱讀測驗（共 **30** 分）：
第一篇（共 **4** 題）

　　Human language is a living thing. Each language has its own biological system, which makes it different from all other languages. This system must constantly adjust to a new environment and new situations to survive and flourish.

When we think of human language this way, it is an easy step to see the words of a language as being like the cells of a living organism—they are constantly forming and dying and splitting into parts as time changes and the language adapts.

There are several specific processes by which new words are formed. Some words come into the language which sound like what they refer to. Words like *buzz* and *ding-dong* are good examples of this process.

Still another way in which new words are formed is to use the name of a person or a place closely associated with that word's meaning. The words *sandwich* and *hamburger* are examples of this word-formation process. The Earl of Sandwich, an English aristocrat, was so fond of gambling at cards that he hated to be interrupted by the necessity of eating. He thus invented a new way of eating while he continued his game at the gambling table. This quick and convenient dish is what we now call a sandwich—a piece of meat between two slices of bread. The hamburger became the best-known sandwich in the world after it was invented by a citizen of Hamburg in Germany.

As long as a language is alive, its cells will continue to change, forming new words and getting rid of the ones that no longer have any use.

41. The passage is mainly about
    (A) the biological system of a living organism.
    (B) the inventors of sandwich and hamburger.
    (C) the development of human cells.
    (D) the changes of a language.

42. A language is a living thing in many ways EXCEPT
    (A) it is similar to the biological system of a living organism.
    (B) it actually has many living cells that split and form constantly.
    (C) it must adjust to new environments to survive.
    (D) its old words die out while new words are constantly added.

43. The word *sandwich* came from
    (A) card games.　　　　　　　(B) a piece of meat.
    (C) a person's name.　　　　　(D) a place in England.

44. How many ways of word-formation are mentioned in the article?
    (A) Two.　　　(B) Three.　　　(C) Four.　　　(D) Five.

第二篇（共 4 題）

Tears are nature's way of making us feel more comfortable. When our eye is made uncomfortable by some small piece of pollution, or when we are peeling onions, or when we are exhausted and "red-eyed" from overwork and late hours, tears form in our eyes to clean and refresh them.

Tears are also a sign of strong emotion. We cry when we are sad and we cry when we are happy.

And tears seem to be uniquely human. We know that animals also experience emotion—fear, pleasure, loneliness—but they do not shed tears. From this, we can conclude that tears are closely related to the emotional and biological makeup of the human species.

Biologically speaking, tears are actually drops of saline fluid produced by a gland in the body. Because salt is an important component, tears may actually constitute the most conclusive evidence that the human animal is the end product of a long evolutionary process that began in the sea.

And it is clear that, in addition to the emotional benefits, the shedding of tears has a specific biological function as well. Through tears, we can eliminate from our body certain chemicals which build up in response to stress and create a chemical imbalance in the body. Crying actually makes us feel better by correcting that imbalance and making us feel good again. And thus the emotional and the biological functions of tears merge into one and make us even more "human" than we would otherwise be.

45. Which of the following is NOT true?
    (A) Tears are a sign of strong emotion.
    (B) Tears are produced by salt.
    (C) Shedding tears is a biological function.
    (D) Tears eliminate chemicals from our bodies.

46. According to the passage, human beings may have originated in
(A) the sea.　　　　　　　　(B) the salt.
(C) chemicals.　　　　　　　(D) animals.

47. Which of the following is NOT a function of tears?
(A) Biological.　　　　　　　(B) Emotional.
(C) Political.　　　　　　　　(D) Chemical.

48. According to the article, which of the following is unique to humans?
(A) The feeling of loneliness.　　(B) The state of feeling good.
(C) The ability to shed tears.　　(D) The feeling of fear.

第三篇（共 4 題）

A long time ago in India there lived a young couple. The young couple had wanted a child very much, and when they finally had a baby, they loved him with all their hearts. However, before the baby was one year old, he became sick and soon died. The young couple cried and cried and could not stop. They would not let anyone bury the child and asked everyone to help them find the medicine that would make their son come back to life again.

The people in the village did not know what to do. They thought the young couple had gone crazy over the death of the baby. The villagers were worried that the young couple would not be able to return to their old way of life if they continued to focus on the death of the baby. One day, a wise man from another village came to the young couple and told them that perhaps they could seek help from the Buddha.

The couple rushed to pay the Buddha a visit. After they explained their reason for visiting, the Buddha nodded and said, "I have what you are looking for. But the medicine is missing one ingredient." "What is the ingredient?" asked the couple anxiously, "We will find it for you!"

"All I need is a handful of mustard seeds," said the Buddha slowly, "but it must come from a family where no one has died. That means no child, no spouse, and no parent has died in the family." The young couple were so anxious to bring the baby back to life that they did not think about the Buddha's words, and set out to look for the mustard seeds. However, after months and months of searching, they came to realize that the Buddha's request was impossible to fulfill.

However, the young couple learned something important during their search for the mustard seeds. They saw that every family they visited had lost someone, be it a child, a parent, or a spouse. All of these families learned to go on with their lives after the loved one's death. The couple saw that death was a part of the life cycle, and as painful as it was for them, it was part of life. The families' stories and talks helped the young couple feel better, and they realized they were not alone. But most importantly, they learned that they could continue to live a normal life after the death of their child.

49. Why did the couple go to see the Buddha?
    (A) They wanted to have their dead child alive again.
    (B) They wanted to have another child.
    (C) They wanted the Buddha to bless the dead child.
    (D) They wanted the Buddha to help them bury the child.

50. The Buddha told the couple to find the mustard seeds from
    (A) families that had never had children.
    (B) families that had never lost a loved one.
    (C) families that had only one child.
    (D) families that were Buddhists.

51. The young couple were unable to find the mustard seeds because
    (A) there was a draught and mustard seeds were difficult to get.
    (B) the couple did not think much about the Buddha's words.
    (C) the searching for the ingredient took many months.
    (D) all of the families had experienced a loved one's death.

52. What is the moral of this story?
    (A) We should always come to the Buddha for help.
    (B) It is possible to bring a dead person back to life.
    (C) Death is natural and is part of our life cycle.
    (D) Happiness is the best medicine for sorrow.

第四篇（共 **3** 題）

> In time of silver rain
> The earth
> Puts forth new life again,
> Green grasses grow
> And flowers lift their heads,
> And over all the plain
> The wonder spreads
> Of life, of life, of life!
>
> In time of silver rain
> The butterflies lift silken wings
> To catch a rainbow cry,
> And trees put forth
> New leaves to sing
> In joy beneath the sky
> As down the roadway passing boys
> And girls go singing, too,
> In time of silver rain
> When spring
> And life are new.

53. The setting of the poem is in
    (A) spring.   (B) summer.   (C) autumn.   (D) winter.

54. The main idea of the poem is
    (A) rain brings silver to the earth.
    (B) rain brings life to the earth.
    (C) rain brings sadness to the earth.
    (D) rain brings rainbow to the earth.

55. In the poem, which of the following words was used to rhyme
with "rain"?
(A) Wings.　　　(B) Pain.　　　(C) Again.　　　(D) Spring.

第二部分：非選擇題

I、**中譯英**（共 10 分）：

下面一段短文中，有五處係以中文呈現，請將其譯成正確、通順、達意且前後
連貫的英文，並使用適當標點符號及大小寫。每題二分。答案請寫在「**非選擇
題答案卷**」上，同時務必分行標示題號。

When people think of conversations, they think of people talking to
each other. What people often forget is that listening is an important part
of keeping a conversation going. Have you ever stopped talking to someone
because you did not think he or she was listening to you? Not paying
attention is (1)中止對話的最快速方法之一。

Listening actually is a lot of work, because it is more than just you
sitting there looking at the person, nodding your head from time to time.
You must let the person know that you have heard him or her. You can use
sounds such as "Mm" or "Ah" or "Oh." You can also add short comments
such as "yes," "really?" or "I didn't know that."

One of the most useful, but maybe also the most difficult listening
skills is to summarize or paraphrase what the person has said. This shows
the person you are not just hearing what he or she said, (2)而是真的（聽）
懂了。 For example, if someone comes to you and tells you a story of (3)
他如何在上學途中被狗咬了， then he found out he had left his homework at
home, so the teacher punished him. At lunch he found out his lunch money
was stolen, and (4)因為他很餓，所以考試考得不好。 You can nod and show
you have heard him, or you can summarize what he has said by saying,
(5)「聽起來你今天很倒霉。」

You can also summarize the feelings the person was communicating by saying "You must feel awful after having all these things happen to you today." If a person feels you are not just listening, but you are listening carefully to his words and feelings, he is more likely to open up and communicate with you even more.

II、英文作文（共 20 分）：

說明：請以 "The Difficulties I Have with Learning English"為題，寫一篇約一百二十個單字的英文作文。文分兩段，第一段寫出在你修習英語過程中某些學習上的困難；第二段說明處理這些困難的經過及結果。答案請寫在「**非選擇題答案卷**」上（內容 5 分，組織 5 分，文法 4 分，用字遣詞 4 分，拼字、大小寫及標點符號 2 分）。

89年大學聯考英文試題詳解

第一部分：單一選擇題

I、對話：5%

1. (**D**) 湯姆：對不起，我似乎找不到我的行李。
   職員：＿＿＿＿＿＿＿＿＿＿
   湯姆：西北航空 007 班機。
   - (A) 先生，您是什麼時候抵達的？　　　(B) 先生，要我爲您效勞嗎？
   - (C) 先生，您的行李是什麼顏色的？
   - (D) <u>先生，您搭的是哪一班飛機？</u>

   luggage (ˈlʌgɪdʒ) *n.* 行李　　　flight (flaɪt) *n.* 班機
   airline (ˈɛrˌlaɪn) *n.* 航空公司

2. (**C**) 比爾：我眞不敢相信！我已經好幾年沒見到你了。
   麥克：對呀，你都在忙些什麼？
   比爾：＿＿＿＿＿＿＿＿＿ 那你呢？
   麥克：我現在是個自由作家。
   - (A) 我要去買一些雜貨。　　　　　(B) 我再兩個星期就要結婚了。
   - (C) <u>我一直都在一家貿易公司上班。</u>　(D) 看見你眞好。

   be up to 忙於～　　free-lance (ˈfriˈlæns) *adj.* 自由投稿的；自由作家的
   grocery (ˈgrosəɪ) *n.* 雜貨

3. (**B**) 南　茜：喂，我要查珍・艾莎帖克的電話號碼。
   接線生：＿＿＿＿＿＿＿＿＿＿
   南　茜：當然，Isateck。Irene 的 I，Susan 的 S，Adam 的 A，Tom 的 T，
   　　　　Eric 的 E，Charles 的 C，Karen 的 K。
   接線生：謝謝，請稍候…。電話號碼是 883-4733。
   - (A) 您貴姓？　　　　　　　　(B) <u>請您再說一遍剛剛那個姓，好嗎？</u>
   - (C) 我不知道您的姓該怎麼拼。
   - (D) 這是個很少見的名字，不是嗎？

   last name 姓（*cf. first name* 名）　　repeat (rɪˈpit) *v.* 重複；重說

4. (**A**)　店員：鞋子合腳嗎？

　　　　瑪麗：它們太鬆了。我要小一號的。

　　　　店員：＿＿＿＿＿＿＿＿＿

　　　　瑪麗：好。

　　　　店員：很抱歉，妳要的尺寸已經賣完了。

　　　　(A) <u>讓我看一看有沒有那個尺寸。</u>

　　　　(B) 可是妳穿起來很好看。

　　　　(C) 我不認為我們有更小號的。

　　　　(D) 妳為什麼不先試穿看看？

　　　loose〔lus〕*adj.* 鬆的　　***sell out*** 賣完了

　　　available〔ə'veləbḷ〕*adj.* 可獲得的　　***try on*** 試穿

5. (**B**)　卡蘿：妳看那件洋裝。真是漂亮。

　　　　茉蒂：＿＿＿＿＿＿＿＿＿

　　　　卡蘿：哎呀！我沒注意到！實在是太貴了！

　　　　(A) 對呀，是很漂亮，而且價格也很合理。

　　　　(B) <u>對呀，可是看看價錢！要新台幣五萬元！</u>

　　　　(C) 對呀，它是很漂亮，可是這種款式不適合我。

　　　　(D) 對呀，很美。你應該把它買下來。

　　　gorgeous〔'gɔrdʒəs〕*adj.* 漂亮的；華麗的

　　　my〔maɪ〕*int.*（表示驚奇）哎呀！

　　　style〔staɪl〕*n.* 風格；款式　　lovely〔'lʌvlɪ〕*adj.* 可愛的；漂亮的

Ⅱ、詞彙及慣用語：15％

6. (**D**)　***Although*** Martha had been away from home *for a long time*, ***when*** she came near her house, everything *suddenly* became <u>familiar</u>.

　　　雖然瑪莎已經離家很久，當她到達她家附近時，突然一切都變得很<u>熟悉</u>。

　　　　(A) functional〔'fʌŋkʃənḷ〕*adj.* 有功能的；有作用的

　　　　(B) impulsive〔ɪm'pʌlsɪv〕*adj.* 衝動的

　　　　(C) emotional〔ɪ'moʃənḷ〕*adj.* 情緒的

　　　　(D) ***familiar***〔fə'mɪljɚ〕*adj.* 熟悉的

7. (**A**)　It was obvious ***that*** *this young artist's latest work was* definitely *much*

better than any other work in the exhibition.

很明顯的，這位年輕藝術家最新的作品，確實比展覽會中其他的作品好很多。

      (A) ***definitely*** (ˈdɛfənɪtlɪ) *adv.* 確實地；當然

      (B) optionally (ˈɑpʃənḷɪ) *adv.* 可選擇地；隨意地

      (C) occasionally (əˈkeʒənḷɪ) *adv.* 偶爾

      (D) initially (ɪˈnɪʃəlɪ) *adv.* 起初

obvious (ˈɑbvɪəs) *adj.* 明顯的　　　latest (ˈletɪst) *adj.* 最新的
work (wɝk) *n.* 作品　　　exhibition (ˌɛksəˈbɪʃən) *n.* 展覽會

8. (**B**)　***Since the contestants were all very good,*** *the competition for the*

first prize was fierce.

因為所有的參賽者都非常棒，所以爭取第一名的競爭很激烈。

      (A) sincere (sɪnˈsɪr) *adj.* 衷心的；誠懇的

      (B) ***fierce*** (fɪrs) *adj.* 激烈的；兇猛的

      (C) radiant (ˈredɪənt) *adj.* 容光煥發的

      (D) efficient (ɪˈfɪʃənt) *adj.* 有效率的

contestant (kənˈtɛstənt) *n.* 參賽者
competition (ˌkɑmpəˈtɪʃən) *n.* 競爭　　***the first prize*** 第一名

9. (**D**)　The company decided to put the plan into operation ***because it was***

the most feasible ***one.***

公司決定實施這項計畫，因為它是最切實可行的。

      (A) addictive (əˈdɪktɪv) *adj.* 使人上癮的

      (B) likable (ˈlaɪkəbḷ) *adj.* 可愛的

      (C) pleasant (ˈplɛznt) *adj.* 令人愉快的

      (D) ***feasible*** (ˈfizəbḷ) *adj.* 可實行的

operation (ˌɑpəˈreʃən) *n.* 運作　　***put ~ into operation*** 實施~

10. (**C**) The owner was demanding. He expected nothing but <u>perfection</u> *from his employees.*

老闆的要求非常高。他對員工唯一的要求就是<u>完美</u>。

   (A) laziness〔'lezɪnɪs〕*n.* 懶惰
   (B) impatience〔ɪm'peʃəns〕*n.* 沒耐心；不耐煩
   (C) ***perfection***〔pɚ'fɛkʃən〕*n.* 完美
   (D) ignorance〔'ɪgnərəns〕*n.* 無知

demanding〔dɪ'mændɪŋ〕*adj.* 過分要求的；苛求的
nothing but 只是 (= *only*)　　employee〔͵ɛmplɔɪ'i〕*n.* 員工

11. (**C**) The reason *for designing the special bus lane* is to <u>facilitate</u> the traffic flow, not to slow it down.

設計公車專用道的原因，是要<u>使</u>交通流量更<u>便捷</u>，而不是要減緩它的速度。

   (A) accommodate〔ə'kɑmə͵det〕*v.* 容納
   (B) discount〔'dɪskaʊnt , dɪs'kaʊnt〕*v.* 打折扣
   (C) ***facilitate***〔fə'sɪlə͵tet〕*v.* 使便利
   (D) influence〔'ɪnfluəns〕*v.,n.* 影響

design〔dɪ'zaɪn〕*v.* 設計　　lane〔len〕*n.* 車道
flow〔flo〕*n.* 流量　　***slow down*** 使減速

12. (**A**) *In many novels and films,* step-mothers are *often* <u>stereotyped</u> *as wicked women.*

在許多小說和電影裡，後母經常被<u>定型</u>爲邪惡的女人。

   (A) ***stereotype***〔'stɛrɪə͵taɪp〕*v.* 使定型
   (B) isolate〔'aɪsḷ͵et〕*v.* 使孤立；隔離
   (C) irritate〔'ɪrə͵tet〕*v.* 激怒
   (D) decorate〔'dɛkə͵ret〕*v.* 裝飾

step-mother〔'stɛp͵mʌðɚ〕*n.* 繼母；後母　　wicked〔'wɪkɪd〕*adj.* 邪惡的

13. (**A**) *Among the high-risk group of heart disease* are people *with a*

preference for fat-rich foods.
比較喜歡吃高脂肪食品的人，是屬於心臟疾病的高危險群。

    (A) **preference** (ˈprɛfərəns) *n.* 偏愛；比較喜歡
    (B) reflection (rɪˈflɛkʃən) *n.* 反射；反射作用
    (C) sympathy (ˈsɪmpəθɪ) *n.* 同情
    (D) frequency (ˈfrikwənsɪ) *n.* 頻率

high-risk (ˈhaɪˈrɪsk) *adj.* 高危險的
fat-rich (ˈfætˈrɪtʃ) *adj.* 含多量脂肪的
※ 本句爲倒裝句，原句爲：People with a…foods are among…disease.

14. (**B**) There was no doubt **that** *the candidate was popular, **because** he*

had won a <u>landslide</u> *victory in the election.*

無疑地，那位候選人十分受歡迎，因爲他在選舉中，<u>贏得壓倒性的勝利</u>。

    (A) helpless (ˈhɛlplɪs) *adj.* 無助的
    (B) **landslide** (ˈlænd͵slaɪd) *n.* (選舉中的) 壓倒性的勝利；山崩
    (C) thoughtful (ˈθɔtfəl) *adj.* 體貼的
    (D) permanent (ˈpɝmənənt) *adj.* 永久的

candidate (ˈkændə͵det) *n.* 候選人　　victory (ˈvɪktərɪ) *n.* 勝利

15. (**D**) Technological changes will <u>inevitably</u> lead to a change *in human*

relationships.
科技上的改變，<u>必然</u>會導致人與人之間關係的改變。

    (A) suspiciously (səˈspɪʃəslɪ) *adv.* 可疑地
    (B) generously (ˈdʒɛnərəslɪ) *adv.* 大方地；慷慨地
    (C) earnestly (ˈɝnɪstlɪ) *adv.* 認眞地
    (D) **inevitably** (ɪnˈɛvətəblɪ) *adv.* 不可避免地；必然

technological (͵tɛknəˈlɑdʒɪkl̩) *adj.* 科技上的

16. (**C**) *After a lengthy discussion*, the experts *finally* came up with

suggestions *for resolving the economic crisis.*

在冗長的討論之後，專家們終於<u>提出</u>解決經濟危機的建議。

(A) set up 設立

(B) catch up with 趕上

(C) **come up with** 提出；想出

(D) give up 放棄

lengthy (ˈlɛŋθɪ) *adj.* 冗長的　　resolve (rɪˈzɑlv) *v.* 解決

economic (ˌikəˈnɑmɪk) *adj.* 經濟的　　crisis (ˈkraɪsɪs) *n.* 危機

17. (**A**) These batteries are not good. <u>*At best*</u> they will last *only for*

two months.

這些電池不怎麼好。它們<u>最多</u>只能用兩個月。

(A) **at best** 最多；充其量

(B) in advance 事先

(C) in contrast with / to~　與~形成對比

(D) at least 至少

battery (ˈbætərɪ) *n.* 電池　　last (læst) *v.* 持續；夠~之用

18. (**C**) The sale *of the company's new product* is *overwhelmingly* good.

It has <u>brought in</u> two million dollars *so far.*

這家公司新產品的銷售出奇地好。到目前為止，它已經<u>賺進</u>了兩百萬元。

(A) carry on 繼續　　　　　　(B) keep up 保持

(C) **bring in** 賺進　　　　　(D) consist of 由~組成

overwhelmingly (ˌovəˈhwɛlmɪŋlɪ) *adv.* 壓倒性地；極大地

so far 到目前為止

19. (**D**)　Einstein was considered one *of the greatest scientists of the 20th century in terms of his influence on the study of physics.*
由愛因斯坦對物理研究的影響看來，他被認爲是二十世紀最偉大的科學家之一。

(A) in exchange for 作爲～的交換
(B) in spite of 儘管　　(C) on behalf of 代表
(D) *in terms of* 由～觀點看來

Einstein〔'aɪnstaɪn〕*n.* 愛因斯坦　　physics〔'fɪzɪks〕*n.* 物理學

20. (**B**)　*When the landlord opened the door,* he looked me *up and down before asking who I was.*
當房東開了門，在問我是誰之前，就上下打量了我一番。

(A) back and forth 來回地
(B) *up and down* 上上下下；到處
(C) to and fro 來回地 (= *back and forth*)
(D) off and on 斷斷續續 (= *on and off*)

landlord〔'lænd‚lɔrd〕*n.* 房東

※ 報上提出這一題有爭議，因爲中文也會説「來回地」打量某人，但是讀者要注意，中英文是不同的，美國人不説 *look sb. back and forth* 或 *look sb. to and fro*，而只説 *look sb. up and down*。

Ⅲ、綜合測驗：20％

第一篇（共 10 題）

People have different ideas *about what exactly is being on time and being late.* These ideas *also* differ *from time to time, and from country to country.* *For example, in the United States,* it is *very* important to be on time *for almost all occasions.*
21
22
23

人們對於何謂準時，以及怎麼樣算是遲到，有不同的看法。這些看法也因時間、因國家，而有不同。例如，在美國，幾乎在所有的場合中，準時都是很重要的。

> exactly〔ɪgˈzæktlɪ〕 *adv.* 確切地　　*on time* 準時
> differ〔ˈdɪfɚ〕 *v.* 不同　　*differ from* A *to* A 每個 A 都不同
> *differ from country to country* 每個國家都不同
> occasion〔əˈkeʒən〕 *n.* 場合

21. (**D**) 依句意，選 (D) *differ from time to time*「每個時間都不同；因時而異」。而 (A) from head to toe「從頭到腳；完全」，(B) differ from hour to hour「每個小時都不同」，(C) from top to bottom「從上到下；徹底地」，則不合句意。

22. (**A**) 依句意，選 (A) *For example*「例如」。而 (B) in addition「此外」，(C) in case「如果；以防萬一」，(D) for good「永遠」(＝*forever*)，則不合句意。

23. (**C**) 在美國，「幾乎在所有的」場合中，準時都是很重要的，選 (C) *almost all*。而 (A) hardly any「幾乎沒有～」(＝*almost no*)，(B) simply none「完全沒有」，均不合句意。(D)「nearly every + 單數名詞」，表「幾乎每一個～」，因為 occasions 為複數名詞，故在此用法不合。

The only time *it is socially underline{acceptable} to be late* is **when** going to a friend's
                                                            24

party. A person *usually* tries to arrive *about 5 minutes underline{after} the invitation
                                                                            25

underline{time}, **so that** the host would have a little extra time *to prepare for the guests.*

This underline{is called} being *"fashionably* late." Any time underline{later than that} is
    26   27

considered impolite, ***because** it keeps the host and other guests underline{waiting}.*
                                                                        28

　　唯一在社交上可被接受的遲到，是去參加朋友的宴會時。通常大家都會比受邀的時間晚五分鐘到，以便讓主人有多一點的時間，為客人做準備。這就是所謂的「時髦的遲到」。如果再晚的話，就會被認為是不禮貌的，因為會讓主人及其他客人等候。

> socially〔'soʃəlɪ〕*adv.* 在社交上
> ***so that*** 以便於　　host〔host〕*n.* 主人
> extra〔'ɛkstrə〕*adj.* 額外的　　guest〔gɛst〕*n.* 客人
> fashionably〔'fæʃənəblɪ〕*adv.* 時髦地；流行地

24. (**A**) 依句意，選 (A) ***acceptable***〔ək'sɛptəbl̩〕*adj.* 可接受的。而 (B) accessible〔æk'sɛsəbl̩〕*adj.* 方便達到的；容易取得的，(C) attainable〔ə'tenəbl̩〕*adj.* 可達到的，(D) admirable〔'ædmərəbl̩〕*adj.* 令人欽佩的，皆不合句意。

25. (**C**) 依句意，主人能有多一點的時間來做準備，所以客人是「比邀請的時間晚到」，故選 (C) ***after***。

26. (**B**) 依句意為被動，選 (B) ***is called***「被稱為」。

27. (**A**) 「比」那個時間「晚」就會被認為不禮貌，故選 (A) ***later***「較晚的」。

28. (**B**) ***keep sb. waiting*** 使某人等候

Being on time goes <u>both</u> ways. One should *also* not arrive *early for*

29

a friend's party, ***because*** it would rush the host. <u>However</u>, ***when*** going to

30

a doctor's appointment, it is *usually* good to arrive *earlier **than** the*

appointment ***because*** there are usually forms ***that*** need to be filled out by

the patient.

準時有好有壞。朋友的宴會，也不應該早到，因爲可能會使主人很緊張繁忙。不過，當和醫生約好時間時，通常最好早一點到，因爲通常會有一些表格病人必須塡寫。

> rush〔rʌʃ〕v. 催促；使緊張繁忙
> appointment〔ə'pɔɪntmənt〕n. 約會　　form〔fɔrm〕n. 表格
> **fill out** 塡寫　　patient〔'peʃənt〕n. 病人

29. (**D**) 依句意，準時「有好有壞」，選 (D) **go both ways**「有好有壞；有利也有弊」(= cut both ways)。

30. (**D**) 前面講太早到的壞處，後面提到看醫生必須要早點到，故句意有轉折，選 (D) **However**「然而」。

第二篇（共 10 題）

When Jerry Siegel and Joseph Shuster were just teenagers they developed that heroic character known as Superman. It was a clever idea to create a

31

person [faster than a speeding bullet **and** able to leap tall buildings in a single

32

bound.] Children everywhere were fascinated by Superman **and** bought

33

hundreds of thousands of comic books with stories of his heroic acts. Soon

34

other products bearing the Superman symbol hit the market, **and** it wasn't

35

36

long **before** the superhero was the star of his own television show.

當傑瑞・席格和約瑟夫・舒斯特才十幾歲時，他們創造出了眾所皆知的英雄人物——超人。創造出一個速度比飛快的子彈還快，而且能夠一躍就跳過高樓的人，是個非常聰明的點子。各地的孩子都對超人非常著迷，並買了數十萬本畫有他英勇行爲故事的漫畫書。很快地，其他印有超人圖案的商品，也在市場上銷售，而不久之後，這位超級英雄就成爲他自己電視節目中的主角。

develop〔dɪˈvɛləp〕v. 發展；創造出
heroic〔hɪˈroɪk〕adj. 英雄的；英勇的
character〔ˈkærɪktɚ〕n. 人物；角色
create〔krɪˈet〕v. 創造　　speed〔spid〕v. 飛馳
speeding〔ˈspidɪŋ〕adj. 飛快的
bullet〔ˈbʊlɪt〕n. 子彈　　leap〔lip〕v. 跳過；越過
single〔ˈsɪŋgl̩〕adj. 單一的　　bound〔baʊnd〕n. 跳躍
fascinate〔ˈfæsn̩‚et〕v. 使著迷
comic book 漫畫書（＝*comics*）
symbol〔ˈsɪmbl̩〕n. 象徵；標誌　　hit〔hɪt〕v. 出現在
star〔stɑr〕n. 明星；主角

31.(**D**) 本句的眞正主詞是不定詞片語 to create…a single bound，故句首
用 It，做爲形式主詞，選 (D)。

32.(**B**) 依句意，超人「能夠」一躍跳過高樓，應選 (B) ***be able to*** 「能夠」。
而 (A) be paid to「被付費去～」，(C) unlikely〔ʌnˈlaɪklɪ〕adj. 不可
能的，(D) force〔fors〕v. 強迫，均不合句意。

33.(**C**) 依句意，「各地的」孩子都對超人非常著迷，選 (C) ***everywhere*** 「到
處；各地」。而 (A) 某處，(B) 沒有一個地方，(D) 無論任何地方，均
不合句意。

34.(**B**) ***hundreds of thousands of*** 數十萬的～（不可寫成 *thousands of*
hundreds of）

35.(**D**) 表「擁有；印有」某個圖案、特徵等，動詞用 ***bear***，選 (D)。
bearing the Superman symbol 是由 *which bore* the Superman
symbol 簡化而來的分詞片語。

36.(**B**) 敘述發生在過去的事實，時態用過去簡單式。
It wasn't long before～ 不久就～

Superman's great popularity should have made his originators *very*
　　　　　　　　　　　　　　 37

rich, ***but*** it didn't. ***Although*** *Mr. Siegel and Mr. Shuster invented the*
　　　　　　　　　　　38

superhero, it was the company *they* worked *for* ***that*** *actually made the money.*
　　　　　　　　　　　　　　　　　　　39

The genius *of the creators* was not rewarded, ***and*** for *most of their lives*
　　　　　　　　　　　　　　　　　　　　　　　　　40

these two men made *barely* enough to survive.

　　超人的大受歡迎，當時應該可以使他的創造者非常有錢，但事實上並沒有。
雖然席格先生和舒斯特先生發明了這位超級英雄，但真正賺錢的，是他們所屬的
公司。這二位創造者的天賦，並沒有得到報酬，而且在他們的大半生中，所賺的
錢幾乎不夠糊口。

　　　　originator〔ə'rɪdʒə,netə〕*n.* 創造者 (= *creator*)
　　　　actually〔'æktʃʊəlɪ〕*adv.* 真正地；實際上
　　　　genius〔'dʒinjəs〕*n.* 天賦；才能
　　　　reward〔rɪ'wɔrd〕*v.* 給予報酬
　　　　barely〔'bɛrlɪ〕*adv.* 幾乎不 (= *hardly*)
　　　　survive〔sə'vaɪv〕*v.* 繼續生存

37. (**A**)　should have + p.p. 「早該～」，表「過去應該發生而未發生」之事。

38. (**C**)　依句意，選 (C) ***Although*** 「雖然」。而 (A) 除非，(B) 因為；自從，
　　　　　(D) 因為，均不合句意。

39. (**D**)　依句意，選 (D) ***work for a company*** 「為某公司工作」。而 (A) look
　　　　　for「尋找」，(B) search for「尋找」，(C) wait for「等待」，均不
　　　　　合句意。

40. (**A**)　***for most of one's life*** 某人的大半生中

IV、閱讀測驗：30 %

第一篇（共 4 題）

Human language is a living thing. Each language has its own biological system, *which makes it different from all other languages.* This system must *constantly* adjust to a new environment and new situations *to survive and flourish.*

人類的語言是有生命的。每一種語言都有自己的生理系統，能使本身和其他的語言不同。這個系統必須不斷地適應新的環境和情況，才能繼續存在，並且變得更興盛。

> living〔ˈlɪvɪŋ〕*adj.* 活著的
> biological〔ˌbaɪəˈlɑdʒɪk!〕*adj.* 生物的
> constantly〔ˈkɑnstəntlɪ〕*adv.* 不斷地　　***adjust to*** 適應
> flourish〔ˈflɝɪʃ〕*v.* 興盛；繁榮

When we think of human language *this way,* it is an easy step to see the words *of a language* as being like the cells *of a living organism*—they are *constantly* forming and dying and splitting *into parts* *as time changes* *and the language adapts.*

當我們以這種方式來思考人類的語言時，很容易就能把語言中的文字，看成是生物的細胞——隨著時間的變化，語言必須適應這些變化時，它們會不斷形成、死亡，以及分裂成好幾個部分。

> step〔stɛp〕*n.* 步驟　　cell〔sɛl〕*n.* 細胞
> organism〔ˈɔrgənˌɪzəm〕*n.* 生物　　form〔fɔrm〕*v.* 形成
> split〔splɪt〕*v.* 分裂　　adapt〔əˈdæpt〕*v.* 適應

There are several specific processes *by which new words are formed.*

Some words come into the language *which sound like what they refer to.*

Words *like buzz and ding-dong* are good examples *of this process.*

　　新字的形成，有好幾個特定的過程。有些字是擬聲字，聽起來就像是所指的東西，也會加入語言中。像是「嗡嗡聲」及「叮咚聲」，就是這種過程很好的例子。

> specific〔spɪ'sɪfɪk〕*adj.* 特定的　　process〔'prɑsɛs〕*n.* 過程
> *refer to* 是指　　buzz〔bʌz〕*n.* 嗡嗡聲
> ding-dong〔'dɪŋ,dɔŋ〕*n.* 叮咚聲

Still another way *in which new words are formed* is to use the name *of a person or a place closely associated with that word's meaning.* The words *sandwich* and *hamburger* are examples *of this word-formation process.* The Earl of Sandwich, *an English aristocrat,* was *so* fond of gambling at cards *that he hated to be interrupted by the necessity of eating.* He *thus* invented a new way *of eating while he continued his game at the gambling table.* This quick and convenient dish is *what we now call* a sandwich—a piece of meat *between two slices of bread.* The hamburger became the best-known sandwich *in the world after it was invented by a citizen of Hamburg in Germany.*

還有另一種造新字的方法，那就是使用與字義有密切關連的人名或地名。「三明治」和「漢堡」就是這種造字過程的例子。三明治伯爵，他是一位英國的貴族，非常喜歡賭紙牌，很討厭因為必須吃東西，而被打斷。因此，他發明了一種可在牌桌上繼續玩牌的新吃法。這種又快又方便的菜餚，就是我們現在所謂的「三明治」——將一片肉夾在兩片麵包之間。有位德國漢堡市的市民，發明了漢堡之後，漢堡就成為全世界最有名的一種三明治。

still〔stɪl〕*adv.* 還有　　closely〔'kloslɪ〕*adv.* 密切地
be associated with 與~有關　　sandwich〔'sændwɪtʃ〕*n.* 三明治
formation〔fɔr'meʃən〕*n.* 形成　　earl〔ɝl〕*n.* 伯爵
aristocrat〔ə'rɪstəˌkræt〕*n.* 貴族　　***be fond of*** 喜歡
gamble〔'gæmbļ〕*v.* 賭博　　cards〔kɑrdz〕*n.pl.* 紙牌遊戲
gamble at cards 賭紙牌　　interrupt〔ˌɪntə'rʌpt〕*v.* 打斷；使中斷
necessity〔nə'sɛsətɪ〕*n.* 需要；必要　　***gambling table*** 賭桌
dish〔dɪʃ〕*n.* 菜餚　　***what we call*** 所謂的　　slice〔slaɪs〕*n.* 片
best-known〔'bɛst'non〕*adj.* 最有名的　　citizen〔'sɪtəzņ〕*n.* 市民

As long as a language is alive, its cells will continue to change, forming new words **and** getting rid of the ones **that** no longer have any use.

只要語言還活著，它的細胞就會繼續改變，會形成新的字，並除去那些已經沒有用的字。

as long as 只要　　***get rid of*** 擺脫；除去

41. (**D**) 本文主要是關於
　　(A) 生物的生理系統。　　(B) 三明治和漢堡的發明者。
　　(C) 人類細胞的發展。　　(D) 語言的變化。

42. (**B**) 語言在很多方面是有生命的，除了
　　(A) 它和生物的生理系統相似。
　　(B) 它真的具有許多會不斷分裂和形成的活細胞。
　　(C) 它必須適應新的環境，才能繼續存在。
　　(D) 它舊的字會逐漸消失，而新的字則不斷地增加。

die out 逐漸消失　　add〔æd〕*v.* 添加

43. (**C**) "sandwich"這個字是來自於

 (A) 紙牌遊戲。   (B) 一片肉。

 (C) <u>一個人的名字。</u>   (D) 英國的一個地方。

44. (**A**) 本文中提到幾種造字的方法？

 (A) <u>兩種。</u> (B) 三種。 (C) 四種。 (D) 五種。

第二篇（共4題）

Tears are nature's way *of making us feel more comfortable.* ***When our*** *eye is made uncomfortable by some small piece of pollution,* ***or when*** *we are peeling onions,* ***or when*** *we are exhausted and "red-eyed" from overwork and late hours,* tears form *in our eyes to clean and refresh them.*

流眼淚是種自然的方式，能讓我們覺得更舒服。當有某個細小的髒東西，使我們的眼睛感到不舒服，或是當我們剝洋蔥，或當我們因為工作過度或熬夜，感到筋疲力盡，而紅著眼睛時，眼睛就會產生淚水，來清潔自己，並消除疲勞。

 some〔sʌm〕*adj.* 某一 pollution〔pəˋluʃən〕*n.* 污染物

 peel〔pil〕*v.* 剝（皮） onion〔ˋʌnjən〕*n.* 洋蔥

 exhausted〔ɪgˋzɔstɪd〕*adj.* 筋疲力盡的

 red-eyed〔ˋrɛdˋaɪd〕*adj.* 紅眼的 overwork〔ˋovɚˏwɝk〕*n.* 工作過度

 late hours 晚睡；熬夜 refresh〔rɪˋfrɛʃ〕*v.* 使提神

Tears are *also* a sign *of strong emotion.* We cry ***when we are sad and*** we cry ***when we are happy.***

And tears seem to be *uniquely* human. We know ***that*** animals also *experience emotion—fear, pleasure, loneliness—****but*** they do not shed tears.* *From this,* we can conclude ***that*** *tears are closely related to the emotional and biological makeup of the human species.*

眼淚也是一種強烈的情緒表現。我們傷心的時候會哭，高興的時候也會哭。而眼淚似乎是人類所特有的。我們都知道，動物也有情緒感受——恐懼、快樂、寂寞——不過牠們不會掉眼淚。由此可知，眼淚和人類情緒上，及生理上的構造，是息息相關的。

sign〔sain〕*n.* 表示；跡象　　emotion〔ɪ'moʃən〕*n.* 情緒

uniquely〔ju'niklɪ〕*adv.* 獨特地；獨一無二地

human〔'hjumən〕*adj.* 人類的

experience〔ɪk'spɪrɪəns〕*v.* 感受；體驗

loneliness〔'lonlɪnɪs〕*n.* 寂寞　　shed〔ʃɛd〕*v.* 流（淚）

conclude〔kən'klud〕*v.* 下結論；斷定　　*be related to*～ 與～有關

makeup〔'mek,ʌp〕*n.* 組成；構造

species〔'spiʃɪz〕*n.* 種　　*human species* 人類

Biologically speaking, tears are *actually* drops *of saline fluid* produced *by a gland in the body*. ***Because*** *salt is an important component*, tears may *actually* constitute the *most* conclusive evidence *that the human animal is the end product of a long evolutionary process* ***that*** *began in the sea.*

生理上來說，眼淚其實是身體的某個腺體，所製造的鹹的水滴。由於鹽是重要的成分，所以眼淚實際上，可能就構成最具決定性的證據，證明人類是從海底開始，經過長久進化過程後的最終產物。

biologically〔,baɪə'lɑdʒɪklɪ〕*adv.* 生物上地

saline〔'selaɪn〕*adj.* 含有鹽分的；鹹的　　fluid〔'fluɪd〕*n.* 液體

gland〔glænd〕*n.* 腺體　　salt〔sɔlt〕*n.* 鹽

component〔kəm'ponənt〕*n.* 成分

constitute〔'kɑnstə,tjut〕*v.* 構成

conclusive〔kən'klusɪv〕*adj.* 決定性的

evidence〔'ɛvədəns〕*n.* 證據

end〔ɛnd〕*adj.* 最後的　　product〔'prɑdəkt〕*n.* 產物

evolutionary〔,ɛvə'luʃən,ɛrɪ〕*adj.* 進化的

And it is clear **that,** *in addition to the emotional benefits, the shedding of tears has a specific biological function as well.* *Through tears,* we can eliminate *from our body* certain chemicals *which build up in response to stress* **and** *create a chemical imbalance in the body.* Crying *actually* makes us feel better *by correcting that imbalance* **and** *making us feel good again.* **And** *thus* the emotional and the biological functions *of tears* merge into one **and** make us *even more* "human" **than** *we would otherwise be.*

而且很明顯地，掉眼淚除了有情緒上的好處之外，還有一個特殊的生理功能。藉由眼淚，我們可以消除體內的某些化學物質，這些化學物質會因為要應付壓力而增加，造成身體的化學成分失調。哭其實能讓我們覺得更舒服，因為它能調整這種失調的狀態，使我們再次感到舒暢。因此，眼淚在情緒上，及生理上的功能合而為一，讓我們比不流淚時，更加「人性化」。

> ***in addition to*** 除了~之外　　benefit (ˈbɛnəfɪt) *n.* 利益；好處
> function (ˈfʌŋkʃən) *n.* 作用；功能　　***as well*** 也 (= *too*)
> eliminate (ɪˈlɪməˌnet) *v.* 除去　　certain (ˈsɝtṇ) *adj.* 某種；某些
> chemical (ˈkɛmɪkḷ) *n.* 化學物質　*adj.* 化學的
> ***build up*** 增強；增加　　***in response to*** 回應~
> stress (strɛs) *n.* 壓力　　imbalance (ɪmˈbæləns) *n.* 失調；不平衡
> correct (kəˈrɛkt) *v.* 修正　　merge (mɝdʒ) *v.* 合併
> otherwise (ˈʌðəˌwaɪz) *adv.* 不是那樣；在不同的情況之下

45. (**B**)　下列何者為非？
　　(A) 眼淚是一種強烈的情緒表現。
　　(B) 眼淚是由鹽製造出來的。
　　(C) 掉眼淚是一種生理作用。
　　(D) 眼淚能除去我們體內的化學物質。

46. (**A**) 根據本文，人類可能是起源自
   　　(A) 海洋。　　　(B) 鹽。　　(C) 化學物質。　　(D) 動物。

   human beings 人類　　originate〔əˈrɪdʒəˌnet〕*v.* 起源於

47. (**C**) 下列何者不是眼淚的功能？
   　　(A) 生理的功能。　　　　　(B) 情緒的功能。
   　　(C) 政治的功能。　　　　　(D) 化學的功能。

48. (**C**) 根據本文，下列何者是人類所特有的？
   　　(A) 寂寞的感覺。　　　　　(B) 心情好的狀態。
   　　(C) 流眼淚的能力。　　　　(D) 恐懼的感覺。

   be unique to 是～所特有的　　state〔stet〕*n.* 狀態

第三篇（共 4 題）

A long time ago in India there lived a young couple. The young couple had wanted a child *very much,* **and** *when they finally had a baby,* they loved him *with all their hearts.* However, *before the baby was one year old,* he became sick **and** *soon* died. The young couple cried and cried **and** could not stop. They would not let anyone bury the child **and** asked everyone to help them find the medicine *that would make their son come back to life again.*

　　很久很久以前，在印度住著一對年輕的夫婦。這對年輕的夫婦一直很想要小孩，當他們終於生了一個小嬰兒之後，便全心全意地疼愛他。然而，嬰兒在滿週歲之前，生了病，很快就死了。這對年輕的夫婦哭個不停。他們不讓任何人埋葬這個小孩，並且四處請求大家，幫他們尋找能讓兒子起死回生的藥。

　　　　couple〔ˈkʌpl̩〕*n.* 夫婦　　***with all one's heart*** 全心全意地
　　　　bury〔ˈbɛrɪ〕*v.* 埋葬　　***come (back) to life*** 復活

The people *in the village* did not know **what** *to do.* They thought *the young couple had gone crazy over the death of the baby.* The villagers were worried **that** *the young couple would not be able to return to their old way of life* **if** *they continued to focus on the death of the baby.* One day, a wise man *from another village* came to the young couple **and** told them **that** *perhaps they could seek help from the Buddha.*

村子裡的人不知道該怎麼辦。他們認為，這對年輕夫婦因為小孩的死，已經發瘋了。村民們擔心，如果這對年輕夫婦，繼續將注意力集中在小孩死去這件事，他們將不能回復到往常的生活方式。有一天，有位另一個村莊的智者，來找這對年輕夫婦，並告訴他們，也許可以尋求佛陀的幫助。

village〔'vɪlɪdʒ〕*n.* 村莊　　**go crazy** 發瘋
villager〔'vɪlɪdʒɚ〕*n.* 村民　　focus〔'fokəs〕*v.* 集中 <*on*>
seek〔sik〕*v.* 尋求　　Buddha〔'budə〕*n.* 佛陀

The couple rushed to pay the Buddha a visit. [**After** *they explained their reason for visiting,*] the Buddha nodded and said, "I have **what** *you are looking for.* **But** the medicine is missing one ingredient." "What is the ingredient?" asked the couple *anxiously,* "We will find it *for you!*"

這對夫婦趕緊去拜訪佛陀。在他們解釋來訪的原因後，佛陀點點頭，說：「我有你們在尋找的東西。但是這個藥少了一種成分。」「什麼成分呢？」這對夫婦焦急地問，「我們會替您找到的！」

rush〔rʌʃ〕*v.* 趕緊　　**pay sb. a visit** 拜訪某人
nod〔nɑd〕*v.* 點頭　　miss〔mɪs〕*v.* 缺少
ingredient〔ɪn'gridɪənt〕*n.* 成分；原料
anxiously〔'æŋkʃəslɪ〕*adv.* 焦急地

"All I need is a handful of mustard seeds," said the Buddha *slowly*, "*but* it must come from a family *where no one has died.* That means *no child, no spouse, and no parent has died in the family.*" The young couple were *so* anxious to bring the baby back to life *that they did not think about the Buddha's words, and* set out *to look for the mustard seeds.* However, *after months and months of searching*, they came to realize *that the Buddha's request was impossible to fulfill.*

　　「我所需要的是一把芥菜子，」佛陀慢慢說道，「但是它必須來自一個都沒有人去世的家庭。也就是說，在這個家庭裡，沒有任何小孩、配偶，以及父母過世。」這對年輕夫婦太急著要讓嬰兒復活，以致於他們並沒有思考佛陀的話，就出發去尋找芥菜子了。然而，經過好幾個月的搜尋之後，他們終於了解，佛陀的要求是不可能達到的。

handful ('hænd,fʊl) *n.* 一把　　mustard ('mʌstəd) *n.* 芥菜
seed (sid) *n.* 種子　　spouse (spaʊz) *n.* 配偶
anxious ('æŋkʃəs) *adj.* 熱切的；渴望的
bring ~ (back) to life 使復活　　*set out* 出發
search (sɜtʃ) *v.,n.* 尋找　　*come to* 變成 (某種狀態)
request (rɪ'kwɛst) *n.* 請求；要求　　fulfill (fʊl'fɪl) *v.* 實現；達成

However, the young couple learned something important *during their search for the mustard seeds.* They saw *that every family they visited had lost someone, be it a child, a parent, or a spouse.* All *of these families* learned to go on with their lives *after the loved one's death.* The couple saw *that* death was a part *of the life cycle, and as* painful *as it was for them,* it was part *of life.* The families' stories and talks helped the young couple

feel better, ***and*** they realized *they were not alone.* ***But most importantly,***

they learned ***that*** *they could continue to live a normal life after the death*

of their child.

　　然而，在尋找芥菜子的過程中，這對年輕夫婦學到一件重要的事。他們知道，每一個他們拜訪過的家庭，都曾經失去某個親人，無論是小孩、父母或是配偶。所有的這些家庭，在他們的親人過世後，都學著要繼續過日子。這對夫婦了解到，死亡只是生命周期的一部分，雖然對他們來說很痛苦，但這就是人生的一部分。這些家庭的故事及談話，讓這對年輕夫婦覺得好多了，而他們也了解到，自己並不孤單。不過最重要的是，他們知道，自己能夠在小孩過世之後，繼續過正常的生活了。

　　* be it a child, a parent, or a spouse. = no matter it is a child, a parent, or a spouse. (詳見文法寶典 p.524, 530)

　　　go on 繼續　　loved (lʌvd) *adj.* 親愛的　　***loved one*** 親人
　　　cycle ('saɪkḷ) *n.* 周期；循環　　painful ('penfəl) *adj.* 痛苦的

49. (**A**) 爲什麼這對夫婦要去見佛陀？
　　　(A) 他們想要讓他們死去的小孩復活。
　　　(B) 他們想再生一個小孩。
　　　(C) 他們想要佛陀祝福這位死去的小孩。
　　　(D) 他們想要佛陀幫他們埋葬小孩。
　　　alive (ə'laɪv) *adj.* 活的　　bless (blɛs) *v.* 爲～祝福

50. (**B**) 佛陀要這對夫婦去哪裏找來芥菜子？
　　　(A) 從來都沒有小孩的家庭。
　　　(B) 從來都沒有失去親人的家庭。
　　　(C) 只有一個小孩的家庭。
　　　(D) 佛教徒的家庭。
　　　Buddhist ('budɪst) *n.* 佛教徒

51. (**D**) 這對年輕的夫婦找不到芥菜子，是因為
  (A) 發生旱災，芥菜子很難取得。
  (B) 這對夫婦沒有仔細思考佛陀說的話。
  (C) 尋找這個成分花了好幾個月的時間。
  (D) <u>所有的家庭都曾經歷過親人的死亡。</u>

  ※ 聯招會的英文試題中，將 drought 誤打為 *draught*。
  drought〔draʊt〕*n.* 旱災

52. (**C**) 本故事的寓意為何？
  (A) 我們應該一直去找佛陀幫助。
  (B) 讓人起死回生是有可能的。
  (C) <u>死亡是自然的，是我們生命周期的一部分。</u>
  (D) 快樂是悲傷的最佳良藥。

  moral〔'mɔrəl〕*n.* 寓意　　sorrow〔'saro〕*n.* 悲傷

第四篇（共 3 題）

In time of silver rain	在銀色的雨中
The earth	地球
Puts forth new life *again*,	再次綻放出新生命，
Green grasses grow	綠草蓬勃
And flowers lift their heads,	花朵昂首，
And over all the plain	在整個平原上
The wonder spreads	滿佈著生命的奇觀！
Of life, of life, of life!	

  put forth 長出；發揮　　grass〔græs〕*n.* 草
  lift〔lɪft〕*v.* 抬起　　plain〔plen〕*n.* 平原
  wonder〔'wʌndɚ〕*n.* 奇景；奇觀

In time of silver rain	在銀色的雨中
The butterflies lift silken wings	蝴蝶展開絲般的翅膀
To catch a rainbow cry,	捕捉彩虹的呼喚，
And trees put forth	樹木萌發出
New leaves to sing	新生的樹葉在歌唱
In joy beneath the sky	在喜悅中，在天空下
As down the roadway passing boys	路過的男孩女孩們
And girls go singing, too,	也在一路歡唱，
In time of silver rain	在銀色的雨中
When spring	當春天
And life are new.	和生命嶄新之時。

silken ('sɪlkən) *adj.* 如絲的　　rainbow ('ren,bo) *n.* 彩虹
roadway ('rod,we) *n.* 公路

53. (**A**) 本詩的背景是在

(A) 春天。　　(B) 夏天。　　(C) 秋天。　　(D) 冬天。

setting ('sɛtɪŋ) *n.* 背景；環境

54. (**B**) 本詩的主旨是

(A) 雨爲地球帶來銀。　　　(B) 雨爲地球帶來生命。
(C) 雨爲地球帶來悲傷。　　(D) 雨爲地球帶來彩虹。

55. (**C**) 在詩中，下列哪一個字被用來和 "rain" 押韻？

(A) Wings　　(B) Pain　　(C) Again　　(D) Spring

rhyme (raɪm) *v.* 押韻

第二部分：非選擇題

I、中譯英：10 %

When people think of conversations, they think of people talking to each other. What people often forget is that listening is an important part of keeping a conversation going. Have you ever stopped talking to someone because you did not think he or she was listening to you? Not paying attention is (1) one of the fastest / quickest ways to end / stop a conversation.

當人們想到對話，就會想到是人們在彼此交談。人們常常忘記，聆聽是讓對話繼續下去的一個重要部分。你曾經因爲認爲某人沒有在聽你說話，而停止和他或她說話嗎？不注意是 (1) 中止對話的最快速方法之一。

Listening actually is a lot of work, because it is more than just you sitting there looking at the person, nodding your head from time to time. You must let the person know that you have heard him or her. You can use sounds such as "Mm" or "Ah" or "Oh." You can also add short comments such as "yes," "really?" or "I didn't know that."

聆聽眞的需要很大的工夫，因爲它不只是你坐在那裡看著某人，偶爾點點頭而已。你必須讓對方知道，你已經聽到他或她說的話。你可以用像「嗯」、「啊」或「喔」這種聲音。你也可以加一些簡短的評論，像是「是的，」、「眞的嗎？」或「我不知道那件事。」

from time to time 偶爾（= sometimes）
comment〔'kɑmɛnt〕n. 評論

One *of the most useful,* **but** *maybe also the most difficult listening skills* is to summarize or paraphrase **what** *the person has said.* This shows the person *you are not just hearing* **what** *he or she said,* (2) **but you really / do understand.** *For example,* **if** *someone comes to you* **and** *tells you a story of* (3) **how he was bitten / bit** *by a dog on his way to school,* *then* he found out *he had left his homework at home,* **so** the teacher punished him. *At lunch* he found out *his lunch money was stolen,* **and** (4) **because he was very hungry,** he didn't *do* well *on / in the exam.* You can nod **and** show *you have heard him,* **or** you can summarize **what** *he has said* [by saying, (5) *"It sounds like today wasn't your day." / "It sounds like you had a bad day today."*]

　　最有用，但可能也是最困難的聆聽技巧之一，就是將對方所說的話做總結，或是再解釋一次。這樣能夠讓對方知道，你不只是聽到他或她所說的話而已，(2) 而是眞的聽懂了。 例如，如果有個人找你，告訴你他的遭遇，(3) 他如何在上學途中被狗咬了，然後發現自己把家庭作業遺忘在家裡，所以老師處罰他。午餐時，他發現自己的午餐費被偷了，而且 (4) 因爲他很餓，所以考試考得不好。 你可以點點頭，讓他知道你聽到他說的了，或者你可以總結他的話，說：(5)「聽起來你今天很倒霉。」

　　　　summarize (ˈsʌməˌraɪz) v. 摘要；做總結
　　　　paraphrase (ˈpærəˌfrez) v. 改述；意譯
　　　　story (ˈstorɪ) n. 詳情；情況　　**do well** 考得好

You can *also* summarize the feelings *the person was communicating by*

saying "You must feel awful after having all these things happen to you

today." If a person feels you are not just listening, but you are listening

carefully to his words and feelings, he is *more* likely to open up *and*

communicate *with you even more.*

　　你也可以總結對方想表達的感覺，說：「今天發生了這些事，你一定覺得心情糟透了。」如果對方感覺到，你不只是聽到了，而且你在仔細聆聽他所說的話，和所表達的感覺，他就更有可能會毫無保留地，和你聊得更多。

> communicate〔kə'mjunə͵ket〕*v.* 傳達；溝通
> awful〔'ɔfḷ〕*adj.* 很糟的
> *be likely to* + V. 可能～
> *open up* 沒有拘束地談；暢談

Ⅱ、作文範例：20%

The Difficulties I Have with Learning English

　　English used to be a piece of cake for me in junior high school. *However*, when I entered senior high school, it turned out to be a headache of mine. I became so frustrated with English that I nearly gave it up. Naturally, when I encountered new words, I consulted a dictionary for their meanings. *But* I found that there were too many words to look up in the time I had; I also got nervous in class, because the teacher spoke too fast for me to follow. My grades in English suffered a sudden decline.

The problem lasted until I had a new English teacher, Ms. Ku, in the second year. She was patient and enthusiastic. She taught us to try to figure out the meanings of the words from the context before looking them up. *In this way*, I found many of the new words were not as difficult as I had thought. In class too, she explained the lessons and grammar as thoroughly as she could and encouraged us to ask any questions we had. By listening attentively and studying hard, I rapidly improved my English. Thanks to Ms. Ku's advice and guidance, I regained my confidence in English. I really appreciate her teachings and I owe my progress to her.

> *a piece of cake* 輕而易舉的事   *turn out* 結果（成為）
> frustrated（'frʌstretɪd）*adj.* 受挫折的
> naturally（'nætʃərəlɪ）*adv.* 理所當然   encounter（ɪn'kaʊntɚ）*v.* 遇到
> consult（kən'sʌlt）*v.* 查閱（字典）   *look up* 查閱（生字）
> nervous（'nɝvəs）*adj.* 緊張的   follow（'falo）*v.* 聽懂
> decline（dɪ'klaɪn）*n.* 下降   *suffer a sudden decline* 一落千丈
> enthusiastic（ɪn,θjuzɪ'æstɪk）*adj.* 充滿熱誠的
> *figure out* 想出   context（'kantɛkst）*n.* 上下文
> grammar（'græmɚ）*n.* 文法   thoroughly（'θɝolɪ）*adv.* 徹底地
> *as~as one can* 儘可能（＝*as~as possible*）
> attentively（ə'tɛntɪvlɪ）*adv.* 專心地
> rapidly（'ræpɪdlɪ）*adv.* 快速地   *thanks to* 由於
> advice（əd'vaɪs）*n.* 勸告   guidance（'gaɪdn̩s）*n.* 指導
> regain（rɪ'gen）*v.* 恢復；重拾（信心）
> appreciate（ə'priʃɪ,et）*v.* 感激   teachings（'titʃɪŋz）*n.pl.* 教導
> *owe* A *to* B 把 A 歸功於 B   progress（'pragrɛs）*n.* 進步

※ 這份試題出得不錯，唯一的缺點是在閱測的 51 題中，把 drought 誤打成 *draught*。
　關於有爭議的第 43 題 "sandwich" 的來源，各有各的說法。考試時，考生應該以
　文章中的說法來選答案。這是答閱讀測驗的密訣。

心得筆記欄

八十八學年度大學聯考英文分數人數統計表

分數	第一類組	第二類組	第三類組	第四類組	分數	第一類組	第二類組	第三類組	第四類組
100	0	0	0	0	50	18751	12649	8966	9038
99	0	0	0	0	49	19813	13378	9443	9519
98	0	0	0	0	48	20805	14026	9856	9936
97	0	0	0	0	47	21907	14754	10303	10386
96	1	1	1	1	46	22964	15439	10755	10841
95	2	3	2	2	45	24064	16170	11218	11305
94	7	4	2	2	44	25195	16904	11678	11767
93	8	10	8	8	43	26324	17606	12109	12201
92	12	16	14	14	42	27493	18393	12608	12701
91	18	28	24	24	41	28714	19139	13067	13163
90	27	38	32	32	40	29896	19865	13490	13590
89	46	60	50	50	39	31098	20660	13962	14066
88	75	85	69	69	38	32186	21428	14428	14536
87	110	106	84	85	37	33332	22195	14891	15003
86	145	138	111	112	36	34515	22913	15332	15446
85	210	184	152	153	35	35706	23683	15811	15926
84	268	243	205	206	34	36909	24469	16300	16418
83	357	319	268	270	33	38112	25245	16806	16927
82	456	394	329	331	32	39301	26060	17312	17439
81	582	500	414	418	31	40481	26848	17795	17925
80	731	603	491	495	30	41691	27638	18296	18429
79	893	738	599	605	29	42904	28377	18776	18911
78	1094	895	724	730	28	44052	29142	19244	19383
77	1303	1061	857	863	27	45224	29856	19674	19818
76	1556	1240	1007	1013	26	46463	30649	20163	20309
75	1831	1440	1164	1170	25	47676	31449	20632	20784
74	2104	1626	1311	1317	24	48894	32149	21051	21206
73	2427	1866	1490	1498	23	50085	32926	21520	21677
72	2808	2145	1706	1715	22	51313	33698	21986	22146
71	3192	2444	1925	1935	21	52443	34443	22443	22605
70	3638	2751	2159	2171	20	53609	35157	22875	23040
69	4101	3055	2391	2408	19	54750	35916	23326	23503
68	4616	3415	2665	2683	18	55888	36668	23787	23971
67	5145	3749	2905	2925	17	57055	37386	24223	24407
66	5684	4102	3164	3185	16	58157	38052	24629	24815
65	6261	4512	3471	3494	15	59308	38754	25040	25233
64	6877	4934	3777	3801	14	60431	39478	25482	25683
63	7531	5366	4107	4132	13	61551	40140	25873	26080
62	8255	5843	4428	4457	12	62684	40771	26246	26455
61	9013	6336	4756	4791	11	63832	41367	26612	26824
60	9763	6811	5085	5124	10	64961	42003	27012	27238
59	10550	7324	5440	5484	9	65981	42560	27361	27594
58	11357	7830	5787	5831	8	67041	43159	27716	27956
57	12215	8387	6167	6214	7	68159	43719	28055	28303
56	13106	8977	6554	6606	6	69215	44267	28398	28658
55	13968	9566	6952	7006	5	70173	44775	28704	28971
54	14851	10149	7341	7405	4	71235	45254	28986	29268
53	15774	10749	7723	7789	3	72351	45762	29284	29594
52	16725	11389	8127	8197	2	73391	46268	29578	29906
51	17705	12003	8538	8609	1	74353	46633	29791	30145
					0	76764	47667	30406	30859

※ 88年大學聯考英文科：高標51分，均標34分，低標17分。

八十八學年度大學暨獨立學院入學考試
英 文 試 題

第一部分：單一選擇題

以下 1～40 題，每題 1 分，41～55 題，每題 2 分。請由每題 4 個備選項中選出一個最適當者，標示在「**答案卡**」上。每答錯一題倒扣題分的⅓，不答不給分。

I、對話（共 5 分）：

1. *Passenger* : I'd like to go to the World Trade Center.
   Taxi Driver : Sure. But it's only a few blocks away.
   Passenger : I know. But ＿＿＿＿＿＿＿＿
   (A) I'll take my time.
   (B) I need to exercise more.
   (C) I'm late for giving a talk.
   (D) I'd like to get there.

2. *Post Office Clerk* : I'm sorry. You can't send this package in this way.
   Customer : What's the matter? The mailing address is clearly marked.
   Post Office Clerk : Yes, but ＿＿＿＿＿＿＿＿＿
   (A) you have enough postage.
   (B) you still need to write the return address.
   (C) you've marked the zip code clearly.
   (D) you haven't asked for my help.

3. (After a meal at a restaurant.)
   Friend 1 : Let me get that.
   Friend 2 : No. ＿＿＿＿＿＿＿＿＿
   Friend 1 : That's not true. You paid.
   Friend 2 : I did not. It's my turn today.
   (A) You picked up the check last time.
   (B) I can't let you spend so much money.
   (C) The meal was awful and we shouldn't pay.
   (D) I don't have my credit card with me.

4. *Flight Attendant* : Excuse me, would you like the chicken or the beef?
   Passenger　　　 : Beef, please.
   Flight Attendant : _____
   Passenger　　　 : No. I'll have coffee instead.
   (A) What would you like to drink?
   (B) Where would you like to have it served?
   (C) How would you like it cooked?
   (D) Would you like some red wine with that?

5. *Bank Teller* : How can I help you today?
   Customer　 : Well, I'd like to cash these checks.
   Bank Teller : OK, everything looks fine except _____
   Customer　 : Oh. Sorry. I'll do it right now.
   (A) these checks are not in US dollars.
   (B) you forgot to sign the back of this check.
   (C) I'll need to see your I.D. card.
   (D) it will take a few minutes to process.

II、詞彙及慣用語（共 15 分）：

6. A person of great _____ usually can achieve his goal.
   (A) affirmation　　(B) information　　(C) determination　　(D) imitation

7. I am in a hurry, so I can only discuss this matter with you
   _____.
   (A) likely　　(B) scarcely　　(C) mainly　　(D) briefly

8. We need your help in order to have _____ funds to promote
   this social welfare program.
   (A) efficient　　(B) sufficient　　(C) proficient　　(D) deficient

9. These questions are _____ easy. I am sure you can answer them.
   (A) tentatively　　(B) protectively　　(C) relatively　　(D) expressively

10. Recent studies on whales have _____ that, they, like humans,
    also have emotions.
    (A) revealed　　(B) remained　　(C) reviewed　　(D) rewarded

11. Discrimination against women is a _____ of human rights.
    (A) suggestion (B) violation (C) reservation (D) demonstration

12. For our family to make both ends meet, it is important to _____ living expenses.
    (A) popularize (B) organize (C) liberalize (D) minimize

13. This couple went to Paris to celebrate their tenth wedding _____ last month.
    (A) ceremony (B) formality (C) anniversary (D) security

14. John is a very _____ person. He often tries to give others the impression that he is a VIP.
    (A) spontaneous (B) tremendous (C) humorous (D) pretentious

15 This scientist is very _____, His original experiments are widely admired.
    (A) imaginative (B) cooperative (C) representative (D) persuasive

16. After you have learned something new, it is important that you try to _____.
    (A) bring it up   (B) let go of it
    (C) get rid of it   (D) put it into practice

17. It is a well-known fact that one's success is _____ one's hard work.
    (A) in the way of   (B) in proportion to
    (C) in the case of   (D) in excess of

18. You messed up everything in the living room. When Mom comes home, you'll have to _____.
    (A) face the music   (B) make your point
    (C) make room for it   (D) hold your horses

19. The speaker's lecture is quite stimulating. It has given us some _____.
    (A) food for thought   (B) pie in the sky
    (C) cloud on the horizon (D) sweetness and light

20. It is hard for a country to _____ between economic development and environmental protection.

(A) save their skin   (B) beat around the bush
(C) strike a balance   (D) hold their ground

Ⅲ、綜合測驗（共 20 分）：

第一篇（共 10 題）

In your conversations with American adults, you should learn that some topics are safe, but others are not. Work and hobbies are good starters for conversations, but ___(21)___ avoid talking about age and money. When you meet an American ___(22)___, it is all right for you to ask "What do you do?" Most Americans are happy to talk about it, because they think they are ___(23)___ by their work. If work does not prove to be a productive topic, try other topics ___(24)___ hobbies. He may get quite excited about a hobby or some hobbies he is currently ___(25)___ with.

The topics of age and money may rapidly ___(26)___ your conversation to an end. Many adult Americans are ___(27)___ about looking young, so they always keep their age a secret. If you carelessly ___(28)___ this topic, they will often feel quite uneasy or upset. Income is also a very sensitive matter. While Americans may spend a lot of time ___(29)___ how much other people make, they don't say so. The reason may be that they think people are paid ___(30)___ their worth, and they don't want to have their worth known by others.

21. (A) by no means   (B) by all means
    (C) by means of   (D) by any means

22. (A) at the first moment   (B) for the first time
    (C) first of all   (D) from the very first

23. (A) defined   (B) referred   (C) controlled   (D) proposed

24. (A) so as   (B) as to   (C) as such   (D) such as

25. (A) involving   (B) involve   (C) involved   (D) involves

26. (A) bring   (B) let   (C) come   (D) make

27. (A) hasty　　　　(B) eager　　　(C) crazy　　　　(D) gentle
28. (A) touch on　　　(B) put on　　　(C) set on　　　(D) come on
29. (A) mastering　　(B) realizing　　(C) wondering　　(D) fulfilling
30. (A) appealing to (B) attending to (C) amounting to　(D) according to

第二篇（共 10 題）

　　E-mail (electronic-mail) as a form of private communication has recently created a new kind of writing with new rules. The ___(31)___ language of e-mail is English. A traditional English letter usually begins ___(32)___ an address, the date and perhaps the address of the addressee. ___(33)___ the e-mail system itself inserts these things, is there any ___(34)___ in putting them in? Traditional letters cannot interact with each other, but with e-mail it is possible ___(35)___ parts of the original letter in the reply. Because of this special feature, an e-mail letter can ___(36)___ be written quickly. So is it necessary to include a greeting and a farewell? Is it rude to ___(37)___? By using the symbols on the keyboard, the writer can ___(38)___ new messages. For example, to *emphasize* a word, or to indicate the writer's attitude, such as ☺ or ☻. ___(39)___, e-mail departs from the norm for writing letters, such as standard spellings and grammar. ___(40)___, an e-mail writer enjoys a great deal of freedom in communicating with anyone in any place of the world at any time.

31. (A) dominant　　(B) maximum　　(C) positive　　(D) relative
32. (A) to　　　　　(B) from　　　　(C) in　　　　　(D) with
33. (A) What if　　　(B) But if　　　(C) As if　　　(D) Not if
34. (A) point　　　　(B) plan　　　　(C) place　　　　(D) part
35. (A) included　　　(B) include　　(C) including　　(D) to include
36. (A) differently　　(B) primarily　(C) consequently　(D) harmoniously
37. (A) let them go　　　　　　　　(B) leave them out
　　(C) lift them up　　　　　　　　(D) lower them down
38. (A) polish　　　　(B) suppose　　(C) delay　　　　(D) convey
39. (A) For one thing　　　　　　　(B) In this way
　　(C) Once and for all　　　　　　(D) Sooner or later
40. (A) On the contrary　　　　　　(B) By contrast
　　(C) As a result　　　　　　　　(D) By the way

Ⅳ、閱讀測驗（共 30 分）：
第一篇（共 3 題）

A few years ago a gifted young conductor, Clive Wearing, was struck by a strange brain disease that virtually destroyed his memory. For him, every moment in time is separated from every other moment.

Otherwise his intellect is not damaged, which makes his condition even more tragic, and he is often deeply depressed. Yet there are two elements of his former, rich life that haven't deserted him. The first is his love for his wife. Every time he sees her, which may be five minutes since he last saw her, he greets her with great joy, welcoming her back into his life as though she had been gone for years.

The second element of his past life that mysteriously remains is music. When his wife first takes him into a room where there is a piano and a small group of singers, he doesn't know what to do. But as soon as the singers start to sing, his face immediately brightens and he begins to sing and conduct a song by Mozart. Somehow love and music have remained whole in his weakened brain. No one can explain why this can be, when the rest of his memory seems to have been destroyed. But somehow in his mind and his heart there is a miraculous survival of love and beauty.

41. The overall tone of this passage is one of
    (A) sadness.   (B) hope.
    (C) forgiveness.   (D) irony.

42. The greatest tragedy of Wearing's illness is that he can no longer
    (A) recognize his family.   (B) appreciate music.
    (C) conduct a group of singers. (D) recall his past.

43. This passage points out that Wearing
    (A) has been away from his wife for a long time.
    (B) didn't learn to play the piano before his illness.
    (C) is sad that part of his memory is lost.
    (D) can only remember Mozart's music.

第二篇（共 3 題）

Books are like people. You may like a person without necessarily wanting to ask him or her home for supper. You may like a book without necessarily wanting to read or possess it. So it is with the books in our shop. We know them all, we like them all, we enjoy their companionship, because to a bookseller a book is not something to read; it is something to handle, something to sell. To a bookseller a good book is something that is well designed and well made, and the handling of it gives him or her great pleasure. I know little and care nothing about weapons, yet I know that in my town there are many people with a passion for tanks. I can recognize a well-designed tank book when I am shown one, and it gives me great pleasure to order it, display it, and even introduce it to a customer with my personal recommendation.

Does it seem wrong that I am prepared to say, "Here is a good book," when I have done no more than glance at it? How can I judge a book about which I know nothing? The answer is that I can because I can get the help of others, including the publisher, the reviewers, and other customers. My personal judgment is confined to the book's production, to its look and feel. I leave it to the experts to judge the contents.

44. This passage states that a bookseller's main concern about a book is its
    (A) contents.   (B) appearance.   (C) cost.   (D) publisher.

45. The author feels that he or she is NOT
    (A) an expert on how well-written a book is.
    (B) a good judge of a book's design.
    (C) someone who recommends books on weapons.
    (D) a person who appreciates having books around.

46. Which of the following statements does the author argue against?
    (A) Booksellers usually charge customers too much for well-produced books.
    (B) Booksellers should take delight in having books around them.
    (C) Booksellers should always read a book before urging a customer to buy it.
    (D) Booksellers should sell only books that have received good reviews.

第三篇（共 4 題）

First-time dog owners may encounter many problems getting to know and train their pets. Sometimes a puppy, or even an older dog, will chew their fingers or bite them. Even in play, this can really hurt. Unfortunately, many pet owners tolerate this in a young dog. However, when the dog gets larger, it is not fun to be bitten by it. Training a dog to never place his teeth on human skin or clothing is an important lesson. From now on, if you feel your dog's teeth while you are playing with him, say "Ouch" in a loud voice and move away from him. He will soon learn that when he bites, you will not play with him anymore.

Another bad habit that many people tolerate in their pets is allowing them to bite and hold on to clothing. Don't let your dog do this to you. When he does something you want him to do, praise him and tell him he's a good dog. You can also give him a treat at the same time he performs the good behavior. Eventually he will learn which kind of behavior is acceptable and which is not. Remember that reward is more effective than punishment. If you reward your dog when he does what you want him to, he will become very well behaved. Also remember that puppies need to chew on something. So give him a sock with a knot tied in it or an old shoe. If he chews the wrong thing, take it away while saying "No" and give him something he can chew. If dogs are trained well, they will truly be your friends for a lifetime.

47. This passage focuses on the topic of
    (A) teaching people how to train dogs.
    (B) showing dog owners how to behave.
    (C) demonstrating good dog behavior.
    (D) explaining why a dog chews on something.

48. According to this passage, many people tend to
    (A) think puppies should be properly trained.
    (B) be too rough towards their dogs.
    (C) give their dogs treats infrequently.
    (D) allow their dogs to behave badly.

49. Based on this passage, which of the following statements is NOT TRUE?
   (A) Our behavior influences our dogs' behavior.
   (B) Dogs enjoy being rewarded by their owners.
   (C) Say nothing even when your dog has bitten you.
   (D) Training a dog takes patience and time.

50. The author thinks that a better way to train a dog is:
   (A) punish him for any mistake he has made.
   (B) reinforce his good behavior with a treat.
   (C) tolerate him no matter what he does.
   (D) always be kind to him and don't scold him.

第四篇（共 5 題）

One day in 1918, something very strange happened at an army camp in America. Their camp had thousands of horses and mules. They disposed of the animals' waste matter by burning it. That day a huge dust storm, along with the burning waste matter, turned the sun completely black. Two days later, men began to complain of having very bad colds. By noon, more than one hundred men were sick. Doctors didn't have the record keeping that we have in modern times to keep track of illnesses, although they knew that many people living close together often gave their diseases to others. In the same month, the United States sent 84,000 soldiers to fight in the war against Germany. Little did they know that they were carrying a disease that would kill as many soldiers as their rifles would. The disease traveled fast, and in just four months, tens of thousands in every part of the world had fallen ill and died.

In those days, many people believed medical science could cure any disease. When they discovered no one had a solution to this deadly disease, people turned toward prevention. The government tried to educate people not to use common cups and utensils. They also told people not to cough or sneeze without covering their mouths. People were also encouraged to wash their hands often and pay attention to personal cleanliness. In this way, they could reduce the chance of infecting someone else or becoming infected themselves. In modern times, we also need to take responsibility to avoid spreading illness.

51. The main idea of this passage is
    (A) to tell us about an important war in human history.
    (B) to describe the hardships of military life in the U.S.
    (C) to demonstrate the advances of medical science.
    (D) to show that disease can spread from person to person.

52. According to this passage, many soldiers fell ill because
    (A) they raised too many horses and mules.
    (B) they didn't want to go to war.
    (C) they all lived very close together.
    (D) they didn't have record keeping.

53. Based on this passage, which of the following is TRUE?
    (A) American soldiers used disease as a weapon to kill the enemy.
    (B) American soldiers enjoyed horse racing at the army camp.
    (C) The Germans were defeated by bad colds in World War I.
    (D) Bad colds spread and killed without regard to borders.

54. Which of the following is NOT a preventive measure?
    (A) Complain to your doctor about a bad cold.
    (B) Don't share cups and utensils with others.
    (C) Cover your mouth when coughing and sneezing.
    (D) Wash your hands as frequently as possible.

55. In modern times, we believe that
    (A) any disease can be cured by medicine.
    (B) everyone should be careful about diseases.
    (C) doctors alone are held responsible for diseases.
    (D) the government can handle any disease.

第二部分：非選擇題

I、中譯英（共 10 分）：

　　下面一段短文共含五個中文句子，請譯成正確、通順、達意且前後連貫的英
　　文。每句二分。答案請寫在「**非選擇題試卷**」上，同時務必分行標示題號。

　　(1) 以年輕人和老年人的睡眠習慣很不相同。

　　(2) 許多年輕人往往很晚還不睡，第二天早上就不能早起。

(3) 老年人通常晚上沒事做，所以很早上床。

(4) 這兩種不同的睡眠習慣，哪一種比較有益健康呢？

(5) 其實，只要睡飽，早睡晚睡都沒關係。

Ⅱ、**英文作文**（共 20 分）：

請以 "A Happy Ending"（快樂的結局）為題，寫一篇約一百二十個單字的英文作文。你可以從你所讀過的故事、看過的電影或親身的體驗中去找題材。描述完快樂的結局以後，並寫幾句你的感想。答案請寫在「**非選擇題試卷**」上。

（內容 5 分，組織 5 分，文法 4 分，用字遣詞 4 分，拼字、大小寫及標點符號 2 分）。

88年大學聯考英文試題詳解

第一部分：單一選擇題

I、對話：5％

1.(**C**) 乘　　　客：我要到世貿。
　　計程車司機：好的，但世貿離這裏只有幾條街。
　　乘　　　客：我知道。但是 _____

　　(A) 我會慢慢來。　　　　　(B) 我需要多運動。
　　(C) 我演講要遲到了。　　　(D) 我想到那裏。

block〔blɑk〕*n.* 街區　　***take one's time*** 慢慢來　　***give a talk*** 演講

※ (A)(B) 不合乎前後句意。(D) 要改成：I'd like to get there ***sooner***.
　 這條題目，有些外國老師會認為答案 (D) 可以。唸成 I'd like to get there.，
　 重讀在 I 上，表示諷刺的意味。會話題答題的祕訣是：在正常情況下，正常人
　 說出有禮貌的話。答案 (D) 的回答，不是在正常情況下，所以是錯誤的答案。
　 我們在家敎班的講義中，常有類似的題目，聯考也常考類似的題目。(C) give a
　 talk「演講」，較少用，但我們在家敎班的模擬試題中考過兩次，一般多用 give
　 a speech。

2.(**B**) 郵局職員：很抱歉，你的包裹這樣沒辦法寄。
　　顧　　客：怎麼了？收件人的地址已標示得很清楚了。
　　郵局職員：是的，但是 _____

　　(A) 你有足夠的郵資。
　　(B) 你還必須寫寄件人地址。
　　(C) 你已經把郵遞區號標示清楚了。
　　(D) 你還沒要求我幫忙。

clerk〔klɜk〕*n.* 職員　　　***mailing address*** 收件人地址
mark〔mɑrk〕*v.* 標示　　　postage〔'postɪdʒ〕*n.* 郵資
return address 寄件人地址　　　***zip code*** 郵遞區號

※ (A) 要改成：You don't have enough postage. (C) 要改成：You haven't
　 marked the zip code clearly. (D) 與前面句意不合。

3.(**A**)（在餐廳用餐後。）
友人甲：我來付帳。
友人乙：不行。_____
友人甲：才不是，是你付的。
友人乙：我沒有。今天輪到我付了。

(A) 上次是你付的帳。　　　　　　(B) 我不能讓你花這麼多錢。
(C) 這餐飯真難吃，我們不該付錢。　(D) 我沒帶信用卡。

meal〔mil〕*n.* 一餐　　***pick up the check*** 付帳

※ (B) 可回答，但是跟下一句不合，(C) 只有開玩笑用，且跟下一句不合。(D) 跟上下句意均不合。

4.(**D**)空服員：對不起，您要雞肉還是牛肉？
乘　客：牛肉。
空服員：_____
乘　客：不，我想要咖啡。

(A) 您想喝什麼？　　　　　　　(B) 您想在哪裏用餐？
(C) 您牛肉要幾分熟？　　　　　(D) 您想要配點紅酒嗎？

flight attendant 空服員　　beef〔bif〕*n.* 牛肉
instead〔ɪn'stɛd〕*adv.* 作爲代替；改換　　serve〔sɝv〕*v.* 上（菜）

※ 這個題目作答很容易，因爲下一句有 No，是 Yes-No Question，只能選 (D)。
如果你知道常識，白肉（如雞肉、魚肉等）配白酒，紅肉（如牛肉、羊肉等）
配紅酒，這條題目就會選答案 (D) 了。

5.(**B**)銀行出納員：要我爲您效勞嗎？
顧　　　客：嗯，我想兌現這些支票。
銀行出納員：好的，看來一切都沒問題，只不過 _____
顧　　　客：噢，很抱歉，我馬上簽。

(A) 這些不是美金支票。　　　　(B) 您忘了在支票背面簽名。
(C) 我必須看看你的身份證。　　(D) 需要幾分鐘的時間處理。

teller〔'tɛlɚ〕*n.* （銀行）出納員　　cash〔kæʃ〕*v.* 兌現
sign〔saɪn〕*v.* 在～簽名　　process〔'prɑsɛs〕*v.* 處理

※ 如果要選 (C)，則必須把後面的 I'll do it right now. 改成 Here you are.
(A)(D) 則與後面 I'll do it right now. 句意不連貫。

II、詞彙及慣用語：15%

6. (**C**) A person *of great determination usually* can achieve his goal.
很有<u>決心</u>的人通常可以達成目標。

      (A) affirmation〔͵æfə'meʃən〕*n.* 斷言；肯定
      (B) information〔͵ɪnfə'meʃən〕*n.* 資訊；消息
      (C) ***determination***〔dɪ͵tɝmə'neʃən〕*n.* 決心
      (D) imitation〔͵ɪmə'teʃən〕*n.* 模仿

achieve〔ə'tʃiv〕*v.* 達到   goal〔gol〕*n.* 目標

7. (**D**) I am in a hurry, *so* I can *only* discuss this matter *with you briefly*.
我在趕時間，所以我只能和你<u>簡短地</u>討論這件事。

      (A) likely〔'laɪklɪ〕*adj.* 可能的
      (B) scarcely〔'skɛrslɪ〕*adv.* 幾乎不
      (C) mainly〔'menlɪ〕*adv.* 主要地
      (D) ***briefly***〔'briflɪ〕*adv.* 簡短地

8. (**B**) We need your help *in order to have sufficient funds to promote this social welfare program.*

我們需要你的協助，才能有<u>足夠的</u>錢來推動這項社會福利計劃。

      (A) efficient〔ə'fɪʃənt〕*adj.* 有效率的
      (B) ***sufficient***〔sə'fɪʃənt〕*adj.* 足夠的
      (C) proficient〔prə'fɪʃənt〕*adj.* 精通的
      (D) deficient〔dɪ'fɪʃənt〕*adj.* 不足的

funds〔fʌndz〕*n. pl.* 錢；基金   promote〔prə'mot〕*v.* 提倡；籌劃
welfare〔'wɛl͵fɛr〕*n.* 福利   program〔'progræm〕*n.* 計劃

※ 你唸唸看：efficient-sufficient-deficient，這些字要一起背才不會搞混。（詳見「英文字根字典」p.262）

9. (**C**) These questions are *relatively* easy. I am sure *you can answer*
them. 這些問題相當容易。我相信你一定能回答。

    (A) tentatively〔'tɛntətɪvlɪ〕*adv.* 試驗性地；暫時地
    (B) protectively〔prə'tɛktɪvlɪ〕*adv.* 保護地
    (C) *relatively*〔'rɛlətɪvlɪ〕*adv.* 相當地；相對地
    (D) expressively〔ɪk'sprɛsɪvlɪ〕*adv.* 意味深長地；表情豐富地

10. (**A**) Recent studies *on whales* have revealed *that, they, like humans,*
also have emotions.
最近對於鯨魚的研究顯示，鯨魚像人類一樣，也有情緒。

    (A) *reveal*〔rɪ'vil〕*v.* 顯示
    (B) remain〔rɪ'men〕*v.* 留下；仍然是
    (C) review〔rɪ'vju〕*v.* 複習
    (D) reward〔rɪ'wɔrd〕*v.* 報酬；獎賞

recent〔'risn̩t〕*adj.* 最近的   whale〔hwel〕*n.* 鯨魚
emotion〔ɪ'moʃən〕*n.* 情感；情緒

11. (**B**) Discrimination *against women* is a violation *of human rights.*
歧視女性是種違反人權的行為。

    (A) suggestion〔səg'dʒɛstʃən〕*n.* 建議
    (B) *violation*〔,vaɪə'leʃən〕*n.* 違反（的行為）
    (C) reservation〔,rɛzə'veʃən〕*n.* 預訂
    (D) demonstration〔,dɛmən'streʃən〕*n.* 示威運動；示範

discrimination〔dɪ,skrɪmə'neʃən〕*n.* 歧視   *human rights* 人權

12. (**D**) *For our family to make both ends meet,* it is important to
minimize living expenses.
為了使我們家能收支相抵，把生活費減至最低是十分重要的。

(A) popularize (ˈpɑpjələˌraɪz) v. 使流行；宣傳
(B) organize (ˈɔrgənˌaɪz) v. 組織
(C) liberalize (ˈlɪbərəlˌaɪz) v. 使自由化
(D) *minimize* (ˈmɪnəˌmaɪz) v. 使減到最低

make both ends meet 使收支相抵　　expense (ɪkˈspɛns) n. 費用

13. (**C**) This couple went to Paris *to celebrate their tenth wedding*

anniversary last month.

這對夫婦上個月去巴黎慶祝他們結婚十週年紀念。

(A) ceremony (ˈsɛrəˌmonɪ) n. 典禮
   wedding ceremony 結婚典禮
(B) formality (fɔrˈmælətɪ) n. 拘泥形式；正式
(C) *anniversary* (ˌænəˈvɝsərɪ) n. 週年紀念
   wedding anniversary 結婚週年紀念
(D) security (sɪˈkjʊrətɪ) n. 安全

couple (ˈkʌpl̩) n. 夫婦

14. (**D**) John is a *very* pretentious person. He *often* tries to give others

the impression *that he is a VIP.*

約翰是個很喜歡裝模作樣的人。他經常想讓別人覺得他是個大人物。

(A) spontaneous (spɑnˈtenɪəs) adj. 自發性的；不由自主的
(B) tremendous (trɪˈmɛndəs) adj. 巨大的
(C) humorous (ˈhjumərəs) adj. 幽默的
(D) *pretentious* (prɪˈtɛnʃəs) adj. 裝模作樣的；虛偽的

impression (ɪmˈprɛʃən) n. 印象；感覺
VIP (ˈviˌaɪˈpi) n. 大人物 (= *very important person*)

15. (**A**) This scientist is *very* imaginative. His original experiments are

widely admired.

這位科學家非常<u>富有想像力</u>。他有創意的實驗，受到大家普遍的讚賞。

　　(A) *imaginative* (ɪˋmædʒəˏnetɪv) *adj.* 富有想像力的
　　(B) cooperative (koˋɑpəˏretɪv) *adj.* 合作的
　　(C) representative (ˏrɛprɪˋzɛntətɪv) *adj.* 代表～的　　*n.* 代表
　　(D) persuasive (pəˋswesɪv) *adj.* 有說服力的

original (əˋrɪdʒənḷ) *adj.* 有創意的

experiment (ɪkˋspɛrəmənt) *n.* 實驗

16. (**D**) *After you have learned something new*, it is important *that you*

try to put it into practice.

在你學完新的事物後，重要的是要<u>把它付諸實行</u>。

　　(A) bring up 撫養長大
　　(B) let go of 放開
　　(C) get rid of 擺脫；除去
　　(D) *put sth. into practice* 把某事付諸實行

17. (**B**) It is a well-known fact *that one's success is in proportion to*

one's hard work.

大家都知道，一個人的成功<u>與</u>他所做的努力<u>成正比</u>。

　　(A) in the way of 妨礙
　　(B) *in proportion to* ～　與～成比例
　　(C) in the case of ～　至於～；就～來說
　　(D) in excess of 超過　　excess (ɪkˋsɛs) *n.* 超過

well-known (ˋwɛlˋnon) *adj.* 有名的；眾所周知的

18. (**A**) You messed up everything *in the living room.* **When Mom comes home**, you'll have to face the music.
你把客廳的東西弄得亂七八糟。等媽媽回到家，你就得<u>接受處罰</u>了。

    (A) *face the music* 面對現實；接受處罰
    (B) make one's point 使別人同意自己的論點
    (C) make room for ~ 讓位給~
    (D) hold *one's* horses 稍安勿躁

mess up 弄亂

19. (**A**) The speaker's lecture is *quite* stimulating. It has given us some food *for thought.*
那位演講者的演講內容十分振奮人心，提供給我們<u>一些值得思考的問題</u>。

    (A) *food for thought* 值得思考的問題
    (B) pie in the sky 空中樓閣；虛幻的承諾
    (C) on the horizon 即將來臨的   horizon (hə'raɪzn) *n.* 地平線
    (D) sweetness and light 和藹可親；友善

lecture ('lɛktʃə) *n.* 演講
stimulating ('stɪmjə,letɪŋ) *adj.* 激勵的；振奮人心的

20. (**C**) It is hard for a country to <u>strike a balance</u> *between economic development **and** environmental protection.*
國家很難在經濟發展與環保之間<u>取得平衡</u>。

    (A) save *one's* skin 平安逃脫
    (B) beat around the bush 拐彎抹角
    (C) *strike a balance* (兩者間) 取得平衡
    (D) hold *one's* ground 堅持立場

economic (,ikə'namɪk) *adj.* 經濟的
environmental protection 環境保護

Ⅲ、綜合測驗：20％

第一篇（共 10 題）

In your conversations with American adults, you should learn *that*
some topics are safe, *but others are not*. Work and hobbies are good
starters *for conversations*, *but* by all means avoid talking about age and
　　　　　　　　　　　　　　　21
money. *When you meet an American for the first time*, it is all right
　　　　　　　　　　　　　　　　　　　22
for you to ask "What do you do?" Most Americans are happy to talk
about it, *because they think they are* defined *by their work*. *If work*
　　　　　　　　　　　　　　　23
does not prove to be a productive topic, try other topics such as
　　　　　　　　　　　　　　　　　　　　　　　24
hobbies. He may get *quite* excited about a hobby *or* some hobbies *he*
is currently involved with.
　　　25

　　和美國成人談話時，你應該要知道，有些話題是不會出錯的，但有些卻不是。
一開始不妨先談工作和嗜好，但是務必要避免談到年齡和金錢。當你和一個美國
人初次見面，問他：「你從事哪一行？」是可以的。大部分的美國人很樂於談論
他們的工作，因為他們認為工作是他們的特色。如果工作不是個很好的話題，那
就試試其他的話題，像是嗜好。談到某種嗜好，或他目前所從事的嗜好，可能會
令他十分興奮。

　　　　　　prove〔pruv〕*v.* 結果是
　　　　　　productive〔prə'dʌktɪv〕*adj.* 有好結果的；有收穫的
　　　　　　currently〔'kɝəntlɪ〕*adv.* 目前

21.(**B**) 依句意，選(B)***by all means*** 「務必」。而(A)by no means「絕不」，
　　　　(C)by means of 「藉由」，及(D)by any means 「無論如何」，均不
　　　　合句意。

22.(**B**)　和一個美國人「初次」見面，選 (B)*for the first time*「生平第一次」。
　　　　而 (A) at the first moment「起初」，(C) first of all「首先；第一點」，
　　　　(D) from the very first「從一開始」，均不合句意。

23.(**A**)　依句意，選 (A)*define*〔dɪˈfaɪn〕*v.* 是～的特色。*be defined by* ～ 特
　　　　色是～（＝*be characterized by* ～）。而 (B) refer〔rɪˈfɝ〕*v.* 提到；
　　　　參考，(C) 控制，(D) propose〔prəˈpoz〕*v.* 提議，均不合句意。

24.(**D**)　依句意，試試其他的話題，「像是」嗜好，選 (D)*such as*「像是」
　　　　（＝like）。而 (A) so as to「為了」（＝*in order to*），(B) as to
　　　　「至於」，不合乎上下文意。(C) as such「就其本身而言」（詳見文
　　　　法寶典 p.535），則不合句意。

25.(**C**)　*be involved with* 與～有關；參與

The topics *of age and money* may *rapidly* bring your conversation
　　　　　　　　　　　　　　　　　　　　　　　　26

to an end. Many adult Americans are crazy about looking young, *so*
　　　　　　　　　　　　　　　　　　27

they *always* keep their age a secret. *If you carelessly touch on this topic*,
　　　　　　　　　　　　　　　　　　　　　　　　　28

they will *often* feel *quite* uneasy or upset. Income is *also* a *very* sensitive

matter. *While Americans may spend a lot of time wondering **how much***
　　　　　　　　　　　　　　　　　　　　　　　　　29

other people make, they don't say so. The reason may be **that** they

think people are paid according to their worth, **and** they don't want to
　　　　　　　　　　　　　　30

have their worth known by others.

年齡和金錢的話題，會使你們的談話很快就結束。許多美國成年人非常渴望能使自己看起來很年輕，所以總是把年齡當作祕密。如果你一不小心在談話中提到這個話題，他們常會覺得非常不自在或生氣。收入也是一件非常敏感的事。雖然美國人可能花很多時間，想知道其他人賺多少錢，但他們卻不會說出來。理由可能是，他們認為，一個人的薪水是依其個人的價值而定，而他們並不想讓別人知道自己的身價。

> uneasy〔ʌn'izɪ〕adj. 不自在的；不安的
> upset〔ʌp'sɛt〕adj. 生氣的　　income〔'ɪn,kʌm〕n. 收入
> sensitive〔'sɛnsətɪv〕adj. 敏感的　　worth〔wɝθ〕n. 價值

26.(**A**) ***bring sth. to an end*** 結束某事

27.(**C**) ***be crazy about*** 渴望；非常喜歡
　　(A) hasty〔'hestɪ〕adj. 匆忙的
　　(B) eager〔'igɚ〕adj. 熱切的；渴望的（其用法為：be eager to-V.「急著要」；
　　　　be eager for「渴望」）
　　(D) gentle〔'dʒɛntl̩〕adj. 溫和的

28.(**A**) (A) ***touch on*** （在談話中）提到（= *mention*）
　　※ touch 原指「碰到」，加上 on 引申為「（談話中）提到」，用法上和 hear「聽
　　　到」，hear from「收到信息」類似。任何及物動詞加上介詞，就形成另外的
　　　意思。
　　(B) put on 穿上　　(C) set on 攻擊（= *attack*）
　　(D) come on （催促對方）趕快；（夜晚、風雨等）來臨

29.(**C**) 依句意，「想知道」別人賺多少錢，選 (C) ***wonder***〔'wʌndɚ〕v. 想知道。
　　而 (A) master〔'mæstɚ〕v. 精通，(B) realize〔'rɪə,laɪz〕v. 了解，(D) fulfill
　　〔ful'fɪl〕v. 履行（義務）；滿足（需要），則不合句意。

30.(**D**) 領多少薪水，是「根據」個人的價值來決定，選 (D) ***according to***「根
　　據」。而 (A) appeal to「吸引」，(B) attend to「注意」，(C) amount
　　to「總計」，則不合句意。

第二篇（共 10 題）

E-mail (electronic-mail) *as a form of private communication* has *recently* created a new kind of writing *with new rules*. The dominant ___31___ language *of e-mail* is English. A traditional English letter *usually* begins with an address, the date *and* perhaps the address *of the addressee*. ___32___ *But if* the e-mail system itself inserts these things, is there any point *in* ___33___ ___34___ putting them in?

　　近來電子郵件（ e-mail ）作為一種私人通訊的形式，已產生了一些新的寫作規則。電子郵件的主要語言是英語。傳統的英文信件，通常一開始就是地址、日期，也許還會有收件人的地址。但如果電子郵件系統本身就已經有這些資料，那麼，把它們寫進去還有什麼意義呢？

　　　　electronic〔ˌɪlɛk'trɑnɪk〕adj. 電子的　　addressee〔ˌædrɛs'i〕n. 收件人
　　　　insert〔ɪn'sɝt〕v. 插入；寫入

31. (**A**)　(A) *dominant*〔'dɑmənənt〕adj. 佔優勢的；主要的
　　　　　　(B) maximum〔'mæksəməm〕adj. 最大的；最高的
　　　　　　(C) positive〔'pɑzətɪv〕adj. 正面的；肯定的
　　　　　　(D) relative〔'rɛlətɪv〕adj. 相對的

32. (**D**)　*begin with* ~　以~為開始

33. (**B**)　前後兩句語意相反，故應用 but 來連接，選 (B) *But if*。而 (A) What
　　　　　　if ~ ？「如果~該怎麼辦？」，(C) As if「就好像」，句意均不合；
　　　　　　(D) Not if 無此用法。

34. (**A**)　依句意，選 (A) *point*，在此作「意義」解。(B) 計劃，(C) 地方，(D) 部
　　　　　　分，均不合句意。

Traditional letters cannot interact *with each other*, *but* *with e-mail* it is

possible *to include* parts *of the original letter* *in the reply*. *Because of*
　　　　　35

this special feature, an e-mail letter can *consequently* be written *quickly*.
　　　　　　　　　　　　　　　　　　36

So is it necessary to include a greeting and a farewell? Is it rude to leave

them out?
37

傳統的信件無法彼此互動，但有了電子郵件，我們就可以把原信的一部分放在回信中。因為有這個特色，所以電子郵件可以很快就寫好。因此，有必要寫上問候語和告別的話嗎？省略不寫會很沒有禮貌嗎？

　　　interact (ˌɪntɚˈækt) v. 互動　　greeting (ˈgritɪŋ) n. 招呼語；問候語
　　　farewell (ˌfɛrˈwɛl) n. 告別語；結語
　　　rude (rud) adj. 沒禮貌的；粗魯的

35. (**D**) it 是虛主詞，後面接不定詞做真正主詞，故選 (D) *to include*。

36. (**C**)　(A) differently (ˈdɪfərəntlɪ) adv. 不同地
　　　　　　(B) primarily (ˈpraɪˌmɛrəlɪ) adv. 主要地
　　　　　　(C) *consequently* (ˈkɑnsəˌkwɛntlɪ) adv. 因此
　　　　　　(D) harmoniously (harˈmonɪəslɪ) adv. 和諧地

37. (**B**)　(A) let go 放開；釋放　　　　(B) *leave out* 漏寫；省略
　　　　　　(C) lift (up) 舉起　　　　　　(D) lower (down) 放下

By using the symbols on the keyboard, the writer can convey new
　　　　　　　　　　　　　　　　　　　　　　　　　　　38

messages. *For example*, to *emphasize* a word, *or* to indicate the

writer's attitude, *such as* ☺ *or* ☹ . *In this way*, e-mail departs from
　　　　　　　　　　　　　　　　　　　　39

the norm *for writing letters*, *such as standard spellings and grammar*. As

a result, an e-mail writer enjoys a great deal of freedom *in communicating*
40

with anyone in any place of the world at any time.

利用鍵盤上的符號，作者可以傳達新的訊息，例如，來*強調*一個字，或是表示作者的態度，如 ☺ 或是 ☹。如此一來，電子郵件就違反了寫信的規範，如標準的拼字及文法。也因此，發電子郵件的人享有很大的自由，可以在任何時候，與世界上任何地方的任何人通信。

> symbol〔ˈsɪmbḷ〕*n.* 符號　　keyboard〔ˈkiˌbord〕*n.* 鍵盤
> indicate〔ˈɪndəˌket〕*v.* 表示　　*depart from* 違反；背離
> norm〔nɔrm〕*n.* 標準；規範　　*communicate with* 通信

38. (**D**) (A) polish〔ˈpɑlɪʃ〕*v.* 擦亮　　(B) suppose〔səˈpoz〕*v.* 以為
　　　　　(C) delay〔dɪˈle〕*v.* 延遲；拖延　　(D) *convey*〔kənˈve〕*v.* 傳達

39. (**B**) (A) for one thing 一則；首先　　(B) *in this way* 如此一來
　　　　　(C) once and for all 最後一次　　(D) sooner or later 遲早

40. (**C**) (A) on the contrary 相反地　　(B) by contrast 對比之下
　　　　　(C) *as a result* 因此　　(D) by the way 順便一提

Ⅳ、閱讀測驗：30 %

第一篇（共 3 題）

A few years ago a gifted young conductor, *Clive Wearing*, was struck

by a strange brain disease **that** virtually destroyed his memory. *For*

him, every moment *in time* is separated *from every other moment*.

幾年前，一位很有天分的年輕指揮家，克萊夫·威耳林，突然得了一種奇怪的腦部疾病，幾乎破壞了他的記憶力。對他而言，時間中的每一瞬間和其他瞬間，都是分開的。

> gifted〔ˈgɪftɪd〕*adj.* 有天分的　　conductor〔kənˈdʌktɚ〕*n.* 指揮家
> virtually〔ˈvɝtʃʊəlɪ〕*adv.* 幾乎（= *almost*）
> strike〔straɪk〕*v.*（疾病）突然侵襲

Otherwise his intellect is not damaged, *which makes his condition even more tragic, and* he is *often deeply* depressed. *Yet* there are two elements *of his former, rich life that haven't deserted him.* The first is his love *for his wife.* *Every time he sees her, which may be five minutes since he last saw her,* he greets her *with great joy,* welcoming her back into his life *as though she had been gone for years.*

除此之外，他的智力並沒有受損，這使得他的情況更悲慘，他經常感到十分沮喪。然而，他以前豐富的生活中，有兩個要素並沒有拋棄他。第一是他對妻子的愛。他每次看見她，可能離上次見到她只有五分鐘，他都會非常高興地和她打招呼，歡迎她回到他的生命中，彷彿她離開了數年之久。

otherwise (ˈʌðəˌwaɪz) adv. 除此之外　　intellect (ˈɪntḷˌɛkt) n. 智力
tragic (ˈtrædʒɪk) adj. 悲慘的　　deeply (ˈdiplɪ) adv. 非常地
depressed (dɪˈprɛst) adj. 沮喪的　　element (ˈɛləmənt) n. 要素
former (ˈfɔrmə) adj. 以前的　　greet (grit) v. 打招呼

The second element *of his past life that mysteriously remains* is music. *When his wife first takes him into a room where there is a piano and a small group of singers,* he doesn't know *what to do.* *But as soon as the singers start to sing,* his face *immediately* brightens *and* he begins to sing and conduct a song *by Mozart.*

第二個從他過去生活中神祕地保留下來的要素，是音樂。當他的妻子初次帶他到一個房間，裏面有一架鋼琴，和一小群演唱者，他不知該怎麼辦。但是當那些演唱者一開始演唱時，他的臉立刻亮了起來。他也開始唱，並指揮了一首莫札特的歌。

mysteriously (mɪsˈtɪrɪəslɪ) adv. 神秘地
brighten (ˈbraɪtn̩) v. 變亮　　conduct (kənˈdʌkt) v. 指揮

Somehow love and music have remained whole *in his weakened brain.* No one can explain *why* this can be, *when* the rest of his memory seems to have been destroyed. *But* somehow *in his mind and his heart* there is a miraculous survival *of love and beauty.*

不知道為什麼，愛和音樂在他衰弱的大腦中，完整地保留著。沒有人能解釋情況為何如此。當時他其餘的記憶似乎都被破壞掉了，但是在他的腦中和心中，愛與美竟奇蹟般地保存下來。

> weaken ('wikən) *v.* 變弱　　somehow ('sʌm,haʊ) *adv.* 不知道為什麼
> miraculous (mə'rækjələs) *adj.* 奇蹟般的
> survival (sə'vaɪvl̩) *n.* 殘存

41. (**B**) 本文整體的語調是充滿 _____ 。

　　　(A) 悲傷　　　(B) 希望　　　(C) 寬恕　　　(D) 諷刺

　　overall (,ovɚ'ɔl) *adj.* 全部的　　tone (ton) *n.* 語調
　　irony ('aɪrənɪ) *n.* 諷刺

　　※ 這條題目有些美國老師會選成 (A)。雖然文章一開始是有悲傷的語調，但最後
　　　一句話，即結尾句，說明了充滿希望。凡是考閱讀測驗時，要特別注意每一
　　　段的第一句，及最後一段的結尾句。結尾句是點出整篇文章的結論。

42. (**D**) 威耳林的病，最悲慘的一點是，他不再能夠

　　　(A) 認得他的家人。　　　　(B) 欣賞音樂。
　　　(C) 指揮一群演唱者。　　　(D) 記得他的過去。

　　no longer 不再　　recognize ('rɛkəg,naɪz) *v.* 認得
　　appreciate (ə'priʃɪ,et) *v.* 欣賞　　recall (rɪ'kɔl) *v.* 記得

43. (**C**) 本文指出，威耳林

　　　(A) 離開他的妻子很久。
　　　(B) 在生病前沒有學過鋼琴。
　　　(C) 因為喪失部分記憶而悲傷。
　　　(D) 只能記得莫札特的音樂。

第二篇（共 3 題）

Books are like people. You may like a person *without necessarily wanting to ask him or her home for supper.* You may like a book *without necessarily wanting to read or possess it.* So it is with the books *in our shop.* We know them all, we like them all, we enjoy their companionship, ***because*** *to a bookseller* a book is not something *to read*; it is something *to handle*, something *to sell. To a bookseller* a good book is something ***that is well designed and well made,*** ***and*** the handling *of it* gives him or her great pleasure.

　　書本就像人。你可以喜歡一個人，而不一定想要請他或她回家吃晚飯。你也可以喜歡一本書，而不一定要讀它或擁有它。我們店裏的書正是如此。我們知道所有的書，喜歡所有的書，也喜歡有它們作伴，因為，對一個書店老板商而言，書不是用來閱讀的，書是用來被經銷、販賣的。對書店老板而言，一本好書就是一樣精心設計、製作良好的東西，把它賣出去，能給予他或她極大的喜悅。

　　　supper (ˈsʌpɚ) *n.* 晚餐　　So it is. （情況）正是如此。
　　　companionship (kəmˈpænjənʃɪp) *n.* 陪伴；友誼
　　　bookseller (ˈbʊkˌsɛlɚ) *n.* 書店老板
　　　handle (ˈhændl̩) *v.* 經銷

I know *little* ***and*** care nothing about weapons, ***yet*** I know ***that*** *in my town there are many people with a passion for tanks.* I can recognize a well-designed tank book *when I am shown one,* ***and*** it gives me great pleasure to order it, display it, ***and even*** introduce it to a customer *with my personal recommendation.*

對於武器，我所知不多，也不感興趣。然而我知道，在我們鎮上有很多人熱愛坦克車。當別人拿一本和坦克車有關的書給我看時，我可以看出它是否設計精美，而我會很樂意訂購它、展示它，甚至也會親自推薦，將它介紹給顧客。

> care about ~ 關心~；對~有興趣
> passion〔'pæʃən〕n. 熱愛　order〔'ɔrdɚ〕v. 訂購
> display〔dɪ'sple〕v. 展示　recommendation〔ˌrɛkəmɛn'deʃən〕n. 推薦

Does it seem wrong *that I am prepared to say, "Here is a good book," when I have done no more than glance at it*? How can I judge a book *about which I know nothing*? The answer is *that I can because I can get the help of others, including the publisher, the reviewers, and other customers*. My personal judgment is confined *to the book's production, to its look and feel*. I leave it to the experts to judge the contents.

當我只是看了它一眼，就準備說：「這是一本好書，」似乎不太對，是嗎？我怎能判斷一本我一無所知的書？答案是我可以，因為我有別人的幫忙，包括出版商、書評家，和其他的顧客。我個人的判斷是侷限於該書的製作，它的外表和感覺。至於書的內容我留給專家來判斷。

> no more than 只是（= only）　glance〔glæns〕v. 看一眼
> publisher〔'pʌblɪʃɚ〕n. 出版商　reviewer〔rɪ'vjuɚ〕n. 書評家
> confine〔kən'faɪn〕v. 限制　be confined to 侷限於
> contents〔'kɑntɛnts〕n. pl. 內容

44.（**B**）本文指出，對於一本書，書店老板最關心的是書的 _____。
　　　(A) 內容　　　　(B) **外表**　　　(C) 成本　　　(D) 出版商
　　state〔stet〕v. 提到；指出　　concern〔kən'sɝn〕n. 關心的事

45.（**A**）作者認為自己並不是
　　　(A) 判斷一本書寫得好不好的專家。　(B) 很會判斷書的設計的人。
　　　(C) 推薦有關武器書籍的人。　　　　(D) 會感激有書在身邊的人。

46. (**C**) 下列哪一個敘述是作者反對的？

　　　(A) 書店老板通常對於製作精美的書，向顧客索取太高的價錢。

　　　(B) 書店老板對於有書在身邊應該感到高興。

　　　(C) 書店老板應該在勸客人買書之前，一定要先讀那本書。

　　　(D) 書店老板應該只賣書評好的書。

　　argue against 反對 (↔ *argue for* 贊成)

　　charge (tʃɑrdʒ) *v.* 收費；索價　　*take delight in* 喜歡

　　urge (ɝdʒ) *v.* 力勸；催促　　review (rɪ'vju) *n.* 評論

第三篇 (共 4 題)

　　First-time dog owners may encounter many problems *getting to know and train their pets. Sometimes* a puppy, *or even* an older dog, will chew their fingers or bite them. *Even in play,* this can *really* hurt. *Unfortunately,* many pet owners tolerate this *in a young dog. However, when the dog gets larger,* it is not fun to be bitten *by it.*

　　第一次養狗的人，可能會在剛開始要了解及訓練狗時，遭遇許多問題。有時候小狗，或甚至較老的狗，會啃主人的手指，或者咬他們。即使是開玩笑，這還是很痛的。不幸的是，許多養狗的人會容許小狗這樣做。然而，當狗長大了，被咬到可就不好玩了。

　　　　encounter (ɪn'kaʊntɚ) *v.* 遭遇　　*get to* ~ 開始要~

　　　　pet (pɛt) *n.* 寵物　　puppy ('pʌpɪ) *n.* 小狗

　　　　chew (tʃu) *v.* 嚼；咬；啃　　*in play* 開玩笑

　　　　tolerate ('tɑlə,ret) *v.* 容許

　　Training a dog *to never place his teeth on human skin or clothing* is an important lesson. *From now on, if you feel your dog's teeth while you are playing with him,* say "Ouch" *in a loud voice and* move away from him. He will *soon* learn *that when he bites, you will not play*

with him anymore.

所以，訓練狗不要把牠的牙齒放到人的皮膚或衣服上，是很重要的一課。從現在起，如果和狗玩的時候，碰到牠的牙齒，你要大叫一聲「哎唷」，並離開牠。這樣牠很快就會知道，如果牠咬你，你就不會再跟牠玩。

feel〔fil〕*v.* 觸摸   ouch〔aʊtʃ〕*interj.* 哎唷

Another bad habit *that many people tolerate in their pets* is allowing

them to bite and hold on to clothing. Don't let your dog do this to you.

When he does something you want him to do, praise him *and* tell him

he's a good dog. You can *also* give him a treat *at the same time he*

performs the good behavior. Eventually he will learn which kind *of*

behavior is acceptable *and* which is not.

另外一個壞習慣就是，很多人會容許他們的狗緊咬著衣服不放。別讓你的狗對你這樣做。當牠完成了你要牠做的事，要誇獎牠，並告訴牠，牠是一隻很乖的狗。你也可以在牠表現好的同時，請牠吃東西。最後牠就會知道，哪種行為是可令人接受的，而哪種不是。

hold on to 緊抓著   praise〔prez〕*v.* 讚美
treat〔trit〕*n.* 款待；請客   perform〔pɚˈfɔrm〕*v.* 做
eventually〔ɪˈvɛntʃʊəlɪ〕*adv.* 最後
acceptable〔əkˈsɛptəbl̩〕*adj.* 可接受的

Remember *that reward is more effective than punishment. If you reward*

your dog when he does what you want him to, he will become *very well*

behaved. *Also* remember *that puppies need to chew on something. So* give

him a sock *with a knot tied in it or* an old shoe.

要記住，獎賞比處罰更有效。如果當你的狗完成了你要求的事，你就獎勵牠，牠就會變得很守規矩。同時還要記住，小狗是需要啃東西的。所以給牠一隻打了結的襪子，或是一隻舊鞋子。

reward〔rɪ'wɔrd〕n. 獎賞；報酬　　effective〔ə'fɛktɪv〕adj. 有效的
punishment〔'pʌnɪʃmənt〕n. 處罰　　sock〔sɑk〕n. 襪子
knot〔nɑt〕n. 結　　tie〔taɪ〕v. 打（結）

If he chews the wrong thing, take it away **while saying** "No" **and** give
him something *he can chew*. *If dogs are trained well*, they will *truly*
be your friends *for a lifetime*.
如果牠啃錯東西，就要跟牠說「不行」，並把東西拿走，再把可以啃的東西給牠。如果能好好訓練，狗真的可以成為你一輩子的朋友。

lifetime〔'laɪf,taɪm〕n. 一輩子；終身

47. (**A**) 本文的主題是
　　　(A) 教導人們如何訓練狗。　　(B) 告訴養狗的人如何守規矩。
　　　(C) 示範狗的良好行為。　　(D) 說明為何狗要啃東西。

focus on 集中於；著重於　　demonstrate〔'dɛmən,stret〕v. 示範

48. (**D**) 根據本文，許多人容易
　　　(A) 認為小狗應該適當地訓練。　(B) 對他們的狗很粗魯。
　　　(C) 很少請他們的狗吃東西。　(D) 容許他們的狗不守規矩。

tend to 容易　　rough〔rʌf〕adj. 粗魯的
infrequently〔ɪn'frikwəntlɪ〕adv. 很少

49. (**C**) 根據本文，下列敘述何者為非？
　　　(A) 我們的行為會影響狗的行為。
　　　(B) 狗喜歡被牠的主人獎勵。
　　　(C) 當你的狗咬你時，什麼話都不要說。
　　　(D) 訓練狗需要耐心和時間。

50. (**B**) 作者認為訓練狗比較好的方法是：

(A) 犯了任何錯誤，都要處罰牠。

(B) 請牠吃東西來強調牠良好的行為。

(C) 無論牠做什麼都要容忍牠。

(D) 永遠對牠好，不要罵牠。

reinforce〔ˌriin'fors〕v. 加強　　scold〔skold〕v. 責罵

第四篇（共 5 題）

One day in 1918, something *very* strange happened *at an army camp in America.* Their camp had thousands of horses and mules. They disposed of the animals' waste matter *by burning it. That day* a huge dust storm, *along with the burning waste matter,* turned the sun *completely* black.

一九一八年的某一天，有個美國軍營發生了一件非常奇怪的事。軍營裏養了好幾千匹馬和騾子。他們以燃燒的方式，來處理這些動物的排泄物。當天，發生了一場巨大的塵暴，連同正在燃燒的排泄物，把陽光完全變黑了。

army camp 軍營　　　mule〔mjul〕n. 騾子
dispose of 處理　　　**waste matter** 排泄物
dust storm 塵暴；沙暴　　turn〔tɜn〕v. 使變成

Two days later, men began to complain of having *very* bad colds. *By noon,* more than one hundred men were sick. Doctors didn't have the record keeping *that we have in modern times* to keep track of illnesses, *although* they knew *that many people living close together often gave their diseases to others.*

兩天後，人們開始抱怨得了重感冒。到了中午，有一百多人都生病了。當時的醫生並沒有像我們現在，有追蹤疾病的病歷紀錄，雖然他們知道，如果有許多人住得很近，常會把疾病傳染給別人。

　　　record keeping 紀錄　　　***keep track of*** 追蹤

In the same month, the United States sent 84,000 soldiers to fight *in the war against Germany. Little* did they know ***that*** *they were carrying a disease* **that** *would kill as many soldiers* **as** *their rifles would.* The disease traveled *fast,* ***and*** *in just four months,* tens of thousands *in every part of the world* had fallen ill and died.

在同一個月，美國派了八萬四千名士兵上戰場，和德國打仗。他們一點也不知道，自己身上的疾病，和他們的來福槍一樣，會殺死很多士兵。那種病蔓延得很快，僅僅四個月，世界各地就有好幾萬人生病和死亡。

　　　soldier〔ˋsoldʒɚ〕*n.* 士兵　　　little〔ˋlɪtl̩〕*adv.* 一點也不
　　　rifle〔ˋraɪfl̩〕*n.* 來福槍
　　　tens of thousands 好幾萬人（比較：*hundreds of thousands* 好幾十萬人）
　　　fall ill 生病

In those days, many people believed *medical science could cure any disease.* **When** *they discovered no one had a solution to this deadly disease,* people turned toward prevention. The government tried to educate people not to use common cups and utensils. They *also* told people not to cough or sneeze *without covering their mouths.*

　　當時有許多人相信，醫學可以治療任何疾病。當人們發現，這致命的疾病沒有解決之道時，他們就只好轉向預防之道。政府試著教育民衆，不要使用公共的杯子和器皿。同時也告訴大家，不要沒掩住嘴巴就咳嗽或打噴嚏。

　　　　prevention〔prɪˋvɛnʃən〕*n.* 預防
　　　　utensils〔juˋtɛnsḷz〕*n.pl.* 器皿；用具
　　　　cough〔kɔf〕*v.* 咳嗽　　　sneeze〔sniz〕*v.* 打噴嚏

People were *also* encouraged to wash their hands *often* **and** pay attention to personal cleanliness. *In this way*, they could reduce the chance *of infecting someone else* **or** *becoming infected themselves*. *In modern times*, we *also* need to take responsibility *to avoid spreading illness*.
人們也被鼓勵，要常洗手和注意個人衛生，這樣就可以減少傳染別人或被傳染的機會。在現代，我們也必須負起避免散播疾病的責任。

　　　　cleanliness〔ˋklɛnlɪnɪs〕*n.* 整潔　　　infect〔ɪnˋfɛkt〕*v.* 傳染
　　　　take responsibility 負起責任

51.(**D**) 本文的主旨是
　　　　(A) 告訴我們關於人類史上一場重要戰爭。
　　　　(B) 描述美國軍人生活的辛苦。
　　　　(C) 說明醫學的進步。
　　　　(D) 明白指出疾病會在人與人之間傳播。

　　hardship〔ˋhɑrdʃɪp〕*n.* 辛苦　　　advance〔ədˋvæns〕*n.* 進步
　　demonstrate〔ˋdɛmənˏstret〕*v.* 說明

52.(**C**) 根據本文，很多士兵生病是因爲
　　　　(A) 他們養了太多的馬和騾子。　　(B) 他們不想去打仗。
　　　　(C) 他們全都住得很近。　　　　　(D) 他們沒有病歷記錄。

　　raise〔rez〕*v.* 飼養

53. (**D**) 根據本文，下列何者為真？

    (A) 美國士兵以疾病為武器殺死敵人。

    (B) 美國士兵喜歡在軍營中賽馬。

    (C) 德國人在第一次世界大戰中，被重感冒打敗。

    <u>(D) 重感冒會散播和致命，不分國界。</u>

without regard to 不顧；不論　　border〔'bɔrdɚ〕 *n.* 邊界

54. (**A**) 下列何者不是一種預防措施？

    <u>(A) 向醫生抱怨你得了重感冒。</u>　(B) 不要和別人共用杯子和器皿。

    (C) 咳嗽和打噴嚏時要掩住嘴巴。　(D) 儘可能常洗手。

preventive〔prɪ'vɛntɪv〕 *adj.* 預防的　　measure〔'mɛʒɚ〕 *n.* 措施

55. (**B**) 在現代，我們認為

    (A) 任何疾病都可以被醫藥治癒。(B) <u>每個人都應該小心疾病。</u>

    (C) 只有醫生對疾病有責任。　　(D) 政府可以處理任何疾病。

alone〔ə'lon〕 *adv.* 僅僅　　hold〔hold〕 *v.* 認為

handle〔'hændḷ〕 *v.* 處理

第二部分：非選擇題

I、中譯英：10%

1. 年輕人和老年人的睡眠習慣很不相同。

The sleeping habits of young people and old people are quite different.

2. 許多年輕人往往很晚還不睡，第二天早上就不能早起。

Many young people often stay up so late that they cannot get up early the next morning.

3. 老年人通常晚上沒事做，所以很早上床。

Old people usually have nothing to do at night, so they go to bed early.

4. 這兩種不同的睡眠習慣，哪一種比較有益健康呢？

Which of these two different sleeping habits is more beneficial to health?

5. 其實，只要睡飽，早睡晚睡都沒關係。

In fact, as long as you get enough sleep, it doesn't matter whether you go to bed early or late.

II、作文範例：20％

A Happy Ending

I like stories with happy endings. They always make me feel good and satisfied when I reach the end of the story. When I was about eight years old, I heard the story *"Snow White and the Seven Dwarfs"* for the first time. This story is about a beautiful princess called Snow White, who was kind and gentle. Her wicked *stepmother* was jealous of her beauty and told a hunter to get rid of her. The hunter *took pity on* her and left her in a forest.

So Snow White lived in the forest with seven dwarfs. When the stepmother found out about this, she disguised herself as an old woman and gave a *poisoned apple* to Snow White. *As soon as* Snow White took a bite of that apple, she *fell asleep* and nobody could wake her up. The stepmother fell down a cliff and died after being chased by the seven dwarfs. As we all know, *"What goes around comes around."* Then a handsome prince kissed Snow White and she woke up from her long sleep. Of course, *they lived happily ever after*. I cannot remember how many times I have read this story since then, but every time I do, it still lifts my spirit. I feel especially touched by the seven dwarfs' love and care for Snow White. It shows that love can overcome all obstacles and *work miracles*.

Snow White 白雪公主　　dwarf〔dwɔrf〕*n.* 侏儒；小矮人
princess〔'prɪnsɪs〕*n.* 公主　　wicked〔'wɪkɪd〕*adj.* 邪惡的
stepmother〔'stɛp,mʌðɚ〕*n.* 繼母　　*be jealous of* 嫉妒
take pity on 同情　　disguise〔dɪs'gaɪz〕*v.* 偽裝
poisoned〔'pɔɪznd〕*adj.* 有毒的　　cliff〔klɪf〕*n.* 懸崖
What goes around comes around. 惡有惡報。
prince〔prɪns〕*n.* 王子　　lift〔lɪft〕*v.* 提振
touched〔tʌtʃt〕*adj.* 感動的
overcome〔,ovɚ'kʌm〕*v.* 克服　　*work miracles* 產生奇蹟

八十七學年度大學暨獨立學院入學考試
英 文 試 題

第一部分：單一選擇題

以下 1～40 題，每題 1 分，41～55 題，每題 2 分。請由每題 4 個備選項中選出一個最適當者，標示在「**答案卡**」上。每答錯一題倒扣**題分**的⅓，不答不給分。

I、對話（共 5 分）：

1. **Student 1**：Did you hear about the new computer virus？It can knock out your entire system.
   Student 2：＿＿＿＿＿＿＿＿＿＿
   Student 1：I hope not. I saved some of my chemistry data on your computer last week！
   (A) My computer is brand-new and it runs well.
   (B) I'll have to check and see if my computer is infected.
   (C) I won't be able to hand in my homework.
   (D) I need to buy some more computer discs.

2. **Sam**：Hi Kate！Glad you could make it to the party.
   Kate：＿＿＿＿＿＿＿＿＿＿
   Sam：You were the first person I thought of.
   (A) Let me give you my coat.
   (B) It looks like the party has already started.
   (C) Thanks for inviting me.
   (D) It's always a pleasure to make a new friend.

3. **Bill**　：I have two tickets for the concert tomorrow night. Would you like to go with me？
   Cherry：Let me check my calendar...sounds good...I'm free.
   Bill　：＿＿＿＿＿＿＿＿＿＿
   (A) OK, so next week I'll get the tickets and give them to you.
   (B) The music is Mozart and Bach.
   (C) Well, that's OK. Maybe next time then.
   (D) Great. I'll pick you up around seven o'clock.

4. **Younger sister** : Who will help me with my homework after you go abroad for studies?

   Older sister : _____

   Younger sister : I don't know if it will be enough.

   (A) The teacher will want you to turn your assignments in on time.

   (B) Just do your best and you'll be fine.

   (C) Mom and Dad can't afford to hire a tutor.

   (D) Your classmates all need to do their homework too.

5. **Melanie** : It's late. I'd better be going.

   Peter : _____

   Melanie : No thanks. I'll just call a taxi.

   (A) Can I give you a lift?   (B) Can I pick up the check?

   (C) Can I lend you the cab fare?   (D) Can I call a taxi for you?

Ⅱ、詞彙及慣用語（共 15 分）：

6. This hotel is quite reasonable. It _____ only NT$ 800 for a single room per night.

   (A) charges   (B) changes   (C) chooses   (D) charts

7. An average person _____ sleeps eight hours a day.

   (A) gradually   (B) partially   (C) mutually   (D) normally

8. Our country has become hi-tech by _____ heavily in electronic industry.

   (A) inspiring   (B) invading   (C) investing   (D) inventing

9. History has had many surprises for us. How events will turn out are often not _____ .

   (A) exchangeable   (B) resistible   (C) predictable   (D) fashionable

10. The economic crisis we are having in Asia now is certainly very _____ to many of us.

   (A) dominating   (B) disturbing   (C) satisfying   (D) imposing

11. A doctor has to _____ your illness before giving you a prescription.

   (A) invent   (B) express   (C) diagnose   (D) inform

12. We are grateful for his _____ in giving a large contribution to our educational foundation.
    (A) generosity　(B) hypothesis　(C) appreciation　(D) experiment

13. At this historic site, you can see some _____ magnificent palaces.
    (A) factually　(B) mutually　(C) legally　(D) immensely

14. He has made a good plan in _____ with marketing strategies.
    (A) ambition　(B) connection　(C) possession　(D) instruction

15. All of us should be concerned with public _____ to make our society a better place.
    (A) mansions　(B) products　(C) contests　(D) affairs

16. The summit meeting between the presidents of those two countries _____ in Paris last week.
    (A) held up　(B) let off　(C) called for　(D) took place

17. Take heart and _____ your goal for as long as it takes.
    (A) hang on to　(B) keep out of　(C) go back on　(D) get it straight

18. This assignment is very boring. I want to _____ as soon as possible.
    (A) begin all over again　(B) take it out
    (C) think it over　(D) get it over with

19. In radio and television call-in programs, there is a lot of _____ between the host and audience.
    (A) hide-and-seek　(B) give-and-take
    (C) do's and don'ts　(D) p's and q's

20. The college _____ is one of the best in our country. You may apply to it for admission.
    (A) in question　(B) out of mind　(C) above your head　(D) in doubt

Ⅲ、綜合測驗（共 20 分）：

　　Before you visit a foreign country, you should find out as much information as possible about its climate, transportation, hotels, restaurants and shopping. For example, if you know ___(21)___ of a particular season

when you plan to visit this country, you can take ___(22)___ suitable
clothes. And if you know ___(23)___ transportation is most convenient
between the two cities you will visit, ___(24)___ will save you much time.
___(25)___ , if you know how much to tip in a hotel or restaurant, you can
___(26)___ some embarrassing situations. ___(27)___ shopping, it is important
that you know when shops are open, ___(28)___ you may be disappointed
at seeing all the shops ___(29)___ . Careful planning and reliable information
will make your trip ___(30)___ enjoyable.

21. (A) that weather   (B) the weather   (C) weather   (D) a weather
22. (A) along   (B) alone   (C) about   (D) around
23. (A) how   (B) that   (C) this   (D) what
24. (A) some   (B) you   (C) it   (D) they
25. (A) Simply   (B) Also   (C) Beside   (D) Only
26. (A) engage   (B) improve   (C) avoid   (D) correct
27. (A) With regard to   (B) On the basis of
    (C) In keeping with   (D) By means of
28. (A) still   (B) yet   (C) then   (D) or
29. (A) closes   (B) closed   (C) close   (D) closing
30. (A) truly   (B) likely   (C) merely   (D) rarely

Most people, young or old, don't know how to plan a healthy diet.
Some people eat too much, and some eat too little. Many people don't eat
breakfast at all except ___(31)___ a cup of coffee, and most people eat a
very heavy and greasy dinner. One important ___(32)___ in a healthy diet
is balance. A balanced diet contains ___(33)___ amounts of food for the
three meals of a day and a variety of foods ___(34)___ vegetables, fruits,
eggs, milk, cereals and meat. For breakfast, which starts you ___(35)___
on a long day's work, you need sufficient food to provide you ___(36)___
enough energy. Lunch is equally important. If you don't store enough
energy at lunchtime for a long afternoon of work, you will ___(37)___
feel tired. But after dinner, normally you relax yourself and don't need
much energy, ___(38)___ it's preferable to have a light dinner. Moreover,
varieties of food give you different kinds of nutrients your body needs.
If your diet lacks variety, you are bound ___(39)___ deficient in nutrition.
Your diet is essential to your health. If you often feel tired or ___(40)___
sick, it's likely that you don't have a balanced diet.

31.	(A) by	(B) from	(C) for	(D) on
32.	(A) factor	(B) reason	(C) cause	(D) manner
33.	(A) numerous	(B) delicate	(C) adequate	(D) liberal
34.	(A) just as	(B) so as	(C) such as	(D) much as
35.	(A) off	(B) up	(C) about	(D) around
36.	(A) for	(B) to	(C) of	(D) with
37.	(A) easily	(B) lazily	(C) entirely	(D) carefully
38.	(A) yet	(B) so	(C) still	(D) though
39.	(A) to make	(B) to have	(C) to do	(D) to be
40.	(A) run	(B) fall	(C) show	(D) rest

IV、閱讀測驗（共 30 分）：

Recent fires have destroyed much of Indonesian forests and pose the latest threat to the survival of the endangered orangutans (red-haired apes). Thirty orangutans fleeing their burning forest home have been killed by villagers, who see the animals as crop raiders. Orangutan mothers have been killed so that their young can be captured and sold into the illegal wildlife pet trade. Orangutan experts continue to receive orangutan infants whose mothers have been killed while searching for food in plantations and fields.

The fires, caused by drought and coupled with fire-setting methods to clear forests, have destroyed more than two million acres. When fire gets into the rainforests' layer of dry peat (partly decayed plant material which covers the soil), it can burn slowly off and on for months or years after the original fire. These fires continue until heavy rainfall soaks the peat through and through. Orangutans once numbered in the hundreds of thousands, but their population has dropped to roughly 25,000 due to fire, the destruction of forests from felling trees for timber and agriculture, and losses linked to the live-animal trade. Before the fires, only two percent of the orangutans' original habitat remained, and now, their habitat has become even smaller.

41. Which of the following is NOT a reason for the decreasing of orangutans in Indonesia?
   (A) The forests have been burned to get land for agriculture.
   (B) Most of orangutans' forests have been destroyed.
   (C) Mother orangutans have been sold into the live-animal business.
   (D) Trees have been cut down for human profits.

42. According to this passage, fires in Indonesia
    (A) will not end until it starts to rain.
    (B) will be eventually put out by human effort.
    (C) will die out in a few days when the trade winds blow.
    (D) will only stop when the peat is totally wet.

43. What is the best title for this passage?
    (A) Fires in Indonesia Keep on Flaming
    (B) Orangutans Are Precious Animals
    (C) Fires Drive Orangutans to Danger
    (D) Orangutans Endanger the Crops of Indonesia

　　A building, as an object that defines and encloses space, reflects the society of its time more than any other art-form. The meaning of a building is expressed as much by the materials in which it is built as by the functions it is designed to perform for a group of people. The vast majority of buildings consist of external walls to keep people out and an interior space covered by a roof to provide shelter for the residents. Their basic shape directly relates to the materials chosen to form that inner space and the functions it is designed to serve.

　　Architecture is essentially the art of compromise. It involves designs to meet the demands of its users within a three-dimensional form. The design of a building is a creative rather than a mathematical process, but unlike other art-forms, it is concerned with a positive search for solutions. There can be no solution without a problem, no problem without limitations, and no limitations without a need. Either a need is automatically met at the outset and there is no problem, or the need is not met because of certain obstacles. Finding out how to overcome these obstacles is the responsibility of an architect.

44. The significance of a building can be found in its
    (A) materials and functions.　　　(B) artistic forms.
    (C) mathematical calculations.　　(D) problems and limitations.

45. Architecture and society
   (A) are limited by mathematical processes.
   (B) pose problems for each other.
   (C) are closely related to each other.
   (D) are frequently in conflict with each other.

46. According to this passage, the job of an architect is to
   (A) make a building as artistic as possible.
   (B) find out the best way to meet the users' needs.
   (C) use the most expensive materials to construct a building.
   (D) satisfy the needs of the users at any cost.

　　Stories are not merely extras in our life. They are vital nourishment in the process of becoming fully human. I remember many books I read in childhood such as *The Secret Garden*, *Peter Pan*, and *Alice in Wonderland*. These books, among others, started me on the road to becoming human and I am awed and grateful.

　　I remember books such as these and I am deeply troubled by publishers whose main goal is to make a profit. These publishers sell only what children say they like to read. However, I don't know of any parents who feed their children only sugared cereals and bubble gum because that is what the children say they like to eat.

　　The best way to cultivate children's tastes is to read to them, starting at birth and keeping on and on. "Let me hear you read it" is a test. "Let me read it to you" is a gift. So as a mother, let me urge you to read your children as many stories as possible. For if we are careless in the matter of nourishing the imagination, the world will pay for it. In fact, we can see that in many cases that the world already has.

　　Some people think that reading stories is a way to kill time when the real world needs tending to. But books show me ways of being, ways of doing, ways of dealing with people and situations and problems that I could never have thought up on my own. I am not killing time; I am trying to understand life.

To illuminate and make whole — I may not be equal to the task, but at least I know how important the task is. Even though people today admire wealth and power, I am grateful to be among those who, reaching to be human, gather their children about the fire and tell them stories.

47. The three books mentioned in the first paragraph of this passage were
    (A) all required reading in English class.
    (B) books that the author found in a public library.
    (C) important to the personal development of the author.
    (D) among the childhood books that the author liked the least.

48. The author criticizes
    (A) publishers for making money by catering to the tastes of children.
    (B) parents for allowing their children to eat only the food they like.
    (C) publishers for selling books which are far too expensive.
    (D) parents for spending too little money on children's books.

49. According to this passage, reading stories is
    (A) a pastime for relaxing oneself.
    (B) a kind of intellectual growth.
    (C) a part of one's schoolwork.
    (D) a way to forget problems.

50. Why does the author persuade parents to read stories to children?
    (A) It is beneficial to children's performance on reading comprehension tests.
    (B) It helps children develop their characters and creative abilities.
    (C) It encourages children to complete their household chores faster.
    (D) It assists children in learning how to read by themselves.

I know science's limitations, but with my worship of science I always let the scientists do the groundwork, having complete confidence in them. I let them discover the physical universe for me — the physical universe that I desire so much to know. Then, after getting as much as possible of the scientist's knowledge, I remember that human beings are greater than the analytical scientist, that the latter cannot tell us everything, cannot tell us about the most important things, the things that make for happiness.

It is instead intuitive thinking that alone can help us attain the truth and wisdom of living. Truly intuitive thinking is always the type of thinking that is sort of warm, emotional, and half-humorous, mixed in part with idealism and in part with delightful nonsense. Great wisdom consists in not demanding too much of human nature, and yet not altogether spoiling it by indulgence. One must try to do one's best and at the same time, one must, when rewarded by partial success or confronted with partial failure, say to oneself, "I have done my best." This is about all the philosophy of living that one needs.

After science has done its groundwork, religion, art, literature, and philosophy must take their rightful place in human life. These things do not seem to tie together with science in the modern world; the specialist has taken over the human being. For science can never replace art, religion, literature and philosophy. Next to knowledge, we must retain, and never lose, a taste for life, a respect for life, a sense of wonder at life, and a proper and reasonable attitude toward life. The taste for life must be simple, the respect for life must be truly profound, the sense of wonder must be fully alive, and the attitude of life must be harmonious and reasonable.

51. According to this passage, which of the following is one of science's limitations?
    (A) Science cannot make us live happily.
    (B) Science cannot discover knowledge.
    (C) Science cannot lead us to success.
    (D) Science cannot give us confidence.

52. According to the author, intuitive thinking is something that
    (A) scientists use to discover knowledge.
    (B) people can do, but animals cannot.
    (C) students can learn in school.
    (D) we need to lead a better life.

53. The author recommends that we should
    (A) be satisfied with moderate achievement.
    (B) avoid failure at all costs.
    (C) ignore human nature.
    (D) drive ourselves to be the best.

54. The author thinks that in the modern world
    (A) a true taste for life depends upon science.
    (B) science is closely related to the humanities.
    (C) harmony can be found among scientists.
    (D) experts have controlled our way of life.

55. What statement best reflects the author's opinion as stated in this passage?
    (A) Science teaches us more about life than art, religion, literature and philosophy.
    (B) Art, religion, literature and philosophy are no less important than science.
    (C) Science should replace religion as a new faith for people today.
    (D) Knowledge of the physical universe gives us wisdom about life.

第二部分：非選擇題

Ⅰ、**中譯英**（共 10 分）：

請將下面五個中文敘述（1～5），譯成正確、通順、達意且前後連貫的英文。每個敘述 2 分。（1～2）、（3）、（4～5）各構成一句。答案請寫在「**非選擇題試卷**」上，同時務必（1～5）分行標示題號。

(1) 以前，我常常到書店去，

(2) 主要是隨便看看一些書。

(3) 有時會買一些小說來讀。

(4) 現在因為忙著準備考試，

(5) 再也沒時間去找小說了。

Ⅱ、**英文作文**（共 20 分）：

請以 Saying "Thank you" and "I'm sorry" frequently will make you a happier person 為起始句，寫一篇約一百二十個單字的英文作文。答案請寫在「**非選擇題試卷**」上。

（內容 5 分，組織 5 分，文法 4 分，用字遣詞 4 分，拼字、大小寫及標點符號 2 分）。

87年大學聯考英文試題詳解

第一部分：單一選擇題

I、對話：5％

1.(**B**) 學生甲：你聽說過新的電腦病毒嗎？它會破壞你整個系統。
  　　學生乙：_____
  　　學生甲：我希望沒有。上禮拜我才將一些化學資料存在你的電腦裏！

  (A) 我的電腦是全新的而且性能很好。
  (B) <u>我得檢查看看我的電腦有沒有被感染。</u>
  (C) 我將無法交作業。
  (D) 我需要再多買一些磁片。

  virus〔'vaɪrəs〕*n.* 病毒　　***knock out*** 破壞
  data〔'detə〕*n.* 資料　　brand-new〔'brænd'nju〕*adj.* 全新的
  infect〔ɪn'fɛkt〕*v.* 感染　　***hand in*** 繳交　　disc〔dɪsk〕*n.* 磁片

2.(**C**) 山姆：嗨，凱特！很高興妳能去參加舞會。
  　　凱特：_____
  　　山姆：妳是我第一個想到的人。

  (A) 讓我把我的外套給你。　　(B) 舞會看來已經開始了。
  (C) <u>謝謝你邀請我。</u>　　(D) 能結交新朋友是件快樂的事。

  make it 成功；辦到

3.(**D**) 比爾：我有兩張明晚音樂會的票。妳想和我一起去嗎？
  　　綺麗：我看一下日曆……聽起來不錯……我有空。
  　　比爾：_____

  (A) 好的，下禮拜我拿到票就會把票給妳。
  (B) 是莫札特和巴哈的音樂。
  (C) 嗯，沒關係。那就下次吧。
  (D) <u>太棒了。我七點左右來接妳。</u>

  calendar〔'kæləndɚ〕*n.* 日曆
  Mozart〔'mozɑrt〕*n.* 莫札特（1756-1791；奧地利作曲家）
  Bach〔bɑk〕*n.* 巴哈（1685-1750；德國的風琴演奏家及作曲家）

4.(**B**) 妹妹：妳出國唸書之後，我做功課時誰來幫我呢？

姊姊：＿＿＿＿＿＿＿＿＿＿＿＿＿＿＿

妹妹：我不知道那樣是不是就足夠了。

(A) 老師會要你按時交作業。　(B) 只要妳盡力就沒問題。

(C) 爸爸媽媽請不起家教。　(D) 你的同學也必須要做功課。

abroad〔əˈbrɔd〕*adv.* 到國外　***turn in*** 繳交（＝*hand in*）

on time 準時　　tutor〔ˈtjutɚ〕*n.* 家庭教師

5.(**A**) 梅蘭妮：時候不早了，我該走了。

彼　得：＿＿＿＿＿＿＿＿＿＿＿＿＿＿＿

梅蘭妮：不用了，謝謝。我叫計程車就好了。

(A) 我能不能送妳？　(B) 我替妳付帳好嗎？

(C) 我可以借妳錢搭計程車嗎？　(D) 我可以替妳叫計程車嗎？

give *sb.* ***a lift*** 讓某人搭便車　***pick up the check*** 替人付帳

cab〔kæb〕*n.* 計程車（＝*taxi*）　fare〔fɛr〕*n.* 車資

Ⅱ、詞彙及慣用語：15％

6.(**A**) This hotel is *quite* reasonable. It charges only NT$ 800 for a single
room *per night*.

這家旅館收費十分合理。單人房每晚只要台幣八百元。

(A) ***charge***〔tʃɑrdʒ〕*v.* 收費　(B) change〔tʃendʒ〕*v.* 改變

(C) choose〔tʃuz〕*v.* 選擇　(D) chart〔tʃɑrt〕*v.* 以圖表表示

reasonable〔ˈriznəbḷ〕*adj.* 合理的　single〔ˈsɪŋgḷ〕*adj.* 單人用的

per〔pɝ〕*prep.* 每一

7.(**D**) An average person *normally* sleeps *eight hours a day*.

一般人通常一天睡八個小時。

(A) gradually〔ˈgrædʒuəlɪ〕*adv.* 逐漸地

(B) partially〔ˈpɑrʃəlɪ〕*adv.* 部分地；不公平地

(C) mutually〔ˈmjutʃuəlɪ〕*adv.* 互相地

(D) ***normally***〔ˈnɔrmḷɪ〕*adv.* 通常（＝*usually*）

8. (**C**) Our country has become hi-tech *by investing heavily in electronic industry.*

我國大量投資電子業，因而躋身高科技的行列。

    (A) inspire〔ɪnˈspaɪr〕*v.* 激勵；給予靈感
    (B) invade〔ɪnˈved〕*v.* 入侵
    (C) ***invest***〔ɪnˈvɛst〕*v.* 投資
    (D) invent〔ɪnˈvɛnt〕*v.* 發明

hi-tech〔ˈhaɪˌtɛk〕*n.* 高科技（ = *high technology* ）
heavily〔ˈhɛvɪlɪ〕*adv.* 大量地
electronic〔ɪˌlɛkˈtrɑnɪk〕*adj.* 電子的

9. (**C**) History has had many surprises for us. How events will turn out are *often* not predictable.

歷史常使我們非常驚訝。事情的結果會如何，常常不是我們可以預料的。

    (A) exchangeable〔ɪksˈtʃendʒəbl̩〕*adj.* 可交換的
    (B) resistible〔rɪˈzɪstəbl̩〕*adj.* 可抗拒的
    (C) ***predictable***〔prɪˈdɪktəbl̩〕*adj.* 可預測的
    (D) fashionable〔ˈfæʃənəbl̩〕*adj.* 時髦的；流行的

turn out 結果（變成）

10. (**B**) The economic crisis *we are having in Asia now* is *certainly very* disturbing to many *of us.*

我們亞洲現在所經歷的經濟危機，必定使我們許多人覺得十分不安。

    (A) dominating〔ˈdɑməˌnetɪŋ〕*adj.* 專制的
    (B) ***disturbing***〔dɪˈstɝbɪŋ〕*adj.* 令人不安的
    (C) satisfying〔ˈsætɪsˌfaɪɪŋ〕*adj.* 令人滿意的
    (D) imposing〔ɪmˈpozɪŋ〕*adj.* 壯觀的；氣勢宏偉的

economic〔ˌikəˈnɑmɪk〕*adj.* 經濟上的
crisis〔ˈkraɪsɪs〕*n.* 危機　　Asia〔ˈeʃə〕*n.* 亞洲

11. (**C**) A doctor has to underline{diagnose} your illness *before giving you a*

prescription.

醫生在替你開藥方之前，必須先診斷你的病。

    (A) invent〔ɪn'vɛnt〕*v.* 發明

    (B) express〔ɪk'sprɛs〕*v.* 表達

    (C) ***diagnose***〔ˌdaɪəg'nos〕*v.* 診斷

    (D) inform〔ɪn'fɔrm〕*v.* 通知

prescription〔prɪ'skrɪpʃən〕*n.* 處方；藥方

12. (**A**) We are grateful for his underline{generosity} in giving a large contribution

to our educational foundation.

我們很感激他，因為他十分慷慨地捐贈許多錢給我們的教育基金。

    (A) ***generosity***〔ˌdʒɛnə'rɑsətɪ〕*n.* 慷慨

    (B) hypothesis〔haɪ'pɑθəsɪs〕*n.* 假說

    (C) appreciation〔əˌpriʃɪ'eʃən〕*n.* 欣賞；感激

    (D) experiment〔ɪk'spɛrəmənt〕*n.* 實驗

contribution〔ˌkɑntrə'bjuʃən〕*n.* 捐獻
foundation〔faʊn'deʃən〕*n.* 基金

13. (**D**) *At this historic site,* you can see some *immensely* magnificent

palaces.

在這歷史遺跡，你可以看到一些非常宏偉的宮殿。

    (A) factually〔'fæktʃʊəlɪ〕*adv.* 事實地；實際地

    (B) mutually〔'mjutʃʊəlɪ〕*adv.* 互相地

    (C) legally〔'liglɪ〕*adv.* 在法律上；合法地

    (D) ***immensely***〔ɪ'mɛnslɪ〕*adv.* 廣大地；非常

historic〔hɪs'tɔrɪk〕*adj.* 有歷史性的   site〔saɪt〕*n.* 地點
magnificent〔mæg'nɪfəsn̩t〕*adj.* 宏偉的
palace〔'pæləs〕*n.* 宮殿

14. (**B**) He has made a good plan *in connection with marketing strategies.*
他已擬定出一個與行銷策略<u>有關</u>的很好的計劃。

    (A) ambition〔æm'bɪʃən〕*n.* 抱負
    (B) ***connection***〔kə'nɛkʃən〕*n.* 連接；關連
      in connection with ~　與~有關
    (C) possession〔pə'zɛʃən〕*n.* 擁有
    (D) instruction〔ɪn'strʌkʃən〕*n.* 教導

marketing〔'mɑrkɪtɪŋ〕*n.* 行銷
strategy〔'strætədʒɪ〕*n.* 策略

15. (**D**) All *of us* should be concerned with public <u>affairs</u> to make our society a better place.
我們大家都應關心公衆的<u>事務</u>，以使我們的社會更好。

    (A) mansion〔'mænʃən〕*n.* （豪華的）宅邸；公寓；大樓
    (B) product〔'prɑdʌkt〕*n.* 產品
    (C) contest〔'kɑntɛst〕*n.* 比賽
    (D) ***affair***〔ə'fɛr〕*n.* 事情

be concerned with 關心

16. (**D**) The summit meeting *between the presidents of those two countries* took place *in Paris last week.*
那兩國元首的高峰會議，上週在巴黎<u>舉行</u>。

    (A) hold up 舉起；使延遲
    (B) let off 讓~下（車、船、飛機）；開（槍）
    (C) call for 需要；呼籲
    (D) ***take place*** 舉行；發生

summit〔'sʌmɪt〕*n.* 峰頂；（政治等的）首腦
summit meeting 高峰會議

17. (**A**) Take heart and <u>hang on to</u> your goal *for as long as it takes.*

振作精神，目標要<u>堅持</u>到底。

　(A) *hang on to* 堅持；緊抓住；不放手
　(B) keep out of 不參加；不捲入
　(C) go back on 違背（諾言）；背叛
　(D) get it straight 把它徹底了解

take heart 振作精神

18. (**D**) This assignment is *very* boring. I want to <u>get it over with</u> *as soon as possible.*

這作業很無聊，我要儘快把它<u>做完</u>。

　(A) begin all over again 再重新開始
　(B) take it out 把它去掉
　(C) think it over 仔細考慮
　(D) *get it over with* 做完；完成

19. (**B**) *In radio and television call-in programs,* there <u>is</u> a lot of <u>give-and-take</u> *between the host and audience.*

在廣播與電視的 call-in 節目中，主持人和聽眾常會<u>交換許多意見</u>。

　(A) hide-and-seek〔'haɪdṇ'sik〕*n.* 捉迷藏
　(B) *give-and-take*〔'gɪvən'tek〕*n.* 交換意見
　(C) do's and don'ts 風俗；規章；法令
　(D) p's and q's （用於片語 mind one's p's and q's 表「言行謹慎」。）

host〔host〕*n.* 主持人

20. (**A**) The college *in question* is one *of the best* in our country.

You may apply to it *for admission.*

我們所談論的大學是我國最好的大學之一。你可以去申請入學。

    (A) *in question* 談論中的

    (B) out of mind （此片語多用於諺語中：Out of sight, out of mind.
        離久情疏；眼不見心不念。）

    (C) above *one's* head 對某人而言太困難而無法理解

    (D) in doubt 懷疑的；未確定的

apply to ~ for … 向～申請…   admission〔əd'mɪʃən〕*n.* 入學許可

Ⅲ、綜合測驗： **20 %**

Before you visit a foreign country, you should find out *as* much

information *as possible* about its climate, transportation, hotels, restaurants

and shopping. For example, *if you know the weather* of a particular
                                      21

season *when you plan to visit this country,* you can take along suitable
                                                    22

clothes. *And if you know **what** transportation is most convenient between*
                        23

the two cities you will visit, it will save you much time.
                       24

      在你要到外國之前，你應該儘量多找一些資料，有關該國的氣候、交通工具、旅館、餐廳及購物等。例如，當你計畫去該國旅行時，如果你知道特定季節的天氣狀況，你就能夠攜帶適當的衣物。又如果你知道，你要去的二個城市之間，何種交通工具最方便，這可以節省你很多時間。

21. (**B**) 指某特定季節的天氣狀況，應用定冠詞 the ，選 (B)。

22. (**A**) along 在此為副詞，表「帶著；連同」之意。而 (B) alone〔ə'lon〕*adv.* 獨自地，(C) 關於，(D) 到處，均不合句意。

23. (**D**)　依句意，「什麼」交通工具最方便，選 (D) what。

24. (**C**)　指前面所提到的整件事，代名詞用 it，選 (C)。

Also, *if you know how much to tip* *in a hotel or restaurant,* you can avoid
　25
some embarrassing situations. *With regard to shopping*, it is important ***that***
　　　　　　　　　　　　　　　　　　27
you know **when** *shops are open,* ***or*** *you may be disappointed* *at seeing all*
　　　　　　　　　　　　　　　　28
the shops closed. Careful planning **and** reliable information will make
　　　　　29
your trip *truly* enjoyable.
　　　　30

此外，如果你知道，在旅館或餐廳中要給多少小費，就可以避免一些尷尬的情況
發生。關於購物方面，要知道商店何時營業，這點很重要，否則你可能會因為看
到所有商店都關門，而感到失望不已。審慎的計畫和可靠的資料，真的會讓你的
旅行非常愉快。

　　　　　　　tip〔tɪp〕v. 給小費　　embarrassing〔ɪmˋbærəsɪŋ〕adj. 尷尬的
　　　　　　　disappointed〔͵dɪsəˋpɔɪntɪd〕adj. 失望的
　　　　　　　reliable〔rɪˋlaɪəbḷ〕adj. 可靠的
　　　　　　　enjoyable〔ɪnˋdʒɔɪəbḷ〕adj. 愉快的

25. (**B**)　依句意選 (B) Also 此外。而 (A) 只是，(C) 在～旁邊，(D) 只有，句意
　　　　　均不合。

26. (**C**)　(A) engage〔ɪnˋgedʒ〕v. 從事　　(B) improve〔ɪmˋpruv〕v. 改善
　　　　　(C) ***avoid***〔əˋvɔɪd〕v. 避免　　(D) correct〔kəˋrɛkt〕v. 改正

27. (**A**)　(A) ***with regard to***～ 關於～　(B) on the basis of～ 根據～
　　　　　(C) in keeping with～ 符合～　(D) by means of～ 藉著～

28. (**D**)　依句意，「否則」你會很失望，選 (D) or。(A) 仍然，(B) 然而，(C) 然後，
　　　　　均不合。

29. (**B**)　形容商店「關閉的」，用 closed，選 (B)。

30. (**A**) (A) *truly*〔'trulɪ〕*adv.* 眞實地　　(B) likely〔'laɪklɪ〕*adj.* 可能的
　　　　 (C) merely〔'mɪrlɪ〕*adv.* 僅僅　　　(D) rarely〔'rɛrlɪ〕*adv.* 很少；不常

Most people, *young or old*, don't know **how** to plan a healthy diet.
Some people eat *too* much, **and** some eat *too* little. Many people don't
eat breakfast at all *except for* a cup of coffee, **and** most people eat a
　　　　　　　　　　　　31
very heavy and greasy dinner. One important factor *in a healthy diet* is
　　　　　　　　　　　　　　　　　　　　32
balance. A balanced diet contains adequate amounts of food *for the three*
　　　　　　　　　　　　　　　　　33
meals of a day **and** a variety of foods *such as* vegetables, fruits, eggs,
　　　　　　　　　　　　　　　34
milk, cereals and meat.

　大部分的人，無論老幼，都不知道如何做一份健康的飲食計畫。有些人吃太多，而有些人吃太少。很多人早餐除了一杯咖啡之外，什麼都不吃，而大部分的人晚餐吃得旣油膩而且又難消化。健康飲食的要素之一，就是均衡。均衡的飲食包含足夠份量的食物，供給一日三餐所需，以及多種食物，例如蔬菜、水果、蛋、牛奶、穀類和肉類。

　　　　diet〔'daɪət〕*n.* 飲食
　　　　heavy〔'hɛvɪ〕*adj.* 油膩難消化的（↔light　*adj.* 輕淡的）
　　　　greasy〔'grizɪ〕*adj.* 油膩的　　*a variety of* ~　各種~
　　　　cereal〔'sɪrɪəl〕*n.* 穀類

31. (**C**) except for ~　除了~之外

32. (**A**) (A) *factor*〔'fæktɚ〕*n.* 因素　　(B) reason〔'rizn̩〕*n.* 理由
　　　　 (C) cause〔kɔz〕*n.* 原因　　　　(D) manner〔'mænɚ〕*n.* 方式

33. (**C**) (A) numerous〔'njumərəs〕*adj.* 很多的
　　　　 (B) delicate〔'dɛləkət〕*adj.* 細緻的
　　　　 (C) *adequate*〔'ædəkwɪt〕*adj.* 足夠的
　　　　 (D) liberal〔'lɪbərəl〕*adj.* 自由的；寬大的

34. (**C**) 舉例說明,選 (C) such as「像是」(= like)。而 (A) 正如,(B) so as to+V,以便於～,(C) 雖然非常～,均不合。

For breakfast, **which** *starts you off on a long day's work,* you need
　　　　　　　　　　　　　　　35

sufficient food *to provide you with enough energy.* Lunch is *equally*
　　　　　　　　　　　　　36

important. **If** *you don't store enough energy at lunchtime for a long*

afternoon of work, you will *easily* feel tired. **But** *after dinner, normally*
　　　　　　　　　　　　　37

you relax yourself **and** don't need much energy, *so* it's preferable to
　　　　　　　　　　　　　　　　　　　38

have a light dinner.

早餐要讓你開始一整天漫長的工作,所以你需要充分的食物,提高你足夠的熱量。
午餐同樣重要。如果你午餐時沒有有儲存足夠的熱量,以維持一下午漫長的工作,
你就會容易覺得疲倦。但在晚餐之後,通常你會放鬆自己,而且不需要很多熱量,
所以晚餐最好吃清淡一點。

> sufficient〔sə'fɪʃənt〕*adj.* 足夠的
> energy〔'ɛnədʒɪ〕*n.* 能量;精力
> equally〔'ikwəlɪ〕*adv.* 同樣地　　store〔stor〕*v.* 儲存
> normally〔'nɔrməlɪ〕*adv.* 通常
> preferable〔'prɛfərəbḷ〕*adj.* 更好的　　light〔laɪt〕*adj.* 清淡的

35. (**A**) *start off* 開始　　*start up* 突然出現;發動 (引擎)

36. (**D**) *provide sb. with sth.* 提供某人某物 (= *provide sth. for sb.*)

37. (**A**) 依句意,「容易」覺得疲倦,選 (A) easily。而 (B) lazily〔'lezɪlɪ〕*adv.* 懶惰地,(C) 完全地,(D) 小心地,均不合句意。

38. (**B**) 前後二句話爲「因果」關係,故連接詞選 (B) so「所以」。而 (A) 然而,(C) 仍然,(D) 雖然,均不合。

Moreover, varieties of food give you different kinds of nutrients *your body needs. If your diet lacks variety,* you are bound to be deficient (39) *in nutrition.* Your diet is essential to your health. *If you often feel tired or fall sick,* it's likely **that** you don't have a balanced diet. (40)

此外，各種不同的食物，能提供你身體所需的各種不同的養分。如果你的飲食缺乏變化，你一定會營養不足。飲食對健康是非常重要的。如果你經常感到疲倦或常生病，可能就是因為你沒有均衡的飲食。

> *varieties of* ~　各種~（ = *a variety of* ~ ）
> nutrient〔′njutrɪənt〕*n.* 養分
> deficient〔dɪ′fɪʃənt〕*adj.* 不足的　　nutrition〔nju′trɪʃən〕*n.* 營養

39.(**D**) *be bound to* + V. 一定~，而由其後的 deficient 為形容詞可知，本題應用 be 動詞，故選 (D)。

40.(**B**) *fall sick* 生病

Ⅳ、閱讀測驗：**30**％

Recent fires have destroyed much *of Indonesian forests* **and** pose the latest threat to the survival *of the endangered orangutans* (red-haired apes). Thirty orangutans *fleeing their burning forest home* have been killed *by villagers,* *who see the animals as crop raiders.* Orangutan mothers have been killed *so that* their young can be captured **and** sold *into the illegal wildlife pet trade.* Orangutan experts continue to receive orangutan infants *whose mothers have been killed* *while searching for food,* *in plantations and fields.*

　　最近幾次的火災，使得印尼境內大片的森林遭到破壞，瀕臨絕種的黑猩猩（紅毛猩猩），生存受到最新的威脅。三十隻黑猩猩在逃離家園時，遭到村民殺害，因為他們視這些猩猩為農作物的掠奪者。黑猩猩媽媽被殺害後，牠們的孩子則被捕捉，賣給非法的野生寵物商。黑猩猩專家們持續收養那些母親在外出到農場或田野覓食時，遭到殺害的黑猩猩寶寶。

pose〔poz〕v. 造成；引起　　threat〔θrɛt〕n. 威脅
survival〔sə'vaɪvḷ〕n. 生存
endangered〔ɪn'dendʒəd〕adj. 瀕臨絕種的
orangutan〔o'ræŋu,tæn〕n. 猩猩　　ape〔ep〕n. 黑猩猩
flee〔fli〕v. 逃走　　villager〔'vɪlɪdʒə〕n. 村民
crop〔krɑp〕n. 農作物　　raider〔'redə〕n. 侵略者
capture〔'kæptʃə〕v. 捕捉　　wildlife〔'waɪld,laɪf〕adj. 野生的
pet〔pɛt〕n. 寵物　　infant〔'ɪnfənt〕n. 幼兒
plantation〔plæn'teʃən〕n. 大農場

The fires, *caused by drought* **and** *coupled with fire-setting methods to clear forests,* have destroyed more than two million acres. **When** *fire gets into the rainforests' layer of dry peat* (*partly decayed plant material* **which** *covers the soil*), it can burn *slowly* off and on *for months or years after the original fire.* These fires continue **until** *heavy rainfall soaks the peat through and through.* Orangutans *once* numbered *in the hundreds of thousands,* **but** their population has dropped to *roughly* 25,000 *due to fire, the destruction of forests from felling trees for timber and agriculture,* **and** *losses linked to the live-animal trade. Before the fires, only* two percent *of the orangutans' original habitat remained,* **and** *now,* their habitat has become *even* smaller.

　　這幾次的大火，是由乾旱所引起，再加上爲清理森林所採行的火燒行爲，已經造成超過二百萬英畝的林地損毀。當火勢延燒至雨林裡的乾泥炭層（覆蓋在土壤表面部分腐爛的植物物質）時，仍會斷斷續續而緩慢地燃燒數月至數年之久。直到降雨完全浸溼乾泥炭層時，火勢才會停止。黑猩猩的數量曾高達數十萬隻，但因爲大火，爲取得木材和農地而砍樹所造成的破壞，以及與活動物買賣有關的損失，使得黑猩猩總數驟降至約剩二萬五千隻。大火發生前，黑猩猩原有的棲息地只剩百分之二，如今，牠們的棲息範圍已變得更小了。

> drought〔ˋdraʊt〕n. 乾旱　　couple〔ˋkʌpḷ〕v. 連接；配合
> acre〔ˋekə〕n. 英畝　　rainforest〔ˋrenˏfɔrɪst〕n. 雨林
> layer〔ˋleə〕n. 層　　peat〔pit〕n. 泥炭
> decay〔dɪˋke〕v. 腐敗　　soil〔sɔɪl〕n. 土壤
> **off and on** 斷斷續續地　　rainfall〔ˋrenˏfɔl〕n. 降雨
> soak〔sok〕v. 浸溼　　**through and through** 徹底地
> number〔ˋnʌmbə〕v. 數目達到
> population〔ˏpɑpjəˋleʃən〕n. 動物的總數
> roughly〔ˋrʌflɪ〕adv. 大約　　**due to** 由於
> fell〔fɛl〕v. 砍伐　　timber〔ˋtɪmbə〕n. 木材
> agriculture〔ˋægrɪˏkʌltʃə〕n. 農業
> link〔lɪŋk〕v. 連結　　original〔əˋrɪdʒənḷ〕adj. 原本的
> habitat〔ˋhæbəˏtæt〕n. 棲息地

41. (**C**)　下列敘述何者<u>不是</u>造成印尼黑猩猩減少的原因？
　　　(A) 爲了取得農業用地，森林因而被燒毀。
　　　(B) 黑猩猩所棲息的森林，大部分已被破壞。
　　　(C) <u>母猩猩被賣給活動物交易商。</u>
　　　(D) 爲了人類的利益，樹木遭到砍伐。

42. (**D**)　根據本文，印尼的火災
　　　(A) 直到開始下雨才會停止。
　　　(B) 最後會因人類的努力而被撲滅。
　　　(C) 季風開始後的數天內會停止。
　　　(D) <u>只有泥炭完全潮溼時，才會停止。</u>

> eventually〔ɪˋvɛntʃʊəlɪ〕adv. 最後　　**put out** 熄滅
> **trade wind** 季風；貿易風（在亞熱帶，北半球從東北、南半球從東南吹向赤道的風。）

43.(**C**) 何者最適合做本文的標題？

    (A) 印尼大火持續延燒   (B) 黑猩猩是珍貴動物

    (C) 大火危害黑猩猩   (D) 黑猩猩危及印尼農作物

flame〔flem〕*v.* 燃燒

A building, *as an object that defines and encloses space*, reflects the society *of its time* more *than* any other art-form. The meaning *of a building* is expressed as much by the materials *in which it is built* *as by the functions it is designed to perform for a group of people*. The vast majority of buildings consist of external walls *to keep people out* *and* an interior space *covered by a roof to provide shelter for the residents*. Their basic shape *directly* relates to the materials *chosen to form that inner space* *and the functions it is designed to serve*.

    建築物是限定和圍住空間的物體，比起其他的藝術形式，它更能反映出當時的社會狀況。建築物的材料，以及為某群人所設計的功能，可表現出建築物本身所代表的意義。大多數的建築物包含外牆，將人群隔絕在外，以及內部的空間，由屋頂覆蓋著，為住戶提供庇護。為形成某種內部空間以及特定功能而選用的建材，會直接影響建築物的基本外形。

    define〔dɪˈfaɪn〕*v.* 定範圍   enclose〔ɪnˈkloz〕*v.* 圍繞；圍起

    vast〔væst〕*adj.* 巨大的   majority〔məˈdʒɔrətɪ〕*n.* 多數

    consist of 包含；由～組成   external〔ɪkˈstɝnl̩〕*adj.* 外部的

    interior〔ɪnˈtɪrɪɚ〕*adj.* 內部的   shelter〔ˈʃɛltɚ〕*n.* 庇護所

    resident〔ˈrɛzədənt〕*n.* 居民   *relate to* 與～有關

    be designed to 為了要～；預定要～

Architecture is *essentially* the art *of compromise*. It involves designs to meet the demands *of its users*, *within a three-dimensional form*. The design *of a building* is a creative **rather than** a mathematical process, **but** *unlike other art-forms*, it is concerned with a positive search *for solutions*. There can be no solution *without a problem*, no problem *without limitations*, **and** no limitations *without a need*. **Either** a need is *automatically* met *at the outset* **and** there is no problem, **or** the need is not met *because of certain obstacles*. Finding out **how** *to overcome these obstacles* is the responsibility *of an architect*.

　　建築本質上是一種妥協的藝術。設計時,必須在三度空間的範圍內,滿足住戶的要求。建築設計是一種發揮創意的過程,而非運算的過程,但是和其他的藝術形式不同,建築設計是積極地尋求解決之道。沒有問題就沒有解決,沒有限制就沒有問題,沒有需要,就沒有限制。不是一開始自然地符合需求,沒有任何問題,就是因為某種阻礙,無法符合需求。找出如何克服這些困難的方法,是建築師的責任。

architecture〔ˋɑrkəˏtɛktʃ⅃〕n. 建築
essentially〔əˋsɛnʃəlɪ〕adv. 本質上
compromise〔ˋkɑmprəˏmaɪz〕n. 妥協
three-dimensional〔ˏθridəˋmɛnʃənəl〕adj. 三度的;立體的
creative〔krɪˋetɪv〕adj. 有創造力的;有創意的
mathematical〔ˏmæθəˋmætɪkl〕adj. 數學的;運算的
be concerned with 與~有關
positive〔ˋpɑzətɪv〕adj. 積極的
automatically〔ˏɔtəˋmætɪklɪ〕n. 自動地
outset〔ˋautˏsɛt〕n. 開始　　obstacle〔ˋɑbstəkl〕n. 阻礙
overcome〔ˏovəˋkʌm〕v. 克服　　architect〔ˋɑrkəˏtɛkt〕n. 建築師

44. (**A**) 建築物的意義在於

    (A) 材料和功能。　　　　(B) 藝術形式。

    (C) 數學計算。　　　　　(D) 問題和限制。

calculation〔͵kælkjə'leʃən〕*n.* 計算

45. (**C**) 建築和社會

    (A) 受限於運算過程。　　(B) 相互造成問題。

    (C) 彼此密切相關。　　　(D) 彼此常互相衝突。

46. (**B**) 根據本文，建築師的工作是

    (A) 盡量讓建築物有美感。

    (B) 找出符合用戶需求的最佳方式。

    (C) 使用最貴的材料來建造。

    (D) 不惜任何代價滿足住戶的需求。

construct〔kən'strʌkt〕*v.* 建造　　***at any cost*** 不惜任何代價

Stories are not merely extras *in our life.* They are vital nourishment *in the process of becoming fully human.* I remember many books *I read in childhood* such as The Secret Garden, Peter Pan, **and** Alice in Wonderland. These books, *among others*, started me *on the road to becoming human* **and** I am awed and grateful.

　　故事不只是生活的添加物，而是我們陶冶人性情操的過程中，不可或缺的養分。我記得許多小時候所讀過的書，如「祕密花園」、「小飛俠」和「愛麗絲夢遊仙境」等。這些書更是我步向人文訓練的開始。我對此又敬畏又感激。

extra〔'ɛkstrə〕*n.* 額外的事物　　vital〔'vaɪtl〕*adj.* 非常重要的

nourishment〔'nɝɪʃmənt〕*n.* 養分；營養品　　***among others*** 尤其

Peter Pan 彼得‧潘（小飛俠）〔英國劇作家 James Barrie 所創造的故事及其主角，一個不肯長大的小孩。〕

awed〔ɔd〕*adj.* 充滿敬畏的　　grateful〔'gretfəl〕*adj.* 感激的

I remember books *such as these* **and** I am *deeply* troubled by publishers *whose main goal is to make a profit.* These publishers sell only **what** children say they like to read. *However,* I don't know of any parents **who** *feed their children only sugared cereals and bubble gum* **because** *that is* **what** *the children say they like to eat.*

我所記得的是像這一類的書。所以我眞搞不懂那些以賺錢爲主要目標的出版商。這些人只賣能迎合小孩子口味的書。但就我所知，沒有任何父母會因爲孩子說喜歡吃甜麥片和泡泡糖，就眞的只餵他們吃那些東西。

publisher (ˊpʌblɪʃɚ) *n.* 出版業者　　profit (ˊprɑfɪt) *n.* 利潤
make a profit 獲得利潤　　sugared (ˊʃʊgɚd) *adj.* 加糖的；甜味的
cereal (ˊsɪrɪəl) *n.* 麥片　　***bubble gum*** 泡泡糖

The best way *to cultivate children's tastes* is to read to them, *starting at birth* **and** *keeping on and on.* "Let me hear you read it" is a test. "Let me read it to you" is a gift. **So** *as a mother,* let me urge you to read your children *as* many stories *as possible.* **For** *if we are careless in the matter of nourishing the imagination,* the world will pay for it. *In fact,* we can see that *in many cases* **that** *the world already has.*

培養孩子興趣最好的方法，是從出生開始，就唸故事給他們聽，而且一直持續下去。用「你來唸這故事」來考考孩子，用「我來唸個故事給你聽」來獎勵孩子。身爲一個母親，我主張唸故事給孩子聽，愈多愈好。因爲，假如我們忽略了想像力的培養，人類世界將會付出代價。事實上，很多例子顯示，世界已經開始付出代價。

cultivate (ˊkʌltəˏvet) *v.* 培養；陶冶　　taste (test) *n.* 愛好；興趣
keep on and on 持續下去　　urge (ɝdʒ) *v.* 極力主張
nourish (ˊnɝɪʃ) *v.* 培育　　case (kes) *n.* 實例

Some people think *that reading stories is a way to kill time* **when** *the real world needs tending to.* **But** books show me ways *of being,* ways *of doing,* ways *of dealing with people* **and** situations **and** problems *that I could never have thought up on my own.* I am not killing time; I am trying to understand life.

有些人認為，當現實世界有事需要處理時，讀故事書不過是打發時間的一種方式。但書本教給我的卻是人生的道理，做事的方法，與人相處之道，以及我自己永遠也想不到的狀況和問題。我可不是在打發時間，我是在試著了解人生。

> **kill time** 打發時間　　**tend to** 照料；注意　　**deal with** 處理
> **think up** 想出（方法）　　**on one's own** 獨自；靠自己

To illuminate and make whole — I may not be equal to the task, **but** *at least* I know **how** important the task is. **Even though** people today admire wealth and power, I am grateful to be among those **who**, *reaching to be human, gather their children about the fire* **and** *tell them stories.*

在此我要完整說明一下 —— 或許我不夠資格扛起這個任務，但至少我了解這個任務有多重要。即使在金錢與權力掛帥的今天，我很慶幸自己是屬於為了追求人性陶冶，而把孩子們集合在火爐邊，說故事給他們聽的人。

> illuminate〔ɪ'lumə,net〕*v.* 說明；闡釋　　**be equal to** 能勝任的
> admire〔əd'maɪr〕*v.* 崇尚　　fire〔faɪr〕*n.* 爐火

47.(**C**) 本文第一段所提到的三本書
　　(A) 都是英文課的指定讀物。
　　(B) 是作者在公立圖書館裏找到的。
　　(C) <u>對於作者的人格發展很重要。</u>
　　(D) 是作者的童年讀物中最不喜歡的。
　required〔rɪ'kwaɪrd〕*adj.* 必須的；指定的

48. (**A**) 作者批評

　　　(A) 出版商爲了賺錢而迎合兒童的喜好。
　　　(B) 父母們放任孩子只吃他們愛吃的食物。
　　　(C) 出版商賣的書貴得離譜。
　　　(D) 父母們花太少錢購買兒童讀物。

　　cater to 迎合

49. (**B**) 根據本文，讀故事書是

　　　(A) 放鬆心情的一種消遣。　　(B) 一種心智上的成長。
　　　(C) 學校功課的一部分。　　　(D) 忘卻煩憂的一種方式。

50. (**B**) 作者爲何鼓勵父母們唸故事給孩子聽？

　　　(A) 這對於孩子考閱讀測驗很有幫助。
　　　(B) 這能幫助孩子發展人格及培養創造力。
　　　(C) 這能激勵孩子做家事更迅速。
　　　(D) 這能幫助孩子學習如何自己閱讀。

　　beneficial〔͵bɛnəˋfɪʃəl〕*adj.* 有益的　　household〔ˋhaʊs͵hold〕*adj.* 家庭的
　　chores〔tʃorz〕*n.*, *pl.* 家庭雜務　　　***household chores*** 家事
　　assist〔əˋsɪst〕*v.* 幫助　　　***by oneself*** 靠自己

I know science's limitations, *but with my worship of science* I *always* let the scientists do the groundwork, *having complete confidence in them.* I let them discover the physical universe *for me*—*the physical universe that I desire so much to know.* Then, *after getting as much as possible of the scientist's knowledge,* I remember *that human beings are greater than the analytical scientist, that the latter cannot tell us everything, cannot tell us about the most important things, the things that make for happiness.*

　　我知道科學有其限制，但基於對科學的崇拜，我總是贊成科學家做基礎研究，並且充分信賴他們。他們替我研究自然界宇宙 —— 而這是我非常渴望了解的。然後在吸取科學家的所有知識之後，我仍會記得，人類本身還是比科學分析家偉大，因後者無法告訴我們所有事情，無法告訴我們最重要的事，即快樂之道。

limitation〔ˌlɪmə'teʃən〕n. 限制；極限
worship〔'wɝʃɪp〕n. 崇拜；敬仰
groundwork〔'graʊndˌwɝk〕n. 基礎
physical〔'fɪzɪkl̩〕adj. 自然界的
analytical〔ˌænl̩'ɪtɪkl̩〕adj. 分析的　　***make for*** 促成；有助於

It is *instead* intuitive thinking ***that*** *alone can help us attain the truth and wisdom of living.* *Truly* intuitive thinking is *always* the type of thinking ***that*** *is sort of warm, emotional, and half-humorous, mixed in part with idealism **and** in part with delightful nonsense.* Great wisdom consists in not demanding too much of human nature, ***and*** yet not altogether spoiling it *by indulgence.* One must try to do one's best ***and*** *at the same time*, one must, ***when*** *rewarded by partial success **or** confronted with partial failure,* say to oneself, "I have done my best." This is about all the philosophy *of living **that** one needs.*

　　相反地，只有直觀思考，才能幫我們達到人生的眞理與智慧。眞正的直觀思考總是有一點溫馨、感情、半詼諧，再結合了部分的理想主義和歡愉式笑鬧的思考方式。這種大智慧在於，對於人性不過分要求，而也不完全地放任驕寵。凡事全力以赴，同時，就算沒有百分之百成功，一定要告訴自己：「我已盡力。」這差不多就是我們所需要的全部人生哲學。

instead〔ɪn'stɛd〕*adv.* 相反地

intuitive〔ɪn'tjuɪtɪv〕*adj.* 直觀的；直覺的

attain〔ə'ten〕*v.* 達到　　***sort of*** 有一點

emotional〔ɪ'moʃən!〕*adj.* 感情的　　***in part*** 部分地（＝*partly*）

idealism〔aɪ'diə,lɪzəm〕*n.* 理想主義

nonsense〔'nɑnsɛns〕*n.* 胡鬧；胡說八道

consist in 在於　　　spoil〔spɔɪl〕*v.* 寵壞

indulgence〔ɪn'dʌldʒəns〕*n.* 放縱

do one's best 盡全力；全力以赴　　reward〔rɪ'wɔrd〕*v.* 獎勵；報酬

partial〔'pɑrʃəl〕*adj.* 部分的　　confront〔kən'frʌnt〕*v.* 面對

After *science has done its groundwork,* religion, art, literature, and philosophy must take their rightful place *in human life.* These things do not seem to tie *together with science in the modern world;* the specialist has taken over the human being. ***For science can never replace art, religion, literature and philosophy.*** *Next to knowledge,* we must retain, ***and*** *never* lose, a taste *for life,* a respect *for life,* a sense *of wonder at life,* ***and*** a proper and reasonable attitude *toward life.* The taste *for life* must be simple, the respect *for life* must be *truly* profound, the sense *of wonder* must be *fully* alive, ***and*** the attitude *of life* must be harmonious and reasonable.

　　在科學做完它該做的研究之後，宗教、藝術、文學和哲學，也必須在人類生活中扮演適當的角色。在現代社會中，這些東西似乎與科學並不密切相關，而學有專精已成為人類的趨勢。但因科學永遠無法取代藝術、宗教、文學和哲學，所以除了科學知識之外，我們必須永遠保留對生命的喜愛、尊敬、驚奇感，以及對於生命抱持適當且合理的態度。單純地喜愛生命，深切地尊敬生命，對生命充滿靈動的驚奇感，並擁有和諧理性的生活觀。

rightful〔'raɪtfəl〕adj. 正當的　　**tie together** 連接起來
specialist〔'spɛʃəlɪst〕n. 專家　　**take over** 接管；佔據
retain〔rɪ'ten〕v. 保留　　wonder〔'wʌndə〕n. 驚奇
profound〔prə'faʊnd〕adj. 深刻的
harmonious〔hɑr'monɪəs〕adj. 和諧的
reasonable〔'riznəbl〕adj. 合理的

51. (**A**) 根據本文，下列何者是科學的侷限之一？
　　　(A) 科學不能使我們生活快樂。
　　　(B) 科學不能發掘知識。
　　　(C) 科學不能使我們走向成功。
　　　(D) 科學不能帶給我們信心。

52. (**D**) 作者認為，直觀式思考是
　　　(A) 科學家用來發掘知識的。
　　　(B) 人類專有而動物所沒有的。
　　　(C) 學生在學校可學到的。
　　　(D) 使生活更美好所必需的。

53. (**A**) 作者建議我們應該
　　　(A) 滿足於一般的成就即可。
　　　(B) 不計一切避免失敗。
　　　(C) 忽視人性。
　　　(D) 驅策自己走向完美。

recommend〔,rɛkə'mɛnd〕v. 建議；推薦
moderate〔'mɑdərɪt〕adj. 普通的；一般的
drive〔draɪv〕v. 驅使

54. (**D**) 作者認為在現代社會中，
　　　(A) 對生活的真正喜愛有賴於科學。
　　　(B) 科學與人文密切相關。
　　　(C) 科學家之間關係和諧。
　　　(D) 專家已宰制了我們的生活方式。

55. (**B**) 下列敘述何者最能反映出本文中作者所表達的意見？
　　　　(A) 科學比藝術、宗教、文學和哲學更能教我們人生的道理。
　　　　(B) 藝術、宗教、文學和哲學是和科學同樣重要的。
　　　　(C) 科學應取代宗教，而成為當今人們的新信仰。
　　　　(D) 關於自然界宇宙的知識帶給我們人生智慧。

　　　no less ～ than … 　與…一樣～　　faith〔feθ〕*n.* 信仰

第二部分：非選擇題

Ⅰ、中譯英：10％

1. 以前，我常常到書店去，
   In the past, I would often go to the bookstore,

2. 主要是隨便看看一些書，
   mostly to $\begin{cases} \text{casually read} \\ \text{browse through} \end{cases}$ some books.

3. 有時會買一些小說來讀。
   Sometimes, I would buy some novels to read.

4. 因為現在忙著準備考試，
   Because I am now busy preparing for the tests,

5. 再也沒時間去找小說了。
   I don't have any more time to look for novels.

Ⅱ、英文作文：20％

　　Saying "Thank you" and "I'm sorry" frequently will make you a happier person. For example, when somebody praises you: "*You're an ace. You're a gem. You're the best of the best,*" don't forget to answer: "*Thank you. Thank you very much. I can't thank you enough.*" Or you may add, "*I appreciate it. I'm much obliged. I'm indebted to you.*" *In this way,* both of *you will feel comfortable and happy.*

Knowing how to make apologies is also important. ***When you've done
something wrong, you should apologize immediately*** and say something
like: "***I blew it. I screwed up. I made a mistake.***" ***Then*** you continue to
say: "***I'm really sorry. I'm extremely sorry. I apologize from the bottom
of my heart.***" Or you can say, "***It's my mistake. It shouldn't have happened.
I won't let it happen again.***" ***Try to use these words as much as possible,
and you will become happy and popular everywhere.***

※ 以上黑體字部份，均取材自學習出版公司出版的「說英文高手①」。

86～88學年度大學聯招各科高低標準對照表

科目 高低標(分)		三民 主義	國文	英文	數學 (自)	歷史	地理	數學 (社)	物理	化學	生物
高 標 準	86學年	41	70	71	55	73	65	58	55	49	63
	87學年	37	66	53	46	65	71	70	58	69	72
	88學年	39	66	51	56	63	56	51	55	59	55
低 標 準	86學年	36	59	53	38	57	50	39	36	32	42
	87學年	30	55	37	31	49	55	46	39	50	52
	88學年	27	45	16	19	31	27	17	20	18	21

※ 資料來源：大學聯招會

八十六學年度大學暨獨立學院入學考試
英 文 試 題

第一部分：單一選擇題

I、**對話**（10％）：下面十個題目（1至10）是日常生活常見的英語對話。每題有一個空格，並各附有四個備選答案。請依照對話內容選出一個最適當的答案，標示在「**答案卡**」上。每題答對得1分，答錯倒扣⅓分，不答不給分。

1. *Student 1*: The teacher is so unfair. I got an F on the exam!
   Student 2: _____ You'll do better next time.
   (A) Isn't it nice?　　　　　　　　(B) Don't be so upset.
   (C) How funny it is!　　　　　　　(D) It sounds right.

2. *Sue*: The party has already started. _____ We're late.
   Sara: OK, I'll be ready in a minute.
   (A) Take your time.　　　　　　　(B) Watch your step!
   (C) Hurry up!　　　　　　　　　　(D) Don't worry.

3. *Wife*: Sweetheart. You'll never believe this. I just won the lottery!
   Husband: _____ I don't believe it.
   (A) Cheer up!　　　　　　　　　　(B) Good work!
   (C) That's awful!　　　　　　　　(D) Good heavens!

4. *Tom*: Do you want to go see a movie tonight?
   Jeff: Sure. Let's ask Jack to go along too.
   Tom: _____
   Jeff: Oh, well then. Let's just go ourselves.
   (A) I haven't asked him yet.　　　(B) He has to work tonight.
   (C) I'm not sure.　　　　　　　　(D) I think he likes Lisa.

5. *Gina*: I love your new pocketbook.
   Cindy: Thanks, John gave it to me.
   Gina: _____
   Cindy: I'll ask him where he got it.
   (A) I wish I could find one just like it. (B) You were lucky to find it.
   (C) That's incredible!　　　　　　(D) It sure looks expensive.

6. **Pete**: My neighbor plays loud music late at night.
  Matt: _____ You really should talk to him about it.
  (A) You've got it right. (B) It's a good point.
  (C) That's annoying. (D) This is tricky.

7. **Passerby 1**: Excuse me, do you have four quarters for a dollar?
  Passerby 2: _____
  Passerby 1: I need to make a phone call.
  (A) Let me look. What do you need?
  (B) Let me see. Are dimes and quarters OK?
  (C) I only have three quarters.
  (D) I'll see what I have. What do you need them for?

8. **Mother**: Why did you leave the water running in the sink?
  Son: I'm sorry. _____
  (A) I should have asked. (B) I guess I forgot to turn it off.
  (C) I meant to ask you first. (D) I thought you wouldn't notice.

9. **Kay**: I'm getting married next month.
  Linda: You are? Congratulations! _____
  Kay: David.
  (A) You deserve it. (B) You're the best friend I ever had.
  (C) What's the problem? (D) Who's the lucky guy?

10. **Caller**: Could I speak to Ms. Johnson please?
  Secretary: _____
  Caller: That's OK. I'll hold.
  (A) I'm sorry. She's in meetings all morning.
  (B) May I take a message?
  (C) She's on the other line.
  (D) May I ask who's calling?

II、**詞彙填空**（10％）：下面十個題目（11至20），每題有一個空格，並各附有四個備選單字。請選擇一個最適合的單字，標示在「**答案卡**」上。每題答對得1分，答錯倒扣⅓分，不答不給分。

11. _____, the drowning boy was saved from the river by a soldier.
  (A) Generally (B) Entirely (C) Fortunately (D) Extensively

12. Many businessmen are under great _____ to gain the largest market share possible.
  (A) pressure (B) fame (C) stage (D) greed

13. I know you've been waiting for a long time. Don't be _____.
The train will arrive on time.
(A) independent　(B) impatient　(C) indifferent　(D) impressive

14. The performance of the musicians has really _____ all of us.
(A) delivered　(B) departed　(C) delighted　(D) deserted

15. The _____ of this empire led to many wars with its neighboring
countries.
(A) expansion　(B) exception　(C) experience　(D) explanation

16. Susan has _____ canceled her plan to study abroad, because she
is now preparing for the college entrance exam.
(A) regularly　(B) apparently　(C) extremely　(D) frequently

17. His personality makes it very difficult to _____ and reach an
agreement with him.
(A) negotiate　(B) liberate　(C) decorate　(D) imitate

18. If you want to speak English without a foreigner's accent, you have to
learn correct _____.
(A) instruction　(B) intention　(C) indication　(D) intonation

19. A _____ person usually can get along with other people well, because
he does not insist on his own opinion.
(A) miserable　(B) noticeable　(C) flexible　(D) capable

20. In a democratic society, we have to _____ different opinions.
(A) participate　(B) compensate　(C) dominate　(D) tolerate

Ⅲ、綜合測驗（10％）：下面一篇短文共有十個空格（21至30），每個空格附有
　　四個備選答案。請仔細閱讀後選出一個最適當的答案，標示在「答案卡」上。
　　每題答對得1分，答錯倒扣⅓分，不答不給分。

　　We really hope that we shall discover more about the link between mind
and body in the future. For example, why can some people control pain
___(21)___ others can't? And why can someone who is mentally very strong
and optimistic hold out ___(22)___ more pressure than a person who is very
nervous? There are many cases like ___(23)___, and they are difficult to

understand. We are ___(24)___ very clever in some ways. We can do many high-tech operations and ___(25)___ , but when it comes to ___(26)___ how the mind and body work ___(27)___ , we are really not very well-informed. ___(28)___ , people in the future will probably look back at medicine today ___(29)___ we look back at medieval medicine. In many ways, we are ___(30)___ very ignorant.

21. (A) where   (B) while   (C) how   (D) then
22. (A) against   (B) across   (C) above   (D) around
23. (A) what   (B) which   (C) these   (D) it
24. (A) entirely   (B) certainly   (C) scarcely   (D) thoroughly
25. (A) so what   (B) so that   (C) so not   (D) so on
26. (A) understanding   (B) understand   (C) understands   (D) understood
27. (A) alright   (B) between   (C) away   (D) together
28. (A) Let's do it   (B) Let's be it   (C) Let's face it   (D) Let's make it
29. (A) if   (B) as   (C) so   (D) just
30. (A) even   (B) ever   (C) hardly   (D) still

IV、**慣用語解釋**（10%）：下面十個題目（31 至 40），每題有一個斜體字慣用語，下面各附有四個備選解釋。請選擇一個最適合的解釋，標示在「**答案卡**」上。每題答對得 1 分，答錯倒扣⅓分，不答不給分。

31. "Let's *go Dutch*," John said to Paul after eating dinner at a restaurant.
    (A) find another restaurant   (B) share expenses
    (C) travel to Holland   (D) leave right away

32. The social workers *called upon* the whole society to help stop drug abuse.
    (A) joined in   (B) went after   (C) appealed to   (D) moved toward

33. A committee was *set up* to study the possibility of strengthening international cooperation.
    (A) determined   (B) organized   (C) accepted   (D) qualified

34. He tried *in vain to* persuade her to enter the speech contest.
    (A) with a great effort   (B) with sympathy
    (C) in disappointment   (D) without any result

35. After thinking about this problem for a long time, I still cannot *come up with* any solution.
    (A) guess   (B) learn   (C) find   (D) sketch

36. Skiing in Taiwan is *out of the question* most of the time because there is very little snow here.
   (A) impossible　(B) no problem　(C) unexpected　(D) without doubt

37. In a democratic society, everyone can *stand up for* his or her human rights.
   (A) charge at　(B) fight for　(C) cope with　(D) do without

38. Mary is *in a good humor*, because today is her birthday.
   (A) rather naughty　　　　　(B) quite humorous
   (C) in a good mood　　　　　(D) being funny

39. Mary and I had a quarrel, so she *turned her back on* me.
   (A) tried to forget　　　　　(B) played a joke on
   (C) stayed away from　　　　(D) made fun of

40. His parents want him to *stand on his own feet* after graduation from college.
   (A) work on land　　　　　(B) become independent
   (C) take a trip　　　　　　(D) run a business

Ⅳ、 **閱讀測驗**（20％）：下面有三篇短文，共有十個問題（41至50），每題附有四個備選答案。請仔細閱讀，把最合文意的一個答案標示在「**答案卡**」上。每題答對得2分，答錯倒扣⅔分，不答不給分。

A fine way to make friends and introduce yourself to your neighbors in Norway is to present them with a simple gift like a cake or a loaf of bread. Such a gift warms their hearts as well as their stomachs. If you give them expensive gifts, they may become suspicious of your intentions.

If you have never baked a cake before, it may take you months to produce a beautiful cake that can stand upright without collapsing. But don't wait for perfection. That moment may never come in this lifetime, and you'll never make any Norwegian friends. Do your best, and when you think your creation is good enough to give away, do just that. Norwegians are not picky people. They don't demand the best bread from a famous bakery or the most beautiful cake imaginable before they say that you pass the test of friendship. They will appreciate your honest gesture of friendship, even if your bread is kind of hard, and the cake looks… "interesting".

41. To make friends with Norwegians, what kind of gift can best show your sincerity ?
   (A) A home-baked cake or loaf of bread.
   (B) A valuable gift such as a Swiss watch.
   (C) The best bread from a famous bakery.
   (D) The most beautiful cake you can think of.

42. When do Norwegian neighbors consider you a friend of theirs ?
   (A) When they first meet you.
   (B) When you are well-dressed.
   (C) When they have received your home-baked cake.
   (D) When someone introduces you to them.

43. "Interesting" in the last sentence means that the cake
   (A) can arouse a person's appetite.
   (B) has a strange shape.
   (C) looks very beautiful.
   (D) must be very expensive.

The telephone call has in many cases replaced the social call in Taiwan, especially in big cities. While dropping in on people uninvited is often a bad idea, you can drop in on them nearly anytime by telephone. You should not, however, wake up the person you're calling. If you have no idea what sort of hours somebody keeps, you should probably try not to call after 10 p.m. or before 8 a.m.

It's nice to inquire "Are you busy ?" when you call. Even if you don't, those who are called may decline to chat if the phone has rung at an inconvenient time. They need only to offer to call back. A large portion of the population now has answering machines, and you should not hesitate to leave a message, making sure to say your own number slowly and clearly.

If you receive messages, you should try to return calls within 24 hours. If you receive a phone call while you have guests at home, you should not chat with the caller too long and neglect your guests. Instead, you should offer to call back at a mutually convenient time.

44. In Taiwan now, it is generally more convenient to get in touch with people by
   (A) visiting them.　　　　　(B) calling them.
   (C) writing them.　　　　　(D) sending a messenger.

45. When the person you call is not home, what should you do if there is an answering machine ?
　　(A) Hang up the phone.　　　　　　(B) Call again.
　　(C) Leave a message on the machine.　(D) Go to visit him.

46. This passage tells you something about good manners for
　　(A) visiting your friends.　　(B) driving cars.
　　(C) playing games.　　　　　(D) calling your friends.

The following is a father's advice to his son/daughter, who has just graduated from high school :

First of all, congratulations on your graduation! Graduation from high school means that a new stage of life is ahead of you. At the beginning of this new stage, I have some advice for you.

Clean your own room and do your own laundry. After you have messed up something, you should learn to clean it up yourself. Cleanliness is indeed close to godliness.

Don't mistake knowledge for wisdom. No matter how much information of knowledge you have accumulated, you'll never make sound judgments if you don't have wisdom. Wisdom comes from imagination and reflection. If you can imagine the possible future outcomes of your present decisions and actions, you can avoid mistakes. And if you can reflect on the mistakes you have made, you can avoid making the same mistakes again and again. Such is wisdom.

Don't complain. When you take up a job, do your best to carry it out. Don't waste time complaining about it, no matter how difficult and boring it is.

Finally, be an early bird. If you get up earlier than the sun, you can watch it rising up slowly into the sky. And the sight of the rising sun will warm your heart and give you energy for the day ahead. Besides, being an early bird, you have plenty of time to take exercise or do a lot of work.

47. The father wants to give his son/daughter some advice, because
　　(A) he/she does not know how to behave himself/herself.
　　(B) the teacher is disappointed at his son's/daughter's performance.
　　(C) another period of life awaits him/her.
　　(D) the father is a philosopher.

48. According to the father, wisdom enables one to
(A) acquire a lot of knowledge.   (B) complain about many things.
(C) avoid one's responsibilities.   (D) evaluate situations correctly.

49. In the opinion of the father, complaining
(A) usually leads to success.   (B) gets you nowhere.
(C) can be appreciated by people.   (D) is a pleasant thing.

50. The father says that being an early bird makes one
(A) energetic and efficient.   (B) clean and happy.
(C) sleepy and tired.   (D) hungry and angry.

第二部分：非選擇題

I、**中譯英**（20％）：下面一段短文共含五個中文句子，請譯成正確、通順、達意且前後連貫的英文。每句四分。答案請寫在「**非選擇題試卷**」上，同時**務必標示題號**。

  1. 我們即將進入二十一世紀。

  2. 那時，人們會活得更長久。

  3. 那的確是個好消息。

  4. 但是會有一個問題：

  5. 更多的老人必須由更少的年輕人奉養。

II、**英文作文**（20％）：下面有兩個英文問題，和你的未來計畫有關，每個問題請用大約六十個英文單字回答。答案請寫在「**非選擇題試卷**」上，同時**務必標示題號**。每題10分（內容2分，組織2分，文法2分，用字遣詞2分，拼字、大小寫及標點符號2分）。

1. Why do you want to enter college ?

2. What else would you do if you should fail to enter college ?

86年大學聯考英文試題詳解

第一部分：單一選擇題

I、對話：**10**％

1.(**B**)　學生 1：老師真是不公平。我考試竟然不及格！
　　　　　學生 2：＿＿＿＿＿＿＿＿＿ 你下次會考得比較好。
　　　　　(A) 這不是很好嗎？　　　　(B) 不要這麼生氣。
　　　　　(C) 多麼有趣啊！　　　　　(D) 聽起來是對的。
　　　　　unfair〔ʌnˋfɛr〕*adj.* 不公平的　　F〔ɛf〕*n.* (學業成績) 不及格
　　　　　upset〔ʌpˋsɛt〕*adj.* 煩亂的；生氣的

2.(**C**)　蘇　　：舞會已經開始了。＿＿＿＿＿＿＿＿＿ 我們遲到了。
　　　　　莎拉：好，我馬上就好。
　　　　　(A) 慢慢來。　　　　　　　(B) 小心腳步。
　　　　　(C) 快一點！　　　　　　　(D) 別擔心。
　　　　　in a minute 馬上　　　*take one's time* 慢慢來

3.(**D**)　妻子：甜心，你一定不會相信。我剛中了彩券。
　　　　　丈夫：＿＿＿＿＿＿＿＿＿ 我不相信。
　　　　　(A) 振作起來！　　　　　　(B) 做得好！
　　　　　(C) 真可怕！　　　　　　　(D) 天啊！
　　　　　lottery〔ˋlɑtərɪ〕*n.* 彩券　　awful〔ˋɔfəl〕*adj.* 可怕的
　　　　　Good heavens! 天啊！；哎呀！

4.(**B**)　湯姆：你今晚要不要去看電影？
　　　　　傑夫：當然要。我們邀傑克一起去吧。
　　　　　湯姆：＿＿＿＿＿＿＿＿＿＿＿＿
　　　　　傑夫：噢，那好。我們自己去。
　　　　　(A) 我還沒問他。　　　　　(B) 他今晚必須工作。
　　　　　(C) 我不確定。　　　　　　(D) 我想他喜歡莉莎。
　　　　　go along 一起去

5.(**A**)　吉娜：我喜歡妳新的手提包。
　　　　辛蒂：謝謝。這是約翰給我的。
　　　　吉娜：＿＿＿＿＿＿＿
　　　　辛蒂：我會問問他在哪買的。
　　　　(A) 我希望能找到那樣的手提包。
　　　　(B) 妳真是幸運能找到這個手提包。
　　　　(C) 真是令人難以置信！
　　　　(D) 那看起來真的很貴。

　　　　pocketbook〔'pakɪt,buk〕*n.* 錢包；手提包
　　　　incredible〔ɪn'krɛdəbḷ〕*adj.* 令人難以置信的

6.(**C**)　彼特：我的鄰居昨天深夜放音樂放得很大聲。
　　　　邁特：＿＿＿＿＿＿　你真的應該和他談一談。
　　　　(A) 你弄對了。　　　　　(B) 這是很好的論點。
　　　　(C) 那真令人生氣。　　　(D) 真奸詐。

　　　　get ~ right 把~弄正；把~弄對　　annoying〔ə'nɔɪŋ〕*adj.* 令人惱怒的
　　　　tricky〔'trɪkɪ〕*adj.* 奸詐的

7.(**D**)　路人 1：對不起，請問你有沒有四個二十五分錢可以跟我換一塊錢？
　　　　路人 2：＿＿＿＿＿＿＿＿＿＿
　　　　路人 1：我要打電話。
　　　　(A) 我看一下。你要什麼？
　　　　(B) 我看看。一角的和二十五分錢可以嗎？
　　　　(C) 我只有三個二十五分錢。
　　　　(D) 我看看我有什麼。你要那些錢做什麼？

　　　　passerby〔'pæsə'baɪ〕*n.* 路人　　quarter〔'kwɔrtə〕*n.* 二十五分錢
　　　　dime〔daɪm〕*n.* 一角；十分

8.(**B**)　母親：你為什麼讓水一直流到水槽裏？
　　　　兒子：抱歉。＿＿＿＿＿＿
　　　　(A) 我早該問的。　　　　(B) 我想我忘了關。
　　　　(C) 我打算要先問妳。　　(D) 我以為妳不會注意到。

　　　　sink〔sɪŋk〕*n.* 水槽　　*turn off* 關掉
　　　　mean to V. 打算~

9.(**D**)　凱　　：我下個月要結婚了。
　　　　　琳達：是嗎？恭禧你！＿＿＿＿＿＿＿＿
　　　　　凱　　：大衛。
　　　　　　　(A) 你活該。　　　　　　　　(B) 你是我最好的朋友。
　　　　　　　(C) 問題是什麼？　　　　　(D) <u>那個幸運的人是誰？</u>
　　　　guy〔gaɪ〕*n.* 男人；傢伙

10.(**C**)　來電者：請問強森小姐在嗎？
　　　　　秘　書：＿＿＿＿＿＿＿＿＿＿＿
　　　　　來電者：沒關係。我不掛斷電話。
　　　　　　　(A) 抱歉，她整個早上都在開會。　(B) 你要留話嗎？
　　　　　　　(C) <u>她在接另一線。</u>　　　　　　(D) 請問你是哪位？
　　　　I'll hold. = I'll hold the line 我電話不掛斷。

II、詞彙填空：10 %

11.(**C**)　*Fortunately*, the drowning boy was saved *from the river by a soldier.*
　　　　<u>很幸運地</u>，這個溺水的男孩被一名軍人從河裏救起。
　　　　　　(A) generally〔'dʒɛnərəlɪ〕*adv.* 一般地；通常
　　　　　　(B) entirely〔ɪn'taɪrlɪ〕*adv.* 完全地
　　　　　　(C) *fortunately*〔'fɔrtʃənɪtlɪ〕*adv.* 幸運地
　　　　　　(D) extensively〔ɪk'stɛnsɪvlɪ〕*adv.* 廣泛地
　　　　drowning〔'draʊnɪŋ〕*adj.* 溺水的

12.(**A**)　Many businessmen are under great <u>pressure</u> to *gain the largest market share possible.*
　　　　許多生意人，為了儘可能得到最大的市場佔有率，都承受巨大的<u>壓力</u>。
　　　　　　(A) *pressure*〔'prɛʃə〕*n.* 壓力
　　　　　　(B) fame〔fem〕*n.* 名聲
　　　　　　(C) stage〔stedʒ〕*n.* 舞台
　　　　　　(D) greed〔grid〕*n.* 貪心
　　　　market share 市場佔有率

13. (**B**) I know you've been waiting *for a long time.* Don't be impatient. The train will arrive *on time.*

我知道你已經等很久了。不要<u>不耐煩</u>。火車會準時到。

(A) independent〔͵ɪndɪˋpɛndənt〕*adj.* 獨立的
(B) *impatient*〔ɪmˋpeʃənt〕*adj.* 不耐煩的
(C) indifferent〔ɪnˋdɪfərənt〕*adj.* 漠不關心的
(D) impressive〔ɪmˋprɛsɪv〕*adj.* 令人印象深刻的

on time 準時

14. (**C**) The performance *of the musicians* has *really* delighted all of us.

音樂家的表演真的<u>使</u>我們都很<u>開心</u>。

(A) deliver〔dɪˋlɪvɚ〕*v.* 遞送　　(B) depart〔dɪˋpɑrt〕*v.* 離開
(C) *delight*〔dɪˋlaɪt〕*v.* 使開心　　(D) desert〔dɪˋzɝt〕*v.* 拋棄

performance〔pɚˋfɔrməns〕*n.* 演出；表演

15. (**A**) The expansion *of this empire* led to many wars *with its neighboring countries.*

這個帝國的<u>擴張</u>引起與鄰近國家的許多戰爭。

(A) *expansion*〔ɪkˋspænʃən〕*n.* 擴張
(B) exception〔ɪkˋsɛpʃən〕*n.* 例外
(C) experience〔ɪkˋspɪrɪəns〕*n.* 經驗
(D) explanation〔͵ɛkspləˋneʃən〕*n.* 解釋

empire〔ˋɛmpaɪr〕*n.* 帝國　　*lead to* 導致；引起

16. (**B**) Susan has apparently canceled her plan to study abroad, *because she is now preparing for the college entrance exam.*

蘇珊<u>顯然</u>取消了出國留學的計劃，因為她現在正在準備大學入學考試。

(A) regularly〔ˋrɛgjələlɪ〕*adv.* 規律地
(B) *apparently*〔əˋpɛrəntlɪ〕*adv.* 顯然；明顯地
(C) extremely〔ɪkˋstrimlɪ〕*adv.* 極端地
(D) frequently〔ˋfrikwəntlɪ〕*adv.* 經常

cancel〔ˋkænsḷ〕*v.* 取消　　abroad〔əˋbrɔd〕*adv.* 到國外

17. (**A**) His personality makes it *very* difficult to negotiate *and* reach an

agreement *with him.*

他的個性使得要與他談判並達成協議很困難。

   (A) *negotiate* 〔 nɪ'goʃɪ,et 〕 *v.* 談判；磋商
   (B) liberate 〔'lɪbə,ret 〕 *v.* 使自由
   (C) decorate 〔'dɛkə,ret 〕 *v.* 裝飾
   (D) imitate 〔'ɪmə,tet 〕 *v.* 模仿

personality 〔,pɝsə'nælətɪ 〕 *n.* 個性   agreement 〔 ə'grimənt 〕 *n.* 協議

18. (**D**) *If you want to speak English without a foreigner's accent,* you

have to learn correct intonation.

如果你英文想說得沒有外國人口音，就必須學習正確的語調。

   (A) instruction 〔 ɪn'strʌkʃən 〕 *n.* 敎導
   (B) intention 〔 ɪn'tɛnʃən 〕 *n.* 意圖
   (C) indication 〔,ɪndə'keʃən 〕 *n.* 指示
   (D) *intonation* 〔,ɪnto'neʃən 〕 *n.* 語調

accent 〔'æksɛnt 〕 *n.* 口音

19. (**C**) A flexible person *usually* can get along with other people *well,*

because he does not insist on his own opinion.

適應力強的人常能和別人好好相處，因爲他不會堅持己見。

   (A) miserable 〔'mɪzərəbḷ 〕 *adj.* 可憐的；悲慘的
   (B) noticeable 〔'notɪsəbḷ 〕 *adj.* 顯著的
   (C) *flexible* 〔'flɛksəbḷ 〕 *adj.* 有彈性的；易適應的
   (D) capable 〔'kepəbḷ 〕 *adj.* 有能力的

get along with 相處   *insist on* 堅持

20. (**D**) *In a democratic society*, we have to tolerate different opinions.
在民主社會裏，我們必須包容不同的意見。

    (A) participate〔pɚˋtɪsə͵pet〕*v.* 參加

    (B) compensate〔ˋkɑmpən͵set〕*v.* 補償

    (C) dominate〔ˋdɑmə͵net〕*v.* 支配；統治

    (D) *tolerate*〔ˋtɑlə͵ret〕*v.* 包容；容忍

democratic〔͵dɛməˋkrætɪk〕*adj.* 民主的

Ⅲ、綜合測驗：10 ％

We *really* hope *that we shall discover more about the link between mind and body in the future. For example*, why can some people control pain *while* others can't? *And* why can someone, *who is mentally very strong and optimistic* hold out against more pressure *than a person who is very nervous?* There are many cases *like these*, *and* they are difficult to understand.

      我們真的希望未來，我們會發現更多有關心靈與身體之間的關聯。例如，為何有些人能控制痛苦，而有些人不能？為何心理堅強、樂觀的人，比緊張的人，能忍受更多的壓力？像這樣的例子很多，而且很難理解。

    link〔lɪŋk〕*n.* 連結；關聯　　mentally〔ˋmɛntl̩ɪ〕*adv.* 心理上

    optimistic〔͵ɑptəˋmɪstɪk〕*adj.* 樂觀的　　pressure〔ˋprɛʃɚ〕*n.* 壓力

    nervous〔ˋnɝvəs〕*adj.* 緊張的

21. (**B**) 前後語氣有轉折，故用 (B) *while*，表「然而」。

22. (**A**) *hold out against* 忍受；抵抗

23. (**C**) 代替前面已提過的複數名詞，用 these，選 (C)。

We are *certainly very* clever *in some ways.* We can do many high-tech
    ₂₄

operations *and so on*, *but* *when* it comes to *understanding* **how** the mind
                    ₂₅   ₂₆

and body work together, we are *really* not *very* well-informed. Let's face it,
                        ₂₇   ₂₈

people *in the future* will *probably* look back at medicine *today* **as** we look
                                                                            ₂₉

back at medieval medicine. In many ways, we are *still* very ignorant.
                                                        ₃₀

在某些方面，我們的確很聰明。我們能夠做許多高科技的工作等等，但一談
到了解心靈和身體如何合作時，我們真的就不太清楚了。讓我們面對事實吧！未
來的人可能會回顧今日的醫學，正如我們回顧中古時代的醫學。在很多方面，我
們仍然是很無知的。

> high-tech〔ˊhaɪˋtɛk〕*n.* 高科技（high technology 的縮寫）
> operation〔͵ɑpəˊreʃən〕*n.* 工作　　**when it comes to ~** 一談到~
> well-informed〔ˊwɛlɪnˊfɔrmd〕*adj.* 消息靈通的；見聞廣博的
> **look back** 回顧
> medieval〔͵midɪˊivḷ,͵mɛd-〕*adj.* 中古的；中世紀的
> ignorant〔ˊɪgnərənt〕*adj.* 無知的

24.(**B**) 依句意，選 (B) ***certainly*** 的確；必然。而 (A) entirely〔ɪnˊtaɪrlɪ〕*adv.* 完
　　　全地，(C) scarcely〔ˊskɛrslɪ〕*adv.* 幾乎不，(D) thoroughly〔ˊθɝolɪ〕*adv.*
　　　徹底地，均不合。

25.(**D**) ***and so on*** 等等（= *and so forth* = *etc.*）而 (A) so what 那又怎麼樣，
　　　(B) so that 以便於，則不合句意。

26.(**A**) ***when it comes to*** $\begin{cases} N \\ V\text{-}ing \end{cases}$ 「一談到~」，to 為介系詞，後須接名詞
　　　或動名詞，故選 (A)。

27.(**D**) ***work together*** 合作

28.(**C**) 依句意，選 (C) ***Let's face it***!「讓我們面對事實吧！」

29. (**B**) 依句意，選 (B) *as*「正如」。

30. (**D**) 依句意選 (D) *still* 仍然。而 (A) 甚至，(B) 曾經，(C) 幾乎不，均不合句意。

IV、慣用語解釋：10 %

31. (**B**) "Let's *go Dutch*," John said to Paul after eating dinner at a restaurant.

　　在餐廳吃完晚飯後，約翰對保羅說：「<u>讓我們各付各的</u>。」

　　　(A) 找另外一家餐廳　　　　　(B) <u>分攤費用</u>
　　　(C) 到荷蘭旅遊　　　　　　　(D) 馬上離開

　　go Dutch 各付各的　　　expense〔ɪk'spɛns〕*n.* 費用
　　Holland〔'hɑlənd〕*n.* 荷蘭

32. (**C**) The social workers *called upon* the whole society to help stop drug abuse.

　　社工<u>呼籲</u>整個社會幫助阻止藥物濫用。

　　　(A) 參加　　　　(B) 追求　　　　(C) <u>呼籲</u>　　　　(D) 往～移動

　　call upon 呼籲　　　drug〔drʌg〕*n.* 藥物；毒品
　　abuse〔ə'bjus〕*n.* 濫用

33. (**B**) A committee was *set up* to study the possibility of strengthening international cooperation.

　　委員會被<u>設立</u>，以研究加強國際合作的可能性。

　　　(A) determine〔dɪ'tɜmɪn〕*v.* 決定；決心
　　　(B) *organize*〔'ɔrgə,naɪz〕*v.* 組織；創立
　　　(C) accept〔ək'sɛpt〕*v.* 接受
　　　(D) qualify〔'kwɑlə,faɪ〕*v.* 使有資格

　　committee〔kə'mɪtɪ〕*n.* 委員會　　　*set up* 設立
　　strengthen〔'strɛŋθən〕*v.* 加強　　　cooperation〔ko,ɑpə'reʃən〕*n.* 合作

34. (**D**) He tried *in vain to* persuade her to enter the speech contest.

　　他勸她參加演講比賽，卻<u>徒勞無功</u>。

　　　(A) 非常努力　　(B) 同情地　　(C) 失望地　　(D) <u>沒有結果</u>

　　in vain 徒勞地　　　persuade〔pə'swed〕*v.* 說服
　　speech contest 演講比賽

35. (**C**) After thinking about this problem for a long time, I still cannot *come up with* any solution.

這個問題我思考了很久，仍想不出解決辦法。

(A) guess 〔 gɛs 〕 *v.* 猜測　　　　(B) 學習

(C) 找到　　　　　　　　　　(D) sketch 〔 skɛtʃ 〕 *v.* 描繪

come up with 想出

36. (**A**) Skiing in Taiwan is *out of the question* most of the time because there is very little snow here.

要在台灣滑雪，大部分時間是不可能的，因為這裏很少下雪。

(A) 不可能的　　　　　　　(B) 沒問題

(C) unexpected 〔 ˌʌnɪkˈspɛktɪd 〕 *adj.* 沒有預料到的

(D) 無疑地

ski 〔 ski 〕 *v.* 滑雪　　***out of the question*** 不可能

out of question 無疑問 (= *without question*)

37. (**B**) In a democratic society, everyone can *stand up for* his or her human rights.

在民主社會中，每個人都能爭取自己的人權。

(A) charge at 進攻　　　　(B) ***fight for*** 為了～而奮鬥

(C) cope with 應付　　　　(D) do without 沒有～也可以

stand up for 維護；爭取　　***human rights*** 人權

38. (**C**) Mary is *in a good humor*, because today is her birthday.

瑪莉心情很好，因為今天是她的生日。

(A) 非常頑皮　naughty 〔 ˈnɔtɪ 〕 *adj.* 頑皮的

(B) 相當幽默　　(C) 心情很好　　(D) 很好笑

in a good humor 心情好 (= *in a good mood*)

39. (**C**) Mary and I had a quarrel, so she *turned her back on* me.

瑪莉和我爭吵，所以她不理我。

(A) 試著忘記　　　　　　　(B) 開～玩笑

(C) 不接近　　　　　　　　(D) 取笑

quarrel 〔 ˈkwɔrəl 〕 *n.* 爭吵　　***turn one's back on*** 不理睬；避開

stay away from 不接近

40.(**B**) His parents want him to *stand on his own feet* after graduation from college.

他的父母希望他大學畢業後能獨立。

(A) 在陸地上工作   (B) 變得獨立
(C) 去旅行   (D) 經營事業

stand on one's ***own feet*** 獨立   ***on land*** 在陸地上
run〔rʌn〕*v.* 經營

V、閱讀測驗：**20 %**

A fine way *to make friends **and** introduce yourself to your neighbors in Norway* is to present them *with a simple gift like a cake or a loaf of bread.* Such a gift warms their hearts ***as well as*** their stomachs. ***If you give them expensive gifts***, they may become suspicious of your intentions.

在挪威，交朋友和向鄰居自我介紹的好方法之一，就是送他們一份簡單的禮物，例如一個蛋糕，或一條麵包。這樣的禮物能溫暖他們的心和胃。如果你送他們昂貴的禮物，他們也許會懷疑你有何企圖。

present〔prɪ'zɛnt〕*v.* 給；贈送   suspicious〔sə'spɪʃəs〕*adj.* 懷疑的
intention〔ɪn'tɛnʃən〕*n.* 意圖

If** you have never baked a cake before*, it may take you months to produce a beautiful cake *that can stand upright without collapsing*. ***But don't wait for perfection. That moment may *never* come *in this lifetime*, ***and*** you'll *never* make any Norwegian friends. Do your best, ***and when** you think your creation is good enough to give away*, do *just* that.

如果你以前從來沒有烤過蛋糕，那麼要做一個漂漂亮亮，又能夠挺立而不會塌下來的蛋糕，可能要花你好幾個月的時間。不過，不要等待完美。那一刻可能一輩子都不會到來，那你就永遠交不到挪威朋友了。盡力就好，當你認為你的作品夠好，可以送人時，就送吧！

bake〔bek〕v. 烘烤　　upright〔'ʌp,raɪt , ʌp'raɪt〕adv. 直立地
collapse〔kə'læps〕v. 倒塌　　perfection〔pə'fɛkʃən〕n. 完美
Norwegian〔nɔr'widʒən〕adj. 挪威的 n. 挪威人
creation〔krɪ'eʃən〕n. 作品；創造　　*give away* 贈送

Norwegians are not picky people. They don't demand the best bread *from a famous bakery* **or** the *most* beautiful cake *imaginable* **before** they say **that** you pass the test *of friendship.* They will appreciate your honest gesture *of friendship,* **even if** your bread is *kind of hard,* **and** the cake looks… "*interesting*".

挪威人並不挑剔。在宣布你已通過友誼測試之前，他們不會要求有名麵包店最好的麵包，或想得到的最美的蛋糕。他們會感激你誠實友誼的表示，即使你的麵包有點硬，蛋糕看起來有點…「有趣」。

picky〔'pɪkɪ〕adj. 挑剔的　　demand〔dɪ'mænd〕v. 要求
bakery〔'bekərɪ〕n. 麵包店
imaginable〔ɪ'mædʒɪnəbḷ〕adj. 可能的；可想像的
appreciate〔ə'priʃɪ,et〕v. 欣賞；感激
gesture〔'dʒɛstʃə〕n. 姿勢；表示　　*kind of* 有點

41.(**A**) 要和挪威人交朋友，何種禮物最能表現你的誠意？
(A) 自己做的蛋糕或一條麵包。　　(B) 昂貴的禮物，像是瑞士的錶。
(C) 有名麵包店最好的麵包。　　(D) 你可以想得到的最美的蛋糕。
sincerity〔sɪn'sɛrətɪ〕n. 誠意
valuable〔'væljʊəbḷ〕adj. 有價值的；貴重的

42.(**C**) 挪威鄰居何時會認為你是他們的朋友？
    (A) 當他們第一次見到你時。 (B) 當你穿著很體面時。
    (C) <u>當他們收到你自己做的蛋糕時。</u>　(D) 當某人把你介紹給他們時。

43.(**B**) 最後一句話中的「有趣」是指，你的蛋糕
    (A) 可以引起食慾。   (B) <u>形狀奇怪。</u>
    (C) 看起來很漂亮。   (D) 一定很貴。

arouse〔ə'rauz〕v. 激起；喚醒 appetite〔'æpə,taɪt〕n. 食慾

The telephone call has *in many cases* replaced the social call *in Taiwan*, *especially in big cities*. ***While dropping in on people uninvited is often a bad idea*,** you can drop in on them *nearly anytime* *by telephone*. You should not, *however*, wake up the person *you're calling*. ***If you have no idea what sort of hours somebody keeps*,** you should *probably* try not to call *after 10 p.m. or before 8 a.m.*

  在台灣，在很多情況之下，電話拜訪已取代了社交拜訪，尤其是在大城市裡。若你未經邀請就貿然地拜訪人家，是不太適宜的，但是你幾乎可以在任何時候打電話，去問候別人。不過你不該因打電話而吵醒對方。如果你不知道對方的生活作息時間，就儘可能不要在晚上十點以後，或早上八點之前，打電話給對方。

  case〔kes〕n. 情況 ***drop in on*** 偶然拜訪
  uninvited〔,ʌnɪn'vaɪtɪd〕adj. 未被邀請的 sort〔sɔrt〕n. 種類

It's nice to inquire "Are you busy?" ***when you call***. ***Even if you don't*,** those ***who are called*** may decline to chat *if the phone has rung at an inconvenient time*. They need *only* to offer to call back. A large portion *of the population now* has answering machines, ***and*** you should not hesitate to leave a message, *making sure to say your own number slowly and clearly*.

當你打電話時,最好問對方:「你忙嗎?」即使你沒有這樣做,而對方又不方便聽電話時,就可以拒絕和你談話,只需要事後回電就好。現在大部分的人,都有電話答錄機,你一定要留言,而且要緩慢而清楚地說出你自己的電話號碼。

> inquire〔ɪnˋkwaɪr〕v. 詢問　　decline〔dɪˋklaɪn〕v. 拒絕
> offer〔ˋɔfɚ〕v. 提議;表示願意
> **answering machine** 電話答錄機
> hesitate〔ˋhɛzəˌtet〕v. 猶豫　　**leave a message** 留話

If you receive messages, you should try to return calls *within 24 hours.*

If you receive a phone call **while** *you have guests at home*, you should

not chat with the caller *too long* **and** neglect your guests. *Instead*, you

should offer to call back *at a mutually convenient time.*

如果你收到留言,應該在二十四小時內回電。如果在你家有訪客時,接到電話,就不應和對方談太久,忽略你的客人。相反的,你應在雙方都方便的時候,再回電給對方。

> neglect〔nɪˋglɛkt〕v. 忽略　　mutually〔ˋmjutʃʊəlɪ〕adv. 相互地

44.(**B**) 在現今的台灣,想要聯絡朋友,通常較方便的方法是
　　　(A) 拜訪他們。　　　　　　　(B) 打電話給他們。
　　　(C) 寫信給他們。　　　　　　(D) 派一位信差。
　　messenger〔ˋmɛsṇdʒɚ〕n. 信差

45.(**C**) 打電話去,對方不在家時,如果有電話答錄機,你該怎麼做?
　　　(A) 掛斷電話。　　　　　　　(B) 再打一次。
　　　(C) 在答錄機中留言。　　　　(D) 去拜訪他。

46.(**D**) 本文告訴你 ＿＿＿＿＿＿＿ 時應有的好禮貌。
　　　(A) 拜訪朋友。　　　　　　　(B) 開車。
　　　(C) 玩遊戲。　　　　　　　　(D) 打電話給朋友。

The following is a father's advice to his son/daughter, who has just graduated from high school :

以下是一位父親，對剛從中學畢業的兒女，所提出的勸告：

First of all, congratulations on your graduation! Graduation *from high school* means *that a new stage of life* is ahead of you. *At the beginning of this new stage*, I have some advice for you.

首先，恭禧你畢業了。從中學畢業，表示你即將迎接另一段新的人生。在這新旅程開始之際，我要給你一些勸告。

stage〔stedʒ〕*n.* 階段

Clean your own room *and* do your own laundry. *After you have messed up something*, you should learn to clean it up *yourself*. Cleanliness is indeed close to godliness.

清理自己的房間，自己洗衣服。弄亂某樣東西之後，要學會自己整理乾淨。整潔就能使人正直。

laundry〔'lɔndrɪ〕*n.* 洗衣服　　*mess up* 弄亂
godliness〔'gɑdlɪnɪs〕*n.* 虔誠；正直

Don't mistake knowledge *for wisdom*. *No matter how* much information *or knowledge you have accumulated*, you'll *never* make sound judgments *if you don't have wisdom*. Wisdom comes *from imagination and reflection*.

If you can imagine the possible future outcomes of your present decisions and actions, you can avoid mistakes. *And if you can reflect on the mistakes you have made,* you can avoid making the same mistakes *again and again.* Such is wisdom.

不要把知識誤認為智慧。不論你累積多少的資訊和知識，如果你沒有智慧，仍然無法做正確的判斷。智慧來自想像和反省。如果你可事先想像，你現在的決定和行為的可能後果，就可以避免錯誤。如果你能檢討所犯的過錯，就可避免一再犯同樣的錯誤。這就是智慧。

> *mistake A for B* 把 A 誤認為 B
> accumulate〔ə'kjumjə,let〕v. 累積
> sound〔saʊnd〕adj. 健全的；正確的
> reflection〔rɪ'flɛkʃən〕n. 反省
> outcome〔'aʊt,kʌm〕n. 結果　　　**reflect on** 反省

Don't complain. *When you take up a job,* do your best to carry it out. Don't waste time *complaining about it, no matter how difficult and boring it is.*

不要抱怨。當你從事一份工作，就盡力把它做好。不論工作是多困難和多無聊，都不要浪費時間發牢騷。

> *take up* 從事　　　*carry out* 完成；實現

Finally, be an early bird. *If you get up earlier than the sun,* you can watch it rising up *slowly into the sky. And* the sight *of the rising sun* will warm your heart *and* give you energy *for the day ahead. Besides, being an early bird,* you have plenty of time *to take exercise or do a lot of work.*

最後，要早起。如果你比太陽早起，就可看到它緩緩升入天空。看著日出，可溫暖你的心，帶給你接下來一天所需的活力。此外，如果早起，就有充足的時間運動，或做很多的工作。

> ***early bird*** 早起的人　　rise〔raɪz〕*v.* 升起
> ***take exercise*** 做運動

47. (**C**) 這位父親，想給他兒女一些建議，因為
　　　(A) 他的兒女守規矩。
　　　(B) 老師對他兒女的表現感到失望。
　　　(C) 另一段人生正等待著他的兒女。
　　　(D) 這位父親是哲學家。

48. (**D**) 根據這位父親的說法，智慧可使一個人
　　　(A) 獲得大量的知識。　　　　(B) 抱怨很多事。
　　　(C) 逃避責任。　　　　　　　(D) 正確地評估情勢。
　　acquire〔ə'kwaɪr〕*v.* 獲得　　evaluate〔ɪ'vælju,et〕*v.* 評估

49. (**B**) 這位父親認為，抱怨
　　　(A) 通常導致失敗。　　　　　(B) 不會使你成功。
　　　(C) 受到人們的喜愛。　　　　(D) 是件愉快的事。

50. (**A**) 這位父親說，早起可使一個人
　　　(A) 充滿活力，而且有效率。　(B) 既整潔又愉快。
　　　(C) 想睡而且疲倦。　　　　　(D) 既飢餓又生氣。
　　energetic〔ɛnə'dʒɛtɪk〕*adj.* 充滿活力的
　　efficient〔ə'fɪʃənt〕*adj.* 有效率的

第二部分：非選擇題

I、中譯英：**20 %**

1. 我們即將進入二十一世紀。

　We are approaching the twenty-first century.

　　* approach〔ə'protʃ〕*v.* 接近

2. 那時，人們會活得更長久。

By that time, people will be able to live longer.

3. 那的確是個好消息。

That certainly is (a piece of) good news.

4. 但是會有一個問題：

However, there will be a problem :

5. 更多的老人必須由更少的年輕人奉養。

More elderly people will have to be taken care of by a smaller number of young people.

* elderly (ˈɛldəlɪ) adj. 年長的　　*take care of* 照顧

Ⅱ、英文作文：**20**％

1.

　　Most people go to university to pursue their interests, or to receive training and qualifications. My main reason for attending college is to pursue knowledge. A university is a place which provides us with a good studying environment. We can further study our interests and sample other subjects, too. Thus we can find what it is that we are truly interested in.

　　Friendship is also something that I want to pursue. Different friends bring different experiences and points of view. I think these are two good goals to pursue, and so I will have to study hard to enter university.

　　　　　　qualifications (ˌkwɑləfəˈkeʃənz) n., pl. 資格
　　　　　　goal (gol) n. 目標　　pursue (pəˈʃu) v. 追求

2.

　　If I failed to enter college, I would be devastated. It wouldn't be the end of the world though, because life holds forth many opportunities for all of us. My choices are limitless. I could join the family business, get a job, or travel, I could do many things, but what I would do is go back to studying, so that I will can be eligible to enter college next year.

devastated (ˈdɛvəsˌtetɪd) *adj.* 被擊垮的
eligible (ˈɛlɪdʒəbḷ) *adj.* 合格的

八十六學年度大學聯考英文分數人數統計表

分數	第一類組	第二類組	第三類組	第四類組	分數	第一類組	第二類組	第三類組	第四類組
100	0	0	0	0	50	44815	35039	24467	24668
99	0	0	0	0	49	45731	35791	24991	25199
98	0	0	0	0	48	46630	36562	25511	25721
97	0	0	0	0	47	47545	37252	25996	26213
96	7	2	1	1	46	48395	38000	26514	26733
95	12	7	4	4	45	49252	38682	26982	27209
94	20	19	14	14	44	50117	39374	27447	27682
93	40	46	36	36	43	50998	40028	27900	28136
92	88	97	79	80	42	51783	40660	28324	28565
91	177	176	143	145	41	52519	41284	28773	29017
90	308	268	215	217	40	53255	41882	29186	29433
89	508	395	306	308	39	54010	42436	29555	29808
88	737	566	445	447	38	54756	42995	29948	30205
87	1066	821	646	650	37	55435	43534	30307	30566
86	1508	1136	893	901	36	56153	43998	30616	30879
85	2078	1545	1206	1215	35	56807	44485	30953	31218
84	2759	2020	1570	1580	34	57475	44938	31282	31551
83	3533	2558	1982	1993	33	58094	45420	31608	31884
82	4441	3158	2426	2440	32	58775	45862	31926	32205
81	5440	3865	2931	2950	31	59472	46284	32209	32492
80	6504	4606	3467	3487	30	60058	46701	32494	32784
79	7664	5422	4058	4083	29	60711	47082	32755	33049
78	8953	6258	4647	4676	28	61267	47460	33027	33324
77	10265	7197	5337	5368	27	61843	47854	33285	33589
76	11621	8187	6038	6079	26	62397	48194	33526	33834
75	13001	9216	6742	6790	25	62976	48517	33734	34045
74	14430	10330	7520	7576	24	63518	48802	33929	34246
73	15845	11469	8335	8396	23	64032	49116	34145	34464
72	17303	12560	9094	9163	22	64554	49399	34327	34648
71	18801	13681	9852	9935	21	65062	49674	34504	34828
70	20346	14802	10600	10686	20	65554	49950	34695	35027
69	21759	15921	11399	11490	19	66046	50210	34860	35198
68	23197	17049	12131	12228	18	66593	50463	35011	35356
67	24597	18270	12996	13103	17	67081	50710	35170	35526
66	25999	19495	13811	13926	16	67556	50944	35330	35700
65	27433	20594	14545	14667	15	67992	51124	35443	35821
64	28790	21686	15273	15400	14	68439	51340	35587	35976
63	30154	22779	16042	16175	13	68902	51553	35724	36122
62	31516	23897	16830	16969	12	69316	51766	35863	36265
61	32773	24934	17539	17686	11	69720	51920	35970	36378
60	34051	26013	18296	18452	10	70174	52118	36104	36516
59	35268	26983	18968	19131	9	70652	52325	36235	36660
58	36414	27960	19596	19765	8	71080	52510	36345	36777
57	37544	28928	20256	20432	7	71415	52638	36427	36863
56	38665	29942	20959	21135	6	71821	52785	36506	36955
55	39788	30841	21566	21745	5	72229	52933	36594	37059
54	40867	31729	22140	22325	4	72605	53117	36692	37168
53	41877	32585	22735	22926	3	72908	53208	36748	37230
52	42904	33447	23364	23559	2	73281	53351	36834	37329
51	43886	34292	23943	24138	1	73661	53510	36921	37425
					0	74400	53805	37089	37635

心得筆記欄

八十五學年度大學暨獨立學院入學考試
英　文　試　題

第一部分：單一選擇題

說明：以下 1－50 題，共 60 分；每題各有一個空格，各附有四個備選答案。請選出一個最適當的答案標示在「答案卡」上。

Ⅰ、**詞彙**（10％）：（1－10題）每題答對得 1 分，答錯倒扣⅓分，不答不給分。

1. The functions of this machine are described ＿＿＿＿＿ in the handbook.
   - (A) steadily
   - (B) precisely
   - (C) extremely
   - (D) forcibly

2. His ＿＿＿＿＿ for power led him into a tragedy.
   - (A) cause
   - (B) fame
   - (C) issue
   - (D) greed

3. The candidate found every way to ＿＿＿＿＿ her election materials to the voters.
   - (A) operate
   - (B) recognize
   - (C) distribute
   - (D) cultivate

4. John is so ＿＿＿＿＿ that he does not accept others' opinions.
   - (A) delicate
   - (B) intimate
   - (C) obstinate
   - (D) considerate

5. Every country needs strong national ＿＿＿＿＿ against enemy invasions.
   - (A) defense
   - (B) balance
   - (C) analysis
   - (D) response

6. At the finish, the winner of the race raised her arms ＿＿＿＿＿ .
   - (A) enormously
   - (B) frequently
   - (C) generously
   - (D) triumphantly

7. He can ＿＿＿＿＿ a motorcycle if he is given all the parts.
   - (A) transmit
   - (B) assemble
   - (C) reform
   - (D) proceed

8. He told me in ＿＿＿＿＿ that he would do everything to help me.
   - (A) action
   - (B) manner
   - (C) earnest
   - (D) progress

9. This exhibition of Chinese paintings is ＿＿＿＿＿ . Indeed, it's the best in ten years.
   - (A) marvelous
   - (B) potential
   - (C) artificial
   - (D) populous

10. Each of these bottles _____ 1,000 cc of mineral water, and it sells for NT$ 50.

(A) attains　　(B) remains　　(C) sustains　　(D) contains

Ⅱ、**對話**（10％）：（11−20題）每題答對得 1 分，答錯倒扣⅓分，不答不給分。

11. Sally : What do you plan to do after the exam?
　　Kathy: _____ How about you?
　　Sally : I'll take some computer lessons.
　　(A) You can say that again!　　(B) I'm all for it.
　　(C) Nothing special.　　(D) I've changed my mind.

12. Jane : Sorry to have kept you waiting.
　　Sue　: _____
　　Jane : In the library. I was trying to finish my homework and just forgot the time.
　　(A) That's OK.　　(B) What are you doing?
　　(C) What's wrong with you?　　(D) Where have you been?

13. Tom　: Don't forget tomorrow night at my home.
　　Bill　: No, I won't. Do you mind if I bring a friend?
　　Tom　: _____
　　Bill　: See you then.
　　(A) Yes, it's a good idea.　　(B) No, you'd better not.
　　(C) Certainly, I do.　　(D) Not at all. You're all welcome.

14. Receptionist : Hello, Kent Restaurant.
　　Ms. Lee　　: How late are you open today?
　　Receptionist : _____
　　Ms. Lee　　: Oh, that's too bad.
　　(A) I'm sorry. We're closed now.　　(B) You can come anytime.
　　(C) We're open very late.　　(D) We open at 11:30 a.m.

15. Mary : Why all this hurry?
　　Beth : I'm rushing to my dancing class.
　　Mary : _____ You sure keep yourself busy.
　　(A) I don't know how you do it.
　　(B) I don't know how much you can do.
　　(C) I don't know how to dance.
　　(D) I don't know how to do it.

16. Bruce : I want to sell my new car. Can you help me?
    Mark : _____
    Bruce : No. I'm quite serious about that.
    (A) Do you mean it?　　　　　　(B) Are you kidding?
    (C) Is that so?　　　　　　　　(D) What a surprise!

17. Andy : Do you know where Steve is?
    Jack : _____
    Andy : Thanks. We planned to go to the movies together, but I
           just couldn't find him.
    (A) I think he lives in Taipei.
    (B) I don't know how to get in touch with him.
    (C) I just saw him in the cafeteria.
    (D) We're in the same school.

18. Carol : Sue, this is Carol. Please tell me how to get to your place.
    Sue   : OK. You take bus number 208 near to your college and get
            off at the railway station, then take bus number 301 heading
            north and get off at the Central Museum. Then you cross the
            street...
    Carol : Please speak slowly. _____
    (A) I can't follow you.　　　　(B) I've no idea.
    (C) Mind your tongue.　　　　　(D) Keep your temper.

19. Alice : Is there a garage sale in the neighborhood today?
    Nancy: Yes. There's one next street. _____
    Alice : Some old furniture, perhaps.
    (A) What can I do for you?
    (B) What do you plan to buy?
    (C) What's the big idea?
    (D) What's on your mind?

20. Kuo-tung : How long did it take you to speak English so fluently?
    Hua-min : Ten years. You have to practice it every day. _____
    Kuo-tung : You're right about it.
    (A) I'd be glad to do it for you.　　(B) Nothing really matters.
    (C) So far so good.　　　　　　　　(D) There's no shortcut.

Ⅲ、 綜合測驗（20％）：（21-40題）每題答對得1分，答錯倒扣⅓分，不答不
給分。

Of course you've been to a library, in your school or your town. You
may ___(21)___ go there regularly to check out books. Libraries are great
places to borrow books, ___(22)___ you want a book to keep, or to give
to someone ___(23)___, a bookstore is the place to go. Most bookstores
have a section for young readers, ___(24)___ you'll find books stacked on
tables and shelves ___(25)___ in the library. Are you looking for *Alice in
Wonderland,* or *The Adventures of Monkey Sun Wu-k'ung*? You'll find all
the books for young readers put together in one place. If you want to buy
a ___(26)___ for a kindergarten friend, check the shelves of picture books.
One of these colorful books might ___(27)___ a perfect present. A bookstore is also a great place ___(28)___ for Mom and Dad. Are they interested
in cameras, gardening, sports, traveling, or music? You'll find books on all
those topics and many more ___(29)___ them. Bookstores are like libraries.
They have something for everyone. And they are just ___(30)___ fun.

21. (A) anyway　　　(B) ever　　　(C) even　　　(D) never
22. (A) but if　　　(B) only if　　　(C) what if　　　(D) as if
23. (A) either　　　(B) else　　　(C) too　　　(D) also
24. (A) which　　　(B) what　　　(C) where　　　(D) while
25. (A) as many　　　(B) more than　　　(C) or so　　　(D) just like
26. (A) book gifted　　　(B) gifted book　　　(C) book gift　　　(D) gift book
27. (A) keep　　　(B) make　　　(C) do　　　(D) come
28. (A) shop　　　(B) shopped　　　(C) to shop　　　(D) shopping
29. (A) except　　　(B) besides　　　(C) beyond　　　(D) between
30. (A) as much　　　(B) as well　　　(C) making such　　　(D) having some

Idioms and proverbs add color to a language, and they also reveal some
of the culture behind the language. ___(31)___ the most interesting example
is the expression "rain cats and dogs." Does it mean that cats and dogs
___(32)___ come down from the sky? Some people in 17th-century England
did believe ___(33)___, since many dead bodies of cats and dogs were
found ___(34)___ around after a heavy fall of rain. ___(35)___, this idiom simply
means "rain very hard." There are two more explanations as to ___(36)___

this idiom came into being. One comes from the Greek word *catadupa*,
____(37)____ "waterfall." People ____(38)____ often thought of waterfalls when it
rained heavily. Since *catadupa* sounds like "cats and dogs," heavy rains
came to be described ____(39)____ falling cats and dogs. ____(40)____ stems
from the belief of ancient weather prophets that rain was caused by the
evil spirits of cats and dogs.

31. (A) Possibly　　　(B) Basically　　　(C) Generally　　　(D) Accidentally
32. (A) fairly　　　　(B) safely　　　　(C) actually　　　　(D) hardly
33. (A) it　　　　　　(B) these　　　　(C) those　　　　　(D) them
34. (A) fooling　　　(B) swimming　　　(C) wandering　　　(D) floating
35. (A) As a result　(B) In fact　　　(C) At last　　　　(D) In addition
36. (A) what　　　　(B) when　　　　(C) how　　　　　(D) where
37 (A) means　　　　(B) meant　　　　(C) meaning　　　　(D) it means
38. (A) the other day (B) in those days (C) for days　　　(D) these days
39. (A) of　　　　　(B) to　　　　　(C) in　　　　　　(D) as
40. (A) The other　　(B) The last　　　(C) The another　　(D) The next

Ⅳ、**閱讀測驗**（20％）：（41－50題）每題答對得2分，答錯倒扣⅔分，不答
　　不給分。

Women are generally more perceptive than men, because they have
"women's intuition." Exactly what it means is hard to explain, but it can
be illustrated by the following female behaviors. Women's intuition can be
found in mothers' caring for their babies. A mother knows what her baby
needs by listening to its cries and observing its body language. Thus, many
women have developed an ability to pick up and understand nonverbal
signals, as well as an accurate eye for small detail. This is why women can
see many things which men fail to notice. A woman can usually see
through her husband's secrets before he realizes it. A husband is often
confused by his wife's unhappy expressions, not knowing what offense he
has given her. It may take a long time and a lot of questions for him to find
out that his wife is upset about a certain unfamiliar perfume on his suit. And
recently it has been found by some experts that in negotiations, women tend
to be more skillful than men, because they are often more tactful and can
use indirect strategies to achieve their goals.

41. According to this passage, the expression "women's intuition" can be better explained in terms of
    (A) general statements.　　　(B) women's views of men.
    (C) women's body language.　(D) concrete examples.

42. Many women are more observant than men, because
    (A) they don't want to be offended.
    (B) they try not to upset others.
    (C) they are sensitive to tiny things.
    (D) they pay much attention to babies.

43. According to this passage, which of the following statements is true?
    (A) A mother understands what her baby needs by feelings.
    (B) A husband can never succeed in cheating his wife.
    (C) Women can run a business better than men.
    (D) A wife usually wants her husband to wear the same perfume.

International Falls, Minnesota, has been called "the Nation's Icebox." The town won the title when a bone-chilling 46 degrees below zero Fahrenheit was recorded in the month of January in 1984. How do the townsfolk feel about living in the coldest spot in America? Most of them are proud. Actually, the title is so important to them that they are angry that Fraser, Colorado, is trying to take it away. Fraser claims that it is colder on average than the Minnesota town. But International Falls has filed for a copyright and now the name "the Nation's Icebox" is legally theirs.

There is more than pride involved in both cities' claim to being coldest. Money is an important factor. Manufacturers of products such as car batteries and flight suits flock to International Falls to test their products against the cold weather. Commercials bring an average of $300,000 per year to the town's economy.

One group that does not always appreciate the cold weather is students. Since winter is cold all the time, schools are almost never closed. Says one resident, "If they closed down every time it got real cold, the kids would be home all winter."

44. The two cities compete for the title of "the Nation's Icebox," because
    (A) many factories donate money only to the coldest town.
    (B) the title brings in financial benefits.
    (C) both cities are in urgent need of money.
    (D) the townsfolk can sell more car batteries and flight suits.

45. Students at International Falls are not always happy about the cold weather, because
    (A) they still have to go to school despite the freezing air.
    (B) the low temperatures inconvenience them.
    (C) it takes them a long time to get to their schools.
    (D) it makes them stay at home all winter.

46. According to this passage, which of the following statements is true?
    (A) Many residents of International Falls would move away because of the cold weather.
    (B) International Falls would lose its title to Fraser within one or two years.
    (C) Fraser, Colorado, has become the coldest spot in the U.S.
    (D) International Falls will continue to hold its title.

The evil reputation of bats is easy to understand. These creatures have been accused of attacking humans and carrying infectious diseases. The fact that they sleep during the day and fly at night also adds to their mystery. However, bats do not attack humans. Actually, there are more deaths each year from pet dog attacks and bees than from bats.

Bats perform an important ecological function throughout the world. They eat millions of harmful insects yearly. In fact, the food a bat eats every night amounts to one quarter of its own body weight. A single colony of Arizona bats observed by scientists eat up to 35,000 pounds of insects every night. That's the equivalent weight of 34 elephants!

Bats may soon disappear from the world. For one thing, they are fast losing their natural homes--caves, abandoned mines, certain kinds of trees. Bats are also in danger from certain chemicals used by farmers to fight destructive insects. Scientists have found that in the State of Arizona alone, the number of bats has declined from 30 million to 30,000 over the past six years. Many people kill bats out of unreasonable fear. Said one bat expert, "The most critical need for bat conservation today is increased public awareness and education."

47. According to this passage, which of the following statements is NOT true?
   (A) Pet dogs are more dangerous than bats.
   (B) Bats are often considered mysterious animals.
   (C) Many people still find bats fearsome.
   (D) In Arizona, bats eat 35,000 pounds of insects every night.

48. Which statement best describes the main idea of this selection?
   (A) Bats are harmful to human beings.
   (B) Bats are becoming an endangered species.
   (C) Bats are frightening and destructive creatures.
   (D) The prejudice against bats is well-grounded.

49. What suggestion is given in this passage to protect bats from dying out?
   (A) Helping them to find new homes.
   (B) Using chemicals to kill insects.
   (C) Making the public learn more about bats.
   (D) Providing them with more insects.

50. The author's attitude toward bats appears to be
   (A) confused.   (B) indifferent.
   (C) optimistic.   (D) sympathetic.

第二部分：非選擇題

I、中譯英（20％）：請將下列五句中文譯成正確、通順、達意，而且前後連貫的英文。每句4分。答案請寫在「非選擇題試卷」上，同時務必標示題號。

1. 每次放假，我都會到台灣某個地方去旅行。
2. 今年春假，我和一些同學搭巴士到墾丁（ Kenting ）國家公園。
3. 我們在那兒待了三天，很欣賞那裡的山林和海洋。
4. 這學期還沒結束，可是我們就在計劃夏天的旅行了。
5. 我們大概會到台灣東部去，因為那兒風景很美。

Ⅱ、**英文作文**(20%)：寫一篇約一百二十字的短文，一段或兩段皆可。文章必須以下面的英文句開頭："You win some; you lose some. That is life."人生中，每一個人都會有得有失。文章中必須舉出你自己有所得（win）又有所失（lose）的一個實例。請寫在「**非選擇題試卷**」上。

　　評分標準：內容5分，組織5分，文法4分，用字遣詞4分，拼字、大小寫及標點符號2分。

85年大學聯考英文試題詳解

第一部分：單一選擇題

I、詞彙：

1. (**B**) The functions *of this machine* are described *precisely in the* handbook.

   這台機器的功能精確地記載於手冊上。

   (A) steadily (ˈstɛdəlɪ) *adv.* 穩定地
   (B) **precisely** (prɪˈsaɪslɪ) *adv.* 精確地
   (C) extremely (ɪkˈstrimlɪ) *adv.* 極端地
   (D) forcibly (ˈforsəblɪ) *adv.* 猛烈地

   function (ˈfʌŋkʃən) *n.* 功能；作用　　handbook (ˈhænd͵bʊk) *n.* 手冊

2. (**D**) His greed *for power* led him into a tragedy.

   他對權力的貪求將他導入悲劇。

   (A) cause (kɔz) *n.* 起因　　(B) fame (fem) *n.* 名聲
   (C) issue (ˈɪʃu , ˈɪʃju) *n.* 發行　　(D) **greed** (grid) *n.* 貪婪

   tragedy (ˈtrædʒədɪ) *n.* 悲劇

3. (**C**) The candidate found every way to distribute her election materials *to the voters*.

   這位候選人找尋各種方法，將她的競選資料分發給選民。

   (A) operate (ˈɑpə͵ret) *v.* 運轉；操作
   (B) recognize (ˈrɛkəg͵naɪz) *v.* 認出；承認
   (C) **distribute** (dɪˈstrɪbjut) *v.* 分發
   (D) cultivate (ˈkʌltə͵vet) *v.* 培養

   candidate (ˈkændə͵det , ˈkændədɪt) *n.* 候選人
   election (ɪˈlɛkʃən) *n.* 選舉　　voter (ˈvotɚ) *n.* 選民；投票者

4. (**C**) John is *so* obstinate *that he does not accept others' opinions.*

　　約翰非常地固執，根本不接受別人的意見。

　　(A) delicate（'dɛləkət , -kɪt）*adj.* 纖細的；優美的
　　(B) intimate（'ɪntəmɪt）*adj.* 親密的
　　(C) *obstinate*（'ɑbstənɪt）*adj.* 固執的
　　(D) considerate（kən'sɪdərɪt , -'sɪdrɪt）*adj.* 體貼的

5. (**A**) Every country needs strong national defense *against enemy*

invasions.

　　每個國家都需要強大的國防，來抵抗敵人的侵略。

　　(A) *defense*（dɪ'fɛns）*n.* 防禦　　*national defense* 國防
　　(B) balance（'bæləns）*n.* 平衡
　　(C) analysis（ə'næləsɪs）*n.* 分析
　　(D) response（rɪ'spɑns）*n.* 回答

enemy（'ɛnəmɪ）*n.* 敵人　　　invasion（ɪn'veʒən）*n.* 侵略

6. (**D**) *At the finish*, the winner *of the race* raised her arms

triumphantly.

　　賽跑結束時，勝利者得意洋洋地舉起雙臂。

　　(A) enormously（ɪ'nɔrməslɪ）*adv.* 巨大地
　　(B) frequently（'frikwəntlɪ）*adv.* 經常
　　(C) generously（'dʒɛnərəslɪ）*adv.* 慷慨地
　　(D) *triumphantly*（traɪ'ʌmfəntlɪ）*adv.* 得意洋洋地

7. (**B**) He can assemble a motorcycle *if he is given all the parts.*

　　如果給他所有的零件，他就能裝配出一輛摩托車。

　　(A) transmit（træns'mɪt）*v.* 傳送；傳達
　　(B) *assemble*（ə'sɛmbl̩）*v.* 裝配
　　(C) reform（rɪ'fɔrm）*v.* 改革
　　(D) proceed（prə'sid）*v.* 前進

8. (**C**) He told me *in earnest* **that** he would *do* everything *to help me.*
他鄭重地告訴我，他會竭盡所能地幫助我。

    (A) action〔'ækʃən〕*n.* 行動

    (B) manner〔'mænɚ〕*n.* 方式

    (C) *earnest*〔'ɜnɪst〕*adj.* 認真的　　*in earnest* 認真地；鄭重地

    (D) progress〔'progrɛs〕*n.* 前進；進步　　in progress 在行進中

9. (**A**) This exhibition *of Chinese paintings* is marvelous. *Indeed*, it's the best *in ten years.*
這次國畫展覽令人驚嘆。的確，這是十年來最棒的一次。

    (A) *marvelous*〔'marvḷəs〕*adj.* 令人驚嘆的

    (B) potential〔pə'tɛnʃəl〕*adj.* 有潛力的

    (C) artificial〔,artə'fɪʃəl〕*adj.* 人造的

    (D) populous〔'papjələs〕*adj.* 人口衆多的

exhibition〔,ɛksə'bɪʃən〕*n.* 展覽

10. (**D**) Each *of these bottles* contains 1,000 cc of mineral water, **and** it sells for NT$ 50.
每個瓶子都裝有 1000 cc 的礦泉水，售價爲新台幣五十元。

    (A) attain〔ə'ten〕*v.* 達到

    (B) remain〔rɪ'men〕*v.* 仍然

    (C) sustain〔sə'sten〕*v.* 支撐；維持

    (D) *contain*〔kən'ten〕*v.* 含有；包含

mineral water 礦泉水

Ⅱ、**對話：**

11. (**C**) 莎莉：考完試後你打算要做什麼？

    凱西：＿＿＿＿＿＿＿＿＿　你呢？

    莎莉：我要參加電腦課程。

    (A) 你說的對極了！　　　　(B) 我完全贊成。

    (C) 沒什麼特別的。　　　　(D) 我改變心意了。

change one's mind 改變心意

12.(**D**) 珍：抱歉讓你久等了。

蘇：_____

珍：圖書館。我努力在趕作業，把時間都給忘了。

(A) 沒關係。　　　　　　　(B) 你在做什麼？

(C) 你是怎麼了？　　　　　(D) 你到哪去了？

13.(**D**) 湯姆：別忘了明晚來我家。

比爾：不，我不會忘的。你介意我帶朋友去嗎？

湯姆：_____

比爾：到時候見。

(A) 是的，那是個好主意。　(B) 不，你最好不要。

(C) 我當然介意。　　　　　(D) 一點也不。歡迎你們。

14.(**A**) 接待員：喂，肯特餐廳。

李小姐：你們今天營業到多晚？

接待員：_____

李小姐：噢，真是糟糕。

(A) 很抱歉。我們現在已經打烊了。

(B) 你隨時都可以來。　　　(C) 我們營業到很晚。

(D) 我們早上十一點半開門。

receptionist〔rɪˈsɛpʃənɪst〕n. 接待員

15.(**A**) 瑪麗：什麼事這麼急？

貝絲：我趕著去上舞蹈課。

瑪麗：_____你真的是讓自己保持忙碌。

(A) 我不知道你是如何辦到的。

(B) 我不知道你有多大能耐。

(C) 我不知道如何跳舞。

(D) 我不知道怎麼做。（若將題目的 You sure keep yourself busy. 改為 How do you keep yourself busy? 則答案應選 D。）

16.(**B**) 布魯斯：我想賣掉我的新車。你能幫我嗎？

馬　克：_____

布魯斯：不，我對這件事相當認真。

(A) 你是當真的嗎？　　　　(B) 你在開玩笑嗎？

(C) 是這樣嗎？　　　　　　(D) 真讓人驚訝！

17. (**C**) 安迪：你知道史蒂夫在哪嗎？

傑克：_____

安迪：謝了。我們打算一起去看電影，可是我就是找不到他。

(A) 我想他住在台北。

(B) 我不知道如何和他連絡。

(C) 我剛剛在自助餐廳看到他。

(D) 我們就讀同一所學校。

get in touch with *sb.* 和某人連絡

cafeteria〔ˌkæfəˈtɪrɪə〕 *n.* 自助餐廳

18. (**A**) 卡蘿：蘇，我是卡蘿。請告訴我怎麼到你那兒。

蘇　：沒問題。你搭學校附近的208路公車到火車站下車，然後搭往北的301路公車，在中央博物館下車。然後過馬路……

卡蘿：請講慢一點。_____

(A) 我跟不上。　　　　　　　(B) 我不知道。

(C) 說話小心。　　　　　　　(D) 克制你的脾氣。

railway〔ˈrelˌwe〕 *n.* 鐵路　　head〔hɛd〕 *v.* 前往

follow〔ˈfɑlo〕 *v.* 聽得懂；跟得上

19. (**B**) 愛麗絲：今天附近有沒有車庫大拍賣？

南　西：有。隔壁街有一場拍賣。_____

愛麗絲：也許買些舊傢俱。

(A) 我能為你效勞嗎？　　　　(B) 你打算買什麼？

(C) 究竟是什麼了不起的計畫？(D) 你在想什麼？

garage sale 車庫大拍賣　　neighborhood〔ˈnebɚˌhud〕 *n.* 附近

the big idea [口] 計畫（常為諷刺用語）

20. (**D**) 國同：你花了多久時間才把英語說得這麼流利？

華敏：十年。必須每天練習。_____

國同：你說的對。

(A) 我很樂意為你效勞。　　　(B) 沒什麼大不了的。

(C) 到目前為止還好。　　　　(D) 這是沒有捷徑的。

fluently〔ˈfluəntlɪ〕 *adv.* 流利地

matter〔ˈmætɚ〕 *v.* 重要；有關係　　***so far*** 至今

shortcut〔ˈʃɔrtˌkʌt〕 *n.* 捷徑

Ⅲ、綜合測驗：

Of course you've been to a library, *in your school or your town.*

You may *even* go there *regularly to check out books.* Libraries are great
　　　　　21

places *to borrow books*, **but if** you want a book to keep, **or** to give to
　　　　　　　　　　　　　　　　22

someone else, a bookstore is the place *to go.* Most bookstores have a
　　　　23

section *for young readers*, **where** you'll find books *stacked on tables and*
　　　　　　　　　　　　　　　24

shelves just like in the library. Are you looking for *Alice in Wonderland,*
　　　　　　25

or The Adventures of Monkey Sun Wu-k'ung? You'll find all the books

for young readers put together in one place.

　　你一定去過圖書館，在你的學校裏或你家附近。你甚至可能定期去借書。圖
書館是借書的好地方，但是如果你想要把一本書保留下來，或是送給別人，你就
要到書局。大部分的書局都有一個區域，專門提供給年輕讀者，在那兒你會發現
書都堆在桌子和架子上，就好像在圖書館一樣。你在找「愛麗絲夢遊仙境」，還
是「西遊記」呢？你會發現，所有適合年輕讀者看的書，都擺在同一個地方。

　　　　　　regularly〔'rɛgjələlɪ〕*adv.* 定期地
　　　　　　check out（辦理手續後）借出　　section〔'sɛkʃən〕*n.* 區域
　　　　　　stack〔stæk〕*v.* 堆積　　shelf〔ʃɛlf〕*n.* 架子（複數形為 shelves）
　　　　　　wonderland〔'wʌndə,lænd〕*n.* 仙境　　adventure〔əd'vɛntʃə〕*n.* 冒險

21.（**C**）依句意，你「甚至」可能定期去借書，選 (C) even。而 (A) 無論如何，(B)
　　　曾經，(D) 從不，均不合句意。

22.（**A**）空格前後語意相反，故應選 (A) but if。而 (B) what if「如果…該怎麼
　　　辦？」，(D) as if「好像」，用法與句意，皆不合。

23.（**B**）依句意，想要把書送給別人，someone 之後應用 else 修飾，選 (B)。

24. (**C**) 關係副詞 where 引導形容詞子句，修飾先行詞 section，選 (C)。

25. (**D**) 依句意，書都堆在架子上，「就好像」圖書館一樣，選 (D) just like。

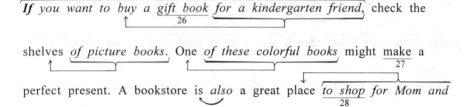

**If** you want to buy a gift book for a kindergarten friend, check the
　　　　　　　　　　　26

shelves _of picture books._ One _of these colorful books_ might make a
　　　　　　　　　　　　　　　　　　　　　　　　　　　　　　27

perfect present. A bookstore is _also_ a great place _to shop for_ Mom and
　　　　　　　　　　　　　　　　　　　　　　　　　　　28

Dad. Are they interested in cameras, gardening, sports, traveling, or

music? You'll find books _on all those topics_ **and** many more _besides_
　　　　　　　　　　　　　　　　　　　　　　　　　　　　　　29

them. Bookstores are like libraries. They have some thing _for everyone._

And they are _just_ as much fun.
　　　　　　　　　　　30

如果你要買書給幼稚園小朋友當禮物，去圖畫書的架子找。買一本這種色彩豐富
的書，可能是個很理想的禮物。書局也是為爸爸媽媽選購禮物的好地方。他們對
照像機、園藝、運動、旅遊或音樂有興趣嗎？所有這些主題的書，你都找得到，
除此之外，還有其他更多的書。書局就像圖書館，每個人要的那裏都有，而且和
圖書館一樣有趣。

　　　　　　　kindergarten (ˈkɪndəˌɡɑrtṇ) n. 幼稚園
　　　　　　　perfect (ˈpɝfɪkt) adj. 完美的　　camera (ˈkæmərə) n. 照像機
　　　　　　　gardening (ˈɡɑrdṇɪŋ) n. 園藝　　topic (ˈtɑpɪk) n. 主題

26. (**D**) 買書當做禮物，此處用名詞 gift 修飾名詞 book，表用途，選 (D)。

27. (**B**) 依句意，圖畫書可以「成為」理想的禮物，應用 make，選 (B)。

28. (**C**) 此處用不定詞片語 to shop，修飾名詞 place。

29. (**B**) 除了前文所提到的多種主題外，還有其他更多，應選 (B) besides 除了～
之外，還有…。(A) except 把～除外，(C) beyond 超過，(D) between 在
～之間，均不合。

30. (**A**) 書局和圖書館「一樣」有趣，選 (A) as much。

Idioms and proverbs add color *to a language*, **and** they *also* reveal some *of the culture behind the language*. *Possibly* the *most* interesting
31
example is the expression "*rain cats and dogs*." Does it mean **that** cats and dogs *actually* come down from the sky? Some people *in 17th-century*
32
England did believe it, *since many dead bodies of cats and dogs* were
33
found *floating* around *after a heavy fall of rain.* *In fact*, this idiom
34   35
simply means "rain very hard."

　　慣用語和諺語增加了語言的特色，也顯露了語言背後的一些文化特質。可能最有趣的例子就是 rain cats and dogs 的這種說法。這句話真的是表示貓和狗會從天而降嗎？有些十七世紀的英國人真的相信會有這種現象，因為他們曾在一場大雨過後，發現貓和狗的屍體在四處漂浮。事實上，這句慣用語只是在表示「雨下得非常大」而已。

　　　　　idiom〔ˋɪdɪəm〕n. 慣用語　　proverb〔ˋprɑvɝb〕n. 諺語
　　　　　add〔æd〕v. 添加　　color〔ˋkʌlɚ〕n. 特色
　　　　　reveal〔rɪˋvil〕v. 顯露　　expression〔ɪkˋsprɛʃən〕n. 說法

31.(**A**) 依句意，選(A)possibly *adv.* 可能地。而(B)基本上，(C)一般而言，
　　　(D)accidentally〔ˌæksəˋdɛntlɪ〕*adv.* 意外地，則不合句意。

32.(**C**) 依句意，選(C)actually〔ˋæktʃʊəlɪ〕*adv.* 真地。而(A)fairly〔ˋfɛrlɪ〕*adv.*
　　　非常地（= *very*），(B)安全地，(D)幾乎不，皆不合句意。

33.(**A**) 依句意，有些十七世紀的英國人相信「貓和狗真的會從天而降」，要代替前面所提過的名詞子句：that cats and dogs … the sky，代名詞須用單數，故選(A)it。

34. (**D**)　大雨過後，發現許多貓和狗的屍體到處「漂浮」，故選 (D) floating 。
　　　　float〔flot〕v. 漂浮。而 (A) fool around 鬼混，(B) 游泳，(C) wander
　　　　〔'wɑndɚ〕v. 流浪，皆不合句意。

35. (**B**)　依句意，選 (B) in fact 事實上。而 (A) 因此，(C) 終於，(D) 此外，皆不合
　　　　句意。

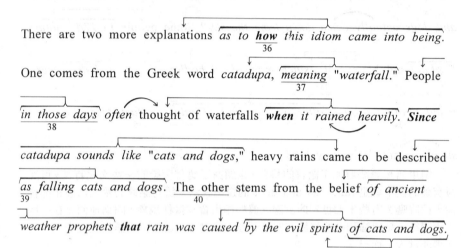

There are two more explanations *as to **how** this idiom came into being.*
36

One comes from the Greek word *catadupa, **meaning** "waterfall."* People
37

in those days often thought of waterfalls **when it rained heavily.** *Since*
38

catadupa sounds like "cats and dogs," heavy rains came to be described
as falling cats and dogs. The other stems from the belief *of ancient*
39　　　　　　　　　　　　　　　　　　　　　　　　40

*weather prophets **that** rain was caused by the evil spirits of cats and dogs.*

至於這個慣用語是如何產生的，還有另外兩種解釋。其一就是來自於希臘字
catadupa，意思就是「瀑布」。當時的人在下大雨時都會想到瀑布。由於 catadupa
聽起來就好像 cats and dogs，因此下大雨就被描述成 falling cats and dogs。
另外一種說法則是起源於古代的天氣預言家，他們認為雨是由貓和狗的邪靈所造
成的。

　　　　　explanation〔͵ɛksplə'neʃən〕n. 解釋
　　　　　come into being 產生　　waterfall〔'wɔtɚ͵fɔl〕n. 瀑布
　　　　　stem from 起源於　　ancient〔'enʃənt〕adj. 古代的
　　　　　prophet〔'prɑfɪt〕n. 預言家

36. (**C**)　依句意，這個慣用語是「如何」產生的，選 (C) how 如何。

37. (**C**)　兩動詞間無連接詞，第二個動詞須改為現在分詞，選 (C) meaning。原句
　　　　是由 ⋯ Greek word catadupa, which means "waterfall."簡化而來的
　　　　分詞構句。

38. (**B**)「當時的」人在下大雨時都會想到瀑布，故選 (B) *in those days* 當時。
　　而 (A) the other day 前幾天，(C) for days 好幾天以來，(D) these days
　　最近，皆不合句意。

39. (**D**) *be described as* ～　被描述成～

40. (**A**) 表特定的兩者，其中一個用 one，另一個則用 the other，選 (A)。而 (B)
　　最後一個，(C) another 之前不可加定冠詞 the，且須用於「三者或三者
　　以上」的情況，(D) 下一個，用法與句意皆不合。

Ⅳ、閱讀測驗：

Women are *generally more* perceptive *than men, because they have*
"*women's intuition.*" *Exactly what* it *means* is hard to explain, *but* it can
be illustrated *by the following female behaviors.* Women's intuition can
be found *in mothers' caring for their babies.* A mother knows *what* her
baby needs *by listening to its cries and observing its body language.*
Thus, many women have developed an ability *to pick up and understand*
nonverbal signals, *as well as* an accurate eye *for small detail.* This is
why women can see many things *which men fail to notice.*

　　一般而言，女人的知覺力較男人敏銳，因為女人擁有「女性的直覺」。其涵義
十分難解釋，不過還是可以透過下列女性的行為來加以說明。當母親在照顧嬰兒
時，女性的直覺就會顯露出來。母親只要聽嬰兒的哭聲、觀察其肢體語言，就能
知道嬰兒的需要。因此，許多的女性已經培養出一種能力，能夠輕易接收並了解
非口語的信號，並且眼光準確，能觀察入微。那就是為什麼女人可以看到很多男
人無法注意到的事物。

perceptive〔pɚˋsɛptɪv〕*adj.* 知覺敏銳的
intuition〔ˌɪntuˋɪʃən〕*n.* 直覺　　illustrate〔ˋɪləstret〕*v.* 說明
care for 照顧　　observe〔əbˋzɝv〕*v.* 觀察　　*pick up* 接收
nonverbal〔nɑnˋvɝb!〕*adj.* 非口語的　　eye〔aɪ〕*n.* 眼光；觀察力

A woman can *usually* see through her husband's secrets *before he realizes it*. A husband is *often* confused *by his wife's unhappy expressions*, *not knowing* **what** offense *he has given her*. It may take a long time **and** a lot of questions for him *to find out* **that** *his wife is upset about a certain unfamiliar perfume on his suit*. **And** recently it has been found *by some experts* **that** *in negotiations*, women tend to be *more* skillful **than** men, **because** *they are often more tactful* **and** *can use indirect strategies* *to achieve their goals*.

女人通常可以在丈夫尚未察覺之前，就看穿他的祕密。丈夫常會對妻子不高興的表情覺得困惑，不知道自己怎麼會惹她生氣。丈夫可能需要很久，而且必須問很多的問題，才能發現，妻子是為了他西裝上某種陌生的香水味而生氣。最近有些專家也發現，在談判交涉時，女人比男人有技巧，因為通常女人比較圓滑，會運用間接的策略來達成她們的目標。

expression〔ɪkˋsprɛʃən〕n. 表情
offense〔əˋfɛns〕n. 冒犯　　**give offense** 使（人）生氣
upset〔ʌpˋsɛt〕adj. 不高興的　　perfume〔ˋpɝfjum〕n. 香水
suit〔sut〕n. 西裝　　negotiation〔nɪˏgoʃɪˋeʃən〕n. 談判
tactful〔ˋtæktfəl〕adj. 圓滑的　　strategy〔ˋstrætədʒɪ〕n. 策略

41.(**D**) 根據本文，「女性的直覺」這種說法，用何種方式解釋比較好？
　　　(A) 一般性的敘述。　　　　　(B) 女人對男人的看法。
　　　(C) 女人的肢體語言。　　　　(D) 具體的例子。
　　in terms of 以～說法　　　concrete〔ˋkɑnkrit, kɑnˋkrit〕adj. 具體的

42.(**C**) 許多女人的觀察力比男人敏銳，那是因為
　　　(A) 女人不想被冒犯。　　　　(B) 女人不想去惹別人生氣。
　　　(C) 女人對小事較敏感。　　　(D) 女人非常注意嬰兒。
　　observant〔əbˋzɝvənt〕adj. 觀察力敏銳的
　　tiny〔ˋtaɪnɪ〕adj. 微小的

43. (**A**) 根據本文，下列敘述何者正確？
    (A) 母親憑感覺就可了解嬰兒的需要。
    (B) 丈夫想騙妻子是無法成功的。
    (C) 女人的事業經營得比男人好。
    (D) 妻子通常會要先生擦同一種香水。

International Falls, Minnesota, has been called "the Nation's Icebox." The town won the title *when a bone-chilling 46 degrees below zero Fahrenheit was recorded in the month of January in 1984.* How do the townsfolk feel about living *in the coldest spot in America*? Most *of them* are proud. *Actually*, the title is *so* important to them *that they are angry that Fraser, Colorado, is trying to take it away.* Fraser claims *that it is colder on average than the Minnesota town.* **But** International Falls has filed for a copyright *and now* the name "*the Nation's Icebox*" is *legally* theirs.

明尼蘇達州的國際瀑布鎮，被稱為「全國（美國）的冰箱」。這個小鎮在一九八四年一月時，記錄到華氏零下四十六度刺骨的低溫，而贏得了這個頭銜。鎮民們對於居住在全美最冷的地方，有何感想呢？他們大部分的人都感到很驕傲。事實上，這個頭銜對他們非常重要，所以當科羅拉多州的弗雷瑟鎮企圖奪走這個頭銜時，他們都非常憤怒。弗雷瑟鎮宣稱，他們的平均溫度比明尼蘇達的國際瀑布鎮冷。但國際瀑布鎮已經申請了版權，所以現在，「全國的冰箱」這個名字，法律上是屬於他們的。

falls〔fɔlz〕*n. pl.* 瀑布　　icebox〔'aɪs‚bɑks〕*n.* 冰箱
bone-chilling〔'bon‚tʃɪlɪŋ〕*adj.* 刺骨的
Fahrenheit〔'færən‚haɪt , 'fɑrən-〕*adj.* 華氏的
townsfolk〔'taʊnz‚fok〕*n. pl.* 市民；鎮民
claim〔klem〕*v.,n.* 宣稱　　***on average*** 平均地
file〔faɪl〕*v.* 申請；提出　　copyright〔'kɑpɪ‚raɪt〕*n.* 版權；著作權
legally〔'ligl̩ɪ〕*adv.* 法律上

There is more than pride *involved in both cities' claim to being coldest.*
Money is an important factor. Manufacturers *of products such as car*
batteries and flight suits flock to International Falls *to test their products*
against the cold weather. Commercials bring an average of $300,000 *per*
year to the town's economy.

　　兩個城鎮都宣稱是最冷的地方,這其中包含的不只是為了誇耀而已,錢是一個重要因素。諸如汽車電瓶、飛行服裝等的製造商,都聚集到國際瀑布鎮,測試他們的產品能否抵抗寒冷的天氣。廣告每年平均為鎮上經濟帶來三十萬美金的收入。

pride〔praɪd〕*n.* 驕傲
involve〔ɪnˈvɑlv〕*v.* 包含;牽涉　　factor〔ˈfæktɚ〕*n.* 因素
manufacturer〔͵mænjəˈfæktʃərɚ〕*n.* 製造商
flight〔flaɪt〕*n.* 飛行　　　suit〔sut, sjut〕*n.* 服裝
flock〔flɑk〕*v.* 聚集　　commercial〔kəˈmɝʃəl〕*n.* 廣告

One group *that does not always appreciate the cold weather* is students.
Since winter is cold all the time, schools are *almost never* closed. Says
one resident, *"If they closed down every time it got real cold,* the kids
would be home *all winter."*

　　不太欣賞寒冷天氣的一群人,就是學生。既然冬天總是很冷,學校就幾乎都不關閉。有位居民說:「如果每次天氣變得真的很冷,學校就關閉,那麼孩子們可能整個冬天都會待在家裏。」

appreciate〔əˈpriʃɪ͵et〕*v.* 欣賞;重視
resident〔ˈrɛzədənt〕*n.* 居民

44. (**B**) 這兩個城鎮為了「全國的冰箱」這個頭銜而競爭，是因為

　　　　(A) 許多工廠只捐錢給最冷的城鎮。

　　　　(B) 這個頭銜帶來金錢上的利益。

　　　　(C) 兩個城鎮都迫切需要錢。

　　　　(D) 鎮民能販賣更多的汽車電瓶和飛行服裝。

　　　compete〔kəm'pit〕v. 競爭　　factory〔'fækt(ə)rɪ〕n. 工廠

　　　donate〔'donet〕v. 捐贈　　***bring in*** 獲利

　　　benefit〔'bɛnəfɪt〕n. 利益　　urgent〔'ɝdʒənt〕adj. 迫切的

45. (**A**) 國際瀑布鎮上的學生，對於寒冷的天氣不是很高興，因為

　　　　(A) 儘管寒氣襲人，他們仍然必須上學。

　　　　(B) 低溫讓他們感到不方便。

　　　　(C) 他們到學校需要很長的時間。

　　　　(D) 寒冷的天氣使他們整個冬天都待在家裏。

　　　freezing〔'frizɪŋ〕adj. 寒冷的

　　　inconvenience〔ˌɪnkən'vinjəns〕v. 使感到不方便

46. (**D**) 根據本文，下列敘述何者為真？

　　　　(A) 許多國際瀑布鎮的居民，會因天氣寒冷而搬走。

　　　　(B) 國際瀑布鎮在一、二年之內，就會把它的頭銜輸給弗雷瑟鎮。

　　　　(C) 科羅拉多州的弗雷瑟鎮已經成為美國最冷的地方。

　　　　(D) 國際瀑布鎮將會繼續保有它的頭銜。

　　　move away 搬走　　hold〔hold〕v. 保有

The evil reputation *of bats* is easy to understand. These creatures have been accused *of attacking humans and carrying infectious diseases.* The fact ***that*** *they sleep during the day* **and** *fly at night* also adds to their mystery. *However*, bats do not attack humans. *Actually*, there are more deaths *each year* *from pet dog attacks and bees* ***than*** *from bats.*

　　蝙蝠會惡名遠播是很容易理解的。攻擊人類、散播傳染病的罪名,長久以來一直加諸在這些蝙蝠身上,而晝伏夜出的特性,也增加了牠們的神祕感。然而,蝙蝠並不會攻擊人類。事實上,每年因寵物狗、蜜蜂的攻擊而導致的死亡,比蝙蝠來得多。

evil (ˈivḷ) *adj.* 邪惡的
reputation (ˌrɛpjəˈteʃən) *n.* 名聲　　bat (bæt) *n.* 蝙蝠
creature (ˈkritʃɚ) *n.* 生物　　accuse (əˈkjuz) *v.* 控告
be accused of 被控以~罪名　　attack (əˈtæk) *v.,n.* 攻擊
infectious (ɪnˈfɛkʃəs) *adj.* 傳染的
mystery (ˈmɪstrɪ , ˈmɪstərɪ) *n.* 神祕

Bats perform an important ecological function *throughout the world*.
They eat millions of harmful insects *yearly*. *In fact*, the food *a bat*
eats every night amounts to one quarter of its own body weight. A single
colony of Arizona bats *observed by scientists* eat up to 35,000 pounds
of insects every night. That's the equivalent weight *of 34 elephants*!

　　在全世界,蝙蝠執行著重要的生態任務,牠們每年吃掉好幾百萬隻害蟲。事實上,一隻蝙蝠一晚的攝食量相當於牠體重的四分之一。據科學家觀察,單單一群亞歷桑那蝙蝠每晚就可吃掉三萬五千磅的昆蟲,其重量相當於三十四頭大象。

perform (pɚˈfɔrm) *v.* 執行
function (ˈfʌŋkʃən) *n.* 任務;作用
ecological (ˌikəˈladʒɪkḷ) *adj.* 生態的
harmful (ˈharmfəl) *adj.* 有害的
insect (ˈɪnsɛkt) *n.* 昆蟲　　amount (əˈmaunt) *v.* 總計
quarter (ˈkwɔrtɚ) *n.* 四分之一
colony (ˈkalənɪ) *n.* 一群(動物或植物)
single (ˈsɪŋgḷ) *adj.* 單一的　　**up to** 多達
equivalent (ɪˈkwɪvələnt) *adj.* 相等的

Bats may *soon* disappear *from the world. For one thing,* they are *fast* losing their natural homes--*caves, abandoned mines, certain kinds of trees.* Bats are *also in danger from certain chemicals used by farmers to fight destructive insects.* Scientists have found **that** *in the State of Arizona alone, the number of bats has declined from 30 million to 30,000 over the past six years.* Many people kill bats *out of unreasonable fear.* Said one bat expert, "The *most* critical need *for bat conservation today* is increased public awareness and education."

蝙蝠可能即將從地球上絕跡。其中一個原因是，牠們的天然居所——洞穴、廢棄的礦坑、某些種類的樹木——正急速在消失，而農人用來撲滅害蟲的一些化學藥品，也讓蝙蝠身陷危機。科學家發現，過去六年來，單單亞歷桑那一州的蝙蝠數量，就已從三千萬減少至三萬。許多人由於無謂的恐懼而殺死蝙蝠。一位蝙蝠專家指出：「今後蝙蝠保育最重要的工作，就是要加強大眾的認知與教育。」

abandoned〔ə'bændənd〕*adj.* 廢棄的　　mine〔maɪn〕*n.* 礦坑
destructive〔dɪ'strʌktɪv〕*adj.* 破壞性的
decline〔dɪ'klaɪn〕*v.* 減低
unreasonable〔ʌn'riznəbḷ, -znəbḷ〕*adj.* 不合理的
critical〔'krɪtɪkḷ〕*adj.* 重要的　　conservation〔͵kɑnsə'veʃən〕*n.* 保育
awareness〔ə'wɛrnɪs〕*n.* 察覺；體認

47. (**D**) 根據本文，下列敘述何者為非？
    (A) 寵物狗比蝙蝠危險。
    (B) 蝙蝠常被認為是神祕的動物。
    (C) 許多人仍認為蝙蝠很可怕。
    (D) 在亞歷桑那州，蝙蝠每晚可吃掉三萬五千磅的昆蟲。
    mysterious〔mɪs'tɪrɪəs〕*adj.* 神祕的
    fearsome〔'fɪrsəm〕*adj.* 可怕的

48. (**B**) 下列敘述何者最能說明本文的主旨？

        (A) 蝙蝠對人類有害。

        (B) <u>蝙蝠即將成為瀕臨絕種的動物。</u>

        (C) 蝙蝠是可怕又具毀滅性的生物。

        (D) 對蝙蝠的偏見是有根據的。

endangered (ɪnˋdendʒəd) *adj.* 瀕臨絕種的

species (ˋspiʃɪz) *n.* 種；類　　prejudice (ˋprɛdʒədɪs) *n.* 偏見

well-grounded (ˋwɛlˋgraʊndɪd) *adj.* 理由充分的

49. (**C**) 本文建議如何保護蝙蝠免於絕種？

        (A) 幫助牠們尋找新的居所。　　(B) 使用化學藥品撲滅昆蟲。

        (C) <u>讓大眾更進一步認識蝙蝠。</u>　　(D) 提供牠們更多昆蟲。

die out （種族）滅絕

50. (**D**) 作者對蝙蝠的態度似乎是

        (A) 困惑的。　　　　　　　　　(B) 漠不關心的。

        (C) 樂觀的。　　　　　　　　　(D) <u>同情的。</u>

appear (əˋpɪr) *v.* 似乎　　indifferent (ɪnˋdɪfərənt) *adj.* 漠不關心的

optimistic (ˏɑptəˋmɪstɪk) *adj.* 樂觀的

sympathetic (ˏsɪmpəˋθɛtɪk) *adj.* 同情的

第二部分：非選擇題

I、中譯英：

1. 每次放假，我都會到台灣某個地方去旅行。

$$\left. \begin{array}{l} \text{Every time} \\ \text{Whenever} \end{array} \right\}$$ there is a vacation, I'll travel somewhere in Taiwan.

2. 今年春假，我和一些同學搭巴士到墾丁（Kenting）國家公園。

This spring vacation, I went with some of my classmates to Kenting National Park by bus.

3. 我們在那兒待了三天，很欣賞那裡的山林和海洋。

We stayed there for three days, appreciating the forests and the sea.

4. 這學期還沒結束，可是我們就在計劃夏天的旅行了。

This semester isn't over yet, but we're already planning our summer vacation travels.

5. 我們大概會到台灣東部去，因為那兒風景很美。

We'll probably go to the east of Taiwan, for the scenery there is very beautiful.

Ⅱ、英文作文：

《範例 1》

You win some; you lose some. That is life. It is important to bear this in mind, especially when you fail. Everyone who has achieved success in life has faced setbacks at one time or another. *Therefore*, to fail is no disgrace, as long as you can learn from experience.

I remember the time I played for my school basketball team. We played with a team from another school, and we didn't think it was a good team. We didn't take our opponents seriously. We were surprised when they beat us because of our unenthusiastic performance. It was very embarrassing, so after that we practiced often and took our opponents seriously. Later we won a tournament. It was a great feeling to have the school principal congratulate us in front of our classmates, and it was a very good learning experience.

> *bear sth. in mind* 把某事牢記在心
> setback〔'sɛt,bæk〕n. 挫敗
> disgrace〔dɪs'gres〕n. 丟臉；恥辱　　*as long as* 只要
> opponent〔ə'ponənt〕n. 對手　　beat〔bit〕v. 打敗
> unenthusiastic〔,ʌnɪn,θjuzɪ'æstɪk〕adj. 不熱心的
> embarrassing〔ɪm'bærəsɪŋ〕adj. 尷尬的
> tournament〔'tɝnəmənt , 'tʊr-〕n. 錦標賽；競賽
> principal〔'prɪnsəpḷ〕n. 校長

《範例 2》

You win some; *you lose some*. *That is life*. Nobody is perfect and expected to win all the time. Even Mohammed Ali has lost in the ring before! Rather than placing emphasis on winning, the wise person will focus on the knowledge gained from competition.

Take myself for example. As a youngster I was a competent athlete, and I participated in many running competitions. I was the best in my school and the pride and envy of many. The winning meant everything, but the glory got to me, and I became slack. I was lazy and didn't train as intensively as before.

Before I knew it I had lost my form and lost competitions. It was only then that I realized the importance of training. I started to train again and promised myself never to be lazy again. By losing I had learnt more things than from winning!

> *Mohammed Ali* 拳王阿里
> ring〔rɪŋ〕*n.*（拳擊的）競技場　　*rather than* 而不要
> *place emphasis on* 強調　　*focus on* 專注於
> competition〔ˌkɑmpəˈtɪʃən〕*n.* 競爭；比賽
> competent〔ˈkɑmpətənt〕*adj.* 有能力的
> athlete〔ˈæθlɪt〕*n.* 運動員　　envy〔ˈɛnvɪ〕*n.* 羨慕的對象
> slack〔slæk〕*adj.* 鬆懈的　　lazy〔ˈlezɪ〕*adj.* 懶惰的
> intensively〔ɪnˈtɛnsɪvlɪ〕*adv.* 密集地
> form〔fɔrm〕*n.*（運動員的）狀況

八十五學年度大學聯考英文分數人數統計表

分數	第一類組	第二類組	第三類組	第四類組	分數	第一類組	第二類組	第三類組	第四類組
100	0	0	0	0	50	19444	15411	11379	11476
99	0	0	0	0	49	20601	16371	12064	12173
98	0	0	0	0	48	21771	17323	12762	12880
97	1	1	0	0	47	22925	18338	13486	13609
96	1	3	1	1	46	24203	19404	14220	14349
95	1	4	2	2	45	25435	20427	14952	15084
94	2	4	2	2	44	26710	21506	15723	15861
93	3	5	2	2	43	27962	22540	16462	16603
92	7	7	4	4	42	29279	23639	17238	17384
91	16	14	8	8	41	30580	24665	17951	18102
90	23	21	13	13	40	31817	25738	18709	18867
89	30	29	20	20	39	33103	26916	19528	19695
88	37	38	27	27	38	34413	27981	20267	20441
87	63	52	39	39	37	35680	29036	21032	21213
86	92	73	57	57	36	36982	30171	21841	22032
85	123	100	79	79	35	38284	31285	22663	22855
84	173	150	121	121	34	39561	32315	23397	23597
83	229	198	166	167	33	40907	33462	24215	24420
82	296	233	210	211	32	42183	34626	25062	25271
81	375	335	272	273	31	43487	35761	25838	26069
80	466	411	330	332	30	44787	36825	26650	26864
79	595	492	389	391	29	46030	37869	27407	27625
78	732	617	487	489	28	47286	38925	28184	28406
77	889	750	593	595	27	48466	39953	28927	29164
76	1059	896	713	715	26	49680	40961	29652	29893
75	1297	1075	860	863	25	50919	41926	30333	30582
74	1564	1309	1036	1039	24	52093	42889	31033	31288
73	1845	1539	1212	1217	23	53317	43803	31685	31949
72	2161	1805	1424	1430	22	54504	44657	32292	32562
71	2523	2096	1656	1664	21	55598	45500	32923	33199
70	2922	2403	1893	1903	20	56725	46334	33533	33816
69	3363	2745	2151	2164	19	57814	47105	34107	34394
68	3856	3120	2437	2450	18	58811	47865	34650	34945
67	4384	3520	2720	2735	17	59801	48594	35187	35488
66	4953	3998	3088	3103	16	60797	49244	35668	35975
65	5562	4497	3445	3464	15	61770	49816	36081	36398
64	6248	5002	3819	3843	14	62672	50375	36480	36805
63	6956	5540	4223	4249	13	63517	50895	36870	37202
62	7717	6124	4641	4673	12	64340	51396	37238	37577
61	8507	6744	5087	5123	11	65137	51872	37585	37929
60	9351	7377	5554	5594	10	65860	52305	37907	38262
59	10197	8048	6054	6097	9	66597	52698	38190	38554
58	11116	8687	6537	6582	8	67321	53041	38444	38817
57	12048	9452	7122	7173	7	67958	53365	38674	39053
56	13017	10187	7635	7690	6	68556	53638	38863	39257
55	14003	10995	8236	8295	5	69184	53951	39094	39500
54	15025	11823	8847	8919	4	69785	54210	39277	39690
53	16079	12680	9450	9528	3	70236	54408	39416	39835
52	17172	13577	10092	10178	2	70765	54630	39574	40007
51	18300	14465	10720	10812	1	71380	54840	39715	40155
					0	72523	55273	40015	40473

八十四學年度大學聯考英文分數人數統計表

分數	第一類組	第二類組	第三類組	第四類組	分數	第一類組	第二類組	第三類組	第四類組
100	0	0	0	0	50	22852	17374	15283	15322
99	0	0	0	0	49	23881	18225	16033	16072
98	0	0	0	0	48	24968	19150	16857	16897
97	0	0	0	0	47	26038	20089	17709	17750
96	0	0	0	0	46	27089	21003	18511	18555
95	0	0	0	0	45	28137	21888	19283	19327
94	0	0	0	0	44	29179	22829	20102	20148
93	2	3	1	1	43	30219	23716	20872	20921
92	3	9	5	5	42	31339	24659	21697	21748
91	4	14	9	9	41	32457	25580	22511	22564
90	15	22	16	16	40	33497	26560	23382	23436
89	25	29	23	23	39	34525	27495	24215	24272
88	32	45	35	35	38	35609	28393	25018	25078
87	52	58	47	47	37	36605	29398	25893	25953
86	91	80	66	66	36	37648	30381	26770	26835
85	114	110	94	94	35	38701	31369	27637	27705
84	196	152	131	131	34	39746	32360	28521	28590
83	269	211	182	183	33	40867	33319	29382	29452
82	383	291	252	253	32	41924	34246	30199	30269
81	524	387	331	332	31	42969	35161	31011	31085
80	674	493	426	427	30	44098	36175	31929	32003
79	861	629	540	541	29	45200	37118	32770	32846
78	1107	794	682	683	28	46263	38066	33624	33705
77	1387	993	857	858	27	47282	38990	34442	34526
76	1709	1215	1053	1054	26	48316	39932	35281	35369
75	2065	1488	1298	1300	25	49297	40870	36114	36204
74	2470	1789	1564	1566	24	50283	41789	36939	37035
73	2954	2150	1882	1884	23	51273	42681	37734	37834
72	3432	2481	2184	2186	22	52281	43579	38544	38646
71	3966	2870	2525	2530	21	53247	44397	39279	39384
70	4549	3257	2874	2877	20	54208	45216	40013	40124
69	5213	3684	3231	3235	19	55198	46002	40711	40827
68	5905	4179	3665	3669	18	56096	46769	41399	41522
67	6608	4738	4156	4162	17	57004	47432	41996	42124
66	7360	5299	4645	4651	16	57843	48118	42603	42735
65	8187	5875	5156	5164	15	58655	48771	43193	43329
64	9032	6522	5723	5732	14	59478	49430	43781	43921
63	9887	7182	6308	6319	13	60296	50009	44297	44440
62	10769	7881	6930	6942	12	61117	50630	44835	44980
61	11713	8580	7552	7566	11	61930	51152	45291	45439
60	12672	9266	8150	8165	10	62705	51725	45795	45949
59	13636	10024	8802	8819	9	63532	52233	46243	46402
58	14623	10773	9454	9475	8	64381	52727	46662	46827
57	15618	11543	10134	10158	7	65129	53159	47030	47197
56	16642	12360	10859	10885	6	65947	53655	47449	47622
55	17668	13138	11544	11572	5	66724	54101	47828	48010
54	18645	13941	12243	12272	4	67603	54548	48190	48378
53	19698	14752	12951	12983	3	68345	54907	48497	48694
52	20782	15624	13715	13750	2	69239	55344	48850	49061
51	21868	16467	14478	14514	1	70161	55744	49166	49402
					0	72279	56702	49875	50144

八十四學年度大學暨獨立學院入學考試
英 文 試 題

第一部份：單一選擇題

I、對話（10％）：下面十個題目（1至10）是日常生活常見的英語對話。每題各有一個空格，並各附有四個備選答案。請依照對話內容選出一個最適當的答案，標示在「答案卡」上。每題答對得1分，答錯倒扣⅓分，不答不給分。

1. Passenger 1：Excuse me. Where can I get on the next train for Tai-chung？
   Passenger 2：Platform 1, right here.＿＿＿＿＿＿because I'm taking the same train.
   (A) I hope you understand it,　　(B) You'd better go early,
   (C) I have no idea,　　　　　　(D) There's no mistake about it,

2. Guest 1：Are you the manager of this hotel？ I've got some com-plaints about your service.
   Guest 2：＿＿＿＿＿＿I'm also looking for the manager. I've got some complaints, too.
   (A) It is very nice of you.
   (B) I'm afraid you must be mistaken.
   (C) I'm glad the manager is here.
   (D) I really appreciate your advice.

3. Teacher：What's your excuse for being late today？
   Student：I had a heartburn this morning and I went to see a doctor.
   Teacher：＿＿＿＿＿＿You have a different excuse each day.
   (A) I wish I were as imaginative as you are.
   (B) How come you always have the same excuse？
   (C) What did the doctor say？
   (D) Do you feel better now？

4. Paul：I've just passed my college entrance exam.
   David：＿＿＿＿＿＿＿＿＿＿
   Paul：I feel so relieved now.
   (A) Well done！　(B) What a pity！　(C) How awful！　(D) Cheer up！

5. Peter： I think I'm going to quit my present job.
   John ： Why? Don't you like it at all?
   Peter：_____ but I can't get along with my boss any more.
   (A) I used to,   (B) Not at all,
   (C) Hardly,   (D) I believe so,

6. Julia： You look worried, Sam. What's the matter?
   Sam ： My computer's broken down. No idea what's wrong with it.
   Julia： _____
   Sam ： Of course, eventually. But I have a paper due tomorrow.
   (A) Can I help you?   (B) Can I fix it for you?
   (C) Can't you get it fixed?   (D) What are you going to do?

7. Tom ： Jack was stopped by the police again for speeding and his
           driver's license was taken away.
   Frank： Good. _____
   Tom ： True. He is such a reckless driver.
   (A) I'm sorry to hear that.   (B) That'll teach him a lesson.
   (C) It's not fair.   (D) How unfortunate for him!

8. Mary ： I've found the right apartment. It's nice and clean.
   Susan： Is it expensive?
   Mary ： _____Only five hundred dollars a month.
   (A) Yes, it is cheap.   (B) Yes, I like it very much.
   (C) No. That's the beauty of it. (D) No. I agree with you entirely.

9. Mother ： I must send out these letters today, but I don't have time.
   Daughter： I'll mail them for you on my way to school.
   Mother ： _____
   Daughter： Don't worry. I won't let you down.
   (A) Thank you very much.   (B) It's a pity that I have to bother you.
   (C) It's very nice of you to help me.   (D) You won't forget, will you?

10. Karen： Mary enjoys playing the violin.
    John ： _____
    Karen： Since she was a little girl.
    (A) Oh, she must be very good.
    (B) Does she? How long has she been playing it?
    (C) Was she good when she was young?
    (D) I wish I could play the violin too.

Ⅱ、詞彙（10％）：下面十個題目（11至20），每題各有一個空格，並各附有四個備選單字。請選擇一個最適合的單字，標示在「答案卡」上。每題答對得1分，答錯倒扣⅓分，不答不給分。

11. My recent trip to Europe has left a＿＿＿＿＿＿impression on me.
   (A) final　　(B) lasting　　(C) forever　　(D) long

12. A＿＿＿＿＿＿of migrant birds flew to our island yesterday.
   (A) flock　　(B) host　　(C) crew　　(D) set

13. Jack fell down while playing tennis and＿＿＿＿＿＿his ankle very badly.
   (A) bent　　(B) crippled　　(C) turned　　(D) twisted

14. These two photographs are too small. Let's have them＿＿＿＿＿＿.
   (A) increased　　(B) formalized　　(C) enlarged　　(D) expanded

15. This museum is famous for its＿＿＿＿＿＿of modern paintings.
   (A) construction　　(B) reduction　　(C) affection　　(D) collection

16. The professor did his best to＿＿＿＿＿＿the students with new ideas.
   (A) witness　　(B) review　　(C) acquaint　　(D) display

17. Their determination to fight to the last man was really＿＿＿＿＿＿.
   (A) admirable　　(B) disposable　　(C) replaceable　　(D) portable

18. All of us must have the＿＿＿＿＿＿that there is no free lunch.
   (A) know-how　　(B) wonder　　(C) dispute　　(D) awareness

19. A large poster in beautiful colors＿＿＿＿＿＿the attention of many people.
   (A) called　　(B) caught　　(C) charted　　(D) caused

20. It rains＿＿＿＿＿＿this summer. The water we've got is not enough for this area.
   (A) frequently　　(B) occasionally　　(C) precisely　　(D) previously

Ⅲ、綜合測驗（20％）：下面兩篇短文共有二十個空格（21至40），每個空格附有四個備選答案。請仔細閱讀後選出一個最適當的答案，標示在「答案卡」上。每題答對得1分，答錯倒扣⅓分，不答不給分。

Effective listening means listening with a third ear. ___(21)___ this I mean trying to listen for the meanings ___(22)___ the words and not ___(23)___ to the words alone. The way words ___(24)___ — loud, soft, fast, or slow — is very important. ___(25)___ a mother says, " Come in now" in a soft, gentle voice, it may mean the kids have ___(26)___ minutes. But when she says, " Come in NOW", ___(27)___ no question about the meaning of the command. ___(28)___ effectively, we have to pay attention to facial expressions, body movement, ___(29)___ to the quality of the other person's voice. These cues are a ___(30)___ part of any message.

21. (A) For   (B) By   (C) With   (D) On
22. (A) behind   (B) beneath   (C) beside   (D) before
23. (A) simply   (B) nearly   (C) calmly   (D) surely
24. (A) speak   (B) spoke   (C) are spoken   (D) have spoken
25. (A) Even   (B) If   (C) Since   (D) Until
26. (A) a little   (B) a longer   (C) a few more   (D) no
27. (A) it has   (B) there comes   (C) it is   (D) there is
28. (A) To speak   (B) To do   (C) To listen   (D) To take
29. (A) as long as   (B) as soon as   (C) as far as   (D) as well as
30. (A) loyal   (B) vital   (C) total   (D) fatal

A hummingbird is a tiny bird with unusual flying abilities. It can fly ___(31)___ up in the air, fly forwards and backwards, and move its wings ___(32)___ fast that it can remain in one spot in the air. ___(33)___ a hummingbird's wingspread is ___(34)___ four inches long on the average, it can rush ___(35)___ the air as swiftly as sixty miles an hour. ___(36)___ hummingbirds can travel far as well as fast is shown ___(37)___ their yearly migrations ___(38)___ the United States and Central and South America.

The hummingbird uses its unique flying abilities ___(39)___ good advantage. When it discovers a flower with nectar, it flies towards the flower and stays in the air in front of the flower to drink from it. After ___(40)___ drinking, it backs away slowly and looks for nectar in another flower.

31. (A) right	(B) near	(C) straight	(D) far
32. (A) so	(B) very	(C) such	(D) too
33. (A) Despite	(B) Concerning	(C) However	(D) Although
34. (A) barely	(B) mainly	(C) likely	(D) chiefly
35. (A) through	(B) out	(C) down	(D) above
36. (A) What	(B) That	(C) Which	(D) Where
37. (A) on	(B) of	(C) at	(D) by
38. (A) from	(B) between	(C) under	(D) againat
39. (A) for	(B) in	(C) on	(D) to
40. (A) finished	(B) to finish	(C) finishing	(D) finish

Ⅳ、閱讀測驗（20％）：下面有三篇短文，共有十個問題（41至50），每題各附
　　有四個備選答案。請仔細閱讀，把最合文意的一個答案標示在「答案卡」上。
　　每題答對得2分，答錯倒扣⅔分，不答不給分。

For the Stone Age people, hunting was an important way to get
food. Stone Age hunters had only crude weapons made of stone and
wood. When they went hunting, their weapons were not powerful enough
to kill big game, so they had to rely more upon their wit than weapons.
Stone Age hunters often cooperated with each other in hunting big game.
Some hunters drove a herd of animals like horses or buffaloes over
steep cliffs, and others waited at the bottom of the cliffs to finish the
kill. Another popular method was to dig a deep pit. The pit was then
covered with branches and dirt. When an animal walked over the pit, it
fell in and was trapped. The hunters rolled heavy stones on the animal
and killed it.

Modern hunters are equipped with powerful weapons, but for most
of them, hunting is more for pleasure than for food. Because many big
animals like lions, tigers and elephants are decreasing in number rapidly,
they can no longer be hunted at will. Nowadays in many countries, hunting
is prohibited in national parks, which preserve wild animals as well as
their natural environments. And even in some countries where hunting
is permitted, a hunter has to get a license for hunting particular game
in a particular season; otherwise he will be punished as a poacher.

41. The Stone Age people showed their wit in hunting big game by
　　(A) throwing stone weapons.　(B) inventing powerful weapons.
　　(C) using bare hands.　(D) working together as a team.

42. According to this passage, for most modern hunters, hunting is
    (A) a form of recreation.　　　　　(B) supported by the government.
    (C) a way to keep wild animals down.　(D) for economic gains.

43. Regarding hunting, there are more restrictions on a modern hunter
    because of
    (A) the limitations of weapons.　　(B) the shortage of manpower.
    (C) the control of governments.　　(D) the lack of cooperation.

    In the eyes of a Western visitor, a temple in Taiwan is very different from a church in the West. The following is a report of this Westerner.

    For a Western church, you can enter the great door in the center and walk straight down the aisle to the altar, but a Taiwanese temple must be entered through the side gates. This leads you right to a large outer courtyard. From here you can see clearly the roof-line of the main wall and doors. The pillars and the roof-line are frequently decorated with dragons. Walking across the outer courtyard, you will reach the main doors leading you to the inner courtyard, and again the doors are not in the center facing the main altar inside the main building, but to the left and right. Painted on the big doors are the fierce guardian spirits in bright and realistic detail. To cross over the doorsill to get into the inner courtyard, you have to lift your foot or you may trip and fall down. Once inside the inner courtyard, you can walk into the main building of the temple and see the images of gods on the altar enclosed within iron bars.

    These architectural details are "security measures" just like those a bank has to keep thieves from breaking in. Some of these measures are aimed at evil spirits, because ghosts cannot lift their feet over barriers, nor can they make 90-degree turns. But the iron bars are apparently there for keeping burglars out.

44. According to this Western visitor, a Taiwanese temple differs from a Western church in that
    (A) the former is older than the latter.
    (B) the former is larger.
    (C) the former has no central passage.
    (D) the former is better decorated.

45. Why is a Taiwanese temple compared to a bank by this Western visitor?
   (A) It is as rich as a bank.
   (B) It is well-protected like a bank.
   (C) It is run as efficiently as a bank.
   (D) It is well-designed as a bank.

46. Based on this article, a Taiwanese temple is partly designed
   (A) to prevent bad spirits and people from entering.
   (B) to welcome worshippers and businessmen.
   (C) to honor government officials and military officers.
   (D) to be a tourist attraction.

   Doctors can be so much concerned with curing diseases that they may fail to notice that sometimes what troubles a patient is not really a disease at all. Dr. Meyer Schwartz described such a case in one of his medical reports.

   Dr. Schwartz was on duty at a hospital one morning a few days after Christmas when a man came in complaining only of "blueness to his face of one hour's duration." He reported no other signs of illness, no itching, dizziness or shortness of breath, and no history of heart disease or bleeding disorders. It was only 10:15 a.m. and all the patient had done that day was shower, shave, and dress. So far, his hands and body were still their normal color, but on both sides of his face, it was distinctly blue up to the cheekbones. Knowing that blue skin might indicate a lack of oxygen in the blood or an undesirable drug reaction, Dr. Schwartz checked the patient thoroughly. Finding nothing else out of the ordinary, he sent the blue man home. At 5:30 p.m. the man called Dr. Schwartz to report that he had "washed his face and the blue came off." He had received blue towels as Christmas gifts and had used one of them that morning for the first time.

47. The blueness to the patient's face was caused by
   (A) shortage of oxygen in the blood.
   (B) a blue washing cloth.
   (C) a serious drug reaction.
   (D) a disease the doctor could not detect.

48. The doctor sent the blue-faced man home after
    (A) washing the patient's face.
    (B) curing the blueness with medicine.
    (C) consulting with other doctors.
    (D) a careful examination of the patient.

49. The main point of this passage is that
    (A) some diseases are often difficult for doctors to recognize.
    (B) doctors are often too careless in their medical treatments.
    (C) doctors may sometimes be misled by a patient's complaints.
    (D) some patients like to play practical jokes on doctors.

50. The cause of the blueness was known only after
    (A) a series of examinations was carried out on the patient.
    (B) the blueness suddenly went away with medication.
    (C) another doctor checked the patient more carefully.
    (D) the patient realized what he had done with his Christmas gifts.

第二部份：非選擇題

I、中譯英（20％）：下面一段短文共含五個中文句子，請譯成正確、通順、達意且前後連貫的英文。每句四分。答案請寫在「非選擇題試卷」上，同時務必標示題號。

1. 台灣的生活最近十年變了很多。

2. 年輕的一代有許多新的生活方式，

3. 和他們父母親那一輩相當不同。

4. 舉個例，很多年輕人喜歡吃美式速食，喝加糖飲料，

5. 而老一輩的大多寧可吃中國菜，喝中國茶。

II、英文作文（20％）：寫一篇大概一百二十個單字左右的英文作文，分成兩段，題目是 "Making Decisions"。第一段的第一句必須是主題句 "Growing up means making my own decisions."第二段的第一句必須是主題句 "The hardest decision that I ever made was_____"，同時自行在空格中填入自己所作的決定。文章請寫在「非選擇題試卷」上。
評分標準：內容5分，組織5分，文法4分，用字遣詞4分，拼字、大小寫及標點符號2分。

84年大學聯考英文試題詳解

第一部分：單一選擇題

I、對話：

1.（**D**）乘客一：對不起，下一班往台中的火車，要在哪裡搭車？

乘客二：在第一月台這裡。＿＿＿＿＿＿因為我也搭同一班車。

　　(A) 我希望你了解，　　　　(B) 你最好早點去，

　　(C) 我不知道，　　　　　　(D) 不會錯的，

platform〔'plæt,fɔrm〕*n.* 月台

　　There is no mistake about it. 這是確實的（不會錯的）。

　　= ***There is no doubt about it.***

　　= ***I am sure.***

　　= ***I am positive.***

2.（**B**）客人一：你是這家飯店的經理嗎？我對於你們的服務有些不滿。

客人二：＿＿＿＿＿＿ 我也在找經理，我也有些不滿的地方。

　　(A) 你真好。　　　　　　　(B) 恐怕你弄錯了。

　　(C) 我很高興經理在這裡。　(D) 我真的很感激你的勸告。

complaint〔kəm'plent〕*n.* 抱怨；不滿

mistaken〔mə'stekən〕*adj.* 錯誤的

3.（**A**）老師：你今天遲到的理由是什麼？

學生：我今天早上胃痛，去看醫生。

老師：＿＿＿＿＿＿＿＿你每天都有不同的理由。

　　(A) 但願我的想像力和你一樣豐富。

　　(B) 為什麼你的理由老是同一個？

　　(C) 醫生怎麼說？

　　(D) 你現在覺得好一點了嗎？

heartburn 〔'hart,bɝn〕*n.* 胃痛（特別指胃酸太多或消化不良所引起）

stomach-ache 胃痛（一般用語）

heart-ache 傷心

imaginative〔ɪ'mædʒə,netɪv〕*adj.* 富想像力的

How come …？ 為什麼…？

4.（**A**）保羅：我剛剛通過大學入學考試。
　　　　大衛：＿＿＿＿＿＿
　　　　保羅：我現在終於鬆了一口氣。
　　　　(A) 做得好！　(B) 真可惜！　(C) 真可怕！　(D) 振作起來！

relieve〔rɪ'liv〕*v.* 鬆一口氣；使放心

　　Well done. 做得好！
　　= ***Good job.***
　　= ***Good show.***
　　= ***Good work.***
　　= ***You did very well.***

　　What a pity ! 多可惜！　　　　　　***Cheer up.*** 振作起來吧！
　　= ***What a shame*** !　　　　　　　　= ***Lighten up.***
　　= ***That's too bad.***　　　　　　　　= ***Pull yourself together.***

5.（**A**）彼得：我想我要辭掉現在的工作。
　　　　約翰：為什麼？你一點也不喜歡這個工作嗎？
　　　　彼得：＿＿＿＿＿＿但是我和我的上司再也相處不來。
　　　　(A) 我以前很喜歡，　　　　(B) 我一點也不喜歡，
　　　　(C) 我幾乎不喜歡，　　　　(D) 我想是的，

used to* + *V. 以前～

6.（**C**）茉莉：你看起來很煩惱，山姆，怎麼回事？
　　　　山姆：我的電腦壞了，我不知道毛病出在哪裡。
　　　　茉莉：＿＿＿＿＿＿
　　　　山姆：最後當然要拿去修理，但是我明天有一份報告要交。
　　　　(A) 我能幫你的忙嗎？　　　　(B) 我可以幫你修理嗎？
　　　　(C) 你不能拿去修理嗎？　　　(D) 你打算怎麼辦？

break down 故障
eventually〔ɪ'vɛntʃʊəlɪ〕*adv.* 最後；終於
due〔dju〕*adv.* 預定的；到期的

7.（**B**）湯　姆：傑克又因為超速被警察攔下來，駕照也被沒收了。
　　　　法蘭克：很好。＿＿＿＿＿＿
　　　　湯　姆：沒錯，他開車很魯莽。
　　　　(A) 聽到這件事我很難過。　　(B) 那樣可以給他一個教訓。
　　　　(C) 這不公平。　　　　　　　(D) 他真不幸！

reckless〔'rɛklɪs〕*adj.* 魯莽的

8. (**C**) 瑪麗：我找到合適的公寓了，又好又乾淨。
　　　蘇珊：貴不貴？
　　　瑪麗：＿＿＿＿＿＿ 一個月才五百元。
　　　(A) 是的，很便宜。　　(B) 是的，我很喜歡。
　　　(C) 不貴，這就是它可愛的地方。　　(D) 不，我完全同意你的看法。

9. (**D**) 母親：今天我必須把這些信寄出去，可是我沒有時間。
　　　女兒：我上學途中幫妳寄。
　　　母親：＿＿＿＿＿＿＿
　　　女兒：別擔心，我不會讓你失望的。
　　　(A) 非常謝謝你。　　(B) 很遺憾我必須麻煩你。
　　　(C) 你真好，願意幫我的忙。　　(D) 你不會忘記吧！

10. (**B**) 凱倫：瑪麗喜歡拉小提琴。
　　　約翰：＿＿＿＿＿＿＿
　　　凱倫：從她小時候開始。
　　　(A) 噢，她一定很好。　　(B) 是嗎？她拉小提琴有多久了？
　　　(C) 她年輕時很好嗎？　　(D) 真希望我也會拉小提琴。

Ⅱ、詞彙：

11. (**B**) My recent trip *to Europe* has left a lasting impression on me.
　　　最近一趟的歐洲之旅讓我留下了永恆的印象。
　　　(A) final〔ˋfaɪnl〕 *adj.* 最後的
　　　(B) ***lasting***〔ˋlæstɪŋ〕 *adj.* 永恆的；持久的
　　　(C) forever〔fəˋɛvə〕 *adv.* 永遠地
　　　(D) long〔lɔŋ〕 *adj.* 長的

12. (**A**) A flock *of migrant birds* flew *to our island yesterday.*
　　　有一群候鳥昨天飛到本島來。
　　　(A) ***flock***〔flɑk〕 *n.* (鳥)羣　　(B) host〔host〕 *n.* 大羣(人)
　　　(C) crew〔kru〕 *n.* 全體工作人員　　(D) set〔sɛt〕 *n.* 組

13. (**D**) Jack fell down ***while*** *playing tennis* ***and*** twisted his ankle *very badly.*
　　　傑克在打網球時跌倒，嚴重地扭傷腳踝。
　　　(A) bend〔bɛnd〕 *v.* 使彎曲　　(B) cripple〔ˋkrɪpl〕 *v.* 使殘廢
　　　(C) turn〔tɝn〕 *v.* 旋轉　　(D) ***twist***〔twɪst〕 *v.* 扭傷

14.(**C**) These two photographs are *too* small. Let's have them enlarged.
　　這兩張相片太小了，我們來把它們放大。
　　　(A) increase〔ɪn'kris〕*v.* 增加　(B) formalize〔'fɔrml,aɪz〕*v.* 正式化
　　　(C) *enlarge*〔ɪn'lɑrdʒ〕*v.* 放大　(D) expand〔ɪk'spænd〕*v.* 擴張

15.(**D**) This museum is famous for its collection *of modern paintings.*
　　這間博物館以現代繪畫的收藏而聞名。
　　　(A) construction〔kən'strʌkʃən〕*n.* 構造
　　　(B) reduction〔rɪ'dʌkʃən〕*n.* 減少
　　　(C) affection〔ə'fɛkʃən〕*n.* 感情
　　　(D) *collection*〔kə'lɛkʃən〕*n.* 收集

16.(**C**) The professor did his best to acquaint the students with new ideas.
　　這名教授盡力讓學生熟悉新知識。
　　　(A) witness〔'wɪtnɪs〕*v.* 目擊　(B) review〔rɪ'vju〕*v.* 複習
　　　(C) *acquaint*〔ə'kwent〕*v.* 使熟悉　(D) display〔dɪ'sple〕*v.* 展示

17.(**A**) Their determination to fight *to the last man* was *really* admirable.
　　他們奮戰到底的決心實在令人欽佩。
　　　(A) *admirable*〔'ædmərəbl〕*adj.* 令人欽佩的
　　　(B) disposable〔dɪ'spozəbl〕*adj.* 用完即丟的
　　　(C) replaceable〔rɪ'plesəbl〕*adj.* 可替代的
　　　(D) portable〔'portəbl, 'pɔr-〕*adj.* 可攜帶的；手提的

18.(**D**) All of us must have the awareness *that there is no free lunch.*
　　我們都必須知道天下沒有白吃的午餐。
　　　(A) know-how〔'no,haʊ〕*n.* 實用知識
　　　(B) wonder〔'wʌndɚ〕*n.* 奇蹟
　　　(C) dispute〔dɪ'spjut〕*n.* 爭論
　　　(D) *awareness*〔ə'wɛrnɪs〕*n.* 察覺；知道

19.（**B**）A large poster *in beautiful colors* caught the attention *of many people.*
一張大型的美麗彩色海報吸引了許多人的注意。
  (A) call〔kɔl〕*v.* 呼喚   (B) **catch**〔kætʃ〕*v.* 吸引（注意）
  (C) chart〔tʃɑrt〕*v.* 製圖 (D) cause〔kɔz〕*v.* 導致

20.（**B**）It rains *occasionally* this summer. The water *we've got* is not
enough for this area.
今年夏天偶爾下個雨，我們的集水量並不夠此地區用。
  (A) frequently〔'frikwəntlɪ〕*adv.* 經常
  (B) **occasionally**〔ə'keʒənlɪ〕*adv.* 偶爾
  (C) precisely〔prɪ'saɪslɪ〕*adv.* 準確地
  (D) previously〔'prɪvɪəslɪ〕*adv.* 以前

Ⅲ、綜合測驗：

  Effective listening means listening *with a third ear.* *By this* I mean
                 21
trying to listen for the meanings *behind the words* *and* not *simply* to
          22   23
the words *alone.*
  有效的傾聽，意味著必須用第三個耳朵去聽。我這麼說的意思，就是要試著
聽出言語背後的含意，而不是只注意字面上的意思。
  effective〔ə'fɛktɪv〕*adj.* 有效的 alone〔ə'lon〕*adv.* 僅僅

21.（**B**）依句意，表「藉著」這種說法，介系詞須用 by，故選(B)。而(A)為了，
  (C)隨著，(D)在…之上，皆不合句意。
  What do you **mean by** this? 這是什麼意思？
    By this I mean …
    = This means …

22.（**A**）依句意，要聽出言語「背後」所隱含的意思，故選(A) behind *prep.* 在…
  之後。而(B) beneath〔bɪ'niθ〕*prep.* 在…之下，(C) beside〔bɪ'saɪd〕
  prep. 在…的旁邊，(D)在…之前，皆不合句意。
    behind the words 言外之意
    = ***between the lines***

23.（ **A** ）依句意，選(A) simply *adv*. 只是 。而(B)幾乎 ，(C) calmly〔'kɑmlɪ〕*adv*.
　　　冷靜地 ，(D)確定地 ，皆不合句意 。

The way *words* <u>*are spoken*</u>—*loud*, *soft*, *fast*, *or slow*— is *very*
　　　　　　　　　24
important. ┌<u>*If* a mother says</u>, "*Come in now*" *in a soft, gentle voice*,┐
　　　　　　　25
it may mean *the kids have* <u>*a few more*</u> *minutes*. *But* *when she says*,
　　　　　　　　　　　　　　　　　26
"Come in NOW", <u>there is</u> no question about the meaning *of the command*.
　　　　　　　　27

說話的方式──大聲、溫和、急促或緩慢──是非常重要的 。如果有位母親用很柔
和的聲音說：「 現在進來 。」，可能就表示孩子們還有幾分鐘的時間 。但是如果她
說：「 **現在**進來 。」，那麼就毫無疑問地 ，是一種命令 。

　　　　gentle〔'dʒɛntl̩〕*adj*. 溫和的　　command〔kə'mænd〕*n*. 命令

24.（ **C** ）依句意，話是被說的 ，故用被動語態：「 be動詞＋過去分詞 」，選(C)
　　　are spoken 。

25.（ **B** ）依句意，選(B) If「 如果 」。而(A)甚至 ，(C)既然 ，(D)直到 ，皆不合句意 。

26.（ **C** ）依句意，如果母親說：「 現在進來 。」時的語氣十分溫和 ，那就表示孩子
　　　「 還有幾 」分鐘的時間 ，故選(C) a few more minutes 。而(A) a little 修
　　　飾不可數名詞 ，在此不合 ，(B)比較長的 ，(D)沒有 ，皆不合句意 。

27.（ **D** ）表「 有；存在 」，須用「 there＋be動詞 」表示 ，故選(D) there is no
　　　question 無疑地（ ＝ *there is no doubt* ）。

To listen effectively, we have to pay attention to facial expressions,
　　　28
body movement, <u>*as well as*</u> to the quality *of the other person's voice*.
　　　　　　　　　29
These cues are a <u>vital</u> part *of any message*.
　　　　　　　30

爲了要有效地傾聽 ，我們必須注意對方臉部表情、身體的動作 ，以及聲音的特質 。
這些暗示在所有的訊息中 ，都是非常重要的一部份 。

　　　　facial〔'feʃəl〕*adj*. 臉部的　　quality〔'kwɑlətɪ〕*n*. 特質
　　　　cue〔kju〕*n*. 暗示；線索

28.(**C**)　依句意，選(C) To listen effectively「爲了要有效地傾聽」。而(A)說，(B)做，(C)拿，皆不合句意。

29.(**D**)　*as well as* 以及。而(A) as long as「只要」，(B) as soon as「一…就～」，(D) as far as「遠至～」，皆不合句意。

30.(**B**)　依句意，選(B) vital〔'vaɪtḷ〕*adj.* 極重要的。而(A) royal〔'rɔɪəl〕*adj.* 皇家的，(C) total〔'totḷ〕*adj.* 全部的，(D) fatal〔'fetḷ〕*adj.* 致命的，均不合句意。

A hummingbird is a tiny bird *with unusual flying abilities*. It can fly *straight* up in the air, *fly forwards and backwards*, *and* move its wings *so* fast *that it can remain in one spot in the air*. *Although a*
₃₂   ₃₃
hummingbird's wingspread is barely four inches long on the average,
₃₄
it can rush <u>through</u> the air *as swiftly as sixty miles an hour*. *That*
₃₅   ₃₆
hummingbirds can travel far as well as fast is shown by their yearly
₃₇
migrations *between* the United States and Central and South America.
₃₈

　　蜂鳥是一種體型嬌小的鳥，有著不凡的飛行能力。牠可以在空中垂直向上、向前、向後飛，而且牠翅膀拍動非常快，所以能夠停留在空中的某一點。雖然蜂鳥的翼幅平均僅有四吋長，牠劃過空中的速度卻高達每小時六十哩。蜂鳥飛行又遠又快的這項事實，可從牠們每年遷移於美國與中南美洲之間，展露無遺。

hummingbird〔'hʌmɪŋˌbɝd〕*n.* 蜂鳥　　spot〔spɑt〕*n.* 點
wingspread〔'wɪŋˌsprɛd〕*n.* 翼幅（兩翼尖端之間的長度）
swiftly〔'swɪftlɪ〕*adv.* 快速地　　migration〔maɪ'greʃən〕*n.* 遷移

31.(**C**)　由空格後提到蜂鳥可以向前、後飛可知，空格中亦指飛行方向，故選(C)
　　　　straight　垂直地。

32.（ **A** ）　*so～that* … 如此～以致於…

33.（ **D** ）　依句意，「雖然」蜂鳥翼幅短，但飛行速度卻很快，選(D) Although。
而(A) despite「儘管」（＝ in spite of）為一介系詞，不可接子句。(B)
concerning 關於，(C)然而，則不合句意。

34.（ **A** ）　(A) *barely*〔ˊbɛrlɪ〕*adv.* 僅僅　　　(B) mainly〔ˊmenlɪ〕*adv.* 主要地
(C) likely〔ˊlaɪklɪ〕*adj.* 可能的　(D) chiefly〔ˊtʃiflɪ〕*adv.* 主要地

35.（ **A** ）　依句意，選(A) rush through the air 衝過、劃過空中。而(B)向外，(C)向
下，(D)在～之上，均不合句意。

36.（ **B** ）　連接詞 that 引導名詞子句 hummingbirds can … fast，做本句的主詞，
選(B)。

37.（ **D** ）　原意為Their yearly migration …shows that hummingbirds can …，
文中將本句改被動，故改為That hummingbirds can … is shown by
their yearly migration…，故選(D)。

38.（ **B** ）　依句意，表「二者之間」，用 between，故選(B)。

The hummingbird uses its unique flying abilities *to good advantage.*
　　　　　　　　　　　　　　　　　　　　　　　　　　　　39
[*When it discovers a flower with nectar,*] it flies towards the flower
and stays *in the air in front of the flower to drink from it.* *After*
finishing drinking, it backs away *slowly and* looks for nectar *in another*
　　　40
flower.

　　蜂鳥充分運用牠獨特的飛行能力。當牠發現一朵有花蜜的花時，牠會飛向那朵
花，然後停留在空中、那朵花的前面，吸取花蜜。吸完之後，牠就慢慢後退離開，
再去尋找其他花的花蜜。

　　　　nectar〔ˊnɛktɚ〕*n.* 花蜜　　*back away* 後退

39.（ **D** ）　*to advantage* 有效地

40.（ **C** ）　介詞After 後在此只能接動名詞 finishing，不可接不定詞或原形動詞。

IV、閱讀測驗：

For the Stone Age people, hunting was an important way *to get food.* Stone Age hunters had only crude weapons *made of stone and wood.* *When they went hunting,* their weapons were not powerful *enough to kill big game, so* they had to rely *more upon their wit than weapons.*

對石器時代的人類而言，狩獵是獲取食物的重要方法。石器時代的獵人只有簡陋的石製或木製的武器可使用。當他們去打獵時，武器的威力並不足以殺死大型的獵物，因此，他們必須仰賴智慧甚於武器。

crude〔krud〕*adj.* 粗糙的;簡陋的　　game〔gem〕*n.* 獵物

Stone Age hunters *often* cooperated with each other *in hunting big game.* Some hunters drove a herd of animals *like horses or buffaloes* over steep cliffs, *and* others waited *at the bottom of the cliffs to finish the kill.* Another popular method was to dig a deep pit. The pit was *then* covered *with branches and dirt. When an animal walked over the pit,* it fell in *and* was trapped. The hunters rolled heavy stones *on the animal and* killed it.

石器時代的獵人常相互合作以獵取大型的獵物。有些獵人將馬或水牛之類的動物群驅趕至陡峭的懸崖，而一些獵人則會在懸崖底下等待完成這次捕殺的行動。另一種普遍的方法是挖掘深洞，然後用泥土與樹枝覆蓋其上，當動物走過時，便會掉落到陷阱裏，然後獵人再滾動巨石，將動物砸死。

cooperate〔ko'ɑpə,ret〕*v.* 合作　　drive〔draɪv〕*v.* 驅趕
herd〔hɝd〕*n.* 群　　buffalo〔'bʌfl,o〕*n.* 水牛
steep〔stip〕*adj.* 陡峭的　　cliff〔klɪf〕*n.* 懸崖
branch〔bræntʃ〕*n.* 樹枝　　dirt〔dɝt〕*n.* 泥土
trap〔træp〕*v.* 以陷阱捕捉　　roll〔rol〕*v.* 滾動

Modern hunters are equipped *with powerful weapons*, **but** *for most of them*, hunting is more for pleasure **than** *for food*. **Because** *many big animals like lions, tigers and elephants* are decreasing *in number rapidly*, they can *no longer* be hunted *at will*.

現代的獵人都配備有強而有力的武器，但是對大部份的獵人而言，打獵多是為了娛樂而非為了獲得食物。由於許多大型動物，像是獅子、老虎、大象等，正在遞減中，已不能再任人隨意地捕殺了。

　　　　　be equipped with～　配備有～　　　*at will*　隨意地

Nowadays in many countries, hunting is prohibited *in national parks*, **which** preserve wild animals **as well as** *their natural environments*. **And** *even in some countries* **where** *hunting is permitted*, a hunter has to get a license *for hunting particular game in a particular season*; **otherwise** he will be punished as a poacher.

目前許多國家規定，國家公園內禁止打獵，這些地區保護野生動物，也保護他們生長的自然環境。即使在一些允許打獵的國家裏，獵人必須取得執照，才能在特定的季節裏獵取特定的動物，否則，他們將因盜獵者的罪名而受到處罰。

　　　　　prohibit〔proˈhɪbɪt〕v. 禁止
　　　　　preserve〔prɪˈzɝv〕v. 保育；保護　　permit〔pɚˈmɪt〕v. 允許
　　　　　poacher〔ˈpotʃɚ〕n. 盜獵者；入侵者

41.(**D**)　石器時代人類在獵取大型獵物時，所展現出來的智慧是
　　　　　(A) 投擲石製的武器。　　　　　(B) 發明有力的武器。
　　　　　(C) 赤手空拳。　　　　　　　(D) 團隊合作。
　　　　　bare〔bɛr〕adj. 赤裸的　*bare hands* 徒手　team〔tim〕n. 團隊

42.(**A**)　根據本文，對大部份的現代獵人而言，打獵是
　　　　　(A) 一種娛樂。　　　　　　　(B) 受政府所支持。
　　　　　(C) 一種減少野生動物的方法。　(D) 為了經濟利益。
　　　　　gain〔gen〕n. 利益

43. (**C**) 關於打獵，現代的獵人所受到的限制較多，因為

　　　(A) 武器的限制。　　　(B) 人力短缺。
　　　(C) 政府的控制。　　　(D) 缺乏合作。

shortage〔ˈʃɔrtɪdʒ〕*n.* 短缺　　manpower〔ˈmænˌpauɚ〕*n.* 人力

In the eyes of a Western visitor, a temple *in Taiwan* is *very* different from a church *in the West*. The following is a report *of this Westerner*.

　　在一位西方遊客的眼中，台灣的寺廟和西方的教堂非常不同。以下就是這位西方人的報導。

temple〔ˈtɛmpl̩〕*n.* 廟

For a Western church, you can enter the great door *in the center* **and** walk *straight down the aisle to the altar*, **but** a Taiwanese temple must be entered *through the side gates*. This leads you *right to a large outer courtyard*. *From here* you can see *clearly* the roof-line *of the main wall and doors*. The pillars and the roof-line are *frequently* decorated *with dragons*.

　　如果是西方的教堂，你可以從正中央的大門進入，然後從走道直接走到祭壇；但台灣的寺廟則必須由邊門進入。一進去就是一個很大的外圍的庭院，從這兒你可以清楚地看到主牆和正門屋頂線。柱子和屋頂線通常都是以龍來裝飾。

aisle〔aɪl〕*n.* 走道　　altar〔ˈɔltɚ〕*n.* 祭壇
courtyard〔ˈkortˌjɑrd, ˈkɔrt-〕*n.* 庭院；天井
roof-line〔ˈrufˌlaɪn, ˈrʊf-〕*n.* 屋頂線　　pillar〔ˈpɪlɚ〕*n.* 柱子

Walking across the outer courtyard, you will reach the main doors *leading you to the inner courtyard*, **and** *again* the doors are not in the center *facing the main altar inside the main building*, **but** *to the left and right*. Painted *on the big doors* are the fierce guardian spirits *in bright and realistic detail*.

穿過外圍庭院，就來到正門，通往裏面中庭，而門仍然不是在中央，能夠面對主廳的主要祭壇，而是通往左右兩側。這些大門上畫的是兇猛的守護神靈，畫得非常仔細，生動而寫實。

  inner〔'ɪnə〕n. 裏面的 fierce〔fɪrs〕adj. 兇猛的
  guardian〔'gɑrdɪən〕adj. 守護的 spirit〔'spɪrɪt〕n. 靈魂
  in detail 仔細地 realistic〔,riə'lɪstɪk, ,rɪə-〕adj. 寫實的

To cross over the doorsill to get into the inner courtyard, you have to lift your foot **or** you may trip and fall down. ***Once inside the inner courtyard***, you can walk into the main building *of the temple and* see the images of gods *on the altar enclosed within iron bars.*
要跨過門檻、進入中庭時，你必須把腳抬起來，否則你可能會被絆倒。一旦進入中庭，你就可以走到寺廟的主廳，並看到祭壇上、圍在鐵欄杆之內的神像。

  doorsill〔'dor,sɪl〕n. 門檻 trip〔trɪp〕v. 絆倒
  enclose〔ɪn'kloz〕v. 圍繞 ***iron bar*** 鐵條；鐵欄杆

  These architectural details are " security measures " *just like those a bank has to keep thieves from breaking in.* Some *of these measures* are aimed at evil spirits, ***because ghosts cannot lift their feet over barriers***, **nor** *can they make 90-degree turns.* **But** the iron bars are *apparently* there for keeping burglars out.
  這些建築上的細節都是「安全措施」，正如銀行中防賊闖入的措施。其中一些是針對惡鬼而設計的，因為鬼無法抬腳跨過障礙，也不能做九十度轉彎。不過那些鐵欄杆，顯然就是為了不讓竊賊闖入而做的。

  architectural〔,ɑrkə'tɛktʃərəl〕adj. 建築的
  detail〔'ditel〕n. 細節 measures〔'mɛʒəz〕n. pl. 措施
  break in 闖入 aim〔em〕v. 瞄準；以⋯為目標
  ghost〔gost〕n. 鬼 barrier〔'bærɪə〕n. 障礙
  apparently〔ə'pærəntlɪ〕adv. 明顯地
  burglar〔'bɝglə〕n. 竊賊

44.（ **C** ）　根據這位西方遊客的說法，台灣的寺廟和西方的教堂不同點在於
　　　　(A) 前者比後者老舊。　　　　　　(B) 前者比較大。
　　　　(C) 前者沒有中央的通道。　　　　(D) 前者裝飾得比較漂亮。

45.（ **B** ）　這位西方遊客爲何將台灣的寺廟比喻成銀行？
　　　　(A) 它和銀行一樣富有。　　　　(B) 它和銀行一樣保護周全。
　　　　(C) 它的經營和銀行一樣有效率。　(D) 它和銀行一樣設計完善。
　　　　be compared to ～ 比喻爲～　　run〔rʌn〕*v.* 經營

46.（ **A** ）　根據本文，台灣的寺廟有部分設計是爲了
　　　　(A) 防止惡鬼和壞人進入。　　　(B) 歡迎拜神者和商人。
　　　　(C) 尊崇政府官員和軍官。　　　(D) 成爲吸引遊客之地。
　　　　worshipper〔'wɜʃəpɚ〕*n.* 禮拜者；崇拜者

Doctors can be *so much* concerned with curing diseases *that* they may
fail to notice **that** sometimes **what** troubles a patient is not really a disease
at all. Dr. Meyer Schwartz described such a case *in one of his medical*
reports.

　　醫生可能會因爲太關心如何治療疾病，以致於沒有注意到，有時候困擾病人的，事實上根本不是一種疾病。梅爾・施瓦茨醫師在他的一份醫學報告中，描述這樣一個病例。

　　　　be concerned with ～ 關心～
　　　　fail to ＋V. 無法～　　case〔kes〕*n.* 病例

　　Dr. Schwartz was *on duty at a hospital one morning a few days after*
Christmas **when** a man came in complaining only of " *blueness to his face*
of one hour's duration." He reported no other signs *of illness*, no itching, dizziness or shortness *of breath*, **and** no history *of heart disease or*
bleeding disorders.

聖誕節過後幾天，有一天早上，當施瓦茨醫師在醫院值班時，有一個人來看病，說他「臉色發青，已持續一個小時」。他說他沒有其他症狀，不會癢、不覺得頭昏、不會喘不過氣，過去也沒有心臟病或不正常出血的紀錄。

on duty 值班中　　duration〔dju'reʃən〕 *n.* 持續期間
itch〔ɪtʃ〕*v.* 癢　　dizziness〔'dɪzɪnɪs〕*n.* 頭昏；暈眩
disorder〔dɪs'ɔrdə〕*n.* (小)病

It was only 10:15 a.m. **and** all *the patient had done that day* was shower, shave, and dress. *So far*, his hands and body were *still* their normal color, **but** *on both sides of his face*, it was *distinctly* blue *up to the cheekbones*. *Knowing **that** blue skin might indicate a lack of oxygen in the blood* **or** *an undesirable drug reaction*, Dr. Schwartz checked the patient *thoroughly*. *Finding nothing else out of the ordinary*, he sent the blue man home.

那時才早上十點十五分，那個病人那天所做的事，只有淋浴、刮鬍子和換衣服。那時他的手和身體仍然是正常的膚色，但是兩邊臉頰却很明顯是青色的。施瓦茨醫師知道，皮膚呈青色可能表示血液中缺氧，或是由於對藥物有不良反應所引起的，他為病人做徹底的檢查，但並沒有發現其他異常的情況，於是要那個臉色發青的病人回家。

so far 到目前為止　　distinctly〔dɪ'stɪŋktlɪ〕*adv.* 清楚地
cheekbone〔'tʃik,bon〕*n.* 頰骨　　indicate〔'ɪndɪ,ket〕*v.* 表示
oxygen〔'ɑksədʒən〕*n.* 氧
undesirable〔,ʌndɪ'zaɪrəbḷ〕*adj.* 不宜的；惹人厭的
thoroughly〔'θʒolɪ〕*adv.* 徹底地；完全地

At 5:30 p.m. the man called Dr. Schwartz to report **that** he had "*washed his face* **and** *the blue came off*." He had received blue towels *as Christmas gifts* **and** had used one of them *that morning for the first time*.

下午五點半時，那個人打電話給施瓦茨醫師，說他「洗臉之後，青色就掉了」。原來聖誕節他收到的禮物是青色的毛巾，那天早上他第一次拿其中一條來使用。

come off 掉落

47. (**B**)　那個病人臉上呈現青色是因為
　　　　(A) 血液中缺氧。　　　　(B) 使用青色的毛巾。
　　　　(C) 嚴重的藥物反應。　　(D) 一種醫生查不出來的疾病。
　　　　detect〔dɪ'tɛkt〕v. 查出

48. (**D**)　醫生要那個臉色發青的人回家之前，先
　　　　(A) 洗了病人的臉。　　　(B) 用藥物治好了他臉上的顏色。
　　　　(C) 和其他醫生討論。　　(D) 替病人做了徹底的檢查。
　　　　consult〔kən'sʌlt〕v. 商量；請教

49. (**C**)　本篇文章的主旨是
　　　　(A) 有些疾病醫生經常很難認定。
　　　　(B) 醫生在做治療時，經常太粗心大意。
　　　　(C) 醫生有時會被病人描述的病狀所誤導。
　　　　(D) 有些病人喜歡對醫生惡作劇。
　　　　practical joke 惡作劇

50. (**D**)　臉色發青的原因是何時確定的？
　　　　(A) 病人做了一連串檢查之後。
　　　　(B) 經由藥物治療，青色突然消失之後。
　　　　(C) 另一位醫生更仔細地檢查病人之後。
　　　　(D) 病人想到他如何使用聖誕禮物之後。
　　　　carry out 進行　　medication〔ˌmɛdɪ'keʃən〕n. 藥物治療

第二部分：非選擇題

Ⅰ、中譯英：

1. 台灣的生活最近十年變了很多。
　　Life in Taiwan has changed quite a lot over the last ten years.

2. 年輕的一代有許多新的生活方式，
　　The younger generation has many ⎰ new ways of living,
　　　　　　　　　　　　　　　　　⎱ new life styles,

3. 和他們父母那一輩相當不同。
　　which are quite different from their parents' generation's.

4. 舉個例，很多年輕人喜歡吃美式速食，喝加糖飲料，

For example, many young people like to eat American fast food and consume sweetened drinks.

5. 而老一輩的大多寧可吃中國菜，喝中國茶。

However, the older generation would rather eat Chinese food and drink Chinese tea.

Ⅱ、英文作文：

Making Decisions

Growing up means making my own decisions. When it comes to the moment of decision, it is I, not my parents or my friends, who must decide what to do and take up the responsibility. Once a decision is made, it is hard to change, so I am always careful when making decisions. Before making a decision, I consider and evaluate all aspects of the situation, which can help me make a better judgement. Once I make up my mind, I do my best to accomplish what I have set out to do.

The hardest decision that I ever made was when I chose to attend senior high school instead of vocational school. My poor family needed me to go to vocational school to help support the family. But my dream was going to high school and then on to university. Stuggling between cold reality and wishful dreams, I was determined to pursue my life-long goal. Though it was very difficult for me to work my way through senior high school, I was satisfied that I could live my life in my own way.

---

when it comes to～ 一提到～　　*take up* 承擔
evaluate〔ɪ'væljʊ,et〕*v.* 評估　　aspect〔'æspɛkt〕*n.* 方面
set out 開始；著手　　vocational〔vo'keʃənl〕*adj.* 職業的
support〔sə'port〕*v.* 維持　　wishful〔'wɪʃfəl〕*adj.* 希望的；渴望的
be determined to 決心　　lifelong〔'laɪf,lɔŋ〕*adj.* 終身的
work one's way through～ 靠工讀唸完～

八十三學年度大學暨獨立學院入學考試
英 文 試 題

第一部分：單一選擇題

Ⅰ、**對話**（10％）：下面十個題目（1至10）是日常生活中常見的英語對話。每題各有一個空白，並各附有四個備選答案。請依照對話內容選出最適當的答案，標示在「答案卡」上。每題答對得1分，答錯倒扣⅓分，不答不給分。

A. 以下第1至第5題，請依各組對話的情境選出適當的句子，將對話完成。

1. Son 　　　: Will it be expensive？
   Mother : ＿＿＿＿＿＿＿＿＿＿＿＿＿＿＿＿
   (A) Oh, really？ 　　　　　(B) Okay.　I understand.
   (C) Don't worry.　I'll pay. 　(D) Oh, don't let me keep you.

2. Alice : Guess what？
   John : ＿＿＿＿＿＿＿＿＿＿＿＿＿＿＿＿
   (A) What？ 　　　　　　(B) Sure.　What can I do for you？
   (C) I'm glad you're having a good time.
   (D) Really？　What a pleasant surprise！

3. Wife 　　: Why didn't you tell me？
   Husband : ＿＿＿＿＿＿＿＿＿＿＿＿＿＿＿＿
   (A) I guess I forgot.
   (B) I'm sorry you have to wait.
   (C) I thought I'd come by to say hello.
   (D) I'd love to, but I have to work until six.

4. Man A : Maybe I could show you the way.
   Man B : ＿＿＿＿＿＿＿＿＿＿＿＿＿＿＿＿
   (A) Oh, thanks.　I like the green one.
   (B) Yes.　I've lived here for years.
   (C) Thanks, but I'm not familiar with this neighborhood.
   (D) No, thanks.　I can get there all right.

5. Man A：_____
　　Man B：Sure. I asked if Mr. Brown would be here tonight.
　　(A) Could you find Mr. Brown for me？
　　(B) Can you tell me how to fill in this form？
　　(C) Could you repeat that question？
　　(D) Did you notice the way he talked？

B. 以下第6至第10題，請依整段對話的前後情境選出適當的句子，將對話完成。

Woman A：That dress looks fantastic on you.
Woman B：I think I look fat in it.　__6__
Woman A：Oh, no. You look very nice. And the color is perfect on you.
Woman B：__7__ I guess I'll take the sweater for now. I can always
　　　　　buy the dress later.
Woman A：__8__ Let me take the sweater up to the cash register for you
　　　　　and write up your bill. But I'd still say the dress does look good on you.
Woman B：__9__ Well, then, I think I'll take it anyway.
Woman A：You can't be wrong with it.　__10__　how are you going to pay？

6. (A) Are you sure？　　　　　　　(B) May I try it on？
　　(C) Don't you agree？　　　　　　(D) Do you have another one？

7. (A) You have good taste.　　　　(B) I don't know.
　　(C) Yes, I see.　　　　　　　　　(D) You bet.

8. (A) Fine.　　　　　　　　　　　(B) No, you're wrong.
　　(C) That's right.　　　　　　　(D) How come？

9. (A) Excuse me.　　　　　　　　　(B) Oh, my goodness.
　　(C) Are you sure？　　　　　　　(D) Excellent！

10. (A) I beg your pardon,　　　　　(B) By the way,
　　(C) Frankly speaking,　　　　　(D) No kidding,

Ⅱ、詞彙（10％）：下面十個題目（11至20），各有一個空格，每題各附四個備選
　　　詞，請選擇最適合的一個，標示在「答案卡」上。每題答對得1分，答錯倒扣
　　　⅓分，不答不給分。

11. The _____ of 18, 13, and 14 is 15.
　　(A) division　　(B) balance　　(C) average　　(D) total

12. There are many _____ that the economy will recover from a recession.
　　(A) indications　(B) organizations　(C) contributions　(D) traditions

13. Intelligence does not _____ mean success. You need diligence as well.
　(A) honestly　　(B) formally　　(C) merely　　(D) necessarily

14. The report says that _____ driving has killed more than 20 persons since June.
　(A) patient　　(B) serious　　(C) thorough　　(D) reckless

15. How can you expect me to _____ exactly what happened twelve years ago?
　(A) remind　　(B) recall　　(C) refill　　(D) reserve

16. The man made a _____ effort to look happy, though deep in his heart he was very sad.
　(A) cheerful　　(B) friendly　　(C) conscious　　(D) laughing

17. Most children find it difficult to _____ the temptation of ice cream, especially on a hot summer day.
　(A) purchase　　(B) resist　　(C) stare at　　(D) accustom to

18. We cannot give you a _____ answer now; there are still many uncertainties on this issue.
　(A) definite　　(B) familiar　　(C) courteous　　(D) hollow

19. The report is much too long — you must _____ it, using as few words as possible.
　(A) strengthen　　(B) destroy　　(C) eliminate　　(D) condense

20. Mary is having a tough time deciding whether to dress _____ or formally for the party tonight.
　(A) individually　　(B) casually　　(C) respectively　　(D) deliberately

Ⅱ、**綜合測驗**（20％）：下面兩篇短文共有二十個空格（21至40），每個空格附有四個備選答案。請仔細閱讀後選出最適當的答案，標示在「答案卡」上。每題答對得1分，答錯倒扣⅓分，不答不給分。

　　Mrs. Smith is an old lady who lives next to a grocery store. She enjoys sitting on her porch and watching people __21__ their shopping at the grocery store. But yesterday she witnessed a very __22__ incident. She saw Judy, her neighbor's youngest daughter, playing with her ball outside __23__ store. Suddenly, Judy stopped playing and __24__ around to see if anyone was looking. The next moment, Mrs. Smith saw Judy __25__ her hand and take a peach from one of the boxes nearby. Judy __26__ ran off down the street. If Mrs. Smith __27__ younger and in better condition, she would have run after her, but __28__ she could do was stare in amazement. Later that evening, when she __29__ her husband about it, he said, "You __30__ have told the owner of the store. That's what I would have done."

21. (A) do   (B) pay   (C) make   (D) deal
22. (A) funny   (B) athletic   (C) enjoyable   (D) upsetting
23. (A) a   (B) the   (C) such   (D) certain
24. (A) saw   (B) watched   (C) noticed   (D) glanced
25. (A) put out   (B) show up   (C) take up   (D) reach for
26. (A) thus   (B) then   (C) though   (D) therefore
27. (A) was   (B) were   (C) would be   (D) had been
28. (A) for   (B) all   (C) that   (D) there
29. (A) told   (B) spoke   (C) talked   (D) discussed
30. (A) ought   (B) would   (C) might   (D) should

　　Most of us have learned to vary our language and our behavior to meet the needs of different circumstances. We may feel free to yell and ___31___ at children when we are angry with them, but we are usually very careful about ___32___ our voices to our bosses or to someone ___33___ . We may tease our friends or joke around with ___34___ , yet we tend to be more serious with strangers. ___35___ , we may accept hugs and ___36___ from other members of our family, but many of us get ___37___ when people we don't know very well touch us. Besides these obvious signals ___38___ which we communicate familiarity, ___39___ are more subtle messages that we send to show whether other people are close friends or whether the relationship is more ___40___ . The subtle changes may include slight differences in language, eye contact, and other forms of nonverbal behavior.

31. (A) hit   (B) look   (C) shout   (D) terrify
32. (A) raising   (B) softening   (C) lowering   (D) hardening
33. (A) anterior   (B) inferior   (C) superior   (D) posterior
34. (A) all   (B) each   (C) many   (D) them
35. (A) Anyway   (B) However   (C) Likewise   (D) Although
36. (A) food   (B) money   (C) kisses   (D) clothing
37. (A) moved   (B) uneasy   (C) pleased   (D) used
38. (A) by   (B) in   (C) for   (D) from
39. (A) thus   (B) they   (C) those   (D) there
40. (A) verbal   (B) distant   (C) obvious   (D) intimate

Ⅳ、**閱讀測驗**（20%）：下面有三篇短文，後面共有十個問題（41至50），每題各
　　附四個備選答案。請仔細閱讀，把最合文意的答案標示在「答案卡」上。每題
　　答對得2分，答錯倒扣⅔分，不答不給分。

When you buy a share of stock, you buy a little part of an incorporated business. The corporation uses your money to help run or expand
its business. If the corporation makes a profit, it sends you a check for
your share of the profit — say $1.00 for each share of the stock. The
money is called a dividend. If the corporation makes a very big profit,
it may decide to make the dividend bigger, say $2.00 for each share of
the stock, and you get more money back even though the amount you invested is the same. But if the corporation doesn't make a profit, your
share earns you nothing. If your stock keeps paying good dividends, people
will want that stock so much that you can sell it for more than you paid
for it. But if that stock never pays a dividend, few people will want to
buy it. If you can sell it at all, you will get much less money than you
paid for it.

41. This passage is taken from an article on
　　(A) gambling.　　(B) mathematics.　　(C) investment.　　(D) banking.

42. A dividend is
　　(A) a one-dollar bill.　　(B) the money you earn from selling your stock.
　　(C) a two-dollar bill.　　(D) a share of the company's profits.

43. The passage contains all of the following ideas except
　　(A) No profits, no dividends.
　　(B) You can make or lose money by selling your shares.
　　(C) You can own part of a business.
　　(D) Don't put all your money into one stock.

For the temporary relief of minor aches and pains, take one capsule
every six hours while symptoms persist. If pain does not respond to one
capsule, two capsules may be used but do not take more than six capsules
in twenty-four hours, unless directed by a doctor. The smallest effective
dose should be used. Take with food or milk if occasional upset stomach
or stomach pain occurs with use.

Do not give this product to children under twelve except under the
advice of a doctor. Do not take this product if you have had a severe
allergic reaction to aspirin.

44. Without a doctor's advice, which of the following persons can <u>not</u> take this product ?
   (A) A very short doctor.   (B) A teenager.
   (C) A baby.   (D) A nurse with minor toothache.

45. If the product upsets your stomach, you may
   (A) take a rest.   (B) take it with milk or food.
   (C) take it with aspirin.   (D) take one capsule every six hours.

46. According to the instructions, if you take one capsule for minor headache at midnight, you may
   (A) take it again at six o'clock in the morning.
   (B) take as many as you want.
   (C) take this product if you are allergic to aspirin.
   (D) take two capsules every hour if one capsule does not work.

   Washington, March 18 — The Clinton administration is studying ways to limit the impact on U.S. business and the mainland Chinese private sector if President Clinton decides to curtail mainland China's trade privileges over human rights issues, senior administration officials said Thursday.

   Rather than making an "all or nothing" decision on revocation of trade privileges, the administration might impose trade sanctions only on certain goods or industries, officials said. The aim would be to maximize the economic impact on the Beijing government, which owns its country's resources and heavy industries, while sparing sectors of the economy not deemed responsible for human rights abuses, officials said.

47. This passage is most probably taken from
   (A) a newspaper report.   (B) a government official's talk.
   (C) an economist's commentary. (D) a teacher's lecture in class.

48. The trade sanction to be imposed on mainland China is planned by
   (A) the Beijing government.   (B) the U.S. government.
   (C) the U.S. businessmen.
   (D) the private sectors of mainland China's economy.

49. According to this passage, the most probable target of the trade
　　sanction would be
　　(A) most of the goods and industries on mainland China.
　　(B) all the resources and industries, state or private, on mainland
　　　　China.
　　(C) the sectors of economy not deemed responsible for human rights
　　　　abuses.
　　(D) the government-owned businesses on mainland China.

50. According to this passage, the aim of the planned trade sanction is
　　(A) to encourage private economy on mainland China.
　　(B) to improve human rights conditions on mainland China.
　　(C) to overthrow the Beijing government.
　　(D) to increase the competitiveness of U.S. business on mainland
　　　　China.

第二部分：非選擇題

Ⅰ、**中譯英**（20％）：下面一段短文共含有五個中文句子，請譯成正確、通順、達
　　意且前後連貫的英文。每句四分，答案請寫在「非選擇題答案卷」上，同時務
　　必標示題號。

1. 我弟弟過去經常整日虛混，一件有意義的事也不做。
2. 現在，他努力用功，並且對未來有明確的計劃。
3. 是什麼使得他在行為和態度上有這樣明顯的改變呢？
4. 是他的高中老師發現了他的潛力，並且不斷地鼓勵他。
5. 弟弟說他會永遠記得並感謝這位老師。

Ⅱ、**英文作文**（20％）：寫一篇大約100到120個單字的英文作文，題目是" A
　　House Is Not a Home "。分成兩段：第一段先解釋 house 和 home 兩個字，
　　及使用上意思可能相同的情況。第二段說明 house 和 home 這兩個字的涵義有
　　何不同。文章請寫在「非選擇題答案卷」上。
　　評分標準：內容5分，組織5分，文法4分，用字遣詞4分，大小寫及標點符
　　　　　　　號2分。

83年大學聯考英文試題詳解

第一部分：單一選擇題

Ⅰ、對話

A.1.（ C ）兒子：會很貴嗎？

母親：_____

  (A) 哦，眞的嗎？　　　　(B) 好，我懂了。

  (C) **別擔心，我來付錢** 。　(D) 別讓我把你耽擱了。

(C)= *Yes, it will, but* don't worry. I'll pay.

  * 如選(A)，則問句應改爲 This will be expensive.

2.（ A ）艾莉絲：猜猜看發生了什麼事？

約 翰：_____

  (A) **什麼事？**　　　　　　(B) 當然。我能爲你做什麼？

  (C) 很高興你玩得很開心。　(D) 眞的嗎？眞令人驚喜！

What a pleasant surprise!（82年台大夜考過）

=What a nice surprise!

3.（ A ）妻子：你爲什麼沒告訴我？

丈夫：_____

  (A) **我想我忘記了。**　　　(B) 很抱歉你必須等。

  (C) 我以爲我會過來打招呼。　(D) 我很樂意，但我必須工作到六點

come by（順路）造訪　(A)= I guess I forgot *to tell you.*

4.（ D ）A：也許我可以帶你去。

B：_____

  (A) 噢，謝謝。我喜歡綠色的。

  (B) 是的，我住在這裏很多年了。

  (C) 謝謝。但我對這附近不熟。

  (D) **不用了，謝謝。我會順利找到那兒的。**

5.（ C ）A：_____

B：當然可以。我是問，布朗先生今晚會在這裏嗎？

  (A) 你可以幫我找布朗先生嗎？

  (B) 你可以告訴我如何填這張表格嗎？　　*fill in* 填寫

  (C) **你可以重覆那個問題嗎？**　(D) 你注意到他講話的方式嗎？

B. Woman A : That dress looks fantastic on you.

Woman B : I think *I look fat in it.* Don't you agree?
6

Woman A : Oh, no. You look *very* nice. *And* the color is perfect on you.

Woman B : I don't know. I guess *I'll take the sweater for now.* I
7
can *always* buy the dress *later.*

Woman A : Fine. Let me take the sweater *up to the cash register for*
8
you and write up your bill. *But* I'd *still* say *the dress does*
look good on you.

Woman B : Are you sure? Well, *then,* I think *I'll take it anyway.*
9

Woman A : You can't be wrong with it. *By the way*, how are you going
10
to pay?

婦人A：妳穿那件洋裝好看極了。

婦人B：我覺得我穿這樣看起來很胖，妳不覺得嗎？

婦人A：不會啊。妳看起來很漂亮，而且顏色也很適合妳。

婦人B：我不知道。我想我現在先買毛衣，洋裝可以以後再買。

婦人A：好。我幫妳拿這件毛衣去結帳。但我還是覺得妳穿那件洋裝真的很好看。

婦人B：妳確定嗎？呃，那麼，我想我還是買好了。

婦人A：妳買這件不會錯的。對了，妳打算如何付錢？

　　　　fantastic〔fæn'tæstɪk〕*adj.* 極好的；絕妙的
　　　　register〔'rɛdʒɪstɚ〕*n.* 收銀機　　　*cash register* 收銀機
　　　　write up 記帳

6.(**C**) (A) 妳確定嗎？　　　　　　(B) 我可以試穿嗎？
　　　　(C) 妳不覺得嗎？　　　　　(D) 妳有沒有另外一件？
　　　　try on 試穿

7.(**B**) (A) 妳很有品味。　(B) 我不知道。　(C) 哦，我明白了。　(D) 當然。

8.(**A**) (A) 好。　(B) 不，妳錯了。　(C) 對。　(D) 為什麼？

9.(**C**) (A) 對不起。　(B) 噢，我的天啊。　(C) 妳確定嗎？　(D) 好極了！

10.(**B**) (A) 對不起，　(B) 對了，　(C) 坦白說，　(D) 別開玩笑，

II、詞彙：

11. (**C**) The average *of 18, 13, and 14* is 15.

    18, 13和14的平均數是 15 。
    (A) division〔dəˈvɪʒən〕*n.* 除法
    (B) balance〔ˈbæləns〕*n.* 平衡
    (C) *average*〔ˈævərɪdʒ〕*n.* 平均數
    (D) total〔ˈtotḷ〕*n.* 總數

12. (**A**) There are many indications *that the economy will recover from*

    a recession.
    有許多跡象顯示，經濟將從不景氣中復甦 。
    (A) *indication*〔ˌɪndəˈkeʃən〕*n.* 跡象
    (B) organization〔ˌɔrgənaɪˈzeʃən〕*n.* 組織
    (C) contribution〔ˌkɑntrəˈbjuʃən〕*n.* 貢獻
    (D) tradition〔trəˈdɪʃən〕*n.* 傳統
    recover〔rɪˈkʌvɚ〕*v.* 復甦　　recession〔rɪˈsɛʃən〕*n.* 不景氣；經濟衰退

13. (**D**) Intelligence does not *necessarily* mean success. You need dili-

    gence *as well.*
    聰明並不一定意謂著會成功，你還需要勤勉 。
    (A) honestly〔ˈɑnɪstlɪ〕*adv.* 誠實地
    (B) formally〔ˈfɔrməlɪ〕*adv.* 正式地
    (C) merely〔ˈmɪrlɪ〕*adv.* 僅僅；祇
    (D) *necessarily*〔ˈnɛsəˌsɛrəlɪ〕*adv.* 必定
    intelligence〔ɪnˈtɛlədʒəns〕*n.* 智力　　*not necessarily* 未必；不一定
    diligence〔ˈdɪlədʒəns〕*n.* 勤勉　　*as well* 也

14. (**D**) The report says *that reckless driving has killed more than 20*

    persons since June.
    報導指出，自六月以來，魯莽的駕駛已經奪走了二十多條人命。
    (A) patient〔ˈpeʃənt〕*adj.* 有耐性的
    (B) serious〔ˈsɪrɪəs〕*adj.* 認眞的
    (C) thorough〔ˈθɝo〕*adj.* 徹底的
    (D) *reckless*〔ˈrɛklɪs〕*adj.* 魯莽的

15. (**B**) How can you expect me to <u>recall</u> *exactly what happened twelve*

years ago ?

你怎麼能期望我完全記得十二年前所發生的事？

    (A) remind 〔rɪ'maɪnd〕 *v.* 提醒　 (B) ***recall*** 〔rɪ'kɔl〕 *v.* 想起

    (C) refill 〔ri'fɪl〕 *v.* 補充　 (D) reserve 〔rɪ'zɜv〕 *v.* 保存

16. (**C**) The man made a <u>conscious</u> effort to look happy, *though deep in*

his heart, he was very sad.

那個人雖然內心深處十分悲傷，卻刻意使自己看起來很快樂。

    (A) cheerful 〔'tʃɪrfəl〕 *adj.* 快樂的

    (B) friendly 〔'frɛndlɪ〕 *adj.* 友善的

    (C) ***conscious*** 〔'kɑnʃəs〕 *adj.* 有意識的

    (D) laughing 〔'læfɪŋ〕 *adj.* 高興的

  * make a conscious effort 意義上等於 make an effort（努力），但

    是現在英語中很少用 make a conscious effort。

17. (**B**) Most children find it difficult to <u>resist</u> the temptation *of ice*

cream, especially on a hot summer day.

大多數小孩發現，要抗拒冰淇淋的誘惑很難，尤其是在炎熱的夏天。

    (A) purchase 〔'pɝtʃəs〕 *v.* 購買　 (B) ***resist*** 〔rɪ'zɪst〕 *v.* 抗拒

    (C) stare at 注視　 (D) accustom to 習慣於

  temptation 〔tɛmp'teʃən〕 *n.* 誘惑

18. (**A**) We cannot give you a <u>definite</u> answer *now*; there are *still* many

uncertainties *on this issue.*

我們現在無法給你明確的答覆；這個問題還有許多不確定之處。

    (A) ***definite*** 〔'dɛfənɪt〕 *adj.* 明確的

    (B) familiar 〔fə'mɪljɚ〕 *adj.* 熟悉的

    (C) courteous 〔'kɝtɪəs〕 *adj.* 有禮貌的

    (D) hollow 〔'halo〕 *adj.* 中空的

  uncertainty 〔ʌn'sɝtṇtɪ〕 *n.* 不確定的事物

  issue 〔'ɪʃʊ, 'ɪʃjʊ〕 *n.* 問題

19.（ **D** ） The report is *much too* long — you must condense it, *using as few words as possible.*

　　這篇報告實在太長了——你必須把它濃縮，字盡量少用。

　　(A) strengthen〔'strɛŋθən〕 *v.* 強化　(B) destroy〔dɪ'strɔɪ〕 *v.* 破壞

　　(C) eliminate〔ɪ'lɪməˌnet〕 *v.* 去除　(D) *condense*〔kən'dɛns〕 *v.* 濃縮

20.（ **B** ） Mary is having a tough time *deciding whether to dress casually or formally for the party tonight.*

　　為了決定今晚的宴會要穿非正式或正式的服裝，瑪麗正在傷腦筋。

　　(A) individually〔ˌɪndə'vɪdʒʊəlɪ〕 *adv.* 個人地

　　(B) *casually*〔'kæʒʊəlɪ〕 *adv.* 非正式地

　　(C) respectively〔rɪ'spɛktɪvlɪ〕 *adv.* 個別地

　　(D) deliberately〔dɪ'lɪbərɪtlɪ〕 *adv.* 故意地

Ⅲ、綜合測驗：

　　Mrs. Smith is an old lady *who lives next to a grocery store.* She enjoys sitting on her porch *and* watching people do their shopping *at the* _____
　　　　　　　　　　　　　　　　　　　　　　　　　　21
grocery store. *But yesterday* she witnessed a very upsetting incident.
　　　　　　　　　　　　　　　　　　　　　　　　　22
She saw Judy, *her neighbor's youngest daughter*, playing with her ball *outside the* store.
　　　　　　　　　　　　23

　　史密斯太太是位年老的婦人，住在一間雜貨店的隔壁。她很喜歡坐在門廊上，看著人們到雜貨店裏買東西。但在昨天，她親眼目睹了一件令她十分心煩的事情。她看見隔壁鄰居的小女兒茉蒂，在雜貨店門口玩球。

　　　　grocery store 雜貨店　　　porch〔portʃ, pɔrtʃ〕 *n.* 門廊

　　　　witness〔'wɪtnɪs〕 *v.* 目擊；看到　　incident〔'ɪnsədənt〕 *n.* 事件

21.（ **A** ） *do one's shopping = go shopping* 購物

22.（ **D** ） 依句意，選(D) *upsetting*〔ʌp'sɛtɪŋ〕 *adj.* 使人心煩的。而(A) funny〔'fʌnɪ〕 *adj.* 滑稽的，(B) athletic〔æθ'lɛtɪk〕 *adj.* 運動（員）的，(C) enjoyable〔ɪn'dʒɔɪəbl̩〕 *adj.* 愉快的，皆不合句意。

23.（ **B** ） 依句意，茉蒂在「那一家」雜貨店門口玩球，指特定的事物，須用定冠詞 the，選(B)。

Suddenly, Judy stopped playing *and* glanced *around* to see *if anyone was*
　　　　　　　　　　　　　　　　24
looking. *The next moment*, Mrs. Smith saw Judy put out her hand *and*
　　　　　　　　　　　　　　　　　　　　　　25
take a peach from one *of the boxes nearby*. Judy *then* ran *off down the*
　　　　　　　　　　　　　　　　　　　　　　　26
street. *If Mrs. Smith* had been *younger and in better condition*, she
　　　　　　　　　　　　　27
would have run after her, *but* all she could do was stare *in amazement*.
　　　　　　　　　　　　　　　28
Later that evening, *when she told her husband about it*, he said, "You
　　　　　　　　　　　　　　　　　　29
should have told the owner *of the store*. That's *what I would have done*."
30

突然間，茱蒂停止玩球，環顧四周，看看是否有人在注意。接著史密斯太太就看到
茱蒂，伸手在附近的盒子中拿了一顆桃子，然後沿著街跑走了。如果史密斯太太年
紀再輕一點，身體再健康一點的話，她就會去追茱蒂，但是這時她只能驚訝地看著
這一切。後來在當天晚上，史密斯太太把這件事告訴她先生。史密斯先生說：「妳
當時應該告訴雜貨店的老闆，換作是我，我一定會這麼做的。」

　　　peach〔pitʃ〕n. 桃子　　　nearby〔'nɪr'baɪ〕adj. 附近的
　　　condition〔kən'dɪʃən〕n. 健康狀態　　stare〔stɛr〕v. 瞪視；注視
　　　amazement〔ə'mezmənt〕n. 驚訝

24.（D）依句意，選(D) *glance around* 環顧四周。glance〔glæns〕v. 匆匆地一看
　　而(A) see v. 看見，(B) watch v. 注視，(C) notice〔'notɪs〕v. 注意，皆不
　　合句意。

25.（A）*put out one's hand* 伸出手。而(B) show up 出現，(C) take up 拾起，
　　(D) reach for（伸手）欲拿～，皆不合句意。

26.（B）依句意，選(B) *then* 然後。而(A)因此，(C)雖然，(D)因此，皆不合句意。

27.（D）表與過去事實相反的假設，if 子句中，動詞須用過去完成式，故選(D)。

28.（B）依句意，選(B) all she could do was... 她所能做的只有…。

29.（A）依句意，選(A)告訴。而(B)說，(C)談話，(D)討論，皆不合用法與句意。

30.（D）表過去應做而未做，須用 should have + p.p.「本該～」，選(D)。

Most of us have learned to vary our language and our behavior *to meet the needs of different circumstances.* We may feel free to yell and shout at children *when we are angry with them,* **but** we are *usually very* careful about raising our voices *to our bosses* **or** *to someone superior.* We may tease our friends **or** joke around with them, *yet* we tend to be *more* serious *with strangers. Likewise,* we may accept hugs and kisses *from other members of our family,* **but** many of us get uneasy *when people we don't know very well, touch us.*

    我們大部分人都學會如何改變我們的語言與行為，以符合不同情況的需要。當我們生小孩子的氣時，可能自然而然地，對他們大吼大叫；但是要對我們的老板或上司提高音量時，我們通常會很小心。我們可能會嘲弄朋友，和他們開玩笑；然而我們對陌生人就會比較嚴肅。同樣地，我們會接受家人的擁抱和親吻；但是不太熟的人碰觸我們時，許多人都會感到不自在。

    circumstance〔'sɝkəm‚stæns〕*n.* 情況
    tease〔tiz〕*v.* 嘲弄   hug〔hʌg〕*n.* 擁抱

31. (**C**) 依句意「大吼大叫」，選(C) shout 。
    (A)打，(B)看著，(D) terrify〔'tɛrə‚faɪ〕*v.* 驚嚇，均不合句意。

32. (**A**) (A) **raise**〔rez〕*v.* 提高   (B) soften〔'sɔfən〕*v.* 軟化；緩和
    (C) lower〔'loɚ〕*v.* 降低   (D) harden〔'hardn̩〕*v.* 變硬

33. (**C**) **superior**〔sə'pɪrɪɚ〕*adj.* 上級的；在上位的
    (A) anterior〔æn'tɪrɪɚ〕*adj.* 前面的   (B) inferior〔ɪn'fɪrɪɚ〕*adj.* 下級的
    (D) posterior〔pas'tɪrɪɚ〕*adj.* 後面的

34. (**D**) 代替前面名詞 friends，用複數代名詞 them，選(D)。

35. (**C**) 依句意選(C) likewise〔'laɪk‚waɪz〕*adv.* 同樣地。
    (A)無論如何，(B)然而，(D)雖然，均不合。

36. (**C**) 依句意，接受家人的擁抱和「親吻」，選(C) kisses 。

37. (**B**) 當不熟的人碰觸我們時，我們會不自在，故選(B) uneasy 不自在的。(A)感動的，(C)高興的，句意不合；(D) get used to 習慣於，用法、句意均錯誤。

Besides these obvious signals by which we communicate familiarity, there
　　　　　　　　　　　　　　　　　　38　　　　　　　　　　　　　　　　　　39
are *more* subtle messages *that we send to show whether other people are*

close friends or whether the relationship is more distant. The subtle
　　　　　　　　　　　　　　　　　　　　　　　　40
changes may include slight differences *in language*, eye contact, *and*

other forms *of nonverbal behavior.*

除了這些明顯的訊號，藉此我們傳遞親密之意外，我們還傳達更微妙的訊息，來顯
示其他人是密友，亦或是關係更加疏遠。這些微妙的改變包括語言上的細微差異、
目光的接觸，以及其他各種非語言的行爲。

　　　　　communicate〔kəˈmjunə,ket〕*v.* 傳遞
　　　　　familiarity〔fə,mɪlɪˈærətɪ〕*n.* 親密　　subtle〔ˈsʌtl̩〕*adj.* 微妙的
　　　　　nonverbal〔nɑnˈvɝbl̩〕*adj.* 非語言的

38.(**A**)「藉」這些訊號以傳遞親密之意，介系詞用 by，選(A)。

39.(**D**) 表示「有～」的句型爲 there＋be 動詞，故選(D)。

40.(**B**) 與密友相對的，即是關係疏遠，故選(B) distant〔ˈdɪstənt〕*adj.* 疏遠的。
　　　　(A) verbal〔ˈvɝbl̩〕*adj.* 言辭上的，(C) 明顯的，(D) intimate〔ˈɪntəmɪt〕
　　　　adj. 親密的，則句意不合。

Ⅳ、閱讀測驗：

When you buy a share of stock, you buy a little part *of an incorpor-*

ated business. The corporation uses your money *to help run or expand*

its business. If the corporation makes a profit, it sends you a check for

your share *of the profit* — *say $ 1.00 for each share of the stock.* The

money is called a dividend. *If the corporation makes a very big profit,*

it may decide to make the dividend bigger, *say $2.00 for each share*

of the stock, and you get more money *back even though the amount you*

invested is the same.

　　當你買了股份，你便是買了一家股份有限公司的一小部份事業。這家公司會用你的錢，來幫助公司經營或拓展事業。如果這家公司獲得利潤，它便會將你應得的那一份用支票寄給你 —— 例如每一股美金一塊錢。這筆錢便稱爲股息。如果公司得到很大的利潤，可能會決定將股息提高，例如每一股美金兩元，那麼即使你所投資的金額一樣，但你所得到的錢卻增多了。

share〔ʃɛr〕n. 股份　　stock〔stɑk〕n. 股票
incorporated〔ɪn'kɔrpə,retɪd〕adj. 股份有限公司的
corporation〔,kɔrpə'reʃən〕n. 股份有限公司
profit〔'prɑfɪt〕n. 利潤　　dividend〔'dɪvə,dɛnd〕n. 股息；紅利
invest〔ɪn'vɛst〕v. 投資

But if *the corporation doesn't make a profit*, your share earns you nothing. **If** *your stock keeps paying good dividends*, people will want that stock so much **that** *you can sell it for more* **than** *you paid for it.* **But**

if *that stock never pays a dividend*, few people will want to buy it.

If *you can sell it at all*, you will get *much* less money **than** *you paid for it.*

　　但是如果這家公司沒有獲利，你的股份就無法幫你賺到錢。如果你的股票能爲你持續帶來優渥的股息，人們就會非常想得到那張股票，而你也可以將它以比你所付的更高價格賣出。但如果這張股票從不曾有股息，想買它的人便很少。既使你能夠賣掉它，你所得的錢會比你所付的錢更少。

41.(　C　) 這段短文是取自於一篇有關＿＿＿＿＿＿的文章。
　　　(A) 賭博　　(B) 數學　　(C) 投資　　(D) 銀行業務
　　　gambling〔'gæmblɪŋ〕n. 賭博
　　　mathematics〔,mæθə'mætɪks〕n. 數學
　　　investment〔ɪn'vɛstmənt〕n. 投資
　　　banking〔'bæŋkɪŋ〕n. 銀行業務

42. (**D**) 股息就是
    (A) 一元紙幣。　　　(B) 賣股票所賺到的錢。
    (C) 二元紙幣。　　　(D) 公司利潤的其中一份。

43. (**D**) 這文章包含了下列所有觀點，不包括
    (A) 沒有利潤就沒有股息。
    (B) 賣掉股份可能會賺錢，也可能賠錢。
    (C) 你可以擁有一部份的事業。
    (D) 別將你所有的錢投資在一張股票上。

For the temporary relief of minor aches and pains , take one capsule every six hours *while symptoms persist. If pain does not respond to one capsule*, two capsules may be used *but* do not take more than six capsules *in twenty-four hours, unless directed by a doctor.* The smallest effective dose should be used. Take *with food or milk if occasional upset stomach or stomach pain occurs with use.*

當症狀持續時，每六個小時服用一顆膠囊，來暫時減輕輕微的疼痛。如果服用一顆膠囊沒有效，可服用兩顆，但二十四小時之內不可服用超過六顆膠囊，除非有醫師指示。應該服用最低的有效劑量，如果服用時胃不舒服或胃痛，可以和食物或牛奶一起服用。

temporary〔'tɛmpəˌrɛrɪ〕*adj.* 暫時的　　relief〔rɪ'lif〕*n.* 緩和
minor〔'maɪnɚ〕*adj.* 輕微的　　capsule〔'kæps!〕*n.* 膠囊
symptom〔'sɪmptəm〕*n.* 症狀　　persist〔pə'zɪst,-'sɪst〕*v.* 持續
respond〔rɪ'spɑnd〕*v.*（對治療等）顯示良好的反應
dose〔dos〕*n.* 服用量　　occasional〔ə'keʒən!〕*adj.* 臨時的

Do not give this product to children *under twelve except under the advice of a doctor.* Do not take this product *if you have had a severe allergic reaction to aspirin.*

　　除非醫生建議，否則別將此藥品給年齡低於十二歲的幼童服用。如果你對阿斯匹靈有嚴重的過敏反應，別服用此藥品。

> advice〔əd'vaɪs〕*n.* 忠告；建議　　severe〔sə'vɪr〕*adj.* 嚴重的
> allergic〔ə'lɝdʒɪk〕*adj.* 過敏的
> reaction〔rɪ'ækʃən〕*n.* 反應　　aspirin〔'æspərɪn〕*n.* 阿斯匹靈

44.(C)　如果沒有醫生的建議，下列何者不可服用此藥？
　　　　(A) 很矮的醫生。　(B) 青少年。　(C) 嬰兒。　(D) 有輕微牙疼的護士。

45.(B)　如果這藥品令你胃不舒服，你可以
　　　　(A) 休息。　　　　　　　　　(B) 和牛奶或食物一起服用。
　　　　(C) 和阿斯匹靈一起服用。　　(D) 每六小時服用一顆膠囊。

46.(A)　根據說明，如果你在午夜因為輕微的牙疼而服用膠囊，你可以
　　　　(A) 早上六點再服用。　　　　(B) 要吃多少就吃多少。
　　　　(C) 服用此藥，如果你對阿斯匹靈過敏的話。
　　　　(D) 每小時服用兩顆，如果一顆膠囊沒有用的話。

　　Washington, March 18 —— The Clinton administration is studying ways to limit the impact *on U.S. business and the mainland* Chinese private *sector if President Clinton decides to curtail mainland China's trade privileges over human rights issues,* senior administration officials said *Thursday.*

　　華盛頓，三月十八日電——政府高級官員週四表示，柯林頓政府正研擬方法，假如柯林頓總統決定因人權問題，削減對中共的貿易優惠，美國將設法減低此舉對美國經濟和中共私人企業所造成的衝擊。

> administration〔əd,mɪnə'streʃən〕*n.* 政府
> impact〔'ɪmpækt〕*n.* 衝擊
> private〔'praɪvɪt〕*adj.* 私有的
> mainland〔'men,lænd,-lənd〕*n.* 大陸
> sector〔'sɛktɚ〕*n.* 部門
> curtail〔kɝ'tel〕*v.* 削減
> privilege〔'prɪvlɪdʒ〕*n.* 優惠；特權
> issue〔'ɪʃju〕*n.* 問題　　official〔ə'fɪʃəl〕*n.* 官員

Rather than making an "all or nothing" decision on revocation of trade privileges, the administration might impose trade sanctions *only on certain goods or industries,* officials said.　The aim would be to maximize the economic impact *on the Beijing government, which owns its country's resources and heavy industries, while* sparing sectors *of the economy not deemed responsible for human rights abuses,* officials said.

　　官員指出，與其在廢除貿易優惠上，做全面否定或肯定的決定，美國政府寧願只對某些貨品和工業採取貿易制裁。官員並表示，其目的是要對擁有該國資源和重工業的北京政府，造成最大的衝擊，而被認為不需為輕視人權一事負責的經濟部門，則得以倖免。

> revocation 〔,rɛvə'keʃən〕 *n.* 廢除
> impose 〔ɪm'poz〕 *v.* 施加
> sanction 〔'sæŋkʃən〕 *n.* 制裁　　aim 〔em〕*n.* 目的
> maximize 〔'mæksə,maɪz〕 *v.* 使～增加到最大極限
> resource 〔rɪ'sors,'risors〕 *n.* 資源　　spare 〔spɛr〕*v.* 赦免
> deem 〔dim〕 *v.* 認為～　responsible〔rɪ'spɑnsəbḷ〕 *adj.* 應負責任的
> abuse 〔ə'bjus〕 *n.* 虐待；苛待

47.(**A**)　這段文章最可能取自於
　　(A) 新聞報導。　　　　　　　　(B) 政府官員的談話。
　　(C) 經濟學者的評論。　　　　　(D) 老師在課堂上的講課。
> economist 〔ɪ'kɑnəmɪst,i-〕 *n.* 經濟學者
> commentary 〔'kɑmən,tɛrɪ〕 *n.* 評論
> lecture 〔'lɛktʃə〕 *n.* 演講；講課

48.(**B**)　對中共的貿易制裁由誰計劃？
　　(A) 北京政府。　　　　　(B) 美國政府。
　　(C) 美國商人。　　　　　(D) 中共經濟機構的私營部門。

49.(D) 根據本文，貿易制裁最可能的對象是

    (A) 中共大部分的貨物和工業。

    (B) 中共所有的能源和工業，無論是國營或私營。

    (C) 被認爲不需爲輕視人權負責的經濟部門。

    (D) 中共政府所屬的企業。

    target〔'tɑrgɪt〕*n.* 對象；目標

50.(B) 根據本文，貿易制裁的目標是

    (A) 鼓勵中共的私人經濟。   (B) 改善中共的人權狀況。

    (C) 推翻北京政府。   (D) 增加美國企業在中國大陸的競爭力。

    overthrow〔,ovɚ'θro〕*v.* 推翻

    competitiveness〔kəm'pɛtətɪvnɪs〕*n.* 競爭力

第二部分：非選擇題

Ⅰ. 中譯英：

1. 我弟弟過去經常整日虛混，一件有意義的事也不做。

    My younger brother used to fool around all day long, not doing anything meaningful.

2. 現在，他努力用功，並且對未來有明確的計劃。

    Now, he is $\begin{Bmatrix} working \\ studying \end{Bmatrix}$ hard; besides, he has a clear plan for the future.

3. 是什麼使得他在行爲和態度上有這樣明顯的改變呢？

    $\begin{Bmatrix} What\ was\ it\ that \\ What \end{Bmatrix}$ made him so obviously change both in behavior and attitude?

4. 是他的高中老師發現了他的潛力，並且不斷地鼓勵他。

    It was his high school teacher $\begin{Bmatrix} who \\ that \end{Bmatrix}$ discovered his potential and kept encouraging him.

5. 弟弟說他會永遠記得並感謝這位老師。

    My younger brother said he would always remember and be grateful to this teacher.

II、英文作文（參考範例）

A House Is Not a Home

"House" and "home" are two words that have similar meanings, which often confuses people. "House" and "home" both refer to places which people live in. However, there is a slight difference between them. "Home" is often referred to as the place that we live in with our families. Sadly, in our society, people can hardly distinguish a home from a house because they often see no difference between them. This confusion can be traced back to the indifference between family members. Therefore, we can tell that love is an important factor in a home.

A home is a shelter, not only for our bodies but also for our minds. Whenever we are depressed, we can go home for comfort. Everyone in the family will do their best to take care of each other and share their happiness as well as sorrow. Without love, a home is merely a house where loneliness is all that can be found. In conclusion, a house can never be a home unless there is love.

slight〔slaɪt〕*adj.* 些微的　　distinguish〔dɪsˈtɪŋgwɪʃ〕*v.* 分辨
be traced back to 追溯　　indifference〔ɪnˈdɪfərəns〕*n.* 冷漠
factor〔ˈfæktɚ〕*n.* 要素　　depressed〔dɪˈprɛst〕*adj.* 沮喪的
sorrow〔ˈsɑro〕*n.* 悲傷　　conclusion〔kənˈkluʒən〕*n.* 結論
in conclusion 總而言之

八十三學年度大學聯考英文分數人數統計表

分數	第一類組	第二類組	第三類組	第四類組	分數	第一類組	第二類組	第三類組	第四類組
100	0	0	0	0	50	18808	14113	12656	12674
99	0	0	0	0	49	19918	14974	13410	13429
98	0	0	0	0	48	21086	15844	14180	14202
97	0	0	0	0	47	22275	16673	14903	14926
96	0	0	0	0	46	23397	17515	15653	15679
95	0	0	0	0	45	24545	18309	16350	16378
94	0	0	0	0	44	25703	19154	17091	17126
93	1	3	3	3	43	26868	20065	17899	17938
92	4	4	4	4	42	28045	20952	18668	18707
91	7	11	10	10	41	29235	21834	19437	19479
90	10	18	16	16	40	30468	22813	20297	20342
89	18	29	26	26	39	31691	23746	21122	21167
88	30	42	37	37	38	32893	24650	21931	21976
87	49	62	56	56	37	34000	25571	22743	22791
86	71	89	81	81	36	35154	26487	23566	23620
85	109	123	112	113	35	36334	27456	24420	24479
84	146	162	150	151	34	37513	28447	25302	25363
83	202	201	186	187	33	38693	29343	26099	26161
82	268	260	242	243	32	39835	30282	26926	26991
81	334	340	316	317	31	41067	31234	27783	27848
80	428	414	386	387	30	42237	32159	28617	28686
79	531	521	485	486	29	43385	33051	29402	29474
78	659	639	597	598	28	44560	33983	30230	30308
77	798	773	721	722	27	45688	34880	31028	31109
76	1011	913	847	848	26	46829	35770	31813	31894
75	1226	1101	1019	1020	25	47944	36655	32584	32671
74	1455	1270	1176	1177	24	49065	37552	33386	33480
73	1708	1492	1377	1378	23	50143	38420	34159	34256
72	2013	1743	1604	1605	22	51185	39253	34893	34994
71	2364	2013	1855	1856	21	52308	40129	35671	35779
70	2720	2321	2139	2140	20	53425	40988	36427	36541
69	3140	2632	2409	2410	19	54524	41892	37242	37364
68	3617	3010	2759	2760	18	55604	42675	37940	38070
67	4137	3377	3093	3095	17	56628	43495	38669	38803
66	4693	3768	3446	3448	16	57626	44264	39346	39489
65	5289	4235	3870	3872	15	58673	45069	40065	40214
64	5911	4698	4275	4278	14	59704	45858	40744	40898
63	6603	5178	4708	4712	13	60817	46614	41399	41558
62	7307	5709	5176	5180	12	61905	47374	42048	42221
61	8110	6308	5717	5722	11	62867	48025	42630	42813
60	8844	6910	6237	6242	10	63845	48710	43234	43426
59	9732	7546	6811	6816	9	64829	49379	43820	44027
58	10580	8202	7395	7402	8	65854	50050	44382	44601
57	11488	8847	7970	7977	7	66759	50602	44862	45086
56	12427	9507	8559	8567	6	67734	51228	45382	45619
55	13441	10169	9140	9151	5	68654	51857	45899	46150
54	14452	10909	9799	9811	4	69598	52474	46402	46677
53	15521	11671	10469	10484	3	70406	52951	46801	47085
52	16628	12462	11173	11188	2	71333	53544	47281	47581
51	17725	13248	11876	11893	1	72329	54125	47741	48061
					0	74335	55270	48576	48973

八十二學年度大學暨獨立學院入學考試
英 文 試 題

第一部分：單一選擇題

Ⅰ、**對話**（10％）：下面十個題目（1至10）是日常生活中常見的英語對話。每題
　各有一個空白，並各附有四個備選答案。請依照對話內容選出一個最適當的答
　案，標示在「**答案卡**」上。每題答對得1分，答錯倒扣⅓分，不答不給分。

1. Peter： I live in a room with two roommates.
   Bob　： Are they easy to live with？
   Peter：＿＿＿＿＿＿＿＿＿＿＿＿＿＿＿＿
   (A) Oh, yes. We get along fine.　　(B) Oh, no. They're very friendly.
   (C) Yes. They're always fighting.　(D) Yes. It's nice to see them.

2. Jack： I've been wanting to get a chance to discuss our homework
   　　　　with you.
   Mark：＿＿＿＿＿＿＿＿＿＿＿＿＿＿＿＿
   (A) Do you want me to go shopping with you？
   (B) So have I. Let's meet at seven o'clock tonight.
   (C) That's fine. I'll see you off.
   (D) Thank you. Then it's settled.

3. Guest： Hi！ I wonder if you have a double room for tonight.
   Clerk：＿＿＿＿＿＿＿＿＿＿＿＿＿＿＿＿
   Guest： Okay, thanks anyway.
   (A) One moment, please. I'll see if there are any flights.
   (B) Sure. Please fill out this form for us.
   (C) Sorry. I'm afraid we have no vacancy at this time.
   (D) How long are you planning to stay here, sir？

4. Tony： My brother's in hospital.
   Suzy： Oh,＿＿＿＿＿＿＿＿＿＿＿＿＿＿＿
   Tony： He has a heart problem.
   (A) he's very sympathetic.　　(B) that's very nice of him.
   (C) is it anything serious？　(D) you really like to crack jokes.

5. Man : I wonder if you could help me. I'm looking for Tandoor
   Restaurant.
   Woman : _____
   Man : Tandoor. It's an Indian restaurant. It's supposed to be around
   here somewhere.
   (A) Of course. You've asked the right person.
   (B) No. I'm looking for my boyfriend.
   (C) I'm sorry. I don't work here.　(D) Sure. What's the name again?

6. Paul : How can I get to the Palace Museum from here?
   David : You can take a number 304 bus in front of our school.
   Paul : How often does the bus leave for the museum?
   David : _____
   (A) Early in the morning.　　(B) In an hour.
   (C) Ten minutes later.　　　(D) Every half an hour.

7. John : Mom, have you seen the blue jacket I was wearing earlier?
   Mom : Yes, I put it in the washer.
   John : _____ My glasses are in the pocket.
   (A) My goodness!　　　(B) No wonder!
   (C) Certainly not!　　(D) Never mind!

8. Mary : My father quit smoking three months ago.
   Sue : _____ I wish my Dad could do that, too.
   (A) Don't worry about that.　(B) I'm very grateful.
   (C) By all means.　　　　　(D) Good for him.

9. Bob : Did you say you like this novel?
   Jim : _____ I said it's not bad.
   (A) Not exactly.　　　(B) I don't see why.
   (C) You're great.　　 (D) That's quite all right.

10. Yung-lin : You must be very excited about going to France for
    schooling.
    Chen-mei : _____ but I'm afraid I can't do well because my
    French is poor.
    (A) Never mind,　　　(B) Well, I ought to be,
    (C) I don't know yet,　(D) Certainly not,

Ⅱ、詞彙（10％）：下面十個題目（11至20），各有一個空格，每題各附四個備選單字，請選擇一個最適合的單字，標示在「**答案卡**」上。每題答對得1分，答錯倒扣⅓分，不答不給分。

11. When a public official is found involved in a _____ , he usually has to resign.
    (A) request　　(B) tension　　(C) scandal　　(D) hardship

12. The transportation in this city is terrible and people have many _____ about it.
    (A) transcripts　　(B) complaints　　(C) accounts　　(D) results

13. Movies, sports and reading are forms of _____ . They help us relax.
    (A) entertainment　　(B) advertisement　　(C) tournament　　(D) commitment

14. After reading for nearly two hours, Carol felt _____ to go out for some fresh air.
    (A) dismissed　　(B) tired　　(C) tempted　　(D) attached

15. A polite person never _____ others while they are discussing important matters.
    (A) initiates　　(B) instills　　(C) inhabits　　(D) interrupts

16. Some students get _____ aid from the government to support their education.
    (A) financial　　(B) vocational　　(C) professional　　(D) intellectual

17. Henry, my old classmate, has _____ a true friend of mine all over the years.
    (A) retained　　(B) remained　　(C) regained　　(D) respected

18. He was very shy, so his smile was barely _____ when he met his teacher.
    (A) deliberate　　(B) extensive　　(C) noticeable　　(D) residential

19. They had not seen each other for years until they met _____ in Taipei last week.
    (A) distinctly　　(B) enormously　　(C) precisely　　(D) accidentally

20. The king was _____ for all his cruelties to the people.
    (A) feverish　　(B) notorious　　(C) spiritual　　(D) generous

Ⅲ、**綜合測驗**（20％）：下面兩篇短文共有二十個空格（21至40），每個空格附有四個備選答案。請仔細閱讀後選出一個最適當的答案，標示在「**答案卡**」上。每題答對得1分，答錯倒扣⅓分，不答不給分。

Each of your fingertips has many tiny lines. Some of these lines ___21___ circles, while the others, arches or loops. If you put ink ___22___ your fingers and roll them onto paper, you will make fingerprints. ___23___ when you are very old, your fingerprints will ___24___ look very much the way they do now.

___25___ thousands of years, people ___26___ that no two people have the same fingerprints. Long, long ago, people used fingerprints ___27___ signatures as a way of identifying ___28___ . About a hundred years ago, fingerprinting began to be used as a way to identify people who ___29___ crimes. Today, we can make computers ___30___ at the fingerprints of people to identify them.

21. (A) form   (B) bend   (C) grow   (D) chart
22. (A) of   (B) on   (C) in   (D) up
23. (A) Although   (B) Until   (C) Even   (D) Unless
24. (A) yet   (B) then   (C) just   (D) still
25. (A) From   (B) For   (C) About   (D) Since
26. (A) knew   (B) had known   (C) know   (D) have known
27. (A) instead of (B) as a result of (C) by means of   (D) on account of
28. (A) these   (B) those   (C) themselves   (D) them
29. (A) committed (B) have committed (C) are committing (D) commit
30. (A) to look   (B) looked   (C) look   (D) looking

When you stand on a beach and look out to sea, the horizon, or skyline, seems curved. This is because our earth is ___31___ like a ball; it measures about 13,000 km ___32___ . The land and water that you can see are ___33___ a small part of the surface of this ball.

___34___ from space the earth is almost ___35___ round and appears to have a smooth surface. The highest mountain ___36___ the land is about 9 km high, and the deepest ocean is about 11 km deep. This is very small compared to the size of the earth.

The earth is ___37___ of many planets in our solar system. ___38___ , it is the only planet which has the ___39___ conditions for human life. Other planets would be too cold or too hot for us to live ___40___ , or the atmosphere would be too poisonous.

31. (A) viewed	(B) played	(C) shaped	(D) seemed
32. (A) along	(B) across	(C) away	(D) above
33. (A) mainly	(B) rarely	(C) likely	(D) only
34. (A) Seen	(B) Moved	(C) Found	(D) Kept
35. (A) broadly	(B) usually	(C) perfectly	(D) partly
36. (A) on	(B) in	(C) to	(D) at
37. (A) the one	(B) one	(C) this one	(D) that one
38. (A) Whatever	(B) However	(C) Whenever	(D) Wherever
39. (A) brief	(B) free	(C) huge	(D) right
40. (A) then	(B) where	(C) over	(D) there

Ⅳ、**閱讀測驗**（20％）：下面有三篇短文，後面共有十個問題（41至50），每題各附四個備選答案。請仔細閱讀，把最合文意的一個答案標示在「**答案卡**」上。每題答對得2分，答錯倒扣⅔分，不答不給分。

　　Besides providing an ideal environment for sea plants and animals to live in, seawater has other valuable properties, one of which is that it constantly moves. And its movements produce energy.

　　The most obvious movements are the waves and the tides. Winds cause the waves, and the gravitational pull of the moon and the sun causes the tides. In places like the Bay of Fundy in Canada, the difference between the high and low tide level can be as much as 40 feet.

　　France and Britain are now trying to use energy in the tides to produce electricity. Waves can produce electricity and some small-scale experiments are taking place to learn more about this. One of the most encouraging areas of research uses the difference between the temperature of seawater at the surface and deep down to produce electricity.

41. One of the valuable properties of seawater is that
　(A) it has no plants in it.
　(B) it pulls the sun and the moon.
　(C) it flows all the time.
　(D) it feeds all kinds of animals.

42. Waves and tides are caused by
　(A) the same forces.
　(B) different forces.
　(C) their own movements.
　(D) plants and animals.

43. According to this passage, which of the following statements is NOT true?
   (A) The temperature difference of seawater can produce electricity.
   (B) The energy in the tides can produce electricity.
   (C) Waves can produce electricity.
   (D) The plants and animals in the ocean can produce electricity.

Greek soldiers sent messages by turning their shields toward the sun. The flashes of reflected light could be seen several miles away. The enemy did not know what the flashes meant, but other Greek soldiers could understand the messages.

Roman soldiers in some places built long rows of signal towers. When they had a message to send, the soldiers shouted it from tower to tower. If there were enough towers and enough soldiers with loud voices, important news could be sent quickly over a long distance.

In Africa, people learned to send messages by beating on a series of large drums. Each drum was kept within hearing distance of the next one. The drum beats were sent out in a special way that all the drummers understood. Though the messages were simple, they could be sent at great speed for hundreds of miles.

In the eighteenth century, a French engineer found a new way to send short messages. In this way, a person held a flag in each hand and the arms were moved to various positions representing different letters of the alphabet. It was like spelling out words with flags and arms.

Over a long period of time, people sent messages by all these different methods. However, not until the telephone was invented in America in the nineteenth century could people send speech sounds over a great distance in just a few seconds.

44. According to this passage, the Roman method of communication depended very much upon
   (A) fine weather.
   (B) high towers.
   (C) the spelling system.
   (D) arm movements.

45. Which method of communication could send messages to the most distant place within the shortest time?

   (A) The Greek method.   (B) The Roman method.

   (C) The African method.   (D) The American method.

46. The African method of communication sent messages

   (A) of a complicated nature.

   (B) over a very short distance.

   (C) by a musical instrument.

   (D) at a rather slow speed.

47. Which method of communication made use of visual signs?

   (A) The French method.   (B) The Roman method.

   (C) The African method.   (D) The American method.

Not many dogs can become movie stars. However, thousands of highly trained dogs in the world today are working in a very honorable profession: they are Seeing-Eye dogs guiding the blind. The first Seeing-Eye dog was a German shepherd named Buddy. In Switzerland, Buddy's owner, Mrs. Dorothy Eustis, was originally training dogs of the German shepherd breed for police work and saving people from dangers. Then in 1927, she wrote an article for the Saturday Evening Post about dogs being trained in Germany to help blinded war veterans. Morris Frank, a young blind American, heard about the article and wrote to Mrs. Eustis to ask if there was such a dog to help him. That letter led Frank to spend five weeks in Switzerland learning to be guided by Buddy. Buddy was with Frank when he returned to the United States. Newspaper reporters were waiting for them in New York. They couldn't believe that a dog could safely guide a blind man through a modern city. Buddy surprised them by leading her master confidently across the streets through the heavy traffic.

48. In the beginning, Mrs. Eustis trained German shepherds

   (A) to be movie stars.

   (B) for scientific experiments.

   (C) to be the eyes for the blind.

   (D) to serve the public.

49. Frank first learned about the guiding dogs
　　(A) from reading newspapers.
　　(B) indirectly from Mrs. Eustis' article.
　　(C) by writing a letter to Mrs. Eustis.
　　(D) from watching television programs.

50. Which of the following statements is NOT true about Buddy?
　　(A) Buddy was a male German shepherd.
　　(B) Buddy was not frightened by the heavy traffic of New York.
　　(C) Buddy was trained by Mrs. Eustis.
　　(D) Buddy came from Switzerland.

第二部分：非選擇題

I、**中譯英**（20％）：下面一段短文共含五個中文句子，請譯成正確、通順、達意
　　且前後連貫的英文。每句四分。答案請寫在「**非選擇題試卷**」上，同時**務必標
　　示題號**。

1. 這個月，我的運氣真是好得我都不敢相信。

2. 月初，我的數學月考考了九十分。

3. 月中，父親送我一部電腦當生日禮物。

4. 前幾天，英語演講比賽我得了第二名。

5. 這輩子，我的運氣從來沒有這麼好過。

II、**英文作文**（20％）：

　　寫一篇大約一百個單字（word）的英文作文，分成兩段，題目是" Near-
　　sightedness "（近視）。第一段的第一句必須是主題句" Near-sightedness
　　is a serious problem among the youth of our country. "。第二段的
　　第一句必須是主題句" I have some suggestions for solving this prob-
　　lem. "。文章請寫在「**非選擇題試卷**」上。

　　評分標準：內容5分，組織5分，文法4分，用字遣詞4分，拼字、大小寫及
　　　　　　　　標點符號2分。

　　　注意：1. 主題句必須抄在每一段第一句的位置。漏寫一個主題句扣2分。
　　　　　　2. 兩段必須分開寫，兩段如合成一段扣2分。

82年大學聯考英文試題詳解

第一部分：單一選擇題

I、對話

1. (**A**)　彼得：我和兩位室友共同住一個房間。

　　　　鮑伯：和他們容易相處嗎？

　　　　彼得：＿＿＿＿＿＿＿＿＿＿＿

　　　　(A) 喔，是的，我們相處的很好。　(B) 喔，不，他們非常友善。

　　　　(C) 是的，他們老是打架。　(D) 是的，看到他們眞好。

　　　　get along 相處

2. (**B**)　傑克：我一直想找個機會，和你討論我們的作業。

　　　　馬克：＿＿＿＿＿＿＿＿＿＿＿

　　　　(A) 你要我和你去購物嗎？　(B) 我也是，我們今晚七點見吧！

　　　　(C) 很好，我會去替你送行。　(D) 謝謝，那麼就說定了。

　　　　see sb. off 爲某人送行　　settle〔ˈsɛtl〕*v.* 決定

3. (**C**)　客人：嗨！不知道你們今晚還有沒有雙人房？

　　　　職員：＿＿＿＿＿＿＿＿＿＿＿

　　　　客人：好吧，還是謝謝你。

　　　　(A) 請稍等，我看看是否還有班機。

　　　　(B) 當然有，請塡寫這張表格。

　　　　(C) 抱歉，恐怕我們現在沒有空房間了。

　　　　(D) 先生，您打算在這裡停留多久？

　　　　fill out 塡寫（表格等）　　vacancy〔ˈvekənsɪ〕*n.* 空房間

4. (**C**)　東尼：我哥哥住院了。

　　　　蘇茜：噢，＿＿＿＿＿＿＿＿＿＿＿

　　　　東尼：他的心臟有問題。

　　　　(A) 他很有同情心。　(B) 他人眞好。

　　　　(C) 嚴重嗎？　(D) 你眞愛開玩笑。

　　　　be in hospital 住院

　　　　sympathetic〔ˌsɪmpəˈθɛtɪk〕*adj.* 有同情心的　　***crack jokes*** 說笑話

5.（ **D** ）男：不知道你能不能幫我的忙。我正在找坦度爾餐廳。

女：_____

男：坦度爾，是一家印度餐廳，應該就在這附近。

　　(A) 當然，你問對人了。　　(B) 不，我在找我的男朋友。

　　(C) 很抱歉，我不在這兒工作。　(D) 當然，再說一次名字好嗎？

be supposed to + *V* 應該～

6.（ **D** ）保羅：從這裡怎麼去故宮博物院？

大衛：你可以在我們學校前面搭 304 號公車。

保羅：開往博物館的公車多久一班？

大衛：_____

　　(A) 一大早。　(B) 再過一小時。　(C) 十分鐘後。　(D) 每半個小時。

* How often …? 「～多久一次？」問頻率，常用 every ～（每～）來回答。

7.（ **A** ）約翰：媽，你有沒有看到，我先前穿的那件藍色夾克？

媽　：有，我把它放進洗衣機了。

約翰：_____ 我的眼鏡在口袋裡。

　　(A) 老天！　　　(B) 難怪！

　　(C) 當然不是！　(D) 沒關係。（用在回答別人的道歉時）

washer〔ˈwɑʃɚ〕*n*. 洗衣機　　*My goodness*！天啊！（表吃驚、憤怒等）

8.（ **D** ）瑪麗：我爸爸三個月前戒煙了。

蘇　：_____ 我希望我爸爸也能這麼做。

　　(A) 別擔心。　(B) 我很感激。　(C) 當然。　(D) 這樣對他很好。

quit〔kwɪt〕*v*. 停止

9.（ **A** ）鮑伯：你說你喜歡這篇小說？

吉姆：_____ 我是說它還不錯。

　　(A) 不完全是。　　　(B) 我不明白為什麼。

　　(B) 你真棒。　　　　(D) 那相當不錯。

* not exactly（不完全是，未必就）是副詞的部份否定（詳見文法寶典 p.658）。

10.（ **B** ）永林：要去法國讀書，你一定很興奮。

珍美：_____ 但恐怕我會做不好，因為我的法語不好。

　　(A) 沒關係。　　　　(B) 呃，我應該很興奮。

　　(C) 我還不知道。　　(D) 當然不會。

II、詞彙

11. (C) *When a public official is found involved in a scandal*, he *usually* has to resign.

　　當公務員被發現涉及醜聞時，通常必須辭職。

　　　(A) request〔rɪˋkwɛst〕*n.* 請求　(B) tension〔ˋtɛnʃən〕*n.* 緊張

　　　(C) *scandal*〔ˋskændḷ〕*n.* 醜聞　(D) hardship〔ˋhɑrdʃɪp〕*n.* 艱難

　　　involve〔ɪnˋvɑlv〕*v.* 捲入　　resign〔rɪˋzaɪn〕*v.* 辭職

12. (B) The transportation *in this city* is terrible *and* people have many complaints *about it*.

　　這都市的交通狀況很糟，人們有許多怨言。

　　　(A) transcript〔ˋtræn͵skrɪpt〕*n.* 成績單

　　　(B) *complaint*〔kəmˋplent〕*n.* 抱怨

　　　(C) account〔əˋkaʊnt〕*n.* 帳目　(D) result〔rɪˋzʌlt〕*n.* 結果

　　　transportation〔͵trænspɚˋteʃən〕*n.* 運輸

13. (A) Movies, sports and reading are forms *of entertainment*. They help us relax.

　　電影、運動和閱讀是娛樂的方式，可幫助我們放鬆心情。

　　　(A) *entertainment*〔͵ɛntɚˋtenmənt〕*n.* 娛樂

　　　(B) advertisement〔͵ædvɚˋtaɪzmənt〕*n.* 廣告

　　　(C) tournament〔ˋtɝnəmənt〕*n.* 比賽

　　　(D) commitment〔kəˋmɪtmənt〕*n.* 委任；承諾

　　　relax〔rɪˋlæks〕*v.* 放鬆

14. (C) *After reading for nearly two hours*, Carol felt tempted to go out for some fresh air.

　　看了將近兩個鐘頭的書之後，卡羅想到外面呼吸一下新鮮空氣。

　　　(A) dismiss〔dɪsˋmɪs〕*v.* 開除；解散　(B) tired〔taɪrd〕*adj.* 疲倦的

　　　(C) *tempt*〔tɛmpt〕*v.* 打動～的心　*feel tempted to* ～　想要～

　　　(D) attach〔əˋtætʃ〕*v.* 附著

15. (D)　A polite person *never* interrupts others *while they are discussing*
　　　important matters.
　　　有禮貌的人絕不會在別人討論重要事情時，從中打斷。
　　　(A) initiate〔ɪ'nɪʃɪ,et〕*v.* 創始
　　　(B) instill〔ɪn'stɪl〕*v.* 灌輸
　　　(C) inhabit〔ɪn'hæbɪt〕*v.* 居住
　　　(D) *interrupt*〔,ɪntə'rʌpt〕*v.* 打斷

16. (A)　Some students get financial aid *from the government* to support
　　　their education.
　　　有些學生獲得政府財務上的幫助，來維持他們的教育。
　　　(A) *financial*〔faɪ'nænʃəl〕*adj.* 財政的
　　　(B) vocational〔vo'keʃənḷ〕*adj.* 職業上的
　　　(C) professional〔prə'fɛʃənḷ〕*adj.* 專業的
　　　(D) intellectual〔,ɪntḷ'ɛktʃʊəl〕*adj.* 智力的

17. (B)　Henry, *my old classmate*, has remained a true friend *of mine all*
　　　over the years.
　　　我的老同學亨利多年來一直是我的忠實朋友。
　　　(A) retain〔rɪ'ten〕*v.* 保留　　(B) *remain*〔rɪ'men〕*v.* 依然
　　　(C) regain〔rɪ'gen〕*v.* 恢復　　(D) respect〔rɪ'spɛkt〕*v.* 尊敬

18. (C)　He was *very* shy, *so* his smile was *barely* noticeable *when he*
　　　met his teacher.
　　　他非常害羞，所以當他遇見老師時，笑容不怎麼明顯。
　　　(A) deliberate〔dɪ'lɪbərɪt〕*adj.* 故意的
　　　(B) extensive〔ɪk'stɛnsɪv〕*adj.* 廣泛的
　　　(C) *noticeable*〔'notɪsəbḷ〕*adj.* 明顯的
　　　(D) residential〔,rɛzə'dɛnʃəl〕*adj.* 居住的
　　　barely〔'bɛrlɪ〕*adv.* 幾乎不

19. (**D**) They had not seen each other *for years* **until** *they met acciden-*
tally in Taipei last week.
他們彼此已好幾年沒見面了，直到上個禮拜才在台北偶然相遇。
(A) distinctly〔dɪ'stɪŋktlɪ〕*adv.* 清楚地
(B) enormously〔ɪ'nɔrməslɪ〕*adv.* 極大地
(C) precisely〔prɪ'saɪslɪ〕*adv.* 精確地
(D) ***accidentally***〔,æksə'dɛntlɪ〕*adv.* 偶然；意外地

20. (**B**) The king was notorious for all his cruelties *to the people.*
這國王因為對人民殘酷而惡名昭彰。
(A) feverish〔'fivərɪʃ〕*adj.* 發熱的
(B) ***notorious***〔no'torɪəs〕*adj.* 惡名昭彰的
(C) spiritual〔'spɪrɪtʃʊəl〕*adj.* 精神的
(D) generous〔'dʒɛnərəs〕*adj.* 慷慨的
cruelty〔'kruəltɪ〕*n.* 殘忍（的行為）

Ⅲ、綜合測驗

Each *of your fingertips* has many tiny lines. Some *of these lines*
form circles, *while* the others, arches *or* loops. *If you put ink* on
—21—   22
your fingers **and** *roll them onto paper*, you will make fingerprints.
Even **when** *you are very old*, your fingerprints will *still* look very
23   24
much the way *they do now.*

　　你的每根手指的指尖上，都有許多細微的線。有些線呈圓形；有些則是弧形
或環形。如果用手指沾點墨水，然後在紙上平壓，就可以印出指紋。即使在你年
紀很大的時候，你的指紋看起來，仍然和現在差不多。

　*第二句中，while the others, arches or loops 是由對等子句 while
the others **form** arches or loops 省略動詞而來。

fingertip〔'fɪŋɚˌtɪp〕*n.* 指尖　　tiny〔'taɪnɪ〕*adj.* 微小的
arch〔artʃ〕*n.* 弧形　　loop〔lup〕*n.* 環形
roll〔rol〕*v.* 壓平　　fingerprint〔'fɪŋɚˌprɪnt〕*n.* 指紋

21.(A) (A) **form** 〔fɔrm〕v. 形成　　(B) bend 〔bɛnd〕v. 彎曲
　　　　 (C) grow 〔gro〕v. 生長　　　 (D) chart 〔tʃɑrt〕v. 製圖

22.(B) 依句意，應是手指上沾墨汁，故介系詞應填 on（在～之上）。

23.(C) even（即使）修飾 when。

24.(D) 根據句意選(D) still 仍然。

For thousands of years, people have known *that no two people have the same fingerprints*. *Long, long ago*, people used fingerprints instead of signatures as a way *of identifying themselves*. *About a hundred years ago*, fingerprinting began to be used as a way *to identify people* **who** *committed crimes*. *Today*, we can make computers look at the fingerprints *of people to identify them*.

　　幾千年以來，人們就知道，每個人的指紋都不一樣。很久很久以前，人們使用指紋，而非簽名，來確認身份。大約一百年前，採集指紋便成了確認罪犯的一種方法。而現在，我們可以使用電腦來檢視人們的指紋，以確認他們的身份。

　　　　signature 〔'sɪgnətʃɚ〕n. 簽名
　　　　identify 〔aɪ'dɛntə,faɪ〕v. 確認
　　　　fingerprinting 〔'fɪŋɚ,prɪntɪŋ〕n. 採集指紋
　　　　crime 〔kraɪm〕n. 罪　　**commit a crime** 犯罪

25.(B)　for＋時間長短，表「一段時間」。

26.(D)　好幾千年以來，人類就知道每個人的指紋都不一樣。表過去到現在持續的狀態或行為，應用現在完成式，故選(D) have known。

27.(A) (A) **instead of** 代替；而不是　　(B) as a result of 由於
　　　　 (C) by means of 藉著　　　　　　 (D) on account of 因為

28.(C)　依句意，應是「確認他們自己的身份」，故須填一反身代名詞，選(C) themselves。

29. (**A**) 依句意，須用過去式動詞，故選(A) committed 。

commit〔kə'mɪt〕v. 犯（罪）

30. (**C**) make 爲使役動詞，而使役動詞＋受詞＋ $\begin{cases} 原形\text{V} \quad 表主動之狀態 \\ \text{V-ing} \quad 表動作之進行 \end{cases}$ ，依句意，使用電腦辨識指紋，是電腦主動進行辨識之動作，而且未強調該動作之進行，故應填原形動詞，選(C) look 。

When you stand on a beach and look out to sea, the horizon, or skyline, seems curved. This is *because our earth is shaped like a ball*; it measures about 13,000 km across. The land and water ***that you can*** 31 see are only a small part *of the surface of this ball*. 32 33

當你站在海灘上眺望大海時，地平線看起來似乎是彎曲不平的。這是因爲地球的形狀像球，其直徑約一萬三千公里。你所看到的陸地和海，只不過是地球表面的一小部份而已。

beach〔bitʃ〕n. 海灘   horizon〔hə'raɪzn〕n. 地平線
skyline〔'skaɪ,laɪn〕n. 地平線（= *horizon*）
curved〔kɜvd〕adj. 彎曲的   measure〔'mɛʒɚ〕v. 大小爲～
surface〔'sɝfɪs〕n. 表面

31. (**C**) (A) view〔vju〕v. 看   (B) play〔ple〕v. 扮演
(C) ***shape***〔ʃep〕v. 造成～形狀   (D) seem〔sim〕v. 似乎

32. (**B**) across〔ə'krɔs〕adv. 以直徑計
而(A) along〔ə'lɔŋ〕prep. 沿著，(C)在遠處，(D)在～之上，皆不合句意。

33. (**D**) (A) mainly〔'menlɪ〕adv. 主要地
(B) rarely〔'rɛrlɪ〕adv. 罕見地
(C) likely〔'laɪklɪ〕adj. 有可能的
(D) ***only***〔'onlɪ〕adv. 只是
依句意選(D) 。

Seen from space the earth is *almost perfectly* round *and* appears to have
34   35
a smooth surface. The highest mountain *on the land* is about 9 km high,
36
and the deepest ocean is about 11 km deep. This is *very* small *compared
to the size of the earth.*

    從太空中看地球，地球幾乎是正圓形，而且地表看起來十分平滑。陸地上最高
的山，高度約九公里，而最深的海洋，深度約十一公里。這和地球的大小相比，非常
地微不足道。

    compare〔kəm'pɛr〕v. 比較

34.(**A**)　Seen from space …是由 When the earth is seen from space …化簡
      而來。而(B)移動，(C)尋找及(D)保持，皆不合句意。

35.(**C**)　(A) broadly〔'brɔdlɪ〕adv. 寬廣地　　(B) usually adv. 通常
      (C) *perfectly*〔'pɝfɪktlɪ〕adv. 完全地　(D) partly〔'partlɪ〕adv. 部份地

36.(**A**)　若人站在陸地上來看，則 in the land 在陸地上，in the mountain 在山
      中，in the rain 在雨中，in the sea 在海中。但本題係從太空中看地球
      上最高的山，是大的接觸，故用 *on the land*。

The earth is one of many planets *in our solar system. However*, it
37   38
is the only planet *which has the right conditions for human life.*　Other
39
planets would be *too* cold *or too* hot for us to live there, *or* the atmos-
40
phere would be *too* poisonous.

    地球是太陽系裏眾多的行星之一。然而，它卻是唯一擁有適合人類生存環境的
行星。其他的行星不是太冷就是太熱，或是大氣層中含有太多有毒氣體，不適合人類居住。

    planet〔'plænɪt〕n. 行星　　*solar system* 太陽系
    conditions〔kən'dɪʃənz〕n.pl. 環境　atmosphere〔'ætməs,fɪr〕n. 大氣
    poisonous〔'pɔɪznəs〕adj. 有毒的

37.(**B**)　one of ～，some of ～前不可加修飾語限定。不可說 *this* one of ～。
      （詳見文法寶典 p. 142）

38.(**B**)　依句意選(B) However 然而。

39.(**D**) (A) brief〔brif〕*adj.* 簡短的　　(B) free〔fri〕*adj.* 自由的
　　　　　 (C) huge〔hjudʒ〕*adj.* 巨大的　(D) **right**〔raɪt〕*adj.* 適合的

40.(**D**) 依句意，選(D) there 那裏。而(A) 那時，(B) 哪裏，(D) 在～之上，皆不合句意。

Ⅳ、閱讀測驗

Besides** providing an ideal environment for sea plants and animals to live in*, seawater has other valuable properties, *one of **which** is that it constantly moves*. ***And its movements produce energy.

海水除了提供海裏動植物理想的生活環境之外，還有其他珍貴的特質。其中之一便是海水會不斷地流動，產生能量。

　　　　valuable〔'væljuəbl̩〕*adj.* 有價值的　property〔'prɑpətɪ〕*n.* 特質;財產
　　　　constantly〔'kɑnstəntlɪ〕*adv.* 不斷地

The most obvious movements are the waves and the tides. Winds cause the waves, ***and*** the gravitational pull *of the moon and the sun* causes the tides. In places *like the Bay of Fundy in Canada*, the difference *between the high and low tide level* can be *as* much *as 40 feet*.

最明顯的運動便是波浪與潮汐。風造成波浪，而日月的引力則造成潮汐。有些地方，像加拿大的芬地灣，漲潮與退潮的差距可高達四十呎。

　　　　gravitational〔ˌgrævə'teʃənl̩〕*adj.* 引力的

France and Britain are *now* trying to use energy *in the tides* *to produce electricity.* Waves can produce electricity ***and*** some small-scale experiments are taking place *to learn more about this*. One *of the most encouraging areas of research* uses the difference *between the temperature of seawater at the surface and deep down* *to produce electricity.*

　　法國和英國目前正嘗試利用潮汐的能量來發電。波浪能產生電子，而一些小規模的實驗正在進行，以對這方面有更深入的瞭解。最有希望的研究範疇之一，是利用海面以及海底深處的溫差來產生電力。

　　　　electricity〔ɪ,lɛk′trɪsətɪ〕*n.* 電力　　***take place*** 舉行；發生

41.（ **C** ）海水珍貴的特質之一是
　　　　(A)沒有植物。　(B)吸引太陽月亮。　(C)一直流動。　(D)養育各種動物。

42.（ **B** ）波浪和潮汐的產生是來自
　　　　(A)同樣的力量。　(B)不同的力量。　(C)自己的移動。　(D)動植物。

43.（ **D** ）根據本文，下列何者為非？
　　　　(A)海水的溫差可產生電力。　　(B)潮汐的能量能產生電力。
　　　　(C)波浪能產生電力。　　　　　(D)海裏的動植物能產生電力。

Greek soldiers sent messages *by turning their shields toward the sun.*
The flashes *of reflected light* could be seen *several miles away.* The enemy did not know **what** *the flashes meant*, **but** other Greek soldiers could understand the messages.

　　希臘士兵要傳遞訊息時，會將他們的盾牌朝向太陽，反射陽光的閃光幾哩外都看得見。敵人不知道這些閃光代表什麼意思，但其他的希臘士兵都能了解。

　　　　shield〔ʃild〕*n.* 盾　　flash〔flæʃ〕*n.* 閃光

　　＊試題中 The flashes reflected light 應改為 The flashes of reflected light。

Roman soldiers *in some places* built long rows *of signal towers.*
***When** they had a message to send*, the soldiers shouted it *from tower to tower.* **If** *there were enough towers* **and** *enough soldiers with loud voices*, important news could be sent *quickly over a long distance.*

　　有些地方的羅馬士兵建了長排的信號塔。當他們要傳消息時，士兵們逐塔大喊，如果有足夠的塔，而聲音大的士兵也夠多的話，重要的消息就可以長距離地快速傳遞。

　　　　row〔ro〕*n.* 排；行列　　tower〔′tauɚ〕*n.* 塔

In Africa, people learned to send messages *by beating on a series of large drums*. Each drum was kept *within hearing distance of the next one*. The drum beats were sent out *in a special way* **that** all the drummers understood. ***Though the messages were simple***, they could be sent *at great speed* *for hundreds of miles*.

在非洲，人們學會以擊打一連串的大鼓，來傳遞消息。鼓與鼓之間都保持鼓聲能被聽見的距離，鼓聲以一種所有鼓手都了解的特殊方法傳出。雖然是簡單的訊息，也可以高速傳遞數百哩遠。

> ***a series of*** 一連串的　　　　drum〔drʌm〕*n.* 鼓
> ***within hearing distance*** 在聽得見的距離內
> drummer〔'drʌmɚ〕*n.* 鼓手　　***at ～ speed*** 以～的速度

In the eighteenth century, a French engineer found a new way *to send short messages*. *In this way*, a person held a flag *in each hand* **and** the arms were moved to various positions *representing different letters of the alphabet*. It was like spelling out words *with flags and arms*.

十八世紀，一位法國工程師發明一種新方法，來傳遞短的訊息。要傳信的人雙手各拿一支旗子，雙臂擺出不同的姿勢來表示不同的字母，這就好像以旗子和手臂把字拼出來一樣。

> represent〔ˌrɛprɪ'zɛnt〕*v.* 表示；代表　　alphabet〔'ælfəˌbɛt〕*n.* 字母

Over a long period of time, people sent messages *by all these different methods*. However, **not until** the telephone was invented in America *in the nineteenth century* could people send speech sounds *over a great distance in just a few seconds*.

長久以來，人們用這些不同的方法來傳遞訊息。然而，一直要到十九世紀，美國發明電話後，人們才能夠在幾秒鐘之內，將說話的聲音傳至遠方。

44.（ **B** ） 根據本文，羅馬人的傳遞方法非常依賴
   (A) 良好的天氣。   (B) 高塔。
   (C) 拼字系統。   (D) 手臂的動作。

45.（ **D** ） 哪一種傳遞方法能在最短的時間內，將消息傳到最遠的地方？
   (A) 希臘人的方法。   (B) 羅馬人的方法。
   (C) 非洲人的方法。   (D) 美國人的方法。

46.（ **C** ） 非洲人的傳遞方法
   (A) 可傳送非常複雜的消息。 (B) 只能短距離地傳送消息。
   (C) 藉著樂器來傳送消息。 (D) 傳送消息的速度很慢。
  of～nature 爲～性質 *musical instrument* 樂器

47.（ **A** ） 哪一種傳遞方法要利用視覺的符號？
   (A) 法國人的方法。   (B) 羅馬人的方法。
   (C) 非洲人的方法。   (D) 美國人的方法。
  visual〔'vɪʒʊəl〕*adj.* 視覺的

  Not many dogs can become movie stars. *However*, thousands of *highly trained* dogs in the world today are working *in a very honorable profession* : they are Seeing-Eye dogs *guiding the blind*.

  沒有多少狗能成爲電影明星，然而在今天，全世界有數千隻訓練精良的狗，在從事一項非常光榮的職業：他們就是引導盲人的導盲犬。

  honorable〔'ɑnərb!〕*adj.* 光榮的 *Seeing-Eye dog* 導盲犬

The first Seeing-Eye dog was a German shepherd *named Buddy*. *In Switzerland*, Buddy's owner, *Mrs. Dorothy Eustis*, was *originally* training dogs *of the German shepherd breed* for police work **and** saving people *from dangers*. *Then in 1927*, she wrote an article *for the Saturday Evening Post* about dogs *being trained in Germany to help blinded war veterans*.

第一隻導盲犬是一隻德國牧羊犬，叫寶弟。寶弟的主人，桃樂絲‧尤西提斯太太，原本在瑞士訓練德國牧羊犬，以協助警方的工作，及救援有危險的人。後來在一九二七年，她為星期六夜間郵報寫了一篇文章，內容是關於在德國被訓練來幫助眼盲的戰後老兵的狗。

> shepherd〔ˈʃɛpɚd〕*n.* 牧羊犬　　originally〔əˈrɪdʒənlɪ〕*adv.* 原本
> breed〔brid〕*n.* 品種　　veteran〔ˈvɛtərən〕*n.* 老兵

Morris Frank, *a young blind American*, heard about the article **and** wrote to Mrs. Eustis to ask **if** *there was such a dog to help him*. That letter led Frank to spend five weeks *in Switzerland learning to be guided by Buddy*. Buddy was with Frank **when** *he returned to the United States*.

墨利斯‧法蘭克，一位眼盲的美國年輕人，聽說了這篇文章，寫信給尤西提斯太太，詢問是否有這樣的狗能幫助他。那封信使得法蘭克在瑞士待了五週，學習如何被寶弟引導，寶弟並跟著他一起回到美國。

Newspaper reporters were waiting for them *in New York*. They couldn't believe **that** *a dog could safely guide a blind man through a modern city*. Buddy surprised them *by leading her master confidently across the streets through the heavy traffic.*

報紙的記者都在紐約等著他們，他們不相信狗能引導盲人安全地在現代都市中穿梭。但寶弟很有信心地帶領牠的主人，穿越交通流量非常大的馬路，讓他們都大吃一驚。

> confidently〔ˈkɑnfədəntlɪ〕*adv.* 有自信地

48.（ **D** ）起初，尤西提斯太太訓練德國牧羊犬，是為了
　　　　(A) 讓牠們成為電影明星。　　(B) 作科學實驗。
　　　　(C) 讓牠們成為盲人的眼睛。　(D) 服務大眾。

49.（ B ） 法蘭克如何知道導盲犬的事？

    (A) 看報紙得知。

    (B) 間接地從尤西提斯太太的文章得知。

    (C) 寫信給尤西提斯太太而得知。   (D) 看電視節目得知。

    indirectly〔ˌɪndəˈrɛktlɪ〕 *adv.* 間接地

50.（ A ） 有關寶弟的敍述下列何者為非？

    (A) 寶弟是隻公的牧羊犬。

    (B) 寶弟並沒有被紐約繁忙的交通嚇到。

    (C) 寶弟是由尤西提斯太太訓練的。   (D) 寶弟來自瑞士。

第二部分：非選擇題

Ⅰ、中譯英

1. 這個月，我的運氣真是好得我都不敢相信。

I $\left\{ \begin{array}{l} \text{can hardly} \\ \text{can't} \end{array} \right\}$ believe $\left\{ \begin{array}{l} \text{(that) I have been so lucky} \\ \text{how lucky I've been} \end{array} \right\}$ this month.

2. 月初，我的數學月考考了九十分。

$\left\{ \begin{array}{l} \text{Earlier} \\ \text{In the beginning of} \end{array} \right\}$ this month, I $\left\{ \begin{array}{l} \text{got 90} \left\{ \begin{array}{l} \text{points} \\ \text{marks} \end{array} \right\} \\ \text{scored 90} \end{array} \right\}$ in the

monthly math $\left\{ \begin{array}{l} \text{exam.} \\ \text{test.} \end{array} \right\}$

3. 月中，父親送我一部電腦當生日禮物。

In the middle of the month, my father gave me a computer as a

birthday $\left\{ \begin{array}{l} \text{present.} \\ \text{gift.} \end{array} \right\}$

4. 前幾天，英語演講比賽我得了第二名。

A few days ago, I $\left\{ \begin{array}{l} \text{won second place} \\ \text{won Second prize} \\ \text{took second place} \\ \text{was second} \\ \text{came in second} \end{array} \right\}$ in the English speech

$\left\{ \begin{array}{l} \text{contest.} \\ \text{competition.} \end{array} \right\}$

5. 這輩子，我的運氣從來沒有這麼好過。

$$\left.\begin{array}{l}\text{So far in my}\\\text{In my entire}\end{array}\right\}\text{life,}\left\{\begin{array}{l}\text{I have never been so lucky.}\\\text{my luck has never been so good.}\end{array}\right.$$

Ⅱ、英文作文

≪範例1≫

Near-sightedness

　　Near-sightedness is a serious problem among the youth of our country. *As a matter of fact*, the number of near-sighted students is increasing every year. Although the government and educators have been paying much attention to this problem, it seems to become more serious year by year.

　　I have some suggestions for solving this problem. *First*, the government should see to it that the lighting in all the classrooms is good enough, or else the school authorities should be punished. *Second*, we must tell all our fellow citizens to avoid incessantly watching TV. *As we know*, television is the most popular form of amusement today, but it can permanently damage our eyes if we watch it too much.

near-sightedness〔'nɪr'saɪtɪdnɪs〕*n.* 近視
as a matter of fact 實際上
educator〔'ɛdʒə,ketɚ〕*n.* 從事教育者
see to 留意　　lighting〔'laɪtɪŋ〕*n.* 照明
authority〔ə'θɔrətɪ〕*n.*(*pl.*)當局
fellow〔'fɛlo〕*n.* 同伴
citizen〔'sɪtəzn〕*n.* 公民
incessantly〔ɪn'sɛsntlɪ〕*adv.* 不斷地
amusement〔ə'mjuzmənt〕*n.* 娛樂
permanently〔'pɝmənəntlɪ〕*adv.* 永久地
damage〔'dæmɪdʒ〕*v.* 損害

≪範例2≫

Near-sightedness

　　Near-sightedness is a serious problem among the youth of our country. The most important reason is that students in Taiwan are required to go through very competitive entrance exams, so they overwork their eyes by studying too intensively. *Besides*, the popularity of TV and video games among teenagers has also contributed to this problem.

　　I have some suggestions for solving this problem. *First*, we should have a healthier approach in preparing for exams — no last-minute intensive rituals. *Second*, young people should be encouraged to do more outdoor activities. *Finally*, school authorities should educate the youth on proper eye care. If we all act now, our next generation will enjoy much better eyesight than we do.

　　　　require〔rɪ'kwaɪr〕*v*. 要求
　　　　competitive〔kəm'pɛtətɪv〕*adj*. 競爭的
　　　　intensively〔ɪn'tɛnsɪvlɪ〕*adv*. 集中地
　　　　popularity〔,pɑpjə'lærətɪ〕*n*. 普遍
　　　　video game 電動玩具
　　　　contribute to 成為～的原因之一
　　　　approach〔ə'protʃ〕*n*. 方法
　　　　ritual〔'rɪtʃʊəl〕*n*. 慣例
　　　　eyesight〔'aɪ,saɪt〕*n*. 視力

八十一學年度大學暨獨立學院入學考試
英 文 試 題

第一部分：單一選擇題

I. **對話**（10%）：下面十個題目（1至10）是日常生活中常見的對話。每題各有一個空格，並各附有四個備選答案。請依照對話內容選出一個最適當的答案，標示在「答案卡」上。每題答對得1分，答錯倒扣⅓分，不答不給分。

1. A: I can't believe it!　I took the math exam, and I got the highest score in my class!
   B: _____ I'm thrilled for you.
   (A) It's a pity.　　　　　　(B) That's great.
   (C) No wonder.　　　　　　(D) You can count on it.

2. A: May I help you?
   B: Yes, please.　I bought this shirt here yesterday.　Two buttons are missing.　Look!
   A: _____
   (A) I'll bring you another suit.
   (B) Don't worry about it.　You can fix them yourself.
   (C) What you said is very interesting.
   (D) I'm sorry.　I'll change it for you.

3. A: When are you coming to New York?
   B: Next Monday evening at nine o'clock.　Can you meet me at the airport?
   A: _____ but I have an appointment with my doctor.
   (A) Certainly,　　(B) Sure,　　(C) I'd like to,　　(D) No problem,

4. A: Would you like some more chicken?
   B: Yes, please.　It's really delicious.
   A: Well, I'm glad you like it.　How about some more rice?
   B: _____
   (A) How nice!　I'd like some more dessert.
   (B) Thanks for the compliment.
   (C) No, thanks.　I'm already too full
   (D) Many thanks.　I can't eat any more rice.

5. A : Extension 312, please.
   B : Engaged. Will you hold on?
   A : No. I'll call back.
   B : Oh, it's free. _____
   (A) I'll tell him you called.   (B) I didn't recognize your voice.
   (C) You have the wrong number.   (D) I'll put you through.

6. A : I'm depressed. I just lost my new car.
   B : _____
   (A) Guess what! You'll buy another.
   (B) I'm sorry to hear that.
   (C) I'd rather you bought a new car.
   (D) It is always nice to drive a new car.

7. A : Which movie are you going to see?
   B : There's nothing good on at the moment. _____ Would you like
       to go to a concert?
   (A) Let's do something different.   (B) Let's take a look at the menu.
   (C) Let's go there right away.   (D) Let's go buy the tickets.

8. A : Excuse me. I'd like to have some information on a tour of Taipei.
   B : Sure. We offer several different tours of Taipei and all of them
       take just one single day.
   A : _____
   (A) That's none of my business.   (B) You're very helpful.
   (C) What can I do for you?   (D) You'll like all of them.

9. A : Say, what do you think of your new work?
   B : It's not bad, but the hours are long.
   A : Oh, _____
   (A) that's really something!   (B) how about that!
   (C) you'll soon get used to it.   (D) you did it again.

10. A : I'm really frustrated. Last semester I failed in two subjects.
    B : Take heart! _____
    (A) The world didn't come to an end.
    (B) You can kill two birds with one stone.
    (C) Better late than never.
    (D) Old dogs cannot play new tricks.

II. **詞彙**（10％）：下面十個題目（11至20），各有一個空格，每題各附四個備選單字。請選擇一個最適合空格的單字，標示在「答案卡」上。每題答對得1分，答錯倒扣⅓分，不答不給分。

11. Two important secrets of long life are regular exercise and ＿＿＿＿ from worry.

　　(A) process 　　(B) freedom 　　(C) motion 　　(D) favor

12. The policemen have ＿＿＿＿＿ the whole area but haven't found the criminal yet.

　　(A) looked 　　(B) improved 　　(C) searched 　　(D) discovered

13. If you want to become a good tennis player, you have to ＿＿＿＿＿ your skill.

　　(A) sharpen 　　(B) increase 　　(C) progress 　　(D) realize

14. Newspapers are ＿＿＿＿＿ with advertisements for all kinds of consumer goods.

　　(A) full 　　(B) filled 　　(C) fitted 　　(D) fixed

15. After spending one hour on this math problem, John still could not ＿＿＿＿＿＿ it.

　　(A) count 　　(B) figure 　　(C) add 　　(D) solve

16. The ＿＿＿＿＿ of the story was when the dog saved the little girl from the bad man.

　　(A) version 　　(B) climax 　　(C) attempt 　　(D) system

17. Tell me what happened at the end of the game. Don't keep me in ＿＿＿＿＿.

　　(A) suspense 　　(B) record 　　(C) memory 　　(D) permission

18. My poor test score does not ＿＿＿＿how much I know about this subject.

　　(A) reflect 　　(B) vanish 　　(C) adapt 　　(D) contain

19. The ＿＿＿＿＿ I have of the principal is that of a very kind and gentle person.

　　(A) aspect 　　(B) effect 　　(C) image 　　(D) message

20. My apartment has one ＿＿＿＿＿ I like. It has a fireplace in the living room.

　　(A) mystery 　　(B) triumph 　　(C) product 　　(D) feature

Ⅲ. 綜合測驗（20％）：下面兩篇短文共有二十個空格（21至40），每個空格附有
四個備選答案。請仔細閱讀後選出一個最適當的答案，標示在「答案卡」上。
每題答對得1分，答錯倒扣⅓分，不答不給分。

Sometimes people are deceived by dress. Once a great scholar went to
a party. As he was very simply ___(21)___ , he could not find admission ___(22)___ .
So he returned home and ___(23)___ his best. He went back to the party and
___(24)___ a warm reception. In the ___(25)___ of dinner he did not eat but
was talking to his clothes. The host came and asked ___(26)___ . The scholar
told him what happened. Since he ___(27)___ for the sake of his dress, he was
talking to his dress. The host ___(28)___ and sought the pardon of the scholar.
Though dress may be, ___(29)___ some extent, useful to judge a person, that
___(30)___ will not be sufficient.

21. (A) dressed   (B) dressed up   (C) wearing   (D) worn out
22. (A) outside   (B) out of   (C) inside   (D) into
23. (A) put up with   (B) put on   (C) took off   (D) pulled over
24. (A) was taken   (B) provided with   (C) was given   (D) was holding
25. (A) sense   (B) case   (C) event   (D) course
26. (A) how was it   (B) what was the matter
    (C) why did he do it   (D) when did he come
27. (A) only admitted   (B) was admitted only
    (C) was only adopted   (D) respected only
28. (A) regretted about it   (B) was pleased
    (C) was sympathized   (D) was disappointing
29. (A) in   (B) on   (C) by   (D) to
30. (A) alone   (B) along   (C) almost   (D) all

A long time ago people lived mostly out-of-doors. They noticed that
plants, animals, insects, and birds sensed the coming of a storm ___(31)___
than people did. All living things ___(32)___ to save their own lives, ___(33)___
they look for shelter ___(34)___ before a storm. When the people of long ago
saw animals seeking shelter, they ___(35)___ , too. The things that make ___(36)___
weather — the air pressure, the amount of water in the air, the temperature, and the wind — have an effect ___(37)___ plants and animals. Their actions
give clues to ___(38)___ . The people of long time ago called these " weather
signs." Those who knew ___(39)___ to read the signs were often as good as
weather services, ___(40)___ predicting is done with modern instruments.

31. (A) easier	(B) sooner	(C) quicker	(D) faster
32. (A) try	(B) have tried	(C) trying	(D) tried
33. (A) but	(B) yet	(C) so	(D) still
34. (A) quite	(B) pretty	(C) ever	(D) just
35. (A) did	(B) made	(C) went	(D) ran
36. (A) by	(B) for	(C) from	(D) up
37. (A) to	(B) on	(C) in	(D) out
38. (A) weather changes		(B) the weather changes	
(C) the weather change		(D) weather change	
39. (A) what	(B) that	(C) how	(D) why
40. (A) which	(B) while	(C) where	(D) when

Ⅳ. **閱讀測驗**（20％）：下面有三篇短文，共有十個問題（41至50），每題各附四個備選答案。請仔細閱讀文章，把最合文意的一個答案標示在「答案卡」上。每題答對得2分，答錯倒扣⅔分，不答不給分。

In some cultures, the act of touching another person is considered very intimate and is therefore reserved for people who know each other very well. In the United States, for example, young children are taught that it is rude to stand too close to people. By the time they are adults, Americans have learned to feel most comfortable when standing at about arm's length away from people to whom they are talking. And many Americans do not touch each other with great frequency while talking (this is particularly true of men). In contrast, other cultures have more relaxed rules regarding touching. For example, it is usual for friends—both men and women—to embrace each other when they meet. When they talk, they generally stand closer than Americans do, and they touch each other more often. They are as much at ease doing this as Americans are with more space between them.

41. Two persons touching each other may be viewed to be

(A) in close relationship in American culture.

(B) rude in all different cultures.

(C) common friends in American culture.

(D) very unfriendly in other cultures.

42. The polite space between two persons talking to each other
    (A) is not very important in American culture.
    (B) is very important in American culture if they are intimate.
    (C) is about arm's length in all cultures.
    (D) varies from culture to culture.

43. According to this passage, different cultural backgrounds
    (A) have little to do with human behaviors.
    (B) influence human interaction.
    (C) show that one people is superior to another.
    (D) have produced the same human behavior.

What comes into your mind when you think about robots? Do you imagine armies of evil metal monsters planning to take over the world? Or, perhaps of mechanical men who have been created as guards or soldiers by a mad genius? Or maybe you think of man-like robots who act, think, and look like human beings. In fact robots like these have more to do with science fiction films than with real life. In the real world robots are machines that do jobs which otherwise have to be done by people. Robots either operate by themselves or under the control of a person.

In a car factory, for example, robot machinery can put together and paint car bodies. On the sea bed remote controlled underwater machines with mechanical arms can perform tasks too difficult for divers. Robot spacecraft can explore the solar system and send back information about planets and stars.

Many robots have computer brains. Some robots are fitted with cameras, sensors, and microphones which enable them to see, to feel, and to hear. And some robots can even produce electronic speech.

All this does not mean that a robot can think and behave like a human being. Present day robots have to be programmed with a good deal of information before they can carry out even simple tasks.

44. Robots in real life
    (A) can behave like human beings.
    (B) have the ability to control the world.
    (C) can act as the evil guards of a tyrant.
    (D) can help us with a lot of work.

45. According to this article, which of the following is <u>NOT</u> true about robots in the real world?
(A) Some robots are as creative as artists.
(B) Some robots can help manufacture cars.
(C) Some robots can see and hear.
(D) Some robots can explore outer space.

46. Robots can perform many tasks for man because
(A) they have intelligence.
(B) they have computer programs stored in them.
(C) they can imitate human beings.
(D) they have the ability to learn new things.

47. The robots in science fiction films and those in real life differ mainly in
(A) mentality.　　　　　　　(B) appearance.
(C) material.　　　　　　　(D) size.

　　Our lives are regulated by many cycles, some external, like day, night, and seasons, and some internal, like the bodily signals that tell us when to sleep, eat, be active, and so forth.　When we travel long distances east or west, we are rapidly transported into a different time zone.　The external signs have changed and we discover, for example, that the sun is rising when we expect to be asleep.　The body becomes confused at the time change and responds by attempting to reset the internal clock to correspond with the new time zone.　The result is "jet lag," a condition characterized by a mental and physical exhaustion and confusion.　Jet lag is a term used to describe what happens when the body's internal clock is no longer matched with the external environment.

48. Our lives have their patterns which are controlled by
(A) the timing of the outside world.
(B) the timing of our bodies.
(C) the outside timing as well as the inner timing.
(D) our moods in the different seasons of the year.

49. We suffer from jet lag when
  (A) we travel to a distant place by boat.
  (B) we fly by the jet plane by night.
  (C) we feel very tired after travelling to many different places.
  (D) the internal rhythm disagrees with the external rhythm.

50. This passage shows that jet lag is
  (A) a normal functioning of the body.　(B) a symptom of bodily adaptation.
  (C) a contagious disease.　　　　　　　(D) a mental disorder.

第二部分：非選擇題

I . 填空（10％）：下面一段文章共有十個空格（1至10），每個空格請填寫一個最適當的單字（word），以使文句合乎文法而且通順。每寫一個正確的單字得1分，不答不給分，答錯不倒扣。

答案請寫在「非選擇題試卷」上；務必標示題號。

　　"Fire is a good servant but a bad master." This is an old English saying.　(1)　does it mean?　(2)　one time people did not know how to　(3)　fire. Then they learned to　(4)　so. They also learned how to use it to　(5)　them warm. They used it to drive　(6)　animals. They also learned how to cook food　(7)　it. Fire was their servant. It　(8)　things for them. But sometimes a building　(9)　fire. And the building may be destroyed and people　(10)　their homes, and even their lives. Fire is not the servant then. It has become their master!

II . 中譯英（10％）：請用最適當的句型將下列兩句話譯成通順而達意的英文。每題5分。答案請寫在「非選擇題試卷」上；務必標示題號。

1. 老實說，一直到昨天我才知道他已經去美國了。

2. 首先，我要說明清楚，我並不反對你的意見。

III . 英文作文（20％）：寫一篇大約100個單字（word）的英文作文，題目是 "Time"。分成兩段：第一段第一句必須是 "Lost time is never found again." 第二段第一句必須是 "Now I have a new plan for using my time wisely." 文章請寫在「非選擇題試卷」上。

> 注意：這兩句主題句不可漏寫，漏寫一個主題句扣兩分。

評分標準：內容4分，組織4分，文法4分，用字遣詞4分，拼字、大小寫及標點符號4分。

81年大學聯考英文試題詳解

第一部分：單一選擇題

I、對話

1. (**B**) A：真不敢相信！我數學考試在班上拿了最高分！

　　　　 B：＿＿＿＿＿＿＿＿＿＿ 我真為你感到興奮 。

　　　　　 (A) 真可惜 。　**(B) 太棒了 。**　(C) 難怪 。　(D) 你放心吧 。

　　　　 math〔mæθ〕n. 數學（＝*mathematics*）　　score〔skor, skɔr〕n. 分數

　　　　 thrill〔θrɪl〕v. 使興奮；使激動　　***count on*** 信賴；依靠

2. (**D**) A：我能為你效勞嗎？

　　　　 B．好的，麻煩你。昨天我在這兒買了這件襯衫。缺兩個鈕扣。你瞧！

　　　　 A：＿＿＿＿＿＿＿＿＿＿

　　　　　 (A) 我給你拿另一套衣服 。（suit 是指套裝，應改為 shirt）

　　　　　 (B) 別擔心 。你自己可以修理 。

　　　　　 (C) 你說的話很有趣 。　**(D) 真抱歉 。我換一件給你 。**

　　　　 button〔'bʌtn̩〕n. 鈕扣　　miss〔mɪs〕v. 缺少

　　　　 suit〔sut〕n. 套裝

3. (**C**) A：你什麼時候要來紐約？

　　　　 B：下週一晚上九點。你可不可以來機場接我呢？

　　　　 A：＿＿＿＿＿＿＿＿＿＿ 但是，我和醫生約好了 。

　　　　　 (A) 當然，　(B) 當然，　**(C) 我很想去，**　(D) 沒問題，

　　　　 meet sb. at the airport 到機場接某人　　appointment〔ə'pɔɪntmənt〕n. 約會

4. (**C**) A：你要不要再來些雞肉？

　　　　 B：好呀！這雞肉真好吃 。

　　　　 A：嗯，很高興你會喜歡。要不要再來些飯？

　　　　　 (A) 真好！我想再吃些點心 。　　(B) 多謝誇獎 。

　　　　　 (C) 不，謝了。我已經太飽了。

　　　　　 (D) 多謝。我吃不下飯了。（表示拒絕時，不可用 Many thanks. 要用 No,

　　　　　　　 thanks. 來表達，肯定的回答，該用肯定的內容。）

　　　　 chicken〔'tʃɪkən, -ɪn〕n. 雞肉　　delicious〔dɪ'lɪʃəs〕adj. 味美的

　　　　 dessert〔dɪ'zɜt〕n. 點心　　rice〔raɪs〕n. 米飯

5.（ D ）A：請轉分機三一二。

　　　　B：講話中。你要不要等一下？

　　　　A：不了。我會再打過來。

　　　　B：噢，線路通了。_____

　　　　(A) 我會告訴他你打電話來過。　　(B) 我認不出你的聲音。

　　　　(C) 你撥錯號碼了。　　(D) 我來幫你接通。

　　　extension〔ɪk'stɛnʃən〕*n.* 分機　　engaged〔ɪn'gedʒd〕*adj.* 佔線的

　　　hold on 不掛斷電話　　recognize〔'rɛkəgˌnaɪz〕*v.* 認出

　　　put *sb.* ***through*** 替某人接通電話

6.（ B ）A：眞難過。我剛剛丢了新車。

　　　　B：_____

　　　　(A) 你知道嗎？你可以買另外一輛了。(B) 聽到這件事，我感到很遺憾。

　　　　(C) 我寧願你買輛新車。　　(D) 開新車總是件很棒的事。

　　　depressed〔dɪ'prɛst〕*adj.* 難過的；沮喪的

7.（ A ）A：你要去看那一部電影？

　　　　B：現在上演的沒什麼好看的。_____ 你想不想去聽音樂會呢？

　　　　(A) 我們做點兒別的事吧。　　(B) 我們來看看菜單。

　　　　(C) 我們馬上就去那兒。　　(D) 我們去買票吧。

　　　concert〔'kɑnsɚt〕*n.* 音樂會　　menu〔'mɛnju，'menju〕*n.* 菜單

8.（ B ）A：對不起。我想詢問一下有關台北旅遊的消息。

　　　　B：好呀。我們提供幾種不同的台北旅遊路線，而且都是一天的旅遊。

　　　　A：_____

　　　　(A) 那不關我的事。　　(B) 你幫了不少忙。

　　　　(C) 我能爲你做些什麼？　　(D) 那些你都會喜歡的。

　　　tour〔tʊr〕*n.* 旅遊　　single〔'sɪŋgḷ〕*adj.* 單一的

9.（ C ）A：嗯，你覺得你的新工作怎麼樣？

　　　　B：還不錯，不過工作時間太長了。

　　　　A：噢，_____

　　　　(A) 眞了不起！　　(B) 眞想不到啊！

　　　　(C) 你很快就會習慣了。　　(D) 你又犯了。

10. (**A**)　A：我眞感到沮喪。上學期我有兩科被當。

B：振作點！＿＿＿＿＿＿＿＿＿＿＿＿＿

(A) 又不是世界末日。　　　(B) 你可以一舉兩得。

(C) 亡羊補牢猶未晚。

(D) 老狗玩不出新把戲；朽木不可雕。

（原諺語爲 You cannot teach an old dog new tricks.）

frustrated〔ˈfrʌstretɪd〕*adj.* 沮喪的　　***take heart*** 振作

come to an end 結束　　trick〔trɪk〕*n.* 把戲；技藝

II、詞彙

11. (**B**)　Two important secrets *of long life* are regular exercise ***and***

freedom *from worry.*

長壽的兩項重要秘訣是，規律的運動以及免於憂慮。

(A) process〔ˈprɑsɛs〕*n.* 過程　(B) ***freedom***〔ˈfridəm〕*n.* 免除；自由

(C) motion〔ˈmoʃən〕*n.* 動作　(D) favor〔ˈfevɚ〕*n.* 恩寵；偏好

regular〔ˈrɛgjəlɚ〕*adj.* 有規律的

12. (**C**)　The policemen have searched the whole area ***but*** haven't found

the criminal *yet*.

警察已經搜尋了整個地區，但是還沒有找到罪犯。

(A) look〔lʊk〕*v.* 看　　　(B) improve〔ɪmˈpruv〕*v.* 改良

(C) ***search***〔sɝtʃ〕*v.* 搜尋　(D) discover〔dɪˈskʌvɚ〕*v.* 發現

criminal〔ˈkrɪmənl̩〕*n.* 罪犯

13. (**A**)　*If you want to become a good tennis player*, you have to

sharpen your skill.

如果你想要成爲優秀的網球選手，你就必須磨練技巧。

(A) ***sharpen***〔ˈʃɑrpən〕*v.* 磨練；使銳利

(B) increase〔ɪnˈkris〕*v.* 增加

(C) ***progress***〔prəˈgrɛs〕*v.* 進步（爲不及物動詞，其後不可加受詞）

(D) realize〔ˈriə,laɪz〕*v.* 了解

14. (B) Newspapers are filled with advertisements *for all kinds of con-sumer goods*.

報紙充滿了各式各樣消費品的廣告 。

(A) full 〔 fʊl 〕 *adj.* 裝滿的(與 of 連用)　(B) **fill** 〔 fɪl 〕 *v.* 使充滿
(C) fit 〔 fɪt 〕 *v.* 安裝　(D) fixed 〔 fɪkst 〕 *adj.* 固定的

be filled with 充滿　　advertisement 〔 ͵ædvɚˈtaɪzmənt 〕 *n.* 廣告
consumer 〔 kənˈsumɚ, -ˈsjumɚ 〕 *n.* 消費者
goods 〔 gʊdz 〕 *n.* 物品

15. (D) *After spending one hour on this math problem*, John still could not solve it.

約翰在這個數學題上已經花了一個小時 ，但是還沒辦法解出來 。

(A) count 〔 kaʊnt 〕 *v.* 計算
(B) figure 〔ˈfɪgjɚ, ˈfɪgɚ 〕 *v.* 估計 (應改爲 figure out)
(C) add 〔 æd 〕 *v.* 加上　(D) **solve** 〔 sɑlv 〕 *v.* 解答

16. (B) The climax *of the story* was **when the dog saved the little girl** *from the bad man*.

這則故事的高潮 ，出現在小狗從壞人手裏救出了小女孩 。

(A) version 〔ˈvɝʒən, ˈvɝʃən 〕 *n.* 譯本
(B) **climax** 〔ˈklaɪmæks 〕 *n.* 高潮
(C) attempt 〔 əˈtɛmpt 〕 *n.* 企圖　(D) system 〔ˈsɪstəm 〕 *n.* 系統

17. (A) Tell me **what** happened at the end of the game. Don't keep me in suspense.

告訴我比賽最後的結果 。別吊我胃口 。

(A) **suspense** 〔 səˈspɛns 〕 *n.* 懸疑 ；不確知的狀態
(B) record 〔ˈrɛkəd 〕 *n.* 記錄　(C) memory 〔ˈmɛmərɪ 〕 *n.* 記憶
(D) permission 〔 pɚˈmɪʃən 〕 *n.* 准許

keep *sb.* **in suspense** 吊某人胃口

18. (**A**) My poor test score does not <u>reflect</u> ***how much*** I *know about this subject.*

　　我考得很差的成績，並不能<u>反映</u>出我對這科的了解有多少。

　　　(A) ***reflect*** 〔rɪˈflɛkt〕*v.* 反映　　(B) vanish〔ˈvænɪʃ〕*v.* 消失

　　　(C) adapt〔əˈdæpt〕*v.* 使適合　　(D) contain〔kənˈten〕*v.* 包含

　　score〔skor, skɔr〕*n.* 分數

19. (**C**) The <u>image</u> *I have of the principal* is that *of a very kind and gentle person.*

　　校長在我心目中的<u>樣子</u>是個非常仁慈而和藹的人。

　　　(A) aspect〔ˈæspɛkt〕*n.* 方面；表情　(B) effect〔əˈfɛkt〕*n.* 效果

　　　(C) ***image***〔ˈɪmɪdʒ〕*n.* 樣子；形象　(D) message〔ˈmɛsɪdʒ〕*n.* 消息

　　principal〔ˈprɪnsəpl〕*n.* 中小學的校長

20. (**D**) My apartment has one <u>feature</u> *I like.* It has a fireplace *in the living room.*

　　我的公寓有一樣<u>特色</u>我很喜歡，它的客廳裏有個壁爐。

　　　(A) mystery〔ˈmɪstərɪ〕*n.* 秘密　　(B) triumph〔ˈtraɪəmf〕*n.* 勝利

　　　(C) product〔ˈprɑdəkt〕*n.* 生產品　(D) ***feature***〔ˈfitʃɚ〕*n.* 特色

　　apartment〔əˈpɑrtmənt〕*n.* 公寓　　fireplace〔ˈfaɪr͵ples〕*n.* 壁爐

Ⅱ、綜合測驗

　　Sometimes people are deceived by dress. Once a great scholar went to a party. ***As he was very simply dressed***, he could not find admission *inside*. ***So*** he returned home ***and*** put on his best. He went *back to the party* and was given a warm reception.

　　有時候人會被衣着給騙了。有一次，某位大學者去參加一個宴會。由於他穿得非常簡樸，竟然不得其門而入。於是他就回家把最好的衣服穿上，他回到宴會，受到熱情的接待。

　　　admission〔ədˈmɪʃən〕*n.* 許可　　reception〔rɪˈsɛpʃən〕*n.* 接待

21.(A) *be simply dressed* 穿得很簡樸
(B)中的 dress up 是「盛裝」之意，不合句意；(C)中的 wear 是及物動詞，之後要接受詞,(D) be worn out 表「疲憊的」，不合句意。

22.(C) 本句是表達這位教授不得其門而「入」，故根據句意，應在空格中填入表「進去」的意思，(C)(D)均有此意，但(D) into 是介詞，之後必須有受詞 the party，而(C) inside 可做副詞用，故選(C)。

23.(B) (A) put up with 忍受　　　　(B) *put on* 穿上
(C) take off 脫下　　　　　(D) pull over 推翻

24.(C) 根據句意，他受到熱情招待，有「被動」的意思，故選(C)was given。(A)無此用法；(B)應改為was provided with;(D)意思不合。

In the course of dinner he did not eat *but* was talking to his clothes. The
　　　　25
host came and asked *what was the matter*. The scholar told him what hap-
　　　　　　　　　　　　　　26
pened. *Since* he was admitted only *for the sake of his dress*, he was talking
　　　　　　　　　　27
to his dress. The host regretted about it *and* sought the pardon of the
scholar. *Though* dress may be, *to some extent*, useful *to judge a*
　　　　　　　　　　　　28　　　　29
person, that *alone* will not be sufficient.
　　　　　　30

在用晚餐的過程中，他不吃東西，只對著衣服講話。主人過來問他怎麼回事。這位學者就把事情的經過告訴他。既然他只是因為衣著的緣故而得以入場，所以他就對著衣服說話。主人為此事感到抱歉，並且請求學者原諒。雖然衣著或多或少可以用來判斷一個人，但僅僅這樣是不夠的。

host 〔host〕 *n.* 主人　　*for the sake of* ～ 為了～的緣故
seek 〔sik〕 *v.* 請求（過去式為 sought〔sɔt〕）
sufficient 〔sə'fɪʃənt〕 *adj.* 足夠的

25.(D) *in the course of* ～ 在～的過程中　(A)意義　(B)案例　(C)事件

26.(B) 本空格在 asked 之後，應填入一名詞子句，而名詞子句若為間接問句，不須倒裝，選項中(A)(C)(D)均經過倒裝，故不合，(B)中的 what 作主詞，所以 was 本來就接在其後，並非倒裝句，故選(B)。

27.（B）根據句意，這位學者是因為穿著的緣故，才「被允許」進入會場，故選 (B)was admitted only，其中 admit 是表「准許進入」。
admit〔əd'mɪt〕v. 准許進入　adopt〔ə'dɑpt〕v. 採納

28.（A）根據句意，這位主人應該為此事感到抱歉才對，故選(A)。
sympathize〔'sɪmpə,θaɪz〕v. 同情

29.（D）*to some extent* 或多或少地（= *to some degree*）

30.（A）alone 當形容詞用，可置於所修飾的名詞或代名詞之後，表「僅僅」。

A long time ago people lived *mostly* out-of-doors. They noticed *that* plants, animals, insects, and birds sensed the coming *of a storm* sooner

31
than people did. All living things try to save their own lives, *so* they

　32　　　　　　　　　　　　　　　　33
look for shelter *just before a storm.*

　　　34

很久以前，人類大多居住在戶外。他們注意到，植物、動物、昆蟲及鳥類可以比人類更早察覺到暴風雨的來臨。所有的生物都試著拯救自己的生命，於是就在暴風雨來之前，尋找遮風避雨的地方。

sense〔sɛns〕v. 察覺　　shelter〔'ʃɛltɚ〕n. 避風雨之處

31.（B）依句意，指「時間」上的「早」，應用 soon，故選(B)。(A)指「程度」上的「容易」，(C)與(D)則指「速度」上的「快」，均不合句意。

32.（A）表一般的「事實」，應用現在簡單式。

33.（C）因兩子句之間為「因果」關係，後面一個子句表「結果」，故連接詞選(C) so。

34.（D）依句意應選(D)，*just before* ～「就在～之前」。(A)(B)(C)均無此用法。

When the people of long ago saw animals seeking shelter, they did, *too.*

　　　　　　　　　　　　　　　　　　　　　　　　　35
The things [*that* make up weather — the air pressure, the amount of water

　　　　　　　36
in the air, the temperature, and the wind] — have an effect *on plants*

　　　　　　　　　　　　　　　　　　　　　　　　　37
and animals.

　　以前的人看到動物在尋找避風雨的地方時，他們也會跟著找。所有構成天氣的事物——氣壓、空氣中的含水量、溫度、以及風——都對植物和動物有所影響。

　　＊ the air pressure … the wind 為插入語，補充說明前面的 the things。

35.（**A**）過去式助動詞 did 用以代表動詞 sought。

36.（**D**）依句意應選(D)，***make up***「構成」。(A)(B)(C)無此用法。

37.（**B**）***have an effect*** (up)***on*** ～　對～有影響

Their actions give clues to weather changes. The people *of long time ago* called these "weather signs." ***Those who knew*** how *to read the signs* were often as good as weather services, where *predicting is done with modern instruments*.

38

39

40

它們的動向暗示了天氣的變化。從前的人稱這些為「天氣預兆」。知道怎樣看懂這些預兆的人，通常跟氣象台一樣行，而氣象台的預測，則是由現代的儀器來完成的。

　　　　clue〔klu〕*n.* 線索；暗示　　　sign〔saɪn〕*n.* 預兆；徵候
　　　　weather services 氣象台；氣象中心　　predict〔prɪˈdɪkt〕*v.* 預測
　　　　instrument〔ˈɪnstrəmənt〕*n.* 儀器；工具

38.（**A**）因「天氣變化」有很多且各種不同的變化，故應以複數表之，且其前不加
　　　　定冠詞 the。

39.（**C**）依句意應選(C) how「如何」，表方法。

40.（**C**）此處的 where，相當於 at which，作關係副詞，引導形容詞子句，修飾前面
　　　　的 weather services。

Ⅳ、閱讀測驗

In some cultures, the act *of touching another person* is considered *very* intimate *and* is *therefore* reserved for people *who know each other very well*. *In the United States, for example*, young children are taught ***that*** it is rude *to stand too close to people*.

　　在某些文化裡，與別人觸碰的舉動被視爲很親密，因此，也只有彼此很熟悉對方的人，才會有這種舉動。例如在美國，大人會告訴小孩，站得離別人太近是不禮貌的。

> intimate〔ˈɪntəmɪt〕*adj.* 親密的
>
> reserve〔rɪˈzɝv〕*v.* 保留；專供　　rude〔rud〕*adj.* 無禮的

By the time they are adults, Americans have learned to feel *most* comfortable **when** *standing at about arm's length away from people to whom they are talking.*　**And** many Americans do not touch each other *with great frequency* **while** *talking* (this is *particularly* true of men).

到了長大成人，美國人已經學會了，當他站在離談話對象前一臂之遙處，他會覺得最自在。很多美國人在談話時都不會常常去碰觸對方（男士尤其如此）。

> adult〔əˈdʌlt, ˈædʌlt〕*n.* 成人　　comfortable〔ˈkʌmfɚtəbl〕*adj.* 舒適的
>
> length〔lɛŋkθ, lɛŋθ〕*n.* 長度　　frequency〔ˈfrikwənsɪ〕*n.* 頻率

In contrast, other cultures have more relaxed rules *regarding touching*. *For example*, it is usual for friends— *both men and women* — to embrace each other *when they meet.* **When** *they talk*, they *generally* stand closer *than Americans do*, **and** they touch each other *more often*. They are as much at ease doing this *as Americans are with more space between them.*

相反地，其他的文化在身體接觸方面的規範比較鬆。例如，不論是男是女，朋友見面時相互擁抱是很平常的事。他們談話時，通常站得比美國人近，也比較常碰觸對方。他們這麼做很自在，就像美國人保持距離一樣。

> ***in contrast*** 相反地　relaxed〔rɪˈlækst〕*adj.* 放鬆的
>
> regard〔rɪˈgɑrd〕*v.* 關於　embrace〔ɪmˈbres〕*v.* 擁抱　***at ease*** 安逸；自在

41. (**A**) 兩個人互碰對方可能被視爲
　　(A) 美國文化中的親密關係。　　(B) 所有不同文化中的無禮。
　　(C) 美國文化中的普通朋友關係。　　(D) 其他文化中非常不友善的表現。

42.（ D ）兩個人談話的禮貌性距離
  (A) 對美國文化而言，不是很重要。
  (B) 對美國文化而言，如果兩人有親密關係，就非常重要。
  (C) 對所有文化而言，都是一臂可及的距離。
  (D) 因文化不同而有差異。

43.（ B ）根據本文，不同的文化背景
  (A) 與人類的行為沒什麼關係。 (B) 影響人們交往的方式。
  (C) 顯示某一民族優於其他民族。 (D) 已產生相同的行為舉止。

What comes into your mind *when you think about robots*? Do you
imagine armies *of evil metal monsters* planning to take over the world?
Or, perhaps of mechanical men *who have been created as guards or soldiers*
by a mad genius? *Or* maybe you think of *man-like* robots *who act, think,*
and look like human beings.

  想到機器人，你會想到什麼？你會不會想像，有許多由邪惡的金屬怪物組成的
軍隊，正企圖征服世界？或者，這些軍隊是由機器人組成，有一位瘋狂的怪才把他
們創造成警衛或軍人？還是你會想到一些無論行為、思想、外貌都和真人一樣的機
器人。

  ＊ of mechanical men …之前省略了 you imagine armies。

  come into* one's *mind 使某人想起 robot〔'robət,'rɑb-〕 n. 機器人
  monster〔'monstɚ〕 n. 怪物 ***take over*** 接收；接管

In fact robots *like these* have more to do with science fiction films *than with real*
life. *In the real world* robots are machines *that do jobs* *which otherwise have to*
be done by people. Robots ***either*** operate *by themselves* *or under the control of a person*.
事實上，這些機器人和科幻電影的關係，要比和現實生活的關係來得密切。在現實
世界中，機器人就是機器，它們做那些不然就得由人們來做的工作。機器人可以自
動操作，或由人控制。

  ***have*~ *to do with*… 和…有關 otherwise〔'ʌðɚ,waɪz〕 adv. 不然的話
  operate〔'ɑpə,ret〕 v. 操作 ***under the control of*** 受~支配

In a car factory, *for example*, robot machinery can put together *and* paint car bodies. *On the sea bed* remote controlled underwater machines *with mechanical arms* can perform tasks *too difficult for divers*. Robot spacecraft can explore the solar system *and* send back information *about planets and stars*.

例如，在汽車工廠裡，機器人裝置可以組合與油漆車身。在海底，具有機械手臂的水底遙控機器，可以完成那些對潛水人員來說太過困難的工作。機械太空船可以探測太陽系，並傳回有關行星與恒星的訊息。

> machinery〔məˈʃinərɪ〕*n.* 機械裝置　　*put together* 組合
> remote controlled〔rɪˈmot kənˈtrold〕*adj.* 遙控的
> perform〔pɚˈfɔrm〕*v.* 做；完成　　diver〔ˈdaɪvɚ〕*n.* 潛水者
> spacecraft〔ˈspesˌkræft,-ˌkrɑft〕*n.* 太空船
> explore〔ɪkˈsplɔr,-ˈsplor〕*v.* 探測　　planet〔ˈplænɪt〕*n.* 行星

Many robots have computer brains. Some robots are fitted with cameras, sensors, *and* microphones *which enable them to see, to feel, and to hear*. *And* some robots can *even* produce electronic speech.

許多機器人具有電腦，有些機器人配備有照相機、感應裝置和麥克風，使它們能看、能感覺、能聽。有些機器人甚至能製造電子合成語言。

> *be fitted with* 裝備～　　sensor〔ˈsɛnsɚ,-sɔr〕*n.* 感應裝置
> microphone〔ˈmaɪkrəˌfon〕*n.* 擴音器；麥克風
> electronic〔ɪˌlɛkˈtrɑnɪk,ə-〕*adj.* 以電子裝置發音的

All this does not mean *that a robot can think and behave like a human being*. Present day robots have to be programmed *with a good deal of information before they can carry out even simple tasks*.

這些並不表示機器人可以像人一樣思考和行為，目前的機器人，即使在做簡單的工作前，也必須先設定程式，輸入許多訊息才行。

> program〔ˈprogræm〕*v.* 製作程式　　*carry out* 實行

44.(**D**) 現實生活中的機器人

    (A) 舉止可以像人類一樣 。   (B) 有能力控制世界 。

    (C) 可以擔任暴君的邪惡護衛 。   (D) 可以幫助我們做許多工作 。

45.(**A**) 根據這篇文章，下列有關現實世界中的機器人哪一項是不正確的？

    (A) 有些機器人像藝術家一樣富創造力 。

    (B) 有些機器人可以協助製造汽車 。

    (C) 有些機器人能看和聽 。   (D) 有些機器人能探測外太空 。

46.(**B**) 機器人能為人類完成許多工作，因為

    (A) 它們有智慧 。   (B) 它們儲存著電腦程式 。

    (C) 它們能模仿人類 。   (D) 它們有能力學習新事物 。

47.(**A**) 科幻電影中的機器人和現實生活的機器人主要差別在於

    (A) 智力 。   (B) 外表 。

    (C) 原料 。   (D) 大小 。

    mentality〔mɛnˈtælətɪ〕*n.* 智力；心性

Our lives are regulated *by many cycles*, some external, *like day,*
night, and seasons, **and** some internal, like the bodily signals *that tell*
us when to sleep, eat, be active, and so forth.

    我們的生命受週而復始的循環現象所調節，有些是外在的，像晝夜及四季；有些是內在的，像身體的一些訊號，告訴我們何時睡覺、吃飯、活動等等。

    regulate〔ˈrɛgjə,let〕*v.* 規定；調節   cycle〔ˈsaɪkl̩〕*n.* 循環
    external〔ɪkˈstɜnl̩〕*adj.* 外在的   internal〔ɪnˈtɜnl̩〕*adj.* 內在的
    and so forth 等等

When we travel long distances *east* **or** *west*, we are *rapidly* transported
into a different time zone. The external signs have changed **and** we discover, *for example,* **that** the sun is rising *when we expect to be asleep.*

當我們做東向或西向的長途旅行時，會快速地移進不同的時區。外界的訊號改變了，譬如，我們會發現，我們覺得應該是睡著的時刻，太陽卻昇起了。

east〔ist〕*adv.* 向東方地　　　west〔wɛst〕*adv.* 向西方地
rapidly〔'ræpɪdlɪ〕*adv.* 快速地
transport〔træns'port, -'pɔrt〕*v.* 運送；運輸
zone〔zon〕*n.* 區域　　　sign〔saɪn〕*n.* 跡象
discover〔dɪ'skʌvə〕*v.* 發現　　　expect〔ɪk'spɛkt〕*v.* 期望
asleep〔ə'slip〕*adj.* 睡著的

The body becomes confused *at the time change* **and** responds *by attempting to reset the internal clock to correspond with the new time zone.* The result is "jet lag," a condition *characterized by a mental and physical exhaustion **and** confusion.*

身體會因為時間改變而不知所措，接下來的反應是，試著重整生理時鐘，來配合新時區。結果會造成「時差症」，其特徵是，心理和身體上的疲乏和混亂。

confused〔kən'fjuzd〕*adj.* 混亂的
respond〔rɪ'spɑnd〕*v.* 反應　　　attempt〔ə'tɛmpt〕*v.* 嘗試
reset〔ri'sɛt〕*v.* 重整；重新放置　　　***internal clock*** 生理時鐘
correspond〔,kɔrə'spɑnd〕*v.* 配合　　　result〔rɪ'zʌlt〕*n.* 結果
jet lag 長時間快速噴射機旅行飛越時區所引起之生理節律上之障礙、疲倦、急躁等徵候；時差症
characterize〔'kærɪktə,raɪz〕*v.* 表特點；以～為特性
mental〔'mɛntḷ〕*adj.* 心理上
physical〔'fɪzɪkḷ〕*adj.* 身體的；生理的
exhaustion〔ɪg'zɔstʃən, ɛg-〕*n.* 疲倦
confusion〔kən'fjuʒən〕*n.* 混亂

Jet lag is a term *used to describe **what** happens **when** the body's internal clock is no longer matched with the external environment.*

「時差症」是一種術語，用來描述當人體的生理時鐘不再與外界環境配合時，所產生的徵狀。

> term〔tɝm〕n. 術語　　describe〔dɪˈskraɪb〕v. 描述
> **no longer** 不再　　match〔mætʃ〕v. 配合
> environment〔ɪnˈvaɪrənmənt〕n. 環境

48.(**C**) 我們的生命有種種形態，受控於
- (A) 外在世界的時間安排。
- (B) 我們身體的時間安排。
- (C) 外在與內在的時間安排。
- (D) 一年四季的不同心情。

49.(**D**) 我們會患「時差症」，當
- (A) 我們乘船到遠方旅遊。
- (B) 我們夜間搭噴射機。
- (C) 我們到很多不同的地方旅遊後，覺得很疲倦。
- (D) 內在與外在的周期性不一。

50.(**B**) 本文顯示「時差症」是
- (A) 身體的正常功能。
- (B) 身體適應的徵候。
- (C) 一種傳染病。
- (D) 一種精神病。

第二部分：非選擇題

Ⅰ、填空

"Fire is a good servant but a bad master." This is an old English saying. <u>What</u> does it mean? *At one time* people did not know how to <u>control</u> fire. *Then* they learned to <u>do</u> so. They also learned how to use it *to keep them warm*. They used it *to drive away animals*. They also learned how to cook food *with it*. Fire was their servant. It <u>did</u> things *for them*.

(標號 1 What、2 At one time、3 control、4 do、5 to keep them warm、6 to drive away animals、7 with it、8 did)

「火是很好的僕人，却是很糟的主人」，這是一句英文的諺語。它是什麼意思呢？曾經有一段時間，人類不懂得如何去控制火，後來他們學會了這麼做。他們也學會了用火來取暖，用火驅走野獸，同時學會用火煮飯。火是他們的僕役，替他們做很多事情。

> servant〔ˈsɝvənt〕n. 僕人

1. ***What*** *does it mean*？ 這是什麼意思？

2. ***At one time*** 曾經有一段時間

3. control （控制）

4. ***do so*** 用來代替前面的 control fire，以避免重覆。

5. ***keep*** *sb*. ***warm*** 取暖

6. ***drive away*** 趕走

7. with 可用來表示「用～」。

8. 表示「做事情」，要用 do things，此處是用在過去式，故 do 要改成 ***did***。

But sometimes a building catches fire. ***And*** the building may be destroyed
　　　　　　　　　　　　　　9
and people lose their homes, and even their lives. Fire is not the servant
　　　　　　　　10
then, It has become their master！

然而有時候建築物會起火，於是這棟建築物可能被毀壞，人們就失去了住所，甚
至性命。這個時候火就不是僕人，它成了人類的主人。

9. 表示「著火」或「起火」，要用 catch fire。本句因爲要和後面一句的時式一
　　致，故空格中塡入現在式 catches 。

10. lose （失去）

II、中譯英

1. 老實說，一直到昨天我才知道他已經去美國了。

　　Frankly speaking, it was not until yesterday that I knew he had
　　gone to the United States.

　＝ To be frank, not until yesterday did I know that he had gone to
　　the United States.

2. 首先，我要說明清楚，我並不反對你的意見。

$$\left\{ \begin{array}{l} \text{First} \\ \text{First of all} \\ \text{To begin with} \\ \text{In the first place} \end{array} \right\} , \text{ I want to make it clear that}$$

$$\text{I} \left\{ \begin{array}{l} \text{am not opposed to} \\ \text{do not} \left\{ \begin{array}{l} \text{oppose} \\ \text{object to} \end{array} \right. \end{array} \right\} \text{ your} \left\{ \begin{array}{l} \text{opinion.} \\ \text{idea.} \end{array} \right\}$$

Ⅲ、英文作文（參考範例）

Time

Lost time is never found again. *In my opinion, time is more precious than money. Why? Because when money is spent, we can earn it back. However, when time is gone, it will never return. This is the reason why we must value time. Now I know that I shouldn't waste time because even an hour is precious.*

Now I have a plan for using my time wisely. I have arranged my schedule so that I can save time. *Furthermore, I won't put off until tomorrow what can be done today. I will make full use of my time to do useful things. As students we must use our time well and not relax our efforts to engage in our studies so as to serve society and our nation in the future.*

＊ 本班考前強迫同學背誦之「萬用作文錦囊妙句」教材，
第八頁 " The Value of Time " 此次完全命中 81 日
大聯考作文題目 " Time "。

八十學年度大學暨獨立學院入學考試
英 文 試 題

第一部分：單一選擇題

I. **對話**（10％）：下面是一段日常生活中常見的對話，共有十個空格(1~10)，
　每個空格附有四個備選答案。請依照對話內容各選出一個最適當的答案，標
　示在「**答案卡**」上，每題答對得1分，答錯倒扣⅓分，不答不給分。

May : Sue, you've been to Hawaii, haven't you?

Sue : Yeah, I spent my winter vacation there with my parents last year.

May : I heard ___1___ .

Sue : Yes. It's just like a paradise.

May : My family are planning ___2___ . I'm really looking forward
　　　to it.

Sue : Oh great! ___3___ .

May : When's a good time to go?

Sue : Well, I wouldn't go in summer. It's kind of hot. It's mild
　　　in winter, but sometimes it can be wet. If you're lucky, ___4___ .
　　　When we're there, it rained for only one afternoon.

May : I think ___5___ . I don't like hot weather. And what would you
　　　recommend me ___6___ ?

Sue : First, you can go to the beach. Then, I think you can visit
　　　some of the other islands.

May : ___7___ . And besides going to the beach, what can we do on
　　　Oahu?

Sue : I think you can see a Hawaiian show. And ___8___ , there's an
　　　aquarium, which is very interesting.

May : What do you think of the sunset cruise off Waikiki?

Sue : Well, some people say it's fun, but ___9___ .

May : By the way, is it easy to get around on the island? Do you
　　　think we should rent a car?

Sue : ___10___ . Public transportation is pretty good, though. There're
　　　plenty of buses, and you can take a bus trip around the whole
　　　island for only 60 cents.

1. (A) it's quite dusty   (B) it's pretty deserted
   (C) it's very beautiful   (D) it's much polluted

2. (A) to leave Hawaii   (B) to invite some friends over
   (C) to get together sometime   (D) to go there next year

3. (A) You'll be there   (B) You'll see me
   (C) You'll love it   (D) You'll do your best

4. (A) you'll arrive on time   (B) you'll have nice weather
   (C) you'll see many things   (D) you'll meet a lot of people

5. (A) I'd like to go in winter   (B) I'd go there in summer
   (C) I'd be there anytime   (D) I'd go with my parents

6. (A) to do there   (B) to be there
   (C) to eat there   (D) to stay there

7. (A) I don't mind   (B) It sounds annoying
   (C) That's a good idea   (D) I don't understand it

8. (A) if you like old things
   (B) if you want to buy fashionable shoes
   (C) if you are fond of fresh flowers
   (D) if you wish to see colorful fish

9. (A) we enjoyed it a great deal   (B) we didn't like it very much
   (C) we took it several times   (D) we found it very pleasant

10. (A) You had better agree with me   (B) It's up to you
    (C) Leave it to me   (D) You should take a bus

Ⅱ. **綜合測驗**（20％）：下面有三段短文，共有二十個空格（11～30），每個空格附有四個備選答案。請仔細閱讀各段文章後，每個空格各選一個最適當的答案，標示在「**答案卡**」上。每題答對得1分，答錯倒扣⅓分，不答不給分。

    Jack was walking   11   the street when he saw a big dog. The dog looked very, very   12   . It kept on barking   13   Jack, so Jack stopped walking. Jack saw a woman   14   near the dog, so he walked up to her and said, " 15   , does your dog bite?" "No," the woman   16   , "my dog doesn't bite."   17   hearing this, Jack continued walking. Suddenly the dog jumped up   18   bit Jack. "Hey!" Jack   19   to the woman, "you said your dog doesn't bite!" "It   20   ," the woman said, "but that's not my dog!"

11. (A) above　　　　(B) over　　　　(C) at　　　　(D) down
12. (A) sad　　　　　(B) mean　　　　(C) just　　　　(D) fit
13. (A) at　　　　　(B) to　　　　　(C) on　　　　　(D) up
14. (A) stood　　　　(B) stands　　　(C) to stand　　(D) standing
15. (A) I'm sorry　　　　　　　　　(B) Excuse me
　　(C) I beg your pardon　　　　　(D) Please forgive me
16. (A) remembered　(B) requested　(C) replied　　　(D) refused
17. (A) On　　　　　(B) From　　　　(C) In　　　　　(D) With
18. (A) then　　　　(B) but　　　　(C) thus　　　　(D) and
19. (A) confirmed　　(B) complained　(C) commanded　(D) conveyed
20. (A) does　　　　(B) did　　　　(C) didn't　　　(D) doesn't

　　For years Italians have suffered with one of the ___21___ postal and telegraph services in Europe. To show ___22___ incompetent the service is, Giorgio Benvenuto, secretary-general of the Italian Labor Union, ___23___ a test a few weeks ago. Benvenuto sent a telegram ___24___ the fourth floor in his office building to an office on the third floor. The telegram was ___25___ four days later.

21. (A) easiest　　　(B) fastest　　　(C) greatest　　(D) slowest
22. (A) such　　　　(B) how　　　　(C) as　　　　　(D) what
23. (A) contested　　(B) constructed　(C) conducted　(D) contained
24. (A) to　　　　　(B) from　　　　(C) in　　　　　(D) at
25. (A) delivered　　(B) canceled　　(C) delayed　　(D) advanced

　　The modern English name didn't come into common use ___26___ the late Middle Ages. Before that, only one name was ___27___ to a person. We now call ___28___ the first name. Because many people received ___29___ first name, they were additionally differentiated by another name, now called the last name. Many of the last names were passed down in ___30___ families.

26. (A) until　　　　(B) with　　　　(C) for　　　　(D) while
27. (A) sent　　　　(B) made　　　　(C) used　　　　(D) given
28. (A) this　　　　(B) which　　　　(C) person　　　(D) family
29. (A) many a　　　(B) the only　　　(C) the same　　(D) more than
30. (A) typical　　　(B) individual　　(C) entire　　　(D) particular

II. **閱讀測驗**（30%）：下面有四段短文，共有十五個題目（31－45），每題附有四個備選答案。請仔細閱讀後，把每題最適當的一個答案標示在「**答案卡**」。每題答對得2分，答錯倒扣⅔分，不答不給分。

One young woman, an only child, chose to live in a college dormitory in order to better learn to live with others. She considered dormitory living to be an invaluable experience. She said that someone "living in the dormitory becomes more involved in college activities. People depend on you to do more, and so do you. You learn to become involved." She went on to say, "You don't have a whole lot of privacy with all those people in one dormitory, but you learn how to get along. After a while, it's like having one big family."

31. The only child chose to live in a college dormitory because
   (A) she would like to be more closely connected with people.
   (B) she found it more convenient to go to classes and the library.
   (C) she would like to enjoy more freedom and independence.
   (D) her family was too big and complicated and she didn't like it.

32. According to the only child, the students living in the dormitory
   (A) learned to cherish their privacy.
   (B) considered dormitory life unbearable.
   (C) shared many common experiences.
   (D) thought little of their experiences.

Drunken driving has become a serious form of murder. Every day about twenty-six Americans on the average are killed by drunk drivers. Heavy drinking used to be an acceptable part of the American masculine image, but the drunken killer has recently caused so many tragedies that public opinion is no longer tolerant.

Twenty states in the United States have raised the legal drinking age to 21, reversing a trend of 1960s to reduce it to 18. After New Jersey lowered it to 18, the number of people killed by 18-to-20-year-old drivers doubled, so the state recently upped it back to 21. Some states are also punishing bars for serving customers too many drinks. As the casualties continue to occur daily, some Americans are even beginning to suggest a national prohibition of alcohol. Reformers, however, think that legal prohibition and raising the drinking age will have little effect unless accompanied by educational programs to help young people develop responsible attitudes about drinking.

33. Drunken driving has become a major problem in America because
    (A) most murderers are heavy drinkers.
    (B) many Americans drink too much.
    (C) most drivers are too young.
    (D) many traffic accidents are caused by heavy drinking.

34. What is the public opinion regarding heavy drinking?
    (A) It's a manly image.
    (B) It can create a relaxing and happy atmosphere.
    (C) Fewer and fewer people can stand it.
    (D) People should be careful in choosing the right drink.

35. According to reformers, the best way to solve the problem of drunken driving is to
    (A) specify the amount drivers can drink.
    (B) couple education with legal measures.
    (C) forbid liquor drinking.
    (D) raise the drinking age.

　　Ten years ago, there were more than 1.3 million elephants in Africa. Over the past ten years, that number has been cut down to around 600,000. African elephants are hunted for their valuable ivory tusks. Most have been killed by poachers. Poachers are hunters who kill animals illegally. An adult elephant eats as much as 300 pounds a day. In their search for food, elephants often move great distances. When they cannot find the grasses they prefer, they may strip the land of trees.

　　Today, the area in which elephant herds live is much smaller than it used to be. Many areas in their path have been turned into farms. And some elephants have been killed by farmers for trampling their crops.

　　What can we do here in our country about a threatened animal that lives so far away? Our government has passed a law to protect it. People cannot import or bring in items made from ivory or any part of the elephant's body.

　　Most countries throughout the world have also stopped ivory imports. It is hoped that the ban on the sale of ivory will help save the African elephant. But the world's largest land animal needs other help. The countries where these animals live are often poor and unable to manage the herds. If the elephant is to survive, this animal is going to need our support for many years to come.

36. The number of elephants in Africa today is
   (A) the same as that ten years ago.
   (B) more than that ten years ago.
   (C) a little less than half of that in 1981.
   (D) a little more than half of that in 1981.

37. African elephants have been killed mainly because
   (A) they eat a lot.
   (B) they have beautiful tusks.
   (C) poachers kill them for fun.
   (D) there are too many of them.

38. The areas where African elephants live are much smaller today because
   (A) they tend to live in herds.
   (B) there are not so many of them today.
   (C) many of these areas have been turned into farms.
   (D) farmers have been killing them to save their crops.

39. It is mentioned in the article that our country has
   (A) officially stopped ivory imports.
   (B) banned the killing of elephants in Africa.
   (C) threatened the elephants that live far away.
   (D) helped the African countries where elephants live.

40. Which of the following statements is true?
   (A) Poachers have a license to hunt for animals.
   (B) Elephants do a lot of good for the farmers in Africa.
   (C) We live too far away to help save the African elephant.
   (D) The African elephant needs the world's support for its survival.

Lincoln College Preparatory Academy, a secondary school for sixth to twelfth graders in Kansas City, Missouri, U.S.A., is proving a little money can grow a long way. About 45 of the 60 staff members at this school are giving $10 of their salaries each month to a college fund for Lincoln graduates who want to become teachers.

"Our area is short of teachers," explains Shirley Johnson, a math teacher who started the fund. "I know it wasn't going to get better unless we did something about it ourselves." Lincoln graduates can be considered for awards if they "maintain a B-or-above average in high school and a C-plus or above in college," says Johnson. "And they have to major in education and want to teach in Kansas City for two years."

Students who change their major from education in college can pay back the award later. If the fund—expected to reach $7,000 or more by May—proves successful, Johnson will introduce her program to other schools later on.

41. The secondary school in Kansas City is proving that
    (A) education funds can be started with small sums.
    (B) money can make anything happen.
    (C) money is more important than education.
    (D) good teachers always have chances to get awards.

42. The total amount of the fund raised each month is about
    (A) seven hundred dollars.
    (B) six hundred dollars.
    (C) five hundred dollars.
    (D) ten dollars.

43. The staff members have contributed to the college fund because
    (A) they want to encourage their graduates to come back to teach.
    (B) they think teaching is a rewarding profession.
    (C) they expect their graduates to become famous scholars.
    (D) their salaries are high and their living expenses are low.

44. One of the conditions for a student to receive the education award is:
    (A) he must be a graduate of a college.
    (B) he must be a graduate of Lincoln College Preparatory Academy.
    (C) he must have outstanding grades in high school and college.
    (D) he must want to teach in Kansas City for at least one year.

45. Who has to pay back the award？
　　(A) Those who maintain a B average in high school.
　　(B) Those who maintain a C-plus average in college.
　　(C) Those who have earned enough money for their education.
　　(D) Those who no longer major in education.

第二部分：非選擇題

　I. 中譯英（20％）

　　下面一段中文短文共含五個句子，請譯成正確通順而達意的英文。每句4分，答錯不倒扣。答案請寫在「**非選擇題試卷**」上，同時務必標示題號。

(1) 我生長在鄉下的一個小村落。

(2) 那時，我家附近有一條清澈的小溪。

(3) 我們常在夏天到那裡游泳、釣魚。

(4) 現在溪水髒得魚都不能活了。

(5) 不知道甚麼時候才能再見到童年的美景。

　II. 英文作文（20％）

　　寫一篇有關鐘或錶的短文，分成兩段：第一段談鐘或錶對我們生活的重要性；第二段談你最喜歡的一個鐘或錶。文章寫在「**非選擇題試卷**」上，長度以不超過100個單字為原則。

　　評分標準：內容4分、組織4分、文法4分、用字遣詞4分、拼字、大小寫及標點符號4分。

80年大學聯考英文試題詳解

第一部分：單一選擇題

I、對話

May： Sue, you've been to Hawaii, haven't you？

Sue： Yeah, I spent my winter vacation there *with my parents last year*.

May： I heard *it's very beautiful*.
　　　　　　　　　　　　1

Sue： Yes. It's just like a paradise.

May： My family are planning to go there next year. I'm *really* looking
　　　　　　　　　　　　　　　　2
　　　forward to it.

Sue： Oh great！ You'll love it.
　　　　　　　　　3

"梅：蘇，你去過夏威夷，對不對？

　蘇：是啊！去年我和父母在那裡度過寒假。

　梅：我聽說那裡很美。

　蘇：是啊，簡直像是人間樂園。

　梅：我們家打算明年要去那裡。我真地好盼望那一天的來到。

　蘇：噢，太棒了，你會喜歡那兒的。"

　　　Hawaii〔hə'waɪ‧i〕*n.* 夏威夷
　　　paradise〔'pærə,daɪs〕*n.* 天堂；樂園
　　　look forward to～ 期待～

1.（C） 根據下一句 Sue 回答 Yes. It's just like a paradise. 可以得知May
　　　　是談到夏威夷的風景很美，故選(C)。

2.（D） May 向 Sue 詢問夏威夷之旅的事，並且說她很期望那一天的來到，可
　　　　見她的家人也打算去夏威夷，故選(D)。

3.（C） Sue 說 Oh great！表示她認為May 要去夏威夷是件好事，根據句意，
　　　　本空格應選(C)You'll love it.

May : When's a good time to go?

Sue : Well, I wouldn't go in summer. It's *kind of* hot. It's mild in

winter, but sometimes it can be wet. If you're lucky, you'll have
<u>nice weather</u>. *When we're there*, it rained for only one afternoon.

May : I think *I'd like to go in winter*. I don't like hot weather. And
5

what would you recommend me <u>to do there</u>?
6

Sue : First, you can go to the beach. *Then*, I think you can visit some

of the other islands.

May : <u>That's a good idea</u>. *And besides going to the beach*, what can we
7

do on Oahu?

Sue : I think you can see a Hawaiian show. And *if you wish to see*
8

colorful fish, there's an aquarium, *which is very interesting*.

"梅：什麼時候去比較好？
蘇：我不會夏天的時候去。夏天天氣變熱的，冬天天氣很溫和,但有時候很會下
   雨。你們如果運氣好的話，會遇到好天氣。我們在那裏的時候，就只有一個
   下午會下雨。
梅：我想我會喜歡冬天去,我不喜歡炎熱的天氣。你要建議我在那兒做些什麼事呢?
蘇：首先，你們可以去海邊，然後，我想你們可以去其他島嶼玩。
梅：這是個好主意。除了去海邊以外，我們在歐胡島還可以做什麼？
蘇：我想你們可以去看一場夏威夷秀。另外，如果你喜歡看彩色魚，那兒有一個
   水族館，非常有趣。"

> ***kind of*** 頗為   wet〔wɛt〕*adj.* 多雨的
> recommend〔ˌrɛkə'mɛnd〕*v.* 建議；推薦
> Oahu〔o'ɑhu〕*n.* 歐胡島（夏威夷第三大島）
> aquarium〔ə'kwɛrɪəm〕*n.* 水族館

4. (B) Sue 在本空格的前後文都在談天氣，故選(B)。

5. (A) May 在下一句說她不喜歡熱天氣，根據此句意，本空格應選(A)。

6.（ **A** ）本句中的what 必須要做之後的不定詞片語中的受詞,在選項中只有(A)(C)
符合此條件，而(C)不符合句意，故選(A)。

7.（ **C** ）對別人的建議表示肯定，可以說 That's a good idea.

8.（ **D** ）本句中提到水族館，所以應選(D)才符合句意。

May : What do you think of the sunset cruise off Waikiki?

Sue : Well, some people say it's fun, but <u>we didn't like it very much.</u>
9

May : By the way, is it easy to get around on the island? Do you

think we should rent a car?

Sue : <u>It's up to you.</u> Public transportation is pretty good, though.
10

There're plenty of buses, ***and*** you can take a bus trip around

the whole island for only 60 cents.

" 梅：你覺得黃昏乘船遊懷基基外海怎麼樣？

蘇：嗯，有些人說很好玩，但是我們不太喜歡。

梅：順便一提的是，環島的交通方便嗎？你覺得我們應該租車嗎？

蘇：那要看你們自己了，不過那兒的公共運輸很不錯，公車很多，你只要花六

毛錢，就可以搭巴士環遊全島。"

cruise〔kruz〕*n.* 乘船巡遊　　off〔ɔf〕*prep.* 在…的海面上
Waikiki〔'waɪ,kiki〕*n.* 懷基基（夏威夷海灘）
transportation〔,trænspɚ'teʃən〕*n.* 運輸
though〔ðo〕*adv.* 但是（置於句尾）

9.（ **B** ）本空格之前有連接詞but,表語意的轉折，故選(B)。

10.（ **B** ）It's up to you. 這就隨你決定了。(C)Leave it to me. 這件事讓我來。

II、綜合測驗

Jack was walking <u>down</u> the street ***when*** *he saw a big dog.*
11
The dog looked very, very <u>mean.</u> It kept on barking <u>at</u> Jack, ***so*** Jack
1213
stopped walking. Jack saw a woman <u>standing</u> near the dog, ***so*** he walked
14
up to her and said, " <u>Excuse me,</u> does your dog bite?" " No, " the
15
woman <u>replied,</u> "my dog doesn't bite."
16

　　"傑克走在街上，他看見一隻大狗，這隻狗看起來非常非常不懷好意，牠不停地向傑克吠，所以傑克停下來不走了。傑克看到一位女士站在那隻狗的旁邊，所以他就走上去並且說：「對不起，請問你的狗會不會咬人？」這位女士說：「不會，我的狗不咬人。」"

　　　　keep on V-ing 不停地～

11. (**D**) down〔daʊn〕*prep.* 沿著
　　　　(A) above 在～之上　　(B) over 在～之下

12. (**B**) mean〔min〕*adj.* 不懷好意的
　　　　(A) sad 沮喪的　　(C) just 公正的　　(D) fit 健康的

13. (**A**) bark ***at*** ～　對著～吠

14. (**D**) 感官動詞之後，可以用現在分詞或原形動詞作受詞補語，本題選項中只有現在分詞，故選(D)。

15. (**B**) 表示要麻煩別人或請人幫忙時，可以先說 Excuse me，故選(B)。

16. (**C**) reply〔rɪ'plaɪ〕*v.* 回答
　　　　(A)想起　　(B)要求　　(D)拒絕

　　On hearing this, Jack continued walking. *Suddenly* the dog jumped
　　　　17
up ***and*** bit Jack. "Hey!" Jack complained to the woman, "you said *your*
　　18　　　　　　　　　　　19
dog doesn't bite!" "It doesn't," the woman said, "*but* that's not my
　　　　　　　　　　20
dog!"

　　"傑克一聽到這句話，就繼續向前走。突然間那隻狗跳起來咬傑克，傑克於是向那位女士抱怨：「你說你的狗不會咬人的！」這位女士回答：「牠的確不咬人，但是那隻並不是我的狗。」"

17. (**A**) ***on V-ing*** 一…就～

18. (**D**) 本空格需要連接詞來連接 jumped up 和 bit，選項中只有(B)(D)是連接詞，根據句意，應選(D)。

19.（ **B** ）　complain〔kəm'plen〕*v.* 抱怨
　　　　(A)證實　　(C)命令　　(D)表達

20.（ **D** ）該女士說她的狗不會咬人，這是一種常態，故用現在簡單式。

For years Italians have suffered with one of the slowest postal and
（21）
telegraph services in Europe.　To show *how incompetent the service is*,
（22）
Giorgio Benvenuto, secretary-general of the Italian Labor Union, conducted a test *a few weeks ago.*　Benvenuto sent a telegram *from the*
（23）　　　　　　　　　　　　　　　　　　　　　　　　　（24）
fourth floor in his office building to an office on the third floor.
The telegram was delivered *four days later.*
（25）

　　"多年來義大利人一直忍受著歐洲最遲緩的郵政和電報服務。為了要顯示這項
服務業是如何地無能，義大利勞工局秘書長班凡魯道幾週前做了一次試驗。班凡魯
道從他辦公大樓的四樓發出一封電報，寄到三樓的一間辦公室。結果這封電報四天
後才送到。"

　　　　　　postal〔'postḷ〕*adj.* 郵政的　　　telegraph〔'tɛlə,græf〕*n.* 電報
　　　　　　telegram〔'tɛlə,græm〕*n.* 電報
　　　　　　incompetent〔ɪn'kɑmpətənt〕*adj.* 無能的
　　　　　　secretary-general *n.* 秘書長

21.（ **D** ）　slowest　最遲緩的
　　　　(A)最容易的　　(B)最快速的　　(C)最偉大的

22.（ **B** ）本空格需要一連接詞，來連接後面的子句，此連接詞同時須為副詞，修飾
　　　　之後的形容詞 incompetent，符合此條件者只有 how，故選(B)。

23.（ **C** ）　***conduct***〔kən'dʌkt〕*v.* 處理；指導
　　　　contest〔kən'tɛst〕*v.* 競爭
　　　　construct〔kən'strʌkt〕*v.* 建造
　　　　contain〔kən'ten〕*v.* 包含

24.（ **B** ）　***from*** … to～　從…到～

25.（ **A** ）　deliver〔dɪ'lɪvə〕*v.* 投遞
　　　　(B)取消　　(C)延後　　(D)使前進

The modern English name didn't come into common use <u>until the late Middle Ages</u>. *Before that*, only one name was <u>given</u> to a person. We
26, 27

now call <u>this</u> the first name. ***Because*** *many people received the same first name*, they were *additionally* differentiated by another name, *now called the last name*. Many of the last names were passed down *in in-dividual families*.
28, 29, 30

"現代的英文名字，要到中世紀末，才被人廣為使用。在那之前，一個人只給一個名字，我們現在稱之為「名」。因為很多人都有相同的名，所以他們就用另一個名來另外區分，這個名現在被稱為「姓」。許多姓在個自的家庭中被傳承下來。"

> ***come into use*** 被使用起來　additionally〔əˈdɪʃənḷɪ〕*adv.* 另外地
> differentiate〔͵dɪfəˈrɛnʃɪ͵et〕*v.* 區分

26.(**A**)　***not ~ until*** … 直到…才~

27.(**D**)　根據句意和文法，應選(D)被給予。(A) be sent to sb. 被送給某人，(B) be made 之後應接不定詞 to V，(C) be used to＋(代)名詞表「習慣於~」，都不合。

28.(**A**)　根據句意，用 this 代替前句中的 only one name，以避免重複。

29.(**C**)　由後面的 differentiated 可知，應選(C)相同的。(A)許多的，(B)唯一的，(D)多過，都與句意不合。

30.(**B**)　由 differentiated 可知，應選(B)個自的。許多同學選(D)特別的，在此不合上下文句意。

Ⅲ、閱讀測驗

One young woman, an only child, chose to <u>live in a college dormitory in order to better learn to live with others</u>. She considered dormitory living to be an invaluable experience.

"一個年輕的女孩，又是獨生女，為了學習與人相處之道，而選擇住進大學宿舍。她認為住宿生活是非常珍貴的經驗。"

> dormitory〔ˈdɔrmə͵torɪ〕*n.*（大學等的）宿舍
> invaluable〔ɪnˈvæljəbḷ〕*adj.* 非常貴重的

She said ***that*** someone " *living in the dormitory* becomes more involved in college activities. People depend on you to do more, ***and*** so do you. You learn to become involved."

" 她說:「住在宿舍裏,可以參與更多的大學活動,大家靠你幫忙,你也靠大家的幫忙,你可學習如何去積極參與。」"

　　　　　　involve〔ɪnˈvɑlv〕*v.* 捲入　　　***be involved in*** 參與;涉入

She went on to say, " You don't have a whole lot of privacy with all those people *in one dormitory,* ***but*** you learn how to get along. *After a while,* it's like having one big family."

她繼續說道:「雖然和許多人同住在宿舍裏,你無法享有太多隱私,但你可學習如何與人相處,不久之後,大家就會像是一家人一樣了。」

　　　　　　privacy〔ˈpraɪvəsɪ〕*n.* 隱私　　　***get along*** 過日子;和好相處

31. (**A**) 這獨生女選擇住進大學宿舍,因為
　　　 (A)她希望多和大家接觸。 (B)她發現上課和去圖書館都更方便。
　　　 (C)她想享有更多的自由和獨立。(D)她的家庭太大又太複雜,她不喜歡。
　　　 connect〔kəˈnɛkt〕*v.* 連接;接觸
　　　 complicated〔ˈkɑmpləˌketɪd〕*adj.* 複雜的

32. (**C**) 根據這獨生女所說的,住在宿舍裏的學生
　　　 (A)學會了珍惜他們的隱私。 (B)無法忍受住宿生活。
　　　 (C)分享許多共同的經驗。(D)認為他們的經驗微不足道。
　　　 cherish〔ˈtʃɛrɪʃ〕*v.* 珍愛　　unbearable〔ʌnˈbɛrəbl̩〕*adj.* 不堪忍受的
　　　 think little of 輕視

　　Drunken driving has become a serious form of murder. *Every day* about twenty-six Americans *on the average* are killed by drunk drivers. Heavy drinking used to be an acceptable part of the American masculine image, ***but*** the drunken killer has *recently* caused *so* many tragedies *that public opinion is no longer tolerant.*

"酒後開車已經成爲一種嚴重的謀殺行爲，每天平均約有二十六個美國人被酒後開車的人撞死。從前，美國人常將酒量好視爲男子氣概的象徵，但近來由於酒後肇事之多，使得大衆輿論再也無法忍受。"

on the average 平均　　masculine ['mæskjəlɪn] *adj.* 有男子氣概的
public opinion 輿論　　tolerant ['tɑlərənt] *adj.* 容忍的

Twenty states *in the United States* have raised the legal drinking age to 21, reversing a trend of 1960s *to reduce it to 18*, *After New Jersey lowered it to 18*, the number of people *killed by 18-to-20-year-old drivers* doubled, *so* the state *recently* upped it back to 21. Some states are *also* punishing bars *for serving customers too many drinks*.

"美國有二十個州已將可以喝酒的法定年齡提高到二十一歲，一反六十年代將年齡降低到十八歲的趨勢。在紐澤西州將法定年齡降低到十八歲之後，被十八到二十歲的年輕人開車撞死的人數增加了一倍，所以該州最近又將它提高回二十一歲。有些州同時還對供應顧客過多酒的酒吧，施與處罰。"

reverse [rɪ'vɝs] *v.* 顛倒；改變　　trend [trɛnd] *n.* 趨勢

As the casualties continue to occur daily, some Americans are even beginning to suggest a national prohibition of alcohol. Reformers, **however**, think **that** legal prohibition and raising the drinking age will have little effect *unless accompanied by educational programs to help young people develop responsible attitudes about drinking.*

"由於每天仍不斷有傷亡事故發生，有些美國人甚至開始主張實施全國性的禁酒。然而，改革者却認爲，除非學校課程能配合，幫助年輕人對喝酒建立起負責任的態度，否則立法禁酒與提高喝酒的法定年齡，成效都不大。"

* unless 所引導的子句，在句意明確時，可省略主詞和 be 動詞，本句中是省略了 legal prohibition and raising the drinking age are。

casualty ['kæʒʊəltɪ] *n.* 傷亡事故
prohibition [,proə'bɪʃən] *n.* 禁酒　　alcohol ['ælkə,hɔl] *n.* 酒
accompany [ə'kʌmpənɪ] *v.* 伴隨

33.（**D**）在美國，酒後開車已經成為一個重大問題，是因為
　　(A) 大多數的殺人凶手都酗酒。
　　(B) 許多美國人飲酒過量。
　　(C) 大多數開車的人都太年輕。
　　(D) 許多交通事故是由喝酒過多所引起。

34.（**C**）輿論對酗酒的看法如何？
　　(A) 那是男子氣概的象徵。
　　(B) 它能創造輕鬆快樂的氣氛。
　　(C) 越來越少人能夠忍受。
　　(D) 人們應該謹慎地選擇合適的酒。

35.（**B**）根據改革者的看法，解決酒後開車問題的最佳辦法是
　　(A)明定開車者的飲酒量。(B)教育與法令相互配合。(C)禁酒。
　　(D) 提高喝酒的年齡。
　　couple～with… 將～和…連在一起

Ten years ago, there were more than 1.3 million elephants in Africa. *Over the past ten years*, that number has been cut down to around 600,000. African elephants are hunted *for their valuable ivory tusks*. Most have been killed by poachers. Poachers are hunters *who kill animals illegally*. An adult elephant eats *as much as* 300 pounds a day. *In their search for food*, elephants often move great distances. *When they cannot find the grasses they prefer*, they may strip the land of trees.

　　"十年前，非洲有一百三十多萬頭大象，過去十年間，這個數字已經減少到六十萬頭左右。非洲象因為珍貴的象牙而遭捕獵，大多數都是被偷獵者所殺，偷獵者就是非法捕殺動物的獵人。成年的大象每天要吃多達三百磅的食物。牠們尋找食物時，通常長途跋涉。當牠們找不到喜歡的草地時，可能將地上樹木的葉子啃光。"

　　cut down 減少　　ivory〔'aɪvərɪ〕*n.* 象牙
　　tusk〔tʌsk〕*n.*（象等的）長牙
　　poacher〔'potʃɚ〕*n.* 偷獵者
　　strip～of… 將～的…剝光

Today, the area *in which elephant herds live* is *much* smaller *than* it used to be. Many areas *in their path* have been turned into farms. *And* some elephants have been killed by farmers *for trampling their crops*.

「今天，象群生存的地區比過去小得多。牠們活動的地區很多都被闢爲農田，有些大象因爲踐踏農作物而被農人殺死。」

herd〔hɝd〕*n.* 獸群　　trample〔'træmpḷ〕*v.* 踐踏

What can we do here in our country about a threatened animal *that lives so far away*? Our government has passed a law *to protect it*. People cannot import or bring in items *made from ivory or any part of the elephant's body*.

「在國內，我們能爲距我們如此遙遠，飽受威脅的動物做些什麼呢？我們的政府已通過一項法令來保護大象。凡是象牙製品或是取自大象身上任何部位的製品，都不可以進口或攜帶入境。」

Most countries *throughout the world* have also stopped ivory imports. It is hoped *that* the ban on the sale of ivory will help save the African elephant. *But* the world's largest land animal needs other help. The countries *where these animals live* are often poor and unable to manage the herds. *If the elephant is to survive*, this animal is going to need our support for many years *to come*.

「全世界大多數國家都禁止象牙進口，希望象牙交易的禁令對挽救非洲象能有所幫助。但這種世界上最大的陸上動物還需要其他援助。這些動物居住的國家通常很貧窮，無法照顧這些象群。大象如果要存活，未來許多年仍需要我們的援助。」

ban〔bæn〕*n.* 禁令

36.（ **C** ） 現在非洲象的數目
　　　　(A) 和十年前一樣。　　　　　　(B) 比十年前多。
　　　　(C) 比一九八一年的半數還少。　(D) 比一九八一年的半數稍多。

37.（ **B** ） 非洲象被獵殺的主因在於
　　　　(A) 牠們的食量大。　　　　　　(B) 牠們有美麗的象牙。
　　　　(C) 偷獵者爲了好玩而獵殺牠們。 (D) 牠們的數量太多。

38.（ **C** ） 今天，非洲象居住的地區縮小了許多，原因是
　　　　(A) 牠們性喜群居。
　　　　(B) 牠們現在的數量沒那麼多。
　　　　(C) 這些地區有許多被闢爲農田。
　　　　(D) 農人不斷捕殺牠們，以挽救作物。

39.（ **A** ） 文中提到，我們國家已經
　　　　(A) 正式禁止象牙進口。
　　　　(B) 禁止殺戮非洲象。
　　　　(C) 威脅了居住在遙遠地方的大象。
　　　　(D) 幫助象群所在的非洲國家。

40.（ **D** ） 下列敘述何者正確？
　　　　(A) 偷獵者擁有獵捕物的執照。
　　　　(B) 大象對非洲農人的用處很大。
　　　　(C) 我們住得太遠了，無法幫忙挽救非洲象。
　　　　(D) 非洲象需要世界的援助，以維持生存。

　　　　Lincoln College Preparatory Academy, a secondary school for sixth to twelfth graders in Kansas City, Missouri, U.S.A., is proving *a little money can grow a long way.* About 45 *of the 60 staff members at this school* are giving $10 of their salaries *each month* to a college fund *for Lincoln graduates* **who** *want to become teachers.*

　　" 林肯大學預備學院是一所位於美國密蘇里州堪薩斯城，供六年級到十二年級生就讀的中學，這所學校證明一點小錢也可以做大事。這所中學的六十名教職員中，約有四十五名每月捐出薪水中的十塊錢，為想成為老師的林肯學院畢業生，成立大學教育基金。"

> preparatory 〔prɪˈpɛrəˌtorɪ〕 adj. 預備的
> academy 〔əˈkædəmɪ〕 n. 學院；（比 university 下一級的）專科學校
> secondary 〔ˈsɛkənˌdɛrɪ〕 adj. 中等的（教育、學校等）
> fund 〔fʌnd〕 n. 基金

"Our area is short of teachers," explains Shirley Johnson, a math teacher *who started the fund*. "I know *it wasn't going to get better unless we did something about it ourselves*." Lincoln graduates can be considered for awards *if they "maintain a B-or-above average in high school and a C-plus or above in college*," says Johnson. "*And* they have to major in education *and* want to teach in Kansas City for two years."

　　"「我們這裡非常缺老師，」發起這項基金的數學老師莎莉·強生解釋道，「我知道除非我們自己採取行動，否則情況不會好轉。」強生老師又說，只要林肯學院的畢業生，「高中平均成績維持在B以上，大學成績在C＋以上，而且必須主修教育，願意到堪薩斯城教書二年者，就有機會獲得獎學金。」"

> award 〔əˈwɔrd〕 n. 獎學金；獎品
> average 〔ˈævərɪdʒ〕 n. 平均分數　　*major in* 主修
> education 〔ˌɛdʒʊˈkeʃən〕 n. 教育學

Students *who change their major from education in college* can pay back the award *later*. *If the fund — expected to reach $7,000 or more by May — proves successful*, Johnson will introduce her program to other schools *later on*.

"在大學中，想改變主修，不唸教育的學生，可在稍後將這筆獎學金退回。如果這項基金——預計在五月前能募達七千美元以上——能成功，強生老師將在日後把她的計畫推廣到別的學校。"

41.（**A**）堪薩斯城的這所中學證明

　　(A) 教育基金可從很小的金額開始募集。

　　(B) 有錢可使鬼推磨。（有錢天下無難事。）

　　(C) 金錢比教育重要。

　　(D) 好老師總是有機會獲得獎金。

　　sum〔sʌm〕*n.* 數額

42.（**C**）這筆基金每個月募集的總額大約是

　　(A) 七百元。(B) 六百元。(C)五百元。(D)十元。

　　total〔'totl〕*adj.* 總共的

43.（**A**）學校教職員捐款給大學教育基金，是因為

　　(A) 他們想鼓勵本校畢業生，回到母校教書。

　　(B) 他們認為教書是一種有所報酬的職業。

　　(C) 他們希望本校畢業生能成為知名學者。

　　(D) 他們的薪水高，但生活開支却很少。

　　contribute〔kən'trɪbjut〕*v.* 捐贈；貢獻

　　rewarding〔rɪ'wɔrdɪŋ〕*adj.* 有所報酬的

　　expense〔ɪk'spɛns〕*n.* 費用；開支

44.（**B**）學生能獲教育獎學金的條件之一是：

　　(A) 他必須是大學畢業生。

　　(B) 他必須是林肯大學預備學院的畢業生。

　　(C) 他必須在高中及大學中有傑出的成績。

　　(D) 他必須願意在堪薩斯城，至少教一年書。

　　outstanding〔aut'stændɪŋ〕*adj.* 傑出的

45.（**D**）誰必須退回這筆獎學金？

　　(A) 高中平均成績保持B的學生。

　　(B) 大學平均成績保持C+的學生。

　　(C) 已經賺足教育費用的學生。

　　(D) 不再主修教育學的學生。

第二部分、非選擇題

I、中譯英

1. 我生長在鄉下的一個小村落。

 I grew up in a small village in the country.

2. 那時，我家附近有一條清澈的小溪。

 At that time, near our house was a clean stream.

 ＊ near our house 在此做主詞補語，置於句首時，be 動詞須放在主詞（ a clean stream ）之前。

3. 我們常在夏天到那裏游泳、釣魚。

 We would often swim and fish there during the summer.

 ＊ would 與副詞 often 連用，表過去重複之習慣。

4. 現在溪水髒得魚都不能活了。

 The stream is now so dirty that no fish can live there.

5. 不知道甚麼時候才能再見到童年的美景。

 I don't know when I'll be able to see that beautiful sight of my childhood again.

II、英文作文（參考範例）

　　It goes without saying that the importance of watches cannot be overemphasized. Why? Because watches play a very important role in our lives today. For example, with watches, we can know the time. Besides, watches can remind us to cherish our time, as a western proverb says, " Time is money." In other words, they are essential to our everyday life.

　　The other day, my parents went to a gift shop near the Chiang Kai-shek Memorial Hall to buy me a watch as a present for my 18th birthday. The watch is transparent. You can see its inner structure clearly. I like its special style very much, and I am wearing it to this year's Joint College Entrance Examination. I sincerely hope this watch can bring me good luck.

　　＊＊ 本篇作文的黑體字部分，完全取材自**學習升大學補習班**與**劉毅英文家教班**的考前機密資料──**英文作文萬用錦囊妙句**。

七十九學年度大學暨獨立學院入學考試

英 文 試 題

第一部分：單一選擇題

I. 綜合測驗（30％）：下面三篇短文共有三十個空格（1～30），每個空格附有
　　四個備選答案。請仔細閱讀後選出一個最適當的答案標示在答案卡上。每題答
　　對得1分，答錯倒扣1/3分，不答不給分。

　　　Many foreigners find that Taiwan is a rather nice place to ___1___
a holiday. They ___2___ that there are many interesting things to do
and to see. They also say that the beaches are ___3___ clean and the
scenery is ___4___ beautiful. Many say that the hotels are ___5___ but
much too expensive. They experiment ___6___ different kinds of Chinese
food and find that Chinese food ___7___ delicious. They are ___8___
with Chinese music and fascinated ___9___ Chinese dancing. Visitors
___10___ many foreign countries say that Chinese people are warm and
friendly.

1. (A) live　　　　(B) spend　　　　(C) fix　　　　(D) stay
2. (A) enjoy　　　(B) admire　　　(C) discover　　(D) dismiss
3. (A) pretty　　　(B) much　　　(C) ever　　　(D) somehow
4. (A) mainly　　　(B) roughly　　(C) briefly　　(D) simply
5. (A) reasonable　(B) comfortable　(C) satisfied　(D) impressed
6. (A) in　　　　(B) at　　　　(C) by　　　　(D) with
7. (A) eats　　　(B) dines　　　(C) tastes　　　(D) tries
8. (A) delightful　(B) delighted　(C) noticing　　(D) noticed
9. (A) in　　　　(B) for　　　　(C) against　　　(D) by
10. (A) in　　　　(B) with　　　(C) about　　　(D) from

　　　More and more people are attracted to the idea of buying on credit and
___11___ credit cards. Having a credit card ___12___ you to carry very little
___13___ , a consideration in big cities where people ___14___ security. Buying
on credit also makes it ___15___ to spread the payments over a ___16___ of
time; of course, there is the ___17___ cost of interest payments. ___18___ the
most attractive yet dangerous ___19___ of the credit system is that you
can buy things ___20___ , at the moment, you haven't the money.

11. (A) doing　　　(B) using　　　(C) selling　　　(D) bringing
12. (A) makes　　　(B) forces　　　(C) enables　　　(D) expects
13. (A) sum　　　(B) cash　　　(C) amount　　　(D) account
14. (A) think about　(B) look up　　(C) hear of　　　(D) do without
15. (A) possible　　(B) valuable　　(C) able　　　　(D) capable
16. (A) point　　　(B) era　　　　(C) stage　　　　(D) period
17. (A) same　　　(B) less　　　　(C) given　　　　(D) added
18. (A) For　　　　(B) But　　　　(C) Although　　　(D) Because
19. (A) variety　　(B) place　　　(C) aspect　　　　(D) sale
20. (A) even if　　(B) as though　　(C) as long as　　(D) so far as

A bag is a flexible container. Many bags are made ___21___ paper, foil, or thin plastic. Such bags are not ___22___ containers — we usually throw them away. We ___23___ bags in several ways, for example, by folding them, by tying them with something, and ___24___ plastic bags, by knotting them or sealing them with heat. Bags also ___25___ in many sizes and may contain different products.

___26___ Americans hear the word "bag," they probably think first of the brown paper bags at the checkstands in American markets. Markets use millions of brown paper bags every year for customers' ___27___. The customers save the bags and use them ___28___ for other purposes. In some other countries, ___29___, people must bring their own bags to the market. String bags are popular for this ___30___.

21. (A) from　　　(B) by　　　　(C) of　　　　　(D) with
22. (A) worthless　(B) durable　　(C) useless　　　(D) portable
23. (A) sell　　　(B) open　　　(C) carry　　　　(D) close
24. (A) for the lack of　　　　　(B) with the exception of
　　(C) at the request of　　　　(D) in the case of
25. (A) come　　　(B) buy　　　(C) weigh　　　　(D) give
26. (A) Because　　(B) Although　(C) Since　　　　(D) When
27. (A) concern　　(B) groceries　(C) homes　　　　(D) servings
28. (A) scarcely　　(B) least　　　(C) again　　　　(D) ever
29. (A) therefore　(B) however　　(C) whereas　　　(D) moreover
30. (A) purpose　　(B) belief　　　(C) claim　　　　(D) area

Ⅱ. **對話**（10％）：下面十題（31～40）是日常生活中常見的英語對話。每題各有一個空白，並各附有四個備選答案。請依照對話的內容選出一個最適當的答案，標示在答案卡上。每題答對得1分，答錯倒扣⅓分，不答不給分。

31. John：Good evening, Jane.
　　Jane：Hi, John. I'm glad you could come.
　　John：_____
　　Jane：No, you're right on time.
　　　　(A) It's my great honor, thanks.
　　　　(B) You're welcome. Am I the first?
　　　　(C) Thanks. Do you have the time?
　　　　(D) I hope I'm not too late.

32. Dan　：Oh, what a nice photograph!
　　May　：_____
　　Dan　：The one above the sofa.
　　May　：Oh, yes. Thank you. That's my parents when they were young.
　　　　(A) Which one do you like best?
　　　　(B) Thank you. It's very kind of you to say so.
　　　　(C) Which one are you talking about?
　　　　(D) Yes, it was taken a few years ago, in Taichung.

33. Mary：Would you like some ice cream?
　　Lucy：No, thanks.
　　Mary：Why not? Don't you like ice cream?
　　Lucy：_____
　　　　(A) No, I don't. But it's too fattening.
　　　　(B) Yes, I do. But I'd rather have a milk shake.
　　　　(C) Yes, I don't. And I think a coke is a better choice.
　　　　(D) No, I do. And on second thought, I like some now.

34. John：_____
　　Jack：In two weeks.
　　John：Are you going to Japan?
　　Jack：No, I'm going to Thailand. I went to Japan two years ago.
　　　　(A) How long have you been here?
　　　　(B) When are you leaving for Thailand?
　　　　(C) How long do you plan to stay in here?
　　　　(D) When is your vacation?

35. Tom : You seem to get lost. Need help ?

　　Joe ：＿＿＿＿＿＿＿＿＿＿＿＿＿＿＿＿

　　　　　(A) Yes, would you please help me with the bag ?

　　　　　(B) Help me find my key, please.

　　　　　(C) Yes, give me a hand please.

　　　　　(D) I'm looking for Chung-shan Road.

36. Luck : ＿＿＿＿＿＿＿＿＿＿＿＿＿＿＿＿＿

　　Mary : Fried shrimp balls.

　　Luck : Great. That's what I was hoping you were going to make.

　　　　　(A) What are you making for dinner ?

　　　　　(B) What is it that you enjoy most ?

　　　　　(C) What are you doing over there ?

　　　　　(D) What's your order, Madam?

37. Tom : Would you like me to water your plants while you're on vacation?

　　Joe ：＿＿＿＿＿＿＿＿＿＿＿＿＿＿＿＿

　　　　　(A) No problem. I was more than glad to do it.

　　　　　(B) Thanks for offering your help, but my brother's going to do it.

　　　　　(C) I appreciate it, but I'm already finished with watering them.

　　　　　(D) Certainly. Watering plants is my favorite pastime.

38. Judy : Jane, would you like some more salad?

　　Jane ：＿＿＿＿＿＿＿＿＿＿＿＿＿＿＿＿

　　Judy : Here you are.

　　　　　(A) Yes, please. It looks very delicious.

　　　　　(B) Thank you. I've had plenty of it.

　　　　　(C) Yes, please. It's really delicious.

　　　　　(D) Thanks. But I really can't.

39. Sam : Brrr! It's cold! ＿＿＿＿＿＿＿＿＿＿＿＿＿

　　Sue ： It's hanging over there next to the door.

　　Sam ： Next to the door? Oh, yes. Thanks.

　　　　　(A) I'm dying for a cup of hot coffee.

　　　　　(B) Have you seen my coat ?

　　　　　(C) Is the heater on ?

　　　　　(D) Why don't we get a heater for the apartment?

40. John : Do you happen to have twenty dollars with you ?

    Jack : _____

    John : I want to buy a notebook.

        (A) How do you want it ?   (B) How much ?

        (C) What for ?   (D) When can you pay me back ?

Ⅱ. **閱讀測驗**（20％）：下面三篇短文共有十個問題（41～50），每題各附四個備選答案。請仔細閱讀文章，把最適合文意的一個答案標示在答案卡上。每題答對得2分，答錯倒扣2/3分，不答不給分。

    What can one boy or girl do to preserve the world's rain forests ? Ask Jiro Nakayama. He's the twelve-year-old leader of a band of school-children in Nagano, Japan, who have already saved 40 acres of forest land in Costa Rica. On their way to and from school, they collect old newspapers and empty aluminum cans for sale to a recycling plant at 63 cents per kilogram. The money they have made, together with donations from parents and neighbors, is sent to the International Children's Rainforest Program, which buys and preserves virgin rain forests at the rate of $50 an acre. So far, Jiro and his friends have raised more than $5,000.

41. The children collect old newspapers and empty aluminum cans because

    (A) they like to play with them.

    (B) they want to save forest land.

    (C) they work for a recycling plant.

    (D) they can make money for their parents.

42. With more than $5,000, how many acres of forest land can Jiro and his friends buy ?

    (A) About 40.   (B) Nearly 50.

    (C) At most 63.   (D) At least 100.

    All the housewives who went to the new supermarket had one great ambition : to be the lucky customer who did not have to pay for her shopping. For this was what the notice just inside the entrance promised.　It said :"Remember, once a week, one of our customers gets free goods.　This may be *your* lucky day!"

For several weeks Mrs. Wang hoped, like many of her friends, to be the lucky customer.　Unlike her friends, she never gave up hope.　The cupboards in her kitchen were full of things which she did not need. In vain her husband tried to dissuade her.　She dreamed of the day when the manager of the supermarket would approach her and say, "Madam, this is *your* lucky day.　Everything in your basket is free."

43. The housewives learned about the offer of free goods
    (A) from their friends.　　　(B) from the manager.
    (C) from television.　　　(D) at the supermarket.

44. Mrs. Wang very much wanted to
    (A) meet the manager.　　　(B) get a free basket of goods.
    (C) please her husband.　　　(D) have a lot of friends.

45. Mrs. Wang's husband tried to
    (A) persuade her to approach the manager.
    (B) talk her into arguing with the manager.
    (C) stop her from buying unnecessary things.
    (D) make her buy more things.

There is one difference between the sexes on which almost every expert and study agree : Men are more aggressive than women.　It shows up in two-year-olds.　It continues through school days and persists into adulthood.　It is even constant across cultures.　And there is little doubt that it is rooted in biology.

If there is a feminine trait that is comparable to male aggressiveness, it is female caring nature.　Feminists have argued that the caring nature of women is not biological in origin, but rather has been drummed into women by a society that wanted to keep them in the home. But the signs that it is at least partly inborn are too numerous to ignore.　Just as tiny infant girls respond more readily to human faces, little girls who have just learned to walk pick up nonverbal cues from others much faster than little boys of about the same age. And grown women are far better than men at interpreting facial expressions : A recent study by University of Pennsylvania brain researcher Ruben Gur showed that they easily read emotions such as anger, sadness and fear. The only such emotion men could pick up was disgust.

46. It is found that men are more aggressive than women
    (A) only when they are two years old.
    (B) during the time they attend school.
    (C) as soon as they have grown up.
    (D) almost throughout their lives.

47. Which feminine trait is comparable to male aggressiveness ?
    (A) Female aggressiveness.
    (B) The caring nature of women.
    (C) The nonverbal cues of women.
    (D) The emotions of anger, sadness and fear.

48. The author of this article believes that female caring nature
    (A) is not rooted in biology.
    (B) has been forced into women by society.
    (C) is at least partly inborn.
    (D) has very few signs.

49. The fact that women can interpret facial expressions better than men is a sign of
    (A) brain research.　　　　(B) female caring nature.
    (C) emotion reading.　　　 (D) nonverbal cues.

50. Which of the following statements is the best summary of this article ?
    (A) Male aggressiveness is generally seen all over the world.
    (B) Caring nature is an inborn trait of women.
    (C) Men can read disgust more readily than women.
    (D) Male aggressiveness and female caring nature are probably rooted in biology.

第二部分：非選擇題

Ⅰ. 翻譯：中譯英（20％）

　　下面一段短文共含有五個中文句子，請譯成正確、通順而達意的英文。每題
4分。答案請寫在「**非選擇題試卷**」上，同時務必標示題號。

1. 昨天早上我出門的時候，天氣相當暖和。

2. 所以我沒有穿毛衣，只穿了一件襯衫。

3. 但是到了下午，氣溫却急速下降了。

4. 雖然晚上比往常早回家，我還是覺得有點不舒服。

5. 今天我不但打噴嚏而且頭痛，我想我最好馬上去看醫生。

Ⅱ. 英文作文（20％）

　　台灣多山，氣候溫和，有很多珍貴的野生動物，但是有些人却濫捕濫殺。請
寫一篇大約一百個英文字（words）的短文。短文分爲兩段：第一段說明台
灣野生動物越來越稀少而濫捕濫殺却不斷發生的情形；第二段討論我們應該
怎麼樣保護野生動物。文章請寫在「**非選擇題試卷**」上。

　　評分標準：內容4分、組織4分、文法4分、用字遣詞4分、拼字、大小寫
　　　　　　　及標點符號4分。

79年大學聯考英文試題詳解

第一部分：單一選擇題

Ⅰ、綜合測驗

Many foreigners find *that* Taiwan is a *rather* nice place *to spend a*
　　　　　　　　　　　　　　　　　　　　　　　　　　　　　1

holiday. They <u>discover</u> *that* there are many interesting things *to do and*
　　　　　　　2

to see. They also say *that* the beaches are *pretty* clean *and* the scenery
　　　　　　　　　　　　　　　　　　　　　　　3

is *simply* beautiful. Many say *that* the hotels are <u>comfortable</u> *but*
　　4　　　　　　　　　　　　　　　　　　　　　　　　　　5

much too expensive.

　　「許多外國人發現台灣是個相當好的度假勝地。他們發覺有很多趣事可以做、可以看。他們還說，海灘很乾淨，風景也美極了。很多人說，飯店很舒適，但是太貴了。」

　　　　beach〔bitʃ〕*n.* 海灘　　　scenery〔'sinərɪ〕*n.* 風景

1.（**B**）(A) live 居住　(B) **spend** 度過　(C) fix 修理　(D) stay 停留（只有答案(B)合句意。）

2.（**C**）(A) enjoy 享受　(B) admire 欽佩　(C) **discover** 發現　(D) dismiss 忘掉

3.（**A**）pretty「非常地」，在此當副詞，修飾 clean。(B) much 是修飾比較級用的，(C) ever 曾經，(D) somehow 以某種方式，均與句意不合。

4.（**D**）(A) mainly 主要地　(B) roughly 大致地　(C) briefly 簡短地
　　　　(D) **simply** 非常地　（只有答案(D)合句意。）

5.（**B**）**comfortable**〔'kʌmfətəbl̩〕*adj.* 舒適的
　　　　(A) reasonable 合理的，只能修飾人或事，不能修飾物。
　　　　(C) satisfied 滿意的，(D) impressed 印象深刻的，均只可修飾人。

They experiment <u>with</u> different kinds *of Chinese food* **and** find *that Chinese*
6

food <u>*tastes*</u> *delicious*.　They are <u>delighted</u> with Chinese music **and** fas-
7   8

cinated *by Chinese dancing*.　Visitors *from many foreign countries* say **that**
9   10

Chinese people are warm and friendly.

"他們嘗試各種中國菜，並發現中國菜很好吃。他們很喜歡中國音樂，還對中國舞蹈感到著迷。來自許多不同國家的觀光客都說，中國人又親切又友善。"

> delicious〔dɪˈlɪʃəs〕*adj.* 美味的
> fascinate〔ˈfæsn̩ˌet〕*v.* 使著迷
> foreign〔ˈfɔrɪn, ˈfɑrɪn〕*adj.* 外國的

6.（ D ）　***experiment with*** 試驗～
(A) experiment in～ 指「在～方面的實驗」，與句意不合。experiment 之後不接 (B) at, (C) by 這兩個介系詞。

7.（ C ）　由主詞補語 delicious 可知，此處缺少一個表示味覺的感官動詞，故選 (C) tastes 嘗起來。其他選項均非感官動詞。

8.（ B ）　（***sb.***）***be delighted with*** ～（某人）對～感到滿意
(A) delightful 令人愉快的, (C) noticing 通知, (D) noticed 被通知的，後面均不加 with，且與句意不合。

9.（ D ）　此處為被動語態，故應選 (D) ***by***。　***be fascinated by*** ～ 對～著迷

10.（ D ）　由句意可知，此處應選表示「來自～」的介系詞，故答案為 (D) from。

　　More and more people are attracted to the idea *of buying on credit*

and <u>*using credit cards*</u>.　Having a credit card enables you to carry very
11   12

little <u>cash</u>, *a consideration in big cities* **where** *people think about security.*
13   14

　　" 以信用貸款購物，以及使用信用卡這個觀念，已經吸引了愈來愈多的人。有了信用卡，身上只需要帶一點現金就夠了，這點在有安全顧慮的大都市中，是件值得考慮的事。"

　　＊ a consideration … security 是由補述用法形容詞子句 *which is* a consideration … security 簡化而成的分詞構句，對前一句話加以補述說明。

> credit〔ˈkrɛdɪt〕 *n.*（經濟上的）信用
> *on credit* 信用貸款　　*credit card* 信用卡
> consideration〔kənˌsɪdəˈreʃən〕 *n.* 要考慮的事
> security〔sɪˈkjʊrətɪ〕 *n.* 安全

11. (**B**) (A) doing 做　(B) *using* 使用　(C) selling 賣　(D) bringing 帶來

12. (**C**) *enable*〔ɪnˈebl̩〕 *v.* 使能夠
　　(A) makes 致使，為使役動詞，需接原形動詞，不可接不定詞。
　　(B) forces 迫使，(D) expects 期待，均與句意不符。

13. (**B**) (A) sum 總數　(B) *cash* 現金　(C) amount 總額　(D) account 帳目

14. (**A**) (A) *think about*（仔細）考慮　(B) look up 查；尋找
　　(C) hear of 聽說　(D) do without 無需；免除

Buying on credit also makes *it* possible *to spread the payments over a*
　　　　　　　　　　　　　　形式受詞 15　　眞　　　正　　　受
period of time; *of course*, there is the added cost *of interest payments.*
　16　　　詞　　　　　　　　　　　　　　　　17
But *the most attractive yet dangerous* aspect *of the credit system* is *that*
　18　　　　　　　　　　　　　　　　　　　　　19
you can buy things *even if*, at the moment, you haven't the money.
　　　　　　　　　　20

　　" 以信用貸款購物還能讓人們在一段時間之內，將貨款分期繳清，當然，款項中還多加了利息的部份。不過，信用制度最吸引人，但卻也最危險的一面在於，就算當時你沒有錢，還是可以買東西。"

> spread〔sprɛd〕 *v.* 延長　　payment〔ˈpemənt〕 *n.* 付款
> interest〔ˈɪntərɪst, ˈɪntrɪst〕 *n.* 利息

15. (**A**) 　*possible*「可能的」，用於修飾事情。

　　　(B) valuable 有價值的，與句意不合。(C) able 能夠的，只用於修飾人。
　　　(D) capable（事物）容許～的，但用法為 be capable of＋Ving。

16. (**D**) 　(A) point 點　　(B) era 時代　　(C) stage 階段　　(D) *period* 期間

17. (**D**) 　利息是另外附加上去的，故選 (D) *added* 增加的。
　　　(A) same 相同的　　(B) less 較少的　　(C) given 既定的

18. (**B**) 　此處需要一個表示語氣轉折的對等連接詞，故選 (B) *But*。
　　　(A) For 因為，與句意不符。(C) Although 雖然，(D) Because 因為，均為
　　　從屬連接詞。

19. (**C**) 　(A) variety 多樣性　　(B) place 場所；地方　　(C) *aspect*〔'æspɛkt〕*n.* 方面
　　　(D) sale 銷售

20. (**A**) 　(A) *even if* 即使（＝*even though*）　　(B) as though 宛如（＝*as if*）
　　　(C) as long as 只要；既然（＝*so long as*）
　　　(D) so far as 像～那麼遠；就～而言（＝*as far as*）

　　　A bag is a flexible container. Many bags are made of paper, foil,
　　　　　　　　　　　　　　　　　　　　　　　21

or thin plastic. *Such* bags are not durable containers — we *usually* throw
　　　　　　　　　　　　　　　　　　　　22

them away.

　　　"袋子是一種會變形的容器。許多袋子是由紙、錫箔或薄塑膠製成的，這種袋
子並非耐用的容器——我們通常會把它們扔掉。"

　　　flexible〔'flɛksəbl̩〕*adj.* 能變形的　　container〔kən'tenə〕*n.* 容器
　　　foil〔fɔɪl〕*n.* 錫箔　　plastic〔'plæstɪk〕*n.* 塑膠

21. (**C**) 　*be made of* ～（由～所製成），指原料製成成品後性質未改變；be made
　　　from～ 則指性質已改變，如：Wine *is made from* grapes.（酒是由葡
　　　萄釀造的。）

22. (**B**) 　根據句意，應選 (B) *durable*〔'djʊrəbl̩〕*adj.* 耐用的
　　　(A) worthless 無價值的　　(C) useless 無用的　　(D) portable 可攜帶的

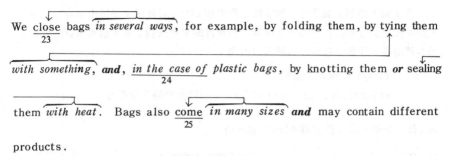

We close bags *in several ways*, for example, by folding them, by tying them
　　23
with something, **and**, *in the case of* plastic bags, by knotting them **or** sealing
　　　　　　　　　　　　24
them *with heat*. Bags also come *in many sizes* **and** may contain different
　　　　　　　　　　　25
products.

「 我們將袋子封起來的方法有好幾種，例如：把它們摺起來，或用某種東西綁起來，
如果是塑膠袋的話，可以打個結，或是加熱封起來。袋子的大小尺寸也有很多種，
可容納不同的物品。」

　　＊副詞片語 in the case of plastic bags 是插入語，修飾全句的動詞 close。

　　　knot〔nɑt〕v. 打結　　　seal〔sil〕v. 密封

23.(**D**) 由 by folding them…heat 可知，此句是在敘述「封閉」袋子的方法，
　　　故選 (D) close。

24.(**D**) (A)正確應為 for lack of 因缺乏～，但亦不合句意。
　　　(B) with the exception of 除～之外
　　　(C) at the request of 應～的要求
　　　(D) *in the case of* 就～的情形而論

25.(**A**) come 在此作「有（某種尺寸）」解，例：The dress **comes** in four
　　　sizes. 這件衣服有四種尺寸。(B)、(C)、(D)均不合句意。

When Americans hear the word "bag," they *probably* think *first* of the
　26
brown paper bags *at the checkstands in American markets*. Markets use
millions of brown paper bags *every year for customers' groceries*. The
　　　　　　　　　　　　　　　　　　　　　　　27
customers save the bags **and** use them again *for other purposes*.
　　　　　　　　　　　　　　　　28

　　"美國人聽到「袋子」這個字時，最先想到的，可能就是超級市場裏，收銀台上的牛皮紙袋。超級市場每年使用數以百萬計的牛皮紙袋，來裝顧客所買的雜貨。顧客將這些袋子保存起來，再做其他用途。"

　　　　brown paper 牛皮紙

　　　　checkstand〔'tʃɛk,stænd〕n.（超級市場的）收銀台

26.（**D**）根據句意，應選(D)When（當～時）。

27.（**B**）***grocery***〔'grosərɪ〕n. 雜貨（常用複數型）
　　　　(A) concern〔kən'sɜn〕n. 關心　(C) homes 家　(D) serving〔'sɜvɪŋ〕n.（餐食等的）一人份，均與句意不合。

28.（**C**）根據句意，應選(C) again。(A) scarcely 幾乎不，(B) least 最少，(D) ever 曾經，均不合句意。

*In some other countries, **however**, people must bring their own bags to the market. String bags are popular for this purpose.*
　　　　　　　　　　　29　　　　　　　　　　　　　　　　　　　　　30

"然而，在其他一些國家中，人們必須自己攜帶袋子去市場，網袋經常做此用途。"

　　　　string bag 網袋

29.（**B**）however（然而）是轉承語，連接前面的句子。
　　　　(A) therefore 因此。(D) moreover 此外，不合句意。(C) whereas 亦作「然而」解，但是連接詞，只能用來連接兩個子句，不可作插入語。

30.（**A**）(A) ***purpose*** 用途　(B) belief 信仰　(C) claim 主張　(D) area 區域

Ⅱ、對話

31.（**D**）約翰：晚安，珍。
　　　　珍　：嗨！約翰。很高興你能來。
　　　　約翰：＿＿＿＿＿＿＿＿＿＿＿＿
　　　　珍　：不，你剛好準時。
　　　　　(A)我很榮幸，謝謝。　　　　　(B)不客氣，我是第一個到的嗎？
　　　　　(C)謝謝，現在幾點鐘？　　　　(D)希望我不算太遲。

32.（ **C** ）丹：喔，這張照片好漂亮啊！

梅：＿＿＿＿＿＿＿＿＿＿＿

丹：沙發上方的那一張。

梅：喔，是的，謝謝你。那是我父母年輕時的照片。

　(A) 你最喜歡哪一張？　　(B) 謝謝，你這麼說人眞好。

　(C) 你說的是哪一張？　　(D) 是的，這張照片是幾年前在台中照的。

33.（ **B** ）瑪麗：你要不要來點冰淇淋？

露西：不，謝了。

瑪麗：爲什麼不要，你不喜歡冰淇淋嗎？

露西：＿＿＿＿＿＿＿＿＿＿＿＿

　(A) 不，我不喜歡，但是冰淇淋太容易使人變胖了。

　(B) 是，我喜歡冰淇淋，但是我比較想吃奶昔。

　(C) 是，我不喜歡，我認爲可樂更好。

　(D) 不，我喜歡，但是重新考慮過後，現在我想吃了。

　＊在 Yes-No 問句的答句中，若答句的內容是肯定句，就配合 Yes；答句
　的內容是否定句，就配合 No，所以答案(C) Yes 之後，應該是 I do，而
　答案(C) No 之後，應改成 I don't 才對。

　fattening〔ˈfætənɪŋ〕*adj.* 容易使人變胖的

　milk shake 奶昔　　*on second thought* 重新考慮之後

34.（ **D** ）約翰：＿＿＿＿＿＿＿＿＿＿＿

傑克：再過兩個禮拜。

約翰：你要去日本嗎？

傑克：不，我要去泰國，我兩年前去過日本了。

　(A) 你在這裏待多久了？　　(B) 你什麼時候去泰國？

　(C) 你打算在這裏待多久？　　(D) 你什麼時候去渡假？

　Thailand〔ˈtaɪlənd〕*n.* 泰國　　*leave for* 前往

35.（ **D** ）湯姆：你似乎迷路了，需要幫忙嗎？

喬　：＿＿＿＿＿＿＿＿＿＿＿

　(A) 好的，能不能請你幫我提這個袋子？　　(B) 請幫我找鑰匙。

　(C) 好的，請幫我一個忙。　　(D) 我在找中山路。

　get lost 迷路　　*give sb. a hand* 幫某人忙

36.（ **A** ）魯克：＿＿＿＿＿＿＿＿＿＿＿＿＿＿＿

　　瑪麗：炸蝦球。

　　魯克：太棒了，我就希望你做這個。

　　　(A) 你晚飯做什麼？　　　　　(B) 你最喜歡什麼？

　　　(C) 你在那裏做什麼？　　　　(D) 這位女士，您要點些什麼荣？

　　shrimp〔ʃrɪmp〕*n.* 蝦

37.（ **B** ）湯姆：你渡假時要不要我替你的植物澆水？

　　喬　：＿＿＿＿＿＿＿＿＿＿＿＿＿＿＿＿＿＿＿＿＿

　　　(A) 沒問題，我非常樂意去做。

　　　(B) 謝謝你伸出援手，但是我弟弟打算替我澆水了。

　　　(C) 很感謝你樂心相助，但是我已經澆完了。

　　　(D) 沒問題，替植物澆水是我最喜歡的消遣。

　　more than 遠超過；非常　　　appreciate〔ə'priʃɪ,et〕*v.* 感謝

　　pastime〔'pæs,taɪm〕*n.* 消遣

38.（ **C** ）茱蒂：珍，要不要再來點沙拉？

　　珍　：＿＿＿＿＿＿＿＿＿＿＿＿＿＿＿

　　茱蒂：沙拉在這兒。　〔由 some *more* salad 可知，Jane 已吃過沙拉，故選(C)。因(A)表
　　　　　　　　　　　　　Jane 尚未吃沙拉，與句意不合。〕

　　　(A) 好的，麻煩你了。沙拉看起來很好吃。　　(B) 謝謝你，我吃很多了。

　　　(C) 好的，麻煩你，沙拉眞是好吃。　　　　　(D) 謝了，但我眞的不能。

39.（ **B** ）山姆：哇！眞是冷！＿＿＿＿＿＿＿＿＿＿＿＿＿

　　蘇　：就掛在門旁邊。

　　山姆：門旁邊？喔，找到了，謝謝。

　　　(A) 我眞想喝杯熱咖啡。　　　(B) 你有沒有看到我的外套？

　　　(C) 暖氣開了嗎？　　　　　　(D) 我們何不在公寓裏裝暖氣？

　　be dying for 渴望　　heater〔'hitɚ〕*n.* 暖氣；電熱器

40.（ **C** ）約翰：你身上有沒有二十塊錢？

　　傑克：＿＿＿＿＿＿＿＿＿＿＿＿＿＿＿

　　約翰：我想買筆記本。

　　　(A) 你希望二十塊怎麼給？（如兩張十塊或四張五塊等）　(B) 多少錢？

　　　(C) 要二十塊做什麼？　　　　　　　　　　　　　　　　(D) 什麼時候還我？

　　happen to 碰巧；偶而

Ⅲ、閱讀測驗

What can one boy or girl do *to preserve the world's rain forests*? Ask Jiro Nakayama. He's the twelve-year-old leader *of a band of school-children in Nagano, Japan, who have already saved 40 acres of forest land in Costa Rica.*

「小男孩或小女孩可以爲保存世界上的雨林做些什麼工作呢？問中山次郎就知道了。他今年十二歲，是日本長野一群學童的領袖。他已經拯救了哥斯大黎加四十英畝的林地。」

　　　　preserve〔 prɪˈzɜv 〕v. 保存　　rain forest 雨林（多雨、樹密的大森林）
　　　　acre〔 ˈekɚ 〕n. 英畝　　Costa Rica〔 ˈkɑstəˈrikə 〕n. 哥斯大黎加

On their way to and from school, they collect old newspapers and empty aluminum cans for sale to a *recycling* plant at 63 cents per kilogram.
「在上下學途中，他們收集舊報紙和空的鋁罐，以每公斤六毛三的價錢賣給廢物處理工廠。」

　　　　aluminum〔 əˈlumɪnəm 〕n.〔化〕鋁　　can〔 kæn 〕n. 金屬罐
　　　　recycle〔 riˈsaɪkḷ 〕v. 處理（廢物）使成爲有用之物
　　　　per〔 pɚ 〕prep. 每一　　kilogram〔 ˈkɪləˌgræm 〕n. 公斤

The money *they have made*, together with donations *from parents and neighbors*, is sent to the International Children's Rainforest Program, *which buys and preserves virgin rain forests at the rate of $50 an acre.*
So far, Jiro and his friends have raised *more than* $5,000.
「他們所賺的錢，再加上父母、鄰居的捐款，一起被送到「國際兒童雨林計劃」去，這個單位以每英畝五十元的價格，買下且保存處女雨林。到目前爲止，次郎和他的朋友已經籌到五千多元了。」

* together with 前後連接兩個主詞，其動詞要與第一個主詞一致（請參考文法寶典 p.400）。

donation〔do'neʃən〕n. 捐款　　virgin〔'vɜdʒɪn〕adj. 未開墾的
rate〔ret〕n. 價格　　**so far** 到目前爲止
raise〔rez〕v. 籌措

41.(B) 這些學童收集舊報紙和空鋁罐是因爲

(A) 他們喜歡玩這些東西。　　　(B) 他們要拯救林地。
(C) 他們爲廢物處理工廠做事。　(D) 他們可以替父母賺錢。

42.(D) 次郎和他的朋友可以用五千多元，買多少英畝的林地？

(A) 大約四十。　　　　　　　(B) 將近五十。
(C) 最多六十三。　　　　　　(D) 至少一百。

All the housewives *who went to the new supermarket* had one great ambition: to be the lucky customer *who did not have to pay for her shopping*. **For** this was **what** the notice *just inside the entrance* promised. It said: "Remember, *once a week*, one *of our customers* gets free goods. This may be *your* lucky day!"

"所有前往這家新超級市場的主婦，都有一個很大的野心：成爲購物不需付費的幸運顧客。因爲這正是張貼在入口處的公告所保證的。公告上寫著：「記住，一週有一次機會，我們的顧客之一可獲得免費商品。今天也許就是**你的**幸運日。」"

* what 用來引導名詞子句，在子句中作 promised 的受詞。

ambition〔æm'bɪʃən〕n. 野心　　shopping〔'ʃɑpɪŋ〕n. 所購之物
entrance〔'ɛntrəns〕n. 入口　　promise〔'prɑmɪs〕v. 保證
notice〔'notɪs〕n. 公告　　　　this〔ðɪs〕n. 今天

For several weeks Mrs. Wang hoped, *like many of her friends*, to be the lucky customer. *Unlike her friends*, she never gave up hope. The cupboards *in her kitchen* were full of things *which she did not need*.

"連續好幾個星期，王太太就像她的許多朋友一樣，希望能成為幸運顧客。但是她和朋友不同的是，她從不放棄希望。她廚房的碗櫃裏堆滿了她不需要的東西。"

cupboard〔'kʌbəd〕*n.* 碗櫃

In vain her husband tried to dissuade her. She dreamed of the day*when the manager of the supermarket would approach her and say, "Madam, this is your lucky day. Everything in your basket is free."*

"她的丈夫試圖勸阻她，但徒勞無功。她夢想著有一天，超級市場的經理會走向她，並且對她說：「女士，今天是你的幸運日，你籃子裏的每樣東西都免費。」"

in vain 徒勞無功　　dissuade〔dɪ'swed〕*v.* 勸阻
approach〔ə'protʃ〕*v.* 走近

43（ﾌ）主婦們得知有免費貨品供應
　　　　(A) 從她們的朋友口中知道。　　(B) 從經理口中知道。
　　　　(C) 由電視知道。　　　　　　　(D) 在超級市場知道。

44.（B）王太太非常想要
　　　　(A) 會見經理。　　　　　　　　(B) 得到一籃免費的商品。
　　　　(C) 取悅她的丈夫。　　　　　　(D) 擁有許多朋友。

45.（C）王太太的丈夫試圖
　　　　(A) 勸她接近經理。　　　　　　(B) 勸她跟經理理論。
　　　　(C) 使她停止購買不需要的東西。　(D) 使她買更多東西。

talk sb. into ～說服某人去～

There is one difference *between the sexes on which almost every expert and study agree*: Men are more aggressive than women. It shows up *in two-year-olds*. It continues *through school days* and persists *into adulthood*. It is *even* constant across cultures. ***And*** there is little doubt *that* it is *rooted in biology*.

"兩性間存在一個差異，這個差異幾乎每一位專家及每一項研究都同意，那就是男性比女性更具侵略性。這種現象在兩歲時就會突顯出來，並延續至學生時代，乃至於成人時期。這種現象甚至在不同的文化裏也保持不變。此現象乃是根植於生物本性這點，幾乎是無庸置疑的。"

aggressive〔əˈgrɛsɪv〕*adj.* 侵略的　　***show up*** 顯眼；揭發

persist〔pɚˈzɪst,-ˈsɪst〕*v.* 持續；堅持

adulthood〔əˈdʌlthʊd〕*n.* 成年　　root〔rut〕*v.* 使生根

biology〔baɪˈɑlədʒɪ〕*n.* 生物

*If there is a feminine trait **that** is comparable to male aggressiveness*, it is female caring nature. Feminists have argued ***that*** the caring nature *of women* is ***not*** biological *in origin*, ***but*** rather has been drummed into women by a society *that wanted to keep them in the home*.

"如果女性也有一項特徵，能與男性的侵略性相匹敵，那就是女性照顧人的天性了。女權主義者辯稱，女性照顧人的天性並非與生俱來的，而是社會硬教給女性的，好讓她們待在家裏。"

feminine〔ˈfɛmənɪn〕*adj.* 婦女的　　trait〔tret〕*n.* 特徵；特性

comparable〔ˈkɑmpərəbl̩〕*adj.* 可相比的

feminist〔ˈfɛmənɪst〕*n.* 女權主義者

biological〔ˌbaɪəˈlɑdʒɪkl̩〕*adj.* 生物的

origin〔ˈɔrədʒɪn〕*n.* 起源；出生

***drum** sth. **into** sb.* 硬教某事給某人

But the signs ***that*** *it is at least partly inborn* are too numerous to ignore.

*Just **as** tiny infant girls respond more readily to human faces*, little girls *who have just learned to walk* pick up nonverbal cues *from others much faster than little boys of about the same age*.

"但是有跡象顯示，女性照顧人的天性多少是與生俱來的，而且這些跡象多得令人無法忽略。正如同小女嬰對人的面孔較有反應一樣，剛學會走路的小女孩，也比大約同年齡的小男孩，更能快速地接收別人非語言的信號。"

> inborn〔'ɪn,bɔrn〕 adj. 天生的；天賦的　　ignore〔ɪg'nɔr〕 v. 忽略
> respond〔rɪ'spɑnd〕 v. 反應　　readily〔'rɛdɪlɪ〕 adv. 毫無困難
> nonverbal〔nɑn'vɝbḷ〕 adj. 非語言的　　cue〔kju〕 n. 信號

And grown women are *far* better than men *at interpreting facial expressions*: A recent study *by University of Pennsylvania brain researcher Ruben Gur* showed **that** *they easily read emotions such as anger, sadness and fear.* The only such emotion *men could pick up* was disgust.

"成年女性在闡釋臉部表情上，也遠優於男性：賓州大學腦部研究員魯賓‧古爾，在最近的一項研究中指出，女性可以輕易地領會到如憤怒、悲傷及恐懼等情緒，而男性可能接收的這類情緒卻只有厭惡。"

> interpret〔ɪn'tɝprɪt〕 v. 解釋；闡明
> Pennsylvania〔,pɛnsḷ'venjə〕 n. 賓夕凡尼亞州(簡稱賓州,位於美東)
> disgust〔dɪs'gʌst〕 n. 厭惡

46.(D) 人們發現男性較女性更具侵略性
　　　　(A) 只在他們兩歲的時候。　　(B) 只在他們求學期間。
　　　　(C) 在他們成人之後。　　　　(D) 幾乎終其一生皆如此。

47.(B) 女性的哪一項特徵可與男性的侵略性相比？
　　　　(A) 女性的侵略性。　　　　(B) 女性照顧人的天性。
　　　　(C) 女性的非語言信號。　　(D) 憤怒、悲傷及恐懼等情緒。

48.(C) 本文作者相信，女性照顧人的天性
　　　　(A) 並非根植於生物本性。　(B) 是社會強加於女性的。
　　　　(C) 多少是與生俱來的。　　(D) 沒什麼跡象可循。

49.(B) 女性比男性更擅長詮釋臉部表情這個事實，是什麼的跡象？
　　　　(A) 腦部研究。　　　　　　(B) 女性照顧人的天性。
　　　　(C) 領會情緒。　　　　　　(D) 非語言信號。

50.（ **D** ）下列哪一項敍述爲本文的最佳摘要？

      (A) 男性的侵略性是全世界普遍的現象。

      (B) 照顧人的天性是女性與生俱來的特質。

      (C) 男性能比女性更輕易領會到厭惡。

      <u>(D) 男性的侵略性與女性照顧人的天性，可能根植於生物本性。</u>

summary〔ˈsʌmərɪ〕 *n.* 摘要

第二部分：非選擇題

Ⅰ、翻譯：中譯英

1. 昨天早上我出門的時候，天氣相當暖和。

  When I left home yesterday morning, the weather was quite warm.

2. 所以我沒有穿毛衣，只穿了一件襯衫。

  Therefore I did not wear my woolen sweater; I only wore a shirt.

3. 但是到了下午，氣溫却急速下降了。

  However the temperature dropped sharply in the afternoon.

4. 雖然晚上比往常早回家，我還是覺得有點不舒服。

  That evening, although I went home earlier than usual, I still felt a little bit uncomfortable.

5. 今天我不但打噴嚏而且頭痛，我想我最好馬上去看醫生。

  Today I am not only sneezing but also have a headache. I think I had better see a doctor at once.

Ⅱ、作文（參考範例）

    It is of general consensus that men should protect all kinds of animals; ***however, people in Taiwan*** lack such an awareness. The number and kinds of wild animals in Taiwan are getting fewer and fewer. What is distressing to note is the fact that despite this consensus, the killings have continued unabated.

To protect wild animals from extinction, *we have the duty to inform our fellow citizens that* all animals are created equal and that we have no right to kill them. *On the other had*, we must also persuade people to stop eating wild animals. Let us keep the wilderness in its pristine state and let these animals continue roaming wild and free.

　　consensus〔kən'sɛnsəs〕*n.* 一致的意見；共識
　　distressing〔dɪ'strɛsɪŋ〕*adj.* 令人苦惱的
　　unabated〔͵ʌnə'betɪd〕*adj.* 不減輕的
　　extinction〔ɪk'stɪŋkʃən〕*n.* 滅亡
　　pristine〔'prɪstin〕*adj.* 原始的　　roam〔rom〕*v.* 漫步

心得筆記欄........................

七十八學年度大學暨獨立學院入學考試
英 文 試 題

第一部分：單一選擇題

I. **對話**（10%）：下面十題（1～10）是日常生活中常見的英語對話。每題各有一個空白，並各附有A、B、C、D四個備選答案。請依照對話的內容選出一個最適當的答案，標示在**答案卡**上。每題答對得1分，答錯倒扣1/3分，不答不給分。

1. Joe : This is heavy！ What's in it？
   Sue : ＿＿＿＿＿＿＿＿＿＿＿＿＿
   A. Thanks. I think I can manage by myself.
   B. My new stereo equipment. I just bought it.
   C. I sure could. I'm glad you're here.
   D. Are you really interested in it？

2. Joe : You play the piano, don't you？ I've heard music coming from your apartment a few times.
   Sue : ＿＿＿＿＿＿＿＿＿＿＿＿＿
   A. Oh, I hope I didn't disturb you.
   B. You will know that, won't you？
   C. I'm not bothering you at all.
   D. You enjoy listening to it, don't you？

3. Joe : By the way, do you know Mr. Walker by any chance？
   Sue : ＿＿＿＿＿＿＿＿＿＿＿＿＿
   A. No, it never happens to me.
   B. I do remember it presently.
   C. As a matter of fact, I do.
   D. Yes, I happen to see him on the way.

4. Joe : My leg is caught！ Can you help me？
   Sue : ＿＿＿＿＿＿＿＿＿＿＿＿＿
   A. Let me see if I can move the desk.
   B. You might need to get some help.
   C. Why do you think I'd help you？
   D. Sure. Just do whatever you like to.

5. May : Excuse me, but I couldn't help noticing your earrings.
   Sue : _____

   A. Oh, they were a present from my parents.
   B. They are very, very beautiful.
   C. Oh, I'm sorry. I've never noticed them myself.
   D. Thank you. You can have them.

6. May : Believe me, Sue, this program can help you with your geography
         course.
   Sue : _____

   A. It's called "A Trip Down the Amazon."
   B. Do you often watch public TV?
   C. Any idea about the program?
   D. Okay, you've talked me into watching it.

7. Lin : Do you mind if I ask you how much you weigh?
   May : _____

   A. In fact, I've been on diet for quite a long time.
   B. Frankly, I've been trying my best to lose weight.
   C. Oh, no. Most people do care about the matter.
   D. Ha, ha. Gee, Americans don't really like to be asked such
      a question.

8. John : What's the matter? You really look down.
   Jack : _____
   John : Well, better luck next time.

   A. I always look up to you.
   B. What a strange coincidence!
   C. I failed an important test.
   D. Me? I never look down upon you!

9. John : We're going hiking this weekend. _____
   Jane : Sure. Where are you going?
   John : Mt. Ali.

   A. What's your plan?
   B. Do you want to come along?
   C. I hope you could've joined us.
   D. How about you?

10. Jack : Bill, do you have the time ?

Bill : _____

Jack : Never mind. Thanks anyway.

    A. Yes, it's half past nine.

    B. Sorry. But I left my watch home.

    C. Of course, I do. The time is 10：30.

    D. Sure. But I'm afraid it's too late for me.

II. **綜合測驗**（30％）：下面一篇對話及兩篇短文共有三十個空格（11～40），
每個空格附有四個備選答案。請仔細閱讀後選出一個最適當的答案來標示在**答
案卡**上。每題答對得1分，答錯倒扣1/3分，不答不給分。

Denise :   If you jog for an hour every day, you're sure to lose weight.

Florence : Could be, ___11___ I've just read a book arguing otherwise.

Patrick :   I ___12___ with Florence. I ruined my knees jogging.

Denise :   Some experts seem to disagree with you ___13___ . Maybe you
didn't wear the ___14___ running shoes.

Florence : Let's face it. The only way to lose weight is to ___15___ less.

Patrick :   Not ___16___ . It's clear from the evidence that heredity is a
factor.

Florence : I try hard to avoid eating red meat and fatty ___17___ .

Denise :   That's no hardship, ___18___ the cost of meat these days.

Patrick :   You may laugh, but I've been thinking of becoming a ___19___ .

Denise :   Oh, Patrick, you ___20___ be out of your mind. You will be
hungry all the time.

11. A. but   B. so   C. for   D. now

12. A. read   B. argue   C. agree   D. disagree

13. A. either   B. there   C. too   D. otherwise

14. A. new   B. old   C. expensive   D. proper

15. A. run   B. exercise   C. eat   D. work

16. A. only   B. fairly   C. possibly   D. necessarily

17. A. food   B. bread   C. fish   D. soup

18. A. taken   B. given   C. offered   D. provided

19. A. jogger   B. sportswoman C. vegetarian   D. cook

20. A. must   B. may   C. will   D. should

    Some reading you select for yourself will be for learning, ___21___
will be for pleasure or recreation. ___22___ your purpose for reading
is not always ___23___ , the way in which you read the ___24___ will differ.

When you read to learn, you should 25 main and supporting ideas, trying to 26 facts and details. You will probably read the material 27 . On the other hand, 28 you read for pleasure, you should try to read much 29 , not worrying about unknown words. Adjusting your reading style to your 30 is an important part of becoming a skillful reader.

21. A. few   B. some   C. all   D. others
22. A. Since   B. From   C. Though   D. But
23. A. clear   B. the same   C. different   D. right
24. A. style   B. purpose   C. interest   D. material
25. A. look up   B. look into   C. look for   D. look through
26. A. remember   B. write   C. supply   D. support
27. A. for pleasure B. on purpose   C. more than once D. for a long time
28. A. as   B. and   C. when   D. so
29. A. faster   B. slower   C. more carefully D. more patiently
30. A. ideas   B. facts   C. learning   D. purpose

There are three ways to take the salt from ocean water: electrodialysis, freezing, and distillation. Electrodialysis is used to desalt 31 that does not have much salt. In this process, an electric charge is sent through the salty water and causes the salt to 32 the water.

Another method of desalinization is freezing. Ice is pure, 33 water. When seawater is frozen, the 34 separates and can be washed off. Finally, the ice can be 35 and used as fresh water.

The oldest and most common way to turn seawater into fresh water is distillation. In this process, the sun provides the 36 for distillation. A piece of plastic covers a few inches of 37 water in a shallow basin while the water 38 with the heat of the sun. The vapor 39 until it hits the plastic top. Then it 40 into fresh water. This method is not very efficient because it does not produce much water quickly enough.

31. A. salt   B. water   C. the sea   D. the ocean
32. A. turn into   B. melt in   C. separate from D. get rid of
33. A. fresh   B. cold   C. salty   D. freezing
34. A. ice   B. water   C. salt   D. material
35. A. heated   B. frozen   C. washed   D. melted
36. A. heat   B. source   C. method   D. possibility

37. A. fresh   B. salty   C. hot   D. frozen
38. A. runs   B. goes   C. melts   D. evaporates
39. A. rises   B. falls   C. appears   D. disappears
40. A. turns   B. changes   C. freezes   D. condenses

Ⅲ. **閱讀測驗**（20％）：下面三篇短文後面共十個問題（41～50），每題各附四
個備選答案。請仔細閱讀文章，把最適合文意的一個答案標示在**答案卡**上。每
題答對得2分，答錯倒扣2/3分，不答不給分。

　　With tears streaming down her face, Miss Sophie Harris pleaded
with the post office worker to help her retrieve two love letters which
she had mistakenly sent to the wrong addresses.

　　Calling it " a matter of life and death," Miss Harris said she had
mixed up letters to her boyfriends and realized the mistake only after
posting them.

　　The post office succeeded in retrieving the letters after notifying
postal authorities in Taichung and Kaohsiung, where the letters had
been sent.

41. How did Miss Harris react when she found that she had sent her let-
ters to the wrong persons?
　　A. She was very much delighted.
　　B. She was greatly amazed.
　　C. She was so upset as to start crying.
　　D. She took it easy and called up her friends for help.

42. If Miss Harris's two letters had been received by the wrong persons,
the consequence would have been
　　A. of vital importance to her.   B. very significant to her.
　　C. disastrous to her.   D. of little value to her.

43. What happened to the two letters at last?
　　A. They got lost in the post office.
　　B. They disappeared somewhere in Taiwan.
　　C. They were recovered and given back to Miss Harris.
　　D. We don't know because the information is not given.

　　On November 24, 1988, a 16-year-old boy with a clean criminal record was strip-searched and sentenced to 25 days in jail for possessing
cigarettes while visiting his grandparents in Idaho.

He spent one night in jail before his grandparents paid his fine.

" I just can't believe this, " Jack Larsen, 16, said late Tuesday night, shortly before being released from the Kootenai County Jail. " Twenty-five days in here for smoking? I was so scared that I didn't sleep at all last night. "

" I knew I wasn't old enough to smoke, " he said. " But I thought I'd just get a small fine. This is so tough here. They even strip-searched me. "

Larsen was released to his grandparents after they borrowed $126.50 to pay his fine. The boy lives in Spokane, Washington, with his father.

" We live on $600 of Social Security a month, " said the boy's grandfather. " But I don't think we can bear leaving him in jail for something like smoking. "

In Idaho, possession of tobacco is illegal for those under 18. Jack has learned a big lesson from this incident.

44. Jack Larsen was arrested and imprisoned because
    A. he smoked illegally.   B. he sold tobacco illegally.
    C. he was strip-searched.   D. he was fined for smoking.

45. How long was Jack actually in jail ?
    A. One night.   B. Three days.
    C. One week.   D. Twenty-five days.

46. How did Jack describe his experience in jail ?
    A. He was so excited as to call his father.
    B. He was too frightened to get any sleep.
    C. He was so worried that he called his grandparents.
    D. It was a fantastic experience that he would never forget.

47. Had Jack committed any kind of crime before ?
    A. Yes. Illegal possession of tobacco.
    B. No, not at all.
    C. Yes, when he was in Washington.
    D. The information is not given.

48. According to the law in Idaho, nobody is allowed to smoke until he is over _____ years old.
    A. 16   B. 18   C. 20   D. 25

　　Money is one of the most important inventions of mankind. Without it a complex, modern economy based on the division of labor and the consequent widespread exchange of goods and services would be impossible.

　　Because many things, ranging from gold to copper to shells, have been used as money, it cannot be defined as some particular object but must instead be defined by the functions it serves — to act as a medium of exchange and a standard of value. A third function of money — as a store of wealth — is something money shares with many other types of objects.

49. Money is an important human invention in that

　　A. it is the consequence of widespread exchange of goods and services.

　　B. it is based on the division of labor.

　　C. it is an indispensable factor in modern economy.

　　D. it ranges from gold to copper to shells.

50. Money is best defined in terms of

　　A. its relation to the division of labor.

　　B. the objects used to represent it.

　　C. the amount of gold it can purchase.

　　D. the purposes it is used for.

第二部分：非選擇題

I. 翻譯：中譯英（20％）

　　下面一段短文共含有五個中文句子，請譯成正確、通順而達意的英文。每題4分。答案請寫在「非選擇題試卷」上，同時務必標示題號。

1. 讀小學的時候，我身體很虛弱，並且常感冒。

2. 自從上了國中以後，我就儘量找機會運動。

3. 雖然功課一直很繁重，我還是每天慢跑半小時。

4. 六年繼續不斷的鍛鍊使我不但更加強壯，而且也長得更高。

5. 現在大家都說他們無法相信我從前又矮又瘦。

II. 英文作文（20％）

　　寫一篇大約八十個英文字（words）的短文，敍述你上學途中看到什麼、聽到什麼、想到什麼。把文章分成兩段，第一段敍述你怎麼樣上學、在上學途中遇到那些人、見到那些事物、景象；第二段就所見所聞敍述你的看法。文章請寫在「非選擇題試卷」上。

　　評分標準：內容4分、組織4分、文法4分、用字遣詞4分、拼字、大小寫及

　　　　　　　標點符號4分。

78年大學聯考英文試題詳解

第一部分：單一選擇題

I. 對話

1. (**B**) 喬：這很重！裏面是什麼東西？

蘇：＿＿＿＿＿＿＿＿＿＿＿

A. 謝謝。我想我能自行處理。　　B. 我的新立體音響。剛買的。

C. 我當然能。很高興你在這兒。

D. 你眞的對它有興趣嗎？

stereo〔ˈstɛrɪo〕*adj.* 立體音響的

2. (**A**) 喬：你會彈鋼琴，對不對？我好幾次聽到，從你公寓傳出來的音樂。

蘇：＿＿＿＿＿＿＿＿＿＿＿

A. 噢，希望沒打擾到你。　　B. 你會知道的，對不對？

C. 我一點也沒有打擾你。　　D. 你喜歡聽，對不對？

3. (**C**) 喬：對了，你認識渥克先生嗎？

蘇：＿＿＿＿＿＿＿＿＿＿＿

A. 不，我從未發生過那件事。　　B. 現在我的確想起來了。

C. 其實，我認得他。　　D. 是的，我湊巧在路上看到他。

by any chance 如果湊巧；萬一　　　***it happens to*** *sb.* 某人發生某事

presently〔ˈprɛzn̩tlɪ〕*adv.* 現在；目前

as a matter of fact 事實上

4. (**A**) 喬：我的腳被絆住了！你能幫我忙嗎？

蘇：＿＿＿＿＿＿＿＿＿＿＿

A. 我看看能不能搬動桌子。　　B. 你可能需要幫助。

C. 爲什麼你認爲我願意幫你？

D. 當然囉。你愛做什麼就做什麼。

5. (**A**) 梅：對不起，我沒辦法不注意到你的耳環。

蘇：＿＿＿＿＿＿＿＿＿＿＿

A. 噢，那是我父母送的禮物。　　B. 它們非常非常美麗。

C. 喔，很抱歉。我自己都沒注意到。

D. 謝謝。你可以擁有它們。

earring〔ˈɪrˌrɪŋ〕*n.* 耳環　　　***can not help*** ＋ *V-ing* 不得不～

6. (D)　梅：相信我，蘇，這個節目對你的地理會有幫助。

　　　　蘇：_____

　　　　　　A. 它叫做「亞馬遜河之旅」。　　B. 你常看公共電視嗎？

　　　　　　C. 對這個節目有何意見？　　　　D. 好吧，你已經說服我去看它了。

　　　　talk sb. into + V-ing 說服某人去做某事

7. (D)　林：如果問你體重多少，你會介意嗎？

　　　　蘇：_____

　　　　　　A. 其實我已經節食很久了。（ on *a diet* 在節食，聯招會的題目中少了 a 。）

　　　　　　B. 老實說，我已經盡力減肥了。

　　　　　　C. 喔，我不介意！大多數的人都很介意這個問題。

　　　　　　　　（ 此處的 no 指 I don't mind，故前後句意不合。）

　　　　　　D. 哈哈！天啊，美國人眞的不喜歡被問到這樣的問題。

　　　　Gee〔dʒi〕*interj.* 天啊！（ 表示強調驚奇的感歎句 ）

8. (C)　約翰：怎麼回事？你看起來眞的很沮喪。

　　　　傑克：_____

　　　　約翰：那麼，祝你下回好運了。

　　　　　　A. 我向來都很尊敬你。　　　　B. 多麼奇怪的巧合啊！

　　　　　　C. 我有個重要考試不及格了。　D. 我？我從來沒有看不起你啊！

　　　　down〔daʊn〕*adj.* 沮喪的　　　*look up to sb.* 尊敬某人

　　　　look down upon sb. 輕視某人

　　　　coincidence〔ko'ɪnsədəns〕*n.* 巧合

9. (B)　約翰：這個周末我們要去遠足。_____

　　　　珍　：好啊！你們要去哪裏？

　　　　約翰：阿里山。

　　　　　　A. 你的計劃如何？　　　　　　B. 要不要一塊兒去？

　　　　　　C. 要是當時你能跟我們一塊兒去就好了。

　　　　　　D. 你有什麼計劃？

10. (B)　傑克：比爾，你知道現在幾點嗎？

　　　　比爾：_____

　　　　傑克：不要緊。不管怎麼說，還是謝謝你。

　　　　　　A. 噢，現在是九點半。　　　　B. 抱歉，我把錶放在家裏。

　　　　　　C. 當然知道。現在是十點半。

　　　　　　D. 當然有空。可是恐怕時間已經太晚了。

　　　　Do you have the time? 現在幾點？

　　　　注意：*Do you have time*? 則是「你有時間嗎？」

Ⅱ. 綜合測驗

Denise： *If you jog for an hour every day*, you're sure to lose weight.

Florence： Could be, ***but*** I've just read a book *arguing otherwise*.
　　　　　　　　　　　　　　11

Patrick： I <u>agree</u> with Florence. I ruined my knees *jogging*.
　　　　　12

"丹 妮 斯：如果你每天慢跑一小時，你的體重一定會減輕。

　佛羅倫斯：可能吧，但是我才剛看過一本書，有不同的說法。

　派 屈 克：我同意佛羅倫斯的話。我因慢跑而傷了膝蓋。"

　　＊ jogging 是由副詞子句 because I jogged 簡化而來的分詞構句，表原因。

　　　　otherwise〔ˈʌðɚˌwaɪz〕*adv.* 不同地　　　ruin〔ˈruɪn〕*v.* 破壞

11.(**A**) 根據前後句意，選用連接詞 but。

12.(**C**) A. read 閱讀　B. argue 爭論　C. ***agree*** 同意　D. disagree 不同意

Denise： Some experts seem to disagree with you *there*. *Maybe* you
　　　　　　　　　　　　　　　　　　　　　13
　　　　didn't wear the <u>proper</u> running shoes.
　　　　　　　　　　14

Florence： Let's face it. The only way *to lose weight* is to <u>eat</u> less.
　　　　　　　　　　　　　　　　　　　　　　　　　　　　15

Patrick： *Not necessarily*. It's clear *from the evidence* ***that*** heredity is
　　　　　　16
　　　　a factor.

"丹 妮 斯：關於這一點，有些專家似乎不同意你的說法。也許你沒有穿適當的慢跑
　　　　　鞋。

　佛羅倫斯：面對事實吧。減輕體重唯一的辦法就是少吃東西。

　派 屈 克：不一定。有證據明白顯示，遺傳也是一個因素。"

　　　　heredity〔həˈrɛdətɪ〕*n.* 遺傳　　factor〔ˈfæktɚ〕*n.* 因素

13.(**B**)　there 在此作「關於那一點」解。其它選項不合句意。

14.(**D**) A. new 新的　B. old 舊的　C. expensive 昂貴的　D. ***proper*** 適當的

15.(**C**) A. run 跑步　B. exercise 運動　C. ***eat*** 吃　D. work 工作

16.(**D**) ***not necessarily*** 未必

　　　　B. fairly〔ˈfɛrlɪ〕*adv.* 公平地

Florence： I try *hard* to avoid eating red meat *and* fatty food.
　　　　　　　　　　　　　　　　　　　　　　　　　　　　17
　Denise： That's no hardship, *given the cost of meat these days.*
　　　　　　　　　　　　　　　18
　Patrick： You may laugh, *but* I've been thinking of becoming a vegetarian.
　　　　　　　　　　　　　　　　　　　　　　　　　　　　　　　19
　Denise： Oh, Patrick, you must be out of your mind.　You will be hun-
　　　　　　　　　　　　　　　 20
　　　　 gry *all the time.*

"佛羅倫斯：我盡量不吃牛、羊肉，以及脂肪過多的食物。
　丹　妮　斯：最近的肉價很貴，那並不難。
　派　屈　克：你大概會笑，我一直想吃素。
　丹　妮　斯：噢，派屈克，你一定是瘋了。你會時時挨餓的。"

　　　　 red meat　紅肉（牛肉、羊肉等）
　　　　 hardship〔'hɑrd‚ʃɪp〕*n.* 艱難　　　*out of one's mind* 發瘋

17.(**A**)　根據句意，應選A. food 來指除了 red meat 以外，其他脂肪過多的食物。
　　　　 C. fatty fish（多脂肪的魚）句意不合。（答案A的food 改成 foods較佳。）

18.(**B**)　given the … days 是由 *if you are* given the … days 簡化而來的分詞構
　　　　 句。A.被拿取，C.被提供，D.被供應，都與句意不合。

19.(**C**)　A. jogger 慢跑者　　B. sportswoman 女運動家
　　　　 C. *vegetarian*〔‚vɛdʒə'tɛrɪən〕*n.* 素食者　　D. cook 廚師

20.(**A**)　表示肯定推測的助動詞，應用must，故選(A)。

　Some reading *you select for yourself* will be for learning, some will
　　　　　　　　　　　　　　　　　　　　　　　　　　　　　　　　21
be for pleasure or recreation. *Since your purpose for reading is not al-*
　　　　　　　　　　　　　　　　　　　　　　　　22
ways the same, the way *in which you read the material* will differ.
　　　 23　　　　　　　　　　　　　　　　　　　　24

　　　 "在你為自己選擇的讀物中，有一些是為了學習之用，有一些則是為了樂趣或消
遣。由於你在不同時候，讀書的目的不盡相同，所以你在閱讀資料時所用的方法，也
會不同。"

　　　　 recreation〔‚rɛkrɪ'eʃən〕*n.* 消遣

21.（ B ）由單數的 Some reading 可知，應選 B. some（reading），some … some 、 some … others 均可形成對照，但 D. others 則是表複數的 other readings，與前面不一致，故只能選 B 。

22.（ A ）根據句意，應選表原因的從屬連接詞 since（既然；因為）。

23.（ B ）B. *the same* 相同的，其他選項句意均不合。

24.（ D ）A. style 風格　B. purpose 目的　C. interest 興趣
　　　　D. *material* 資料

When you read to learn, you should look for main and supporting ideas,
　　　　　　　　　　　　　　　　　　25
trying to remember facts and details. You will probably read the materi-
　　　　　26
al *more than once*.
　　27

"當你是為了學習而讀書時，你應該找出主要及次要的意旨，並試著記住事實和細節。你可能會不止一次閱讀這份資料。"

* trying to … details 是由對等子句 and（*you should*）try to … details 簡化而來的分詞構句，表連續的動作。

supporting〔sə'pɔrtɪŋ〕*adj.* 支持的；協助的

25.（ C ）A. look up 查出　B. look into 調查　C. *look for* 尋找
　　　　D. look through 看穿

26.（ A ）A. *remember* 記住　B. write 寫　C. supply 供給　D. support 支持

27.（ C ）*more than once* 不止一次
　　　　A. for pleasure 為樂趣　B. on purpose 故意地
　　　　D. for a long time 很久

On the other hand, *when* you read *for pleasure*, you should try to read
　　　　　　　　　　　　　28
much faster, *not worrying about unknown words*. Adjusting your reading
　　　29
style to your purpose is an important part *of becoming a skillful reader*.
　　　　　　　30

"另一方面，當你只是爲了樂趣而讀書時，就應該試著讀快一點，不要管不認得的字。根據你的目的來調整讀書方法，是成爲高明的讀者的一個重要因素。"

adjust〔ə'dʒʌst〕v. 調整　　**adjust ～ to**… 調整～使適合…
skillful〔'skɪlfəl〕adj. 精湛的

28. (**C**)　A. as 如～一樣　B. and 和　C. **when** 當～時　D. so 所以

29. (**A**)　A. **faster** 較快　B. slower 較慢　C. more carefully 更加小心
　　　　　　D. more patiently 更有耐心

30. (**D**)　A. ideas 概念　B. facts 事實　C. learning 學習　D. **purpose** 目的

There are three ways *to take the salt from ocean water*: electrodialysis, freezing, *and* distillation. Electrodialysis is used to desalt water
　　　　　　　　　　　　　　　　　　　　　　　　　　　　　　　　　31
that does not have much salt.

"從海水中除去鹽的方法有三種：電滲析法、冷凍法、以及蒸餾法。電滲析法用於除去含鹽量不高的水。"

electrodialysis〔ɪ,lɛktrodaɪ'æləsɪs〕n. 電滲析法
distillation〔,dɪstl̩'eʃən〕n. 蒸餾
desalt〔dɪ'sɔlt〕vt. 除去（海水之）鹽分

31. (**B**)　water〔'wɑtɚ〕n. 水
　　　　　　A. salt 鹽，C. the sea 海洋，D. the ocean 海洋，均不合句意。

In this process, an electric charge is sent *through the salty water* *and*
causes the salt to separate from the water.
　　　　　　　　　　　　　32
"在此過程中，電荷被送入鹽水中，使得鹽從水中分離出來。"

electric charge 電荷

32. (**C**)　**separate from** 分離
　　　　　　A. turn into 使變成，B. melt in 融入，D. get rid of 去掉，均不合句意。

Another method of desalinization is freezing. Ice is pure, fresh
water.
　　　　　　　　　　　　　　　　　　　　　　　　　　　　　　　33

　　"另外一種除去鹽份的方法爲冷凍法。冰是純淨的淡水。"

　　desalinization〔di,sælinəˈzeʃən〕n. 除去鹽份

33.(**A**) fresh〔frɛʃ〕adj. 淡的

　　B. cold 冷的，C. salty 有鹽份的，D. freezing 冰凍的，均與上下文句
　　意不合。

When *seawater is frozen*, the <u>salt</u> separates **and** can be washed off.
　　　　　　　　　　　　　　　34

　　"當海水結冰時，鹽份就會脫離，並且可以清洗掉。"

34.(**C**) salt〔sɔlt〕n. 鹽

　　A. ice 冰，B. water 水，D. material 物質，均不合句意。

Finally, the ice can be <u>melted</u> **and** used as fresh water.
　　　　　　　　　　　　35

　　"最後，就可以把冰融解，當作淡水使用了。"

35.(**D**) be melted 被融解

　　A. be heated 被加熱，B. be frozen 被冰凍，C. be washed 被清洗，
　　均與句意不合。

　　The oldest and most common way *to turn seawater into fresh water*

is distillation.　*In this process*, the sun provides the <u>heat</u> *for distillation*.
　　　　　　　　　　　　　　　　　　　　　36

　　"將海水變成淡水，最古老也是最普通的方法，就是蒸餾。在此過程中，太陽
提供了蒸餾所需的熱力。"

36.(**A**) heat〔hit〕n. 熱力

　　B. source〔sors , sɔrs〕n. 泉源，C. method〔ˈmɛθəd〕n. 方法，
　　D. possibility〔,pɑsəˈbilətι〕n. 可能性，均不合句意。

A piece of plastic covers a few inches of <u>salty</u> water *in a shallow basin*
　　　　　　　　　　　　　　　　　　　37

while the water <u>*evaporates*</u> with the heat of the sun.　The vapor <u>rises</u>
　　　　　　　　　38　　　　　　　　　　　　　　　　　　　　39

<u>*until* *it hits the plastic top.*</u>

" 在淺盆中注入幾吋深的鹽水，當水隨著太陽的熱力蒸發時，拿一塊塑膠板，將盆蓋住。蒸氣會上升，一直到碰到塑膠板為止。"

plastic〔'plæstɪk〕n. 塑膠　　shallow〔'ʃælo〕adj. 淺的
vapor〔'vepɚ〕n. 蒸氣

37.(**B**) salty〔'sɔltɪ〕adj. 有鹽份的
　　　　A. fresh 清淡的，C. hot 熱的，D. frozen 冰凍的，均不合句意。

38.(**D**) evaporate〔ɪ'vepə,ret〕v. 蒸發
　　　　A. run 跑，B. go 去，C. melt 融化，均不合句意。

39.(**A**) rise〔raɪz〕vi. 上升
　　　　B. fall 掉落，C. appear 出現，D. disappear 消失，均不合句意。

Then it condenses into fresh water.　The method is not very efficient
　　　　40

because it does not produce much water *quickly enough.*

" 然後蒸氣就會凝結成為淡水。這方法並不十分有效，因為不能快速生產夠多的水。"

40.(**D**) condense〔kən'dɛns〕v. 凝結
　　　　A. turn 轉變，B. change 改變，C. freeze 凍結，均不合句意。

Ⅲ. 閱讀測驗

With tears streaming down her face, Miss Sophie Harris pleaded with

the post office worker to help her retrieve two love letters *which she*

had mistakenly sent to the wrong addresses.

" 蘇菲‧哈瑞絲小姐帶著兩行熱淚，請求郵局的工作人員，幫她尋回兩封地址錯誤的情書。"

stream〔strim〕v. 流　　plead〔plid〕vi. 懇求
retrieve〔rɪ'triv〕vt. 尋回

Calling it "a matter of life and death," Miss Harris said she had

mixed up letters *to her boyfriends* **and** realized the mistake *only after*

posting them.

"哈瑞絲小姐認爲這是一件「攸關生死的事」,她說她把寄給男友們的信件搞混了,等到寄出之後才發現錯了。"

* Calling it … death," 爲一分詞構句,原句爲 She (= Miss Harris) called it "a matter of life and death," and 在此表附帶狀況 (詳見文法寶典 p. 460)。

The post office succeeded in retrieving the letters after notifying postal authorities *in Taichung and Kaohsiung,* **where the letters had been** *sent.*

"郵局通知台中與高雄的郵政主管單位之後,順利地找回信件。台中與高雄正是信件誤投之處。"

41.(**C**) 哈瑞絲小姐發現她將信件送錯人時,有何反應?

　　　A. 她十分高興。　　　　　　　B. 她十分吃驚。

　　　C. 她很難過,並開始哭泣。

　　　D. 她一點也不緊張,打電話向她的朋友求助。

　　　　　delighted〔dɪˋlaɪtɪd〕*adj.* 高興的

　　　　　amazed〔əˋmezd〕*adj.* 吃驚的　　**take it easy** 不緊張

42.(**C**) 如果哈瑞絲小姐的兩封信,被不該收到的人收到了,結果將會是

　　　A. 對她十分重要。　　　　　　B. 對她非常重要。

　　　C. 對她而言很悲慘。　　　　　D. 對她而言毫無價值。

　　　　　disastrous〔dɪzˋæstrəs, -ˋɑs-〕*adj.* 悲慘的

43.(**C**) 最後,這兩封信怎麼了?

　　　A. 在郵局遺失了。　　　　　　B. 在台灣的某處消失了。

　　　C. 被找到,而且歸還給哈瑞絲小姐。

　　　D. 因爲資料上沒有說明,所以我們不知道。

On November 24, 1988, a 16-year-old boy *with a clean criminal record* was strip-searched **and** sentenced to 25 days in jail *for possessing cigarettes* **while** *visiting his grandparents in Idaho.*

"一九八八年十一月二十四日,一個沒有犯罪紀錄的十六歲男孩,被脫光衣服搜身,並且判拘留二十五天,因爲他在拜訪愛達荷州的祖父母時,身上帶有香煙。"

criminal〔'krɪmən̩ḷ〕 *adj*. 犯罪的

strip-search〔'strɪp,sɝtʃ〕 *v*. 脫光衣服搜身

be sentenced to 被判決

Idaho〔'aɪdə,ho, 'aɪdɪ,ho〕 *n*. 愛達荷州（美國西北部之一州）

He spent one night *in jail* ***before*** *his grandparents paid his fine*.

"I just can't believe this," Jack Larsen, 16, said *late Tuesday night, shortly before being released from the Kootenai County Jail*. "Twenty-five days in here for smoking? I was *so* scared ***that*** *I didn't sleep at all last night*."

"在他祖父母付清罰款之前，他在拘留所待了一個晚上。

「我實在不能相信這件事，」星期二深夜，從庫特內郡拘留所被釋放出來之前不久，十六歲的傑克‧萊森這麼說。「只是抽煙就要在這裏關二十五天？昨夜我嚇得連覺都睡不著。」"

fine〔faɪn〕 *n*. 罰款　　release〔rɪ'lis〕 *vt*. 釋放

county〔'kaʊntɪ〕 *n*. 郡

"I knew I wasn't old *enough to smoke*," he said. "***But*** I thought I'd *just* get a small fine. This is *so* tough *here*. They *even* strip-searched me."

Larsen was released to his grandparents ***after*** *they borrowed $126.50 to pay his fine*. The boy lives in Spokane, Washington, *with his father*.

"「我知道我還不夠大，不能抽煙，」他說道。「但是我認為我只要繳一點罰款就解決了。這裏的做法真是太粗暴了。他們甚至脫光我的衣服搜身。」

萊森的祖父母向別人借了一百二十六元五角來付清罰款，將他保釋出獄。這個男孩和他的父親住在華盛頓的斯波堪城。"

"We live on $600 of Social Security a month," said the boy's grandfather. "***But*** I don't think we can bear leaving him in jail *for something like smoking*."

In Idaho, possession of tobacco is illegal for those *under 18*. Jack has learned a big lesson *from this incident*.

「「我們靠一個月六百元的養老金過活，」男孩的祖父這麼說。「但是我認為，我們不能忍受，讓他為了像抽煙這樣的事，而待在拘留所。」

在愛達荷州，未滿十八歲的少年持有煙草是違法的。傑克已從這次事件中，學到了很大的教訓。"

> Social Security 社會保障制度（包括失業保險、社會醫療、養老金等）
> illegal 〔ɪ'ligl̩〕 *adj.* 違法的　　　　*learn a lesson* 學到教訓
> incident 〔'ɪnsədənt〕 *n.* 事件

44.（ A ）傑克‧萊森被拘捕坐牢是因為
　　　(A) 他違法抽煙。　　　　　　　(B) 他違法販賣煙草。
　　　(C) 他被脫衣搜身。　　　　　　(D) 他抽煙被罰款。

45.（ A ）傑克實際上在拘留所裏待多久？
　　　(A) 一個晚上。　(B) 三天。　　(C) 一個星期。　(D) 二十五天。

46.（ B ）傑克如何形容他在拘留所裏的經驗？
　　　(A) 他興奮得打電話給他的父親。　(B) 他害怕得無法睡覺。
　　　(C) 他擔心得打電話給他的祖父母。
　　　(D) 那是一個他將永難忘記的奇異經驗。
　　　　　fantastic 〔fæn'tæstɪk〕 *adj.* 奇異的

47.（ B ）傑克以前犯過罪嗎？
　　　(A) 有，違法持有煙草。　　　　(B) 不，一次也沒有。
　　　(C) 有，當他在華盛頓的時候。　(D) 資料中沒有提到。

48.（ B ）根據愛達荷州的法律，年滿 _____ 歲以前不准抽煙。
　　　(A) 十六歲　　(B) 十八歲　　(C) 二十歲　　(D) 二十五歲

Money is one of the most important inventions of mankind. *Without* it a complex, modern economy *based on the division of labor* **and** the consequent widespread exchange of goods and services would be impossible.

"金錢是人類最重要的發明之一。如果沒有金錢，那麼建立在分工上的複雜現代化經濟，以及隨之而起的普遍貨物交換和服務業，都是不可能的。"

invention〔ɪn'vɛnʃən〕*n.* 發明　　division of labor 分工

consequent〔'kɑnsə,kwɛnt〕*adj.* 跟隨發生的

widespread〔'waɪd'sprɛd〕*adj.* 普遍的

Because many things, ranging from gold to copper to shells, have been used as money, it cannot be defined as some particular object *but* must *instead* be defined by the functions *it serves* — to act as a medium of exchange *and* a standard of value. A third function of money — as a store of wealth — is something *money shares with many other types of objects*.

　　"因為從金到銅，以至於貝類等許多物質，都曾經被當成錢來使用，所以錢不能用某種特定的物品來界定，而應該以它所提供的功能來下定義——也就是做為交換媒介和價值標準的功能。錢的第三個功能——當做財富的儲存——則是與其他許多類型物品共有的。"

　　＊ ranging from … shells 是由補述用法的形容詞子句 which range from … shells 簡化而來的分詞構句。

　　range〔rendʒ〕*v.* 延及　　copper〔'kɑpə〕*n.* 銅

　　medium〔'midɪəm〕*n.* 媒介　　share〔ʃɛr〕*v.* 共有

49.（**C**）錢是人類一項重要的發明，乃是因為

　　(A) 它是普遍的貨物交換和服務業的結果。

　　(B) 它建立在分工的基礎上。

　　(C) 它是現代經濟中不可或缺的因素。

　　(D) 它的範圍從金、銅，以至於貝類都有。

　　　　indispensable〔,ɪndɪs'pɛnsəbḷ〕*adj.* 不可或缺的

50.（**D**）錢最好是以＿＿＿＿＿來定義。

　　(A) 它和分工的關係

　　(B) 代表它的物品

　　(C) 它能購買的黃金數目

　　(D) 它被使用的目的

　　　　in terms of 以～之觀點　　represent〔,rɛprɪ'zɛnt〕*vt.* 代表

　　　　purchase〔'pɝtʃəs〕*vt.* 購買

第二部分：非選擇題

Ⅰ. 翻譯：中譯英

1. 讀小學的時候，我身體很虛弱，並且常感冒。

   When I *was* **in** *elementary school*, my body was very weak **and** I

   often caught colds.

   > elementary school 小學

2. 自從上了國中以後，我就盡量找機會運動。

   Beginning with junior high (*school*), I *continuously* looked for oppor-

   tunities *involving* ⎰ *physical activity.*
   ⎱ *exercise.*

3. 雖然功課一直很繁重，我還是每天慢跑半小時。

   Even though *my studies took up a great deal of my time*, I continued

   to jog *for half an hour every day.*

4. 六年繼續不斷的鍛鍊使我不但更加強壯，而且也長得更高。

   Six years of nonstop physical conditioning has made me **not only**

   stronger, **but also** taller.

   > ＊physical conditioning 不要寫成 *exercise*，否則句意會變成「日夜不停在
   > 運動」。
   >
   > condition〔kən'dɪʃən〕*vt*. 訓練

5. 現在大家都說他們無法相信我從前又矮又瘦。

   Now, people say **that** they cannot believe **that** I was *once* very small

   and thin.

Ⅱ. 英文作文（參考範例）

　　Since I am a commuter, I go to school by bus every day.　One day
I walked to the bus stop as usual.　When I finally got on the bus, the
air was very bad.　What was worse was that the traffic was very heavy.

It took me almost one and a half hours to reach my destination. After getting off the bus, I was soaked to the bone.

The experience taught me the importance of the rapid transportation system. During rush hour, we waste a lot of time which we can use to do lots of work. *Therefore*, I think the government should set up the rapid transportation system as soon as possible. Only by doing so can we ease the traffic jams and let ourselves live a more convenient life.

> commuter〔kə′mjutɚ〕 *n.* 通勤者
> *be soaked to the bone* "全身濕透"
> *rapid transportation system* 捷運系統　　*rush hour* 交通擁擠時間

心得筆記欄 ....

七十七學年度大學暨獨立學院入學考試
英 文 試 題

第一部分：複選題

發　音（5%）

　　下面 1 至 5 題，每題有五個英文單字，找出其中畫線部分的母音或子音發音相同的，標示在答案卡上。每題相同的母音或子音最少兩個，最多五個。每題全對得 1 分，答錯倒扣 1/25 分，不答不給分。

　　例：(A) b<u>oo</u>k　(B) lam<u>b</u>　(C) B<u>o</u>b　(D) b<u>ee</u>　(E) b<u>ee</u>n　答案：A B C D E ■ □ ■ ■ ■

1. (A) b<u>a</u>th　(B) m<u>ea</u>t　(C) br<u>ea</u>k　(D) t<u>a</u>ke　(E) M<u>i</u>ss
2. (A) c<u>oo</u>k　(B) p<u>oo</u>r　(C) p<u>u</u>sh　(D) g<u>oo</u>d　(E) f<u>oo</u>t
3. (A) <u>o</u>nly　(B) al<u>o</u>ne　(C) al<u>o</u>ng　(D) <u>ow</u>n　(E) h<u>o</u>me
4. (A) f<u>i</u>sh　(B) u<u>s</u>ual　(C) plea<u>s</u>e　(D) pea<u>c</u>e　(E) deci<u>s</u>ion
5. (A) lo<u>ng</u>er　(B) foreig<u>n</u>er　(C) si<u>ng</u>er　(D) fi<u>ng</u>er　(E) a<u>ng</u>ry

第二部分：單一選擇題

一、對　話（5%）

　　下面 6 至 10 題是簡單的對話，各自獨立。每題各有一個空白，並各附四個備選答案。請依照對話的內容，選出一個最適當的答案標示在答案卡上。每題答對得 1 分，答錯倒扣 1/3 分，不答不給分。

6. Peter : Let's go to the movies tonight.

　John : But I have to prepare for tomorrow's math exam.

　Peter : _____, let's go! You won't flunk it!

　(A) Great　(B) Oh, no　(C) Of course　(D) Come on

7. Manager : This is a challenging job. Who wants it?

　David : _____

　(A) I'll take it.　(B) It's a good idea.　(C) You bet!　(D) No sweat!

8. Guest : I brought this painting from my country. I hope you like it.

　Host : _____

　(A) It's a pity.　(B) No wonder.　(C) That's exactly what I want !
　(D) Let's face it.

9.　Daddy : This is a birthday present for you.

　　Daughter : _____

　　(A) What's the problem ?　　　　(B) Oh, what a surprise !

　　(C) I can't help it !　　　　　　(D) I'm afraid so.

10. Student : How come I always make a lot of mistakes in speaking English?

　　Teacher : Don't worry too much about mistakes._____

　　(A) Might is right.　　　　　　(B) Practice what you preach.

　　(C) Practice makes perfect.　　(D) Pride goes before a fall.

二、綜合測驗　（20%）

　　下面三段文章，共有二十個空白（11 至 30），每個空白附有四個備選答案。
仔細閱讀各段文章後，選出一個最適當的答案標示在答案卡上。每題答對得1
分，答錯倒扣1/3分，不答不給分。

　　Nowadays, most cameras are very easy to use. In the 1800s,＿＿11＿＿,
photography was much more difficult. In the first＿＿12＿＿, the cameras
were large and＿＿13＿＿. Also photographers needed to＿＿14＿＿glass plates
and chemicals with them＿＿15＿＿their cameras. They used the plates and
chemicals to develop their pictures. In those days, photographers had to
develop their pictures＿＿16＿＿after they took them. Some of the chemicals
smelled very＿＿17＿＿and burned holes in clothing. One chemical, silver
nitrate,＿＿18＿＿the photographers' fingers turn black. Photography was
＿＿19＿＿easy task. Therefore, most photographers＿＿20＿＿professionals.

11. (A) however　　　(B) moreover　　　(C) anyway　　　(D) accordingly

12. (A) time　　　　(B) place　　　　(C) point　　　　(D) year

13. (A) small　　　　(B) big　　　　　(C) light　　　　(D) heavy

14. (A) carry　　　　(B) use　　　　　(C) cause　　　　(D) find

15. (A) more than　　(B) instead of　　(C) in addition to　(D) with a view to

16. (A) right　　　　(B) left　　　　　(C) quick　　　　(D) fast

17. (A) pretty　　　　(B) worse　　　　(C) bad　　　　　(D) ugly

18. (A) got　　　　　(B) forced　　　　(C) made　　　　(D) burned

19. (A) not　　　　　(B) rather　　　　(C) none　　　　(D) no

20. (A) are　　　　　(B) were　　　　　(C) have been　　(D) had been

An extremely wealthy man was greeted one evening by his young daughter who announced, "Daddy, ___21___ my dog today."

"___22___" asked the father. "For how much?"

"___23___ —ten thousand dollars！"

"Really? ___24___ the money."

"Oh, I didn't get any money," replied the daughter. "I got 2 five-thousand-dollar cats ___25___ it."

21. (A) I'll sell　　(B) I'd sold　　(C) I'm selling　　(D) I sold
22. (A) You're kidding,(B) Sold your dog?　(C) Wait a minute！　(D) Don't fool me.
23. (A) I don't know　(B) Very expensive　(C) You won't believe it(D) It's worth it
24. (A) Who paid　　(B) Show me　　(C) Did you count　　(D) Cash
25. (A) for　　　　　(B) on　　　　　　(C) at　　　　　　　(D) by

Ai-mei : Mom, I think I've ___26___ with a cold. I'm not well enough to go to Wen-lan's birthday party tonight.

Mother : ___27___ worry about it. I'll give her a ring and explain. I'm sure she'll understand.

Ai-mei : But I wanted so much to go. I've been ___28___ all week.

Mother : I know exactly ___29___, dear. Why don't we throw a party for your birthday which is next month, and invite Wen-lan over？

Ai-mei : Thanks, mom. That's very thoughtful ___30___ you."

26. (A) caught up　　(B) come down　　(C) brought up　　(D) fallen down
27. (A) You won't　　(B) Won't you　　(C) You don't　　(D) Don't you
28. (A) looked forward to it　　　　(B) looked forward to go
　　(C) looking forward to it　　　　(D) looking forward to go
29. (A) how to feel　(B) how you feel　(C) what to feel　(D) what you feel
30. (A) of　　　　　(B) for　　　　　(C) by　　　　　(D) from

三、閱讀測驗 （20%）

下面四篇文章共有十個題目（ 31 至 40 ），每題各附四個備選答案。仔細閱讀文章以後，把最適合文意的一個答案標示在答案卡上。每題答對得 2 分，答錯倒扣 2/3 分，不答不給分。

Seahorses live in warm, shallow water where there is lots of sea grass. They can change their color to match the colors of the grass, so it is very hard to see them. Their coloring protects them. This is called protective coloring. In warm weather, they spend their time mostly about a meter below the surface of the water. When it gets cold, they go down to about seven meters below the surface. At this depth, the temperature of the water does not change very much. When there is a storm, the seahorse holds onto a piece of grass with its tail. Then it cannot be carried to the shore.

31. It is not easy to see seahorses because
    (A) they are very small.
    (B) their color may become very much like those of the grass.
    (C) they live in warm, shallow water.
    (D) they can hide themselves in the depths of water.

32. Which of the following sentences best states the main idea of the above passage?
    (A) Seahorses can change their color.
    (B) Seahorses like to stay in shallow water.
    (C) Seahorses have their ways of protecting themselves.
    (D) In cold weather, seahorses do not live in shallow water.

The marathon is a race with a long history. It was first run over two thousand years ago in Greece by just one runner. The race became a part of the ancient Olympics. The first marathon in the United States took place almost one hundred years ago. It was held in New York City. The year was 1896. Another marathon was run in that same year in Boston. But these races did not get a lot of attention at that time. There were not many runners then. And only a few were willing--or able--to run a race of more than 26 miles.

But in recent years jogging has become a very popular sport. People who at one time could barely run a few yards to catch their morning buses are now jogging. Many people run one or two miles a day. And marathon running appeals to many of them. The number of marathons has grown to keep pace with the new public interest. Now, a marathon is run somewhere in the United States every week of the year.

33. Which of the following sentences best states the main idea of the
    above passage?
    (A) The marathon is a Greek sport.
    (B) The marathon was already quite popular in the United States about
        one hundred years ago.
    (C) Jogging is a popular sport.
    (D) The marathon is more popular in the United States now than it was
        in the nineteenth century.

34. About how many marathons are held in the United States every year?
    (A) Fifty.　　(B) Forty.　　(C) Thirty.　　(D) Twenty.

35. The first marathons held in the United States in 1896 didn't have many
    runners because
    (A) the prizes were too few and they were not attractive enough.
    (B) the marathons were held in the areas where the weather was too cold.
    (C) not many people could run that long and very few people paid atten-
        tion to them.
    (D) most people preferred jogging to running marathons.

　　Human beings wouldn't be human if they didn't wonder about the world
around them. Many thousands of years ago, when mankind was still primitive, men must have looked out of caves and wondered about what they
saw. What made the lightning flash? Where did the wind come from? Why
would winter start soon and why would all the green things die? And then
why did they all come back to life the next spring?

　　Man wondered about himself, too. Why did men get sick sometimes?
Why did all men get old and die eventually? Who first taught men how to
use fire and how to weave cloth?

　　There were any number of questions but there were no scientific
answers. These were the days before science; before men had learned to
experiment in order to determine the hows and whys of the universe.

　　What early man had to do was to invent what seemed to be the most
logical answers. And the concepts of "god" and "demon" were created to
account for the various phenomena in the world. For example, the lightning seemed, perhaps, the huge deadly spear of a god, and disease could
be the result of invisible arrows fired by a demon.

36. Primitive men asked many questions about the world because

(A) they were frightened. (B) they were curious about the world.

(C) they were rather dumb. (D) they were uneducated.

37. Primitive men before the scientific age

(A) could find no answers at all to their questions about man and the world.

(B) were able to find scientific answers based upon logic.

(C) were not inventive enough in giving answers to their questions.

(D) managed to answer their questions in their own logical way.

38. The best title for the above passage is

(A) The World Views of Primitive Men. (B) Man and Nature.

(C) Primitive Society and the World. (D) Disease and Lightning.

　　In most modern industrial countries, "Keeping up with the Joneses" is the main concern of most people. In other words, people want to improve their standard of living. They want to have as much as their neighbors ("the Joneses") and, if possible, even more. This and other features of life in a modern industrial society have some serious results. Keeping up with the Joneses naturally causes a great deal of stress and nervous tension. People worry about whether they have as much money and as many material things as other people have.

　　The stress, nervous tension and worry cause a good deal of illness. Some doctors in these industrial countries estimate that as many as 50% of their patients are not suffering from real physical illnesses at all. Instead, they are suffering from illnesses with physical symptoms but mental causes.

39. " Keeping up with the Joneses" means

(A) competing with one's neighbors in raising the living standard.

(B) making the Joneses happy.

(C) making friends with the Joneses.

(D) putting pressure on the Joneses.

40. The competitive life in a modern industrial society has brought about
    (A) many physical illnesses without mental disorders.
    (B) many mental illnesses without physical symptoms.
    (C) many mental illnesses with physical symptoms.
    (D) many physical illnesses caused by poverty.

第三部分：非選擇題

一、填　充　（10％）

下面的文章中有十個空格（1至10），在每一個空格中填一個適當的英文字（word）。每一個正確的字得1分。答案請寫在「非選擇題答案卷」上，同時務必標示題號。

My neighbor across the street is having a garage sale. Let's go there and look at all the items for sale.

There are a lot of things for sale today. There are some clothes over ___1___. There are some dresses, shoes, hats, and sweaters. Under the table ___2___ a box of books. There are a lot of books. Here is an interesting book ___3___ photography.

Look at this! Here is a picture of Aunt Lucy. ___4___ wants to buy this old thing? Maybe someone likes to collect old pictures.

On this table there are some items for the ___5___: some dishes, some cups, four old spoons, a coffee pot, and a pan.

Look at the old woman near the coffee pot. Her dress is very old, and her sweater has holes. She wants to ___6___ the coffee pot, but she does not seem to have much ___7___. The coffee pot costs $4.00, but my friend ___8___ it to her for only $1.50.

Now the old woman is walking ___9___. Look! She is getting into that big, expensive car. Look at my neighbor's face. He is very surprised.

Garage sales are interesting, but sometimes the people ___10___ garage sales are even more interesting.

二、中譯英　（20％）

下面一段短文共有五個中文句子，請譯成通順而達意的英文，每句4分。答案請寫在「非選擇題答案卷」上，同時務必標示題號。

1. 英語是一種重要的語言，所以很多人都在學習。

2. 許多中國學生認為學習說英語很難。

3. 但是只要經常練習，任何困難都可以克服。

4. 會背課本上的對話，並不表示會說英語。

5. 最重要的是，要能用英語說自己想說的話。

三、英文作文　（20％）

寫一篇大約八十個英文字（words）的英文作文，說明樹木對人類的重要。第一段描述樹木對人類的益處，第二段說明如何保護樹木，每段約四十個字。文章寫在「非選擇題答案卷」上，並參考下面的評分標準：

拼字與標點（4％），遣詞用字（4％），文法（4％），組織（4％），內容（4％）。

77年大學聯考英文試題詳解

第一部分：複選題

發音

1.（　**C D**　）(A) b<u>a</u>th〔bæθ〕*n*. 洗澡；浴室　(B) m<u>ea</u>t〔mit〕*n*. 肉
(C) br<u>ea</u>k〔brek〕*v*. 打破　(D) t<u>a</u>ke〔tek〕*v*. 拿
(E) M<u>i</u>ss〔mɪs〕*n*. 小姐

2.（**A B C D E**）(A) c<u>oo</u>k〔kʊk〕*v*. 烹調　(B) p<u>oo</u>r〔pʊr〕*adj*. 貧窮的
(C) p<u>u</u>sh〔pʊʃ〕*v*. 推　(D) g<u>oo</u>d〔gʊd〕*adj*. 好的
(E) f<u>oo</u>t〔fʊt〕*n*. 腳

3.（　**A B D E**　）(A) <u>o</u>nly〔'onlɪ〕*adj*. 唯一的　(B) al<u>o</u>ne〔ə'lon〕*adj*. 單獨的
(C) al<u>o</u>ng〔ə'lɔŋ〕*prep*. 沿著　(D) <u>o</u>wn〔on〕*vt*. 擁有
(E) h<u>o</u>me〔hom〕*n*. 家

4.（　**B E**　）(A) f<u>i</u>sh〔fɪʃ〕*n*. 魚　(B) u<u>s</u>ual〔'juʒʊəl〕*adj*. 通常的
(C) plea<u>s</u>e〔pliz〕*v*. 使快樂　(D) pea<u>c</u>e〔pis〕*n*. 和平
(E) deci<u>s</u>ion〔dɪ'sɪʒən〕*n*. 決定

5.（　**A D E**　）(A) lon<u>g</u>er〔'lɔŋgɚ,'lɑŋgɚ〕*adj*. 比較久的
(B) forei<u>g</u>ner〔'fɔrɪnɚ,'fɑrɪnɚ〕*n*. 外國人
(C) sin<u>g</u>er〔'sɪŋɚ〕*n*. 歌者　(D) fin<u>g</u>er〔'fɪŋgɚ〕*n*. 手指
(E) an<u>g</u>ry〔'æŋgrɪ〕*adj*. 生氣的

第二部分：單一選擇題

一、對話

6.（**D**）彼得：今天晚上我們去看電影吧。
約翰：但是我得準備明天的數學考試。
彼得：＿＿＿＿＿＿＿，走吧！你不會當掉的！
(A) 太棒了　　(B) 哦，不　　(C) 當然　　　(D) <u>好啦</u>
come on "（做懇懇語）好啦，請啦"

7.（**A**）經理：這是一份富有挑戰性的工作。誰想做？
大衛：＿＿＿＿＿＿＿＿＿
(A) <u>我願意接受。</u>　(B) 是個好主意。　(C) 當然！　　(D) 輕而易舉！

8.（**C**）客人：我在我的國家買了這幅畫，但願你會喜歡。

主人：_____

(A) 眞可惜。　　　　　　　　(B) 難怪。

(C) 那正是我想要的！　　　　(D) 讓我們面對它吧。

9.（**B**）父親：這是給妳的生日禮物。

女兒：_____

(A) 是什麼問題呢？　　　　　(B) 哦，眞叫人驚喜的禮物！

(C) 我沒有辦法！　　　　　　(D) 恐怕會如此！

10.（**C**）學生：爲什麼在講英文的時候，我老是犯一大堆錯誤？

老師：不要太擔心犯錯。_____

(A) 強權卽是公理。　　　　　(B) 說得到要做得到。

(C) 熟能生巧。　　　　　　　(D) 驕者必敗。

　　　　might〔maɪt〕*n.* 強權　　preach〔pritʃ〕*vi.* 說教

二、綜合測驗

Nowadays, most cameras are *very* easy to use. *In the 1800s , however*,
photography was *much* more difficult. ***In the first place***, the cameras were
large ***and*** heavy. *Also* photographers needed to carry glass plates ***and***
chemicals *with them in addition to their cameras*. They used the plates
and chemicals *to develop their pictures*.

　　"現在大部分的照相機使用起來都非常簡便。然而，在一八〇〇年代，攝影却
困難多了。首先，當時的照相機又大又重。而且除了相機之外，攝影者還得隨身帶
著玻璃感光版和化學藥品。他們使用感光版和化學藥品來沖洗照片。"

　　　　nowadays〔'nauə,dez〕*adv.* 現今　　camera〔'kæmərə〕*n.* 照相機
　　　　photography〔fə'tɑgrəfɪ〕*n.* 攝影（術）
　　　　photographer〔fə'tɑgrəfə,fo-〕*n.* 攝影者
　　　　plate〔plet〕*n.*〔攝〕感光版　　chemical〔'kɛmɪkl〕*n.* 化學藥品
　　　　develop〔dɪ'vɛləp〕*vt.*〔攝〕顯影；沖洗

11.（**A**）(A) 然而　　　　(B) 此外　　　　(C) 無論如何

　　　(D) accordingly〔ə'kɔrdɪŋlɪ〕*adv.* 於是

12.（ **B** ）　***in the first place***　"首先"

13.（ **D** ）　(A) 小　　　　(B) 大　　　　(C) 輕　　　　(D) 重

14.（ **A** ）　***carry*** *sth.* ***with*** *sb.*　"隨身帶著～"

15.（ **C** ）　(A) 超過　　　(B) 代替　　　(C) 除了～之外　(D) 爲了

In those days, photographers had to develop their pictures *right after*

16

they took them. Some of the chemicals smelled very bad *and* burned holes

17

in clothing. One chemical, silver nitrate, made the photographers'

18

fingers turn black. Photography was no easy task. *Therefore*, most pho-

19

tographers were professionals.

20

"當時，攝影者一拍完照，就得沖洗照片。有些化學藥品的味道很難聞，而且會把衣服燒破洞。有種化學藥品叫做硝酸銀，會弄黑攝影者的手指。攝影絕不是簡單的工作。因此，大多數的攝影者都是專業的。"

　　＊ silver nitrate 是 One chemical 的同位語。

　　　　nitrate〔'naɪtret〕*n.* 硝酸鹽　　***silver nitrate***〔化〕硝酸銀
　　　　professional〔prə'fɛʃənl〕*n.* 從事專門職業的人

16.（ **A** ）　(A) 馬上；即刻　　(B) 左邊的　　(C) 快的　　(D) 快的

17.（ **C** ）　(A) 漂亮的　　　(B) 更糟的　　(C) 令人不愉快的　(D) 醜的

18.（ **C** ）　使役動詞 make ＋受詞＋原形動詞。（詳見文法寶典 p. 421）
　　　　(A) get，(B) force，(D) burn 沒有上述的句型。

19.（ **D** ）　no 加在 be 動詞的補語（名詞）或其他形容詞之前，作「絕不是」解。
　　　　例：He is ***no*** scholar.（他根本不是個學者。）
　　　　(A) *not* → not an

20.（ **B** ）　本題敘述過去的事實，故用過去式。

An *extremely* wealthy man was greeted *one evening* by his young

daughter *who announced*, " *Daddy*, *I sold my dog today.*"

21

"<u>Sold your dog?</u>" asked the father. "For how much?"
 ₂₂

"<u>You won't believe it</u> — ten thousand dollars！"
 ₂₃

"Really？<u>Show me</u> the money."
 ₂₄

"Oh，I didn't get any money," replied the daughter. "I got 2 five-

thousand-dollar cats <u>for</u> it."
 ₂₅

　　"有天晚上，大富翁的小女兒迎接他回家，並且對他說：「爸爸，我今天把狗

賣掉了。」

　　「賣狗？」這父親接著問：「賣了多少錢？」

　　「你不會相信的——賣了一萬元！」

　　「眞的？把錢拿給我看。」

　　「哦，我沒拿錢，」這女兒回答說：「我拿它換了兩隻價值五千元的貓。」"

　　　　extremely〔ɪk'strimlɪ〕adv. 非常地　greet〔grit〕vt. 迎接

　　　　announce〔ə'naʊns〕vt. 宣告

21.（**D**）敘述過去發生的事，故用過去式。

　　　　(A) 未來式，(B)過去完成式，(C)現在進行式，都不合句意。

22.（**B**）(A) 你在開玩笑吧，　(B) 賣狗？　　(C) 等一會兒！　(D) 不要騙我。

23.（**C**）(A) 我不知道　　(B) 非常貴　　(C) 你不會相信的　(D) 它很值得

24.（**B**）(A) 誰付(錢)呢　(B) 拿給我看　　(C) 你有數(錢)嗎 (D) 兌現

25.（**A**）for 在此表示「交換」，相當於 *in exchange of* 。

Ai-mei : Mom, I think I've <u>come down</u> with a cold. I'm not well *enough*

　　　　 <u>　　　26　　　</u>

　　　　 to go to Wen-lan's birthday party tonight.

Mother : <u>Don't you</u> worry about it. I'll give her a ring **and** explain. I'm
　　　　　 ₂₇

　　　　 sure she'll understand.

"艾美：媽，我想我已經感冒了。我不太舒服,今天晚上沒辦法去參加文蘭的生日宴

　　　　會。

　　母親：妳不用擔心。我會打電話向她解釋。我相信她會了解。"

　　　　ring〔rɪŋ〕n. 打電話

26. (**B**) (A) 趕上　　　　(B) 病倒　　　　(C) 養育　　　　(D) 倒下

27. (**D**) Don't you ＋原形動詞… .〔不可寫成 *You don't* ＋原形動詞… .〕本題是祈使句的否定句型,保留主詞 you,是為了引起對方注意。(詳見文法寶典 p.358)

Ai-mei : **But** I wanted *so much* to go. I've been looking forward to it
28
all week.

Mother : I know *exactly* **how** you feel, dear. Why don't we throw a party
29
for your birthday, **which is next month, and** invite Wen-lan over?

Ai-mei : Thanks, mom. That's *very* thoughtful of you."
30

"艾美:但是我很想去。我整個星期都在盼望它的來臨。

　母親:親愛的,我很清楚妳的感受。妳的生日就在下個月,我們何不也辦個生日宴會,邀請文蘭過來呢?

　艾美:謝謝媽。妳那麼做實在很週到。"

28. (**C**) look forward to(盼望)後面必須接代名詞、名詞或動名詞。而且根據句意,應用現在完成進行式。

29. (**B**) (A)如何感覺,不合句意;(C)(D)中的 feel 是不及物動詞,不可接 what 為受詞,故選(B)。

30. (**A**) be thoughtful of "(為他人)設想週到"

三、閱讀測驗

Seahorses live in warm, shallow water *where there is lots of sea grass*.
They can change their color *to match the colors of the grass*, *so* it is *very*
hard to see them. Their coloring protects them. This is called protective
coloring. *In warm weather*, they spend their time *mostly about a meter*
below the surface of the water.

"海馬生活在溫暖的淺水中，那兒有許多的海草。牠們能夠改變身體的顏色來配合海草的顏色，所以要看到牠們非常困難。變色保護牠們。這就叫保護色。天氣暖和時，牠們大部分的時間都待在水面下一公尺的地方。"

seahorse〔'si,hɔrs〕*n.* 海馬　meter〔'mitɚ〕*n.* 公尺

When *it gets cold*, they go down to about seven meters *below the surface*.

At this depth, the temperature of the water does not change very much.

When *there is a storm*, the seahorse holds onto a piece of grass *with its tail*. *Then* it cannot be carried to the shore.

"天氣變冷，牠們就沈到水面下大約七公尺的地方。在這個深度，水溫的改變並不大。有暴風雨的話，海馬就用尾巴鉤住一根海草，那麼牠就不會被帶到岸上去了。"

31.（**B**）想看到海馬並不容易是因為

　　(A) 牠們很小。

　　(B) 牠們身體的顏色可以變得和海草的顏色很相近。

　　(C) 牠們生活在溫暖的淺水中。　　(D) 牠們可以把自己藏身在深水中。

32.（**C**）下列何者最能說明上面這段文章的主旨？

　　(A) 海馬可以改變身體的顏色。　　(B) 海馬喜歡待在淺水中。

　　(C) 海馬有保護自己的方法。

　　(D) 天氣冷的時候，海馬就不住在淺水中。

The marathon is a race *with a long history*. It was *first* run *over two thousand years ago* *in Greece* *by just one runner*. The race became a part of the ancient Olympics. The first marathon *in the United States* took place *almost one hundred years ago*. It was held *in New York City*.

"馬拉松是一項歷史悠久的賽跑。最早起源於兩千多年以前的希臘，跑者只有一個。這種賽跑後來成為古代奧林匹克運動會的一部分。美國最早的馬拉松，大約是在一百年前舉行的。地點在紐約市。"

marathon〔'mærə,θɑn,-θən〕*n.* 馬拉松

Olympics〔o'lɪmpɪks〕*n.pl.* 奧林匹克運動會

The year was 1896. Another marathon was run *in that same year* *in Boston*.
But these races did not get a lot of attention *at that time*. There were
not many runners *then*. *And* only a few were willing — or able — to run a
race *of more than 26 miles.*

"時間是一八九六年。同年在波士頓也有另一項馬拉松開跑。但是這些賽跑在當時並未受到太多的注意。跑者並不多。而且只有少數人願意——或是能夠——跑二十六哩以上。"

But *in recent years* jogging has become a *very* popular sport. People
who *at one time could barely run a few yards to catch their morning
buses* are *now* jogging. Many people run *one or two miles a day*. *And*
marathon running appeals to many of them. The number of marathons has
grown to keep pace with the new public interest. Now, a marathon is run
somewhere in the United States every week of the year.

"但是近幾年來，慢跑成為很受歡迎的運動。以前想趕上早班公車，跑個幾碼幾乎都不行的人，現在也在慢跑。很多人一天跑個一兩哩。而且其中很多人對馬拉松跑步很有興趣。馬拉松比賽的數目隨著大眾對它的注意而增加。如今，馬拉松在美國每個星期都舉行。"

jog〔dʒɑg〕*vi.* 慢跑　　*keep pace with* "與～並駕齊驅"

33.（ D ）下列何者最能說明上面這段文章的主旨？
　　(A) 馬拉松是希臘的運動。
　　(B) 馬拉松大約在一百年前，就已經在美國廣受歡迎。
　　(C) 慢跑是一般的運動。
　　(D) 馬拉松現在在美國比十九世紀時更受人歡迎。

34.（ A ）美國每年大約舉行多少次的馬拉松？
　　(A) 五十。
　　(B) 四十。
　　(C) 三十。
　　(D) 二十。

35.（**C**）一八九六年，美國舉行第一次的馬拉松比賽，跑者不多是因爲 _____
　　　　(A) 獎品太少，而且不夠吸引人。
　　　　(B) 馬拉松在天氣酷寒的地方舉行。
　　　　(C) 沒有多少人能跑那麼遠，而且沒什麼人注意他們。
　　　　(D) 大多數的人比較喜歡慢跑，而不喜歡跑馬拉松。

Human beings wouldn't be human *if they didn't wonder about the world around them*. Many thousands of years ago, **when** mankind was still primitive, men must have looked out of caves **and** wondered about **what** they saw. What made the lightning flash? Where did the wind come from? Why would winter start *soon* **and** why would all the green things die? **And** then why did they all come back to life *the next spring*?

　　「如果人們不對周遭世界感到好奇，就不算是人類。在數千年前，原始人的時代，人們一定會從洞穴裏往外看，想知道自己所見的一切。閃電爲什麼閃爍？風從那裏來？冬天爲什麼會這麼快開始，草木又爲什麼枯死？下一個春天來臨時，爲什麼一切又復甦了？」

* Human beings *wouldn't be* ～ if they *didn't* ‥‥. 是與現在事實相反的假設，所以主要子句動詞部份是would＋原形動詞，條件子句是過去式。（詳見文法寶典 p. 361）

* when mankind was still primitive 在關係副詞 when 前加逗點，表示是補述的對等子句，用來補充說明前一句話的句意，而非形容詞子句。（詳見文法寶典 p. 244）

* men must have looked ～ saw 中，must have＋過去分詞，表示過去肯定的推測。（詳見文法寶典 p. 319）

　　wonder about ～「對～感到好奇；想知道～」
　　mankind〔mæn'kaɪnd〕*n.* 人類（當單數用）
　　primitive〔'prɪmətɪv〕*n.* 原始人　　flash〔flæʃ〕*vi.* 閃爍；閃光

Man wondered about himself, too. Why did men get sick *sometimes*? Why did all men get old **and** die *eventually*? Who *first* taught men how to use fire **and** how to weave cloth?

"人們也對自己感到好奇。爲什麼有時候人會生病？爲什麼人會變老，最後死亡？第一個教我們用火、織布的人是誰？"

> eventually〔ɪˈvɛntʃʊəlɪ〕*adv.* 最後　　weave〔wiv〕*vt.* 織

There were *any number of* questions **but** there were no scientific answers. These were the days *before science*; **before** *men had learned to experiment* *in order to determine the hows and whys of the universe.*

"問題有很多，只是缺少科學的解答。這是科學以前的時代，是人們尚未學會實驗，以解答宇宙運行方法及理由的時代。"

any number of "無論多少；無數的"

What early man had to do was to invent **what** seemed to be the most logical answers. **And** the concepts *of "god" and "demon"* were created *to account for the various phenomena in the world.* **For example**, the lightning seemed, *perhaps*, the huge deadly spear *of a god*, **and** disease could be the result *of invisible arrows fired by a demon.*

"原始人該做的事即發明似乎是最合邏輯的解答。「神」與「魔鬼」的概念便因應而生，以解釋世上各種現象。例如：閃電或許很像神致命的大矛。而疾病就是魔鬼發出的無形箭。"

> * fired by a demon 是由形容詞子句which were fired by a demon 簡化而成的分詞片語，修飾 arrows。
>
> concept〔ˈkɑnsɛpt〕*n.* 概念　　demon〔ˈdimən〕*n.* 魔鬼
> **account for** "解釋"
> phenomena〔fəˈnɑmənə〕*n. pl.* 現象（單數形是 phenomenon）
> spear〔spɪr〕*n.* 矛　　invisible〔ɪnˈvɪzəbḷ〕*adj.* 看不見的
> arrow〔ˈæro〕*n.* 箭　　fire〔faɪr〕*vt.* 發射

36.（ **B** ）原始人類對世界有許多疑問，因爲 ————

　　　(A) 他們受驚嚇。　　　　　　　(B) 他們對世界好奇。
　　　(C) 他們相當遲頓。　　　　　　(D) 他們未受教育。

37.（**D**）科學時代之前的原始人類 ＿＿＿＿＿＿＿＿＿＿

  (A) 完全不能解答自己對人、對世界的疑問。

  (B) 能找出有邏輯基礎的解答。

  (C) 解答疑問時創意不足。 (D) 嘗試以自己的邏輯方式回答問題。

   base on～ " 以～爲基礎 "

38.（**A**）以上這段文章最佳標題是 ＿＿＿＿＿＿＿＿＿＿

  (A) 原始人的世界觀。 (B) 人與大自然。

  (C) 原始社會與世界。 (D) 疾病與閃電。

 In most modern industrial countries，"keeping up with the Joneses" is the main concern *of most people*. *In other words*, people want to improve their standard *of living*. They want to have *as* much *as their neighbors* ("*the Joneses*") *and*, if possible, even more.

  " 大部份現代工業國家中，大多數人最關心的事是「與隔壁的張三李四並駕齊驅」。換句話說，人們想提升生活水準。他們想要與鄰居（張三李四）同樣富有，如果可能的話，要比他們更富有。"

  ＊ Jones 是相當普遍的姓氏，所以 the Joneses（姓氏的複數形表某姓氏一家人）用來泛指一般世人、鄰人，類似中國人所謂的「張三李四」。

  ＊ if possible 是由 if it is possible，因句意明確，省略主詞和 be 動詞而來的（詳見文法寶典 p.645）。

   industrial〔ɪn'dʌstrɪəl〕*adj.* 工業的 ***keep up with***～ " 跟上～ "

   concern〔kən'sɝn〕*n.* 關心的事 ***in other words*** " 換句話說 "

This and other features of life *in a modern industrial society* have some serious results. Keeping up with the Joneses *naturally* causes *a great deal of* stress and nervous tension. People worry about *whether* they have *as* much money *and as* many material things *as other people have*.

  " 現代工業社會，這種和其他生活的特徵，產生一些嚴重後果。與張三李四並駕齊驅，自然引起很大的壓力與精神緊張。人們擔心他們的財富與物質享受是否跟他人一樣多。"

feature〔′fitʃɚ〕*n.* 特徵　　　stress〔strɛs〕*n.* 壓力

tension〔′tɛnʃən〕*n.* 緊張

The stress, nervous tension and worry cause a good deal of illness. Some doctors *in these industrial countries* estimate **that** as many **as** *50%* *of their patients* are not suffering from real physical illnesses at all. *Instead*, they are suffering from illnesses *with physical symptoms but mental causes.*

　　" 這種壓力、精神緊張及擔憂造成很多的疾病。許多這些工業國家的醫生估計，多達百分之五十的病人，根本沒有生理上的疾病。相反地，他們的病雖有生理上的症狀，却起因於心理因素。"

　　　　estimate〔′ɛstə,met〕*vt.* 估計　　　symptom〔′sɪmptəm〕*n.* 症狀

39.（**A**）「與張三李四並駕齊驅」意指＿＿＿＿＿＿＿＿＿＿

　　　(A) 在提升生活水準上與鄰人一較長短。(B) 使鄰居高興。

　　　(C) 與鄰居結交朋友。　　　　　　　　(D) 對鄰居施加壓力。

40.（**C**）現代工業社會競爭的生活引起＿＿＿＿＿＿＿＿＿＿

　　　(A) 許多生理疾病，但沒有造成心理失調。

　　　(B) 許多心理疾病，但沒有生理症狀。

　　　(C) 許多心理疾病，但有生理症狀。

　　　(D) 許多貧困造成的生理疾病。

第三部分：非選擇題

一、填　充

　　My neighbor *across the street* is having a garage sale. Let's go there *and* look at all the items *for sale*. There are a lot of things *for sale* today. There are some clothes over there. There are some dresses, shoes, hats, and sweaters. Under the table is a box of books. There are a lot of books. Here is an interesting book *on photography*.

1

2

3

"對街的鄰居正在舉辦車庫舊貨出售。讓我們過去，看看出售的物品。今天有很多東西出售。那邊有些衣物，包括衣服、鞋子、帽子及毛衣。桌下有一盒書。裏面有許多書籍。這是一本有關攝影的書，內容很有意思。"

1. over ***there*** "在那邊"

2. 本句是倒裝句，將補語部份 Under the table 倒裝至句首，加以強調。句中尚缺少動詞，主詞是 a box，所以用單數的動詞 ***is***。

3. 介系詞 ***on*** 表示「有關；論及」。

Look at this! Here is a picture *of Aunt Lucy*. Who wants to buy this
　　　　　　　　　　　　　　　　　　　　　　　　　　4
old thing? Maybe someone likes to collect old pictures.

On this table there are some items *for the kitchen* : some dishes, some
　　　　　　　　　　　　　　　　　　　　　　　5
cups, four old spoons, a coffee pot, ***and*** a pan.

"看看這個東西。這是露西姑姑的照片。誰想買這老古董？或許有人喜歡收集舊照片。

這張桌上有些廚房用具：一些盤子、杯子、四根舊湯匙、一個咖啡壺和一個平底鍋。"

　　　　pot〔pɑt〕*n.* 壺、罐、瓶等　　　pan〔pæn〕*n.* 平底鍋

4. 本句是問句，買東西的動作者一定是人，所以填入疑問詞***Who***。

5. 盤、杯、鍋等都是廚房用具，故填 ***kitchen***。

Look at the old woman *near the coffee pot*. Her dress is very old, ***and***
her sweater has holes. She wants to buy the coffee pot, ***but*** she does not
　　　　　　　　　　　　　　　6
seem to have much money. The coffee pot costs $4.00, ***but*** my friend
　　　　　　　　　　　7
sells it to her for only $1.50.
8

"看那位站在咖啡壺旁邊的老婦人。她的衣服很舊，毛衣也有破洞。她想買咖啡壺，但是她的錢似乎不夠。咖啡壺賣四塊，但我的朋友只賣她一塊半。"

6. 根據前後句意判斷，老婦人想「買」咖啡壺，所以填 ***buy***。

7. 買咖啡壺需要錢，故填***money***。

8. 老婦人想買咖啡壺，作者的朋友就「賣」給她。因為主詞是第三人稱單數，
   時式是現在式，所以填 ***sells*** 。

Now the old woman is walking <u>away</u>. Look！She is getting into that
9
big, expensive car. Look at my neighbor's face. He is very surprised.

Garage sales are interesting, ***but*** sometimes the people *at garage*
10
sales are even more interesting.

　　" 現在老婦人走開了。你看！她坐進一輛豪華大車裏。看看我鄰居的表情。
他感到非常驚訝 。

　　車庫舊貨出售實在有趣 ，但有時參加的人更有趣 。"

9. walk ***away*** " 走開 "

10. ***at*** a ～ sale　" 在～清倉大廉售時 "

二、中譯英

1. 英語是一種重要的語言，所以很多人都在學習 。
   English is an important language, so many people are learning it.

2. 許多中國學生認為學習說英語很難 。
   Many Chinese students think that it is rather difficult for them to
   learn to speak English.

3. 但是只要經常練習，任何困難都可以克服 。
   But as long as they practice it constantly, they will be able to
   overcome any difficulty.

4. 會背課本上的對話，並不表示會說英語 。
   Being able to learn the dialogues in the textbooks by heart does not
   mean being able to speak English.

5. 最重要的是，要能用英語說自己想說的話 。
   Above all, they should be able to express themselves in English.

三、英文作文（參考範例）

　　Trees play a very important role in our lives today. We could even go so far as to say that we cannot do without them. Trees produce oxygen we inhale and take in carbon dioxide we exhale. They are good for our health. **What's more**, trees can beautify the environment, making our world a more comfortable place to live in.

　　Since we know that trees are so indispensable to us, we should try our best to keep them from destruction. **First of all**, we should not fell trees at random. The law on tree protection has to be strictly obeyed. **Then**, we should plant as many trees as possible. Only by doing so will we have a better world to inhabit.

　　　　go so far as to-V “甚至～”　　　oxygen〔'ɑksədʒən〕*n*. 氧
　　　　inhale〔ɪn'hel〕*vt*. 吸入　　*carbon dioxide* 二氧化碳
　　　　exhale〔ɛks'hel, ɪg'zel〕*vt*. 呼出　　　fell〔fɛl〕*vt*. 砍伐
　　　　at random “隨便地”

　　心得筆記欄

七十六學年度大學暨獨立學院入學考試
英 文 試 題

第一部分：單一選擇題

I.**對話**（5％）：下面五題（1～5）是生活中常用的英語對話，各自獨立。每題各
各有一個空白，並各附A、B、C、D四個備選答案。請依照對話的內容，選
出一個最適當的答案，並按規定標示在答案卡上。每題答對得1分，答錯
倒扣⅓分。不答不給分。

1. Mr. Smith : Excuse me, sir. I'm writing a research paper on Chinese
culture.

　　　　　　　Do you mind answering a few questions？

　Dr. Chang : _____

　(A) Certainly.　　　　　　　　(B) No, of course not.

　(C) By all means.　　　　　　　(D) Yes, please.

2.　Jack : Hello. Is this Star Supermarket？

　Voice : No. I'm afraid you've called the wrong number.

　Jack : Is this three-two-one, double nine-three-one？

　Voice : No. This is three-one-two, double nine-three-one.

　Jack : _____

　Voice : That's all right.

　(A) Oh, I'm sorry.　　　　　　(B) Are you sure？

　(C) No! That's impossible!　　　(D) May I speak to Dr. Edison？

3. Dr. Armstrong : Good afternoon, Mr. Goodman.

　　　　　　　　　How are you feeling today？

　Mr. Goodman : Not very well.

　Dr. Armstrong : _____

　Mr. Goodman : I have a sore throat, and my whole body aches.

　(A) What's the matter with you !

　(B) You must have been ill.

　(C) What can I do for you？

　(D) What seems to be wrong with you？

4. Clerk : Can I help you, sir?

   John : Yes. I want to buy a blue shirt, size fourteen.

   Clerk : I have several in your size.

   _____

   John: Yes, of course.

(A) How do you like it?   (B) Why don't you buy it?

(C) Do you want to try on one of these?

(D) They must be very cheap.

5.   Susan : Mother, can I go to the National Theater to see "Gone with the Wind"?

  Mother : _____

  Susan : What do you mean?

  Mother : You may go only if you have finished your homework.

(A) It depends.

(B) I happened to see the movie today.

(C) I'll be glad to.

(D) What do you think of Clark Gable?

II. 綜合測驗（15％）：下面兩段文章，共有十五個空白（6～20）；每個空白附有四個備選答案。請在仔細閱讀各段文章後，選出一個最適當的答案，並標示在答案卡上。每題答對得1分，答錯倒扣⅓分。不答不給分。

Dick McDonald, the ___6___ of McDonald's fast-food chain, tells a story about his mother.

She was from Ireland, and to an Irish mother a job is important-- mechanic, butcher, police officer, artist, barber, anything that provides a regular pay check. My brothers and I always worked for ourselves, and this ___7___.

Years ___8___, and we were very successful with our restaurants. "Your sons have their name on buildings and in TV commercials," said one of Mother's friends. "I'll bet you're really ___9___."

"I guess so," Mother replied. "But I still wish they ___10___ good, steady jobs."

6. (A) finder   (B) fender

   (C) founder   (D) feeder

7. (A) drove her crazy   (B) makes her mad
   (C) enrages her   (D) got her very excited

8. (A) flying out of sight   (B) broke down
   (C) let her down   (D) went by

9. (A) worrying about them   (B) proud of them
   (C) anxious about them   (D) shattered to pieces

10. (A) have   (B) are having
    (C) have had   (D) had

The seashore may be simply described as a land that meets the sea, but for many of us it is rather a special place. Perhaps this is because we like to ___11___ a holiday there — bathing, playing on the sand, walking on the beach, looking for treasure or wildlife ___12___ simply sitting in a deckchair doing nothing in particular.

But if we go back about 300 years we would find that ___13___ had even heard of seashore holidays, while bathing in the sea would have seemed a very strange thing to ___14___. The few people who could ___15___ a holiday would most likely visit a spa town, which had wells or mineral springs ___16___ waters waters were believed to be ___17___ for people, either for drinking or for bathing in. At first, hot springs were ___18___ for bathing, but then some doctors suggested that bathing in cold water might be just ___19___ good. It was much later that the idea of a family holiday at the seaside became popular. People had discovered that bathing in the sea and taking the air were more ___20___ in the summer.

11. (A) cost   (B) waste   (C) took   (D) spend
12. (A) and   (B) or   (C) but   (D) for
13. (A) we   (B) everyone   (C) nobody   (D) many
14. (A) do   (B) say   (C) put   (D) bathe
15. (A) affect   (B) afford   (C) affront   (D) affirm
16. (A) its   (B) their   (C) whose   (D) those
17. (A) good   (B) bad   (C) taken   (D) thought
18. (A) allowed   (B) rejected   (C) favored   (D) arranged

19. (A) as   (B) so   (C) very   (D) too

20. (A) fresh   (B) crowded   (C) economical   (D) pleasant

Ⅱ. **閱讀測驗**（30％）：下面四段文章後面，各有若干題目（21～22，23～25，26～30 及 31～35）。每題各附四個備選答案。請在仔細閱讀文章後，把最適合文意的一個答案標示在答案卡上。每題答對得 2 分；答錯倒扣⅔分；不答不給分。

In the 1960s a leading British newspaper, the <u>Daily Mirror</u>, ran an article about the office of the future. In the 1980s, it said, machines will do all the office work. There will be machines to record and then type the boss's letters. Machines will be able to put away letters and papers in order and then find the paper that is needed. There will be no more secretaries; they will be unnecessary.

21. When was the newspaper article written?
   (A) In 1960.
   (B) Sometime between 1960 and 1969.
   (C) In the 1980s.
   (D) It isn't mentioned in the passage at all.

22. The <u>Daily Mirror</u> article said that
   (A) machines will do everything in the house.
   (B) machines will forecast the news.
   (C) machines will replace secretaries.
   (D) machines will translate one language into another.

" Move your head a bit to the left, would you?"
   Carrie did as she was told. She was quite an experienced artist's model by now and knew exactly what Pamela wanted.
   " Why didn't you dance with Richard at the party?" said Carrie. "You know the poor boy likes you."
   " Keep still a minute."
   Pamela's concentration was total. She hadn't really heard Carrie. The phone rang downstairs. Pamela didn't hear it.
   " Can you answer that?" shouted Carrie.
   " No," came a voice from downstairs.

That was Julia, Pamela's younger sister. She was cutting out a dress pattern. The phone was always for Pamela anyway.

" Oh, no!" said Pamela under her breath, glaring at the empty tube. Carrie started to speak, but Pamela was already moving to the door.

23. Which part of the text tells you that Pamela was painting Carrie?
    (A) " Move your head a bit to the left, would you?" Carrie did as she was told.
    (B) She was quite an experienced artist's model by now and knew exactly what Pamela wanted.
    (C) "Why didn't you dance with Richard at the party?" said Carrie. " You know the poor boy likes you."
    (D) " Oh, no!" said Pamela under her breath, glaring at the empty tube.

24. Which part of the text tells you that Pamela was very interested in what she was doing?
    (A) " Keep still a minute."
    (B) The phone rang downstairs.
    (C) She was cutting out a dress pattern.
    (D) Pamela's concentration was total.

25. Which part of the text tells you that Pamela was popular?
    (A) Pamela was already moving to the door.
    (B) She hadn't really heard Carrie.
    (C) The phone was always for Pamela anyway.
    (D) " No," came a voice from downstairs.

In the United States, 30 percent of the adult population has a "weight problem." To many people, the cause is obvious: we eat too much. But scientific evidence does little to support this idea. Going back to the America of 1910, we find that people were leaner than today, yet they ate more food. In those days people worked harder physically, walked more, used machines much less, and didn't watch television.

Several modern studies, moreover, have shown that fatter people do not eat more on average than thinner people. In fact, some investigations, such as a 1979 study of 3,545 London office workers, report that, on balance, fat people eat less than slimmer people.

Studies show that slim people are more active than fat people. A study by a research group at Stanford University School of Medicine found the following interesting fact:

The more the men ran, the greater loss of body fat.

The more they ran, the greater their increase in food intake.

Thus, those who ran the most ate the most, yet lost the greatest amount of body fat.

26. What kind of physical problem do many adult Americans have?
    (A) They are too slim.   (B) They work too hard.
    (C) They are too fat.   (D) They lose too much body fat.

27. Based upon the statistics given in the article, suppose there are 500 adult Americans, about how many of them will have a "weight problem"?
    (A) 30 .   (B) 50 .   (C) 100 .   (D) 150 .

28. Is there scientific evidence to support that eating too much is the cause of a "weight problem"?
    (A) Yes, there is plenty of evidence.
    (B) Of course, there is some evidence to show this is true.
    (C) There is hardly any scientific evidence to support this.
    (D) We don't know because the information is not given.

29. In comparison with the adult American population today, the Americans of 1910
    (A) ate more food and had more physical activities.
    (B) ate less food but had more activities.
    (C) ate less food and had less physical exercise.
    (D) had more weight problems.

30. What have modern medical and scientific researches reported to us?
    (A) Fat people eat less food and are less active.
    (B) Fat people eat more food than slim people and are more active.
    (C) Fat people eat more food than slim people but are less active.
    (D) Thin people run less, but have greater increase in food intake.

A young eastern Nigerian had a job as a driver for an American visitor. The Nigerian took the American from Lagos to Contonou, the sleepy capital of French-speaking Dahomey, eighty miles (128 kilometers) away. Once there, the Nigerian was shocked to discover that without help he could not even bargain with his fellow Africans over the price of a pineapple. The Dahomeans spoke Yoruba and a bit of French. He spoke Ibo and rather good English. The American visitor, who could speak the two European languages, was needed to bridge the gap.

Advocates of African languages say that barriers like that will be broken by depending on local tongues rather than on English and French. Kenya, for example, is encouraging the use of Swahili as a substitute not only for English but also for Kikuyu and Luo. These are two languages used in certain parts of Kenya.

No African language has met with much success in becoming a national language. But some uniformity has been started by transistor radios and by people who move from place to place. For example, traders carry the Lingala dialect up and down the Congo River.

The schools, which still reach only a small number of African children, teach mainly in European languages. But there, too, a strong group of teachers prefer to use the African language, especially in the primary grades.

" The moment you're trying to explain something complicated —math, for example — you have to slip into the tribal language. You must do this or you know the child won't follow you," said a teacher in Liberia, where English is the teaching language.

In spite of the wishes of the groups pressuring for the official use of African languages, few African leaders have gone along with the trend. They feel that too few Africans know any one tribal language. They believe that there is little choice but to use European languages.

As a West African politician put it: "English is an imperfect way of communicating here. But it's still better than any of the other choices open to us."

31. The young eastern Nigerian communicated with the American visitor in

(A) Ibo.　　　(B) English.　　　(C) Yoruba.　　　(D) French.

32. The American visitor could bargain with the Dahomeans because
   (A) he was a foreigner.   (B) he used gestures.
   (C) he spoke Yoruba.   (D) he spoke French.

33. Transistor radios and traders in Africa have helped make African
   languages become more similar because
   (A) they have promoted African economy.
   (B) they have encouraged nationalism.
   (C) they have brought people into closer contact with one another.
   (D) they have discouraged the use of European languages.

34. According to a teacher in Liberia, the African language should be used
   instead of the European language because
   (A) school children cannot understand difficult ideas explained in the
      European language.
   (B) the teachers themselves do not speak European languages well enough.
   (C) the teachers think the African language is superior to the European
      language.
   (D) the African language contains more mathematic concepts than the
      European language.

35. Many African leaders are of the opinion that European languages still
   cannot be replaced by African languages because
   (A) many teachers oppose tribal languages.
   (B) European languages are necessary for international trading.
   (C) European languages have higher social status.
   (D) no African tribal language has enough speakers to make it a national
      language.

第二部分：非選擇題

  I. **填充**（10％）：根據提示的第一個字母或第一個及最後一個字母，在每格中
    填一個完整的英文單字。把這個完整的單字寫在「非選擇題試卷」上。

    Advertising is now big b 1 , and there are people who e 2
their living by writing and presenting advertisements. S 3 h people
do not actually make soap powder or baked beans or motor cars, b 4
they prepare advertising matter for those that d 5 . Thus a
manufacturer will often go to an advertising agency and ask the people

t　6　e to handle all the publicity that will e　7　e him — he hopes —
to sell more of his g　8　　. In return, he pays the agency f　9　　
their services. The newspaper, magazine or television channel w　10　e
the advertisement appears also has to be paid.

II. 翻譯：中譯英（20％）

下面一段短文共有五個中文句子，請譯成正確、通順而達意的英文。每
題4分，各題前後半句各佔2分。答案請寫在「非選擇題試卷」上。

1. 很多學生都不太注意讀書的方法，以致於浪費許多寶貴的時間。

2. 他們讀英文讀了好幾年，還是看不懂相當容易的文章。

3. 其實，只要方法正確，英文的閱讀能力並不難培養。

4. 在老師還沒有講解課文之前，一定要自己先讀兩三遍。

5. 不要讀太難的文章，也不要遇到生字就立刻查字典。

III. 作文（20％）：

一般說來，中國學生的功課負擔，無論是上課時間或家庭作業，都比美國學
生為重。請寫一篇八十字（Words）左右的短文，來敘述你對功課沈重的看
法。文章寫在「非選擇題試卷」上，並參考下面的評分標準。

評分標準：拼字與標點（4％），遣詞用字（4％），文法（4％），組織
（4％），內容（4％）。

76年大學聯考英文試題詳解

第一部分：單一選擇題

I．對話

1. （ B ）史密斯先生：對不起，先生，我正在寫一份有關中國文化的研究報告。
   您介意回答一些問題嗎？

   陳　博　士：_____

   (A) 當然（介意）。　　　　　　(B) 不，當然不介意。
   (C) 當然（介意）。　　　　　　(D) 是的，請問。

2. （ A ）傑　　　克：喂，請問是星星超級市場嗎？

   回話者：不是，恐怕您打錯了。

   傑　　　克：這裏是 321-9931 嗎？

   回話者：不是，這裏是 312-9931。

   傑　　　克：_____

   回話者：沒關係。

   (A) 哦，抱歉。　　　　　　　　(B) 你確定嗎？
   (C) 不！那是不可能的！　　　　(D) 我可以跟艾德森博士說話嗎？

3. （ D ）阿姆斯壯醫生：午安，古德曼先生。你今天覺得如何？

   古德曼先生：不太好。

   阿姆斯壯醫生：_____

   古德曼先生：我喉嚨痛，又全身痠痛。

   (A) 你怎麼搞的！（如把 " ！" 改爲 " ？" 則正確，參照文法寶典 p.38）
   (B) 你一定病了。
   (C) 我能爲你效勞嗎？　　　　　(D) 你似乎有什麼不舒服吧？

4. （ C ）店員：先生，有何爲您效勞？

   約翰：是的，我想買一件藍襯衫，十四吋大的。

   店員：我有許多您要的尺寸。_____

   約翰：好，當然要。

   (A) 您覺得這件如何？　　　　　(B) 您爲何不把它買下來？
   (C) 您想試穿其中的一件看看嗎？　(D) 它們必定很便宜。

5. （ **A** ）蘇珊：媽，我可以去國家戲院看「亂世佳人」嗎？

　　母親：＿＿＿＿＿＿＿＿＿＿＿＿＿＿＿＿＿

　　蘇珊：妳的意思是什麼？

　　母親：只有做完你的家庭作業，你才可以去。

(A) 看情形而定。　　　　　　(B) 我今天碰巧也去看電影。

(C) 我很樂意去。　　　　　　(D) 你覺得克拉克蓋博怎麼樣？

Ⅱ. 綜合測驗

Dick McDonald, the **founder** _of McDonald's fast-food chain_, tells a
story _about his mother_.
₆

She was from Ireland, **and _to an Irish mother_** a job is important—
mechanic, butcher, police officer, artist, barber, anything **_that provides
a regular pay check_**. My brothers and I always worked for ourselves,
and this drove her crazy.
₇

　　"狄克‧麥當勞，麥當勞速食連鎖店的創始人，說了一則有關他母親的故事。

　　她來自愛爾蘭；對一個愛爾蘭的母親而言，工作是重要的——技工、屠夫、警官、藝術家、理髮師，任何能供給定期薪水支票的工作。我的兄弟和我，總是為我們自己工作，這件事使她發怒。"

* the founder … chain 為插入的名詞片語，表 Dick McDonald 的同位語。
* and this … crazy 中的 this 表 My brothers … ourselves。

　　founder 〔ˈfaʊndɚ〕 _n._ 創始人；建立者
　　fast-food chain "速食連鎖店"　　　Ireland 〔ˈaɪrlənd〕 _n._ 愛爾蘭
　　Irish 〔ˈaɪrɪʃ〕 _adj._ 愛爾蘭的　　　butcher 〔ˈbʊtʃɚ〕 _n._ 屠夫
　　barber 〔ˈbɑrbɚ〕 _n._ 理髮師　　　pay check "薪水支票"
　　$\begin{cases} \textbf{\textit{drive sb. crazy}} = \textbf{\textit{drive sb. mad}} \text{ "使某人發怒"} \\ = \textbf{\textit{send sb. mad}} = \textbf{\textit{make sb. mad}} = \textbf{\textit{enrage sb.}} \end{cases}$

6. （ **C** ）(A)發現者；拾獲者　　　　　(B)防禦物；防禦者
　　　　　　(C)創始人；建立者　　　　　(D)餵養者；給食器

7. (**A**) (A) 使她發怒
　　　　(B) 使她發怒（根據句意，動詞須用過去式）
　　　　(C) 使她發怒（理由同(B)）　　　(D) 使她非常興奮

Years <u>went by</u>, ***and*** we were *very* successful <u>***with our restaurants***</u>.
　　　　　8

" Your sons have their name on buildings ***and*** in TV commercials,"said

one of Mother's friends. "I'll bet you're *really* <u>proud of them.</u>"
　　　　　　　　　　　　　　　　　　　　　　　9

　" I guess so," Mother replied. "***But*** I *still* wish they <u>had</u> good,
　　　　　　　　　　　　　　　　　　　　　　　　　　10

steady jobs."

　　"經過幾年，我們的餐廳非常成功。「妳的孩子們讓自己的名字留在各建築物和電視的商業廣告上。」母親的一位朋友說道。「我相信妳十分以他們為傲。」

　　「我也這麼想，」母親回答說，「不過，我還是希望他們有良好、固定的工作。」

* I guess so 的 so, 表 I am really proud of them。
* S＋wish（*that*）＋S＋過去式動詞，表與現在相反的假設法。（詳見文法寶典 p.368 ）

　　go by "（時間）消逝；過去"
　　commercial 〔kəˊmɝʃəl〕 *n*. 無線電或電視的商業廣告
　　{ ***be proud of*** "以～為榮；以～自傲"
　　{ ＝ ***take pride in*** ＝ ***pride oneself on***

8. (**D**) (A) 飛到看不見　　　　　(B) 損壞
　　　　(C) 令她失望　　　　　　(D) 消逝
　　　　out of sight "看不見"　　　***break down*** "損壞；崩潰"
　　　　let sb. down "令某人失望"

9. (**B**) (A) 為他們擔心　　　　　(B) 以他們為榮
　　　　(C) 為他們憂慮　　　　　(D) 破成碎片
　　　　shatter 〔ˊʃætə〕 *vt*. 使破滅；使粉碎

10. (**D**) 根據句意，得知與現在事實相反，所以用 had。

The seashore may be *simply* described as a land *that meets the sea,* *but* for many of us it is *rather* a special place. *Perhaps* this is *because* we like to spend a holiday *there* — bathing, playing *on the sand,* walking
11
on the beach, looking for treasure or wildlife or *simply* sitting *in a* 12
deckchair doing nothing *in particular.*

"海岸可能只被簡單地描述爲與海相交的一塊陸地，但是，對我們之中許多人而言，那是非常特別的地方。也許這是因爲我們喜歡在那裏渡假——泡水、在沙上玩耍、在海灘散步、尋找寶藏或野生動物、或只是坐在帆布睡椅上，不做什麼特別的事。"

* doing …表示與 sitting …同時在進行的動作。(詳見文法寶典 p.453)

　　wildlife 〔'waɪld,laɪf〕 *n.* 野生生物

　　deckchair 〔'dɛk,tʃɛr〕 *n.* 帆布睡椅(可以折疊之坐臥兩用椅)

11. (**D**) spend (花費)的句型： *sb.* + **spend** + **時間** + *(in)* + **V-ing**
　　(A) cost 作「花費」解時，通常以事物爲主詞。
　　(B) waste (浪費)在此不合句意。
　　(C) take (花費)多以 It 爲其形式主詞，後接眞正主詞——不定詞片語。而且 like to 之後也應接原形動詞，而非過去式。

12. (**B**) 根據句意，應選 or。

But *if we go back about 300 years* we would find *that* nobody had
13
even heard of seashore holidays, *while* bathing *in the sea* would have seemed a very strange thing *to do*. The few people *who could afford*
14 15
a holiday would *most likely* visit a spa town, *which had wells or mineral springs* whose *waters were believed to be good for people,* *either for*
16 17
drinking *or for bathing in.*

　　" 但是，假如我們回溯到大約三百年前，我們會發現，甚至沒有人聽說過海濱渡假，而在海裏泡水似乎是十分奇怪的事。極少數能夠渡假的人，很可能會去一個有礦泉名勝的城鎮，該地有井或礦泉，其水質無論飲用，或是在裏面浸泡，都相信對人有益。"

* while 在此是作對等連接詞用，連接 nobody had … holidays 和 bathing in … say 兩個對等子句，作「而」解，語氣上和 and 幾乎相同。
* which had wells … bathing in 是補述用法的形容詞子句，補充說明 a spa town 。

　　　　go back " 回溯；追溯 "　　　　spa 〔spɑ, spɔ〕 *n.* 礦泉名勝；礦泉
　　　　mineral spring " 礦泉 "

13.（ **C** ）根據上下文，應選(C) nobody（沒有人）。

14.（ **A** ）根據句意，應選(A) do 。

15.（ **B** ）(A) affect 〔əˊfɛkt〕 *vt.* 影響　　(B) ***afford*** 〔əˊford, əˊfɔrd〕 *vt.* 力足以　　(C) affront 〔əˊfrʌnt〕 *vt.* 當面侮辱　　(D) affirm 〔əˊfɝm〕 *vt.* 斷言；證實

16.（ **C** ）關係代名詞whose引導形容詞子句，修飾wells 和 springs 。(A) its, (B) their, (D) those 都缺少連接詞的功用，故不合。

17.（ **A** ）good 在此作「有益的；適宜的」解。

At first, hot springs were favored for bathing, ***but then*** some doctors
　　　　　　　　　　　　　　18
suggested ***that*** bathing *in cold water* might be *just as* good. It was
　　　　　　　　　　　　　　　　　　　19
much later ***that*** the idea *of a family holiday at the seaside* became

popular. People had discovered ***that*** bathing in the sea and taking the

air were more pleasant *in the summer.*
　　　　　　　20

　　" 起初，溫泉有利於浸泡，但是當時有些醫生建議，在冷水裏浸泡也可能一樣有益。更後來，全家在海邊渡假的觀念，變為普及起來。人們已經發現，炎炎夏日中，在海裏浸泡，到戶外透透氣，更令人愉快。"

* 第二句中的 It 是加強語氣的用法，其句型結構如下：

> **It was** ＋所要加強的部分＋ **that** ＋其餘部分　　（詳見文法寶典 p.115）

take the air " 到戶外透透氣 "

18. （ **C** ） (A) allow〔ə'laʊ〕*vt.* 允許　　(B) reject〔rɪ'dʒɛkt〕*vt.* 拒絕
　　　(C) *favored*〔'fevəd〕*adj.* 有利的
　　　(D) arrange〔ə'rendʒ〕*vt.* 整理；安排

19. （ **A** ）…might be just as good.
　　　＝…might be just *as* good *as bathing in hot springs（might be good）*.
　　　也就是 good 之後省略了句意明確的從屬子句。(as…as～ "和～一樣…")

20. （ **D** ） (A) fresh〔frɛʃ〕*adj.* 新鮮的　　(B) crowded〔'kraʊdɪd〕*adj.* 擁擠的
　　　(C) economical〔,ikə'nɑmɪkl̩〕*adj.* 節省的
　　　(D) *pleasant*〔'plɛznt〕*adj.* 愉快的

Ⅲ. 閱讀測驗

In the 1960s a leading British newspaper, the Daily Mirror, ran an article *about the office of the future.* *In the 1980s*, it said, machines will do all the office work. There will be machines *to record and then type the boss's letters*. Machines will be able to put away letters and papers in order *and then* find the paper *that is needed*. There will be no more secretaries; they will be unnecessary.

　　" 在一九六〇年代，一家主要的英國報紙「每日寫眞」，刊載了一篇關於未來辦公室的文章。文章內容是說，在一九八〇年代，機器將處理所有的辦公室業務。將會有用來記錄，然後打老闆信件的機器。機器將能夠有條不紊地貯存書信和報告，並且能找到所需要的文件。將不會再有祕書了，因爲他們沒有可用之處。"

　　　leading〔'lidɪŋ〕*adj.* 主要的　　mirror〔'mɪrə〕*n.* 寫眞
　　　run〔rʌn〕*vt.* 刊載　　　*put away* " 貯存

21.（ **B** ）報紙上這篇文章是何時寫成的？

    (A) 在一九六〇年。

    (B) 在一九六〇年至一九六九年之間的某一時間。（1960s 指 1960 ～ 1969）

    (C) 在一九八〇年代。   (D) 這段文字完全沒有提到。

22.（ **C** ）這篇「每日寫眞」的文章認爲 _____

    (A) 機器將可處理家裏的所有事情。(B) 機器將可預測消息。

    (C) 機器將代替祕書。   (D) 機器將把一種語言翻成另一種語言。

    forecast〔for'kæst〕*vt.* 預測   translate〔'trænslet〕*vt.* 翻譯

"Move your head *a bit to the left*, would you?"

Carrie did *as she was told*. She was *quite* an experienced artist's

model *by now* **and** knew *exactly* what Pamela wanted.

"Why didn't you dance *with Richard at the party*?" said Carrie.

"You know the poor boy likes you."

"Keep still *a minute*."

「「麻煩你把頭向左偏一點好嗎？」

凱莉照著她被吩咐的話做，她目前是一位很有經驗，爲藝術家工作的模特兒，她非常懂得白梅拉所要求的。

「在舞會裏，你爲什麼不和理查跳舞？」凱莉說。「你曉得那個窮男孩喜歡你。」

「再保持一分鐘不動。」"

   * Move to the left 等於 move left；前面的 left 爲名詞，後面的 left 爲副詞。

     by now "此刻已經"

Pamela's concentration was total. She hadn't *really* heard Carrie. The phone rang *downstairs*. Pamela didn't hear it.

"Can you answer that?" shouted Carrie.

"No," came a voice *from downstairs*.

"白梅拉的注意力很集中，她實際上沒有在聽凱莉說話；樓下電話響了，白梅拉也沒聽見。

「你接一下電話好嗎？」凱莉嘆著。

「不要。」樓下傳來一個聲音。"

concentration〔͵kɑnsn̩'treʃən, -sɛn-〕*n.* 注意力；專心

answer the telephone "接電話"

That was Julia, Pamela's younger sister. She was cutting out a dress pattern. The phone was *always* for Pamela *anyway*.

"Oh, no!" said Pamela *under her breath*, glaring at the empty tube.

Carrie started to speak, ***but*** Pamela was *already* moving to the door.

"那是白梅拉的妹妹茉莉亞。她正在裁製一件衣服的式樣。無論如何電話總是找白梅拉的。

「噢，糟糕。」白梅拉望著空的顏料管，輕聲地說道。凱莉要開始叫時，白梅拉已經到門口。"

* glaring at … tube 是由 and she was glaring at … tube 省略而來。對等子句改成分詞構句時，若主詞相同，則保留一主詞即可，即 and ＋主詞＋ V ＝ Ving 。（詳見文法寶典 p.459）

cut out "裁製"   ***dress pattern*** "衣服的式樣"

under one's breath "輕聲地"

tube〔tjub〕*n.* 裝顏料的小管

23.（ **B** ）本文中那個部分告訴你，白梅拉正在畫凱莉？

   (A)「麻煩你把頭向左偏一點好嗎？」 凱莉照著她的話做了。

   (B) 她目前是一位很有經驗,為藝術家工作的模特兒,她非常懂得白梅拉所要求的。

   (C)「在舞會裏,你為什麼不和理查跳舞?」凱莉說，「你曉得那個窮男孩喜歡你。」

   (D)「噢，糟糕。」白梅拉望著空的顏料管，輕聲地說道。

24.（ **D** ）本文中那個部分告訴你，白梅拉對她所做的事非常有興趣？

   (A)「再保持一分鐘不動。」   (B) 樓下的電話響了。

   (C) 她正在裁剪一件衣服的式樣。   (D) 白梅拉的注意力很集中。

25.（ **C** ）本文中那個部分告訴你，白梅拉人緣好？

  (A) 白梅拉已經走到門口了。

  (B) 她聽凱莉說話。

  (C) <u>無論如何電話總是找白梅拉的。</u>

  (D)「不要。」樓下傳來一個聲音。

In the United States, 30 percent *of the adult population* has a "weight problem." *To many people*, the cause is obvious: we eat too much. *But* scientific evidence does little *to support this idea*.

  「在美國，百分之三十的成人人口中都有「體重的困擾」。對許多人來說，原因很明顯：我們吃太多了。但是科學的證據並不怎麼支持這種想法。」

  adult〔ə'dʌlt,'ædʌlt〕*n.* 成人 obvious〔'ɑbvɪəs〕*adj.* 明顯的
  evidence〔'ɛvədəns〕*n.* 證據

Going back to the America of 1910, we find *that* people were leaner *than today*, *yet* they ate more food. *In those days* people worked *harder physically*, walked *more*, used machines *much less*, *and* didn't watch television.

「回溯到一九一〇年的美國，我們發現，那時候的人們比現在的人瘦，然而，他們吃更多食物。那時候人們在體力上比較操勞，步行多，甚少使用機器，而且不看電視。」

  * Going back … 1910 是 When we go back … 1910 而來的分詞構句。

  go back「回溯」 lean〔lin〕*adj.* 瘦的
  physically〔'fɪzɪkḷɪ〕*adv.* 體力上地

Several modern studies, *moreover*, have shown *that* fatter people do not eat more *on average* *than thinner people*. *In fact*, some investigations, such as a 1979 study of 3,545 London office workers, report *that*, *on balance*, fat people eat less *than slimmer people*.

"一些現代的研究更進一步地顯示，一般而言，肥胖者吃得不會比瘦者多。事實上，有些調查，例如一項一九七九年對於倫敦三千五百四十五名辦公人員的研究指出，歸根結底，肥胖者比瘦者吃得還少。"

> **on** (**the** 或 **an**) **average**　"一般而言"
> investigation 〔ɪn,vɛstə'geʃn〕 *n.* 調查
> **on balance**　"將一切情形都考慮到；歸根結底"
> slim 〔slɪm〕 *adj.* 纖細的

Studies show **that** slim people are more active **than fat people**.

A study **by a research group** **at Stanford University School of Medicine**

found the following interesting fact:

The more the men ran, the greater loss of body fat.

The more they ran, the greater their increase in food intake.

Thus, those **who ran the most** ate the most, **yet** lost the greatest

amount of body fat.

"研究顯示，瘦者比胖者好動。史丹佛大學醫學院的一個研究團體所提出的一項調查中，發現下列有趣的事實：

人們愈常跑步，體內脂肪失去得也愈多。

人們愈常跑步，食物攝取量就愈大。

因此，凡是最常跑步的人吃得最多，但是也失去最多的體內脂肪。"

> School of Medicine　"醫學院"
> intake 〔'ɪn,tek〕 *n.* 吸收量

26. (C)　很多美國成年人都有什麼身體上的困擾？
　　(A) 他們太瘦。　　　　　　　(B) 他們工作得太辛苦。
　　(C) 他們太胖。　　　　　　　(D) 他們失去太多體內脂肪。

27. (D)　根據文中的統計結果，假如有五百位美國成年人，其中大約有多少人會有「體重的困擾」？
　　(A) 三十。　　(B) 五十。　　(C) 一百。　　(D) 一百五十。
　　statistics 〔stə'tɪstɪks〕 *n.* 統計；統計表

28.（ **C** ）有沒有科學證據支持這種看法，認爲吃太多造成「體重問題」？
　　(A) 有的，有很多的證據。
　　(B) 當然，有某些證據顯示這種看法是正確的。
　　(C) 幾乎沒有任何科學證據支持這種看法。
　　(D) 因爲沒有資料，所以我們無法得知。

29.（ **A** ）和今天的美國成人人口比較起來，一九一〇年的美國人 ＿＿＿＿＿＿＿
　　(A) 吃得多，身體的活動也多。　　(B) 吃得少，但活動多。
　　(C) 吃得少，身體的運動也少。　　(D) 有較多的體重困擾。

　　　in comparison with "與～比較"

30.（ **A** ）現代醫學和科學的研究爲我們報導了些什麼？
　　(A) 肥胖者食物吃得少，而且比較不好動。
　　(B) 肥胖者吃的食物比瘦者多，而且比較好動。
　　(C) 肥胖者吃的食物比瘦者多，但是比較不好動。
　　(D) 瘦者較少跑步，食量却增加。

　A young eastern Nigerian had a job *as a driver for an American visitor*. The Nigerian took the American *from Lagos to Contonou, the sleepy capital of French-speaking Dahomey, eighty miles* (128 *kilometers*) *away*.

　"一個東奈及利亞的年輕人，擔任一位美國遊客的司機。這個奈及利亞人載這位美國人，從拉哥斯到八十英里（一百二十八公里）外的柯都努，講法語的達荷美共和國的靜寂之都。

　＊ as 在此當介系詞用，作「擔任」解。

　　　Nigerian〔naɪˈdʒɪrɪən〕*n.* 奈及利亞人
　　　Lagos〔ˈlɑgəs, ˈlegəs〕*n.* 拉哥斯（Nigeria 共和國之首都）
　　　Cotonou〔ˌkotəˈnu〕*n.* 柯都努（聯考試卷上誤爲 *Contonou*）
　　　Dahomey〔dəˈhomɪ〕*n.* 達荷美（非洲幾內亞灣沿岸之一共和國）

Once (*the Nigerian was*) *there*, the Nigerian was shocked to discover *that without help* he could not even bargain *with his fellow Africans over the price of a pineapple*.

"一到了那裏，這個奈及利亞人就驚訝地發現，如果沒有幫助，他甚至無法和他的非洲同胞議定鳳梨的價錢。"

　　* Once 是連接詞，作「一…就；當…的時候」解，引導一個省略了句意明確的主詞(the Nigerian)和 be 動詞(was)的副詞子句，修飾 shocked，表時間。

　　　　bargain 〔'bɑrgɪn〕 vi. 議價；爭論價錢

　　　　pineapple 〔'paɪn,æpl̩〕 n. 鳳梨

The Dahomeans spoke Yoruba **and** a bit of French. He spoke Ibo **and** *rather* good English. The American visitor, **who** **could speak the two** **European languages**, was needed to bridge the gap.

"達荷美人講猶魯巴語和一點法語。他講伊伯語和相當好的英語。這位美國遊客就需要來作為溝通歧異的橋樑，因為他會講兩種歐洲語言。"

　　* who could … language 是補述用法的形容詞子句，其意義相當於表原因的副詞子句 because he could … language 。（詳見文法寶典 p.163）

　　　　Yoruba 〔'jɔrubə, 'jorubɑ〕 n. 猶魯巴語（西非沿岸，尼日河和達荷美河之間的一支種族語言）

　　　　Ibo 〔'ibo〕 n. 伊伯語（蘇丹西部方言的一支）

　　　　bridge 〔brɪdʒ〕 vt. 度過；克服　　gap 〔gæp〕 n. 歧異；漏洞

Advocates *of African languages* say **that** barriers *like that* will be broken by depending on local tongues rather than on English and French. Kenya, **for example**, is encouraging the use of Swahili as a substitute **not only** for English **but also** for Kikuyu and Luo. These are two languages *used in certain parts of Kenya*.

　　"非洲的語言提倡者說，像那樣的障礙，要靠當地母語，而非英語或法語來破除。例如，肯亞正鼓勵使用斯華西里語，不僅用它來取代英語，而且取代基古猶語和魯歐語。這些是在肯亞某些地方所使用的兩種語言。"

　　* used in …Kenya 是由形容詞子句 which are used …Kenya 簡化而來的分詞片語，修飾 languages 。

advocate 〔'ædvəkɪt〕 n. 提倡者；擁護者
barrier 〔'bærɪə〕 n. 障礙
Kenya 〔'kɛnjə, 'kinjə〕 n. 肯亞共和國 (在非洲東部)
Swahili 〔swɑ'hilɪ〕 n. 斯華希里語 (北班圖的語言，是使用於中東非的混合國
際語言)
substitute 〔'sʌbstə,tjut〕 n. 代替物
Kikuyu 〔kɪ'kuju〕 n. 基古猶語　　　Luo 〔'luo〕 n. 魯歐語

No African language has met with much success *in becoming a national language*. **But** some uniformity has been started by transistor radios **and** by people *who move from place to place*. **For example**, traders carry the Lingala dialect *up and down the Congo River*.

"沒有一種非洲語言能很成功地成為國家的語言。但是電晶體收音機和到處遷徙的人們，已經開創了某種統一。例如，貿易商操著林哥拉方言往返剛果河。"

meet with " 得到 "　　　uniformity 〔,junə'fɔrmətɪ〕 n. 一致；統一
transistor 〔træn'zɪstə〕 n. 電晶體
dialect 〔'daɪə,lɛkt〕 n. 方言　　　*up and down* " 往返；來回 "
Congo 〔'kɑŋgo〕 n. 剛果河 (非洲中部一大河，注入大西洋)

The schools, **which still reach only a small number of African children**, teach *mainly* in European languages. **But there, too**, a strong group of teachers prefer to use the African language, *especially in the primary grades*.

"學校，依舊只普及於少數非洲學童，而且主要以歐洲語言教學。可是在那兒也是一樣，大多數的老師較喜歡使用非洲語言，特別是在小學一到三年級。"

primary 〔'praɪ,mɛrɪ,-mərɪ〕 adj. 初級的；基本的
primary grades " 〔美〕小學一至三年級 "

" **The moment** you're trying to explain something complicated —
math, **for example** — you have to slip into the tribal language. You must
do this **or** you know the child won't follow you," said a teacher *in
Liberia*, **where** English is the teaching language.

「你一試著要解釋複雜的事情時——例如，數學——你就得脫口說出種族語言。你必須這麼做，否則，如你所知的，孩子會聽不懂你的話。」一位賴比瑞亞的老師說道，在那裏，英語是教學語言。"

* The moment（一…就）是名詞當連接詞用，後面可接 that，但通常省略。
（詳見文法寶典 p.496）

> complicated〔'kɑmplə‚ketɪd〕 adj. 複雜的
> **slip into** " 不留神的說出 "
> tribal〔'traɪbḷ〕 adj. 種族的；部落的
> Liberia〔laɪ'bɪrɪə〕 n. 賴比瑞亞（非洲西部之一國）

*In spite of the wishes of the groups pressuring for the official use
of African languages*, few African leaders have gone along with the
trend. They feel **that** too few Africans know any one tribal language.
They believe **that** there is little choice but to use European languages.

雖然有團體施加壓力，希望官方使用非洲語言，但是很少非洲領導人物同意這種趨勢。他們認為太少非洲人知道任何一種種族語言。他們相信，除了使用歐洲語言之外，幾乎沒有選擇。

> official〔ə'fɪʃəl〕 adj. 官方的；正式的
> **go along with** " 同意；贊成 "   trend〔trɛnd〕 n. 趨勢；傾向

As a West African politician put it: "English is an imperfect way
of communicating here. **But** it's *still* better **than** any of the other
choices open to us."

　　"誠如一位西非政治家所說的:「英語在這裏並不是很完美的溝通方法。可是它比任何其他開放給我們的選擇更好。」"

　　　　as … put it "誠如～所說"　　*open to* "開放給～"

31. (**B**) 這位東奈及利亞年輕人和這位美國遊客溝通是用
　　　(A) 伊伯語。　　　　　　　　(B) 英語。
　　　(C) 猶魯巴語。　　　　　　　(D) 法語。

32. (**D**) 這位美國遊客能和達荷美人議價是因為
　　　(A) 他是個外國人。　　　　　(B) 他使用手勢。
　　　(C) 他會講猶魯巴語。　　　　(D) 他會講法語。

33. (**C**) 在非洲的電晶體收音機和貿易商已經幫助非洲語言變得更相似是因為
　　　(A) 他們已經促進非洲經濟。　(B) 他們已經鼓勵民族主義。
　　　(C) 他們已經使人與人間的關係更密切。
　　　(D) 他們已經不敢再使用歐洲語言。

34. (**A**) 依據賴比瑞亞的老師之言,非洲語言應用來取代歐洲語言,因為
　　　(A) 學童無法了解用歐洲語言解釋的困難觀念。
　　　(B) 老師本身無法把歐洲語言說得很好。
　　　(C) 老師認為非洲語言優於歐洲語言。
　　　(D) 非洲語言比歐洲語言包含更多的數學觀念。

35. (**D**) 許多非洲領導人物認為,歐洲語言還是無法被非洲語言所取代,是因為
　　　(A) 許多老師反對種族語言。
　　　(B) 歐洲語言對國際貿易是必須的。
　　　(C) 歐洲語言擁有更高的社會地位。
　　　(D) 沒有一種非洲的種族語言,有足夠會說的人,使它成為國家語言。
　　　　status 〔'stetəs〕 *n.* 地位;聲望

第二部分:非選擇題

Ⅰ. 填充

　　Advertising is now big <u>business</u>, and there are people [*who earn*
　　　　　　　　　　　　　1　　　　　　　　　　　　　　　2
their living by writing and presenting advertisements.] <u>Such</u> people do not
　　　　　　　　　　　　　　　　　　　　　　　　　3
actually make soap powder or baked beans or motor cars, <u>but</u> they
　　　　　　　　　　　　　　　　　　　　　　　　　4
prepare advertising matter for those *that* <u>do.</u>
　　　　　　　　　　　　　　　　　　5

"廣告現在是一門大行業，有人就靠寫廣告和提供廣告謀生。這樣的人實際上並不製造肥皂粉、烘焙豆或汽車，而是替那些從事該行業的人準備廣告事宜。

1. business（行業；業務）

2. ***earn** one's **living*** "謀生"

3. Such（這樣的）

4. not … ***but*** ～　（不是…而是～）

5. <u>do</u> 作代動詞用，在此代替make soap …motor cars, 避免重複。

   present [prɪ'zɛnt] *vt.* 提出　　soap powder "肥皂粉；清潔粉"
   bean [bin] *n.* 豆　　motor car "〔英〕汽車（=〔美〕automobile)"

Thus a manufacturer will ***often*** go to an advertising agency ***and*** ask the people <u>there</u> to handle all the publicity [*that will* <u>*enable*</u> *him* — he
　　　　　　　　　　　　　　　　6　　　　　　　　　　　　　7
hopes — *to sell more of his* <u>*goods*</u>.] *In return*, he pays the agency <u>for</u>
　　　　　　　　　　　　　　　　8　　　　　　　　　　　　　　　　9
their services. The newspaper, magazine or television channel <u>where *the</u>
　　　　　　　　　　　　　　　　　　　　　　　　　　　　　10
advertisement appears also</u> has to be paid.

"因此，製造業者會常去廣告代理機構，要求那裏的人處理所有的宣傳廣告，他希望那會使他賣出更多的貨品。他則付給廣告代理機構服務費，作為回報。廣告所出現的地方——報紙、雜誌或電視頻道，也都得付費。"

＊ he hopes 是主要子句形式的插入語，that will … goods 等於是它的受詞。

6. there（= at the advertising agency）

7. ***enable*** *sb.* *to-V* "使某人能～"

8. goods（貨品）

9. ***pay*** *sb.* ***for*** *sth.* "付錢給某人以報答～"

10. 關係副詞where 引導形容詞子句，分別修飾 newspaper, magazine 和 channel。

    manufacturer [ˌmænjə'fæktʃərə] *n.* 製造業者
    agency ['edʒənsɪ] *n.* 代理店
    publicity [pʌb'lɪsətɪ] *n.* 宣傳；廣告
    in return "作為回報"　　channel ['tʃænl̩] *n.* 頻道

II. 翻譯：中譯英

1. 很多學生都不太注意讀書的方法，以致於浪費許多寶貴的時間。

   Many students pay *so* little attention to their study methods ***that*** *they waste much of their precious time.*

   precious 〔'prɛʃəs〕 *adj.* 寶貴的

2. 他們讀英文讀了好幾年，還是看不懂相當容易的文章。

   They have been studying English *for many years*, ***but*** they still cannot understand *rather* easy articles.

3. 其實，只要方法正確，英文的閱讀能力並不難培養。

   In reality, ***as long as their methods are correct***, their ability in reading English is not difficult *to cultivate.*

   in reality "其實；實際上"　　cultivate 〔'kʌltə,vet〕 *vt.* 培養

4. 在老師還沒講解課文之前，一定要自己先讀兩三遍。

   Before the teacher lectures on a lesson, they must read it *two or three times in advance.*

   lecture 〔'lɛktʃə〕 *vi.* 講課　　***in advance*** "預先；事前"

5. 不要讀太難的文章，也不要遇到生字就立刻查字典。

   They should ***neither*** read too difficult an article, ***nor*** consult a dictionary ***as soon as*** *they run into new words.*

   consult 〔kən'sʌlt〕 *vt.* 參考；查閱　　***run into*** "偶然遇到"

III. 英文作文（參考範例）

Ever since I became a high school student, I have had to cope with various kinds of examinations and quizzes. My high school teachers always told me that I would pass the entrance examination and enter a famous school, so long as I did well in these tests.

I remember that I had to spend long nights sitting up to study all parts of tests that came my way. I just could not but study harder and harder as was expected of me. *As a result*, it seemed that those tests had been an important part of my high school days.

No doubt, there are still many other high school students like me. To relieve high school students of their heavy study burdens, the authorities concerned should take measures to improve our educational system.

cope with "應付"　　various 〔'vɛrɪəs〕 *adj.* 種種不同的

quiz 〔kwɪz〕 *n.* 測驗；小考　　*so long as* "只要"

sit up "熬夜"　　*come one's way* "發生（在某人身上）"

cannot but ｜原形動詞　"不得不"

as a result "結果"　　*no doubt* "無疑地"

relieve 〔rɪ'liv〕 *vt.* 減輕　　burden 〔'bɝdn̩〕 *n.* 負擔

the authorities concerned "有關當局"

take measures to-V　　"採取措施～"

＊聯考的英文作文，如果沒有特別要求，最好寫成三段：第一段相當於「起」，第二段包含「承」或「轉」，第三段則是「合」。三段一氣呵成，自是佳作。

心得筆記欄

七十五學年度大學暨獨立學院入學考試
英　文　試　題

第一部分：單一選擇題

I. 對話（5%）：下面五題（1～5）是簡單的對話，各自獨立。每題各有一個空白，
　　並各附A、B、C、D四個備選答案。請依照對話的內容，選出一個最適當的
　　答案，並標示在答案卡上。每題答對得1分，答錯倒扣⅓分，若不答則不給分。

1. Mary： You must be able to speak several languages.
　　John：＿＿＿＿＿＿＿＿＿＿
　　(A) French, I guess.　　　　　(B) No, neither.
　　(C) That's a problem.　　　　(D) Yes, I'd say five.

2. Mary： I guess I'll stay home.
　　John：＿＿＿＿＿＿＿＿＿＿
　　(A) So you are.　　　　　　(B) Me too.
　　(C) You guess so.　　　　　(D) I will.

3. Mary： Would you mind opening the door for me?
　　John：＿＿＿＿＿＿＿＿＿＿
　　(A) I'd be glad to·　　　　(B) I probably will.
　　(C) Don't open it.　　　　(D) Don't do that.

4. Mary： I wonder if I could use your telephone.
　　John：＿＿＿＿＿＿＿＿＿＿
　　(A) I wonder how.　　　　　(B) I don't know.
　　(C) Well, of course.　　　(D) No wonder, here it is.

5. Mary： Tom told me that you collect stamps.
　　John：＿＿＿＿＿＿＿＿＿＿
　　(A) Who told you that?　　　(B) I don't think so.
　　(C) Does he collect stamps?　(D) Yes, I do. Do you?

II. 綜合測驗（20%）：下面兩段文章，共有二十個空白（6～25），每個空白附有
　　四個備選答案。請仔細閱讀各段文章後，選出一個最適當的答案，並標示在
　　答案卡上。每題答對得1分，答錯倒扣⅓分，若不答則不給分。

At that time the high-school entrance examinations were just __6__ the corner, and I figured I'd get through them all right. I believed I would __7__ high enough to __8__ for a provincial high school.

Unfortunately, my name did not appear on the list of successful __9__ . This news was met __10__ indifference by my family except Mother. In our home, everyone __11__ his own business--no one had anything to do with anyone else. Only Mother had something to say; she called me to her bed, "I won't scold you, but I want you to make __12__ of yourself...." I tried and tried to __13__ what she meant __14__ this, finally __15__ that she didn't want me to be yet another burden on Elder Brother, for her illness was already a heavy burden to him.

6. (A) in   (B) by   (C) around   (D) over
7. (A) get   (B) mark   (C) score   (D) record
8. (A) qualify   (B) competent   (C) certify   (D) eligible
9. (A) nominees   (B) examinees   (C) members   (D) examiners
10. (A) by   (B) in   (C) with   (D) for
11. (A) noticed   (B) regarded   (C) concerned   (D) minded
12. (A) use   (B) something   (C) anything   (D) anyone
13. (A) reason with (B) figure out (C) see through   (D) point out
14. (A) by   (B) for   (C) with   (D) in
15. (A) had realized (B) have realized (C) realizing (D) realize

Mexico, the largest nation in the region, provides a good example of life in Middle America. Although Mexico is a large country, __16__ 12 percent of its land is good for farming. __17__ 40 percent is good grazing land. The __18__ of the land is hills and mountains, dry, high plateaus, or wet coastal regions.

The mountains are too __19__ to farm. The high plateau in the middle of Mexico would be good farmland if it had more __20__ . The coastal areas receive so much __21__ that the land often becomes waterlogged. For all of these reasons, Mexicans must take care of the good farmland they have. Yet good farming has not always been possible in Mexico.

For many centuries, Mexican farmers had __22__ traditional crops. These __23__ corn, beans, and squash. However, when the Spanish arrived in the 1500's, they tried to __24__ new ideas. They thought new plants such as onions, turnips, sugarcane, and bananas would __25__ well in the warm, tropical climate. But the Mexicans wished to continue with their old ways.

16.	(A)	only	(B)	for	(C)	even	(D)	with
17.	(A)	Other	(B)	Another	(C)	The other	(D)	All
18.	(A)	best	(B)	place	(C)	height	(D)	rest
19.	(A)	warm	(B)	mild	(C)	steep	(D)	good
20.	(A)	farmers	(B)	hills	(C)	water	(D)	cattle
21.	(A)	rain	(B)	wind	(C)	fog	(D)	sunshine
22.	(A)	used	(B)	grown	(C)	seen	(D)	missed
23.	(A)	produced	(B)	combined	(C)	substituted	(D)	included
24.	(A)	introduce	(B)	replace	(C)	mistake	(D)	abandon
25.	(A)	be	(B)	do	(C)	plant	(D)	receive

Ⅲ. 閱讀測驗（ 25％ ）：

甲（5％）：下面的對話後面有五個題目（ 26～30 ），每題各附四個備選答案。請
　　　　　仔細閱讀對話後，把最適合文意的一個答案標示在答案卡上。每題答
　　　　　對得1分，答錯倒扣⅓分，若不答則不給分 。

WOMAN： Just put it in there, will you?

　MAN： Here, by the cupboard?

WOMAN： Yes, that's it. Would you mind unpacking it? I've hurt my
　　　　 shoulder. I can't lift anything.

　MAN： Well, OK then. It's just in a cardboard box, really. The
　　　　 rest of this stuff is just padding. For protection. OK. There
　　　　 you are. One <u>Easiwash</u> washing machine. Ready for use.

WOMAN： How does it work?

　MAN： The instructions are here somewhere....

WOMAN： I hate machines.

　MAN： It tells you what to do. There's a little booklet of instruc-
　　　　 tions。It's here somewhere. ... Oh here we are.

WOMAN： I suppose it's all right when you get used to it but I find
　　　　 new machines so intimidating, don't you? My husband's the
　　　　 same. He's hopeless with machinery.

　MAN： The instructions tell you exactly what to do. Look. There're
　　　　 diagrams, in color and everything.

WOMAN： Yes. I can't understand a thing. What's the difference
　　　　 between 'synthetic' and 'non-synthetic' material? Actually
　　　　 my husband usually does the washing. He's an angel.

26. The man is
    (A) repairing the washing machine.
    (B) delivering the washing machine.
    (C) taking the washing machine away.
    (D) selling the washing machine.

27. The woman can't lift anything
    (A) because she is too weak.
    (B) because she doesn't know how to.
    (C) because she has an injury.
    (D) because she hates machines.

28. The woman's husband
    (A) likes new machines.
    (B) does less washing than she.
    (C) is disappointed in washing machines.
    (D) also finds new machines difficult to handle.

29. The man in the above dialogue
    (A) cannot find the instructions at all.
    (B) temporarily cannot find the instructions.
    (C) has forgot to bring the instructions with him.
    (D) has misplaced the instructions somewhere.

30. The woman can't understand
    (A) the instructions.
    (B) the man.
    (C) her husband.
    (D) anything.

乙（20％）：下面兩段文章後面各有五個題目（31～35及36～40），每題各附四
　　　　　個備選答案。請仔細閱讀文章後，把最適合文意的一個答案標示在
　　　　　答案卡上。每題答對得2分，答錯倒扣⅔分，不答則不給分。

　　Families have always changed. For example, once the family was
the world. In other words, at one time everything a person did took
place within the family. The family was a child's only school. One
worshiped only within the family. The rules set up by the family were
the only laws one had to obey, and the family was the only means one
had to settle a dispute. The family is still the "world" in some

cultures. But in many cultures, these former functions of the family have largely been taken over by other institutions, such as schools, churches, and governments.

In the past, families changed in other ways. Some scientists believe that when people obtained food by hunting animals and gathering roots and plants, the nuclear family was the rule. The family had to be small in order to move around and live off the land. When people settled in one place and began to farm to obtain food, they found that they needed more hands to do the work. The extended family developed in some cultures. Now in addition to their children, people lived together with their parents and even grandparents.

How are families changing today? The number of nuclear families seems to be increasing everywhere in the world. The number of extended families is declining. One reason for this seems to be that in many cultures today people are leaving farms and villages to find jobs in the city. Extended families are hard to maintain when people have to be free to move in order to find work.

31. During the time when the family was the world,

   (A) people traveled all over the world.

   (B) children were educated at home.

   (C) only a few people went to church.

   (D) disputes could hardly be settled.

32. In many cultures today,

   (A) the family is the world.

   (B) the family is not an institution.

   (C) the family does not have any functions.

   (D) the family has lost many of the functions it used to have.

33. The nuclear family was the rule because

   (A) the family had to move around to find enough food.

   (B) people didn't know many ways of hunting animals.

   (C) people needed many hands to do farming.

   (D) the extended family had not been invented yet.

34. The reason why many people are leaving farms to find jobs in the city is
    (A) that there are more and more nuclear families in the world.
    (B) that extended families are hard to maintain.
    (C) that people do not like to settle down.
    (D) not stated in the above article.

35. Which of the following is true?
    (A) Although the nuclear family developed before the extended family, the latter is gaining more and more popularity everywhere in the world.
    (B) The most important reason why people are leaving villages is that they do not enjoy living together with their parents or grandparents.
    (C) Different types of families have developed as different ways of life are adopted.
    (D) Families change because tides and fashions always change.

The Yangtze River is not the longest, the widest, or the mightiest river in the world. But in one sense it is the most important river, because it serves more people than any other. In every way the Yangtze is China's life stream.

The Yangtze isn't just a trade river, a highway along which goods are picked up and distributed. It is an agricultural river as well. Networks of irrigation ditches stretch out from it to millions of tiny garden-size farms. There men and women work endlessly with ancient hand tools--planting, transplanting, fertilizing, weeding, harvesting, raising the family's food, and raising the nation's food.

The river begins somewhere high in the area north of Tibet, hurtling down from a three-mile height. It surges and tumbles for hundreds of miles, roars through canyons, and picks up tributaries. Only in the last 1,000 miles of its 3,200-mile journey does the Yangtze become the sunny and cheerful river that is China's blessing.

36. Where does the Yangtze River begin its journey to the sea?

　　(A) Somewhere in the central part of Tibet.

　　(B) Somewhere in the western part of Tibet.

　　(C) Somewhere in the region south of Tibet.

　　(D) Somewhere in the area north of Tibet.

37. How many miles does the river travel?

　　(A) one thousand miles.

　　(B) thirty-two hundreds miles.

　　(C) thirty-two hundred miles.

　　(D) thirty-two thousand miles.

38. The upper part of the Yangtze River

　　(A) flows through wide plains.

　　(B) rushes down from high mountains.

　　(C) is good for navigation.

　　(D) is more valuable to China than the lower part.

39. The Yangtze River is

　　(A) primarily a trade river.

　　(B) not only a trade river but an agricultural river.

　　(C) a very famous river mainly because it surges and tumbles for
　　　　hundreds of miles.

　　(D) not the longest river in the world, but it is the widest and
　　　　mightiest one.

40. From this article we have learned that

　　(A) the Yangtze River is China's source of strength.

　　(B) a big dam should be built to hold the waters back in the
　　　　Yangtze gorges.

　　(C) many people will certainly be starved without the foods produced
　　　　in the Yangtze basin.

　　(D) millions of tiny garden-size farms along the river are often
　　　　flooded.

第二部分：多重選擇題（10%）

下面五題（41～45）是簡單的對話，每題各有一個空白，並各附A、B、C、D、E 五個備選答案，其中至少有一個爲對的答案。請依照對話的內容，選出正確的 答案，並標示在答案卡上。對此五個備選的答案，考生的選擇若符合標準答案， 則可各獲0.4分；若不符合標準答案，則倒扣0.4分；完全不作答則視同放棄， 不給分。例如：設某題標準答案爲CDE,而考生答案爲BCD,則CD填對，共得 0.8分；E應填而未填，倒扣0.4分；B不應填而填，倒扣0.4分；A不應填， 未填爲對，得0.4分；則該題可得0.4分。

41. Mary : How long had you been studying before you gave up?
　　Helen : _____
　　(A) I have studied for five years.
　　(B) Five years.
　　(C) I don't remember clearly.
　　(D) Before I gave up I had been studying for five years.
　　(E) I had given up for five years already.

42. John : Don't you like to eat American food?
　　George : _____
　　(A) Yes, I don't like to eat American food.
　　(B) No, I like very much to eat American food.
　　(C) No, because American food is too expensive.
　　(D) No, I prefer to have noodles in a Chinese restaurant.
　　(E) No, American food is not really to my taste.

43. Teacher : Why didn't you hand in the paper yesterday?
　　Student : _____
　　(A) I'm sorry I forget.
　　(B) I must apologize for it.
　　(C) Because I had not finished writing the paper.
　　(D) I thought I was supposed to hand it in today.
　　(E) Please forgive me for it. I promise to hand in my next paper in time.

44. X : My father is not at home right now.
　　Y : _____
　　(A) Could you tell me when he will get home?
　　(B) Don't you remember I called this morning?
　　(C) May I leave a message with you?
　　(D) What can I do for you?
　　(E) May I take a message for him?

45. Woman：Please tell me some of your working experiences.

　　 Man：Frankly, I never worked before. I've been unemployed since I graduated from the university.

　　Woman：I see. The job market is very bad indeed.

　　 Man：I sincerely hope I can have the opportunity to work for your company.

What are these two persons doing?

(A) Discussing their working experiences.

(B) Talking about the market.

(C) Discussing the problem of unemployment.

(D) Holding a job interview.

(E) Talking about university life.

第三部分：非選擇題

I. 翻譯：中譯英（20％）

　　　　下面一段短文共有五個中文句子，請譯成正確、通順而達意的英文。每題4分，而各題都分前後兩個半句，各佔2分。答案請寫在「非選擇題試卷」上。

(1) 每天早晨有一位穿綠色制服的人（2％），把信件送到我們的社區來（2％）。

(2) 無論是晴天或下雨（2％），天天都可以看到他（2％）。

(3) 如果有掛號信要送給我們（2％），他就會在門口按一下鈴（2％）。

(4) 他認識我們附近的每一個人（2％），而我們每一個人也都認識他（2％）。

(5) 有時候我在上學的途中遇到他（2％），他就以微笑跟我打招呼（2％）。

II. 英文作文（20％）

用英文簡要敘述你上街買東西的經驗。全文分為兩段。第一段〔約三十個詞（words）〕說明買東西（例如：書籍、衣服、禮物等）的理由、商店的所在地、往返的交通工具等。第二段（約五十個詞）敘述買東西的經過情形、東西是否買成功、買了以後是否感到滿意等。文長以80個詞為度，不要太長或太短，並參考後面的評分標準。文章寫在「非選擇題試卷」上。

評分標準：拼字與標點（4％），遣詞用字（4％），文法（4％），組織（4％），內容（4％）。

75年大學聯考英文試題詳解

第一部份：單一選擇題

I. 對話（5％）

1. （ **D** ）瑪麗：你一定會說幾種語言。

　　　約翰：＿＿＿＿＿＿＿＿＿＿＿

　　　　(A) 我猜是法文。

　　　　(B) 不，我兩種都不會。（neither 作「二者中沒有一個」解，因此(B)句意不對）

　　　　(C) 那是個問題。

　　　　(D) 是的，我會說五種。

2. （ **B** ）瑪麗：我想我會待在家裏。

　　　約翰：＿＿＿＿＿＿＿＿＿＿＿

　　　　(A) 是的，你是。　　　　　(B) 我也是。

　　　　(C) 你想是如此吧。　　　　(D) 我會的。

3. （ **A** ）瑪麗：請你幫我把門打開，好嗎？

　　　約翰：＿＿＿＿＿＿＿＿＿＿＿

　　　　(A) 我很樂意。　　　　　　(B) 我大概會去開。

　　　　(C) 不要把它打開。　　　　(D) 不要那樣做。

4. （ **C** ）瑪麗：我想知道我是否可以借用你的電話。

　　　約翰：＿＿＿＿＿＿＿＿＿＿＿

　　　　(A) 我想知道那怎麼用。　　(B) 我不知道。

　　　　(C) 好，當然可以。　　　　(D) 難怪，它在這裏。

5. （ **D** ）瑪麗：湯姆告訴我說，你有集郵。

　　　約翰：＿＿＿＿＿＿＿＿＿＿＿

　　　　(A) 誰告訴你的？　　　　　(B) 我不認為如此。

　　　　(C) 他有集郵嗎？

　　　　(D) 是的，我有。你有嗎？

Ⅱ. 綜合測驗:

　　At that time the high-school entrance examinations were *just* <u>around</u>
₆

the corner, *and* I figured I'd get through them *all right.* I believed I

would <u>score</u> *high enough* to <u>qualify</u> *for a provincial high school.*
₇　　　　　　　　　　₈

　　"那時候中學入學考試就在眼前，我想我會順利地通過。我相信我的分數會

夠高，有資格進省立中學。"

　　* At that time (＝ Then) 是表時間的副詞片語，修飾 were。對等連接詞

　　　and 連接 At that... corner 和 I figured... right 兩子句，其中 I'd...

　　　right 是省略 that 的名詞子句，做 figured 的受詞。to qualify...

　　　school 是表結果的不定詞片語，修飾 enough，enough 又修飾 high 。

　　　（詳見文法寶典 p. 417 ）

　　　　entrance examination "入學考試"

　　　　figure〔'fɪgjɚ,'fɪgɚ〕*vt.* 想；認爲　　　*get through* "（考試）及格"

　　　　provincial〔prə'vɪnʃəl〕*adj.* 省的

6.（ **C** ）*around the corner* "快來到；在轉角處"

　　　(A) in the corner "在角落"　　　(B)(D) 則無此用法。

7.（ **C** ）(A) get "得到；變成"　　　　(B) mark "加符號"

　　　(C) <u>score "得到分數"</u>　　　　(D) record "記錄"

8.（ **A** ）(A) *qualify*〔'kwɑlə,faɪ〕*vi.* 取得資格（與 for 連用）

　　　(B) competent〔'kɑmpətənt〕*adj.* 能幹的；勝任的

　　　(C) certify〔'sɝtə,faɪ〕*vi.* 證明；保證

　　　(D) eligible〔'ɛlɪdʒəbl〕*adj.* 合格的

　　Unfortunately, my name did not appear on the list *of successful*

<u>*examinees*</u> . This news was met <u>*with*</u> *indifference by my family except*
₉　　　　　　　　　　　　　₁₀
Mother.

　　"不幸地，我的名字並沒有出現在上榜者的名單上。我的家人，除了母親以

外，都對這個消息漠不關心。"

＊ Unfortunately 是副詞，置於句首修飾 my name... examinees 全句
（詳見文法寶典 p. 268）。of successful examinees 是形容詞片語，修飾
list。with indifference 是副詞片語，修飾 met。

　　unfortunately〔ʌn'fɔrtʃənɪtlɪ〕 *adv*. 不幸地
　　indifference〔ɪn'dɪfərəns〕 *n*. 漠不關心；不重視

9.（ B ）(A) nominee〔‚nɑmə'ni〕 *n*. 被提名的候選人；被任命者
　　　　　(B) ***examinee***〔ɪg‚zæmə'ni, ɛg-〕 *n*. 應試者
　　　　　(C) 團體中之成員。
　　　　　(D) examiner〔ɪg'zæmɪnɚ, ɛg-〕 *n*. 主考者；檢查者

10.（ C ）***with indifference*** "漠不關心地；冷淡地"

In our home, everyone minded his own business — no one had anything
　　　　　　　　　　　　　11
to do with anyone else. *Only* Mother had something to say；she
called me to her bed, "I won't scold you, *but* I want you to make
something of yourself...."
　12
"在我們家裏，每個人管自己的事——大家彼此無關。只有母親有話要說；她把
我叫到她的床邊，說道：「我不會責備你，但是，我要你重視自己…。」"

　＊ In our home 是表地方的副詞片語，修飾 minded。長劃（——）在此引導總
　　括全句意義的用語（詳見文法寶典p. 43）。副詞 Only 修飾 Mother（副詞修飾
　　名詞，詳見文法寶典p. 228）。半支點（；）在此用來連接沒有連接詞的兩個有
　　密切關係的獨立子句（詳見文法寶典 p. 41）。

　　have anything to do with "與～有任何關係"
　　scold〔skold〕 *vt.*, *vi.* 責罵；責備

11.（ D ）(A) notice〔'notɪs〕 *vt*. 注意；通知
　　　　　(B) regard〔rɪ'gɑrd〕 *vt*. 視為；當作
　　　　　(C) concern〔kən'sɝn〕 *vt*. 關係；使關心
　　　　　(D) ***mind one's own business*** "管自己的事"

12.（ B ）***make something of*** "重視～"

I tried and tried to figure out what she meant by this, *finally*
　　　　　　　　　　　　　―――
　　　　　　　　　　　　　13　　　　　　　　　14
realizing *that* she didn't want me to be *yet* another burden on
―――――
15
Elder Brother, *for* her illness was *already* a heavy burden to him.
"我一再試著去理解她這句話的含意，終於了解，她不要我成爲大哥的另一個負
擔，因爲她的病對他來說，已經是個沈重的負擔了。"

* and 連接兩個 tried，表「重複」或加強語氣（詳見文法寶典 p.466）。what
she … this 是名詞子句，做 figure 的受詞。finally realizing that …
him 是由對等子句 and I finally realized that … him 簡化而來的分詞
構句，表示和 tried and tried 動作的連續（詳見文法寶典 pp. 459〜460）。對
等連接詞 for 在 that 子句中，連接兩個對等子句，第一個子句表結論，第
二個子句則說明產生該結論的原因（詳見文法寶典 p.477）。

13. (**B**)　(A) reason with + *sb*. "向某人說理"
　　　　　　　(B) *figure out* "理解；解決"
　　　　　　　(C) see through "看透；貫徹"　　(D) point out "指出"

14. (**A**)　mean A *by sth*. "藉著某事來表達A"，例：What did he *mean*
　　　　　　　by 'coward'？（他所謂「懦夫」是什麼意思？）
　　　　　　　(B) mean A for *sb*. "打算將A給某人"，不合。 (C)(D) 則無此用法。

15. (**C**)　選(C) realizing 的理由，請見本段的文法解析。
　　　　　　　(A) 是過去完成式，(B) 是現在完成式，(D) 則是現在式，三者與 tried
　　　　　　　and tried 的過去式不一致，故不合。

Mexico, the largest nation *in the region*, provides a good example
of life *in Middle America*. **Although** Mexico is a large country, *only*
　　　　　　　　　　　　　　　　　　　　　　　　　　　　　　　　　――――
　　　　　　　　　　　　　　　　　　　　　　　　　　　　　　　　　16
12 percent of its land is good for farming. Another 40 percent is
　　　　　　　　　　　　　　　　　　　　　　　　―――――
　　　　　　　　　　　　　　　　　　　　　　　　17
grazing land. The rest *of the land* is hills and mountains, dry,
　　　　　　　　　　　―――
　　　　　　　　　　　18
high plateaus, *or* wet coastal regions.

"墨西哥，中美洲最大的國家，提供了一個該地區生活的好實例。雖然墨西
哥是個大國，但是其土地只有百分之十二適於耕作。另外百分之四十是很好的放
牧地。其他土地則是丘陵和山地、又乾又高的臺地，或是潮濕的海岸區。"

* the largest … region 是 Mexico 的同位語。in Central America 是形容詞片語，修飾 life。Although 引導表讓步的副詞子句，修飾 is。選擇連接詞 or 在此作「或」解，連接 hills and mountains 等 (詳見文法寶典 p. 473)。

Mexico〔'mɛksɪˌko〕*n.* 墨西哥　　region〔'ridʒən〕*n.* 地方；區域
provide〔prə'vaɪd〕*vt.* 供給；供應
farming〔'fɑrmɪŋ〕*n.* 農業；耕作
grazing〔'grezɪŋ〕*n.* 放牧；牧場　　grazing land " 放牧地 "
plateau〔plæ'to〕*n.* 臺地；高原　　coastal〔'kostḷ〕*adj.* 海岸的

16. (**A**)　(A) 只有。　　(B) 因為。　　(C) 甚至。　　(D) 附有。

17. (**B**)　another 指的是「另外任何一個的」，因此至少有三個才能用；如果只有兩個時，就只能用 the other。本題因有三部分（ 12 percent；40 percent；the rest），故選(B) another。 (A)(D) 則句意不合。

18. (**D**)　(A) 最好的部分。　　(B) 地方。　　(C) 高度。　　(D) 剩餘 (其前須有 the)。

The mountains are *too* steep *to farm*. The high plateau *in*
　　　　　　　　　　　　　　19
the middle of Mexico would be good farmland *if it had more* water.
　　　　　　　　　　　　　　　　　　　　　　　　20

"那些山地太陡峭而無法耕作。墨西哥中部的高原，如果有更多的水，將會是很好的農地。"

* 不定詞 to farm 修飾副詞 too，表否定的結果 (詳見文法寶典 p. 415)。in the middle of Mexico 是形容詞片語，修飾 plateau。The high … more water 是表示與現在事實相反的假設，由 if 引導表條件的副詞子句，修飾 be (詳見文法寶典 p. 361)。

farmland〔'fɑrmˌlænd〕*n.* 農地

19. (**C**)　(A) 溫暖的。　　　　　　　　(B) mild〔maɪld〕*adj.* 溫暖的
　　　　　　(C) *steep*〔stip〕*adj.* 陡峭的　(D) 好的。

20. (**C**)　(A) 農夫。　　　　　　　　　(B) 丘陵。
　　　　　　(C) 水。　　　　　　　　　　(D) cattle〔'kætḷ〕*n.* 牛
　　　　　　上段提到 dry, high plateaus，可聯想到 water 對於該地區之重要性。

The coastal areas receive *so* much rain *that the land often becomes*
　　　　　　　　　　　　　　　21
waterlogged. *For all of these reasons*, Mexicans must take care of

the good farmland *(which) they have.* *Yet* good farming has *not al-*

ways been possible *in Mexico.*

"海岸區的雨水下得太多，以致於土地往往變得泥濘不堪。基於這些理由，墨西哥人必須照顧他們所擁有的良好農地。但是在墨西哥却未必可有良好的農作。"

　＊ that 引導副詞子句修飾前面的相關副詞 so，表前面原因的結果，so 則修飾其後的much（詳見文法寶典 p. 516）。For all … reasons 是副詞片語修飾 take。they have 是省略 which 或 that 的形容詞子句，修飾 farmland。Yet（但是）與 but 同義，是表反義的副詞連接詞，用來連接其前後的句子（詳見文法寶典 p. 471）。

　　　waterlogged〔'wɔtɚ,lɑgd〕*adj.*（地）被水浸透了的；泥濘的
　　　Mexican〔'mɛksɪkən〕*n.* 墨西哥人
　　　take care of "看護；照料"　　　***not always*** "不一定總是；未必"

21.（ **A** ）(A) 雨水。　　　(B) 風。　　　(C) 霧。　　　(D) 日光。

For many centuries, Mexican farmers had grown traditional crops.
　　　　　　　　　　　　　　　　　　　　　　22
These included corn, beans, and squash.
　　　　　23

　"好幾百年以來，墨西哥的農夫一直種植傳統的農作物。這些包括玉蜀黍、豆類、和南瓜。"

　＊ For many centuries 是副詞片語，修飾 grown，表時間。

　　　Mexican〔'mɛksɪkən〕*adj.* 墨西哥的
　　　traditional〔trə'dɪʃənl〕*adj.* 傳統的
　　　bean〔bin〕*n.* 豆；豆類　　　squash〔skwɑʃ〕*n.* 南瓜

22.（ **B** ）(A) 使用。　　(B) 種植。　　(C) 看見。　　(D) 錯失。

23.（ **D** ）(A) produce〔prə'djus〕*vt.* 生產　　(B) combine〔kəm'baɪn〕*vt.* 聯合
　　　　　　(C) substitute〔'sʌbstə,tjut〕*vt.* 以～代替
　　　　　　(D) ***include***〔ɪn'klud〕*vt.* 包括

However, **when** *the Spanish arrived in the 1500's*, they tried to <u>introduce</u>
                                              24

new ideas. They thought new plants **such as** onions, turnips, sugarcane,

and bananas would <u>do</u> *well in the warm, tropical climate*. **But** the Mex-
                                25

icans wished to continue *with their old **ways***.

「然而，當西班牙人在十六世紀抵達時，就試著引入新的觀念。他們認為像洋葱、蘿蔔、甘蔗和香蕉等新植物，在這溫暖的熱帶氣候會長得很好。但是墨西哥人希望持續他們古老的方式。」

  * However 是轉承語，連接前面的句子。when 引導表時間的副詞子句，修飾 tried。new plants … climate 是省略 that 的名詞子句，做 thought 的受詞。such as（像；如）是用來解釋的連接詞，表舉例（詳見文法寶典 p.478）。in the … climate 是副詞片語，修飾 do。with their old ways 也是副詞片語，修飾 continue，其中的 with 表示工具、媒介，作「用～；以～」解（詳見文法寶典 p.606）。

    Spanish〔'spænɪʃ〕*n.* 西班牙人（集合名詞，須加定冠詞）
    onion〔'ʌnjən〕*n.* 洋葱   turnip〔'tɝnɪp〕*n.* 蘿蔔；蕪菁
    sugarcane〔'ʃʊgɚ,ken〕*n.* 甘蔗   tropical〔'trɑpɪkl〕*adj.* 熱帶的

24.（ A ）(A) 引入；介紹。   (B) replace〔rɪ'ples〕*vt.* 代替
         (C) 誤會。   (D) abandon〔ə'bændən〕*vt.* 放棄

25.（ B ）(A) 是。   (B) *do vi.*（植物）成長（＝grow）
         (C) plant *vt.* 種植（主詞為人） (D) 收到。

Ⅲ. 閱讀測驗（25%）：

甲（5%）：

Woman : Just put it in there, will you ?

  Man : Here, by the cupboard ?

Woman : Yes, that's it. Would you mind unpacking it ? I've hurt my
            shoulder. I can't lift anything.

  Man : Well, OK then. It's just in a cardboard box, really. The rest
            of this stuff is just padding. For protection. OK. There you
            are. One <u>Easiwash</u> washing machine. Ready for use.

"女：就放在那裏面，好嗎？

男：這兒，放在碗櫥旁邊嗎？

女：對，就是那兒。請把它打開拿出來好嗎？我的肩膀受傷了。我什麼東西都抬不起來。

男：嗯，好吧。這只不過是放在一個硬紙板的盒子裏。其他的物品只是一些塡塞物。作保護用的。好了，你瞧。一臺易洗牌洗衣機　隨時都可以啟用。"

* 在肯定祈使句後面的附加問句，若表示「請求」，用 will you。

* Would you mind＋V-ing…？＝Would you please＋V（原形）…？作「請…好嗎？」解，表示謙恭的請求，實際上是省略了條件子句的假設法，比 will 客氣。（詳見文法寶典 p. 308）

　　cupboard〔'kʌbəd〕n. 碗櫥（ p 不發音）

　　unpack〔ʌn'pæk〕vt. 開箱取出　　cardboard〔'kɑrd͵bord〕n. 硬紙板

　　stuff〔stʌf〕n. 物品；材料　　padding〔'pædɪŋ〕n. 塡塞物

　　protection〔prə'tɛkʃən〕n. 保護

Woman : How does it work ?

　Man : The instructions are here somewhere....

Woman : I hate machines.

　Man : It tells you what to do. There's a little booklet of instructions. It's here somewhere. ... Oh here we are.

"女：它如何操作？

男：說明書在這裏某個地方…

女：我討厭機器。

男：它會告訴你做些什麼。有一本說明的小冊子。在這裏某個地方。…哦，找到了。"

* somewhere 是副詞，作「在某處」解。what to do 是名詞片語，作 tell 的直接受詞。

　　instruction〔ɪn'strʌkʃən〕n. 指示；說明　　booklet〔'bʊklɪt〕n. 小冊子

Woman : I suppose it's all right *when you get used to it* **but** I find new machines *so* intimidating, don't you ? My husband's the same. He's hopeless with machinery.

　Man : The instructions tell you *exactly* what to do. Look. There're diagrams, *in color* and everything.

"女：我想當你習慣它的時候就好了，但是我覺得新機器蠻嚇人的，不是嗎？我先生也有同樣的感覺。他對機器毫無辦法。

男：這些說明告訴你該怎麼做。看，有圖表，彩色的，還有種種事項。"

* when … it 是表時間副詞子句，修飾 is。intimidating 是受詞補語，補充說明 machines。複句的附加問句是以主要思想的子句爲準（不一定是主要子句），而主要子句是 I suppose（think，consider, believe...)時，附加問句不能以主要子句爲準，因爲 don't I？這類的疑問句沒有意義。（詳見文法寶典 p.7）。但此處 don't you？表示 don't you find new machines so intimidating？之意。

　　intimidating〔ɪn'tɪmə,detɪŋ〕adj. 嚇人的
　　hopeless〔'hoplɪs〕adj. 毫無辦法；絕望的
　　machinery〔mə'ʃinərɪ〕n. 機器（總稱）
　　diagram〔'daɪə,græm〕n. 圖表

Woman : Yes. I can't understand a thing. What's the difference between 'synthetic' and 'non-synthetic' material? *Actually* my husband usually does the washing. He's an angel.

"女：是的，但我有一項不懂。「合成衣料」和「非合成衣料」有什麼差別？事實上是我先生經常洗衣服。他是一個可愛的人。"

　　synthetic〔sɪn'θɛtɪk〕adj. 合成的；人造的
　　non-synthetic〔,nɑnsɪn'θɛtɪk〕adj. 非合成的

26.（ B ）這個男人正在
　　　　(A) 修理洗衣機。　　　　　　(B) 把洗衣機送來。
　　　　(C) 把洗衣機搬走。　　　　　(D) 出售洗衣機。

27.（ C ）這個女人什麼都抬不起來
　　　　(A) 因爲她太虛弱了。　　　　(B) 因爲她不知道怎麼抬。
　　　　(C) 因爲她受傷了。　　　　　(D) 因爲她討厭機器。

28.（ D ）這個女人的先生
　　　　(A) 喜歡新的機器。　　　　　(B) 比她較不常洗衣服。
　　　　(C) 對洗衣機很失望。　　　　(D) 也覺得新的機器難以操作。

29.（ **B** ）上列對話中的那個男人

(A) 根本找不到說明書。　　(B) 暫時找不到說明書。

(C) 忘記把說明書帶在身上。　(D) 誤將說明書放在某處。

misplace〔mɪs'ples〕*vt.* 誤放

30.（ **A** ）這個女人無法瞭解

(A) 那說明。　　　　　　(B) 這個男人。

(C) 她的先生。　　　　　(D) 任何一件事。

乙（20％）：

Families have *always* changed. ***For example***, *once* the family was the world. ***In other words***, *at one time* everything *a person did* took place *within the family*. The family was a child's only school. One worshiped only *within the family*.

　"家庭始終在改變。例如，從前家庭就是世界。換句話說，一度人所做的每件事，都發生在家裏。家庭是小孩唯一的學校。一個人也只能在家中拜拜。"

　＊ a person did 是形容詞子句，省略了 that，修飾 everything。within … family 是表地方的副詞片語，修飾 took。

　　in other words " 換句話說 "　　　***at one time*** " 曾經；一度 "

　　take place " 發生；舉行 "（不用被動）

　　worship〔'wɝʃəp〕*n.,vt.,vi.* 禮拜；崇拜

The rules *set up by the family* were the only laws *one had to obey*, ***and*** the family was the only means *one had to settle a dispute*. The family is still the " world "*in some cultures*. ***But in many cultures***, these former functions of the family have *largely* been taken over by other institutions, ***such as*** schools, churches, and governments.

"家庭所訂立的規矩是唯一必須遵守的法則，而且家庭是解決爭論的唯一方法。在某些文化中，家庭仍然還是「世界」。但是在許多文化中，家庭原先的功能，已經大量被其他像學校、教堂和政府的事業機構給接管。"

* set … family是分詞片語，修飾rules，實際上是形容詞子句省略了which were而來(詳見文法寶典p. 457)。one … obey是形容詞子句，省略了that (or which)。one had … dispute 也是形容詞子句，省略了that；that在子句中作 had 的受詞。

> **set up** "訂立；設立"　　　means〔minz〕n. 方法；工具
> settle〔'sɛtl〕vt. 解決　　dispute〔dɪ'spjut〕n. 爭論
> former〔'fɔrmɚ〕adj.早先的；原先的　　function〔'fʌŋkʃən〕n.作用；功能
> **take over** "接管"　　institution〔ˌɪnstə'tjuʃən〕n. 事業機構

In the past, families changed *in other ways.* Some scientists believe **that when** people obtained food *by hunting animals and gathering roots and plants,* the nuclear family was the rule. The family had to be small *in order to move around and live off the land.*

"過去，家庭以其他方式改變。一些科學家們相信，當人們靠狩獵、收集根莖類和農作物來獲得食物時，一貫採核心家庭。這種家庭勢必很小，以便四處遷移和靠土地為生。"

* in … ways是副詞片語，修飾 changed。that … rule是名詞子句，作 believe 的受詞。by … plants是副詞片語，修飾 obtained，表方法。
* in order … land是不定詞片語當副詞用，修飾 be，表目的。

> obtain〔əb'ten〕vt.獲得　　root〔rut〕n. 植物的根；根莖類
> nuclear family "核心家庭"　　**live off** "靠…為生"

When people settled *in one place* and began to farm *to obtain food,* they found **that** they needed more hands *to do the work.* The *extended* family developed *in some cultures. Now in addition to their children,* people lived together *with their parents and even grandparents.*

"當人們在一處安頓下來，開始爲了要獲得食物而耕作時，他們發覺需要更多的人手來做這件工作。一些文化就產生了大家庭。這時候除了小孩以外，人們還和他們的父母，甚至祖父母都住在一起。"

* in one place 是副詞片語，修飾 settled。to obtain food 是不定詞片語，修飾 farm，表目的，to 相當於 in order to。that … work 是名詞子句，作 found 的受詞。

　　settle〔ˈsɛtḷ〕vt. 安頓　　farm〔fɑrm〕vt., vi. 種植；耕作
　　extended family "大家庭"　　*in addition to* "除了…以外還…"

How are families changing today? The number *of nuclear families* seems to be increasing *everywhere in the world*. The number of *extended* families is declining.

"今天的家庭如何改變？核心家庭的數量似乎世界各地都在增加中。大家庭的數量則在減少。"

* seem 是不完全不及物動詞，沒有受詞，但需主詞補語。而 seem 和主詞補語間的 to be 可省略。

　　decline〔dɪˈklaɪn〕vi. 減少；下降

One reason *for this* seems to be *that in many cultures today* people are leaving farms and villages *to find jobs in the city*. Extended families are hard *to maintain* *when people have to be free to move in order to find work*.

"這種情況的一個原因可能是今天在許多文化中，人們爲了在城市中找尋工作，而離開了農田和村落。當人們爲了找工作而必須自由遷移之時，大家庭很難再保持下去。"

* that … city 是名詞子句，作主詞補語。to … city 是不定詞片語當副詞用，修飾 leaving，表目的。
* to maintain 是不定詞片語當副詞用，修飾 hard，而且要用主動語態。
　　（詳見文法寶典 p. 425）

　　maintain〔menˈten；mənˈten〕vt. 保持；維持

31. （ **B** ） 在家庭就是世界的這段時間，

    (A) 人們到世界各地旅遊。   (B) <u>孩子們在家受教育。</u>
    (C) 只有一些人去教堂。   (D) 爭論幾乎無法解決。

32. （ **D** ） 今天在許多文化中，

    (A) 家庭就是世界。   (B) 家庭不是一種事業機構。
    (C) 家庭沒有任何功能。
    (D) <u>家庭失去了許多它以前所具有的功能。</u>

33. （ **A** ） 核心家庭是規範，因為

    (A) <u>這種家庭必須四處遷移來找尋足夠的食物。</u>
    (B) 人們不知道許多狩獵的方法。
    (C) 人們需要許多的人力來務農。   (D) 大家庭尚未被發明。

34. （ **D** ） 許多人為了在城市中找工作，而離開農田和村落的原因是

    (A) 世界上的核心家庭越來越多。   (B) 大家庭很難再保持下去。
    (C) 人們不喜歡定居。   (D) <u>上述文章並未提到。</u>

35. （ **C** ） 下列何者正確？

    (A) 雖然核心家庭發生在大家庭之前，但是後者在世界各地越受到歡迎。
    (B) 人們為何離開村落最重要的原因，就是他們不喜歡和父母或祖父母住在一起。
    (C) <u>當不同的生活方式被採行時，就發展出不同種類的家庭。</u>
    (D) 家庭改變是因為潮流和時尚始終在改變。

    The Yangtze River is not the longest, the widest, *or* the mightiest river *in the world*. **But in one sense** it is the most important river, **because** *it serves more people* **than** *any other. In every way* the Yangtze is China's life stream.

    "長江並不是世界上最長、最寬或是最強大的河流。但就某一方面來說，它是最重要的河，因為它所照顧的人比其他任何一條河流多。在每個方面，長江是中國的生命源流。"

* because … other 是副詞子句，修飾 is，表直接的原因。than 是表差異的連接詞，引導省略 serves people 的副詞子句，修飾 more。

> Yangtze〔'jæŋ,tsɪ〕n. 長江；揚子江（亦作 Yangtse；Yangtse Kiang）
> mighty〔'maɪtɪ〕adj. 強大的　　　sense〔sɛns〕n. 方面；意義
> serve〔sɜv〕vt. 為…效勞；服務

The Yangtze isn't just a trade river, a highway *along which goods are picked up and distributed.* It is an agricultural river as well. Networks of irrigation ditches stretch out *from it to millions of tiny garden-size farms.*

"長江不只是一條商業河流，一條沿河將貨物收集和分配的水道。它也是一條農業河流。灌溉渠網從長江伸展到數百萬菜園般大小的小農田。"

* a highway … distributed 是作 a trade river 的同位語，其中 along … distributed 是形容詞子句，修飾 highway。

> highway〔'haɪ,we〕n. 水道；公路　　**pick up** "（車船）中途搭載"
> distribute〔dɪ'strɪbjʊt〕vt. 分配
> agricultural〔,ægrɪ'kʌltʃərəl〕adj. 農業的
> network〔'nɛt,wɜk〕n. 網；網狀物　　irrigation〔,ɪrə'geʃən〕n. 灌溉
> ditch〔dɪtʃ〕n.（灌溉用）渠，溝
> stretch〔strɛtʃ〕vt., vi. 伸展；張開

There men and women work endlessly *with ancient hand tools* — planting, transplanting, fertilizing, weeding, harvesting, raising the family's food, **and** raising the nation's food.

"在那兒，男女都以古代的手工具，無止境地工作──種植、移植、施肥、除草、收割、栽培家庭的食糧、栽培國家的食糧。"

* with … tools 是副詞片語，修飾 work。長劃（──）是引導總括或附加全句之意義的用語。（詳見文法寶典 p. 43）

tool〔tul〕*n.* 工具　　transplant〔træns'plænt〕*vt.* 移植

fertilize〔'fɝtl͵aɪz〕*vt.* 施肥　　weed〔wid〕*vt.* 除草

harvest〔'hɑrvɪst〕*vt.* 收割；收穫　　raise〔rez〕*vt.* 栽培；養育

The river begins *somewhere high in the area north of Tibet*, hurt-

ling down from a three-mile height. It surges and tumbles *for hun-*

dreds of miles, roars through canyons, **and** picks up tributaries. *Only*

in the last 1,200 mile of its 3,200-mile journey does the Yangtze be-

come the sunny and cheerful river **that is China's blessing.**

"這條河發源於西藏北部的某處高地，從三英里的高度急衝而下。它洶湧翻滾數百哩長，怒吼穿過峽谷，滙集許多支流。在長江三千二百英里的行程中，只有在最後的一千英里，它才是一條輝耀、令人喜悅的中國的幸福之河。"

* hurtling … height 是分詞構句，本句可改爲一個對等子句，和原句主要子句並立：The river begins somewhere high in the area north of Tibet, and hurtles down from a three-mile height.（詳見文法寶典 p.457）

* for … miles 是副詞片語，修飾 surges 和 tumbles。Only … blessing是副詞片語放在句首的倒裝句，原句應爲：The Yangtze becomes the sunny and cheerful river that is China's blessing only in the last 1000 miles of its 3200-mile journey；其中 that … blessing 是形容詞子句，修飾 river。

Tibet〔tɪ'bɛt〕*n.* 西藏地方　　hurtle〔'hɝtl〕*vi.* 急動；猛撞

surge〔sɝdʒ〕*vi.* 起伏；洶湧　　tumble〔'tʌmbl〕*vi.* 翻滾

roar〔ror；rɔr〕*vi.* 怒吼；怒號　　canyon〔'kænjən〕*n.* 峽谷

tributary〔'trɪbjə͵tɛrɪ〕*n.* 支流　　blessing〔'blɛsɪŋ〕*n.* 幸福；恩賜

36.（ **D** ）長江從那裏啓程，而流入海洋？

(A) 在西藏中央部份的某處。　　(B) 在西藏西部的某處。

(C) 在西藏南區的某處。　　(D) 在西藏北部的某處。

region〔'ridʒən〕*n.* 區域；地方

37. （ C ）這條河行經多少英里？

    (A) 一千英里。

    (B) 三千二百英里。（名詞修飾名詞應該用單數形，所以應改為
        thirty-two hundred miles）

    (C) 三千二百英里。　　　　　(D) 三萬二千英里。

38. （ B ）長江的上游部分

    (A) 流經寬廣的平原。　　　　(B) 從高山上急衝而下。

    (C) 利於航行。

    (D) 對中國的價值比下游部分大。

    rush〔rʌʃ〕vt., vi. 急衝　　navigation〔ˏnævəˈgeʃən〕n. 航海；航行

39. （ B ）長江

    (A) 主要是商業河流。

    (B) 不但是商業河流，也是農業河流。

    (C) 是很有名的河流，主要因為它洶湧翻滾數百哩長。

    (D) 不是世界上最長的河，卻是世界上最寬、最強大的河流。

40. （ A ）從這篇文章我們知道

    (A) 長江是中國力量的泉源。

    (B) 應該建造一個大水壩來阻止長江三峽的水。

    (C) 沒有長江流域所生產的食物，許多人一定會挨餓。

    (D) 沿河數百萬像菜園大小般的小農田時常被淹沒。

    source〔sors, sɔrs〕n. 泉源　　　dam〔dæm〕n. 水壩

    gorge〔gɔrdʒ〕n. 峽谷（the Yangtze Gorges "長江三峽"）

    starve〔stɑrv〕vt., vi. 使饑餓

    basin〔ˈbesṇ〕n. 流域；盆地（the Yangtze basin 長江流域）

第二部分：多重選擇題

41. （ BCD ）瑪麗：在你放棄前，你研讀了多久？

    海倫：＿＿＿＿＿＿＿＿＿＿＿＿＿

        (A) 我已經研讀了五年。

          （時式不對，應把完成式改為過去完成進行式）

        (B) 五年。　　　　　(C) 我記不清楚了。

        (D) 在我放棄前，我已研讀了五年。

        (E) 我已經放棄有五年之久。（答非所問，故不選）

42. (　**C D E**　) 約翰：你不喜歡吃美式食品嗎？

喬治：＿＿＿＿＿＿＿＿＿＿＿＿＿

(A) 是的，我不喜歡吃美式食品。(答案應把 Yes 改爲 No)

(B) 不，我非常喜歡吃美式食品。(答案應把 No 改爲 Yes)

(C) 是的，因爲美式食品太貴了。

(D) 是的，我還是比較喜歡在中國餐館吃麵條。

(E) 是的，美式食品實在不合我的胃口。

noodle〔'nudḷ〕*n*. 麵條（常用複數形）

to one's taste "合某人的胃口"

43. (　**B C D E**　) 老師：你昨天爲什麼沒交報告？

學生：＿＿＿＿＿＿＿＿＿＿＿＿＿

(A) 對不起，我忘記了。(時式不對，故不選)

(B) 我必須爲這件事道歉。(C) 因爲我還沒把報告完成。

(D) 我以爲今天才要交報告。

(E) 請原諒我。我答應下次準時交。

hand in "繳交；呈遞"　　apologize〔ə'pɑlə,dʒaɪz〕*vi*. 道歉

44. (　**A C**　) X：我父親現在不在家。

Y：＿＿＿＿＿＿＿＿＿＿＿＿＿

(A) 你能告訴我他什麼時候會到家？

(B) 你難道不記得今天早上我打過電話來嗎？

(C) 我可以留個話給你嗎？ (D) 我能替你做什麼嗎？

(E) 我可以替他帶給口信嗎？

45. (　**D**　) 女：請告訴我一些你的工作經驗。

男：坦白說，我以前從來沒有工作過。自從大學畢業後就沒有工作。

女：我知道了。工作市場實在是不好。

男：我很誠懇地希望我能有這個機會，爲你的公司效力。

這兩個人在做什麼？

(A) 討論他們的工作經驗。 (B) 談論市場。

(C) 討論失業的問題。　　 (D) 進行求職面談。

(E) 談論大學生活。

unemployment〔͵ʌnɪm'plɔɪmənt〕*n*. 失業

第三部分：非選擇題

Ⅰ. 翻譯：中譯英

(1) 每天早晨有一位穿綠色制服的人，把信件送到我們的社區來。

Every morning a man $\begin{Bmatrix} in \\ wearing \\ dressed\ in \end{Bmatrix}$ *a green uniform* delivers

letters to our community.

uniform〔'junə,fɔrm〕*n.* 制服

community〔kə'mjunətɪ〕*n.* 社區

(2) 無論是晴天或下雨，天天都可以看到他。

$\begin{Bmatrix} Rain\ or\ shine, \\ \textbf{\textit{Whether}}\ it\ rains\ or\ shines, \end{Bmatrix}$ he can be seen *every day*.

rain or shine "不論晴雨"

(3) 如果有掛號信要送給我們，他就會在門口按一下鈴。

If there are any registered letters for us, he will ring the doorbell.

registered〔'rɛdʒɪstəd〕*adj.* 掛號的

(4) 他認識我們附近的每一個人，而我們每一個人也都認識他。

He knows everyone *in our* $\begin{Bmatrix} vicinity \\ neighborhood \end{Bmatrix}$ *and*

$\begin{Bmatrix} vice\ versa. \\ everyone\ of\ us\ also\ knows\ him. \end{Bmatrix}$

vicinity〔və'sɪnətɪ〕*n.* 附近；近處

vice versa〔'vaɪsɪ 'vɝsə〕*adv.* 〔拉丁文〕反之亦然

(5) 有時候我在上學的途中遇到他，他就以微笑跟我打招呼。

Sometimes I meet him on my way to school, ***and*** he greets me *with a smile*.

greet〔grit〕*vt.* 打招呼

Ⅱ. 英文作文（參考範例）

My mother's birthday was just around the corner, and I wanted to give her a big surprise, so I walked to the Far Eastern Department Store on Jen Ai Road to buy a gift for her.

At first I just had a random look around the different departments, but later I was deeply attracted to a beautiful blouse. It was pale pink with a lace collar. Although it was very expensive, I did not care about the price as long as Mother liked it. As was expected, she was surprised and gave me a warm embrace on her birthday.

department store " 百貨公司；百貨商店 "
random〔'rændəm〕*adj.* 隨便的；無目的的
blouse〔blaʊs, blaʊz〕*n.* 女上衣；女襯衫　　lace〔les〕*n.* 花邊
embrace〔ɪm'bres〕*n.* 擁抱

我母親的生日就快到了，我想要給她一個很大的驚喜，所以，我走路到仁愛路上的遠東百貨公司去買一份禮物給她。

起初，我只是隨意看看各個部門，後來我深深地給一件漂亮的女襯衫吸引住。它是淡淡的粉紅色，帶有花邊的領子。雖然很昂貴，但是我並不在意價錢，只要母親喜歡它。如所預料的，在母親生日那天，她很驚喜，而且給我一個溫馨的擁抱。

七十四學年度大學暨獨立學院入學考試
英文試題

第一部分：單一選擇題

I. 綜合測驗㈠（含用詞、成語、語法、文意、推理等）（20％）

說明：下面兩段文章，共有二十個空白，編號1～20，每個空白附有四個答案。
請仔細閱讀各段文章後，選出一個最適當的答案，並標示在答案卡上。每
題答對得1分，答錯倒扣1/3分，若不答則不給分。

　　Six feet＿＿1＿＿and weighing between 400 and 500 pounds, a
grown male gorilla is 10 to 14 times as powerful as the strongest
man. ＿＿2＿＿up, thick arms flung to the sky, he seems much like
King Kong, the super gorilla of the movies. But we have learned
that gorillas would rather use their power and frightening display to
avoid trouble, ＿＿3＿＿to make it.

　　＿＿4＿＿government is simple. Each tribe has a male boss, who
is more or less undemanding. Sometimes the boss does assert his
right to the choicest food, the favorite companion, or the driest spot
＿＿5＿＿it is raining. In general,＿＿6＿＿, he leaves the others
well alone. Intelligence and a way for＿＿7＿＿along seem to count
as much as strength in deciding who becomes — and＿＿8＿＿— ape-king.
As long as the old king holds his job, his subjects turn＿＿9＿＿him
to decide everything — when to search for food or where to camp,
＿＿10＿＿instance.

1. (A) high　　　　(B) tall　　　　(C) round　　　　(D) long

2. (A) Standing　　(B) Stand　　　(C) Stood　　　　(D) To stand

3. (A) and　　　　(B) not　　　　(C) but　　　　　(D) only

4. (A) His　　　　(B) Its　　　　(C) Her　　　　　(D) Their

5. (A) whether　　(B) where　　　(C) when　　　　(D) why

6. (A) yet　　　　(B) instead　　 (C) however　　　(D) accordingly

7. (A) going　　　(B) coming　　 (C) running　　　(D) getting

8. (A) keeps　　　(B) remains　　(C) retains　　　(D) makes

9. (A) on　　　(B) for　　　(C) at　　　(D) to
10. (A) for　　　(B) by　　　(C) on　　　(D) among

　　What is ___11___ that a teacher most wants in his students ? Attentiveness ? A good memory ? Diligence ? Certainly these are the qualities commonly ___12___ with "good student" in the ___13___ mind. And certainly, too, these are the qualities that most ___14___ to teacher comfort.

　　But the best student I ever had, ___15___ I remember the most wistfully, was a talkative, lazy day-dreamer. Sometimes he turned assignments in ___16___, and a few he never ___17___ around to doing at all. Actually, my admiration for him was ironic, ___18___ I have never liked the name Ronald, ___19___ suggests to me the assumed name of a movie star. But he made one whole year of my ___20___ experience a delight.

11. (A) there　　(B) they　　(C) it　　(D) that
12. (A) associate　(B) associated　(C) associates　(D) associating
13. (A) popular　(B) proper　(C) inner　(D) educated
14. (A) contribute　(B) contributed　(C) contributes　(D) contributing
15. (A) a one　　(B) the one　　(C) the ones　　(D) these ones
16. (A) early　　(B) behind　　(C) ahead　　(D) late
17. (A) gave　　(B) looked　　(C) sent　　(D) got
18. (A) so　　　(B) still　　(C) because　　(D) though
19. (A) who　　(B) which　　(C) what　　(D) that
20. (A) teaching　(B) teacher　　(C) teach　　(D) taught

Ⅱ. 綜合測驗⑵（含詞彙、語法、語用、標點等）（5%）

　　說明：下面五題（21～25）各有一個空白，並各附 A、B、C、D 四個答案，其中只有一個答案是正確的。請選出這個正確的答案，並標示在答案卡上。每題答對得 1 分，答錯倒扣 1 / 3 分，若不答則不給分。

21. Before _____, ask yourself where your interest lies.
　　(A) making up your mind　　(B) make any decision
　　(C) deciding your mind　　(D) out of your mind

22. Whether_____travel today is much more convenient than, say, fifty years ago.
　(A) by land, sea, or air
　(B) by land, sea, or air,
　(C) by land or sea, or air
　(D) by land or sea, air,

23. The classic handbook on writing, *The Elements of Style* by W. Strunk, Jr., and E. B. White,_____: " To achieve style, begin by affecting none."
　(A) advise　(B) to advise　(C) advises　(D) advising

24. After several visits, _____.
　(A) he not only liked the girl but the family too
　(B) he not only liked the girl, and liked the family too
　(C) he liked not only the girl but the family too
　(D) not only the girl, and the family liked him too

25. When you apply for a job, the prospective employer would like to know_____.
　(A) who is the boss
　(B) where to get the application forms
　(C) when you have the qualifications
　(D) whether you meet the requirements

Ⅱ. 閱讀測驗（20%）

說明：下面兩段文章後面各有五個題目（26～30及31～35），每題各附四個答案。請仔細閱讀文章後，把最適合文意的一個答案標示在答案卡上。每題答對得2分，答錯倒扣2/3分，不答則不給分。

　Nobody likes to stay home on a public holiday—especially when the weather is fine. Last August, the Joneses decided to spend the day in the country. The only difficulty was that millions of other people had exactly the same idea. They moved out of the city slowly behind a long line of cars, but at last they came to a quiet country road and, after some time, stopped at a lonely farm. They had brought plenty of food with them and they got it out of the car. Now everything's ready, so they sat down near a path at the foot of a hill. It was very peaceful in the cool grass—until they heard bells ringing at the top of the hill. What they saw made them pick up their things and run back to the car as quickly as possible. There were about two hundred sheep coming towards them down the path!

26. On a public holiday many people like to_____.
    (A) stay home　　　　　　　　　(B) have fine weather
    (C) go out into the country　　　(D) have exactly the same idea

27. The Joneses lived_____.
    (A) in the country　(B) in a city　(C) on a farm　(D) on a hill

28. They could not move fast because_____.
    (A) the weather was bad　　　　(B) they did not have a good car
    (C) they brought too much food
    (D) there were too many cars on the road

29. They went to the farm to_____.
    (A) have a picnic　(B) take a rest　(C) play a game　(D) watch animals

30. The reason why they ran back to the car was that_____.
    (A) it started to rain　　　　　(B) the farm was too crowded
    (C) they wanted to get food out of the car
    (D) many sheep were coming towards them

Some doctors write neatly and clearly, but most doctors do not. They write very quickly and untidily. Druggists have lots of practice in reading doctors' notes, but sometimes doctors write so badly that even the druggist cannot read them.

One day a lady wrote a letter to a doctor inviting him to have dinner at her house. The doctor wrote a reply, but he wrote so carelessly that the lady could not read it.

"What shall I do?" she said to her husband anxiously. "I don't know if he is going to come or not. And I don't want to phone him and say that I can't read his writing."

Her husband frowned thoughtfully. Then he had an idea.

"Take it to the druggist," he said. "He will be able to read it easily."

"Thank you," said his wife gratefuliy. "That's a very good idea."

She went to the drugstore and gave the doctor's note to the drug-gist. The druggist looked at it very carefully. Then he got his glasses and looked at the note more closely.

"Could you wait a moment, Madam?" he said politely. He went to the back of his store. After a few minutes he returned, smiling cheerfully and carrying a large bottle. He gave the bottle to the lady.

"Take one spoonful before every meal," he said !

31. Most of the notes written by doctors are _____.

(A) neatly　　(B) badly　　(C) easy to read　　(D) hard to read

32. The doctor in the story wrote a note to the lady to _____.

(A) answer her letter　　　　(B) reject her invitation

(C) accept her invitation　　(D) have dinner at her house

33. The lady took the note to the druggist because _____.

(A) she was sick　　　　(B) she could not read it

(C) her husband needed some medicine

(D) her husband was anxious to know its content

34. Who suggested that the lady take the note to the druggist?

(A) The doctor.　　　　(B) The druggist.

(C) The lady's husband.　　(D) The lady herself.

35. The druggist _____.

(A) read the note easily　　(B) read the note correctly

(C) did not give the right medicine

(D) thought the note was a prescription

第二部分：多重選擇題（10％）

說明：下面五題（36～40）是簡單的對話。每題各有一個空白，並各附A、B、C、D、E五個備選答案，各自獨立，唯其中至少有一個爲對的答案。請依照對話的內容，選出正確的答案，並標示在答案卡上。對此五個備選的答案，考生的選擇若符合標準答案，則可各獲0.4分，若不合標準答案，則倒扣0.4分，完全不作答視同放棄不給分。例如：設某題標準答案爲CDE，然考生之答案爲BCD，則CD填對，共得0.8分；E應填而未填，倒扣0.4分；B不應填而填，倒扣0.4分；A不應填未填爲對，得0.4分；則該題可得0.4分。

36. Chang San : When does the library open on Saturday ?

Wang Wu :＿＿＿＿＿＿＿＿＿＿＿＿＿＿＿＿＿＿＿

(A) Eight-thirty in the morning, if I remember correctly.

(B) It closes at six in the afternoon.

(C) It opens Monday through Saturday.

(D) It is not open on Sunday, I believe.

(E) I don't know. Why don't we check with the librarian ?

37. John : Thank you, Mrs. Smith. You've been such a big help !

Mrs. Smith :＿＿＿＿＿＿＿＿＿＿＿＿＿＿＿＿＿＿＿

(A) Yes, I did.   (B) You're welcome, John.

(C) Certainly not. (D) Oh, not at all. (E) My pleasure.

38. George's mother : Please remember to mail those letters for me
on your way to school.

George :＿＿＿＿＿＿＿＿＿＿＿＿＿＿＿＿＿＿＿

(A) Certainly, Mom.   (B) Sure, you can count on me.

(C) But, Mom, it's Sunday today and I'm staying home !

(D) Yes, please, will you ?

(E) But Father has already taken care of them.

39. Mei-li : The final exam is coming. Aren't you nervous ?

Ta-hua :＿＿＿＿＿＿＿＿＿＿＿＿＿＿＿＿＿＿＿

(A) Why should I ? In fact, I rather like exams.

(B) Yes, I am not nervous at all.

(C) No. — I am well prepared for it.

(D) Yes, and that's why I hate those exams.

(E) No. I've been so nervous lately that I hardly get any sleep.

40. Customer :＿＿＿＿＿＿＿＿＿＿＿＿＿＿＿＿＿

Shop attendant : That's right. Two thousand and five hundred.
It's of the highest quality.

(A) How much do I owe you ?   (B) Is this a shirt ?

(C) What kind of shirt is it ?   (D) What is the quality ?

(E) Two thousand and five hundred dollars for a shirt ?

第三部分：非選擇題（填充、翻譯及英文作文）

I. 填充題：（10%）

說明：下面這段文章共有十個空白，編號(a)至(j)。每個空白內均應填入一個字，纔能使語法正確、文意清楚。請依照上下文的意思，按順序把各空白內應填的字，連同編號，寫在「非選擇題試卷」上。答對每一空白得1分，答錯或不答則不給分。

Margaret Bourke-White was the first photographer for *Fortune* magazine. Later she became ___(a)___ of the first photographers for *Life*. ___(b)___ a result of her photo essays in *Life*, she became famous. Her name was ___(c)___ known than any other photographer's.

Surprisingly, Margaret chose her career almost ___(d)___ accident. She started college with the idea ___(e)___ becoming a scientist. But she found ___(f)___ necessary to support herself. She turned to taking pictures. From ___(g)___ moment she fell under the spell of photography, she was obsessed by ___(h)___ she and the camera could do together. "After I found the camera," she once said, " ___(i)___ never really felt like a whole person unless I ___(j)___ planning pictures or taking them."

II. 翻譯：中譯英（15%）

說明：把下面五題，譯成正確通順的英文，並按順序連同題號寫在「非選擇題試卷」上。每題3分。

(a) 這一篇文章值得仔細閱讀。

(b) 中國字很難寫嗎？

(c) 那一位戴黃帽子的外國人是誰？

(d) 天氣一天比一天熱起來了。

(e) 我不是告訴過你，我到車站的時候他們已經走了嗎？

III. 英文作文：（20%）

說明：用英文簡要敍述一件在高中階段一直想做卻沒有做到，因而想在進大學以後儘情去做的休閒活動（例如旅遊、運動、看電影、聽音樂、讀自己所喜愛的書等）。把文章分爲兩段：第一段說明高中階段未能做到的原因；第二段敍述進大學後如何去做這一件事。文章以80字爲度，不要太長或太短，寫在「非選擇題試卷」上。

74年大學聯考英文試題詳解

第一部份：（單一選擇題）

Ⅰ. 綜合測驗 ㈲

Six feet __tall__ and weighing between 400 and 500 pounds，a grown
         1

male gorilla is 10 to 14 times *as* powerful *as the strongest man*.

     "一隻成熟的公的大猩猩身長六呎，重量在四百到五百磅之間。牠的力量是最強壯的人的十到十四倍大。"

* Six feet tall…500 pounds 是省略了 Being 的分詞構句，可視爲由表原因的副詞子句 Since a grown male gorilla is six feet tall and weighs…簡化而來。倍數的表示法：～ times as $\left\{ \begin{array}{l} adj. \\ adv. \end{array} \right\}$ as… "是…的～倍"（詳見文法寶典 p.182）。

    weigh〔we〕*vi.* 重（若干）   gorilla〔gə′rɪlə〕*n.* 大猩猩

1.（**B**）tall 可用以指身高、物高。
    (A) high 指物的高，如 The tower is forty feet high.（這塔高四十呎。）
    (C) round 圓的，句意不合。
    (D) long 指距離、長度的長，不用以指高度。

Standing up, *thick arms flung to the sky*, he seems much like King Kong,
     2

the super gorilla of the movies.

"牠站直的時候，粗壯的手臂甩到空中，像極了電影裡的超級大猩猩「金剛」。"

* Standing up 是分詞構句，可視爲由表時間的副詞子句 When he stands up 簡化而來。thick arms flung to the sky 是獨立分詞構句，可視爲由對等子句 and his thick arms are flung to the sky 簡化而來。對等子句改爲表附帶狀態的獨立分詞構句時，and 可用 with 來代替，形成 "with ＋受詞 ＋分詞" 的形態。with 可以省略，受詞前的所有格代名詞，句意明確時可省略（詳見文法寶典 p.226）。the super… movie 是 King Kong 的同位語。

  … and his thick arms are flung to the sky

  → with his thick arms flung to the sky

  → thick arms flung to the sky   fling〔flɪŋ〕*vt.* 摔；抛

                       （flung 爲其過去式、過去分詞）

2. (**A**) 空格後有一完整的子句 he seems …用逗點分隔開，所以句首應該用
分詞來形成分詞構句。這個分詞構句的主詞是 he，站著時應該是主動
的，所以用現在分詞 standing。
　　(B) 用 Stand 則成爲祈使句，句意不合，且缺少連接詞。
　　(C) 應改爲現在分詞。
　　(D) To stand up 爲表目的的副詞片語，句意不合。

But we have learned **that** gorillas would rather use their power and
frightening display *to avoid trouble, not to make it.*
　　　　　　　　　　　　　　　　　　　　　3

"但是我們知道，大猩猩寧可用牠們的威力，並展現嚇人的樣子，來避免麻煩，
而不是要製造麻煩。"

　　* But 是轉承語，連接前面的句子。that gorillas … it 是名詞子句，作
　　learned 的受詞。to avoid trouble, not to make it 是不定詞片語當
　　副詞用，修飾 use，表目的。not 前省略了 and（and的省略詳見文法寶典 p.649）
　　display〔dɪˈsple〕*n.* 展示

3. (**B**) (A) and 意爲「並且製造麻煩」　(C) but 意爲「但是製造麻煩」
　　(D) only 意爲「只是製造麻煩」，均不合句意。

　Their government is simple. Each tribe has a male boss, *who is*
　　4
more or less undemanding.

"猩猩的政府很單純。每個羣體有位公的首領，這首領不大要求什麼。"

　　* who … undemanding 是補述用法的形容詞子句，用以補充說明 boss。
　　undemanding〔ˌʌndɪˈmændɪŋ〕*adj.* 無要求的

4. (**D**) 「猩猩的政府」指全體猩猩，而不是一隻猩猩，所以要用複數代名詞
　　their。

Sometimes the boss does assert his right *to the choicest food, the favorite companion, or the driest spot* __when__ *it is raining.*
　　　　　　　　　　　　　　　　　　5

"有時候首領確實會維護牠的權利，以得到最好的食物，最喜愛的同伴，或是在
下雨時有最乾燥的地方。"

＊does 是用來加強語氣。to the … raining 是形容詞片語，修飾 right。when it is raining 是副詞子句，修飾省略了的 assert。

assert〔ə'sɝt〕vt. 維護

5. (C) (A) 用 whether 意爲「是否下雨」，句意不合。

(B) where 爲關係副詞，引導形容詞子句修飾 spot，意爲「最乾燥的下雨的地方」，句意不合。

(D) 用 why 意爲「爲什麼下雨」，句意不合。

In general, however, he leaves the others well alone.
　　　　　　6

"不過一般說來，牠一點都不管別人。"

＊In general "一般說來" 是副詞片語，修飾 leaves。however 是轉承語，連接上面的句子，可放在句首、句中或句尾。

leave sb. alone "不干涉某人"　　well〔wɛl〕*adv.* 完全地

6. (C) (A) yet 作「但是」解時爲連接詞，而空格中應塡副詞。

(B) instead「相反地」句意不合。

(D) accordingly「因此」句意不合。

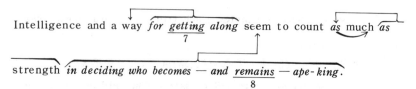

Intelligence and a way *for getting along* seem to count *as* much *as*
　　　　　　　　　　　　7

strength *in deciding who becomes — and remains — ape-king*.
　　　　　　　　　　　　　　　　　8

"在決定誰成爲，並且繼續當猩猩王的時候，智慧和處世的作風，似乎和體力一樣重要。"

＊in deciding … ape-king 是副詞片語，修飾 seem，其中兩個長劃括起 and remains，表示語氣的轉折。

count〔kaʊnt〕*vi.* 有重要性

ape-king〔'ep,kɪŋ〕*n.* 猴王

7. (D) ***get along*** "相處"

(A) go along "前進"　　(B) come along "來"　　(C) run along "跑來"，均不合句意。

8. (B)　remain + $\begin{cases} \text{n} \\ \text{adj} \\ \text{Ving} \end{cases}$ "繼續;保持"

　　(A)　keep 作 "繼續;保持" 解時,後面只能接形容詞或現在分詞;keep
　　　　後面若接名詞則為及物動詞,意為 "飼養;保存" 等,句意不合。

　　(C)　retain "保有",句意不合。

　　(D)　make "使做",句意不合。

As long as the old king holds his job, his subjects turn to him *to decide*
　　　　　　　　　　　　　　　　　　　　　　　　　　　　　　　9

everything — when to search for food or where to camp, *for instance*.
　　　　　　　　　　　　　　　　　　　　　　　　　　　10

"只要老王在位,牠的臣民就要依賴牠決定一切 —— 例如什麼時候去找食物,到
那裡紮營。"

　　* As long … job 是副詞子句,修飾 turn。長劃引導附加全句意義的語句。
　　　when to search for food 和 where to camp 是疑問副詞加不定詞,等
　　　於名詞片語 (詳見文法寶典 p. 241)。

　　　　subject〔'sʌbdʒɪkt〕*n.* 臣民　　camp〔kæmp〕*vi.* 紮營

9. (D)　***turn to*** "求助於"

　　　　(A) turn on "打開",句意不合　(B) turn for　(C) turn at 均無此用法

10. (A)　***for instance*** "例如"

What is it *that* a teacher most wants *in his students*?　Attentive-
　　　　11

ness?　A good memory?　Diligence?

　　"老師究竟最希望學生怎樣?專心聽講?記憶力好?用功?"

　　　　attentiveness〔ə'tɛntɪvnɪs〕*n.* 注意

11. (C)　that … students 為形容詞子句,先行詞為 what,what 為疑問代名
　　　　詞,在句中當補語,因此本句缺少主詞。而動詞 is 是單數,所以主詞
　　　　用單數。(D) that 是指示代名詞,前面並無所指,不可選。故選(C)的 it,
　　　　而形成 It is … that 的強調句型,其公式為 | It is +所強調的部分+
　　　　that +其餘部分 | (詳見文法寶典 p. 115)。本句強調的部分是未知的
　　　　what。所以用問句形式 What is it that … ? 改為普通語氣時則為
　　　　What does a teacher most want in his students?

Certainly these are the qualities *commonly associated with* " *good student* "
　　　　　　　　　　　　　　　　　　　　　12

in the popular mind.
　　　　　13

" 當然，這些特質是一般人心目中常和「好學生」聯想在一起的 。"

12.（ **B** ）　*associate* A *with* B " 把 A 和 B 聯想在一起 " 改成被動為 A *be asso-*
　　　　ciated with B

　　　　這句主詞、動詞、受詞都具備了，所以空格中應填形容詞。又因為「聯
　　　　想」是「被人聯想的」，所以用過去分詞。commonly associated
　　　　with … mind 是由 which are commonly associated with … mind 省
　　　　略而來的分詞片語，當形容詞用，修飾 qualities 。

13.（ **A** ）(A) *popular* 一般的　　(B) proper 適當的　　(C) inner 內在的
　　　　(D) educated 受過教育的，根據句意應選 (A) 。

And , *certainly* , *too* , these are the qualities *that most contribute to*
　　　　　　　　　　　　　　　　　　　　　　　　　　　　14

teacher comfort.

" 這些特質當然也是最令老師欣慰的 。"

　　　＊ 題句 teacher comfort 改為 a teacher's comfort 較佳 。

　　　　contribute to " 助於 ; 促成 "

14.（ **A** ）　that 是關係代名詞，引導形容詞子句，修飾先行詞 qualities ，在子句
　　　　中又作主詞。因為主要子句的動詞是現在式，qualities 為複數，故形
　　　　容詞子句的動詞要用現在式複數形 。

But the best student *I ever had* , the one *I remember the most wist-*
　　　　　　　　　　　　　　　　　　　15

fully , was a talkative, lazy day-dreamer.

　　" 但是我所有過的最好的學生，最令我懷念的，是個愛講話的，懶惰的幻
想家 。"

　　　＊ I remember … wistfully 是省略了 that 的形容詞子句，修飾 one 。the
　　　one … wistfully 是 student 的同位語 。

　　　　wistfully〔 ˈwɪstfəlɪ 〕*adv.* 渴望地

15. （ **B** ）空格後的形容詞子句有限定作用，因此要定冠詞 the，又因爲 student
　　　是單數的，所以塡 the one 。

Sometimes he turned assignments in *late*, *and* a few he *never* got
　　　　　　　　　　　　　　　　　　　16　　　　　　　　　　　　17
around to doing *at all*.

"有時候他遲交作業，而有的作業他根本從不找時間去做 。"

　　　＊ a few…all 是受詞放在句首的倒裝句，用以强調受詞，原句應爲 he never
　　　　got around to doing a few at all. （詳見文法寶典 p.635）

　　　　turn ～ in "交出～"

16. （ **D** ）根據上句說這個學生懶惰，故應該是遲交作業。則⑷⒞句意不合。
　　　　⑻ behind 作 "落後" 解時，多爲副詞轉作形容詞的用法，如 He is
　　　　behind in his work. 而不作純粹的副詞，修飾動詞 。

17. （ **D** ）***get around to*** ＋（動）名詞 "找時間去做～"
　　　　⑷ gave　⒞ sent 均無此用法。⑻ look around "到處觀看"，句意不合。

Actually, my admiration *for him* was ironic, ***because*** I have never liked the
　　　　　　　　　　　　　　　　　　　　　　　　18
name Ronald, *which* suggests to me the assumed name of a movie star.　***But***
　　　　　　　19
he made one whole year *of my teaching experience* a delight.
　　　　　　　　　　　　　　　20

"實際上，我對他的稱讚只是諷刺，因爲我從沒喜歡過隆納德這個名字，它讓我
想起一位電影明星的化名。但是他使我一整年的教學經驗很愉快 。"

　　　＊ because … star 是副詞子句，修飾動詞 was，表原因；其中 which …
　　　　star 是補述用法的形容詞子句，用以補充說明 Ronald 。

　　　　ironic〔 aɪˈrɑnɪk 〕*adj.* 諷刺的
　　　　suggest〔 səˈdʒɛst 〕*vt.* 使想到
　　　　assumed〔 əˈsumd , əˈsjumd 〕*adj.* 假裝的
　　　　assumed name "化名"

18. （ **C** ）⑷ so 所以　⑼ though 雖然，均不合句意。⑻ still "仍然" 爲副
　　　　詞，句意、用法均不合。

19. （ **B** ）空格前有逗點，因此後面是補述用法的形容詞子句，先行詞 the name Ronald 非人，因此關代用 which 。

　　(A) who 先行詞爲人，故不合　(C) what　(D) that 均不可用以引導補述用法的形容詞子句。

20. （ **A** ）　teaching experience "教學經驗"

II. 綜合測驗 (乙)

21. （ **A** ）*Before making up your mind*, ask yourself *where* your interest lies.

　　"在你做決定之前，問問自己的興趣何在 。"

　　* Before是介系詞，後面應接動名詞。"決定"的片語爲 *make up one's mind* ，故選(A)。(C) deciding your mind 沒有這種用法。(B) (D) 文法不對 。

22. （ **B** ）*Whether* by land, sea, or air, travel today is *much more* convenient *than* (*it was*), say, fifty years ago.

　　"不論坐車、坐船或坐飛機，今天旅遊比譬如說五十年前方便多了。"

　　* Whether by … air 是省略了 it is 的副詞子句，修飾 is，表讓步。whether 後的主詞和主要子句主詞相同時，主詞和 be 動詞可以省略（詳見文法寶典 p.525）。say 在此作 "譬如說"解(= let us say)，表示假設或估計。對等連接詞 or 連接文法作用相同的單字時，應放在最後一個之前（詳見文法寶典 p.465）。本句爲避免將 air travel （空中旅行）看爲一體，因此中間用逗點分隔開來 。

23. （ **C** ）The classic handbook *on writing*, *The Elements of Style by W. Strunk, Jr., and E.B. White,* advises : " *To achieve style,* begin *by affecting none.* "

　　"古典的寫作手冊，由小 W. 斯窗克和 E.B. 懷特寫的「風格的要素」勸道：「要建立風格，首先就不裝作是任何人。」"

　　* *The Elements* … White 是 handbook 的同位語。句子的核心主詞是 handbook ，受詞是整個引句，所以空格中缺少動詞；又因爲主詞是

單數的，所以選(C) advises 。

Jr. 即 junior 的縮寫，意為 " 年少的 " 。

affect〔əˈfɛkt〕*vt.* 假裝

24.（ C ） ***After several visits***, he liked ***not only*** the girl ***but*** the family ***too*** .

" 拜訪幾次後，他不僅喜歡上那女孩，也喜歡全家人。 "

* not only ～$\begin{cases} \text{but (also)} \\ \text{but ～too} \\ \text{but ～as well} \end{cases}$ " 不但～而且～ " ，這是對等連接詞，

其後連接的字詞文法作用須相同。

25.（ D ） ***When you apply for a job***, the prospective employer would like to know ***whether*** you meet the requirements.

" 你求職的時候，未來的老板會想知道你是否符合要求。 "

* (A) 誰是老板　(B) 到那裡拿申請表　(C) 你什麼時候有資格，句意均不合。

prospective〔prəˈspɛktɪv〕*adj.* 未來的

employer〔ɪmˈplɔɪə〕*n.* 老板

employee〔ˌɛmplɔɪˈi, ɪmˈplɔɪ‧i〕*n.* 職員

meet〔mit〕*vt.* 符合

Ⅱ. 閱讀測驗

Nobody likes to stay home ***on a public holiday*** — ***especially when*** the weather is fine. ***Last August***, the Joneses decided to spend the day ***in the country***. The only difficulty was ***that*** millions of other people had exactly the same idea.

" 沒有人喜歡假日待在家裡——尤其是天氣好的時候。去年八月，瓊斯一家決定要到鄉下度假。唯一的困難是，另有數百萬人想法剛好相同。 "

* 長劃引導的 especially … fine 是附加全句的副詞子句，修飾 stay 。

They moved out of the city *slowly behind a long line of cars*, **but at last** they came to a quiet country road **and**, *after some time*, stopped at a lonely farm.

"他們尾隨一長列車子，慢慢地出城，不過終於來到一條安靜的鄉間道路，又過了一會兒，在一個孤立的農場停了下來。"

* 這個句子包含三個對等子句，用 but 和 and 來連接。第三個子句中，after some time 是插入的副詞片語，用逗點分隔開。

They had brought plenty of food *with them and* they got it out of the car. *Now* everything's ready, **so** they sat down *near a path at the foot of a hill*.

"他們帶有很多吃的東西，就把食物拿下車。這時一切都準備好了，他們便在山腳的小徑旁坐下。"

* near … hill 是副詞片語，修飾 sat。

It was very peaceful *in the cool grass —* **until** *they heard bells ringing at the top of the hill*. **What** they saw made them pick up their things **and** run back to the car *as quickly as possible*. There were about two hundred sheep coming towards them *down the path*!

"涼爽的草地上，一切都很祥和——直到他們聽見山頂的鈴聲響起。他們看到的景象，使他們儘快拿起東西，跑回車裡。大約有兩百隻羊沿著小徑下來，走向他們！"

* until … hill 前用長劃，表示文意的突然變化，until … hill 是副詞子句，修飾 was。

$$\begin{cases} as \sim as \ possible \ \text{"儘可能} \sim \text{"} \\ = as \sim as \ one \ can \end{cases}$$

26.（ C ）假日時，很多人喜歡　　　　　　。
　　　(A) 待在家裡　(B) 有好天氣　(C) 到鄉下去　(D) 有一模一樣的想法

27.（ **B** ） 瓊斯一家住在 _____ 。

    (A) 鄉下　　(B) 城裡　　(C) 農場　　(D) 山上

28.（ **D** ） 他們動不快，因為 _____ 。

    (A) 天氣不好　　　　　　　(B) 他們的車子不好

    (C) 他們帶了太多吃的東西　　(D) 路上車太多了

29.（ **A** ） 他們去農場 _____ 。

    (A) 野餐　　(B) 休息　　(C) 比賽　　(D) 觀看動物

30.（ **D** ） 他們跑回車子是因為 _____ 。

    (A) 開始下雨　　　　　　　(B) 農場太擠

    (C) 他們想把吃的東西從車裡拿出來　(D) 很多羊正走向他們

Some doctors write *neatly and clearly*, *but* most doctors do not. They write *very quickly and untidily*. Druggists have lots of practice *in reading doctors' notes*, *but sometimes* doctors write *so* badly *that even the druggist cannot read them.*

    "有的醫生寫字整齊又清楚，但是大部分的醫生並不是這樣的。他們寫得很快又亂七八糟。藥劑師經常看醫生的條子，但是有時候醫生寫得太亂了，以致於連藥劑師也看不懂。"

    * in reading doctors' notes 是形容詞片語，修飾 practice。so~that
    "如此~以致於"是相關連接詞，that 所引導的副詞子句修飾 so，表結果。

    untidily〔ʌnˈtaɪdɪlɪ〕*adv.* 亂七八糟地
    druggist〔ˈdrʌɡɪst〕*n.* 藥劑師
    practice〔ˈpræktɪs〕*n.* 熟練；實習

One day a lady wrote a letter to a doctor *inviting him to have dinner at her house.* The doctor wrote a reply, *but* he wrote *so* carelessly *that the lady could not read it.*

    "一天，一位女士寫了封信給醫生，邀請他去她家吃晚飯。醫生寫了張回條。但是他寫得太草了，所以這位女士看不懂。"

"What shall I do？" she said to her husband *anxiously*.　"I don't know *if* he is going to come or not.　And I don't want to phone him and say *that* I can't read his writing."

"「我該怎麼辦？」她著急地對丈夫說。「我不知道他要不要來。而我又不想打電話給他，說我看不懂他的字。」"

* if … not 是名詞子句，作 know 的受詞。if 可和 whether 通用，引導名詞子句作動詞的受詞，但後面有 or not 時，只可用 whether，不可用 if，題句錯誤（詳見文法寶典 p.485）。

　　phone〔 fon 〕 *vt.* 打電話給（某人）

Her husband frowned *thoughtfully*.　*Then* he had an idea.

"Take it to the druggist," he said.　"He will be able to read it *easily*."

"Thank you," said his wife *gratefully*.　"That's a very good idea."

"她的丈夫皺著眉頭仔細想了想。然後有了個主意。
「拿給藥劑師，」他說。「他很容易看懂。」
「謝謝你，」他的太太感激地說。「那真是個好主意。」"

* frown〔 fraʊn 〕 *vi.* 皺眉
  thoughtfully〔 'θɔtfəlɪ 〕 *adv.* 深思地
  have an idea "有個主意"
  gratefully〔 'gretfəlɪ 〕 *adv.* 感激地

She went to the drugstore *and* gave the doctor's note to the druggist.　The druggist looked at it *very carefully*.　*Then* he got his glasses *and* looked at the note *more closely*.

"她到藥房去，把醫生的條子拿給藥劑師。藥劑師很仔細地看。然後又拿出眼鏡，看得更近些。"

* drugstore〔'drʌg,stor 〕 *n.* 藥房
  closely〔 'kloslɪ 〕 *adv.* 接近地；密切地

　　" Could you wait a moment, Madam？ " he said *politely*.　He went to the back of his store.　*After a few minutes* he returned, smiling *cheerfully and* carrying a large bottle.　He gave the bottle to the lady.

　　" Take one spoonful before every meal, " he said！

　　"「太太，請你等一下好嗎？」他很有禮貌地說。他去店的後面。幾分鐘後回來，高興地笑著，拿了個大瓶子。他把瓶子拿給女士。

　　「每餐前服用一湯匙。」他說！

＊　After a few minutes 是副詞片語，修飾 returned。smiling cheerfully, carrying a large bottle 是兩個分詞構句，由 and 來連接，表附帶狀態。

　　politely〔pə'laɪtlɪ〕*adv.* 禮貌地

　　the back of ～　"～的後部"

　　spoonful〔'spun,fʊl〕*n.* 一匙

31.（ D ）醫生寫的紙條多半 ＿＿＿＿＿。

　　　　(A) 整潔　　　　　　　　　(B) 壞（badly 是副詞,此處應填形容詞,且句意不對）
　　　　(C) 容易看　　　　　　　　(D) 不容易看

32.（ A ）故事中醫生寫了張紙條給女士，為了 ＿＿＿＿＿。

　　　　(A) 回她的信　　　　　　　(B) 拒絕她的邀請
　　　　(C) 接受她的邀請　　　　　(D) 去她家吃晚飯

33.（ B ）這位女士把紙條拿給藥劑師，因為 ＿＿＿＿＿。

　　　　(A) 她生病了　　　　　　　(B) 她看不懂
　　　　(C) 她丈夫需要一些藥　　　(D) 她丈夫急著知道內容

34.（ C ）誰建議女士把條子拿給藥劑師？

　　　　(A) 醫生　　(B) 藥劑師　　(C) 女士的丈夫　　(D) 女士自己

35.（ D ）藥劑師 ＿＿＿＿＿。

　　　　(A) 很容易看了條子　　　　(B) 正確地看了條子
　　　　(C) 給的藥不對　　　　　　(D) 以為紙條是張藥方

　　prescription〔prɪ'skrɪpʃən〕*n.* 藥方

第二部份:(多重選擇)

36.(　**A E**　)張三:圖書館星期六什麼時候開?

王五:＿＿＿＿＿＿＿＿＿＿＿

(A) 早上八點三十分,如果我記的沒錯。

(B) 下午六點關。　　(C) 從星期一開到星期六。

(D) 我相信星期天沒開。

(E) 我不知道。我們何不向圖書管理員查詢呢?

check with sb. "向某人查詢"

37.(　**B D E**　)約翰:謝謝你,史密斯太太。你幫了個大忙!

史密斯太太:＿＿＿＿＿＿＿＿＿＿

(A) 是的,我是。　　(B) 不客氣,約翰。

(C) 當然不。　　(D) 哦,不客氣。

(E) 這是我的榮幸。

38.(　**A B C E**　)喬治的媽媽:你上學的時候,請記得幫我寄那些信。

喬治:＿＿＿＿＿＿＿＿＿＿

(A) 一定的,媽。　　(B) 沒問題,包在我身上。

(C) 不過,媽,今天是星期天,我要待在家裡。

(D) 好的,請,好嗎?　　(E) 不過爸爸早就辦了。

count on "依賴"

39.(　**A C D**　)美莉:快要期末考了。你不緊張嗎?

大華:＿＿＿＿＿＿＿＿＿＿

(A) 我為什麼要緊張?事實上,我相當喜歡考試。

(B) 是的,我一點也不緊張。(應把 Yes 改成 No)

(C) 不緊張,我準備得很好。

(D) 緊張啊,那就是我討厭考試的原因。

(E) 不緊張。我最近太緊張了,所以都沒睡什麼。(應把 No 改成 Yes)

40.(　**E**　)顧客:＿＿＿＿＿＿＿＿＿＿

店員:對。兩千五百元。這是品質最好的。

(A) 我要付你多少錢?　　(B) 這是件襯衫嗎?

(C) 這是什麼樣的襯衫?　　(D) 品質是怎樣的?

(E) 一件襯衫要兩千五百元?

第三部份：（非選擇題）

I. 填充題

Margaret Bourke-White was the first photographer *for Fortune*

magazine. *Later* she became <u>one</u> of the first photographers *for Life*.
(a)

"瑪格麗特·褒克·懷特是「財星」雜誌的第一位攝影師。後來她成爲「生活」雜誌最早的攝影師之一。"

a. 根據句意是「其中之一」，故用 one of the ＋複數名詞的形式。

<u>*As a result of her photo essays in Life*</u>, she became famous. Her name
(b)

was <u>better</u> known than any other photographer's.
(c)

"她由於「生活」上的攝影文章而出名。她的名字比其他任何一位攝影師更廣爲人知。"

b. $\begin{cases} \textbf{\textit{as a result of}} \text{ "由於"} \\ = \textbf{\textit{on account of}} \end{cases}$

c. "廣爲人知" 是 be well known。空格後有 than，所以用比較級 be better known。

Surprisingly, Margaret chose her career *almost by accident*. She
(d)

started college *with the idea of becoming a scientist*. *But* she found <u>it</u>
(e)   (f)

necessary to support herself. She turned to taking pictures.

"令人驚訝的是，瑪格麗特選擇職業幾乎純屬偶然。她剛上大學就想當科學家。但是她發現得自食其力，就開始攝影。"

d. *by accident* "偶然地"（＝ *by chance*）

e. *the idea of* V-ing "欲做～的想法"，idea 後的介詞應用 of。

f. find 爲及物動詞，缺少受詞，to support herself 是不定詞片語，爲眞正的受詞，故塡 it 作形式受詞。

　　turn to "開始"

From the moment she fell under the spell of photography, she was ob-
     (g)

sessed *by **what** she and the camera could do together.* " After I found
     (h)

the camera, " she *once* said, " I *never really* felt like a whole person
     (i)

***unless** I **was** planning pictures or taking them.* "
     (j)

「 從她迷上攝影開始，她和相機能一起做的事，就把她迷住了。「我發現相機之後，」她曾經說，「除非我在計畫照片，或是拍攝它們，否則我從不真的覺得像個完整的人。」」

g. she was … together 是個完整的子句，From 是介系詞，而非連接詞，所以 From … photography 應為副詞片語，修飾 obsessed。she fell … photography 是省略了 when 的形容詞子句，修飾 moment。「那一刻」指特定的一刻，因此要填定冠詞 the。

h. by 後面要接受詞，she … together 子句中 do 缺少受詞，所以填複合關係代名詞 what (＝ the things that)，引導名詞子句，作 by 的受詞，在子句中又作 do 的受詞。

i. 主要子句缺少主詞，故填 I。

j. 空格後是現在分詞，根據句意是過去正在發生的事，故填 was，構成過去進行式。也可將 planning 和 taking 視為動名詞，則空格裡填 started 和 began 也可以。

    under the spell of " 被～迷住 "

    obsess〔əb'sɛs〕*vt.* 迷住 （ 聯招會誤拼為 obssess ）

Ⅱ. 翻譯：中譯英

  ⒜ 這篇文章值得仔細讀。

    This article is
       worth reading carefully.
       worthy of being read carefully.
       worthy to be read carefully.

    be worth ＋ V-ing " 值得～ "
    ＝ be worthy of ＋ V-ing
    ＝ be worthy to-V

(b) 中國字很難寫嗎？

Are Chinese characters $\begin{Bmatrix} difficult \\ hard \end{Bmatrix}$ to write ?

Is it $\begin{Bmatrix} hard \\ difficult \end{Bmatrix}$ to write Chinese characters ?

* Chinese characters "中國字"

(c) 那一位戴黃帽子的外國人是誰？

Who is that foreigner $\begin{Bmatrix} wearing \\ with \end{Bmatrix}$ a yellow hat ?

(d) 天氣一天比一天熱起來。

$\begin{Bmatrix} It \\ The\ weather \end{Bmatrix}$ is getting hotter and hotter *every day*.

* 比較級＋and＋比較級，表 "越來越～"（詳見文法寶典 p.202）

(e) 我不是告訴過你，我到車站的時候他們已經走了嗎？

Didn't I tell you *that* they had $\begin{Bmatrix} gone \\ left \end{Bmatrix}$ $\begin{Bmatrix} by\ the\ time \\ when \end{Bmatrix}$

I $\begin{Bmatrix} got\ to \\ arrived\ at \end{Bmatrix}$ the station ?

* that 引導名詞子句，作 tell 的直接受詞；子句中 by the time … station 是副詞子句，修飾 gone。

Ⅲ. 英文作文（參考範例）

　　Since I became a senior high school student, I have been interested in Chinese classical novels. They are the fruits of our ancestors' wisdom. I like reading them. *However*, preparing for the Joint College Entrance Examination prevented me from doing so.

　　I think that I have done well in this entrance examination and I will likely enter college. If so, I will have much time to enjoy those novels I like best. While in college, I will devote myself to reading as long as I have some spare time.

classical〔'klæsɪkl̩〕*adj.* 古典的
ancestor〔'ænsɛstə〕*n.* 祖先
prevent A ***from*** + V-ing " 阻止A～；使A不能～ "
$\begin{cases} \textit{\textbf{devote oneself to}} + (動)名詞 " 專注於～ " \\ = \textit{\textbf{be devoted to}} + (動)名詞 \end{cases}$
spare〔spɛr〕*adj.* 多餘的

　　自從我成為高中生以後，我就一直對中國古典小說有興趣。它們是祖先智慧的結晶，我喜歡閱讀它們。然而，準備大學聯考使我無法這麼做。

　　我想，我在這次入學考試裏表現不錯，有可能進入大學就讀。如果這樣的話，我將有很多時間來享受那些我最喜愛的小說。在大學裏，只要我有一些閒暇時間，我就會全心投入閱讀。

七十三學年度大學暨獨立學院入學考試
英 文 試 題

注意：1.本學科測驗包括綜合測驗、閱讀測驗、翻譯及英文作文。請務必把握作答時間。
　　　2.除作文外，共 64 題。測驗題（1-54）答在答案卡上；翻譯（55-64）和作文答在作文及翻譯試卷內。
　　　3.測驗題（1-54）全爲單一選擇題。

I. 綜合測驗：（含讀音、拼字、用字、文法、文意等）（30％）

　　說明：下面三段文章，共有三十個空白，編號 1-30，每個空白含有四個可能的答案。請仔細閱讀各段文章後，選出一個最適當的答案，並將其標示在答案卡上。每題答對得 1 分，答錯倒扣 1／3 分，若不答則不給分。

　　A good teacher is many things to many people. I suppose everyone has his definite ideas about____(1)____ a good teacher is. As I____(2)____ back on my own experience, I find the teachers that I respect and think about the most are those who demanded the most____(3)____ from their students.

　　I think of one teacher in ____(4)____ that I had in high school. I think he was a good teacher because he was a very strict person. He just____(5)____ no kind of nonsense____(6)____ all in his classroom. I remember very vividly a sign over his classroom door. It was a simple sign that____(7)____, "laboratory—in this room the first five letters of the word____(8)____, not the last seven." In other____(9)____, labor for him was more important than____(10)____.

1. (A) how　(B) that　(C) who　(D) what
2. (A) figure　(B) figured　(C) look　(D) was looking
3. (A) dicipline　(B) disciprine　(C) dissepline　(D) discipline
4. (A) peculiar　(B) particular　(C) curio　(D) curiosity
5. (A) endure　(B) intoliet　(C) tolerated　(D) toils
6. (A) at　(B) after　(C) in　(D) to
7. (A) told　(B) spoke　(C) said　(D) talked
8. (A) is stressed　(B) put stress　(C) emphasize　(D) are emphasized
9. (A) mind　(B) words　(C) opinion　(D) hands
10. (A) absorbs　(B) library　(C) auditory　(D) oratory

Although milk is an important part of our everyday diet, cows give milk in the first place to feed to their calves. Usually a cow has her first calf_____(11)_____ she is about two years old. After calving, a cow gives milk for about 300 days _____(12)_____ during this time she will give a total of about 900 gallons before she_____(13)_____dry. The following year she will have_____(14)_____calf and then_____(15)_____to give milk again, as before. Modern breeds of dairy cattle now give more milk than their calves _____(16)_____ , so there is always plenty for human_____(17)_____. Young calves are given_____(18)_____ of their mothers' milk but they are also given_____(19)_____made from milk powder._____(20)_____possible they are given solid foods such as concentrates, hay or grass.

11. (A) that   (B) who   (C) what   (D) when
12. (A) and   (B) but   (C) for   (D) since
13. (A) walks   (B) runs   (C) does   (D) makes
14. (A) a   (B) one   (C) another   (D) the other
15. (A) try   (B) stop   (C) continue   (D) cease
16. (A) have   (B) need   (C) play   (D) can
17. (A) moderation   (B) recreation   (C) assumption   (D) consumption
18. (A) none   (B) some   (C) all   (D) lot
19. (A) milk   (B) hay   (C) grass   (D) meat
20. (A) As good as   (B) As well as   (C) As fast as   (D) As soon as

A thundershower lasting for two hours yesterday temporarily relieved a six-month long_____(21)_____in the Kaohsiung area. The Taiwan Water Company also announced yesterday_____(22)_____postponement of a second stage of water rationing originally scheduled to begin today.

The sky was dark and cloudy in Kaohsiung City as the day_____(23)_____. Local residents all had a forewarning it was going to rain. At around 10:00,_____(24)_____. Soon it was raining_____(25)_____. Although_____(26)_____ were forced to take cover, they were all pleased,_____(27)_____the rain had come in the nick of time.

It was the first_____(28)_____rainfall within half a year in this southern port city. As a result, the originally scheduled water restrictions _____(29)_____.

_____(30)_____ from 9：00 this morning, the water supply to swimming pools and fountains will be resumed, together with irrigation of trees and flowers on streets.

21. (A) drought　　　(B) draft　　　(C) drift　　　(D) draught
22. (A) a limit　　　(B) a limiting　　　(C) indefinable　　　(D) an indefinite
23. (A) lighted　　　(B) broke　　　(C) opened　　　(D) initiated
24. (A) sky began to rain　　　　　(B) sky began raining
　　(C) it began raining　　　　　(D) it rain began
25. (A) cat and dog　　(B) cats and dogs　　(C) cats and dog　　(D) dogs and cats
26. (A) passer-by　　(B) passer-bys　　(C) passing-bys　　(D) passers-by
27. (A) saying　　　(B) say　　　(C) said　　　(D) to say
28. (A) noteworth　　(B) noteworthy　　(C) note worthy　　(D) noteworthing
29. (A) were cancellations　　　　(B) cancelled
　　(C) were cancelled　　　　　(D) were cancelling
30. (A) Start　　　(B) To start　　　(C) Started　　　(D) Starting

II. 閱讀測驗：

　第一部分（5％）

　　說明：下面各題（31－35）是簡單的對話，請按語意和習慣用法選出最適當的答
　　　　　話，並將其標示在答案卡上。每題答對得1分，答錯倒扣1/3分，若不答
　　　　　則不給分。

31. Jane：Hello, Tom.　How are you？
　　Tom：_____
　　(A) I'm fine, thanks.　How do you do？　(B) Thank you.　How do you do？
　　(C) I am a new student.　　　　　　　(D) Fine, thanks.　How are you？

32. Tom：May I speak to Jane, please？
　　Jane：_____
　　(A) Here is Jane.　　　　　　(B) This is Jane speaking.
　　(C) Here I am.　　　　　　　(D) Keep talking.

33. Jane：I went to the opera last night.
　　Tom：_____
　　(A) Oh, what was the operation about？　(B) Which way did you go？
　　(C) Did you enjoy it？　　　　　　　(D) Which band did you invite？

34. Jane： What would you like to drink？

　　Tom：＿＿＿＿＿＿＿＿＿＿＿＿＿＿

　　(A) Yes, I always have tea for breakfast.

　　(B) Well, can I get you anything else？

　　(C) I think many people drink too much.

　　(D) I'll have the same again, please.

35. Jane： Thank you for the present. It was just what I wanted.

　　Tom：＿＿＿＿＿＿＿＿＿＿＿＿＿＿

　　(A) What did you want？　　　(B) I'm sorry you didn't like it.

　　(C) I am glad you like it.　　(D) Was it a present？

第二部分（13％）

說明：下面各題（36－48），各有四個可能的解釋性答案。請把其中最正確的一
　　　個，標示在答案卡上。每題答對得1分，答錯倒扣1／3分，若不答則不
　　　給分。

36. Jack went to school in spite of the cold weather.

　　(A) It being cold, Jack did not go to school.

　　(B) Jack went to school because the weather was cold.

　　(C) Although the weather was cold, Jack still went to school.

　　(D) Jack went to school because of the cold weather.

37. Education is the only alternative to lives of poverty and ignorance.

　　(A) Education is necessary for lives of poverty and ignorance.

　　(B) One needs education if he wants to live in poverty and ignorance.

　　(C) Education can help us to differentiate poverty from ignorance.

　　(D) If you do not want to live in poverty and ignorance, you must
　　　　receive education.

38. The lecture Mr. Simpson delivered the other day is not only enter-
　　taining but also informative.

　　(A) Mr. Simpson's talk is funny but informal.

　　(B) Mr. Simpson's presentation is interesting and instructive.

　　(C) Mr. Simpson's speech is amusing and informal.

　　(D) Mr. Simpson's lecture is dry but inspiring.

39. John : Do you mind my asking you some questions about your family ?

    Paul : Certainly not.

    (A) Paul is willing to answer John's question.

    (B) Paul is not willing to answer John's question.

    (C) Paul is not interested in answering John's question.

    (D) Paul refused to answer John's question.

40. Jane : Have you finished your paper yet ?

    Bill : Oh, yes. It's far from being satisfactory, though.

    Jane : It serves you right.

    Bill : I know. I've learned my lesson.

    (A) Bill's paper was well written.

    (B) Bill will never forget his unsatisfactory homework.

    (C) Bill learned a lot from each lesson.

    (D) Bill failed to have his paper finished in time.

41. Tom is trying out for a team. He has to know how to throw and catch a ball. He has to be able to hit a ball with a bat. He has to be a fast runner. What team is Tom trying out for ?

    (A) Football.　　　　　　(B) Basketball.

    (C) Baseball.　　　　　　(D) Tennis.

42. Peter : How is the article you're reading ?

    David : It's no more than an average piece.

    David considers the article＿＿＿＿＿＿.

    (A) excellent　　　　　(B) very impressive

    (C) awful　　　　　　(D) unimpressive

43. Mr. Wang deserves great credit for establishing an updated general hospital.

    (A) Mr. Wang has to pay more bills for setting up a new hospital.

    (B) Mr. Wang should be applauded for founding a modern hospital.

    (C) Mr. Wang has been given approval to set up a brand-new hospital.

    (D) Mr. Wang has been trusted to found a modern hospital.

44. Heart disease continues to decline but still tops the list of the 15 leading killers, a group that causes 89% of all American deaths.

(A) Although heart disease continues to decline, it still causes more American deaths than any other disease.

(B) About 89% of all American deaths are caused by heart disease.

(C) As heart disease continues to decline, it is no longer the first of the 15 leading killers.

(D) About 89% of all American deaths are caused by the diseases other than heart disease in the list of the 15 leading killers.

45. Until the 1950's most of the people of Georgia were farmers. Many crops are still raised, but now only a fifth of the people earn their living by farming. Today most Georgians live in cities and towns and work in factories. They make such things as cotton cloth, peanut butter, boats, automobiles, lumber, and paper.

Which sentence best gives the main idea of the paragraph?

(A) More people have become farmers since 1950.

(B) Many important products come from Georgia.

(C) Most Georgians live in villages nowadays.

(D) Today most of the people of Georgia work in factories.

下面三題（46－48）根據下文作答。

Mandy found a wallet that had ten dollars in it. "I must find the owner," she thought. "The person who lost it will be glad to get the money back." Mandy looked through the wallet but couldn't find a name or address. Suddenly she had an idea. She took the wallet to a police station.

A few days later, a young man phoned Mandy. "Thank you for being so honest," said the man.

Mandy smiled a big smile. "You're welcome," she said.

46. What was Mandy's problem?

(A) She wanted a new wallet.   (B) She needed ten dollars.

(C) She was unhappy.

(D) She didn't know how to return the wallet.

47. How did Mandy solve her problem?

　(A) She called the owner.

　(B) She took the wallet to a police station.

　(C) She waited for a few days.

　(D) She kept the wallet.

48. Why did Mandy want to return the wallet?

　(A) She wanted to meet the person who lost it.

　(B) She thought the owner would like to get the money back.

　(C) She was looking forward to a phone call.

　(D) She wanted to show off.

第三部分（12％）

說明：下面各題（49－54），各附四個答案，請仔細閱讀下列文章後，把最適合
　　　文意的 個答案標示在答案卡上。每題答對得2分，答錯倒扣2/3分，
　　　若不答則不給分。

　　When the Westinghouse Science Talent Search Team named its top
achievers in 1983, the grand prize went to Paul Ning, then 16.

　　Paul Ning is not a native-born American. He is the son of a diplomat from the Republic of China on Taiwan. Ning came to the United
States at the age of three. By 11, he was constructing a simple wind
tunnel to study the relationship between speed and pressure. Now a
senior at the superb Bronx High School of Science in New York City,
Ning feels, " You have to be aggressive in your studies to really understand what you're doing. " Adds his mother : " He always tries to prove
to us and to himself that he is the best. "

　　Out of 40 Westinghouse finalists, nine, including Ning, were born
in Asia and three others were of Asian descent. This story has reminded us of the fact that some 10％ of Harvard University's freshman
class is Asian American. While no more than 15％ of California high
school graduates are eligible for admission to the University of California system, about 40％ of Asian Americans qualify.

　　Most educators believe that Asian scholastic achievement has much
to do with breeding and nurture. Many Asian American children have
also well-educated parents who are always on the school's side. In

addition, most Asians regard education as the best avenue to recognition and success through which they pay the indefinite debt to parents. Also, this is a way of showing filial piety. As a result, it is no wonder that Asian American children usually do a far better job than their classmates.

49. Where is Paul Ning's birthplace?
(A) New York City.   (B) Somewhere in the United States.
(C) Somewhere other than the United States.
(D) Somewhere other than Asia.

50. When did Paul Ning come to the United States?
(A) 1968.   (B) 1970.   (C) 1971.   (D) 1978.

51. Which of the following expressions can best describe the characteristics of Paul Ning?
(A) An intelligent youngster of extreme confidence.
(B) An intelligent youngster who is offensive but confident.
(C) A diligent youngster who is very outspoken.
(D) An industrious youngster who is disagreeable.

52. About what percent of the students qualified for admission to the University of California system are non-Asian Americans?
(A) 15%.   (B) 40%.   (C) 50%.   (D) 60%.

53. What causes the Asian American children to be so successful in their studies?
(A) Respect for education and elders.
(B) Wealthy parents.
(C) Excellent learning facilities.
(D) Better intelligence and health.

54. What is the attitude of the parents of Asian Americans toward the education of their children?
(A) They pay little attention to it.
(B) They are concerned about their children's education.
(C) They hardly worry about it.
(D) The information is not given in this article.

Ⅲ. 翻譯：英譯中（ 10％ ）

　　說明：把下面五題，譯成中文，並依題號順序，寫在試卷內。每題2分。

55. He indicated approval with a nod.

56. I am convinced of the value of keeping diary.

57. As far as traffic safety is concerned, most drivers in Taipei should be re-educated.

58. Given encouragement and help, he would not have failed.

59. A strong national defense is the most certain guarantee of peace and freedom.

Ⅳ. 翻譯：中譯英（ 10％ ）

　　說明：把下面五題，譯成正確的英文，並依題號順序，寫在試卷內。每題2分。

60. 運動對健康有益 。

61. 我的腳踏車上禮拜天被偷了 。

62. 大多數的學生都不曉得如何使用圖書館 。

63. 我在今天的報紙上看到一則很有趣的新聞 。

64. 要學好英文，必須下功夫 。

Ⅴ. 英文作文：（ 20％ ）

　　說明：請用下面的題目作文，以80字爲度，不要太多或太少。請寫在試卷內。

　　題目：How I Spent Yesterday Evening

73年大學聯考英文試題詳解

I. 綜合測驗

A good teacher is many things *to many people*. I suppose everyone has his definite ideas *about* **what** *a good teacher is*.

"對很多人來說，好老師是很重要的。我想每個人對怎樣是好老師，都有明確的看法。"

* to many people 是副詞片語，修飾 is。everyone … is 是省略了 that 的名詞子句，作 suppose 的受詞。what 是複合關係代名詞，引導名詞子句，作 about 的受詞；what 在子句中又作主詞補語。

thing〔θɪŋ〕*n.* 重要的事物（nothing "無關緊要的事物"，something "重要的事物"）

definite〔'dɛfənɪt〕*adj.* 明確的

1. （ **D** ）(A) how 是關係副詞，沒有代名作用，在子句中不能做補語。

(B) 關代 that 不能作介系詞的受詞，且缺少先行詞。

(C) 用 who 則意為"一個好的老師是誰"，句意不合。

As I underline{look back on my own experience}, I find the teachers *that I respect and think about the most* are those *who demanded the most* discipline *from their students.*

"當我回顧自己的經歷，發現我最尊敬、最常想到的老師，是那些對學生要求最嚴格的老師。"

* As … experience 是副詞子句，修飾 find，表時間。that I respect … about the most 是形容詞子句，修飾其先行詞 teachers。who … students 是形容詞子句，修飾其先行詞 those。

look back "回顧"　　demand〔dɪ'mænd〕*vt.* 要求

discipline〔'dɪsəplɪn〕*n.* 紀律

2. **(C)** 這題考時式和動詞片語。主要子句的動詞 find 是簡單現在式，副詞子句的時式應該一致 (詳見文法寶典 p. 354)。(B) 過去式，(D) 過去進行式，均不合。(A) figure 作不及物動詞，意爲 " 計算 ; 料想 "，且沒有 figure back 的用法。

3. **(D)** 這題考拼字，(A)(B)(C)都是錯誤的拼法。

I think of one teacher *in particular* *that* I had in *high school*. I think he was a good teacher *because he was a very strict person*. He *just* tolerated no kind of nonsense *at all in his classroom*.

　　" 我特別想念我的一位高中老師。因爲他是個很嚴格的人，所以我認爲他是好老師。在課堂上，他一點也不容忍胡鬧。"

　　* in particular 是副詞片語，修飾 think。that I … school 是形容詞子句，修飾 teacher。because … person 是副詞子句，修飾 think，表原因。

　　　in particular " 特別地 " (= particularly)

4. **(B)** (A) peculiar 〔 pɪˈkjuljɚ 〕 *adj*. 奇異的
　　　(C) curio 〔 ˈkjʊrɪ‚o 〕 *n*. 古玩
　　　(D) curiosity 〔 ‚kjʊrɪˈɑsətɪ 〕 *n*. 好奇心

5. **(C)** 這題考用字和時式，因爲是過去發生的事，故應用過去式。
　　　(A) endure 〔 ɪnˈdjʊr 〕 *vt*. 忍耐 ; 忍受，時式不合，且 endure 是指長時間忍受痛苦或不幸，亦不適用於本句。
　　　(B) 沒有這個字。
　　　(C) ***tolerate*** 〔 ˈtɑlə‚ret 〕 *vt*. 容忍
　　　(D) toil 〔 tɔɪl 〕 *vt*. 以苦工完成工作，意思與時式均不合。

6. **(A)** (A) ***at all*** " 全然 "　　前面常有否定詞 not，no 等，表示 " 一點也不 "。
　　　(B) after all " 畢竟 "
　　　(C) in all " 合計 "
　　　(D) to all " 對所有的人 "

I remember *very vividly* a sign *over his classroom door*. It was a simple sign *that said*, "*laboratory — in this room the first five letters of the word are emphasized, not the last seven.*" *In other words*, labor *for him* was more important than oratory.

"我記得很清楚，他的教室門上有一張牌子。那是張簡單的牌子，上面寫著：「研究室——在這個房間裡，著重這個字的前五個字母，而不是後七個字母。」換句話說，對他而言，努力比雄辯重要。"

* 第一句中 over his classroom door 是形容詞片語，修飾 sign。第二句中 that said … seven."是形容詞子句，修飾 sign。In other words 是轉承語，連接上面的句子。

vividly〔ˈvɪvɪdlɪ〕*adv*. 清楚地　　laboratory〔ˈlæbrə͵torɪ〕*n*. 研究室
in other words "換句話說"　　labor〔ˈlebɚ〕*n*. 工作；努力
oratory〔ˈɔrə͵torɪ〕*n*. 雄辯；修辭

7. (**C**) say, tell, talk, speak 中，只有 say 後面可接直接引句（詳見文法寶典 p.299）。

8. (**D**) 主詞是 letters，故動詞要用複數，且為被動語態，故選 are emphasized。

　　(A) → are stressed, stress〔strɛs〕*vt*. 著重　*n*. 強調
　　(B) → are put stress on
　　(C) → are emphasized

　　$\begin{cases} \textit{lay emphasis on "強調"} \\ = \text{put emphasis on} \\ = \text{place emphasis on} \end{cases}$ $\begin{cases} = \text{lay stress on} \\ = \text{put stress on} \\ = \text{place stress on} \\ = \text{emphasize} \end{cases}$

9. (**B**) *in other words* 是慣用語，其他字沒有這種用法。
　　(D)有關 hand 的慣用語是 on the other hand "另一方面"

10. (**D**) (A) 吸收（是動詞）　　(B) 圖書館
　　(C) auditory〔ˈɔdə͵torɪ, -͵tɔrɪ〕*n*. 聽衆

Although milk is an important part of our everyday diet, cows give

milk *in the first place to feed to their calves.*

　　"雖然牛奶是我們日常飲食中重要的一部分，但是母牛產牛奶，首先是要餵牠們的小牛。"

　　* Although … diet 是副詞子句，修飾 give，表讓步。in the first place 是副詞片語，修飾 give。to feed … calves 是不定詞片語當副詞用，修飾 give，表目的。

　　　　diet〔ˊdaɪət〕*n.* 飲食　　*in the first place* "首先"

　　　　calf〔kæf, kɑf〕*n.* 小牛（複數為 calves）

Usually a cow has her first calf *when she is about two years old. After*

calving, a cow gives milk *for about 300 days and during this time* she

will give a total of about 900 gallons *before she runs dry.*

　　"通常母牛在兩歲左右生第一隻小牛。產下小牛後，母牛大約產奶三百天。而在牠奶流完以前的這段期間，總產量將近九百加侖。"

　　* when … old 是副詞子句，修飾 has，表時間。After calving 和 for about 300 days 是副詞片語，均修飾第一個 gives。and 連接兩個對等子句 After … days 和 during … dry。during this time 是副詞片語，before … dry 是副詞子句，共同修飾 give。

　　　　calf〔kæf, kɑf〕*n.* 小牛；犢

　　　　calve〔kæv, kɑv〕*vt., vi.* 產（犢）

　　　　gallon〔ˊgælən〕*n.* 加侖

11.（**D**）表時間的副詞子句，用 when 來引導；其他答案均不合。

12.（**A**）and 是表累積的對等連接詞，連接兩對等子句。
　　　　(B) but 是表反義的連接詞，(C) for 是解釋性的連接詞，均不合句意。
　　　　(D) since 是表原因的從屬連接詞，句意、文法均不合。

13.（**B**）(A) 走　(B) 流　(C) 做　(D) 使

The following year she will have another calf *and then* continue to give

milk *again, as before*.

"翌年她又會生一隻小牛，然後會像以前一樣繼續再產牛奶。"

　　* and 連接兩個對等子句，第二個子句中，省略了和前面相同的助動詞will。

14. （ **C** ）　another ＝ one more（詳見文法寶典 p.140）

　　(A)(B) 均意為 " 一 "　　(D)（二者之中的）另一個

15. （ **C** ）　(A)試圖　　(B)停下來　　(C)**繼續**　　(D)停止

Modern breeds *of dairy cattle now* give *more* milk *than their calves need*,

so there is *always* plenty for human consumption.

"現代品種的乳牛，目前產的牛奶超過牠們的小牛所需，因此一直有大量牛奶供人
類消耗。"

　　* than … need 是形容詞子句，修飾 milk。

　　　breed〔brid〕*n.* 種　　dairy cattle " 乳牛 "

16. （ **B** ）　(A) 有　　(B) **需要**　　(C) 遊戲　　(D) 能（產）

17. （ **D** ）　(A) moderation〔͵mɑdə'reʃən〕*n.* 適度
　　　　　　　(B) recreation〔͵rɛkrɪ'eʃən〕*n.* 娛樂
　　　　　　　(C) assumption〔ə'sʌmpʃən〕*n.* 假定
　　　　　　　(D) *consumption*〔kən'sʌmpʃən〕*n.* 消耗

Young calves are given some of their mothers' milk *but* they are *also*

given milk *made from milk powder*. *As soon as* possible they are given

solid foods such as concentrates, hay *or* grass.

"人們讓小牛喝母牛的奶，但也給牠們喝奶粉沖的牛奶。而且儘早給牠們固體的食
物，例如濃縮物、乾草或青草。"

　　* made … powder 是形容詞片語，修飾 milk。As soon as possible 是副詞
　　　片語，修飾全句。

　　　as～as possible ＝ as～as one can " 儘量 "
　　　concentrate〔'kɑnsn͵tret〕*n.* 濃縮物　　hay〔he〕*n.* 乾草

18.（ **B** ）　(A) 沒有，由 also 可知是錯誤的。

　　　　　　(C) 全部，由於 but 是表反義的連接詞，故知不是 " 全部 " 。

　　　　　　(D) → lots 或 a lot

19.（ **A** ）　(A) 牛奶　　(B) 乾草　　(C) 靑草　　(D) 肉

20.（ **D** ）　(A) 儘量好　　(B) 儘量好　　(C) 儘量快（指運動、動作）　　(D) 儘量早

A thundershower *lasting for two hours yesterday temporarily* relieved a six-month long drought *in the Kaohsiung area.*

　　" 昨天持續兩小時的一場雷雨，暫時解除了高雄地區長達六個月的久旱。"

　　＊ lasting … yesterday 是形容詞片語，修飾 thundershower 。in … area 是形容詞片語，修飾 drought 。

　　　　thundershower〔ˊθʌndəˌʃaʊə〕*n.* 雷雨

21.（ **A** ）　(A) *drought*〔draʊt〕*n.* 久旱　　　(B) draft〔dræft〕*n.* 通風

　　　　　　(C) drift〔drɪft〕*n.* 漂流　　　　(D) draught〔dræft〕= draft

The Taiwan Water Company *also* announced *yesterday* an indefinite postponement *of a second stage of water rationing originally scheduled to begin today.*

" 台灣自來水公司昨天也宣布，將原定今天開始的第二階段限制供水，延到不確定的日期。"

　　＊ originally … today 是形容詞片語，修飾 rationing 。

　　　　postponement〔postˊponmənt〕*n.* 延期

　　　　rationing〔ˊreʃənɪŋ〕*n.* 配給

22.（ **D** ）　(A) 一個限制

　　　　　　(B) 限制的

　　　　　　(C) indefinable〔ˌɪndɪˊfaɪnəbl̩〕*adj.* 無法下定義的

　　　　　　(D) indefinite〔ɪnˊdɛfənɪt〕*adj.* 不明確的

The sky was dark **and** cloudy *in Kaohsiung City* **as** the day broke.
Local residents all had a forewarning (*that*) it was going to rain. *At*
around 10 : 00 it began raining. *Soon* it was raining cats and dogs.

　　" 天剛亮的時候，高雄市的天空烏雲密佈。當地居民都有預感要下雨了。十點
左右，天開始下雨了。很快就大雨傾盆了。"

　　* as the day broke 是副詞子句，修飾 was，表時間。it was going to
　　rain 是省略了 that 的名詞子句，作 forewarning 的同位語。

　　　　resident〔ˈrɛzədənt〕*n.* 居民
　　　　forewarning〔forˈwɔrnɪŋ, fɔr-〕*n.* 事先之警告

23. (**B**)　表示 " 破曉 " 的動詞要用 break 或 dawn。
　　　　(A) 變亮　(C) 開始　(D) 發起；創造（沒有不及物動詞的用法）

24. (**C**)　中文裡的 " 天開始下雨 "，天是指 " 天氣 "，而非 " 天空 "，要用非人
　　　　稱的 it（詳見文法寶典 p.111），故不能用 sky 做主詞。(D) 沒有意義。
　　　　(C) it began raining 也可說 it began to rain。

25. (**B**)　*rain cats and dogs* " 傾盆大雨 " 是固定用法的成語，cats 和 dogs
　　　　都用複數，且 cats 在前，dogs 在後。

Although passers-by were forced to take cover, they were all pleased,
saying the rain had come *in the nick of time*.

" 儘管路人們被迫避雨，他們都很高興，說雨來得正是時候。"

　　* Although … cover 是副詞子句，修飾 were，表讓步。saying … time 是
　　　分詞構句，表附帶的狀態，可改為對等子句 and said …（詳見文法寶典 p.460）。

　　　　take cover " 躲避 "
　　　　$\begin{cases} \textit{in the nick of time} \text{ " 正是時候 "} \\ = \textit{just in time} \end{cases}$

26. (**D**)　passer-by " 路人 " 是複合名詞，變成複數形時，要將其主要字改為複
　　　　數（詳見文法寶典 p.79）。

27. (**A**) (B) say 缺少連接詞，且時式不對。

(C) → and said

(D) 不定詞片語可表目的、理由、條件、結果、原因，均不合乎句意，且其間不應用逗點分隔。

It was the first <u>noteworthy</u> rainfall *within half a year in this southern port city*. *As a result*, the originally scheduled water restrictions <u>were cancelled</u>.

"這是這個南部港市半年來第一場顯著的降雨。因此原定的供水限制被取消了。"

* within half a year 和 in this southern port city 是副詞片詞片語，修飾 was。

noteworthy〔'not,wɜðɪ〕*adj.* 顯著的；值得注目的
port〔port,pɔrt〕*n.* 港口　　*as a result* "因此"

28. (**B**) (A)(C)(D)均無此種拼法。

29. (**C**) 這題要用被動語態，所以選(C)的 be＋p.p.。

<u>Starting</u> from 9：00 this morning, the water supply *to swimming pools and fountains* will be resumed, *together with irrigation of trees and flowers on streets*.

"從今天早上九點開始，將恢復游泳池與噴泉的供水，和街上花樹的澆灌。"

* 本句是分詞構句，可改爲對等子句 The water supply to swimming pools and fountains will start from … morning，and it will be resumed，together … streets（詳見文法寶典 p.459）。together with … street 是副詞片語，修飾主要子句。

fountain〔'faʊntn̩,-tɪn〕*n.* 噴泉
resume〔rɪ'zum,-'zɪum,-'zjum〕*vt.* 再開始
irrigation〔,ɪrə'geʃən〕*n.* 灌溉

30. (**D**) 見文法說明。

　　(A) 以動詞起首，為祈使句，句意不合，且兩個子句缺連接詞。

　　(B) 置於句首的不定詞片語表目的或條件，在此句意不合。

　　(C) 過去分詞為首的分詞構句表被動，不合句意。

Ⅱ. 閱讀測驗

第一部份

31. (**D**) 　Jane : Hello, Tom. How´are you？

　　　　　Tom : Fine, thanks. How are´you？

　　　" 珍：哈囉，湯姆。你好嗎？

　　　　湯姆：好，謝謝。你好嗎？"

　　* How are you？是已經認識的朋友見面時的寒暄。回答方式如題句。How do you do？則是初識的人見面時的招呼，回答只要說 How do you do？而不要加上 fine，或 thanks。

　　　(C) "我是個新學生。"句意不相干。

32. (**B**) 　Tom : May I speak to Jane, please？

　　　　　Jane : This is Jane speaking.

　　　" 湯姆：請找珍聽電話好嗎？

　　　　珍：我就是珍。"

　　　(A) 珍來了。　　　(C) 我到了。　　　(D) 繼續說。

33. (**C**) 　Jane : I went to the opera *last night*.

　　　　　Tom : Did you enjoy it？

　　　" 珍：我昨晚去看歌劇。

　　　　湯姆：你喜歡它嗎？"

　　　(A) 哦，是關於什麼的手術？

　　　(B) 你走那條路？

　　　(D) 你邀請那個樂隊？

　　　opera〔ˊɑpərə〕*n.* 歌劇　　operation〔͵ɑpəˊreʃən〕*n.* 手術
　　　band〔bænd〕*n.* 樂隊

34. (**D**)　Jane : What would you like to drink？

　　　　　Tom : I'll have the same again, please.

　　　　"　珍：你想要喝什麼？

　　　　　湯姆：請再給我同樣的。"

　　　　　　　(A) 是的，我早餐一向喝茶。

　　　　　　　(B) 嗯，要我帶給你別的東西嗎？

　　　　　　　(C) 我認為很多人酒喝得太多了。

35. (**C**)　Jane : Thank you for the present.　It was just what I wanted.

　　　　　Tom : I am glad you like it.

　　　　"　珍：謝謝你的禮物。那正是我想要的。

　　　　　湯姆：我很高興你喜歡它。"

　　　　　　　(A) 你想要什麼？　　　　　(B) 你不喜歡它。

　　　　　　　(D) 那是一件禮物嗎？

第二部份

36. (**C**)　Jack went to school *in spite of the cold weather*.

　　　　"雖然天氣冷，傑克還是去上學。"

　　　　　　　(A) 天氣冷，因此傑克沒去上學。

　　　　　　　(B) 因為天氣冷，所以傑克去上學。

　　　　　　　(C) 雖然天氣冷，但傑克還是去上學。

　　　　　　　(D) 因為天氣冷，所以傑克去上學。

37. (**D**)　Education is the only alternative *to lives of poverty and ignorance*.

　　　　"不過貧窮無知生活，教育是唯一的選擇。"

　　　　　　　(A) 對貧窮和無知的生活來說，教育是必須的。

　　　　　　　(B) 一個人如果想生活在貧窮和無知中，就需要教育。

　　　　　　　(C) 教育能幫助我們辨別貧窮和無知。

　　　　　　　(D) 如果你不想活在貧窮和無知中，必須受教育。

　　　　* to lives … ignorance 是形容詞片語，修飾 alternative。

　　　　　alternative〔ɔl'tɝnətɪv, æl'tɝnətɪv〕*n.* 二者擇一；選擇的事物

　　　　　differentiate〔͵dɪfə'rɛnʃɪ͵et〕*vt.* 辨別

38. (**B**) The lecture *Mr. Simpson delivered the other day* is **not only** entertaining **but also** informative.

"辛普森先生幾天前發表的演講,不僅有趣,且有益。"

   (A) 辛普森先生的談話有趣,但是不正式。

   (B) 辛普森先生發表的談話有趣而且有益。

   (C) 辛普森先生的演講有趣而且不正式。

   (D) 辛普森先生的演講乏味,但是能鼓舞人。

* Mr. Simpson … day 是省略了 which 或 that 的形容詞子句,修飾 lecture。

    deliver〔dɪ'lɪvɚ〕*vt.* 發表　　*the other day* "幾天前"

    entertaining〔,ɛntɚ'tenɪŋ〕*adj.* 有趣的

    informative〔ɪn'fɔrmətɪv〕*adj.* 有益的;供給知識的

    presentation〔,prɛzn̩'teʃən〕*n.* 發表

    instructive〔ɪn'strʌktɪv〕*adj.* 有益的;供給知識的

    inspiring〔ɪn'spaɪrɪŋ〕*adj.* 鼓舞的

39. (**A**) John : Do you mind my asking you some questions *about your family*?

    Paul : Certainly not.

"約翰:你介意我問你一些關於你家庭的問題嗎?

保羅:當然不介意。"

   (A) 保羅願意回答約翰的問題。　　(B) 保羅不願回答約翰的問題。

   (C) 保羅對回答約翰的問題不感興趣。

   (D) 保羅拒絕回答約翰的問題。

* *Do you mind my asking* ~ ? = *Do you mind if I ask* ~ ?

40. (**B**) Jane : Have you finished your paper *yet*?

    Bill : Oh, yes. It's *far from* being satisfactory, *though*.

    Jane : It serves you right.

    Bill : I know. I've learned my lesson.

" 珍：你的論文寫完了嗎？

比爾：噢，是的。但是它一點也不令人滿意。

珍：你活該。

比爾：我知道。我已經得到教訓了。"

　(A) 比爾的論文寫得很好。

　(B) 比爾永遠不會忘記他不令人滿意的家庭作業。

　(C) 比爾從每一課學到了很多。

　(D) 比爾未能及時完成他的論文。

　far from " 一點也不 "

　It serves you right. " 你活該。"

　learn one's lesson " 從經驗中獲取教訓 "

41.（ **C** ） Tom is trying out for a team.　He has to know how to throw and catch a ball.　He has to be able to hit a ball *with a bat*. He has to be a fast runner.　What team is Tom trying out for？

" 湯姆正試圖加入一個球隊。他得知道如何投球、接球。他得能用棒子擊球。他得跑得很快。湯姆試圖加入什麼球隊？"

　(A) 橄欖球。　　(B) 籃球。　　(C) 棒球。　　(D) 網球。

　try out for " 試圖加入；參加競爭 "

42.（ **D** ） Peter : How is the article you're reading？

David : It's *no more than* an average piece.

David considers the article_____.

" 彼得：你正在讀的文章如何？

大衞：那只是普通的文章。

大衞認為那文章_____。

　(A) 好極了　　　　　　(B) 給人的印象很深刻

　(C) 糟糕　　　　　　　(D) 平淡

　no more than = only " 只 "

　piece〔pis〕*n.* 一篇作品（詩、散文等）

　unimpressive〔͵ʌnɪmˋprɛsɪv〕*adj.* 平淡的；給人印象不深的

43. (**B**)　Mr. Wang deserves great credit *for establishing an updated general hospital.*

"王先生建立一所新式的綜合醫院，應得很大的光榮 。"

(A) 王先生得為建立一所新醫院，付更多帳單 。

(B) 王先生應該為建立一所現代化的醫院受到稱讚 。

(C) 王先生已被允許，建立一所全新的醫院 。

(D) 王先生已被委託，去建立一所現代化的醫院 。

* for … hospital 是副詞片語，修飾 deserves 。

　　credit〔ˈkrɛdɪt〕*n.* 光榮

　　updated〔ʌpˈdetɪd〕*adj.* 最新的

　　general hospital "綜合醫院"

　　set up "建立"　　applaud〔əˈplɔd〕*vt.* 稱讚

44. (**A**)　Heart disease continues to decline **but** still tops the list *of the 15 leading killers*, a group *that causes 89% of all American deaths.*

"心臟病繼續減少，但仍高居十五大死因之首，百分之八十九的美國人死亡，是由這十五大死因引起的 。"

(A) 雖然心臟病繼續減少，它仍比其他任何疾病，引起更多的美國人死亡 。

(B) 大約百分之八十九的美國人死亡，是由心臟病引起的 。

(C) 隨著心臟病繼續減少，它不再是十五大死因之首 。

(D) 大約百分之八十九的美國人死亡，是由十五大死因中，心臟病以外的疾病所引起的 。

* a group … deaths 是 killers 的同位語，that … deaths 是形容詞子句，修飾 group 。

　　heart desease "心臟病"

　　decline〔dɪˈklaɪn〕*vi.* 減低　　top〔tɑp〕*vt.* 為～的頂點

　　leading〔ˈlidɪŋ〕*adj.* 領先的

　　killer〔ˈkɪlɚ〕*n.* 殺手（在此指疾病、意外等致死的原因）

45.（ D ）*Until the 1950's* most of the people *of Georgia* were farmers. Many crops are *still* raised, *but now* only a fifth *of the people* earn their living *by farming*. *Today* most Georgians live *in cities and towns* *and* work *in factories*. They make *such* things *as* cotton cloth, peanut butter, boats, automobiles, lumber, and paper.

Which sentence best gives the main idea *of the paragraph*？

"1950 年以前，喬治亞州的人大部分是農民。現在仍然種植很多農作物，但是只有五分之一的人務農。今天，大部分的喬治亞州人住在城鎮，而且在工廠裡工作。他們製造棉布、花生醬、船、汽車、木材和紙等。"

那一句最能指出本段的主旨？

(A) 自1950年起，有更多的人成為農夫。
(B) 許多重要的產品來自喬治亞州。
(C) 現在喬治亞州人大半住在村落裡。
(D) 今天喬治亞州人多半在工廠裡工作。

Georgia〔'dʒɔrdʒə, -dʒjə〕*n*. 喬治亞（美國南部之一州）
peanut butter " 花生醬 "
automobile〔'ɔtəmə,bil, ,ɔtə'mobil〕*n*. 汽車
lumber〔'lʌmbɚ〕*n*. 木材

46～48

Mandy found a wallet *that had ten dollars in it*. "I must find the owner," she thought. "The person *who lost it* will be glad to get the money back." Mandy looked through the wallet *but* couldn't find a name or address. *Suddenly* she had an idea. She took the wallet *to a police station*.

"曼蒂撿到了一個皮夾，裡面有十元。她想：「我得找到它的主人。掉了皮夾的人一定會很高興拿回錢。」曼蒂徹底檢查皮夾，但是找不到姓名或住址。忽然她有了個主意，把皮夾送到警察局。"

* that … it 是形容詞子句，修飾 wallet。who lost it 是形容詞子句，修飾 person。

wallet〔′wɑlɪt〕n. 皮夾；錢袋　　***look through*** "徹底審查"

A few days later, a young man phoned Mandy. "Thank you for being so honest," said the man.

Mandy smiled a big smile. "You're welcome," she said.

"幾天後，一個年輕人打電話給曼蒂，他說：「謝謝你這麼誠實。」
曼蒂開心地笑了。她說：「不客氣。」"

* smile a big smile 是同系動詞、同系受詞所形成的片語(詳見文法寶典 p.280)。

46. (D) 曼蒂有什麼困難？

(A) 她想要一個新的皮夾。　　(B) 她需要十元。

(C) 她不快樂。　　(D) 她不知道怎樣歸還皮夾。

47. (B) 曼蒂如何解決她的困難？

(A) 她打電話給失主。　　(B) 她把皮夾拿到警察局去。

(C) 她等了幾天。　　(D) 她留下了皮夾。

48. (B) 曼蒂為什麼想歸還皮夾？

(A) 她想認識失主。　　(B) 她想失主想拿回錢。

(C) 她期待一通電話。　　(D) 她想炫耀。

show off "炫耀"

第三部份

When the Westinghouse Science Talent Search Team named its top achievers in 1983, the grand prize went to Paul Ning, then 16.

"西屋科學才藝探查小組公布1983年最高成就者姓名時，大獎歸於當時十六歲的寧保羅。"

* When … 1983 是副詞子句，修飾 went，表時間。in 1983 是形容詞片語，修飾 achievers。

name〔nem〕vt. 說出～的名字

achiever〔ə′tʃivɚ〕n. 有成就的人

Paul Ning is not a native-born American.　He is the son *of a diplomat from the Republic of China on Taiwan*.　Ning came to the United States *at the age of three*.

「寧保羅不是土生土長的美國人。他是來自中華民國台灣的一位外交官的兒子。他三歲的時候到了美國。」

* of a … Taiwan是形容詞片語，修飾 son。at the age of three 是副詞片語，修飾 came。

By 11, he was constructing a simple wind tunnel *to study the relationship between speed and pressure*.

「十一歲的時候，他就造一個簡單的風洞，來研究速度和壓力間的關係。」

* to study … pressure 是不定詞片語當副詞用，修飾 constructing，表目的。

　　wind tunnel　「風洞」（用來測定風壓對飛機或汽車等之作用）

Now a senior *at the superb Bronx High School of Science in New York City*, Ning feels, "You have to be aggressive *in your studies to really understand what you're doing*." Adds his mother: "He *always* tries to prove *to us and to himself* that he is the best."

「寧現在是紐約市一流的布隆克斯科學高中的四年級生。他覺得：「你對研究必須積極，以真正了解你在做的東西。」他的母親補充說：「他總是試著向我們和他自己證明他是最優秀的。」」

* to really … doing 是不定詞片語當副詞用，修飾 be，表目的。that he is the best 是名詞子句，作 prove 的受詞。

　　senior〔ˈsinjɚ〕*n.*（大學或四年制中學的）四年級生
　　superb〔suˈpɝb, sə-〕*adj.* 極好的；上等的
　　Bronx〔brɑŋks〕*n.* 布隆克斯（紐約市之一區）
　　aggressive〔əˈgrɛsɪv〕*adj.* 積極的；進取的

Out of 40 Westinghouse finalists, nine, *including Ning*, were born in Asia **and** three others were of Asian descent.

　"西屋的四十名決選者中，包括寧在內，有九個人生在亞洲，另外有三個人是亞洲人的後裔。"

　* Out of … finalists 是形容詞片語，修飾主詞，爲強調而倒裝於句首。

　　　finalist〔'faɪnḷɪst〕*n.* 獲決賽權者
　　　descent〔dɪ'sɛnt〕*n.* 出身

This story has reminded us of the fact **that** some 10% *of Harvard University's freshman class* is Asian American. **While** no more than 15% of California high school graduates are eligible for admission *to the University of California system*, about 40% of Asian Americans qualify.

　"這個故事提醒我們一個事實，就是大約百分之十的哈佛大學新生是亞裔美人。雖然只有百分之十五的加州高中生，夠格進入加州大學系統，卻有大約百分之四十的亞裔美人有資格進入。"

　* that … American 是名詞子句，作 fact 的同位語。While 引導副詞子句，修飾 qualify，表讓步。

　　　remind sb. of sth. "提醒某人某事"
　　　eligible〔'ɛlɪdʒəbḷ〕*adj.* 合格的　　qualify〔'kwɑlə,faɪ〕*vi.* 合格

Most educators believe **that** *Asian scholastic achievement has much to do with breeding and nurture*. Many Asian American children have also well-educated parents *who are always on the school's side*.

　"多數教育家相信亞洲人的學術成就，和教養很有關係。許多亞裔美人也有受過良好教育的父母，他們總是站在學校的一邊。"

　* that … nurture 是名詞子句，作 believe 的受詞。who … side 是形容詞子句，修飾 parents。

　　　scholastic〔sko'læstɪk〕*adj.* 學術的　　achievement〔ə'tʃivmənt〕*n.* 成就
　　　have much to do with "和～很有關係"
　　　breeding〔'bridɪŋ〕*n.* 教育　　nurture〔'nɝtʃɚ〕*n.* 養育；教養

In addition, most Asians regard education as the best avenue *to recogni-* *tion and success through **which** they pay the indefinite debt to parents*.

"此外,大多數的亞洲人認為,教育是獲得讚譽和成功最好的途徑;而他們可藉著讚譽和成功,來報答父母無限的恩情。"

* to recognition … parents 是形容詞片語,修飾 avenue;其中 through which … parents 是形容詞子句,修飾 recognition 和 success。

  avenue〔'ævə,nju〕 *n.* 方法;途徑　　recognition〔,rɛkəg'nɪʃən〕 *n.* 讚譽
  indefinite〔ɪn'dɛfənɪt〕 *adj.* 無限制的

Also, this is a way *of showing filial piety.*　***As a result***, it is no wonder *that Asian American children usually do a far better job **than** their* *classmates*.

"而且,這是表現孝道的一種方式。因此,難怪亞裔美籍的小孩,常表現得遠比他們的同學好。"

* 第二句中 it 是形式主詞,that … classmates 是真正主詞,其中 than their classmates 是省略了 do 的形容詞子句,修飾 job。

  filial〔'fɪlɪəl,-ljəl〕 *adj.* 子女的;孝順的
  piety〔'paɪətɪ〕 *n.* 孝順;恭敬　　filial piety "孝道"

49. (**C**) 寧保羅的出生地點是那裡?

　　(A) 紐約市。　　　　　　　　(B) 美國某地。
　　(C) 美國以外的某個地方。　　(D) 亞洲以外的某個地方。

50. (**B**) 寧保羅什麼時候到美國的?

　　(A) 1968 年。　(B) 1970 年。　(C) 1971 年。　(D) 1978 年。

51. (**A**) 下列何者敘述最能描述寧保羅的特色?

　　(A) 極自信的聰明少年。　　　(B) 無禮但有自信的、聰明的少年。
　　(C) 非常坦白勤勉的少年。　　(D) 勤勉但脾氣不好的少年。

　　youngster〔'jʌŋstə〕 *n.* 少年　　offensive〔ə'fɛnsɪv〕 *adj.* 無禮的
　　outspoken〔'aʊt'spokən〕 *adj.* 坦白的
　　disagreeable〔,dɪsə'griəb!〕 *adj.* 脾氣不好的;不為人喜愛的

52. (　) 夠格進加州大學系統的非亞洲人的百分比大約是多少？

　　　(A) 百分之十五。　　　　　(B) 百分之四十。

　　　(C) 百分之五十。　　　　　(D) 百分之六十。

　　（文中只提到①加州高中生有 15 ％ 可入大學，②亞裔學生中有 40 ％ 可入大學。並未提及可入大學的亞裔學生佔 15 ％ 中的多少，故題不明，無法做答。）

53. (A) 什麼使亞裔美籍小孩在課業上那麼成功？

　　　(A) 尊重教育和長者。　　　(B) 富有的父母。

　　　(C) 最佳的學習設備。　　　(D) 較好的智慧和健康。

　　facility〔fə'sɪlətɪ〕n.(pl.) 設備

54. (B) 亞裔美籍父母對他們小孩教育的態度怎樣？

　　　(A) 他們極少注意。　　　　(B) 他們關心孩子的教育。

　　　(C) 他們幾乎不擔心它。　　(D) 本文未提及。

　　pay attention to "注意"

Ⅲ. **翻譯**：英譯中

55. He indicated approval *with a nod*.
　他點頭表示贊同。

　　　indicate〔'ɪndə,ket〕*vt.* 表示；說
　　　approval〔ə'pruvl̩〕*n.* 贊成　　nod〔nɑd〕*n.* 點頭

56. I am convinced of the value *of keeping diary.*
　我深信寫日記的價值。

　　　be convinced of "深信；確信"
　　　keep a diary "寫日記"（原題遺漏 a）

57. *As far as traffic safety is concerned*, most drivers *in Taipei* should be re-educated.
　就交通安全而言，台北的駕駛員大部分應該再教育。

　　　as far as～be concerned "就～而言"
　　　re-educate〔ri'ɛdʒə,ket〕*vt.* 再教育

58. *Given encouragement and help*, he would not have failed.
　　假如他曾經受到鼓勵和幫助，就不會失敗了。

　　　* Given … help 是由副詞子句 If he had been given encouragement and
　　　　help 簡化而來的分詞構句，修飾 failed，表條件。本句是與過去事實相反
　　　　的假設。

　　　　　encouragement〔ɪnˋkɝɪdʒmənt, ɛn-〕*n.* 鼓勵

59. A strong national defense is the most certain guarantee *of peace*
　　and freedom.
　　堅強的國防是和平與自由最可靠的保證。

　　　　　national defense " 國防 "
　　　　　guarantee〔͵gærənˋti〕*n.* 保證；擔保

IV. 翻譯：中譯英

60. 運動對健康有益。

　　Exercise is good for (*your*) health.
　　Exercise is good for the health.

　　　　　be good for " 對～有益 "

61. 我的脚踏車上禮拜天被偷了。

　　I had my bicycle stolen *last Sunday*.
　　My bicycle was stolen *last Sunday*.

　　　* have＋受詞（物）＋ p.p. " 某物被～了 "

62. 大多數的學生都不曉得如何使用圖書館。

　　Most (*of the*) students do not know ⎰*how* to use a library.
　　　　　　　　　　　　　　　　　　　　　⎱*how* to make use of a library.

　　　　　make the use of " 使用；利用 "

63. 我在今天的報紙上看到一則很有趣的新聞。

I read an interesting $\begin{cases} \text{item} \\ \text{piece} \end{cases}$ of news *in today's paper*.

　　* 表示「一則新聞」用 an *item* of news 或 a *piece* of news。

64. 要學好英文，必須下功夫。

To learn English well, you have to take (*great*) pains.

If you want to learn English well, you have to take (*great*) pains.

　　* take (*great*) pains 也可用 make (*great*) efforts 代替。

　　　take pains "努力；費力"　　　*make efforts* "努力；奮力"

V. 英文作文（參考範例）

How I Spent Yesterday Evening

(一) *Last night*, after dinner, I sat comfortably in front of the T.V. and watched the news. Thinking that I did well in yesterday's examination, I felt like relaxing a little.

A short time later, I entered my room, took out my books and brushed up on my Chinese, English and the Three Principles of the People. These subjects are the topics of today's examination. *At about ten thirty*, my mother brought me a glass of milk and asked me to go to bed early.

After reviewing those subjects, I went to bed and had a nice sleep.

brush up on " 溫習" (= review)

我如何度過昨晚

昨天晚上，吃過晚飯後，我舒服地坐在電視前看新聞。想到我昨天考得不錯，就想要輕鬆一下。

過了一會兒，我走進房內，拿出書本，開始溫習國文、英文和三民主義。這些都是今天要考的科目。大約十點半，媽媽替我帶來一杯牛奶，要我早點上牀。

複習完那些科目後，我就上牀睡了美好的一覺。

㈡　It was the evening before the start of my college entrance examination. I felt nervous but also excited because I knew my exam would very soon be over.

To relax myself, I thought of how hard I had studied especially in the last few months. I tried to reassure myself that I had done enough preparation.

At nine o'clock I went to bed and had a good night's sleep. *As a result* I did not find the examination too difficult.

reassure〔,riə'ʃʊr〕*vt.* 再保證

大學入學考試開始的前一個傍晚，我覺得很緊張，但是也很興奮，因為我知道考試很快就會結束了。

為了放鬆自己，我想到我一直多麼用功，尤其是過去的幾個月以來。我試著再向自己保證，已經準備充分了。

九點鐘我上牀睡覺，並且一晚都睡得很好。因此我不覺得考試太難。

* 第一篇適合第一類組考生，第二篇適合第二類組考生。

心得筆記欄

七十二學年度大學暨獨立學院入學考試
英 文 試 題

※ 本學科除作文外，共有 50 題。測驗題（1-40）答在答案卡上；翻譯（41-50）
和作文答在作文及翻譯試卷內。

Ⅰ、拼字（5％）（多重選擇題）

說明：下列 1-5 題，每題 5 個英語單字，其中至少有兩個是拼對的。把拼對的單字標出在答案卡上。一題全對得 1 分，答錯倒扣 1/25 分，不答者 0 分。

例：(A) eletronic　　(B) prayor　　(C) suckle　　(D) knot　　(E) trust

答案：A B C D E
　　　□ □ ■ ■ ■

1. (A) agressive　　　(B) sugestive　　　(C) agreeable　　　(D) sufferable
　 (E) sluggish

2. (A) convenient　　 (B) obedient　　　 (C) expereince　　 (D) reimburse
　 (E) primier

3. (A) contemptable　 (B) irresponsable　(C) adolescent　　 (D) independant
　 (E) indispensable

4. (A) maintainance　 (B) insistence　　 (C) elevator　　　 (D) barometer
　 (E) photographor

5. (A) surrender　　　(B) suspicius　　　(C) volunter　　　(D) embarrass
　 (E) ambassador

Ⅱ、發音（5％）（多重選擇題）

說明：下列 6-10 題，每題 5 個英語單字，每個單字中有一個或二個字母畫有底線。找出畫有底線的字母發音相同的各個單字，然後在答案卡上將正確的答案標出。一題全對得 1 分，答錯倒扣 1/25 分，不答者得 0 分。

例：(A) joke　　(B) get　　　(C) gentle　　(D) job　　　(E) sing

答案：A B C D E
　　　■ □ □ ■ □

6. (A) bomb　　(B) autumn　　(C) damp　　(D) come　　(E) hymn

7. (A) height　(B) island　　(C) sign　　(D) quit　　(E) gigantic

8. (A) precious (B) scene (C) psalm (D) vision (E) lose
9. (A) tidy (B) express (C) yield (D) perceive (E) unique
10. (A) admiral (B) passage (C) foundation (D) academic (E) astonish

Ⅲ、綜合測驗（單一選擇題）

第一部分（10％）

說明：11－20題，每題有一個空白，四個答案。按句法句義，這些答案只有一個是正確的。請把正確答案，標示在答案卡上。每題1分，答錯者倒扣⅓分，不答者0分。

11. The coast was undefended and _____ open to attack.
    (A) lie (B) lay (C) laid (D) lain

12. Please be _____ .
    (A) sit (B) sat (C) set (D) seated

13. The boy's wayward behavior _____ his mother many a sleepless night.
    (A) cost (B) took (C) spent (D) robbed

14. There is no _____ when they can be here today.
    (A) saying (B) talking (C) speaking (D) telling

15. _____ being a fine day last Sunday, we went mountain climbing.
    (A) For (B) It (C) As (D) The weather

16. The waiter took a very long time _____ us.
    (A) treating (B) awaiting (C) serving (D) dealing

17. The explorers set out _____ their hazardous journey into the unknown.
    (A) to (B) on (C) for (D) along

18. I would appreciate it if you could finish this work _____ May.
    (A) by (B) until (C) prior (D) up to

19. Oh, Jane, you've broken still another glass. You ought _____ when you washed it.
    (A) be careful (B) to careful
    (C) to be careful (D) to have been careful

20. Mr. Wang bought that piece of land near the shore with a view to _____ a summer house there.
    (A) build (B) be built (C) having built (D) building

第二部分（20％）

說明：下面兩段文章，各有五個空白，應填的字各有號碼，每個號碼包含四個答案，選出最合適的一個答案，標示在答案卡上。每題2分，答錯者倒扣⅔分，不答者0分。

Large ___(21)___ of people nowadays might define a holiday as "traveling to another part of the country or of the world for a week or two once or twice a year." ___(22)___ me personally a holiday does not necessarily require a lot of travel. ___(23)___. In fact, for the past twenty years, it has meant no travel at all, because I would define a holiday as "a period of time in which you do something completely different from your normal ___(24)___." So, by my definition, a holiday means roughly the same as a complete change. And that might ___(25)___, as long as it is not the same kind of work that one does the rest of the time.

21. (A) crowds　　(B) numbers　　(C) mass　　(D) amounts
22. (A) But for　　(B) Yet with　　(C) Whereas　　(D) Although
23. (A) Reversely　　(B) Contradictorily
　　(C) On the other hand　　(D) Quite the opposite
24. (A) routine　　(B) life　　(C) schedule　　(D) time
25. (A) work　　(B) even work　　(C) be in the works　　(D) even be work

The thing I remember most vividly about my early childhood was the very first time I ___(26)___ to the seaside. I know it was a gloriously hot day, but I ___(27)___ if I said I had a clear recollection of the journey to the coast. My parents have often told me that I was sick most of the way. Fortunately I have no ___(28)___ at all of those unpleasant hours. But I shall never forget running down the hot sand and into the "big pond", as I called it. It was the Atlantic, and although the day was hot, the ___(29)___ was extremely cold. It was the shock of that first voluntary baptism, I know, which has to this day ___(30)___ me very wary of bathing in the sea.

26. (A) took　　(B) turned　　(C) was taken　　(D) was called
27. (A) lied　　(B) would lie　　(C) am lying　　(D) would be lying
28. (A) reminder　　(B) memory　　(C) recognition　　(D) thought
29. (A) pebbles　　(B) beach　　(C) sea　　(D) shore
30. (A) continued　　(B) caused　　(C) stayed　　(D) made

IV、閱讀能力（單一選擇題）

第一部分（10%）

說明：下面31-35題，各有四個可能的解釋性答案。請把其中最正確的一個，在答案卡上標出。每題2分，答錯者倒扣⅔分，不答者0分。

31. He has completely abandoned himself to despair.
    (A) He has forgotten his despair.
    (B) He has been very much in despair.
    (C) He has been too busy to despair.
    (D) He has totally given up despair.

32. The statement made by the witness ties in with the evidence the police already had.
    (A) The statement of the witness and the evidence collected by the police are one and the same.
    (B) What the witness said is one thing and what the police had already is another.
    (C) The witness's statement has no bearing on the evidence discovered by the police.
    (D) The witness's statement and the police's evidence are closely connected.

33. Tom should have known better when he asked her to go out with him, her parents being so very old-fashioned.
    (A) Tom did not ask her to go out with him because he did not know her better than he actually did.
    (B) Knowing that she would not go out with him anyway since her parents were known to be old-fashioned, Tom did not ask her.
    (C) She refused to go out with Tom.
    (D) She went out with Tom in spite of her parents' strong objection.

34. Tom : There's been a steady increase in the number of cars on the road.
    Jane : Yes, and it's high time the Government does something about it.
    Jane thinks that
    (A) the government has managed to control the increase of cars.
    (B) immediate action is called for to control the growth.
    (C) it takes time for the Government to reduce the number of cars.
    (D) the Government should find the right time to get some of the old cars off the roads.

35. Few of the people in adult-education classes across the nation seem to miss the traditional trappings of colleges or the prestige that usually is attached to instruction from professors loaded with academic honors. Most such people are

(A) looking for teachers who have experience rather than credentials.

(B) taking courses solely to gain a college degree.

(C) in a better position to judge which of the professors are academically qualified.

(D) regretful that they did not have their chance of college trappings and prestigious professors when they were young.

第二部分 (10 %)

說明：下面 36～40 題，各附四個答案，請在仔細閱讀全段文字後，把最適合文義的一個答案，在答案卡上標出。每題2分，答錯者倒扣⅔分，不答者0分。

In the development of literature, prose generally comes late. Verse is more effective for oral delivery and more easily retained in the memory. It is therefore a rather remarkable fact that English possessed a considerable body of prose literature in the ninth century, at a time when most other modern languages in Europe had barely developed a literature in verse. This unusual accomplishment was due to the inspiration of one man, King Alfred the Great, who ruled from 871 to 899. When he came to the throne, Alfred found that the learning which in the previous century had placed England in the forefront of Europe had greatly decayed. In an effort to restore his country to something like its former state, he undertook to provide for his people certain books in English, books which he deemed most essential to their welfare. In preparation for this task, he set about in mature life to learn Latin.

36. According to the information given above, King Alfred may most properly be regarded as the father of English

(A) poetry.　　　　　　　　(B) learning.

(C) prose.　　　　　　　　 (D) literature.

37. The writer suggests that the earliest poetry in England was
   (A) written in very difficult language.
   (B) not intended to be read silently.
   (C) never really popular with the public.
   (D) less original than later poetry.

38. According to the text given, England's learning had brought it to the forefront of Europe in the
   (A) seventh century.　　　　(B) eighth century.
   (C) ninth century.　　　　 (D) tenth century.

39. The writer believes that at the time of King Alfred most of the other modern languages of Europe had
   (A) their own literature in both verse and prose.
   (B) a literature in prose but not in verse.
   (C) neither a prose nor a verse literature.
   (D) a literature in verse but not in prose.

40. We may conclude from what we have been told that the books which King Alfred considered so very important were
   (A) already available in another language.
   (B) written largely in verse.
   (C) later translated into Latin, which he took so much pains to learn.
   (D) original with the king himself.

V、翻譯：英譯中（10％）

說明：把下面五題，譯成中文，並依題號順序，寫在試卷內。每題 2 分。

　例：I will back you up.
答案：我會支持你。

41. His arguments left me cold.

42. Always pick up your own litter after a picnic.

43. When a child, you must go by the wishes of your parents.

44. Most high school students are weighed down with exams.

45. He came of a line of people who knew a spade when they saw one.

VI、翻譯：中譯英（10％）

說明：把下面五題，譯成正確的英文，並依號碼順序，寫在試卷內。每題2分。

46. 我們必須尊敬長者。
47. 我恐怕他會反對我們的計劃。
48. 你能肯定他從不說謊嗎？
49. 貧而無諂，不如富而好禮。
50. 那五位男子和一位女子，是爲了投奔自由纔奪機（highjacked an airplane）的。

VII、英文作文：（20％）

說明：請用下面的題目作文，以80字爲度，不要太多或太少。寫在試卷內。

題目： A Taxi Ride

72年大學聯考英文試題詳解

I、**拼字：選出拼對的（多重選擇題）**

1. (**C D E**)　(A) *agressive* → aggressive〔ə'grɛsɪv〕*adj.* 具侵略性的
   (B) *sugestive* → suggestive〔səg'dʒɛstɪv, sə'dʒɛ-〕*adj.* 暗示的
   (C) *agreeable*〔ə'griəbḷ〕*adj.* 愉快的；和藹可親的
   (D) *sufferable*〔'sʌfərəbḷ〕*adj.* 可忍受的
   (E) *sluggish*〔'slʌgɪʃ〕*adj.* 遲緩的

2. (**A B D**)　(A) *convenient*〔kən'vinjənt〕*adj.* 方便的
   (B) *obedient*〔ə'bidɪənt〕*adj.* 服從的
   (C) *expereince* → experience〔ɪk'spɪrɪəns〕*n. , v.* 經驗
   (D) *reimburse*〔ˌriɪm'bɝs〕*vt.* 賠償
   (E) *primier* → premier〔'primɪɚ〕*n.* 首相；總理

3. (**C E**)　(A) *contemptable* → contemptible〔kən'tɛmptəbḷ〕*adj.* 卑鄙的
   (B) *irresponsable* → irresponsible〔ˌɪrɪ'spɑnsəbḷ〕
   　　adj. 不負責任的；沒有責任的
   (C) *adolescent*〔ˌædḷ'ɛsṇt〕*adj.* 青春期的　*n.* 青少年
   (D) *indepandent* → independent〔ˌɪndɪ'pɛndənt〕*adj.* 獨立的
   (E) *indispensable*〔ˌɪndɪs'pɛnsəbḷ〕*adj.* 不可缺少的

4. (**B C D**)　(A) *maintainance* → maintenance〔'mentənəns〕*n.* 維持
   (B) *insistence*〔ɪn'sɪstəns〕*n.* 堅持
   (C) *elevator*〔'ɛləˌvetɚ〕*n.* 電梯
   (D) *barometer*〔bə'rɑmətɚ〕*n.* 氣壓計
   (E) *photographor* → photographer〔fə'tɑgrəfɚ〕*n.* 攝影師

5. (**A D E**)　(A) *surrender*〔sə'rɛndɚ〕*vi. , vt.* 投降
   (B) *suspicius* → suspicious〔sə'spɪʃəs〕*adj.* 可疑的
   (C) *volunter* → volunteer〔ˌvɑlən'tɪr〕
   　　n. 志願者　*vt.* 自動申請　*vi.* 自願做
   (D) *embarrass*〔ɪm'bærəs〕*vt.* 使困窘
   (E) *ambassador*〔æm'bæsədɚ〕*n.* 大使

Ⅱ、發音：選出發音相同者（多重選擇題）

6. (**ABDE**) (A) bomb〔 bɑm 〕 *n.* 炸彈（字尾為 mb 的 b 不發音）

　(B) autumn〔ˊɔtəm 〕 *n.* 秋天（字尾為 mn 時的 n 不發音）

　(C) damp〔 dæmp 〕 *adj.* 潮濕的

　(D) come〔 kʌm 〕 *vi.* 來

　(E) hymn〔 hɪm 〕 *n.* 聖歌（字尾為 mn 時的 n 不發音）

7. (**ABCE**) (A) height〔 haɪt 〕 *n.* 高度

　(B) island〔ˊaɪlənd 〕 *n.* 島嶼
　　（ s 不發音的字還有 isle〔 aɪl 〕，debris〔ˊdebri , dəˊbri 〕）

　(C) sign〔 saɪn 〕 *n.* 標誌

　(D) quit〔 kwɪt 〕 *vt.* 停止　　*vi.* 辭職

　(E) gigantic〔 dʒaɪˊgæntɪk 〕 *adj.* 巨大的

8. (**B C**) (A) precious〔ˊprɛʃəs 〕 *adj.* 珍貴的（ ci ，ce 的 c 讀 /ʃ/ ）

　(B) scene〔 sin 〕 *n.* 風景；現場

　(C) psalm〔 sɑm 〕 *n.* 讚美詩（ ps 或 pn 為字首的 p 不發音）

　(D) vision〔ˊvɪʒən 〕 *n.* 視力；看法（母音加 sion 讀 /ʒən/ ）

　(E) lose〔 luz 〕 *vt.* 失去　*vi.* 失敗
　　（ s 之前為母音字母，之後亦為母音字母或 y 時，讀 /z/ ）

9. (**CDE**) (A) tidy〔ˊtaɪdɪ 〕 *adj.* 整齊的

　(B) express〔 ɪkˊsprɛs 〕 *vt.* 表達　*n.* 快車

　(C) yield〔 jild 〕 *vi.* , *vt.* 生產　*n.* 收穫（量）

　(D) perceive〔 pɚˊsiv 〕 *vt.* 察覺

　(E) unique〔 juˊnik 〕 *adj.* 獨一無二的

10. (**D E**) (A) admiral〔ˊædmərəl 〕 *n.* 海軍總司令

　(B) passage〔ˊpæsɪdʒ 〕 *n.* 通行；走道

　(C) foundation〔 faʊnˊdeʃən 〕 *n.* 基礎

　(D) academic〔ˌækəˊdɛmɪk 〕 *adj.* 學術的

　(E) astonish〔 əˊstɑnɪʃ 〕 *vt.* 使驚訝

Ⅲ、綜合測驗（單一選擇題）

第一部分

11.（**B**）那海岸未設防，而處於易受攻擊的狀態。

　* lie〔laɪ〕「處於（某種狀態）」，是不完全的不及物動詞，其過去式
　是 lay；open to attack 是主詞補語，其中 to attack 是副詞片語，
　修飾 open。須注意本答案易和另一慣用語 lay oneself open to「使
　自己易受…；使自己暴露…」混淆，其中的 lay，作「使得」解，是
　不完全的及物動詞。

　　　(A) 須改為過去式 lay。
　　　(C) laid 是 lay〔le〕的過去式，作「放置；產卵」解，不合句意。
　　　(D) lain〔len〕是 lie 的過去分詞，不可單獨作主要動詞用。

　　　undefended〔͵ʌndɪ'fɛndɪd〕*adj.* 未設防的

12.（**D**）請坐。

$$
\begin{cases}
\textit{be seated } 坐下 \\
= \textit{seat oneself}（seat 是反身動詞，在主動語態中要接反身代名詞，\\
\quad 詳見文法寶典 p.281。）\\
= \textit{sit down} \\
= \textit{take one's seat} \\
= \textit{take}（\textit{or have}）\textit{a seat} \\
= \textit{take}（\textit{or have}）\textit{a chair}
\end{cases}
$$

13.（**A**）那男孩任性的行為，使得他母親多夜失眠。

　* 主詞 (*sth.*) + cost + *sb.* + *sth.*（時間、金錢、勞力等）；cost
　在此作「使受損失；犧牲」解。

　　　(B) take 的句型應是：
　　　　It + takes + (*sb.*) + *sth.*（時間或勞力）+ to + 原形動詞
　　　(C) spend 的句型應是：

$$
\begin{cases}
主詞 (\textit{sb.}) + spend + 時間 + (\textit{in}) + Ving \\
主詞 (\textit{sb.}) + spend + 金錢 + on + \textit{sth.}
\end{cases}
$$

　　　（cost，take，spend 的用法詳見文法寶典 p.299）
　　　(D) rob「搶劫」，後面須接 of，且與句意不合。

　　　wayward〔'wewəd〕*adj.* 任性的；頑強的

14. (**D**) There is no telling **when** *they can be here today.*

無法得知他們今天將在何時到達。

* when 引導的名詞子句，作動名詞 telling 的受詞。其他答案用法不合。

$$\begin{cases} \textbf{There is no} + 動名詞（片語）\cdots是不可能的 \\ = \textbf{It is impossible to} + 原形動詞（詳見文法寶典 p.439） \\ = \textbf{No one can} + 原形動詞 \\ = \textbf{We cannot} + 原形動詞 \end{cases}$$

15. (**B**) 上星期日天氣很好，我們去爬山。

* It being a fine day last Sunday 是獨立分詞構句，其意義上的主詞 It 和主要子句的主詞 we 不同，故不可省略。（見文法寶典 p.462）

(A) being … Sunday 是分詞構句，因 we 不能做其意義上的主詞，故應保留表示天氣的 It 為其意義上的主詞，形成獨立分詞構句。

(C) 若用 As，須改為 As it was a fine day last Sunday, …。

(D) 若用 The weather，須改為 The weather being fine last Sunday, …。

16. (**C**) 那侍者花了很長的時間侍候我們。

* 本句亦可寫為：The waiter took a very long time *to serve* us.（take 的用法參照第 13 題 (B)）

(A) treat〔trit〕*vt.* 對待；請客。主人接待客人可以用 treat，但侍者對客人通常用 serve，不用 treat。

(B) await〔ə'wet〕*vt.* 等待

多用於表示等待抽象的事物，例如：await one's decision「等待某人的決定」；await one's instruction「等待某人的指示」。

(C) serve〔sɝv〕*vt. , vi.* 服務；侍候

(D) deal〔dil〕*vi.* 交易；對待（作此義解時，需和 with 連用）

17. (**C**) The explorers set out on their hazardous journey *into the unknown.*

探險家開始到未知之地的冒險旅行。

* *set out on a journey*（*or* trip, tour）「出發去旅行」on 可表示目的，含有「從事於」的意思，後面常接 gusiness，errand，journey，trip 之類的字。如：He was sent *on* an errand.。（詳見文法寶典 p.594）into the unknown 是形容詞片語，修飾 journey。

(A) set out to＋V 打算；企圖

(C) set out for＋地點 「動身前往（某地）」，例如：Marian set out for Canada yesterday.

(D) 無 set out along 的用法。

explorer〔ɪkˈsplorɚ〕*n.* 探險家

hazardous〔ˈhæzədəs〕*adj.* 危險的；冒險的

18. (**A**) I would appreciate it *if you could finish this work by May.*

如果你能在五月前將此工作完成，我會十分感激的。

* by 「最遲在…之前」，表示某事最遲在某期限前完成，須與非持續性動作的動詞（如 start，reach，finish 等）連用，如：I will start *by* 6 o'clock.（詳見文法寶 p.613）

(B) until 「直到」，表某件事持續到某時為止，須與持續性動詞（如 wait，go on 等）連用（詳見文法寶典 p.491）。

(C) prior〔ˈpraɪɚ〕*adj.* 在前的；若表「在…之前」則須與 to 連用。

(D) up to＝until，並無「最遲在…之前」的含意，其慣用語如下：up to the present，up to then，up to now。

19. (**D**) *Oh, Jane,* you've broken still another glass. You ought to have been careful *when you washed it.*

喔，珍，妳又打破另一個玻璃杯了。妳在清洗時應更加小心的。

* 「ought to（＝should）have＋過去分詞」表過去該做而未做的事（詳見文法寶典 p.320）。Oh 是感嘆詞，Jane 是稱呼主格，都是和句子其他部分沒有文法關連的獨立語（詳見文法寶典 p.19）。still 是副詞，置於動詞前後，表動作與狀態的持續（詳見文法寶典 p.249）。

(A) ought to＋V，其中 to 不可省略，且不合句中需要的假設法。

(B) 缺少動詞，且不合句中需要的假設法。

(C) 應改為(D)的形式。

20. (**D**) Mr. Wang bought that piece of land *near the shore with a view to building a summer house there.*

王先生買了那塊濱海的土地，是為了要在那兒造一棟夏季別墅。

* ***with a view to = with an eye to***「為了」，其中 to 是介詞，須接
動名詞為受詞，表目的（詳見文法寶典 p.514）。near the shore 是形
容詞片語，修飾 land；with … there 是副詞片語，修飾 bought，表
目的。

(C) having built 是完成式的動名詞，表比主要動詞先發生的動作
或狀態，故與句意不合。

$$
\left\{
\begin{array}{l}
\textit{with a view to 為了} \\
\textit{= with an eye to} \\
\textit{= with the view of}
\end{array}
\right.
\qquad
\left\{
\begin{array}{l}
\textit{= with the purpose of} \\
\textit{= for the sake of} \\
\textit{= for the purpose of}
\end{array}
\right.
$$

summer house 夏季別墅

第二部分

Large numbers of people *nowadays* might define a holiday as "traveling
to another part *of the country or of the world for a week or two once
or twice a year.*"

目前有許多人可能給假期下的定義是：一年一兩次到某國家或世界的另一部
分，去旅遊一兩個星期。

* nowadays 是副詞，作形容詞用，修飾 people（副詞代替形容詞詳見文法寶
典 p.228）；***define*** A ***as*** B「把 A 定義為 B」，as 之後的 traveling …
year 作受詞補語（詳見文法寶典 p.500）；of the … world 是形容詞片語，
修飾 part；for … year 是由兩個副詞片語組成：for a week or two
(*weeks*)和 once (*a year*) or twice a year，修飾 traveling。

nowadays〔'navə,dez〕*adv.* 現今；目前
define〔dɪ'faɪn〕*vt.* 下定義；詳細說明
mass〔mæs〕*n.* 塊；大多數；大量
amount〔ə'maʊnt〕*n.* 總數；數量總計　*vi.* 總計

21.(**B**) ***large numbers of = a large number of = a great number of = a
good many of = many***「許多的」是表數的形容詞（片詞）。crowd，
mass 表「許多的」，應寫作 a crowd of 和 a mass of。amount 表「數
量」，其後只能接不可數名詞，如：a large amount of work；a
small amount of sugar。

But *for* me personally a holiday does *not necessarily* require a lot of travel.
Quite the opposite.
但是，對我個人而言，假期未必需要許多旅遊。而且是完全相反。

* But 在此作轉承語，連接前面的句子。for me personally 是副詞片語，
  修飾其後的句子。not necessarily「未必」，是表部分否定的副詞片語
  （詳見文法寶典 p.658）。Quite the opposite 是省去 it is 的省略句。

　　personally〔ˈpɝsn̩lɪ〕*adv.* 親自地；就本人而言
　　necessarily〔ˈnɛsəˌsɛrəlɪ, ˌnɛsəˈsɛrəlɪ〕*adv.* 必要地；必然地
　　opposite〔ˈɑpəzɪt〕*n.* 相反的人或物　*adj.* 相反的
　　whereas〔hwɛrˈæz〕*conj.* 然而　　reversely〔rɪˈvɝslɪ〕*adv.* 顛倒地
　　contradictorily〔ˌkɑntrəˈdɪktərɪlɪ〕*adv.* 矛盾地；對立地
　　on the other hand 另一方面

22. (**A**) yet with，其中 with 雖可接 me 作受詞，但不合句意；whereas「然
　　　　而」，although「雖然」均是連接詞，須接子句。

23. (**D**) Reversely，Contradictorily，On the other hand 只是單字或片語，
　　　　和答案的省略句不同，不能接句點。

In fact, *for the past twenty years,* it has meant no travel at all, ***because***
I would define a holiday as " *a period of time* in **which** *you do something*
completely different from your normal routine. "
事實上，過去二十年來，假期一直意謂著完全不旅行，因為我給假期下的定義是：
一段你做些完全不同於你的例行工作的時期。

* ***In fact***「事實上」是副詞片語，修飾全句，for...years 也是副詞片語，
  修飾 meant，表時間；because 引導的副詞子句，修飾 meant，其中 of
  time 和 in which … routine，分別是形容詞片語和子句，修飾 period；
  completely different … routine 是形容詞片語，修飾 something。

　　mean〔min〕*vt.* 意謂著　　normal〔ˈnɔrml̩〕*adj.* 正常的；正規的
　　routine〔ruˈtin〕*n.* 例行公事；日常工作
　　schedule〔ˈskɛdʒul〕*n.* 時間表

24. (**A**) (A) 例行工作。(B) 生活 (C) 時間表 (D) 時間，本答案用 normal routine 而不用 normal life，主要是和前文 do something 相對稱。routine 意指「例行公事」，剛好和 something 相對。

So, *by my definition*, a holiday means *roughly* the same **as a complete change**. **And** that might *even be work* **as long as** it is not the same kind of work **that** one does the rest of the time.

因此，依照我的定義，假期大致上意指一種完全的改變。而且，只要它和人其餘時間所做的工作不相同，那甚至可以是工作。

* *So*「因此」，在此作轉承語，連接前面的句子。by my definition 是副詞片語，修飾其後的句子。roughly 是副詞，修飾 same（詳見文法寶典 p.228），as … change 是形容詞片語，修飾 same。And 是對等連接詞，在此作轉承語，連接前面的句子。*as long as* = *if only*「只要」，引導的副詞子句，修飾 be，表條件（詳見文法寶典 p.520），其中 that one … time 是形容詞子句，修飾 work。of the time 是形容詞片語，修飾 rest。

   definition〔͵dɛfəˈnɪʃən〕*n.* 定義　　roughly〔ˈrʌflɪ〕*adv.* 大致上；大約
   complete〔kəmˈplit〕*adj.* 完全的

25. (**D**) even be work，even「甚至」是副詞，修飾 be，might 在此不是 may 的過去式，而是對現在或未來的推測，可能性比 may 小，其後接原形動詞 be（might 的用法詳見文法寶典 p.317）；work 是抽象名詞，不須加冠詞。

The thing *I remember most vividly about my early childhood* was the very first time *I was taken to the seaside.*

有關我童年記憶最深刻的事情，正是我頭一遭被帶到海邊去。

* I remember … childhood 是省略 that 或 which 的形容詞子句，修飾 thing；I was … seaside 是省略 when 的形容詞子句，修飾 time。（詳見文法寶典 p.243）

   vividly〔ˈvɪvɪdlɪ〕*adv.* 生動地；鮮明地
   childhood〔ˈtʃaɪld͵hʊd〕*n.* 童年　　seaside〔ˈsi͵saɪd〕*n.* 海邊

26. (**C**) take 作「帶領；引導」解，句中主詞 I 是被帶領者，故須用被動語態。was called「被召喚」，雖是被動語態，但不合句意。

I know it was a *gloriously* hot day, **but** I would be lying *if I said I had a clear recollection of the journey to the coast.* My parents have *often* told me **that** *I was sick most of the way.*

我知道那是一個極愉快的熱天，但是，如果我說我對那次海濱之旅記憶清楚的話，我是在撒謊。我的父母時常告訴我，一路上我大半時候都不舒服。

> * but 連接的另一對等子句，其中 if … coast 是副詞子句，修飾 lying，是表與現在事實相反的假設法；of the … coast 是形容詞片語，修飾 recollection。 that…way 是名詞子句，作 told 的直接受詞，其中 most of the way 是副詞片語，修飾 was。
>
> > gloriously〔ˊglorɪəslɪ,ˊglɔr-〕*adv.* 極愉快地；光榮地
> > recollection〔͵rɛkəˊlɛkʃən〕*n.* 記憶；回憶

27. (**D**) 「If＋主詞＋過去式…，主詞＋would＋原形動詞…」是表與現在事實相反的假設法（詳見文法寶典 p.361），本答案不選 would lie，而選 would be lying，是表說話當時正在進行的動作。

Fortunately I have no memory at all *of those unpleasant hours.* **But** I shall *never* forget running down the hot sand and into the "big pond", **as** *I called it.*

幸好，我對那些不愉快的時刻，一點也沒有印象。但是我絕不會忘記跑下熱沙灘，進入我所謂的「大池塘」的情形。

> * Fortunately 是副詞，修飾全句，of … hours 是形容詞片語，修飾 memory。But 是轉承語，連接前面的句子。as I called it 是補述用法的形容詞子句，修飾 big pond as 在子句中，作受詞補語。（詳見文法寶典 p.160）
>
> > memory〔ˊmɛmərɪ〕*n.* 記憶　　unpleasant〔ʌnˊplɛznt〕*adj.* 使人不愉快的
> > pond〔pɑnd〕*n.* 池塘　　reminder〔rɪˊmaɪndɚ〕*n.* 提醒物；提醒者
> > recognition〔͵rɛkəgˊnɪʃən〕*n.* 認識；認出

28. (**B**)　(A) 提醒物　　(B) 記憶　　(C) 認識　　(D) 思想

It was the Atlantic, ***and although*** *the day was hot*, the sea was *extremely* cold.

那是大西洋，而雖然當日天氣很熱，但是海水卻非常冷。

> * and 連接的另一對等子句之中，although 引導的副詞子句，修飾 was，
> 表讓步。
>
>> Atlantic〔ət'læntɪk〕*n.* 大西洋
>> extremely〔ɪk'strimlɪ〕*adv.* 非常地；極端地

29. (**C**)　(A) pebble〔'pɛbḷ〕*n.* 小圓石
　　　　　(B) beach〔bitʃ〕*n.* 海邊
　　　　　(C) 海
　　　　　(D) shore〔ʃor，ʃɔr〕*n.* 海岸

It was the shock *of that first voluntary baptism, I know,* ***which*** *was to this day* made *me very wary of bathing in the sea.*

我知道那第一回自動洗禮的震撼，到今天還使我在海裡游泳非常小心。

> * It was … which 是表加強語氣的用法（詳見文法寶典 p.115）。I know 是
> 插入語，可當作全句的主要子句來看，插入語以外的部分，等於主要子
> 句的受詞，可寫成 I know it was the shock of that first voluntary
> baptism which …（詳見文法寶典 p.650）；to this day 是副詞片語，修飾
> made。in the sea 是副詞片語，修飾 bathing，表地點。
>
>> shock〔ʃɑk〕*n.* 震撼；震動
>> voluntary〔'vɑlən,tɛrɪ〕*adj.* 自動的；志願的
>> baptism〔'bæptɪzəm〕*n.* 洗禮
>> wary〔'wɛrɪ，'werɪ，'wærɪ〕*adj.* 小心的；警覺的
>> bathing〔'beðɪŋ〕*n.* 游泳；沐浴
>> cause〔kɔz〕*vt.* 起因於；致使

30. (**D**) made「使得」是不完全及物動詞，接形容詞片語 wary … sea 作受詞補語。continued「繼續」，stayed「停留」，caused「致使」都是完全及物動詞，不需接受詞補語。

IV、閱讀測驗：（單一選擇題）

第一部分

31. (**B**) He has *completely* abandoned himself to despair.
　　　他徹底地自暴自棄。

　　　　　(A) 他忘記了他的絕望。　　　(B) 他非常絕望。
　　　　　(C) 他忙得沒有時間絕望。　　(D) 他完全放棄了絕望。

　　＊ *abandon oneself to* = *addict oneself to*「沈溺於～」，abandon，addict 是反身動詞，to 是介系詞，須接名詞或動名詞為受詞。類似的還有：*accustom oneself to*；*adapt oneself to*；*address oneself to* 等。（詳見文法寶典 p.281）

　　　　despair〔dɪˋspɛr〕*n.* 絕望　　*abandon oneself to despair* 自暴自棄

32. (**D**) The statement *made by the witness* ties in with the evidence *the police already had.*
　　　證人的陳述，和警方已經掌握的證據有關連。

　　　　　(A) 證人的陳述和警方收集的證據完全相同。
　　　　　(B) 證人所言是一回事，警方已經掌握的證據又是一回事。
　　　　　(C) 證人的陳述和警方發現的證據無關。
　　　　　(D) 證人的陳述和警方的證據有密切的關連。

　　＊ made…witness 是分詞片語，作形容詞用，修飾 statement；the police already had 是省略 which 或 that 的形容詞子句，修飾 evidence。

　　　　statement〔ˋstetmənt〕*n.* 陳述　witness〔ˋwɪtnɪs〕*n.* 證人
　　　　tie in with 與…有關連　　evidence〔ˋɛvədəns〕*n.* 證據
　　　　…*one thing*,…*another* (thing)　…是一回事，…是另一回事
　　　　⎰ *one and the same* 完全相同
　　　　⎱ = *the very same*
　　　　have no bearing on 與～無關　　bearing〔ˋbɛrɪŋ〕*n.* 關係

33. (**D**) Tom should have known better *when he asked her to go out with him, her parents being so very old-fashioned.*

邀請她一起外出的時候，湯姆就應該知道那是不對的，因為她的父母非常的守舊。

　　(A) 湯姆沒有邀請她一起外出，因為他實際上並不了解她。
　　(B) 湯姆知道因為她父母是有名的守舊者，她無論如何也不會和他一起出去，所以沒有邀請她。
　　(C) 她拒絕和湯姆一起外出。
　　(D) 她不顧父母的強烈反對，而和湯姆一起外出。

＊「should＋have＋過去分詞」表過去應該做而未做(詳見文法寶典 p.311)；when 引導的副詞子句，修飾 known，表時間；her parents … old-fashioned 是表理由的對等子句 for her parents were …簡化而來的獨立分詞構句。(詳見文法寶典 p.462)

　　know better 知道～是不對的；不致於笨到～
　　old-fashioned〔'old'fæʃənd〕*adj.* 老式的；守舊的
　　objection〔əb'dʒɛkʃən〕*n.* 反對

34. (**B**) Tom：There's been a steady increase *in the number of cars on the road.*

Jane：Yes, and it's high time the Government does something about it.

Jane thinks ***that*** *immediate* action is called for to *control the growth.*

湯姆：馬路上汽車的數量在持續地增加。
　珍：是啊，現在政府也該拿點辦法來管管了。

珍認為 ＿＿＿＿＿＿＿＿＿＿

　　(A) 政府已經在控制汽車的增加。
　　(B) 要求政府緊急行動以控制汽車的增加。
　　(C) 政府減少汽車的數量是要花時間的。
　　(D) 政府應該找恰當的時候，使某些老舊的汽車離開公路。

* in … road 是形容詞片語，修飾 increase；其中 on the road 又作形容詞片語，修飾 cars。「it's high time＋直說法現在式」為口語的用法。to … growth 為副詞片語，修飾 called，表目的。

steay (ˈstɛdɪ) *adj.* 持續的；穩定的
increase (ˈɪnkris , ˈɪŋk-) *n.* 增加　　***call for*** 要求；需要
immediate action 緊急行動　　reduce (rɪˈdjus) *vt.* 減少

35 (**A**) Few of the people *in adult-education classes across the nation* seem to miss the traditional trappings *of colleges* *or* the prestige *that usually is attached to instruction from professors loaded with academic honors.* Most such people are looking for teachers *who have experience rather than credentials.*

全國接受成人教育的人之中，極少人似乎會懷念大學傳統的虛飾，或通常與有學術榮譽教授教導有關的聲望。多數這樣的人 _____

(A) 與其說在找有資格的老師，不如說在找有經驗的老師。
(B) 上課只為了學位。
(C) 較適合評審教授的學術資格。
(D) 惋惜他們年輕的時候，沒有上大學接受名教授教導的機會。

* in adult … nation 是形容詞片語，修飾 people；of colleges 是形容詞片語，修飾 trappings，or 連接 trappings 和 prestige，作 miss 的受詞；that 引導的形容詞子句，修飾 prestige，其中 from … honors 是形容詞片語，修飾 instruction；loaded … honors 是形容詞片語，修飾 professors。who 引導形容詞子句，修飾 teachers。

adult (əˈdʌlt , ˈædʌlt) *adj.* 成人的；成長的
miss (mɪs) *vt.* 惋惜　　traditional (trəˈdɪʃənḷ) *adj.* 傳統的
trappings (ˈtræpɪŋz) *n.,pl.* 裝飾物　　prestige (ˈprɛstɪdʒ) *n.* 聲望
prestigious (prɛsˈtɪdʒɪəs) *adj.* 享有聲望的
attach (əˈtætʃ) *vt.* 附屬；繫上
instruction (ɪnˈstrʌkʃən) *n.* 教導；教育
academic (ˌækəˈdɛmɪk) *adj.* 學術的；學校的
honors (ˈɑnəz) *n.,pl.* 榮譽　　credential (krɪˈdɛnʃəl) *n.* 學歷
solely (ˈsollɪ) *adv.* 只是　　qualify (ˈkwɑləˌfaɪ) *vt.* 使有資格

第二部分

In the development of literature, prose *generally* comes late. Verse is
more effective *for oral delivery* and *more easily* retained *in the memory.*

在文學的發展中，散文通常來得較遲。韻文對於口頭傳誦較爲有效，而且更
容易保留在記憶裡。

* In … literature 是副詞片語，修飾 comes。for oral delivery 是副詞片語，
  修飾 effective。 in the memory 也是副詞片語，修飾 retained，表地點。

> literature〔'lɪtərətʃɚ〕n. 文學　　prose〔proz〕n. 散文
> verse〔vɜs〕n. 韻文；詩　　effective〔ə'fɛktɪv,ɪ-〕adj. 有效的
> oral〔'orəl,'ɔrəl〕adj. 口頭的　　retain〔rɪ'ten〕vt. 保留
> memory〔'mɛmərɪ〕n. 記憶

It is *therefore* a *rather* remarkable fact *that English possessed a considerable body of prose literature in the ninth century, at a time* when *most
other modern languages in Europe had barely developed a literature in
verse.*

因此，這是一個頗爲值得注意的事實，即英國文學在第九世紀的時候，擁有相當
數量的散文，而同時大多數其他的歐洲現代語文，幾乎尚未發展韻文文學。

* therefore「因此」在此作轉承語，連接前面的句子。It 是形式主詞，其後
  的 that 子句，才是眞主詞；in … century 是副詞片語，修飾 possessed，
  表時間；at a time … verse 是 in … century 的同位語，其中 when … verse
  是形容詞子句，修飾 time（詳見文法寶典 p.242）；in Europe 和 in verse
  是形容詞片語，分別修飾其前的 languages 和 literature。barely「幾乎
  不」是副詞，修飾 developed。

> remarkable〔rɪ'mɑrkəbḷ〕adj. 值得注意的
> possess〔pə'zɛs〕vt. 擁有
> considerable〔kən'sɪdərəbḷ〕adj. 相當多的
> barely〔'bɛrlɪ〕adj. 幾乎不；僅
> body〔'bɑdɪ〕n. 數量　　*at a time* 同時

This unusual accomplishment was due to the inspiration *of one man,* King

Alfred the Great, **who** ruled *from 871 to 899.*

這種非凡的成就是由於一個人鼓吹的結果 —— 阿佛烈大帝，在位期間是西元 871 年到 899 年。

* of one man 是形容詞片語，修飾 inspiration， King … Great 是 man 的同位語， who 引導的是補述用法的形容詞子句，其中 from … 899 是副詞片語，修飾 ruled，表時間。

unusual〔ʌn'juʒʊəl〕*adj.* 非凡的；罕有的
accomplishment〔ə'kɑmplɪʃmənt〕*n.* 完成；成就

$$\begin{cases} \textbf{\textit{due to}} \ (\text{一般書上說只可放在 be 動詞後，事實上可放在句首}) \\ = \textbf{\textit{owing to}} \\ = \textbf{\textit{thanks to}} \ (\text{通常用於表好的原因，如用於壞的原因時，則含諷刺意味}) \\ = \textbf{\textit{because of}} \ \text{因為；由於} \end{cases}$$

inspiration〔͵ɪnspə'reʃən〕*n.* 靈感；鼓吹的人或事
Alfred〔'ælfrɪd〕*n.* 阿佛烈（人名）

When he came to the throne, Alfred found *that* the learning [*which* in

the previous century had placed England in the forefront of Europe] had

greatly decayed.

即位的時候，阿佛烈發現，前一世紀使得英國領先歐洲的學術，已經大為衰微。

* when 引導的副詞子句，修飾 found； that … decayed 是名詞子句，作 found 的受詞，其中 which … Europe 是形容詞子句，修飾 learning， in … century 和 in … Europe 是副詞片語，都修飾 placed，分別表時間和地點。

throne〔θron〕*n.* 王位；寶座
come to the throne 即位；登基
learning〔'lɝnɪŋ〕*n.* 學術；學問
previous〔'privɪəs〕*adj.* 先前的
forefront〔'for͵frʌnt , 'fɔr-〕*n.* 最前部；最前線
decay〔dɪ'ke〕*vi.* 衰退；衰微

In an effort to restore his country to something like its former state, he undertook to provide *for his people* certain books *in English,* books ***which*** he deemed most essential to their welfare. *In preparation for this task,* he set about *in mature life* to learn Latin.

在努力使他的國家恢復至昔日情況時候，他著手供給人民某些英文書藉，他認為這些書對人民的福祉至關重要。爲了準備這項工作，他成年即開始學習拉丁文。

* In … state 是副詞片語，修飾 undertook，其中 to restore … state 是形容詞片語，修飾 effort；to provide … welfare 是不定詞片語，當名詞用，作 undertook 的受詞，其中 certain books … welfare 是名詞片語，當 provide 的受詞，由於太長而倒裝至副詞片語 for his people 之後（詳見文法寶典 p.639）；books which … welfare 是前面的 books 的同位語，其中 which 引導的形容詞子句，修飾 books。In … task 和 in mature life 是副詞片語，修飾 set，分別表目的和時間。

effort〔ˋɛfət〕n. 努力　　restore〔rɪˋstor , -ˋstɔr〕vt. 恢復；重建
undertake〔͵ʌndəˋtek〕vt. 從事；著手
deem〔dim〕vt. , vi. 認為　essential〔əˋsɛnʃəl〕adj. 必要的；基本的
welfar〔ˋwɛl͵fɛr , -͵fær〕n. 福祉；福利
set about 開始；著手　　mature〔məˋtjʊr , -ˋtʃʊr〕adj. 成熟的

36. (**C**) 根據上文，阿佛烈王可能最適合被當作英國 ＿＿＿＿＿＿＿ 之父。

  (A) 詩　　　　(B) 學術　　　　(C) <u>散文</u>　　　　(D) 文學

37. (**B**) 作者暗示最早的英國詩 ＿＿＿＿＿＿＿。

  (A) 以非常難的語言寫成。　　(B) <u>不是要被靜靜地閱讀。</u>
  (C) 從未真正在坊間流行過。　　(D) 比後來的詩缺少創意。

intend〔ɪnˋtɛnd〕vt. 打算
original〔əˋrɪdʒənḷ〕adj. 獨創的；原來的

38. (**B**) 根據本文，英國學術在 ＿＿＿＿＿＿＿ 居於歐洲領先地位。

  (A) 七世紀　　(B) <u>八世紀</u>　　(C) 九世紀　　(D) 十世紀

39. (**D**) 作者相信阿佛烈王在位的時候，其他的歐洲現代語言 ＿＿＿＿＿＿＿＿＿ 。

　　　　(A) 有自己的韻文和散文。　　　(B) 有散文但沒有韻文。

　　　　(C) 旣無散文也無韻文。　　　　(D) 有韻文但沒有散文。

40. (**A**) 從告訴我們的事情中，我們可以推論，阿佛烈王認爲非常重要的書籍

　　　　(A) 已用於另一種語言中。

　　　　(B) 大半是用韻文寫的。

　　　　(C) 後來被譯成他費盡苦心去學習的拉丁文。

　　　　(D) 是國王本人獨創的。

　　　　available〔əˋveləbḷ〕*adj.* 可獲得的；可用的

V、英譯中：

41. His arguments left me cold.

　　他的論點並沒有說動我。

　　　　　　　argument〔ˋɑrgjəmənt〕*n.* 理由；論點

　　　　　　　leave a person cold（ *or* ***cool*** ）使人不起反應；使人不感興趣

42. *Always* pick up your own litter *after a picnic.*

　　每次郊遊後，一定要把自己的垃圾撿起來。

　　　　　　pick up 拾起　　litter〔ˋlɪtɚ〕*n.* 垃圾；雜物

43. *When* a child, you must go by the wishes *of your parents.*

　　小孩子要聽父母的話。

　　或孩童時代，一切要依父母的期望行事。

　　* When a child 是由副詞子句省略了主詞和 be 動詞 *you are*，而形成的
　　　副詞片語。（詳見文法寶典 p.462,645 ）

　　　　　　go by 遵照

44. Most high school students are weighed down with exams.

　　大部分高中生都被考試壓得喘不過氣來。

　　　　　　be weighed down with 被～壓迫；被～壓得喘不過氣來

45. He came of a line of people *who knew a spade* *when they saw one.*
他出身於世代務農之家。

* 本句直譯爲：他出身於凡是見到鋤頭，就懂得鋤頭用法的那些人的家族。
可引申爲：「他出身於農家」。

> *come of* 出身於　spade〔sped〕*n.* 鏟子；鋤頭
> *a line of people* 一系列的人（同一祖先下來的）

VI、中譯英：

46. 我們必須尊敬長者。
We must respect our elders.
We must respect the elderly.

47. 我恐怕他會反對我們的計劃。
I am afraid he might oppose our plan.

> *oppose oneself to* 反對
> = *be opposed to*
> = *oppose* (*vt.*)
> = *have an objection to*
> = *object to*

48. 你能肯定他從不說謊嗎？
Are you sure he never lies?
Are you sure he has never told lies?
Are you sure he has never lied?

49. 貧而無諂，不如富而好禮。
One would rather be rich and courteous *than poor, though unfawning.*
Being rich and polite is better *than being poor without flattery.*
One should rather be wealthy and courteous *than be poor and disdain flattery.*

> *would rather* A *than* B 寧願 A 而不願 B
> courteous〔'kɜtɪəs〕*adj.* 有禮貌的
> unfawning〔ʌn'fɔnɪŋ〕*adj.* 不奉承的
> disdain〔dɪs'den〕*vt.* 輕視；瞧不起

50. 那五位男子和一位女子，是為了投奔自由纔奪機 (highjacked an airplane) 的。

Those five men and one woman highjacked an airplane so as to

(or in order to) seek freedom.

不定詞片語 so as to seek freedom 作副詞用，修飾 highjacked，表目的。

highjack〔ˈhaɪˌdʒæk〕 *vt.* 劫持

VII、**作文**：（參考範例）

A Taxi Ride

One afternoon, I, as usual, left my school after the classes were over. My intention was to go home by bus as I always do, but it was unusual in that every bus was crowded with many students and tourists. ***After second thoughts***, I decided to take a taxi for a change.

A few minutes later I finally caught up with a taxi. You may feel it is strange that I had to "catch up with" a taxi. The reason was that my school is situated in the suburbs where taxis are rarely seen.

However, my biggest surprise was that the taxi driver was my classmate in junior high school. On my way home we talked a lot and had a good time. He said that it was really his lucky day to be able to meet me and so he insisted on driving me home for free.

After I had said good-bye to my friend and had arrived home, I was reminded of a proverb which states : "It's a small world."

一次搭計程車的經驗

一天下午，如往常般，上完課我離開了學校。本來打算和以前一樣搭公車回家，可是奇怪的是，每輛公車都擠滿學生與觀光客。三思後，我決定改搭計程車。

幾分鐘以後，我終於逮著一部計程車。也許你會對我必須「逮著」一部計程車而感到奇怪。理由是我的學校位於很少見到計程車的郊區。

然而，最令我驚訝的是，那個計程車司機居然是我的國中同學。在回家的路上，我們談了許多也很愉快。他說那天真幸運能遇到我，所以堅持免費載我回家。

我跟他道過再見回到家後，想起一句諺語：「這個世界真小啊！」

七十一學年度大學暨獨立學院入學考試
英 文 試 題

※ 本學科除作文外，共有 45 題。測驗題（1–35）答在答案卡上；翻譯（36–45）和作文答在作文及翻譯試卷內。

I、拼字（5%）：（多重選擇題）

說明：下列 1–5 題，每題 5 個英語單字，其中至少有兩個是拼錯的。把拼錯的單字標出在答案卡上。一題全對得 1 分，答錯倒扣 1/25 分；不答者得 0 分。

例：(A) remain　(B) progress　(C) studing　(D) fortunete　(E) glory

答案：A B C D E
(填塗格)

1. (A) beleive　　(B) creat　　(C) seperate　　(D) perceive　　(E) proceed
2. (A) gymnasium (B) grammer　(C) begger　　(D) deligent　　(E) immense
3. (A) sergant　　(B) grocery　(C) recompanse (D) excede　　(E) ingenous
4. (A) descendant (B) immitate　(C) edible　　(D) guerrila　　(E) evidance
5. (A) shield　　(B) disciple　(C) desease　　(D) fragrence　(E) pesimism

II、發音（5%）：（多重選擇題）

說明：下列 6–10 題，每題 5 個英語單字，每個單字中有一個或二個字母畫有底線。找出畫有底線的字母中發音相同的字母，然後在答案卡上將正確的答案標出。一題全對得 1 分，答錯倒扣 1/25 分；不答者得 0 分。

例：(A) column　(B) mountain　(C) knight　(D) resign　(E) nine

答案：A B C D E
(填塗格)

6. (A) pose　　(B) wood　　(C) choose　　(D) blue　　(E) shoot
7. (A) pen　　　(B) pain　　(C) pan　　　(D) make　　(E) captain
8. (A) whole　　(B) which　　(C) home　　(D) ghost　　(E) phase
9. (A) barber　(B) chamber　(C) bribery　　(D) bomber　(E) club
10. (A) resist　(B) sign　　(C) vision　　(D) reserve　(E) pressure

Ⅲ、習慣用法、詞彙、文法（20％）：（單一選擇題）

說明：下面是一段有 10 個空白的文章，文章下面是 10 個選擇題，各有四個答案，
選出其中最恰當的一項，在答案卡上標出。這選出的一項，如填入空白，
便可以使該一句子的前後文意思完整，文法正確，也合乎習慣。每題 2 分；
答錯的倒扣⅔分。

Teachers of English who want to be responsible yet realistic about teaching usage and mechanics to today's writing students face a chronic ___(11)___ . What should our priority be? Should we insist that we distinguish between lie and lay or sit and sat, and that we use a singular pronoun after everybody? If we do, we risk ___(12)___ as if we ___(13)___ the posture of the protectors of pure English ___(14)___ the barbarians who will corrupt the language if we relax our ___(15)___ . On the other hand, if we take the attitude that ___(16)___ students to generate content and organize it in a coherent pattern should be our major goal ___(17)___ surface features are comparatively unimportant, we open ourselves ___(18)___ from readers who are genuinely ___(19)___ good English. There are people who claim that we are not doing our job. And they imply that in their day English teachers were a different breed who had standards and ___(20)___ no one left their classrooms without being able to write.

11. (A) matter   (B) instruction   (C) dilemma   (D) failure

12. (A) looking   (B) to look   (C) in looking   (D) for looking

13. (A) presume   (B) regard   (C) are assuming   (D) are having

14. (A) turning off   (B) holding off   (C) calling off   (D) taking off

15. (A) care   (B) watch   (C) vigilance   (D) attention

16. (A) help   (B) helping   (C) be of help to   (D) in helping

17. (A) and which   (B) that   (C) which   (D) and that

18. (A) for attack   (B) with attack   (C) to attack   (D) on attack

19. (A) concerned about   (B) concerned to
    (C) concerned in   (D) concerned on

20. (A) saw that   (B) saw to it that
    (C) took it that   (D) had it that

Ⅳ、閱讀能力：(單一選擇題)

第一部分 (20 %) 說明：下面 21－30 題，或附問題，或問要點，各附四個答案，請把其中最正確的一個，在答案卡上標出。每題 2 分；答錯的倒扣⅔分。

21. John : Excuse me. I've got to go now.

    Paul : But it's only 9 : 30.

    John : Yes. But I have to check in one hour before departure time, 11 : 45.

    How much more time does John have before he checks in?
    (A) 75 minutes   (B) One hour
    (C) Half an hour   (D) Two hours and fifteen minutes

22. Peggy : What do you think of Dr. Peterson's speech?

    Jane : What he says makes sense. How about you?

    Peggy : I can't agree more with you.

    What do Peggy and Jane think of Dr. Peterson's speech?
    (A) They do not like it
    (B) Both of them like it.
    (C) Peggy likes it but Jane does not.
    (D) Jane thinks that the speech makes no sense.

23. For hundreds of years cases of supernatural happenings have been reported with strange similarity from all over the world. But only in the last century has any serious study been made of these apparently fanciful stories.
    (A) Scientists have been studying the supernatural for centuries.
    (B) It is only since 1901 that hauntings have been reported.
    (C) These stories are strange because they are similar.
    (D) There is nothing new about ghost stories; however, research into them is a relatively recent development.

24. Nothing was further from her intention than to destroy my faith.
    (A) She never intended to destroy my faith.
    (B) She came close to destroying my faith.
    (C) She had no further intention than to destroy my faith.
    (D) Nothing was more on her mind than the destruction of my faith.

25. A home painted with an inferior grade of paint will need repainting
   in a third of the time that the same job with a better grade of paint
   would have lasted.
   As is the case with many other items, a cheap paint is often
   (A) a work saver.　　　　　(B) impossible to use.
   (C) a waste of money.　　　(D) a good investment.

26. Braille is a system of raised dots arranged on the page so that blind
   persons can read by feeling the dots with their fingers. Because many
   books and magazines are available in braille, blind people can now do
   their own reading and need not depend on
   (A) people who know braille.　(B) people who can see.
   (C) people who can read.　　　(D) people who own books.

27. Judging that the couple were Orientals, I addressed them in Chinese.
   They replied in near-perfect French that they did not speak Japanese. As
   the conversation went on, I learned that they were Vietnamese.
   The writer spoke to the man and wife
   (A) first in Vietnamese and then in French.
   (B) first in Japanese and then in French.
   (C) first in Chinese and then in Vietnamese.
   (D) first in Chinese and then in French.

28. Wife : How did you find Mary?
   John : She was no more virtuous than intelligent.
   According to John, Mary was
   (A) less virtuous than intelligent. (B) intelligent, but not virtuous.
   (C) virtuous, but not intelligent. (D) neither virtuous nor intelligent.

29. In the evolution of the human jaw, scientists find progressively greater
   grinding capacity, suggesting a diet of rough roots.
   The writer points out that
   (A) scientists suggest a diet of rough roots for humans.
   (B) as civilization progresses, the grinding capacity of the human jaw
      always improves.
   (C) man lived on rough roots to protect his jaw.
   (D) there is a causal connection between diet habits and the evolution
      of the human jaw.

30. Cautious scientists remember that supposedly extinct volcanoes have produced some of the world's most devastating eruptions.
(A) The devastating effect of volcanic eruptions must be kept in mind.
(B) Scientists are cautious when it comes to predicting volcanic eruptions.
(C) Not all extinct volcanoes are truly dead.
(D) Volcanic eruptions are without exception devastating.

第二部分（10％）說明：下面31-35題，各附四個答案，來解釋下文的意義。選出一個最符合下文意義的答案，標出在答案卡上。每題2分；答錯的倒扣⅔分。

In seeking to solve their problems, social scientists encounter greater resistance than physical scientists. By that I do not mean to belittle the great accomplishments of physical scientists, who have been able, for example, to determine the structure of the atom without seeing it. That is a tremendous achievement; yet in many ways it is not so difficult as what social scientists are expected to do. The conditions under which social scientists must work would drive a physical scientist frantic. Here are five of those conditions. He can make few experiments; he cannot measure the results accurately; he cannot control the conditions surrounding the experiments; he is often expected to get quick results with slow-acting economic forces; and he must work with people, not with inanimate objects.

31. According to this author, social scientists
(A) make more contributions to society than physical scientists.
(B) have solved more problems than physical scientists.
(C) are no more important than physical scientists.
(D) face more obstacles than physical scientists in their research.

32. A physical scientist would find the restrictions imposed upon social scientists
(A) difficult for him to manage.　(B) quite easy to cope with.
(C) similar to those in his own field.
(D) helpful to his scientific exploration.

33. "That" after "By" in the second sentence refers to
(A) "resistance" in the first sentence.
(B) the first sentence as a whole.
(C) "to belittle the great accomplishments of physical scientists" in the second sentence.
(D) "the structure of the atom" in the second sentence.

34. The discovery of the structure of the atom by physical scientists is
    (A) a great feat of theirs.
    (B) their greatest achievement.
    (C) not so remarkable as the accomplishments of social scientists.
    (D) more valuable than what social scientists have ever accomplished.

35. The five conditions under which a social scientist must work are characterized by
    (A) precision, efficiency, and testability.
    (B) rigidity, accuracy, and explicitness.
    (C) flexibility, variability, and vagueness.
    (D) objectivity, aloofness, and exactitude.

Ｖ、翻譯：英譯中（10％）

說明：下面 36~40 題，都附有不完整的中文句子，各有一個空格，所填字數不限，但必須在句子裡規定的位置，同時要使中、英文句句意相符合。答案要寫在試卷內，務請抄錄全句，並請在填入的字下面劃線。每題 2 分；未抄全句每題扣 0.5 分。

　　例：I will back you up. 我會 ＿＿＿＿＿＿＿＿ 。
答案：我會支持你。

36. Regarding this accident, I am not supposed to make any comments.
    關於這件意外，我 ＿＿＿＿＿＿＿＿ 表示任何意見。

37. In an examination, students are often hard put to find the right answers.
    考試的時候，學生往往 ＿＿＿＿＿＿＿＿ 正確的答案。

38. He never goes to a bookstore without buying some books.
    他每次進書店，＿＿＿＿＿＿＿＿ 。

39. I cannot and will not accept your proposal.
    我不能接受你的建議，＿＿＿＿＿＿＿＿ 。

40. Everything scared me in those days, and still does.
    那時候，件件事都令我驚慌失措，＿＿＿＿＿＿＿＿ 。

VI、**翻譯**：中譯英（10％）

說明：下面 41-45 題，是把中文句子譯成英文。請按中文句意，把各題括號裡的字做適當排列（其中有一或二字是多餘的），使中、英文句句意相同。爲方便計分，請把英文全句抄在試卷內，並請在填入的字下面畫線。每題 2 分，未抄全句每題扣 0.5 分。

例：他有了今天的地位，全仗他工作勤奮。

He is where he is（working, hard, by, with）

答案：He is where he is <u>by</u> <u>working</u> <u>hard</u>.

41. 約有 150 個學生，在昨天考試時缺考。

About 150 students（were, absented, from, themselves）the sitting for yesterday's examinations.

42. 她的嫻靜和職業上的能幹都同樣令人懷念。

She is remembered for her quiet charm（as, more, as, much）for her professional competence.

43. 一分又一分鐘終於在嘀嗒聲中過去了，他還是想不出答案來。

The minutes finally ticked away, and he still failed to（come, to, with up）an answer.

44. 約翰的車子，不幸偏偏在很偏僻的地方拋了錨。

John's car（came, to, happen, had）break down on him in a most out of the way place.

45. 二十歲以上的人，佔全部人口的百分之三十。

People over twenty years of age（compose, of, up, make）30% of the total population.

VII、**作文**：（20％）以 80 字爲度，請勿過少或過多。

題目：The National Flag and I

71年大學聯考英文試題詳解

I、拼字：選出拼錯者（多重選擇題）

1. (**A B C**)　(A) *beleive* → *believe* 〔 bɪˈliv 〕 *vt.* 相信　　*vi.* 信仰
　　　　　　(B) *creat* → *create* 〔 krɪˈet 〕 *vt.* 創造；建立
　　　　　　(C) *seperate* → *separate* 〔ˈsɛpə.ret, -prɪt 〕 *vt. , vi.* 分離
　　　　　　(D) perceive 〔 pɚˈsiv 〕 *vt.* 感覺
　　　　　　(E) proceed 〔 prəˈsid 〕 *vi.* 進行；進展

2. (**B C D**)　(A) gymnasium 〔 dʒɪmˈnezɪəm 〕 *n.* 體育館
　　　　　　(B) *grammer* → *grammar* 〔ˈgræmɚ 〕 *n.* 文法
　　　　　　(C) *begger* → *beggar* 〔ˈbɛgɚ 〕 *n.* 乞丐
　　　　　　(D) *deligent* → *diligent* 〔ˈdɪlədʒənt 〕 *adj.* 勤勉的
　　　　　　(E) immense 〔 ɪˈmɛns 〕 *adj.* 廣大的

3. (**A C D E**)　(A) *sergant* → *sergeant* 〔ˈsɑrdʒənt 〕 *n.* （陸軍）中士；（空軍）下士
　　　　　　(B) grocery 〔ˈgrosɚɪ 〕 *n.* 雜貨店
　　　　　　(C) *recompanse* → *recompense* 〔ˈrɛkəm.pɛns 〕 *vt.* 報酬；賠償
　　　　　　　　n. 酬金；補償金
　　　　　　(D) *excede* → *exceed* 〔 ɪkˈsid 〕 *vt. , vi.* 超過
　　　　　　(E) *ingenous* → *ingenious* 〔 ɪnˈdʒinjəs 〕 *adj.* 智巧的；靈敏的
　　　　　　　或 *ingenuous* 〔 ɪnˈdʒɛnjʊəs 〕 *adj.* 天真的；坦白的

4. (**B D E**)　(A) descendant 〔 dɪˈsɛndənt 〕 *n.* 後裔
　　　　　　(B) *immitate* → *imitate* 〔ˈɪmə.tet 〕 *vt.* 模仿
　　　　　　(C) edible 〔ˈɛdəbḷ 〕 *adj.* 可食用的
　　　　　　(D) *guerrila* → *gue(r)rilla* 〔 gəˈrɪlə 〕 *n.* 游擊隊（通常用複數）；
　　　　　　　游擊隊隊員
　　　　　　(E) *evidance* → *evidence* 〔ˈɛvədəns 〕 *n.* 證據

5. (**C D E**)　(A) shield〔ʃild〕*n.* 盾
　　　　　　　(B) disciple〔dɪˋsaɪpl̩〕*n.* 門徒
　　　　　　　(C) *desease* → ***disease***〔dɪˋziz〕*n.* 疾病
　　　　　　　(D) *fragrence* → ***fragrance***〔ˋfregrəns〕*n.* 香味
　　　　　　　(E) *pesimism* → ***pessimism***〔ˋpɛsəˏmɪzəm〕*n.* 悲觀主義

Ⅱ、**發音：選出發音相同者**

6. (**C D E**)　(A) pose〔poz〕*n.* 姿勢
　　　　　　　(B) wood〔wʊd〕*n.* 木材
　　　　　　　(C) choose〔tʃuz〕*vt. , vi.* 選擇
　　　　　　　(D) blue〔blu〕*n.* 藍色；憂鬱（常作複數）
　　　　　　　(E) shoot〔ʃut〕*vt.* 射擊

　　　　＊ oo 一律讀 /u/，在 k 前的 oo 一律讀 /ʊ/，其他讀 /ʊ/ 的重要字
　　　　　有 good, stood, wood, wool, woolen, hoot, foot, childhood

7. (**B D**)　(A) pen〔pɛn〕*n.* 鋼筆　　　(B) pain〔pen〕*n.* 疼痛
　　　　　　(C) pan〔pæn〕*n.* 平底鍋　　(D) make〔mek〕*vt.* 製造
　　　　　　(E) captain〔ˋkæptɪn〕*n.* 船長

8. (**A C**)　(A) whole〔hol〕*adj.* 全部的
　　　　　　(B) which〔hwɪtʃ〕*pron.* 何者　*adj.* 哪一個；哪些
　　　　　　(C) home〔hom〕*n.* 家
　　　　　　(D) ghost〔gost〕*n.* 鬼
　　　　　　(E) phase〔fez〕*n.* 局面；階段

9. (**ABCE**)　(A) barber〔ˋbɑrbɚ〕*n.* 理髮師
　　　　　　　(B) chamber〔ˋtʃembɚ〕*n.* 臥房
　　　　　　　(C) bribery〔ˋbraɪbərɪ〕*n.* 賄賂
　　　　　　　(D) bomber〔ˋbɑmɚ〕*n.* 轟炸機
　　　　　　　(E) club〔klʌb〕*n.* 俱樂部

　　　　＊ 字尾 mb 的 b 不發音，例如：comb〔kom〕, tomb〔tum〕,
　　　　　climber〔ˋklaɪmɚ〕等，如果字尾本來就是 ber，而不是由 mb
　　　　　加上 er，則 b 要發音，如 lumber〔ˋlʌmbɚ〕, number〔ˋnʌmbɚ〕。

10. (**A D**) (A) resist〔rɪ'zɪst〕 *vt.*,*vi.* 抵抗
   (B) sign〔saɪn〕 *n.* 符號 *vt.*,*vi.* 簽名
   (C) vision〔'vɪʒən〕 *n.* 視力;看法
   (D) reserve〔rɪ'zɝv〕 *vt.* 保留;預訂
   (E) pressure〔'prɛʃɚ〕 *n.* 壓力

Ⅲ、習慣用法、詞彙、文法（單選）

Teachers *of English* **who** *want to be responsible yet realistic about*
 主詞
teaching usage and mechanics to today's writing students face a chronic
                                                            動詞
dilemma.

　　想負責而又想兼顧實際的英文老師,在教導今日學生寫作的慣用方法和技巧
時,都會面臨一個常見的困境。

* who … students 是形容詞子句,修飾 teachers,其中 about … students
  又作副詞片語,修飾 responsible 和 realistic,其中 to … students 亦作
  副詞片語,修飾 teaching。

   realistic〔,riə'lɪstɪ,,rɪə-〕 *adj.* 實際的　　usage〔'jusɪdʒ〕 *n.* 慣用法
   mechanics〔mə'kænɪks〕 *n.* 技巧;機械學
   chronic〔'krɑnɪk〕 *adj.* 慣常的;長期的

11. (**C**) (A) 事情
   (B) instruction〔ɪn'strʌkʃən〕 *n.* 教導
   (C) **dilemma**〔də'lɛmə,daɪ-〕 *n.* 困境
   (D) 失敗

What should our priorities be? Should we insist **that** we (*should*) distinguish between lie and lay or sit and sat, **and that** we (*should*) use a
singular pronoun after everybody?

什麼是我們該優先考慮的事情呢?我們要不要堅持區別 lie 和 lay 或 sit 和 sat,
以及要不要堅持在 everybody 之後使用單數代名詞呢?

* insist 之後的 that 子句用假設法動詞，should 省略和不省略均可（詳見文法寶典 p.372 ）；and 連接兩個 that 子句，作 insist 的受詞。

priority〔praɪˈɔrətɪ,-ˈɑr-〕*n.* 優先
singular〔ˈsɪŋgjələ〕*adj.* 單數的

If we do, we risk looking *as if* we are assuming the posture of the

protectors of pure English holding off the barbarians *who will corrupt*

the language if we relax our vigilance.

如果我們堅持的話，我們就冒著看起來像是採取純正英語保護者姿態的危險，對抗那些若是我們鬆懈警戒，就會敗壞語言的野蠻人。

* If we do 是副詞子句，修飾 risk，其中 do＝insist ；as if 引導的子句，在 look，seem 等動詞之後，可依句意需要，不用假設法，而接直說法（詳見文法寶典 p.371 ）；holding … barbarians 是分詞片語，當受詞補語；who … vigilance 是形容詞子句，修飾 barbarians，其中 if … vigilance 是副詞子句，修飾 corrupt，表條件。

assume〔əˈsjum〕*vt.* 採取
posture〔ˈpɑstʃ⋅〕*n.* 姿勢；態度
assume the posture of 採取～態度
vigilance〔ˈvɪdʒələns〕*n.* 警戒

12.(**A**) risk「冒～之險」須接動名詞為受詞，故選 (A)。（詳見文法寶典 p.436 ）

13.(**C**) (A) presume〔prɪˈzum〕*vt.* 假定　(B) 認為　(C) 採取　(D) 有

14.(**B**) (A) turn off 關掉　　　(B) *hold off* 對抗
　　　　　(C) call off 取消　　　(D) take off 起飛；脫掉

15.(**C**) care, watch, attention, vigilance 雖都有「注意，留心」的意思，但 vigilance 尤指為某一理由或目標而特別警戒，故 (C) 最合句意。

*On the other hand, **if** we take the attitude **that** helping students to generate content and organize it in a coherent pattern should be our major goal **and that** surface features are comparatively unimportant, we open ourselves to attack from readers who are genuinely concerned about good English.*

從另一方面來說，假如我們採取另一種態度 — 我們最主要的目標是幫助學生寫出內容，並用有條理的形式加以組織，並且認爲表面的特點是比較不重要的 — 那我們又易遭受誠心關切純正英語的讀者的攻擊。

* On the other hand「從另一方面來說」是副詞片語，修飾全句；if…unimportant 是副詞子句，修飾 open，其中 and 連接兩個名詞子句，that…goal 和 that … unimportant 作 attitude 的同位語；who … English 是形容詞子句，修飾 readers。

> generate〔'dʒɛnə,ret〕*vt.* 產生；造成
> coherent (ko'hɪrənt) *adj.* 一致的；連貫的
> feature〔'fitʃ〕*n.* 特點；外貌
> genuinely〔'dʒɛnjuɪnlɪ〕*adv.* 誠心地；眞正地
> ***be concerned about*** 關切

16. (**B**) that helping … goal 是名詞子句，其中 helping … pattern 是動名詞片語作主詞。（詳見文法寶典 p.427 ）

17. (**D**) attitude 接兩個 that 子句作同位語，第二個 that 子句需要 and 連接，且 that 不能省略。

18. (**C**) ***open oneself to*** + N (= be open to + N)「易遭受…」，故選 (C)。

19. (**A**) (A) 關切
　　　　　　(B) be concerned to 一心希望
　　　　　　(C) be concerned in 從事；與～有關
　　　　　　(D) 無此用法

There are people 「*who claim that we are not doing our job. And* they imply *that in their day English teachers were a different breed* 「*who had standards and saw to it that no one left their classrooms without being able to write.*」

有一些人認為我們沒有盡責任。而且他們暗示說，以前他們的英文老師和我們是不同類型的人，他們有自己的標準，而且留心務必使離開他們教室的學生，都能寫作。

　　* who claim … job 是形容詞子句，修飾 people。 And 是對等連接詞，在此用於句首，作轉承語，連接前面的句子；who had … write 是形容詞子句，修飾 breed。

　　　　breed〔brid〕*n.* 類型；種　　standard〔ˈstændəd〕*n.* 標準

20. (**B**) *see to it that* = see that「留意…」，是慣用語，其中 that 子句是 it 的同位語（詳見文法寶典 p.481）；本題雖然 (A)(B) 皆可，但 see that 較口語，且有時易被誤解成 that 引導名詞子句作 see 的受詞，故在此選 (B) 較適當。

Ⅳ、閱讀能力（單選）

第一部分

21. (**A**) John : Excue me. I've got to go now.

　　　　 Paul : But it's only 9:30.

　　　　 John : Yes. But I have to check in *one hour before departure time, 11:45.*

　　　　 How much more time does John have **before** *he checks in*?

約翰：對不起。我得走了。

保羅：可是才九點半。

湯姆：是的，但是我得在出發時間十一點四十五分的前一小時辦理登記。

約翰在辦理登記前，還有多少時間？

　　　(A) 七十五分鐘。　　　　(B) 一小時。
　　　(C) 半小時。　　　　　　(D) 兩小時十五分鐘。

*　　11 時 45 分　　　　　　　　10 時 45 分
　　－　1 時　　　　　　　　　－　9 時 30 分
　　―――――――――――　　　―――――――――――
　　10 時 45 分 ― check in 的時間　　　1 時 15 分 ＝ 75 分

　　$\begin{cases} \textit{\textbf{got to}} \ 必須 \\ = \textit{\textbf{have}} \ (\textit{got}) \ \textit{\textbf{to}} \end{cases}$　　\textit{\textbf{check in}} 辦理登記

22. (**B**) Peggy : What do you think of Dr. Peterson's speech?

　　　Jane　 : *What* he says makes sense. How about you?

　　　Peggy : I can't agree more with you.

　　　What do Peggy and Jane think of Dr. Peterson's speech?

　　　佩姬：你認爲彼得森博士的演講怎樣？
　　　珍　：他說得很有道理。你認爲呢？
　　　佩姬：我再同意不過了。

　　　佩姬和珍認爲彼得森博士的演講如何？

　　　(A) 她們不喜歡它。　　　　(B) 她們都喜歡它。
　　　(C) 佩姬喜歡，但珍不喜歡。　(D) 珍認爲這演講沒意義。

* 本題重點在 *I can't agree more with you.*（我再同意不過了。）
　也就是：我非常同意你；我完全同意你。67 年日大也出現過：
　I couldn't agree more.

　　　make sense 合道理；有意義

23. (**D**) *For hundreds of years* cases *of supernatural happenings* have

　　been reported *with strange similarity from all over the world.*

　　But only in the last century has any serious study been made

　　of these apparently fanciful stories.

　　數百年來，世界各地都有超自然事件的傳說，而這些傳說有奇怪的相似
　　之處。但是只有在上個世紀，人們才認眞研究這些似乎是想像的故事。

(A) 幾個世紀以來，科學家一直在研究超自然的事情。

(B) 只有從 1901 年起，才有人報導鬼魂出沒。

(C) 這些故事很奇怪，因為它們很相似。

(D) 鬼故事沒什麼新鮮的，但是對它們的研究是最近的事。

* For hundreds of years 是副詞片語，修飾全句。of supernatural happenings 是形容詞片語，修飾 cases。with strange similarity 和 from all over the world 是副詞片語，共同修飾 reported。But 是轉承語，連接上面的句子。Only … century 是副詞片語，only + 副詞（片語、子句）放在句首，後面的助動詞和主詞要倒裝。（詳見文法寶典 p.631）

supernatural〔͵supɚˈnætʃrəl〕*adj.* 超自然的；神奇的
report〔rɪˈport〕*vt.* 傳說　　apparently〔əˈpɛrəntlɪ〕*adv.* 似乎
fanciful〔ˈfænsɪful, -fəl〕*adj.* 想像的
haunting〔ˈhɔntɪŋ, ˈhɑntɪŋ〕*n.*（鬼魂）出沒

24. (**A**) Nothing was further from her intention *than to destroy my faith.*
　　沒有一件事比摧毀我的信念，更遠離她的意圖。

　　(A) 她從未打算摧毀我的信念。

　　(B) 她幾乎摧毀了我的信念。

　　(C) 除了摧毀我的信念外，她沒有更進一步的意圖。

　　(D) 沒有什麼事比摧毀我的信念，更放在她的心上了。

* than … faith 是省略了 was 的副詞子句，修飾 further，表比較。

　intention〔ɪnˈtɛnʃən〕*n.* 意圖

25. (**C**) A home *painted with an inferior grade of paint* will need repainting *in a third of the time* *that the same job with a better grade of paint would have lasted.*

As is the case with many other items, a cheap paint is often

_____ .

用較差的油漆所漆的房子,在用較好的油漆所能維持的三分之一時間內,就需要重漆。

如常見於許多其他事項的情形,便宜的油漆常是 ＿＿＿＿＿＿＿＿ 。

    (A) 省工的東西   (B) 沒辦法用的

    (C) <u>浪費錢</u>   (D) 一個好的投資

* painted … of painted 是省略了 which is 的形容詞子句,修飾 home。in a third … lasted 是副詞片語,修飾 need;其中 that … lasted 是形容詞子句,修飾 time。

    inferior〔ɪnˈfɪrɪɚ〕*adj.* 較劣的

    as is (*often*) ***the case with*** ~ 如(常見於)~ 的情形

    item〔ˈaɪtəm〕*n.* 項目

26. (**C**) Braille is a system *of raised dots arranged on the page* ***so that*** blind persons can read *by feeling the dots with their fingers.*

Because many books and magazines are available in Braille, blind people can *now* do reading ***and*** need not depend on ＿＿＿＿＿＿.

點字法是一種在書頁上安置凸出小點的方法,使盲人可以用手指觸摸這些小點來閱讀。因爲許多書籍和雜誌都有點字本,盲人現在可以自己閱讀而不需要依賴 ＿＿＿＿＿＿＿ 。

    (A) 懂得點字法的人。   (B) 看得見的人。

    (C) <u>能閱讀的人</u>。   (D) 擁有書的人。

* so that 引導的副詞子句,修飾 arranged,表目的,其中 by … fingers 是副詞片語,修飾 read。

盲人不懂點字法,需要能閱讀的人告訴他各種知識。答案 (B) 盲人平時固然需要看得見的人幫助他生活,但看得見的人未必識字、能夠閱讀,因此 (B) 不正確。

    Braille〔brel〕*n.* 點字法   dot〔dɑt〕*n.* 小點

27. (**D**) *Judging that the couple were Orientals,* I addressed them in Chinese. They replied in near-perfect French *that they did not speak Japanese. As the conversation went on,* I learned *that they were Vietnamese.*

The writer spoke to the man and wife ＿＿＿＿＿＿＿＿＿ .

由於判斷這對夫婦是東方人，我就用中文和他們說話。他們用幾近完美的法語回答說，他們不說日語。繼續談下去的時候，我才知道他們是越南人。

作者用 ＿＿＿＿＿＿＿ 和這對夫婦交談。

    (A) 先是越南話，後來是法語

    (B) 先是日語，後來是法語

    (C) 先是中文，後來是越南話

    (D) 先是中文，後來是法語

* Judging … Orientals 是由表原因的副詞子句變來的分詞構句，修飾 addressed。 As … on 是副詞子句，修飾 learned，表時間。

    Oriental〔͵orɪˈɛntḷ,͵or-〕*n.* 東方人

    address〔əˈdrɛs〕*vt.* 對～說話

    Vietnamese〔vi͵ɛtnɑˈmiz,-ˈmis,-nə-〕*n.* 越南人；越南語言

28. (**D**) Wife : How did you find Mary?

John : She was no more virtuous than intelligent.

According to John, Mary was ＿＿＿＿＿＿＿＿＿

太太：你覺得瑪麗如何？

約翰：她既沒有美德，又不聰明。

根據約翰，瑪麗 ＿＿＿＿＿＿＿＿＿

    (A) 與其說有美德，不如說聰明。

    (B) 聰明，但沒有美德。

    (C) 有美德，但是不聰明。

    (D) 既沒有美德，也不聰明。

find〔faɪnd〕*vt.* 覺得   ***no more … than*** ～ 既不…，也不～

29. (D) *In the evolution of the human jaw,* scientists find *progressively greater* grinding capacity, *suggesting a diet of rough roots.*

The writer points out that _____

科學家發現，在人類顎骨的進化中，研磨的能力日益增強，這暗示了人類吃粗糙根莖的食物。

作者指出 _____

　　(A) 科學家建議人們吃粗糙根莖的食物。
　　(B) 隨著文明的進步，人類顎骨的研磨能力一直在增強。
　　(C) 人類賴粗糙根莖爲食，以保護他的顎骨。
　　(D) 飲食習慣和人顎骨的進化有因果關係。

　* In the … jaw 是副詞片語，修飾 find。suggesting … roots 是由補述用法的形容詞子句 which suggests …省略而來的分詞構句。

　　evolution〔͵ɛvə'luʃən, -'lju-〕*n.* 進化；演化
　　jaw〔dʒɔ〕*n.* 顎
　　progressively〔prə'grɛsɪvlɪ〕*adv.* 日益增多地
　　grinding〔'graɪndɪŋ〕*adj.* 研磨的
　　capacity〔kə'pæsətɪ〕*n.* 能力
　　diet〔'daɪət〕*n.* 飲食
　　causal〔'kɔzḷ〕*adj.* 關於因果的

30. (C) Cautious scientists remember *that supposedly extinct volcanoes have produced some of the world's most devastating eruptions.*
懼重的科學家記得，被認爲的死火山曾造成世上最具毀滅性的爆發。

　　(A) 人們必須記住火山爆發毀滅性的結果。
　　(B) 說到預測火山爆發，科學家都很懼重。
　　(C) 並非所有的死火山都眞的死了。
　　(D) 火山爆發沒有例外的，都具有毀滅性。

　* that … eruptions 是名詞子句，作 remember 的受詞。

cautious〔'kɔʃəs〕*adj.* 慎重的
supposedly〔sə'pozɪdlɪ〕*adv.* 也許；推想上
extinct〔ɪk'stɪŋkt〕*adj.* 熄滅了的
extinct volcano 死火山
devastating〔'dɛvəs,tetɪŋ〕*adj.* 毀滅性的；破壞的
eruption〔ɪ'rʌpʃən〕*n.* 爆發　　***keep ~ in mind*** 記住

第二部分

In seeking to solve their problems, social scientists encounter greater resistance ***than** physical scientists.*

在尋找解決問題的方法時，社會科學家遭遇了比自然科學家更大的阻力。

　　* In … problems 是副詞片語，修飾 encounter，表時間。

encounter〔ɪn'kaʊntɚ〕*vt.* 遭遇
resistance〔rɪ'zɪstəns〕*n.* 阻力；抵抗
physical science 自然科學；物理學

By that I do not mean to belittle the great accomplishments *of physical scientists,* **who** have been able, *for example, to determine the structure of the atom without seeing it.*

我這麼說，並不是意謂著輕視自然科學家的卓越成就，舉例來說，他們能在看不見的情形下，決定原子的結構。

　　* By that 是副詞片語，修飾 mean；who 引導作補述用法的形容詞子句，修飾 scientists（詳見文法寶典 p.161），其中 for example「例如」是副詞片語，修飾 been。

belittle〔bɪ'lɪtl̩〕*vt.* 輕視
determine〔dɪ't3mɪn〕*vt.* 決定
accomplishment〔ə'kɑmplɪʃmənt〕*n.* 成就
atom〔'ætəm〕*n.* 原子

That is a tremendous achievement; *yet in many ways* it is not *so* difficult *as what* social scientists are expected to do (*is*).

那是一項驚人的成就，但是在許多方面，這並不比社會科學家應做的事情困難。

* yet「但是」，與 but 同義，連接另一對等子句，其中 in many ways 是副詞片語，修飾 is ；so … as 是表比較的連接詞，as 連接的副詞子句中省略 is （詳見文法寶典 p.507 ），what … do 是名詞子句，作主詞。

　　tremendous〔trɪ'mɛndəs〕*adj.* 驚人的；巨大的

The conditions *under which social scientists must work* would drive a physical scientist frantic. Here are five *of those conditions.*

社會科學家工作上必須處的情況，會使一位自然科學家發狂。在此舉出那些情況中的五種。

* under … work 是形容詞子句，修飾 conditions 。 Here 置於句首，主詞是名詞時，主詞和動詞須倒裝。（詳見文法寶典 p.250,643 ）

　　drive〔draɪv〕*vt.* 驅使　　frantic〔'fræntɪk〕*adj.* 發狂的

He can make few experiments; he cannot measure the results accurately; he cannot control the conditions *surrounding the experiments;* he is *often* expected to get quick results *with slow-acting economic forces; and* he must work *with people, not with inanimate objects.*

他只能做極少的實驗；他不能精確地估計結果；他不能控制環繞那些實驗的情況；在遲緩的經濟援助之下，他經常被要求儘快地得到結果；而且他必須和人而不是和無生物一起工作。

* 句中的半支點(;)是分隔集合句中的子句（詳見文法寶典 p.41 ）。surrounding the experiments 是分詞片語，作形容詞用，修飾 conditions ；with … forces 是副詞片語，修飾 get ；not …objects 在此作副詞片語，修飾 work 。 slow-acting「遲緩的」是「形容詞＋現在分詞」組合而成的複合形容詞。（詳見文法寶典 p.451 ）

measure〔'mɛʒɚ〕*vt.*, *vi.* 估計；測量
accurately〔'ækjərɪtlɪ〕*adv.* 精確地
surround〔sə'raund〕*vt.* 環繞；包圍
inanimate〔ɪn'ænəmɪt〕*adj.* 無生命的

31. (**D**) 根據本文作者，社會科學家

　　(A) 比自然科學家對社會貢獻更大。
　　(B) 比自然科學家解決了更多的問題。
　　(C) 和自然科學家同樣不重要。
　　(D) 在研究方面比自然科學家面臨更多的障礙。

make contributions to 對…有貢獻
no more … than ～ 和～一樣不…　　obstacle〔'abstəkl〕*n.* 障礙

32. (**A**) 自然學家會發現，加諸於社會科學家身上的限制

　　(A) 他難以處理。
　　(B) 相當容易應付。
　　(C) 和他自己的範圍內的限制相似。
　　(D) 有助於他的科學探討。

restriction〔rɪ'strɪkʃən〕*n.* 限制　　*cope with* 應付

33. (**B**) 第二句中的 "By" 之後的 "that" 指

　　(A) 第一句中的「阻力」。
　　(B) 第一句的整個句子。
　　(C) 第二句中的「輕視自然科學家的卓越成就」。
　　(D) 第二句中的「原子的結構」。

34. (**A**) 自然科學家發現原子的結構是

　　(A) 他們的一項偉大的成就。
　　(B) 他們最偉大的成就。
　　(C) 不如社會科學家的成就那麼顯著。
　　(D) 比社會科學家所完成的事情更有價值。

feat〔fit〕*n.* 偉大的事業；功績
remarkable〔rɪ'markəbl〕*adj.* 顯著的

35. (**C**) 社會科學家工作上必然遭遇的五種情況，其特徵爲

　　　　(A) 精確，效率，和可試驗性。
　　　　(B) 彈性，準確，和明確。
　　　　(C) 彈性，易變，和不明確。
　　　　(D) 客觀，超然，和精密。

characterize〔'kærɪktə,raɪz〕*vt.* 以…爲特徵
testability〔tɛstə'bɪlətɪ〕*n.* 可試驗性
rigidity〔rɪ'dʒɪdətɪ〕*n.* 嚴格；堅硬
explicitness〔ɪk'splɪsɪtnɪs〕*n.* 明確
flexibility〔,flɛksə'bɪlətɪ〕*n.* 彈性；易曲性
variability〔,vɛrɪə'bɪlətɪ〕*n.* 易變
vagueness〔'vegnɪs〕*n.* 不明確；模糊
objectivity〔,ɑbdʒɛk'tɪvətɪ〕*n.* 客觀
aloofness〔ə'lufnɪs〕*n.* 超然；不關心
exactitude〔ɪg'zæktə,tjud,-,tud〕*n.* 精密

V、翻譯：英譯中

36. *Regarding this accident*, I am not supposed to make any comments.
　　關於這件意外，我不應該表示任何意見。

　　　* *be supposed to* 應該
　　　　例：To tell you the truth, I don't know what I *am supposed to* do.
　　　　　　（老實說，我不知道應該做什麼。）〔66夜大〕

37. *In an examination*, students are often hard put to find the right answers.
　　考試的時候，學生往往很難找到正確的答案。

　　　* *be hard put* (*to it*) 極爲困難
　　　　例：He *is hard put to it* trying to solve the problem.
　　　　　　（他在解決這個問題上，遭到頗大的困難。）〔67夜大〕

38. He *never* goes to a bookstore *without* buying some books.
　　他每次進書店，一定買一些書。

　　　* 否定字＋without「每…必～」（「雙重否定」，詳見文法寶典 p.661）

39. I cannot **and** will not accept your proposal.
我不能接受你的建議，<u>也不願意接受你的建議</u>。

　　* will 表意志，故譯作「願意」。

40. Everything scared me in those days, **and** still does.
那時候，件件事都令我驚慌失措，<u>現在仍然如此</u>。

　　* does 代替前面出現過的動詞片語。原句 = Everything … days, and everything still scares me now.

　　　in those days 那時候

VI、翻譯：中譯英

41. 約有 150 個學生，在昨天考試時缺考。

About 150 students <u>absented themselves from</u> the sitting for yesterday's examinations.

$\begin{cases} \textbf{\textit{absent}} (vt.) \textbf{\textit{ oneself from}} \text{ 缺席於 (注意動詞唸 (æb'sɛnt) 形容詞唸 ('æbsṇt))} \\ = \textbf{\textit{be absent}} (adj.) \textbf{\textit{ from}} \end{cases}$

sitting ('sɪtɪŋ) n. 就座；入席

42. 她的嫻靜和職業上的能幹都同樣令人懷念。

She is remembered *for her quiet charm* ***as much as*** *for her professional competence.*

　　as much as 與～同樣；與～同量
　　competence ('kɑmpətəns) n. 能力

43. 一分又一分鐘終於在嘀嗒聲中過去了，他還是想不出答案來。

The minutes *finally* ticked away, **and** he still failed to <u>come up with</u> an answer.

　　tick (tɪk) vi. 作嘀嗒聲　　***fail to*** 未能
　　$\begin{cases} \textbf{\textit{come up with}} \text{ 想出} \\ = \textbf{\textit{think of}} \end{cases}$

44. 約翰的車子，不幸偏偏在很偏僻的地方拋了錨。

John's car <u>had to</u> break down on him in a most out of the way place.

> ***had to*** 偏偏（＝ *must*）（表示發生了不希望發生的事；參照文法寶典 p.319）
> ***break down*** 拋錨　　***out of the way*** 偏僻的

45. 二十歲以上的人，佔全部人口的百分之三十。

People *over twenty years of age* <u>make up</u> 30% of the total population.

> { ***make up*** 構成
> ＝ compose

* 本題用 compose 也可以，但題目中說明有一、二個字是多餘的，如填
　compose 要刪三個字，故不合適。

VII、英文作文（參考範例）

The National Flag and I

Whenever I see our national flag, it makes me think of all the things it stands for.

For instance, the flag is the symbol of our nation's power and independence, when I see the flag blowing in the wind, I feel proud to be a citizen of the R.O.C.

I am also proud because I know our flag stands for peace, justice and fraternity among men. ***All told***, I love our national flag very much, and will protect it at all times.

fraternity〔frəˋtɝnətɪ〕*n.* 博愛

國旗與我

每當我看到我們的國旗，它便使我想到它所代表的一切。

舉例來說，國旗是國家權力和獨立的象徵。當我看到國旗在風中飄揚，我以身為一個中華民國的國民為傲。

因為我知道我們的國旗象徵人與人之間的和平、正義和博愛，因此我也引以為傲。總之，我很愛我們的國旗，而且任何時候都會保護它。

七十學年度大學暨獨立學院入學考試
英 文 試 題

※本學科除作文外共有45題。測驗題（1－35）答在答案卡上；翻譯（36－45）
和作文答在作文及翻譯試卷內。

I. 發音（5％）（多重選擇題）

說明：下列1至5題，每題有五個英語單字，每個單字中有一個或數個字母畫有
底線。那幾個畫底線字母的發音是相同的？請在答案卡上將正確的答案標
出。一題全對得1分；答得有錯倒扣1/25分；不答者，得0分。

例：fi<u>sh</u>　　<u>s</u>ee　　<u>t</u>ension　　<u>ch</u>air　　<u>sh</u>e
　　A　　　　B　　　　　C　　　　　D　　　　E

答案：
A B C D E
■ □ ■ □ ■

1.　<u>o</u>ccur　　p<u>o</u>t　　L<u>o</u>ndon　　ab<u>o</u>ut　　<u>o</u>nion
　　A　　　　B　　　　C　　　　　D　　　　E

2.　w<u>a</u>lk　　t<u>o</u>ld　　she<u>ll</u>　　nai<u>l</u>　　<u>l</u>ook
　　A　　　B　　　　C　　　　D　　　E

3.　t<u>a</u>pe　　b<u>e</u>d　　s<u>a</u>d　　s<u>ay</u>s　　m<u>e</u>n
　　A　　　B　　　C　　　D　　　E

4.　lam<u>b</u>　　clim<u>b</u>　　bac<u>k</u>　　tom<u>b</u>　　lam<u>p</u>
　　A　　　　B　　　　C　　　　D　　　E

5.　si<u>g</u>n　　<u>g</u>eneral　　<u>j</u>udge　　be<u>gg</u>ar　　<u>j</u>ealous
　　A　　　　B　　　　　C　　　　D　　　　E

II. 重音（5％）（單一選擇題）

說明：以下6至10題，每題有A、B、C、D四個畫線部份，但是其中只有一
個是該句的主重音。請在答案卡上將該主重音標出。每題1分。

例：Peter always tries to help other people. He's the <u>nicest</u> <u>man</u> in
　　　　　　　　　　　　　　　　　　　　　　A　　　B　　C

the <u>world</u>.　答案：
　　　D

A B C D
□ ■ □ □

6.　" Did you see a cat？" " No. <u>I</u> <u>saw</u> <u>a</u> <u>dog</u>. "
　　　　　　　　　　　　　　　　A　B　C　D

7. There is a little girl. When she is good, <u>she</u> <u>is</u> <u>very</u> <u>good</u>. But
       A B   C   D

   when she is bad, she is horrible.

8. John has nothing to do now. Give <u>him</u> a <u>ball</u> to <u>play</u> <u>with</u>.
       A   B   C D

9. Your plan to have an outing to Shihmen Dam is no good. I've got <u>a</u>
                                           A B

   <u>better</u> <u>idea</u>.
    C   D

10. I'm not sure whether Paul is right or not, but <u>I'm</u> certain <u>that</u> <u>you</u>
                                            A   B   C

    are <u>right</u>.
       D

Ⅲ. 習慣用法、字彙、文法（ 20％ ）（ 單一選擇題 ）

　　說明：下列11至20題，每題中有一個空白，選出四個答案中最恰當的一項，填
　　　　　入空白，便可使該句意思完整，文法正確，合乎習慣。每題2分。

　　例：A government must collect taxes in order to meet its_____.

　　　　(A) regulations　　　　　　　(B) constructions

　　　　(C) satisfactions　　　　　　 (D) obligations

　　答案：A　B　C　D
　　　　　□　□　□　■

11. He'll never know if nobody tells him. That_____to reason.

　　(A) sounds　　　(B) seems　　　(C) stands　　　(D) stays

12. As a_____I only mind my own business.

　　(A) way　　　(B) rule　　　(C) method　　　(D) thought

13. No_____your father was mad at you! Look at your report card.

　　(A) wonder　　　(B) matter　　　(C) surprise　　　(D) surprising

14. A man is_____to be successful if only he will do his best.

　　(A) bound　　　(B) ought　　　(C) ascertained　　 (D) assuring

15. The office is open Monday_____Saturday, and closed on Sundays.

　　(A) since　　　(B) through　　　(C) until　　　(D) also

16. Nations all over the world today are trying their best to_____with
    the energy crisis.

　　(A) solve　　　(B) survive　　　(C) tackle　　　(D) cope

17. In many modern cities, Taipei _____, congestion and air pollution have become real problems.

　(A) includes　　(B) include　　(C) included　　(D) including

18. That was a close call: you _____ hit by the car.

　(A) could have been　　　(B) can have been

　(C) could be　　　　　　(D) can be

19. Don't worry. If he said he _____ help you, he will.

　(A) shall　　(B) will　　(C) would　　(D) ought

20. Facts and figures, even when _____, can often be misleading.

　(A) accurate　　(B) mistaken　　(C) detailed　　(D) careful

Ⅳ. 閱讀能力（單一選擇題）Part A（20%）

　說明：下列21至30題每題附有四個答案解釋該題意義。選出其中與題目意義最
　　　　接近的一個答案。每題2分。

　例：Paul spared nothing to entertain his guests.

　　(A) Paul provided little entertainment for his guests.

　　(B) Paul's guests were not well entertained.

　　(C) Nothing was prepared by Paul to entertain his guests.

　　(D) Everything that Paul could get hold of was offered for the
　　　　pleasure of his guests.

　答案：A B C D
　　　　□ □ □ ■

21. If one thing characterizes China more than anything else, it is Confucianism.

　(A) Confucianism is the most important philosophy in China.

　(B) Confucianism can best represent the Chinese way of life.

　(C) It is necessary to know Confucianism in order to understand
　　　China.

　(D) In China, other philosophies are not so important as Confucianism.

22. Nothing could be in greater contrast to France than Germany.

　(A) France and Germany are as different from each other as can be.

　(B) France is not much different from Germany.

　(C) France is a greater country than Germany.

　(D) Germany is superior to France.

23. The uniqueness of this university lies in its liberal spirit.
    (A) This university, among others, possesses liberal spirit.
    (B) This university as well as others has liberal spirit.
    (C) The liberal spirit of this university is different from that of other universities.
    (D) What makes this university different from others is its liberal spirit.

24. The combined effects of energy shortage and insufficient capital have damaged the economy of many a developing country.
    (A) Many a developing country is beginning to feel the pinch of energy shortage and insufficient capital.
    (B) Energy shortage and insufficient capital are no great problems for the economy of many a developing country.
    (C) Energy shortage and insufficient capital have seriously affected the economy of many a developing country.
    (D) Many a developing country will never recover from the damage caused by energy shortage and insufficient capital.

25. The academic record of John has not in some ways been a proud one.
    (A) John has had outstanding academic performance.
    (B) John's academic record has left something to be desired.
    (C) John is proud of his academic record.
    (D) John has done his best to improve his academic performance.

26. The large task of feeding today's world population is hard to imagine.
    (A) It is difficult to conceive the population of the world today.
    (B) To provide food for today's world population is beyond man's ability.
    (C) The difficulty of supplying food to today's world population is not easy to estimate.
    (D) Today's world population is too large for us to feed.

27. Cells are the units from which all but the simplest living organisms are built.
    (A) Most of the simplest living organisms are made of cells.
    (B) All living organisms except the simplest ones are composed of cells.
    (C) Cells are the basic building materials for all the simplest living organisms.
    (D) The simplest living organisms together with others are all made of cells.

28. It was the success of the simplest tools that started the whole trend of human evolution.
    (A) Not until man started to use tools was the entire course of human evolution set.
    (B) The successful use of tools was the direct result of human evolution.
    (C) Man's use of tools was not directly related to his evolution.
    (D) Human evolution was brought about by something other than the use of tools.

29. As communications improve in the future, so the need for transportation will decrease.
    (A) The need for transportation in the future will be in proportion to the improvement of communications.
    (B) The improvement of communications in the future will heighten the importance of transportation.
    (C) The development of communications and that of transportation will go hand in hand in the future.
    (D) In the future, transportation will gradually lose ground as communications are better developed.

30. One man's meat is another man's poison.
    (A) What you like may not be what I like.
    (B) One must be careful these days because meat may be poisonous.
    (C) Meat is as dangerous as poison because they can both make you sick.
    (D) There is no difference between meat and poison.

Part B (10%)

說明：下列 31 至 35 題每題附有四個答案解釋下文的意義。選出一個最符合下文意義的答案。每題 2 分。

　　If education is the transmission of civilization, we are unquestionably progressing. Civilization is not inherited; it has to be learned and earned by each generation anew; if the transmission should be interrupted for one century, civilization would die, and we should be savages again. So our finest contemporary achievement is our unprecedented expenditure of wealth and toil in the provision of higher education for all. Once colleges were luxuries, designed for the male half of the leisure class; today universities are so numerous that he who runs may become a Ph.D. We may not have excelled the selected geniuses of the past, but we have raised the level and average of knowledge beyond any age in history.

31. We are making progress in education because
    (A) colleges have become more luxurious.
    (B) college education is designed for only a small number of people.
    (C) a lot of money and work unheard of in the past has been invested in college education.
    (D) we have produced many geniuses.

32. Civilization is passed down from one generation to another
    (A) through automatic biological processes.
    (B) through the efforts of each new generation。
    (C) through the contributions of geniuses.
    (D) through the increase of knowledge.

33. The author thinks that the purpose of education is
    (A) to produce diploma holders.
    (B) to give geniuses opportunities to do creative work.
    (C) to increase the wealth and power of a country.
    (D) to preserve the life of civilization.

34. If civilization should discontinue for one hundred years,
    (A) it would be easily revived.
    (B) it would perish.
    (C) it would be created again.
    (D) it would be made better.

35. Since there are so many universities today,
    (A) anybody has the opportunity to get the highest academic degree.
    (B) many geniuses will be produced.
    (C) the quality of students has lowered.
    (D) they have drained many a country of its wealth and manpower.

Ⅴ. 翻譯：中譯英（ 10％ ）

　　說明：下面中文譯成英文的題目中，每一個英文句子都附有一定數目的空格，每格限填一個字，就可使中、英兩句的意思相符合。答案必須寫在試卷內，而且要抄錄原英文全句，填入的字下面要畫線。每題2分。

　　例：他之有今天的地位，全仗工作勤奮。

　　　　He is where he is by_____ _____ .

　　答案：He is where he is by <u>working</u> <u>hard</u>.

36. 他是你最好的朋友，再怎麼說也不會出賣你。

As your best friend, he will be＿＿＿＿＿ ＿＿＿＿＿person to betray you.

37. 比這個更有趣的故事，我從來沒有聽說過。

A more interesting story I ＿＿＿＿＿ ＿＿＿＿＿ ＿＿＿＿＿.

38. 你昨天打電話來的時候，我們正在吃午飯。

We＿＿＿＿＿ ＿＿＿＿＿lunch when you called on the phone yesterday.

39. 告訴孩子們，他們如果不守規矩，就得不到禮物。

Tell the children to＿＿＿＿＿ ＿＿＿＿＿they are not getting any presents.

40. 我整天都研究這樁問題，到現在還沒解決。

I ＿＿＿＿＿ ＿＿＿＿＿ ＿＿＿＿＿ ＿＿＿＿＿ the problem all day, but it is not solved yet.

VI. 翻譯：英譯中（ 10％ ）

說明：下面的英文題目，都附有不完整的中文句子，各有一個空格。每個空格所填字數不限，但必須在句子裡規定的位置，同時要使中文句和英文句的意思相符合。答案要把全句抄錄在試卷內，所填的字下面要畫線。每題 2 分。

例：John is so stubborn there is no reasoning with him.

　　約翰執拗萬分，＿＿＿＿＿。

答案：約翰執拗萬分，<u>不可理喻</u>。

41. The way our drivers drive, we cannot be too careful when crossing the streets.

我們的司機們那種開車的方式，使我們過街的時候＿＿＿＿＿。

42. People are beginning to realize the importance of their cultural heritage.

大家開始了解到他們自己的＿＿＿＿＿。

43. You may pick whatever takes your fancy.

你 ＿＿＿＿＿就揀甚麼。

44. If he persists in laziness, he might as well withdraw from school.

如果他堅持懈怠下去，＿＿＿＿＿。

45. You have to admit that what he says makes perfect sense.

你得承認，他的話 ＿＿＿＿＿。

Ⅶ. 英文作文（20％）

說明：利用下面的主旨句（topic sentence）作為第一句，寫一段 60 到 80 個字的英文作文（主旨句九字不算），同時要在下面所列的十二項詞彙（vocabulary）裡至少選用十項在你的作文裡。詞彙在作文裡的次序不拘，時式也沒有限制。但詞彙少用一項就要扣 2 分，少用兩項扣 4 分；依此類推。詞彙的字數算在作文的字數裡，而且所選的詞彙下必須畫線。

Topic sentence：I have long hoped to become a college student.

Vocabulary： 1. make up my mind　　2. as early as　　3. specialize

4. on the one hand　　5. on the other　　6. enable

7. after all　　8. moreover　　9. do my best

10. lose heart　　11. certainly　　12. success

70年大學聯考英文試題詳解

Ⅰ. **發音**：選出發音相同者（多重選擇題）

1. （**ACD**）(A) <u>o</u>ccur〔ə'kɝ〕 vi. 發生；出現

   (B) p<u>o</u>t〔pɑt〕 n. 壺；罐

   (C) Lond<u>o</u>n〔'lʌndən〕 n. 倫敦

   (D) <u>a</u>bout〔ə'baut〕 prep. 關於；近於

   (E) <u>o</u>nion〔'ʌnjən〕 n. 洋葱

2. （**BCDE**）(A) wa<u>l</u>k〔wɔk〕 vi. 步行；散步

   (B) to<u>l</u>d〔told〕 vt., vi.（tell的過去式及過去分詞）說；講

   (C) she<u>ll</u>〔ʃɛl〕 n. 殼，外觀

   (D) nai<u>l</u>〔nel〕 n. 釘子　vt. 用釘釘牢

   (E) <u>l</u>ook〔luk〕 vt. 看；注意；看似～　vt. 注視

   ＊alk 中的 l 不發音。

3. （**BDE**）(A) t<u>a</u>pe〔tep〕 n. 帶；磁帶

   (B) b<u>e</u>d〔bɛd〕 n. 牀

   (C) s<u>a</u>d〔sæd〕 adj. 悲哀的；憂愁的

   (D) s<u>ay</u>s〔sɛz〕 vt. 說

   (E) m<u>e</u>n〔mɛn〕 n.（man 的複數形）男人

4. （**ABD**）(A) lam<u>b</u>〔læm〕 n. 小羊；羔羊

   (B) clim<u>b</u>〔klaɪm〕 vt., vi. 攀登

   (C) <u>b</u>ack〔bæk〕 n. 背後；後面

   (D) tom<u>b</u>〔tum〕 n. 墳墓

   (E) lam<u>p</u>〔læmp〕 n. 燈

   ＊字尾 mb 的 b 不發音。

5. （**BCE**）(A) si<u>g</u>n〔saɪn〕 n. 記號　vt., vi. 簽字

   (B) <u>g</u>eneral〔'dʒɛnərəl〕 adj. 普遍的

   (C) <u>j</u>ud<u>g</u>e〔dʒʌdʒ〕 vt. 審判　n. 法官

   (D) be<u>gg</u>ar〔'bɛgɚ〕 n. 乞丐

   (E) <u>j</u>ealous〔'dʒɛləs〕 adj. 嫉妒的

Ⅱ. 重音：

6.（ **D** ）"Did you see a cat?" "No, I saw a dog."
　　　　　　　　　　　　　　　　　A　B　C　D

"「你看到一隻貓了嗎?」「不。我看到一隻狗。」"

* dog 與 cat 對比，故 dog 要重讀。

7.（ **C** ）There is a little girl. When she is good, she is very good.
　　　　　But when she is bad, she is horrible.　　A　B　C　　D

"有個小女孩。她好的時候非常好；壞的時候很可怕。"

* 副詞＋形容詞時，通常重音在形容詞上，但此處為了強調，以和前面的 good 區分，故 very 要重讀。

8.（ **B** ）John has nothing to do now. Give him a ball to play with.
　　　　　　　　　　　　　　　　　　　B　　　C　　D

"約翰現在沒事做。給他個球玩。"

* nothing 和 ball 對比，故重音在 ball 上。

9.（ **C** ）Your plan to have an outing to Shihmen Dam is no good.
　　　　　I've got a better idea.
　　　　　　　A　B　C　　D

"你去石門水庫遠足的計畫不好。我有個比較好的主意。"

* no good 與 better 對比，故重音在 better 上。

　　　outing〔'aʊtɪŋ〕n. 遠足；短途旅行

10.（ **C** ）I'm not sure whether Paul is right or not, but I'm certain
　　　　　that you are right.　　　　　　　　　　　　　　A
　　　　　B　C　　D

"我不確定保羅對不對，但我確定你是對的。"

* Paul 和 you 對比，故重音在 you 上。

Ⅲ. 習慣用法、字彙、文法：

11.（ **C** ）He'll never know *if nobody tells him*. That stands to reason.

"如果沒有人告訴他，他永遠不會知道。那是理所當然的。"

* *stand to reason* "理所當然；合理"　例: *It stands to reason* that I should decline the offer.(我拒絕那項提議是理所當然的。)

(A)(B)用 sounds 和 seems，應把 to reason 改為 reasonable，作主詞補語，意為 "似乎合理"。

12.（ **B** ）*As a rule* I *only* mind my own business.

"一般說來，我只管自己的事。"

* *as a rule* "一般說來；通常"，是副詞片語，修飾全句。

(A) as a way "當作一種方式"，(C) as a method "當作一種方法"

(D) as a thought "當作一種想法"，均不合乎句意。

$\left\{ \begin{array}{l} \textbf{\textit{mind one's own business}} \text{ "管自己的事；不管閒事"} \\ = \textbf{\textit{mind one's own affairs}} \\ = \textbf{\textit{go about one's business}} \end{array} \right.$

13.（ **A** ）No wonder your father was mad at you! Look at your report card.

"難怪你爸爸生你的氣！看看你的成績單。"

* *no wonder* "難怪"，是由（*It is*）*no wonder*（*that*）省略而來的。

(A) no matter "無論什麼"，句意不合。且後面要接疑問代名詞或疑問副詞。(B) 沒有 no surprise 的用法。

(C) → It is not surprising that

be mad at "對～生氣"　　report card "成績單"

14.（ **A** ）A man is bound to be successful *if only he will do his best.*

"一個人只要肯盡力而為，就必定會成功。"

* if only 引導副詞子句，修飾 is，表條件；其中 will 表「願意」（詳見文法寶典 p. 328）。*be bound to* ＋ V "必定"。

(A) ought to "應該"，前面不需加 is。

(C) ascertain〔͵æsəˈten〕*vt.* 探知

(D) assuring〔əˈʃʊrɪŋ〕*adj.* 令人確信的（通常不用來修飾人）

do one's best "盡力而為"

15.（ **B** ）The office is open *Monday through Saturday, and*（*is*）closed *on Sundays.*

"這辦公室星期一到星期六都開著，星期天關閉。"

* and 連接兩個對等子句，第二個子句中省略了動詞 is 。through
" 一直到（並包括）某時間 "（詳見文法寶典 p. 598）。

  (A) since " 從～以來 " (C) until " 到～爲止 " (D) also " 也 "

16. (**D**) Nations *all over the world today* are trying their best *to cope*
with the energy crisis.

 " 今日世界各國都在盡全力，以應付能源危機。"

* all over the world 是形容詞片語，修飾 Nations 。to cope … crisis 是不定詞片語當副詞用，修飾 trying，表目的。

  (A) solve " 解決 "，是及物動詞，後面直接接受詞。
  (B) survive〔sɚ'vaɪv〕*vt.,vi.* 殘存；生還
  (C) tackle〔'tæk!〕*vt.*解決；處理 (D) *cope with* " 應付 "

  try one's best " 盡力而爲 " energy crisis " 能源危機 "

17. (**C**) *In many modern cities*, Taipei <u>included</u>, congestion and air
pollution have become real problems.

 " 在許多現代化的城市裏，台北包括在內，擁擠和空氣污染已成爲眞正
的問題。"

* Taipei included 是插入的獨立分詞構句，可改爲對等子句，放在句
尾：…, and Taipei is included.

  (A)(B) 都應該用過去分詞。
  (D) 如要用現在分詞 including，則應改爲 including Taipei，是由
   補述用法的形容詞子句 which include Taipei 簡化而來的形容
   詞片語（詳見文法寶典 p. 457）。

18. (**A**) That was a close call : you <u>could have been</u> hit by the car.

 " 那眞是千鈞一髮：你本來會被車子撞的。"

* 由前面的動詞 was，可知是過去的事；又根據句意，可知與過去事實
相反，故用假設法 could have＋p.p. 。

  (B) can have＋p.p. 表示對過去的推測，但不是假設法。
  (C) could be 表與現在事實相反的假設。
  (D) can be 表對現在的推測。

  close call " 千鈞一髮 "

19. (**C**) Don't worry. *If he said he would help you*, he will (*help*).

　　"別耽心。如果他說過要幫助你，他就會這麼做。"

　　* If 所引導表條件的副詞子句，修飾 help；子句中 he would help
　　you 是省略了 that 的名詞子句，作 said 的受詞。因為 said 是過去式，
　　所以空格裡要填過去式助動詞 would（詳見文法寶典 p. 351）。

　　　(A)(B)(D)時式均不合。

20. (**A**) Facts and figures, *even when accurate*, can *often* be misleading.

　　"事實和數字即使是精確的，仍常常可能導致錯誤。"

　　* even when (*they are*) accurate 是插入的副詞子句，修飾 be，子
　　句中省略了主詞和動詞。

　　　(A) 精確的　　(B) 錯誤的　　(C) 詳細的　　(D) 小心的

　　　figure〔'fɪgɚ〕 *n.* 數字
　　　misleading〔mɪs'lidɪŋ〕 *adj.* 導致錯誤的

Ⅳ. 閱讀能力

Part A

21. (**B**) *If one thing characterizes China more than anything else*, it is
　　Confucianism.

　　"如果有一件事比其他事情更能描述中國的特性，那就是儒家思想。"

　　　(A) 儒家思想是中國最重要的哲學。
　　　(B) 儒家思想最能代表中國的生活方式。
　　　(C) 為了瞭解中國，認識儒家思想是必要的。
　　　(D) 在中國，其他的哲學不如儒家思想那麼重要。

　　* If 引導的副詞子句，修飾 is，表條件，其中 more … else 是副詞片
　　語，修飾 characterizes。

　　　characterize〔'kærɪktə,raɪz〕 *vt.* 描述；以…為特性
　　　Confucianism〔kən'fjuʃənɪzm̩〕 *n.* 儒家思想；孔子思想
　　　more than "超過；比…更甚"

22. (**A**) Nothing could be in greater contrast to France ***than Germany.***

"沒有任何事物比德國更異於法國。"

 (A) 法國和德國彼此大不相同。

 (B) 法國和德國沒什麼不同。

 (C) 法國比德國大。

 (D) 德國優於法國。

 * than Germany 是省略了 is in contrast to France 的副詞子句，修飾 greater。

 in contrast to (*or with*) "與～顯然有別；與～成對比"

 as ～ as can be "至爲；極爲"

23. (**D**) The uniqueness *of this university* lies in its liberal spirit.

"這所大學的獨特點，在於它的自由精神。"

 (A) 這所大學在其他衆多學校之中，保有自由精神。

 (B) 這所大學和其他的一樣，有自由精神。

 (C) 這所大學的自由精神異於其他大學的。

 (D) 使這所大學異於其他大學的，就是它的自由精神。

 uniqueness〔ju'nɪknɪs〕*n.* 獨特   { ***lie in*** "在於"

 among others "在其他衆多之中"   { = ***consist in***

24. (**C**) The combined effects *of energy shortage and insufficient capit-*

al have damaged the economy *of many a developing country.*

"能源短缺和資金不足的雙重影響，損害了許多開發中國家的經濟。"

 (A) 許多開發中的國家已開始感到能源短缺和資金不足的危急。

 (B) 能源短缺和資金不足，對許多開發中國家的經濟不是大問題。

 (C) 能源短缺和資金不足，嚴重影響許多開發中國家的經濟。

 (D) 許多開發中的國家絕不會從能源短缺和資金不足的損害中復原。

* of … capital 是形容詞片語，修飾 effects；of many … country
也是形容詞片語，修飾 economy；many a ＋單數名詞（詳見文法
寶典 p.167）。

> effect〔ə'fɛkt, ı-, -ɛ-〕 n. 影響
> shortage〔'ʃɔrtıdʒ〕 n. 短缺；不足
> insufficient〔ˌınsə'fıʃənt〕 adj. 不充足的
> capital〔'kæpətl̩〕 n. 資金；首都　　damage〔'dæmıdʒ〕 vt. 損害
> developing country "開發中國家"
> pinch〔pıntʃ〕 n. 危急；困難　　 *recover from* "從～復元"

25. （ **B** ） The academic record *of John* has not *in some ways* been a proud
one.

"約翰的學業成績，在某些方面並不值得驕傲。"

(A) 約翰學業成績傑出。　　　(B) 約翰的學業成績有待加強。
(C) 約翰以他的學業成績爲傲。
(D) 約翰已盡力改善他的學業成績。

* *in some ways* "在某些方面"，是副詞片語，修飾 been。

> outstanding〔aʊt'stændıŋ〕 adj. 傑出的
> performance〔pɚ'fɔrməs〕 n. 成績；表現
> *leave something to be desired* "有待加強；有些缺點"
> *leave nothing to be desired* "毫無缺點"
> *leave much to be desired* "缺點很多"

26. （ **C** ） The large task *of feeding today's world population* is hard
to imagine.

"供給食物給今天世界人口的龐大工作，是難以想像的。"

(A) 很難想像今天世界的人口。
(B) 供給食物給今天世界的人口，超過人的能力範圍。
(C) 供給食物給今天世界人口的困難，不容易估計。
(D) 今天世界人口太多，所以我們無法供給食物。

＊ of feeding … population 是形容詞片語，修飾 task 。

conceive〔kən'siv〕*vt.* 想像

27. （ **B** ） Cells are the units *from* ***which*** *all but the simplest living organisms are built.*

"細胞是除了最簡單生物外，一切生物的構成單位。"

(A) 多數最簡單生物是由細胞構成的。

(B) 除了最簡單的生物外，一切生物都是由細胞構成的。

(C) 細胞是所有最簡單生物的基本構成物質。

(D) 最簡單的生物和其他的生物，都是由細胞構成的。

＊ from which … built 是形容詞子句，修飾 units，which 在子句中又作 from 的受詞。but 在此可視為連接詞或介詞（詳見文法寶典 p.565）。

cell〔sɛl〕*n.* 細胞　　unit〔'junɪt〕*n.* 單位

organism〔'ɔrgən͵ɪzəm〕*n.* 生物；有機體

⎧ ***be made up of*** " 由～所組成"
⎨ ＝ ***be composed of***
⎩ ＝ ***consist of***

28. （ **A** ） ***It was*** the success *of the simplest tools* ***that*** started the whole trend of human evolution.

"最簡單工具的成功，才開始了整個人類進化的趨勢。"

(A) 直到人類開始使用工具，人類整個進化的過程才開始。

(B) 工具使用的成功，是人類進化的直接結果。

(C) 人類使用工具，和其進化沒有直接的關係。

(D) 人類的進化是由某件不同於工具的使用的事所引起的。

＊本句是 It was … that 的強調句型，所強調的部分是 the success of the simplest tools（詳見文法寶典 p.115）。

trend〔trɛnd〕*n.* 趨勢

evolution〔͵ɛvə'luʃən〕*n.* 進化

bring about " 引起；導致"　　 ***other than*** "與～不同"

29. （ D ） **As** communications improve **in the future**, so the need **for**

transportation will decrease.

"正如未來的通訊會改善一樣，所以運輸的需要將會減少。"

    (A) 未來運輸的需要，將和通訊設備的改善成正例。

    (B) 未來通訊設備的改善，會增強運輸的重要性。

    (C) 未來通訊設備和運輸的發展會並行。

    (D) 將來隨著通訊設備改善得更好，運輸會漸漸失去它的地位。

 * As … so "正如…，所以" 是相關連接詞，as 引導副詞子句，修
飾相關副詞 so，前後兩個子句有對比的關係。

    communication〔kə͵mjunə'keʃən〕 *n.* 通訊設備

    transportation〔͵trænspɚ'teʃən〕 *n.* 運輸

    in proportion to "與~成比例"（未說明時，通常指正比）

    heighten〔'haɪtn̩〕 *vt.* 提高；增強

    hand in hand "手牽手；共同地"

    lose ground "落伍；失勢"

30. （ A ） One man's meat is another man's poison.

"對甲是肉，對乙是毒；人各有所好。"

    (A) 你喜歡的東西未必就是我喜歡的。

    (B) 人近來必須小心，因為肉可能有毒。

    (C) 肉和毒藥一樣危險，因為兩者都可能使你生病。

    (D) 肉和毒藥沒有差別。

 *題句是英國諺語，相似的尚有：Everyone to his taste. "人
各有所好。"；Tastes differ. "人人品味不同。"；Beauty
is in the eye of the beholder. "情人眼裏出西施。"等（詳
見英文諺語 p.535）。

    poison〔'pɔɪzn̩〕 *n.* 毒藥

    poisonous〔'pɔɪznəs〕 *adj.* 有毒的

    ⎧ **these days** "近來；近日"

    ⎨ = **of late** = lately

    ⎩ = recently

Part B

If education is the transmission of civilization, we are *unques-*
tionably progressing.

「假如教育是傳播文明，我們無疑地是在進步。」

* If 引導的副詞子句，progressing，表條件。

transmission〔træns'mɪʃən〕*n.* 傳播
unquestionably〔ʌn'kwɛstʃənəblɪ〕*adv.* 無疑地
progress〔prə'grɛs〕*vi.* 進步

Civilization is not inherited ; it has to be learned **and** earned *by each*
generation anew ; *if the transmission should be interruped for one cen-*
tury, civilization would die, **and** we should be savages again.

「文明不是繼承而來的，每一代必須重新學習來得到它。萬一文明的傳播中斷了
一世紀，文明將會滅亡，而且我們也將再做野蠻人。」

* 句中的半支點（；）是連接沒有連接詞，但關係密切的子句（詳見文法寶典
p. 41）。anew "重新" 是副詞，修飾 learned 和 earned；if … century
是副詞子句，修飾 die 和 be，表條件；其中「should＋原形動詞」是表
與未來事實相反的假設（詳見文法寶典 p. 363）；and 連接兩個對等子句，作
假設法的主要子句。

inherit〔ɪn'hɛrɪt〕*vt.* 繼承　　anew〔ə'nju,ə'nu〕*adv.* 再；重新
interrupt〔‚ɪntə'rʌpt〕*vt.* 使中斷
civilization〔‚sɪvḷə'zeʃən,‚sɪvlaɪ-〕*n.* 文明
savage〔'sævɪdʒ〕*n.* 野蠻人

So our finest contemporary achievement is our unprecedented
expenditure *of wealth and toil in the provision of higher*
education for all.

「因而我們現在最卓越的成就，就在於我們花費史無前例的財力和人力，以提供
大眾接受更高等的教育。」

* So " 因而；因此 " 是副詞性連接詞，在此作轉承語，連接前面的句子。
  of … toil 和 in … all 是介詞片語，作形容詞用，共同修飾 expenditure，
  其中 for all 是形容詞片語，修飾 education。

> fine〔faɪn〕*adj.* 卓越的
> contemporary〔kən'tɛmpə͵rɛrɪ〕*adj.* 現代的
> unprecedented〔ʌn'prɛsə͵dɛntɪd〕*adj.* 無前例的；空前的
> expenditure〔ɪk'spɛndɪtʃɚ〕*n.* 費用
> toil〔tɔɪl〕*n.* 辛勞工作　　provision〔prə'vɪʒən〕*n.* 供應

Once colleges were luxuries, *designed for the male half of the*

liesure class; *today* universities are *so* numerous *that* he who

runs *may* become a Ph. D.

" 大學一度是奢侈品，只是為有閒階級的男性而設計的。今天，大學非常多，以
致努力的人都可能成為博士。"

* Once " 一度 " 是副詞，修飾 were；designed … class 是由補述用法的形
  容詞子句 which were designed … 簡化而來，也可改為對等子句 and
  were designed … 。其中 of … class 是形容詞片語，修飾 male half " 男
  性 " 。so … that " 如此…以致 " 是從屬連接詞，so 是副詞，修飾 numerous, that … Ph. D. 是副詞子句，修飾 so，表結果（詳見文法寶典 p.516），
  其中 who runs 是形容詞子句，修飾 he 。

> luxury〔'lʌkʃərɪ〕*n.* 奢侈品
> male〔mel〕*adj.* 男性的　　*n.* 男性
> numerous〔'njumərəs〕*adj.* 極多的
> Ph. D. = Doctor of Philosophy " 博士學位 "

We may not have excelled the selected geniuses *of the past,* *but* we have

raised the level and average *of knowledge beyond any age in history.*

" 我們可能不優於過去所精選的天才，但是我們已將一般的知識水準，提昇到遠
超過歷史上任何時代的程度。"

*　but 連接兩個對等子句 We … past 和 we … history, beyond … history
　是副詞片語，修飾 raised 。

　　excel〔ɪk'sɛl〕*vt*. 優於；勝過

31.（ **C** ）在教育方面，我們正在進步，因為＿＿＿＿＿

　　　　(A) 大學已變得更奢侈。

　　　　(B) 大學教育只是為少數人而設計的。

　　　　(C) 過去不曾聽說的大量金錢和人力，已投資在大學教育上。

　　　　(D) 我們已產生了許多天才。

32.（ **B** ）文明是＿＿＿＿＿而一代傳一代。

　　　　(A) 藉自然的生物演變過程　　(B) 藉每一新生代的努力

　　　　(C) 藉天才的貢獻　　　　　　(D) 藉知識的增加

33.（ **D** ）作者認為教育的目的是＿＿＿＿＿

　　　　(A) 製造持有文憑的人。　　　(B) 給天才創作的機會。

　　　　(C) 增加國家的財富和力量。　(D) 保存文明的生命。

　　　　diploma〔dɪ'plomə〕*n*. 文憑

34.（ **B** ）萬一文明中斷一百年，＿＿＿＿＿

　　　　(A) 它很容易復甦。　　　　　(B) 它會毀滅。

　　　　(C) 它會再被創造。　　　　　(D) 它會變得更好。

35.（ **A** ）由於今天有這麼多大學，＿＿＿＿＿

　　　　(A) 任何人都有機會得到最高學位。

　　　　(B) 將有許多天才產生。

　　　　(C) 學生的素質已經降低。

　　　　(D) 使得許多國家的財富及人才枯竭。

　　　　academic degree “學位”　　　drain〔dren〕*vt*. 使乾竭

Ⅴ. 翻譯：中譯英

36. 他是你最好的朋友，再怎麼也不會出賣你。

　　As your best friend, he will be the last person *to betray you*.

　* **the last** ＋名詞 " 最不可能的～；最不願意的～ " (詳見文法寶典p.199，664)例：

That's **the last** thing I should expect him to do.

(那是我認爲他最不可能做的一件事。)

Health is **the last** thing that wealth can buy.

(健康絕非財富所能買。)

37. 比這個更有趣的故事，我從來沒有聽說過。

A more interesting story I have never heard.

　* A more interesting story 是 heard 的受詞，爲強調而倒裝置句首。

　（詳見文法寶典 p.635)。原句爲：

I have never heard a more interesting story (**than this**).

38. 你昨天打電話來的時候，我們正在吃午飯。

We were having (**or** eating) lunch **when you called on the phone yesterday.**

　* when … phone 是副詞子句，修飾 having。表示過去某一時候正在進行的

　動作，用過去進行式。

39. 告訴孩子們，他們如果不守規矩，就得不到禮物。

Tell the children to behave **or** they are not getting any presents.

　* to behave … presents 是不定詞片語，作名詞用，當 Tell 的直接受詞；可

　改爲 that 子句：that they must behave，or they are not …

　　　　　　　＝ that if they do not behave，they are not …

　behave (**oneself**) " 守規矩 "

40. 我整天都研究這樁問題，到現在還沒解決。

I have been working on the problem **all day**，**but** it is not

solved **yet**.

　* 表示從過去某時間開始，一直繼續到現在仍在進行的動作，用現在完成

　進行式 (詳見文法寶典 p.349)。

　work on " 繼續工作 "

Ⅵ. 翻譯：英譯中

41. The way *our drivers drive*, we cannot be too careful *when crossing the streets*.

    我們的司機們那種開車的方式，使我們過街的時候愈小心愈好（再怎麼小心也不為過）。

    * The way our drivers drive 之前省略了 Owing to " 由於 " 。

    　cannot ~ too " 無論~也不為過 " 與 *cannot ~ over-* ＋ V 意思相同。

    　例：The virtue in enlarging one's reading *cannot be over-emphasized.* （擴大個人閱讀範圍的價值，再怎麼被強調也不為過。） 67日大

42. People are beginning to realize the importance *of their cultural heritage.*

    大家開始了解到他們自己的文化遺產的重要性。

    　　　cultural〔'kʌltʃərəl〕*adj.* 文化的　　　heritage〔'hɛrətɪdʒ〕*n.* 遺產

43. You may pick *whatever* takes your fancy.

    你喜歡什麼就揀什麼。

    * 複合關係代名詞 whatever 引導名詞子句，作 pick 的受詞。

    　take (or strike, catch, suit, please) one's fancy " 討某人喜歡 "

44. *If he persists in laziness*, he might as well withdraw from school.

    如果他堅持懈怠下去，倒不如退學算了。

    * If … laziness 是副詞子句，修飾 withdraw，表條件。

    　might as well ＋ V " 不妨~；最好~ "
    　＝ *had better* ＋ V

45. You have to admit *that what* he says makes perfect sense.

    你得承認，他的話很有道理。

* that 是從屬連接詞，引導名詞子句，作 admit 的受詞；子句中，what he says 作主詞。

make sense " 合道理 "

perfect 〔ˊpɝfɪkt 〕 *adj.* 全然的；徹底的

Ⅶ. 英文作文（參考範例）：

I have long hoped to become a college student. I made up my mind to be a college student and specialize in English as early as two years ago. On the one hand, it is a universal language; on the other, it enables us to understand the world better. Moreover, to know another foreign language means to possess another fortune. So, I have done my best to work hard to fulfill my ambition. Though I have encountered many difficulties, I'll never lose heart. And success will certainly come to me after all.

　　長久以來我就希望成為大學生。早在兩年前，我就下定決心要成為一個大學生，而且專攻英文。一方面，它是世界性的語言；另一方面，它能使我們更瞭解這個世界。此外，懂得另一種外國語言意味著擁有一項財富。所以，我已經盡力用功，以達成我的志向。雖然我遭遇了許多困難，我決不灰心。最後成功一定會到來。

心得筆記欄

六十九學年度大學暨獨立學院入學考試
英 文 試 題

I. 拼字

說明：下列 1 至 10.題，每題中有五個單字，其中有一個字的拼法是錯的。找出
這個拼法錯誤的單字。每題 1／2 分。5％。

例：(A) four　　　　　(B) fourth　　　　　(C) fourty
(D) fortieth　　　(E) fourteen

答案：(C)

1. (A) punish　　(B) own　　　　(C) adequite　　(D) quarantee
(E) respond

2. (A) hyphen　　(B) temprature　(C) calculate　(D) strengthen
(E) avoid

3. (A) aproove　　(B) genuine　　(C) immature　(D) offend
(E) destroy

4. (A) traffic　　(B) disturb　　(C) revenge　　(D) petroleum
(E) cooporate

5. (A) judgment　(B) temporary　(C) illegal　　(D) limmited
(E) challenge

6. (A) security　(B) emphasize　(C) welfare　　(D) overthrow
(E) stuborn

7. (A) propriety　(B) technique　(C) obedient　(D) prosperus
(E) intolerable

8. (A) obstinate　(B) opposition　(C) convincing　(D) shedule
(E) ripe

9. (A) career　　(B) taxi　　　(C) mission　　(D) completion
(E) pronounciation

10. (A) imitate　　(B) frightn　　(C) weapon　　(D) phenomenal
(E) niece

II. 重音

說明：下列 11. 至 15. ，每題有 A、B、C 三項，是 X 與 Y 兩人間連貫的對話。每項
項中有兩個音節分別標明為 1 與 2 ，主重音如不讀在 1 則必讀在 2 。請在
A、B、C 三項中選出主重音位置與其他兩項不同之一項。如下例 A 項的
主重音讀在 help ，B 項的主重音讀在 door ，C 項的主重音讀在 all ，應
$\quad\quad\quad\quad$ 2 $\quad\quad\quad\quad\quad\quad\quad\quad\quad\quad$ 1 $\quad\quad\quad\quad\quad\quad\quad\quad\quad\quad$ 2
選 B 為答案。每題 1 分。5％。

例：(A) X：Need some help ?
$\quad\quad\quad\quad\quad\quad\quad\quad$ 1 $\quad$ 2

$\quad$ (B) Y：Would you mind opening the door for me ?
$\quad\quad\quad\quad\quad\quad\quad\quad\quad\quad\quad\quad\quad\quad\quad\quad$ 1 $\quad\quad$ 2

$\quad$ (C) X：Not at all.
$\quad\quad\quad\quad\quad\quad$ 1 $\quad$ 2

答案：(B)

11. (A) X：Have you told them ?　　　　(B) Y：Of course not.
$\quad\quad\quad\quad\quad\quad$ 1 $\quad$ 2 $\quad\quad\quad\quad\quad\quad\quad\quad\quad\quad$ 1 $\quad$ 2

$\quad$ (C) X：Better keep it between us.
$\quad\quad\quad\quad\quad\quad\quad\quad\quad\quad$ 1 $\quad\quad$ 2

12. (A) X：Is it possible ?　　　　　　(B) Y：It's got to be.
$\quad\quad\quad\quad\quad$ 1 $\quad$ 2 $\quad\quad\quad\quad\quad\quad\quad\quad\quad\quad\quad$ 1 $\quad$ 2

$\quad$ (C) X：You take too much for granted.
$\quad\quad\quad\quad\quad\quad\quad\quad\quad\quad\quad$ 1 $\quad\quad$ 2

13. (A) X：Are you traveling on your own ?
$\quad\quad\quad\quad\quad\quad\quad\quad\quad\quad$ 1 $\quad\quad$ 2

$\quad$ (B) Y：My daughter's with me.
$\quad\quad\quad\quad\quad$ 1 $\quad\quad\quad$ 2

$\quad$ (C) X：Is she the one with the pigtails ?
$\quad\quad\quad\quad\quad\quad\quad\quad\quad\quad\quad\quad\quad$ 1 $\quad$ 2

14. (A) X：Time to get up, John.　　　　(B) Y：It's only six o'clock.
$\quad\quad\quad\quad\quad\quad\quad\quad$ 1 $\quad$ 2 $\quad\quad\quad\quad\quad\quad\quad\quad\quad\quad\quad\quad$ 1 $\quad$ 2

$\quad$ (C) X：We've got work to do.
$\quad\quad\quad\quad\quad\quad\quad\quad$ 1 $\quad\quad$ 2

15. (A) X：It can't be done.
　　　　　　　　　1　　2

(B) Y：You're talking nonsense.
　　　　　　　　　1　　　　2

(C) X：Try it yourself, then.
　　　　　　　　　1　　　2

Ⅲ. 習慣用法、字彙、文法

說明：下列16.至25.題，每題中有一個空白，選出四個答案中最恰當的一項，填
　　　入空白後則句義完整，文法正確，合乎習慣用法。每題2分。20%。

例：She is in the garden _____ some flowers.

(A) picking　　　(B) taking　　　(C) doing　　　(D) wanting

答案：(A)

16. Rarely _____ such nonsense.

(A) I have heard　　　　　　　(B) have I heard

(C) I do hear　　　　　　　　(D) don't I hear

17. Every night John studied hard and did his homework _____ 11：30 p.m.

(A) at　　　(B) since　　　(C) until　　　(D) for

18. John was too much _____ with the thought of passing examinations.

(A) preoccupied　　(B) withdrawn　　(C) indebted　　(D) concern

19. The supply of oil, the most important source of energy in the world today, is _____ short.

(A) making　　　(B) running　　　(C) doing　　　(D) letting

20. Mencius's mother was known for her moving from place to place in order to find for her son more suitable _____.

(A) surrounding　　　　　　　(B) surroundings

(C) circumstance　　　　　　　(D) circumstances

21. What you have heard is a lie, and a malicious lie _____.

(A) at that　　　(B) like that　　　(C) at all　　　(D) in all

22. The priest is yelling at the little boy. That _____ as a strange thing for him to do.

(A) seemingly appears　　　　(B) appeals to me

(C) strikes me　　　　　　　(D) has the impression

23. It is an＿＿＿＿＿fact that the greatest problem facing the world today is that of how to avoid a nuclear war.
　　(A) illuminating
　　(B) indifferent
　　(C) unsuspected
　　(D) unquestionable

24. In the 18th century there were only two classes : the working class and the upper class. But later the＿＿＿＿＿new middle class began to play an important role in western society.
　　(A) declining　　(B) moving　　(C) appearing　　(D) emerging

25. John was the only man not struck down by the flu. While all of us were choking and sneezing and using up sackfuls of paper handkerchiefs, he remained in complete possession of his human dignity, looking the＿＿＿＿＿of health.
　　(A) picture　　(B) condition　　(C) perfection　　(D) idol

Ⅳ. 寫作測驗

　　說明：下列 26.至 30.題，每題有若干短句，今按其綜合意義重寫成一個句子。新句
　　　　　中有一空白，試在四個答案中選一個最合適的填入空白，以使文法正確，句
　　　　　意完整。每題 2 分。10 ％。

　　例：I don't like John. I don't like Peter.
　　　I like
　　　(A) nobody
　　　(B) none other than John and Peter
　　　(C) either John or Peter
　　　(D) neither John nor Peter
　　答案：(D)

26. They began to work. They were absorbed in their work. The job was finished immediately.
　　They set themselves to work with such concentration that the job was finished＿＿＿＿＿.
　　(A) in no time
　　(B) at all
　　(C) without time
　　(D) at any time

27. I am going to tell you just that. Nothing more. As things stand now, you'd better know no more than that.

At the moment, you need to know _____.

(A) nothing about the truth　　(B) less than what you already know

(C) no more than what you have already been told

(D) more than what's good for you _____.

28. People sometimes see strange objects in the sky. Reports of these were first recorded more than 200 years ago. Research on them began late. For more than 200 years sightings of strange objects in the sky had been reported in different parts of the world, but it was _____ recent times that these began to receive some serious attention.

(A) still　　　(B) in between　　　(C) never before　　　(D) not until

29. I cannot give you an answer this moment. I'll let you know my decision in two weeks. Please don't make me decide now. If you want me to decide now, I have to refuse your offer.

_____, then I'm afraid I'll have to turn down your offer.

(A) Granted you're curious about my decision

(B) If you wish to press for an answer now

(C) Much as I would like to accept your generosity

(D) Realizing that the earlier a decision is made the better

30. We don't know much about the sea. Technical information concerning the wealth under the sea is insufficient. Our knowledge is still poorer about how to make the best use of its resources at a minimum of cost.

We simply do not know enough about the sea as it is, _____.

(A) in addition, we are equally unaware of what wealth it holds for us

(B) much less how to explore and use it efficiently

(C) on top of which, we have been deprived of a rich store of knowledge about its resources and how to tap them

(D) beyond that, a non-familiarity with it provides us with nothing but ignorance

V. 中譯英

說明：下列 31. 至 35. 題每題有一句中文，下隨四種英譯。選出其中最恰當的一種。每題 2 分。10％。

31. 大家都喜歡好天氣。

　(A) People like good weather.　　(B) People like good weathers.

　(C) People like a good weather.　(D) People like the weather well.

32. 他們在一小時以前就應該已經會面了。

　(A) They should meet an hour ago.

　(B) They would have met an hour ago.

　(C) They should have met an hour ago.

　(D) They are supposed to meet an hour ago.

33. 他的境況比三年前好得多。

　(A) It has been three years since he achieved success.

　(B) He is far better off now than he was three years ago.

　(C) His conditions have been improved over the last three years.

　(D) It was only three years ago that he found himself at a total loss.

34. 人的年事愈高，愈難抗拒疾病。

　(A) Old people fall easy victims to failing health.

　(B) The aged are especially easy to contract disease.

　(C) As the years pass, elderly people lose their power to fight off diseases.

　(D) One's resistance to the attack of disease grows up with the years.

35. 耐心再好，總不會永無止境。

　(A) The more patient you are, the less likely you are to reach infinity.

　(B) A patient man can go a long way.

　(C) There are endless possibilities for a patient man.

　(D) There is always a limit to one's patience.

VI. 英譯中

說明：下列 36. 至 40. 題每題是一句英文，附有四種中譯。選出其中最恰當的一個。每題 2 分。10％。

36. She said she was through with singing.

　(A) 她說她唱歌唱得太久了。　　(B) 她說她不再唱歌了。

　(C) 她說她唱歌唱煩了。　　　　(D) 她說她要從頭再開始唱。

37. It takes rich imagination to be an inventor.

　(A) 財富，想像力和發明家三位一體。

　(B) 有想像力的發明家隨時能發跡。

　(C) 做一個發明家需要具備豐富的想像力。

　(D) 有想像力，有錢，才能做個成功的發明家。

38. I will make a special point of seeing you before I leave for Taipei.

　(A) 我上台北的目的就是要來看你。

　(B) 到台北後，我一定特地來看你。

　(C) 我特別要強調的一點是我一定會陪你去台北。

　(D) 去台北前我一定會先來看你。

39. Speaking the language the way you do, you can pass for a native.

　(A) 聽你講話，別人會認為你是當地人。

　(B) 你的語言才能勉強及格。

　(C) 你的鄉音太重，人家一聽就知道你是外鄉人。

　(D) 你的英文講得太好了，簡直可以冒充美國人。

40. What is simpler than that ?

　(A) 還有更簡單的事呢！　　　(B) 那也還簡單。

　(C) 那是再簡單不過了。　　　(D) 不致於那麼簡單吧？

Ⅶ. 閱讀能力　　PART A.

　說明：下列 41.至 55.題每題附隨的四個答案解釋該題意義，其中只有一個是對
　　　　的。選出這個正確的答案。每題 2 分。30 ％。

　例：It's time you had a haircut.

　　(A) you finally had a haircut.

　　(B) It's too late for a haircut.

　　(C) You'd better go to the barber-shop now.

　　(D) Take your time. There's no hurry.

　答案：(C)

41. Mary said to John " Look what you did to my dress ! "

　(A) Mary thanked John for the dress he had bought for her.

　(B) Mary was excited about the dress ; it looked rather nice.

　(C) Mary blamed John for his ruining her dress.

　(D) In Mary's opinion John would some day become a good tailor.

42. John said before he took the examination, " We've learned enough to pass our exams. "
   (A) John showed confidence.
   (B) John passed the exam.
   (C) John failed the exam.
   (D) John was uncertain.

43. I believe <u>that</u> that was what he said.
   The word " that " underlined in the sentence is
   (A) a determiner.
   (B) an adverb.
   (C) a conjunction.
   (D) a pronoun.

44. The job is much more than child's play.
   The job is
   (A) easy.
   (B) not as easy as you might think.
   (C) to present a play for children.
   (D) to present a play for adults.

45. He is not the man that he was.
   (A) He has a new job.
   (B) He has moved to another city.
   (C) He has changed his name.
   (D) He is a changed man.

46. I am going to wash my hands of the whole thing.
   (A) My hands are dirty ; I'm going to wash them.
   (B) My hands need washing.
   (C) I will not be responsible for it any longer.
   (D) I will start the whole thing as soon as I get myself cleaned.

47. Friendship redoubles joys, and cuts griefs in halves.
   Friendship, among other things, means that
   (A) people can be too easily saddened.
   (B) there is a lesser degree of sorrow when it comes to you because someone will share it with you.
   (C) your joys are doubly hard to find.
   (D) there will be walls whichever way you turn.

48. The greatest happiness of the greatest number is the foundation of legislation.

To write laws for a nation, the basic consideration is

(A) what is best for the greatest happiness.

(B) a life of subsistence for the greatest number of people.

(C) the quality of happiness for the well-to-do.

(D) the well-being of the majority.

49. John wrote them for information a week ago but they are still holding out on him.

(A) There has been no response to John's inquiry.

(B) They are holding the letter for John.

(C) They wrote John promptly in answer to his letter.

(D) They showed no hesitation in their eagerness to respond.

50. In the USA, restaurants with any pretensions to being high class almost always have lists of imported wines far longer than their list of native ones.

These restaurants are likely to have in stock

(A) more native wines than imported ones.

(B) more foreign wines than native ones.

(C) only imported wines.

(D) only native wines.

51. Poor countries with a rich cultural heritage are finding that priceless bits and pieces of their past keep disappearing, only to appear on the market of the West.

In more precise terms, these bits and pieces of the poor countries' past refer particularly to

(A) old coins.

(B) ancient history.

(C) art objects.

(D) ancient timepieces.

52. Judging of the speech contest will be carried out by persons appointed by the college president, the decision of such judges being final.

(A) The college president is responsible for the judging.

(B) The college president is invested with the power to make the final decision.

(C) The judges work independently.

(D) The judges reach their decisions with the final approval of the college president.

53. The rescue mission was on the point of taking off, when weather conditions made it necessary to call it off.

(A) The mission was successful.

(B) It was necessary for the mission to go ahead despite bad weather.

(C) Weather conditions made it imperative to stop the mission before it even started.

(D) The mission took on the stormy weather valiantly. No casualties were reported.

54. Every man who is high up loves to think that he has done it all himself ; and the wife smiles, and lets it go at that.

(A) Wives of great men usually know better.

(B) Wives do not contribute to the making of great men.

(C) Behind every wife there is a dutiful husband.

(D) Men in high positions know full well that they cannot have become what they are without the help of their wives.

55. " Rain is possible but not probable before evening. " " It's possible that it will rain if the wind changes, but with such a cloudless sky it doesn't seem probable. "

From the two examples given above, we may draw the conclusion that

(A) what is possible may not be probable.

(B) what is probable, after all, may not possibly happen.

(C) the words " possible " and "probable" may be used interchangeably.

(D) what is possible and what is probable refer to almost the same degree of possibility ; if there is any difference, it is negligible.

PART B.

說明：下列56.至60.題每題附隨的四個答案解釋下文意義，其中只有一個是對的。選出這個正確的答案。每題2分。10％。

Human and political freedom has never existed and cannot exist without a large measure of economic freedom. Those of us who have been so fortunate as to have been born in a free society tend to take freedom for granted, to regard it as the natural state of mankind. It is not-- it is a rare and precious thing. Most people throughout history, most people today, have lived in conditions of tyranny and misery, not of freedom and prosperity. The clearest demonstration of how much people value freedom is the way they vote with their feet when they have no other way to vote.

56. Political freedom

(A) comes before economic freedom.

(B) is dependent on economic freedom.

(C) has nothing to do with economic freedom.

(D) determines economic freedom, but not the way round.

57. Freedom

(A) is a natural state of mankind.

(B) is something precious and rare.

(C) to thoes born in a free society is something beyond reach.

(D) to those born in a not so free society is often taken for granted.

58. Which of the following can be regarded as a natural pair, by which it is meant that they are closely associated with each other ?

(A) tyranny and prosperity

(B) tyranny and freedom

(C) freedom and misery

(D) misery and tyranny

59. Most people in the world today

    (A) are in want of freedom.

    (B) enjoy total freedom.

    (C) lead a prosperous life.

    (D) have rid themselves of miseries.

60. When people have to vote with their feet they

    (A) move on to greener pastures.

    (B) are required to put down their foot as a sign indicating approval.

    (C) are required to stamp their feet as a sign indicating disapproval.

    (D) are forced to give up their freedom.

69年大學聯考英文試題詳解

Ⅰ. 拼字：

1. (C)　2. (B)　3. (A)　4. (E)　5. (D)　6. (E)　7. (D)　8. (D)　9. (E)　10. (B)

Ⅱ. 重音：

11. (C)　12. (B)　13. (A)　14. (B)　15. (C)

Ⅲ. 習慣用法、字彙、文法：

16. (B)　17. (C)　18. (A)　19. (B)　20. (B)　21. (A)　22. (C)　23. (D)　24. (D)　25. (A)

〔解析〕

16. 否定副詞 rarely 放句首時，主詞和動詞的位置與疑問句同。

18. *be preoccupied with* ～ " 一心一意地～ "

19. *run short* " 短缺 "

20. surroundings 和 circumstances 均指環境，但 surroundings 強調四周的事物，circumstances 則指較抽象的情況，如經濟情況，事情的前後因果關係等。

21. at that ＝ besides " 並且 "

22. (A) 外表似乎　(B) 引起我的興趣　(C) 使我突然想起　(D) 以爲～

23. (A) 照明的　(B) 漠不關心的　(C) 沒有嫌疑的　(D) 無可置疑的

24. (A) 衰敗的　(B) 移動的　(C) 英文中沒有 appear 加 ing 用以修飾名詞的用法。(D) 興起的。

25. the picture of health " 健康的化身；十分健康 "

Ⅳ. 寫作測驗：

26. (A)　27. (C)　28. (D)　29. (B)　30. (B)

〔解析〕

26. *in no time* ＝ *at once* " 立刻 "

27. *as things stand* " 依據現況 "　*no more than* " 僅僅只要 "　*at the moment* ＝ now

28. *not until* ～＋倒裝句 " 直到～才… "

29. *turn down* ＝ reject, refuse " 拒絕；擱置 " (A) 即使你對我的決定好奇 (B) 如果你現在逼著要有答覆　(C) 雖然我很喜歡接受受你的慷慨　(D) 了解到早做決定早好。

30. *make the best use of* "充分利用" 　　at a minimum of "以最少的～"
　　(B) *much less = let alone = not to mention*，更不用說如何有效地去開發
　　及利用它。　(A) 除此之外，我們也一樣不知道海底爲我們保存了什麼。　(C)
　　最重要的，我們已被剝奪掉有關其資源，及如何開發它們的大量知識。　(D)
　　不只那樣，對其不熟悉的狀況，使得我們只擁有無知而沒有其它的東西。

Ⅴ. 中譯英：

31.(A)　　32.(C)　　33.(B)　　34.(C)　　35.(D)

Ⅵ. 英譯中：

36.(B)　　37.(C)　　38.(D)　　39.(A)　　40.(C)

Ⅶ. 閱讀測驗：
　　Part A.

41.(C)　42.(A)　43.(C)　44.(B)　45.(D)　46.(C)　47.(B)　48.(D)　49.(A)　50.(B)

51.(C)　52.(C)　53.(C)　54.(A)　55.(A)

　　Part B.

56.(B)　　57.(B)　　58.(D)　　59.(A)　　60.(A)

中譯：

　　沒有相當大的經濟自由，就從來沒有過、也不可能有人類及政治的自由。我們
這些有幸能生長在一個自由社會中的人，常常容易認爲自由是件理所當然的東西，
視自由爲人類的自然生活狀態。事實卻不是如此──自由是個稀有而寶貴的東西，
古今大多數人都生活在暴政及悲慘的狀況下，而不是生活在自由及繁榮中。要證明
有多少人重視自由，最清楚的方法，就是看有多少人在無法用其它方式投票時，他
們就用腳投票（在沒有投票權時，就搬到別的地方去）。

〔解析〕

a large measure of "相當的；大部分的"

take ～ for granted "視～爲當然"　　precious〔'prɛʃəs〕*adj.* 寶貴的

tyranny〔'tɪrənɪ〕*n.* 暴政　　prosperity〔prɑs'pɛrətɪ〕*n.* 繁榮；成功

demonstration〔,dɛmən'streʃən〕*n.* 證實

六十八學年度大學暨獨立學院入學考試
英 文 試 題

I. 重音

說明：下列 1. 至 5. 題每題的四項中各有兩個音節標有不同底線。按照一般英語
　　　口語習慣，不強調特別意義時，四項中三項的主重音均在底線相同的音
　　　節上。另一項的主重音則在相異音節上，請在答案卡上標出。每題 1 分。

例：(A) tech<u>no</u>logy　　　　　　(B) Good Luck !
　　(C) Mind your manners　　　(D) post office
答案：(D)

1. (A) in the middle of the road　　(B) smoke-bomb
　　(C) during office hours　　　　(D) task force

2. (A) High Street　　　　　　　(B) nineteen eighty-four
　　(C) nerve-center　　　　　　(D) a lover of horror films

3. (A) fit for a prince　　　　　　(B) photographer
　　(C) gravestone　　　　　　　(D) Bob Hope

4. (A) astronomy　　(B) mischievous　　(C) rigidities
　　(D) they were buried alive

5. (A) Peter : Excuse me, could you tell me the time, please.
　　(B) John : Certainly ! It's exactly ten past two.
　　(C) Mary : Your watch is fast-- it's nearly ten to two.
　　(D) John : You know, your watch loses.

II. 拼法

說明：下列 6. 至 10. 題，每題中有五個單字，其中有一個字的拼法是錯的。找出
　　　這個拼法錯誤的單字。每題 1 分。

例：(A) picnicing　(B) benevolence　(C) exhibition　(D) necessity
　　(E) pronunciation
答案：(A)

6. (A) forty　(B) musician　(C) government　(D) changable　(E) license

7. (A) solenm (B) reminiscence (C) committee (D) receive
   (E) calendar

8. (A) seize (B) forehead (C) nineth (D) hygiene (E) dying

9. (A) sincerety (B) exaggerate (C) tailor (D) preferred
   (E) preceding

10. (A) maintenance (B) imitate (C) occurence (D) conscientious
    (E) foreign

Ⅲ. 應對

　　說明：下列11.至15.題，每題有一句話，後隨四句回答，答話中有一句不恰當。
　　　　　請找出這句不恰當的答話。每題 2 分。

　　例：Why did you come so late ?

　　　　(A) I was caught in a terrible traffic jam.

　　　　(B) Are you sure you have the correct time ?

　　　　(C) Didn't you feel the same lately ?

　　　　(D) I'm sorry. Really, I am.

　　答案：(C)

11. You'd better go now.

　　(A) Just as you wish.　　　　(B) Go and see what you can do.

　　(C) Whatever you say.　　　　(D) There's no rush.

12. How prices have gone up !

　　(A) You're telling me !

　　(B) We can hardly make ends meet.

　　(C) It's going to be worse, I expect.

　　(D) The price comes to two fifty.

13. That was a smart move you made.

　　(A) Nothing to brag about, really.

　　(B) It's very kind of you.

　　(C) How kind of you to make room for me.

　　(D) I wasn't the one who made the move.

14. May I borrow one of your books?
    (A) Check it in at the other end of the counter, please.
    (B) You're perfectly welcome.
    (C) How long do you need it?
    (D) Which one do you want?

15. I wonder what's going to be the outcome.
    (A) May the best man win.
    (B) Very much depends on John's insistence on his proposals.
    (C) I was pleased to have the honor.
    (D) No use being too pessimistic about it.

Ⅳ. 習慣用法、文法、字彙

說明：下列16.至30.題，每題中有一個空白。選出四個答案中最恰當的一項，填
　　　入空白後則句義完整，文法正確，並合乎習慣用法。每題1分。

例：My mind was a _____ blank.
　　　(A) completely　　(B) total　　(C) entire　　(D) sum

答案：(B)

16. John likes to keep track, in a general sort of _____ , of all
    new developments in the natural sciences.
    (A) way　　　(B) ways　　　(C) a way　　　(D) the way

17. True, he was sixteen and she was nineteen. But he was old for his
    age and she looked_____ for hers.
    (A) young　　　(B) old　　　(C) elder　　　(D) youngest

18. This is exactly what happened. _____ my word for it.
    (A) Take　　　(B) Make　　　(C) Ask　　　(D) Believe

19. Roman law is one of the greatest systems _____ ever existed.
    (A) which is　　(B) which are　(C) that has　　(D) that have

20. Earlier in the book I wrote about the necessity of the arms race.
    I must_____write a word about its evils.
    (A) at here　　(B) today　　(C) this moment　(D) now

21. I don't know very much about modern architecture; to be quite frank, I don't_____admire most of the examples I've seen of architecture today.

    (A) much   (B) more   (C) very   (D) too

22. Are you going on for the rest of your life teaching, or are you going to do other things; are there other ambitions that you want to _____?

    (A) make   (B) fulfil   (C) work   (D) strive

23. _____that can endure uncomplainingly a long period of suffering is perhaps the noblest.

    (A) Courage   (B) Courages   (C) The courage   (D) The courages

24. Although too much leisure may lead people to a wasteful life, everyone has a right_____a minimum amount of leisure time.

    (A) with   (B) to   (C) on   (D) for

25. Over two thousand years ago, men discovered a method of_____water from one level to another by means of the vacuum pump.

    (A) rising   (B) raising   (C) laying   (D) making

26. In the sentence, " The size of the room is 12 ×14", the sign " ×" is to read "_____".

    (A) times   (B) cross   (C) by   (D) and

27. With a view_____ a quick profit, the firm was reduced to sacrificing control over the quality of their products.

    (A) to make   (B) to making   (C) to be making   (D) to have made

28. If the radiator of my car begins to leak and I am far from a garage. I may be able to stop the leak with chewing gum. This will be_____perhaps, but only for a time, in an emergency.

    (A) affected   (B) affecting   (C) effectuated   (D) effective

29. Many conventional laboratory instruments are so large or heavy that they cannot be used in space research, so special_____ versions have been developed.

    (A) deflated   (B) depressed   (C) compressed   (D) minaturized

30. Then he is off on some special topic, and I am once more _____ ,
    able to contribute no more than a monosyllable of agreement here
    and there ; though it does occur to me that I am perhaps valued just
    as much as a listener as a participant in the conversation.
    (A) quite at home　　　　　　　(B) out of my depth
    (C) brought to the realization　(D) aware of my usefulness

Ⅴ. 中譯英
　　說明：下列31.至35.題，每題畫有底線部分的文字，有四種英譯，選出其中最恰
　　　　　當的一種。每題2分。

31. 據說他考試沒及格。
    (A) Word has spread like bush fire that
    (B) Everyone knows that
    (C) We have been told that　　(D) It is widely circulated that

32. 「字典借一下好嗎？」「不行。」小妹嘟著嘴說。
    (A) Nothing doing.　　　　　　(B) Not going.
    (C) No bargaining.　　　　　　(D) Don't dream.

33. 我完全同意你的看法，改革首重檢討。
    (A) You have my complete confidence
    (B) You have fully convinced me
    (C) I am entirely with you
    (D) I whole-heartedly agree to assume the view

34. 不必擔心，我們會竭盡全力支持你。
    (A) all that has to be done is done
    (B) we'll go all out to support you
    (C) we have done the best we could to keep you from harm
    (D) to the best of our ability we shall not desert you

35. 由於電力供應中斷的緣故，公共設施均已癱瘓。
    (A) public buildings are paralyzed
    (B) facilities suffered a severe setback
    (C) utilities are deemed no longer adequate
    (D) services have ground to a halt

Ⅵ. 英譯中

說明：下列36.至40.題，每題畫有底線部分的文字，有四種中譯，選出其中最恰當的一種。每題2分。

36. All friends have deserted him because <u>he has got a loose tongue.</u>
    (A) 他是個話匣子。　　　　　　(B) 他口吃。
    (C) 他口無遮攔。　　　　　　　(D) 他講話口齒不清，有個大舌頭。

37. " You are always apologizing. When will you learn to be more confident of yourself ?
    " I'm sorry, but I promise I'll..." " <u>There you go again !</u>"
    (A) 你還是要往那邊走！　　　　(B) 你又走了！
    (C) 你又去了！　　　　　　　　(D) 你又來了！

38. In any automobile accident, <u>it is almost always the car in back which is at fault.</u>
    (A) 在每次車禍中，幾乎總是後面的車子找麻煩。
    (B) 在每次車禍中，幾乎總是後面的車子有過失。
    (C) 在每次車禍中，幾乎總是後面的車子要賠償。
    (D) 在每次車禍中，幾乎總是後面的車子受損壞。

39. You keep asking me questions of which I don't know the answers myself.
    It is said, you know, <u>some questions are best left unanswered.</u>
    (A) 有些問題的答案不知道也罷。
    (B) 有些問題最好不問。
    (C) 沒有答案的問題仍舊是問題。
    (D) 還有一些剩下來沒有答覆的問題。

40. After years of patient waiting for a court action to condemn the criminals, the victims and their families grew apprehensive and finally decided <u>to take the law into their own hands.</u>
    (A) 以奉公守法為己任。　　　　(B) 成為一群目無法紀之徒。
    (C) 自尋暴力途徑，以圖復仇。　(D) 感謝庭上能法外施恩。

Ⅶ. 閱讀能力

說明：細讀下列41.至55.題，每題後隨的四個答案或者解釋題義，或者申論重點。
其中三個答案和原題本意一致。請選出一個不符合原題意義的答案。每
題2分。

例： If only you told me the truth.

(A) you didn't tell me the truth.

(B) you chose to keep the truth.

(C) I could have done something to help if you had told
me the truth.

(D) I was glad you lied to me.

答案：(D)

41. They required us to follow too many rules.

(A) Not enough rules were made.

(B) There were more rules than necessary.

(C) We were made to follow rules some of which were actually
uncalled-for.

(D) We felt a little resentful that we should be made to appear
so obedient.

42. Whatever else John does, he never goes back on his word.

(A) John is as good as his word.

(B) John never breaks his word.

(C) John is sometimes a little careless of what he says.

(D) John has managed so far to keep all his promises.

43. A : Excuse me, sir. May I draw your attention to the regulations?

B : The regulations?

A : Yes, sir. Haven't you read the regulations which are put up
round the place? That notice for example. It says "No Litter".

B : Yes, I know but I'm not the sort of person who drops litter.
Anyway, I can't see the litter you're complaining about. (A
points to the paper bag along one of the benches by the
path.) Oh, I see. But the man who dropped that bag has
just gone away.

(A) The scene where the conversation takes place may be a public park.

(B) A could very well be a park-keeper.

(C) The fact that B first said, " I can't see the litter you're complaining about," and then added, "The man who dropped that bag has just gone away," gives us no cause at all to suspect if B was being totally consistent.

(D) B might have been telling the truth when he said, " I'm not the sort of person who drops litter."

44. They didn't stop to rest at each station because it would have slowed them down.

(A) Stopping to rest at each station would have slowed them down.

(B) It would have slowed them down to stop to rest at each station.

(C) Much as they would like to stop to rest at each station, they thought better of it.

(D) It was essential that they should stop to rest at each station; otherwise it would have slowed them down.

45. All went well for a while, until one day the farmer's fortune turned again.

(A) The farmer was not doing badly for a while.

(B) The farmer would soon find himself in a tight spot.

(C) The farmer had good fortune all along, and it stayed that way till he became very old.

(D) The farmer had known worse times.

46. It used to be said that a man who had read Montaigne was not the man he was before he had read Montaigne.

(A) It makes a lot of difference if you have read Montaigne.

(B) Montaigne's influence as a writer is beyond dispute.

(C) You could hardly imagine what mark Montaigne could leave on you once you start reading him.

(D) It does not matter if you have read Montaigne or if you have not read Montaigne, the point to bear in mind being that he is simply too much for the ordinary man to understand.

47. John has been a nodding acquaintance of mine for the last seven years.

   (A) I know John only slightly.

   (B) John and I are no close friends.

   (C) I have known John intimately for the last seven years.

   (D) When passing in the streets, John and I would exchange nothing more than a nod upon recognition.

48. You remind me of someone who has a problem and who simply hopes it will go away. TV won't go away and the sooner you learn to live with it, the better.

   (A) TV does somehow present a problem.

   (B) TV is here to stay.

   (C) You'd better face the fact and deal with your problem as well as you can.

   (D) Problems can be gotten over if you can learn to ignore them.

49. Beggars cannot be choosers.

   (A) A man without any means is wise to be choosy.

   (B) One cannot afford to refuse whatever is offered him when his luck has run out.

   (C) When a man is begging, he does not ask what he is going to get.

   (D) Beggars are not in a position to turn down even the smallest amount in charity.

50. Sometimes one event can have a chain of consequences. Remember the night John couldn't go to sleep until early morning? If he had not set his alarm by mistake, his whole day might have been different.

   (A) John overslept.

   (B) As a consequence of missetting his alarm, John had a hard time catching up with some of his lost sleep.

   (C) The alarm didn't go off at the time John had expected it would.

   (D) If John had a good night's sleep and gotten up as he had planned, things would not have happened the way they did.

51. The year 1984 will be the beginning of the end of all wars.
   (A) There will be no more wars after 1984.
   (B) Eternal peace will come upon the world in 1984.
   (C) Nineteen eighty-four will be remembered as the year which ends all wars.
   (D) Something will happen in 1984 which will start an endless war among countries all over the world.

52. You cannot escape your conscience, wherever you may be, even on a desert island ; if you try to make a desert island.
   (A) A guilty man will bear the weight of his guilt wherever he goes.
   (B) A man with a burden on his conscience will find peace only when he is all alone by himself.
   (C) To the best of our knowledge, there is no such thing as a desert island that can be found in existence, as far as our wish to find a haven from our conscience is concerned.
   (D) Not even when we have succeeded in keeping ourselves completely isolated can we rest with a clean conscience once we have done somebody wrong.

53. The lesson we have to learn is that our dislike for certain person does not give us any right to injure our fellow creatures, however odious they may be. As I see it, the social rule must be " live and let live ".
   (A) It is perfectly within our right to bring harm, either physically or spiritually, to those with whom we are displeased.
   (B) Peaceful co-existence is the best solution to social differences.
   (C) However hideous we think some of our fellow creatures are, we should never contemplate doing anything to hurt them.
   (D) Every person has the right to lead a way of life which, though seeming strange and unpleasant to others, pleases himself.

54. The playwright and poet William Shakespeare is generally ac-
knowledged to be the greatest writer in the history of English
literature. However, much of his life is not well documented.
A few dates and events are known certainly, others have been
pieced together from evidence, and still others are only a matter of conjecture.

(A) Not everything we know about Shakespeare is supported by historical evidence.

(B) A few stories about Shakespeare could very well be the product
of somebody's wild imagination.

(C) That Shakespeare is the greatest writer in the history of English literature lacks unanimous acknowledgement.

(D) We have well-kept records, meticulously compiled and carefully
preserved, to show the life of William Shakespeare, the greatest English writer in history.

55. Our face is where we think of ourselves as being on show; it is
the part we hide when ashamed, and lose when in disgrace.

(A) Our face is lost when we suffer loss of respect.

(B) To try to escape recognition, the first thing we do is to quickly cover our face up.

(C) Our normal reaction when discredit is brought to our name
is to put our face on show.

(D) An instinctive reaction to the revelation of our shame is to try
to dig a hole in the ground for ourselves to hide in.

Ⅷ. 閱讀能力

說明：下列56.至60.題，復述下面一段文字的幾處重點。每題的四個答案中有一
個是錯的，請選出這個錯誤的答案。每題3分。

Why should there be a general feeling that a civilized society
is superior to an uncivilized one? What is the essential difference
between them? The civilized person is a person belonging to a
stable and ordered society. The subsistence of law and order is
the first essential of civilization. You may remember the story
of the shipwrecked sailors who, after tossing for weeks on un-

charted seas, caught sight, at last, of an island with something --was it a tree?--standing up on the horizon. As they drew near, they made out what it was--a gibbet. " Thank God!" exclaimed one of them. " It's a civilized country." Well, in a country where you may be executed by the hangman, you are at least unlikely to be scalped by savages or eaten by cannibals.

And it is only in a society where law and order prevail, and where the exchange of goods and the organization of labor are facilitated by a monetary system, that the arts and sciences can flourish, and that nations, like individuals, can develop to the full their peculiar gifts and potentialities.

If we want to see the process of civilization actually at work, we need only look around us. Every child starts life as, literally, a primitive man. Then, by contact with others, and by learning from the civilized world around him and accepting its order and its rules, he becomes gradually less and less of the little barbarian, the little savage, that he was when he was born. He learns the conventions imposed by communal life, its decencies and its artifices, its pretences and its disciplines, how to dress, how to say " please" and " thank you", how to control himself, how to pretend to pay regard to others, how really to pay regard to others, how to read and write, and the meaning of money. In short, he becomes a civilized man.

56. A civilized society is generally considered to be one

(A) which enjoys the fruits of education and research.

(B) which does its best to see that every man is equal before the law.

(C) where resistance to rule is dealt with by repressive measures.

(D) where law and order comes before the private gains of a privileged few.

57. The story of the shipwrecked sailors reminds us that
    (A) not everything in a civilized society is pleasant.
    (B) it is sometimes necessary to use the death sentence to maintain law and order.
    (C) it is better to live in a society where peace is maintained by an unyielding legal system than to be left to certain death at the hands of force and brutality.
    (D) we have much to thank for living in a civilized society where savages and cannibals are executed by hanging.

58. Full development of our talents and potentialities is possible only in a society where
    (A) individuals have easy access to intellectual pastimes and artistic refinements.
    (B) people must choose to gain complete freedom at the expense of law and order.
    (C) advancement can be achieved within a general social framework of equal opportunity for all.
    (D) commerce flourishes in an orderly manner.

59. Every child, when born into the world, is in a sense literally
    (A) a civilized man.   (B) a primitive.
    (C) a barbarian.   (D) a savage.

60. In the process of growing up in a civilized society, the child
    (A) learns to conform.
    (B) cannot help but sometimes lose a freshness of vision.
    (C) is lucky if he can keep himself from losing his innocence.
    (D) is constantly exposed to influences not altogether desirable, all of which will inevitably lead him to ruin.

68年大學聯考英文試題詳解

Ⅰ. 重音：

1. (A)　2. (B)　3. (C)　4. (B)　5. (C)

Ⅱ. 拼法：

6. (D)　7. (A)　8. (C)　9. (A)　10. (C)

Ⅲ. 應對：

11. (B)　12. (D)　13. (C)　14. (A)　15. (C)

〔解析〕

11. (B) 去看看你能做些什麼。　(D) 不急。

12. (D) 價錢總共二元五角。　(A) 用不著你說！　(B) 我們幾乎入不敷出了。

13. (C) 你讓位給我實在太好了！　(A) 說眞的，沒什麼好誇口的。

14. (A) 請你到櫃枱的那邊登記。　15. (C) 很高興能有這份榮幸。

Ⅳ. 習慣用法、文法、字彙：

16. (A)　17. (A)　18. (A)　19. (C)　20. (D)　21. (A)　22. (B)　23. (C)　24. (B)　25. (B)
26. (C)　27. (B)　28. (D)　29. (D)　30. (B)

〔解析〕

16. in a general sort of way = in a general way = orainarily = usually

19. 句中 that 的先行詞顯然是 systems，而不是前面的 one，選(D)似乎更合理。
(C)是美國最近的用法。

20. now 和前面的 Earlier 相對。　21. 修飾動詞 admire 應該用 much。

23. 因主詞後有形容詞子句限定，故要有定冠詞。

27. *with a view to* 的 to 是介系詞，後接動名詞。

29. (A) 洩輪胎的氣　(B) 沮喪的　(C) 壓縮過的　(D) 小型的

30. out of my depth = beyond my depth = beyond my comprehension
" 非能力所及；無法理解"

Ⅴ. 中譯英：

31. (C)　32. (A)　33. (C)　34. (B)　35. (D)

〔解析〕

31. We have been told = We hear = They say = People say = It is said "據說"

32. *Nothing doing* "不行"　　33. *be with sb.* "同意某人"

34. *go out* "盡全力～"　　35. *grind to a halt* "慢慢停止"

Ⅵ. 英譯中：

36.(C)　37.(D)　38.(B)　39.(A)　40.(C)

〔解析〕

40. *take the law into one's own hands* "（不依法律）私行制裁"

Ⅶ. 閱讀能力：

41.(A)　42.(C)　43.(C)　44.(D)　45.(C)　46.(D)　47.(C)　48.(D)　49.(A)　50.(B)

51.(D)　52.(B)　53.(A)　54.(D)　55.(C)

〔解析〕

42. He never *goes back on* his word. "他從不食言。"

45. *in a tight spot* = in a tight corner = in a tight place "處於困境"

47. *nodding acquaintance* "點頭之交"

53. *live and let live* "和平共存"

Ⅷ. 閱讀能力：

56.(C)　57.(D)　58.(B)　59.(A)　60.(D)

中譯：

　　為什麼一般人會覺得文明比未開化的社會優越呢？他們二者間有什麼重大的不同呢？文明人屬於穩定而有秩序的社會，而文明的第一要件是法律和秩序的存在。你或許記得船隻遇難中的一些水手的故事，他們在航海圖上沒記載的茫茫大海中漂流幾週後，終於發現一個島嶼，島上好像有什麼東西豎立在地平線上——是一棵樹嗎？當他們靠近時，才發現原來是個絞架。「謝天謝地！」其中有人高呼著，「這是一個文明的國度。」在一個可能被絞刑官處死的國度裏，至少不會被野蠻人活剝頭皮或被食人族吃掉。

　　只有在一個施行法律和有秩序的社會中，在一個有貨幣制度促進貨物交易，和勞工組織的社會中，人文和科學才得以發展。而那樣的國家就如同個人一樣，才能將其特殊才能和潛力發展到極限。

　　如果我們想明白文明過程的實際發展，只要看一下四周即可。每一個小孩子實際上都像原始人般開始他的生命。然後藉著與他人的接觸，藉著從周圍文明不斷地學習，並接受社會的秩序與法則。於是，他才逐漸地脫離他出生時那種小野人的狀態。他從社會生活中學習社會的習俗、禮儀、技巧、虛偽、規律，也學到如何穿著，如何說「請」和「謝謝你」，如何自我控制，如何對人表示虛偽，或誠心的尊敬，如何讀書，寫字，以及金錢的意義。總之，他變成了一個文明人。

〔解析〕

subsistence〔səb'sistəns〕 *n.* 存在；生存

shipwrecked〔'ʃip,rɛkt〕 *adj.* 船舶失事的

toss〔tɔs〕 *vi.* 搖蕩　　uncharted〔ʌn'tʃɑrtɪd〕 *adj.* 海圖上未記載的

gibbet〔'dʒɪbɪt〕 *vt.* 絞台　　execute〔'ɛksɪ,kjut〕 *vt.* 處死

hangman〔'hæŋmən〕 *n.* 劊子手

scalp〔skælp〕 *vt.* 剝去～的頭皮　　cannibal〔'kænəbl〕 *n.* 食人肉的野蠻人

prevail〔prɪ'vel〕 *vt.* 盛行　　facilitate〔fə'sɪlə,tet〕 *vt.* 使便利

monetary〔'mʌnə,tɛrɪ〕 *adj.* 貨幣的　　peculiar〔pɪ'kjuljə〕 *adj.* 特殊的

potentiality〔pə,tɛnʃɪ'ælətɪ〕 *n.* 潛力　　***at work*** "在起作用；在產生影響"

impose〔ɪm'poz〕 *v.* 加諸於　　communal〔'kɑmjunl〕 *adj.* 社區的

decency〔'disṇsɪ〕 *n.* (*pl.*)禮儀；正當的行為　　artifice〔'ɑrtəfɪs〕 *n.* 技巧

pay regard to sb. "尊重某人"　　***in short*** "總之"

六十七學年度大學暨獨立學院入學考試
英 文 試 題

※本學科共 60 題

第一部份：多重選擇題

以下 1 至 15 題，共計十五題為多重選擇。

I. 發音

説明：下列 1 至 5 題，每題有五個英語單字，每個單字中有一個或數個字母畫有底線，那幾個畫底線字母的發音是相同的？每題 1 分。

1. (A) mention　　　(B) suggestion　　　(C) gesture
   (D) capture　　　(E) churn

2. (A) jam　　　(B) decision　　　(C) huge
   (D) gin　　　(E) caution

3. (A) convince　　　(B) connect　　　(C) consider
   (D) combine（v.）　　　(E) conflict（n.）

4. (A) moons　　　(B) chose　　　(C) loose
   (D) toes　　　(E) edges

5. (A) learned（adj.）　　　(B) markedly　　　(C) sorted
   (D) marched　　　(E) wretched

II. 文法

説明：下列 6 至 10 題每題有一個句子，其中畫有底線的字在文法上作何用途？四個答案中有一個或多個是正確的。選出正確答案。每題 1 分。

6. She follows him wherever he goes.
   (A) 是疑問詞
   (B) 是副詞，修飾 " follows "
   (C) 是副詞，修飾 " goes "
   (D) 是關係副詞

7. It was raining hard, which kept us indoors.
   (A) 是關係代名詞
   (B) 指 " raining "
   (C) 指 " It "
   (D) 指 " It was raining hard "

8. John sat up all night <u>reading a novel</u>.
 (A) 是動名詞片語　　　　　　　　(B) 是 " sat up " 的受詞
 (C) 是現在分詞片語　　　　　　　(D) 修飾 " John " , 作爲主詞補語

9. I am afraid that <u>that</u> won't do.
 (A) 是連接詞　　　　　　　　　　(B) 是代名詞
 (C) 是 " won't do " 的主詞　　　　(D) 在句中絕對是多餘的

10. At different times in the <u>past</u> parts of the body from the head to the feet have been kept covered, out of a sense that it was not decent to be seen with a bare head or an uncovered ankle.
 (A) 是形容詞 , 冠以 " the " 共作名詞用
 (B) 修飾 " parts "
 (C) 屬於一個介系詞片語 , 整個片語修飾 "times "
 (D) 冠以 " the " , 共作 in 的受詞

Ⅱ. 句義、文法

說明：下列11至15題每題句中有一個空白，五個答案中有二個或多個可以用來
　　　填入空白，使句義完整，並合乎習慣用法。每題1分。

11. John was _____ the daily routine of managing the factory.
 (A) not interesting　　(B) disinterested　　(C) not interested in
 (D) uninterested with　　(E) uninterested in

12. Mother was so glad to see me after all these years that soon I was _____ tightly in her arms.
 (A) hold　　　　　　(B) holding　　　　(C) to be holding
 (D) held　　　　　　(E) being held

13. Every afternoon at three when Mary was about to start her violin lessons, I _____ go out for a walk.
 (A) would　　　　　(B) used　　　　　(C) used to
 (D) was used to　　　(E) got used to

14. I would like to try, _____ you agree to give me a free hand.
 (A) provide for　　　(B) provided that　　(C) as long as
 (D) whether　　　　(E) if

15. Nobody would say anything about how the window was broken. Peter, the most accident-prone among the boys, when asked, denied _____ anything to do with it.

   (A) having   (B) having had   (C) have

   (D) have to be having   (E) has to be had

第二部份：單一選擇題

以下16至60題，為四選一或五選一之單一選擇題，每題僅有一個正確答案。請在答案卡上將正確答案標出。

Ⅳ. 重音

   說明：下列16至20題，每題有一組字的四個音節畫有底線，按照英語口語習慣，在說出這組字時最重的變調音節是那一個音節？每題1分。

16. You may believe his whole story. But I didn't believe a word he said.
                                             A   B C D

17. Peter：" Is this 321-1234 ? "

   John　：" No, I'm afraid you have the wrong number. This is three

         two one-- one one three four. "
                 A   B   C   D

18. It's useless writing him a letter now. Even a telegram wouldn't
                                    A   B

   reach him in time.
    C   D

19. Peter : " I'm still undecided whether to accept the invitation or

          not. "

   John : " I wouldn't accept it if I were you. "
            A   B C D

20. " I didn't realize that to get over one's loss could be so difficult, "
                                  A   B   C   D

   she said in an emphatic tone.

Ⅴ. 詞類

說明：下面一段文字中，有五個空白，依序標明的號碼是 21 至 25。後面跟隨著和這些號碼相應的 21 至 25 題中，各有四個答案。請選一個對的答案。每題 2 分。

The ancestral apes already had large and high-quality brains. They had good eyes and efficient ___(21)___ hands. They inevitably had some degree of social organization. With strong pressure on them to increase their prey-killing power, vital changes began to take place. They became more upright, and were fast, better runners. Their hands became strong, efficient weapon- ___(22)___ . Their brains became more complex, and developed into brighter, quicker ___(23)___ — makers. But these developments did not follow one another in a major, set sequence, minute advances ___(24)___ made first in one quality and then in another, each urging the other on. A hunting ape, a killer ape, was in the ___(25)___ .

21. (A) grasp　　(B) grasped　　(C) grasping　　(D) grasper
22. (A) holders　　(B) holds　　(C) holdings　　(D) held
23. (A) decision　　(B) decisive　　(C) decided　　(D) deciding
24. (A) be　　(B) being　　(C) been　　(D) beings
25. (A) makes　　(B) made　　(C) maker　　(D) making

Ⅵ. 字彙

說明：下面 26 至 30 題，每題中有一個空白。五個答案中，只有一個用來填入空白在意義上最為妥當。找出這個最恰當的答案。每題 2 分。

26. Collecting stamps is much more than a hobby to me ; it is my_____ .

(A) side line　　(B) outside interest　　(C) passion

(D) wonder　　(E) concern

27. Modern technology has finally succeeded in _____ a bomb that destroys people but does no harm to buildings.

(A) rearing　　(B) raising　　(C) organizing

(D) developing　　(E) discovering

28. It was still too early to enter the dining-room, and the guests, hanging about in _____ of two or three, with nothing really serious to talk about, exchanged pleasantries.

   (A) teams   (B) gangs   (C) groups

   (D) herds   (E) mobs

29. Attention is not the same thing as concentration. Concentration is _____ ; attention, which is total awareness, excludes nothing.

   (A) recognition   (B) perception   (C) reception

   (D) all-inclusiveness   (E) exclusion

30. " What are heavy? Sea-sand and sorrow;

   What are brief? Today and tomorrow;

   What are frail? Spring blossoms and youth;

   What are deep? The ocean and truth."

   The four lines on the left appear in a verse which expresses a feeling of _____.

   (A) tenderness   (B) sorrow   (C) indifference

   (D) misunderstanding   (E) triumph

Ⅶ. 寫作測驗

   說明：下列31至35題，每題含有若干短句。今按各短句之綜合原意重寫成一個較長的句子。新句中有一個空白，試在四個答案中找出一個最適合填入空白的答案。每題2分。

   例： It was about midnight. They brought the flashlight. They placed it beside the sleeping bag. The sleeping bag was inside the tent.

   It was about midnight _____ they brought the flashlight and placed it beside the sleeping bag inside the tent.

   (A) which   (B) when   (C) where   (D) who

  答案：(B)

31. The rain is over. You must not stay any longer.

   You must not stay longer _____ the rain is over.

   (A) when   (B) that   (C) now that   (D) as for

32. One of the women left. A little later, she came back, carrying a chair. She put it down before me.

   One of the women left and then returned with a chair＿＿＿＿she put down before me.

   (A) that which　　　　　　(B) which

   (C) with which　　　　　　(D) of that

33. I don't like the books you sent me. I dislike all of them. The one I most dislike is The Utter Failure.

   I like none of the books you sent me,＿＿＿＿The Utter Failure.

   (A) among them all　　　　(B) best of all

   (C) worst of all　　　　　(D) least of all

34. He didn't tell me much. His words were full of wisdom.

   ＿＿＿＿he told me was full of wisdom.

   (A) A little　　　　　　　(B) What little

   (C) Not much　　　　　　(D) The much

35. Despite the pilot's sharp eyesight, the ground was invisible to him because of the heavy fog. However, by listening to ground communications, he could visualize the situation.

   Even though visibility was very bad, the pilot could still grasp the situation＿＿＿＿ground communications.

   (A) with a view to　　　　(B) with respect to

   (C) on good terms with　　(D) with the aid of

VIII. 中譯英

　　說明：下列36至40題，每題是一句中文，後隨四種英譯，選出其中最符合英語
　　　　　習慣的一個正確譯法。每題2分。

36. 他惜錢如命。

   (A) Money is more important to him than life.

   (B) He is as tight-fisted as one can be.

   (C) He places as much importance on money as he does on life.

   (D) He pities life in the same way he loves money.

37. 他守口如瓶。
   (A) His mouth is sealed.
   (B) His mouth is as tight as a bottle.
   (C) Your secret won't pass through his mouth.
   (D) He watches his mouth the same way he watches over his bottle.

38. 多讀對學習語言有令人想不到的效果。
   (A) To read, to read voluminously, has less effect on the language learner than you could imagine.
   (B) In learning languages, incredible results can be achieved by reading as much as you can.
   (C) The virtue in enlarging one's reading cannot be over-emphasized.
   (D) For a foreign language learner, the shortest cut to success is constant reading.

39. 過分重視文法細則對學習外語學生的進展有害無益。
   (A) To attach undue importance to the finer shades of grammar rules may impede, rather than help, the progress of a foreign language learner.
   (B) It is not beneficial, but harmful to a foreign language student, if an unnecessary heavy load is put on special rules in grammar.
   (C) If a foreign language learner looks too much to grammatical subtleties, he may find it harmful, not helpful.
   (D) Too much importance unnecessarily laid on detailed grammar rules is a pest, not a cure, for the foreign language learner.

40. 限制太多，缺乏彈性，不如聽其自然。
   (A) To listen to the call of nature may compensate for the limitations that have been put on and the freedom that has been taken away.
   (B) Too many restrictions, too little flexibility; why don't you just let things take their own course.
   (C) Instead of maintaining strict control or giving too much elbow room, we simply leave things as they are.
   (D) There is too much limitation, not enough elasticity; it would be better to let them stick to their own fancy and make their own rules.

IX. 英譯中

說明：下列41至45題，每題是一句英文，後隨四種中譯，選出其中最恰當的一種。每題2分。

41. We knew nothing about the American Japan policy.

   (A) 有關美國對日政策我們毫不知情。　　(B) 有關日本對美政策我們毫不知情。

   (C) 有關美日政策我們毫不知情。　　(D) 有關日美政策我們毫不知情。

42. They voiced their disapproval to a man.

   (A) 他們不贊成這個人。　　(B) 他們說不出贊成這個人的理由。

   (C) 他們異口同聲一致反對。　　(D) 只有一個人不贊成他們的意見。

43. His bravery was beyond the call of duty.

   (A) 他的英勇使他忘却職責。　　(B) 他的英勇遠超職責所求。

   (C) 責任呼喚著他，要具備勇氣。　　(D) 責任提醒他，要有超人勇氣。

44. I knew what this money was for; it was to get me started on my own.

   (A) 我知道這筆錢的用途是要我獨個兒走。

   (B) 我知道這筆錢的用途是要幫我自立。

   (C) 我知道這筆錢的用途是要使我單獨開始。

   (D) 我知道這筆錢的用途是要助我走上旅途。

45. I would that we had more of it left.

   (A) 我真希望能剩給它多一點。　　(B) 我真希望能省下來多給它一點。

   (C) 我真希望盡量多節省一點。　　(D) 我真希望多剩下一點。

X. 閱讀能力

A. 說明：下列46至55題每題有四個答案，或解釋該題的意義，或申論其重點。其中三個答案和原題文字所述一致；請選出一個和題目原意最離譜的答案。每題2分。

   例： Correct me if I am wrong.

   (A) What I'm going to say might not be accurate.

   (B) I'll be only too happy to have you correct my mistake.

   (C) I've been continuously making mistakes.

   (D) I have doubts about the information I have, but I am willing to tell you about it.

   答案： (C)

46. If you really like it so much, you can have it for nothing.
   (A) The more you want it, the less chance you will ever get it.
   (B) I'll be glad to give it to you as a gift if you have really taken a fancy to it.
   (C) If you like it, you can have it. It won't cost you a penny.
   (D) You can have it for free if you really want it so badly.

47. Peter : " These documents contain our country's top military secrets."
   John : " Don't worry. I don't intend to let them out of my sight. "
   John _____
   (A) is well aware of his responsibility.
   (B) agrees to keep close watch over the documents.
   (C) cannot see anything.
   (D) is duly concerned with the safe-keeping of the papers.

48. Peter : " Perseverence is what makes people succeed. "
   John : " I couldn't agree more."
   John _____
   (A) agrees with Peter.
   (B) upholds the belief in perseverence.
   (C) is willing to go along with Peter.
   (D) has reservations.

49. He all but broke the record.
   (A) He almost broke the record.　　(B) He didn't break the record.
   (C) He at last broke the record.　　(D) He nearly broke the record.

50. I didn't like to tell her a deliberate lie, nor to ask her to mind her own business.
   (A) She had been sticking her nose into other people's business.
   (B) I had already made up my mind to be as polite as I could; however, I didn't have a very high regard for her.
   (C) I told her that she was a liar, and that she was meddling in affairs not her own.
   (D) I thought it might hurt her feelings by telling her the truth. So, I held myself back.

51. I can see quite clearly your argument now. You have certainly driven your point home.

   (A) You fail to convince me.

   (B) I have no more doubts as to your suggestions.

   (C) I am quite prepared to accept your proposals.

   (D) Basically, I believe we'll all agree to do things your way.

52. If our world is to survive in any sense that makes survival worth while, it must learn to create, not to destroy.

   (A) Learning to create brings meaning to existence.

   (B) Destruction makes it pointless for the world to go on.

   (C) If countries continue with their headlong rush into the arms race, there is little purpose for human survival.

   (D) It has become more and more difficult for the individual to survive in the world.

53. All animals, and probably other organisms such as trees, or even the universe itself, must in the nature of things wear out.

   (A) All living things have a limited life span.

   (B) Everything dies in the universe but the universe itself.

   (C) It is a universal truth that organic existence is never immortal.

   (D) The universe may one day be reduced to nothingness.

54. The minor writers go very well with illustrations. But the better ones come over too strongly to need pictures.

   (A) Illustrations are drawings that help make the reader understand and appreciate what the writer is trying to get across.

   (B) The average writer could always use illustrations to help him reach the reader.

   (C) Illustrations in a book are necessary if the writer hopes to gain greater status and renown in the literary world.

   (D) Truly accomplished writers avoid using illustrations.

55. A man is innocent until he is proven guilty.

(A) An accused person is guilty only after he has been proven so.

(B) A criminal brought before a court of law should be regarded innocent until the court has decided otherwise.

(C) The spirit of the law is to give a defendant the benefit of the doubt. In other words, the defendant is not considered guilty of the crime he has been accused of unless sufficient evidence establishes that he has indeed committed such a crime.

(D) Whatever crime he has been accused of, the man brought to trial, before a sentence is passed, should be considered dangerous and harmful to the community, and be treated accordingly.

B. 說明：56 至 60 題是針對下面一段文字所提出的幾個問題。請細讀下文後，在每題的四個答案中選出一個最恰當的答案。每題 2 分。

But the very question, "What do you believe？", expecting a shapely "ism" for an answer, is a Western question. My host, a retired ambassador, at lunch, gave a scholar's answer, a diplomat's answer, and a slightly mocking answer, i.e., a Confucian answer : " The Chinese are Confucian when we are in office, making the wheels turn; Taoist when we are out of office, and have time for nature, obscurity and contemplating waterfalls; and Buddhist when we are about to die and our fading wits turn to our next life. "

56. The retired ambassador was

(A) a man well read in Aristotle and Socrates.

(B) a renowned scholar acquainted with the skills of political double talk.

(C) responding to a question concerning man, his relation with the state, and perhaps even more, his religious conviction.

(D) apparently not very philosophical in his interpretation of the question.

57. According to the retired ambassador, we, as a people, are
    (A) extremely religious.   (B) constantly shifting in our beliefs.
    (C) uncertain what faith we pursue.
    (D) reasonable and practical men, ready to accommodate our neighbors and national institutions, having complete freedom, moreover, to indulge in our fancies.

58. We are Confucian when we are in office, in the sense that we may
    (A) work at the mill, and obey the master's teaching.
    (B) be a servant of the state, making the functions of government move smoothly along.
    (C) all become scholar officials, devoting our learning to the administration of government, in the meantime climbing up the ladder in officialdom.
    (D) be perfect models of high morals.

59. Taoism is a philosophical teaching or religion which
    (A) encourages people to involve themselves in community life.
    (B) warns people not to fall into worldly sins; otherwise, they will be punished by being condemned to Hell in their after life.
    (C) advises people to lead a simple life, not to interfere with the course of natural events.
    (D) puts more importance on the desires and cravings of man than on the attainment of a happy existence in harmony with the Way of Heaven.

60. When we are about to die, we are generally
    (A) just as sharp-witted as we used to be.
    (B) more concerned with what we are to become than what we have been.
    (C) left with the choice to convert to Buddhism and thus save our souls or not to convert to Buddhism and thus go to Hell.
    (D) unwilling to let go the thought of all the things we are going to leave behind.

67年大學聯考英文試題詳解

Ⅰ. 發音：

1. (B)(C)(D)(E)　　2. (A)(C)(D)　　3. (A)(B)(C)(D)　　4. (A)(B)(D)　　5. (A)(B)(C)(E)

Ⅱ. 文法：

6. (C)(D)　　7. (A)(D)　　8. (C)(D)　　9. (B)(C)　　10. (A)(C)(D)

〔解析〕

6. wherever 是複合關係副詞，修飾 goes（詳見文法寶典 p.245）。

7. 此爲補述用法。which 是關係代名詞，用來代表 It was raining hard。在補述用法中，關係代名詞前必須加逗點，而且不可用 that 代替。（詳見文法寶典 p.152, 161）

Ⅲ. 句義、文法：

11. (C)(E)　　12. (D)(E)　　13. (A)(C)　　14. (B)(C)(E)　　15. (A)(B)

〔解析〕

11. uninterested " 不感興趣的"，和 interested 介系詞均用 in；disinterested " 公平的。

13. (A) will 的過去式。　　(B) used "使用"，與句意不合。　　(C) used to ＋原形動詞，"（過去）習慣於"　　(D)(E) was used to, get used to 後面接 V-ing 或名詞，不接原形動詞。

15. deny 後面的動詞形式，須用 - ing。(A),(B) 皆可，只是(B)的時間比(A)早。

Ⅳ. 重音：

16. (B)　　17. (B)　　18. (A)　　19. (A)　　20. (C)

Ⅴ. 詞類：

21. (C)　　22. (A)　　23. (A)　　24. (B)　　25. (D)

中譯：

　　人類之祖猿已經有大而且高等的頭腦。他們有視力艮好的眼睛和抓力很強的雙手，他們必然有某種程度的社會組織。由於急迫需要增強牠們捕殺獵物的能力，牠們開始產生重大的變化。牠們變得更直立，跑得更快更好。牠們的雙手強而有力，能有效地握住武器。牠們的頭腦日益複雜，發展成能更聰明更迅速地下決定。這些演變不是一個接一個，循著一個明顯而固定的順序發生。某一特徵做了微小的進步，然後另外的特徵也做了稍微的進步，一個促進另一個。一隻獵猿——一隻殺手猿——就這樣地成長醞釀著。

〔解析〕

24. (B) 獨立分詞構句，表附帶說明＝… , and minute advances were made …
　（詳見文法寶典 p. 462）

25. (D) in the making "在成長中；在醞釀中"

Ⅵ. 字彙：

26. (C)　　27. (D)　　28. (C)　　29. (E)　　30. (B)

〔解析〕

26. (A) 副業　(B) 附帶的興趣　(C) <u>熱愛的事物</u>　(D) 不可思議之事　(E) 關心的事

27. (A) 養育　(B) 舉起；飼育　(C) 組織　(D) <u>發展</u>　(E) 發現

28. (A) 有組織的隊伍　(B) 成群的惡徒　(C) <u>人群</u>　(D) 獸群　(E) 暴民

29. (A) 承認　(B) 理解　(C) 接受　(D) 無所不包　(E) <u>排除</u>

30. (A) 溫柔　(B) <u>哀傷</u>　(C) 冷漠　(D) 誤會　(E) 勝利

Ⅶ. 寫作測驗：

31. (C)　　32. (B)　　33. (D)　　34. (B)　　35. (D)

〔解析〕

31. (A) when "當～時" 表未來，不合。　(B) 用 that 意爲「說到雨已停這件事」
　(C) 既然　(D) 爲介詞片語，不可接子句。

32. which 在此作關係代名詞，代替前面先行詞 chair 作後面動詞 put 的受詞。

33. ***least of all*** "尤其不；最不"

34. (B) what little ＝ all the little "僅有的一點點"　(A)與(C)都不能引導名詞子句　(D) 與原文不符。

Ⅷ. 中譯英：

36. (C)　　37. (A)　　38. (B)　　39. (A)　　40. (B)

Ⅸ. 英譯中：

41. (A)　　42. (C)　　43. (B)　　44. (B)　　45. (D)

〔解析〕

42. ***to a man*** "一致；全體"　　44. ***on one's own*** "獨力；靠自己"

Ⅹ. 閱讀能力：

A. 46.(A)　47.(C)　48.(D)　49.(C)　50.(C)　51.(A)　52.(D)　53.(B)　54.(C)　55.(D)

〔解析〕

49. *all about* "幾乎；差點"　*break the record* "打破紀錄"

50. (A) *stick one's nose into others' business* "干涉別人的事"

51. *drive ～ home* "使～被清楚了解"

B. 56.(C)　57.(D)　58.(B)　59.(C)　60.(B)

中譯：

　　但是「你相信什麼？」這個期待有美好「主義」答案的問題，是個西式的問題。午餐時，主人是個退休的大使，午餐時對這問題給了一個學者的回答、一個外交家的回答、以及一個略帶嘲諷的回答，也就是一種儒家的回答：「我們中國人執政時是儒家，推動社稷的巨輪。在野時就變成道家，徜徉自然，過著默默無聞，寄懷山水的生活。臨死時又成為佛家，衰退的心智轉向來世。」

〔解析〕

shapely〔'ʃeplɪ〕*adj.*樣子好看的　　ambassador〔æm'bæsədə〕*n.* 大使

mocking〔'mɑkɪŋ〕*adj.* 嘲弄的

Confucian〔kən'fjuʃən〕*adj.* 孔子的；儒家的　*n.* 儒家學者

in office "在位；當政"　　out of office "在野"

Taoist〔'tauɪst,'dauɪst〕*adj.* 道教的　*n.* 道教信徒

obscurity〔əb'skjurətɪ〕*n.*默默無聞

contemplate〔kən'tɛmplet〕*vt.,vi.* 沈思；打算

waterfall〔'wɔtə,fɔl〕*n.* 瀑布　　Buddhist〔'budɪst〕*adj.*佛教的　*n.*佛教徒

fade〔fed〕*vt.,vi.* 衰弱；褪色

心得筆記欄

六十六學年度大學暨獨立學院入學考試
英 文 試 題

第一部份：多重選擇題（以上 1～10 題，共計十題爲多重選擇。）

Ⅰ. 發音

說明：下列 1 至 5 題，每題有五個英語單字，每個單字中有一個或數個字母畫有底線，問那幾個畫底線字母的發音是相同的？請在答案卡上將正確的答案標出。答對者，得題分 1 分；答錯者，倒扣 1／30 分；不答者，得 0 分。

例：(A) rou<u>gh</u>　　(B) <u>th</u>ough　　(C) <u>Ph</u>ilosophy　　(D) lea<u>f</u>　　(E) li<u>v</u>e

答案：(A)(C)(D)

1. (A) sal<u>e</u>s　　(B) rich<u>e</u>s　　(C) spac<u>e</u>　　(D) cow<u>s</u>　　(E) ob<u>s</u>erve
2. (A) h<u>e</u>　　(B) beli<u>e</u>ve　　(C) s<u>i</u>ck　　(D) p<u>eo</u>ple　　(E) s<u>ee</u>
3. (A) b<u>ay</u>　　(B) m<u>a</u>ke　　(C) s<u>a</u>ck　　(D) t<u>e</u>st　　(E) ob<u>ey</u>
4. (A) p<u>u</u>t　　(B) m<u>u</u>te　　(C) n<u>u</u>t　　(D) c<u>u</u>t　　(E) fl<u>u</u>te
5. (A) c<u>ow</u>　　(B) pl<u>ough</u>　　(C) c<u>ough</u>　　(D) thr<u>ew</u>　　(E) thor<u>ough</u>

Ⅱ. 文法

說明：下列 6 至 10 題每題有一個句子，其中畫有底線的字在文法上作什麼用？四個答案中有一個或多個是正確的。找出正確的答案。答對者得題分 2 分，答錯者倒扣 1／7；不答者，得 0 分。

例：This is a picture in <u>which</u> we can all rejoice.

(A) 作 " rejoice " 的直接受詞　　(B) 是關係代名詞，指 " picture "
(C) 作 " in " 的受詞　　(D) 是疑問詞

答案：(B)(C)

6. I would never think of <u>doing</u> such a thing.

(A) 是形容詞　　　　　　　　(B) 是動名詞
(C) 作 " of " 的受詞　　　　　(D) 作 " I " 的主要動詞

7. She asked me <u>who</u> I thought would be invited.

(A) 是代名詞，指 " she "　　(B) 是代名詞，指 " me "
(C) 是 " thought " 的主詞　　(D) 是 " would be invited " 的主詞

8. During the busiest hours, some of the telephones in the office jingled <u>unanswered</u>.

  (A) 作 " the telephones " 的主要動詞

  (B) 是過去分詞

  (C) 作主詞補語（ subject complement ）

  (D) 作受詞補語（ object complement ）

9. John is likely to be the next mayor. All my friends say <u>so</u>.

  (A) 是代名詞   (B) 是形容詞

  (C) 作 " say " 的受詞

  (D) 指 " John is likely to be the next mayor. "

10. Nevertheless he has to make judgments in which the time he is to give to science <u>must be weighed</u> against the rival attractions of food and the pursuit of happiness.

  (A) 是 " Judgments " 的主要動詞   (B) 是 " time " 的主要動詞

  (C) 是 " science " 的主要動詞   (D) 是 " attractions " 的主要動詞

第二部份：單一選擇題（以下 11 至 60 題，每題有 A、B、C、D 四個答案。請在答案卡上將正確答案標出。答對者，得題 1 分；答錯者，倒扣題分 1 / 3；不答者得 0 分。）

Ⅱ. 重音

  說明：下列 11 至 15 題每題中有一組字的四個音節畫有底線，假設在說這組字時最重的音節只可能是這個畫線音節之一，問：按一般英語習慣，這四個音節中那一個的重音最重？每題 1 分。

  例： John found this novel very interesting. But <u>Paul</u> <u>found</u> <u>it</u> <u>very</u> boring.
                                     A   B   C D

  答案：(A)

11. I don't remember the exact words he said. But I am pretty sure <u>he</u>
                                                    A

  didn't <u>call</u> you <u>a</u> <u>liar</u>.
       B   C   D

12. "Did Paul buy a new car ? " " No, <u>he</u> <u>bought</u> a <u>used</u> <u>car</u>. "
                              A   B   C   D

13. "What do you want ? " " <u>I</u> want <u>some</u> <u>drinking</u> <u>water</u>. "
                      A   B   C   D

14. "We are not making much progress." "Don't you think we might as
                                                                    A
well give up the idea?"
       B   C   D

15. "Was it Nancy Brown whom I saw you were talking to just a moment
ago?" "No, it wasn't Nancy Brown, it was her twin sister. Helen
                                                                    A
Brown is her name."
  B   C   D

Ⅳ. 句法

　　說明：下列16至20題每題有一個空白，所附四個答案文字的字序皆不同，其中
　　　　　只有一個可填入空白，符合習慣用法。找出正確的答案。每題2分。

　　例： Do you know_____?
　　　　(A) Where is the City Hall　　　(B) the City Hall is where
　　　　(C) is where the City Hall　　　(D) where the City Hall is
　　答案：(D)

16. _____ succeed in doing anything.
    (A) Only by working hard we can　　(B) By only working hard we can
    (C) Only by working hard can we　　(D) By only working hard can we

17. You shouldn't have refused,_____ of you to have spoken so frankly.
    (A) was it neither wise　　　　(B) neither was it wise
    (C) it was wise neither　　　　(D) wise was it neither

18. She bought the house for fifty-thousand dollars three years ago, but
now it is worth _____ that amount.
    (A) double more than　　　　(B) more than double
    (C) more double than　　　　(D) double than more

19. I admit it was stupid of me_____what you hinted at.
    (A) have not to understood　　(B) have to not understood
    (C) to not have understood　　(D) not to have understood

20. _____to participate, I might have won the grand prize.
    (A) Had had I the chance　　(B) I had had the chance
    (C) The chance had I had　　(D) Had I had the chance

V. 字詞解釋

說明：下列21至30題，每題畫有底線的文字在答案中有四個不同的解釋，其中只有一個是最適當的。找出正確的答案。每題1分。

例：At long last, unfortunately, all his efforts were in vain.

    (A) fruitless　　(B) helpful　　(c) beneficial　　(D) forgotten

答案：(A)

21. The traffic accident was underlined witnessed by two high school students.

    (A) discovered　　(B) avoided　　(C) prevented　　(D) seen personally

22. It is incredible that an experienced diplomat like him should have made such a mistake at this international conference.

    (A) unbelievable　　(B) unreasonable　　(C) appropriate　　(D) expectable

23. His proposal was dismissed by the committee as impractical.

    (A) evaluated　　(B) rejected　　(C) regarded　　(D) considered

24. In this ever changing world, we must be prepared to face all kinds of challenges.

    (A) difficulties　　(B) tests　　(C) confusion　　(D) troubles

25. What the lawyer has said is irrelevant to this case.

    (A) inapplicable　　(B) significant　　(C) interesting　　(D) important

26. Scientists have succeeded in collecting uranium from sea waters in what is believed to be the first such successful experiment, the government announced today.

    (A) demanding payment for　　　　(B) compiling

    (C) obtaining　　　　　　　　　　(D) digging up

27. Some reports of the fire have given an exaggerated impression of the damage that has been caused.

    (A) a false　　　　　　　　　　　(B) an overstated

    (C) a misleading　　　　　　　　　(D) an unfortunate

28. There are some things in life we had better not pay any attention to.

    (A) might as well close our eyes to　(B) can not see

    (C) often fail to understand　　　　(D) cannot afford to ignore

29. John, shy and slow and lazy, didn't seem to be cut out for journalism.

    (A) didn't really like　　　　　　(B) was naturally fond of

    (C) was not really fit for　　　　　(D) was not satisfied with

30. As it happened, he never got to the point of playing the game at all；
    he <u>lost himself</u> in the study of it, watching the errors of the players.

    (A) failed to succeed   (B) gave up

    (C) ruined himself   (D) became absorbed

Ⅵ. 句義、文法、習慣用法

    說明：下列31至35題每題句中有一空白，所附四個答案中有三個可以填入空白，
          使句義完整合理，文法正確，並合乎習慣用法。找出不適合填入空白的一
          個答案。每題1分。

    例： I'll come＿＿＿＿.

        (A) right away   (B) immediately   (C) yesterday   (D) to see you

    答案：(C)

31. John will go abroad＿＿＿＿.

    (A) soon   (B) recently

    (C) in the near future   (D) for schooling

32. Albert Einstein, a＿＿＿＿physicist, died in 1955.

    (A) outstanding   (B) famous   (C) prominent   (D) distinguished

33. As far as education is concerned, we should＿＿＿＿creativity rather
    than memory.

    (A) emphasize   (B) place emphasis on

    (C) stress   (D) emphasize on

34. He was so funny that I＿＿＿＿.

    (A) couldn't but break into a roar of laughter

    (B) had a hard time not to burst out laughing

    (C) couldn't keep a straight face

    (D) was certain he was pulling a long face at me

35. I think the time is rapidly approaching when Tatung will have exploited
    its present markets to the full and should very soon be thinking＿＿＿＿
    diversification.

    (A) in the direction of   (B) of a departure from

    (C) in terms of   (D) seriously about

Ⅶ. 中譯英

說明：下列 36 至 40 題每題是一句中文，後隨四種英譯，其中只有一句是最恰當的。找出這一句最恰當的英譯。每題 2 分。

例：無論做什麼事情，他總是盡力而爲。

(A) He always spends his extreme power whatever he is doing.

(B) Whatever he does he always does his best.

(C) He does everything to the best of his knowledge.

(D) He never does things in halves.

答案：(B)

36. 他們是天生的一對。

(A) They were born a couple.

(B) They are a couple by birth.

(C) They were meant for each other.

(D) They are a well-made couple by nature.

37. 大火燒了十小時才撲滅了。

(A) The great fire was finally brought under control after ten hours.

(B) The fire wasn't extinguished until it last ten hours.

(C) The blaze raged on for ten hours before it was finally put out.

(D) The big fire has not been put out until it burned for ten hours.

38. 據說他上次考試沒有及格。

(A) The report says he did not qualify for the final examination.

(B) It is suggested that he is not to pass the next examination.

(C) He is said to have failed in the last examination.

(D) They say he did not come out too well in the exam given last time.

39. 天曉得他下次會說些什麼。

(A) Heaven knows what he'll say next.

(B) Heaven knows that which he will tell next time.

(C) Nobody but Heaven knows whether he'll speak again.

(D) What will say again cannot escape Heaven's prediction.

40. 在那兒抽煙的人是我爸爸。

(A) The smoking person is my father over there.

(B) The person smoking over there is my father.

(C) My father is smoking over there.

(D) My father is the smoking person over there.

Ⅷ. 英譯中

說明：下列41至45題，每題是一句英文，後隨四種中譯，其中只有一種最恰當。
　　　找出最恰當的中譯。每題2分。

例： It pays to be honest.

(A) 要做個老實人就得花錢。　　　(B) 錢買不到誠實。

(C) 做老實人不會吃虧。　　　　　(D) 誠實自有其代價。

答案：(D)

41. John's criticism amounts to nothing.

(A) 約翰的批評無中生有。　　　(B) 約翰的批評不明是非。

(C) 約翰的批評達到無意義的程度。　(D) 約翰的批評毫無意義。

42. I don't quite enjoy his company.

(A) 我覺得在他的公司裏毫無樂趣。　(B) 他的公司使我不十分快樂。

(C) 我不太喜歡和他在一起。　　　　(D) 我不喜歡他的伴侶。

43. He is not above asking questions.

(A) 他不恥下問。　　　　　　(B) 他不屑發問。

(C) 他一再地發問。　　　　　(D) 別怕他問問題。

44. If he had never done much good in the world, he had never done much
harm.

(A) 他在世上固然沒做過太多善事，但他也沒有做過什麼惡事。

(B) 假如他沒有在世界上做過很多好事，那是因爲他沒有做過太多傷天害理的事。

(C) 他既不行善，又不行惡。　　　(D) 他行善不足，行惡有餘。

45. The pilot of a China Airlines plane reported sighting what looked
like three small uncharted islets near Guam in the pacific.

(A) 華航飛機的一名駕駛員報告說他在太平洋中關島附近曾看到三個像小島的東
　　西，顯然是尚未發現的新島。

(B) 華航駕駛員報導，太平洋關島附近出現三個以前地面上沒有的島。

(C) 華航的一位飛行員報告，在太平洋關島附近看到三個尚未發現的新生島。

(D) 一架華航飛機的駕駛員報告，在太平洋關島附近看到三個似乎是地圖上尚未
　　標明的小島。

IX. 釋義

說明：下列 46 至 55 題每題所附的四個答案，或解釋這段文字的意義，或對提出
的問題提供解答，其中只有一個答案是正確的。找出這個正確的答案。每
題 2 分。

例：The man most Americans would place beside George Washington as
the very greatest of their nation's leaders is Abraham Lincoln. If
Washington is often thouht of as the "Father" of nation, Lincoln
is quite often thought of as its preserver.

(A) To most Americans, Lincoln is greater than Washington.

(B) Lincoln is the greatest of all the leaders of the U.S.

(C) Lincoln as well as Washington is thought of as the "Father" of
the U.S.

(D) Lincoln is often considered the person who kept America united.

答案：(D)

46. If you have a weakness, make it work for you as a strength; and if
you have a strength, don't abuse it into a weakness.

(A) You should change weaknesses into strengths and strengths into
weaknesses.

(B) You should have strengths as well as weaknesses.

(C) You should develop a weakness into a strength and prevent a strengt?
from developing into a weakness.

(D) All persons must have strengths and weaknesses.

47. "When the well is dug, Abe can go to school," said Abe's stepmother.
Abe's eyes brightened. "You mean I can really go to school and learn
to read?" he asked.

(A) Abe felt bitter.   (B) Abe felt overjoyed.

(C) Abe felt calm.   (D) Abe felt shocked.

48. "Did you disobey me and go in swimming again?" Mother asked. "Yes,
I'm guilty," said Tom. "But I didn't do it on purpose. A lamb was
about to drown, and I went in after it!" "Well, that's reason enough
" replied Mother. The underlined sentence implies that

(A) She thought he had done right.

(B) She thought he had acted foolishly.

(C) She had heard too many excuses.

(D) She did not believe him.

49. Those who have fewest regrets are those who take each moment as it
comes for all that it is worth.
(A) They are wisest who plan in advance for the future.
(B) It is better to live in the past than in the future.
(C) They are wisest who live most fully in the present.
(D) Living only in the present is a foolish policy.

50. You will have more satisfaction and fun out of life if you always look
on the bright side of things. And your friends will tell others with
pride that you are a man who is always cheerful and pleasant to be with.
(A) Your life will be more enjoyable if you are optimistic.
(B) Your friends like you because you are proud.
(C) Your friends are proud of you because you are bright.
(D) You will have more fun out of life if you have lots of friends who
are always cheerful and pleasant.

51. It is said that the great German poet Goethe got quite excited when
he learned that two little baby songbirds which had got lost were found
next day in the nest of robins who fed these lost little birds along
with their own youngsters. In such an incident, Goethe saw great hope
for the future development of human beings.
(A) Goethe believed that humans, like animals, are capable of kindness
and compassion.
(B) Goethe realized that the animal world is more human than the world
of men.
(C) Goethe believed that man yearns to care for animals.
(D) Goethe regretted that birds cannot distinguish among themselves.

52. The Tao Yuan International Airport, now being built, is one of our
ten major construction projects. In view of our increasing tourist
business, the importance of the new airport cannot be overemphasized.
(A) The new international airport must be completed as soon as possible.
(B) The new international airport is extremely important to our
increasing tourist business.
(C) Building a new international airport is the most important of our
ten major construction projects.
(D) We should not overemphasize the importance of the new international
airport.

53. No one can avoid being influenced by advertisements. Much as we may pride ourselves on our good taste, we are no longer free to choose the things we want, for advertising exerts a subtle influence on us. In their efforts to persuade us to buy this or that product, advertisers have made a close study of human nature and have classified all our little weaknesses.

(A) In spite of our good taste, we still may be forced by advertisements to buy what we do not want.

(B) Our good taste will guide us to buy the things we want despite advertisements.

(C) Advertisers have often neglected human nature.

(D) Advertisers tend to overlook our little weaknesses.

54. Ending air pollution is not going to be cheap. However, since many scientists tell us that a normal, healthy person can live about five weeks without food and five days without water, but only five minutes without air, it may be well worth the price.

(A) We can lower the price of food by going without it for five weeks.

(B) A lot of money can be saved because man can live five weeks without food.

(C) Ending air pollution is expensive, but it may be worth the money that we have to spend on it, because clean air is so important to us.

(D) That a person can live five weeks without food shows how healthy people are today.

55. The hopeful question is sometimes asked, "If insects can become resistant to chemicals, could human beings do the same thing?" Theoretically they could; but since this would take hundreds or even thousands of years, the comfort to those living now is slight. Resistance is not something that develops in an individual; it is something that develops in a population after several or many generations.

(A) In practice, it is possible for man to become resistant to chemicals within his lifetime.

(B) People living now may feel optimistic for the possibility of developing resistance to chemicals.

(C) Theoretically, man being so different from insects, can never develop resistance to chemicals as they do.

(D) Man's resistance to chemicals will not come about within one generation.

X. 閱讀能力

　　說明：下列 56 至 60 題，細讀下文。按照文義，每題的四個答案中只有一個是正
　　　　　確的。找出這個正確的答案。

　　Has it ever struck you that what the tourist considers most picturesque about a country the local resident often thinks shameful and
unprogressive？ The average visitor to the Middle East finds camels
fascinating: either they attract him strongly or they repel him strongly,
but in any case, he finds them romantic and full of local color. If
however, he talks enthusiastically about camels to a local acquaintance,
hoping to gain favor in his sight thereby, he will almost certainly be
disappointed. He will be met with blank incomprehension of his view-point,
or even hostility to it.

　　It seems to be a fact that familiarity breeds contempt, and that
those who seek excitement and romance cannot see it at home, under
their noses, but only in distant lands. The Middle Easterner traveling
abroad enjoys seeing cowboys and Indians in America, old castles and
cathedrals in France, and Gypsies in Spain. It is not because they are
unprogressive that he enjoys these sights；his pleasure is not mixed with
feelings of superiority, just as the European or American visitor to the
Middle East is fascinated by camels and veiled women and ancient buildings, not because they make him feel how rich and clever he is by contrast, but because they are strange and remote and mysterious, arousing
in him feelings of curiosity which are deeply rooted in man's nature.

56. The average visitor to the Middle East finds camels fascinating because
　(A) they are usually regarded as something shameful and unprogressive
　　　by the local resident.
　(B) they are strange creatures which to his mind stand for what is ro-
　　　mantic and what is local color.
　(C) of their powers of endurance.
　(D) they can go in the desert at long stretches without water and
　　　without food.

57. When a visitor to the Middle East talks enthusiastically to a local
acquaintance about camels, he is
   (A) trying to impress upon the local acquaintance his general knowledge
   of animals.
   (B) anticipating disappointment.
   (C) hoping to gain esteem in the eyes of the local acquaintance.
   (D) attempting to attract attention from the local acquaintance.

58. A tourist from the Middle East would most likely enjoy seeing
   (A) camels.   (B) veiled women.
   (C) ancient Middle Eastern buildings.
   (D) cowboys in America.

59. Romance and excitement to the tourist are often identified with alien
things in distant lands. He is attracted to them because they
   (A) make him feel superior.
   (B) make him realize how rich he is.
   (C) open for him the door to progress.
   (D) arouse in him a sense of curiosity.

60. If we accept that familiarity breeds contempt as a matter of fact,
then we may say quite safely that
   (A) tourists from technologically advanced countries, such as the U.S.
   and Great Britain, may find it a waste of their time to be led on
   a guided tour of the chemical factories in Kaohsiung.
   (B) tourists from Western countries would show no interest whatever to
   the exhibits at the Palace Museum in Taipei or the ritual dances
   performed by the Highland Troupe in Hualien.
   (C) no tourist from a Western country will be interested in veiled
   women and ancient buildings in a Middle East country, least of all
   in camels.
   (D) tourists who seek excitement can always find it in front of their
   own doors.

66年大學聯考英文試題詳解

I. 發音：

1. (A)(D)(E)　　2. (A)(B)(D)(E)　　3. (A)(B)(E)　　4. (C)(D)　　5. (A)(B)

II. 文法：

6. (B)(C)　　7. (D)　　8. (B)(C)　　9. (A)(C)(D)　　10. (B)

〔解析〕

6. *think of* ＋動名詞 " 想做～ "，動名詞 doing 當 of 的受詞。

7. I thought 是插入句。who 為疑問代名詞作 would be invited 的主詞。

8. unanswered 為過去分詞（＝形容詞）作主詞補語，修飾主詞 some。

III. 重音：

11. (D)　　12. (C)　　13. (C)　　14. (C)　　15. (A)

IV. 句法：

16. (C)　　17. (B)　　18. (B)　　19. (D)　　20. (D)

〔解析〕

16. only 在句首，後接副詞片語或副詞子句時，主要子句中的助動詞和主詞要對調。這種句法和否定副詞放在句首的情形相類似。（詳見文法寶典 p.631 ）

17. neither 或 nor 在句首時，後面的主詞和動詞要倒裝。

19. 不定詞否定是 not ＋ to ＋ *v.*

20. 與過去事實相反的假設，其條件子句用 if ＋主詞＋ had ＋過去分詞，若省略 if，則 had 要放在主詞前。（詳見文法寶典 p.362 ）

V. 字詞解釋：

21. (D)　22. (A)　23. (B)　24. (B)　25. (A)　26. (C)　27. (B)　28. (A)　29. (C)　30. (D)

VI. 句義、文法、習慣用法：

31. (B)　32. (A)　33. (D)　34. (D)　35. (B)

〔解析〕

31. recently ＝ lately ＝ *of late* " 近來；最近 "，常和「現在完成式」或「過去式」並用。

32. 母音開頭的字之前不可用 a 修飾，須用 an 。

33. emphasize = *place emphasis on* = stess "強調"

34. *have a hard time*(*in*)＋～*ing*；但 have a hard time not to＋原動(詳見文法寶典

35. a departure from diversification "違反多樣化"　　　　　　　　p.444)。

Ⅶ. 中譯英 :

36.(C)　　37.(C)　　38.(C)　　39.(A)　　40.(B)

〔解析〕

36. be born 和 by birth 均表 "天生的" ，a couple 是一對夫妻 ，因此(A)和(B)
　不合 ，因為不可能生下來就是夫妻 。 (D) *by nature* 是指與生俱來的本性 ，
　也與句意不符 。

37. (A) 表火勢暫時被控制 ，並未表示已撲滅了 。 (B) last 應改作 lasted 。 (C)
　blaze "大火" ，*rage on* "繼續旺盛地燒" ，*put out* "撲滅" (D) has
　not been put out 應改為 was not put out 。

38. (A) the report says "報告上說" did not qualify "沒資格" (B) it is
　suggested "有人建議" (C) He is said～ "據說他～" (D) They say
　"據說" *come out* "(考試的)結果是" ，did not come out too well :
　成績不太好 ，但沒有到不及格的程度 。

40. over there 修飾 smoking ，應接在 smoking 之後 ，所以(A)和(D)錯誤 。 (C)
　"我的父親正在那兒抽煙 。"句意不合 。

Ⅷ. 英譯中 :

41.(D)　　42.(C)　　43.(A)　　44.(A)　　45.(D)

〔解析〕

41. *amount to* "等於～ ；結果是～ "

Ⅸ. 釋義 :

46.(C)　47.(B)　48.(A)　49.(C)　50.(A)　51.(A)　52.(B)　53.(A)　54.(C)　55.(D)

Ⅹ. 閱讀能力 :

56.(B)　　57.(C)　　58.(D)　　59.(D)　　60.(A)

中譯 :

　　你是否曾經想到 ，觀光客心目中認為某一國家中最獨特而有趣的事物 ，當地人
却視為羞恥和落後 ？到中東去的一般觀光客發現駱駝很吸引人 ，牠們不是強烈地吸
引著遊客 ，就是使遊客強烈地感到厭惡 ，但是無論如何 ，他發現駱駝富於浪漫氣息

和地方色彩。然而，假使他興致勃勃地和當地熟人談到有關駱駝的事，希望藉此獲得對方贊同他的看法，那他幾乎必定要失望，他將會遭遇到對他的觀點茫然不解，或甚至敵對的反應。「熟悉易生輕侮」這句話似乎是事實，那些尋求刺激和浪漫氣息的人絕不可能在自己的家鄉，在自己的眼前看到它，而只能在遠方找到。到國外旅行的中東人士喜歡看美國牛仔和印地安紅人，法國的古堡和大教堂，西班牙的吉普賽人。他並不是因為這些景物是落伍的才喜歡看；他的喜悅並沒摻雜優越感，這正如一個歐美人士到中東去遊覽，被駱駝、蒙著面紗的女人和古老的建築物所吸引，並非因為這些景物在相形之下，使他覺得自己多麼富有和聰慧，而是因為這些景物是陌生、遙遠而神秘的，而激起了他深植於人性中的好奇心。

〔解析〕

picturesque〔,pɪktʃə'rɛsk〕adj. 獨特而有趣的；美麗的

repel〔rɪ'pɛl〕vt. 厭惡　　enthusiustically〔ɪn,θjuzɪ'æstɪklɪ〕adv. 熱心地

thereby〔ðɛr'baɪ〕adv. 藉以　　**meet with** ～ "嘗到～的經驗"

blank〔blæŋk〕adj. 空虛的；茫然的

incomprehension〔,ɪnkɑmprɪ'hɛnʃən〕n. 不了解

hostility〔hɑs'tɪlətɪ〕n. 敵意　　contempt〔kən'tɛmpt〕n. 輕視

under one's **nose** "在某人面前"　　cathedral〔kə'θidrəl〕n. 大教堂

Gypsy〔'dʒɪpsɪ〕n. 吉普賽人　　superiority〔sə,pɪrɪ'ɔrətɪ〕n. 優越感

veiled〔veld〕adj. 戴面紗的　　remote〔rɪ'mot〕adj. 遙遠的

心得筆記欄

六十五學年度大學暨獨立學院入學考試
英 文 試 題

※ 本學科共有60題

第一部份：多重選擇題

I. 重音

第1～5題：請在每組五個字、辭、或片語中選出重音落在同號碼音節的項目。
讀法以常用習慣爲準，不强調特別意義。每題2分。

例：(A) <u>bas-ic Eng-lish</u>　(B) <u>ex-a-min-er</u>　　(C) <u>fi-nal re-sult</u>
　　　　1　2　3　4　　　　　1　2　3　4　　　　　　1　2　3　4

　　　(D) <u>top of the class</u>　(E) <u>well-done in-deed</u>　答案：(C)(D)(E)
　　　　1　2　3　4　　　　　1　2　3　4

1. (A) <u>Miss John-son</u>　(B) <u>guar-an-tee</u>　(C) <u>o-ver-look</u>(v.)
　　　　1　2　3　　　　　1　2　3　　　　　1　2　3

　　(D) <u>right on time</u>　(E) <u>ap-ple pie</u>
　　　　1　2　3　　　　　1　2　3

2. (A) <u>af-ter-thought</u>　(B) <u>wed-ding bells</u>　(C) <u>un-der-pay</u>
　　　　1　2　3　　　　　1　2　3　　　　　1　2　3

　　(D) <u>cof-fee cup</u>　(E) <u>half emp-ty</u>
　　　　1　2　3　　　　　1　2　3

3. (A) <u>A, B, C</u>　(B) <u>vit-a-min</u>　(C) <u>watch-mak-er</u>
　　　　1　2　3　　　　　1　2　3　　　　　1　2　3

　　(D) <u>stock mar-ket</u>　(E) <u>sur-face mail</u>
　　　　1　2　3　　　　　1　2　3

4. (A) <u>try a-gain</u>　(B) <u>in New York</u>　(C) <u>out of breath</u>
　　　　1　2　3　　　　　1　2　3　　　　　1　2　3

　　(D) <u>cold com-fort</u>　(E) <u>bus tick-et</u>
　　　　1　2　3　　　　　1　2　3

5. (A) <u>Heav-en for-bid</u>　(B) <u>en-gage-ment ring</u>　(C) <u>art col-lect-or</u>
　　　　1　2　3　4　　　　　1　2　3　4　　　　　1　2　3　4

　　(D) <u>de-fense bud-get</u>　(E) <u>be nice to her</u>
　　　　1　2　3　4　　　　　1　2　3　4

第二部份：單一選擇題

Ⅱ. 應對

第 6 ～ 10 題，每題有一句甲說的話，後隨四句乙的回話，其中有一句較不恰當。請選出這個較不恰當的答話。每題 2 分。

例：How old is she？

 (A) Why don't you ask her yourself？

 (B) In the early thirties, I believe.

 (C) Probably about the same as you and me.

 (D) She looks much younger than her age.

答案：(D)

6. Why did you come so late？

 (A) I was caught in a traffic jam. (B) Does it really matter？

 (C) She's not late. (D) My watch is out of order.

7. Where on earth is my book？

 (A) Which one？

 (B) The blue one？

 (C) It must be John who lent you the book.

 (D) Are you looking for the one under your arm？

8. The examination was quite easy.

 (A) Did you come out top of the class again？

 (B) I'm afraid I'm going to be sacked this time.

 (C) Some of the questions weren't so difficult.

 (D) Intelligence test results are sometimes not quite so reliable.

9. Nice to see you again. You're quite a stranger these days. Been away or something？

 (A) It's my pleasure to have met you, Mr. Smith.

 (B) Yes, quite frequently. Not that I liked it though.

 (C) No, at least not recently.

 (D) I scarcely see you these days myself. And I really missed our little game of bridge.

10. I suppose you couldn't remember anything else that happened that year?

An earthquake, or something like that?

(A) No, I don't think there was an earthquake. Wait a moment……

(B) To have a poor memory is sometimes a blessed thing; while most people have to live with their nightmares of the past, you may enjoy undisturbed peaceful sleep.

(C) A natural disaster like that should have left its deep scars. No, I don't think it was an earthquake.

(D) All I could remember that happened that year was that John was killed in a car accident.

Ⅲ. 文法、字彙、習慣用法

第 11～40 題，請選出最恰當的一項，填入空白，使句義完整，符合習慣用法。每題 1 分。

例：He _____ twenty this coming March.

(A) may be　(B) has been　(C) will turn　(D) was

答案：(C)

11. He's been quite helpful, _____?

(A) isn't he　　(B) is he　　(C) hasn't he　　(D) he has

12. They turned _____ my offer.

(A) away　　(B) off　　(C) up　　(D) down

13. Keep an eye on the children for me while I _____.

(A) go to shop　　　　　(B) go shopping

(C) am doing some shopping　(D) will be doing some shopping

14. To feel spring near _____ hand is an indescribable joy in itself.

(A) at　　(B) on　　(C) in　　(D) by

15. _____ the painting, he gave a sigh of relief.

(A) Finishing　　　　(B) Has finished

(C) Being finished　　(D) Having finished

16. John said he would get the repairs to the house over and done _____
    _____ by today.

    (A) with　　　(B) for　　　(C) in　　　(D) up

17. The building which housed the police headquarters was a well-made
    structure of stone, three _____ high.

    (A) story　　(B) stories　　(C) stairs　　(D) level

18. If you sell your rice now you will be playing your hand very badly.
    Wait _____ the price goes up.

    (A) until　　(B) still　　(C) for　　(D) so that

19. The quarrel between my neighbors is becoming serious.
    It's time I took a hand in it and _____ to stop it.

    (A) try　　(B) to try　　(C) trying　　(D) tried

20. It's _____ asking Mr. Smith to help you. He's a stony-hearted old
    man.

    (A) not good　　　　　(B) no useful

    (C) no use　　　　　(D) an utter failure

21. Whatever Mr. Brown does, he does it with an eye to _____ more
    money.

    (A) make　　(B) be making　(C) making　　(D) have made

22. A writer does not usually decide to write a simple sentence or a
    compound-complex sentence ; he expresses himself in sentences that
    _____ naturally to him.

    (A) come　　(B) comes　　(C) has come　　(D) coming

23. His ambitious attempt failed because several things _____ .

    (A) came to light　　　(B) defeated him

    (C) stood in his way　　(D) were kept from him

24. In the mountains of Taiwan, the _____ remains below that of the
    cities on the plains.

    (A) level of life　　　　(B) standard of living

    (C) level of living　　　(D) standard of life

25. He_____enjoy seeing movies when he was a younger man. Now he has turned to other kinds of relaxation because the movies today are so full of violence.

   (A) used to   (B) was used to

   (C) was to   (D) got used to

26. The reason_____I was feeling happy that morning was that the examination was over and we were going to have our long holiday.

   (A) for   (B) because   (C) of   (D) why

27. We are all familiar with the delicious fruits of some trees, but how many know the stages of development which are passed_____before the fully ripened fruit is formed?

   (A) up   (B) over   (C) by   (D) through

28. Food, drink, clothing, and a roof over one's head--these are the daily necessities that no one can_____without.

   (A) be   (B) do   (C) make   (D) endure

29. _____twelve can be divided by 2, 3, 4 and 6.

   (A) Number   (B) A number   (C) The number   (D) Numbers

30. _____the fact that the measuring instruments were defective, the experiment was a failure.

   (A) Due to   (B) Owing   (C) Viewing   (D) According to

31. He was dressed in a quiet grey suit and looked very well bred and _____a gentleman.

   (A) all over him   (B) every inch

   (C) with due respect   (D) to no appearance

32. Even in the last years of his life, when his illness had_____and was killing him inch by inch, Lawrence could still laugh, on occasion, with something of the old and exuberant gaiety.

   (A) lost ground   (B) given way to a promising cure

   (C) knocked him down cold   (D) got the upper hand

33. _____, for instance, the electric blanket; on many a grey autumn evening when the trees are bare and the rain patters on the pane, have I thought of my electric blanket, and know that when night falls I shall rush into its arms.

(A) Say　　　　(B) Take　　　(C) Speaking of　(D) As

34. The customer called the waiter and complained that the soup was cold, adding that it ought to have been served in a hot dish, and that the waiter _____ better than to have served it like that.

(A) should know　　　　　(B) would know

(C) should have known　　　(D) must have known

35. Theories regarding the shape of the earth have changed. _____ it was believed that it was flat, although ideas about the exact shape varied.

(A) At the first (B) In the outset (C) In the beginning (D) On the initial

36. Like the children of Hamelin to the piper, they came rushing, _____ the sound of our approach, from doorways and alleyways and from behind houses, to line up by the road and cheer.

(A) on　　　　　(B) to　　　　(C) at　　　　(D) beyond

37. In the course of an incredibly short time, the seas round about us were flung up to _____ of fifteen feet, while single crests were hissing twenty and twenty-five feet above the trough of the sea.

(A) a height　　(B) a length　　(C) an altitude　(D) a tallness

38. The forces of the outer world are in league with those of the living body; natural catastrophes, earth and sky, weather and war, dead matter and our fellow creatures, all can wound us, can _____ the seeds of pain.

(A) blow　　　(B) grow　　　(C) cause　　　(D) sow

39. He was never a leader, because he had never liked to _____ in the firm he worked with or anywhere else. He was not even a conspicuous figure there, because he never wanted to be different from the crowd.

(A) put his nose　　　　(B) find his footing

(C) stick his neck out　　(D) snap his fingers at others

40. During the last decade a change has taken place in our conception of open spaces in relation to the urban and regional _____. The value of the landscape parks of the city was indisputable; they served as barriers against the spread of the city as an ugly unbroken mass.

(A) environment (B) situation (C) circumstance (D) condition

Ⅳ. 翻譯

A. 第41～45題，每題有一句英文，其後是四句中譯。試選出最恰當的答案。每題 2 分。

例：Mind your own business.

　　(A) 小心照顧你的事業。　　　(B) 記住你自己的事業。
　　(C) 少管閒事。　　　　　　 (D) 要多照顧自己。　　答案：(C)

41. There's no way of knowing where the man came from, let alone identifying him by name.

(A) 他來處沒有路，也只有他沒名沒姓。

(B) 不知他來自何處，只有他一個人叫這個名字。

(C) 無法知曉他的來踪，更不必提他的名字了。

(D) 不知道他從那裏來，只知道叫這個名字的人是獨自來的。

42. He lives next door to us but one.

　　(A) 他住在我們隔壁第二家。　　(B) 只有他一個人住在我們隔壁。
　　(C) 我們隔壁只有他一家住。　　(D) 他是我們的緊鄰。

43. See to it that my instructions are followed to the letter.

(A) 瞧吧，我的指令會隨信後傳達。

(B) 我的建議將見諸文字，收到後尚請過目。

(C) 信將隨指令後傳達，你會看到的。

(D) 務必徹底按照我交待的話去做。

44. Houses which fail to satisfy these minimum requirements are to be pulled down.

(A) 不能滿足最低要求的房子將被拖倒。

(B) 凡是不符合最低要求的房子一律拆除。

(C) 最低限度應該拆除不能使人滿意的房子。

(D) 雖然你失敗了，可是你有房子住，應當覺得滿足。

45. Come, come. Let's not quarrel any more.
    (A) 來吧，來吧。我們別再吵了。
    (B) 好了，好了。你們再也不可以吵下去了。
    (C) 來，來。要不要讓我再吵兒點你看？
    (D) 算了，算了。我們別再吵啦。

B. 第46～50題，每題有一句中文，後隨四句英譯，試選出最恰當的一個答案。
   每題2分。

   例：固習難改。
       (A) Fixed habits are difficult to change.
       (B) Long habits are not easy to forget.
       (C) Old habits die hard.
       (D) It's not easy to leave one's habits behind.　　答案：(C)
   （注意：以上英譯皆什九差不離；因英語中有現成成語，故捨A、B、D而取C。）

46. 你該不會在挖苦人吧？
    (A) You are not being sarcastic.
    (B) Do you mean to be sarcastic?
    (C) You certainly don't sound sarcastic to me.
    (D) Do I detect a note of sarcasm in your voice?

47.「你說什麼都行。」
    (A) "Whatever you say will be alright."
    (B) "What do you say?"
    (C) "Whatever you say."
    (D) "Tell me what you said and everything will come out fine."

48. 請你幫個忙，我很想見見他。
    (A) Could you please do me a favor? I'd like very much to see him.
    (B) Please help me so that I could meet him.
    (C) Help me. I think I want to have a look at him.
    (D) I could be some help if I may talk to him.

49. 他們默默苦幹。
    (A) They worked on in speechlessness.
    (B) They worked laboriously, talking to nobody.
    (C) They labored on in wordless silence.
    (D) They toiled in such a manner as if they were mutes.

50. 爲達到目的而不擇手段。

(A) No method is selected if it doesn't help to achieve the objective.

(B) The end justifies the means.

(C) The means justifies the end.

(D) Any method is right if it helps to reach the aim.

V. 閱讀能力

第51～60題，每段文字後有四個句子，或釋義，或解答，其中只有一個是正確的。請選出這個正確的項目。每題3分。

例： I enjoy the present enormously. I regret the past only in so far as it respresents for me my lost youth, which is, believe me, an intolerable loss.

(A) The present to me is more important than the past.

(B) My greatest regret for my past is that I could never be young again.

(C) Let us eat and drink, for tomorrow we die.

(D) It is a great burden for me to have to face my future.

答案：(B)

51. I don't think you'll like to hear what I'm going to say, any more than I shall like telling you.

(A) I think you would not be too unwilling to listen to what I'm going to say.

(B) However willing and anxious I wish to tell you about it, you would probably refuse to listen.

(C) It's painful for me to have to tell you about this.

(D) You're not going to like it, but I'm glad to get it off my chest anyway.

52. We have found in her a good daily help.

(A) She asked us to find for her a daily help and we did.

(B) She didn't want any help from us, but we nevertheless gave it to her.

(C) Everyday we helped her a little with her work.

(D) She's proven herself a useful person for us to have around.

53. I've heard nothing from him for a very long time.

   (A) He hasn't spoken to me for a very long time.

   (B) He hasn't written any letter to me for a long time.

   (C) Nobody has told me anything about him for a long time.

   (D) We are no longer on speaking terms.

54. He asked the manager if he should go ahead with the project.

   (A) He asked the manager if it was all right for him to go ahead with the project.

   (B) He wondered if the manager had gone ahead with the project as he had asked him to.

   (C) He was rather unhappy about the manager's delay in performing his duties, so he prompted him.

   (D) He was always a very cautious man. Whenever he took a step, it was one taken at the urge of his superiors.

55. The only white people who came to our house were welfare workers and bill collectors. It was almost always my mother who dealt with them, for my father's temper, which was at the mercy of his pride, was never to be trusted.

   (A) My father was too proud a negro and too quick-tempered a man to deal with our white visitors.

   (B) No white people ever came to visit us because we were black. The only ones who cared to come to our house were those from whom we had borrowed money.

   (C) Being proud and having nothing to hide, my father was always glad to see the white social welfare workers.

   (D) Knowing father as mother did, she would never think of letting him talk to any of our guests, black or white, for he could lecture on the subject of racial prejudice for hours on end.

56. If life is to be lived again it must be lived on the same unknown terms in order to be worth living.

(A) If we are to live this life again, it would be extremely fascinating tracing once more the same old steps we have taken.

(B) Our feeling, in spite of all the fascinations we have experienced, is against repeating the same life all over again.

(C) Life is worth living again if only we could learn what would happen at every turn of a corner.

(D) We would come to this world, as we have done before, like wanderers out of eternity, not seeking any new adventure, because we have already known.

57. British universities, which are extremely jealous of their independence, are proud of the machinery they have set up for getting money from the Treasury without strings. No questions about universities can be asked in Parliament because no minister is responsible for them (the Minister of Education has no responsibility for or control over the universities.)

(A) British universities cannot easily obtain money without the help of the Ministry of Education.

(B) British universities are jealous of the financial independence of certain universities in some other countries.

(C) The British Ministry of Education has no authority whatever over the universities.

(D) The British Parliament asks no questions of the universities. All the questions to be asked are asked by the Ministry of Education.

58. A passenger who makes a journey or a portion of a journey in a class of carriage superior to that for which the ticket held is available will be required to pay for such journey or portion of journey the the difference between the fare for the class of carriage used and that for which the ticket held is available. " Will be required to pay " is predicate to

(A) a passenger.　　　　(B) a journey.

(C) a class of carriage.　　(D) the ticket.

59. The above passage, put into plain language, means:
   (A) A passenger travelling second-class on a first-class ticket must be refunded the difference in fare.
   (B) A passenger travelling second-class on a first-class ticket need not be refunded the difference in fare.
   (C) A passenger travelling first-class on a second-class ticket must pay the difference in fare.
   (D) A passenger travelling first-class on a second-class ticket need not pay the difference in fare.

60. A conversation should not be a market where one sells and another buys. Rather, it should be a bargaining back and forth, and each person should be both merchant and buyer.
   (A) A conversation should be a speech or a lecture to be listened to with patience and attention.
   (B) A conversation should be a two-way affair.
   (C) One must be good at bargaining to be a good conversationalist.
   (D) Merchants and buyers have to be well versed in the art of conversation to be successful at bargaining.

65年大學聯考英文試題詳解

I. 重音：

1. (B)(C)(D)(E)　2.(A)(B)(D)　3.(B)(C)(D)(E)　4.(A)(B)(C)　5.(B)(D)(E)

〔第 1 題答案引起爭論，因 ′apple píe 有兩個重音〕

II. 應對：

6. (C)　7. (C)　8. (B)　9. (A)　10. (B)

〔解析〕

8. (A) *come out top* "佔上首席 "　(B) *be sacked* " 被當了 "

9. You're quite a stranger " 好久不見了 "

III. 文法、字彙、習慣用法：

11. (C)　12. (D)　13. (B)或(C)　14. (A)　15. (D)　16. (A)　17. (B)　18. (A)　19. (D)　20. (C)

21. (C)　22. (A)　23. (C)　24.(B)　25.(A)　26. (D)　27. (D)　28.(B)　29. (C)　30. (A)

31. (B)　32. (D)　33. (B)　34. (C)　35. (C)　36. (C)　37. (A)　38. (D)　39. (C)　40. (A)

〔解析〕

12. *turn down* = reject "拒絕 "　13. *keep an eye on* " 看守；監視 "

14. *at hand* = *near at hand* = *close at hand* " 近處；在附近 "

16. *get sth. over* " 完成 "　18. *play one's hand badly* " 沒有聰明地做 "

19. It's (*high*) time ＋主詞＋ $\begin{cases} should ＋原形動詞 \\ were \\ V-ed \end{cases}$ 因 took 為過去式，故用 tried 。

20. It is no use (or no good) asking ～

= It is of no use (= useless) to ask ～

= There is no use (in) asking ～（詳見文法寶典 p. 441 ）

21. *with an eye to* " 為了 "　to 是介系詞，後接動名詞。

22. 關係代名詞 that 的先行詞是 sentences ，因此動詞用 come 而不用 comes 。

23. *stand in one's way* "阻礙某人"　24. standard of living "生活水準"

25. *used to* ＋原形動詞　表過去的習慣，*be used to* ＋ $\begin{cases} 動名詞 & "習慣於" \\ 名詞 & （詳見文法寶典 \\ 代名詞 & p. 324） \end{cases}$

26. the reason ＋why 子句　"～的理由"

27. *pass through* " 經歷 "　28. *do without* " 不用；不需 "

29. 特指 " twelve " 這個數字,所以用 " the number ",A be divided by B
　　" A 被 B 除 "

30. *due to* " 由於 " 　　31. *every inch* " 徹頭徹尾的 "

32. *get the upper hand* " 佔上風 "

33. *take ～ for instance* " 舉～為例 "

34. should have ＋過去分詞　表示應做而未做。

35. *in the beginning* = *at first* " 起初 "

36. *at the sound of* " 一聽到～ "

37. height 指一般的高度,altitude 指海拔。

38. *sow the seeds of* ～ " 播～的種子 "

39. *stick one's neck out* " 做出危險的事 "

40. (A) (自然的)環境　(B) 情況　(C) (事物的)情況;環境 (常用複數形)　(D) 條件

Ⅳ. 翻譯:

41. (C)　42. (A)　43. (D)　44. (B)　45. (D)　46. (D)　47. (C)　48. (A)　49. (C)　50. (B)

〔解析〕

43. *See to* " 注意 "　*to the letter* " 嚴格地 "

45. Come, come " 算了,算了 "

46. a note of ～ in *one's* voice " 某人有～的語調 "

48. do one a favor " 幫忙某人 "

Ⅴ. 閱讀能力:

51. (C)　52. (D)　53. (B)　54. (A)　55. (A)　56. (B)　57. (C)　58. (A)　59. (C)　60. (B)

〔解析〕

53. (D) *on speaking terms* " 友好 "

57. *be jealous of* " 妒忌;盡心保護 (自己的權力等)"
　　without strings " 無附帶條件 "

58. portion 〔'porʃən, 'pɔr-〕 *n.* 部分
　　carriage 〔'kærɪdʒ〕 *n.* 乘用車;(四輪)馬車　*superior to* " 優於 "
　　available 〔ə'veləbḷ〕 *adj.* 有效的;近便的

60. bargaining 〔'bɑrɡɪnɪŋ〕 *n.* 交易　　*back and forth* " 來回地;往復地 "

六十四學年度大學暨獨立學院入學考試
英 文 試 題

I.重音

A.第1～5題，請依照上下文的意思，把讀音最重的一個字選出來。每題2分
（五選一）

例： I am not reading a magazine; I am reading a book.
　　　　　　　　　　　　　　　 A B   C   D   E

　　答案：(E)

1. The truth is that all the buildings are tall, not just some of them.
　　　　　　　　　　　　　　　　　　　　　　　 A   B   C   D   E

2. A horse like that won't win anything; you need a race horse to do the job.
　　　　　　　　　　　　　　　　　　　　　　　　 A   B   C D   E

3. You are working too hard. Why don't you take a day or two off?
　　　　　　　　　　　　　　　　　　　 A   B C   D   E

4. I really don't think John liked to go to the party.　He went there
　　　　　　　　　　　　　　　　　　　　　　　　　　　　　　 A

because he had to.
　 B　　C　 D　E

5. Tom used to be the best batter of the team, but last week he never
batted even once in the game.
　　　　 A   B   C   D   E

B.第6～10題，請選出重音落於相同號碼之各組。讀法以一般情況為準，不強調任
何特別意義。每題2分（多重選擇）

例：(A) but- ter- fly　　　(B) char-ac-ter　　　(C) in-dus-try
　　　　 1   2   3　　　　　　 1   2   3　　　　　　 1   2   3

　　(D) can-dle light　　　(E) smart stu-dent　　　答案：(A)(B)(C)(D)
　　　　 1   2   3　　　　　　 1   2   3

6. (A) I'm sor-ry
      1   2 3

   (B) for-get it
       1   2 3

   (C) af-ter you
       1   2 3

   (D) safe-ty belt
       1   2   3

   (E) no smo-king
       1   2   3

7. (A) post of-fice
       1   2 3

   (B) tax-i-cab
       1 2 3

   (C) I hate it
       1 2   3

   (D) book re-view
       1   2   3

   (E) bar-ber shop
       1   2   3

8. (A) see you la-ter
       1   2   3 4

   (B) cam-e-ra man
       1   2 3   4

   (C) tour-ist ho-tel
       1   2   3   4

   (D) wea-ther bu-reau
       1   2   3   4

   (E) po-lice sta-tion
       1   2   3   4

9. (A) Eng-lish u-sage
       1   2   3 4

   (B) speed-y re-treat
       1   2 3   4

   (C) din-ing room door
       1   2   3   4

   (D) re-turn tick-et
       1   2   3   4

   (E) be-yond rea-son
       1   2   3   4

10. (A) de-part-ment store
        1   2   3   4

    (B) mos-qui-to net
        1   2   3 4

    (C) a gram-mar book
        1   2   3   4

    (D) desk cal-en-dar
        1   2   3 4

    (E) a pound of meat
        1   2   3   4

Ⅱ. 用字

第11～15題，請依照上下文的意思，選一正確答案，使句義完整合理。每題2分。（五選一）

例：The teacher told her ＿＿＿＿＿＿ to hand in their homework.

(A) husband (B) son (C) friend (D) student (E) pupils

答案：(E)

11. No man can be a good teacher unless he has feelings of warm ＿＿＿＿＿＿ toward his pupils.

(A) sentiment (B) passion (C) admiration
(D) affection (E) adoration

12. Mr. Chiang Kai-shek_____Mr. C.K. Yen as the president of the Republic of China.

(A) proceeded　　　(B) preceded　　　(C) projected

(D) promoted　　　(E) proved

13. I like dogs quite well, though usually on condition that I have trained them myself and that I know their_____and they know mine.

(A) moods　　　(B) ideas　　　(C) tastes

(D) hearts　　　(E) concepts

14. The police told the people_____on the road to hurry, for they are blocking the traffic.

(A) loitering　　　(B) stalking　　　(C) strutting

(D) riding　　　(E) scampering

15. A man who is apt to be moved by sudden_____acts first and thinks afterwards.

(A) decision　　　(B) impulse　　　(C) aspiration

(D) inspiration　　　(E) meditation

Ⅲ　造句

第16～25題乃未完成的句子，每句後有五個項目，請用其中二項、三項或四項填充，使該句成為完整合理的文句。每題2分。（多重選擇）

例：If I were you, I _____ the same thing.

　　(A) will　　(B) would　　(C) had done　　(D) do　　(E) wanted to do

答案：(B)(D)

16. They got over that difficulty_____of different approaches.

(A) in order to　　　(B) by trying　　　(C) have tried

(D) try　　　(E) a number

17. Shortly afterwards, the little boy scout became_____alone in the woods.

(A) terrified　　　(B) to　　　(C) to be scared

(D) of being　　　(E) left

18. The news agency finally agreed to supply the latest news _____.
    (A) if　　　　　　　　(B) whomever　　　　(C) was requested
    (D) asked　　　　　　(E) for them

19. Under no circumstances _____ to stay up late, since you are in poor health.
    (A) doctor　　　　　(B) should　　　　　(C) has order
    (D) you　　　　　　(E) be allowed

20. Most people don't like the way the commercials are shown on television, and _____.
    (A) nor　　　　　　(B) am　　　　　　(C) I
    (D) don't　　　　　(E) either

21. Those _____ the university considered themselves very lucky.
    (A) were　　　　　(B) admitted　　　　(C) admitting
    (D) attended　　　(E) to

22. Disheartened by poor health and discouraged by lack of work, he finally _____.
    (A) was　　　　　(B) took　　　　　(C) to
    (D) begging　　　(E) a beggar

23. Investigator Hsu demanded that the murder suspect _____.
    (A) to be brought　　(B) be brought　　(C) brings
    (D) himself　　　　　(E) to his office immediately

24. If you _____ every day, you'll find yourself improving.
    (A) keep　　　　　(B) toward　　　　(C) practices
    (D) with　　　　　(E) practicing

25. A person _____ pleases nobody.
    (A) who　　　　　(B) is used to　　　(C) tries to
    (D) please　　　　(E) everybody

Ⅳ. 文法

A. 第26～30題，每題有四句話，其中只有一句的文法是正確的，請把這句選出來。每題1分。（四選一）

例：(A) John comes here last week. (B) John has come here last week.
　　(C) John came here last week.　(D) John will come here last week.
　　答案：(C)

26. (A) A pretty young waitress wore a scarf around her neck which hung
　　　down to her waist.
　　(B) Around the neck of a pretty young waitress wore a scarf which
　　　hung down to her waist.
　　(C) Hung down to her waist, a pretty waitress wore a scarf around
　　　her neck.
　　(D) A pretty waitress wore around her neck a scarf which hung down
　　　to her waist.

27. (A) As he tries hard, however, he'll never succeed.
　　(B) However hard he tries, he'll never succeed.
　　(C) It doesn't matter he tries however hard, he'll never succeed.
　　(D) He tries however hard, he'll never succeed.

28. (A) It was not until the beginning of the 20th century that people
　　　became aware of pollution problems.
　　(B) When it came to the beginning of the 20th century that people
　　　became aware of pollution problems.
　　(C) Until the beginning of the 20th century, people became aware of
　　　pollution problems.
　　(D) Not until the beginning of the 20th century that people became
　　　aware of pollution problems.

29. (A) Do you have any idea whom that magnificent house with a big yard
　　　belongs to?
　　(B) Do you have any idea who does that magnificent house with a big
　　　yard belongs to?
　　(C) Do you have any idea to whom does that magnificent house with
　　　a big yard belongs?
　　(D) Do you have any idea that that magnificent house with a big yard
　　　belongs to whom?

30. (A) Whoever might he be, I wouldn't tolerate such an insult.

　　(B) No matter who he might be, I wouldn't tolerate such an insult.

　　(C) Never mind whoever might be he, I wouldn't tolerate such an insult.

　　(D) Might he be whoever, I wouldn't tolerate such an insult.

B. 第 31～35 題，請選出一項，填入空白，使句義完整，文法無誤。每題1分。
（四選一）

　　例： I arrive＿＿＿＿＿school on time every morning.

　　　　(A) at　　　　(B) on　　　　(C) in　　　　(D) up

　　答案：(A)

31. Don't go away ＿＿＿＿ you have told me what actually happened.

　　(A) since　　　(B) then　　　(C) after　　　(D) until

32. Do you know enough English to carry＿＿＿＿a conversation in English?

　　(A) up　　　　(B) out　　　　(C) down　　　　(D) on

33. I've got quite enough work to do without letting myself ＿＿＿＿
for more.

　　(A) on　　　　(B) in　　　　(C) up　　　　(D) into

34. You'll soon get used to ＿＿＿＿early morning walks. It does wonderful things to your health.

　　(A) take　　　(B) taking　　(C) be taking　　(D) be taken

35. "What has happened to John?" "I don't know. He ＿＿＿＿lost."

　　(A) may have gotten　　　　　(B) might get

　　(C) can have gotten　　　　　(D) could get

Ⅴ　應對

　　第36～40題中，每題開頭的句子是甲說的話，假設你是乙，請在四項中選擇一項，使與甲所說的話在意義上連貫起來。每題2分。（四選一）

　　例： Do you have to go?

　　　　(A) Good-bye　　　　　　(B) Yes, I have to.

　　　　(C) See you later.　　　　(D) I'll be back in no time.

　　答案：(B)

36. Are you sure John knows what he is doing?
    (A) I am pretty sure he does.　(B) I'm sure he is.
    (C) He is sure.　(D) I am not responsible.

37. Did the doctor tell him to quit smoking cigarettes, or did he do it
    on his own?
    (A) Yes, he did.　(B) It was his own decision.
    (C) Cigarette-smoking is bad for the lungs.
    (D) The doctor advised him to smoke a pipe instead.

38. It isn't the first meeting Mary missed, is it?
    (A) She missed the meeting.　(B) She did not feel well.
    (C) Yes, it isn't.　(D) No, it isn't.

39. The new manager doesn't seem to respect my feelings.
    (A) Which is that?　(B) How is that?
    (C) Where is that?　(D) When is that?

40. Why did he go to such a country for a sight-seeing tour?
    (A) He went there for advanced studies.
    (B) He has been working very hard and he deserves a vacation.
    (C) I haven't the slightest idea.
    (D) He took a lot of pictures on the tour.

Ⅵ. 翻譯

A. 第41～45題中，每題有一句英文，底下有四句中文，請把與英文句子最接近的
   中文句子選出來。每題1分。（四選一）

   例：Stop talking so loudly, please.
       (A) 請大聲講話。　(B) 請停止講話。
       (C) 請別大聲講話。　(D) 請別停止講話。
   答案：(C)

41. That incident made his hair stand on end.
    (A) 那件事使他栽了跟斗。　(B) 那件事使他怒髮衝冠。
    (C) 那件事使他毛骨悚然。　(D) 那件事使他費盡腦汁。

42. Oh, boy! Can't you just mind your own business?

　　(A) 噢，孩子！你能不管你自己的生意嗎？

　　(B) 孩子！你不能自己做自己的事嗎？

　　(C) 咳！你不能只管你自己的事嗎？

　　(D) 啊呀，孩子！你管得了自己的事嗎？

43. As far as the problem of violence on television is concerned, I don't see eye to eye with you.

　　(A) 關於電視上暴力的問題，我和你均有同感。

　　(B) 對於電視上暴力的問題，我和你看法不同。

　　(C) 談到電視上暴力的問題，我們越扯越遠了。

　　(D) 我不能眼看著你沈溺於電視上的暴力節目。

44. You should always put a little money aside for a rainy day.

　　(A) 你該經常預備點錢，以備不時之需。

　　(B) 你該經常把錢分開，以免帳目不清。

　　(C) 你該經常準備零錢，免得找不開。

　　(D) 你該一點一滴的把錢存起來，避免浪費。

45. Familiarity breeds contempt.

　　(A) 了解就會滿足。　　　　　(B) 輕視之心，自家庭中養成。

　　(C) 謙受益，滿招損。　　　　(D) 過度親密，易啟侮慢之心。

B. 第 46～50 題中，每題有一句中文，底下有四句英文，請把與中文句子最接近與合乎文法的英文句子選出來。每題1分。（四選一）

　　例：蘇珊是瑪麗的繼母。

　　　　(A) Susan is Mary's stepmother.

　　　　(B) Susan is Mary's second mother.

　　　　(C) Susan is Mary's adopted mother.

　　　　(D) Susan is Mary's continued mother.

　　答案：(A)

46. 籃子裏有幾個你可以吃的梨子。

　　(A) There are in the basket some pears which you can eat.

　　(B) There are some pears in the basket which you can eat.

　　(C) The basket has some pears which you can eat.

　　(D) You can eat some of the pears in the basket.

47. 你能來與不能來，有什麼關係？

　(A) What difference is there if you can come or not?

　(B) What's the difference between your ability to come or not?

　(C) Whether you can come or not does not make difference, does it?

　(D) What difference does it make whether you can come or not?

48. 在星期五以前把你的車子修好是絕對必要的。

　(A) You are absolutely necessary to have your car fixed before Friday.

　(B) Before Friday is absolutely necessary to have your car repaired.

　(C) Having repaired your car is absolutely necessary in front of Friday.

　(D) It is absolutely necessary to have your car fixed before Friday.

49. 他的誠實大部份得自父親的遺傳。

　(A) The majority of his honesty was a heritage from his father.

　(B) His honesty chiefly inherited from his father.

　(C) His honesty was largely a heritage from his father.

　(D) The major part of his honesty was a heritage from his father.

50. 假如他今天來的話，她就全勤了。

　(A) She has attended all the classes, if she comes today.

　(B) She will have attended all the classes, if she shows up today.

　(C) She attends all the classes should she appears today.

　(D) Were she coming today, she will attend classes everyday.

Ⅶ. 閱讀能力

第51～60題，每題有一段文字，請在閱讀後，在四項答案中選擇一項最正確的。
每題2分。（四選一）

例：Leigh Hunt, a well-known author, says that our world is divided
into two parts: the world that we can measure with line and rule,
and the world that we feel with our hearts and imagination.

According to the above passage, which of the following statements
is true?

　(A) Leigh Hunt is a traveler.

　(B) Our world is divided into two parts.

　(C) Leigh Hunt is a famous mathematician.

　(D) Our world cannot be divided.

答案：(B)

51. As a birthday present a rod and reel had just been received. I could scarcely wait to go fishing with my friends. Indeed, the more I thought about it the more eager I became. Having finally started, my brother and I went to the corner to get Tom, my second cousin. Unfortunately, Tom couldn't go with us. Later, when we stopped at the store to get something to put in our lunch baskets, we met Peter playing with the twins. I asked them if they wanted to join us. They all said yes. So we went to the lake together.

How many people went fishing?

(A) 4   (B) 5   (C) 6   (D) 7

52. A general feature of modern society is the gap that separates the adult from the young, and it is most painfully felt between parents and children.

In this paragraph, we are talking about the gap between _____.

(A) families   (B) society   (C) parents   (D) generations

53. A great many stunts were played by all the guests at the party. Each person was given several sheets of paper, every one of which was numbered. At a given signal everybody entered an adjoining room, in the center of which stood a table loaded with many different kinds of articles. Those who took part were allowed three minutes during which they could try to remember what was on the table. At the end of the three minutes, the players returned to the first room and wrote on the sheets of paper as many of these articles as they could recall. The longest list won.

The game that all the guests played was a _____.

(A) memory game   (B) treasure hunt

(C) hide-and-seek   (D) writing game

54. Economy was the golden rule of Coolidge—economy of words, economy of money, economy of action, economy of emotions—in short, economy of everying but thought.

Coolidge believed that _____.

(A) nothing should be economical except thinking

(B) thinking was an exception to the rule of economy

(C) actually, doing things could be more economical than thinking

(D) nothing could be more economical than thinking

55. Mrs. Smith is a boardinghouse owner; and more often than she takes
in roomers, she lets rumors out. She's a firm believer in using the facilities at hand. If one of her roomers raises his voice above the par-
titions of his room, before he can take back his words, she has an
officer of the law on him. She says she believes in peace at all costs,
so she is a most devoted client of the city police force.
Which of the following statements about Mrs. Smith is true?
(A) Instead of spreading rumors herself, she lets her roomers
    do it.
(B) She loves peace as long as it doesn't cost much.
(C) She never hesitates to go to the police station when her roomer
    raises his voice.
(D) She loves her roomers as well as rumors.

56. In today's world the strides taken to build our civilization are rarely
the result of a single gifted talent. The lonely inventor working in his
basement and the scientific genius isolated in his ivory tower have
vanished and they are replaced by corps of skilled research teams in
modern air-conditioned buildings.
According to this passage, which statement is true?
(A) Team work is an important factor in building our modern
    civilization.
(B) The scientific genius has to be isolated in order to concentrate on
    his work.
(C) A gifted talent is the least helpful to our modern civilization.
(D) The ivory tower has taken the place of air-conditioned buildings in
    building modern civilization.

57. Perhaps the most obvious way in which birds differ from men in their
behaviour is that they can do all that they have to do, including some
quite complicated things, without ever being taught. Flying, to start
with, is an activity which, for all its astonishing complexity of balance and aeronautical adjustment comes untaught to birds.

Which of the following statements about the birds is true?

(A) Birds learn to fly when they are very young, and they take their lessons from their parents.

(B) Birds, like men, can do all the things that they have to do without ever being taught.

(C) Birds are like men in that they regard flying as an activity of astonishing complexity of balance and of aeronautical adjustment.

(D) Young birds very frequently make their first flight by instinct and without guidance from elder birds.

58. Although he was a great orator and a great statesman, his powers as a speaker and his insights as a politician were declining. It was the first time in his twelve years as leader of the party that he delivered a speech to his party members without receiving a standing ovation.

(A) For the last twelve years, he was applauded every time he delivered a speech to the party members. Last time was an exception.

(B) After having served as leader of the party for twelve years, he gave a farewell speech to the party and he proved that he was still a great orator.

(C) He delivered speeches to his party for twelve years and each time he received a standing ovation.

(D) For all those twelve years as leader of the party, he was warmly received each time he gave a speech to his party for he was a great statesman.

59. With a glance at the clock, which rivalled Greenwich in exactitude, but which had a mysterious and disconcerting habit of hurrying when she wanted it to loiter, Mary hastened away to the bathroom and gave a knock on the bedroom door as she passed.

In Mary's estimation the main flaw with the clock was that it

(A) told time in a way contrary to her wishes.

(B) was unreliable mechanically.

(C) couldn't be compared in accuracy to the Greenwich clock.

(D) chimed too loudly that it disturbed Mary and hastened her.

60. The theory that a college student knows what he should need and that he can exercise sound judgment when he has the opportunity to choose the courses that he will study during his college days does not work out in practice.

Too often a college student picks courses because the professor is personable or handsome, or his requirements are easy to meet, or he is prone to give high marks even to mediocre students ,or he cracks a lot of jokes while class is in session. The truth is that courses should be taken and studied on the basis that they contribute comprehensively and substantially to the development in intellect and personality.

What is the author's attitude toward the taking of courses in colleges ?

(A) He favors elective courses.

(B) He does not favor elective courses.

(C) Courses should be chosen on the basis that the professor is a celebrity on the campus.

(D) Students in colleges are capable of sound evaluation and therefore they should be allowed the largest possible freedom in choosing courses of study.

64年大學聯考英文試題詳解

Ⅰ. 重音：

A. 1. (C)　2. (A)　3. (E)　4. (D)　5. (B)

B. 6. (A)(B)(E)　7. (A)(B)(D)(E)　8. (B)(C)(D)　9. (A)(E)　10. (A)(B)(C)

Ⅱ. 用字：

11. (D)　12. (B)　13. (A)　14. (A)　15. (B)

〔解析〕

11. (A) 情緒　(B) 熱情　(C) 讚歎；讚美　(D) 感情；愛心　(E) 愛慕

12. (A) 前進　(B) 在～之前　(C) 計劃　(D) 促進　(E) 證明

13. (A) 脾氣　(B) 主意　(C) 嗜好　(D) 心臟　(E) 觀念

14. (A) 閒逛　(B) 昂首濶步　(C) 趾高氣昂地走　(D) 騎　(D) 急奔

15. (A) 決定　(B) 衝動　(C) 抱負　(D) 靈感　(E) 沈思

Ⅲ. 造句：

16. (B)(E)　17. (A)(D)(E)　18. (A)(D)　19. (B)(D)(E)　20. (C)(D)(E)　21. (B)(E)　22. (B)(C)(D)

23. (B)(E)　24. (A)(E)　25. (A)(C)(D)(E)

〔解析〕

16. *get over* ＝ overcome "克服"，by ～ "藉著～"，*a number of* ＝ many "許多"　(A)(D)(E)文法沒問題，但句意不合理。

17. *leave ～ alone* "將～單獨留下；不理會"

18. if asked 即 if it was asked 的省略。

19. *under no circumstances* ＝ *in no way* ＝ *by no means* "決不"，此否定副詞片語放在句首，其後用倒裝句（詳見文法寶典 p.629）。

20. I don't either ＝ nor (*neither*) do I

21. 此句原為 Those who were admitted to ～　省略了關係代名詞 who 及 were。

22. *take to* ＋ V-ing "耽於～"

23. demmand (suggest, order …) ＋ that ＋ S. ＋ (*should*) ＋原形動詞
　　（詳見文法寶典 p. 372）

24. keep ＋ V-ing "繼續做～"

25. who tries to please everybody 是形容詞子句，修飾先行詞 A person。
   (B) is used to 後面應接名詞。

Ⅳ. 文法：

A. 26.(D)　27.(B)　28.(A)　29.(A)　30.(B)

〔解析〕

26. which 引導的形容詞子句修飾先行詞 scarf，故應緊接其後。

28. "直到…，才～" 有四種句型：It is (was) not until ＋ $\begin{Bmatrix} 子句 \\ 時間 \end{Bmatrix}$ that ～.

   ＝ Not until ＋ $\begin{Bmatrix} 子句 \\ 時間 \end{Bmatrix}$ ＋倒裝句. ＝ Only when ＋子句 ＋倒裝句

   ＝ not ～＋ until ＋ $\begin{Bmatrix} 子句 \\ 時間 \end{Bmatrix}$.（詳見文法寶典 p.492）

29. 疑問句中的名詞子句，其排列為疑問代名詞＋主詞＋動詞。

B. 31.(D)　32.(D)　33.(B)　34.(B)　35.(A)

〔解析〕

32. *carry on* ＝ manage "進行"

33. *let ～ in for* ＝ *involve in* "使陷入（麻煩，困難等）"

34. *get used to* "對～變習慣"　後接動名詞（詳見文法寶典 p.324）。

35. may have ＋過去分詞　表對過去的猜測（詳見文法寶典 p.316）。

Ⅴ. 應對：

36.(A)　37.(B)　38.(D)　39.(B)　40.(C)

〔解析〕

39. (B) 怎麼會這樣呢？那是怎麼回事呢？

40. (C) 我一點也不知道。

Ⅵ. 翻譯：

41.(C)　42.(C)　43.(B)　44.(A)　45.(D)

〔解析〕

41. *make one's hair stand on end* "令某人毛骨悚然"

42. Oh, boy！"啊！真是！"　表感歎。

43. *as far as～be concerned* "就～而論"
   see eye to eye (*with*) "同意"

44. **put aside** = **lay aside** = save = deposit "節省"
for a rainy day "備不時之需"

A. 46.(A)　47.(D)　48.(D)　49.(C)　50.(B)

〔解析〕

46. (B) which you can eat 修飾 basket，句意不合。 (C) 無生物，"有～"用
There are(is)～較好。 (D) 文法對，但不合題意。

48. necessary 用非人稱主詞，一般爲 it 或事物。

49. (A) The majority of 之後通常接人 (B) 應用被動 (D) "誠實的主要部分"不合
題意。

50. **show up** = appear "出現"

Ⅶ. 閱讀能力：

51.(B)　52.(D)　53.(A)　54.(B)　55.(C)　56.(A)　57.(D)　58.(A)　59.(A)　60.(B)

〔解析〕

51. reel〔ril〕n. 捲輪　　twin〔twɪn〕n. 雙胞胎

53. **a great many** "許多"　　adjoining〔ə'dʒɔɪnɪŋ〕adj. 鄰近的；隔壁的
take part (**in**) "參加"　　recall〔rɪ'kɔl〕vt. 記起

54. golden rule "金科玉律"　　**in short** "總之"

55. **take in** "接收；容納"　　rumor〔'rumɚ〕n. 謠言
facility〔fə'sɪlətɪ〕n. 設備　　**at hand** "手邊的"
partition〔par'tɪʃən〕n. 隔牆　　client〔'klaɪənt〕n. 訴訟委託人

56. isolate〔'aɪsl̩,et〕vt. 使孤立　　ivory tower 象牙塔
vanish〔'vænɪʃ〕vi. 消失

57. aeronautical〔,ɛrə'nɔtɪkl̩〕adj. 航空的

58. decline〔dɪ'klaɪn〕vi. 衰退　　standing ovation "起立的喝采"

59. rival〔'raɪvl̩〕vt. 匹敵　　exactitude〔ɪg'zæktə,tjud〕n. 精密
loiter〔'lɔɪtɚ〕vi. 徘徊　　estimation〔,ɛstə'meʃən〕n. 意見
disconcerting〔,dɪskən'sɝtɪŋ〕adj. 令人驚慌失措的

60. pick courses "選課"　　requirement〔rɪ'kwaɪrmənt〕n. 需要；要求
mediocre〔'midɪ,okɚ〕adj. 平常的　　**crack** a lot of **jokes** "說很多笑話"
in session "正在上課(開庭)"
comprehensively〔,kɑmprɪ'hɛnsɪvlɪ〕adv. 廣博地
substantially〔səb'stænʃəlɪ〕adv. 實際上地
intellect〔'ɪntl̩,ɛkt〕n. 智力

六十三學年度大學暨獨立學院入學考試
英 文 試 題

I. pronunciation （發音 10％）

下面十題，每題列有五個單字；每一單字部份字母下劃有底橫線，其中有兩個單字的底橫線部份，讀音相同。請將這兩個單字找出。按照規定作答。本題為重選擇。每題1分。

例：(A) <u>a</u>ct　(B) <u>a</u>rt　(C) <u>a</u>te　(D) t<u>a</u>ll　(E) t<u>a</u>ct　　　答案：(A)(E)

1. (A) po<u>s</u>e	(B) loo<u>s</u>e	(C) le<u>s</u>ion	(D) garri<u>s</u>on	(E) man<u>s</u>ion
2. (A) p<u>ear</u>	(B) b<u>ear</u>d	(C) h<u>ear</u>d	(D) h<u>ear</u>th	(E) <u>ear</u>l
3. (A) vill<u>ai</u>n	(B) <u>ai</u>sle	(C) s<u>ai</u>d	(D) h<u>ai</u>l	(E) st<u>ai</u>d
4. (A) w<u>ar</u>d	(B) c<u>ar</u>ry	(C) <u>ar</u>ea	(D) st<u>ar</u>ry	(E) l<u>ar</u>d
5. (A) bl<u>oo</u>d	(B) br<u>oo</u>d	(C) g<u>oo</u>d	(D) c<u>oo</u>perate	(E) c<u>oo</u>p
6. (A) buff<u>a</u>lo	(B) ex<u>a</u>lt	(C) <u>a</u>pex	(D) cr<u>a</u>m	(E) <u>a</u>ltitude
7. (A) pl<u>ough</u>	(B) dr<u>ough</u>t	(C) thr<u>ough</u>	(D) b<u>ough</u>t	(E) c<u>ough</u>
8. (A) disg<u>u</u>ise	(B) sk<u>u</u>ll	(C) b<u>u</u>ll	(D) <u>u</u>tensil	(E) g<u>u</u>ll
9. (A) f<u>o</u>cus	(B) p<u>o</u>d	(C) w<u>o</u>lf	(D) w<u>o</u>men	(E) st<u>o</u>le
10. (A) ba<u>l</u>m	(B) cha<u>l</u>k	(C) ba<u>l</u>d	(D) sa<u>l</u>ute	(E) ga<u>l</u>l

II. Vocabulary （字彙）10％

下面十個未完成句子，每句係解釋該句之中的某一個單字。每句後所附的五個用以完成句子的項目之中，按照句意只有一個是正確的。請將此正確項目選出。按照規定作答。本題為單一選擇。每題1分。

例：A <u>generous</u> person is one that is _____ .

(A) outspoken　　　(B) outstanding　　　(C) open-handed
(D) good-hearted　　(E) simple-minded　　答案：(C)

11. An incredibly easy job is one that is _____ .

(A) very easy　　　(B) very difficult　　　(C) not very easy
(D) not very difficult　　(E) neither easy nor difficult

12. A notorious person is one that is _____.
   (A) well-known for some good quality
   (B) well-known for some bad quality
   (C) little-known for some good quality
   (D) little-known for some bad quality
   (E) known for some unknown quality

13. "Superficial knowledge" means knowledge that is _____.
   (A) thorough　　　(B) deep　　　(C) unnecessary
   (D) first-rate　　　(E) shallow

14. A hospitable family is one that _____.
   (A) entertains patients　　(B) has a host
   (C) owns a hospital　　(D) welcomes guests
   (E) puts on a hostile look to everyone

15. A parallel case is one that is _____.
   (A) contrary　　　(B) similar　　　(C) dissimilar
   (D) constant　　　(E) variable

16. To abandon a career is to _____.
   (A) enjoy it　　　(B) take it easy　(C) give it up
   (D) give it out　　　(E) give it in

17. Simultaneous events are events that occur _____.
   (A) at the same time　　(B) at various times　(C) in ancient times
   (D) in modern times　　(E) successively

18. A man of integrity is one that acts _____.
   (A) treacherously　　(B) unfaithfully　　(C) dishonestly
   (D) honestly　　(E) unfairly

19. To substantiate a theory is to _____.
   (A) oppose it　　(B) disprove it　　(C) undervalue it
   (D) favor it　　(E) verify it

20. To recapitulate a discussion is to _____.
   (A) memorize it　　(B) monopolize　　(C) summarize it
   (D) capitalize it　　(E) sympathize with it

Ⅱ. Grammar and Idioms（文法及成語）20%

下面十個未成句子，每句後所附五個用以完成該句的項目之中，必須選擇按順序排列的二項或三項，方可使該句成一通順而有意義的句子。請將適當項目選出。按照規定作答。本題為多重選擇。每題2分。

例：Mr. Brown said that he ＿＿＿＿ writing that letter.
(A) had nothing　(B) had　(C) to do　(D) with　(E) to　　答案：(A)(C)(D)

21. His wife wants him to do ＿＿＿＿ that old hat.
(A) out　　(B) away　　(C) from　　(D) upon　　(E) with

22. He spoke English so well that I ＿＿＿＿ that he was an American.
(A) took it (B) as　　(C) for　　(D) granted (E) being granted

23. He was unable to get ＿＿＿＿ the group what he meant.
(A) used　　(B) across (C) along　　(D) with　　(E) to

24. Mary once played a mean trick on John, and now John wants to ＿＿＿＿ her.
(A) make　　(B) get　　(C) even with (D) good　　(E) up for

25. The maid quit because Mrs. Jones kept ＿＿＿＿ with her work.
(A) finding　(B) criticizing　(C) fault (D) faults　(E) out

26. Mr. Carr is ＿＿＿＿ rash statements.
(A) giving to (B) given to　　(C) in to (D) making　(E) make

27. While eating lunch on the lawn, ＿＿＿＿.
(A) the speeding cars　　　(B) the children were　　　(C) amused
(D) the children　　　(E) by the speeding cars

28. Our neighbors were threatening that they ＿＿＿＿ play such loud music.
(A) would call the police　　(B) will call the police
(C) if we　　　(D) continued to
(E) will continue to

29. The children were told that on no account ＿＿＿＿ the door to strangers.
(A) they were　　　(B) were they　　　(C) to open
(D) opening　　　(E) to opening

30. _____ so many flights of steps, she was completely out of breath.

 (A) since (B) after (C) she (D) runing (E) running up

IV. Writing Ability （寫作能力）20 %

　　下面十個句子，每句有五處劃底橫線部份，其中有一處在寫作造句上是錯誤的。請將該錯誤的項目選出。按照規定作答。本題為單一選擇。每題二分。

例：The neighbors having promised to take care of your dog while you are
　　 (A)　　　　 (B)　　　　 (C)　　　　　　　　　　　　　　 (D)

　　away on vacation.
　　　　 (E)

　　答案：(B)

31. The money being stolen and we had no chance of getting it back, so I
　　　　　 (A)　　　　　　　　　　　　　　　 (B)

　　explained to her that there was no use crying over spilt milk.
　　　　 (C)　　　　　　　　　　　　　　 (D)　　 (E)

32. I'd like to get all the informations you have on a man named Evans who
　　　　 (A)　　　　　　 (B)　　　　　　 (C)　　　　　　　　　　 (D)

　　used to work in your office.
　　 (E)

33. Since we don't want to run short of food in the trip, we are carrying
　　　　　 (A)　　 (B)　　　 (C)　　　　　　　 (D)

　　extra rations in our knapsacks.
　　　　　　 (E)

34. I should ask the superintendent of our building to fix the leak in our
　　 (A)　　　　　　　　　　　　　　　　　 (B)　　　　　　 (C)

　　faucet, and he said he would see to it today.
　　　　　　　　　　　 (D)　　 (E)

35. During these hot summer spells I began to pine for the cool woods and
　　 (A)　　　　　　　 (B)　　　　　 (C)　　　　　　 (D)

　　those evenings spending out in the open.
　　　　　　　　 (E)

36. Just as they were getting ready to leave, a messenger brought them the
　　 (A)　　　　 (B)　　　　　　　　　　　　　　 (C)

　　telegram canceled the arrangements for the trip.
　　　　　　 (D)　　　　 (E)

37. The doctor <u>says</u> that there is nothing <u>the</u> matter <u>with</u> John, but I can't
　　　　(A)　　　　　　　　　　　　　　(B)　　　　(C)

　　help <u>worry</u> <u>about</u> that constant pain in his side.
　　　　(D)　(E)

38. The newspaper <u>predicted</u> that we <u>would have</u> sunny weather, but it <u>is</u>
　　　　　　　　　(A)　　　　　　　(B)　　　　　　　　　　　(C)

　　already <u>begining</u> to cloud <u>over.</u>
　　　　　(D)　　　　　(E)

39. <u>Learn</u> to dive <u>before learning</u> to swim <u>well</u> seems to me <u>to be putting</u>
　　(A)　　　　　(B)　　　　　　　(C)　　　　　　　(D)

　　the cart <u>before</u> the horse.
　　　　　(E)

40. She <u>had</u> scarcely <u>recovered</u> <u>from</u> one stroke when <u>she</u> <u>was suffering</u> an-
　　　(A)　　　　(B)　　(C)　　　　　　　　(D)　　(E)

　　other.

V. Translation （翻譯）20 %

下面十句中文，各有五種英文翻譯，其中只有一種在文法和意義上是正確的。請將正確的翻譯項目選出。按照規定作答。本題為單一選擇。每題二分。

41. 我衝到門口，卻發現門鎖著的。
　　(A) I rushed to the door, and discover that it was locked.
　　(B) I rushed to the door, then discovered that it was locked.
　　(C) I rushed to the door, to discover that it was locked.
　　(D) I rushed to the door, only to discover that it was locked.
　　(E) I rushed to the door, and then discovered that it was locked.

42. 任何人都不能單獨生存。
　　(A) Anyone can't live alone.　　　　(B) No one can live alone.
　　(C) Everyone can't live alone.　　 (D) All men can't live alone.
　　(E) No one can be a loner.

43. 你說他什麼時候會來？
　　(A) When did you say he would come?　 (B) You said when he would come?
　　(C) When did you say would he come?　 (D) You said when would he come?
　　(E) When would you say for him to come?

44. 我想約翰已經走了，是嗎？
    (A) I think John has left, has he?
    (B) I think John must have left, haven't I?
    (C) I think John has left, hasn't he?
    (D) I think John must have left, don't I?
    (E) I think John has left, doesn't he?

45. 我的書比你的多兩倍。
    (A) My books are as twice many as yours.
    (B) My books are as many twice as yours.
    (C) My books are as many as twice yours.
    (D) My books are twice as many as yours.
    (E) My books are as many as yours twice.

46. 畢爾生病了，必須在床上躺到星期一。
    (A) Bill is sick and will have to remain in bed until Monday.
    (B) Bill is sick and will request to lie in bed until Monday.
    (C) Bill is sick and will have to remain on bed through Monday.
    (D) Bill is sick and will require to remain in bed until Monday.
    (E) Bill is sick and will have to lay in bed until Monday.

47. 他已經畢業十年了。
    (A) He was a graduate student ten years ago.
    (B) He has been a graduate for 10 years.
    (C) He has graduated 10 years ago.
    (D) It has been 10 years since he graduated.
    (E) It has been 10 years since he is a graduate student.

48. 瑪麗長得美，可是不夠高。
    (A) Mary is beautiful, but she is not nearly tall enough.
    (B) Mary is beautiful, but she is not nearly so tall.
    (C) Mary is beautiful, but she is not enough tall nearly.
    (D) Mary is beautiful, but she is nearly enough tall.
    (E) Mary is beautiful, but she is not sufficient tall.

49. 幣值低落，物價就上漲。
    (A) As the value of money drops, prices rise.
    (B) As the value of money drops, the price is rising.
    (C) As the value of money drops, then prices rise.
    (D) As the value of money drops, then prices raise.
    (E) As the value of money drops, prices arise.

50. 那是一輛漂亮的汽車。不知道是誰的。
   (A) That's a nice-looking car. I wonder it belongs to whom.
   (B) That is a nice-looking car. I wonder whom it belongs to.
   (C) That is a nice-looking car. I wonder who belongs to it.
   (D) That is nice-looking car. I wonder whose car it belongs to.
   (E) That is a nice-looking car. I wonder who belongs to the car.

Ⅵ· Reading comprehension （閱讀能力）20 %
   下面一篇選文，後面列有十題，每題所附五個答案之中，根據該文內容，只有一個
   是正確的。請於詳讀該文後，將正確答案選出，按照規定作答。本題為單一選擇。
   每題二分。

We have recently heard a great deal about the bad effects of computers on our social and economic institutions. In industry, computers mean automation, and automation means unemployment. The United States, with its extravagant investment in computers, is plagued by unemployment for unskilled workers; it is frequently argued that these facts are causally related. Already computers have begun to displace workers whose tasks are simple and repetitive: clerical workers, workers, on assembly lines, and the like. The variety of jobs formerly done only by humans that the machine can perform more rapidly, accurately, and economically increases with each new generation of computers. If we follow this trend, say the pessimists, we are faced with the prospect of mass unemployment for all but a handful of highly trained, highly intelligent professionals, who will then be more influential and overworked than they are now. Only recently a distinguished English physicist predicted that within twenty years electronic engineers might have to become conscientious objectors in order to prevent these machines from wrecking our social and economic institutions.

According to the prophets of doom, our situation is hopeless. The computer is already stirring up industrial strife as management desires and labor resists the effects of automation. The gap between advanced and developing nations will increase, thus heightening international tensions. All the industrial and commercial machinery of production and distribution of commodities will have to be taken over by the state, which will lead inevitably to tighter economic controls or even dictatorship. And so on and on runs this hopeless catalogue. Little wonder that some have thrown up their hands in dismay and proposed that we must somehow find a way to stop, or at least slow, the pace of this technological nightmare.

What can we do about it? It is foolish to dream of reversing history. We cannot pass laws forbidding science and technology. The computing machines are here, and they will not merely stay; they will grow bigger, faster, and more useful every year. They will grow because engineers want to build them, soldiers want to enlist them in new weapons systems, politicians want their help in the process of government. In short, they will flourish because they enable us to accomplish tasks that could never before have been undertaken, no matter how many unskilled laborers we might have set to work. Computers will continue to amplify our intelligence for just the same reason that engines continue to amplify our muscles. The question we must ask is not whether we shall have computers or not have computers, but rather, since we are going to have them, how can we make the most humane and intelligent use of them?

51. The author maintains that _____.

    (A) computers will continue to have bad effects on our social and economic institutions

    (B) computers will continue to cause mass unemployment

    (C) computers will lead to technological progress

    (D) computers will slow down technological progress

    (E) computers are here to stay, but there is no cause for pessimism

52. In the first paragraph, "conscientious objectors" most nearly means _____.

    (A) persons who refuse to do something because of moral reasons

    (B) objects which are foremost in the minds of the engineers

    (C) machines that can prevent computers from ruining us

    (D) clerical workers that are being displaced by computers

    (E) pessimists who find the whole situation hopeless

53. In the first paragraph, "wrecking" could be replaced correctly by _____.

    (A) changing   (B) destroying   (C) affecting

    (D) hurting   (E) stoning

54. In the second paragraph, "the gap" refers to _____.

    (A) social gap   (B) generation gap   (C) technological gap

    (D) international gap   (E) commercial gap

55. The phrase "technological nightmare" in the second paragraph most probably refers to _____.

(A) the author's view about computer technology

(B) the pessimists' view about computer technology

(C) the reader's view about computer technology

(D) the engineers' view about computer technology

(E) the unskilled laborers' view about computer technology

56. In the second paragraph, "industrial strife" refers to _____.

(A) the bitter conflict between pessimists and optimists

(B) the bright outlook for future technology

(C) the tension between advanced and developing countries

(D) the antagonism between management and labor

(E) the dismal future for the unskilled laborers

57. According to the article, which of the following best characterizes the author's attitude towards the computer?

(A) extreme pessimism　(B) extreme optimism　(C) cautious optimism

(D) cautious pessimism　(E) patriotism

58. Why does the author suggest that the computer will continue to grow and flourish?

(A) Because it is foolish to reverse history.

(B) Because no laws can forbid science and technology.

(C) Because engines amplify our muscles.

(D) Because computers can be and have been put to good use.

(E) Because the job of engineers is to build computers.

59. What seems to have been the chief concern of the author?

(A) The fact that computers are here to say.

(B) The fact that the computers have caused industrial strife.

(C) Whether we are able to build bigger and faster computers.

(D) Whether social and economic institutions will remain intact.

(E) Whether we can make the most humane and intelligent use of the computers.

60. What would be the best title for this article?

(A) Man and Machine.　　(B) Computers and Laborers.

(C) Management and Labor.　　(D) Computer and Conscience.

(E) Prophets and pessimists.

63年大學聯考英文試題詳解

Ⅰ. 發音：

1. (B)(D)　　2. (C)(E)　　3. (D)(E)　　4. (D)(E)　　5. (B)(E)　　6. (D)(E)　　7. (A)(B)　　8. (B)(E)
9. (A)(E)　　10. (C)(E)

Ⅱ. 字彙：

11. (A)　　12. (B)　　13. (E)　　14. (D)　　15. (B)　　16. (C)　　17. (A)　　18. (D)　　19. (E)　　20. (C)

〔解析〕

11. incredibly = unbelievably 難以令人相信的　　12. notorious 聲名狼籍的
13. superficial = shallow 膚淺的　　14. hospitable 好客的
15. parallel 平行的；同樣的；類似的　　16. abandon = *give up* " 放棄 "
17. simultaneous 同時發生的　　18. integrity 正直；廉潔
19. substantiate = verify 證實　　20. recapitulate = summarize 摘錄要點

Ⅲ. 文法與成語：

21. (B)(E)　　22. (A)(C)(D)　　23. (B)(E)　　24. (B)(C)　　25. (A)(C)　　26. (B)(D)　　27. (B)(C)(E)
28. (A)(C)(D)　　29. (B)(C)　　30. (B)(E)

〔解析〕

21. *do away with* = *get rid of* = discard " 丟棄 "
22. *take* ～ *for granted* " 視～爲當然 "
23. *get across* (*to*) ～ = *make* ～ *understood* " 使～了解；傳達給～ "
24. *get even with* ～ = *take revenge on* ～ " 向～報復 "
25. *find fault with* = *complain of* = *complain about* = criticize " 挑剔；批評 "
26. *be given to* = *be addicted to* " 耽於；有～習慣 "
27. *be amused by* = *amuse oneself by* " 以～爲娛樂 "
28. 因主要子句是過去式，故作受詞的名詞子句要改爲以過去式爲主的句型 。
29. 否定副詞片語 *on no account* 置於句首，後面句子要用倒裝句型 。
30. flights of steps " 許多層階梯 "　　*out of breath* " 喘著氣 "

Ⅳ. 寫作能力：

31. (A)　　32. (B)　　33. (C)　　34. (A)　　35. (E)　　36. (D)　　37. (D)　　38. (D)　　39. (A)　　40. (E)

〔解析〕

31. being 改為 was　　32. information 為不可數名詞，不可加 s 。

33. ***on the trip*** " 在旅行中 "　　34. 改為 asked　　35. 改為 spent

36. 改為 cancelling　　37. ***can't help*** " 不得不 "　應接動名詞。

38. 改為 beginning　　39. 改為 To learn 或 Learning　　40. 改為 suffered

V . 翻譯 :

41.(D)　42.(B)　43.(A)　44.(C)　45.(D)　46.(A)　47.(D)　48.(A)　49.(A)　50.(B)

〔解析〕

41. ***only to*** ＋動詞原形，表失望的結果。

48. enough 可以放在名詞之前或之後，但必須放在形容詞或副詞之後。

VI . 閱讀能力 :

51.(E)　52.(A)　53.(B)　54.(D)　55.(B)　56.(D)　57.(C)　58.(D)　59.(E)　60.(A)

中譯 :

　　我們最近聽到很多有關電腦對我們社會和經濟結構的不良影響。在工業界，電腦就是自動化，自動化也就等於失業。美國由於在電腦方面投資甚巨，因此對無技術的工人失業感到頭痛；常常有人辯說，這些事實是互為因果關係的。電腦已開始取代做簡單及反覆性工作的工人：書記員、裝配線上的裝配員等等。很多以前由人做的工作，隨著新生代的電腦的出現，能由機器更迅速、更精確及更經濟地來做。悲觀者說，假使照這種趨勢下去，我們會面臨到了少數受過高度訓練，及高深學養的專業人員之外，其他人都會大量失業的問題。那些少數人會比現在更有影響力，而其工作量也會過度。不久以前英國一位有名的物理學家預測，二十年內電子工程師將會為了阻止機器破壞我們的社會和經濟結構，而成為本著良心做事的反對者。

　　根據世界末日的預言家的看法，我們的情況是毫無希望。電腦已激起了工業爭鬥，因為經營者渴望自動化的影響，而工人抵擋它的影響。先進國家與開發中的國家之間的隔閡會越來越深，這樣一來，就會增加了國際間的緊張。一切工業上及商業上的生產機械，以及貨品的銷售，將必由政府來接管，不可避免地會導致更嚴厲的經濟控制或甚至獨裁。這種毫無辦法的條目就一直延續下去，難怪有些人已經驚慌地舉手投降，並提議說我們無論如何必須找方法來阻止，或者至少減緩這個技術惡魔的腳步。

　　對它我們該怎麼辦呢？夢想使歷史倒轉是愚不可及的事。我們也不能立法來阻止科學及技術。電腦已出現，而且它們不會只是停留不前；它們會每年越來越大，越來越快，越來越有用地發展下去。它們會進步，因為工程師們要製造它們，軍人要把它們列入新的武器系統，政治家要利用它們來幫忙處理政事。總而言之，它們會苤莊，因爲它們能使我們完成以前我們不管用多少無技術的人力也無法完成的工作。電腦會繼續擴大我們的智慧，正如機械會繼續增進我們的體力一樣。我們所必須提出的問題，不是我們要不要有電腦，而是旣然我們要擁有電腦，我們該如何對它們做最人道最聰明的使用？

〔解析〕

a great deal "許多"　　institution〔,ɪnstə'tjuʃən〕n. 機構

industry〔'ɪndəstrɪ〕n. 工業　　automation〔,ɔtə'meʃən〕n.自動操作；自動化

unemployment〔,ʌnɪm'plɔɪmənt〕n. 失業

extravagant〔ɪk'strævəgənt〕adj.過量的　　plague〔pleg〕vt. 使苦惱

causally〔'kɔzlɪ〕adv. 因果地　　repetitive〔rɪ'pɛtɪtɪv〕adj. 重覆的

clerical〔'klɛrɪkl̩〕adj. 抄寫的　　assembly line "裝配線"

the like "性質相似之物"　　variety〔və'raɪətɪ〕n. 種種；多樣性

formerly〔'fɔrməlɪ〕adv. 從前　　perform〔pə'fɔrm〕vt.,vi. 實行；執行

accurately〔'ækjərɪtlɪ〕adv. 正確地　　generation〔,dʒɛnə'reʃən〕n.代；產生

trend〔trɛnd〕n. 趨勢　　pessimist〔'pɛsəmɪst〕n. 悲觀主義者

prospect〔'prɑspɛkt〕n. 期望的事物　　a handful of "一把；一撮"

professional〔prə'fɛʃənl̩〕n. 專家　　influential〔,ɪnflʊ'ɛnʃəl〕adj.有影響力的

distinguished〔dɪ'stɪŋgwɪʃt〕adj. 卓越的；顯著的

physicist〔'fɪzəsɪst〕n. 物理學家　　predict〔prɪ'dɪkt〕vt. 預言

electronic〔ɪ,lɛk'trɑnɪk〕adj. 電子的

conscientious〔,kɑnʃɪ'ɛnʃəs〕adj. 本良心行事的

objector〔əb'dʒɛktə〕n. 反對者　　*prevent from ~* "防止~"

wreck〔rɛk〕vt.,vi. 破毀　　prophet〔'prɑfɪt〕n. 預言家

doom〔dum〕n. 惡運　　*stir up~* "激起~"

strife〔straɪf〕n. 爭吵　　gap〔gæp〕n. 裂縫；歧異

advanced nations "先進國家"　　developing nations "開發中國家"

tension〔'tɛnʃən〕n. 緊張　　machinery〔mə'ʃinərɪ〕n. 機器

distribution〔,dɪstrə'bjuʃən〕n.分配　　commodity〔kə'mɑdətɪ〕n.商品；日用品

take over "接管；接收"　　inevitably〔ɪn'ɛvətəblɪ〕adj. 不可避免的

dictatorship〔dɪk'tetə,ʃɪp〕n. 獨裁　　catalogue〔'kætə,lɔg〕n. 目錄

throw up "拋上"　　dismay〔dɪs'me〕n. 驚慌；不安

propose〔prə'poz〕vt.,vi. 提議；提出　　reverse〔rɪ'vɝs〕vt.,vi. 顚倒

forbid〔fə'bɪd〕vt. 阻止；妨礙　　enlist〔ɪn'lɪst〕vt.,vi. 使入伍；獲得

weapon〔'wɛpən〕n. 武器　　politician〔,pɑlə'tɪʃən〕n. 政治家

flourish〔'flɝɪʃ〕vt.,vi. 繁榮　　amplify〔'æmplə,faɪ〕vt. 擴大；放大

muscle〔'mʌsl̩〕n. 肌(肉)　　humane〔hju'men〕adj.合乎人道的；有人情的

六十二學年度大學暨獨立學院入學考試
英 文 試 題

㈠以下共20題（從1到20）每題一分：

一、下面有十句，每句中有一詞組（片語）劃有底橫線。每句後列有四個項目，其中有一個項目，在意義上和該詞組（片語）在句中的意義最爲接近。請將這一項目找出，按注意事項的規定作答。（10％）

例： He <u>ran into</u> an old friend at the party yesterday.

(A) went　　　(B) met　　　(C) broke　　　(D) knew

答案： (B)

1. I was all <u>at sea</u> on the first day of my new job.

(A) crazy　　(B) puzzled　　(C) excited　　(D) free

2. Stage fright <u>accounted for</u> her bad performance.

(A) resulted from　　　　　(B) was due to
(C) explained the cause of　　(D) compensated for

3. Those boys have got quite <u>out of hand</u> since their parents went away.

(A) well-behaved　　　　(B) out and away
(C) not handy　　　　　(D) out of control

4. He <u>made up</u> the story which you thought was true.

(A) invented　(B) was told of　(C) made good　(D) discovered

5. His speech <u>touched off</u> a political debate in Congress.

(A) attacked　(B) followed　(C) started　(D) discussed

6. <u>By and large</u>, George's plan has a good deal in common with Nelson's.

(A) in general　(B) gradually　(C) by and by　(D) partially

7. She <u>left out</u> an important detail in her report.

(A) described　(B) omitted　(C) exposed　(D) revealed

8. We have decided to leave tomorrow, so I must <u>set about</u> my packing now.

(A) put down　(B) send　(C) arrange　(D) start

9. A new machine has been <u>set up</u> in the laboratory.
(A) organized   (B) repaired   (C) ordered   (D) installed

10. You have to <u>look through</u> these bills and check each item before you pay.
(A) examine   (B) expect   (C) be through with   (D) watch carefully

二、下面每組四句。在意義上，各句間並無任何關係。在語法（文法）上，則四句中有一句是錯的。請將這錯的一句找出，按規定作答。（10％）

例：(A) That is a book.   (B) Are you a student?
(C) He are writing.   (D) I don't know.
答案：(C)

11. (A) I plan to work full time, besides attending school at night.
(B) I saw him reading book a little while ago.
(C) He said he would look forward to seeing you.
(D) One of the two girls is short, but the other is tall.

12. (A) Everyone who sees the building is impressed by its magnificence.
(B) He was still sleeping when I got up.
(C) The servant put out the fire, doesn't he?
(D) His arms are longer than mine.

13. (A) New York City is larger than any city in Central America.
(B) I asked him what was he doing.
(C) Need she copy this sentence ten times?
(D) I didn't expect you to come so soon.

14. (A) No matter how high the pay, workers refuse to be treated like machines.
(B) You aren't interested in skating, and I am not, either.
(C) "George will probably break his promise." "I hope not."
(D) I've not finished my work, and neither he did.

15. (A) Were he able to go with us, we could make a team of four.
(B) The chairman requested that the report be completed by the end of the week.
(C) If he had not lost the money, he could buy the furniture last night.
(D) I don't know his answer yet, but he should have made up his mind by now.

16. (A) It's high time that he begins to think how to do with the money.
    (B) We must design work to fit people, but not the other way around.
    (C) Today's workers are much better trained than those of any previous generation.
    (D) Of course they don't want there to be a third world war.

17. (A) Did your friend offer lending you a few hundred dollars?
    (B) Which of you is Mr. Brown?
    (C) Didn't I tell you my shoes wanted cleaning?
    (D) Do you remember meeting Jack at the airport two years ago?

18. (A) What little chances there were for education were turned to account.
    (B) The twin sisters look so much alike that we never know which is which.
    (C) Today growth rates of from 5 to 10 percent per year are not uncommon in some areas of the world.
    (D) I cut me when shaving this morning.

19. (A) The sisters were arguing when I brought them the telegram.
    (B) She dropped her handkerchief but she did not aware of it.
    (C) Neither of the applicants has received any further notice.
    (D) Mr. Jones had already begun the work before our arrival.

20. (A) All that our men were able to do was completed on Thursday.
    (B) Did you realize that it was Miss Day who called?
    (C) Don't you think the new office girl seems to be extraordinarily timidly?
    (D) I did not ask him what there was in that box.

㈡以下共40題（從21到60）每題二分：

三、下面每組四句。在意義上，各句間並無任何關係。在標點、大小寫、拼字方面，
    則四句中有一句是錯的。請將這一句找出，按規定作答。（6％）

例：(A) It is late.   (B) Is it a dog?

    (C) What are they doing?   (D) I am sorry.

    答案：(D)

21. (A) However, it won't be finished until the end of July.

(B) May be he'll gladly accept your invitation.

(C) It is truly said that time is more important than money.

(D) "Is it a girls' school?" he said.

22. (A) In August 1970 Mr. Stone visited his first cousin in New York City.

(B) Both Uncle Webb and his friend were altogether ignorant of the event.

(C) I saw a dog scratching it's right ear.

(D) The price of the furniture is reasonable, but I don't like the color.

23. (A) I received the telegram at 3 p.m. yesterday.

(B) Wednesday, November 21, is our fortieth anniversary.

(C) The president can't make the decision; it is up to the board of directors.

(D) He lived at 47, Nanking W. road, Taipei, Taiwan, The Republic of China.

四、下面等號左方的句子都有一處空白,因而句意也不完整。其後所列四個項目中有一個項目最爲適當,不僅可使該句完整,而且在句意上可與等號右方的句子相等。請將這最適當的項目找出,按規定作答。(10％)

例：He is ＿＿＿＿ son.= She is his mother.

(A) my　　(B) their　　(C) her　　(D) your

答案：(C)

24. Business has ＿＿＿＿Mr. Stone here.

= Mr. Stone has come here on business.

(A) brought　　(B) driven　　(C) fetched　　(D) taken

25. The story made my hair stand ＿＿＿＿.

= I was frightened by the story.

(A) at rest　　(B) on end　　(C) on head　　(D) on guard

26. That's one possibility that can't be ＿＿＿＿out.

= That is something we must bear in mind.

(A) called　　(B) realized　　(C) borne　　(D) ruled

27. Both brothers fell overboard, and _____escaped drowning.

  = Both brothers fell over the side of the boat into the water and were almost drowned.

  (A) narrowly　　(B) almost　　(C) mostly　　(D) nearly

28. That's the _____thing I should expect him to do.

  = It seems most improbable that he will do it.

  (A) most　　　(B) least　　　(C) last　　　(D) hardest

五、下面每題四個項目中只有一個項目，在發音方面，含有與其前劃有底橫線部份相同的發音。請將這樣的一個項目找出，按規定作答。（ 10 ％）

例：a s<u>u</u>bject　(A) up　(B) full　(C) blue　(D) united
答案：(A)

29. a hou<u>s</u>ing problem

  (A) see　　　(B) this　　　(C) as　　　(D) sing

30. a l<u>ea</u>d pencil

  (A) head　　(B) leaf　　(C) leader　　(D) great

31. the min<u>u</u>test details

  (A) knit　　(B) use　　(C) nut　　(D) utmost

32. He r<u>ea</u>d it yesterday

  (A) break　　(B) meat　　(C) neat　　(D) knelt

33. He never b<u>ow</u>s to anyone.

  (A) bowl　　(B) crow　　(C) brown　　(D) blown

六、下面每題四個項目中，只有一個，在意義上和其前句中劃有底橫線單字的意義相同。請將這一項目找出，按規定作答。（ 10 ％）

例：I want to buy a <u>watch</u>.

  (A) timepiece　　(B) guard　　(C) look　　(D) wake

  答案：(A)

34. I sat up with a <u>start</u> when I saw a snake crawling near my feet.

  (A) shout　　(B) shriek　　(C) beginning　　(D) surprise

35. Don't you think it a matter of <u>moment</u> to choose between liberty and slavery?

    (A) importance   (B) momentum   (C) time   (D) while

36. He is so strong that you are no <u>match</u> for him.

    (A) game   (B) rival   (C) marriage   (D) bridegroom

37. You have no <u>grounds</u> for complaint.

    (A) lands   (B) earth   (C) chances   (D) reasons

38. That set of reference books is a rich <u>mine</u> of information.

    (A) gold   (B) underground   (C) source   (D) my

七、下面每題四個項目中只有一個項目，足以說明前面那句話通常是在什麼情形之下使用的。請將這一項目找出，按規定作答。（ 10％ ）

例："Good morning."

    (A) When you sleep.   (B) When you study.

    (C) When you meet your friend in the morning.

    (D) In the afternoon.

    答案：(C)

39. "Well, I've got to get along."

    (A) When you have passed an examination.

    (B) When you want to leave because you have something to do elsewhere.

    (C) When you want to start a quarrel.

    (D) When you want to make room for someone in a crowded bus.

40. "I wish you many happy returns of the day."

    (A) It is said on somebody's birthday.

    (B) It is said when someone has opened a new shop.

    (C) To someone who is going abroad.

    (D) When a person is expected to recover from an illness soon.

41. "I'm sorry I don't quite follow you."

    (A) To someone when you don't understand what he says.

    (B) To someone when it is unpleasant to go with him.

    (C) When you begin to fall behind someone in a race.

    (D) When you disagree with someone.

42. "Please make yourself at home."

  (A) To someone who wants to go home.

  (B) When a teacher tells his class to do some homework at home.

  (C) To a visitor in your home when you want him to feel at ease.

  (D) When you meet a friend in his home.

43. "Here you are."

  (A) To someone when you come to the end of a journey.

  (B) To someone when you bring him what he is looking for.

  (C) When you want someone to know his mistake.

  (D) When you want someone to stay here.

八、本題是中譯英的一種測驗，需要翻譯的五題均已標明號碼（從44到48）並劃有底
　　橫線。中文之後列有各組英文句子，以供各題譯文選擇之用。請仔細閱讀該文後，
　　按照（例1）的方法選出最適當的答案。（10％）
　　大約是十點左右。（例1）火車靠站停車的震動把我搖醒了。
　　「先生，這是什麼地方？」（44）我問鄰座的旅客。
　　他看了看窗外朦朧燈光下的月台，沒有回答。
　　「我們還沒有到新竹站嗎？」我再問他。
　　「是的，還沒有到。」（45）他用肯定的語氣回答我。
　　「到新竹還有多久？」（46）
　　「大約三十分鐘，」他說。
　　我心裏想這一定是竹南站。（47）不久火車又開動了。
　　「第一次到新竹嗎？」他看到我開始收拾行李，他問我。
　　「是的。」
　　「希望你，玩得很愉快。」（48）

例：(A) It was about six o'clock.　　(B) It was about 10 o'clock.

　　(C) It was about right.　　(D) It was about three o'clock.

　　答案：(B)

44. (A) "Where is this place, sir?"　　(B) "What a station?"

　　(C) "What station do we arrive. sir?"　　(D) "Where are we now, sir?"

45. (A) "Yes, we don't."　　(B) "No, we haven't."

　　(C) "Yes, we haven't yet."　　(D) "No, we weren't."

46. (A) "How much longer will it take to get to Hsin-chu?"
   (B) "How much time will pass to get to Hsin-chu?"
   (C) "What time is there to get to Hsin-chu?"
   (D) "How much yet to get to Hsin-chu?"

47. (A) I thought in my mind that there is Chu-nan.
   (B) My mind told me Chu-nan is here.
   (C) I know certainly Chu-nan.
   (D) I said to myself that it must be Chu-nan.

48. (A) "I hope you to have a good play there."
   (B) "Wishing you play around there well."
   (C) "I hope you'll have a good time."
   (D) "I would like you play well."

九、下面一段文字中有六處空白，均經標明題號（從49到54）。其後六組英文是供各題填空之用。請於細讀該文後，按照（例1）的方法，選出最適當的答案。（12％）

　　The inhabitants of (例1) earth are divided not only by race, nation or religion, but also, (49) , by their position in time. Examining the present populations of the globe, we find a tiny group who still live on hunting as men did thousands of years ago. Others, the vast majority of mankind, depend not on hunting, but on agriculture. They live, in many respects, as their (50) . These two groups taken together (51) perhaps 70 percent of all living human beings. They are the people of the past.

　　By contrast, somewhat more than 25 percent of the earth's population can be found (52) . They lead modern lives. They are products of the first half of the twentieth century, molded by (53) , brought up with lingering memories of their own country's agricultural past. They are, in effect, (54) .

例：(A) a　(B) one　(C) only　(D) the
　　答案：(D)

49. (A) in a sense　(B) in color　(C) in no way　(D) in an instant

50. (A) circumstances　　　　　　 (B) ancestors did centuries ago
　　 (C) living conditions　　　　　 (D) descendants want them to do

51. (A) are consisting　　　　　　　(B) are composed
　　 (C) consist　　　　　　　　　　(D) compose

52. (A) in the agricultural societies　(B) where mechanization is yet unknown
　　 (C) in the industrialized societies (D) in primitive ways of life

53. (A) engineers and technicians　　(B) mechanization and mass education
　　 (C) radio and television　　　　 (D) electricity and atomic energy

54. (A) the people of the world　　　(B) the citizens of the world
　　 (C) the slaves of machinery　　 (D) the people of the present

十、下面一段文字之後，列有六個問題（從55到60），每題有四個答案，其中只有一
　　個是對的。請於詳讀該文後，將正確的答案找出，按規定作答。（12％）

　　Like most people, I was brought up to look upon life as a process of
getting.　It was not until in my late thirties that I made this important
discovery : giving-away makes life so much more exciting. You need not worry
if you lack money. This is how I experimented with giving-away.　If an
idea for improving the window display of a neighborhood store flashes to me,
I step in and make the suggestion to the store-keeper.　If an incident occurs, the story of which I think the local Catholic priest could use, I call
him up and tell him about it, though I am not a Catholic myself.　One discovery I made about giving-away is that it is almost impossible to give a-
way anything in this world without getting something back, though the return often comes in an unexpected form.　One Sunday morning the local post
office delivered an important special delivery letter to my home, though it
was addressed to me at my office.　I wrote the postmaster a note of appreciation.　More than a year later I needed a post-office box for a new business I was starting.　I was told at the window that there were no boxes
left, and that my name would have to go on a long waiting list.　As I was
about to leave, the postmaster appeared in the doorway.　He had overheard
our conversation.　"Wasn't it you that wrote us that letter a year ago about
delivering a special delivery to your home?"　I said it was.　"Well, you
certainly are going to have a box in this post office if we have to make one
for you.　You don't know what a letter like that means to us. We usually
get nothing but complaints."

55. We understand that _____.

   (A) the author was brought up to look upon life as a process of getting in the same way as most people

   (B) he liked most people who were brought up that way

   (C) because most people were brought up that way, the author was, too

   (D) he liked most people as they looked upon life in the same way

56. At first the author looked upon life as a process of getting. He formed this view of life probably because _____.

   (A) of most people   (B) he was similar to most people in looks

   (C) of his early education   (D) he was brought up to like most people

57. The author makes the suggestion to the store-keeper _____.

   (A) in writing   (B) in person

   (C) in the window display   (D) about the neighborhood

58. The letter the author received was addressed _____.

   (A) correctly   (B) incorrectly

   (C) to the author's home   (D) to the local post office

59. When the author needed a post-office box, _____.

   (A) his name was put on a waiting list

   (B) he wrote the postmaster a note of appreciation

   (C) many had applied for post-office boxes before him

   (D) he asked the postmaster to make one for him

60. In reply to the postmaster's question, the author said _____.

   (A) it was the special delivery   (B) it was the post-office box

   (C) it was the note of appreciation he wrote

   (D) it was he

62年大學聯考英文試題詳解

(甲)

Ⅰ. 成語解釋：

　　1.(B)　2.(C)　3.(D)　4.(A)　5.(C)　6.(A)　7.(B)　8.(D)　9.(D)　10.(A)

〔解析〕

1. *at sea* = *at a loss* = puzzled " 茫然的 "

2. *account for* = explain " 說明～ "

3. *out of hand* = *out of control* " 失去控制的 "

4. *make up* = invent " 編造 "　　5. *touch off* = start " 觸發 "

6. *by and large* = *in general* " 大體上 "

7. *leave out* = omit " 遺漏掉 "　　8. *set about* = start " 開始 "

9. *set up* = install " 安裝起來 "　　10. *look through* = examine " 細查 "

Ⅱ. 文法：

　　11.(B)　12.(C)　13.(B)　14.(D)　15.(C)　16.(A)　17.(A)　18.(D)　19.(B)　20.(C)

〔解析〕

11. reading book 改為 reading a book 。

12. doesn't he 改為 didn't he 。　　13. was he 改為 he was 。

14. he did 改為 has he 。　　15. could buy 改為 could have bought 。

16. (A) begins 改為 began 或 should begin 。

17. lending 改為 to lend 。　　18. me 改為 myself 。

19. did 改為 was 。　　20. timidly 改為 timid 。

(乙)

Ⅲ. 挑錯：

　　21.(B)　22.(C)　23.(D)

〔解析〕

21. May be 改為 Maybe 。　　22. it's 改為 its 。

23. 47 後的逗點去掉，road 改為 Road，The Republic 改為 the Republic 。

Ⅳ. 代換：

　24. (A)　25. (B)　26. (D)　27. (A)　28. (C)

〔解析〕

　26. **rule out** = reject "排除"

　27. **narrowly escape** = **have a narrow escape** = **have a close call**
　　 "倖免於難"

　28. **the last** ～ "最不～的"

Ⅴ. 發音：

　29. (C)　30. (A)　31. (B)　32. (D)　33. (C)

Ⅵ. 字義：

　34. (D)　35. (A)　36. (B)　37. (D)　38. (C)

〔解析〕

　35. **of moment** = **of importance** "重要的"

　36. match = rival "對手；敵手"　　37. grounds = reasons "理由"

　38. mine = source "資源"

Ⅶ. 會話解釋：

　39. (B)　40. (A)　41. (A)　42. (C)　43. (B)

〔解析〕

　39. **get along** = leave "離開"

　41. I don't quite follow you. "我不太明瞭你的意思"

　42. Please make yourself at home. "請不用拘束"

　43. Here you are. "您要的東西在此"

Ⅷ. 翻譯：

　44. (D)　45. (B)　46. (A)　47. (D)　48. (C)

Ⅸ. 選擇：

　49. (A)　50. (B)　51. (D)　52. (C)　53. (B)　54. (D)

〔解析〕

　51. (A) consist 不能用進行式　(B)(C)後都須加 of

　54. the people of the present "現代人" 和上一段的 the people of the
　　 past 相對應。

Ⅹ. 閱讀測驗：

55. (A)　56. (C)　57. (B)　58. (A)　59. (C)　60. (D)

中譯：

　　和大部分的人一樣，我從小被教養成把人生視為一種求取的過程的觀念。一直到年近四十，我才有了這個重大的發現：那就是施予使得生命更多彩多姿。如果你沒錢也不用擔心。下面就是我實驗施予的方法。如果我突然想到附近一家商店櫥窗的擺設需要改進，我就走進店裏向老闆建議。如果有偶發事件，而該事件的經過我認為可供當地天主教神父講道時使用，我就打電話告訴他這個故事，雖然我並不是一個天主教徒。關於施予，我有一個發現，那就是在這個世界上，只要你有所付出，不可能沒有回報的，雖然這種回報往往令人意想不到。一個星期天早上，當地郵局把一封重要的限時信件送到我家來，雖然信上寫的是我辦公室的地址。於是我寫了一封謝函給郵局局長。一年多以後，為了開創一個新事業，我需要一個郵政信箱。在窗口的地方，郵局的職員告訴我已經沒有剩餘的信箱了，即使登記，也要等很久。當我正要離去時，郵局局長在門口出現了。他無意中聽到我們的談話。他問我：「你不就是那位為了送遞限時信而到府上而寫一封謝函給我們的先生嗎？」我說：「是的。」接著局長說：「那麼我們郵局一定要給你一個信箱，就是沒有也要為你做一個。你不知道像你寫的那封信對我們是多麼重要。因為通常我們收到的都是些抱怨的信。」

〔解析〕

bring up "教養；養育"　　***look upon … as ～*** "把…視為～"
giving-away 施予　　experiment〔ɪkˈspɛrəmənt〕*vi*. 實驗
flash〔flæʃ〕*vi*. 閃過；掠過　　***make the suggestion to*** *sb*. "向某人建議"
Catholic〔ˈkæθəlɪk〕*adj*. 天主教的　　priest〔prist〕*n*. 牧師
call up "打電話（給某人）"　　special delivery letter 限時專送
postmaster 郵局局長　　appreciation〔ə,priʃɪˈeʃən〕*n*. 感激
doorway 門口　　overhear〔,ovɚˈhɪr〕*vt*. 無意聽到
complaint〔kəmˈplent〕*n*. 抱怨

心得筆記欄

六十一學年度大學暨獨立學院入學考試
英　文　試　題

I.　PART　A

下面每行之首均爲動詞，其後接有四個單音節的字。這四個字中，有一個字的母音發音（子音不計）和行首動詞過去式的母音發音相同，此字卽該答案。請把它找出來，利用它的代表字母，依照注意事項的規定作答，（ 10％ ）。

例：(1) write：(A) beef　　　(B) see　　　(C) no　　　(D) desk

答案：(1) (C)

1.　mean：(A) scene　　(B) lay　　(C) lie　　(D) dealt

2.　steal：(A) weak　　(B) go　　(C) still　　(D) do

3.　eat：(A) doll　　(B) paid　　(C) said　　(D) heat

4.　find：(A) soul　　(B) sign　　(C) ought　　(D) foul

5.　seek：(A) both　　(B) law　　(C) ground　　(D) bowl

6.　sing：(A) chalk　　(B) lock　　(C) fault　　(D) lack

7.　put：(A) hut　　(B) cool　　(C) cook　　(D) grew

8.　shoot：(A) boat　　(B) show　　(C) hot　　(D) tool

9.　beat：(A) beast　　(B) breast　　(C) belt　　(D) dawn

10.　win：(A) none　　(B) town　　(C) tone　　(D) want

PART　B

下面每行起首一字的部份字母爲斜體，其後列有四個字，其中一個包含和斜體部份發音相同的發音，此字卽該題答案。請把它找出來，利用它的代表字母，依照規定作答。（ 10％ ）

例：11. li*fe*：(A) have　　(B) is　　(C) pen　　(D) laugh

答案：11. (D)

11.　too*th*：(A) worthy　　(B) these　　(C) author　　(D) rhythm

12.　loo*se*：(A) base　　(B) lose　　(C) rose　　(D) cause

13. t*i*ny： (A) aid　(B) wild　(C) yield　(D) skinny

14. hu*ge*： (A) ugly　(B) singer (C) gift　(D) journey

15. church*es*： (A) establish　(B) pieces　(C) longest　(D) possess

16. sw*ea*t： (A) strength　(B) pear　(C) beer　(D) break

17. seat*ed*： (A) tedious　(B) needed　(C) kicked　(D) sawed

18. p*o*se： (A) dose　(B) release　(C) please　(D) decease

19. h*a*lt： (A) fowl　(B) aunt　(C) awful　(D) adult

20. laugh*ed*： (A) head　(B) mended　(C) allowed (D) sent

Ⅱ.

下面每一括弧中列有四個項目。請依照文意，選擇一個最適當的項目，按照規定作答。（ 20 ％ ）

21. An honest person will be rightly annoyed when he (A) is accused of stealing；(B) recovers from his illness；(C) keeps a promise；(D) comes to class on time.

22. David replied, " About six years ago. " The question he answered was probably " 〔(A) How long have you studied English？(B) When will it take place？(C) When did the old sailor die？(D) How old are you？ 〕 "

23. When John was asked whether he would like to have tea or coffee, he answered " 〔(A) Yes；(B) No, you don't；(C) I hope we do；(D) Either will do. 〕 "

24. There is little vegetation in the desert because of the small amount of 〔(A) atmosphere；(B) sand；(C) moisture；(D) air pollution. 〕

25. If you hazard a guess, it means you 〔(A) are not sure you know the answer；(B) are almost right；(C) have certainly made a grammatical mistake；(D) are almost worng. 〕

26. It is not safe to get out of a car〔(A) unless it is in motion；(B) until it has come to a stop；(C) after you have opened the window；(D) before the traffic light turns red. 〕

27. No one seemed to be able to get enough money， 〔(A) one way or another ; (B) on and off ; (C) now or never ; (D) off and on. 〕

28. He stopped me from telling her the secret by 〔(A) judging from the fact ; (B) means of hard work ; (C) putting his finger to his lips ; (D) virtue of thrift. 〕

29. We believe Mr. Smith will contribute to this cause of charity 〔(A) because he doesn't think it is a worthy one ; (B) ever since he came here two years ago ; (C) just as you were pleased to see him ; (D) because he is generous and public-minded. 〕

30. Fixing water pipes is the job of a 〔(A) mason ; (B) plumber ; (C) carpenter ; (D) electrician. 〕

31. Respectable people are those who 〔(A) pay respects to others ; (B) consider themselves extremely important ; (C) deserve respect ; (D) do their work respectively. 〕

32. When asked whether he had seen Bob, George answered, " 〔(A) Yes, I have. Haven't you ? (B) Nor have I ; (C) Certainly, he had seen Bob ; (D) Of course, I will. " 〕

33. Diplomats need to become familiar with the foreign countries 〔(A) when they retire ; (B) where there is a high degree of civilization ; (C) which are highly industrialized ; (D) in which they serve. 〕

34. An object shaped like a ball with a map of the earth on it is called a 〔(A) glove ; (B) globe ; (C) grave ; (D) grove. 〕

35. In a rocky field all efforts to 〔(A) look for stones ; (B) raise a good crop of rice ; (C) look out for a storm ; (D) wait for the sun to rise 〕 will be in vain.

36. I have been to the airport to 〔(A) send for ; (B) let in ; (C) let down ; (D) see off 〕 a friend of mine to Japan.

37. He has missed several classes, so he is working hard to 〔(A) keep up ; (B) take back ; (C) make up for ; (D) fill in 〕 lost time.

38. Health is the last thing that 〔(A) patients seriously think of ; (B) wealth can buy ; (C) most people want to have ; (D) counts. 〕

39. They did not turn up at my party ; I was sure 〔(A) they wanted to stay within my sight ; (B) I was out of sight ; (C) they were in sight ; (D) they wanted to keep out of my sight. 〕

40. Alice : " Did you hand him the letter yesterday ? " Mary : " No, I 〔(A) had it sent ; (B) took it ; (C) brought it ; (D) carried it 〕 to him.

Ⅲ. 下面每一括弧中，列有四個項目。請依照語法（文法），選擇一個最適當的項目，依照規定作答。（ 20 ％ ）

41. George hasn't made up his mind, 〔(A) has ; (B) does ; (C) doesn't (D) isn't 〕 he ?

42. He was greatly surprised at it. 〔(A) So I was ; (B) So was I ; (C) I wasn't also ; (D) I either wasn't. 〕

43. My brother used to 〔(A) be timid ; (B) timid ; (C) have been timid ; (D) being timid 〕 when he was a schoolboy.

44. When the summer vacation began, all the students (A) returned home ; (B) went back to home ; (C) came back to home ; (D) got to home. 〕

45. The retiring teacher made a speech 〔(A) which ; (B) what ; (C) that; (D) in which 〕 she thanked the class for the gift.

46. We demanded that he 〔(A) pays ; (B) pay ; (C) paid ; (D) has paid 〕 the bill by the end of the month.

47. Atomic energy plays an 〔(A) increasing ; (B) increasingly; (C) increasely; (D) increased 〕 important role in industry.

48. I cannot find my ticket ; I 〔(A) lose ; (B) maybe lose ; (C) must have lost ; (D) needn't have lost 〕 it.

49. China is the birthplace of kites , 〔(A) from that ; (B) from there (C) from where ; (D) from here 〕 kite-flying spread to Korea, Japan Thailand and India.

50. John : " Is Tom a good artist ? " Mary : " No, he isn't. I don't think 〔 (A) little ; (B) some ; (C) any ; (D) much 〕 of him.

51. The policeman stopped the man to search 〔 (A) him a hidden weapon ; (B) him of a hidden weapon ; (C) a hidden weapon on him ; (D) him for hidden weapon. 〕

52. The whole area was flooded because it 〔 (A) rains ; (B) has rained ; (C) had been raining ; (D) was raining 〕 for weeks.

53. Our sales 〔 (A) have been dropping ; (B) had been dropping ; (C) have been dropped ; (D) are dropping 〕 for months, so we are now in great financial difficulties.

54. If you 〔 (A) talked ; (B) were talking ; (C) could talk ; (D) had talked 〕 with George yesterday morning, you would not be so angry now.

55. He wrote letter after letter, and it was well past midnight when he finished 〔 (A) to write ; (B) written ; (C) having written ; (D) writing 〕 the last one.

56. 〔 (A) Dissatisfactory ; (B) Not being satisfied ; (C) Having not satisfied ; (D) Dissatisfying 〕 with his report, I told him to write it all over again.

57. In order to be heard over the noise of the large crowd, he tried to talk 〔 (A) in the loudest voice possible, (B) in the loudest voice possibly ; (C) in the possible voice loudest ; (D) in the possibly voice loudest. 〕

58. He exclaimed " 〔 (A) Never I met with such ; (B) I never met with such ; (C) Never have I met with such a ; (D) Never I have met with a such 〕 kind man before ! "

59. He tried to give me some explanations, but I insisted 〔 (A) him pay ; (B) that he pays ; (C) on his paying ; (D) on him pay 〕 the debt immediately.

60. 〔 (A) In case of ; (B) While ; (C) As ; (D) During 〕 on a trip, I always have my camera ready.

Ⅳ. 下面每一括弧中,列有四個項目,請依照前面中文句意,選擇一個最適當的,按照規定作答。(15%)

他的誠實不容有懷疑的餘地。

= His honesty leaves 61. 〔(A) never, (B) no , (C) nothing , (D) few 〕 62. 〔(A) background, (B) land, (C) surplus, (D) room 〕for doubt.

過去十年中,大城市的人口大為增加。

= During the past 63. 〔(A) score, (B) ten, (C) decade, (D) teens 〕 populations of large cities 64. 〔(A) have greatly increased ; (B) largely raised ; (C) have much added ; (D) greatly added.〕

我們抵達的時候,天已經黑了,更糟糕的是,我們忘掉了地址。

= It was dark when we got there. 65. 〔(A) To make matter worse ; (B) To make matters worse ; (C) Worse as it might ; (D) Worse as matter was 〕, we forgot the address.

但我們離去的時候,比來的時候更為失望。

= But we went away more disappointed than 66. 〔(A) we came ; (B) we were ; (C) we had been (D) when we came !〕

他說他寧可死不受辱。

= He said he 67. 〔(A) would rather die than suffer ; (B) chose death to ; (C) would prefer death before ; (D) would die rather than 〕 disgrace.

火延燒到二樓時,老人有生命的危險。

= When the fire had spread to the second floor, 68. 〔(A) the old man had a life's danger ; (B) the old man's life was in danger ; (C) the old man had a dangerous life ; (D) the old man's life was dangerous.〕

我想要知道他長相如何。

= I wanted to know 69. 〔(A) how he looked like ; (B) what appearance he looked ; (C) how he grew ; (D) what he looked like.〕

當我們在討論春假旅行時,我提議說:『坐飛機怎麼樣?』

= When we were discussing the trip for the spring vacation, I suggested, 70." 〔(A) Taking a plane somehow?(B) Taking a plane, anyhow? (C) How about going there by air ? (D) How to go there by air ? 〕"

父親勸我不要和背後說人家壞話的人交朋友。

= Father advised me not to 71. 〔(A) make friend with；(B) make friends with；(C) strike friendship of；(D) strike acquaintance at〕anyone who 72. 〔(A) talks bad；(B) says long and short；(C) tells about；(D) speaks ill〕of others behind their backs.

我看他不高興，所以我就問他有什麼地方不對勁。

= I saw he was in low spirits, so I asked him 73. 〔(A) if there was anything the matter with him；(B) whether was there anything matter with him；(C) if he had any matter with him；(D) what matter he had with him.〕

考試成績沒有達到老師的期望。

= The results of the examination 74. 〔(A) fell short of；(B) did not arrive to；(C) were not due to；(D) did not reach at〕the teacher's expectations.

雖然貧窮，他們依然知足而快樂。

= Though poor, they were 75. 〔(A) none the better；(B) none other than；(C) none the less；(D) still much as〕content and happy.

Ⅴ. 下面三段文字之後，列有十五個問題，每題有四個答案，其中只有一個是對的。請於詳讀該文後，將正確的答案找出來，按照規定作答。（ 15 ％）

Talk with anybody in the management of a business that serves the public, and you will find that the average citizen growls but seldom complains when something goes wrong in his daily life. He will likely argue with a ticket-seller or a city employee, but will not go to the trouble of sending an orderly complaint to officials, with names, dates, facts. Least of all does he suspect that he owes a duty to the community in such matters. Sometimes he holds his anger long enough to write to the newspapers. He tells them stories, trying to relieve his feelings by vague scolding. His letter gives no names, dates or facts upon which somebody anxious to set things right could act.

An editor could not get to sleep in his apartment because some fellow across the area was busy hammering at a night job of home carpentry. In desperation he telephoned to the police with very little hope of relief. To his astonishment the police were interested, and thanked him. Within a few minutes a policeman appeared and told the disturber to stop.

It really pays to stop growling and to make complaints instead. But before complaining, get all the facts. And the next best step is forget to grow angry.

76. According to the author, the fact that the average ciziten growls, but seldom complains is 〔(A) familiar to；(B) argued by；(C) made up by；(D) well-known because of 〕 anybody in the management of a business that serves the public.

77. The first sentence in the first paragraph actually means that 〔(A) only you can talk and；(B) anyone can talk and；(C) it is imperative for you to talk and；(D) no one is to talk, so you will〕 find out.

78. The average citizen growls 〔(A) as seldom as；(B) as frequently as；(C) far oftener than；(D) more infrequently than 〕 he complains.

79. By " the average citizen " the author means 〔(A) " the average aged citizen；(B) half the citizens "；(C) " the usual type of citizen"; (D) " every other citizen. "〕

80. " A city employee " means " a person 〔(A) who is in the pay of the city；(B) whose employment is in the city；(C) who works in the city；(D) who employs people of the city.〕 "

81. According to the author, the average citizen will 〔(A) not find it a great trouble to send；(B) not go to the length of sending；(C) be in trouble if he sends；(D) not go if it is troublesome to send 〕 an orderly complaint to officials.

82. For the average citizen to suspect that he owes a duty to the community in such matters is 〔(A) at least what he does；(B) nevertheless what he does；(C) to say the least of what he would do；(D) something he would never do.〕

83. The author seems to think that the average citizen is 〔(A) suspected of a duty；(B) susceptible to an obligation；(C) under an obligation；(D) bound by an oath of duty〕to the community in such matters.

84. For what particular reason does the average citizen owe a duty to the community in such matters？〔(A) Because he suspects so；(B) Probably because he growls；(C) Because it pays to stop growling；(D) The author hasn't given any.〕

85. Sometimes the average citizen holds his anger 〔(A) too long as to decide to；(B) too long not to；(C) as long as not to decide to；(D) too long to〕write to the newspaper.

86. When the average citizen writes to the newspaper to tell them stories, he is trying to 〔(A) provide an outlet for；(B) hold back；(C) make light of；(D) stir up〕his feelings.

87. An editor could not get to sleep because 〔(A) he couldn't tell the fellow to stop to hammer at a night job；(B) he had received a letter in the newspaper office；(C) his next-door neighbor was busy hammering at a night job；(D) he was disturbed.〕

88. The editor 〔(A) was so astonished as to call；(B) was in despair when he called；(C) despaired of calling；(D) called to the astonishment of〕the police.

89. According to the author, people 〔(A) will find it to their advantage to；(B) are paid to；(C) have to pay to；(D) will find it fruitless to〕stop growling and make complaints instead.

90. The author means 〔(A)" Before people complain, you should get all the facts " ; (B)" Complain, and you get all the facts " ; (C)" It is not until you get all the facts that you should complain"; (D)" It is before you have all the facts that you should complain ".〕

Ⅵ. PART A

下面每組四句，其中只有一句在標點（包括大小寫）方面最爲妥善。請把這樣的一句找出來，按照規定作答。（ 7％ ）

91. (A) The nurses husband isn't a medical doctor.
    (B) The nurse's husband isn't a medical doctor.
    (C) The nurses' husband isn't a medical doctor.
    (D) The nurse' husband isn't a medical doctor.

92. (A) Colored designs' can be baked into china.
    (B) Colored designs can be baked into China.
    (C) Colored designs' can be baked into China.
    (D) Colored designs can be baked into china.

93. (A) " George , " she asked, " don't you want to join us for dinner " ?
    (B) " George , " she asked, " don't you want to join us for dinner ? "
    (C) " George , " she asked, " Don't you want to join us for dinner " ?
    (D) " George , " she asked, " don't you want to join us for dinner ? "

94. (A) She was born in Taichung, Taiwan, the Republic of China, at 10 a.m., on May 20, 1945, wasn't she ?
    (B) She was born in Taichung, Taiwan, the Republic of China, at 10 A.M., on May 20, 1945, wasn't she ?
    (C) She was born in Taichung, Taiwan, the Republic of China, at 10 A.M., on May 20, 1945, wasn't she ?
    (D) She was born in Taichung, Taiwan, the republic of China, at 10 a.m., on May 20, 1945, wasn't she ?

95. (A) Robert asked her : what she was doing there.
    (B) Robert asked her what she was doing there.
    (C) Robert asked her what was she doing there ?
    (D) Robert asked her, what she was doing there.

96. (A) I suggest, Mr. chairman that 3 per cent of the profit should be given to the sales'man.

   (B) I suggest Mr. chairman that 3 per cent of the profit should be given to the salesman.

   (C) I suggest, Mr. Chairman, that 3 per cent of the profit should be given to the salesman.

   (D) I suggest, Mr. Chairman that 3 per cent of the profit should be given to the salesman.

97. (A) Why, it's my umbrella, not yours !

   (B) Why, it's my umbrella not yours !

   (C) Why, it's my umbrella not yours.

   (D) Why, it's my umbrella, not yours.

PART B 下面每組各有四段短文，其中只有一段，在句法排列方面，表達最為妥善。請把這樣的一段找出來，按照規定作答。（3％）

98. (A) But he developed the game in the United States, and it is there that it has become the most popular indoor sport through the winter months. Basketball is a sport that can be called truly American. The man who invented it, J.A. Naismith, was born in Canada.

   (B) Basketball is a sport that can be called truly American. The man who invented it, J.A. Naismith, was born in Canada. But he developed the game in the United States, and it is there that it has become the most popular indoor sport through the winter months.

   (C) But he developed the game in the United States, and it is there that it has become the most popular indoor sport through the winter months. The man who invented it, J.A. Naismith, was born in Canada. Basketball is a sport that can be called truly American.

   (D) The man who invented it, J.A. Naismith, was born in Canada. Basketball is a sport that can be called truly American. But he developed the game in the United States, and it is there that is has become the most popular indoor sport through the winter months.

99. (A) Everything ······ glass, iron, water, and even your own body ···
    is made of atoms. These tiny particles are called atoms.
    All objects are made up of tiny particles which cannot be
    seen even with the best microscopes.

   (B) These tiny particles are called atoms. Everything ··· glass,
    iron, water, and even your own body ··· is made of atoms.
    All object are made up of tiny particles which cannot be
    seen with the best microscopes.

   (C) These tiny particles are called atoms. All objects are made
    up of tiny particles which cannot be seen even with the best
    microscopes. Everything ··· glass, iron, water, and even your
    own body ··· is made of atoms.

   (D) All objects are made up of tiny particles which cannot be
    seen even with the best microscopes. These tiny particles
    are called atoms. Everything ··· glass, iron, water, and even
    your own body ··· is made of atoms.

100. (A) Fireflies are natural light sources, too. The greatest natural
    source of light is the sun. Others in the heavens are the
    stars, the planets, and lightning. Though not very bright, they
    are interesting to scientists, who study them for their secrets
    of " cold " light.

   (B) Others in the heavens are the stars, the planets, and light-
    ning. The greatest natural source of light is the sun. Fire-
    flies are natural light sources, too. Though not very bright,
    they are interesting to scientists, who study them for their
    scerets of " cold " light.

   (C) The greatest natual source of light is the sun. Others in the
    heavens are the stars, the planets, and lightning. Fireflies
    are natural light sources, too. Though not very bright, they
    are interesting to scientists, who study them for their secrets
    of " cold " light.

   (D) Fireflies are natural light sources, too. Though not very bright,
    they are interesting to scientists, who study them for their
    secrets of " cold " light. Others in the heavens are the stars,
    the planets and lightning. The greatest natural source of
    light is the sun.

61年大學聯考英文試題詳解

Ⅰ. 音標：Part A

1.(D)　2.(B)　3.(B)　4.(D)　5.(B)　6.(D)　7.(C)　8.(C)　9.(A)　10.(A)

　　　Part B

11.(C)　12.(A)　13.(B)　14.(D)　15.(B)　16.(A)　17.(B)　18.(C)　19.(C)　20.(D)

Ⅱ. 文意選擇：

21.(A)　22.(C)　23.(D)　24.(C)　25.(A)　26.(B)　27.(A)　28.(C)　29.(D)　30.(B)

31.(C)　32.(A)　33.(D)　34.(B)　35.(B)　36.(D)　37.(C)　38.(B)　39.(D)　40.(A)

〔解析〕

21. annoy 不高興　(A) *be accused of* ～ "被控～罪"

22. 回答時若用副詞 ago 表過去時間，則用過去簡單式發問。

23. 用 whether 問，表兩者選一，所以要選(D)隨便那樣都行。

25. *hazard a guess* "碰運氣猜"

27. *one way or another* "無論如何"　(B)斷斷續續地　(C)現在不做就沒機
　　會了　(D) 同(B)

28. *stop sb. from* V-*ing* "阻止某人做～"

30. plumber〔'plʌmɚ〕*n.* 鉛管工人

35. rocky field "多岩石地區"　　　*in vain* "無用的"

36. *see off* "送別"　(A)延請　(B)讓入；放入　(C)放低；使失望

37. *make up for*～ "彌補～"　(A)維持　(B)收回　(D)填

38. the last thing～ "最不可能～的"

39. *turn up* ＝ appear "出現"　　　*keep out of one's sight* "不讓某人看見"

40. have＋受詞＋過去分詞，表示被動含意（詳見文法寶典 p. 305）。

Ⅱ. 文法：

41.(A)　42.(B)　43.(A)　44.(A)　45.(D)　46.(B)　47.(B)　48.(C)　49.(C)　50.(D)

51.(D)　52.(C)　53.(A)　54.(B)　55.(D)　56.(B)　57.(A)　58.(C)　59.(C)　60.(B)

〔解析〕

42. So was I.＝I was, too. "我也是。"

43. *used to* "過去習慣於"，後接原形動詞。

44. home為副詞，其前不可加to。

47. *play an important role* "扮演重要角色"

48. must have＋過去分詞，本題表示對過去事情作肯定的推測。

49. 此題包括兩個子句，必須用關係代名詞，that之前不能加介系詞，故選(C)。

50. *think little of sb.* "輕視某人"　　51. *search A for B* "爲找B搜查A"

53. 因有for months，應用完成式或完成進行式，因主要子句是現在式，故條件子句用現在完成進行式；drop "下跌"作不及物動詞時，形式上雖無主動，但表被動意義。（詳見文法寶典p.388）

54. 從主要子句中的would可知此句爲對過去事實假設，故條件子句要用had＋過去分詞。（詳見文法寶典p.362）

55. finish後接名詞或動名詞作受詞。

56. 否定分詞構句，not應置於分詞之前。

57. possible和loudest共同修飾voice，(A)也可寫成the loudest possible voice。

58. 否定副詞never在句首，須將助動詞移於主詞之前。

59. 介詞後若用動名詞作受詞，則其前代名詞必須改成所有格。

60. while on a trip是從while I am on a trip省略而來。

Ⅳ. 句意選擇：

61. (B)　62. (D)　63. (C)　64. (A)　65. (B)　66. (A)　67. (A)　68. (B)　69. (D)　70. (C)

71. (B)　72. (D)　73. (A)　74. (A)　75. (C)

〔解析〕

61. 62. *leave no room for doubt* "沒有懷疑的餘地"

65. *to make matters worse* "更糟的是"

67. *would rather*＋原形動詞＋*than*＋原形動詞　"寧願～而不願～"

70. *How(What) about*＋(動)名詞…? 是用來徵詢對方的意見。

71. 72. *make friends with sb.* "和某人交朋友"

　　　speak ill of sb. "說某人的壞話"

　　　behind one's back "在某人背後"

73. 間接疑問句的問句以敘述句的形式表示。

74. *fall short of* "沒有達到"　　75. *none the less* "仍然"

Ⅴ. 閱讀測驗：

76. (A)　77. (B)　78. (C)　79. (C)　80. (A)　81. (B)　82. (D)　83. (C)　84. (D)　85. (B)

86. (A)　87. (D)　88. (B)　89. (A)　90. (C)

中譯：

　　如果你跟一位經營大眾服務業的人談天，你將會發現，一般的市民在日常生活中遭到麻煩時，都在發牢騷，但卻很少提出抗議。他很可能會跟個售票員或是一位市府的雇員爭吵，但卻不肯麻煩去遞送一份有條理的抗議給有關的官員，並寫明姓名、日期、事實。他們根本就沒想到，他在這件事上，對社會負有責任。有時，他將抑制了很久的憤怒，寫一封信給報紙，他向這些報紙述說他的事情，並想以含糊不明的責難來宣洩他的感受。他的信也不寫姓名、日期與事實，而這些東西正是急切想要把這些事情處理好的人所要依藉來採取行動的。

　　有位編輯在他的公寓中無法入睡，因為住在他家對面的人，正忙著敲敲打打趕夜工做家庭木製品。在絕望中，他向警方打了個電話，但對事情的解決也沒抱多大希望。令他驚訝的是，警方很感興趣，並向他道謝。不到幾分鐘，一位警察出現，要那位擾人清夢者停止。

　　停止發牢騷而以提出抗議代之實在是值得的。但在提出抗議之前要先收集所有的事實。而最好的下一步是──不要生氣。

〔解析〕

serve〔sɝv〕*vt.,vi.* 服務　　growl〔graʊl〕*vi.* 發牢騷

employee〔ˏɛmplɔɪˊi〕*n.* 受雇人員　　vague〔veg〕*adj.* 含糊不清的

scolding〔ˊskoldɪŋ〕*n.* 責難；叱責　　anxious〔ˊæŋkʃəs〕*adj.* 急切的

editor〔ˊɛdɪtɚ〕*n.* 編輯　　hammer〔ˊhæmɚ〕*vt.* 搥打

carpentry〔ˊkɑrpəntrɪ〕*n.* 木製品　　desperation〔ˏdɛspəˊreʃən〕*n.* 絕望

relief〔rɪˊlif〕*n.* 減輕　　***to one's astonishment*** " 令某人驚訝的是～ "

Ⅵ. 標點：Part A

91. (B)　92. (D)　93. (D)　94. (A)　95. (B)　96. (C)　97. (A)

　　　　　Part B

98. (B)　99. (D)　100. (C)

心得筆記欄

六十學年度大學暨獨立學院入學考試
英 文 試 題

I. 下面各句都有一個不完整的字，必須補充所缺的字母，才能使句意通達。所缺
   字母的母音發音部分，和句首括弧中單字的母音發音，必須相同（子音不計）。
   請將適當的字想出來，把它填寫在試卷上。（10％）
   注意：答案必須將每一個字完全拼出，否則不予計分。
   　　　答案不得填寫在下面的空格內，必須填在試卷內。

   例：（sheep）Students learn English at school; they don't
   　　t＿＿＿＿＿ch it.

   答案：teach

1. （buy）The frightened bird flew out of s＿＿＿＿＿t.

2. （heir）Life is often comp＿＿＿＿＿d to a voyage.

3. （love）My uncle and c＿＿＿＿＿sins will all come to my father's birthday party tomorrow.

4. （earth）He is the best s＿＿＿＿＿geon in town to operate on
   a case like this.

5. （tool）Fr＿＿＿＿＿t contains a lot of vitamin C.

6. （dawn）He is leaving Taiwan to travel abr＿＿＿＿＿d.

7. （sold）This beautiful guidebook is published by the Tourist
   Bur＿＿＿＿＿.

8. （late）They l＿＿＿＿＿d down their arms and surrendered.

9. （ease）He was eager to s＿＿＿＿＿ze the opportunity.

10. （wash）I had a q＿＿＿＿＿rel with him last night and we
    were both angry.

Ⅱ. 把下面每字中最重讀的音節找出來，將它的標號填寫在試卷內。（10％）

例：beau-ti-ful
　　　(1)　(2)　(3)

答案：(1)

1. av-er-age
　　(1) (2) (3)

2. pa-tri-ot-ic
　　(1) (2) (3) (4)

3. dem-o-crat
　　(1) (2) (3)

4. at-mos-phere
　　(1) (2) (3)

5. mo-not-o-nous
　　(1) (2) (3) (4)

6. char-ac-ter-is-tic
　　(1) (2) (3) (4) (5)

7. ca-reer
　　(1) (2)

8. dis-trib-ute
　　(1) (2) (3)

9. ge-og-ra-phy
　　(1) (2) (3) (4)

10. a-rith-me-tic
　　(1) (2) (3) (4)

Ⅲ. 下面每一空白，需要一個適當的字，才能使等號兩邊句意相符。每空白只准用一個字。（20％）

例：Jack is ___(1)___ father. = Mary ___(2)___ Jack's daughter.

答案：(1) Mary's　(2) is

There isn't much work for me to do today. = ___(1)___ have ___(2)___ work to do today.

I had hardly begun to move when George grasped my arm. = Hardly ___(3)___ ___(4)___ begun to move when George caught ___(5)___ by the arm.

This car must be washed. = This car needs ___(6)___ .

I don't have a good opinion of him. = I don't ___(7)___ much ___(8)___ him.

Everyone likes John because he is a very obedient boy. = John is ___(9)___ an obedient boy ___(10)___ everyone likes him.

Mr. Day is expected ___(11)___ ___(12)___ arrived by now. = ___(13)___ is expected that Mr. Day has arrived by now.

It was ___(14)___ until 1960 that he managed to finish his college work. = He ___(15)___ able to finish his college work earlier ___(16)___ 1960.

All these procedures are ___(17)___ no means unfamiliar to you. = You are certainly familiar ___(18)___ all these procedures.

Do you mind my ___(19)___ ? = Do you mind ___(20)___ 1 smoke ?

Ⅳ. Part A 下面每句必須刪除一個字，才能使語法正確，請將應該刪除的字找出來，將它填寫在試卷內。（ 10％ ）

注意：每句只准刪除一個字，否則不予計分。

例：He came here on yesterday.

答案：on

1. He is sure of that the meeting is over.

2. This is the book which I've been looking for it.

3. Henry went to home, but I didn't.

4. Soon the traveller fell into asleep under the tree.

5. The news of his failure disappointed in all of us.

6. He asked me that if the next bus would leave in an hour.

7. Never did he answer to my letter immediately.

8. Surprisingly, even such an educated people as those professors were indifferent to the moral principle of chastity.

9. Many cities will run in short of water again this summer.

10. When he traveling in Europe, he met my uncle.

　Part B 下面每組都有a,b 兩句，句意各不相連。不過每一 b 句中都缺少一個字，必須從a 句中找出來。請將找出來的字填寫在試卷內。（ 7％ ）

例：a. This is a book.

　　b. What ___(1)___ his name ?

答案：(1) is

a. We accomplished the task without difficulty.

b. He likes his coffee with sugar and cream, I like mine ___(11)___ .

a. Janet hasn't bought a ticket, and nor have I.

b. I ___(12)___ no idea of what is going on there.

a. We often hear people say time is money.

b. He cannot write Chinese well, to ___(13)___ nothing of English.

a. It is a good thing to begin learning a language in childhood.

b. He says that he's leaving the country for ___(14)___ .

a. Did he rise from the seat to set the clock?

b. Before long the rainy season will ⒂ in.

a. This has brought it to a successful end.

b. I'm hopeful everything will turn out all right in the ⒃ .

a. The pen may be on the desk or in the drawer.

b. I helped her ⒄ with her overcoat.

Ⅴ. 下面一段文字內有十五個括弧，每一個括弧內有四個項目。請在其中選擇一個最適合以下文意及語法的項目，將它的標號填寫在試卷內。（ 15 % ）

　　English has been(1)（ 1. largely, 2. mostly, 3. widely, 4. very）taught in South America (2)（ 1. for, 2. since, 3. in, 4. through）more than twenty-five years, and (3)（ 1. much, 2. few, 3. many, 4. good ）thousands of people have (4)（ 1. learn, 2. studied, 3. worked, 4. acquired）a good knowledge of (5)（ 1. a, 2. some, 3. the, 4. its）language. What (6)（ 1. must, 2. need, 3. do, 4. ought）they do (7)（ 1. with, 2. at, 3. for, 4. on）this (8)（ 1. hard-earned, 2. hardly-earn, 3. hard-earning, 4. hardly-earning）treasure? A few go on reading; many keep up an elementary level by teaching; but perhaps the majority (9)（ 1. let, 2. make, 3. have, 4. allow）their English to rust away through disuse, a lame ending to ten or twelve years of hard (10)（ 1. works, 2. work, 3. reader, 4. readings）. The time has come, I think, (11)（ 1. payed, 2. pay, 3. paid, 4. to pay）serious attention to the next stage in our English teaching, (12)（ 1. being offered, 2. to offer, 3. offer, 4. offered）classes in which the students themselves can take (13)（ 1. place, 2. part, 3. proud, 4. price）(14)（ 1. so that, 2. in order that, 3. as much, 4. so as）to keep their English alive and make them feel that their long years of study (15)（ 1. have not been wasted, 2. have not been spent, 3. was not wasted, 4. is not passed.）

Ⅵ. 下面有十句中文句子，每句後有四句英文譯句，請依照中文句意，找出最適當的英文譯句，將句首標誌的字母填寫在試卷內。（ 10 % ）

　　例：我愛我的國家。

　　　(a) I love my country. (b) I love your country. (c) I like my country. (d) I like a country.

　　答案：(a)

1. 我不會游泳，他也不會游泳。

   (a) I can't swim, and he can't too. (b) I can't swim, neither he can't. (c) I can't swim and he can't, either. (d) I can't swim, and neither does he.

2. 自從前年以來，羅勃先生已經環遊世界兩次。

   (a) Mr. Robert has gone the world around twice since the year before last. (b) Mr. Robert goes around the earth again since before the last year. (c) Mr. Robert has visited around the globe twice two years since. (d) Mr. Robert has been around the world twice since the year before last.

3. 在實驗期間，我明白了三項事實。

   (a) Three truths were known to me for the experiments. (b) I became clear to three truthful things when the experiments. (c) During the experiments, three facts became clear to me. (d) While the experiments, I proved three things truly.

4. 它並沒有我想像的那樣困難。

   (a) It is not so hard as I thought it would be. (b) It is as hard as I thought it would be. (c) It is not so hard as I thought it be. (d) It is so hard that I thought it would not be so.

5. 死亡總是可怕的，但以海上的死亡最為恐怖。

   (a) Any death but that at sea is most dreadful. (b) Death is at all times terrible but never so much so as at sea. (c) Death always fears, but deaths at sea are most terrible. (d) There is nothing but death at sea that is always horrible.

6. 嬰兒給隆隆的雷聲嚇壞了，哇的一聲哭起來。

   (a) To its astonishment to hear a roaring thunder, the baby began to cry. (b) Frightened at a roaring thunder, the baby burst out crying. (c) Scaring a roaring thunder, the baby burst out crying. (d) A roaring thunder in fright made the baby cry out.

7. 因為他懶惰他才失敗。

   (a) His idleness owed to his failure. (b) His failure resulted in his idleness. (c) He failed, thanks to his idleness. (d) It was because he was idle that he failed.

8. 當她的父親提着鳥籠走進房間的時候，她並沒有抬頭看。

(a) Carrying a bird cage, she didn't look up when her father entered the room. (b) She didn't see up, carrying a bird cage, when her father entered into the room. (c) When her father went into the room, she raised her head, carrying a bird cage. (d) She didn't look up when her father entered the room, carrying a bird cage.

9. 他的錢被偷了。

(a) He had his money stolen. (b) He was stolen his money. (c) His money was robbed. (d) Someone stole him his money.

10. 眞遺憾他們沒有趕上火車。

(a) How a pity they missed the train. (b) We are pitiful that they were late for the train. (c) It is sorry that they failed to catch the train. (d) It is a pity that they missed the train.

Ⅶ. 下面兩段文字之後，列有九個問題，每題設有四個答案，其中只有一個是對的，請於詳讀該文後，將正確答案的號碼填寫在試卷內。（18％）

There is no man-made pump that can compete in efficiency with the human heart. It is able to run a hundred years and more, without the loss of even a few minutes for repairs; it tolerates for days at a time an enormous overload; it keeps on going though sped up to three or four times its normal pace; if its valves leak, it increases its efforts to make up for the leaks, and still does good work. It is a double force pump built of very powerful muscle, with the most remarkable control system known.

Even this efficient machine needs care. Among other things, there is the rapid pace of present-day life, to which may be attributed much of the increase in the death rate from heart disease in recent years. Hearts today are as good as those of yesterday, except for the changed conditions under which they are forced to labor. Certain methods of exercise use up the reserve of the heart with undue rapidity. One of the most serious is the common custom, indulged in by many men who spend most of their

time at desks, of trying to get a month's exercise in a single
day. The same sort of strain takes place in comparatively young
men who, splendidly trained athletes in college, have then let all
training go. In the course of ten years or so they acquire a fine
income, a family, and probably thirty or forty pounds of overweight. They decide that something must be done. If exercise
is taken in moderation and gradually increased, the results usually will be excellent. Often, however, the same vigor is used
right at the start that was the habit of college days, and trouble
is almost certain.

1. The author means that (1) there is no man-made pump to rival
   the human heart in efficiency; (2) there is no man-made pump
   to compete with the human heart's inefficiency; (3) there is
   competition between a man-made pump and the human heart;
   (4) there is no efficient competition between the human heart
   and a man-made pump.

2. How can the human heart run? (1) It is able to run a hundred
   yards and more; (2) It is able to run; (3) It is able to run for
   a few minutes without repairs; (4) It is able to run continuously for a very long period of time.

3. According to the author, the human heart can (1) tolerate an enormous overload at a certain time; (2) tolerate an enormous overload
   for days at a time; (3) endure an enormous overload at once; (4)
   endure an enormous overload for days on end.

4. According to the author the control system of the human heart is
   (1) most remarkable and well-known; (2) the most remarkable one
   known to man; (3) the most remarkable one known in the story;
   (4) a well-known system that is remarkable.

5. The rapid pace of present-day life [(1) has a lot to answer for; (2)
   is attributable to much of; (3) may be attributed to much of; (4) is
   among other things attributable to much of] the increase in the
   death rate from heart disease in recent years.

6. Does the author think that hearts today are as good as those of yesterday? (1) Yes, they are; (2) Yes, he does; (3) No, they aren't; (4) Yes, he is.

7. In the clause "under which they are forced to labor", the word they refers to (1) hearts of yesterday; (2) some people not mentioned in the story; (3) hearts today; (4) many men who spend most of their time at desks.

8. The "comparatively young men" (1) splendidly trained athletes in college; (2) trained athletes splendidly in college; (3) received splendid training under the same sort of strain at college; (4) were splendidly trained athletes at college.

9. In the course of ten years or so, the "comparatively young men" (1) are sure to have 30 or 40 pounds of overweight; (2) are likely to weigh over 30 or 40 pounds; (3) are likely to weigh 30 or 40 pounds heavier than they should; (4) are probably over 30 or 40 pounds in weight.

60年大學聯考英文試題詳解

I. 單字：

1. sight（**out of sight** "看不到"）
2. compared（**be compared to** "被比喻爲"）
3. cousins 堂（表）兄弟姐妹　　4. surgeon 外科醫生
5. Fruit 水果　　6. abroad 在國外
7. Bureau（the Tourist Bureau "觀光局"）　　8. laid 放（**lay down** 放下）
9. seize〔siz〕*vt.,vi.* 抓住；把握　　10. quarrel 吵架

II. 標重音：

1.(1)　2.(3)　3.(1)　4.(1)　5.(2)　6.(4)　7.(2)　8.(2)　9.(2)　10.(2)

III. 代換：

(1) I　(2) little　(3) had　(4) I　(5) me　(6) washing　(7) think
(8) of　(9) such　(10) that　(11) to　(12) have　(13) It　(14) not　(15) wasn't　(16) than　(17) by　(18) with　(19) smoking　(20) if

IV. Part A：刪去多餘的字

1. of　2. it　3. to　4. into　5. in　6. that　7. to　8. an
9. in　10. he

〔解析〕

1. that 子句不可直接作介詞 of 的受詞（詳見文法寶典 p.480）。
2. which 是 for 的受詞，不需再加受詞 it。
3. home 在動詞後，當副詞用，不可加介詞。
4. **fall asleep** "睡著"
5. disappoint 爲及物動詞，直接加受詞，不需加介詞。
6. if 引導名詞子句接在 ask 後，等於連接詞 whether，故不需再加連接詞 that（詳見文法寶典 p. 485）。
7. answer 爲及物動詞，直接接受詞，不需另接介詞 to。
8. people 在本題中作「人們」解，不可加表單數的冠詞 an。
9. **run short of** "缺乏"

10. 副詞子句在句意明確時，可改為「連接詞＋分詞」的句型，其主詞與主要子句的主詞相同時，必須省略，故本題要刪去he。本句＝When he was traveling in…

Part B：由a句中選一字填入b句

11. without　12. have　13. say　14. good　15. set　16. end　17. on

Ⅴ. 選擇：

1. (3)　2. (1)　3. (3)　4. (4)　5. (3)　6. (3)　7. (1)　8. (1)　9. (4)　10. (2)

11. (4)　12. (2)　13. (2)　14. (4)　15. (1)

Ⅵ. 翻譯選擇：

1. (c)　2. (d)　3. (c)　4. (a)　5. (b)　6. (b)　7. (d)　8. (d)　9. (a)　10. (d)

〔解析〕

1. 否定句中用 either 代替 too 。(b)(d)中，後半句應改為 neither can he 。

2. has been 在此表經驗。the year before last " 前年 "

3. 三項事實是 three facts，不可用 truths 或 truthful things 。

4. *not so … as* " 不像～一樣… "　it would be 是名詞子句，作 thought 的受詞，因 thought 是過去式，名詞子句也應用過去式。

5. (b)中，at all times ＝ always, so much so ＝ so terrible 。(a)任何不是在海上的死亡不是最可怕的(c) Death 後面不可用主動動詞 fears (d)只有在海上的死亡總是可怕的。

6. (b)原為 As it was frightened at a … ＝ Being frightened at a … , Being 可省略。(c) Scaring 應改為 Scared at 。

7. It was because … that …中的 it 是做加強語氣用，本句相當於 Because he was idle，he failed。（詳見文法寶典 p.115 ）

8. carrying 為現在分詞，放在 entered 之後，表示與 entered 同時的動作，carrying 放在其他位置，則句意不合。

9. have＋受詞＋過去分詞，表被動經驗。（詳見文法寶典 p.387.）

10. It is a pity that～ " 真可惜，～ "，It is sorry 其主詞是人，而非 It 。

Ⅶ. 閱讀測驗：

1. (1)　2. (4)　3. (2)(4)　4. (2)　5. (1)　6. (2)　7. (3)　8. (4)　9. (3)

中譯：

　　沒有人造幫浦能在效率上與人的心臟相匹敵。心臟能夠活動一百年，甚至更久，不須為了修理而停頓片刻；它能一次忍受超量的重載達數天之久；即使將心跳速度驟增到正常速度的三、四倍，它仍能繼續工作；如果心瓣有缺口，它會加強其本身的跳動力量來填補缺口，而且仍能工作良好。心臟是由強有力的肌肉所構成的一種雙倍力量的幫浦，具有人們所知的最驚人的控制系統。

　　即使像這樣有效率的機器仍需要照料。尤其現代生活的快速步調，是造成近年來心臟病死亡率大為增加的主因。今日人類的心臟與過去的同樣健全，只不過它們工作的狀況卻改變了。某些運動的方式由於過度的快速而耗盡了心臟的潛能，其中最嚴重的一種就是許多終日伏案的人所沈迷的共有習慣，想在一天之內得到一個月的運動量。同樣過度使用心臟的習慣發生在比較年輕的人身上，他們曾在大學時代受過良好的體育訓練，然後又將所有的訓練放棄。經過十年左右，他們獲得了良好的收入，成了家，體重或許會超過三四十磅，他們決定要做運動。假使運動做得適當，且漸漸增加，其結果通常會是良好的。但常常在開始時所使用的體力與在大學時代所慣常使用的一樣，所以不幸的結果差不多也是一定的。

〔解析〕

man - made pump "人造幫浦"

compete in …… with ～ "在（某方面）和～競爭"

efficiency〔ə'fɪʃənsɪ, ɪ-〕*n.* 效率　　tolerate〔'tɑlə,ret〕*vt.* 寬容；忍耐

overload〔'ovɚ,lod〕*n.* 過重負擔；超載　　***keep on*** + Ving "繼續（做某事）"

speed up "加速"　　valve〔vælv〕*n.* 活瓣；活門

leak〔lik〕*vt.,vi.* 漏洞　　***make up for*** "補償；賠償"

muscle〔'mʌsḷ〕*n.* 肌肉　　***attribute to*** "歸因於"

death rate "死亡率"→ heart disease "心臟病"

use up "用光；用完"　　reserve〔rɪ'zɝv〕*n.* 儲存

except for ～ "除～以外；若無"　　undue〔ʌn'dju〕*adj.* 過度的；不當的

rapidity〔rə'pɪdətɪ〕*n.* 速度　　***indulge in*** ～ "耽迷於"

strain〔stren〕*n.* 拉緊；過勞　　***take place*** "發生"

comparatively〔kəm'pærətɪvlɪ〕*adv.* 相當地

splendidly〔'splɛndɪdlɪ〕*adv.* 極佳地；輝煌地

athlete〔'æθlit〕*n.* 運動家　　***let*** ～ ***go*** "使～走；放手"

in the course of ～ "在～中"　　overweight 超重

in moderation "適度的"　　vigor〔'vɪgɚ〕*n.* 精力；活力

at the start "起初"

心得筆記欄

五十九學年度大學暨獨立學院入學考試
英 文 試 題

I. 下面每句中有一個斜體字，句後列有四個單音節字，請在四個單音節字中，把凡是和該斜體字重讀音節母音讀法相同的找出來，把它的標號填寫在試卷內。（ 10％ ）

注意：(1)所謂相同，係指母音讀法而言，子音讀法不計。

　　　(2)答案不全者（ 如下例中，若僅填②③ ）不予計分。

例： 1. He is *absent* today.

① see　　　② hat　　　③ add　　　④ sat

答案： ②③④

1. This car broke the world's *record* for speed.

① head　　② cord　　③ core　　④ peak

2. They want to *record* your speech on magnetic tape.

① red　　② net　　③ pound　　④ lord

3. He is in the *export* business.

① port　　② ax　　③ let　　④ pork

4. We did not *permit* him to use the machine.

① give　　② stir　　③ build　　④ purse

5. Both of them are *progressing* in their studies.

① fold　　② heart　　③ great　　④ sweat

6. That is an *insult*.

① solve　　② guilt　　③ sit　　④ ink

7. He is a man of bad *conduct*.

① done　　② lot　　③ duck　　④ change

8. A large area of waste land without water or trees is a *desert*.

① deed　　② friend　　③ nurse　　④ sir

9. He paid the tax under *protest*.

① test　　② road　　③ home　　④ met

10. She is a *perfect* wife.

① earth   ② fact   ③ bird   ④ ear

Ⅱ. 下面每組兩句，每句缺少一個字，請想出兩個發音相同而拼法不同的字，分別按照其標號，填寫在試卷內。（12%）

例：America was discovered ___①___ Columbus.

He went to the post office to ___②___ some stamps.

答案：① by   ② buy

1. Give me a ___①___ of paper.

They have to make a choice between war and ___②___.

2. Two and ___③___ make three.

My sister ___④___ the first prize last night.

3. There are seven days in a ___⑤___.

He had to lie in bed because he was too ___⑥___ to walk.

4. He has lost his left arm, so he can only use his ___⑦___ arm.

He has no pen to ___⑧___ with.

5. I gave him six apples and he ___⑨___ them all.

Twelve minus four is ___⑩___.

6. Stop when the traffic light is ___⑪___.

I ___⑫___ this poem before, but I can't remember it now.

Ⅲ. 下面每組缺少一個字，請想出一個適當的字，使每組中等號前兩字間的關係和等號後兩字間的關係相同。把你想出的字，按照其標號，填寫在試卷內。（13%）

例：book : books = pen : ①

I : my = he : ②

答案：① pens   ② his

large   : larger = bad   : ①

exclude : include = export : ②

door   : doors   = child   : ③

uncle : aunt   = nephew : ④

John   : John's = it   : ⑤

begin	:	began	=	prefer	:	⑥
send	:	sending	=	write	:	⑦
me	:	mine	=	her	:	⑧
honesty	:	honest	=	thirst	:	⑨
glad	:	gladly	=	easy	:	⑩
play	:	player	=	create	:	⑪
two	:	second	=	nine	:	⑫
care	:	careful	=	courage	:	⑬

Ⅳ. 下面每一空白，須要一個適當的字，才能使句法完整，而符合下面翻譯及句法
　 變換的要求，每空格祇許填寫一字。

A. 翻譯：10％

　例：　1. 這是我的書。

　　　　　This is ＿①＿ book.

　　　　2. 昨夜沒有下雨。

　　　　　It did not rain ＿②＿ night.

　答案：　① my　　　② last

1. 不曉得（這件事的）結局如何。

　 There is ＿①＿ knowing ＿②＿ this will come out.

2. 一放學，他們就去游泳。

　 As ＿③＿ as school ＿④＿ over, they went ＿⑤＿.

3. 我所怕的是，你假裝知道其實你所不知道的。

　 What I am afraid ＿⑥＿ is that you pretend to know ＿⑦＿ you

　 really ＿⑧＿.

4. 不論晴雨，運動會將於明晨九時正開始。

　 The athletic meeting will begin, ＿⑨＿ or ＿⑩＿ at nine o'clock

　 sharp tomorrow morning.

B. 句法變換：10％

　例：　John taught ＿①＿ English. = Mary was taught English ＿②＿

　　　　John.

　答案：　① Mary　　　② by

5. He makes mistakes every time＿⑪＿speaks English. = He＿⑫＿ speaks English＿⑬＿making mistakes.

6. It was＿⑭＿hot that we could not fall＿⑮＿, though we were sleepy. = The heat made＿⑯＿impossible for＿⑰＿to sleep, though we felt＿⑱＿sleeping.

7. It is a＿⑲＿that I don't know the answer. = I wish I＿⑳＿the answer; it is too bad I don't.

V. 下面每一括弧內有四個項目，請根據上下文意思及結局，選擇一個最適當的項目，將它的標號，填寫在試卷內。（20％）

1. He held on to the rope with all his might and wouldn't（① let, ② gave, ③ broke, ④ break）it go.

2. Don't let me ever（① gain, ② obtain, ③ possess, ④ catch）sight of you in my room again, or I'll give you a good beating.

3. It goes without（① talking, ② telling, ③ saying, ④ mentioning）that knowledge is important.

4. A few days rest in a quiet country will（① make, ② have, ③ do, ④ get）you a lot of good.

5. The campers gathered some wood and（① light, ② built, ③ burned, ④ put）a fire to keep off wild animals at night.

6. The boys were told to（① make, ② do, ③ put, ④ finish）the beds after getting up.

7. The man（① hit, ② struck, ③ draw, ④ rubbed）a match and lighted a cigarette.

8. I'll（① go, ② pay, ③ take, ④ give）a visit to a friend of mine next week.

9. It（① needed, ② spent, ③ took, ④ used）me two hours to get there.

10. His speech might（① bring, ② induce, ③ call, ④ give）rise to arguments.

11. The short supply did not（① catch, ② meet, ③ follow, ④ answer）the increasing demand.

12. He worked hard enough to（① give, ② buy, ③ earn, ④ purchase）a decent living for his family.

13. It doesn't（① say, ② make, ③ work, ④ turn）any difference to me whether you are rich or poor.

14. She（① told, ② said, ③ spoke, ④ talked）me that she would not go.

15. I（① see, ② think, ③ look, ④ believe）no reason why this cannot be done right away.

16. My friend said he would attend the meeting but he failed to show（① out, ② on, ③ in, ④ up）.

17. The fire broke out at ten and was not put（① out, ② across, ③ off, ④ up）until midnight.

18. None of us objected to（① invite, ② inviting, ③ invited, ④ have invited）George to the birthday party.

19. Before he came, I'd finished（① to read, ② to have read, ③ reading, ④ read）the whole book.

20. They warned him not（① made, ② making, ③ make, ④ to make）any noise.

Ⅵ. 下面三段文字之中，列有十五個問題，每題設有四個答案，其中只有一個是對的，請於詳讀該文後，將正確答案的號碼，填寫在試卷內。（10％）

　　Gregory wandered among the smaller rocks where the Martha had wrecked upon the sunken reef ten weeks before. He was the only survivor. For two months he had lived almost entirely upon crabs. This time, however, the crabs were wanting. The tempest had driven them into their solitary retreats and they had not yet taken courage to venture abroad.

　　As Gregory was trying to make up his mind to be content with something else, a little noise at his feet aroused his attention. A large crab, startled by his approach, had just dropped into a pool.

　　He chased the crab along the base of the rock; but the crab moved fast, and suddenly disappeared. It had buried itself somewhere under the rock. As he suspected, there was an opening in which the creature had evidently taken refuge.

1. Why did Gregory wander? Because_____

　① he wanted to find something to eat.

　② he wanted to find out where the Martha had wrecked.

　③ he was among the smaller rocks.

　④ he would like to take a walk.

2. The place where Gregory was_____

　① was accessible by rail.

　② was not conveniently accessible to tourists.

　③ was not accessible to crabs.

　④ was accessible by car.

3. If Gregory had died,_____

　① there would not have been any rocks.

　② there would not have been a shipwreck.

　③ there would not have been any crabs.

　④ there would have been no such story.

4. The reef was_____

　① above the surface of the water.

　② sinking beneath the waves.

　③ below the surface of the water.

　④ sunk by a storm.

5. Gregory_____

　① had barely escaped death.　　② had perished.

　③ had survived with the Martha.

　④ had survived with other people.

6. For two months Gregory_____
   ① had eaten only crabs.
   ② had eaten anything except crabs.
   ③ had eaten nothing but crabs.
   ④ had hardly eaten anything other than crabs.

7. Before the time when Gregory wandered among the smaller rocks, apparently_____
   ① crabs had not been available.
   ② the demand of crabs had been greater than the supply.
   ③ crabs had been wanting.
   ④ there had been no lack of crabs.

8. What had happened to the crabs this time?
   ① A tempest had made their retreats solitary.
   ② A tempest had driven them out of sight.
   ③ A tempest had turned them into rocks.
   ④ They had been given a treat again.

9. When Gregory wandered about, the crabs_____
   ① had not the courage to go overseas.
   ② had not yet taken courage to venture overseas.
   ③ had not yet been bold enough to go out.
   ④ did not dare to go into their retreats.

10. When he heard the noise, Gregory_____
    ① had already made up his mind.
    ② had not yet quite made up his mind.
    ③ did not want to make up his mind.
    ④ no longer wanted to make up his mind.

11. The phrase "startled by his approach" can be replaced by_____
    ① "which startled by his approach".
    ② "it had startled by his approach".
    ③ "which had been startled by his approach".
    ④ "it had been startled by his approach".

12. Probably the crab would not have moved if Gregory_____
    ① had not come near where it was.
    ② had not made up his mind yet.
    ③ had not found something to eat.
    ④ had not been content with something else.

13. Because the crab moved fast, it_____
    ① had not appeared suddenly.
    ② did not appear to be sudden.
    ③ suddenly vanished.
    ④ suddenly dropped into the pool.

14. Though it had disappeared, Gregory knew the crab_____
    ① had gone under the rock.
    ② had been dead and buried at the foot of the rock.
    ③ was hidden among the reef.
    ④ was behind the rock.

15. This passage describes_____
    ① where a person can catch crabs.
    ② why crabs are scared by human beings.
    ③ what a shipwreck is.
    ④ how a survivor from a shipwreck is looking for food.

Ⅶ. 下面有一組對話中，僅有答句，沒有問句，按照所規定字數（不准多用或少用）
　　寫在試卷內，本題所用問句，第一個字必須爲疑問詞，其起首字母並已註明。
　　（ 10 ％ ）

　　例： A：＿＿＿＿①＿＿＿＿ ？
　　　　　規定三字，起首字母W
　　　　B： My name is John.

　　答案： ① What's your name？

　1. A：＿＿＿＿①＿＿＿＿ ？（ 6 ％ ）
　　　　規定六字，起首字母H
　　　B： I come here twice a month.

　2. A：＿＿＿＿②＿＿＿＿ ？（ 4 ％ ）
　　　　規定四字，起首字母H
　　　B： I come by train.

59年大學聯考英文試題詳解

Ⅰ. 發音：

1.（1）　2.（4）　3.（3）　4.（1,3）　5.（4）　6.（2,3,4）
7.（2）　8.（2）　9.（2,3）　10.（1,3）

Ⅱ. 同音異義字：

(1) piece　(2) peace　(3) one　(4) won　(5) week　(6) weak　(7) right
(8) write　(9) ate　(10) eight　(11) red　(12) read

Ⅲ. 類比：

(1) worse　(2) import　(3) children　(4) niece　(5) its　(6) preferred
(7) writing　(8) hers　(9) thirsty　(10) easily　(11) creator　(12) ninth
(13) courageous

Ⅳ. 翻譯填充及代換：

A：(1) no　(2) how　(3) soon　(4) was　(5) swimming　(6) of　(7) what　(8) don't　(9) rain　(10) shine

B：(11) he　(12) never　(13) without　(14) so　(15) asleep　(16) it　(17) us　(18) like　(19) pity or shame　(20) knew

Ⅴ. 選擇：

1.①　2.④　3.③　4.③　5.②　6.①　7.②　8.②　9.③　10.④
11.②　12.③　13.②　14.①　15.①　16.④　17.①　18.②　19.③　20.④

〔解析〕

1. *let go* " 放鬆 "　　2. *catch sight of* " 看見 "
3. It goes without saying that～" 不用說，～ "
4. *do one good* " 對某人有益處 "　　5. *build a fire* " 生火 "
6. *make the bed* " 舖床 "　　7. *strike a match* " 擦火柴 "
8. *pay a visit to* " 拜訪或訪問 "
9. It takes＋*sb.*＋時間＋to＋原形動詞 " 某人花費多少時間做某事 "（詳見文法寶典p.299）
10. *give rise to* " 引起 "　　11. *meet the demand* " 滿足需求 "
12. *earn* 〔*get, make*〕*a living* " 謀生

13. It doesn't **make** any **difference to sb.** "對某人無關緊要"

14. tell 是授與動詞，後接間接受詞和直接受詞，say，speak，talk 均非授與動詞（詳見文法寶典 p.278）。

15. I see no reason "我看不出有任何理由"　　16. **show up** "出席；出現"

17. **put out** "撲滅；熄火"

18. **object to** "反對"，to是介系詞，後面須接動名詞（詳見文法寶典 p.446）。

19. finish 後只可接動名詞。（詳見文法寶典 p.436）

20. warn 爲一使役動詞，後接不定詞。

VI. 閱讀測驗：

1. (1)　　2. (2)　　3. (4)　　4. (3)　　5. (1)　　6. (4)　　7. (4)　　8. (2)　　9. (3)　　10. (2)

11. (3)　　12. (1)　　13. (3)　　14. (1)　　15. (4)

中譯：

　　格列高里徘徊在那些小岩石中，那裡就是十週前瑪沙號撞上暗礁的地方。他是唯一的生還者。兩個月以來，他幾乎完全靠螃蟹爲生。然而這個時候，螃蟹正缺乏，暴風雨將牠們驅趕至僻遠的隱蔽地，牠們還不敢出來冒險。

　　當格列高里正試著下定決心用別的東西來滿足胃口時，在他脚邊小小的雜聲引起他的注意。一隻大螃蟹，因他的接近而驚嚇得正好掉進水池裡。

　　他沿著岩石底下追趕，但螃蟹爬得很快，突然就不見了。牠藏身在岩石下某個地方。正如他所懷疑的，這隻動物很顯然已經逃進一個洞裡去了。

〔解析〕

Gregory 人名　　Martha "瑪沙號（船名）"

wreck〔rɛk〕vt.,vi.遇難；破毀　　sunken reef〔rock〕"暗礁"

survivor〔sə'vaɪvɚ〕n.殘存者；生還者

live upon〔**on**〕"以～爲主食；靠～過活"

crab〔kræb〕n.蟹　　want〔wɑnt〕vi.缺少

tempest〔'tɛmpɪst〕n.大風暴；暴風雨　　**drive into** "趕進"

solitary〔'sɑlə,tɛrɪ〕adj.僻遠的　　retreat〔rɪ'trit〕n.隱蔽地；避難所

take courage "鼓起勇氣"　　**make up one's mind** "決心"

approach〔ə'protʃ〕n.接近　　bury〔'bɛrɪ〕vt.埋藏；隱匿

chase〔tʃes〕vt.,vi.追趕　　**take refuge in** "避難到；逃進"

VII. 問句：

1.: How often do you come here ?

2.: How do you come ?

心得筆記欄

五十八學年度大學暨獨立學院入學考試
英 文 試 題

I. 下面每組有四個字，斜體字母的發音，有相同的，有不同的（或有二、三個相同；或四個全同；或四個全不同）。將斜體字母發音相同的字的號碼，填入試卷上該題空白內。若四個字的這幾個字母發音全部不同，則請寫「×」號。（10％）

例：　1 2　　① talk*ed*　　② *t*ired　　③ *d*id　　④ *th*ank

　　　1 2 3 4　① m*a*ke　　② p*a*y　　③ f*a*ce　　④ persu*a*de

　　　×　　　① g*e*t　　② b*a*d　　③ s*i*t　　④ f*ee*t

1. ① p*o*lice　　② s*u*ppose　　③ p*a*rticular　　④ comp*a*rable

2. ① compl*e*te　　② p*eo*ple　　③ mach*i*ne　　④ m*ea*n

3. ① bec*o*me　　② c*o*nsider　　③ c*o*mmon　　④ *a*bove

4. ① s*o*ap　　② s*a*w　　③ m*o*ve　　④ b*u*lletin

5. ① hands*o*me　　② p*a*rty　　③ Chin*a*　　④ b*a*nana

6. ① b*oo*ts　　② f*oo*d　　③ g*oo*d　　④ f*oo*l

7. ① forei*gn*　　② amo*ng*　　③ si*ng*le　　④ thi*n*k

8. ① plea*s*ure　　② come*s*　　③ ca*s*e　　④ *z*oo

9. ① s*ch*eme　　② *sh*ake　　③ *c*ure　　④ *ch*est

10. ① sm*oo*th　　② *th*eir　　③ mo*n*th　　④ clo*th*e

II. 下面每題缺少一個字，其首尾字母均已標明，請在試卷上該題的空白內，填入這個完整的字（包括已標明的字母在內）。（15％）

例：　People who give instruction to students are t＿＿＿＿＿＿rs.

答案：　teachers

1. Students often work too hard when an examination comes up: some s_____t up late, some don't go to sleep until early in the morning; and a few have no sleep at all, which is bad for their health.

2. To help meet expenses, many housewives r_____se chickens at home, for the sale of eggs often brings in a useful profit.

3. The weather was so hot that we wore n_____t to nothing.

4. Money in this matter is not absolutely necessary, we can very well do w_____t it.

5. Some people suffering from color blindness cannot tell the d_____e between red and green.

6. You are j_____ing to conclusions, you haven't heard me through yet.

7. The ship was lost at sea, reports said, and nobody was expected to su_____e for more than thirty minutes in that freezing temperature.

8. I cannot help you by giving you money; I can give you n_____g but friendship.

9. A m_____ge is a scene that isn't there, caused by light moving through different kinds of hot air and found often in desert regions.

10. We just couldn't understand why a man of his background and education is given to such inf_____e habits of a small child.

11. If you are driving from Taipei to Keelung and not taking the McArthur Highway, you will have to pass through two t_____ls on the way.

12. He is no amateur photographer, he is a pr_____l.

13. One who studies grammar, teaches grammar, and writes about grammar, is called a g_____n.

14. One who p_____es medicine is called a physician.

15. Both the Americans and the Russians are in the heat of developing something to protect themselves against possible attacks of ballistic missiles. This development is known as the a_____ i-ballistic-missile system.

Ⅲ. 下面各句代表某甲講的一句話。後面接著是四個不同的句子；其中有三個可以用某甲的回話，有一個則不適用。試將這一個不適用的回話找出來，把它的號碼填在試卷上該題的空白內。（10%）

例1. Good morning.
　　① Good morning.　　　　② Beautiful day, isn't it?
　　③ I'm not feeling quite well.　④ You're early today.

例2. What's your name?
　　① Haven't I told you before?　② They call me Tom.
　　③ It's Tom.　　　　　　④ Everybody knows Tom.

答案：　1. ③　　2. ④

注意：本題不要你選擇對的答案，而是要你選擇一個錯的答案。

1. Thank you very much indeed.
　　① It's the least I could do.　② Glad to have been of help.
　　③ Please forgive me.　　　④ I thank you.

2. By the way, where do you live?
　　① Don't tell me.　　　　② Still the same old place.
　　③ Twenty minutes from the school.
　　④ I'm not going to tell you.

3. Is it raining?
　　① It is at the moment.　　② It's simply pouring down.
　　③ Why don't you look out the window for yourself?
　　④ One never knows.

4. How far is it to Taipei?

  ① All depends on which way you go.

  ② About a quarter of an hour's drive.

  ③ There's plenty of time.　④ Don't ask me, I'm new here.

5. May I use your phone?

  ① By all means.　② Go right ahead.

  ③ Not at all.

  ④ It's out of order, I'm sorry to say.

6. Haven't we met somewhere before?

  ① At the party, last Saturday.

  ② No. I don't think it's likely.

  ③ You're old friends, aren't you?

  ④ Have we?

7. When did you last see him?

  ① Sometime last year, I think. ② He was a wonderful fellow.

  ③ Haven't seen him for ages.　④ I'm not so sure.

8. Time to get up.

  ① But it's only half past six.　② Get up yourself!

  ③ Go away! Let me alone!　④ You lazy bone!

9. I just don't believe it.

  ① Nor do I.　② So do I.

  ③ Nobody does.　④ What's so unbelievable?

10. Must I eat it all?

  ① I'm already too full.　② I'm afraid so.

  ③ Stop whenever you want to.　④ Who's going to force you?

Ⅳ. 下面各題，各有三種假定是與原意相同的說法，但其中只有一種在意義與文法
上都是正確的，請把這一種說法的標號寫在試卷上。（10％）

例：I lost a watch. That watch was a birthday present.

　① The watch I lost was a birthday present.

　② The birthday present was a watch I lost.

　③ A birthday present which I lost was a watch.

答案：①

1. Are you sure that he will come here?

　① Are you sure for his coming here?

　② Are you sure of his coming here?

　③ Are you sure at his coming here?

2. He is a student and is now eighteen years old.

　① He is an 18 year old student.

　② He is an 18 years old student.

　③ He is an 18-year-old student.

3. He was forgetful. He forgot even my name.

　① He was so forgetful as to forget my name.

　② He was such forgetful that he forgot my name.

　③ He was as forgetful as forgot my name.

4. Hearing him speak English, I thought of Mr. Tao, my high school
teacher of English.

　① His English made me think up Mr. Tao, my high school teacher
of English.

　② His English reminds me of Mr. Tao, my high school teacher of
English.

　③ His English reminded me of Mr. Tao, my high school teacher of
English.

5. I like cats. She doesn't care so much for them as I do.
　① I like cats better than she.
　② I like cats better than her.
　③ Cats are better liked by me than she.

6. He told me not to forget the lesson I had just learned.
　① He said, " Forget not the lesson you had just learned."
　② He said, " You don't forget the lesson you had just learned."
　③ He said, " Don't forget the lesson you have just learned."

7. They had finished their work, so they went home.
　① Work done, they went home.
　② They finishing their work, they went home.
　③ Work having done, they went home.

8. When he was thirteen years old, he went with his parents to live in America.
　① When aging 13, he went with his parents to live in America.
　② In the age of 13, he went with his parents to live in America.
　③ At 13 he went with his parents to live in America.

9. " Do you watch TV often?" asked my friend.
　① My friend asked that whether I watched TV often.
　② My friend asked whether I watched TV often.
　③ My friend asked whether I watched TV often?

10. I have written a book. Someone is going to print it for me.
　① I am going to print my book.
　② I am going to have my book printed.
　③ I am going to have printed my book.

Ⅴ. 下列各題，請按上下文意思，從每個括弧中選擇一個最恰當的字或片語，並按
　　標號，填寫在試卷上，"×"號表示不須加填任何字，但仍須將此筆號寫在試
　　卷上，需大寫處，必須大寫。（ 25 % ）

　　例： 1. (do, be, is) brave！Let us　2.（ remain, remaining, to
　　　　　remain) aware 3.（ about, ×, of) our task and not grumble.

　　答案： 1. Be　　2. remain　　3. of

A.　Just for 1.（ the, a, ×) fun I'm going to tell you each person's
　　first wish when the examinations are over. Lee and Liu long more
　　than anything 2.（ to, for, at) a hot bath and 3.（ want, wanting,
　　wants) to stay in it for 4.（ half hour, one half hour, half an
　　hour), Chang wants 5.（ mostly, most, at most) to go and eat a
　　hearty meal at a restaurant. Chao thinks of nothing but 6.（ see,
　　to see, seeing) a movie. As for me, I just want to sleep a 7.
　　(sound, heavy, big) sleep.

B.　It rained heavily all morning. The rain stopped at two o'clock
　　and I went out 8.（ for, for a, for the) walk. There 9.（ had,
　　arose, was) a cold wind 10.（ blowing, was blowing, blew), so I put
　　11.（ up, upon, on) my heaviest and warmest coat.

C.　12.（ on, ×, in) one night last week while I was doing my homework
　　in my room, my cousin came in and asked me 13.（ ×, that,
　　whether) I could 14.（ lend to, lend, borrow) him the Chinese
　　novel I bought a few days before. I gave him the book, but de-
　　manded that he 15.（ must return, return, returned) it to me in a
　　week, for I knew he was in 16.（ an, a, ×) habit of keeping 17.（lent,
　　borrowed, other men's) books.

D. As the storm passed away and 18.(terribly nothing, terrible
nothing, nothing terrible) happened, I stopped 19.(worrying, to
worry, worry). Then, 20.(to find, found, finding) that it 21.(had
got, got, was getting) late, I put out the light and went to bed.

E. The years hurried onward and now he was an aged man. But not in
vain had he 22.(grew, grown, to grow) old; more numerous than
the white hairs on his head 23.(was, be, were) the wise thoughts in
24.(×, the, his) mind. 25.(beside, beside this, besides) he was
loved and respected by all.

Ⅵ. 下面的一篇短文，其後列有十項說明，每項包含四個不同的完成方式；請細讀
該文之後把最好的一個完成方式的標號，填寫在試卷上。(20 %)

The Greeks of the classical period habitually divided the human
family into Hellenes and barbarians. The preclassical Greek, Homer for
instance, did not speak of "barbarians" in this way; not because he was
more polite than his descendants, but because this difference had not
then fully declared itself. It was not, in fact, a matter of politeness
at all. The Greek word "barbaros" does not mean "barbarian" in the
modern sense ; it is not a term of contempt. It does not mean people
who live in caves and eat their meat raw. It means simply people who
make noise like "bar bar" when they speak instead of talking Greek. If
you did not speak Greek, you were a "barbarian" whether you belonged
to some wild tribe, or to one of the civilized cities in the East. People
who did not speak Greek were all regarded as "barbarians." But was it
only because they did not use the Greek language? No, for the fact
that the "barbarian" did not speak Greek was a sign of a more serious
difference. It meant that they did not live or think like a Greek. Their
whole attitude toward life seemed different.

1. The word barbarians in the modern sense means people_____

    (a) whose way of life is uncivilized.

    (b) whose food is inferior.　　(c) who live in the jungle.

    (d) who have never been to school.

2. The word barbarians in ancient Greek_____

    (a) is a term of disrespect.

    (b) refers to foreigners who did not speak Greek.

    (c) means people who understood little Greek art.

    (d) means enemies of the Greek citizens.

3. Hellenes_____

    (a) were a wild tribe with Helen as the Queen.

    (b) was the name of a Greek city.

    (c) were barbarians in every sense of the word.

    (d) were Greeks.

4. Homer_____

    (a) was a polite gentleman.　　(b) was not very polite.

    (c) is a great man in modern Greece.

    (d) belonged to ancient Greece.

5. " Bar bar " was_____

    (a) a kind of noise.　　(b) a term of contempt.

    (c) a strange language.

    (d) what foreign languages sounded like to the preclassical Greeks.

6. People who live in caves and eat their meat raw are_____

    (a) barbarians.　　(b) barbaros.

    (c) old-fashioned.　　(d) civilized.

7. If you do not speak Greek,_____

  (a) it simply means that you do not know the Greek language.

  (b) it means that you speak another language.

  (c) it means that you cannot appreciate the Greek way of life.

  (d) it makes a serious difference.

8. It is difficult to understand a foreigner's attuide toward life_____

  (a) until you can live and think like him.

  (b) unless he is polite to you.

  (c) until you make him speak your language.

  (d) unless you are polite to him.

9. To an early Greek, you would be_____

  (a) a barbarians if you lived in caves and ate raw meat.

  (b) a barbarians unless you speak his language.

  (c) a civilized man if you came from a civilized city.

  (d) a wild man if you came from a wild tribe.

10. The short essay above tells us two things, namely,_____

  (a) the importance of mastering a language, the meaning of words is subject to change.

  (b) the importance of learning classical Greek; "barbaros" at one time was not a term of contempt.

  (c) better not live in caves, avoid eating raw meat.

  (d) study Homer; be polite.

Ⅶ. 把下列三句譯成英文，寫在試卷上。（ 10％ ）

1. 我只有四十塊錢借給你。

2. 臺北的交通問題很嚴重。

3. 我要等她來了才能離開這裏。

58年大學聯考英文試題詳解

Ⅰ. 發音：

1.（1234）或（124）　2.（1234）　3.（24）　4.（×）　5.（134）

6.（124）　7.（234）　8.（24）　9.（13）　10.（124）

Ⅱ. 單字：

1. sit　2. raise　3. next　4. without　5. difference　6. jumping

7. survive　8. nothing　9. mirage　10. infantile　11. tunnels　12. professional　13. grammarian　14. practices　15. anti

〔解析〕

1. *sit up late* " 晚睡；熬夜 "　　2. *raise* chicken " 養雞 "

3. *next to nothing* " 幾乎沒有 "　　4. *do without* " 無需 "

5. *tell difference between* ～ " 辨別～之間的差別 "

6. *jump to conclusion* " 輕率作結論 "

7. survive〔sə'vaɪv〕*vt., vi.* 生還　　8. *nothing but* ＝ only

9. mirage〔mə'rɑʒ〕*n.* 海市蜃樓；幻想

10. infantile〔'ɪnfən͵taɪl, -təl, -tɪl〕*adj.* 嬰兒的；像小孩似的

11. tunnel〔'tʌn!〕*n.* 隧道　　12. professional 職業的；從事專業的人

13. grammarian〔grə'mɛrɪən〕*n.* 文法家　　14. *practice medicine* " 行醫 "

15. anti－ballistic－missile system " 反彈道飛彈系統 "

Ⅲ. 會話：

1.③　2.①　3.④　4.③　5.③　6.③　7.②　8.④　9.②　10.①

Ⅳ. 句意測驗：

1.②　2.③　3.①　4.③　5.①　6.③　7.①　8.③　9.②　10.②

〔解析〕

1. be sure ＋ that 子句 ＝ be sure of ＋ V-ing

2. 由名詞和形容詞所構成的名詞修飾語，其名詞不可用複數形。如：a 200-foot-high hill（二百呎高的山）〔不可用 feet〕

3. *so* ～ *as to* ～ " 如此～以致於～ " 表程度及結果。

4. 原句為過去式，故用 reminded of 。　*think up* " 想出（計畫）"

5. *care for* " 喜歡 "　*not so much* ～ *as* A " 不如 A 那麼～ "

6. not ＋不定詞改為直接敍述句時，應用 Don't 開頭的命令句。

7. 此句改為 Work（having been）done, they went home 。

8. at 13 ＝ at the age of thirteen

9. ① 同時用 that whether，連接詞重覆不可。 ③ 原來的問句改為名詞子句後是肯定句的形式，不應加問號。

10. have ＋受詞（*sth.*）＋過去分詞 " 要某物被～ " 表被動。

Ⅴ. 選擇：

1. × 2. for 3. want 4. half an hour 5. most 6. seeing 7. sound 8. for a 9. was 10. blowing 11. on 12. × 13. whether 14. lend 15. return 16. a 17. borrowed 18. nothing terrible 19. worrying 20. finding 21. was getting 22. grown 23. were 24. his 25. Besides

Ⅵ. 閱讀測驗：

1. (a) 2. (b) 3. (d) 4. (d) 5. (a) 6. (a) 7. (d) 8. (a) 9. (b) 10. (a)

中譯：

　　古代時期的希臘人習慣上把人類分成 Hellenes（希臘人）和 barbarians（不會說希臘話的人）。在遠古時代的希臘人，例如荷馬，並沒有用這種口吻提到 " barbarians "。不是因為荷馬比他的子孫更有禮貌，而是因為這種區分在當時並沒有充分表露出來。事實上，那決不是禮貌不禮貌的問題，希臘字 " barbaros " 並不含有現代意義中的「野蠻人」的意思，它並不是一個輕蔑的字眼，也不是指住在山洞裏吃生肉的野蠻人。它僅僅是指那些在說話時只會發出 " bar bar " 的吵聲，而不會說希臘話的人。如果你不說希臘話，你就是個 " barbarian "，不論你是屬於某一野蠻部落，或是屬於東方某一文明城市。凡是不說希臘話的人都被認為是 "barbarians"。然而就只是因為他們不使用希臘語嗎？不是的，事實上不說希臘語是個更嚴重差別的象徵：這意味著他們不像希臘人一樣地生活或思想。他們對人生整個態度似乎都不同。

〔解析〕

classical period " 古典時代 "　　　habitually〔hə'bɪtʃʊəlɪ〕*adv.* 習慣地;慣常地

Hellene〔'hɛlin〕*n.*（古代的）希臘人　　barbarian〔bɑr'bɛrɪən〕*n.* 野蠻人

Homer〔'homɚ〕*n.* 荷馬（古希臘詩人）　　descendant〔dɪ'sɛndənt〕*n.* 子孫;後裔

be regarded as ～ " 被認為是～ "

Ⅶ. 翻譯：

1. I have only forty dollars to lend you.

2. The traffic problems in Taipei are very serious.

3. I won't leave here until she comes.

五十七學年度大學暨獨立學院入學考試
英 文 試 題

I. VOCABULARY SPELLING AND WORD ORDER（15％）

Part I. 在下面每一個英文句子內，有幾個未拼完全的字，請把它們完全拼出來，並寫在試卷上。

A. The chart which shows the w.....ks（星期）and the m.....s（月份）
① ②

is a c...l...r.（月份牌）
③

B. His p...p...se（目的）in st.....ng（攻讀）so hard was to become
④ ⑤

well ed...c....（教育）
⑥

C. If you go on the e...r...s（特快）train, you must r...s...ve（定座）
⑦ ⑧

your seats in a...dv...e.（預先）
⑨

Part II. 下面每句中的字和片語，分成五組。請把它們組織成一個句子。

例： On your paper you find：

a motion picture you did go to see?
① ② ③ ④ ⑤

答案： ③②④⑤①

10. be glad I would if could return my son.
① ② ③ ④ ⑤

11. to see me who came the stranger yesterday was Mr. Chén.
① ② ③ ④ ⑤

12. Sophia said Alice would like that a tall man to marry.
    ①   ②   ③ ④   ⑤

13. people love John, to smoke why do you understand?
  ①   ②   ③ ④ ⑤

14. coffee George neither Frank nor could drink.
  ① ②   ③ ④ ⑤

15. that Chinese people have good teeth all my teacher said.
  ①   ②   ③   ④   ⑤

Ⅱ. CONVERSATION AND IDIOM（15％）

A. 在下面八句中，每句各有四個答案。把正確答案的標號寫在試卷上。

  例：When someone says " Goodbye " to you, you should answer
    ① Yes.   ② No.   ③ Hello.   ④ Goodbye.

答案：④

1. You should answer "No, thanks," when someone says：
 ① Will you have a cup of coffee?
 ② Thank you very much.   ③ Please don't open the door.
 ④ Did he say, " Thank you"?

2. When should you say "Good Night" to anyone ?
 ① At ten in the morning.
 ② When you arrive at the house for dinner.
 ③ When you are going to bed.
 ④ When you meet each other in the evening.

3. A boy may answer "Certainly, Sir."
 ① When Mrs. Johnson says, " Please open the door. "
 ② When his teacher says," Please don't open your books."
 ③ When his father's friend says, " I'm sorry."
 ④ When his uncle says, " Please excuse me."

4. While you are taking this examination, you aren't talking to your neighbor, are you?

　① Yes, I'm not.　　　　② No, I don't.

　③ No, I'm not.　　　　④ No, it isn't.

5. What do you wish to become when you finish your education?

　① I'll go to the U.S.A.　　② Chemistry.

　③ Do business.　　　　④ A doctor.

6. How shall we go to town?

　① Let's go to the movies.　② Let's go by taxi.

　③ Let's go at 5:30.　　④ To go shopping.

7. Where are you going?

　① I'm going to class.　② I'll go to my class.

　③ I'll go to English class.　④ I shall go to English class.

8. What's the matter with your sister?

　① At home.　　　② She lies on the bed.

　③ She has a bad cold.　④ She sick today.

B. 下面三個中文句子，已譯成英文。對每句若干字和片語，有四個不同的英文譯文。把最恰當的英文譯寫在試卷上。

　例：　他是我父親。

　　　　1（He, She, You, It）is my　2（brother, sister, father, mother）.

　答案：　1 He　　2 father

1. 醫生告訴我留心我的身體。

　The doctor told me　9.（to take care of, taking care on, taking care of, do take care）10.（my body, me, mine, myself）.

2. 他臉上常帶笑容。

　11.（He, The face, On his face, His face）is always　12.（wears a smile, smiling, smiles, wearing a smile）.

3. 在你就寢前，勿忘關電燈。

Don't forget to 13. (close, turn, turn on, put out) the light
14. (before, after, until, while) you 15. (asleep, sleeps, go to
sleep, wake).

II. COMPREHENSION (15%)

Part I. 仔細讀過下面這段英文，然後爲每一個問題選擇一個適當的答案，寫
在試卷上。

One of the most remarkable things about the Chinese is their power
of winning the love of foreigners. Almost all Europeans like China,
both those who come only as tourists and those who live there for many
years. And the Chinese, even those who suffer misfortune, show an excellent indifference to the excitement of the foreigners. Gradually,
after observing this, strange new ideas creep into the minds of the
foreigners. They begin to wonder if it is really wise to guard against
future misfortune. The foreigner sees that the Chinese answer this
question in the negative. The Chinese choose to face suffering with
great calm, and they also develop a wonderful power for civilized enjoyment.

QUESTION	ANSWERS
1. Do the Chinese people show anything re-markable?	Yes / No
2. Do the Europeans hate China?	Yes / No
3. Do Chinese think it is really wise to guard against future misfortune?	Yes / No
4. Don't the Chinese choose to fight against suffering?	Yes / No
5. Can the Chinese people enjoy life?	Yes / No
6. Is the writer of the passage speaking for or against the Chinese?	For / Against

Part II. 仔細讀過 A. B. C. D. 四句，並按照英文指示回答。

A.　My aunt is not like my father, but she likes him very much.
　　Write the answers to the following questions after the right numbers
　　on your ANSWER SHEET.

　7.　My father and my aunt look alike, don't they?　　Yes / No
　8.　Do we know whether my father likes my aunt or　　Yes / No
　　　not?
　9.　On your ANSWER SHEET write the two words
　　　which tell how my aunt likes my father.

B.　If he studies, he always passes.

　10.　Do we know whether or not he studies or passes?　Yes / No

C.　If James listened, he would understand what Mary is now saying.

　11.　Which one is talking now, Mary or James?（One word）
　12.　Does James understand what Mary is saying?　　Yes / No
　13.　What is James doing?
　　　Copy the right answer from the list below.
　　　He is talking. He is listening. We don't know.
　　　He is understanding.

D.　Write the best word from each list on your ANSWER SHEET.

　14.　Fast is to slow as tall is to: hight, small, short, little.
　15.　Grass is to green as sugar is to: taste, sweet, coffee, food.

Ⅳ.　GRAMMAR（25%）
　　說明：下列各題，請照中文的意思，從每個括弧中選擇一個最恰當的字或片
　　　　語，加上必要的標點，並把它按照標號，填寫在試卷上。" X "號表
　　　　示不須加填任何字。

例：　我的母親把她的衣服給了我了。

　　　1.（My, Your, Our, The）mother gave 2.（at, on, to, X）me
　　　3.（him, I, me, her）dress.

答案：　1. My　　2. X　　3. her

A. 我的父親昨天很快的吃了他的早餐，因爲我的姑母恐怕他誤了火車。

Yesterday my father 1.（ate, has, eats, takes）2.（her, the, his,
a）breakfast 3.（to, very, much, more）4.（swift, fastly, quickly,
rapid）because my aunts 5.（are, was, is, were）afraid of 6.（he,
her, his, him）7.（miss, to miss, missed, missing）the train.

B. 我的母親很願意給許多的勸告；但她常說，我們不聽她的任何話。

There 8.（have, is, had, are）9.（a lot of, any, many, a, an）
10.（advices, advice）11.（which, whose, who, whom）my mother
would very much 12.（like, likes, liking, liked）to give, but she
always 13.（say, speaks, talks, says）that we do not listen 14.（to,
at, on, X）any words of 15.（her, him, his, hers）.

C. 如果我的父親現在在此地，他會叫我們怎樣做，但他既不在此地，我們必須
好自爲之。

If my father 16.（were, is, would be, be）here now, he 17.（tells,
told, to tell, would tell）us 18.（what, how, why, where）19.（do,
to do, doing, does）; but since he is not here, we must 20.（do,
does, doing, to do）the best we can.

D. 我的母親問我當她叫我的時候，我爲什麼不答應。

My mother asked me 21.（that, how, why, X）22.（didn't you,
haven't I, I didn't, you don't）answer when she called me.

E. 那是我所聽過的最美的音樂。

That is 23.（beautifuler, more beautiful, the most beautiful,
beautiful, a most beautiful）music 24.（that, than, like, as）I
25.（never, have ever, had never, have never）heard.

V. READING (20 %)

說明：仔細讀過下面的一篇文章，然後再作答案。

It was only in the Eighteenth Century that people in Europe began to think that mountains are beautiful.

Before that time, they were feared by the inhabitants of the plain, and especially by the townsmen, to whom they were wild, dangerous place in which one was lost or killed by terrible animals. Townsmen saw, in their cities, the victory of Man over Nature, of civilization, order, peace and beauty over what was wild, cruel, disorderly and ugly.

Slowly, however, many of the people who were living comfortably in this town civilization began to grow tired of it. Man has many desires, some of which fight against others; one of these is to explore the Unknown, to look for mystery, for things which the reason cannot explain, for sights and sounds which produce in one a thrill of fear.

So, in the Eighteenth Century, people began to turn away from the man-made town to the untouched country, and particularly, to places where it was dangerous, rough and disorderly. Wild rocks and high mountains began to take their place in poems and novels, and the Lake District in North-west England, with its mountains and lakes, became a popular place for a holiday.

Then, mountain-climbing began to grow popular as a sport. To some people, there is something enormously attractive about setting out to conquer a mountain: a struggle against Nature is finer than a battle against other human beings. And then, when you are at the top of a giant mountain, after a long and difficult climb, what a satisfactory reward it is to be able to look down over everything within sight! At such times, you feel nobler and purer than you can ever feel down below.

Part A. 在試卷上那個對的標號後面，寫出回答每個問題最好的一個字。

1. This passage is written about people living in what part of the world?

Answer：　China, America, Europe, Africa.

2. What is this passage mainly about？(or) What would be the best title for this passage？

Answer：The Sea, Cities, Civlization, Mountains.

3. Which of the following desires of man is mentioned in this passage. The desire for

Answer：food, mystery, clothes, housing.

4. In the Eighteenth Century what did people begin to write poems and novels about？

Answer：order, towns, rocks, man.

5. Where is the Lake District？In

Answer：the 18th Century, England, the North-east, Sun Moon Lake.

Part B. 在試卷上那個對的標號後面，寫出對每個問題最好答案的號數。

6. Which of these was NOT afraid of the mountains before the 18th Century?
   ① The townsmen.
   ② The people who lived in the plains.
   ③ Most of the people who lived in Europe.
   ④ The animals.

7. Before the 18th Century why did the people in Europe fear the mountains? Because they thought the mountains
   ① were beautiful.
   ② were killed by terrible animals.
   ③ were dangerous places.
   ④ showed the victory of man over nature.

8. Which of these desires of man is NOT mentioned? The desire to
   ① make a living and raise a family.
   ② explore the unknown.
   ③ see and hear things which frighten us.
   ④ search for things we cannot explain.

9. What new feelings did men begin to have in the 18th Century?
   ① They began to enjoy the town civilization.
   ② They began to be tired of an easy life.
   ③ They began to fear the inhabitants of the plain.
   ④ They began to want everything to be comfortable.

10. How does the passage say a mountain-climber feels when he
    reaches the top of a mountain?
    ① Not as pure as down below.
    ② Tired and dirty.
    ③ That the climb has been too long and difficult.
    ④ Rewarded.

Ⅵ. TRANSLATION（10%）

說明：把下列四句譯成英文。

1. 沒有知識，你不能當教員。
2. 人生和夢一樣，沒有多少歡樂。
3. 你應該好好利用你的寶貴光陰。
4. 他們都是別處來的生人。

57年大學聯考英文試題詳解

Ⅰ. 單字及字彙：

Part Ⅰ.

A. **1.** weeks　　**2.** months　　**3.** calendar

B. **4.** purpose　　**5.** studying　　**6.** educated

C. **7.** express　　**8.** reserve　　**9.** advance

Part Ⅱ.

10. 2,1,3,5,4 or 3,5,4,2,1　　**11.** 3,2,1,4,5　　**12.** 1,3,2,5,4　　**13.** 2,5,4,1,3

14. 3,4,2,5,1　　**15.** 5,1,4,2,3

Ⅱ. 會話及慣用語：

A. **1.** (1)　**2.** (3)　**3.** (4)　**4.** (3)　**5.** (4)　**6.** (2)　**7.** (1)　**8.** (3)

B. **9.** to take care of　　**10.** myself　　**11.** He　　**12.** wearing a smile（或
smiling）　**13.** put out　　**14.** before　　**15.** go to sleep

10. 當及物動詞或介系詞的受詞與主詞指同一人或物時，該用反身代名詞（詳見文
法寶典p.117）。

13. *put out*"熄滅"　　**15.** *go to sleep*"就寢"　　asleep 是形容詞或副詞。

Ⅲ. 文意測驗：

Part Ⅰ.

1. Yes　**2.** No　**3.** No　**4.** No　**5.** Yes　**6.** For

Part Ⅱ.

A. **7.** No　　**8.** No　　**9.** very much

B. **10.** No　　**11.** Mary　　**12.** No　　**13.** We don't know.　**14.** short　　**15.** sweet

Ⅳ. 文法：

A. **1.** ate　　**2.** his　　**3.** very　　**4.** quickly　　**5.** were　　**6.** his　　**7.** missing

B. **8.** is　　**9.** a lot of　　**10.** advice　　**11.** which　　**12.** like　　**13.** says
14. to　　**15.** hers

C. **16.** were　　**17.** would tell　　**18.** what　　**19.** to do　　**20.** do

D. **21.** why　　**22.** I didn't

E. **23.** the most beautiful　　**24.** that　　**25.** have ever

〔解析〕

A. (1) 因有 yesterday，故選 ate 。　(2) 四字均為副詞。too作「太」解，不合句意；much須修飾比較級，最高級的形容詞及副詞；more 修飾形容詞或副詞形成比較級，此處不可用，故選 very，修飾形容詞或副詞原級。　(4) quickly 為副詞，修飾 ate 。　(7) be afraid of＋V-ing 故選 missing 。

B. advice作「勸告」解時，無複數，且其前不可加 a(n)，故(8) 選 is　(9) 選 a lot of　(10)選 advice 。advice是先行詞，故(11) 選 which 。　(12) 前有 would，故選動詞原形 like 。　(13) 主詞為 she, always 為副詞，故選 says，因為 speaks 和 talks 後均不可接 that 子句。　(15) hers＝her words 。

C. 此題前半部為與現在事實相反的假設，其條件子句動詞要用簡單過去式，主要子句要用 should（would, could, might）＋原形動詞（詳見文法寶典 p. 361），故(16) 選 were，　(17) 選 would tell 。　(18) what 為代名詞，可作(19) to do 的 do 的受詞，其餘 how, why, where 皆副詞，不可當 do 的受詞。　(20) 前有 must，故選動詞原形 do 。

D. (21) why "為什麼" 引導名詞子句，作 asked 的直接受詞。名詞子句作受詞時，主詞在前，動詞在後，又 asked 為過去式，故(22) 選 I didn't 。

E. (23) beautiful 是三音節的形容詞，其比較級及最高級，應在其前加 more, the most,（詳見文法寶典 p. 196）故選 the most beautiful 。　(24) 先行詞 music 有最高級形容詞修飾時，關係代名詞要選 that 。且 that 子句內，不可用副詞 never，故(25) 選 have ever 。

Ⅴ. 閱讀測驗：

Part A：

1. Europe　2. Mountains　3. Mystery　4. Rocks　5. England

Part B：

6. (4)　7. (3)　8. (1)　9. (2)　10. (4)

中譯：

直到十八世紀，歐洲的人民才開始認為山是美麗的。

在此之前，平地居民都畏懼山，特別是都市的居民，山對他們是荒涼、危險之地，在山中一個人會迷失或被猛獸吞噬。都市人在他們的城市中，看到了人類征服自然的勝利，文明、秩序、安寧與美麗征服野蠻、殘酷、混亂與醜惡的勝利。

有許多人，雖正舒適地過着都市文明的生活，但却漸漸地開始厭倦這種生活。人類有許多慾望，且其中有些是互相抵觸的。去探險未知的世界，去探求秘密，去探求不可用理性解釋的事情，去探求視覺上或聽覺上使人產生恐懼的事事物物，都是那些互相抵觸的慾望之一。

　　所以在十八世紀時，人們開始從人為的鎮市中，轉向未經接觸過的鄉間，特別是到那些危險、崎嶇、混亂的地方。天然的懸岩及高大的山脈開始在詩及小說中取得它們的地位，英格蘭西北部的「湖區」擁有許多湖山勝景，就成為當時的渡假勝地。

　　然後，登山漸漸開始成為流行的運動。出發去征服一座高山對某些人有着相當大的吸引力：反抗自然的奮鬥，比反抗其他人類的戰爭要來得好，並且當你經過一段長途而艱辛的攀爬，登上了一座巍巍山巔向下俯視時，一切景物盡入眼簾，是多麼令人心滿意足！此時此刻，你會感到比在平地所感到的更為高貴，更為清澈。

〔解析〕

inhabitant〔ɪnˊhæbətənt〕n. 居民　　　plain〔plen〕n. 平地
wild〔waɪld〕adj. 野蠻的　　　victory over～ "戰勝～的勝利"
civilization〔ˏsɪvḷaɪˊzeʃən〕n. 文明　　　**grow tired of**～ "漸漸對～生厭"
fight against～ "和～戰鬥"　　　explore〔ɪkˊsplor,-ˊsplɔr〕vt.,vi. 探討
thrill〔θrɪl〕n. 毛骨悚然的感覺
untouched〔ʌnˊtʌtʃt〕adj. 未著手的；原封不動的
attractive〔əˊtræktɪv〕adj. 吸引人的　　　**set out** "開始；著手"
giant〔ˊdʒaɪənt〕adj. 巨大的　　　reward〔rɪˊwɔrd〕n. 報酬
look down "俯視"　　　noble〔ˊnobḷ〕adj. 高貴的；崇高的

Ⅵ. 翻譯：

1. (1) Without knowledge, you cannot be a teacher.
   (2) You can't become a teacher without knowledge.

2. (1) Life is just like a dream, without much pleasure〔fun, joy〕in it.
   (2) Life may be compared to a dream in which we find little pleasure.

3. (1) You should make good use of your valuable time.
   (2) You should make the best use of your precious time.

4. (1) They are all strangers from other places.
   (2) All of them are strangers from other places.

五十六學年度大學暨獨立學院入學考試
英 文 試 題

I. 發　音（15％）

A. 下面每個多音節字的後面列有四個單音節字。請在四個單音節字中，把凡是和前面多音節的字重讀音節母音讀法相同的字找出來，把它的標號填寫在試卷內。

注意：(1)所謂相同係指母音讀法而言，子音讀法不計。

　　　 (2)答案不全者（如下面例1中，若僅填1, 3），不予計分。

例：　1.　father　：　① dark　② fair　③ far　④ car

　　　 2.　above　 ：　① took　② but　③ lose　④ say

　　　 3.　central ：　① sent　② son　③ can　④ set

答案：　1. ①, ③, ④　　 2. ②　　 3. ①, ④

1.	natural　:	① catch	② pack	③ crab	④ pray
2.	engage　:	① end	② aim	③ beach	④ at
3.	appreciate:	① leave	② art	③ bee	④ add
4.	October　:	① fruit	② coal	③ caught	④ top
5.	errand　:	① sand	② term	③ head	④ said
6.	country　:	① count	② new	③ court	④ blood
7.	literature:	① lie	② smell	③ quit	④ small
8.	bamboo　:	① foot	② soup	③ am	④ cool
9.	taller　:	① tail	② learn	③ sought	④ half
10.	barbarous :	① barn	② bare	③ war	④ bank

B. 下面每組四字中用底橫線標明的讀音部份，有的相同，有的不同。請將含有讀音相同的字找出來，把它的標號填寫在試卷內。

注意：答案不全者（如下面例1中，若僅填1, 3）不予計分。

例：　1.　① cake　② sentenc<u>e</u>　③ k<u>e</u>y　④ coo<u>k</u>

　　　 2.　① <u>ch</u>air　② <u>sh</u>are　③ <u>h</u>air　④ <u>s</u>ugar

答案：　1. ①, ③, ④　　 2. ②, ④

11. ① bu<u>s</u>y　　② <u>z</u>oo　　③ <u>s</u>ure　　④ time<u>s</u>
12. ① si<u>d</u>e　　② dea<u>d</u>　　③ walke<u>d</u>　　④ di<u>d</u>
13. ① enou<u>gh</u>　② <u>th</u>ought　③ sa<u>f</u>e　　④ brea<u>th</u>
14. ① na<u>t</u>ion　② s<u>ch</u>ool　③ <u>ch</u>emistry　④ <u>ch</u>eer
15. ① <u>g</u>uess　② sin<u>g</u>er　③ bri<u>dg</u>e　　④ lan<u>g</u>uage

Ⅱ. 下面每句含有一個未完全拼出的字，該字起首和結尾的字母已經標明。請按句意將該字的完整形式填寫在試卷內。（15％）

　例： 1. My father's father is my g__(1)__r.
　　　 2. The sun rises in the e__(2)__t.

　答案： 1. <u>grandfather</u>　　2. <u>east</u>

A. The merchant is now in great f__(1)__l difficulty because he has lost all his money.

B. The machine operates by itself; it is a__(2)__c.

C. Whenever Jane looks in the m__(3)__r she is pleased with her own image.

D. Fifteen minutes is q__(4)__r of an hour.

E. One can drive from Taichung to Hualien by the cross-island h__(5)__y.

F. A k__(6)__n is a room where food is prepared.

G. John wanted to know the girl very much, so he asked me to i__(7)__ce him to her.

H. Mr. Jones, who is always ready to give money to help those who need it, is known as the most g__(8)__s person in the neighborhood.

I. At that time the government was too weak to p__(9)__ct the people from being attacked by the enemy.

J. Diamonds and precious stones are j__(10)__s.

K. After the peace treaty was signed, the enemy troops were prepared to w__(11)__w from the country.

L. We usually eat l__(12)__h at noon.

M. When he had tried many times without success, he lost all his hope and gave up any further attempt in d⎽⎽(13)⎽⎽r.

N. People who live in a city are called the i⎽⎽(14)⎽⎽ts of the city.

O. One who kills a person unlawfully and on purpose is a m⎽⎽(15)⎽⎽r.

Ⅱ. 下面每題含有一個空白，其後列有四個項目。請按照句意及文法結構，在四個項目中選擇一個最爲適當的項目，將它的標號填寫在試卷內。（15％）

例： This⎽⎽⎽⎽⎽⎽⎽a book.

　　① will　　　② are　　　③ am　　　④ is

答案： ④

1. Would you mind fixing my bicycle? "⎽⎽⎽⎽⎽⎽.I'll fix it for you right now."

　　① Yes, I will　② I would　　③ Certainly not ④ I do

2. Do you know the reason⎽⎽⎽⎽⎽⎽he didn't come?

　　① which　　　② why　　　③ what　　　④ whether

3. Let's start right now,⎽⎽⎽⎽⎽⎽?

　　① shall we　　② won't we　　③ do we　　　④ don't we

4. ⎽⎽⎽⎽⎽⎽you please tell me your address?

　　① Do　　　　② Can　　　③ Shall　　　④ Would

5. I remember⎽⎽⎽⎽⎽⎽the house about an hour ago.

　　① to see him leave　　　② to see him to leave

　　③ to see him leaving　　④ seeing him leave

6. ⎽⎽⎽⎽⎽⎽of the three daughters in the family has got married yet.

　　① None　　　② No　　　③ One　　　④ Some

7. When we were in high school, Jim often helped me⎽⎽⎽⎽⎽⎽my mathematics.

　　① with　　　② through　　③ by　　　　④ to

8. By the time you graduate, I shall have been_____here for five years.
   ① work
   ② worked
   ③ working
   ④ to be working

9. " You speak very good English." "_____."
   ① No, thanks
   ② With pleasure
   ③ You are welcome
   ④ Thank you

10. A man is usually judged by_____he does.
    ① what
    ② however
    ③ that
    ④ which

11. _____people in Taiwan earn a wage high enough for a comfortable life.
    ① Most of
    ② Most
    ③ The most of
    ④ The most

12. The radio is getting on my nerves. Please_____.
    ① turn off it
    ② turn it off.
    ③ close off it
    ④ close it off.

13. _____came to see me?
    ① Who you think
    ② Do you think who
    ③ Who do you think
    ④ Whom do you think

14. _____do you think of the new teacher?
    ① How about
    ② How
    ③ What like
    ④ What

15. A secondhand bookstore is a bookstore which sells_____.
    ① secondhand book
    ② secondhand books
    ③ a secondhand book
    ④ the secondhand book

Ⅳ. 下面左邊有十五個未完成的句子，請在右邊選擇適當的項目以完成之，並將代表該項目的大寫字母（如 A 或 B 或 C 等）填寫在試卷內。（15％）

注意： (1) 在選擇項目時，句意與文法並重。

(2) 右邊有二十個項目，其中有五個是沒有用的。

1. This is one of the largest rooms

2. Is it education that makes (us)

3. Running at the full speed of one mile a minute,

4. Did the two boys look so much alike

5. We found her

6. Everything is

7. Your cousin does not insist on

8. She would have told you her age

9. She has decided to make you

10. She will feel hurt

11. Jack could not swim, and

12. I knocked at the door, but

13. Rich as he is,

14. They do not know which girl

15. No sooner had they heard the news

A. fixing the TV set in the basement last night.

B. had you asked her.

C. just as we left it.

D. if you ask her age.

E. what we are?

F. which took place yesterday, didn't it?

G. that I've ever slept in.

H. than they rushed out into the street.

I. whose book we have read?

J. where to go, does she?

K. forget one's own name.

L. postpone the trip until she hears from them.

M. their car crashed into a tree.

N. hearing no one answer it, I concluded that the house was deserted.

O. Bob is going to marry next week.

P. it is getting dark.

Q. he has never spent a cent on charity.

R. to kill two birds with one stone, does he?

S. that no one could tell them apart?

T. neither could Mary.

V. 下面每一空白，須填一適當的字，方可使等號兩邊的句意相同。(20％)
   注意：(1) 有些空白所應填寫的字，其第一個字母已經標明。
         (2) 每一空白只准填寫一個字。所填寫的字必須按照號碼填寫在試卷內。

A. Although the enemy resisted stubbornly, our army occupied the
   town according to the original schedule.
   = In __(1)__ __(2)__ the enemy's s__(3)__ r__(4)__ , our army
   occupied the town __(5)__ originally __(6)__ .

B. Must I get someone to paint the walls?
   = Is __(7)__ necessary __(8)__ __(9)__ to h__(10)__ the walls __(11)__ ?

C. The problem is more complicated than I thought.
   = I __(12)__ e__(13)__ the problem to __(14)__ so complicated.

D. This idea, though good, must be tried out.
   = The idea, though good, needs t__(15)__ out.

E. He has bought a lot of furniture.
   = He has bought many a __(16)__ of furniture.

F. He has such a lot of things to do today that he cannot go to the
   party.
   = He has __(17)__ __(18)__ w__(19)__ to do today that he cannot
   a__(20)__ the party.

VI. 下面的一篇文字，其後列有十個問題，每題附四個答案，其中只有一個是對
    的。請於細讀該文之後，把正確答案的標號，填寫在試卷內。(20％)

Old Henry Ford retired from business after the war, at the age of
81, and moved to Dearborn.

Here, a few months before his death in April, 1947, he took a walk
through his gardens one day, holding the hand of one of his little great-
grandsons. Suddenly the boy dropped something carelessly on the grass.

"What was that?" inquired Henry Ford.

"Nothing. Just a penny."

Without a word the old man bent down and searched the grass for the coin until he found it. Then he handed it back to the little boy.

" Grandfather," said the boy after a while as they were walking on, "is it true that you are the richest man that ever lived?"

" I guess so. "

" Then why did you stop to look for my penny?"

" My dear boy," replied Henry Ford, " if you were alone on a desert island, all the paper money in the world wouldn't do you any good. But a penny. There you have metal-copper. You could hammer out a spearhead or sharpen it into a tool. That penny is important because it doesn't represent something, as paper money does; it is something. So don't drop your penny again. You never know when you'll be on a desert island."

1. Henry Ford died :
   ① at the age of 81.   ② before the war.
   ③ in April, 1947.   ④ late in 1947.

2. The little boy dropped :
   ① Henry Ford's hand.   ② a copper coin.
   ③ a bank note or bill.   ④ nothing.

3. Henry Ford did not :
   ① find the penny.   ② look for the penny.
   ③ give the penny to the boy. ④ keep the penny.

4. " I guess so. " means :
   ① " No. "
   ② " I think that is probably true. "
   ③ " I don't think so. "   ④ " That is not true. "

5. The boy asked Henry Ford the two questions, because :
   ① he was surprised that a rich man cared about a penny.
   ② he was surprised that an old man should care about money.
   ③ he wanted the money back.
   ④ he wanted to give Henry Ford the penny.

6. Henry Ford says that paper money is :
   ① useless on a desert island.　② useful on a desert island.
   ③ useless anywhere.　④ always worth less than a coin.

7. Henry Ford says that a penny would be valuable on a desert island because :
   ① you could buy something with it.
   ② you could make something with it.
   ③ you could save it and become rich.
   ④ you could give it to someone else.

8. Henry Ford says that the important difference between a penny and paper money is that :
   ① you can buy more with paper money.
   ② paper money is more convenient than metal money.
   ③ copper costs more than paper.
   ④ a penny has value while a $100.00 bill only represents value.

9. The lesson that Henry Ford wanted to teach the boy was :
   ① "Don't waste money."
   ② "Save your pennies and you will be rich like me."
   ③ "Take care of useful material."
   ④ "Don't depend on other people."

10. The story shows that Henry Ford was probably a :
    ① great traveller.　② great politician.
    ③ great explorer.　④ great leader of industry.

56年大學聯考英文試題詳解

Ⅰ. 發音：

A. 1.(1)(2)(3)　2.(2)　3.(1)(3)　4.(2)　5.(3)(4)　6.(4)　7.(3)　8.(2)(4)
　　9.(3)　10.(1)

B. 11.(1)(2)(4)　12.(1)(2)(4)　13.(1)(3)　14.(2)(3)　15.(3)(4)

Ⅱ. 單字：

(A) financial〔fə′nænʃəl,faɪ-〕adj.財務的　　(B) automatic 自動的
(C) mirror 鏡子　(D) quarter 四分之一；一刻鐘
(E) highway 公路　　(F) kitchen 廚房
(G) introduce〔,ɪntrə′djus〕vt.介紹；引入　　(H) generous 慷慨的
(I) protect〔prə′tɛkt〕vt. 保護　　(J) jewels〔′dʒuəlz,′dʒɪuəlz〕n. 珠寶
(K) withdraw〔wɪð′drɔ,wɪθ-〕vt.,vi. 撤退　　(L) lunch 午餐
(M) despair 絕望　(N) inhabitants 居民　　(O) murderer 兇手

Ⅲ. 選擇：

1.(3)　2.(2)　3.(1)　4.(4)　5.(4)　6.(1)　7.(1)　8.(3)　9.(4)　10.(1)
11.(2)　12.(2)　13.(3)　14.(4)　15.(2)

〔解析〕

1. Would you mind …?是表客氣的請求，其回答常用 Certainly not，意爲
　"當然不反對"。

2. reason 後通常接 why，當關係副詞，引導形容詞子句，修飾 reason 。

3. Let's 引出的祈使句，其附加問句用 " shall we？"（詳見文法寶典 p.6,7）。

5. remember ＋ V-ing 表動作已發生，若加不定詞，則表動作尚未發生。
　（詳見文法寶典 p.435 ）

6. None 表三者以上的全部否定，在此爲代名詞，當 has got married 的主詞。
　因 yet 通常用在否定或疑問句中，依此題句意要配合一個否定字，而 One 和
　Some 是肯定意思，No 爲形容詞、副詞，不爲主詞。

8. 此句要用未來完成進行式。By the time " 到…時 " 爲表時間的連接詞 。

11. most作「大多數」解時，不加冠詞（ 詳見文法寶典 p.205 ）。　(1) 改爲 most of
　　the people 。

14. What是 think 的受詞。(1) How about 後接名詞或動名詞。(2) How是副詞，不
　　能當受詞 。

Ⅳ. 配合：

　1. G　　2. E　　3. M　　4. S　　5. A　　6. C　　7. J　　8. B　　9. L　　10. D
　11. T　12. N　13. Q　14. O　15. H

Ⅴ. 代換：

　1. spite　2. of　3. stubborn　4. resistance　5. as　6. scheduled　7. it　8. for　9. me　10. have　11. painted　12. hardly　13. expected　14. be　15. trying　16. piece　17. so　18. much　19. work　20. attend

Ⅵ. 閱讀測驗：

　1. (3)　2. (2)　3. (4)　4. (2)　5. (1)　6. (1)　7. (2)　8. (4)　9. (3)　10. (4)

　中譯：

　　戰後，老亨利福特在八十一歲時退休，並且移居到第波恩。

　　在第波恩，一九四七年四月，他去世前的幾個月，有一天，他牽著他的一個小曾孫的手，散步穿過他的花園。忽然，這孩子不小心掉了一樣東西在草地上。

　　「什麼東西掉了？」亨利福特問。

　　「沒有什麼，只是一分錢。」

　　這位老人一言不發就彎下腰去找那一分錢銅幣，終於找到了。然後將它交還給他的小孫子。

　　「祖父」，那小孩子繼續向前走了一會兒說，「你是當今世上最有錢的人，是真的嗎？」

　　「我想是吧。」

　　「你為什麼要停下來找我的一分錢呢？」

　　「好孩子」，亨利福特回答說，「如果你一個人身處在一座荒島上，世界上所有的紙幣對你都不會有任何好處，但一分銅幣對你却有用處。在那裡你有了金屬──銅，你就可以把它錘成矛頭，或把它磨成工具，那一分錢重要，是因為它不像紙幣只代表著某種價值，它本身就是一種價值。所以不要再丟了你的一分錢，你決不會知道何時會處身在荒島上。」

　〔解析〕

　Henry Ford　美國汽車製造者（ 1863 － 1947 ）

　retire〔rɪˋtaɪr〕*vt.,vi.* 退休

　Dearborn〔ˋdɪrbən,-ˏbɔrn〕*n.* 第波恩（美國密西根州東南的一個城市）

　bend down "彎下腰"　　***search for*** "尋找"

　a desert island "荒島"　　paper money "紙幣；鈔票"

　metal-copper "金屬銅"　　***hammer out*** "用鎚打成器；鎚平"

　spear-head "矛頭；槍尖"

五十五學年度大學暨獨立學院入學考試
英 文 試 題

Ⅰ. 對下面 1, 2, 3, 4, 5, 6, 7 各題，在每題四個答案之中，選擇一個最恰當的
答案，把它的標號填寫在試卷內。對下面 8, 9, 10, 11, 12, 13, 14, 15
各題，在每題四個答案之中，選擇其中一個你認為對於這句中文是最恰當的
英文譯句，把它的標號填寫在試卷內。（15％）

例： 1. When someone says "Good morning" to you, you should
answer：
①Good morning.　　　　　②Fine, thanks.
③Yes.　　　　　　　　　④Good night.

2. 鳥在多天飛向南方。
①Birds flies south in winter.
②Birds fly to south in winter.
③Birds fly south winter.
④Birds fly south in winter.

答案：1. 1　　　2. 4

1. When you answer "Yes" to old Mrs. Smith, it is polite to say：
①Yes, Mrs. Smith.　　　②Yes, Sir.
③Yes.　　　　　　　　　④Not at all.

2. When someone thanks you for opening the door, you should answer：
①Don't thank.　　　　　②Certainly.
③You're welcome.　　　　④No thanks.

3. When someone asks you to open the door, you should say：
①Not at all.　　　　　　②Certainly.
③Good.　　　　　　　　④You're welcome.

4. When someone says, "Please don't open the window." you should say：
①All right，I won't.　　　②Not at all.
③Yes, Sir.　　　　　　　④No thanks.

5. When someone says you are a very good student, you should say:
   ①Where, where.　　　　　②You're welcome.
   ③Thank you.　　　　　　④Of course.

6. When your friend says, "Shall we go to the movies tonight?" and
   you do not want to go, you should say:
   ①No, let's not.　　　　　②Yes, I can't.
   ③Yes, let's.　　　　　　④Of course.

7. When someone asks you; "Is there no earlier train?" and there
   isn't any earlier train, you answer:
   ①Of course.　　　　　　②Yes.
   ③No.　　　　　　　　　④Surely.

8. 我伯父的兩個孩子都是男孩子。
   ①My uncle's both children are boys.
   ②My uncle's children both boys.
   ③Both my uncle's children are boy.
   ④Both my uncle's children are boys.

9. 在這屋裏有一些桌子。
   ①This room have several desks.
   ②There are several desks in this room.
   ③There have several desks in this room.
   ④In this room have several desks.

10. 昨天下很大的雨。
    ①Yesterday rained very hard.
    ②Yesterday have very hard rain.
    ③It fell very large rain yesterday.
    ④It rained very hard yesterday.

11. 去年他和她結了婚。
    ①He married with her last year.
    ②He married her last year.
    ③He married her in last year.
    ④He marry her last year.

12. 她的孩子是昨天出生的。

①Her baby was born yesterday.

②She borned her baby yesterday.

③Her baby born yesterday.

④Her baby born on yesterday.

13. 這是我從來未見過的最長的一列火車。

①It is the longest train I have never seen.

②It is longest train than I ever saw.

③It is the longest train than I have never seen.

④It is the longest train I have ever seen.

14. 我的父親在這新的銀行大廈工作。

①My father works in the new bank house.

②My father work in the new bank house.

③My father walks in the new house.

④My father works in the new bank building.

15. 我在四年以前來到這裏。

①I came here before four years.

②I came here four years go.

③Four years before I came here.

④Ago four years I came here.

II. 下面每句都缺少一個字，該字起首及最後的字母已經標明。請將適當的字想出來，把它填寫在試卷上。

注意：1.答案必須將每一個字完全拼出，否則不予計分。

　　　2.答案不得填寫在下面每句的空白內，必須填寫在試卷內。（15%）

例：My father's father is my g_____r.

答案：grandfather.

1. People who rely on others are not i_____nt.

2. Gold or silver is a m_____l, but wood or paper is not.

3. Christopher Columbus was famous for his d_____ry of America.

4. Cameras are used to take p_____hs.

5. To Chinese students English is a f_____n language.

6. A room which has no furniture in it is not f_____d.

7. The number between 47 and 49 is f_____t.

8. The o_____e of "black" is "white".

9. A r_____t is a place where meals can be bought and eaten.

10. To a_____d a meeting is to be present at it.

11. To talk someone into doing something is to p_____de him to do it.

12. To do something in some other way is to do it o_____e.

13. "Do you know her?" "No, I don't. I am not ac_____d with her at all."

14. "Did he ac_____e your letter?" "Yes, he did. He said he had received my letter."

15. "What medicine has the doctor told you to take?" "He has pre_____d no medicine. He only advised me to take a good rest."

Ⅲ. 請將下面每題中的五個項目組成一句通順的句，並將各項目的標號按組成的順序填寫在試卷內。請特別注意大小寫及標點符號。〔20%〕

　　例：grandfather.　father's father　my　My　is
　　　　　1　　　　　　　2　　　　　　 3　4　5
　　答案：42531

1. Jack put on　new shoes; nor　Jane cannot put on her　his.　can
　　　1　　　　　2　　　　　　　　3　　　　　　　4　　5

2. the book is　as　not useful.　it is,　Interesting
　　　1　　　　2　　3　　　　　4　　　5

3. Our class　and what time　does begin?　begins at eight ten,　yours
　　　1　　　　　2　　　　　　3　　　　　4　　　　　　　5

4. Mr. Smith　the results.　announced　Chairman of the Board;　As
　　　1　　　　　2　　　　　3　　　　　4　　　　　　　　　5

5. is He　more money than　needed.　has borrowed
　　1 2　　　3　　　　　　4　　　　　5

6. an best　Usually　about his own books.　author knows
　　1　2　　　3　　　　4　　　　　　　　　5

7. John　asked where to go;　"I don't know."　When　replied,
　　1　　　2　　　　　　　　3　　　　　　　4　　　5

8. to interest　new　nothing　me.　There's
　　　1　　　　2　　　3　　　4　　　5

9. I hope I can borrow money, so I haven't some . got any
  1   2   3 4 5

10. you have made the often same How mistake !
  1   2 3 4 5

Ⅳ. 在下面各題，左面的一個字之後，列有四個單音節字，在這四個單音節字之中，找出一個含有與左面用粗體字標明部分相同讀音的字，請把它的標號填寫在試卷內。（10％）

 例：1. **ma**n：① run　② ran　③may　④ rain

   2. b**e**d：① but　② talk　③ take　④ did

 答案：1. ②　　2. ④

1.	**e**nough	: ① fill	② ghost	③ gun	④ hat
2.	b**i**g	: ① pen	② pin	③ pan	④ pine
3.	s**ai**d	: ① laid	② dead	③ side	④ mad
4.	br**i**ght	: ① bread	② bring	③ write	④ fit
5.	s**a**le	: ① fail	② ran	③ sell	④ sight
6.	**c**ircle	: ① cry	② kind	③ church	④ sang
7.	me**ch**anical	: ① shut	② city	③ school	④ such
8.	h**ea**d	: ① made	② died	③ eat	④ bed
9.	l**o**w	: ① now	② law	③ roar	④ boat
10.	the**se**	: ① zero	② this	③ Nell	④ sell

Ⅴ. 對下面問題，請照中文的意思，從每個括弧中選擇一個最恰當的字，並且加上必要的標點符號，都把它按照標號填寫在試卷內。（20％）

 例：你的新書給我了嗎？

   1. （Was / is /Did /Has）you 2. （give /given/gave/Give）

   3. （I/my /mine /me）your new 4. （book /coat /hat /suit）

 答案：1. Did 2. give 3. me 4. book？

A. 他向來是個懶惰的人，所以他現在沒有錢，也沒有食物。

  1. （He/She /They /We） 2. （do/did/has/have）always been

  3. （a such/such a）lazy man 4. （so/that）now he hasn't

  5. （any/some）money or 6. （food/foods）

  7. （too/either）

B. 你有什麼傢俱可以借給我們嗎？

  8.　（Are /Have /Has / Is）there any

  9.　（furniture / furnitures）of　　10.　（your / yours）you can

  11.　（borrow/ lend）　　　　　　12.　（I / us / you）

C. 如果昨天醫生不在那裏，那些可憐的嬰孩全都會死亡。

  If the doctor

  13.　（did not be / had not been /was not /would not be）there yesterday,

  14.　（the all poor, little /all the poor, little /all the little; poor / the all little poor）babies

  15.　（was dead /would be died /would dead /would have died）

D. 史密斯先生問他女兒他的鞋子在那裏，當她回答說是在衣櫥間，他叫她立刻去取來。

  Mr. Smith asked his daughter

  16.　（if / that /where /whether）

  17.　（are his shoes /his shoes were /my shoes are /was his shoes）, and when she answered

  18.　（if /that /where /whether）they

  19.　（are / be / have /were）in the closet, he told her

  20.　（get /gets /got / to get）them at once.

Ⅵ. 下面的一篇文字，其後列有十個問題，每題附五個答案，其中只有一個是對的，請於詳讀該文後，將正確答案的標號填寫在試卷內。（20％）

  In our attic, neatly arranged in a wooden box are the back numbers of The Reader's Digest for about ten years.

  The other day I went to the attic to look for a fishing rod. I saw the box and remembered I had wanted to look up some articles in the Digest that bore on a speech I was making. I sat down on the floor and went to work. In a short time I found that instead of merely reading the articles on my subject I was reading at random. Before I knew it a couple of hours had passed and the light from the window in the roof was too dim to read more.

What stands out in my mind as I think back over the experience is the fun I had. Every time I finished an article which was off my main course, and which I shouldn't then have taken time to read, I thought I would read only one other...... well, at least only one and the short item that followed it. Then another subject aroused my interest and lured me on.

Finally I felt I was wasting time. To break the spell I dipped into an issue ten years back. But here the interest was even greater. A forgotten world came into being...... not in vague memory but with touches of unmistakable reality. I was astonished to find how much of the past decade I had actually forgotten and how much more I remembered only vaguely.

1. Where is the attic?
   (1) Neatly arranged in a wood.　(2) Neatly arranged in a box.
   (3) Neatly arranged in the writer's wooden box.
   (4) In the writer's house.　(5) Nowhere.

2. The writer felt the need of looking up some articles_____
   (1) when he was making a speech.
   (2) when he remembered fishing.　(3) until he saw the box.
   (4) until he remembered.　(5) even before he saw the box.

3. Some articles in the Digest_____
   (1) carried a speech he was making.
   (2) had something to do with the speech he was making.
   (3) were boring.　(4) bored.
   (5) were boring speeches.

4. The writer_____
   (1) was going to make a speech possibly a few days after he saw the box.
   (2) was making a speech while he was going to the attic.
   (3) made a speech before he saw the box.
   (4) was going to make a speech that had been printed in the Digest.
   (5) was going to make a speech for the Digest.

5. In a short time the writer found that
   (1) he was fishing instead of reading.
   (2) he was merely reading the articles on his subject.
   (3) he was reading without definite purpose.
   (4) he was looking at articles of furniture at random.
   (5) he was sitting instead of reading.

6. The light from the window became too dim
   (1) a couple of hours before the writer could read any more.
   (2) before a couple of hours had passed.
   (3) in a couple of hours.
   (4) before he had passed a couple of hours in the attic.
   (5) after he knew it.

7. What shouldn't the writer have taken time to read?
   (1) His main subject.　　　　(2) His finished article.
   (3) Definite and indefinite articles.
   (4) Articles that did not concern his subject of investigation.
   (5) The word "which" in the English language.

8. What did the writer want to do every time when he finished an
   article of his main course ?
   (1) He thought he would read little more than one more article.
   (2) He thought he would stop reading.
   (3) He thought he would stop to read.
   (4) He wanted to be lured on.
   (5) He wanted to read nothing more.

9. What did the writer do when he felt he was wasting time ?
   (1) He put a ten-year old issue into water.
   (2) He dipped the magazine into water.
   (3) He sprinkled the magazine with water drops.
   (4) He dipped the magazine into the box.
   (5) He picked out a ten-year old issue of the magazine.

10. A forgotten world came into being when the writer
   (1) did not like his vague memory.
   (2) was clearly reminded of the past.
   (3) touched on important events in the past ten years in his speech.
   (4) remembered his main subject.
   (5) knew how much time he had wasted.

55年大學聯考英文試題詳解

Ⅰ. 選擇：

1.① 　2.③ 　3.② 　4.① 　5.③ 　6.① 　7.③ 　8.④ 　9.② 　10.④
11.② 　12.① 　13.④ 　14.④ 　15.②

Ⅱ. 單字：

1. independent 獨立的 　　2. metal 金屬的
3. discovery〔dɪˈskʌvərɪ〕n. 發現 　　4. photographs 照片
5. foreign〔ˈfɔrɪn,ˈfarɪn〕adj. 外國的 　　6. furnished 佈置的
7. forty-eight 48 　　8. opposite〔ˈɑpəzɪt〕n. 相反的事物
9. restaurant〔ˈrɛstərənt,-,rɑnt〕n. 飯館 　　10. attend 參加
11. persuade〔pəˈswed〕vt. 說服；勸 　　12. otherwise 用別的方法；不那樣
13. acquainted 認識；熟悉
14. acknowledge〔əkˈnɑlɪdʒ〕vt. 承認收到（信件等）；函謝
15. prescribed 開藥方

Ⅲ. 句子重組：

1. 32514 　　2. 52413 　　3. 14253 　　4. 54132 　　5. 25314 　　6. 31524
7. 42153 　　8. 53214 　　9. 35214 　　10. 42135

Ⅳ. 發音：

1.① 　2.② 　3.② 　4.③ 　5.① 　6.④ 　7.③ 　8.④ 　9.④ 　10.①

Ⅴ. 翻譯：

A. 1. He 　2. has 　3. such a 　4. that 　5. any 　6. food 　7. either.
B. 8. Is 　9. furniture 　10. yours 　11. lend 　12. us？
C. 13. had not been 　14. all the poor, little 　15. would have died.
D. 16. where 　17. his shoes were 　18. that 　19. were 　20. to get

Ⅵ. 閱讀測驗：

1.④ 　2.⑤ 　3.② 　4.① 　5.③ 　6.③ 　7.④ 　8.① 　9.⑤ 　10.②

Ⅶ. 中譯

　　大約有十年的過期讀者文摘，整齊地排在閣樓上的一隻木箱中。

　　前兩天我上閣樓去找一根釣魚竿，一看見那箱子就想起，我本想在文摘中找幾篇與我所要作的演講有關的文章。我坐在地板上著手工作，一會兒以後，我發現我並不是在讀有關我講題的文章，而是在隨便地讀。在我察覺之前，幾個小時已經過去了，而且從屋頂的窗戶中射進來的陽光也太暗而不能再讀。

　　當我仔細回想這種經過時，突現在我腦海中的是我所得到的樂趣。每次當我讀完一篇與我的主題無關的文章時，而且那篇文章我當時本不應該費時去讀的，我就想到我只打算再讀一篇，至少只讀一篇以及接着的那一個短篇，但是另一篇的主題又引起了我的興趣而吸引住我。

　　最後，我認為我是在浪費時間，為了破除這種誘惑力，我抽出十年前的一期。但這一期裡趣味更加濃厚，一個被遺忘的世界產生了，不是產生在模糊不清的記憶中，而是與明顯的現實結合在一起。我很驚訝地發現，過去十年我其實忘了這麼多東西，而有更多的只是依稀記得而已。

〔解析〕

attic〔'ætɪk〕n. 頂樓；閣樓　　　back number "過期的出版物"

neatly〔'nitlɪ〕adv. 整潔地　　The Reader's Digest "讀者文摘"

look for "尋找"　　fishing rod "釣魚竿"　　*look up* "查；往上看"

bear on～ "與～有關"　　*go*〔*fall, get*〕*to work* "著手工作(讀書)"

instead of～ "代替～"　　　*at random* "隨便地；漫無目的地"

a couple of "兩個；一些"　　dim〔dɪm〕adj. 微暗的；不清楚的

stand out "引人注目；突出"　　*at least* "至少"

arouse〔ə'raʊz〕vt. 喚醒；激起　　*lure one on*～ "誘惑某人～"

waste〔west〕vt.,vi. 浪費　　spell〔spɛl〕n. 咒語；魅力

dip into "取出；看一看；探究"　　vague〔veg〕adj. 模糊的；不清楚的

unmistakable〔,ʌnmə'stekəb!〕adj. 不可能弄錯的；明顯的

decade〔'dɛked, dɛk'ed〕n. 十年

心得筆記欄

五十四學年度大學暨獨立學院入學考試
英 文 試 題

Ⅰ. 下面 每個多音節字的後面列有四個單音節字。請在這四個單音節字中，找出一個與前面多音節字之重音節母音讀法相同的字，把它的標號填寫在試卷內。

　　注意：所謂相同係指母音讀法而言，子音讀法不計。（10%）

　　例：remember：① cream　②man　③ bend　④ bird　　答案：3

1. reality　　　：① ran　　②real　　③ rail　　④ right
2. contribute　：① ton　　②tribe　　③ rib　　④ blue
3. politics　　：① pole　②paul　　③ lit　　④ lot
4. country　　：① count　②cart　　③ cup　　④ cope
5. Persuade　：① term　②pure　　③ break　④ fat
6. genius　　：① Jane　②geese　③ news　④bus
7. variety　　：① wild　②chief　③ seize　④ bare
8. America　：① smell　②mere　③ burn　④ mark
9. government　：① learn　②lock　③ lack　④ luck
10. creature　：① great　②greet　③ rate　④ church

Ⅱ. 請將下面每題中的五個項目組成一句通順的句子，並將各項目的標號按組成的順序填寫在試卷內。請特別注意大小寫及標點符號。（10%）

　　例：John bought Is this book the yesterday？
　　　　　1　　　　　2　　　　3　　　4　　　5

　　答案：2 4 3 1 5

1. do you know where is John, Mary going？
　　　　1　　　　　　2　　　3　　　4　　5

2. Tom Should be found guilty, I would have hanged. him
　　1　　　2　　　　　3　　　　　　4　　　　5

3. "Miss Lee，" "I've a perfect right I said, I like！" to read whatever
　　　1　　　　　　　2　　　　　　　3　　　　4　　　　　5

4. our soldiers Like they win the fame of and sailors courage.
       1   2   3   4   5

5. this time of Restless again, the mountains. Jack will probably think
    1   2   3   4
an expedition to
    5

Ⅲ. 下面每一句內遺漏兩個字，這兩個字列在句子的後面。請找出這兩個字在句中原來的位置。答案的寫法是將所遺漏的字連同原來位置的前後兩字，共三字，依次填寫在試卷內。（20％）

   例：Anyone does not look like them considered a foreigner.

     (a) who   (b) is

   答案：(a) Anyone who does   (b) them is considered

   注意：每一答案之三字中，如有任何一字拼寫錯誤，或次序顛倒，即不予計分。

       (a)(b)兩組答案顛倒，亦不予計分。

1. The early afternoon we play tennis the hottest time of the day.
   (a) when   (b) is

2. It the good students that studying their lessons, not the poor ones.
   (a) is   (b) are

3. Those rather foolish servants have broken many of only eight brilliant blue tea cups. (a) two   (b) the

4. John says he will believe in ghosts he sees one. (a) not   (b) until

5. What color Mr. Jones have his country house last summer?
   (a) did   (b) painted

6. She was much afraid of the teacher of the principal.
   (a) more   (b) than

7. The man wearing the brown suit the captain elected the team last year. (a) was   (b) by

8. Mary knows a lady has a friend cook's son won a prize at school.
   (a) who   (b) whose

9. If that earthquake lasted for a few more minutes, there would have great damage and loss of life. (a) had   (b) been

10. Librarians all over the country report that more books being borrowed now than before. (a) are   (b) ever

IV. 下面有二十個句子，每句都有一個空白，每一空白處需要填入一個適當的介係詞（Preposition）或副詞（adverb）。答案請填寫在試卷內。(20%)

注意：每一空白處只可填寫一個字，多則不予計分，拼錯之字亦不予計分。

1. We hit _____ a new road back to town while we were out for a ride Sunday.
2. None of his friends could put _____ with his rudeness.
3. They had to call _____ the game because of the storm.
4. He spent too much for the trip and ran out _____ money before the vacation ended.
5. She was not able to go through _____ her plan to study in a university.
6. They were fed up _____ her complaints.
7. The burglar broke into the house and made away _____ two thousand dollars.
8. He has to wind _____ his business before he leaves here.
9. To begin _____ , Chinese and Japanese are not related languages; and there is not much similarity between the two.
10. He always took _____ his bed at the first sign of a cold.
11. Although it rained in the morning , it turned _____ to be good day for the trip.
12. They boarded the ship which was bound _____ Singapore.
13. The weather bureau says the typhoon is heading towards Japan but we can not rule _____ the possibility of its hitting our island.
14. He said he would refer my application _____ the board for approval.
15. Before we left , we reminded him _____ his appointment with the examiner.
16. He is well versed _____ English literature.
17. I can give you no answer until I have talked her _____ accepting the job.
18. The scientist said he felt greatly indebted _____ all his associates for his new discovery.
19. It seemed that he was not convinced _____ his ignorance.
20. He argued with his superior, but his argument amounted _____ nothing.

Ⅴ. 下面一段文字內有二十個方括弧，每一方括弧內有四個項目，請在其中選擇
一個適合上下文意及文法結構的項目，並將該項目的標號，填寫在試卷內。
（20％）

　　A girl who (1)〔 ① to dream ② dream of ③ dreams of ④ dreamed〕
becoming a concert pianist does not simply sit and wait (2)〔 (1) toward
② for ③ on ④ until〕 that wonderful, magic moment comes when she
suddenly becomes an artist. She begins at the beginning. She takes piano lessons. She (3)〔 ① does ② makes ③ plays ④ gives〕 finger exercises.
She (4)〔 ① keep practicing ② keeps upon practicing ③ keeps to practicing
④ keeps on practicing〕, for she knows that she cannot learn everything
at once and that she can continue to learn and (5)〔 ① progressed
② progress ③ progressing ④ progressive〕 only by constantly applying
herself. So it is (6)〔 ① as ② like ③ with ④ such〕 writing. (7)〔 ① The best
way ② The best of way ③ Best way ④ The best ways〕 to learn to writer
is, of course, by writing. Both writing and rewriting (8)〔 ① careful
② carefulness ③ carefully ④ carelessly〕 in light of comments and criticism
are essential. Studying rules (9)〔 ① are ② were ③ is ④ have been〕 helpful,
but until (10)〔① such ② so ③ such a ④ such as〕 rules are applied, they can
(11)〔 ① of not value ② not of value ③ not value ④ of no value〕 to you.
Certainly rules themselves never taught (12)〔 ① anyone ② anyone else
③ anybody else ④ the other〕 to write. You must (13)〔 ① do ② made ③ making
④ make〕 a conscientious effort to avoid (14)〔 ① to repeat ② repeating
③ repeated ④ to be repeated〕 the same errors time after time. You can
never afford to be lazy, because writing is a (15)〔 ① demand ② demanding
③ demanded ④ to demand〕 craft and good writing is carefully (16)〔 ① plan
② planning ③ be planned ④ planned〕 writing. Moreover, good writing can't
be learned in a day. (17)〔 ① Like playing ② As playing ③ Like to play ④ As
to play〕 the piano, good writing is an acquired skill (18)〔 ① that require
② what requires ③ that requires ④ which require〕 constant practice
(19)〔 ① maintain ② to be maintained ③ is maintained ④ has maintained〕
at a high level. Fortunately, the more you write, the more (20)〔① rewarded
② reward ③ rewarding ④ to reward〕 and enjoyable writing it becomes.

Ⅵ. 下面一段文字之後列有十個問題，每題的括弧內設有四個答案，其中只有一個
　　是對的，請於詳讀該文後，將正確答案的標號填寫在試卷內。（20％）

As the Ice Age came to an end, and mile after mile of Europe was
retrieved from frosty desolation, the hunting men of the south came
drifting northwards through the thick forests of beech and oak, with
their flint arrows and spears in pursuit of game. Man had entered upon
his long struggle with nature. Peril and want sharpened his wits and gave
him reliance. He learned to spin, to weave, to clothe himself against
the cold. By degrees he perfected his weapons against the wild beasts
of the forests, exchanging stone for bronze, and bronze for iron. The
sail, the wheel, the domestication of animals, three of the most
important inventions in human history, belong to this unrecorded
period. Gradually the hunter acquired the arts of stock keeping and
farming, so that thousands of years before the dawn of history a
peasantry was settled upon the soil of Europe, and there, for century
after century, bent to the unchanging cycle of the season, sowing,
ploughing and reaping, tending the ox, the goat, the sheep, and the pig,
practicing with such skill as they might command the arts and crafts
of weaving and building, carving and pottery, and, since religion well-
nigh universal, worshipping nature in its manifold forms.

1. Before the hunting men came, Europe_____
　　① had been deserted.　　② had been a frosty desert.
　　③ had been in ruins.
　　④ had been a desert retrieved from frost.

2. The hunting men went_____
　　① from north.　　② north.
　　③ south.　　④ south of Europe.

3. The hunting men came_____
　　① drifting on water.
　　② without caring where they were going.
　　③ floating on water.
　　④ by boat through bushes.

4. The men came _____

① in pursuit of a game.　② to play games.

③ in pursuit of recreation.　④ to chase wild animals.

5. The hunter _____

① acquired works of art of stock-keeping.

② acquired the art of taking stock.

③ learned to take stock.

④ learned to raise and keep cattle.

6. His weapons _____

① were completed by and by.

② were perfectly made in some degree.

③ were perfected by and by.

④ were made perfect little by little.

7. Stone _____

① exchanged bronze for iron.　② was replaced by bronze.

③ was changed into bronze and then into iron.

④ exchanged bronze.

8. There _____ settled upon the soil of Europe.

① was a body of peasants　② was a farmer

③ were many peasants

④ was a kind of peasant-like farmer

9. The _____ to the unchanging cycle of the seasons.

① peasantry bowed down in deference

② peasantlike farming class was submitted

③ peasantry was subjected　④ peasantry was very attentive

10. The primitive men _____ the ox, the goat, the sheep, and the pig.

① took care of　② were tending toward

③ were attended with　④ attended with

54年大學聯考英文試題詳解

Ⅰ. 發音：

1. ①　2. ③　3. ④　4. ③　5. ③　6. ②　7. ①　8. ①　9. ④　10. ②

Ⅱ. 句子重組：

1. 3 1 4 2 5　2. 2 1 3 5 4　3. 1 3 2 5 4　4. 2 1 4 3 5　5. 2 4 1 5 3

Ⅲ. 插字：

1. (a) afternoon *when* we　(b) tennis *is* the
2. (a) It *is* the　(b) that *are* studying
3. (a) Those *two* rather　(b) of *the* only
4. (a) will *not* believe　(b) ghosts *until* he
5. (a) color *did* Mr. Jones　(b) house *painted* last
6. (a) much *more* afraid　(b) teacher *than* of
7. (a) suit *was* the　(b) elected *by* the
8. (a) lady *who* has　(b) friend *whose* cook's
9. (a) earthquake *had* lasted　(b) have *been* great
10. (a) books *are* being　(b) than *ever* before

Ⅳ. 填充：

1. on (*or* upon) 2. up　3. off　4. of　5. with　6. with　7. with
8. up　9. with　10. to　11. out　12. for　13. out　14. to　15. of
16. in　17. into　18. to　19. of　20. to

〔解析〕

1. *hit on*〔*upon*〕"巧遇"　　2. *put up with* "忍受"
3. *call off* "取消"　　4. *run out of* "用盡"
5. *go through with* "完成"　　6. *feed up with* "飽受；厭倦"
7. *make away with* "拿走；偷"　　8. *wind up* "結束"
9. *to begin with*（獨立不定詞）"首先；第一（點）"
10. *take to one's bed* "病倒；臥病"

11. *turn out* "轉變；變成"　　12. *be bound for* "開往"

13. *rule out* "排除；拒絕承認"　　14. *refer ～ to～* "提交～給～"

15. *remind sb. of sth.* "提醒某人某事"

16. *be versed in* "精通於"　　17. *talk sb. into sth.* "說服某人某事"

18. *be indebted to sb.* "感激某人"

19. *be convinced of* "相信"　　20. *amount to* "等於"

Ⅴ. 選擇：

(1) ③　(2) ④　(3) ①　(4) ④　(5) ②　(6) ③　(7) ①　(8) ③　(9) ③　(10) ①

(11) ④　(12) ①　(13) ④　(14) ②　(15) ②　(16) ④　(17) ①　(18) ③　(19) ②　(20) ③

Ⅵ. 閱讀測驗：

1. ④　2. ②　3. ②　4. ④　5. ④　6. ④　7. ②　8. ①　9. ③　10. ①

中譯：

當冰河時代結束，歐洲大陸一哩一哩地從冰凍的荒地中解救出來的時候，南方的獵人們，帶着他們追逐獵物用的石製的弓箭和長矛，穿過濃密的櫸木和橡樹的森林，向北漫無目的地進行。人類早已開始與大自然作長期的搏鬥。「冒險與需要」磨練了人類的才智，而給了人類信心。漸漸地人類改善了他們的武器，以對抗森林中的野獸，他們用銅製武器代石製武器，又用鐵器代銅器。人類歷史上最重要的三大發明，舟、車、馴養獸類，都是屬於這個無歷史記載的時代。漸漸地，獵人學得了飼養家畜和農業的技術，所以在有歷史記載以前的幾千年，一群農民就定居在歐洲的土地上，在那裡，一世紀接一世紀地順從著四季不變的循環，播種、耕種、收割、看守牛、山羊、羊及豬，以他們可以使用的技巧，練習紡織、建築、雕刻、和製陶器的藝術及技術，並且因為宗教幾乎很普遍，就以各種不同的宗教形式來崇拜自然。

〔解析〕

Ice Age "冰河時代"　　*come to an end* "終止；結束"

retrieve〔rɪˈtriv〕*vt.,vi.* 恢復

frosty〔ˈfrɔstɪ,ˈfrɑstɪ〕*adj.* 下霜的；凍寒的

desolation〔,dɛsļˈeʃən〕*n.* 荒蕪；荒涼　　drift〔drɪft〕*vt.,vi.* 盲目前進

northwards〔ˈnɔrθwədz〕*adv.* 向北地；往北地

beech〔bitʃ〕*n.* 櫸木　　oak〔ok〕*n.* 橡樹

flint〔flɪnt〕*n.* 燧石；火石　　*in pursuit of ～* "為追求～"

game〔gem〕*n*. 獵物　　　peril〔'pɛrəl〕*n*. 危險；危難

want〔wɔnt, wɑnt〕*n*. 需求（之物）

sharpen〔'ʃɑrpən〕*vt., vi*. 使敏銳；使聰明

reliance〔rɪ'laɪəns〕*n*. 依賴；寄託　　　spin〔spɪn〕*vt., vi*. 紡紗

weave〔wiv〕*vt., vi*. 編織　　　clothe〔kloð〕*vt*. 給～穿衣

by degrees "漸漸地；逐漸"　　　bronze〔brɑnz〕*n*. 青銅

domestication〔də,mɛstə'keʃən〕*n*. 馴服

stock-keeping "家畜的飼養"　　　dawn〔dɔn〕*n*. 黎明；開始

peasantry〔'pɛzəntrɪ〕*n*. 小農；農民　　　*bend to* ～ "順從～；適應～"

plough〔plaʊ〕*vt., vi*. 耕；犂（＝plow）

reap〔rip〕*vt*. 收割　　　tend〔tɛnd〕*vt., vi*. 照料；看護

carving〔'kɑrvɪŋ〕*n*. 雕刻（術）　　　pottery〔'pɑtərɪ〕*n*. 製陶（術）

well-nigh〔'wɛl'naɪ〕*adv*. （古）幾乎（＝almost）

manifold〔'mænə,fold〕*adj*. 種種的；多方面的

心得筆記欄

五十三學年度大學暨獨立學院入學考試
英 文 試 題

Ⅰ. 下面每組四字中的斜體部份所代表的發音有相同的，有不相同的。如果彼此完全相同，答案是1,2,3,4；如果彼此完全不同，答案是0；如果第一和第四相同，答案是1,4；餘類推。答案填寫在試卷內。（10％）

例：1. (1) br*ea*k　　(2) l*ea*f　　(3) br*ea*th　　(4) s*a*me
　　2. (1) *so*　　　(2) c*oa*t　　(3) n*o*te　　(4) sn*ow*
　　3. (1) bl*oo*d　　(2) s*oo*t　　(3) t*u*ne　　(4) t*o*ne

答案：1. (1)(4)　　2. (1)(2)(3)(4)　　3. 0

1. (1) pol*i*ce　　(2) rec*ei*ve　　(3) k*e*y　　(4) p*eo*ple
2. (1) t*y*pe　　(2) ch*ie*f　　(3) t*ie*　　(4) fr*ie*nd
3. (1) sou*th*ern　　(2) brea*th*ing　　(3) *th*en　　(4) *th*in
4. (1) ca*n*　　(2) si*ng*　　(3) tha*n*k　　(4) pi*n*k
5. (1) *sh*ip　　(2) hi*v*e　　(3) ma*ch*ine　　(4) p*ai*d
6. (1) *eigh*t　　(2) h*eigh*t　　(3) b*uy*　　(4) th*ei*r
7. (1) p*u*sh　　(2) p*u*ll　　(3) f*u*ll　　(4) p*u*t
8. (1) wait*ed*　　(2) laugh*ed*　　(3) rubb*ed*　　(4) caugh*t*
9. (1) *ch*eap　　(2) pa*tch*　　(3) *ch*aracter　　(4) ma*ch*ine
10. (1) t*ou*ch　　(2) b*u*t　　(3) t*o*n　　(4) d*oe*s

Ⅱ. 下面每題含有一個未完全拼出的字，該字的第一個字母和最後一個字母已經標示出來，請按句意將該字的完整形式填寫在試卷內。（20％）

例：London is the c_____l of England.

答案：capital

1. The food we eat is digested mostly in the s_____h.
2. This story is an English translation ; the o_____l is in French.
3. Spain, Germany, and Italy are E_____n countries.
4. Cars, ships, and airplanes are different means of t_____n.
5. Books and magazines are often referred to as m_____l food.
6. An i_____s person is a hard-working person.

7. The fine arts generally include painting, s_____e, and architecture.

8. Twins often show great r_____e in character as well as in appearance.

9. That man committed s_____e; that is to say, he killed himself.

10. If you have no a_____e, you don't enjoy the pleasure of eating.

11. The a_____e is the air surrounding the earth.

12. A student of p_____s studies the science and art of government.

13. The a_____c year 1964-65 lasts from August 1,1964 to July 31, 1965.

14. Drivers of cars, buses, or trucks must obey t_____c rules.

15. The words in an English dictionary are arranged in a_____l order.

16. The collective name for beds, desks, tables, and chairs is f_____e.

17. An i_____t of a place is a person living in that place.

18. Arithmetic, algebra, and geometry are branches of m_____s.

19. He has c_____e he will win; in other words, he feels sure he will win.

20. I have a camera; let me take a p_____h of you.

Ⅱ. 下面每一句中間遺漏兩個字，這兩個字列在句子的後面。請找出這兩個字在句中原來的位置。答案的寫法是將所遺漏的字連同原來位置的前後兩字，共三字，依次填寫在試卷內。

例：The examination was long for us finish in an hour. (A) to (B) too
答案：(A) us to finish (B) was too long
注意：每一答案之三字中，如有任何一字拼寫錯誤，或次序顛倒，即不予計分。

1. The mayor was a nice person I enjoyed the visit. (A) such (B) that

2. The large drawer in the papers were kept locked up. (A) was (B) which

3. The fellow recommended the committee know my name. (A) does (B) by

4. Did you tell Martha letters she mail right away? (A) should (B) which

5. How pleasant thing it to go swimming on a hot day! (A) is (B) a

6. The sound of her own steps her fear that some strange was following behind her. (A) being (B) made.

7. Anyone seeing the circus sure to find a big event in his life. (A) it (B) is

8. The teacher have insisted that boy learn all the words by heart. (A) the (B) shouldn't

9. The symbols used by dictionaries aids to pronunciation called phonetic symbols. (A) are (B) as

10. None the boys Tom and Frank are waiting for their friends. (A) of (B) are

Ⅳ. 下面一段文字之後列有十個問題，每題的括弧內設有四個答案，其中只有一個是對的。請於詳讀該文後，將正確的答案號碼填寫在試卷內。(10%)

All men would necessarily have been equal had they been without wants. It is the misery attached to our species which places one man in subjection to another; inequality is not the real grievance, but dependence. It is of little consequence for one man to be called His Highness and another His Holiness, but it is hard for me to be the servant of another. A numerous family has cultivated a good soil, two small neighboring families live on lands unproductive and barren. It will therefore be necessary for the two poor families to serve the rich one, or to destroy it. This is easily accomplished. One of the two indigent families goes and offers its services to the rich one in exchange for bread; the other makes attacks upon it and is conquered. The serving family is the origin of domestics and laborers; the one conquered is the origin of slaves. It's impossible in our melancholy world to prevent men living in society from being divided into two classes, one of the rich who command, the other of the poor who obey, and these two are subdivided into various others, which have also their respective shades of difference.

1. According to the author, human inequality was due to the fact that all men
   (1) had been without wants.　　(2) had wants.
   (3) were born unequal.　　(4) had grievance.

2. The author is concerned mainly with the question of
   (1) farming.　　(2) family life.　　(3) equality.　　(4) labor.

3. The two small families
   (1) become slaves.
   (2) become masters over the third family.
   (3) represent the class that obeys.　(4) are dependent upon each other.

4. "Consequence here means
   (1) logical sequence .
   (2) as a result.
   (3) agreement .
   (4) importance.

5. According to the passage, the real human grievance is
   (1) equality.　　(2) dependence .　　(3) inequality .　　(4) independence.

6. According to the passage, the family which try to destroy the rich become
   (1) slaves.　　(2) servants.　　(3) masters .　　(4) conquerors .

7. The other poor family
   (1) destroy the large family.
   (2) have no wants.
   (3) become servants .
   (4) are conquered by the rich.

8. According to the author, the division of people into social classes is
   (1) desirable.　　(2) avoidable .　　(3) impossible .　　(4) inevitable.

9. " Indigent " means
   (1) poor .　　(2) angry.　　(3) small .　　(4) diligent.

10. According to the author, the two big classes _____ divided up again into sub-classes.
    (1) must not be
    (2) cannot be
    (3) are not necessarily
    (4) are

Ⅴ. 下面一段文字內有二十個方括弧，每一方括弧內有四個項目，請在其中選擇一個適合上下文意及文法結構的項目，並將該項目的號碼，填寫在試卷內。(20％)

　　(1) 〔① Some time ② Sometimes ③ Sometime ④ sometimes 〕 it is a heartbreaking experience for a fisherman (2) 〔① made ② to do ③ to make ④ get 〕 his prize catch of the year. (3) 〔① Of course ② In the course of ③ In due course ④ Of the course 〕, I do not mind (4) 〔① wait ② waited ③ waiting for ④ waiting 〕 patiently all day without (5) 〔① get ② getting ③ to get ④ had got 〕 a nibble, but to catch a seventeen-inch trout and then (6) 〔① was pressed ② pressed ③ be forced ④ to force〕 to give up such

a beauty is certainly the (7)〔① heighten ② high ③ height ④ highly〕of an angler's misfortune. (8)〔① Lates ② Later ③ Latter ④ Last〕spring early one Saturday morning Sam Lewis and I drove to Brush Creek. We had planned the trip (9)〔① during ② for ③ since ④ at〕over a week. We (10)〔① have determined ② to determine ③ were determined ④ to be determined〕to be the first to toss our (11)〔① baited ② baiting ③ to bait ④ bait〕hooks into the water. That vapor of early morning, drab and gray, (12)〔① just begin ② just beginning ③ has just begun ④ was just beginning〕to rise from the water (13)〔① how ② what ③ when ④ why〕we arrived. (14)〔① To select ② To elect ③ Choose ④ Selection〕our favorite spot took (15)〔① but ② mere ③ a few ④ few〕a moment. (16)〔① Baited ② Having baited ③ Bait ④ To be baited〕my hook with a fat, juicy worm, I threw it into the water. Gradually the sun arose and spread a warm (17)〔① to glow ② flame ③ growth ④ glow〕over the water, but its heat did not appear to penetrate (18)〔① deep enough ② enough deep ③ enough deeply ④ so deep〕to wake the fish. After a short time, when nothing (19)〔① happen ② happened ③ was happened ④ chanced〕, I began to lose my enthusiasm. The cold damp air of the morning (20)〔① fast ② as soon as ③ had sooner ④ soon〕chilled all my interest.

Ⅵ. 下面左邊有二十個未完成的句子，請在右邊選擇適當的項目以完成之，並將代表適當項目的字母(如 A 或 B 或 C 等)填寫在試券內。(20%)

注意：(1)在選擇適當項目時，句意須與文法並重。

　　　(2)右邊有二十三個項目，其中有三個是沒有用的。

1. He said he would deny whatever.
2. When the airplane will arrive
3. He seems different from
4. Little is known
5. The television is a newly
6. Have the boys
7. Never have I
8. For three days and three nights
9. The man put on his glasses in order

(A) invented machine.
(B) to see better.
(C) in the dignity of manual labor.
(D) they said.
(E) with the similarities of things.
(F) the same color as that one.
(G) have nothing to do with religion.
(H) closing the window?
(I) as a professor.
(J) unable to come.

10. My father believed
11. The White House was accustomed
12. I know a place
13. Baseball is played by girls
14. My sister has a dress
15. Many people earn their living
16. I don't eat beef,
17. I have just finished
18. Do you mind
19. The university offered him a job
20. Science is concerned

(K) and neither does she.
(L) of George Washington as a boy.
(M) to receiving about 5 thousand letters a day.
(N) by working with their hands.
(O) what he used to be.
(P) is not known yet.
(Q) where we can have a quiet talk.
(R) been in such a hurry.
(S) the storm continued.
(T) do the problems.
(U) with sadness in her eyes.
(V) typing my paper.
(W) as well as by boys.

53年大學聯考英文試題詳解

Ⅰ. 發音：

1. (1)(2)(3)(4)　　2. (1)(3)　　3. (1)(2)(3)　　4. (2)(3)(4)　　5. 0　　6. (2)(3)　　7. (1)(2)(3)(4)

8. (2)(4)　　9. (1)(2)　　10. (1)(2)(3)(4)

Ⅱ. 單字：

1. stomach〔'stʌmək〕n. 胃　　　2. original〔ə'rɪdʒənḷ〕n. 原文

3. European 歐洲的　　4. transportation〔,trænspə'teʃən〕n. 運輸

5. mental 精神的　　6. industrious〔ɪn'dʌstrɪəs〕adj. 勤勉的

7. sculpture 雕刻　　8. resemblance 相似；類似

9. suicide〔'suə,saɪd,'sɪu-〕n.自殺　　10. appetite〔'æpə,taɪt〕n. 胃口

11. atmosphere〔'ætməs,fɪr〕n. 大氣　　12. politics 政治學

13. academic〔,ækə'dɛmɪk〕adj. 學校的　　14. traffic 交通

15. alphabetical〔,ælfə'bɛtɪkḷ〕adj. 字母的　　16. furniture 傢俱

17. inhabitant〔ɪn'hæbətənt〕n. 居民　　18. mathematics〔,mæθə'mætɪks〕n.數字

19. confidence 信任；自信　　20. photograph〔'fotə,græf〕n. 照片

Ⅲ. 插字：

1. (a) was *such* a　　(b) person *that* I

2. (a) kept *was* locked　　(b) in *which* the

3. (a) committee *does* know　　(b) recommended *by* the

4. (a) she *should* mail　　(b) Martha *which* letters

5. (a) it *is* to　　(b) pleasant *a* thing

6. (a) strange *being* was　　(b) steps *made* her

7. (a) find *it* a　　(b) circus *is* sure

8. (a) that *the* boy　　(b) teacher *shouldn't* have

9. (a) pronunciation *are* called　　(b) dictionaries *as* aids

10. (a) None *of* the　　(b) for *are* their

Ⅳ. 閱讀測驗：

1. (2)　　2. (3)　　3. (3)　　4. (4)　　5. (2)　　6. (1)　　7. (3)　　8. (4)　　9. (1)　　10. (4)

中譯：

如果所有的人生來就無虞匱乏的話，他們一定都是生而平等的。但是使一個人臣服於另一個人，卻是附屬於我們人類的悲慘命運。眞正造成苦況的原因不是不平等，而是依賴。一個人是否被尊稱爲 His Highness（殿下）或 His Holiness（陛下）並無關緊要，但要我做別人的僕人卻是敎人難以忍受。一個人口衆多的家庭，耕種著一塊艮好的土地，兩個附近的小家庭都靠著無生產力而又貧瘠的土地爲生。所以這兩家窮戶若不服役於這富戶，就要毀滅這富戶，這是必然的，這也很容易達成。這兩個貧苦人家之一就去貢獻他的勞力給這富戶，以換取糧食；另一家則去搶刼富戶而遭逮捕；這服務的貧戶就是佣人及勞工的起源，這被捕戶就是奴隸的起源。在我們悲慘的世界中，要阻止生活在社會的人類分成兩級是不可能的，一級是發號司令的富人，另一級是服從的窮人，而這兩級中又再分成各種不同的其他的級，那些級也有他們各別不同的陰暗面。

〔解析〕

want〔wɑnt, wɔnt〕 n. 缺乏；需求之物　　misery〔'mɪzərɪ〕 n. 痛苦；悲慘
attach〔ə'tætʃ〕 vt., vi.附上；使附屬
species〔'spiʃiz, -ʃiz〕 n. 種　　our species ＝人類
subjection〔səb'dʒɛkʃən〕 n.服從；隸屬　　inequality〔͵ɪnɪ'kwɑlətɪ〕 n.不平等
grievance〔'grivəns〕 n. 苦狀；抱怨的原因
of little conseqence "不大重要的"　　cultivate〔'kʌltə͵vet〕 vt.耕種；培植
unproductive〔͵ʌnprə'dʌktɪv〕 adj. 無生產力的　　barren〔'bærən〕adj. 貧瘠的
indigent〔'ɪndədʒənt〕 adj. 貧窮的　　service(s)〔'sɝvɪs(ɪz)〕 n. 效勞；貢獻
in exchange for " 交換"　　*make an attack on* "攻擊"
domestic〔də'mɛstɪk〕 n. 僕人　 adj. 家庭的
melancholy〔'mɛlən͵kɑlɪ〕 adj. 憂鬱的；悲哀的　 n. 憂鬱
prevent～ from～ "阻止～免於～"　　subdivide〔͵sʌbdə'vaɪd〕vt.,vi.細分；再分
respective〔rɪ'spɛktɪv〕 adj.各別的；各自的
shade〔ʃed〕 n. 陰暗；陰影部分

Ⅴ. 選擇：

1.② 　2.③ 　3.① 　4.④ 　5.② 　6.③ 　7.③ 　8.④ 　9.② 　10.③
11.① 　12.④ 　13.③ 　14.① 　15.① 　16.② 　17.④ 　18.① 　19.② 　20.④

Ⅵ. 配合：

1.(D) 　2.(P) 　3.(O) 　4.(L) 　5.(A) 　6.(T) 　7.(R) 　8.(S) 　9.(B) 　10.(C)
11.(M) 　12.(Q) 　13.(W) 　14.(F) 　15.(N) 　16.(K) 　17.(V) 　18.(H) 　19.(I) 　20.(E)

五十二學年度大學暨獨立學院入學考試
英 文 試 題

I. 下面每組四字中的劃線部份所代表的發音如果彼此完全相同，答案是 1, 2, 3, 4；如果彼此完全不同，答案是 0；如果第二和第三相同，答案是 2, 3；餘類推。答案填寫在試卷內。（ 10 ％ ）

例：　1. (1) g<u>o</u>　　　(2) kn<u>o</u>w　　(3) b<u>oa</u>t　　(4) n<u>o</u>te
　　　2. (1) d<u>oo</u>r　　(2) t<u>e</u>n　　　(3) t<u>i</u>me　　(4) c<u>a</u>n
　　　3. (1) h<u>i</u>ve　　(2) <u>d</u>idn't　　(3) le<u>d</u>　　　(4) <u>f</u>ive

答案：　1. <u>1, 2, 3, 4</u>　　　2. <u>2, 3</u>　　　3. <u>0</u>

1. (1) <u>Th</u>omas　　(2) as<u>k</u>ed　　(3) si<u>tt</u>ing　　(4) <u>r</u>ead
2. (1) sou<u>th</u>　　(2) <u>th</u>ink　　(3) ba<u>th</u>ing　　(4) brea<u>th</u>less
3. (1) r<u>ai</u>n　　(2) s<u>ai</u>d　　(3) p<u>ai</u>d　　(4) m<u>a</u>d
4. (1) tele<u>ph</u>one　(2) Ste<u>ph</u>en　(3) o<u>f</u>　　(4) o<u>v</u>er
5. (1) m<u>ou</u>th　　(2) s<u>ou</u>l　　(3) <u>ou</u>ght　　(4) s<u>ou</u>thern
6. (1) g<u>e</u>t　　(2) dr<u>e</u>ss　　(3) <u>a</u>ny　　(4) fr<u>ie</u>nd
7. (1) <u>s</u>ugar　　(2) ma<u>ch</u>ine　　(3) <u>ch</u>eck　　(4) <u>sh</u>oe
8. (1) pr<u>e</u>tty　　(2) b<u>u</u>sy　　(3) b<u>ui</u>lding　　(4) t<u>i</u>ll
9. (1) m<u>a</u>de　　(2) s<u>a</u>d　　(3) pl<u>ea</u>d　　(4) b<u>a</u>de
10. (1) bl<u>oo</u>d　　(2) f<u>oo</u>t　　(3) t<u>o</u>n　　(4) m<u>oo</u>n

II. 下面每題缺少一個字，該字的第一個字母和最後一個字母已經標示出來，請按句意將該字的完整形式填寫在試卷內。（ 20 ％ ）

注意：凡拼法錯誤，或單複數寫錯者一律不予計分。

例：　Look up the word in a d_____y if you don't know what it means.

答案：　dictionary

1. She knows a great many English words; so we say she has a large v_____y.

2. A d_____t is a doctor who looks after teeth.

3. George Washington was elected P_____t of the United States of America in 1789.

4. Mary's husband died two years ago; and she has been a w_____w since then.

5. A p_____r is a teacher who teaches in a college or university.

6. Abraham Lincoln (1809-1865) lived in the nineteenth c_____y in America.

7. An o_____n is a child who has lost one or both of its parents by death.

8. The nurse took my t_____e and told me I had no fever.

9. Nearly 1,000,000 people live in Taipei. The p_____n of Taipei is very large.

10. People in the world speak more than 1,000 different l_____s ; English is but one of them.

11. An e_____t is a huge animal which has a long trunk and two ivory tusks.

12. Washington D.C. is the c_____l of the United States of America.

13. She likes to read Shakespeare's plays. Shakespeare is her f_____e author.

14. Asia is the largest c_____t in the world.

15. Students in the first year in a college or university are called f_____n.

16. It's raining hard. May I borrow your u_____a?

17. My friend was badly hurt in a traffic a_____t yesterday.

18. Pure water is a transparent, colorless, and tasteless compound of hydrogen and o_____n.

19. May I use your t_____r to type the letter?

20. A k_____n is a school that educates children from 4 to 6 years old.

Ⅲ. 下面每一括弧中都有一個字，請根據句意及文法，將那個字的適當詞類（Part of speech）的形式填寫在試卷內。（20％）

注意：(1) 所填的字必須完全正確拼出，否則不予計分。

　　　(2) 僅在動詞後加 ing 者不予計分。

　　　(3) 單複數形式錯誤者亦不予計分。

例：　1. It is（danger）to drive to fast.

　　　2. The land here is very（produce）.

答案：　1. dangerous　　　2. productive

1. Please finish the two（assign）by Saturday.

2. The moon produced a（reflect）on the water.

3. His（refuse）to accept their offer was a surprise to us.

4. He had to stay home during his father's（ill）.

5. A few people saw the（wise）of this idea.

6. The chairman made his decision with（reluctant）.

7. The failure was due to his（careless）.

8. After their（marry）, the couple moved to New York.

9. We did not accept the（invite）because we won't be here next week.

10. He talked a great deal about ambition, and I think he was（ambition）himself.

11. A good system of education is the（found）of democracy.

12. After his father's death, he became the（own）of the farm.

13. Jane's（behave）was about the same on all occasions.

14. The program was bitterly（critic）by the public.

15. We had a（wonder）time when we were in Taichung.

16. He has a strong feeling of（superior）.

17. What are the important（qualify）of a good teacher?

18. Brown is an American by（nation）.

19. A rich person is not（necessary）intelligent.

20. My uncle advised me to（special）in history.

Ⅳ. 下面一則文字之後列十個問題，每題的括弧內設有四個答案，其中只有一個是對的。請於詳讀該文後，將正確的答案號碼填寫在試卷內。（10％）

Books are for reading, but man must bring to their reading a desire to learn and a power of assimilation. Reading a book without assimilating it is like eating a meal without digesting it. Reading should be active, not passive.

When students first go to a library, they may be puzzled as to what to read of all the different subjects. Well, Bacon tells you to look at weak places in your armour; and shows you how to fill up the gaps in your knowledge. On the other hand it is no good just trying to fill your mind with knowledge. Knowledge in itself is often useless. A mind overloaded with knowledge is like a room too full of furniture; a man cannot walk about freely in it, and look out of the windows. It is much better to concentrate on a few subjects which interest you and to deal lightly with the others, than to march stably and heavily through the whole range of learning, like a silly tourist going through a museum and not missing a single object. If you try to master every subject you may become very wise, but you will be very inhuman and you will probably lose all your friends. So you must learn to pick and choose, and you must also learn to browse in a library like a camel browsing in the pasture. If you watch a camel grazing, you will see that although he is supposed to be one of the most stupid animals in creation, he has at least one of the characteristics of the cultured man, the power to pick and choose. A student looking for mental food in a library should take the camel as his model.

1. The author thinks that every one must _____
   ① read as many books as he can.
   ② try to read books on all the different subjects.
   ③ just read books on subjects that interest him.
   ④ overload his mind with knowledge.

2. To "browse" means to _____
  ① read carefully.
  ② read here and there in a library.
  ③ read in the pasture.　　　④ digest a book or books.

3. A cultured man is similar to a camel because _____
  ① neither of them concern themselves with knowledge.
  ② the man assimilates books as a camel digests food.
  ③ both have the ability to select.
  ④ neither of them can be considered wise.

4. The term "mental food" as found in a library refers to _____
  ① books.　　　② pasture.　　　③ brain.　　　④ culture.

5. In the second paragraph the author primarily discusses _____
  ① how to select furniture.
  ② how to select reading materials.
  ③ how to master every subject.
  ④ why books must be assimilated.

6. To read a book intelligently a reader must _____
  ① agree entirely with its author.
  ② try to assimilate it.
  ③ disagree entirely with its author.　　　④ be a tourist.

7. The author thinks that it is _____
  ① necessary　　　② very good　　　③ not good
  ④ not interesting　　to try to master every subject.

8. The power of assimilation is a very important factor in _____
  ① reading books.　　　② writing books.
  ③ grazing in the pasture.　　　④ visiting a museum.

9. Bacon advises us to _____
   ① study our armour.　　② look at our armour.
   ③ master all the different subjects.
   ④ study what we don't know.

10. The author advises us _____
   ① to overload our mind with knowledge.
   ② not to overload our mind with knowledge.
   ③ to walk about in our mind.
   ④ to look out of the windows of our mind.

Ⅴ. 下面每題有一個空白，每一空白，設有四個答案，其中只有一個是對的。請將對的答案號碼填寫在試卷內。（20％）

例： Mr. Johnson will _____ go.
　　　① unable.　　② unable to　　③ be unable　　④ be unable to
答案：④

1. There aren't many people _____ in that village.
   ① living　　　② are living　　　③ live　　　④ lived

2. Our teacher _____ that lesson to us last time.
   ① explains　　　　② explained
   ③ has explained　　④ hasn't explained

3. _____ members came to the meeting this week than last week.
   ① Few　　　② A few　　　③ Fewer　　　④ Lesser

4. The man _____ today left this message for you.
   ① called　　② has called　　③ who calls　　④ who called

5. Did your friend mention what _____ said to him?
   ① has his father　　　② his father has
   ③ had his father　　　④ his father had

6. There will_____no charge for the lecture in the auditorium.
   ① to be   ② to have   ③ be   ④ have

7. Would you recommend that your friend_____to this university to study?
   ① comes   ② come   ③ came   ④ would come

8. Bill would have taken more photographs if he_____more film.
   ① had had   ② has had   ③ should have   ④ would

9. Can you see_____blowing the bugle?
   ① who is   ② whom is   ③ who   ④ whom

10. It's getting quite late. We'd better_____home very soon.
    ① going   ② to be going   ③ go   ④ to go

11. Your tent blew in the storm, but theirs_____.
    ① didn't   ② wasn't   ③ weren't   ④ hadn't

12. John and I will wait right here_____you get back.
    ① so that   ② that   ③ until   ④ for

13. Miss Smith makes_____her own clothes by hand.
    ① the most of ② most of   ③ the most   ④ most

14. We_____when Joe came early.
    ① had surprised   ② were surprising
    ③ surprised   ④ were surprised

15. We put the corn_____the birds could find it easily.
    ① which   ② where   ③ of which   ④ there

16. Those men should_____that work two days ago.
    ① finish   ② finished   ③ had finished ④ have finished

17. I always think that people_____that are a menace to society.
　① like　　　　② are like　　　③ do like　　　④ look like

18. Pete tied the knot_____the horse couldn't loosen it.
　① which　　　　　　　　　② in which
　③ so tight that　　　　　　④ very tight

19. Jim is not quite_____as his sister.
　① good as a student　　　　② as good a student
　③ as a good student　　　　④ an as good student

20. _____is extremely dangerous.
　① Cars at very high speeds driving
　② At very high speeds driving cars
　③ Cars driving at very high speeds
　④ Driving cars at very high speeds

Ⅵ. 下面有二十個問句，請在右邊選擇每一問句之最適當的回答，並將代表各回答
　　之字母（如A或B或C等）填寫在試卷內。（20％）
　　注意：下面有二十三個回答，其中有三個是無用的。

1. What did the doctor say about　　(A) Seven feet eleven inches.
　 Ed's sickness?
　　　　　　　　　　　　　　　　(B) In their garage.
2. What flavor ice cream does
　 Jack like?　　　　　　　　　　(C) By taxi.

　　　　　　　　　　　　　　　　(D) Three loaves.
3. What kind of car does Mr.
　 Green have?　　　　　　　　　(E) Beautifully.

　　　　　　　　　　　　　　　　(F) Strong.
4. Why do you need so much
　 money?　　　　　　　　　　　(G) A Ford.

　　　　　　　　　　　　　　　　(H) Ninety kilograms.
5. Whose coats are those over
　 there?　　　　　　　　　　　　(I) To buy a television set.

　　　　　　　　　　　　　　　　(J) Chocolate.

6. Where do the Wilsons keep their car?

7. Which course of study are you working on?

8. How did Bob get to the airport?

9. How does one learn a foreign language?

10. How often do you have physics class?

11. How much bread did they bring for the picnic?

12. How much did the transportation cost?

13. How much does Tom's father weigh?

14. How well does Mr. Lee speak English?

15. How long did it take you to drive there?

16. How tall is the new building going to be?

17. How many brothers does Betty have?

18. How far is it to the museum?

19. How do most Americans like their coffee?

20. How can I find out what's playing at the movies?

(K) George's cousins.

(L) Nothing serious.

(M) Algebra.

(N) About five blocks.

(O) By looking in the newspaper.

(P) By repetition.

(Q) I hope not.

(R) Every other weekday.

(S) Far from it.

(T) Ten stories.

(U) Sixty dollars.

(V) Two hours and a half.

(W) None.

52年大學聯考英文試題詳解

I. 音標：

1. (1)(2)(3)　　2. (1)(2)(4)　　3. (1)(3)　　4. (2)(3)(4)　　5. (0)　　6. (1)(2)(3)(4)

7. (1)(2)(4)　　8. (1)(2)(3)(4)　　9. (2)(4)　　10. (1)(3)

II. 單字：

1. vocabulary〔vəˈkæbjəˌlɛrɪ, vo-〕n. 字彙　　2. dentist 牙醫

3. President 總統　　4. widow 寡婦

5. professor 教授　　6. century 世紀

7. orphan〔ˈɔrfən〕n. 孤兒　　8. temperature 體溫

9. population 人口　　10. languages 語言

11. elephant 大象　　12. capital 首都

13. favorite 最喜愛的　　14. continent 洲

15. freshmen 大學一年級學生　　16. umbrella 雨傘

17. accident 意外　　18. oxygen〔ˈɑksədʒən〕n. 氧

19. typewriter 打字機　　20. kindergarten〔ˈkɪndəˌgɑrtn̩〕n. 幼稚園

III. 詞類變化：

1. assignments　　2. reflection（ or reflexion ）　　3. refusal　　4. illness　　5. wisdom　　6. reluctance（ or reluctancy ）　　7. carelessness　　8. marriage　　9. invitation　　10. ambitious　　11. foundation　　12. owner　　13. behavior（ or behaviour ）　　14. criticized　　15. wonderful　　16. superiority　　17. qualifications　　18. nationality　　19. necessarily　　20. specialize

IV. 閱讀測驗：

1. ③　　2. ②　　3. ③　　4. ①　　5. ②　　6. ②　　7. ③　　8. ①　　9. ④　　10. ②

中譯：

　　書是用來閱讀的，但我們必須對閱讀有一種求知的欲望與吸收的能力，讀書不能吸收，就好像吃飯不能消化一樣。閱讀必須是主動而不是被動的。

　　當學生第一次上圖書館時，他們也許會因為科目繁多而不知道應該閱讀那些。那麼，培根告訴你注意你本身的弱點，並指示你如何填補知識上的缺陷。在另一方面，只是盡量使你的腦筋百科雜陳，也是無益的，知識本身往往是沒有用的。一個有太多知識的頭腦，就好像一間充塞過多傢俱的房間，使人不能自由地在房中走動，也不能從窗戶往外觀望。與其堅決而沉悶地去讀一切學問，如同一個愚笨的觀光者走遍一所博物館，一物不遺地去參觀每一陳列品，遠不如專心地研讀幾種你有興趣的科目，而稍微閱覽其他的科目。如果你嘗試要精通每一種科目，你也許會變得很聰明，但你將是一點人情味都沒有，而且可能會失去所有的朋友。所以你必須懂得挑選與抉擇，同時你也必須懂得在圖書館裡，要像駱駝在草原裡吃嫩枝一樣從容地瀏覽，倘若你看一隻駱駝在吃草，你將會明白，雖然牠在動物界被人們認為是最笨的動物之一，但牠至少具有文明人類的特質，即有選擇的能力。凡在圖書館裡尋找精神食糧的學生，應以駱駝作為典範。

〔解析〕

assimilation〔ə,sɪml̩ˈeʃən〕n. 吸收；同化
digest〔dəˈdʒɛst, daɪˈdʒɛst〕vt., vi. 消化　　passive〔ˈpæsɪv〕adj. 被動的；消極的
Bacon〔ˈbekən〕n. 培根（英國作家及哲學家）　　armo(u)r〔ˈɑrmə〕n. 甲冑
fill up "填補；填滿"　　gap〔gæp〕n. 缺口；縫隙
overload〔ovəˈlod〕vt. 使裝載過重　vi. 裝載過重　　**concentrate on** "專心於"
march〔mɑrtʃ〕vi. 前進；發展　　sternly〔ˈstɝnlɪ〕adv. 堅決地；嚴厲地
inhuman〔ɪnˈhjumən, -ˈjumən〕adj. 不近人情的
browse〔brɑʊz〕vt., vi. 食；瀏覽　　pasture〔ˈpæstʃɚ, ˈpɑs-〕n. 草地；牧場
graze〔grez〕vi. 吃青草　vt. 放牧　　suppose〔səˈpoz〕vt. 以為；假定
characteristic〔ˌkærɪktəˈrɪstɪk〕n. 特性　adj. 特性的

Ⅴ. 選擇：

1. ①　2. ②　3. ③　4. ④　5. ④　6. ③　7. ②　8. ①　9. ①　10. ③
11. ①　12. ③　13. ②　14. ④　15. ②　16. ④　17. ①　18. ③　19. ②　20. ④

〔解析〕

2. last time 表過去發生的確定時間，所以用過去簡單式的動詞。

7. suggest, recommend, propose＋that…(should)＋原形動詞（詳見文法寶典 p. 372）

10. had better 後接原形動詞。

Ⅵ. 配合：

1. (L)　2. (J)　3. (G)　4. (I)　5. (K)　6. (B)　7. (M)　8. (C)　9. (P)　10. (R)
11. (D)　12. (U)　13. (H)　14. (E)　15. (V)　16. (T)　17. (W)　18. (N)　19. (F)　20. (O)

心得筆記欄

五十一學年度大學暨獨立學院入學考試
英 文 試 題

I. 下面有二十個句子，每一句都有一個空白處需要填入一個適當的介系詞（ preposition ）或副詞（ adverb ）。答案請填寫在試卷內。（ 20% ）

注意：每一空白處只可填一個字，多則不予計分 。

1. The pictures we took last week didn't come_____very well.

2. I fell_____in my work last week and I still haven't caught up with the class.

3. The letters "U.S.A." stand_____the United States of America.

4. This tie seems to go_____all my suits.

5. The advisory group is made _____of three professors and an assistant.

6. On the way home we had to take a taxi because our car broke_____.

7. They have to put_____the trip to Taichung until next month.

8. All the children looked_____to seeing the clown of the circus.

9. The thieves broke_____his house and got away with a lot of valuables.

10. He said he would bring this matter_____for discussion in the next meeting.

11. You can depend on him; I have never known him to go back_____his word.

12. The work calls_____a man who has had both training and experience.

13. He picked_____quite a bit of French while he was in Europe.

14. He is the only person who succeeded in working_____the puzzles and became the prize winner.

15. The president eventually turned_____his application on account of his poor health.

16. He has a philosophy to cope_____frustration and defeat.

17. Do you care_____some more tea?

18. I didn't want to become mixed_____in that affair.

19. They tore down the old house and put_____a new one.

20. The audience was carried_____by the splendid performance of the actor.

Ⅱ. 下面每一括弧中都有一個字,請根據句意及文法,將那個字的適當詞類(part of speech)填寫在試卷內。(20%)

注意:(1)所填的字必須完全正確拼出,否則不予計分。

(2)僅在動詞後加- ing者不予計分。

例:1 My uncle is an (influence) architect.

2 Fred is the best (music) in our class.

答案:1 influential   2. musician

The road to success lies through① (able) and perseverance.

The foundation of all ②(know) is our own direct ③(person) experience.

It may be that the result of the ④ (explore) will be ⑤ (disappoint) and failure.

The sun had risen, and it was already ⑥ (uncomfortable) warm.

The most ⑦ (enjoy) time of life is ⑧ (young).

An illness during his ⑨ (child) made him very ⑩ (depend) on his parents.

A cultivated person may ⑪ (occasion) enjoy barbaric music.

Just as John was telling about the ⑫ (mystery) noise, the lights went out.

This snake kills and eats other ⑬ (poison) snakes.

He pretended that he was ⑭ (friend) with his Indian captors.

Every member of the United Nations is responsible for the success of the ⑮ (organize).

Benjamin Franklin, a great statesman and writer, was also an important ⑯ (science) in America.

An anecdote is a brief incident which leads to a ⑰ (humor) climax.

My father is an eye ⑱ (special).

She is working as a ⑲ (library) in the Lincoln ⑳ (Memory) Library.

Ⅲ. 下面左邊有二十個未完成的句子,請在右邊選擇適當的項目以完成之,並將代表適當項目的字母(如A或B或C等)填寫在試卷內。(20%)

注意:(1)在選擇適當項目時,句意須與文法並重。

(2)右邊有二十三個項目,其中有三個是沒有用的。

1. All my hopes and plans were

2. At the peak of his career

3. From the air Chinatown appears

4. I didn't know him well

(A) enough to call him a friend.

(B) to the beauty of the room.

(C) if you had tried harder.

(D) who are seldom in trouble.

5. The candle lights added greatly　(E) shattered by the bad news.

6. American women are not thought (F) as a cluster of pagoda roofs.

7. You would have succeeded　　　(G) the athlete won many contests.

8. He would rather go without food (H) my fall that saved me.

9. I had lunch with a friend　　　(I) did I think of the invitation.

10. I have never been as homesick　(J) by the time we get home.

11. It was what had caused　　　(K) of as a weak subservient sex.

12. Not until I lay in bed　　　　(L) just back from a trip to Japan.

13. How to be a better man　　　(M) than give up the car.

14. The peasants, at long last,　　(N) goes a hand-painted silk banner.

15. The more I thought about it,　(O) for him to swim against it.

16. Mother will have supper ready　(P) as I was at that moment.

17. There seems no point in　　　(Q) was always on his mind.

18. To the winner of the game　　(R) choosing maids is very complex.

19. The child asked questions that　(S) were given their own land.

20. The current was too strong　　(T) the more ashamed I became.

　　　　　　　　　　　　　　　(U) talking about that matter now.

　　　　　　　　　　　　　　　(V) only a doctor could answer.

　　　　　　　　　　　　　　　(W) which one you like best.

Ⅳ. 下面一段文字內有二十個方括弧，每一方括弧內有四個單字，請在其中選擇一個
　　適合上下文意及文法結構的字，並將該字的號碼，填寫在試卷內。（20％）

　　Parents and teen-agers often disagree about the amount of freedom
and responsibility that the young people are (1)〔① should ② to ③ ought
④ must〕have. The teen-ager often wants to be (2)〔① like ② likely ③ free
④ freely〕to choose his own friends, select his own (3)〔① causes ② courses
③ tests ④ grades〕in school, plan for his own vocational　(4)〔① future
② season ③ succession ④ afterwards〕, (5)〔① earn ② borrow ③ spell ④ fight
〕and spend his own money and generally (6)〔① walk ② jump ③ kick ④ run
〕his own life in a more independent (7)〔① fashion ② nation ③ style
④ shape〕(8)〔① whose ② how ③ than ④ where〕many parents are able to
(9)〔① allow ② appeal ③ disagree ④ worry〕. Most problems between teenagers and their parents (10)〔① bring ② find ③ ride ④ yield〕best to
(11)〔① join ② joint ③ joins ④ joining〕planning and (12)〔① deciding ② decisive
③ decision ④ decide〕making. With it any (13)〔① giving ② gives ③ gave

④ given 〕 family disagreements are ⑭ 〔 ① agreed ② aroused ③ avoided ④ happened 〕 and problems are solved when all of the persons ⑮ 〔 ① have ② with ③ had ④ take 〕 interest in the situation ⑯ 〔 ① settle ② intend ③ share ④ suggest 〕 in working it out. ⑰ 〔 ① For ② Despite ③ Hence ④ As 〕 parents and young people learn how to get through to each other and ⑱ 〔 ① think ② develop ③ engage ④ argue 〕 skills in understanding and ⑲ 〔 ① being ② are ③ is ④ be 〕 understood, even the most difficult problems are ⑳ 〔 ① doubled ② maintained ③ necessitated ④ relieved 〕.

Ⅴ. 下面是一則文字，其後列有二十個問題，每題的括弧內設有四個答案，其中只有一個是對的。請於詳讀該文後，將正確的答案號碼填寫在試卷內。(20%)

Piloting an airplane is an exacting technical job involving great responsibility for life and property. Emergencies which test the pilot's judgment and skill are a constant possibility.

During flights, the pilot's primary task is, of course, to operate the controls of the plane. Other typical flight duties include keeping close watch on the multitude of instruments and operating the radio. How these duties are divided between the captain (or first pilot) and the first officer (or co-pilot) is determined by the former, who has complete authority over the plane, crew, passengers, and cargo while in the air. The co-pilot acts as his assistant and is regarded as a "captain in training."

Both captain and co-pilot have extensive ground duties. Before each flight, they must study weather maps and reports for the region where they will be flying, in consultation with the company meteorologist. In cooperation with the airline dispatcher, they prepare the flight plan of the route to be followed. The pilots also make a pre-flight check on the condition and loading of the aircraft and the functioning of engines and instruments. If the captain is not satisfied with the "airworthiness" of the planes or the weather conditions, the flight is cancelled, normally by mutual agreement between the captain and the dispatcher. However, if such agreement cannot be reached, the captain may refuse to take off, and according to air custom, he may not be overruled in this decision even by the president of his company.

1. Piloting is _____ job.
   ① not an exacting
   ② a more technical than exacting
   ③ an exacting technical
   ④ an easy

2. The job of piloting an airplane demands that a pilot have _____
   ① authority and " airworthiness ".
   ② judgment and skill.
   ③ emergencies.
   ④ possibility.

3. The pilot has _____ during flights.
   ① one duty only
   ② the duty of loading
   ③ no assistants
   ④ many duties

4. The _____ is regarded as a " captain in training."
   ① first pilot
   ② oldest passenger
   ③ co-pilot
   ④ radio operator

5. " Crew " here means _____
   ① the past tense of " crow ".
   ② sail to and fro.
   ③ a group of persons engaged upon a particular work.
   ④ an aircraft.

6. To operate _____ of the plane is the pilot's most important duty during flights.
   ① the radio   ② the crew   ③ the controls   ④ the cargo

7. _____ the captain and co-pilot must study weather maps and reports for the place where they will be flying.
   ① Before each flight
   ② After each flight
   ③ During each flight
   ④ After taking off

8. The co-pilot is _____
   ① the captain.
   ② the first officer.
   ③ the dispatcher.
   ④ one of the passengers.

9. Who does the captain have to consult with about the weather?
   ① The company president
   ② The company meteorologist
   ③ The crew
   ④ The airline

10. According to air custom, the captain can refuse to take off _____
 ① only when he gets the president's permission.
 ② only when the dispatcher agrees with him.
 ③ even when the dispatcher does not agree with him.
 ④ for no reason at all.

11. "Overrule" means _____
 ① decide against.　　　　② spread over quickly.
 ③ run over.　　　　　　 ④ be in mutual agreement.

12. The _____ decides on how flight duties are to be divided.
 ① first officer　② first pilot　③ crew　④ former

13. If the pilot refuses to take a plane off, the president of the company may _____
 ① overrule the captain's decision.
 ② not overrule the captain's decision.
 ③ make new air customs.　　④ prepare the flight plan.

14. Flight duties are divided between the captain and the _____
 ① meteorologist.② radio operator.③ dispatcher.　④ co-pilot.

15. Both captain and co-pilot _____
 ① have authority.　　　　② have ground duties.
 ③ can cancel a flight.　　 ④ can give commands.

16. "Pre-flight" means _____ the flight.
 ① during　　② in　　③ after　　④ before

17. The co-pilot acts as the captain's _____
 ① assistant.　② superior.　③ consultant.　④ guide.

18. The _____ has complete authority over the whole plane while in the air.
 ① first officer　　　　② president of the company
 ③ captain　　　　　　④ dispatcher

19. It is the duty of _____ to prepare the flight plan of the route to be followed.

   ① the captain and the president

   ② the captain and the meteorologist

   ③ the dispatcher and the meteorologist

   ④ the captain, the first officer and the dispatcher

20. Which word is a noun?

   ① Flight   ② Extensive   ③ Cancelled   ④ Mutual

51年大學聯考英文試題詳解

Ⅰ. 填充：

1. out　2. behind　3. for　4. with　5. up　6. down　7. off
8. forward　9. into　10. forward　11. on(*or* from)12. for　13. up
14. out　15. down　16. with　17. for　18. up　19. up　20. away

〔解析〕

1. *come out* "顯現；(相片等的)顯像"　2. *fall behind* "落後"
3. *stand for* "代表"　4. *go with* "適合；相配"
5. A *be made up of* B "A由B組成"　6. *break down* "故障；拋錨"
7. *put off* "延期"　8. *look forward to* "期待；盼望"
9. *break into* "闖入；侵入"　10. *bring forward* "提出"
11. *go back on*〔from〕"食言；背叛"　12. *call for* "要求；需要"
13. *pick up* "(無人教而)學得；拾起"　14. *work out* "解出(問題)；計算出"
15. *turn down* "拒絕(駁回)；轉小"　16. *cope with* "對抗；克服"
17. *care for* "想要"　18. *be mixed up* "牽連；有關係"
19. *put up* "蓋(房子)"　20. *be carried away* "深受感動；大受影響"

Ⅱ. 詞類轉換：

① ability　② knowledge　③ personal　④ exploration　⑤ disappointment　⑥ uncomfortably　⑦ enjoyable　⑧ youth　⑨ childhood　⑩
dependent　⑪ occasionally　⑫ mysterious　⑬ poisonous　⑭ friendly
⑮ organization　⑯ scientist　⑰ humorous　⑱ specialist　⑲ librarian　⑳ Memorial

Ⅲ. 配合：

1. (E)　2. (G)　3. (F)　4. (A)　5. (B)　6. (K)　7. (C)　8. (M)　9. (L)　10. (P)
11. (H)　12. (I)　13. (Q)　14. (S)　15. (T)　16. (J)　17. (U)　18. (N)　19. (V)　20. (O)

Ⅳ. 選擇：

(1)②　(2)③　(3)②　(4)①　(5)①　(6)④　(7)①　(8)③　(9)①　(10)④
(11)②　(12)③　(13)④　(14)③　(15)①　(16)③　(17)④　(18)②　(19)①　(20)④

V. 閱讀測驗:

1. ③ 2. ② 3. ④ 4. ③ 5. ③ 6. ③ 7. ① 8. ② 9. ② 10. ③

11. ① 12. ② 13. ② 14. ④ 15. ② 16. ④ 17. ① 18. ③ 19. ④ 20. ①

中譯:

　　駕駛飛機是項費神費力且技術性的工作,同時對生命和財產要負很大的責任。考驗駕駛員的判斷能力和技術的各種緊急事件經常可能發生。

　　在飛行期間,駕駛員最主要的工作當然是操縱飛機,其他典型的飛行責任,包括密切注意各種的儀器及操縱無線電,這些責任在正駕駛與副駕駛之間如何分配,由正駕駛決定。在飛行的時候,正駕駛有全權管理飛機、機員、旅客及貨物,副駕駛員充當他的助手,並且被當作是「訓練中的機長」。

　　正駕駛員和副駕駛員都有廣泛的地面任務。在每次飛行以前,他們必須要研究氣候、地圖以及他們要飛往地區的報告,和該公司的氣象人員磋商。他們與航線的調度負責人合作,以準備飛行所經路線的計劃。駕駛員也要作一次飛行前的檢查,以了解飛機的情況和載貨量,以及引擎和儀器的性能。如果正駕駛認為各種計畫未「達安全飛行的標準」或氣候惡劣,飛行即可取消,此種決定通常要駕駛員和航線調度負責人彼此的同意,但如果此種同意不能達成,駕駛員可以拒絕起飛。而且依照飛行慣例,在此種決定方面,他甚至可以不受該公司總裁的批駁。

〔解析〕

pilot〔'paɪlət〕vt. 駕駛;引導　　exacting〔ɪg'zæktɪŋ, ɛg-〕adj.費時費力的

responsibility〔rɪ,spɑnsə'bɪlətɪ〕n.責任;職責　　property〔'prɑpətɪ〕n. 財產

emergency〔ɪ'mɝdʒənsɪ〕n. 緊急;急變(複數 emergencies)

primary〔'praɪ,mɛrɪ, -mərɪ〕adj.主要的;首要的　　**keep watch** " 監視 "

multitude〔'mʌltə,tjud〕n.眾多;大批　　captain〔'kæptɪn〕n. 正駕駛

the first officer " 副駕駛 "　　**have authority over**～ " 有權力指揮～ "

crew〔kru〕n. (船上或飛機上的)全體工作人員

co-pilot〔ko'paɪlət〕n.(飛機的)副駕駛員

extensive〔ɪk'stɛnsɪv〕adj.廣泛的;廣大的

consultation〔,kɑnsḷ'teʃən〕n. 磋商

meteorologist〔,mitɪə'rɑlədʒɪst〕n. 氣象學家

dispatcher〔dɪ'spætʃɚ〕n.調度負責人;派遣者　　pre-flight " 飛行前 "

aircraft〔'ɛr,kræft, 'ær-〕n. 航空器(飛機、飛艇、飛船的總稱)

be satisfied with " 滿意;喜歡 "

airworthiness〔'ɛr,wɝðɪnɪs〕n.達到安全飛行的標準狀況

mutual〔'mjutʃʊəl〕adj.互相的;共同的　　**take off** " 起飛 "

president〔'prɛzədənt〕n.主席;董事長　　overrule〔,ovɚ'rul〕vt.,vi.不准;批駁

心得筆記欄

五十學年度大學暨獨立學院入學考試
英 文 試 題

I. 下列各句內共有二十個空白，每一空白需要填入一個適當的介系詞（ preposition ）。答案請填寫在試卷內。（ 20％ ）

注意：每一空白只可填一個介系詞，多則不予計分。

　　Mr. Johnson said he was ___(1)___ favor ___(2)___ doing the work right away. ___(3)___ best, he is only a temporary substitute ___(4)___ the other one. It's always better to study vocabulary ___(5)___ connection ___(6)___ reading. Do you think she threw those papers away ___(7)___ purpose or ___(8)___ accident？ We had to postpone the picnic ___(9)___ account ___(10)___ the bad weather. I don't know why he insists ___(11)___ blaming me ___(12)___ all his troubles. I'm not familiar ___(13)___ his name, but his face seems familiar ___(14)___ me. It is a mean thing to make friends ___(15)___ a view ___(16)___ using them. ___(17)___ my opinion, traveling ___(18)___ airplane is much more interesting. His poor health prevented him ___(19)___ catching up ___(20)___ the other people.

II. 在下面每一括弧內有一字，請按照句意將那個字變爲適當的詞類（ parts of speech ）填寫在試卷內。（ 20％ ）

注意：必須拼寫正確，否則不予計分。

例：The explorers needed (protect) for their legs.

答案：*protection*

　　The snakes in the tall grass were very (danger).

答案：*dangerous*

1. He did (loose) his tie in order to breathe better.
2. It was a courageous (decide) to refuse the offer.
3. The presidential (elect) took place last month.
4. The native's (loyal) was important to the expedition.

5. He wasn't expected to (voluntary) to do the work.
6. (Apparent), he felt little pain from the injury.
7. The students are very (respect) to their teachers.
8. The sentry gave them (warn) of the approaching attack.
9. They have expressed their (approve) of the plan.
10. He worked out a (system) method of regulating clocks.
11. What caused the (disaster) accident was a mystery.
12. The men of the wrecked ship (urgent) needed help.
13. They noticed the (disappear) of the shining object.
14. The (fail) of the project disappointed the scientists.
15. The leader did not want to (angry) the mob.
16. They lost their course in the (storm) weather.
17. English (pronounce) is very different from that of Chinese.
18. During the (interrupt), no business took place.
19. People always remember him for his (modest).
20. (Attract) girls often have trouble with crazy suitors.

Ⅲ. 下面左邊有二十個未完成的句子，請在右邊選擇適當的項目以完成之，並將代表適當項目的字母（如A，B，C……等）填寫在試卷內。（ 20％ ）。
  注意：①在選擇項目時，句意與文法並重。
      ②右邊有二十三個項目，其中有三個是沒有用的。
  左邊未完成句子

1. The stranger told the little boy
2. None of the men in the room had
3. She was screaming while Jim and Joe
4. The brown dog that lived in Nelson's
5. Jane was actually very anxious to
6. What puzzled the police especially
7. She said her husband was in the habit
8. The man jumped into the car and
9. The lawyer arrived carrying some papers
10. The best-seller story was neither
11. Mr. Norris lengthened his poems by
12. His boss would raise his salary

13. He never showed us the piece of cloth
14. Mother said girls should not interfere
15. When the dancing stopped, Dick joined
16. In spite of Bill's larger size, Tom
17. The sound like thunder turned out to be
18. The old man knew the woods as well
19. The travelers found a large tree under
20. The worker can't promise to finish

右邊的項目

(A) begin to work on her wedding clothes.
(B) of returning home after midnight.
(C) signed by the owner of the factory.
(D) which they could take a rest.
(E) drove on to the highway by himself.
(F) was no doubt the stronger of the two.
(G) a group of men at one end of the porch.
(H) in order to cover themselves.
(I) was how the murder was committed.
(J) back yard was called Bobby.
(K) painting the house by Thursday.
(L) eaten anything for several days.
(M) as the wild creatures living there.
(N) the waves striking the shore.
(O) that he had a collection of old stamps.
(P) cutting a few lines in half yesterday.
(Q) that he carried in his pocket.
(R) were struggling for possession of the gun.
(S) as bright as a sun rises in the east.
(T) a biography nor an autobiography.
(U) with their parents' wishes.
(V) if he would not resign.
(W) green hat with feathers on it.

Ⅳ. 下面一段文字內有二十個方括弧〔 〕，每一方括弧內有四個單字，其中只有一個適合上下文意。請將該適合上下文意之字的號碼，填寫在試卷內。（20％）

One of the most important features that (1) 〔 ① produce ② overcome ③ forbid ④ distinguish 〕 man from animals is the (2) 〔 ① ability ② machine ③ soul ④ case 〕 to laugh. People who have (3) 〔 ① practiced ② achieved ③ demanded ④ investigated 〕 the phenomenon have offered many (4) 〔 ① turkeys ② tanks ③ theories ④ escapes 〕 to explain human laughter. (5) 〔 ① Miners ② Scholars ③ Farmers ④ Marbles 〕 in the field of (6) 〔 ① economics ② psychology ③ archaeology ④ engineering 〕, for example, have done research on the (7) 〔 ① subject ② career ③ passage ④ adventure 〕 of what makes people laugh. But, as usually happens, the (8) 〔 ① followers ② visitors ③ experts ④ hunters 〕 disagree, and there is much (9) 〔 ① fixture ② alliance ③ nature ④ controversy 〕 in the field. Some people (10) 〔 ① perform ② exhaust ③ claim ④ experiment 〕 that human (11) 〔 ① beings ② mankind ③ kingdom ④ millions 〕 laugh at things which are (12) 〔 ① strange ② capable ③ wealthy ④ patient 〕 to their experience. Others feel that people laugh at what they (13) 〔 ① smoothly ② secretly ③ punctually ④ savagely 〕 believe to be their own (14) 〔 ① witnesses ② tenderness ③ weaknesses ④ usefulness 〕. Humor often depends on (15) 〔 ① protest ② crisis ③ mission ④ knowledge 〕 of certain words or even on an (16) 〔 ① understanding ② intervening ③ advertising ④ entertaining 〕 of a particular cultural (17) 〔 ① barnyard ② background ③ blackmail ④ temperature 〕. There are, of course, many different (18) 〔 ① minerals ② sources ③ forests ④ pounds 〕 of humor, but the important (19) 〔 ① welcome ② organ ③ found ④ fact 〕 is that all people (20) 〔 ① apply ② attend ③ share ④ manage 〕 the great pleasure of laughter.

Ⅴ. 下面是一則文字，其後列有二十個問題，每題的括弧內設有四個答案，其中只有一個是對的。請於詳讀該文後，將正確的答案號碼填寫在試卷內。（20％）

This remarkable man went to a log-cabin school until he was 12 years old. That was the end of his formal education. In spite of this, he became the most famous literary figure of his generation. He received honorary degrees from Oxford and Yale. People speak of him as the best known humorous writer of all times. He also brought realism and western local color to American fiction. He started to write articles in 1861 and made millions by writing short stories and books like *Tom Sawyer* and

Huckleberry Finn, etc. His real name was Samuel Langhorne Clemens, but he is better known all over the world as Mark Twain.

Mark Twain was born in a tiny two-room cabin in a small Missouri village near the Mississippi in 1835. At that time, Andrew Jackson was the president of the country. Abraham Lincoln was still a young farm laborer in Illinois. The first railroad had been built seven years before and the economic collapse, called the Panic of 1837, still lay ahead.

In the tiny two-room cabin Mark Twain lived with his parents, four brothers and sisters and a slave girl. As a baby he was not healthy and was not expected to live through the first winter. But his mother, from whom he inherited his genius for humor, took such tender care of him that he managed to survive. As a boy, he caused his parents much trouble by playing practical jokes on all his friends and neighbors. He hated to go to school and he constantly ran away from home.

1. Mark Twain came of_____family.
   ① a rich ② a well-educated
   ③ a poor ④ an Indian

2. Mark Twain is the pen name of_____
   ① Andrew Jackson. ② Abraham Lincoln.
   ③ Tom Sawyer. ④ Samuel Langhorne Clemens.

3. "Survive" here means_____
   ① to remain alive after the death of some one.
   ② to continue to live. ③ to restore to life.
   ④ to inspect or examine formally.

4. The first railroad was built in_____
   ① 1828. ② 1835. ③ 1837. ④ 1842.

5. In 1835 Abraham Lincoln was_____
   ① the president of the United States.
   ② the most famous American writer.
   ③ a young man working on a farm in the state of Illinois.
   ④ a lawyer.

6. " Figure " here means_____
   ① a person of distinction.　　② a number.
   ③ a device.　　④ a picture.

7. Mark Twain_____a lot of money by writing.
   ① earned　　② saved　　③ lost　　④ borrowed

8. Oxford and Yale are names of_____
   ① famous writers.　　② Mark Twain's books.
   ③ Mark Twain's friends.　　④ universities.

9. Mark Twain got his sense of humor from_____
   ① Mr. Clemens.　　② Mr. Jackson.
   ③ Mrs. Clemens.　　④ Tom Sawyer.

10. The Mississippi is a_____
    ① village.　　② river.　　③ mountain.　　④ state.

11. Mark Twain was from_____
    ① Missouri.　　② Illinois.　　③ New York.　　④ Yale.

12. The Panic of 1837 was caused by_____
    ① a political collapse.　　② a religious movement.
    ③ an economic reformation.　　④ an economic depression.

13. Mark Twain ran away from home because he hated_____
    ① his neighbors.　　② their tiny cabin.
    ③ school.　　④ literature.

14. Mark Twain was best known for his_____
    ① honorary degrees.　　② humor.
    ③ money.　　④ health.

15. He introduced_____into American fiction.
    ① formal education　　② humor
    ③ the eastern states　　④ the West

16. His_____brought much trouble to his home.
    ① laziness   ② humorous books
    ③ practical jokes on his friends and neighbors
    ④ love affairs

17. Without his mother's_____,Mark Twain would have died before he
    was one year old.
    ① care   ② humor   ③ genius   ④ anxiety

18. _____people lived in the tiny two-room cabin where Mark Twain
    was born.
    ① 12   ② 7   ③ 10   ④ 8

19. Mark Twain started his writing career when he was_____years old.
    ① 12   ② 20   ③ 36   ④ 26

20. Mark Twain became a very famous writer_____
    ① because he was the most highly educated figure of his time.
    ② because he belonged to the same generation as Lincoln.
    ③ in spite of his father's wealth.
    ④ in spite of his little formal education.

50年大學聯考英文試題詳解

Ⅰ. 填充：

① in　② of　③ At　④ for　⑤ in　⑥ with　⑦ on　⑧ by　⑨ on　⑩ of　⑪ on　⑫ for　⑬ with　⑭ to　⑮ with　⑯ to　⑰ In　⑱ by　⑲ from　⑳ with

Ⅱ. 詞類轉換：

1. loose 或 loosen　2. decision　3. election　4. loyalty　5. volunteer　6. Apparently　7. respectful　8. warning　9. approval　10. systematic　11. disastrous　12. urgently　13. disappearance　14. failure　15. anger　16. stormy　17. pronunciation　18. interruption　19. modesty　20. Attractive

Ⅲ. 配合：

1. (O)　2. (L)　3. (R)　4. (J)　5. (A)　6. (I)　7. (B)　8. (E)　9. (C)　10. (T)　11. (P)　12. (V)　13. (Q)　14. (U)　15. (G)　16. (F)　17. (N)　18. (M)　19. (D)　20. (K)

Ⅳ. 選擇：

(1)④　(2)①　(3)④　(4)③　(5)②　(6)②　(7)①　(8)③　(9)④　(10)③　(11)①　(12)①　(13)②　(14)③　(15)④　(16)①　(17)②　(18)②　(19)④　(20)③

Ⅴ. 閱讀測驗：

1. ③　2. ④　3. ②　4. ①　5. ③　6. ①　7. ①　8. ④　9. ③　10. ②　11. ①　12. ④　13. ③　14. ②　15. ①　16. ③　17. ①　18. ④　19. ④　20. ④

中譯：

　　這位著名的人物進了一所簡陋的木造學校，一直到十二歲爲止，那是他正式教育的結束。雖然這樣，他却成爲他那一代中最有名的文學人物。他接受牛津和耶魯兩大學的榮譽學位，人們都說他是古今最有名的幽默作家。他也把寫實主義及西部的地方色彩帶到美國的小說裡。他於 1861 年開始寫作，並以寫短篇故事和像「湯姆歷險記」和「頑童歷險記」等一類的書賺了幾百萬。他的本名是 Samuel Langhorne Clemens，但却以馬克吐溫的筆名而舉世聞名。

　　馬克吐溫於 1835 年出生在靠近密西西比河的密蘇里的一個小村子中，一個只有兩個房間的小木屋裏。當時安德魯・傑克遜是美國總統，林肯還是伊利諾州的一個農場的青年勞工，第一條鐵路在七年前建築起來了，但經濟崩潰，史稱 1837 年的經濟恐慌仍橫置於前。

　　馬克吐溫和他的父母，四個兄弟姊妹與一個黑奴女孩，住在那棟只有兩個房間的小木屋中。當他是個嬰兒時，身體很不健康，甚至沒有人預料他會活過第一個冬天。但是他的母親（從她那裡他繼承了幽默的天賦）非常小心地照顧他，而使他設法活下來。當他是個孩子的時候，他經常對他的朋友和鄰居要鬼把戲，而給他父母惹來許多麻煩。

　　他很討厭上學，並且時常逃家。

〔解析〕

remarkable〔rɪ'mɑrkəbḷ〕 *adj.* 值得注意的；顯著的

log cabin " 木造小屋 "　　formal〔'fɔrmḷ〕 *adj.* 正式的

in spite of " 雖然 "　　literary〔'lɪtə,rɛrɪ〕 *adj.* 文學的

figure〔'fɪgjɚ,'fɪgɚ〕 *n.* 人物；數字　　honorary degree " 名譽學位 "

Oxford〔'ɑksfəd〕 *n.* 牛津；牛津大學　　Yale〔jel〕 *n.* 耶魯大學

humorous〔'hjumərəs,'ju-〕 *a.* 風趣的；有幽默感的

realism〔'riəl,ɪzəm,'rɪəl-〕 *n.* 寫實主義

fiction〔'fɪkʃən〕 *n.* 小說；虛構　　article〔'ɑrtɪkḷ〕 *n.* 文章；論文

Mark Twain〔'mɑrk'twen〕 *n.* 馬克吐溫(1835-1910)（美國作家 Samuel L. Clemens 的筆名）

laborer〔'lebərɚ〕 *n.* 勞工；工人　　railroad〔'rel,rod〕 *n.* 鐵路；軌道

collapse〔kə'læps〕 *vt.,vi.* 倒塌；崩潰

inherit〔ɪn'hɛrɪt〕 *vt.,vi.* 繼承；遺傳　　genius〔'dʒinjəs〕 *n.* 天才；天賦

run away from ~ " 從~逃出 "　　practical joke " 鬼把戲 "

心得筆記欄

四十九學年度大學暨獨立學院入學考試
英 文 試 題

I. 下面二十題，每題包含一個成語（idiom），即加( )之字。每一成語設有四個解釋，其中只有一個是對的。請將對的答案號碼填寫在試卷內（20％）

例如：You can have this book（for nothing）. ① worthless　② free of charge　③ without substance　④ meaningless

答案：②

1. It is very easy to（find fault with）the work of others. ① complain about　② make fun of　③ make a fool of　④ praise.

2. I'll（get even with）him for his insulting remarks. ① be on an equal standing with　② get along with　③ get the better of　④ take revenge on.

3. The heavy spring rains（brought about）the flood. ① happened　② caused to happen　③ brought to an end　④ reared.

4. This project will（call for）a lot of money and man power. ① yield　② visit　③ require　④ telephone.

5. I refuse to（put up with）his actions any longer. ① support　② approve　③ criticize　④ tolerate.

6. After running up so many flights of steps, she was completely（out of breath）. ① panting　② dying　③ dead　④ laughing.

7. Did Mr. Wilson（get over）his cold quickly？① pass over　② move over　③ recover from　④ call upon.

8. Our two-week vacation（compensated for）a year of hard work. ① deserved　② made up for　③ made use of　④ increased.

9. The Smiths have bad luck, but they always（make the best of）everything. ① accept cheerfully　② do efficiently　③ understand thoroughly　④ enjoy heartily.

10. In his easy-going character, Jim seems to (take after) his father. ① like　② follow　③ resemble　④ pursue.

11. The king was (surprised rather than annoyed). ① not surprised but annoyed　② not annoyed but surprised　③ either surprised or annoyed　④ neither surprised nor annoyed.

12. He said that he (had nothing to do with) writing that letter. ① had a good time at　② had no time to do　③ had no freedom to do　④ had no connection with.

13. It's (up to you) whether we should take action or not. ① depend on you　② decide on you　③ for you to decide　④ for you to take action.

14. We have to (do away with) the old system before adopting the new one. ① abolish　② establish　③ finish　④ punish.

15. Just as he was going to point out the falling star to us, he (lost sight of) it. ① became blind　② ceased to see　③ stopped to see　④ lost the power of seeing.

16. If he doesn't (have his own way), he gets very angry. ① go somewhere　② have an obstruction　③ make a special effort　④ do as he wishes.

17. Should you (look down upon) him just because his family is poor? ① despise　② examine　③ observe　④ inquire about.

18. Only the (well-to-do) can afford to own homes in that exclusive district. ① skillful　② intelligent　③ honest　④ wealthy.

19. The story was (anything but) funny. ① exceedingly　② nothing short of　③ not at all　④ just.

20. We (reminded) him (of) his appointment in the afternoon. ① minded　② caused to remember　③ recalled　④ minded again.

Ⅱ. 下面二十題，每題有一個空白，每一空白設有四個答案，其中只有一個是對的請將對的答案號碼填寫在試卷內（ 20％ ）

　　例如：My friend promised _____ the book very soon. ① will return　② to return　③ return　④ returning

　　答案：②

1. Mr. Meyer knows _____. ① what does that word mean ② what means that word ③ what that word means ④ what meaning has that word.

2. We are looking forward _____ our friends next week. ① to see ② to seeing ③ to be seeing ④ shall see.

3. Mr. Johnson's suit is not _____ color as yours. ① as ② so ③ like ④ the same.

4. These machines ought _____ once a year. ① to be inspected ② to inspect ③ be inspected ④ inspect.

5. It is difficult _____. ① to speak correctly English for me ② for me to speak correctly English ③ for me to speak English correctly ④ to speak English correctly for me.

6. It _____ me two hours to find your new house. ① cost ② took ③ spent ④ occupied.

7. "How often do you go to the theater?" "_____." ① Twice a week. ② By bus. ③ With friends. ④ Probably Monday.

8. We _____ more than the normal amount of rain so far this year. ① will have ② are having ③ having had ④ have had.

9. She speaks the language _____ better now. ① considering ② considerable ③ considerably ④ considerately.

10. Is the river _____ through that town very large? ① flows ② that flows ③ that flowing ④ which flowing.

11. We didn't know _____ had suggested that plan to them. ① whom ② who ③ that ④ with whom.

12. This is _____ I recommend for you to do. ① what ② that ③ which ④ about which.

13. Would you please put the book _____ it belongs? ① to whom ② to which ③ into which ④ where.

14. If I had had enough time, I _____ to the meeting with you. ① would go ② would have gone ③ has gone ④ were to go.

15. He is _____ busy man that he really needs a secretary. ① so
    ② so a ③ such ④ such a.

16. When Catherine _____ back from school, give her the message.
    ① comes ② will come ③ is coming ④ coming.

17. I enrolled in this course _____ my English. ① will improve
    ② for improve ③ to improve ④ in order to improving.

18. I can't imagine how _____ about it. ① could they know possibly
    ② could they possibly know ③ they could possibly know ④ possibly they could know.

19. I think that you are _____ that shelf. ① enough tall to reach
    ② tall to reach enough ③ tall to enough reach ④ tall enough
    to reach.

20. He allowed himself _____ . ① two years to finish it completely
    ② to finish it two years completely ③ completely to finish it
    two years ④ to finish it completely two years.

Ⅲ. 下面十題係測驗句義（ sentence meaning ）瞭解能力，每一句話的意義設有
    四個解釋，其中只有一個是對的。請將對的答案號碼填寫在試卷內。（ 10％ ）

    例如：Miss Jones does not sing well. ① She does not sing at all.
          ② She is not interested in singing. ③ She is not particularly
          good at singing. ④ She will never learn to sing.
    答案：③

 1. Grandfather is too old to work. ① He still works hard because he
    is old. ② He does not work any longer because he is too old.
    ③ He is so old that he has to work. ④ He has worked so hard that
    he has become old.

 2. Bill said to Tom : " Unless you leave immediately, I will call a po-
    liceman. " ① Bill wanted Tom to leave. ② Bill wanted Tom to
    stay. ③ Bill wanted Tom to call a policeman. ④ Tom wanted
    Bill to call a policeman.

3. That student speaks English fluently in spite of his limited vocabulary. ① He knows a great many English words. ② He does not know many English words. ③ He knows all English words.

4. If it rains tomorrow, we will not go swimming. ① We are sure it will rain tomorrow. ② We are sure it will not rain tomorrow. ③ We are not sure whether it will rain or not tomorrow. ④ We are sure we will not go swimming anyhow.

5. When we were going to class, a stranger asked a group of students who taught them English. ① We asked the students something. ② We asked the stranger something. ③ The stranger asked the students something. ④ The students asked the stranger something.

6. John says, " Somebody must have opened my drawer. " ① John has found something was wrong with his drawer. ② John has found he had a different drawer. ③ John is ordering somebody to open his drawer.

7. Bill says, " I shall never forget seeing the President. " ① Bill has never seen the President and will rememder to see him. ② Bill has never seen the President and will not forget him. ③ Bill has seen the President and will forget him. ④ Bill has seen the President and will never forget the seeing of him.

8. If John had seen Mary, he would have spoken to her. ① John saw Mary and spoke to her. ② John saw Mary but didn't speak to her. ③ John didn't see Mary but spoke to her. ④ John didn't see Mary and didn't speak to her.

9. Not knowing exactly what to do, the zoo keeper simply gave the hawk a snake. The phrase " not knowing exactly what to do " describes ① nobody ② the zoo keeper ③ the hawk ④ the snake.

10. Ruth asks Mary : " If you took a trip to Europe, which countries would you visit ? " The question indicates that Mary ① has recently taken a trip to Europe ② is taking a trip to Europe right now ③ will take a trip to Europe pretty soon ④ has never taken a trip to Europe and so far has made no plans to do so.

Ⅳ. 下面十題，每題解釋一個英文單字。每題後所給的一個字母，就是那單字的第一個字母，請將那個字完全拼出來，寫在試卷內。注意必須完全正確拼出，不可略去題目上所給的字母，並且詞類（ parts of speech ）必須正確，否則不予計分。（ 10% ）

　　例如： to move or go forward.　　　　　　　　　　a ……
　　答案： advance.

　1. a doctor who performs operations.　　　　　　　　s ……
　2. make or think out something new ; devise for the first
　　　time.　　　　　　　　　　　　　　　　　　　　i ……
　3. having to do with machinery or tools.　　　　　　m ……
　4. a building or place for the keeping and exhibition of
　　　works of art, scientific specimens, etc.　　　　　m ……
　5. made by human skill or labor (opposed to natural)　a ……
　6. a place where meals are served to customers.　　　r ……
　7. a person who plays the piano.　　　　　　　　　　p ……
　8. what is contained in something.　　　　　　　　　c ……
　9. give (a person) notice of possible danger, evil, harm, or
　　　anything unfavorable.　　　　　　　　　　　　w ……
　10. a highly unpleasant or annoying thing or person.　　n ……

Ⅴ. 下列各句括弧中的字，大多數都是詞類（ parts of speech ）用錯了的，但也有並無錯誤的。請將詞類用錯的字改正（ 注意不可改變原字基本意義 ）填寫在試卷內；詞類並無錯誤的字，也要抄寫在試卷內，否則不予計分。（ 20% ）

　　例如： Jimmy could hardly speak for (nervous).
　　答案： nervousness

　1. A scholar should not give in to the (tempt) to be lazy.
　2. A little (encourage) often brings out the best in even the most
　　　stubborn child.
　3. When we look back over the accomplishments of Benjamin Franklin,
　　　it is (obviously) that he was a man of great genius.
　4. The salesman bothered me every day with (request) to buy his
　　　magazine.

5. Those who have suffered are usually (sympathy) towards suffering.

6. Mrs. Brown said she was more (likely) to go to London than Paris.

7. One must work hard in order to run a (success) business.

8. Jimmy should (apology) for his rudeness to me.

9. In many countries it is (custom) to give flowers to people who are sick.

10. Mr. Young seemed to take his friend's (advise) in bad humor.

11. Even the most (industry) student sometimes gets tired of studying.

12. Attempts to (economy) by eating poor food often end up in serious illness.

13. A (chemistry) course in college usually consists of two hours of lecture and one of laboratory.

14. Beauty is not (necessary) a sign of a good personality.

15. Some apples look more (delicious) than they taste.

16. Old Professor Jones spends his time reading nothing but (detect) stories.

17. It is difficult for a son to always live up to the (expects) of his parents.

18. A visit to the zoo will (acquaintance) you with many kinds of animals.

19. If you can afford to travel to Europe, it will (rich) your education.

20. Music is regarded by many people as an essential part of a (religion) ceremony.

Ⅵ. 下面是一則文字，其後列有二十個問題，每題設有四個答案，其中只有一個是對的。請於詳讀該文後，將正確的答案號碼填寫在試卷內。(20 %)

A prominent American professor decided to try to split the very core of an atom. He built a powerful machine called a cyclotron. Into this machine he fed electrical particles and made them travel around in a circle, faster, faster, faster, faster. When they were going faster than anything known except the speed of light, they were shot through an opening against a metal plate. There was a flare of weird blue light.

The professor had ripped apart the stubborn atom. The professor survived because he split only a few atoms and because he had built a very thick wall between himself and the explosions.

The cyclotron split the very core of atoms, but the power required was too great, greater than the power produced. If only one atom would explode the next, and that one the next and so on in a chain！

Under the Hitler regime a German racial court decided that Madame Lise Meitner had Jewish blood in her veins and therefore must stop her scientific researches. But when she left Germany, she carried with her a great secret. She had an idea that uranium was just such a mineral as scientists wanted. If so, the controlled explosions of a thimbleful would run an automobile until it wore out. Ten pounds of it would blast a hole in the earth one mile deep and thirty miles across, and would kill every living thing for 100 miles around. After Germany expelled her, Madame Meitner worked for the United States and its allies.

1. Particles were shot through an opening in a ① machine ② metal plate ③ metal tube ④ piece of plate glass.

2. The light mentioned in the story was ① green ② red ③ blue ④ yellow.

3. The story says that the atom is ① cooperative ② powerful ③ stubborn ④ swift.

4. The thick wall was built for ① observation ② explosion ③ splitting ④ protection.

5. What was it that travelld faster, faster？ ① a machine ② particles ③ light ④ a shot.

6. （① A few ② Many ③ Dozens of ④ No) atoms were split in this experiment.

7. The machine the professor built was ① weak ② heavy ③ poor ④ powerful.

8. In order to protect himself and others while experimenting a scientist must use great ① strength ② caution ③ force ④ speed.

9. What kind of particles were fed into the machine? ① electrical ② chemical ③ biological ④ scientific.

10. Madame Meitner was a ① charwoman ② German ally ③ scientist ④ spy.

11. The court was ① Jewish ② scientific ③ atomic ④ racial.

12. Lise Meitner was very ① young ② beautiful ③ wise ④ rich.

13. How much uranium would run an automobile as long as its parts lasted? ① one grain ② several grains ③ half a thimbleful ④ a thimbleful.

14. How deep a hole would one pound of uranium blast in the earth? ① one mile ② one-half mile ③ one-quarter mile ④ one tenth mile.

15. How big a hole would twenty pounds of uranium blast in the earth? ① 30 ② 60 ③ 90 ④ 120 miles across.

16. Who profited most from Madame Meitner's wonderful mind? ① Hitler ② Hitler's allies ③ Hitler's enemies ④ the Germans.

17. The power required to split the atoms with the cyclotron was ① not so great as ② greater than ③ as great as ④ as much as the power produced.

18. Madame Meitner's great secret was that ① she had Jewish blood in her veins ② Germany possessed controlled explosions ③ uranium could split the cyclotron ④ uranium could make the atoms explode in a chain.

19. Madame Meitner was driven out of Germany because she ① was partly Jewish ② had German blood in her veins ③ knew a great secret ④ was too old.

20. A nation's intolerance usually results in its ultimate ① gain ② loss ③ success ④ prosperity.

49年大學聯考英文試題詳解

I. 成語選擇：

1.①　2.④　3.②　4.③　5.④　6.①　7.③　8.②　9.②　10.③

11.②　12.④　13.③　14.①　15.②　16.④　17.①　18.④　19.③　20.②

II. 選擇：

1.③　2.②　3.④　4.①　5.③　6.②　7.①　8.④　9.③　10.②

11.②　12.①　13.④　14.②　15.④　16.①　17.③　18.③　19.④　20.①

III. 句意測驗：

1.②　2.①　3.②　4.③　5.③　6.①　7.④　8.④　9.②　10.④

IV. 單字：

1. surgeon〔'sɝdʒən〕*n.* 外科醫師　　2. invent 發明

3. mechanical〔mə'kænɪkl̩〕*adj.* 機械的　　4. museum 博物館

5. artificial〔,ɑrtə'fɪʃəl〕*adj.* 人造的　　6. restaurant 飯店

7. pianist〔pɪ'ænɪst〕*n.* 鋼琴家

8. contents〔'kɑntɛnts, kən'tɛnts〕*n.* 內容　　9. warn 警告

10. nuisance〔'njusn̩s〕*n.* 令人討厭的人或物

V. 詞類測驗：

1. temptation　2. encouragement　3. obvious　4. requests

5. sympathetic　6. likely　7. successful　8. apologize

9. customary　10. advice　11. industrious　12. economize

13. chemistry　14. necessarily　15. delicious　16. detective

17. expectations　18. acquaint　19. enrich　20. religious

VI. 閱讀測驗：

1.①　2.③　3.③　4.④　5.②　6.①　7.④　8.②　9.①　10.③

11.④　12.③　13.④　14.④　15.②　16.③　17.②　18.④　19.①　20.②

Ⅶ.　中譯：

　　一位著名的美國教授，決定設法分裂原子核，他建造起一座有力的機器稱爲磁力加速器，在這個機器裡面他通以電質點，並且使那些電質點在一個圓圈中愈來愈快地繞圈轉動，當它們進行到比除光的速度以外任何知名的東西都快時，他就將那些電質點經過一個孔射向一塊金屬板，就會有一道奇異的藍色閃光出現。

　　這位教授已經分裂開堅固的原子，他經歷危險之後仍然活着，是因爲他只分裂幾個原子，而且在他自己和爆炸之間，他已建造了一座很厚的牆。

　　磁力加速器分裂原子的極核所需的力量非常大，大得比所產生的力量還要大，只要有一個原子就會爆開第二個原子，第二個原子又會爆開第三個原子，像一條鎖鏈般的一直繼續下去。

　　在希特勒的政權統治之下，一個德國的種族法庭判決麥特納夫人有猶太血統，因而得停止她的科學研究。當她離開德國的時候，她帶走了一極大的秘密，她有一種觀念，認爲鈾正是科學家們所需要的礦物。如果是這樣，只要控制一點點鈾的爆炸力就可開動一輛汽車，直到它耗盡，十磅的鈾會在地上炸成一個深一哩寬三十哩的窟窿，並且會殺死周圍 100 哩以內的一切生物，德國人驅逐麥特納夫人後，她就爲美國及其同盟國效勞了。

〔解析〕

prominent〔'pramənənt〕*adj.* 著名的；主要的

core〔kor〕*n.* 核心；果心　　atom〔'ætəm〕*n.* 原子；微粒

cyclotron〔'saɪklə,tran,'sɪklə-〕*n.* 旋轉磁力加速器

electrical〔ɪ'lɛktrɪkḷ〕*adj.* 電的；用電的

particle〔'partɪkḷ〕*n.* 分子；微粒

metal〔'mɛtḷ〕*n.* 金屬　　plate〔plet〕*n.*（金屬）板

flare〔flɛr〕*n.* 搖曳的火焰；閃光　　weird〔wɪrd〕*adj.* 怪異的；奇異的

rip〔rɪp〕*vt.,vi.* 裂開；扯開　　stubborn〔'stʌbən〕*adj.* 硬的；倔強的

explosion〔ɪk'sploʒən〕*n.* 爆炸　　chain〔tʃen〕*n.* 鏈子；一連串

Hitler〔'hɪtlə〕*n.* 希特勒　　regime〔rɪ'ʒim〕*n.* 政體；政權

racial〔'reʃəl〕*adj.* 種族的；民族的　　Jewish〔'dʒuɪʃ,'dʒuɪʃ〕*adj.* 猶太人的

vein〔ven〕*n.* 血管；靜脈　　research〔'risɝtʃ,rɪ'sɝtʃ〕*n.* 研究；調查

uranium〔jʊ'reniəm〕*n.* 鈾　　mineral〔'mɪnərəl〕*n.* 礦物

thimbleful〔'θɪmbḷ,fʊl〕*n.*（酒等）極少量

automobile〔'ɔtəmə,bil,,ɔtə'mobil〕*n.* 汽車

blast〔blæst〕*vt.,vi.* 炸毀；爆炸　　expel〔ɪk'spɛl〕*vt.* 驅逐；逐出

ally〔'ælaɪ,ə'laɪ〕*n.* 同盟者；盟邦

心得筆記欄

四十八學年度大學暨獨立學院入學考試
英 文 試 題

❶ Spelling 拼字：（20％）

下面有二十個字，每字列有四種拼法，其中只有一種拼法是對的。請將對的那個號碼填寫在試卷的空白內。

例如：① fammly　② family　③ famiely　④ farmily　　　　　答案爲②

1. ① exquisit　② exquisite　③ exquissite　④ exquissiit

2. ① envairoment　② envirenment　③ enviroment　④ environment

3. ① nucleous　② nuclius　③ neucleus　④ nucleus

4. ① legitimite　② ligitimate　③ legitimate　④ legetimate

5. ① cooporation　② corperation　③ corparation　④ corporation

6. ① interprete　② inturpret　③ interpret　④ interprit

7. ① primmitive　② primitive　③ primative　④ primetive

8. ① tremandous　② tremendus　③ tremendous　④ trimendous

9. ① efficiency　② eficiency　③ effaciency　④ efficncy

10. ① machanical　② mechinical　③ mechnnical　④ mechanical

11. ① nusance　② nuisanse　③ nuisance　④ nuisence

12. ① guarantee　② garantee　③ guarrantee　④ guarentee

13. ① vacuum　② vaccuum　③ vaccum　④ vacuam

14. ① exclimation　② exclamation　③ exclamasion　④ exclemsion

15. ① parrallel　② paralell　③ parallel　④ parallell

16. ① alocohol　② alcohol　③ alkohol　④ alcohole

17. ① reutine　② routine　③ routene　④ routeen

18. ① mosquito　② mospueto　③ maspuito　④ musquito

19. ① temporameut ② tenperament ③ tamperament ④ temperament

20. ① ocurrence ② occurence ③ occurrence ④ occurrance

❷ Syntax 造句法：（ 20％ ）

下面有二十題，每題包括四個答案，其中只有一個是正確的。請把正確答案的號碼寫在試卷內。

例如： Mary was there, but her three brothers ① don't ② didn't
③ wasn't ④ weren't　　　　　　　　答案④

1. He asked ① to the people for money ② for money to the people
③ the people for money ④ money to the people.

2. How much ① do you cost the books ? ② do the books cost ?
③ the books cost you ? ④ do cost the books ?

3. Alice likes the flowers and Jane ① does too ② likes too
③ is too ④ is like too

4. No, thank you. I have ① some ② any ③ other ④ anything.

5. The man ① I saw ② what I saw ③ which I saw ④ of whom I
saw　was happy.

6. Dick went ① late yesterday there ② there late　yesterday
③ yesterday late there ④ yesterday there late.

7. The gentleman ① had the tailor a coat made ② had the tailor
make a coat ③ had the tailor made a coat ④ had made a coat
the tailor

8. If he ① were coming ② would come ③ should come ④ were come
late, give him the message.

9. The book ① belonged ② belongs ③ is belonging ④ belonging to
Mary is lost.

10. He wasn't going to the movies, ① wasn't he ? ② was he ?
③ wouldn't he ④ didn't he ?

11. Didn't Mary go to Hongkong ? Yes, she ① didn't ② wasn't ③ did
④ was.

12. Weren't you in class yesterday ? No, I ①weren't ②wasn't ③were ④was.

13. Henry was sick yesterday and ①delayed ②lost ③absenced ④missed his classes.

14. The people at the party ①had ②made ③did ④took a good time.

15. The man is ①taking ②giving ③getting ④letting his hair cut.

16. We turned ①on ②down ③over ④up the radio to make it louder.

17. The pens of the students are all ①like ②same ③alike ④resemble.

18. He ①talked ②spoke ③told ④said that he was coming at six o'clock.

19. What do you usually eat ①by ②in ③for ④on breakfast ?

20. The teachers were ①pleased ②pleasing ③pleasant ④please with the student's progress.

❸ Parts of Speech 詞類：（ 20％ ）

　　下面有二十個單字，有些是動詞（ verb ），有些是形容詞（ adjective ）把它們的抽象名詞（ abstract noun ）填寫在試卷內。每題答案只寫一字，並須拼寫正確，否則不予計分。

　　例如： occupy　　　答案是 occupation　　　clever　　　答案是 cleverness

1. destroy	2. exist	3. strong	4. refuse
5. discover	6. wise	7. maintain	8. entertain
9. certain	10. probable	11. repeat	12. complain
13. satisfy	14. conclude	15. persevere	16. divide
17. describe	18. define	19. similar	20. revolve

❹ Vocabulary 字彙：（ 20％ ）

　　下面二十題，每題解釋一個英文單字。每題後所給的一個字母就是那個單字的第一個字母。你應把那個單字完全拼出來寫在試卷內。

　　注意：必須完全正確拼出，不可略去題目上所給的字母，並且詞類（ Parts of Speech ）必須正確，否則不予計分。

例如：one fourth; half of a half.　　　　　　　　　　q……
答案是：quarter

1. something said or done to make somebody laugh.　　j……

2. always the same; not changing.　　　　　　　　　c……

3. a person who loves and loyally supports his own country.　p……

4. one of the six great masses of land on the earth.　c……

5. fearful that a person one loves may love someone else
   better or may prefer someone else.　　　　　　　j……

6. speak very softly and low.　　　　　　　　　　w……

7. whatever is produced by a cause.　　　　　　　　e……

8. give up the wish to punish or get even with, pardon.　f……

9. person who carries a message or goes on an errand.　m……

10. form of energy that can produce light, heat, magnetism,
    and chemical changes.　　　　　　　　　　　　e……

11. praise too much or beyond what is true; praise
    insincerely.　　　　　　　　　　　　　　　　f……

12. a musical performance in which several musicians or
    singers take part.　　　　　　　　　　　　　c……

13. instrument for showing directions, consisting of a needle
    that points to the magnetic north.　　　　　　c……

14. a sharing of another's sorrow or trouble.　　　　s……

15. room or building fitted with apparatus for conducting
    scientific investigations, experiments, tests; etc.　l……

16. doing no wrong; free from sin or wrong.　　　　i……

17. put off till later; delay.　　　　　　　　　　p……

18. an official force for keeping order and arresting people
    who break the law.　　　　　　　　　　　　p……

19. the distinctive clothes worn by the members of a
    group when on duty; by which they may be recognized
    as belonging to that group.   u ⋯⋯

20. person who writes letters, keeps records, etc; for
    a person, company, club, etc.   s ⋯⋯

❺ Comprehension 閱讀能力：（ 20 % ）

　　本題是一則文字，其後列有二十個句子，每句包括四個答案，其中只有一個是
正確的。應於仔細閱讀後，將正確的答案號數寫在試卷內。

　　While touring through Washington with his family, Joe was fascinated by
a helicopter（ 直升機 ）he saw hovering just above a clump of trees. He
wondered whether the pilot was preparing to deliver something needed in
an emergency or whether he was studying a suspicious condition.

　　Joe urged his father to drive toward the clump of trees. As the car
approached it, the family saw signs advertising fresh cherries and they
decided to buy some.

　　By this time the helicopter had disappeared from view. Still reflecting
about its movements, Joe discussed the matter with his father. The latter
suggested that they call it to the attention of the person who was selling
the cherries.

　　At the cherry orchard Joe noticed that many of the trees were colored
a brilliant red with clusters of ripe fruit. The owner of the orchard ex—
tended a small box of sweet cherries to his customers and invited them to
taste the fruit.

　　He explained Joe's observation in this way. "After a shower at this
time of year, a helicopter dried out my 13-acre orchard in about a half
hour. The pilot charged me $87.00 an acre and saved my $15,000 crop
from splitting. Some of my neighbors who call me crazy took a 50 percent
loss last year. I lost only about 10 percent. Now I buy a breeze to protect my crop."

1. Joe was taking a trip through Washington ① by himself ②with
   his father and possibly his mother ③with his father only
   ④with his father and his father's friend.

2. What interested Joe was ① a hovering ② a clump ③ a helicopter ④ a number of trees.

3. What the pilot was actually doing Joe was ① not sure at all ② fairly sure ③ pretty sure ④ absolutely sure.

4. The person who drove the car was ① Joe's mother ② Joe himself ③ Joe's father ④ Joe's father's friend.

5. As the car approached the orchard, the family found ① advertisements selling cherries ② Joe selling cherries ③ the pilot selling cherries ④ everybody selling cherries.

6. They decided to buy some ① signs ② cherries ③ acres ④ trees.

7. The helicopter disappeared ① as Joe was watching it ② as Joe's father was watching it ③ as Joe's mother was watching it ④ without noticing any of them.

8. ① Because ② After ③ Since ④ Before, the helicopter had disappeared from view, Joe was still reflecting about its movements.

9. Joe discussed with his father ① the scenery near the orchard ② the freshness of the cherries ③ the attractiveness of the advertisements ④ the movements of the helicopter.

10. Joe and his father agreed that they would tell the owner of the orchard ① to take notice of the helicopter ② or take care of the helicopter ③ to take hold of the helicopter ④ to stay away from the helicopter.

11. Many of the cherry trees were colored a brilliant red because ① the owner had painted them red ② their fruit is red ③ there had been a red shower ④ the weather was getting frosty.

12. In the cherry orchard ① trees were ripe ② the cherries were ripe ③ the colors were ripe ④ the clusters were ripe.

13. The owner of the orchard offered to his customers ① some cherries ② some small cherries ③ some small boxes ④ many small boxes of cherries.

14. The customers were ① required ② requested ③ reminded ④ implored to taste fruit.

15. Joe told the orchard owner his observation of ① the cherries ② the shower ③ the customers ④ the helicopter.

16. At this time of year as stated in the story, a shower makes the cherries ① taste better ② grow bigger ③ red ④ split.

17. The helicopter was hired ① to reap the cherries ② to make dried cherries ③ to make the wet cherries dry ④ to drive out insects from the orchard.

18. For his service the pilot charged the orchard owner about ① seven dollars altogether ② ninety-one dollars altogether ③ fifteen thousand dollars altogether ④ fifty dollars altogether.

19. Some of the neighbors of the orchard owner called him crazy because ① they didn't believe in hiring a helicopter ② they had lost 50 percent of their crop ③ they envied his prosperity ④ they regretted that they hadn't hired a helicopter.

20. To protect his crop the orchard owner now buys a breeze ① from the woods ② from the customers ③ from the pilot ④ from his neighbors.

48年大學聯考英文試題詳解

❶拼字：

1. ②　2. ④　3. ④　4. ③　5. ④　6. ③　7. ②　8. ③　9. ①　10. ④
11. ③　12. ①　13. ①　14. ②　15. ③　16. ②　17. ②　18. ①　19. ④　20. ③

〔註釋〕

1. exquisite〔 ˊɛkskwɪzɪt, ɪkˊs-〕 adj. 精美的
4. legitimate〔 lɪˊdʒɪtəmɪt 〕 adj. 合法的；正當的
5. corporation〔 ˌkɔrpəˊreʃən 〕 n. 團體；公司
6. interpret〔 ɪnˊtɝprɪt 〕 vt. 解釋；闡明
7. primitive〔 ˊprɪmətɪv 〕 adj. 原始的
13. vacuum〔 ˊvækjʊəm 〕 n. 真空

❷造句法：

1. ③　2. ②　3. ①　4. ①　5. ①　6. ②　7. ②　8. ③　9. ④　10. ②
11. ③　12. ②　13. ④　14. ①　15. ③　16. ④　17. ③　18. ④　19. ③　20. ①

〔解析〕

1. ask ＋人＋ for ＋事物（詳見文法寶典 p.280）

4. 肯定句用 some 表 "一些"，否定句或疑問句則用 any。

5. The man（whom）I saw was happy.

6. 副詞的順序：地方＋狀態＋次數＋時間（詳見文法寶典 p.269）

7. have ＋人＋原形動詞 " 命～，叫～（去做）"（詳見文法寶典 p.305）

8. 「If ＋ S. ＋ should ＋**原形動詞，祈使句**」是表可能性極小的假設法，should 在此作「萬一」解。

14. **have a good time** " 玩得愉快 "

15. get ＋受詞＋過去分詞，表「使役」（詳見文法寶典 p.387）

16. **turn up** " 將（收音機等的音量）開大 "

　① turn on " 打開（燈、收音機等）"

　② turn down " 將（收音機等的音量）轉小 "

　③ turn over " 翻倒 "

❸詞類：

1. destruction　　2. existence　　3. strength　　4. refusal
5. discovery　　6. wisdom　　7. maintenance　　8. entertainment
9. certainty　　10. probability　　11. repetition　　12. complaint
13. satisfaction　　14. conclusion　　15. perseverance　　16. division
17. description　　18. definition　　19. similarity　　20. revolution

❹字彙：

1. joke　　2. constant　　3. patriot　　4. continent　　5. jealous
6. whisper　　7. effect　　8. forgive　　9. messenger　　10. electricity
11. flatter　　12. concert　　13. compass　　14. sympathy　　15. laboratory
16. innocent　　17. postpone　　18. police　　19. uniform　　20. secretary

❺閱讀能力：

1. ②　2. ③　3. ①　4. ③　5. ①　6. ②　7. ④　8. ②　9. ④　10. ①
11. ②　12. ②　13. ①　14. ②　15. ④　16. ④　17. ③　18. ①　19. ①　20. ③

〔註釋〕

tour〔tʊr〕vt., vi. 旅行；遊歷　　fascinate〔'fæsn̩,et〕vt. 使迷惑；使著迷
hover〔'hʌvɚ,'hɑvɚ〕vi. 翱翔；盤旋　　clump〔klʌmp〕n. 草叢；樹叢
pilot〔'paɪlət〕n. 飛機駕駛員　　emergency〔ɪ'mɝdʒənsɪ〕n. 緊急事件
suspicious〔sə'spɪʃəs〕adj. 可疑的　　urge〔ɝdʒ〕vt. 力勸；力請
advertise〔'ædvɚ,taɪz, ,ædvɚ'taɪz〕vt. 登～的廣告
reflect〔rɪ'flɛkt〕vi. 思考　　orchard〔'ɔrtʃɚd〕n. 果園
cluster〔'klʌstɚ〕n. 串；束；叢　　ripe〔raɪp〕adj. 成熟的
extend〔ɪk'stɛnd〕vt. 給與　　*dry out* "使～變乾"
split〔splɪt〕vi. 裂開　　breeze〔briz〕n. 微風

說英文高手
與傳統會話教材有何不同?

1. 我們學了那麼多年的英語會語,為什麼還不會説?

我們所使用的教材不對。傳統實況會話教材,如去郵局、在機場、看醫生等,勉強背下來,哪有機會使用?不使用就會忘記。等到有一天到了郵局,早就忘了你所學的。

2. 「説英文高手」這本書,和傳統的英語會話教材有何不同?

「説英文高手」這本書,以三句爲一組,任何時候都可以説,可以對外國人説,也可以和中國人説,有時可自言自語説。例如:你幾乎天天都可以説:What a beautiful day it is! It's not too hot. It's not too cold. It's just right. 傳統的英語會話教材,都是以兩個人以上的對話爲主,主角又是你,又是別人,當然記不下來。「説英文高手」的主角就是你,先從你天天可説的話開始。把你要説的話用英文表達出來,所以容易記下來。

3. 爲什麼用「説英文高手」這本書,學了馬上就會説?

書中的教材,學起來有趣,一次説三句,不容易忘記。例如:你有很多機會可以對朋友説:Never give up. Never give in. Never say never.

4. 傳統會話教材目標不明確,一句句學,學了後面,忘了前面,一輩子記不起來。「説英文高手」目標明確,先從一次説三句開始,自我訓練以後,能夠隨時説六句以上,例如:你説的話,別人不相信,傳統會話只敎你一句:I'm not kidding. 連這句話你都會忘掉。「説英文高手」敎你一次説很多句:

I mean what I say.
I say what I mean.
I really mean it.

I'm not kidding you.
I'm not joking with you.
I'm telling you the truth.

你唸唸看,背這六句是不是比背一句容易呢?
能夠一次説六句以上英文,你會有無比興奮的
感覺,當説英文變成你的愛好的時候,你的目
標就達成。

全省各大書局均售 ◎ 書180元 / 錄音帶四卷500元

✌「**説英文高手**」爲劉毅老師最新創作,是學習出版公司轟動全國的暢銷新書。
已被多所學校採用爲會話教材。本書適合高中及大學使用,也適合自修。

四十七學年度大學暨獨立學院入學考試
英 文 試 題

❶ Spelling 拼字：（10％）

　　下面有二十個字，每字有四種拼法，其中只有一種拼法是對的。請將對的那個號碼填寫在試卷的空白內。

例如：① fammily　② family　③ famiely　④ farmily　　答案為②

1. ① receipt　② receit　③ reciet　④ recept

2. ① execussion　② excecution　③ excution　④ execution

3. ① squirrell　② spuirrel　③ squirrel　④ squirel

4. ① attitude　② atitude　③ atittude　④ alitude

5. ① expierance　② expireince　③ experience　④ expereince

6. ① oxyjen　② oxygen　③ oxigen　④ oxygene

7. ① typhoon　② taiphoon　③ typhone　④ typhon

8. ① oppotunity　② oportunity　③ opportunity　④ apportunity

9. ① signatur　② signiture　③ signture　④ signature

10. ① embassy　② ambassy　③ embasy　④ ambasy

11. ① duplicate　② doublicate　③ doublecate　④ douplicate

12. ① material　② matterial　③ matteral　④ materal

13. ① fundaion　② foundation　③ foodation　④ fondition

14. ① remembrence　② rememberence　③ rememberance　④ remembrance

15. ① serous　② serious　③ sereous　④ sirious

16. ① agression　② agretion　③ aggression　④ aggrestion

17. ① comittee　② committee　③ committy　④ commitee

18. ① penitrate　② penetrante　③ penetrate　④ pennitrate

19. ① explanition　② expranation　③ explaination　④ explanation

20. ① interrupt　② insterrupt　③ interupt　④ interrupte

❷ Vocabulary 字彙：（ 10 ％ ）

　　下面是單字求解釋，或是從解釋推求單字。每題有四個答案，其中只有一個是對的。請將對的那個號碼填寫在試卷的空白內。

　　例如：boy　①女孩　②男孩　③女人　④男人　　　　答案為②

1. homesick ①在家生病　②家常生的病　③厭家　④想家

2. hospitality ①醫院的管理　②醫道　③待客之道　④護理學

3. ivory ①旅行　②象牙　③幕　④發怒

4. jewel ①猶太教　②猶太的　③珠寶　④液汁

5. virtually ①實際上　②道德的　③誠懇的　④愚笨

6. inconspicuous ①愚笨的　②不顯著的　③不合作的　④不可愛的

7. 纖細的 ① slender　② network　③ impregnable　④ grizzly

8. 忘恩 ① ingratitude　② disfavor　③ forgetfulness　④ hate

9. 暫時的 ① temporary　② timely　③ preliminary　④ punctual

10. 沒收 ① confine　② accept　③ compel　④ confiscate

11. 繡花的 ① flourished　② flowered　③ embroidered　④ knit

12. 休息 ① depose　② doze　③ rest　④ remain

13. 炸彈 ① bomb　② pomp　③ shot　④ pump

14. lack ① good fortune　② a bird　③ a lake　④ want

15. rascal ① a foolish person　② an immoral person　③ a lonely person ④ a poor person

16. rapid ① brave　② sick　③ strong　④ quick

17. kinsman ① a minister　② a relative　③ a soldier　④ a goodhearted person

18. temple ① a palace　② an official building　③ a religious building ④ a tall building

19. consequence ① result ② getting together ③ repetition ④ ability to speak well

20. shallow ① a tree ② not deep ③ pale ④ a bird

❸ Phrases and Idioms 片語與成語：（20％）

下面有二十個問題，每題有四個答案，其中只有一個是正確的，請將正確的那個號碼寫在答案紙上。

例： to get away ①走入　②離開　③到達　④耗費　　　答案爲②

1. I took him at his word ①我相信他的話　②我把他的話用筆記下來 ③我把他的話牢牢記住　④我模仿他的說話

2. a means to an end ①其意義在達到某種目的　②達到某種目的之手段 ③黔驢技窮一想不出別的方法來了　④一個意義一個目的

3. to put up with ①放在一起　②住在　③說謊話　④忍受

4. to catch sight of him ①瞥見他　②捉住他　③想起他　④研究的

5. in every respect ①十分尊敬　②在每一方面　③雖然如此 ④每人的自尊心

6. at his mercy ①由他支配　②由於他的慈悲心　③他抹煞良心 ④與他情商

7. to make a bed ①整理牀褥　②安居樂業　③久病不起　④隨遇而安

8. walk of life ①人生之變遷　②各行職業　③生命力之發旺　④死亡

9. homeward bound ①爲家庭所束縛　②向回家的路上走　③恰中要害 ④歸心如箭

10. It gets on my nerves ① 它使我心煩意亂　②它提高我的警覺 ③它對我神經有益　④它使我高興

11. The meeting is about over ①這個會討論的事情很多　②這個會有很多人參加　③這個會快要散了　④這個會常常舉行

12. 發財　① to get the money ② to develop the resources ③ to make a fortune ④ to roll in wealth

13. 突然　① from sudden ② all of a sudden ③ for a sudden ④ by a sudden

14. 假定它是如此 ① to assume it is so ② to believe it to be so
③ to admit the fact ④ to make it a rule

15. 不妨一試 ① never mind ② to try in every way ③ to take a chance
④ trial and error

16. 不論如何 ① not to ask how ② no matter how ③ without method
④ to have no idea

17. 未來之時 ① time to come ② time not to come ③ time that has
come ④ time that is come

18. 產卵 ① to make eggs ② to grow eggs ③ to lay eggs ④ to develop
eggs

19. 下決心 ① to lay down a decision ② to keep the determination
③ to decide one's mind ④ to make up one's mind

20. 我處之泰然 ① I take it easy ② I take it easily ③ I am absorbed
in thought ④ I am in a good humor

❹ Translation 翻譯：（20％）

下面每一空白，要用一個適當的英文字，才能把中文句意，適當地表達出來。
答案須寫在試卷上，每一空白只准用一個字。

父親是化學家，照父親的意思，他兒子也該幹父親的那一行。
The father was a chemist, and ① was intended that the boy should
② in his father's footsteps.

我那可憐的朋友遭遇到很不幸的事情，他的獨生兒子死了。
My poor friend had the great grief of ③ his ④ son.

根據此等理由，我們應當祝賀他實驗的成功。
On these grounds he ⑤ to be ⑥ on the success of his experiment.

我們養狗，為的是晚上防止盜賊和流浪漢進我們的屋子。
We ⑦ dogs to guard our house at night ⑧ thieves and tramps.

我一想到我可能出什麼樣的亂子，不禁毛骨悚然。
It gives me the cold shivers when I think ⑨ might have become ⑩
me.

我等候了十五分鐘，這在我看來，好像是十五個鐘頭那麼長。

I waited for fifteen ⑪ , and they seemed ⑫ same hours to me.

除了死亡以外，沒有東西可以使這對夫婦分開。

⑬ but ⑭ can part this couple.

二十個國家已經接受邀請，願意出席會議。

Twenty nations have ⑮ ⑯ to attend the Congress.

女人當選爲此一委員會的委員，這是第一次。

For the first ⑰ a woman was ⑱ into the committee.

他有說俏皮話的本領，同時又不傷害別人的感情。

He has the knack of ⑲ witty ⑳ hurting other people's feelings.

❺ Correction 改錯：（20％）

　　下面有二十個劃有底橫線的字，多數是錯的。將它們改正後填入試卷的空白內。每空白只准填一個字。如原來的字並無錯誤，你也要將該字抄入該空白內。如原來的字是不應該有的，則該號碼的空白可以不塡。

A publisher must have the courage to *publishing* ① a good book in the face of a *know* ② financial loss.

The book inspired him *with* ③ an enthusiasm that *take* ④ the form of a letter of admiration to the author.

In 1916 Dr. Hu Shih *break* ⑤ all tradition by *wrote* ⑥ a poem in the spoken language.

His *mean* ⑦ of *rising* ⑧ money was not quite honest. *Asked* ⑨ *if* ⑩ he had any bad habit, she replied that he was a heavy smoker.

He was often called "the Little Tyrant", but few people knew so well *that* ⑪ I did *that* ⑫ much truth there was in that phrase.

I might have saved *me* ⑬ the trouble, if I *have* ⑭ known that the key was all the time in my pocket.

It would *use* ⑮ him twenty minutes to get back to the house, if he walked *fastly* ⑯ . I know you have many ideas, but you need not *to* ⑰ trouble *to* ⑱ remember them now.

The ⑲ police would act on the possibility of there *was* ⑳ foul play.

❻ Comprehension 閱讀能力：（20％）

　　本題是一則文字，其後列有十個問題，每個問題有四個答案，其中只有一個是正確的。應於仔細閱讀後，將正確的答案號碼填在試卷內。

　　Herodotus is the historian of the glorious fight for liberty in which the Greeks conquered the overwhelming power of Persia. They won the victory because they were free men defending their freedom against a tyrant and his army of slaves.

　　Herodotus was born about the time when the Persian Army, under the command of the nephew of King Darius was marching on Athens. The fight must often have been described to him by men who had taken part in it. He explains the strategy clearly. The Athenian formation was the exact reverse of the enemy's who trusted to their center, leaving their wings to inferior troops. The Athenian commander threw his chief strength into the wings. The center was weak so that the Persians easily broke through it and rushed on in pursuit. Then the Athenian wings closed in behind, shutting off the enemy from their ships and cutting them down. The defeat was complete.

　　It was an incredible battle and an incredible victory. How could it happen like that the little band of defenders were victors over the mighty power of Persia ? We do not understand. But Herodotus understood, and so did Greeks. A free democracy resisted a slave-supported tyranny. Mere numbers were powerless against the spirit of free men fighting to defend their freedom. The price was the independence or the enslavement of Greece. The result made it sure that Greeks never would be slaves.

　1.　Did Herodotus see the battle ?
　　　① No, he did not see it.　　　② Yes, he saw it.
　　　③ He was in the navy, so he did not see the actions of the army.
　　　④ He was in the army, so he did not see the actions of the navy.

　2.　What was the principal reason for the defeat of the Persian army?
　　　① The Persian commander was a stupid and cowardly person.
　　　② The Persians did not choose the right place to engage the enemy.
　　　③ The weather was against the Persians.
　　　④ The Persian army were an army of slaves, while those who defeated them were free men.

3. Was Athens safe all through the battle ?
　①Yes, because it was defended by freedom-loving people.
　②Yes, because the Persians were repulsed in the very beginning.
　③No, it might have been taken by the Persians, if the latter had put more strength to the wings.
　④It was taken by the Persians but later it was recovered by the Greeks.

4. How did the Athenians win the battle ?
　①They had a better navy, which was the decisive factor in the battle.
　②They gave ground at first, and then they attacked from behind.
　③They avoided battle at first, but later they surrounded the Persians and cut them down.
　④The Persians hated their king and refused to fight, so the Athenians won the battle easily.

5. Which side had more troops — the Persians or the Greeks ?
　①The Persians.　　　　　　　②The Greeks.
　③Numerically, both sides were about equal.
　④The Greeks were weaker as first, but later were reinforced.

6. Why is the battle called "incredible"?
　①Because everybody thought the Persians had a better chance to win.
　②Because it was very foolish of the Persians to attack the Greeks.
　③Because the Persian king never trusted his army of slaves.
　④Because the Athenian commander had a strategy which nobody thought could bring him victory.

7. Why is the fight called "glorious"?
　①Because it was celebrated by such a great historian as Herodotus.
　②Because it was the most important battle in ancient history.
　③Because the Greeks fought bravely, and their victory meant a victory for a freedom-loving people.
　④Because the battle was a good example of Athenian strategy.

8. What happened immediately after the battle ?

　　① Persia was conquered.

　　② Persia became a democracy like Athens.

　　③ The Persians suffered such a severe defeat that they could not launch another attack.

　　④ The Persians sent their navy to attack the Greeks from the south.

9. What is Herodotus' conviction as a historian ?

　　① He thought Persia was too weak to attack Greece.

　　② He understood the importance of a large army.

　　③ He believed that Athens could never be conquered.

　　④ He did not believe that a battle could be won by "mere numbers" alone.

10. How was the fighting strength of the Persians ?

　　① They were poor soldiers; since they were slaves, they did not like to fight.

　　② Only the troops under the king's nephew were well-equipped and fought bravely.

　　③ The troops in the center were stronger than those in the wings.

　　④ Their wings were stronger than those of the Greeks, but were defeated because their center fell back.

47年大學聯考英文試題詳解

❶ 拼字：

1. ①　2. ④　3. ③　4. ①　5. ③　6. ②　7. ①　8. ③　9. ④　10. ①
11. ①　12. ①　13. ②　14. ④　15. ②　16. ③　17. ②　18. ③　19. ④　20. ①

〔註釋〕

2. execution〔,ɛksɪ'kjuʃən〕*n.* 實現；執行

3. squirrel〔'skwɜ˞əl, skwɜ˞l〕*n.* 松鼠

10. embassy〔'ɛmbəsɪ〕*n.* 大使館

11. duplicate〔'djupləkɪt, -, ket〕*adj.*；*n.* 完全相同的；副本

16. aggression〔ə'grɛʃən〕*n.* 進攻；侵略

18. penetrate〔'pɛnə,tret〕*vt.* 透過；貫穿

❷ 字彙：

1. ④　2. ③　3. ②　4. ③　5. ①　6. ②　7. ①　8. ①　9. ①　10. ④
11. ③　12. ③　13. ①　14. ④　15. ②　16. ④　17. ②　18. ③　19. ①　20. ②

❸ 片語與成語：

1. ①　2. ②　3. ④　4. ①　5. ②　6. ①　7. ①　8. ①　9. ②　10. ①
11. ③　12. ③　13. ②　14. ①　15. ③　16. ②　17. ①　18. ③　19. ④　20. ①

❹ 翻譯：

① it　② follow　③ losing　④ only　⑤ ought　⑥ congratulated　⑦ keep
⑧ against　⑨ what　⑩ of　⑪ minutes　⑫ as 或 so　⑬ Nothing　⑭ death
⑮ accepted　⑯ invitations　⑰ time　⑱ elected　⑲ being　⑳ without

❺ 改錯：

① publish　② known　③ with　④ took　⑤ broke　⑥ writing　⑦ means
⑧ raising　⑨ Asked　⑩ if　⑪ as　⑫ how　⑬ myself　⑭ had　⑮ take
⑯ fast　⑰ ✕　⑱ to　⑲ The　⑳ being

〔解析〕

① *have the courage to* ＋原形動詞 "有勇氣～"

② known "已知的"　　　③ with ～ "懷著～；具有～"

④ 前有過去式 inspired，故用 took。　⑤ in 1916 為過去時間，故用簡單過去式。

⑥ by ＋動名詞 表示方式或方法。　⑦ means "方法；手段"

⑧ *raise money* "籌款"　　　⑪ *so ～ as* … "像…一樣～"

⑫ *how much* "多少"

⑮ It takes ＋人＋時間 "花費某人多少時間"（詳見文法寶典 p. 299）

⑯ fast 形容詞和副詞同字。　⑰ need 為助動詞，之後須接原形動詞。

⑳ of 後接名詞作用的字詞，故在此須接一名詞片語。there be～ 的名詞形式為 there being ～。

❻閱讀能力：

1. ①　2. ④　3. ③　4. ②　5. ①　6. ①　7. ③　8. ③　9. ④　10. ③

〔註釋〕

Herodotus〔hə'rɑdətəs〕*n.* 希羅多德（希臘的歷史學家）

glorious〔'glorɪəs, 'glɔr-〕*adj.* 光榮的；壯麗的

conquer〔'kɔŋkɚ〕*vt., vi.* 征服；擊敗

overwhelming〔,ovɚ'hwɛlmɪŋ〕*adj.* 壓倒性的；不可抵抗的

defend ～ against ～ "保衞～抵抗～"

under（*the*）*command of ～* "在～的指揮下"

march〔mɑrtʃ〕*vt., vi.* 行進；進軍

take part in "參加；貢獻"

strategy〔'strætədʒɪ〕*n.* 兵法；戰略

formation〔fɔr'meʃən〕*n.* 組成；成立

reverse〔rɪ'vɝs〕*n.* 顛倒；相反

inferior〔ɪn'fɪrɪɚ〕*adj.* 下方的；劣等的

wing〔wɪŋ〕*n.* 翼；（軍隊之）翼

throw A into ～ "使A投身於～"

break through "突破；克服"

rush〔rʌʃ〕*vt., vi.* 突擊；匆促行事

pursuit〔pɚ'sut, -'sjut〕*n.* 追趕；追擊

shut off "切斷；隔絕"

incredible〔ɪn'krɛdəbḷ〕*adj.* 不可信的

enslavement〔ɪn'slevmənt〕*n.* 奴役；束縛

四十六學年度大學暨獨立學院入學考試
英　文　試　題

❶ Accentuation：標重音（10％）

　　下面有十個字，音節均已分開，每音節以號碼表明，請指出各字的重音所在，將標的重音節的號碼填寫在試卷的空白內。

〔例如〕

$\frac{\text{I-}}{1}\frac{\text{tal-}}{2}\frac{\text{ian}}{3}$　一字重音在第二音節，應將「2」字填寫在試卷的空白內。

(1) $\frac{\text{ge-}}{1}\frac{\text{og-}}{2}\frac{\text{ra-}}{3}\frac{\text{phy}}{4}$

(2) $\frac{\text{ad-}}{1}\frac{\text{jec-}}{2}\frac{\text{tive}}{3}$

(3) $\frac{\text{ex-}}{1}\frac{\text{cel-}}{2}\frac{\text{lent}}{3}$

(4) $\frac{\text{ter-}}{1}\frac{\text{ri-}}{2}\frac{\text{to-}}{3}\frac{\text{ry}}{4}$

(5) $\frac{\text{pi-}}{1}\frac{\text{an-}}{2}\frac{\text{o}}{3}$

(6) $\frac{\text{pho-}}{1}\frac{\text{to-}}{2}\frac{\text{graph}}{3}$

(7) $\frac{\text{am-}}{1}\frac{\text{bas-}}{2}\frac{\text{sa-}}{3}\frac{\text{dor}}{4}$

(8) $\frac{\text{or-}}{1}\frac{\text{i-}}{2}\frac{\text{gin}}{3}$

(9) $\frac{\text{an-}}{1}\frac{\text{ni-}}{2}\frac{\text{ver-}}{3}\frac{\text{sa-}}{4}\frac{\text{ry}}{5}$

(10) $\frac{\text{Lin-}}{1}\frac{\text{coln}}{2}$

❷ Translation：翻譯（10％）

　　下面每一空白要用一個適當的英文字，才能把中文句意適當地表達出來，所有的答案均須寫在試卷上。每一空白只准用一個字。

He cannot bear __(1)__ laughed __(2)__ .
他不能忍受被人嘲笑。

The difficulty lies __(3)__ the __(4)__ that we have no money.
困難在我們沒有錢。

He __(5)__ sooner die __(6)__ do this.
他寧死也不願做這事。

If a man was great while living, he becomes ten fold __(7)__ when __(8)__ .
假如一個人活着的時候是偉大的，則他死後更加十倍偉大。

It does not __(9)__ whether there is only coffee or tea. __(10)__ will do.
只有咖啡或只有茶都沒有關係隨便那一樣都行。

❸Correction：改錯（20％）

下面二十個劃有橫線的字，有的有錯，有的沒錯，將它們改正後填入試卷空白內
，每空白只准填一個字。如原來的字並無錯課，你也要將該字抄入該空白內。

1. You and me __(1)__ divided it between __(2)__ us.

2. The earthquake and fire laid __(3)__ in ruin __(4)__ the nation's capital
   and its most important seaport.

3. This is the most unusual book we had __(5)__ read for __(6)__ months.

4. Nations are not to be judges __(7)__ by their size any more than
   individual __(8)__ .

5. Even in Spanish __(9)__ the study of English became a recognized
   necessary. __(10)__

6. The qualities he has revealed have established his position as one
   of the greatest British Minister __(11)__ who has __(12)__ ever held office

7. I will do as I please for __(13)__ all your oppose __(14)__ .

8. We glorify patriotism because the patriotism __(15)__ thinks first of
   his country and latter __(16)__ of himself.

9. As a people __(17)__ the Chinese cling strong __(18)__ to tradition.

10. You would __(19)__ brush your teeth during __(20)__ going to bed.

❹Explanation：解釋：（30％）

下面每條有四個解釋，其中只有一個是正確的，將標記這一正確解釋的號碼，
填入試卷內。

1. well off ①好好地離開 ②一路順風 ③富裕 ④死裏逃生。

2. 結束一場辯論 ① to close a debate ②to stop a quarrel
   ③ to stop a mouth ④ to silence an argument.

3. 緊張 ① tent ② intent ③ tense ④ intend.

4. He deserted his wife ①他對太太冷淡 ②他溺愛他的太太
   ③他遺棄他的太太 ④他暗殺他的太太。

5. 維持家庭生計　① to support one's family　② to bring up one's family
   ③ to breed one's family　④ to look after one's family.

6. 半小時　① half hour　② half an hour　③ half of hour　④ half the hour.

7. rely　① to tell a lie　② to take and carry farther　③ to lie down
   again　④ to depend.

8. by no means　① 沒有意義　② 沒有辦法　③ 決不　④ 並不下賤。

9. 衣服　① cloth　② clother　③ cloths　④ clothes.

10. sample　① 簡單　② 樸素　③ 例子　④ 樣品。

11. 在耶穌聖誕節的早晨　① at Christmas morning　② in Christmas morning
    ③ on Christmas morning　④ at the morning of Christmas.

12. 火車乘客　① train passengers　② railway passengers　③ locomotive
    passengers　④ fire-engine passengers.

13. 孩子們遊戲的鬧聲　① the sound of children at play　② the noise of
    children at play　③ the voice of children at play　④ the echo of
    children at play.

14. out of date　① 新出的　② 日期不詳　③ 不守信用的　④ 陳舊的。

15. annual　① 取消　② 佈告　③ 一年一度的　④ 環狀的。

16. 數學：① mathemetics　② mathmatic　③ mathematics　④ mathemetic.

17. 理髮店　① barbar　② parlour　③ parlor　④ barber's

18. 手製的　① made by hand　② made with hand　③ made with the hand
    ④ made by the hand.

19. 他像他父親　① He looks alike his father　② he looks after his father
    ③ he takes after his father　④ he takes resemblance of his father.

20. 無意中遇見　① to come across　② to see in an extraordinary way
    ③ to come without idea　④ to look unexpectedly.

21. He is sick of doing nothing：① 他因太懶而生病　② 他因生病而一事不做
    ③ 他的大毛病是一點事也不肯做　④ 他因一事不做而厭煩。

22. to put off until tomorrow：① 延至明天　② 一直到明天才停　③ 一直放
    到明天　④ 暫時丟開，到明天再說。

23. He's leaving for where he was：①他就要到他以前的所在地去　②他離開他以前的什麼地方　③他已經離開此地到從前的地方去了　④他已經離開他的舊地。

24. She did as he told her：①她做像他告訴她　②當他告訴她的時候她就做　③他要告訴她的時候她已做了　④她遵照他的吩咐而行事。

25. I cannot tell A from B：①我不能把B的話告訴A　②我辨不出誰是A誰是B　③A是B地的人，但是我不能把這點事實告訴人　④由於B的關係，我不能告訴A。

26. appeal：①一片梨　②大聲一響　③上訴一次　④一片切下的果皮。

27. sock：①短襪　②浸入水　③布袋　④足球。

28. He is difficult to please：①他不輕易喜歡　②他這人是很難討好的　③他是個不容易請得來的人　④他很困難因而想取樂解悶。

29. smitten：① struck ② young cats ③ threw out from the mouth ④ the flesh of young sheep as food.

30. pretend：① make believe ② tell a lie ③ misunderstand ④ false.

❺ Comprehension：閱讀能力（ 30 % ）

本題是一段文字，其後列有十五個問題，每個問題，有四個答案，其中祇有一個是正確的。應於仔細閱讀後，將正確的答案號碼填在試卷內。

It was evening and early summer, and after her supper Mrs. Wang had climbed the dike steps, as she did every day, to see how high the river had risen. She knew what the river would do. And one by one the villagers had followed her up the dike, and now they stood staring down at the malicious yellow water, curling along like a lot of snakes, and biting at the high dike banks.

She gazed at the river a moment. That river — it was full of good and evil together. It would water the fields when it was curbed and checked, but then if an inch were allowed it, it would crash through like a roaring dragon. That was how her husband had been swept away — careless, he was, about his bit of the dike. He was always going to mend it, always going to pile more earth on top of it, and then in a night the river rose and broke through. He had run out of the house, and she had climbed on the roof with the child and had saved herself and it while he was drowned. Well, they had pushed the river back again behind its dikes, and it had stayed there this time. Every day she herself walked up and down the length of the dike for which the village was responsible and examined it. The men laughed and said, "If anything is wrong with the dikes, Granny will tell us."

It had never occurred to any of them to move the village away from the river. The Wangs had lived there for generations, and some had always escaped the floods and had fought the river more fiercely than ever afterward.

1. What was the dike made of ?
    ① Water.　② Earth.　③ Metal.　④ Wood.

2. Why is the water called malicious ?
    ① Because it was full of snakes.　② Because it was now rising.
    ③ Because it could do much harm to the villagers
    ④ Because so many people were staring down it.

3. When did the river become beneficial to the people ?
    ① When it was curbed and checked.
    ② When all the snakes in it were killed.
    ③ When the water was rising.
    ④ When Mrs. Wang was taking a walk on its banks.

4. What is the meaning of the river's "biting at the high dike banks" ?
    ① The river, of course, had no teeth, but the snakes could make holes in the dike.　② The roaring dragon must have a very large mouth.
    ③ The water's pressure on the dike was tremendous.
    ④ The villagers always pushed the river back behind its dikes.

5. "She knew what the river would do." What did she really know then ?
    ① She knew that the river would water the fields.
    ② She knew that the river was something beautiful to look at.
    ③ She knew that the river would bring her husband back to her.
    ④ She knew that the river would break through again if the villagers were careless.

6. How was the husband when Mrs. Wang was looking at the river ?
    ① He was following her.　② He was piling earth on top of the dike.
    ③ He was dead.　④ He was laughing.

7. When did she climb on the roof ?
   ① When she had a quarrel with her husband.
   ② In the night when the river rose and broke through.
   ③ When she would like to see the river more clearly.
   ④ Every day after her supper she would climb on the roof.

8. How was her child ?
   ① Her child was dead.
   ② Her child was nearly killed the night when the river rose and broke through.
   ③ She always hid her child away from her husband.
   ④ Her child was piling earth on top of the dike.

9. Did the villagers respect her ?
   ① No, they did not, for wherever she went they would follow her and laugh at her.
   ② Yes, they did, for she was an experienced old woman.
   ③ They had respected her once, but they now respected her no more since her husband was dead.
   ④ They never respected her as much as they respected her husband.

10. What was on the villagers' minds when they were following Mrs. Wang up the dike ?
    ① They would follow her because she was a beautiful woman.
    ② They were curious to know what she was doing up there.
    ③ They would help her and bring her husband back to her.
    ④ They would listen to her opinion as to how high the water would rise.

11. What was the most important thing in the life of the Wangs ?
    ① To run away whenever there was a flood.
    ② To keep the river in its course.
    ③ To take a walk now and then and enjoy themselves.
    ④ To leave the village and move to the city.

12. What kind of people were the Wangs ?
    ① Lazy.   ② Cruel.
    ③ Hard-working .   ④ Superstitious.

13. Would the villagers be safe from the flood if they were all careful and kept a vigilant watch over the dike ?
　① Yes, they would.
　② No, not necessarily safe, for the river was very long and it might break through at any point above or below the village.
　③ The villagers believed that they were safe so long as the gods were not angry.
　④ The villagers did not care much about their own safety.

14. Would many people be killed if there was a flood ?
　① Few people would be killed.
　② Almost all the villagers would be killed.
　③ Only women and children would be killed.
　④ Those who had not fled to places of safety would be killed.

15. Why did the Wangs not move the village away from the river ?
　① Because they loved the river.
　② Because none had ever made such a suggestion to them.
　③ Because the government forbade it.
　④ Because their ancestors forbade it.

46年大學聯考英文試題詳解

❶ 標重音：

(1) 2　(2) 1　(3) 1　(4) 1　(5) 2　(6) 1　(7) 2　(8) 1　(9) 3　(10) 1

〔註釋〕

(2) adjective〔'ædʒɪktɪv〕n.〔文法〕形容詞

(4) territory〔'tɛrə,torɪ, -,torɪ〕n. 土地；領土

(7) ambassador〔æm'bæsədə〕n. 大使

(8) origin〔'ɔrədʒɪn, 'ɑr-〕n. 起源

(9) anniversary〔,ænə'vɝsərɪ〕n. 周年；周年紀念

❷ 翻譯：

(1) being　(2) at　(3) in　(4) fact　(5) would　(6) than　(7) greater
(8) dead　(9) matter　(10) Either

❸ 改錯：

(1) I　(2) between　(3) laid　(4) ruins　(5) have　(6) in　(7) judged
(8) individuals　(9) Spain　(10) necessity　(11) Ministers　(12) have
(13) for　(14) opposition　(15) patriot　(16) last　(17) people
(18) strongly　(19) should　(20) before

〔解析〕

(3)(4) *lay in ruins* "使成廢墟"

(5) 依句意「這是我們幾個月以來讀過的最不尋常的一本書」，和動詞 is 來判斷，
　　要用現在完成式。

(9) Spain〔spen〕n. 西班牙
　　Spanish〔'spænɪʃ〕n., adj. 西班牙語（的）；西班牙人（的）

(11) one of ＋複數名詞

(12) who 的先行詞 Ministers 是複數，故用複數動詞 have。

(13)(14) *for all* "儘管～" opposition〔,ɑpə'zɪʃən〕n. 反對

(15) patriot〔'petrɪət〕n. 愛國者
　　patriotism〔'petrɪətɪzəm〕n. 愛國心；愛國精神

❹解釋：

1. ③　2. ①　3. ③　4. ③　5. ①　6. ②　7. ④　8. ③　9. ④　10. ④

11. ③　12. ②　13. ②　14. ④　15. ③　16. ③　17. ④　18. ①　19. ③　20. ①

21. ④　22. ①　23. ①　24. ④　25. ②　26. ③　27. ①　28. ②　29. ①　30. ①

❺閱讀測驗：

1. ②　2. ③　3. ①　4. ③　5. ④　6. ③　7. ②　8. ②　9. ②　10. ④

11. ②　12. ③　13. ①　14. ②　15. ②

〔註釋〕

dike〔daɪk〕n. 堤防；溝渠　　　stare〔stɛr〕vi. 凝視

malicious〔məˈlɪʃəs〕adj. 惡意的　　　curl〔kɝl〕vt., vi. 捲曲

gaze at "凝視"　　　curb〔kɝb〕vt. 抑制

roaring〔ˈrorɪŋ〕adj. 咆哮的；怒號的

pile〔paɪl〕vt., vi. 堆積

drown〔draʊn〕vi. 溺水；淹死（作此義解時，常用被動）

granny〔ˈgrænɪ〕n.〔俗〕奶奶；老太婆

generation〔ˌdʒɛnəˈreʃən〕n.（家族中的）一代；一世

vigilant〔ˈvɪdʒələnt〕adj. 警戒的；注意的

心得筆記欄

四十五學年度大學暨獨立學院入學考試
英 文 試 題

❶ Explanation 解釋：

下面每條有四個解釋，其中只有一個是對的。將標記這一個解釋的數字填入試卷
为。

1. 忠告：(1) consul　(2) council　(3) console　(4) counsel

2. 良心：(1) consciousness　(2) conscience　(3) conscious　(4) conscientious

3. 雕像：(1) stature　(2) status　(3) statue　(4) statute

4. 去請醫生來：(1) to ask a doctor　(2) to please a doctor　(3) to take a doctor　(4) to fetch a doctor

5. 似乎有些困難：(1) Seemingly there has some difficulty　(2) There seems to have some difficulty　(3) There seems to be some difficulty　(4) There are some seeming difficulties

6. confine：(1)相信　(2)監禁　(3)確證　(4)使符合

7. invert：(1)惰性　(2)發明　(3)反對　(4)顛倒

8. mortal：(1)有道德的　(2)不免一死的　(3)模範的　(4)三合土的

9. in the long run：(1)長跑　(2)正在長跑　(3)畢竟　(4)最後目的

10. to account for：(1)解釋　(2)計算　(3)賬目　(4)表示

11. stop to smoke：(1)不吸煙　(2)停下來吸煙　(3)戒煙　(4)禁止吸煙

12. You cannot study too hard：(1)你儘管用功好了　(2)你不能太用功　(3)你不宜太用功　(4)你不是不能用功的

13. leave out：(1) go out　(2) omit　(3) stop　(4) go away

14. reputation：(1) fame　(2) well-known　(3) degree　(4) title

15. looked for：(1) found　(2) sought　(3) got　(4) saw

16. 野蠻的舉動：(1) a savage act　(2) a savageous act　(3) a savagely act　(4) a savageously act

17. 較劣下的：(1) more bad (2) worst (3) inferior (4) degrading

18. senior：(1)年較長的 (2)西班牙人稱先生 (3)參議員 (4)有罪的人

19. most children：(1)最多的孩子 (2)最高級的孩子 (3)大多數的孩子 (4)數目不小的一群孩子

20. strove：(1) a fireplace (2) hunger (3) a strong stick (4) struggled

❷ Choice of words 選字：

（a, at, by, in, of, on, the, to, with）

　　從上面括弧中選擇一個適當的字，使用在下面句子的空白內。答案必須寫在試卷上。

注意：(1)同一個字可以使用一次以上。

　　　(2)每一空白只准填一個字。

　　　(3)有些空白不須填寫，但必須在空白內作（×）的記號。

例：He goes ___①___ school every ___②___ day.　　答案：① to ② ×

1. I can't see ①　what respect this has any bearing ②　the problem we are discussing.

2. He is the sort of ③　man ④　whom it is no use arguing.

3. He will stay ⑤　his friend's until he finds ⑥　house of his own.

4. What ⑦　fun we had when we were at ⑧　seaside.

5. Did he inform the post office ⑨　the change of his address?

6. Tom dropped ⑩　to see us ⑪　his way ⑫　home from ⑬　theater.

7. There is ⑭　dirt on his clothes and ⑮　dirty mark on his cheek

8. Almost all the houses in Taiwan are lit ⑯　electricity.

9. I am not sure ⑰　his success, but I am sure ⑱　that he will do his best.

10. He will end up ⑲　prison, if he doesn't change his ways.

11. He usually put the children ⑳　bed at about eight o'clock in the evening.

❸Definition 定義：

下面有六條定義。寫出每條定義所指的字，填在試卷上。每答案只准填一個字。

例：house or place where one was born.　　　　答案：home

1. an area of land without trees or water, often covered with sand.

2. move along by turning over and over.

3. a very slender tool, sharp at one end, and with a hole or eye to pass a thread through, used in sewing.

4. amount paid on anything sent by mail.

5. hard growth, usually curved and pointed, on the heads of cattle, sheep, goats, and some other animals.

6. Plane area enclosed within three straight lines.

❹Correction 改錯：

下面十個劃有底橫線的字，有的有錯，有的無錯。將它們改正後填入試卷的空白內。每空白只准填一個字。假如原來的字並無錯誤，你也要將該字抄寫填入該空白內。

例：He goes to (1) school every days (2).

答案：(1) to　(2) day

1. He told me that he has (1)　been to the station to see his friend of (2).

2. A gram is one thousands (3)　of a kilogram.

3. Give this to whoever (4)　you think can do the work well.

4. The commitee (5)　has possibly (6)　decided to sieze (7)　the first opportunity of saling (8)　all the steal (9)　and gold to raise the releif (10)　fund.

Substitution 換字：

下面每一空白，要用一個適當的字，才能使每組中兩句的意義相同。所有的答案均寫在試卷上。每一空白只准填一個字。

例：I do not fear the dog.＝ I (1) (2) afraid of the dog.

答案：(1) am　(2) not

1. It is not necessary for him to bring an umbrella. ＝ He (1) not bring an umbrella.

2. It pays to study that language. = That language is _____ studying.

3. Will you please tell me its width ? = Do you _(3)_ telling me how _(4)_ _(5)_ _(6)_ ?

4. He likes white clothes. = He is _(7)_ of _(8)_ himself _(9)_ white.

5. She was quite alone. = She was all _(10)_ herself.

❻ Translation 翻譯：

下面每一空白，要用一個適當的英文字，才能把中文句意，適當地表達出來，所有的答案均須寫在試卷上。每一空白只准用一個字。

例：這是一本書 This _(1)_ a _(2)_ . 答案：(1) is (2) book

1. 虎不能游泳。

_(1)_ cannot swim.

2. 這決不是女子的手帕。一定是個男子的。

This _(2)_ not be a woman's _(3)_ . It _(4)_ be a _(5)_ .

3. 恐怕他不能準時趕到這裏吧。

I am afraid he won't _(6)_ _(7)_ to get here on time.

4. 鈴一響他就衝下樓來。

No _(8)_ had the bell rung _(9)_ he rushed downstairs.

5. 我們正要離家的時候，天下起雨來了。

Just as we _(10)_ _(11)_ the house, it began to rain.

6. 你不贊成把你頭髮剪得如此短嗎？

Do you object to _(12)_ your hair _(13)_ so short ?

7. 你步行到博物館要多少時間？

How _(14)_ does it _(15)_ you to get to the museum on _(16)_ ?

8. 假如他昨天買蛋，買了五十個，而不是買了兩打的話，就不會有錢剩下買牛了。

_(17)_ he bought fifty eggs _(18)_ of two _(19)_ yesterday there would have _(20)_ no money left for the beef.

❼ Comprehension 閱讀能力：

本題是一段文字，其後列有二十五個問題，每個問題有四個答案，其中祇有一個是正確的。考生應於仔細閱讀後，將正確答案號碼填在試卷內。

He was what we would call a Bohemian; that is, he was a careless dresser, scorned regular employment, had no permanent address and was vague about money. But Franz Schubert possessed two attributes that set him apart from other Bohemians: he was a genius, and he had work to do. There was music to be written, and if he had to starve in the process of writing it, he did not mind it. Thanks to the good offices of a group of friends who were devoted to him and believed in his genius, he escaped actual starvation; but his existence was a precarious one. He "boarded around" so to speak, staying with any friend who could give him a place to write and a place to sleep. Legend has it that when he was put up for the night he frequently went to bed wearing his spectacles so that he could set to work immediately should an idea for a melody awaken him. That melody, when it arrived, was more than likely to be the setting for a song poem.

A.　Where was Schubert born ?
  (1) He was born in a place called Bohemia.
  (2) He never told anybody where he was born.
  (3) Nobody knows where he was born.
  (4) Nothing is said here about where he was born.

B.　How was he dressed ?
  (1) He did not care much how he was dressed.
  (2) He liked fine clothes, but he could not afford them.
  (3) He was smartly dressed.
  (4) He hated fine clothes.

C.　What was his work ?
  (1) He worked in an office.
  (2) He composed music.
  (3) He was a genius, so he did not have to work.
  (4) His friends supported him, so he did not have to work.

D.　How did his friends help him ?
  (1) They got him a job in an office.
  (2) They did not help him, because they believed a man of genius needed no help.
  (3) They let him sleep in their house.
  (4) They simply prayed for him.

E. How rich was Schubert ?
   (1) He possessed a large fortune.
   (2) He had been a rich man, but he gave all his money away to his friends.
   (3) The office where he worked gave him a good pay.
   (4) He was never rich.

F. How did he sleep according to popular belief ?
   (1) He slept very badly because he often had nothing to eat before he went to bed.
   (2) He slept badly because even in his sleep he would be thinking about his music.
   (3) He slept well always when his friend gave him a place to sleep.
   (4) He slept well only in the daytime, for at night he must work.

G. How was his eyesight ?
   (1) He had poor eyesight.   (2) He had fine eyesight.
   (3) He could see in the daytime, but at night he was almost blind.
   (4) He was a blind man.

H. From what did he suffer most in his life ?
   (1) His heartless friends.   (2) His bad sleep.
   (3) His hard work.   (4) His poverty.

I. Where did he live ?
   (1) In a cottage, for he was poor.
   (2) Most time he lived aboard a ship.
   (3) He changed his dwelling place very often.
   (4) He lived in a foreign country, for he could not stay in his own country.

J. How did he die ?
   (1) Nothing is said here about his death.
   (2) He died of starvation.
   (3) Nobody knows how he died.
   (4) He died in his sleep.

K. What did his friends think of him ?

   (1) He was born with some special talent.

   (2) He owed his achievement to sheer hard work.

   (3) He composed music in a scientific manner.

   (4) He was a model scholar.

L. What are Bohemians like as a rule ?

   (1) They wear fashionable clothes.

   (2) They are good office workers.

   (3) They like to live in the same house for a long time.

   (4) They are happy-go-lucky with their money.

45年大學聯考英文試題詳解

❶解釋：

1. (4)　2. (2)　3. (3)　4. (4)　5. (3)　6. (2)　7. (4)　8. (2)　9. (3)　10. (1)

11. (2)　12. (1)　13. (2)　14. (1)　15. (2)　16. (1)　17. (3)　18. (1)　19. (3)　20. (4)

❷選字：

① in　② on　③ ×　④ with　⑤ at　⑥ a　⑦ ×　⑧ the　⑨ of　⑩ in或by

⑪ on　⑫ ×　⑬ the　⑭ ×　⑮ a　⑯ by　⑰ of　⑱ ×　⑲ in　⑳ to

〔解析〕

① in～respect "在～方面"　② have bearing on "與～有關"

③ the sort of 之後的單數普通名詞不加冠詞。　④ argue with *sb.* "與某人爭論"

⑦ *have fun* "開心；玩耍"　⑧ 指某特定的海邊，故要加 the。

⑨ *inform sb. of sth.* "通知某人某事"　⑩ *drop in* "偶然來訪"

⑪⑫ on *one's* way home "回家的路上"（home 在此是副詞，故其前不加冠詞）

⑬ 指建築物本身或場所時，爲普通名詞，要加冠詞。

⑭ dirt（污垢，污物）爲不可數名詞，不加冠詞。

⑯ by 在此表示 "用～；靠～"　⑰ *be sure of*～ "確定～"

⑱ that 引導的名詞子句，不可作介詞 of 的受詞，故省略 of。

⑲ *in prison* "在獄中"　⑳ *put〔or get〕*A *to bed* "安置(小孩等)睡覺"

❸定義：

1. desert〔'dɛzət〕*n.* 沙漠　2. roll〔rol〕*vt.*,*vi.* 滾動　3. needle〔'nidḷ〕*n.* 針

4. postage〔'postɪdʒ〕*n.* 郵資　5. horn〔hɔrn〕*n.* 牛、羊頭上的角

6. triangle〔'traɪ,æŋgḷ〕*n.* 三角形

❹改錯：

(1) *has* → had（因 told 爲過去式）　(2) *of* → off（*see sb. off* "給某人送行"）

(3) *thousands* → thousandth（one thousandth "千分之一"）　(4) 無誤

(5) *commitee* → committee　(6) *possibly* → probably〔probably "很可能(most
likely)"的發生機率遠較 possibly "也許(perhaps)"爲高，根據句意，
用 probably 較合理。〕　(7) *sieze* → seize　(8) *saling* → selling

(9) *steal* → steel（鋼）　⑽ *releif* → relief（a relief fund "救濟基金"

❺換字：

(1) need　(2) worth　(3) mind　(4) wide　(5) it　(6) is　(7) fond

(8) dressing (clothing)　(9) in　　(10) by

❻翻譯：

(1) Tigers　(2) can　(3) handkerchief　(4) must　(5) man's　(6) be　(7) able

(8) sooner　(9) than　(10) were　　(11) leaving　(12) having　(13) cut　(14) long

(15) take　(16) foot　(17) Had　　(18) instead　(19) dozen　(20) been

❼閱讀能力：

A(4)　B(1)　C(2)　D(3)　E(4)　F(2)　G(1)　H(4)　I(3)　J(1)　K(1)　L(4)

〔註釋〕

Bohemian〔boˈhimiən,-mjən〕 *n.* 狂放者；玩世不恭者

dresser〔ˈdrɛsə〕 *n.* 穿衣者　　a careless dresser "衣著隨便的人"

scorn〔skɔrn〕 *vt.;n.* 輕蔑；瞧不起

vague〔veg〕 *adj.* 模糊的；茫然的

attribute〔ˈætrə,bjut〕 *n.* 性質；本性

set apart from～ "使與～有區別"

offices〔ˈɔfɪsɪz, ˈɑfɪsɪz〕 *n.* 幫助；服務

precarious〔prɪˈkɛrɪəs〕 *adj.* 不安定的；危險的

board〔bord,bɔrd〕 *vt.* 寄膳；寄宿

Legend *has it* (＝says) that ～ "傳說～"

legend〔ˈlɛdʒənd〕 *n.* 傳說；傳奇　　*put up* "留宿"

spectacles〔ˈspɛktəkḷz〕 *n.* 眼鏡

… *should* an idea for a melody awaken him.

＝… *if* an idea for a melody *should* awaken him.

　（假設語氣中，if的省略，詳見文法寶典 p.365）

setting〔ˈsɛtɪŋ〕 *n.* 〔音樂〕作曲；譜曲

dwelling〔ˈdwɛlɪŋ〕 *n.* 住宅；寓所

happy-go-lucky〔ˈhæpɪ,goˈlʌkɪ〕 *adj.* 隨遇而安的

心得筆記欄............

★ 電腦統計歷屆聯考單字 ★

abandon (63,75,85年)

ability (47,51,52,70,81,84,85,87,89年)

aboard (45年)

abolish (49年)

abroad (59,60,62,66年)

abruptly (90年)

absolutely (48,58,64年)

absorb (47,66,69,73年)

abuse (66,83,86年)

academic (53,70,72年)

academically (72年)

academy (80年)

accent (49,86年)

accept (47,52,54,62,66,67,68,69,71,83,85年)

acceptable (80,88,89年)

access (68年)

accessible (59,89年)

accident (50,52,65,66,67,68,71,74,80年)

accidentally (82,85年)

accommodate (67,89年)

accompany (80年)

accomplish (53,60,63,67年)

accomplishment (71,72年)

accord (61年)

according (78,82,83,84,88,89,90年)

accordingly (67,74,77年)

account (77,79,82年)

accumulate (86年)

accuracy (64,71年)

accurate (67,70,85年)

accurately (63,71年)

accuse (61,67,85年)

accustom (83年)

accustomed (53年)

ache (76,83年)

achieve (50,65,67,68,69,74,85,88.90年)

achievement (70,71,73,87年)

achiever (73年)

acknowledge (55,68,90年)

acknowledgment (68年)

acquaint (49,55,67,84年)

acquaintance (61,66,68年)

acquire (54,60,86年)

acre (48,79,87年)

across (49,59,77,79,82,86,90年)

act (45,61,63,64,66,71,81,89年)

action (49,68,72,81,85,86,90年)

active (52,76,81年)

activity (64,76,80年)

actor (51,90年)

actual (45年)

actually (48,55,61,64,68,72,74,75,76,78,85,89,90年)

adapt (81,89年)

adaptation (81年)

add (51,56,61,65,79,81,85,89年)

addictive (89年)

addition (73,75,89,90年)

additionally (80年)

address (56,61,62,71,73,78年)

addressee (88年)

adequate (68,69,87年)

adjective (46年)

adjoining (64年)

adjust (78,89年)

adjustment (64年)

administration (67,83年)

admirable (84,89年)

admiral (72年)

admiration (47,74年)

admire (68,79,87,88年)

admission (73,81,87年)

admit (47,64,66,70,81年)

adolescent (72年)

adopt (49,75,81年)

adoration (64年)

adult (64,69,72,76,80,81,88年)

adulthood (79年)

advance (57,67,80,88年)

advanced (63,64,66,90年)

advancement (68年)

advantage (61年)

adventure (50,65,85年)

adverb (69年)

advertise (48,50年)

advertisement (48,66,76,81,82年)

advertiser (66年)

advertising (66,76年)

advice (49,57,83,84,86,90年)

advise (52,55,61,64,67,74年)

advisory (51年)

advocate (76年)

aeronautical (64年)

affair (50,51,65,67,87年)

affect (63,68,70,74,76年)

affection (64,84年)

affirm (76年)

affirmation (88年)

afford (45,49,54,66,68,76,87,90年)

affront (76年)

afraid (77,78,84年)

Africa (80,82,90年)

African (76,82年)

afterthought (65年)

afterward(s) (46,51,64,90年)

against (86,88,90年)

aged (58,69年)

agency (64,76年)

aggression (47年)

aggressive (72,73,79年)

agree (78,79年)

agreeable (72年)

agreement (51,53,68,86年)

agricultural (62,75,90年)

agriculture (62,87年)

ahead (86年)

aid (53,61,67,82年)

aim (56,65,83,84年)

air-conditioned (64年)

aircraft (51年)

airline (51,66,89年)

airplane (53年)

airport (52,62,66,81年)

aisle (63,84年)

alarm (68,90年)

alcohol (48,80年)

algebra (52,53年)

alien (66年)

alike (48,56,57,62年)

alive (50,60,87,89,90年)

allergic (83年)

alleyways (65年)

alliance (50年)

allow (46,51,60,61,64,76,78,87,88,90年)

ally (49年)

almost (81,89年)

alone (45,47,56,63,64,68,77,81,84,87,88,89年)

along (59,74,75,77,81,82,87年)

aloofness (71年)

alphabet (82年)

alphabetical (53年)

already (69,90年)

alright (86年)

altar (84年)

alternative (73年)

although (72,73,75,79,82,83,84,89年)

altitude (63,65年)

altogether (62,68,87年)

aluminum (79年)

amateur (58年)

amazed (78年)

amazement (83年)

Amazon (78年)

ambassador (46,67,72年)

ambition (52,68,79,87年)

ambitious (52,65年)

America (58年)

American (58年)

among (68,87,90年)

amount (49,51,54,61,66,68,72,76,78,79,80,81,83,87,88年)

amplify (63年)

amused (63年)

amusing (73年)

analysis (85年)

analytical (37年)

analyze (90年)

ancestor (46,62年)

ancestral (67年)

ancient (58,66,69,75,77,85年)

anecdote (51年)

anew (70年)

angel (75年)

angler (53年)

animal (89,90年)

ankle (67,84年)

anniversary (46,62,88年)

announce (55,66,73,77年)

annoy (61,80年)

annoyed (49年)

annoying (86年)

annual (46年)

answering (86年)

antagonism (63年)

antennae (90年)

anterior (83年)

anticipate (66年)

anxiety (50,90年)

anxious (50,61,65,74,76,89年)

anxiously (74,89年)

anyway (65,72,76,77,78,82,83,85年)

apart (56年)

apartment (78,79,81,84年)

ape (67,74,87年)

apex (63年)

apologize (49,68,75年)

apparatus (48年)

apparently (59,67,71,84,86年)

appeal (46,51,69,77,88,90年)

appear (59,61,62,64,67,69,75,76,78,82,85年)

appearance (53,61,65,81,88,90年)

appetite (53,86年)

applaud (64,73年)

appliance (90年)

applicant (62年)

application (51,54,74年)

apply (50,54,62,74,87年)

appoint (69年)

appointment (49,54,81,89年)

appreciate (56,58,67,72,79,84,85,86,88年)

appreciation (62,87年)

apprehensive (68年)

approach (48,50,59,64,65,66,79年)

appropriate (66年)

approval (50,54,69,73年)

approve (49,69年)

aquarium (80年)

arch (82年)

archaeology (50年)

architect (87年)

architectural (84年)

architecture (53,68,87年)

area (73,75,77,79,80,82,84年)

argue (45,51,54,61,62,63,78, 79,88年)

argument (46,54,59,67,72年)

arise (53,63年)

aristocrat (89年)

Aristotle (67年)

arithmetic (53,60年)

arm (68,82年)

armor (52年)

army (47,56,81,88年)

around (64,65,73,74,75,87年)

arouse (51,55,59,66,86年)

arrange (53,55,62,71,76年)

arrangement (63年)

arrest (48,78年)

arrival (62年)

arrive (75,89年)

arrow (54,77年)

art (54,90年)

art-form (87年)

article (50,55,64,73,75,76,79,80, 81,82,83,89年)

artifice (68年)

artificial (49,85年)

artist (81,89年)

artistic (68,87年)

ascertain (70年)

ashamed (51,68年)

Asia (73,87年)

Asian (73年)

asleep (57,59,81年)

aspect (79,81年)

aspiration (64年)

aspirin (83年)

assemble (85年)

assembly (63年)

assert (74年)

assign (52年)

assignment (52,74,87年)

assimilate (52年)

assimilation (52年)

assist (87年)

assistant (51年)

associate (54,69,74,89年)

assume (47,68,71,74年)

assumption (73年)

assure (70年)

astonish (55,61,72年)

astonishing (64年)

astonishment (60年)

astronomy (68年)

Athens (47年)

athlete (51,60年)

athletic (59,83年)

Atlantic (72年)

atmosphere (60,61,80,82年)

atom (49,61,71年)

atomic (49,61,62年)

attach (53,67,82年)

attack (47,50,53,56,58,62,69,71, 72,85年)

attain (35,87年)

attainable (89年)

attainment (67年)

attempt (49,56,65,66,81年)

attend (47,50,55,59,64,79,88年)

attendant (74,88年)

attention (48,59,60,65,66,67,69, 71,73,77,84,85,88,90年)

attentive (54年)

attentiveness (74年)

attic (55年)

attitude (47,58,63,64,71,73,80, 85,87,88年)

attract (66,79,90年)

attraction (66,84年)

attractive (50,77,79,90年)

attractiveness (48年)

attribute (45,60年)

audience (51,87年)

auditorium (52年)

auditory (73年)

author (47,52,55,60,62,63,70,79, 85,87,88年)

authority (51,65,78年)

autobiography (50年)

automatic (56,70年)

automatically (87年)

automation (63年)

automobile (49,68,73年)

autumn (89年)

available (59,65,71,72,89年)

avenue (73年)

average (60,61,66,67,70,73,76, 80,83,84,85,87年)

avoid (51,54,58,66,67,69,74,78, 86,87,88年)

avoidable (53年)

await (72,86年)

awaken (45年)

award (80,90年)

aware (67年)

awareness (67,84,85年)

awe (87年)

awful (61,73,86,88,89年)

ax (59年)

baby (90年)

background (50,58,61,81年)

backseat (90年)

backwards (84年)

bade (52年)

badly (52,67,84年)

bait (53年)

bake (61,76,86年)

bakery (86年)

balance (64,76,83,85,87年)

bald (63年)

ballistic (58年)

balm (63年)

bamboo (56年)

ban (80年)

band (47,79年)

bank (46,84年)

banking (83年)

banner (51年)

baptism (72年)

bar (84年)

barbarian (58,68,71年)

barbaric (51年)

barbarous (56年)

barber (46,64,71,76年)

bare (54,56,65,67,84年)

barely (59,72,77,84,89年)

bargain (65,68,76年)

bark (80年)

barn (56年)

barometer (72年)

barren (53年)

barrier (65,76,84年)

base (59,88年)

basement (56,64年)

basic (87,90年)

basically (67,85年)

basin (78年)

basis (64,87年)

basket (64,79年)

bat (64,85年)

bath (58,77年)

bathe (52,72,76年)

bathroom (64年)

batter (64年)

battery (85,89,90年)

battery-powered (90年)

battle (47年)

bay (82年)

beach (56,72,76,79,80,82年)

bean (75,76年)

bear (46,68,78,89年)

beard (63年)

beast (54,61年)

beat (59,61,82年)

beautiful (90年)

beauty (53,84年)

bee (77,85年)

beech (54年)

beef (45,53年)

beer (61年)

beg (64,68年)

beggar (64,68,70,71年)

begin (90年)

beginning (90年)

behalf (89年)

behave (52,81,86年)

behavior (52,64,72,81,83,85,88年)

behind (74,84年)

belief (45,67,79,85年)

believe (66,77,78,79,82,89,90年)

belittle (71年)

bell (45年)

below (77年)

bend (56,82,84年)

beneath (59,84,89年)

beneficial (46,67,87,90年)

benefit (67,85,89,90年)

benevolence (68年)

beside (84,87年)

besides (58,62,80,82,85,86年)

best-known (89年)

best-seller (50年)

bet (76,77年)

betray (70年)

better (90年)

beyond (85年)

bill (56,61,65,73,83年)

biography (50年)

biological (49,70,79,89年)

biologically (89年)

biology (79,90年)

birth (90年)

birthplace (61,73年)

bite (46,80,88年)

bitter (63,66年)

bitterly (52年)

blackmail (50年)

blame (69,90年)

blank (66,68年)

blanket (65年)

blast (49年)

blaze (66年)

bleed (84年)

bless (89,90年)

blessing (75年)

blind (45,82年)

block (52,64,88年)

blood (52,63,84年)

bloom (90年)

blossom (67年)

blow (52,58,87年)

blush (90年)

board (45,54,55,62年)

boardinghouse (64年)

bodily (81年)

Bohemian (45年)

bold (59年)

bomb (47,67,68,72年)

bomber (71年)

bone-chilling (85年)

booklet (75年)

bookseller (88年)

bookstore (85年)

boot (58年)

border (88年)

boring (90年)

borrow (51,52,54,55,58,65,68,78,85年)

bother (49,84年)

bottle (85年)

bottom (84年)

bound (89年)

boundary (90年)

bow (54,62,90年)

bowl (61,62年)

brag (68年)

Braille (71年)

brain (52,67,79,81,88年)

branch (53,84年)

brand-new (73,87年)

brave (47年)

bravely (47,67年)

bread (52,53,55,78,86,89年)

breast (61年)

breath (56,65,76,84年)

breathe (50,53年)

breathing (90年)

breathless (52年)

breed (46,64,66,71,73,90年)

breeze (48年)

bribery (71年)

bridegroom (62年)

bridge (65年)

brief (51,67,82年)

briefly (79,88年)

bright (55,61,63,66,67年)

brighten (66,88年)

brilliant (48,54,90年)

Britain (66,82年)

British (65,76年)

broadly (82年)

bronze (54年)

brood (63年)

browse (52年)

brush (46年)

brutality (68年)

bubble (87年)

Buddha (89年)

Buddhism (67年)

Buddhist (67,89年)

budget (65年)

buffalo (63,84年)

bugle (52年)

building (89年)

bull (63年)

bullet (89年)

bulletin (58年)

burden (65,68,75年)

bureau (60,64年)

burglar (54,84年)

burn (88年)

burst (66年)

bury (59,68,89年)

bush (54,68年)

businessman (86年)

butcher (76年)

butterfly (64,89年)

button (81年)

buzz (89年)

cab (87年)

cabin (50年)

cafeteria (85年)

cage (60年)

calculate (69年)

calculation (87年)

calendar (57,64,68,87年)

calf (73年)

call (90年)

call-in (87年)

calm (57,66年)

calmly (84年)

camel (52,66年)

camera (53,55,61,64,74,77,81,85,90年)

camp (74,88年)

camper (59年)

campus (64年)

cancel (51,63,73,80,86年)

candidate (85,89年)

candle (51年)

candlelight (64年)

candy (90年)

cannibal (68年)

canyon (75年)

capable (50,64,79,86年)

capacity (71年)

capital (46,52,70,76年)

capitalize (63年)

capsule (83年)

captain (51,54,71年)

captor (51年)

capture (67,87年)

card (88,89年)

care (50,60,85,90年)

career (50,51,60,63,69,74年)

carefully (89年)

careless (52,87年)

carelessly (56,88年)

carelessness (52年)

cargo (51年)

caring (79年)

carpenter (61年)

carpentry (61年)

carriage (65年)

carry (60,61,64,76,77,79,90年)

cart (54,63年)

carve (54年)

case (58,60,66,71,84,86,87,90年)

cash (77,79,83年)

castle (66年)

casually (83年)

casualty (69,80年)

catalogue (63年)

catastrophe (65年)

catch (77,84,89年)

cater (87年)

cathedral (66年)

Catholic (62年)

cattle (45,54,75年)

causal (71年)

causally (63年)

cause (61,62,63,65,66,70,72,73,76,77,78,80,82,84,85,87年)

caution (49,67年)

cautious (63,65,71年)

cave (58,77,85年)

cease (49,73年)

celebrate (47,88,90年)

celebration (90年)

celebrity (64年)

cell (70,89年)

central (62,75,84,85年)

century (52,54,62,64,69,70,71, 72,75,77,82,85,89,90年)
cereal (87年)
ceremony (49,88年)
certain (50,60,65,68,70,72,76,83, 85,87,89,90年)
certainly (56,57,62,67,68,70,74, 75,79,81,82,85,86,87,90年)
certify (75年)
chain (68,76年)
chairman (52,55,61,62年)
chalk (61,63年)
challenge (66,69,90年)
challenging (77年)
chamber (71年)
chance (90年)
change (66,89,90年)
changeable (68年)
channel (76年)
character (49,53,64,87,89年)
characteristic (52,60,73,90年)
characterize (63,70,81年)
charge (48,52,78,87年)
charity (56,61,68年)
charm (71年)
chart (57,82,84,87年)
charwoman (49年)
chase (54,59年)
chastity (60年)
chat (86年)
cheaper (90年)
check (46,51,76,83,84,87,88,89年)
checkstand (79年)
cheek (45年)
cheekbone (84年)
cheer (56,65,86年)
cheerful (66,75,83年)
cheerfully (49,74年)
chemical (49,66,77,85,89,90年)
chemist (47年)
chemistry (49,56,57,87年)

cherish (80年)
cherry (48年)
chest (58,65年)
chew (68,88年)
chicken (58,81年)
chief (47,53,54,63年)
chiefly (64,84年)
child (90年)
childhood (51,60,72,87年)
chill (53年)
chime (64年)
chocolate (52年)
choice (74,76年)
choke (69年)
choose (57,64,68,71,80,87年)
choosy (68年)
chore (87,90年)
chronic (71年)
church (54,55,61,75年)
churn (67年)
cigarette (59,64,78年)
cinematography (90年)
circle (49,55,82年)
circulate (68年)
circumstance (64,65,69,83年)
circus (51,53年)
citizen (58,61,62,89年)
civilization (57,61,64,68,70年)
civilized (57,58,68年)
claim (50,71,79,85年)
class (65,69年)
classic (74年)
classical (58年)
classify (66年)
classmate (82,87年)
classroom (90年)
clause (60年)
clean (68,89,90年)
cleanliness (86,88年)
clear (72,78,87,89年)
clearly (47,84,86年)

clerical (63年)
clerk (88,89年)
clever (66,86,89年)
client (64年)
cliff (84年)
climate (75,87年)
climax (51,81年)
climb (90年)
close (68,89年)
closely (72,74,80,87,89年)
closet (55年)
cloth (50,73,77,84年)
clothe (54,58年)
clothes (46,77,87年)
clothing (77,83年)
cloud (88年)
cloudless (69年)
cloudy (73年)
clown (51,90年)
clue (81年)
clump (48年)
cluster (48,51年)
coal (56年)
coast (72年)
coastal (75年)
co-existence (68年)
coherent (69,71年)
coin (56年)
coincidence (78年)
collapse (50,86年)
collect (66,72,75,77,79年)
collection (50,84年)
collective (53年)
collector (65年)
college (52,64,69,70,74,80,85, 86,87,90年)
colony (85年)
colorful (80年)
coloring (77年)
colorless (52年)
combine (67,70,75年)

comfort (66,74年)
comfortable (56,57,79,89年)
comic (89年)
command (51,53,54,80,84,90年)
commander (47年)
comment (54,71,89年)
commentary (83年)
commerce (68年)
commercial (63,64,76,85,90年)
commit (50,53,67,78年)
commitment (82年)
committee (47,53,66,68,86年)
commodity (63年)
common (58,60,78,80,81,88,90年)
commonly (74年)
communal (68年)
communicate (76,83,89,90年)
communication (70,82,88,90年)
community (61,67年)
companion (74年)
companionship (88年)
company (48,51,66,73,89,90年)
comparable (58,79年)
comparatively (60,71年)
compare (60,64,90年)
comparison (76年)
compass (48年)
compassion (66年)
compel (47年)
compensate (67,86年)
compete (60,77年)
competence (71年)
competent (75年)
competition (60,89,90年)
competitive (77年)
competitiveness (83年)
compile (66,68年)
complain (48,61,65,80,82,84, 86,88年)
complaint (48,54,61,62,84年)
complement (66年)

complete (47,51,54,58,62,66,67, 68,69,72,87年)
completely (49,63,68,72,88,90年)
completion (69年)
complex (51,65,67,78年)
complexity (64年)
complicated (64,76,80,82年)
compliment (81年)
component (89年)
compose (45,62年)
composition (90年)
compound (52,65年)
comprehension (87年)
comprehensively (64年)
compress (68年)
compromise (87年)
compute (63年)
computer (63,81,85,87,90年)
conceive (70年)
concentrate (64,73,90年)
concentration (67,69,76年)
concept (64,76,77年)
conception (65年)
concern (63,67,69,75,77,88,90年)
concerned (53,73,87年)
concerning (67,69,84年)
concert (48,54,87年)
conclude (48,56,72,89年)
conclusion (48,58,69年)
conclusive (89年)
concrete (85年)
condemn (67,68年)
condense (78,83年)
condition (48,51,60,62,65,69,71, 80,81,82,83,88年)
conduct (48,59,80,88年)
conductor (88年)
conference (66,68,69,73,87年)
confident (68,73年)
confidently (82年)
confine (45,47,88年)

confirm (80年)
confiscate (47年)
conflict (63,67,87年)
conform (68年)
confront (87年)
Confucian (67年)
Confucianism (70年)
confuse (85年)
confused (81,85年)
confusion (66,81年)
congestion (70年)
congratulate (47年)
congratulation (86年)
congress (47,62年)
conjecture (68年)
conjunction (69年)
connect (67,72,80年)
connection (50,71,87年)
conquer (47,53年)
conqueror (53年)
conscience (45,63,68年)
conscientious (45,54,63,68年)
conscious (45,83,90年)
consciousness (45年)
consequence (47,53,68,78年)
consequent (78年)
consequently (88年)
conservation (85年)
consider (52,58,61,64,66,67,68, 72,73,80,81,85,86,89年)
considerable (49,72年)
considerably (49年)
considerate (49,85,90年)
consideration (69,79年)
consist (62,87年)
console (45年)
conspicuous (65年)
constant (48,51,54,63,67,79年)
constantly (54,67,68,82,89年)
constitute (89年)
construct (73,80,87年)

construction (66,84年)

consult (84年)

consultant (51,90年)

consultation (51年)

consumer (81,90年)

consumption (73年)

contact (68,76,83,90年)

contagious (81年)

contain (49,60,67,76,79,80,81,83,85,87年)

container (79年)

contemplate (67,68年)

contemporary (70年)

contempt (58,64,66年)

contemptible (72年)

content (49,59,61,71,74,88年)

contest (51,69,80,86,87年)

contestant (89年)

continent (48,52年)

continue (54,63,73,80,87,89,90年)

continuously (60,67年)

contract (69年)

contradictorily (72年)

contrary (63,64,88年)

contrast (62,70,88年)

contribute (64,68,69,74,80年)

contribution (70,71,83,87年)

control (60,81,86,87,88,90年)

controversy (50年)

convenient (56,87,89年)

conveniently (59年)

convention (68年)

conventional (68,90年)

conversation (88,89年)

convert (67年)

convey (80,88年)

conviction (47,67年)

convince (67,68年)

convincing (69年)

cook (78年)

coop (63年)

cooperate (63,69,84年)

cooperation (51,84,86年)

cooperative (49,88年)

cope (54,71,90年)

co-pilot (51年)

copper (56,78年)

copyright (85年)

cord (59年)

core (49,59年)

corn (52,75年)

corner (64年)

corporation (48,83年)

corps (64年)

correct (67,68,86,87,89年)

correctly (49,62,63,74,86年)

correspond (81年)

corrupt (71年)

cost (90年)

costly (90年)

cottage (45年)

cotton (73年)

cough (63,66,88年)

council (45年)

counsel (45年)

count (54,56,61,74,77,81,90年)

counter (68年)

country (60,61,62,64,66,67,68,70,74,75,77,80,83,86,87,90年)

couple (52,66,71,87,88,89年)

courage (54,59,68年)

courageous (50,59年)

course (46,49,50,51,52,53,55,60,64,65,67,70,72,78,81,90年)

court (49,56,67,68,90年)

courteous (83年)

courtyard (84年)

cousin (52,56,58,60,62,64年)

cover (45,78,84,87年)

cow (66,73,90年)

cowardly (47年)

cowboy (66年)

crab (56,59年)

crack (64,82年)

craft (54年)

cram (63年)

crash (46,56年)

craving (67年)

crawl (62年)

crazy (62,89,90年)

cream (60年)

create (59,67,70,71,77,80,81,88,89,90年)

creation (52,86年)

creative (70,81,87年)

creativity (66年)

creator (59,89年)

creature (54,59,65,66,68,85,90年)

credential (72年)

credit (73,79,88年)

creep (57年)

crest (65年)

crew (51,84年)

crime (67,78,82年)

criminal (68,78,81年)

cripple (84年)

crisis (50,70,87,89,90年)

critic (52年)

critical (85年)

criticism (54,66年)

criticize (49,52,63,87年)

crop (48,61,73,75,80,87年)

cross (70,85年)

crouch (90年)

crow (51,62年)

crowd (62,65,72,74,76年)

crude (84年)

cruel (46年)

cruelty (82年)

cruise (80年)

cue (79,84年)

cultivate (53,85,87年)

cultivated (51年)

cultural (50,69,70年)

culture (52,75,76,79,81,85年)

cunningly (90年)

cupboard (75,79年)

current (51年)

currently (88年)

curtail (83年)

curved (45,82年)

custom (51,60年)

customary (49年)

customer (48,49,65,74,79,80,88年)

cycle (54,81,89年)

cyclotron (49年)

daily (61,65,67,76,90年)

dairy (73年)

damage (61,66,70,88年)

damp (53,72年)

dare (59年)

dash (90年)

curb (46年)

cure (58,65,84,88年)

curio (73年)

curiosity (66,73年)

curious (46年)

curl (46年)

data (87年)

date (61,68年)

daughter (55,56,69,77,86年)

dawn (54,61年)

day-dreamer (74年)

deadly (77,88年)

deal (61,63,72,83,87年)

death (89,90年)

debate (46,62年)

debt (61,73年)

decade (55,61,65,90年)

decay (72,87年)

decease (61年)

deceive (81年)

decency (68年)

decent (59,67年)

decide (83,90年)

decision (47,50,51,64,67,69,77,83,86年)

decisive (47,51,67年)

deckchair (76年)

declare (58年)

decline (64,69,73,75,85,86年)

decorate (84,86,89年)

decrease (70,84,87年)

deed (59年)

deem (68,72,83年)

deeply (53,66,87年)

defeat (47,51,65,88年)

defective (65年)

defend (47,89年)

defendant (67年)

defender (47年)

defense (65,73,85年)

deference (54年)

deficient (87,88年)

define (48,72,78,87,88年)

definite (55,73,83,90年)

definitely (55,73,83,89年)

definition (48,72年)

deflate (68年)

degrading (45年)

degree (45,50,54,61,67,69,70,72,84,85年)

delay (48,65,80,88年)

deliberate (67,82年)

deliberately (83年)

delicate (85,87年)

delicious (79,81年)

delight (74,86,88年)

delighted (78年)

delightful (79,87年)

deliver (64,73,75,80,86年)

delivery (62,72年)

demand (50,51,54,58,59,61,64,66,73,86,87,89年)

demanding (54年)

democracy (47,52年)

democrat (60年)

democratic (86年)

demon (77年)

demonstrate (88年)

demonstration (69,88年)

dentist (52年)

deny (53,67年)

depart (86,88年)

department (64年)

departure (66,71年)

depend (46,71,76年)

dependence (53年)

dependent (51,53,69年)

depose (47年)

depress (68,81,88年)

depression (50年)

deprive (69年)

depth (77年)

desalt (78年)

descendant (58,62,71年)

descent (73年)

describe (47,48,59,62,73,76,78,81,84,85,88年)

description (48年)

desert (45,46,54,56,58,59,61,66,68,80,86,88年)

deserted (56年)

deserve (49,61,64,73,86年)

design (61,62,70,84,87,88,89年)

desirable (53,68年)

desire (52,57,67,70,87年)

desolation (54年)

despair (56,61,72年)

desperate (90年)

desperation (61年)

despise (49年)

despite (51,67,69,84,85年)

dessert (81年)

destroy (48,53,63,67,69,71,81,83,87,88年)

destruction (48,67,71,87年)
destructive (85年)
destructively (90年)
detail (62,70,78,84,85年)
detailed (67年)
detect (65,84年)
detective (49年)
determination (47,84,88年)
determine (53,69,71,77,86年)
determiner (69年)
devastating (71年)
develop (51,57,58,61,66,67,68, 70,72,75,77,80,85,87,89年)
developing (63,70年)
development (58,64,65,66,67, 68,71,72,87,88,89,90年)
device (50,90年)
devise (49年)
devote (67年)
devoted (64年)
diagnose (87年)
diagram (75年)
dialect (76年)
dialogue (75年)
diamond (56年)
diary (73年)
dictatorship (63年)
diet (71,73,87年)
differ (64,78,81,89年)
difference (53,56,59,64,65,68, 69,75,82年)
different (52,58,68,78,79,81,83, 87,89,90年)
differentiate (73,80年)
differently (88年)
difficult (70,71,83,86,89,90年)
difficulty (70,74年)
dig (66,68,84年)
digest (52,53年)
dignity (53,69,90年)

dike (46年)
dilemma (71年)
diligence (74,83年)
diligent (53,71,73年)
dim (55年)
dime (86年)
dimensional (87年)
dine (79年)
ding-dong (89年)
dip (55年)
diploma (70年)
diplomat (61,66,67,73年)
direct (51,70,83,90年)
direction (66,90年)
directly (70,87年)
director (62,90年)
dirt (45,84年)
disagree (50,51,62,78,81年)
disagreeable (73年)
disagreement (51年)
disappear (48,59,69,78,85年)
disappoint (50,81年)
disappointed (60,61,66,75, 86,87年)
disappointment (51,86年)
disapproval (67,69年)
disastrous (50,78年)
disc (87年)
disciple (71年)
discipline (68,73年)
disconcert (64年)
discontinue (70年)
discount (89年)
discourage (64,76年)
discover (48,62,66,67,72,76,79, 81,84,86,87,88,90年)
discovery (48,54,55,62年)
discredit (68年)
discrimination (88年)
discuss (52,62,75,82,88年)

discussion (89,90年)
disease (60,69,71,73,77,81,84, 85,88,89年)
disfavor (47年)
disgrace (61,68年)
disguise (63年)
disgust (79年)
dish (77,89年)
dishearten (64年)
dishonestly (63年)
disinterested (67年)
dislike (67,68年)
dismal (63年)
dismay (63年)
dismiss (66,79,82年)
disobey (66年)
disorder (77,81,84年)
dispatcher (51年)
displace (63年)
display (62,74,84,88,90年)
displeased (68年)
disposable (84年)
dispose (88年)
disprove (63年)
dispute (75,84年)
disrespect (58年)
dissimilar (63年)
dissuade (79年)
distance (80,81,82,90年)
distant (66,81,82,83年)
distillation (78,50年)
distinctive (48年)
distinctly (82,84年)
distinguish (50,66,71年)
distinguished (63,66年)
distract (90年)
distraction (90年)
distribute (60,75,85年)
distribution (63年)
district (49年)

disturb (61,64,69,78,87,90年)
disturber (61年)
disuse (60年)
ditch (75年)
dive (63年)
diver (81年)
diversification (66年)
divide (46,48,51,58,62,90年)
dividend (83年)
division (48,53,78,83年)
dizziness (84年)
do's and don'ts (87年)
document (67,68年)
domestic (53年)
domestication (54年)
dominant (88年)
dominate (86,87年)
donate (85年)
donation (79年)
doom (63年)
doorsill (84年)
doorway (62,65年)
dormitory (80年)
dose (61,83年)
dot (71年)
double (51,60,66,67,76,80年)
doubt (61,67,79,87,89年)
down (78年)
downstairs (45,76年)
doze (47年)
dozen (45年)
drab (53年)
draft (73年)
dragon (46,84,90年)
drain (70年)
draught (89年)
draw (59,68,90年)
drawer (49,53,60年)
drawing (67年)
dreadful (60年)
dream (90年)

dress (53,77,81,89年)
drift (54,73年)
drive (59,71,81,84年)
drop (87,89年)
drought (63,73,87,89年)
drown (46,62年)
drowning (86年)
drug (84,86年)
druggist (74年)
drugstore (74年)
drum (82年)
drummer (82年)
duck (59年)
due (53,84年)
duly (67年)
dumb (77年)
duplicate (47年)
durable (79年)
duration (84年)
during (90年)
dust (88年)
dusty (80年)
dutiful (69年)
duty (51,61,65,67,90年)
dwelling (45年)
eager (60,64,88年)
eagerness (69年)
earl (63,89年)
earlier (90年)
early (90年)
earn (83年)
earnest (85年)
earnestly (89年)
earth (46,53,60,90年)
earthquake (46,54,65年)
easily (69年)
east (50,66,90年)
eastern (76年)
easy-going (49年)
echo (46年)
ecological (85年)

economic (50,63,69,71,83,84,87,88,89年)
economical (64,76年)
economically (63年)
economics (50年)
economist (83年)
economize (49年)
economy (70,76,78,83,85年)
edge (67,90年)
edible (71年)
editor (61年)
educate (52,73,75,88年)
educated (60,74年)
education (52,70,82,85年)
educational (80,87,90年)
effect (48,63,67,70,71,80,81年)
effective (68,72,83,84,88,90年)
effectively (84年)
effectuate (68年)
efficiency (48,60,71年)
efficient (60,67,78,86,88,89,90年)
efficiently (49,69,84年)
effort (54,60,61,66,70,72,83,86,87,90年)
either (61,62,64,66,68,78,85,89年)
elasticity (67年)
elbow (67年)
elder (64,68,73年)
elderly (69,90年)
elect (47,52,53,54年)
election (50,85,89年)
elective (64年)
electric (65,78年)
electrical (49年)
electrician (61年)
electricity (45,48,62,82年)
electrodialysis (78年)
electronic (63,81,87年)
electronic-mail (88年)
element (74,88年)
elementary (60年)

elevator (72年)

eligible (73,75年)

eliminate (83,89年)

else (90年)

E-mail (88年)

embarrass (72年)

embarrassing (87年)

embassy (47年)

embrace (81年)

embroider (47年)

emerge (69年)

emergency (48,51,68年)

emotion (79,88,89年)

emotional (87,89年)

emperor (90年)

emphasis (66年)

emphasize (66,69,73,88年)

emphatic (67年)

empire (86年)

employ (61年)

employee (61,89年)

employer (74年)

employment (45,61年)

empty (79年)

enable (63,70,79,86年)

enclose (45,84,87年)

encounter (71,88年)

encourage (76,80,83,87,88年)

encouragement (49,73年)

encouraging (82年)

end (47,89,90年)

endangered (85,87年)

endless (68,69年)

endlessly (75年)

endurance (66年)

endure (68,73年)

enemy (49,56,58,82,85,88,90年)

energetic (86年)

energy (48,61,62,69,70,82,86,87,90年)

engage (47,51,56,81,87年)

engagement (65年)

engine (51,63年)

engineer (62,63,82年)

England (57,85,89年)

enjoy (90年)

enjoyable (51,54,66,83,87年)

enjoyment (57年)

enlarge (67,84年)

enlist (63年)

enormous (60年)

enormously (65,76,82,85年)

enough (90年)

enrich (49年)

enroll (49年)

enslavement (47年)

entertain (48,50,63年)

entertaining (73,90年)

entertainment (48,82,90年)

enthusiasm (47,53年)

enthusiast (90年)

enthusiastic (90年)

enthusiastically (66年)

entire (68,70,80,87年)

entirely (52,59,68,84,86,87年)

entrance (75,79,90年)

environment (48,65,81,82,84,89年)

environmental (88,90年)

environmentalist (90年)

envy (48年)

equal (47,49,53,68,87年)

equality (53年)

equally (69,87年)

equip (47年)

equipment (78年)

equivalent (85年)

era (79年)

errand (56年)

error (47,54,66年)

eruption (71年)

escape (46,50,59,62,66,68年)

especially (76,83,86年)

essay (58,74年)

essential (49,54,68,72,87年)

essentially (87年)

esson (52,56,58,68,73年)

establish (46,49,61,67,73年)

esteem (66年)

estimate (70,77年)

estimation (64年)

eternal (68年)

eternity (65年)

Europe (54,80,84年)

European (53,57,66年)

evaluate (66年)

evaluation (64年)

evaporate (78年)

even (68年)

event (55,62,63,67,68,81,87年)

eventual (90年)

eventually (51,77,84,87,88年)

everyday (73年)

everything (90年)

everywhere (89年)

evidence (67,68,71,72,76,78,89年)

evidently (59年)

evil (46,49,68,81,85年)

evolution (70,71年)

evolutionary (89年)

evolve (90年)

exact (47,65,66年)

exacting (51年)

exactitude (64,71年)

exactly (49,68,74,75,76,77,83,85,89年)

exaggerate (66,68年)

exalt (63年)

exam (90年)

examination (75,84,90年)

examine (46,49,50,62,75,90年)

examiner (54,65,75年)

example (47,68,75,89,90年)

exceed (49,71年)

excel (70年)

excellent (46,57,60,73,83,90年)

except (49,59,64,70,75,83,85,
87,89,90年)

exception (47,64,71,79,86年)

excess (88年)

exchange (53,54,67,68,78,
89,90年)

exchangeable (87年)

excited (62,82年)

excitement (57,66年)

exclaim (61,68年)

exclamation (48年)

exclude (59,67年)

exclusion (67年)

exclusive (49年)

excuse (66,84,90年)

execute (68年)

exercise (60,64,76,78,81,
88,90年)

exert (66年)

exhaust (50,89年)

exhaustion (81年)

exhibit (66年)

exhibition (49,68,85,89年)

exist (48,68,69年)

existence (45,48,67,68年)

expand (83,84年)

expansion (86年)

expect (58,62,67,68,71,79,80,81,
83,89,90年)

expectable (66年)

expectation (49,61年)

expedition (50,54年)

expel (49年)

expenditure (70年)

expense (58,68,80,86,88,90年)

expensive (84,86年)

experience (65,72,74,75,78,80,
86,89年)

experienced (46,66,76年)

experiment (48,49,50,60,62,65,
66,71,77,79,82,87,88年)

expert (50,78,79,85,87,88,
89,90年)

explain (47,48,50,52,57,63,76,77,
80,85,88,89年)

explanation (47,61,85,86年)

explicitness (71年)

exploit (66年)

exploration (51,71年)

explore (57,69,81年)

explorer (56,72年)

explosion (40年)

export (59年)

expose (50,57,62,68年)

express (65,67,72,87年)

expression (73,79,84,85,90年)

expressively (88年)

exquisite (48年)

extend (48,75年)

extension (81年)

extensive (51,82年)

extensively (86年)

extent (81年)

external (81,87年)

extinct (71年)

extinguish (66年)

extra (63,87,89年)

extraordinarily (62年)

extraordinary (46年)

extravagant (63年)

extreme (63,73年)

extremely (52,61,65,66,67,72,77,
85,86年)

exuberant (65年)

eyesight (45,67年)

face (65,66,69,90年)

facial (79,84年)

facilitate (68,89年)

facility (64,68,73年)

factor (47,52,64,78,85,87年)

factory (50,66,67,73,81,85年)

factually (87年)

fad (67年)

Fahrenheit (85年)

fail (55,60,65,66,69,73,78,81,90年)

failure (50,51,52,60,65,67,71,87年)

fair (84年)

fairly (48,78,85年)

faith (71,87年)

fall (65,77,78,85,89年)

false (46,66年)

fame (45,54,85,86年)

familiar (61,83,89年)

familiarity (64,66,83年)

family (90年)

famous (06,74,75,80,84,86年)

fanciful (71年)

fancy (67,70年)

fantastic (78,83年)

fare (65,87年)

farewell (64,88年)

farming (53,73,75年)

farmland (75年)

farther (46年)

fascinate (48,79,89年)

fascinating (65,66年)

fascination (65年)

fashion (51,75年)

fashionable (45,80,87年)

fashionably (89,90年)

fast (90年)

fast-food (76年)

fat (76年)

fatal (84年)

fat-rich (89年)

fatten (79年)

fatty (78年)

faucet (63年)

fault (61,63,68年)

favor (63,64,66,76,81年)

favorite (52,53,74,79,90年)

fear (53,57,79,85,89年)

fearful (48年)

fearsome (85年)

feasible (89年)

feat (71年)

feather (50年)

feature (64,71,77,81,88年)

February (90年)

feed (82,87,90年)

feeling (89年)

feet (82年)

fell (87年)

fellow (53,58,61,65,68,76年)

female (85,90年)

feminine (79年)

feminist (79年)

fertilize (75年)

fetch (45年)

fever (52年)

feverish (82年)

few (90年)

fiction (50,81年)

field (46,50,61,71,87年)

fierce (84,89年)

fiercely (46年)

fight (46,47,51,57,84,85,89年)

fighting (82年)

figure (50,65,70,73,75,81年)

filial (73年)

fill (81,89年)

film (52,68,81,89,90年)

final (66,69,74,84年)

finalist (73年)

finally (78,89,90年)

financial (47,56,61,65,82年)

find (90年)

fine (78年)

finger (71,77,88年)

fingerprint (82年)

fingertip (82年)

finish (52,57,58,59,61,62,65,69, 72,73,75,76,84,85年)

fire (77年)

fire-engine (46年)

firefly (61年)

fireplace (45,81年)

firm (64,68年)

first-class (65年)

first-rate (63年)

fisherman (53年)

fit (48,55,62,68,80,81年)

fix (56,63,64,79,81,84年)

fixed (81年)

fixture (50年)

flame (53,87年)

flare (49年)

flash (62,77,82年)

flashlight (67年)

flatter (48年)

flavor (52年)

flaw (64年)

flee (46,87年)

flesh (46年)

flexibility (67,71年)

flexible (79,86年)

flight (49,51,63,82,85,88,89年)

fling (74年)

flint (54年)

float (54年)

floating (85年)

flock (84,85年)

flood (46,49,61,75年)

flourish (47,63,68,89年)

flow (89年)

flower (90年)

flu (69年)

fluently (49,85年)

fluid (89年)

flunk (77年)

flute (66年)

focus (63,88,89,90年)

fog (67,75年)

foil (79年)

fold (46,59,79年)

follow (46,49,51,53,55,59,62,63, 65,67,76,85年)

follower (50,90年)

following (64,73,75,76,77,80, 81,82,83,84,85,86,87,88,89年)

fond (89年)

food (90年)

foolishly (66年)

foot (59年)

footstep (47年)

forbade (90年)

forbid (46,50,63,65,80年)

force (48,49,53,58,60,65,66,68,71, 77,79,82,89年)

forced (69年)

forcibly (85年)

forecast (76年)

forefront (72年)

forehead (68年)

foreign (45,52,55,58,61,67,68, 69,87年)

foreigner (58,76,77,79,86年)

foreign-language (90年)

foremost (63年)

forest (50,54,79,87,90年)

forewarning (73年)

forget (57,58,61,72,78,85,86,89年)

forgetful (58年)

forgetfulness (47年)

forgive (48,58,75,80年)

forgiveness (88年)

form (48,54,62,65,74,80,82,83, 87,89年)

formal (50年)

formality (88年)

formalize (84年)

formally (50,83年)

formation (47年)

former (51,72,75,84,88年)
formerly (63年)
fortunate (69年)
fortunately (54,72,86年)
fortune (45,47,74年)
forwards (84年)
foul (47,61年)
found (52,73年)
foundation (51,52,69,72,87年)
founder (76年)
fountain (73年)
fowl (61年)
fragrance (71年)
frail (67年)
framework (68年)
France (70,82年)
frank (68年)
frankly (66,75,78,83年)
frantic (71年)
free (90年)
freedom (64,67,69,73,81,88年)
free-lance (89年)
freely (52年)
freeze (78,85年)
freezing (58,78年)
French (82年)
frequency (81,89年)
frequently (84,85,86,87,88,90年)
fresh (48,76,78,80,82年)
freshman (52,73年)
freshness (48,68年)
friendly (51,79,82,83,90年)
friendship (58,61,69,86年)
fright (62年)
frighten (57,62,69,74,77,82,90年)
frightened (60,78年)
frightening (85年)
frost (54年)
frosty (48,54年)
frown (74年)
frozen (78年)

fruitless (61年)
frustrate (81年)
frustration (51年)
fulfill (68,88,89年)
fully (66,68,87年)
function (51,67,75,78,81,85,87,89年)
functional (89年)
fund (45,80,88年)
fundamental (90年)
funny (83,86,90年)
furnished (55年)
furniture (52,53,55,56,62,85,90年)
further (56,62,71年)
future (51,57,63,65,66,76,86,90年)
gaiety (65年)
gain (49,66,67,68,84,86年)
gall (63年)
gallon (73年)
gamble (89年)
gambling (83年)
game (54,84年)
gang (67年)
gap (52,63,64,76年)
garage (52,68,77,85年)
garden (56,87年)
gardening (85年)
gasoline (90年)
gate (84年)
gather (59,75,87年)
gaze (46年)
gee (78年)
geese (54年)
general (66,68,70,73,80,85年)
generally (51,53,67,68,72,81,85,86年)
generate (71年)
generation (46,50,62,63,64,66,70年)
generosity (69,87年)
generous (56,61,63,82年)

generously (85,89年)
genius (45,49,50,54,64,70,81,89年)
gentle (81,84,88年)
genuine (69年)
genuinely (71年)
geography (46,60,78年)
geometry (53年)
German (49,66,82年)
Germany (49,53,70,82,88,89年)
gesture (67,76,86年)
ghost (54,55,71,84年)
gibbet (68年)
gift (61,67,68,84,86,90年)
gifted (64年)
gigantic (72年)
give (90年)
given (64,70年)
glad (58年)
gladly (59年)
glance (64,83,88年)
gland (89年)
glare (76年)
glasses (53年)
globe (60,61,62年)
glorious (47年)
gloriously (72年)
glove (61年)
glow (53年)
goal (71,85,87,88,90年)
goat (45,54年)
godliness (86年)
gold (55年)
golden (64年)
good-hearted (47,63年)
goods (68,75,78,79,81,83年)
gorge (75年)
gorgeous (89年)
gorilla (74年)
government (54,63,66,67,68,72,74,75,80,82,83,84,88年)
grade (51,71,76,80年)

grader (80年)

gradually (54,57,60,62,68, 70,87年)

graduate (56,63,73,75,80,86年)

graduation (86年)

grain (49年)

gram (45年)

grammar (58,64,67,71,88年)

grammarian (58年)

grammatical (61,67年)

grand (66,73年)

grandparents (75年)

grasp (60,67年)

grass (56,73,74,77,80,89年)

grateful (82,87年)

gratefully (74年)

grave (61年)

gravestone (68年)

gravitational (82年)

gray (53,65年)

graze (52年)

grazing (75年)

greasy (87年)

Greece (47,58,77年)

greed (85,86年)

greedy (90年)

Greek (47,58,77,82,85年)

greet (54,77,88,90年)

grief (47,69年)

grievance (53年)

grinding (71年)

grizzly (47年)

grocery (71,79,83,89年)

ground (47,51,62,67,68年)

groundwork (87年)

group (89,90年)

grove (61年)

grow (61,89,90年)

growl (61年)

grown (74,79年)

growth (53,62,72,87年)

Guam (66年)

guarantee (48,65,69,73年)

guard (47,57,81年)

guardian (84年)

guerrilla (71年)

guess (56,75,83,86年)

guest (64,65,67,86,89,90年)

guidance (64年)

guide (51,66,82年)

guidebook (60年)

guilt (59,68年)

guilty (54,66,67,68年)

gull (63年)

gum (68,87年)

gun (55年)

gurgling (90年)

guy (86年)

gymnasium (71年)

gypsy (66年)

habit (47,58,60,64,65,71,88年)

habitat (87年)

habitually (58年)

hail (63年)

halt (61,68年)

hamburger (89年)

hammer (56,61年)

handbook (74,85年)

handful (63,89年)

handkerchief (45,62,69年)

handle (75,76,88,90年)

hand-painted (51年)

handsome (58,64年)

handy (62,90年)

hang (54,67,68,79年)

hangman (68年)

happen (58,66,68,69,78,81,89年)

happening (71年)

happiness (87年)

happy-go-lucky (45年)

harbor (90年)

hard (90年)

harden (83年)

hardly (59,60,68,73,74,75,76,84, 85,86,89,90年)

hardship (78,82,88年)

hard-working (46,53年)

harm (49,68年)

harmful (67,85年)

harmonious (87年)

harmoniously (88年)

harmony (67,87年)

harvest (75年)

hasten (64年)

hasty (88年)

hate (45,47,74,75,89年)

haunting (71年)

Hawaii (80年)

hawk (49年)

hay (73年)

hazard (61年)

hazardous (72年)

head (54年)

heading (85年)

headlong (67年)

headquarters (65年)

health (73,90年)

healthy (66,87年)

hear (86,90年)

heart (59,60,64,73,81,82,83,84, 87,89年)

heartbreaking (53年)

heartburn (84年)

hearth (63年)

heartily (49年)

heartless (45年)

hearty (58年)

heat (53,58,59,61,78年)

heater (79年)

heaven (61,65,66,67,86年)

heavily (52,58,85,87年)

heavy (49,60,67,75,77,78,80,82, 83,85,87年)

heed (90年)

height (53,65,72,75年)

heighten (53,63,70年)

helicopter (48年)

hello (89年)

help (90年)

helpful (81年)

helpless (89年)

hence (51年)

herd (67,80,84年)

heredity (70年)

heritage (64,69,70年)

heroic (89年)

hesitate (64,86,90年)

hesitation (69年)

hidden (61年)

hide (68,90年)

hide-and-seek (64,87年)

hideous (68年)

highly (49,50,53,61,63,82年)

high-risk (89年)

high-tech (86年)

highway (56,58,75年)

hiking (78年)

hill (74,75年)

hint (66年)

hire (48,87年)

hiss (65年)

historian (47年)

historic (87年)

historical (68年)

history (47,52,54,63,68,69,70,77, 84,87,90年)

hit (54,89年)

hi-tech (87年)

Hitler (49年)

hive (52,53年)

hobby (67,88年)

hold (69,75,77年)

holder (70年)

hole (45,68,77年)

holiday (79,90年)

hollow (83年)

home-baked (86年)

Homer (58年)

home-security (90年)

homesick (47,51年)

homework (58,62,69,76,82,85, 87,89年)

honest (47,49,59,61,73,86年)

honestly (63,83年)

honesty (59,64年)

honor (68,72,79,84年)

honorable (82年)

honorary (60年)

hook (53年)

hopefully (90年)

hopeless (63年)

horizon (68,82,88年)

horn (45年)

horrible (60,70年)

horror (68年)

hospitable (63年)

hospital (63,73,82,84,90年)

hospitality (47年)

host (63,67,81,84,87,89,90年)

hostile (63年)

hostility (66年)

house (65年)

household (87,90年)

housewife (58,79年)

housing (62年)

hover (48年)

however (59,66,67,68,71,77,83, 84,87,89年)

hug (83年)

huge (52,61,67,77,82年)

human (69,70,77,81,82,85,87,88, 89,90年)

human beings (89年)

humane (63年)

humanist (90年)

humanity (87年)

hummingbird (84年)

humor (47,50年)

humorous (51,86,87,88年)

hunger (45,90年)

hunt (64年)

hunting (67,84年)

hurry (58年)

hurt (52,88年)

hurtle (75年)

husband (69,74,75,79,83,85年)

hut (61年)

hydrogen (52年)

hygiene (68年)

hymn (72年)

hyphen (69年)

hypothesis (87年)

I.D. card (88年)

Ice Age (54年)

icebox (85年)

ideal (82年)

idealism (87年)

identical (90年)

identify (65,66,82年)

idiom (85年)

idle (60年)

idleness (60年)

idol (69年)

ignorance (54,69,73,89年)

ignorant (62,86年)

ignore (66,68,79,87年)

illegal (69,78,87年)

illegally (78,80年)

illness (51,77,87,88年)

illuminate (69,87年)

illustrate (85年)

illustration (67年)

image (56,80,81,84年)

imaginable (86年)

imagination (68,69,87年)

imaginative (84,88年)

imagine (49,67,70,81,86,90年)
imbalance (89年)
imitate (68,69,71,81,86年)
imitation (88年)
immature (69年)
immediate (72年)
immediately (61,64,69,88年)
immense (71年)
immensely (87年)
immoral (47年)
immortal (67年)
impact (83年)
impatience (89年)
impatient (86年)
impede (67年)
imperative (61,69年)
imperfect (76年)
implore (48年)
imply (66,71年)
impolite (89年)
import (59,69,80年)
importance (58,62,66,70,78年)
important (52,56,66,73,78,81,82,84,87,89,90年)
importantly (89年)
impose (68,83,87年)
impossible (89年)
impractical (66年)
impregnable (47年)
impress (66,79年)
impressed (62年)
impression (66,69,84,88年)
impressive (73,86年)
imprison (78年)
improbable (62年)
improve (49,62,64,69,70,71,77,81,83,87,90年)
improvement (70,90年)
impulse (64年)
impulsive (89年)
inanimate (71年)

inapplicable (66年)
inborn (79年)
inch (46,78,84,90年)
incident (51,62,64,66,78,83年)
include (53,59,70,75,83,88年)
including (64,73年)
inclusive (67年)
income (60,88年)
incompetent (80年)
incomprehension (66年)
inconspicuous (47年)
inconvenience (85年)
inconvenient (86年)
incorporated (83年)
incorrectly (62年)
increase (49,60,61,63,67,70,72,75,76,81,83,84,85,90年)
increasing (59年)
increasingly (61年)
incredible (47,66,67,86年)
incredibly (63,65年)
indebted (54,69年)
indeed (64,65,67,75,85,86年)
indefinable (73年)
indefinite (55,73年)
independence (51,53,65,80年)
independent (55,72,86年)
independently (69年)
indescribable (65年)
India (61,89年)
Indian (66,82年)
indicate (49,69,73,84,88年)
indication (83,86年)
indifference (57,67,75年)
indifferent (60,69,85,86年)
indigent (53年)
indirect (85年)
indirectly (82年)
indispensable (72,78年)
indisputable (65年)
individual (46,66,67,68,80年)

individually (83年)
Indonesia (87年)
Indonesian (87年)
indoor (61年)
indoors (67年)
indulge (60,67年)
indulgence (87年)
industrial (63,77年)
industrialized (61,62年)
industrious (49,53,73年)
industry (56,61,63,64,83,87年)
inequality (53年)
inevitable (53年)
inevitably (63,67,68,89年)
infant (79,87年)
infantile (58年)
infect (87,88年)
infectious (85年)
inferior (45,47,58,71,83,90年)
infinity (69年)
influence (66,68,81,88,89年)
influent (63年)
inform (45,87年)
informal (73年)
information (62,63,67,69,72,73,76,78,81,86,87,88年)
informative (73年)
infrequently (61,88年)
ingenious (71年)
ingratitude (47年)
ingredient (89年)
inhabit (82年)
inhabitant (53,56,57,62年)
inherit (50,64,70年)
inhuman (52年)
initial (65年)
initially (89年)
initiate (73,82年)
injure (68年)
injury (50,75年)
injustice (90年)

ink (82年)
inner (74,81,84,87年)
innocence (68年)
innocent (48,67年)
inquire (49,56,86年)
inquiry (69年)
insect (48,66,81,85年)
insert (88,90年)
inside (81年)
insight (64年)
insincerely (48年)
insist (53,56,61,71年)
insistence (68,72年)
inspect (49,50年)
inspiration (64,72年)
inspire (47,87年)
inspiring (73年)
install (62,90年)
instead (45,61,64,67,74,77,78,86,87年)
instill (82年)
instinct (64年)
instinctive (68年)
institution (63,67,75,90年)
instruction (65,71,72,75,83,86,87年)
instructive (73年)
instrument (51,65,68,81,82年)
insufficient (69,70年)
insult (59,64年)
insulting (49年)
intact (63年)
intake (76年)
integrity (63年)
intellect (64,88年)
intellectual (68,82,87年)
intelligence (63,65,73,74,81,83年)
intelligent (49,52,63,71,73年)
intelligently (52年)
intend (46,47,51,67,71,90年)

intent (46年)
intention (71,86年)
interact (88年)
interaction (81年)
interchangeably (69年)
interest (55,74,77,78,79年)
interested (67,85年)
interesting (55,66,67,79年)
interfere (50,67年)
interior (87年)
internal (81年)
international (63,66,76,79,85,86年)
interpret (48,79年)
interpretation (67年)
interrupt (47,70,82,89年)
interruption (50年)
intervene (50年)
interview (75年)
intimate (81,83,85年)
intimately (68年)
intimidating (75年)
intolerable (65,69年)
intolerance (49年)
intonation (86年)
introduce (56,75,80,86,88,90年)
intuition (85年)
intuitive (87年)
invade (87年)
invaluable (80年)
invasion (85年)
invent (49,53,61,62,75,77,82,84,87,89年)
invention (54,78年)
inventive (77年)
inventor (64,69,89年)
invert (45年)
invest (69,70,83,87年)
investigate (50年)
investigation (48,55,76年)
investigator (64年)

investment (63,71,83,90年)
invisible (67,77年)
invitation (51,52,62,67,89年)
invite (52,73,77,80,87年)
involve (67,80,82,85,87,88年)
Ireland (76年)
Irish (76年)
iron (54,61,84年)
ironic (74年)
irony (88年)
irregular (90年)
irrelevant (66年)
irresponsible (72年)
irrigation (73,75年)
irritate (89年)
island (50,68,72,80,84年)
islet (66年)
isolate (89年)
isolated (64,68年)
issue (55,83,85年)
Italian (80年)
Italy (53年)
itching (84年)
item (55,62,71,77,80年)
ivory (47,52,64,80年)
jacket (82年)
Jade (90年)
jail (78年)
jam (67,68年)
Japan (61,79年)
jaw (71年)
jealous (48,65,70年)
jet lag (81年)
jewel (47,56年)
Jewish (49年)
jingle (66年)
job (90年)
jog (77,78年)
join (51,78年)
joint (51年)
joke (82,83年)

journalism (66年)

journey (61,62,65,72,75年)

joy (69,88,89年)

judge (46,56,70,71,81,88年)

judgment (64,66,69,86,88年)

juicy (53年)

jump (51,58年)

jungle (58年)

justify (65年)

keen (90年)

keyboard (88年)

kick (51,61年)

kidding (85年)

killer (67年)

kilogram (45,52,79年)

kindergarten (52,85年)

kingdom (50年)

kinsman (47年)

kite (61年)

knack (47年)

knapsack (63年)

kneel (62年)

knit (47,62年)

knock (56,64年)

knot (52,79,88年)

know (60,90年)

know-how (84年)

knowledge (50,51,52,57,59,60,63,66,68,69,70,86,87年)

Korea (61年)

lab (90年)

labor (49,53,60,63,68,78,80年)

laboratory (48,49,62,68,73年)

laborer (50,53,63年)

laboriously (65年)

lack (47,54,59,61,62,64,68,79,84,87年)

ladder (67年)

lake (90年)

lamb (66,70,77年)

lame (60年)

lamp (70年)

land (66,86年)

landlord (89年)

landscape (65年)

landslide (89年)

lane (89年)

language (52,60,71,75,83,85,88,89年)

largely (60,72,75年)

last (53,54,66,71,73,74,89年)

last name (89年)

lasting (84年)

late (58,68,89年)

lately (74,90年)

later (47,53,62,64,67,69,72,73,74,76,80,83年)

latest (64,87,89年)

Latin (72年)

latter (47,48,53,64,84,87年)

laugh (61年)

laughter (66年)

launch (47年)

laundry (86年)

lawn (63,90年)

lawnmower (90年)

lawn-mowing (90年)

lawyer (66年)

lay (46,50,55,60,61,63,67,68,71,72年)

layer (87,90年)

lazily (87年)

laziness (50,70,89年)

lazy (46,49,54,55,58,66,74年)

lead (52,62,87,89年)

leading (73,76年)

leaf (62,89年)

league (65年)

leak (60,63,68年)

lean (76年)

leap (89年)

learned (67年)

least (58,61,64,66,79年)

lecture (49,52,65,73,83年)

left (76年)

legal (68,80年)

legally (85,87年)

legend (45,90年)

legislation (69年)

legitimate (48年)

leisure (68,70,90年)

lend (55,58,87年)

length (46,65,81年)

lengthen (50,90年)

lengthy (89年)

lesson (90年)

letter (51,82,90年)

level (54,60,65,68,70,82年)

liar (66年)

liberal (70,87年)

liberalize (88年)

liberate (86年)

liberty (47,62年)

librarian (51,54,74年)

library (52,80,85年)

license (68,80,84年)

lie (51,59,61,72,74年)

life (90年)

lifetime (66,88年)

lift (75,84,89年)

light (45,55,58,59,73,77,82年)

lightning (61,77年)

likable (89年)

likely (45,49,51,58,61,66,69,76,82,84,87年)

likewise (83年)

limit (69,83,87,90年)

limitation (67,84,87年)

limited (49,67年)

limousine (90年)

line (90年)

linger (62年)

link (86,87年)

lips (61年)
liquor (80年)
lit (68年)
literally (68年)
literary (50,67年)
literature (54,56,68,72,87年)
little (90年)
live (90年)
livestock (90年)
living (52,59,65,66,70,89年)
load (51,64,67,72年)
loaf (52,86年)
lobster (90年)
local (50,62,66,73,76年)
lock (54,63年)
locomotive (46年)
log-cabin (50年)
logic (77年)
logical (53,77年)
loiter (64年)
loneliness (89年)
lonely (47,64,74年)
longer (90年)
loop (82年)
loose (50,61,63,67,68,89年)
loosen (50,52年)
lord (59年)
loss (49年)
lot (54年)
lottery (86年)
loved (89,90年)
lovely (89年)
lover (90年)
lower (66,70,80,83,90年)
low-power (90年)
loyal (84年)
loyally (48年)
loyalty (50年)
luck (54年)
luggage (89年)
lumber (73年)

lung (64,90年)
lure (55年)
luxurious (70年)
luxury (70年)
machine (52,53,58,60,62,63,75,76,81,85,86年)
machinery (49,63,65年)
mad (52,81年)
madam (49,79年)
magazine (71,76年)
magic (54年)
magnetic (48,59年)
magnetism (48年)
magnificence (62年)
magnificent (64,87年)
maid (51,63年)
mail (53,65,74,84年)
main (55,64,73,77,78,84,87,89年)
mainland (83年)
mainly (53,75,76,79,80,81,82,84,89,90年)
maintain (48,51,54,63,67,68,75,80,90年)
maintenance (48,68,72年)
major (64,66,67,71,80年)
majority (60,62,64,69,87年)
makeup (89年)
male (70,74,79,82年)
malicious (46,69年)
manage (60,67,71,72,77,78年)
management (61,63年)
manager (65,77,79,84年)
manifold (54年)
mankind (50,62,69,78年)
manly (80年)
man-made (60年)
manner (65,68,85,86,87年)
manners (68年)
manpower (70,84年)
mansion (63,87年)
mantic (66年)

manual (53年)
manufacture (81年)
manufacturer (76,85年)
marathon (77年)
marble (50年)
march (47,52,67年)
mark (45,54,64,88年)
markedly (67年)
market (66,69,75,79,86,87,89,90年)
marriage (52,62,90年)
marry (52,55,89,90年)
marvelous (85年)
masculine (80年)
mason (61年)
mass (48,62,63,65,72年)
mass-produced (90年)
master (53,58,67,81,82,88年)
match (77,81,90年)
mate (90年)
material (52,70,75,76,77,78,81,85,87年)
materialize (90年)
mathematical (87年)
mathematics (53,56,76,83,90年)
matter (64,70,76,78,81,82,84,85,88,90年)
mature (72年)
maximize (83年)
maximum (88年)
maybe (78,81,89年)
mayor (53,66年)
meal (49,52,58,74,87年)
mean (47,50,61,63,80,84,85,89年)
meaning (87,89年)
means (47,53,61,65,68,75,76年)
measure (65,68,69,71,80,82,84,88年)
meat (58,62,64,70,73,77,87,89,90年)
mechanic (71,76年)
mechanical (48,49,55,81年)

mechanically (64年)

mechanization (62年)

meddle (67年)

medical (61,76,84,88,90年)

medication (84,90年)

medicine (55,58,76,84,86, 89,90年)

medieval (86年)

mediocre (64年)

meditation (64,90年)

medium (78年)

meet (64,74年)

meeting (52,59,86,87,90年)

melancholy (53年)

melody (45年)

melt (78年)

member (51,52,64,75,80,83年)

memorial (51年)

memorize (63年)

memory (55,62,64,65,72,74, 81,88年)

menace (52年)

mend (46,61年)

mental (52,53,77,81年)

mentality (81年)

mention (49,52,57,59,67,76,80, 87,89,90年)

merchant (56,65年)

mere (47,53,54年)

merely (55,63,83,87年)

merge (89年)

mess (88年)

message (48,49,52,75,81,82,83, 84,86,88年)

messenger (48,63,86年)

metal (46,49,55,56,81年)

meteorologist (51年)

meter (77年)

method (47,50,60,65,78,82,84, 87,90年)

meticulously (68年)

Mexican (75年)

Mexico (75年)

microphone (81,90年)

microscope (61年)

middle (66,68,69,75,80,90年)

midnight (50,59,83年)

might (77年)

mighty (47,75,90年)

migrant (84年)

migration (84年)

mild (75,80年)

mile (82年)

military (67,84,88年)

milk (90年)

mill (67年)

million (74,80,89年)

mind (52年)

mine (62,85年)

miner (50年)

mineral (49,50,76,85年)

miniaturize (68年)

minimize (88年)

minimum (65,68,69年)

minister (46,47,65年)

ministry (65年)

minor (67,83年)

minus (59年)

minute (62,67,89,90年)

miraculous (88年)

mirage (58年)

mirror (56,76年)

mischievous (68年)

miserable (86年)

misery (53,69年)

misfortune (53,57年)

mislead (84年)

misleading (66,70年)

misplace (75年)

miss (52,60,64,65,72,75,89年)

missile (58年)

missing (81,89年)

mission (50,69年)

mistake (75,78,86,88年)

mistaken (70,84年)

misunderstand (46年)

misunderstanding (67年)

mix (87年)

mixed (51,66年)

mob (50,67年)

mocking (67年)

model (45,52,67,76年)

moderate (87,90年)

moderation (60,73年)

modern (58,77,78,80,82,84, 87,88年)

modesty (50年)

moisture (61年)

mold (62年)

mom (77年)

moment (46,54,62,65,68,74,76, 82,83,86,89年)

momentum (62年)

monetary (68年)

monopolize (63年)

monosyllable (68年)

monotonous (60年)

monster (81年)

month (89年)

mood (64,81,90年)

moral (60,63,67,89,90年)

moreover (54,67,70,76,77, 79,87年)

mortal (45年)

mosquito (48,64年)

mostly (60,62,77,81年)

motion (61,81年)

motor (76年)

motorcycle (85年)

mountain (90年)

mouth (90年)

move (52,56,58,59,68,69,74,82, 83,90年)

movement (48,50,82,84年)

movie (90年)

Mozart (88年)

Mt. (90年)

mule (88年)

multiply (90年)

multitude (51年)

murder (50,64,80年)

murderer (56,80年)

muscle (60,63年)

museum (45,49,52,66,82,84,85年)

music (90年)

musical (48,82年)

musician (68,86年)

mustard (89年)

mute (65,66年)

mutual (51年)

mutually (86,87年)

mysterious (51,64,66,85,90年)

mysteriously (88年)

mystery (50,57,81,85,90年)

nail (70年)

name (82年)

namely (58年)

narrowly (62年)

nation (52,62,63,69,70,75年)

national (67,73,76,80,84,85年)

nationalism (76年)

nationality (52年)

native (50,69,73年)

natural (65,68,69,84,85,89年)

naturally (65,66,77年)

nature (66,67,79,82,87,89,90年)

naughty (86年)

navigation (75年)

navy (47年)

nearby (83,90年)

nearly (62,67,68,79,82,84,86,89年)

nearsightedness (82年)

neatly (55,74年)

necessarily (46,49,52,53,72,78, 83,88年)

necessary (52,58,73年)

necessitate (51年)

necessity (46,65,68,89年)

neck (64年)

nectar (84年)

need (90年)

needle (45,48年)

needy (90年)

negative (57年)

neglect (66,86年)

negligible (69年)

negotiate (86年)

negotiation (85年)

negro (65年)

neighbor (48,57,63,65,67,77,79, 83,86,90年)

neighborhood (62,83,85年)

neighboring (53,86年)

neither (52,53,56,57,60,62,63, 66,75,89,90年)

nephew (47,59年)

nerve (68年)

nervous (74,77,86年)

nest (66年)

net (59,64年)

network (47,75年)

nevertheless (65,66年)

nibble (53年)

nick (73年)

niece (69年)

nightmare (63,65年)

nitrate (77年)

noble (68年)

nod (73,89年)

nodding (68年)

noise (58,61,90年)

noisy (90年)

nominee (75年)

none (53,67,73,77年)

non-familiarity (69年)

nonsense (69,73,87年)

nonverbal (79,83,85年)

norm (88年)

normal (49,60,66,68,72,81, 84,89年)

normally (51,87年)

north (48,54,75,89年)

northward (54年)

nose (90年)

note (52,62,65,74,90年)

notebook (79,90年)

noteworthy (73年)

nothing (90年)

nothingness (67年)

notice (48,49,50,62,75,78,79,81, 83,84,85,86,89,90年)

noticeable (82,86年)

notify (78年)

notorious (63,82年)

noun (51年)

nourish (87年)

nourishment (87年)

novel (67,82,89,90年)

nowadays (72,73,77,84年)

nowhere (86,89年)

nuclear (69,75年)

nucleus (48年)

nuisance (48,49年)

number (55,64,65,67,69,72,75,76, 77,80,81,82,84,85,87,89,90年)

numerically (47年)

numerous (53,58,70,79,87年)

nurture (73年)

nut (66年)

nutrient (87年)

nutrition (87年)

oak (54年)

oath (61年)

obedient (60,69,72年)

obey (53,75年)

object (45,50,52,61,63,66,69,71, 78,87年)

objection (72年)

objective (65年)

objectivity (71年)

objector (63年)

obligation (61年)

obscurity (67年)

observant (85年)

observation (48,49年)

observe (49,57,66,85年)

obsess (74年)

obstacle (71,87年)

obstinate (69,85年)

obstruction (49年)

obtain (66,75年)

obvious (49,64,76,82,83,89年)

occasion (52,65,89年)

occasional (83年)

occasionally (51,84,89,90年)

occupy (49,56年)

occur (62,63,68,70,80,83年)

occurrence (48,68年)

ocean (82年)

odious (68年)

offend (69,85年)

offense (85年)

offensive (73年)

offer (48,50,52,53,60,65,68,69, 78,79,81,90年)

office (76年)

officer (51,64,76,84年)

official (47,48,61,76,82,83,84年)

officialdom (67年)

officially (80年)

old-fashioned (58,72年)

Olympics (77年)

omit (45,62年)

once (90年)

onion (70,75,89年)

open-handed (63年)

opening (59年)

opera (73年)

operate (51,56,60,81,85,90年)

operation (49,73,86,89年)

operator (51,89年)

opinion (46,60,69,73,80,85, 86,87年)

opportunity (45,47,60,64,68, 70,75年)

oppose (63,76年)

opposite (55,72年)

opposition (46,69年)

optimism (63年)

optimist (63年)

optimistic (66,85,86年)

optionally (89年)

oral (72年)

orangutan (87年)

orator (64年)

oratory (73年)

orchard (48年)

order (49,53,64,68,79,88,90年)

orderly (61,68年)

ordinary (84年)

organ (50年)

organic (67年)

organism (67,70,89年)

organization (51,67,68,83年)

organize (62,67,71,86,88,90年)

oriental (71年)

origin (46,53,79年)

original (53,56,72,87,88年)

originally (73,82年)

originate (89年)

originator (89年)

orphan (52年)

other (90年)

otherwise (55,67,76,81,84, 88,89年)

ouch (88年)

ought (60,61年)

outcome (68,86年)

outer (81,84年)

outing (70年)

outlet (61年)

outlook (63年)

outset (65,87年)

outside (67,81年)

outspoken (63,73年)

outstanding (63,66,70,80年)

ovation (64年)

overall (88年)

overboard (62年)

overcoat (60年)

overcome (50,87年)

overemphasize (66年)

overhear (62年)

overjoyed (66年)

overload (52,60年)

overlook (65,66年)

overrule (51年)

overseas (59年)

oversleep (68年)

overstate (66年)

overthrow (69,83年)

overweight (60年)

overwhelming (47年)

overwhelmingly (89年)

overwork (63,89年)

owe (60,61,74,83年)

owner (88,89,90年)

ox (54年)

oxygen (47,52,84年)

ozone (90年)

p's and q's (87年)

pace (60,63年)

pacific (66年)

pack (56,62年)

package (88年)

padding (75年)

page (71年)
pagoda (51年)
pain (63,71,83,86,90年)
painful (65,89年)
painfully (64年)
painkiller (90年)
pain-relieving (90年)
paint (54,71年)
painting (84,85年)
pair (69年)
palace (47,66,82,87年)
pale (47年)
pan (55,71,77年)
pane (65年)
panic (50年)
paper (90年)
paradise (80年)
paragraph (52,73,87年)
parallel (48,63年)
paralyze (68年)
paraphrase (89年)
pardon (48,81年)
Paris (88年)
parliament (65年)
parlor (46年)
part (90年)
partial (87年)
partially (62,87,90年)
participant (68年)
participate (66,86年)
particle (49,61年)
particular (51,58,61,73,78,84,87,90年)
particularly (81年)
partition (64年)
partly (79,82,87年)
party (64年)
pass (86,89年)
passage (50,53,57,72,76,77,81,82,84,85,86,87,88,89年)
passenger (46,51,65,84,88年)

passer-by (73年)
passion (64,67,88年)
passive (52年)
past (51,68,78年)
pastime (68,79,87年)
pasture (52,69年)
patch (53年)
path (74,80年)
patience (65,69,88年)
patient (50,61,63,69,77,78,83,84,89,90年)
patiently (53年)
patriot (46,48年)
patriotic (60年)
patriotism (46年)
patter (65年)
pattern (81年)
pay (45,52,61,62,76,89,90年)
payment (66,79年)
peace (59,64,68,73,77,90年)
peaceful (65,68,74,90年)
peach (83年)
peak (51,59,90年)
peanut (73年)
pear (61,63,64年)
pearl (90年)
peasant (51,54年)
peasantry (54年)
peat (87年)
pebble (72年)
peculiar (68,73年)
peel (89年)
penetrate (47,53年)
penny (56,67年)
per (79,85,87年)
perceive (71,72年)
percent (61,62,73,75,76,87年)
perception (67年)
perceptive (85年)
perfect (59,70,71,77,83,85年)
perfection (69,86,89年)

perfectly (54,68,82年)
perform (49,50,63,65,66,81,85,87,88,90年)
performance (48,51,62,70,86,87,90年)
perfume (85年)
perhaps (60,64,67,68,76,77,81,88,89年)
peril (54年)
period (54,58,60,68,72,79,82,90年)
perish (59,70年)
permanent (45,89年)
permission (51,81年)
permit (59,84,90年)
perseverance (48,51,67年)
persevere (48年)
Persia (47年)
persist (70,79,83年)
person (71,81,83,90年)
personable (64年)
personal (51,87年)
personality (49,64,86年)
personally (66,72年)
persuade (54,55,66,79,86,87年)
persuasive (88年)
pessimism (63,71年)
pessimist (63年)
pessimistic (68年)
pest (67年)
pet (85,87,88年)
petroleum (69年)
phase (71年)
phenomena (77年)
phenomenal (69年)
phenomenon (50年)
philosopher (86年)
philosophical (67年)
philosophy (51,70,87年)
phonetic (53年)
photo (74年)

photograph (52,53,55,79,84年)
photographer (68,72,74,77年)
photography (74,77年)
phrase (49,59年)
physical (71,76,77,81,87,90年)
physically (68,76年)
physician (58年)
physicist (63,66年)
physics (89年)
pianist (49,54年)
piano (88年)
pick (64,70年)
picky (86年)
picture (90年)
picturesque (66年)
piece (59,61,68,73,89年)
piety (73年)
pigtail (69年)
pile (46年)
pillar (84年)
pilot (48,51,66,67年)
pin (55年)
pinch (70年)
pine (55,63年)
pineapple (76年)
pink (53年)
pipe (61,64年)
piper (65年)
pit (84年)
pity (59,67,77,84年)
place (90年)
plague (63年)
plain (57,65,89年)
plane (45,66年)
planet (61,81,82年)
plant (75,79,81,82,90年)
plantation (87年)
planting (90年)
plastic (78,79年)
plate (49,77,90年)
plateau (75年)

platform (84年)
play (52,90年)
player (90年)
playwright (68年)
plead (52,78年)
pleasant (48,53,66,68,76,80,83,89年)
pleasantry (67年)
please (61,64,79年)
pleased (68,73,81,83年)
pleasure (50,53,56,57,58,65,66,74,78,84,87,88,89,90年)
plenty (73年)
plough (54,63,66年)
plumber (61年)
plus (80年)
poacher (80,84年)
pocket (47,50年)
pocketbook (86年)
pod (63年)
poem (45,50,59,89年)
poet (66,68年)
poetry (72年)
point (66,71,79,86年)
pointed (45年)
pointless (67年)
poison (70年)
poisonous (51,70,82年)
pole (54年)
police (48,53年)
policy (66,67年)
polish (88年)
polite (55,58,67,81年)
politely (74年)
political (50,62,67,69,89年)
politician (56,63,64年)
politics (53,54年)
pollute (80年)
pollution (61,64,66,70,89年)
pool (73年)
poor (90年)

popular (61,76,77,79,84,89,90年)
popularity (75,89年)
popularize (88年)
population (52,61,62,66,70,71,76,86,87年)
populous (85年)
porch (50,83年)
pork (59年)
port (59,73年)
portable (79,84年)
portion (65,86年)
pose (61,63,71,87年)
position (46,62,68,69,82年)
positive (87,88年)
possess (45,49,59,61,70,72,78,88年)
possession (50,69,78,87年)
possibility (51,54,78,86年)
possible (86,88,89年)
possibly (85年)
post (78,82,88年)
postage (45,88年)
postal (78,80年)
poster (84年)
posterior (83年)
postmaster (62年)
postpone (48,50,56年)
postponement (73年)
posture (71年)
pot (77年)
potential (85,90年)
potentiality (68年)
pottery (84年)
pound (49,50,59,60,64,74,85年)
pour (58年)
poverty (45,73,77,90年)
powder (73,76年)
power (47,49,52,64,66,67,69,70,85,87年)
powerful (49,60,74,84年)
practical (50,67,84,90年)

practice (54,58,64,74,77,85,90年)

praise (48,49,88,90年)

pray (45,56年)

preach (77年)

precarious (45年)

precede (64年)

preceding (68年)

precious (56,57,69,72,87年)

precise (69年)

precisely (82,84,85年)

precision (71年)

preclassical (58年)

predator (90年)

predicate (65年)

predict (63,71,81年)

predictable (87年)

prediction (66年)

prefer (48,59,61,68,76,77,80,90年)

preferable (87年)

preference (89年)

prejudice (65,85年)

preliminary (47年)

premier (72年)

preoccupied (69年)

preparation (72年)

prepare (51,56,66,67,74,76,88,89,90年)

preschool (90年)

prescribe (55年)

prescription (74,87年)

present (62,64,65,66,68,69,70,73,76,77,78,81,84,85,86,90年)

presentation (73年)

presently (78年)

preserve (68,70,79,84年)

president (50,51,52,62,64,69,83,87,90年)

presidential (50年)

press (53,69年)

pressure (67,71,73,76,81,86年)

prestige (72年)

prestigious (72年)

presume (71年)

pretend (46,51,59,68年)

pretense (68年)

pretension (69年)

pretentious (88年)

pretty (52,64,66,77,79,80,81,89年)

prevail (68年)

prevent (50,53,63,66,90年)

prevention (88年)

preventive (88年)

previous (62,72年)

previously (84年)

prey (67年)

price (60,62,63,65,66,68,76,89,90年)

priceless (69年)

pride (65,66,77,85年)

priest (62,69,90年)

primarily (52,75,88,90年)

primary (51,76年)

primitive (48,54,62,68,77年)

prince (68年)

principal (47,54,81年)

principle (60年)

print (55,58年)

prior (72年)

priority (71年)

prison (90年)

privacy (80年)

private (68,83,88年)

privilege (68年)

prize (53,54,59,66,73,77,89年)

probability (48年)

probable (48,69年)

probably (52,54,60,62,67,75,78,79,83,86年)

problem (81,90年)

procedure (60,90年)

proceed (64,71,85年)

process (45,62,63,68,70,78,81,87,88,89年)

produce (48,50,52,70,75,78,81,82,86,89,90年)

product (62,66,68,73,79,81,83,85,87,89,90年)

production (63,90年)

productive (88年)

profession (80,82年)

professional (63,71,77,82年)

professor (49,51,52,53,60,64,72,84年)

proficient (88年)

profit (49,58,61,68,83,87,90年)

profound (87年)

program (78,79,80,81,82,87,90年)

progress (54,59,63,66,67,70,81,85年)

progressive (54年)

progressively (71年)

prohibit (84年)

prohibition (80年)

project (49,50,64,65年)

prominent (49,66年)

promise (50,63,68,75,79年)

promising (65年)

promote (64,76,88,90年)

prompt (65年)

promptly (69年)

prone (67年)

pronoun (69,71年)

pronunciation (53,68,69年)

proper (74,78,87年)

properly (72,88年)

property (51,82,90年)

prophet (63,85年)

proportion (88年)

proposal (66,67,68,71年)

propose (63,88年)

propriety (69年)
prose (72年)
prospect (63年)
prospective (74年)
prosperity (48,49,69年)
prosperous (69年)
protect (48,49,56,58,77,80,84,85,90年)
protection (49,75,88,90年)
protective (77年)
protectively (88年)
protector (71年)
protest (50,59年)
proud (60,65,66,70,85,90年)
prove (60,64,67,73,80,88年)
proverb (85年)
provide (61,69,75,76,78,81,82,87,90年)
provided (78年)
provincial (75年)
provision (70年)
psalm (72年)
psychology (50年)
publicity (76年)
publicize (90年)
public-minded (61年)
publish (47,60年)
publisher (87,88年)
pull (53,82年)
pump (47,60,68年)
punctual (47年)
punctually (50年)
punish (48,49,67,69,80,84,88,89年)
punishment (88年)
pupil (64年)
puppy (88年)
purchase (59,78,83年)
pure (52,54,57,71,78年)
purpose (57,66,67,70,78,79,90年)
purse (59年)
pursue (49,67年)

pursuit (66年)
push (46,53,77年)
puzzle (50,51,52年)
puzzled (62年)
qualification (52,74年)
qualified (72年)
qualify (52,66,73,75,86年)
quality (46,63,67,68,69,70,74,84年)
quarrel (46,60,62,65,86年)
quarter (49,56,58,85,86年)
queen (58年)
quest (63年)
quick (71年)
quick-tempered (65年)
quiet (53,59,71,74年)
quit (56,63,72,82,84年)
quite (59,62,64,65,66,67,68,71,72,76,77,78,80,82,86,87年)
race (62,64,67,68,77,85,88年)
racial (49,65年)
radiant (89年)
radiator (68年)
radio (90年)
rage (66年)
raider (87年)
rail (54,59年)
railroad (50年)
railway (46,85年)
rainbow (89年)
rainfall (73,87年)
rainforest (79,87年)
raise (54,57,61,63,64,67,68,70,71,73,75,77,79,80,83,85年)
randomly (90年)
range (52,78,90年)
rapid (47,60,90年)
rapidity (60年)
rapidly (63,66,81,84,88年)
rare (69年)
rarely (64,69,82,87,90年)

rascal (47年)
rash (63年)
rate (54,60,62,79,90年)
rather (63,65,69,72,74,76,77,79,82,86,90年)
ration (63,73年)
raw (58年)
reach (57,80,86,87年)
react (78年)
reaction (68,83,84年)
read (90年)
readily (79年)
reading (60,78年)
realism (50年)
realistic (71,84年)
reality (54,55年)
realization (68年)
realize (62,66,67,69,70,75,78,81,84,85,88,89,90年)
really (75,76,79,90年)
reap (48,54年)
rear (49,67年)
reason (56,63,70,74,75,87,89,90年)
reasonable (62,67,79,87年)
recall (49,64,83,88年)
recapitulate (63年)
receipt (47年)
receive (50,55,62,64,68,69,73,75,78,80,84,86,87,88,90年)
recent (60,69,71,77,79,84,87年)
recently (63,65,66,80,85,90年)
reception (67,81年)
receptionist (85年)
recession (83年)
reckless (83,84年)
recognition (67,68,72,73年)
recognize (48,81,84,85,88,90年)
recollection (72年)
recommend (49,52,53,80,87,88年)
recommendation (88年)

recompense (71年)

record (69,70,76,78,81,85,88年)

recording (90年)

recover (61,62,63,70,78,86年)

recovery (90年)

recreation (54,73,78,84年)

recycle (79年)

red-eyed (89年)

redouble (69年)

reduce (49,67,68,72,80,88,90年)

reduction (84年)

re-educate (73年)

reef (59年)

reel (64年)

refer (58,63,69,88,89年)

reference (62年)

refill (83年)

refinement (68年)

reflect (48,52,81,82,87年)

reflection (52,86,89年)

reform (85年)

reformation (50年)

reformer (80年)

refresh (89年)

refuge (59年)

refund (65年)

refusal (48,52年)

refuse (47,48,50,51,52,62,63,65,
66,69,72,73,80年)

regain (82年)

regard (49,58,64,66,67,68,69,71,72,
75,81,87,88年)

regarding (65,71,80,84年)

regime (49年)

region (51,58,75年)

regional (65年)

register (83年)

regret (48,65,66,81年)

regretful (72年)

regretfully (90年)

regular (45,76,81,90年)

regularly (85,86年)

regulate (50,81年)

reimburse (72年)

reinforce (47,88年)

reject (66,74,76年)

relate (63,87年)

related (54年)

relation (65,67,78年)

relationship (73,81,83,89年)

relative (47年)

relatively (71,88年)

relax (71,81,82,87年)

relaxing (80年)

release (61,78,90年)

reliable (65,87年)

reliance (54年)

relief (45,61,65,83年)

relieve (51,61,73,84,90年)

religion (53,54,62,67,87年)

religious (47,49,50,67年)

reluctance (52年)

reluctant (52年)

rely (46,84,90年)

remain (47,63,65,69,74,82,84,85,
87,88,90年)

remark (49年)

remarkable (50,57,60,71,72,90年)

remember (65,68,71,74,75,78,
80,87年)

remembrance (47年)

remind (48,49,54,55,58,68,
73,83年)

reminder (72年)

reminiscence (68年)

remote (66,81年)

remove (90年)

renown (67年)

renowned (67年)

rent (80年)

repaint (71年)

repair (60,62,64,65,75,90年)

repeat (48,54,65,83,89年)

repel (66年)

repetition (47,48,52年)

repetitive (63年)

replace (63,64,75,76,86,87年)

replaceable (84年)

reply (47,55,56,61,71,74,76,77,
80,88年)

report (71,83,84,90年)

reporter (82年)

represent (56,65,70,78,82年)

representative (88年)

repressive (68年)

republic (61,62,64,73年)

repulse (47年)

reputation (45,85年)

request (48,49,62,63,64,79,80,
82,89年)

require (49,54,63,65,69,72,90年)

required (87年)

requirement (64,65,74年)

rescue (69年)

research (49,64,68,69,71,76,79,
82,90年)

researcher (79,90年)

resemblance (46,53年)

resemble (48,49,90年)

reservation (67,88年)

reserve (57,60,71,81,83年)

reset (81年)

resident (66,73,85,87年)

residential (82年)

resign (50,82年)

resist (47,56,63,71,83年)

resistance (66,68,69,71年)

resistant (66年)

resistible (87年)

resolution (90年)

resolve (89年)

resource (47,69,83年)

respect (46,58,61,62,64,65,67,C8, 73,81,82,87年)

respectable (61年)

respectful (50年)

respective (53年)

respectively (61,83年)

respond (67,69,79,81,83年)

response (69,85,89,90年)

responsibility (51,65,67,86, 87,88年)

responsible (64,69,71,80年)

rest (47,59,68,72,75年)

restaurant (49,55,75,82,85, 86,87年)

restless (54年)

restore (50,72,90年)

restriction (67,71,73,84年)

result (47,55,61,64,67,70,71,73, 74,77,81,82,90年)

resume (73年)

retain (72,74,82,87年)

retire (56,61,67年)

retreat (59,64,90年)

retrieve (54,78年)

return (58,62,73,86,88,89,90年)

reveal (46,62,85,88年)

revelation (68年)

revenge (69年)

reverse (47,63,80年)

reversely (72年)

review (64,84,88年)

reviewer (88年)

revive (70年)

revocation (83年)

revolution (48年)

revolve (48年)

reward (54,57,87,88,89年)

rewarding (54,80年)

rewrite (54年)

rhyme (89年)

rhythm (61,81年)

rib (54年)

rice (61,65,81年)

rid (89年)

ride (54,77,83,86年)

rifle (88年)

rightful (87年)

rightly (61年)

rigidity (68,71年)

ring (45,74,76,77,86年)

ripe (48,69年)

ripen (65年)

rise (46,50,51,53,59,60,61,63,68, 78,81,86年)

risk (71,89年)

ritual (66年)

rival (60,62,66年)

river (90年)

roadway (89年)

roar (46,55,60,66,75年)

rob (72年)

robin (66年)

robomowe (90年)

robot (81,90年)

robotic (90年)

rocky (61年)

rod (55,64年)

role (61,69年)

roll (45,47,84,90年)

roman (68,82年)

romance (66年)

romantic (66年)

Rome (90年)

roof (51,55,84,87年)

roommate (82年)

root (71,75,79年)

rope (59年)

rough (71,88年)

roughly (72,79,87年)

round (82年)

route (51年)

routine (48,67,72年)

row (82年)

rub (53,59,90年)

rude (81,88年)

rudeness (49,54年)

ruin (46,54,63,66,68,69,78年)

rule (72,88年)

rumor (64年)

run (49,76,83,90年)

rush (45,63,65,67,68,75,84,85,89 年)

Russian (58年)

rust (60年)

sack (65,66年)

sackful (69年)

sacrifice (68年)

sadden (69年)

sadness (53,89年)

safe (46,61年)

safely (82,85年)

safety (64,90年)

sail (54年)

sailor (68年)

salad (79年)

salary (50,80年)

sale (55,58,61,79,89年)

saline (89年)

salt (78,89年)

salty (78年)

salute (63年)

sample (46年)

sanction (83年)

sand (45年)

sandwich (89年)

sarcasm (65年)

sarcastic (65年)

satisfaction (48年)

satisfactory (73年)

satisfied (61,79年)

satisfy (48,87年)

satisfying (87年)

savage (45,68,70年)

savagely (50年)

save (46,48,50,56,66,67,79,86,
87.00年)

saver (71年)

saw (61年)

saying (81年)

scale (82年)

scalp (68年)

scamper (64年)

scandal (82年)

scarce (86年)

scarcely (63,64,65,79,88,90年)

scare (59,64,71,90年)

scared (78年)

scarf (64年)

scary (90年)

scene (58,61,72年)

scenery (48,90年)

schedule (56,69,72,73,90年)

scheme (58年)

scholar (45,49,50,67,80,81年)

scholastic (73年)

schoolboy (61年)

schooling (82年)

schoolwork (87年)

science (53,63,66,68,73,77,81,87,
88,90年)

scientific (45,48,49,64,71,76,
77,82年)

scientist (66,71,74,85,87,88,
89,90年)

scold (61,75,88年)

score (61,75,81,90年)

scorn (45年)

scout (64年)

scratch (62年)

scream (50年)

sculpture (53年)

sea (90年)

seahorse (77年)

seal (67,79年)

seaport (46年)

search (56,61,74,78,80,81,87,89年)

seashore (76年)

seaside (45,72,76年)

season (87年)

seat (57,61,72年)

seawater (78,82年)

secondary (80年)

second-class (65年)

secondhand (56年)

secret (49,61,67,81,85,87,88,90年)

secretary (48,80年)

secretly (50年)

section (85年)

sector (83年)

security (69,78,79,84,88年)

seed (65,89年)

seek (45,61,65,66,71,81,89年)

seem (45,49,54,58,61,62,63,69,74,
75,76,77,78,79,82,88,89年)

seeming (68年)

seemingly (45,69年)

seize (45,54,60,68年)

select (51,52,53,65,70,78年)

selection (53,85年)

self (90年)

sell (90年)

send (89,90年)

senior (45,73,83年)

sense (50,58,66,67,68,70,75,81,
87,90年)

sensitive (85,88年)

sensor (81,90年)

sentence (67,68,78年)

sentiment (64年)

sentry (50年)

separate (64,71,78,88,90年)

sequence (53,67年)

sergeant (71年)

series (82年)

serious (52,58,69,71,82,83,84,85年)

seriously (61,66,70年)

servant (53,54,62,67,81年)

serve (49,61,75,78,82,87,90年)

service (76,78,80,84,90年)

serving (79年)

session (64年)

set (61,62,67,68,69,70,84,89,90年)

setback (68年)

setting (45,89年)

settle (51,54,75,82年)

several (61,75,79,81,82,90年)

severe (47,68,83年)

severely (90年)

sewing (45年)

shade (53,67,90年)

shake (79年)

Shakespeare (52,68年)

shallow (47,63,77,78年)

shame (59,68年)

shameful (66年)

shape (51,61,65,82,86,87,90年)

shapely (67年)

share (50,51,78,80,83,86,88年)

shark (90年)

sharp (45,59,67年)

sharpen (54,56,81年)

sharp-witted (67年)

shatter (51,76年)

shave (62,84年)

shed (89,90年)

sheer (45年)

sheet (64年)

shelf (49,85年)

shell (70,78,90年)

shelter (81,87年)

shepherd (82年)

shield (71,82年)

shift (67,90年)

shipwreck (59,68年)

shiver (47年)

shock (66,72,76年)

shoot (61,71年)

shooting (90年)

shore (50,72,77年)

short (90年)

shortage (70,84年)

shortcut (67,85年)

shortly (64,78年)

shortness (84年)

shot (47,49年)

shoulder (75年)

shout (82,83年)

show (90年)

shower (48,84年)

shriek (62年)

shrimp (79年)

shut (55年)

shy (66,82年)

sick (88年)

sigh (65年)

sight (55,60,66,76,86,90年)

sighting (69年)

sightseeing (64年)

sign (48,49,50,56,58,61,69,70,71,
72,73,79,81,84,89,90年)

signal (64,81,82,83,85,90年)

signature (47,82年)

significance (87年)

significant (66,78年)

silence (46,65年)

silently (72年)

silk (51年)

silken (89年)

silly (52年)

silver (55,77,89年)

similar (48,63,71,76,89,90年)

similarity (48,53,54,71年)

simple (63,86,90年)

simple-minded (63年)

simply (54,58,76,79,81,84,85,
87,89年)

simultaneous (63年)

sin (48,67年)

sincere (89年)

sincerely (75年)

sincerity (68,86年)

singer (88年)

single (52,58,60,64,65,81,85,87,
89,90年)

singular (71年)

sink (59,86年)

site (87年)

situation (51,63,65,67,86,87,89年)

size (89年)

skate (62年)

sketch (86年)

ski (86年)

skill (51,54,67,89年)

skilled (64年)

skillful (49,78,85年)

skin (88年)

skinny (61年)

skull (63年)

sky (89年)

skyline (82年)

slave (47,50,53,62年)

slavery (62年)

sleepless (72年)

sleepy (59,86年)

slender (45,47年)

slice (89年)

slight (64,66,83年)

slightly (67,68年)

slim (76年)

slip (76年)

slow (90年)

slowly (89年)

sluggish (72年)

small (90年)

smart (64,68年)

smartly (45年)

smitten (46年)

smoker (47年)

smooth (58,82年)

smoothly (50,67年)

snake (46,49,51,62年)

sneeze (69,88年)

soak (87年)

soap (58,76年)

social (53,63,65,67,68,71,76,78,
86,88,90年)

socially (89年)

society (52,62,64,68,69,77,79,
86,87,90年)

sock (46,88年)

Socrates (67年)

soft (84年)

soften (83年)

soil (53,54,87年)

solar (81,82年)

soldier (54,63,81,82,86,88,90年)

solely (72年)

solemn (68年)

solemnly (90年)

solid (73年)

solitary (59年)

solution (68,86,87,88,90年)

solve (59,70,71,73,80,81,82年)

somehow (61,63,68,79年)

sometime (76年)

sometimes (53,90年)

somewhat (62年)

somewhere (78,89年)

sore (76年)

sorrow (48,67,69,89年)

sort (45,60,67,68,86,87年)

soul (50,52,61,67年)

sound (53,86,89,90年)

soup (56,65,78年)

source (50,61,62,69,75,78年)

south (47,52,54,75,84年)

southern (52,53,73年)

sow (54,65年)

spa (76年)

space (68,81年)

spacecraft (81年)

spade (72年)

Spain (46,53,66年)

span (67年)

Spanish (46,75年)

spare (83年)

spear (54,77年)

special (62,68,85,89年)

specialist (51,87年)

specialize (52,70年)

species (53,85,89,90年)

specific (89年)

specify (80年)

specimen (49年)

spectacle (45年)

spectacular (90年)

speed (52,59,73,82,89年)

speeding (63,84年)

speedy (64年)

spell (55,63,74,82,89年)

spelling (82,88年)

spend (90年)

spill (63年)

spin (54年)

spirit (47,67,70,84,85年)

spiritual (82年)

spiritually (68年)

splendid (51年)

splendidly (60年)

split (48,49,89年)

spoil (87年)

spontaneous (88年)

spoon (77年)

spoonful (74年)

sport (85,90年)

sportswoman (78年)

spot (53,84,85年)

spouse (89年)

spread (51,53,61,64,68,79,88,89年)

spring (76年)

sprinkle (55年)

spy (49年)

squash (75年)

squirrel (47年)

stable (68年)

stably (52年)

stack (85年)

staff (80,90年)

stage (60,62,65,73,79,86年)

stair (65年)

stairway (90年)

stalk (64年)

stamp (50,69,75年)

stand (80年)

standard (65,71,78,88年)

standing (64年)

star (89年)

stare (46,83年)

starry (63年)

start (90年)

startle (59年)

starvation (45年)

starve (45,75年)

state (48,50,63,67,69,72,75,77,
80,83,85,87,89,90年)

statement (63,64,72,80,82,85,
87,88年)

statesman (51,64年)

statistics (76年)

statue (45年)

stature (45年)

status (45,76年)

statute (45年)

stay (90年)

steadily (85年)

steady (72,76年)

steal (61,89年)

steel (45年)

steep (75,84年)

stem (85年)

step (46,53,61,62,63,89年)

stepmother (66,89年)

stereo (78年)

stereotype (89年)

stick (45,67年)

stimulate (88年)

stir (59,63年)

stock (54,65,69,83年)

stomach (53,83,86年)

stony-hearted (65年)

store (78,81,87年)

storm (77,88年)

stormy (50年)

straight (45,66,84,87,90年)

strain (60年)

stranger (83年)

strategy (47,85,87年)

stream (75,78,90年)

strength (48,49,61,66,74,75年)

strengthen (69,83,86年)

stress (66,73,77,89,90年)

stretch (66,75年)

strict (67,73年)

stride (64年)

strife (63年)

strike (46,50,61,66,69,88年)

string (65,79,90年)

strip (78,80年)

strive (68年)

stroke (63年)

strove (45年)

structure (65,71年)

struggle (45,50,54年)

strut (64年)

stubborn (49,69,70年)

stubbornly (56年)

studio (90年)

study (64,87,89,90年)

stuff (75年)

stunt (64年)

stupid (52,66年)

style (51,78,89年)

subdivide (53年)

subject (50,52,54,55,65,66,74,81年)
submit (54年)
subservient (51年)
subsistence (68,69年)
substantially (64年)
substantiate (63年)
substitute (50,75,76,90年)
subtle (66,83年)
subtlety (67年)
succeed (51,66,67,68年)
success (70,76,83,90年)
succession (51年)
successively (63年)
sudden (59,64年)
suddenly (54,56,59,73,80, 83,89年)
suffer (45,49,57,61,63,68,81年)
sufferable (72年)
suffering (49,57,68,63,67,81, 87年)
sufficient (88,90年)
sugar (52,60,87年)
sugarcane (75年)
suggest (61,66,71,74,76,80,90年)
suggestion (67,82,85,88,89,90年)
suggestive (72年)
suicide (53年)
suit (49,51,54,81,85年)
suitable (69,87年)
suitor (50年)
sum (68,79,80年)
summarize (63,89年)
summary (79年)
summit (87年)
sunken (59年)
sunny (75年)
sunset (80年)
sunshine (75年)
super (74年)
superb (73,90年)
superficial (63,90年)

superhero (89年)
superintendent (63年)
superior (51,52,54,65,66,68,70, 76,83年)
superiority (52,66年)
superman (89年)
supermarket (76,79年)
supernatural (71年)
superstitious (46年)
supper (46,88年)
supply (59,64,69,70,73,78年)
support (45,46,48,49,68,74,76, 78,80,82,84年)
suppose (58,65,73,75,76,88年)
supposedly (71年)
sure (90年)
surely (84年)
surface (59,65,71,77,82年)
surge (75年)
surgeon (49,60年)
surplus (61年)
surprise (52,56,61,62,70,77,82, 83,85,87年)
surprised (49,77年)
surprising (70年)
surprisingly (60,74年)
surrender (60,72年)
surround (47,71年)
surrounding (53,69年)
survival (67,80,87,88年)
survive (58,59,67,70,80,89年)
survivor (59年)
suspect (59,61,64年)
suspense (81年)
suspicious (48,72,86年)
suspiciously (89年)
sustain (85年)
swear (90年)
sweat (59,61,77年)
sweater (77,83年)
sweetheart (86年)

swift (49年)
swiftly (84年)
swim (90年)
swimmer (90年)
Swiss (86年)
Switzerland (82年)
symbol (53,88,89年)
sympathetic (49,82,85年)
sympathize (63,81年)
sympathy (48,86,89年)
symptom (77,81,83年)
synthetic (75年)
system (52,58,60,68,71,81,82,87, 88,89,90年)
systematic (50年)
tackle (70年)
tactful (85年)
tail (56,77年)
tailor (48,68,69年)
Taiwanese (84年)
talent (45,64,68年)
talk show (90年)
talkative (74年)
tank (50,88年)
Taoism (67年)
Taoist (67年)
tap (69年)
tape (59,70年)
target (83年)
task (63,63,70,72,77,81,87年)
taste (64,66,75,79,87年)
tasteless (52年)
tax (59年)
taxi (88年)
teach (90年)
teaching (67年)
team (54,62,64,67,73,84年)
tear (78,89年)
tease (83年)
technical (51,60年)
technician (62年)

technique (69,90年)

technological (63,89年)

technologically (66年)

technology (63,67,68,90年)

tedious (61年)

teenager (51,83,89年)

teeth (88年)

telegram (62,63,67,80年)

telegraph (80年)

television (90年)

tell (90年)

teller (88年)

temper (65,85年)

temperament (48年)

temperature (50,52,58,69,77,81, 82,85年)

tempest (59年)

temple (47,84年)

temporarily (73,75年)

temporary (47,50,69,83年)

tempt (82年)

temptation (49,83年)

tend (54,83,87,88,90年)

tenderness (50,67年)

tennis (81,84年)

tense (46,51年)

tension (63,77,82年)

tent (46,52,67年)

tentatively (88年)

term (54,56,58,66,67,69,81,89年)

terms (78年)

terrible (58,68年)

terribly (58年)

terrify (64,83年)

territory (46年)

testability (71年)

text (72,76年)

Thailand (61,79年)

theater (45,49,76年)

theoretically (66年)

theory (50,63,64,65年)

thereby (66年)

therefore (49,77,79,81,90年)

thick (54,74年)

thief (47,51年)

thimbleful (49年)

thin (53年)

think (90年)

thinking (87年)

third (90年)

thorough (63,66,83,86年)

thoroughly (49,84年)

though (74,78,81,90年)

thought (51,64,69,72年)

thoughtful (77,89年)

thoughtfully (74年)

thousand (77年)

thread (45年)

threat (87年)

threaten (63,80年)

thrift (61年)

thrill (81年)

throat (76年)

throne (72年)

through (70,78,89年)

throughout (69,79,80,85,90年)

thunder (50,60年)

thundershower (73年)

thus (67,76,80,85,89年)

tide (75,82年)

tidy (72年)

tie (51,52,53,79,87,88年)

tiger (90年)

tight (63,67年)

tightly (67年)

timber (87年)

time (90年)

timely (47年)

timepiece (69年)

timid (61年)

timidly (62年)

timing (81年)

tiny (61,62,75,79,82,84,85年)

tip (87年)

title (45,63,85,87年)

tobacco (78年)

toil (65,70,73年)

tolerant (80年)

tolerate (49,60,64,73,86,88年)

tomb (70年)

ton (52,53,54年)

tone (61,67,88年)

tongue (68,76,85年)

tool (45,56,61,70,75年)

toothache (83年)

topic (68,85,88年)

toss (53,68年)

total (68,69,73,76,80,83,84年)

totally (72,87年)

touch (55,83年)

tough (78,83年)

tour (48,66,81年)

tourist (52,57,60,64,66,84年)

tournament (82年)

toward(s) (49,54,63,64,73,74, 84,88年)

towel (84年)

tower (64,82年)

townsfolk (85年)

trace (65年)

track (68,88年)

trade (75,83,87,88,89年)

trader (76年)

trading (76,89年)

tradition (46,47,83年)

traditional (72,75,88,90年)

traffic (52,89年)

tragedy (80,85,88年)

tragic (88年)

train (88年)

trait (79年)

tramp (47年)

trample (80年)

transcript (82年)

transistor (76年)

translate (72,76年)

translation (53年)

transmission (70年)

transmit (85年)

transparent (52年)

transplant (75年)

transport (81年)

transportation (52,53,70,80, 82,87年)

trap (72,84年)

travel (49,88年)

traveling (85年)

treacherously (63年)

treasure (60,64,76年)

treasury (65年)

treat (59,62,88年)

treatment (84,90年)

treaty (56年)

tree (90年)

tremendous (46,48,71,88年)

trend (63,70,76,80年)

trial (47,67,90年)

triangle (45年)

tribal (76年)

tribe (54,58,74年)

tributary (75年)

trick (81年)

tricky (86年)

trip (78,84年)

triumph (67,81年)

triumphantly (85年)

trivial (90年)

troop (47,56年)

tropical (75年)

trouble (90年)

troubled (87年)

troublesome (61年)

trough (65年)

trout (53年)

truck (53年)

truly (60,61,62,67,87,88年)

trunk (52年)

truthful (60年)

try (90年)

tube (49,76,90年)

tumble (75年)

tunnel (58,73年)

turkey (50年)

turnip (75年)

tusk (52,80年)

tutor (87,90年)

twice (49,63年)

twin (53,62,64,66年)

twist (84年)

type (52,53,76,78,87,90年)

typewriter (52年)

typhoon (47,54年)

typical (51,80,90年)

tyranny (47,69年)

tyrant (47,81年)

ugly (61,65,77年)

ultimate (49年)

umbrella (52年)

unable (53,89年)

unanimous (68年)

unaware (69年)

unbearable (80年)

unbelievable (58,66年)

unbroken (65年)

uncertain (67,69年)

uncertainty (83年)

uncharted (66,68年)

uncivilized (58,68年)

uncomfortable (89年)

uncomfortably (51年)

uncommon (62年)

uncomplainingly (68年)

uncovered (67年)

undecided (67年)

undefended (72年)

undemanding (74年)

underground (62,90年)

underline (66,69年)

underpay (65年)

understand (83,84,85,86, 87,90年)

understanding (90年)

undertake (63,72年)

undervalue (63年)

underwater (81,90年)

undesirable (84年)

undisturbed (65年)

undue (60年)

uneasy (83,88年)

uneducated (77年)

unemployed (75年)

unemployment (63,75年)

unequal (53年)

unexpected (62,86年)

unexpectedly (46年)

unfair (86年)

unfairly (63年)

unfaithfully (63年)

unfamiliar (60,85年)

unfavorable (49年)

unforgettable (90年)

unfortunate (66,84年)

unfortunately (64,75,88年)

unfriendly (81年)

uniform (48年)

uniformity (76年)

unimportant (71年)

unimpressive (73年)

uninterested (67年)

uninvited (86年)

unique (72,84,89,90年)

uniqueness (70年)

unit (70年)

universal (54,67年)

universe (50,67,77,87年)

university (52,53,54,64,65,70, 73,75,76,79,90年)

unknown (57,65,78年)

unlawfully (56年)

unless (49,61,64,67,74,80,82, 83,89年)

unlike (79,87年)

unlikely (89年)

unmistakable (55年)

unnecessarily (67年)

unnecessary (63,79年)

unpack (75年)

unpleasant (62,68,72,90年)

unprecedented (70年)

unproductive (53年)

unprogressive (66年)

unquestionable (69年)

unquestionably (70年)

unreasonable (66,85年)

unrecorded (54年)

unreliable (64年)

unsafe (90年)

unskilled (63年)

unsuspected (69年)

untidily (74年)

unusual (72,84,89年)

unwilling (65,67年)

unyielding (68年)

updated (73年)

uphold (67年)

upped (80年)

upper (69,75年)

upright (67,86年)

upset (78,83,85,86,88年)

uranium (49,66年)

urban (65年)

urge (48,65,67,87,88年)

urgent (85年)

urgently (50年)

usage (64,71年)

use (90年)

useful (81,89,90年)

useless (79年)

user (90年)

usual (61,77,81,90年)

usually (89年)

utensil (63,88年)

utility (68年)

utmost (62年)

utter (65,67年)

vacancy (82年)

vacation (61,79,80年)

vacuum (48,68年)

vacuum-cleaner (90年)

vague (45,55,61年)

vaguely (55年)

vagueness (71年)

Valentine (90年)

valiantly (69年)

valuable (56,57,71,75,79,80,82, 86,90年)

value (56,60,63,69,73,78年)

valued (68年)

vanish (59,64,81年)

vapor (53,78年)

variability (71年)

variable (63年)

variety (54,63,79,87,90年)

various (53,63,77,82年)

vary (65,81,83年)

vast (62,87年)

vegetable (87年)

vegetarian (78年)

vegetation (61年)

veil (66年)

vein (49年)

venture (59年)

verbal (83年)

verify (63年)

verse (65,67,72年)

version (68,81年)

veteran (82年)

victim (68,69年)

victor (47年)

victory (47,89年)

view (48,63,67,68,77,82,85,90年)

viewpoint (66年)

vigilance (71年)

vigilant (46年)

vigor (60年)

village (46,50,52,73,75,89年)

villager (46,87,89年)

villain (63年)

violation (88年)

violence (64年)

violin (67,84,90年)

violinist (90年)

VIP (88年)

virgin (79年)

virtually (47,88年)

virtue (61,67年)

virtuous (71年)

virus (87年)

vision (68,71,72年)

visit (90年)

visitor (84,90年)

visual (82年)

visualization (90年)

visualize (67年)

vital (64,67,78,84,87年)

vitamin (60,65年)

vividly (72,73,90年)

vocabulary (49,50,52,51年)

vocational (82年)

voice (67,88年)

volcanic (71年)

volcano (71年)

voluminously (67年)

voluntary (72年)

volunteer (50,72年)

vote (69年)

voter (85年)

voyage (60年)

wage (56年)

waist (64年)

waitress (64年)

wake (53,57年)

wall (90年)

wallet (73年)

wander (59,85年)

wanderer (65年)
wanting (59年)
war (88年)
ward (63年)
warm (64,77,79,81,86,87年)
warn (49,59,67,90年)
wary (72年)
washer (82年)
waste (59,88年)
wasteful (68年)
waterfall (67,85年)
waterlogged (75年)
wave (59,82年)
way (90年)
wayward (72年)
weak (52,59,61,75,90年)
weaken (88年)
weakness (50,66年)
wealth (50,61,69,70,78,87年)
wealthy (49,50,73,77,90年)
weapon (61,63,67,69,84,88年)
wear (54,58,64,81,82,85年)
weather (51,58,63,64,65,69,73,74,77,80,81,82,85,87年)
weave (54,77年)
wedding (65,88年)
weed (75年)
weekday (52年)
weekend (78,90年)
weigh (52,60,66,74,78,79年)
weight (60,68,76,78,85年)
weird (49年)
welfare (65,69,72,88,90年)
well-behaved (62年)
well-being (69,90年)
well-done (65年)
well-dressed (86年)
well-educated (50年)
well-grounded (85年)
well-informed (86年)

well-known (45,60,63,88年)
well-made (66年)
well-nigh (54年)
well-to-do (49,69年)
west (69,81,84年)
western (50,67,69,75,89年)
westerner (84年)
whale (88年)
whatever (78年)
wheel (54,67年)
whereas (72,79年)
wherever (89年)
whether (48,55,56,57,59,61,63,66,67,70,74,77,83年)
while (90年)
whisper (48年)
whole (51,52,58,59,61,67,68,69,71,74,80,86,87,90年)
wholeheartedly (68年)
wicked (89年)
wicken (89年)
widely (60,68,88,90年)
widespread (78年)
widow (52年)
width (45年)
wife (69,90年)
wild (54,58,59,61,68年)
wildlife (76,87年)
willing (67,73,77年)
win (90年)
wind (75,82,87年)
window (90年)
wing (47,84,89年)
wingspread (84年)
winner (51,85年)
wire (90年)
wisdom (48,52,67,86,87年)
wise (48,49,52,57,66,68,89年)
wisely (81年)
wistfully (74年)

wit (54,84年)
withdraw (56,69,70年)
within (75,82,86,90年)
witness (50,66,72,83,84年)
witty (47年)
women (90年)
wonder (48,52,57,63,65,67,68,70,73,75,77,81,82,84,87,88,89年)
wonderful (49,52,54,58,64年)
wonderland (85,87年)
wood (46,48,50,55,63,64年)
wooden (55年)
work (90年)
world (88,90年)
worldly (67年)
worm (53年)
worried (84,89年)
worry (78,89年)
worship (54,75,87年)
worshipper (84年)
worth (56,65,66,77,88,90年)
worthless (79年)
worthwhile (67年)
worthy (61年)
wound (65年)
wreck (59,63年)
wrecked (50年)
wretch (67年)
yard (50,77年)
yearly (85年)
yearn (66年)
yell (69,83年)
yield (49,51,61,72年)
young (90年)
youngster (66,73年)
youth (51,82年)
zero (55,85年)
zip code (88年)
zone (81年)

★ 電腦統計歷屆聯考成語 ★

a chain of (68年)
a close call (70年)
a couple of (55年)
a good deal of (77,81年)
a great deal of (52,77, 80,88年)
a great many (52,90年)
a handful of (89年)
a long time ago (89年)
a lot of (56,59,60,70,72,88年)
a matter of life and death (78年)
a number of (48,64,70,76年)
a rainy day (64年)
a series of (82,84年)
a variety of (87年)
abandon *oneself* to (72年)
above *one's* head (87年)
according to (45,51,53,56,60, 61,63,64,65,67,71,72,76,80,81,85,86, 87,88,89,90年)
account for (45,62,77年)
acquaint *sb.* with (49年)
across the country (90年)
across the nation (72年)
act as (51,72,81年)
add to (85年)
adjust to (78,89年)
afford to (68,87年)
after all (69,70年)
again and again (86年)
agree to (64,67年)
agree with (51,52,67,80,84年)
ahead of (86年)
aim at (84年)
all but (63,67,70年)
all of a sudden (47年)
all over (87年)

all over again (65年)
all over the world (50,68, 70,71,75,79年)
all the better (90年)
all the time (78,82,85年)
along with (66年)
among other things (60,69年)
among others (70,87年)
amount to (54,66,85,88年)
an early bird (86年)
and so forth (81年)
and so on (49,86年)
anything but (49年)
appeal to (69,77,86,88,90年)
appear to (53,59年)
apply for (62,74年)
apply *oneself* (54年)
apply to (87年)
argue against (88年)
argue with (45,54年)
around the corner (75年)
as a consequence of (68年)
as a matter of fact (66,78年)
as a result (53,73,85,88年)
as a result of (74,82,90年)
as a rule (45,70年)
as a whole (71年)
as far as (84年)
as far as~be concerned (64,66,68,79,90年)
as for (58年)
as good as (81年)
as if (85,88年)
as is the case with (71年)
as long as (49,61,64,67,72,74, 79,84,87,89年)

as many as (83年)
as much (87年)
as much as (68,80,81,82年)
as soon as (73,79,84,88年)
as soon as possible (66年)
as such (88年)
as the years pass (69年)
as though (79,88年)
as to (52,61,67,85,88年)
as well (75,83,89年)
as well as (53,64,66,70,73,81, 84,85,86,90年)
as~as anyone can be (67,70年)
as~as it is (89年)
as~as possible (74,83,87年)
ask about (73年)
ask for (88年)
associate with (89年)
at a minimum of cost (69年)
at a time (60,72年)
at all (69,83年)
at all costs (64,87年)
at any cost (87年)
at any time (69,88年)
at best (50,89,90年)
at birth (87年)
at ease (62,81年)
at every turn of a corner (65年)
at fault (68年)
at first (47,62,65,76年)
at full speed (56年)
at great speed (82年)
at hand (64,65年)
at high speeds (52年)
at last (61,68,74,78,85年)

at least (52,55,61,63,65,68,79, 80,87,89,90年)

at night (45年)

at noon (56年)

at once (54,55,60年)

at one time (75,81年)

at *one's* mercy (47年)

at random (55年)

at rest (62年)

at sea (58,60,62年)

at that moment (51年)

at that time (50,77,90年)

at the age of (58,73年)

at the beginning (54年)

at the end (81年)

at the expense of (68年)

at the finish (85年)

at the first moment (88年)

at the first sight (54年)

at the foot of a hill (74年)

at the hands of (68年)

at the mercy of (65年)

at the moment (69,79,81年)

at the peak of (51年)

at the rate of (79年)

at the request of (79年)

at the same time (63, 87,88年)

at the start (60年)

at this time (82年)

at will (84年)

at work (68年)

attach importance to (67年)

attempt to (66年)

attend school (62年)

attend to (88年)

away from (88,89年)

back and forth (65,89年)

back sb. up (71,72年)

bark at (80年)

based on (78,88年)

based upon (77年)

be able to (51,54,60,61,62,63, 71,73,74,75,76,87,89,90年)

be about to (67年)

be above V-ing (66年)

be absented from (71年)

be absorbed in (66,69年)

be accessible to (59年)

be accused of (61,67,85年)

be accustomed to (83年)

be acquainted with (55,67年)

be afraid of (54年)

be all for (85年)

be allergic to (83年)

be amused by (63年)

be angry with (83年)

be anxious about (76年)

be anxious to (89年)

be apt to (64年)

be associated with (69,89年)

be at home (68年)

be attached to (72年)

be attended with (54年)

be aware of (62,64,67,68年)

be based on (76,78,84年)

be beyond *one's* ability (70年)

be born with (45年)

be bound for (54年)

be bound to (70,87年)

be capable of (64,66年)

be careful about (88年)

be carried away (51年)

be caught in (65,68年)

be characterized by (71年)

be close to (11,86年)

be closely connected with (72年)

be comparable to (79年)

be compared to (57,60,82, 84,90年)

be composed of (70,71年)

be concerned with (53, 67,84,87年)

be concerned about (73年)

be confined to (88年)

be confronted with (87年)

be connected with (80年)

be content with (59年)

be convinced of (54,73年)

be crazy about (88,90年)

be curious about (77年)

be cut out for (66年)

be delighted with (79年)

be dependent on (69年)

be deprived of (69年)

be devoted to (45年)

be different from (50,65, 66,70,72,84,89,90年)

be divided into (53,90年)

be dressed in (65年)

be dying for (79年)

be eager to (60年)

be eligible for (73年)

be equal to (87年)

be equipped with (84年)

be excited about (69年)

be exposed to (68年)

be faced with (63,90年)

be familiar to (11年)

be familiar with (50,61,65, 83年)

be famous for (55,84年)

be fascinated by (66,79,89)

be filled with (81年)

be finished with (79年)

be fit for (66年)

be fitted with (81年)

be fond of (66,80,89年)

be forced to (69,89年)

be free from (48年)

be full of (46,65,66,67,79,81年)

be given to (63年)
be going to (73年)
be good at (65年)
be good for (75年)
be grateful for (87年)
be grateful to (87年)
be ignorant of (62年)
be imposed on (83年)
be impressed by (62年)
be in a good humor (86年)
be in a good mood (86年)
be in a hurry (53年)
be in agreement (51年)
be in conflict with (87年)
be in danger (61年)
be in favor of (50年)
be in low spirits (61年)
be in office (67年)
be in proportion to (70年)
be in sight (61年)
be in the habit of (50年)
be in trouble (51年)
be in use (90年)
be in want of (69年)
be indebted to (54年)
be indifferent to (60年)
be indulged in (60年)
be inferior to (90年)
be interested in (62,66,73, 76,78年)
be involved with (88年)
be jealous of (65年)
be known as (56,58,89)
be known for (50,63,69年)
be known to (60年)
be likely to (60,66,69,89,90)
be mad at (70年)
be made from (80年)
be made of (46,61,70,71, 79,84年)
be made up of (51年)

be meant for (66年)
be met with (66年)
be mixed up (51年)
be mixed with (66年)
be of little value (78年)
be of the opinion that (76年)
be on a diet (78年)
be on a trip (61年)
be on an equal standing with (49年)
be on good terms with (67年)
be on *one's* mind (71年)
be on speaking terms' (65年)
be on the point of (69年)
be opposed to (49年)
be popular with (72年)
be preoccupied with (69年)
be prone to (64年)
be proud of (65,66,70,76,90年)
be put to use (63年)
be qualified for (73年)
be ready to (56年)
be referred to as (53年)
be regarded as (51,58,66, 72年)
be related to (70,87,89年)
be reminded of (55年)
be replaced by (59,64,76年)
be responsible for (51,65, 69,83,88,90年)
be rooted in (66年)
be said to (66年)
be satisfied with (51,66,87年)
be sensitive to (85年)
be separated from (88年)
be shattered to pieces (76年)
be short of (80年)

be sick of (46年)
be similar to (52,62,71, 89,90年)
be sold out (89年)
be subject to (58年)
be superior to (65,68,70, 76,81年)
be supposed to (52,69,71, 75,82年)
be sure of (45,58,60年)
be sure to (60年)
be susceptible to (61年)
be suspicious of (86年)
be taken from (83年)
be the same as (49年)
be thoughtful of (77年)
be through with (69年)
be tired of (57年)
be to V. (65年)
be translated into (72年)
be true of (81年)
be unable to (63,80年)
be unable to (89年)
be unaware of (69年)
be under control (66年)
be unique to (89年)
be unlikely to (68,89年)
be up to *sb.* (49,62,80,89年)
be used to V-ing (55,64, 65,67,78,82年)
be versed in (54年)
be viewed to be (81年)
be weighed down with (72年)
be willing to (67,73年)
be worn out (81年)
be wrong with *sb.* (85年)
bear on (55年)
bear *sth.* in mind (62年)
beat around the bush (88年)

because of (54,61,63,67,73,84, 85,87,88,90年)

begin with (88年)

behind *one's* back (61年)

believe in (48,54年)

belong to (48,49,50,54,58,63, 64,68年)

bend down (56年)

bend to (54年)

beyond reach (69年)

biologically speaking (89年)

bits and pieces (69年)

blame *sb.* for *sth.* (50年)

bow down (54年)

break down (51,71,76,84年)

break in (84年)

break into (51,66年)

break *one's* promise (62年)

break out (59年)

break the law (48年)

break the record (59,67年)

break through (46,47年)

bring about (49,70,77年)

bring back to life (89年)

bring forward (51年)

bring harm to (68年)

bring in (85,89年)

bring out (49,90年)

bring *sb.* back to life (89年)

bring *sth.* to an end (49, 88年)

bring to (85年)

bring up (46,62,77,88,89,90年)

build a fire (59年)

build up (89年)

burst out (66年)

but for (72年)

by air (61年)

by all means (58,76,82,88年)

by and by (54,62年)

by and large (62,90年)

by any chance (78年)

by any means (88年)

by birth (66年)

by contrast (62,66,88年)

by degrees (54年)

by heart (53年)

by itself (56年)

by mail (45年)

by means of (68,82,87,88年)

by mistake (68年)

by name (65年)

by nature (66年)

by no means (46,88年)

by now (60,62年)

by *oneself* (50,68,81,87年)

by rail (59年)

by telephone (86年)

by the end of (61年)

by the time (51,56,81年)

by the way (78,80,83,88年)

by this time (48年)

call back (81,86年)

call for (49,51,72,87年)

call off (54,69,71年)

call on (90年)

call on the phone (70年)

call the police (63年)

call up (78年)

call upon (49,86年)

can't agree more with (71年)

cannot be overemphasized (66,67年)

cannot be too~ (45,70年)

cannot help but V. (68年)

cannot help V. (63年)

cannot help V-ing (78年)

care about (46,56,78,88年)

care for (51,58,66年)

care to (65年)

carry on (64,89年)

carry out (69,81,84,86,90年)

carry *sth.* with *sb.* (77年)

catch fire (81年)

catch sight of (47,59,68年)

catch up (77,89年)

catch up with (51,68,89年)

change *one's* mind (85年)

charge at (86年)

chat with (86年)

check in (68,71年)

check out (85年)

check with (74年)

Cheer up! (84,86年)

clean up (86年)

cling to (46年)

come about (66年)

come across (46年)

come along (78年)

come back to life (77,89年)

come by (83年)

come down (77,85年)

come from (89年)

come in (79年)

come into being (55,85年)

come into *one's* mind (81年)

come into use (80年)

come near (89年)

come of (72年)

come off (84年)

come on (77,88年)

come out (51,59,65,66年)

come over (67年)

come to (68,89年)

come to a stop (61年)

come to an end (54,81年)

come to light (65年)

come to realize (89年)

come to *sb.* for help (89年)
come to the throne (72年)
come true (90年)
come up (58,89年)
come up with (86,89年)
come upon (68年)
commit a crime (67年)
communicate with (88年)
compensate for (49,62,67年)
compete with (60年)
complain about (49,86年)
complain of (88年)
concentrate on (52,64年)
concern about (71年)
consist in (87年)
consist of (48,49,87,89年)
consult with (51年)
continue with (75年)
contribute to (61,64,69年)
cope with (51,70,71,86,90年)
correspond with (81年)
count on (81,90年)
couple with (87年)
cover up (68年)
crack jokes (64年)
crash into (56年)
credit card (79年)
cry over (63年)
cut down (47,80,87年)
cut in half (50年)
cut out (76年)
dare to (59年)
dash off (90年)
deal with (52,65,68,87年)
define A as B (72年)
deliver a speech (64年)
depart from (88年)
depend on (49,50,51,56,58,62,
68,76,80,82,87年)
die of (45年)
die out (85,87,89年)

differ from (64,84年)
differ from country to
country (89年)
differentiate A from B
(73年)
disagree about (51年)
disagree with (62,78年)
discuss with (88年)
dispose of (88年)
distinguish between (71年)
do as *sb.* wishes (49年)
do away with (49,63年)
do business (57年)
do exercise (54年)
do good to (66,80年)
do harm to (46,66,67年)
do *one's* best (68,70,80,84,
86,87年)
do research (50年)
do *sb.* a favor (65年)
do *sb.* good (56,59年)
do *sb.* wrong (68年)
do something about (72年)
do without (58,65,79,86年)
do wrong (48年)
dozens of (49年)
draw the conclusion (69年)
dream of (54,63,79年)
dress up (81年)
drive away (81年)
drive *one's* point home
(67年)
drive out (48,49年)
drive *sb.* crazy (76年)
drive *sb.* to (87年)
drop in (45,86年)
drop in on (86年)
drum *sth.* into *sb.* (79年)
drunken driving (80年)
dry out (48,73年)
due to (53,61,62,65,72,87年)

earn a living (59年)
earn *one's* living (53,73,76年)
either A or B (76,81,87年)
emphasize on (66年)
enable *sb.* to V. (81年)
end up (45,49年)
enough to (59年)
enter college (86年)
enter upon (54年)
even if (79,86,90年)
even more (88,89年)
even though (87年)
every time (55,59年)
every walk of life (47年)
except for (60,87年)
exchange for (54年)
experiment with (79年)
face the music (88年)
fail in (66,81年)
fail to (59,60,65,66,67,71,73,84,
85,86,90年)
fall asleep (60年)
fall back (47年)
fall behind (51,62年)
fall down (77,84年)
fall ill (88年)
fall short of (61年)
fall victim to (69年)
far from (68,73年)
feed on (90年)
feed to (73年)
feed up with (54年)
feel tempted to (82年)
fight for (86年)
fight off (69年)
figure out (75年)
fill in (61,83年)
fill out (82,89年)
fill up (52年)
find fault with (49,63年)
find *one's* footing (65年)

find out (52,59,61,85,87,89年)

first name (80年)

first of all (86,88年)

focus on (88,89年)

follow in (47年)

food for thought (88年)

for a lifetime (88年)

for a long time (78,89年)

for a rainy day (64年)

for a time (68年)

for ages (58年)

for all (46年)

for all times (90年)

for example (50,71,75,76,77,79, 81,86,87,88,89,90年)

for free (67年)

for fun (58年)

for good (89年)

for instance (58,65,74年)

for lack of (79年)

for nothing (67年)

for one thing (85,88年)

for pleasure (78,84年)

for sale (77,79年)

for the first time (49,84, 88年)

for the purpose of (90年)

for the sake of (81年)

for year (89年)

forget V-ing (49年)

frighten away (90年)

from culture to culture (81年)

from head to toe (89年)

from now on (88年)

from person to person (88年)

from place to place (69,76 年)

from the very first (88年)

from this (89年)

from time to time (89年)

from top to bottom (89年)

garage sale (77年)

get across (63,67年)

get along (62,80,82年)

get along with (49,84,86年)

get away with (51年)

get even with (48,49,63年)

get in touch with sb. (85,86年)

get lost (79年)

get married (89,90年)

get off (61,85年)

get on (84年)

get on one's nerves (47, 56年)

get out (90年)

get over (49,64,67,68,87年)

get rid of (63,78,88,89年)

get sb. nowhere (86年)

get sth. off one's chest (65年)

get sth. over (65年)

get sth. straight (87年)

get the better of (49年)

get the upper hand (65年)

get through (75年)

get tired of (49年)

get up (58,59,62,69,86年)

get used to (64,75,81年)

give a talk (88年)

give away (45,86年)

give back to (78年)

give birth to (90年)

give ground (47年)

give in (63年)

give in to (49年)

give off (90年)

give out (63年)

give rise to (59年)

give sb. a hand (67,79年)

give sb. a lift (87年)

give up (48,51,53,56,63,66,69, 72,75,79,89年)

give way to (65年)

go a long way (69年)

go abroad (62,66,87年)

go after (86年)

go ahead (69年)

go ahead with (65年)

go all out (68年)

go along (86年)

go along with (67,76年)

go away (45,68年)

go back (76年)

go back on (51,87年)

go back to (76年)

go both ways (89年)

go by (72,76年)

go crazy (89年)

go Dutch (86年)

go for a walk (67年)

go hand in hand (70年)

go off (68年)

go on (60,62,67,68,71,80,89年)

go on an errand (48年)

go on with (89年)

go out (45,51,59,72年)

go overseas (59年)

go somewhere (49年)

go through (52,90年)

go through with (54年)

go to (73年)

go to a movie (90年)

go to church (75年)

go to Hell (67年)

go to sleep (68年)

go to the movies (57年)

go to war (88年)

go up (65,68年)

go well with (67年)

go with (51年)

go without (51,66年)
go wrong (61年)
good for him (82年)
Good heavens! (86年)
Good work! (86年)
ground to a halt (68年)
grow up (69,79,84年)
Guess what! (81,83年)
had better (68,80,84,85,87年)
hand in (75,87年)
hang on to (87年)
hang up (86年)
happen to (64,76,78,79,89年)
has~in common (62年)
have a close call (62年)
have a good chance of (90年)
have a good time (48,49,62,83年)
have a hard time (66,68年)
have a look at (65年)
have a loose tongue (68年)
have a narrow escape (62年)
have a talk (53年)
have access to (68年)
have an appointment with (81年)
have an effect on (81年)
have bearing on (45年)
have connection with (49年)
have effect on (63,67年)
have fun (45年)
have little to do with (81年)
have more to do with (81年)
have much to do with (73年)
have no bearing on (72年)

have no idea (84,86年)
have nothing to do with (49,53,69年)
have *one's* own way (49年)
have something to do with (55,67,75年)
have to (90年)
have trouble (in) +V-ing (90年)
hazard a guess (61年)
hear about (82,87年)
hear from (56年)
hear of (76,79年)
help *sb.* with *sth.* (78,79,81,87年)
here and there (52,68,90年)
Here it is. (75年)
Here we are. (75年)
Here you are. (79年)
hint at (66年)
hit on (54年)
hold back (61,67年)
hold off (71年)
hold office (46年)
hold on (81年)
hold on to (88年)
hold *one's* ground (88年)
hold *one's* horses (88年)
hold out (86年)
hold out on *sb.* (69年)
hold up (87年)
homeward bound (47年)
how about (61,71,78,85年)
How come ? (77,83,84年)
How~about? (89年)
hundreds of thousands of (89年)
hunt for (80年)
Hurry up! (86年)
I beg your pardon. (80,83年)

I'd say. (75年)
I've no idea. (85年)
if only (70年)
if possible (77年)
if~or not (74年)
impose upon (71年)
in a chain (49年)
in a hurry (88年)
in a minute (86年)
in a sense (62,68年)
in a short time (55年)
in addition (69,73,85,89年)
in addition to (75,77,89,90年)
in advance (66,89年)
in all (69年)
in an effort to (72年)
in an instant (62年)
in ancient times (63年)
in and out (90年)
in answer to (69年)
in case (89年)
in case of (61年)
in comparison with (76年)
in contrast (81,89年)
in danger (85年)
in despair (56,72年)
in doubt (87年)
in effect (62年)
in excess of (88年)
in exchange for (89年)
in existence (68年)
in fact (72,74,78,81,85,87年)
in fright (60年)
in front of (64,66,84年)
in general (62,74年)
in halves (69年)
in harmony with (67年)
in herds (80年)
in itself (52,65年)
in keeping with (87,90年)
in light of (54年)

in many cases (86年)
in moderation (60年)
in modern times (63,88年)
in motion (61年)
in need of (85,90年)
in no time (69年)
in no way (62年)
in *one's* care (90年)
in *one's* day (71年)
in *one's* opinion (50年)
in *one's* way (65年)
in order (53,76年)
in order that (60年)
in order to (49,50,61,63,64,65,69,70,75,77,80,88,90年)
in other words (53,67,73,75,77年)
in part (87年)
in particular (73,76年)
in person (62年)
in play (88年)
in practice (64,66年)
in praise of (90年)
in prison (45年)
in proportion to (88年)
in pursuit of (47,54年)
in question (87年)
in relation to (65年)
in response to (89,90年)
in return (76年)
in return for (90年)
in ruins (46,54年)
in secret (90年)
in session (64年)
in short (63,64,68年)
in some ways (70年)
in spite of (49,50,65,66,72,73,76,89年)
in terms of (66,78,85,89年)
in that (78,84年)
in the air (51年)

in the beginning (47,65,82年)
in the case of (79,88年)
in the course of (81年)
in the daytime (45年)
in the distance (90年)
in the east (58年)
in the eyes of (84年)
in the first place (73,77年)
in the future (66,70,86年)
in the long run (45年)
in the meantime (67年)
in the middle of (90年)
in the name of (90年)
in the near future (66年)
in the neighborhood (56年)
in the nick of time (73年)
in the open (63年)
in the opinion of (86年)
in the past (66,70,75年)
in the present (66年)
in the same way (62年)
in the way of (88年)
in the world (67,69年)
in this way (48,58,82,88年)
in those days (71,77,88年)
in time (67,73,75年)
in vain (58,61,79,86年)
in view of (66年)
in ~ manner (45年)
in ~ respect (45,47年)
in ~ sense (58年)
in ~ way (88年)
inform *sb.* of *sth.* (45年)
insist on (50,56,61,86年)
instead of (55,58,64,67,76,77,82年)
intend to (67,71,72年)
interfere with (67年)
involve *oneself* in (67年)
~is one thing, ···is another (72年)

It goes without saying that~ (59年)
it is a pity that~ (60年)
It is believed that~ (65,90年)
It is no use V-ing (45年)
It is said that~ (66,90年)
It occurs to me that~ (68年)
It's a pity. (81年)
It's high time~ (72年)
It's my turn. (88年)
jet lag (81年)
join in (86年)
Judging from~ (61年)
jump to conclusion (58年)
keep a promise (61年)
keep a secret (88年)
keep a straight face (66年)
keep an eye on (65年)
keep close watch over (67年)
keep from (84年)
keep it up (90年)
keep off (59年)
keep on (54,60,80年)
keep *one's* temper (85年)
keep order (48年)
keep out (84,87年)
keep out of *one's* sight (61年)
keep pace with (77年)
keep *sb.* from (68年)
keep *sb.* in suspense (81年)
keep *sb.* out (87年)
keep *sb.* waiting (85年)
keep *sth.* in mind (71年)
keep track (68年)
keep track of (88年)
keep up (60,61,89年)
keep up with (77,89年)

keep up with the
Joneses (77年)

kill *oneself* (53年)

kill time (87年)

kill two birds with one
　stone (56年)

kind of (80年)

knock at (56年)

knock out (87年)

knock *sb*. down (65年)

know better (69,72年)

know nothing about (67年)

know of (87年)

last name (80年)

later on (80年)

laugh at (46年)

lay importance on (67年)

lead a～life (67,69年)

lead *sb*. to V. (68年)

lead to (51,63,84,86,87,89年)

learn a lesson (73,78年)

learn about (79年)

least of all (67年)

leave a message (86年)

leave a message with *sb*.
　(75年)

leave behind (65,67年)

leave for (46,69,79,82年)

leave no room for doubt
　(61年)

leave out (45,62,88年)

leave something to be
　desired (70年)

leave～alone (64,74年)

Legend has it that～ (45年)

less…than～ (71,90年)

let alone (65年)

let down (61年)

let go (59,67,88年)

let go of (88年)

let in (61年)

let it go at that (69年)

let off (87年)

let *sb*. down (76,84年)

let things take their own
　course (67年)

lie in (46,70年)

lift up (88年)

line up (65年)

listen to (46,65,67,78,85,89年)

little by little (54年)

Little did they know
　that～ (88年)

live a～life (89年)

live on (53,62,71,78年)

live up to (49年)

live upon (59年)

lock up (53年)

look after (46,52年)

look around (68年)

look at (46,52,70,74,77,89年)

look back (49,86年)

look back on (73年)

look down upon (49,78年)

look for (45,52,55,56,59,60,61,
　62,65,72,76,78,79,81,82,84,85,89年)

look forward to (49,51,62,
　73,77,80年)

look into (78年)

look on the bright side
　of things (66年)

look out (52,61,77,82年)

look through (62,73,78年)

look up (55,60,78,79,90年)

look up to (78年)

look upon～as (62年)

lose ground (65,70年)

lose heart (70年)

lose sight of (49年)

lose weight (78年)

lost *oneself* in (66年)

lots of (74年)

lower down (88年)

made up for (49年)

made up *one's* mind (62年)

major in (80年)

make a fool of (49年)

make a fortune (47年)

make a living (57,59年)

make a mistake (88年)

make a point of (69年)

make a profit (83,87年)

make a speech (55,61年)

make an effort (49年)

make attack upon (53年)

make away with (54年)

make believe (46年)

make both ends meet
　(88年)

make contributions to
　(71年)

make decisions (84年)

make difference (58年)

make ends meet (68年)

make for (87年)

make friends with (50,61,
　77,86,87年)

make fun of (49,86年)

make good use of (57年)

make it (87年)

make light of (61年)

make mistakes (59,66,67年)

make money (65,89年)

make noise (58年)

make *one's* decision (52年)

make *one's* hair stand
　on end (64年)

make *one's* point (88年)

make *oneself* at home
　(62年)

make out (68年)

make progress (66,70年)

make room for (62,68,88年)

make sense (70,71年)

make sure (86,90年)

make the bed (47,59年)

make the best of (49年)

make the best use of (57, 69年)

make the decision (62,69年)

make turn (84年)

make up (61,62,71,81年)

make up for (60,61年)

make up one's mind (59, 61,67,70,74年)

make use of (49,63年)

make whole (87年)

many a (56,70,80年)

mean to (65年)

meet one's needs (83,87年)

meet the demand (59年)

meet with (61,76年)

merge into (89年)

mess up (86,88年)

might as well (66,70年)

mind one's tongue (85年)

mistake A for B (86年)

mix up (78年)

more and more (67年)

more or less (74年)

more than (67,79,88,89,90年)

most of the time (86年)

move along (67年)

move around (75年)

move away (85年)

move on (69年)

much less (69年)

much more (62,69年)

must have (65,77年)

My goodness! (82年)

narrow escape (62年)

neither A nor B (49,57,63, 71,72年)

Never mind. (78,82年)

never…without～ (71年)

next to (79,87年)

next to nothing (58年)

no doubt (50,89年)

no less than (87年)

no longer (59,65,66,68,73,80, 81,84,88,89年)

no matter (86,88年)

no matter how (63,90年)

no more than (69,73,88年)

no more…than～ (71年)

no problem (86年)

no sooner…than～ (56年)

No sweat! (77年)

no wonder (70,73,75,82年)

none of one's business. (81年)

none the less (61年)

not A but B (49年)

not always (75,85年)

not any longer (67,69年)

not at all (51,58,66,72,74,76,77, 78,84,85年)

Not exactly. (82年)

not necessarily (46,53,72, 88年)

not only…but also～ (62, 73,74,76年)

not so much…as～ (58年)

not so…as～ (60年)

not the way round (69年)

not～any longer (49年)

not…until～ (51,54,58,62,64, 68,69,70,78,82,87年)

nothing but (58,59,89年)

now and then (46年)

now or never (61年)

now that (67年)

object to (45,59年)

occur to (46年)

of all times (50年)

of course (46,50,51,53,54,55,61, 62,75,76,78,79,84,85年)

of no value (54年)

of one's time (50年)

off and on (61,87,89,90年)

on account of (50,51,82年)

on and off (61年)

on and on (87年)

on another line (86年)

on average (76,85年)

on behalf of (89年)

on business (62年)

on condition that (64年)

on duty (48,84年)

on earth (65年)

on end (60,62,65年)

on guard (62年)

on head (62年)

on no account (63年)

on occasion (65年)

on one's mind (51,85年)

on one's own (67,69,87年)

on one's way (84年)

on one's way home (45年)

on one's way to school (74年)

on purpose (50,56,66,78年)

on second thought (79年)

on show (68年)

on the average (80,84年)

on the basis of (87年)

on the basis that (64年)

on the campus (64年)

on the contrary (88年)

on the one hand (70年)

on the other hand (52,70, 71,72,78年)

on the way (58,78年)

on the way home (51年)

on time (45,61,65,79,80,86,87, 89年)

on top of (69年)
on vacation (63,79年)
once and for all (88年)
once more (65年)
one day (56,67,89年)
one way or another (67年)
one…the other~ (53年)
only if (85年)
only to (63年)
open up (89年)
or so (60,85年)
originate in (89年)
other than (59,70,73年)
ought to (65,70,72年)
out of (65年)
out of breath (49,63,65年)
out of date (46年)
out of hand (62年)
out of mind (87年)
out of office (67年)
out of one's depth (68年)
out of one's mind (67,74,78年)
out of order (58,65年)
out of sight (59,60,61,76年)
out of the ordinary (84年)
out of the question (86年)
out of the way (71年)
owe sth. to sb. (45,60,61年)
pass a law (80年)
pass away (58年)
pass down (70,80年)
pass for (69年)
pass over (49年)
pass through (65,67年)
pay a visit to (59,89年)
pay attention (60,89年)
pay attention to (66,73,77,84,85,88,89,90年)
pay back (80年)
pay for (73,79,83,87年)

pay regard to (68年)
pay sb. a visit (89年)
pay sb. back (79年)
pen name (50年)
perform operation (49年)
persist in (70年)
pick out (55年)
pick sb. up (87年)
pick up (72,74,75,79,85,87,90年)
pick up the check (87,88年)
pie in the sky (88年)
place emphasis on (66,67年)
plan for (51年)
play a joke on (86年)
play a trick (63年)
play an important part in (90年)
play an important role (61年)
play one's hand badly (65年)
play practical jokes on (50,84年)
play with (79年)
plenty of (74,76,79,80,86年)
point out (49,71,75,88年)
point to (48年)
practice medicine (58年)
prefer to (77年)
prepare for (86,89年)
prepare oneself for (90年)
prevent sb. from (50,53,63,84年)
pride oneself on (66年)
provide sb. with sth. (69年)
provide sth. for sb (67,70年)
provided that (67年)
pull down (65年)
pull over (81年)
put aside (64年)
put away (76年)

put down (62,69年)
put forth (89年)
put in (88年)
put into operation (89年)
put off (46,48,51年)
put on (55,62,63,67,81,88年)
put one's nose into (65年)
put out (58,59,62,66,83,87年)
put pressure on (77年)
put sb. through (81年)
put sb. to bed (45年)
put sth. into practice (88年)
put to death (90年)
put up (45,51年)
put up with (47,49,54,81年)
put~into operation (89年)
quite the opposite (72年)
rage on (66年)
rain cats and dogs (73,85年)
range from A to B (78,90年)
rather than (49,66,67,72,76,83,87年)
reach for (83年)
receive education (73年)
recent times (69年)
recover from (49,63,70年)
refer to (52,54,58,60,63,69,71,89年)
reflect on (86年)
regard A as B (64,69,73年)
rely on (55,90年)
remember to V. (49年)
remind sb. of sth. (49,54,58,68,73年)
report for duty (90年)
result from (62年)
result in (49,60,90年)
return calls (86年)
rich as he is (56年)
rid sb. of sth. (69年)

ride out (90年)

right away (50,53,59,81,86年)

right now (49,56,75,88年)

rip apart (49年)

rise up (86年)

rule out (54,62年)

run a business (85,86年)

run after (83年)

run away from (50年)

run off (83年)

run out (68年)

run out of (46,54年)

run over (51年)

run short (69年)

run short of (60,63年)

run through (90年)

run up (49年)

rush into (65年)

rush on (47年)

rush out (56年)

rust away (60年)

save one's skin (88年)

scare away (90年)

search A for B (61年)

search for (57,74,89年)

see A as B (87,63,89年)

see eye to eye with (64年)

see off (61年)

see sb. off (45,82年)

see that (89年)

see through (75,85年)

see to (63年)

see to it that~ (65,71年)

sell out (89年)

send back (81年)

send for (61年)

send out (84年)

separate from (78年)

serve as (64,65年)

serve sb. right (73年)

set about (62,72年)

set on (88年)

set out (72,89年)

set out to (89年)

set sb. apart from (45年)

set to (63年)

set up (62,65,73,75,86,89年)

settle down (75年)

settle upon (54年)

share sth. with sb. (69年)

shortly before (78年)

should have (65,86年)

show off (73,90年)

show up (59,64,79,83年)

shut off (47年)

sit down (74年)

sit up (58,62,67年)

slow down (63,89年)

snap one's fingers at sb. (65年)

so as to (60,69年)

so far (49,79,84,89,90年)

So far so good. (85年)

so long as (46年)

so that (60,62,65,86,87,89年)

so to speak (45年)

so what (86年)

so~that (47,49,54,66,68,70,74, 78,84,85年)

so…as to~ (58,78年)

so…as~ (47年)

some day (69年)

sooner or later (88年)

sort of (86,87年)

speak ill of (61年)

speak of (50,58年)

speak up (90年)

Speaking of~ (65年)

speed up (60,90年)

spend~on (56年)

stamp one's foot (69年)

stand for (51,66年)

stand on end (64年)

stand on one's own feet (86年)

stand out (55,90年)

stand to reason (70年)

stand up (68年)

stand up for (86年)

standard of living (77年)

start off (87年)

start on (87年)

stay away from (48,86年)

stay up (64年)

stem from (85年)

stick one's neck out (65年)

stick one's nose into (67年)

stick to (67年)

still another (89年)

stir up (61,63年)

stop sb. from V-ing (61,79年)

stop to V. (56年)

strike a balance (88年)

strike a match (59年)

strike down (69年)

study abroad (86年)

subjection to (53年)

succeed in (51,66,68,78,85年)

such as (66,67,75,76,79,85,86, 87,88,89,90年)

such~that (56,69年)

such…as~ (68,89年)

suffer from (58,77,81年)

sweep away (46年)

sweetness and light (88年)

sympathize with (63年)

take a day off (64年)

take a fancy to (67年)

take a hand in (65年)

take a look at (89年)

take a look at sth. (81,89年)

take a message (75年)
take a photograph (53年)
take a rest (50,55,74,83年)
take a step (65年)
take a trip (48,49,86年)
take a walk (46,56,59年)
take action (49年)
take after (46,49年)
take away (67,75,84,85,88年)
take back (61年)
take back *one's* words
　(64年)
take care (57年)
take care of (48,50,54,56,63,
74,75年)
take courage (59年)
take courses (64,72年)
take cover (73年)
take delight in (88年)
take exercise (86年)
Take heart ! (81,87年)
take hold of (48年)
take in (64年)
take interest in (51年)
take it (83年)
take it easy (63,78年)
take lessons (85年)
take notice of (48年)
take off (51,69,71,81年)
take office (90年)
take on (69年)
take *one's* fancy (70年)
take *one's* temperature
　(52年)
take *one's* time (88年)
take out (87,90年)
take over (63,75,81,87,90年)
take pains to (72年)
take part in (47,48,64年)
take photographs (55年)
take pictures (51,64,74年)

take place (50,56,60,61,65,67,
75,77,82,87年)
take refuge (59年)
take responsibility (88年)
take revenge on (49年)
take *sth.* for granted (63,
69年)
take *sth.* in bad humor
　(49年)
take the examination (57,
69,81年)
take the place of (90年)
take time (55年)
take up (83,86年)
Take your time. (86年)
take~for instance (65年)
talk about (64,67,75,79,88年)
talk into (78,79年)
talk *sb.* into V-ing (54,
55年)
teach *sb.* a lesson (84年)
tear down (51年)
tell A from B (46年)
tell a lie (46年)
tell apart (56年)
tell difference between~
　(58年)
tend to (80,85,88,90年)
tens of thousands (88年)
thanks to (45,60,90年)
that is (45年)
that is to say (53年)
the former (51年)
the last~ (61,62年)
the more…the less~ (67年)
the more…the more~
(51,54,64,68年)
the other day (55,73,85年)
the other way around
(62年)
the same as (72年)

the same way (67年)
the sooner~the better
　(68年)
there is (89年)
there is no doubt that
　(89年)
There is no telling~ (72年)
There you are. (75年)
these days (78,85年)
think about (45,51,73,79,81,
86,89年)
think little of (61,80年)
think much of (61年)
think of (45,51,58,61,65,66,68,
71,73,76,78,80,81,85,86,87,89年)
think over (55,87年)
think up (58,87年)
those who (86年)
through and through (87年)
throughout history (69年)
throw a party (77年)
throw away (50,79年)
throw into (47年)
throw out (46年)
throw up (63年)
tick away (71年)
tie in with (72年)
time after time (54年)
to and fro (51,89,90年)
to be frank (68年)
to begin with (54年)
to come (80年)
to good advantage (84年)
to make matters worse
　(61年)
to *one's* astonishment
　(61年)
to *one's* taste (75年)
to say the least of (61年)
to some extent (81年)
to start with (64年)

to the best of *one's*
knowledge (68年)
to the best of *one's*
ability (68年)
to the full (66年)
to the letter (65年)
together with (73,75,79,87年)
too ～ to … (47,49,55,56,61,67,70,
72,75,78,82,90年)
touch off (62年)
touch on (55,88年)
try on (83,89年)
try *one's* best (70,78年)
try out (56,73年)
try to (49,60,64,88,90年)
turn down (48,51,65,68,69年)
turn in (87年)
turn into (59,78,80年)
turn off (56,71,86年)
turn on (48,57年)
turn *one's* back on (86年)
turn out (50,54,60,87年)
turn over (48年)
turn *sth.* to account (62年)
turn to (65,67,74,88年)
turn up (48,61年)
under no circumstances
(64年)
under *one's* nose (66年)
under the control of
(81年)
up and down (76,89年)
up to (72,84,85,90年)
upon recognition (68年)

use up (60,69年)
used to (53,61,63,64,65,67,75,
80,81,84年)
wait for (82,86,89年)
wake up (86年)
walk about (52年)
walk down (80年)
walk up and down (46年)
walk up to (80年)
warn off (90年)
wash off (78年)
wash *one's* hands of
(69年)
watch over (67年)
Watch your step! (86年)
wear a smile (57年)
wear out (49,67年)
weather bureau (54年)
Well done! (84年)
well off (46年)
What a pity! (84年)
what about (61年)
What do you think of ～
(56年)
What for? (79年)
what if (85,88年)
what we call (45年)
what's the matter with ～
(57年)
when it came to ～ (64,71,
86年)
whether ～ or (46年)
whether ～ or not (49,63,67年)
Why don't you? (89年)

wind up (54年)
with a great effort (86年)
with a view to (50,67,68,
72,77年)
with all one's hearts (50,
67,68,72,77,89年)
with an eye to V-ing
(65年)
with regard to (87年)
with respect to (67年)
with the aid of (67年)
with the exception of
(79年)
without any result (86年)
without doubt (86年)
without exception (71年)
without regard to (88年)
wonder about (77年)
work for (89年)
work on (50,52,65,70年)
work out (50,51,64年)
worry about (73,76,77,82年)
would like (61,74,88年)
would rather (51,79年)
would rather V. than V.
(46,61,74年)
write up (83年)
yell at (69年)
yield to (51年)
You bet! (77,83年)
You can never tell. (90年)
You can say that again!
(85,90年)
You're kidding. (77年)

心得筆記欄

劉毅英文「99年學科能力測驗」15級分名單

姓 名	學 校	班 級	姓 名	學 校	班 級	姓 名	學 校	班 級
林述亨	建國中學	332	胡格瑄	大同高中	301	邱韋舜	延平中學	313
陳韋華	政大附中	123	林唯中	師大附中	1188	吳承恕	延平中學	313
陳　文	麗山高中	302	范芷韻	板橋高中	301	沈哲民	東山高中	三忠
杜思璉	北一女中	312	邱群壹	延平中學	303	朱柏樺	中正高中	302
彭紀堯	永平高中	607	管偉傑	建國中學	303	許昱萱	板橋高中	307
林彥儒	建國中學	302	邱意晴	北一女中	三良	渡邊裕美	中山女中	318
吳偉立	板橋高中	301	牛文昀	北一女中	三溫	黃嗣翔	建國中學	312
李　曜	師大附中	1191	陳藝瑄	北一女中	三射	邱于容	景美女中	三良
林政達	市立大同	303	林承勳	建國中學	311	廖芳儀	市立大同	309
黃柏璇	北一女中	309	尤珮榕	板橋高中	301	詹凱傑	建國中學	313
劉金樺	師大附中	1203	李孟翰	師大附中	1202	李元甫	建國中學	304
盧廷羲	中和高中	310	張瑪恩	中正高中	305	黃麗瑾	中山女中	306
羅偉力	師大附中	1207	陳　齊	北一女中	三莊	林勁甫	市立大同	302
陳緒承	建國中學	301	吳其錚	北一女中	三莊	利采穎	北一女中	三射
張若芃	中山女中	三忠	趙子宇	師大附中	1186	趙人平	建國中學	320
盧昆賢	延平中學	310	陳威全	成功高中	324	賴昱凱	建國中學	320
譚偉平	中山女中	三智	向峻毅	成功高中	324	黃柏瑋	建國中學	318
林世傑	建國中學	310	李冠瑩	北一女中	三御	楊祐瑋	中正高中	317
黃子芬	北一女中	三恭	蔡友蓮	北一女中	三毅	李　蘋	市立大同	310
方　齊	建國中學	332	趙君豪	建國中學	312	李卉瑄	師大附中	1187
邱凱琳	延平中學	308	夏定遠	建國中學	308	徐子芸	景美女中	三恭
周泓儒	錦和高中	602	陳宥瑄	中山女中	三公	張緹好	景美女中	三智
楊凱傑	師大附中	1197	鄭雅文	中和高中	311	林志翰	建國中學	309
黃博嵩	建國中學	330	顏大爲	建國中學	332	廖宸偉	延平中學	313
林品硯	成功高中	301	謝政諺	建國中學	308	高嘉蓮	北一女中	三義
林俊吉	建國高中	308	林志叡	建國中學	319	張向晴	內湖高中	308
胡珮瑜	中山女中	三仁	黃咸恆	建國中學	329	張　良	辭修高中	301
王媛萱	麗山高中	302	何維傑	建國中學	329	高立瀚	辭修高中	301
陳永傑	成功高中	312	葉芝岑	北一女中	三和	何其安	中山女中	321
鍾孟雲	大同高中	313	辛　瓔	北一女中	三公	彭詩惟	北一女中	322
林函蓁	中山女中	三忠	曾思評	師大附中	1207	趙思涵	北一女中	三平
吳宗奇	建國中學	306	陳柏君	建國中學	321	張家銘	東山高中	三仁
劉庭維	建國中學	320	黃詩雯	中山女中	三敏	蔡文凱	薇格高中	三丁
李巧云	師大附中	1192	莊博涵	北一女中	三讓	陳心儀	市立大同	304
黃詩穎	北一女中	三良	張宇任	建國中學	313	梁明垣	重考生	重考生
彭碩平	延平中學	305	廖聿婕	政大附中	321	李俊毅	進修生	進修生
林詩穎	北一女中	三善	林士生	建國中學	303	楊凱傑	建國中學	327
劉芳彣	華僑高中	三問	李家萱	景美女中	三義	曾紀華	建國中學	332
高珮倫	中山女中	三義	徐婉盷	松山高中	302	許凱翔	建國中學	318
曾泰輯	建國中學	302	王孟捷	建國中學	329	佘佳穎	北一女中	三善
藍德郁	中山女中	三簡	陳柏鈞	東山高中	三忠	林庭安	師大附中	1192
林潔昕	松山高中	308	林恩莉	北一女中	三愛	唐震華	麗山高中	304
許翎鈺	北一女中	三檢	陳重宇	建國中學	320	巨筑瑄	忠明高中	304
黃道陽	延平中學	311	林明慧	中山女中	312	楊喬誌	台中一中	304
廖偉丞	延平中學	311	韋佳妍	北一女中	三書	王予君	衛道高中	三辛
劉芳瑜	新莊高中	303	莊雅喬	延平中學	310	楊博鈞	台中一中	323

劉毅英文家教班成績優異同學獎學金排行榜

姓　名	學　校	總金額	姓　名	學　校	總金額	姓　名	學　校	總金額
蕭芳祁	成功高中	166150	李冠瑩	北一女中	51000	李宗鴻	成功高中	29400
陳柏瑞	建國中學	158300	楊宗燁	建國中學	49000	許益誠	成功高中	29400
曾昱豪	師大附中	152800	張宇任	建國中學	48800	黃毓雯	育成高中	29400
羅培瑞	延平高中	147500	陳彥華	景美女中	47800	楊玄詳	明志國中	29300
林明億	建國中學	136200	陳亭熹	北一女中	47600	溫育菱	景美女中	29300
江冠廷	建國中學	135300	顏汝翊	北一女中	47300	盧廷羲	中和高中	29100
翁御修	師大附中	130600	徐大鈞	建國中學	46400	林育勳	松山高中	28900
潘貞諭	北一女中	130300	白子洋	建國中學	46100	陳韋華	政大附中	28800
賴宣佑	恆毅國中部	128850	桑孟軒	板橋高中	45400	郭柏宏	中和高中	28500
張矩嘉	台中一中	127800	鄭婷云	師大附中	44100	王孟琦	景美女中	28300
張凱閎	建國中學	126700	王楚薇	松山高中	43500	楊竣翔	建國中學	27800
王泓琦	中山女中	126200	陳瑋欣	北一女中	43400	蘇傳堯	師大附中	27500
陳萱庭	景美女中	124400	李元甫	建國中學	43300	徐子瑜	內湖高中	27300
陳加宜	台中女中	119100	蔡佳君	中山女中	42600	黃珮瑄	中山女中	27050
王冠宇	建國中學	117100	林　立	建國中學	42500	石佩昀	中和高中	26900
張寧珊	北一女中	117000	林琬娟	北一女中	41950	吳則緯	成功高中	26900
邵祺皓	建國中學	116400	張瀚疄	中正高中	41700	陳虹君	內湖高中	26600
薛宜婷	北一女中	116000	賴映儒	延平高中	41300	賴奕丞	明倫高中	26500
楊蕙寧	中崙高中	114900	劉芳彣	華僑高中	39800	林鈺恆	中和高中	26400
葉書偉	師大附中	114900	利采穎	北一女中	39600	李宜靜	惠文高中	26400
呂育昇	建國中學	114200	呂學宸	師大附中	39500	郭琪華	天母國中	26200
林怡萱	北一女中	113300	董怡萱	中山女中	38000	謝孟哲	延平高中	26200
林則方	明倫高中	110800	王安佳	建國中學	38000	林述亨	建國中學	26200
洪培綸	成功高中	108100	胡錚宜	清水高中	37800	張立昀	北一女中	25667
沈奕均	北一女中	108000	陳緯倫	格致高中	36000	林俊瑋	建國中學	25600
林采蓁	古亭國中	105300	范瑜庭	明倫高中	35800	謝家綺	新莊國中	25600
蘇亦稜	台中女中	104100	鍾孟雲	大同高中	35250	黃堂榮	延平高中	25500
陳允禎	格致高中	102800	谷宜臻	北一女中	34300	鄭晧云	松山高中	25100
吳珞瑀	中崙高中	97700	林渝軒	建國中學	33767	藍德郁	中山女中	24900
李宛霖	中山女中	94000	白善尹	建國中學	33500	吳函儒	中正高中	24600
林妍君	薇閣國中部	89650	蘇郁涵	大理高中	33100	許曄苓	百齡高中	24600
王　千	清水國中	84800	胡芝嘉	北一女中	32300	葉芝岑	北一女中	24500
陳亭甫	建國中學	84500	胡格瑄	大同高中	32200	劉彥廷	成功高中	24500
陳麒中	建國中學	80200	洪珮瓊	中山女中	32200	黃煜鈞	建國中學	24500
林彥儒	建國中學	72100	林品硯	成功高中	32100	簡均哲	重考生	24500
張博雄	板橋高中	67800	謝畢宇	景美女中	31900	張政格	三民高中	24400
黃詩穎	北一女中	63000	楊鈺涵	景美女中	31800	張若芃	中山女中	24400
蕭丞晏	建國中學	60400	徐仲爲	建國中學	31700	張薇貞	景美女中	24400
王劭予	建國中學	59150	陳永傑	成功高中	31500	黃柏璇	北一女中	24300
李家偉	成功高中	56400	陳志愷	成功高中	31100	施恩潔	北一女中	24300
王俊升	建國中學	56400	廖家可	師大附中	31100	邱柏霖	東山高中	24200
宋瑞祥	建國中學	56300	陳光炫	建國中學	31000	練子立	海山高中	24200
徐偉傑	建國中學	55900	李　洋	師大附中	30900	吳孟哲	成淵高中	24100
莫斯宇	建國中學	55600	陳冠勳	中正高中	30400	謝彥輝	建國中學	24100
曾昱誠	建國中學	54700	杜佳勳	景美女中	30400	彭郅瑜	建國中學	24000
張家偉	師大附中	54100	洪辰宗	師大附中	30300	林敬傑	成功高中	23900
丁哲浩	建國中學	53600	陳瑞邦	成功高中	30200	吳怡萱	永春高中	23800
何維傑	建國中學	53200	李留凱	建國中學	30100	葉昱祥	東山高中	23700
謝伊妍	北一女中	52700	李佳穎	成功高中	30000	蔡家軒	成功高中	23600
林唯中	師大附中	52400	紀乃慈	衛理女中	30000	蔡雅婷	松山高中	23600
蔡書旻	格致高中	52300	林湧達	師大附中	29900	辛亞潔	大同高中	23500
蔡景匀	內湖高中	51300	邵偉桓	大直高中	29850	江林濚	永平高中	23500

姓 名	學 校	總金額	姓 名	學 校	總金額	姓 名	學 校	總金額
吳俊賢	松山高中	23500	邱耀賢	格致高中	19700	范照松	南山高中	17400
許四融	建國中學	23500	高浩正	建國中學	19600	連庭蔚	建國中學	17400
張峻毓	永春高中	23400	林 均	建國中學	19600	鄭雅恩	萬芳高中	17400
周佳翰	延平高中	23400	王悅溶	樹林高中	19500	林勁甫	大同高中	17300
賴映君	靜修女中	23400	陳庭安	台中女中	19500	何宇屏	陽明高中	17300
邱逸雯	縣立三重	23300	吳岱軒	北一女中	19400	楊凱任	西松高中	17200
潘 寬	成功高中	23200	林庭萱	松山高中	19400	許凱翔	建國中學	17200
邵世儒	成功高中	23000	郭貞里	北一女中	19250	俞乙立	建國中學	17200
林瑜眞	中崙高中	22700	許瑋庭	建國中學	19250	羅予平	中山女中	17100
石 崴	建國中學	22700	魏雲杰	成功高中	19200	薛宜茹	北一女中	17100
陳韻安	北一女中	22500	陳璿宇	建國中學	19200	洪詩涵	中和女中	17000
陳皓琳	三民高中	22400	黃嗣翔	建國中學	19200	馬向恩	成功高中	17000
陳冠綸	成功高中	22200	呂旻珊	大直高中	19000	賈其蓁	百齡高中	17000
陳羿伶	華江高中	22200	高煒哲	成功高中	18800	張書瑜	明倫高中	17000
許翎鈺	北一女中	22100	賴冠宏	大安高工	18700	樊 毓	建國中學	17000
陳奕潔	延平高中	22100	歐銘仁	成功高中	18700	楊其儒	師大附中	17000
李孟蘋	景美女中	22100	劉珮沂	和平高中	18700	張景翔	師大附中	17000
黃安芷	松山高中	22000	范綱晉	師大附中	18700	黃詩芸	自強國中	16900
鄭惟仁	建國中學	22000	李家萱	景美女中	18600	張育銓	成功高中	16700
吳宇晴	中山女中	21900	林琬芸	陽明高中	18600	廖峻傑	建國中學	16667
薛羽彤	北一女中	21834	吳姿萱	北一女中	18550	李亭毅	內湖高中	16600
韋佳妍	北一女中	21800	李韋綸	東山高中	18500	洪健雄	成功高中	16600
范芷韻	板橋高中	21700	劉欣明	台中女中	18467	姜德婷	延平高中	16600
曾泓祥	建國中學	21700	劉欣明	台中女中	18467	陳冠宇	明倫高中	16600
李國維	建國中學	21700	邱群童	延平高中	18400	胡庭翰	建國中學	16600
楊肇焓	建國中學	21700	楊旻豪	建國中學	18400	劉冠廷	建國中學	16500
許瑋峻	延平高中	21600	蔡竺君	中山女中	18300	吳崇豪	成功高中	16400
林伯霖	板橋高中	21600	陳重宇	建國中學	18300	呂咏儒	建國中學	16400
陳彥伶	大同高中	21300	陳嘉敏	北一女中	18200	李語荃	北一女中	16300
李柏逸	建國中學	21200	賴科維	延平高中	18200	陳致宇	建國中學	16300
林育如	大同高中	21000	劉彥甫	南湖高中	18200	許佳萱	華江高中	16300
曾煜凱	成淵高中	20800	江文育	永平高中	18000	劉金樺	師大附中	16250
劉承翰	建國中學	20800	莊珞妤	百齡高中	18000	高嘉蓮	北一女中	16200
高立穎	板橋高中	20700	劉仁偉	板橋高中	18000	張逸軒	建國中學	16200
吳沛蓁	新莊高中	20700	徐永安	建國中學	18000	江昱嫻	北一女中	16100
林雨潔	中山女中	20600	李仁豪	大直高中	17900	陳威任	南湖高中	16100
吳其璇	延平高中	20600	劉詩瑜	中崙高中	17900	吳連哲	建國中學	16100
郭清怡	師大附中	20600	李今純	松山高中	17900	劉 湛	建國中學	16000
王子豪	師大附中	20500	吳冠宏	建國中學	17900	鍾佩廷	北一女中	15900
呂佳璟	中山女中	20450	阮柏勛	華江高中	17900	賴梵予	松山高中	15900
陳奕仲	建國中學	20400	張向晴	內湖高中	17900	張宜平	中和高中	15800
陳 文	麗山高中	20300	陳岱廷	北一女中	17800	何宸瑩	北一女中	15800
賴俊銘	成功高中	20100	曹瑞哲	成功高中	17800	顏大爲	建國中學	15800
洪廷瑋	成功高中	20000	陳奕儒	建國中學	17700	姚政徹	景美女中	15800
陳彥同	建國中學	20000	王彥方	松山高中	17600	張博淵	延平高中	15700
陳冠芸	華江高中	20000	邱麗文	中山女中	17500	詹凱傑	建國中學	15700
張雅鈞	中山女中	19900	張乃云	中山女中	17500	鄭景文	師大附中	15700
王宣鈞	延平高中	19900	林宛倫	北一女中	17400	賴彥誠	師大附中	15600
陳彥賓	成淵高中	19700	張弘毅	成功高中	17400	余欣華	泰山高中	15600

※ 因版面有限，尚有許多領取高額獎金的同學無法列出，歡迎同學到班查詢。

劉毅英文教育機構

學費最低・效果最佳
www.learnschool.com.tw

台北新教室：台北市許昌街17號6F（火車站前・麥德大樓）
台北本部：台北市重慶南路一段10號7F（火車站前・台企大樓）
台中總部：台中市三民路三段125號7F（加州健身中心樓上）
新竹群益補習班：新竹市東大路一段95號（蘇永年數學）
豐原教室：台中縣豐原市圓環東路一段16號5F（黃漢邦數學）

TEL：（02）2389-5212
TEL：（02）2361-6101
TEL：（04）2221-8861
TEL：（03）522-8351
TEL：（04）2525-5222

Editorial Staff

● 主編 / 劉　毅

● 校訂 / 謝靜芳・蔡琇瑩・石支齊・蔡文華
　　　　張碧紋・林銀姿

● 校閱 / Laura E. Stewart・Andy Swarzman
　　　　Ted Pigott

● 封面設計 / 白雪嬌

● 打字 / 黃淑貞・曾怡禎・紀君宜

歷屆大學聯考英文試題全集（珍藏本）

主　　編 / 劉　毅

發 行 所 / 學習出版有限公司　　　　☎ (02) 2704-5525

郵 撥 帳 號 / 0512727-2 學習出版社帳戶

登 記 證 / 局版台業 2179 號

印 刷 所 / 裕強彩色印刷有限公司

台 北 門 市 / 台北市許昌街 10 號 2 F　　☎ (02) 2331-4060

台灣總經銷 / 紅螞蟻圖書有限公司　　　☎ (02) 2795-3656

美國總經銷 / Evergreen Book Store　　☎ (818) 2813622

本公司網址　www.learnbook.com.tw

電 子 郵 件　learnbook@learnbook.com.tw

售價：新台幣六百八十元正

2010 年 5 月 1 日新修訂

ISBN 957-519-599-X　　　　　　版權所有·翻印必究